QUICKSILVER

Neal Stephenson is the author of the novels *The System of the World*, *The Confusion*, *Quicksilver*, *Cryptonomicon*, *Snow Crash*, *The Diamond Age*, and *Zodiac*. He lives in Seattle. *Quicksilver* was the winner of the 2003 Arthur C Clarke award.

'The Baroque Cycle [is] a stunning 3,000-page trilogy about 17th century scientists that will defy any category, genre, precedent or label – except for genius . . . You'll wish it were longer. Its scope is galactically vast and encompasses the lives of noblemen, vagabonds and, above all, thinkers . . . Stephenson has a once-in-a-generation gift: he makes complex ideas clear, and he makes them funny, heart-breaking and thrilling.' *Time*

'Rip-roaring stories . . . Stephenson digs up the Internet's deepest roots and makes them epic.' *Word*

'It's always a joy to discover something new that excites you, and it's a terrific bonus to realize that there's plenty more of this superlative work just over the horizon . . . *Quicksilver* exceeds not only expectations, but also hope. A triumph.' *Starburst*

'Stephenson studs his book with . . . moments of wonder, spectacle and derring-do' *Independent on Sunday*

'A true delight to read despite the fact it weighs in at a back-breaking 900+ pages . . . Stephenson is an amazing talent . . . Incredibly detailed, informed and engrossing. If you want a book that challenges, educates, stimulates and at times makes you laugh out loud (and let's face it, who wouldn't?) then go get *Quicksilver* and find yourself a comfy chair.' *Outland*

'This is meandering with a fierce purpose; elaborate scene-setting on a grand stage, conjuring a time and place so completely that when the cycle is complete, the full gravity – literally – of the changes being wrought will be felt . . . Stephenson [has an] irrepressible sense of humor – he wants us to have as much fun reading as he obviously did writing.' *Village Voice*

'Sprawling, irreverent and ultimately profound' *Newsweek*

'[A] warm, loamy novel of ideas, adventure, science and politics . . . The great trick of *Quicksilver* is that it makes you ponder concepts and theories you initially think you'll never understand, and it's greatest pleasure is that Stephenson is such an enthralling explainer . . . Stephenson's new machine is a wonderment to behold.'
Entertainment Weekly

'Neal Stephenson rewrites history – for the dark prince of hacker fiction, looking backward is another way of seeing the future.' *Wired*

'*Quicksilver* is the first novel in a projected trilogy as epic in scope as Asimov's Foundation series, and it tosses its three main characters into the bubbling cauldron of science and intrigue that Stephenson, like a mad alchemist, has cooked up in his lab . . . [A] swashbuckling pirate battle, for example, dares any reader to put down the novel and gives *Quicksilver* . . . the decadent pacing of a beach thriller.'
Men's Journal

'The joy of entering *le monde Stephenson* is that of surrender. Give up any and all preconceived notions of historical consistency, linear scientific progress, and fail-safe happy endings, and you'll enjoy the ride . . . you'll be begging for more.' *Pages*

Also by Neal Stephenson

neal
stephenson

Quicksilver

VOLUME ONE
OF THE
BAROQUE CYCLE

arrow books

Published in 2004 by Arrow Books

5 7 9 10 8 6

Map of 1667 London reproduced with changes courtesy of
Historic Urban Plans, Inc.

Refracting sphere illustration from the facsimile edition of
Robertt Hooke's *Philosophical Experiments and Observations*,
edited by W. Derham. Published by Frank Cass & Co.,
Ltd., London, 1967

Flea illustration from Robert Hooke's 1665 *Micrographia*
reprinted by permission of Octavo, www.octavo.com

Illustrations from Isaac Newton's 1729 *Mathematical Principles of
Natural Philosophy* courtesy of Primary Source Microfilm

First published in the UK in 2003 by William Heinemann

Arrow Books
The Random House Group Limited
20 Vauxhall Bridge Road, London SW1V 2SA

Random House Australia (Pty) Limited
20 Alfred Street, Milsons Point, Sydney
New South Wales 2061, Australia

Random House New Zealand Limited
18 Poland Road, Glenfield
Auckland 10, New Zealand

Random House (Pty) Limited
Isle of Houghton, Corner Boundary Road & Carse O'Gowrie,
Houghton, 2198, South Africa

The Random House Group Limited Reg. No. 954009

www.randomhouse.co.uk

A CIP catalogue record for this book
is available from the British Library

Papers used by Random House are natural, recyclable products
made from wood grown in sustainable forests. The manufacturing
processes conform to the environmental regulations
of the country of origin

ISBN 0 09 941068 0

Printed and bound in Great Britain by
Cox & Wyman Ltd, Reading, Berkshire

To the woman upstairs

Contents

Invocation

State your intentions, Muse. I know you're there.
Dead bards who pined for you have said
You're bright as flame, but fickle as the air.
My pen and I, submerged in liquid shade,
Much dark can spread, on days and over reams
But without you, no radiance can shed.
Why rustle in the dark, when fledged with fire?
Craze the night with flails of light. Reave
Your turbid shroud. Bestow what I require.

But you're not in the dark. I do believe
I swim, like squid, in clouds of my own make,
To you, offensive. To us both, opaque.
What's constituted so, only a pen
Can penetrate. I have one here; let's go.

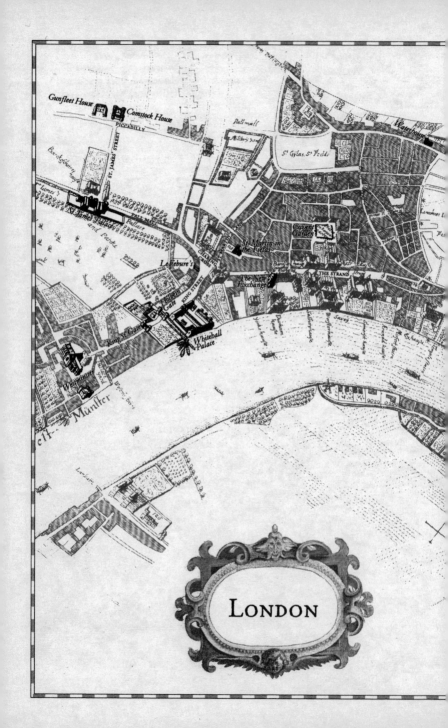

LONDON

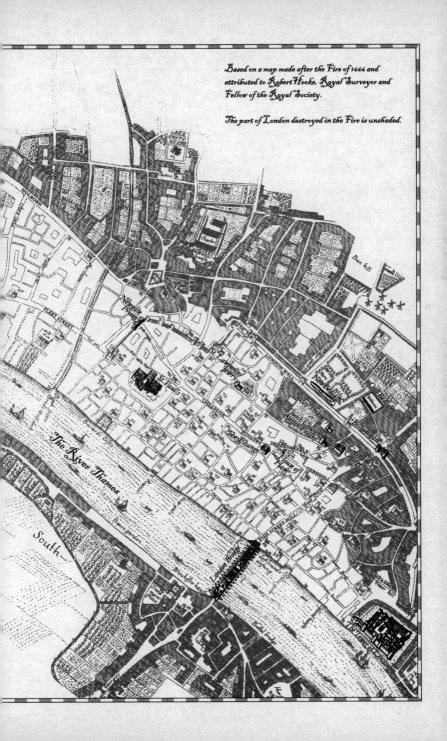

Based on a map made after the Fire of 1666 and attributed to Robert Hooke, Royal Surveyor and Fellow of the Royal Society.

The part of London destroyed in the Fire is unshaded.

HOLBORN

Bun hill

FLEET STREET

Newgate Prison

St Andrew's Holborn

LONDON WALL

St Paul's

CHEAPSIDE

New Bedlam

Old Bedlam

Dutch Church

French Church

Bishopsgate

The Change

THREADNEEDLE

The River Thames

House of

CORNHILL

Bear garden

South

Fish Street Hill

Blackfriars

London Bridge

The Tower of London

BOOK ONE

Quicksilver

Those who assume hypotheses as first principles
of their speculations . . . may indeed form an
ingenious romance, but a romance it will still be.
　　　　　　　　　　　　　—ROGER COTES,
　　　　　PREFACE TO SIR ISAAC NEWTON'S
　　　　　　　　　Principia Mathematica,
　　　　SECOND EDITION, 1713

Boston Common

ENOCH ROUNDS THE CORNER JUST as the executioner raises the noose above the woman's head. The crowd on the Common stop praying and sobbing for just as long as Jack Ketch stands there, elbows locked, for all the world like a carpenter heaving a ridge-beam into place. The rope clutches a disk of blue New England sky. The Puritans gaze at it and, to all appearances, think. Enoch the Red reins in his borrowed horse as it nears the edge of the crowd, and sees that the executioner's purpose is not to let them inspect his knotwork, but to give them all a narrow—and, to a Puritan, tantalizing—glimpse of the portal through which they all must pass one day.

Boston's a dollop of hills in a spoon of marshes. The road up the spoon-handle is barred by a wall, with the usual gallows outside it, and victims, or parts of them, strung up or nailed to the city gates. Enoch has just come that way, and reckoned he had seen the last of such things—that thenceforth it would all be churches and taverns. But the dead men outside the gate were common robbers, killed for earthly crimes. What is happening now on the Common is of a more Sacramental nature.

The noose lies on the woman's gray head like a crown. The executioner pushes it down. Her head forces it open like an infant's dilating the birth canal. When it finds the widest part it drops suddenly onto her shoulders. Her knees pimple the front of her apron and her skirts telescope into the platform as she makes to collapse. The executioner hugs her with one arm, like a dancing-master, to keep her upright, and adjusts the knot while an official reads the death warrant. This is as bland as a lease. The crowd scratches and shuffles. There are none of the diversions of a London hanging: no catcalls, jugglers, or pickpockets. Down at the other end of the Common, a squadron of lobsterbacks drills and marches round the base of a hummock with a stone powder-house planted in its top.

An Irish sergeant bellows—bored but indignant—in a voice that carries forever on the wind, like the smell of smoke.

He's not come to watch witch-hangings, but now that Enoch's blundered into one it would be bad form to leave. There is a drum-roll, and then a sudden awkward silence. He judges it very far from the worst hanging he's ever seen—no kicking or writhing, no breaking of ropes or unraveling of knots—all in all, an unusually competent piece of work.

He hadn't really known what to expect of America. But people here seem to do things—hangings included—with a blunt, blank efficiency that's admirable and disappointing at the same time. Like jumping fish, they go about difficult matters with bloodless ease. As if they were all born knowing things that other people must absorb, along with færy-tales and superstitions, from their families and villages. Maybe it is because most of them came over on ships.

As they are cutting the limp witch down, a gust tumbles over the Common from the North. On Sir Isaac Newton's temperature scale, where freezing is zero and the heat of the human body is twelve, it is probably four or five. If Herr Fahrenheit were here with one of his new quicksilver-filled, sealed-tube thermometers, he would probably observe something in the fifties. But this sort of wind, coming as it does from the North in the autumn, is more chilling than any mere instrument can tell. It reminds everyone here that if they don't want to be dead in a few months' time, they have firewood to stack and chinks to caulk. The wind is noticed by a hoarse preacher at the base of the gallows, who takes it to be Satan himself, come to carry the witch's soul to hell, and who is not slow to share this opinion with his flock. The preacher is staring Enoch in the eye as he testifies.

Enoch feels the heightened, chafing self-consciousness that is the precursor to fear. What's to prevent them from trying and hanging *him* as a witch?

How must he look to these people? A man of indefinable age but evidently broad experience, with silver hair queued down to the small of his back, a copper-red beard, pale gray eyes, and skin weathered and marred like a blacksmith's ox-hide apron. Dressed in a long traveling-cloak, a walking-staff and an outmoded rapier strapped 'longside the saddle of a notably fine black horse. Two pistols in his waistband, prominent enough that Indians, highway-men, and French raiders can clearly see them from ambuscades (he'd like to move them out of view, but reaching for them at this moment seems like a bad idea). Saddlebags (should they be searched) filled with instruments, flasks of quicksilver, and stranger matters—some, as they'd learn, quite dangerous—books in Hebrew, Greek, and Latin pocked with the occult symbols of Alchemists and Kabalists. Things could go badly for him in Boston.

But the crowd takes the preacher's ranting not as a call to arms but a signal to turn and disperse, muttering. The redcoats discharge their muskets with deep hissing booms, like handfuls of sand hurled against a kettledrum. Enoch dismounts into the midst of the colonists. He sweeps the robe round him, concealing the pistols, pulls the hood back from his head, and amounts to just another weary pilgrim. He does not meet any man's eye but scans their faces sidelong, and is surprised by a general lack of self-righteousness.

"God willing," one man says, "that'll be the last one."

"Do you mean, sir, the last witch?" Enoch asks.

"I mean, sir, the last hanging."

Flowing like water round the bases of the steep hills, they migrate across a burying ground on the south edge of the Common, already full of lost Englishmen, and follow the witch's corpse down the street. The houses are mostly of wood, and so are the churches. Spaniards would have built a single great cathedral here, of stone, with gold on the inside, but the colonists cannot agree on anything and so it is more like Amsterdam: small churches on every block, some barely distinguishable from barns, each no doubt preaching that all of the others have it wrong. But at least they can muster a consensus to kill a witch. She is borne off into a new burying ground, which for some reason they have situated hard by the granary. Enoch is at a loss to know whether this juxtaposition— that is, storing their Dead, and their Staff of Life, in the same place—is some sort of Message from the city's elders, or simple bad taste.

Enoch, who has seen more than one city burn, recognizes the scars of a great fire along this main street. Houses and churches are being rebuilt with brick or stone. He comes to what must be the greatest intersection in the town, where this road from the city gate crosses a very broad street that runs straight down to salt water, and continues on a long wharf that projects far out into the harbor, thrusting across a ruined rampart of stones and logs: the rubble of a disused sea-wall. The long wharf is ridged with barracks. It reaches far enough out into the harbor that one of the Navy's very largest men-of-war is able to moor at its end. Turning his head the other way, he sees artillery mounted up on a hillside, and bluecoated gunners tending to a vatlike mortar, ready to lob iron bombs onto the decks of any French or Spanish galleons that might trespass on the bay.

So, drawing a mental line from the dead criminals at the city gate, to the powder-house on the Common, to the witch-gallows, and finally to the harbor defenses, he has got one Cartesian number-line—what Leibniz would call the Ordinate—plotted out: he understands what people are afraid of in Boston, and how the churchmen and the generals keep the place in hand. But it remains to be seen what can be plotted in the space above and below. The hills of Boston are skirted by endless flat marshes that fade, slow as twilight, into Harbor or River, providing blank empty planes on which men with ropes and rulers can construct whatever strange curves they phant'sy.

Enoch knows where to find the Origin of this coordinate system, because he has talked to ship's masters who have visited Boston. He goes down to where the long wharf grips the shore. Among fine stone sea-merchants' houses, there is a brick-red door with a bunch of grapes dangling above it. Enoch goes through that door and finds himself in a good tavern. Men with swords and expensive clothes turn round to look at him. Slavers, merchants of rum and molasses and tea and tobacco, and captains of the ships that carry those things. It could be any place in the world, for the same tavern is in London, Cadiz, Smyrna, and Manila, and the same men are in it. None of them cares, supposing they even know, that witches are being hanged five minutes' walk away. He is much more comfortable in here than out there; but he has not come to be comfortable. The particular sea-captain he's looking for—van Hoek—is not here. He backs out before the tavern-keeper can tempt him.

Back in America and among Puritans, he enters into narrower streets and heads north, leading his horse over a rickety wooden bridge thrown over a little mill-creek. Flotillas of shavings from some carpenter's block-plane sail down the stream like ships going off to war. Underneath them the weak current nudges turds and bits of slaughtered animals down towards the harbor. It smells accordingly. No denying there is a tallow-chandlery not far upwind, where beast-grease not fit for eating is made into candles and soap.

"Did you come from Europe?"

He had *sensed* someone was following him, but *seen* nothing whenever he looked back. Now he knows why: his doppelgänger is a lad, moving about like a drop of quicksilver that cannot be trapped under the thumb. Ten years old, Enoch guesses. Then the

boy thinks about smiling and his lips part. His gums support a rubble of adult teeth shouldering their way into pink gaps, and decid-
uous ones flapping like tavern signs on skin hinges. He's closer to
eight. But cod and corn have made him big for his age—at least by
London standards. And he is precocious in every respect save social
graces.

Enoch might answer, *Yes, I am from Europe, where a boy addresses
an old man as "sir," if he addresses him at all.* But he cannot get past
the odd nomenclature. "Europe," he repeats, "is that what you name
it here? Most people *there* say *Christendom.*"

"But we have Christians *here.*"

"So this *is* Christendom, you are saying," says Enoch, "but, obviously to you, I've come from somewhere *else.* Perhaps Europe *is* the
better term, now that you mention it. Hmm."

"What do other people call it?"

"Do I look like a schoolmaster to you?"

"No, but you talk like one."

"You know something of schoolmasters, do you?"

"Yes, sir," the boy says, faltering a bit as he sees the jaws of the
trap swinging toward his leg.

"Yet here it is the middle of Monday—"

"The place was empty 'cause of the Hanging. I didn't want to
stay and—"

"And what?"

"Get more ahead of the others than I was already."

"If you are ahead, the correct thing is to *get used to it*—not to
make yourself into an imbecile. Come, you belong in school."

"School is where one learns," says the boy. "If you'd be so kind
as to answer my question, sir, then I should be learning something,
which would mean I *were* in school."

The boy is obviously dangerous. So Enoch decides to accept the
proposition. "You may address me as Mr. Root. And you are—?"

"Ben. Son of Josiah. The tallow-chandler. Why do you laugh,
Mr. Root?"

"Because in most parts of Christendom—or Europe—tallow-
chandlers' sons do not go to grammar school. It is a peculiarity
of . . . your people." Enoch almost let slip the word *Puritans.* Back
in England, where Puritans are a memory of a bygone age, or at
worst streetcorner nuisances, the term serves well enough to lam-
poon the backwoodsmen of Massachusetts Bay Colony. But as he
keeps being reminded here, the truth of the matter is more complex. From a coffeehouse in London, one may speak blithely of
Islam and the Mussulman, but in Cairo such terms are void. Here

Enoch is in the Puritans' Cairo. "I shall answer your question," Enoch says before Ben can let fly with any more. "What do people in other parts call the place I am from? Well, Islam—a larger, richer, and in most ways more sophisticated civilization that hems in the Christians of Europe to the east and the south—divides all the world into only three parts: their part, which is the *dar al-Islam*; the part with which they are friendly, which is the *dar as-sulh,* or House of Peace; and everything else, which is the *dar al-harb,* or House of War. The latter is, I'm sorry to say, a far more apt name than Christendom for the part of the world where most of the Christians live."

"I know of the war," Ben says coolly. "It is at an end. A Peace has been signed at Utrecht. France gets Spain. Austria gets the Spanish Netherlands. We get Gibraltar, Newfoundland, St. Kitts, and—" lowering his voice "—the slave trade."

"Yes—the *Asiento.*"

"Ssh! There are a few here, sir, opposed to it, and they are dangerous."

"You have Barkers here?"

"Yes, sir."

Enoch studies the boy's face now with some care, for the chap he is looking for is a sort of Barker, and it would be useful to know how such are regarded hereabouts by their less maniacal brethren. Ben seems cautious, rather than contemptuous.

"But you are speaking only of *one* war—"

"The War of the Spanish Succession," says Ben, "whose cause was the death in Madrid of King Carlos the Sufferer."

"I should say that wretched man's death was the *pretext,* not the cause," says Enoch. "The War of the Spanish Succession was only the second, and I pray the last, part of a great war that began a quarter of a century ago, at the time of—"

"The Glorious Revolution!"

"As some style it. You *have* been at your lessons, Ben, and I commend you. Perhaps you know that in that Revolution the King of England—a Catholic—was sent packing, and replaced by a Protestant King and Queen."

"William and Mary!"

"Indeed. But has it occurred to you to wonder *why* Protestants and Catholics were at war in the first place?"

"In our studies we more often speak of wars *among* Protestants."

"Ah, yes—a phenomenon restricted to England. That is natural, for your parents came here because of such a conflict."

"The Civil War," says Ben.

"Your side won the Civil War," Enoch reminds him, "but later came the Restoration, which was a grievous defeat for your folk, and sent them flocking hither."

"You have hit the mark, Mr. Root," says Ben, "for that is just why my father Josiah quit England."

"What about your mother?"

"Nantucket-born sir. But her father came here to escape from a wicked Bishop—a loud fellow, or so I have heard—"

"Finally, Ben, I have found a limit to your knowledge. You are speaking of Archbishop Laud—a terrible oppressor of Puritans—as some called your folk—under Charles the First. The Puritans paid him back by chopping off the head of that same Charles in Charing Cross, in the year of our lord sixteen hundred and forty-nine."

"Cromwell," says Ben.

"Cromwell. Yes. He had something to do with it. Now, Ben. We have been standing by this millstream for rather a long while. I grow cold. My horse is restless. We have, as I said, found the place where your erudition gives way to ignorance. I shall be pleased to hold up my end of our agreement—that is, to teach you things, so that when you go home to-night you may claim to Josiah that you were in school the whole day. Though the schoolmaster may give him an account that shall conflict with yours. However, I do require certain minor services in return."

"Only name them, Mr. Root."

"I have come to Boston to find a certain man who at last report was living here. He is an old man."

"Older than you?"

"No, but he might *seem* older."

"How old is he, then?"

"He watched the head of King Charles the First being chopped off."

"At least threescore and four then."

"Ah, I see you have been learning sums and differences."

"And products and dividends, Mr. Root."

"Work this into your reckonings, then: the one I seek had an excellent view of the beheading, for he was sitting upon his father's shoulders."

"Couldn't have been more than a few years old then. Unless his father was a sturdy fellow indeed."

"His father was sturdy in a sense," says Enoch, "for Archbishop Laud had caused his ears and his nose to be cut off in Star Chamber some two decades before, and yet he was not daunted, but kept up his agitation against the King. Against all Kings."

"He was a Barker." Again, this word brings no sign of contempt to Ben's face. Shocking how different this place is from London.

"But to answer your question, Ben: Drake was not an especially big or strong man."

"So the son on his shoulders was small. By now he should be, perhaps, threescore and eight. But I do not know of a Mr. Drake here."

"Drake was the father's *Christian* name."

"Pray, what then is the name of the family?"

"I will not tell you that just now," says Enoch. For the man he wants to find might have a very poor character among these people—might already have been hanged on Boston Common, for all Enoch knows.

"How can I help you find him, sir, if you won't let me know his name?"

"By guiding me to the Charlestown ferry," Enoch says, "for I know that he spends his days on the north side of the River Charles."

"Follow me," says Ben, "but I hope you've silver."

"Oh yes, I've silver," says Enoch.

THEY ARE SKIRTING A KNOB of land at the north end of the city. Wharves, smaller and older than the big one, radiate from its shore. The sails and rigging, spars and masts to his starboard combine into a tangle vast and inextricable, as characters on a page must do in the eyes of an unlettered peasant. Enoch does not see van Hoek or *Minerva*. He begins to fear that he shall have to go into taverns and make inquiries, and spend time, and draw attention.

Ben takes him direct to the wharf where the Charlestown Ferry is ready to shove off. It is all crowded with hanging-watchers, and Enoch must pay the waterman extra to bring the horse aboard. Enoch pulls his purse open and peers into it. The King of Spain's coat of arms stares back at him, stamped in silver, variously blurred, chopped, and mangled. The Christian name varies, depending on which king reigned when each of these coins was hammered out in New Spain, but after that they all say D. G. HISPAN ET IND REX. By the grace of God, of Spain and the Indies, King. The same sort of bluster that all kings stamp onto their coins.

Those words don't matter to anyone—most people can't read them anyway. What does matter is that a man standing in a cold breeze on the Boston waterfront, seeking to buy passage on a ferry run by an Englishman, cannot pay with the coins that are being stamped out by Sir Isaac Newton in the Royal Mint at the Tower of

London. The only coinage here is Spanish—the same coins that are changing hands, at this moment, in Lima, Manila, Macao, Goa, Bandar Abbas, Mocha, Cairo, Smyrna, Malta, Madrid, the Canary Islands, Marseilles.

The man who saw Enoch down to the docks in London months ago said: "Gold knows things that no man does."

Enoch churns his purse up and down, making the coins-fragments fly, hoping to spy a single pie-slice—one-eighth of a Piece of Eight, or a bit, as they are called. But he already knows he's spent most of his bits for small necessaries along the road. The smallest piece he has in his purse right now is half of a coin—four bits.

He looks up the street and sees a blacksmith's forge only a stone's throw away. Some quick work with a hammer and that smith could make change for him.

The ferryman's reading Enoch's mind. He couldn't see into the purse, but he could hear the massive gonging of whole coins colliding, without the clashing tinkle of bits. "We're shoving off," he is pleased to say.

Enoch comes to his senses, remembers what he's doing, and hands over a silver semicircle. "But the boy comes with me," he insists, "and you'll give him passage back."

"Done," says the ferryman.

This is more than Ben could have hoped for, and yet he *was* hoping for it. Though the boy is too self-possessed to say as much, this voyage is to him as good as a passage down to the Caribbean to go a-pirating on the Spanish Main. He goes from wharf to ferry without touching the gangplank.

Charlestown is less than a mile distant, across the mouth of a sluggish river. It is a low green hill shingled with long slender hay-mows limned by dry-stone fences. On the slope facing toward Boston, below the summit but above the endless tidal flats and cattail-filled marshes, a town has occurred: partly laid out by geometers, but partly growing like ivy.

The ferryman's hefty Africans pace short reciprocating arcs on the deck, sweeping and shoveling the black water of the Charles Basin with long stanchion-mounted oars, minting systems of vortices that fall to aft, flailing about one another, tracing out fading and flattening conic sections that Sir Isaac could probably work out in his head. *The Hypothesis of Vortices is pressed with many difficulties.* The sky's a matted reticule of taut jute and spokeshaved tree-trunks. Gusts make the anchored ships start and jostle like nervous horses hearing distant guns. Irregular waves slap curiously at the lapping clinkers of their hulls, which are infested with barefoot jacks paying pitch and oakum into troublesome seams. The ships appear to glide this way and that as the ferry's movement plays with the parallax. Enoch, who has the good fortune to be a bit taller than most of the other passengers, hands the reins to Ben and excuses his way around the ferry's deck trying to read the names.

He knows the ship he's looking for, though, simply by recognizing the carved Lady mounted below the bowsprit: a gray-eyed woman in a gilded helmet, braving the North Atlantic seas with a snaky shield and nipples understandably erect. *Minerva* hasn't weighed anchor yet—that's lucky—but she is heavy-laden and gives every appearance of being just about to put to sea. Men are walking aboard hugging baskets of loaves so fresh they're steaming. Enoch turns back toward the shore to read the level of the tide from a barnacled pile, then turns the other way to check the phase and altitude of the moon. Tide will be going out soon, and *Minerva* will probably want to ride it. Enoch finally spies van Hoek standing on the foredeck, doing some paperwork on the top of a barrel, and through some kind of action-at-a-distance wills him to look up and notice him, down on the ferry.

Van Hoek looks his way and stiffens.

Enoch makes no outward sign, but stares him in the eye long enough to give him second thoughts about pushing for a hasty departure.

A colonist in a black hat is attempting to make friends with one of the Africans, who doesn't speak much English—but this is no hindrance, the white man has taught himself a few words of some African tongue. The slave is very dark, and the arms of the King of Spain are branded into his left shoulder, and so he is probably Angolan. Life has been strange to him: abducted by Africans fiercer than he, chained up in a hole in Luanda, marked with a hot iron to indicate that duty had been paid on him, loaded onto a ship, and sent to a cold place full of pale men. After all of that, you'd think that nothing could possibly surprise him. But he's astonished by whatever this Barker is telling him. The Barker's punching at the air and becoming quite exercised, and not just because he is inarticulate. Assuming that he has been in touch with his brethren in London (and that is a very good assumption), he is probably telling the Angolan that he, and all of the other slaves, are perfectly justified in taking up arms and mounting a violent rebellion.

"Your mount is very fine. Did you bring him from Europe?"

"No, Ben. Borrowed him in New Amsterdam. New *York*, I mean."

"Why'd you sail to New York if the man you seek's in Boston?"

"The next America-bound ship from the Pool of London happened to be headed thither."

"You're in a terrible hurry, then!"

"I shall be in a terrible hurry to toss you over the side if you continue to draw such inferences."

This quiets Ben, but only long enough for him to circle round and probe Enoch's defenses from another quarter: "The owner of this horse must be a very dear friend of yours, to lend you such a mount."

Enoch must now be a bit careful. The owner's a gentleman of quality in New York. If Enoch claims his friendship, then proceeds to make a bloody hash of things in Boston, it could deal damage to the gentleman's repute. "It is not so much that he is a friend. I'd never met him until I showed up at his door a few days ago."

Ben can't fathom it. "Then why'd he even admit you to his house? By your leave, sir, looking as you do, and armed. Why'd he lend you such a worthy stallion?"

"He let me in to his house because there was a riot underway, and I requested sanctuary." Enoch gazes over at the Barker, then sidles closer to Ben. "Here is a wonder for you: When my ship reached New York, we were greeted by the spectacle of thousands of slaves—some Irish, the rest Angolan—running through the streets with pitchforks and firebrands. Lobsterbacks tromping after them in leapfrogging blocks, firing volleys. The white smoke of their muskets rose and mingled with the black smoke of burning warehouses to turn the sky into a blazing, spark-shot melting-pot, wondrous to look at but, as we supposed, unfit to support life. Our pilot had us stand a-loof until the tide forced his hand. We put in at a pier that seemed to be under the sway of the redcoats.

"Anyway," Enoch continues—for his discourse is beginning to draw unwanted notice—"that's how I got in the door. He lent me the horse because he and I are Fellows in the same Society, and I am here, in a way, to do an errand for that Society."

"Is it a Society of Barkers, like?" asks Ben, stepping in close to whisper, and glancing at the one who's proselytizing the slave. For by now Ben has taken note of Enoch's various pistols and blades, and matched him with tales his folk have probably told him concerning that fell Sect during their halcyon days of Cathedral-sacking and King-killing.

"No, it is a society of philosophers," Enoch says, before the boy's phant'sies wax any wilder.

"Philosophers, sir!"

Enoch had supposed the boy should be disappointed. Instead he's thrilled. So Enoch was correct: the boy's dangerous.

"*Natural* Philosophers. Not, mind you, the other sort—"

"Unnatural?"

"An apt coinage. *Some* would say it's the unnatural philosophers that are to blame for Protestants fighting Protestants in England and Catholics everywhere else."

"What, then, is a Natural Philosopher?"

"One who tries to prevent his ruminations from straying, by hewing to what can be observed, and proving things, when possible, by rules of logic." This gets him nowhere with Ben. "Rather like a Judge in a Court, who insists on facts, and scorns rumor, hearsay, and appeals to sentiment. As when your own Judges finally went up to Salem and pointed out that the people there were going crazy."

Ben nods. Good. "What is the name of your Clubb?"

"The Royal Society of London."

"One day I shall be a Fellow of it, and a Judge of such things."

"I shall nominate you the moment I get back, Ben."

"Is it a part of your code that members must lend each other horses in time of need?"

"No, but it is a rule that they must pay dues—for which there is *ever* a need—and this chap had not paid his dues in many a year. Sir Isaac—who is the President of the Royal Society—looks with disfavor on such. I explained to the gentleman in New York why it was a Bad Idea to land on Sir Isaac's Shit List—by your leave, by your leave—and he was so convinced by my arguments that he lent me his best riding-horse without further suasion."

"He's a beauty," Ben says, and strokes the animal's nose. The stallion mistrusted Ben at first for being small, darting, and smelling of long-dead beasts. Now he has accepted the boy as an animated hitching-post, capable of performing a few services such as nose-scratching and fly-shooing.

The ferryman is more amused than angry when he discovers a Barker conspiring with his slave, and shoos him away. The Barker identifies Enoch as fresh meat, and begins trying to catch his eye. Enoch moves away from him and pretends to study the approaching shore. The ferry is maneuvering around a raft of immense logs drifting out of the estuary, each marked with the King's Arrow—going to build ships for the Navy.

Inland of Charlestown spreads a loose agglomeration of hamlets conjoined by a network of cowpaths. The largest cowpath goes all the way to Newtowne, where Harvard College is. But most of it just looks like a forest, smoking without being burned, spattered with muffled whacks of axes and hammers. Occasional musket shots boom in the distance and are echoed from hamlet to hamlet— some kind of system for relaying information across the countryside. Enoch wonders how he's ever going to find Daniel in all that.

He moves toward a talkative group that has formed on the center of the ferry's deck, allowing the less erudite (for these must be Harvard men) to break the wind for them. It is a mix of pompous sots and peering quick-faced men basting their sentences together with bad Latin. Some of them have a dour Puritan look about them, others are dressed in something closer to last year's London mode. A pear-shaped, red-nosed man in a tall gray wig seems to be the Don of this jury-rigged College. Enoch catches this one's eye and lets him see that he's bearing a sword. This is not a threat, but an assertion of status.

"A gentleman traveler from abroad joins us. Welcome, sir, to our humble Colony!"

Enoch goes through the requisite polite movements and utterances. They show a great deal of interest in him, a sure sign that not much new and interesting is going on at Harvard College. But the place is only some three-quarters of a century old, so how much can really be happening there? They want to know if he's from a Germanic land; he says not really. They guess that he has come on some Alchemical errand, which is an excellent guess, but wrong. When it is polite to do so, he tells them the name of the man he has come to see.

He's never heard such scoffing. They are, to a man, pained that a gentleman should've crossed the North Atlantic, and now the Charles Basin, only to spoil the journey by meeting with *that* fellow.

"I know him not," Enoch lies.

"Then let us prepare you, sir!" one of them says. "Daniel Waterhouse is a man advanced in years, but the years have been less kind to him than you."

"He is correctly addressed as Dr. Waterhouse, is he not?"

Silence ruined by stifled gurgles.

"I do not presume to correct any man," Enoch says, "only to be sure that I give no offense when I encounter the fellow in person."

"Indeed, he is accounted a Doctor," says the pear-shaped Don, "but—"

"Of what?" someone asks.

"Gears," someone suggests, to great hilarity.

"Nay, nay!" says the Don, shouting them down, in a show of false goodwill. "For all of his gears are to no purpose without a *primum mobile*, a source of motive power—"

"The Franklin boy!" and all turn to look at Ben.

"Today it might be young Ben, tomorrow perhaps little Godfrey Waterhouse will step into Ben's shoes. Later perhaps a rodent on a tread-mill. But in any case, the *vis viva* is conducted into Dr. Waterhouse's gear-boxes by—what? Anyone?" The Don cups a hand to an ear Socratically.

"Shafts?" someone guesses.

"Cranks!" another shouts.

"Ah, excellent! Our colleague Waterhouse is, then, a Doctor of—what?"

"Cranks!" says the entire College in unison.

"And so devoted is our Doctor of Cranks to his work that he quite sacrifices himself," says the Don admiringly. "Going many days uncovered—"

"Shaking the gear-filings from his sleeves when he sits down to break bread—"

"Better than pepper—"

"And cheaper!"

"Are you, perhaps, coming to join his Institute, then?"

"Or foreclose on't?" Too hilarious.

"I have heard of his Institute, but know little of it," Enoch Root says. He looks over at Ben, who has gone red in the neck and ears, and turned his back on all to nuzzle the horse.

"Many learned scholars are in the same state of ignorance—be not ashamed."

"Since he came to America, Dr. Waterhouse has been infected with the local influenza, whose chief symptom is causing men to found new projects and endeavours, rather than going to the trouble of remedying the old ones."

"He's not entirely satisfied with Harvard College then!?" Enoch says wonderingly.

"Oh, no! He has founded—"

"—and *personally endowed*—"

"—and laid the cornerstone—"

"—corner-log, if truth be told—"

"—of—what does he call it?"

"The Massachusetts Bay Colony Institute of Technologickal Arts."

"Where might I find Dr. Waterhouse's Institute?" Enoch inquires.

"Midway from Charlestown to Harvard. Follow the sound of grinding gears 'til you come to America's smallest and smokiest dwelling—"

"Sir, you are a learned and clear-minded gentleman," says the Don. "If your errand has aught to do with Philosophy, then is not Harvard College a more fitting destination?"

"Mr. Root is a Natural Philosopher of note, sir!" blurts Ben, only as a way to prevent himself bursting into tears. The way he says it makes it clear he thinks the Harvard men are of the Unnatural type. "He is a Fellow of the Royal Society!"

Oh, dear.

The Don steps forward and hunches his shoulders like a conspirator. "I beg your pardon, sir, I did not know."

"It is quite all right, really."

"Dr. Waterhouse, you must be warned, has fallen quite under the spell of Herr Leibniz—"

"—him that stole the calculus from Sir Isaac—" someone footnotes.

"—yes, and, like Leibniz, is infected with Metaphysickal thinking—"

"—a throwback to the Scholastics, sir—notwithstanding Sir Isaac's having exploded the old ways through very clear demonstrations—"

"—and labors now, like a possessed man, on a Mill—designed after Leibniz's principles—that he imagines will discover new truths through *computation!*"

"Perhaps our visitor has come to exorcise him of Leibniz's daemons!" some very drunk fellow hypothesizes.

Enoch clears his throat irritably, hacking loose a small accumulation of yellow bile—the humour of anger and ill-temper. He says, "It does Dr. Leibniz an injustice to call him a mere metaphysician."

This challenge produces momentary silence, followed by tremendous excitement and gaiety. The Don smiles thinly and squares off. "I know of a small tavern on Harvard Square, a suitable venue in which I could disabuse the gentleman of any misconceptions—"

The offer to sit down in front of a crock of beer and edify these wags is dangerously tempting. But the Charlestown waterfront is drawing near, the slaves already shortening their strokes; *Minerva* is fairly straining at her hawsers in eagerness to catch the tide, and he must have results. He'd rather get this done discreetly. But that is hopeless now that Ben has unmasked him. More important is to get it done *quickly*.

Besides, Enoch has lost his temper.

He draws a folded and sealed Letter from his breast pocket and, for lack of a better term, brandishes it.

The Letter is borrowed, scrutinized—one side is inscribed "Doktor Waterhouse—Newtowne—Massachusetts"—and flipped over. Monocles are quarried from velvet-lined pockets for the Examination of the Seal: a lump of red wax the size of Ben's fist. Lips move and strange mutterings occur as parched throats attempt German.

All of the Professors seem to realize it at once. They jump back as if the letter were a specimen of white phosphorus that had suddenly burst into flame. The Don is left holding it. He extends it towards Enoch the Red with a certain desperate pleading look. Enoch punishes him by being slow to accept the burden.

"*Bitte, mein herr* . . ."

"English is perfectly sufficient," Enoch says. "Preferable, in fact."

At the fringes of the robed and hooded mob, certain nearsighted faculty members are frantic with indignation over not having been able to read the seal. Their colleagues are muttering to them words like "Hanover" and "Ansbach."

A man removes his hat and bows to Enoch. Then another.

They have not even set foot in Charlestown before the dons have begun to make a commotion. Porters and would-be passengers stare quizzically at the approaching ferry as they are assailed with shouts of "Make way!" and broad waving motions. The ferry's become a floating stage packed with bad actors. Enoch wonders whether any of these men really supposes that word of their diligence will actually make its way back to court in Hanover, and be heard by their future Queen. It is ghoulish—they are behaving as if Queen Anne were already dead and buried, and the Hanovers on the throne.

"Sir, if you'd only *told* me 'twas Daniel Waterhouse you sought, I'd have taken you *to* him without delay—and without all of this *bother*."

"I erred by not confiding in you, Ben," Enoch says.

Indeed. In retrospect, it's obvious that in such a small town, Daniel would have noticed a lad like Ben, or Ben would have been drawn to Daniel, or both. "Do you know the way?"

"Of course!"

"Mount up," Enoch commands, and nods at the horse. Ben needn't be asked twice. He's up like a spider. Enoch follows as soon as dignity and inertia will allow. They share the saddle, Ben on Enoch's lap with his legs thrust back and wedged between Enoch's knees and the horse's rib-cage. The horse has, overall, taken a dim view of the Ferry and the Faculty, and bangs across the plank as soon as it has been thrown down. They're pursued through the streets of Charlestown by some of the more nimble Doctors. But Charlestown doesn't *have* that many streets and so the chase is brief. Then they break out into the mephitic bog on its western flank. It puts Enoch strongly in mind of another swampy, dirty, miasma-ridden burg full of savants: Cambridge, England.

"INTO YONDER COPPICE, then ford the creek," Ben suggests. "We shall lose the Professors, and perhaps find Godfrey. When we were on the ferry, I spied him going thither with a pail."

"Is Godfrey the son of Dr. Waterhouse?"

"Indeed, sir. Two years younger than I."

"Would his middle name, perchance, be William?"

"How'd you know that, Mr. Root?"

"He is very likely named after Gottfried Wilhelm Leibniz."

"A friend of yours and Sir Isaac's?"

"Of mine, yes. Of Sir Isaac's, no—and therein lies a tale too long to tell now."

"Would it fill a book?"

"In truth, 'twould fill *several*—and it is not even finished yet."

"When shall it be finished?"

"At times, I fear *never*. But you and I shall hurry it to its final act to-day, Ben. How much farther to the Massachusetts Bay Colony Institute of Technologickal Arts?"

Ben shrugs. "It is halfway between Charlestown and Harvard. But close to the river. More than a mile. Perhaps less than two."

The horse is disinclined to enter the coppice, so Ben tumbles off and goes in there afoot to flush out little Godfrey. Enoch finds a place to ford the creek that runs through it, and works his way round to the other side of the little wood to find Ben engaged in an apple-fight with a smaller, paler lad.

Enoch dismounts and brokers a peace, then hurries the boys on by offering them a ride on the horse. Enoch walks ahead, leading it; but soon enough the horse divines that they are bound for a timber building in the distance. For it is the *only* building, and a faint path leads to it. Thenceforth Enoch need only walk alongside, and feed him the odd apple.

"The sight of you two lads scuffling over apples in this bleak gusty place full of Puritans puts me in mind of something remarkable I saw a long time ago."

"Where?" asks Godfrey.

"Grantham, Lincolnshire. Which is part of England."

"How long ago, to be exact?" Ben demands, taking the empiricist bit in his teeth.

"That is a harder question than it sounds, for the way I remember such things is most disorderly."

"Why were you journeying to that bleak place?" asks Godfrey.

"To stop being pestered. In Grantham lived an apothecary, name of Clarke, an indefatigable pesterer."

"Then why'd you go *to* him?"

"He'd been pestering me with letters, wanting me to deliver certain necessaries of his trade. He'd been doing it for years—ever since sending letters had become possible again."

"What made it possible?"

"In my neck of the woods—for I was living in a town in Saxony, called Leipzig—the peace of Westphalia did."

"1648!" Ben says donnishly to the younger boy. "The end of the Thirty Years' War."

"At *his* end," Enoch continues, "it was the removal of the King's head from the rest of the King, which settled the Civil War and brought a kind of peace to England."

"1649," Godfrey murmurs before Ben can get it out. Enoch wonders whether Daniel has been so indiscreet as to regale his son with decapitation yarns.

"If Mr. Clarke had been pestering you *for years*, then you must have gone to Grantham in the middle of the 1650s," Ben says.

"How can you be that old?" Godfrey asks.

"Ask your father," Enoch returns. "I am still endeavouring to answer the question of *when* exactly. Ben is correct. I couldn't have been so rash as to make the attempt before, let us say, 1652; for, regicide notwithstanding, the Civil War did not really wind up for another couple of years. Cromwell smashed the Royalists for the umpteenth and final time at Worcester. Charles the Second ran off to Paris with as many of his noble supporters as had not been slain yet. Come to think of it, I *saw* him, and them, at Paris."

"Why *Paris*? That were a *dreadful* way to get from Leipzig to Lincolnshire!" says Ben.

"Your geography is stronger than your history. What do you phant'sy would be a *good* way to make that journey?"

"Through the Dutch Republic, of course."

"And indeed I *did* stop there, to look in on a Mr. Huygens in the Hague. But I did not *sail* from any Dutch port."

"Why not? The Dutch are ever so much better at sailing than the French!"

"But what was the first thing that Cromwell did after winning the Civil War?"

"Granted all men, even Jews, the right to worship wheresoever they pleased," says Godfrey, as if reciting a catechism.

"Well, naturally—that was the whole *point*, wasn't it? But other than *that*—?"

"Killed a great many Irishmen," Ben tries.

"True, too true—but it's not the answer I was looking for. The answer is: the Navigation Act. And a sea-war against the Dutch. So you see, Ben, journeying via Paris might have been *roundabout*, but it was infinitely *safer*. Besides, people in Paris had been pestering me, too, and they had more money than Mr. Clarke. So Mr. Clarke had to *get in line,* as they say in New York."

"Why were so many pestering you?" asks Godfrey.

"Rich Tories, no less!" adds Ben.

"We did not begin calling such people Tories until a good bit later," Enoch corrects him. "But your question is apt: what did *I* have in Leipzig that was wanted so badly, alike by an apothecary in Grantham and a lot of Cavalier courtiers sitting in Paris waiting for Cromwell to grow old and die of natural causes?"

"Something to do with the Royal Society?" guesses Ben.

"Shrewd try. Very close to the mark. But this was in the days before the Royal Society, indeed before Natural Philosophy as we know it. Oh, there were a few—Francis Bacon, Galileo, Descartes— who'd seen the light, and had done all that they could to get everyone else to attend to it. But in those days, most of the chaps who were curious about how the world worked were captivated by a rather different approach called Alchemy."

"My daddy hates Alchemists!" Godfrey announces—very proud of his daddy.

"I believe I know *why*. But this is 1713. Rather a lot has changed. In the æra I am speaking of, it was Alchemy, or nothing. I knew a lot of Alchemists. I peddled them the stuff they needed. Some of those English cavaliers had dabbled in the Art. It was the gentlemanly thing to do. Even the King-in-Exile had a laboratory. After Cromwell had beaten them like kettledrums and sent them packing to France, they found themselves with nothing to pass the years except—" and here, if he'd been telling the story to adults, Enoch would've listed a few of the ways they *had* spent their time.

"Except what, Mr. Root?"

"Studying the hidden laws of God's creation. Some of them—in particular John Comstock and Thomas More Anglesey—fell in with Monsieur LeFebure, who was the apothecary to the French Court. They spent rather a lot of time on Alchemy."

"But wasn't it all stupid nonsense, rot, gibberish, and criminally fraudulent nincompoopery?"

"Godfrey, you are living proof that the apple does not fall far from the tree. Who am I to dispute such matters with your father? Yes. 'Twas all rubbish."

"Then why'd you go to Paris?"

"Partly, if truth be told, I wished to see the coronation of the French King."

"Which one?" asks Godfrey.

"The same one as now!" says Ben, outraged that they are having to waste their time on such questions.

"The big one," Enoch says, "*the* King. Louis the Fourteenth. His formal coronation was in 1654. They anointed him with angel-balm, a thousand years old."

"Eeeyew, it must have stunk to high heaven!"

"Hard to say, in France."

"Where would they've gotten such a thing?"

"Never mind. I am drawing closer to answering the question of *when*. But that was not my whole reason. Really it was that *something was happening*. Huygens—a brilliant youth, of a great family in the Hague—was at work on a pendulum-clock there that was astonishing. Of course, pendulums were an old idea—but he did something simple and beautiful that fixed them so that they would actually tell time! I saw a prototype, ticking away there in that magnificent house, where the afternoon light streamed in off the Plein—that's a sort of square hard by the palace of the Dutch Court. Then down to Paris, where Comstock and Anglesey were toiling away on— you're correct—stupid nonsense. They truly wanted to learn. But they wanted the brilliance of a Huygens, the audacity to invent a whole new discipline. Alchemy was the only way they knew of."

"How'd you cross over to England if there was a sea-war on?"

"French salt-smugglers," says Enoch, as if this were self-evident. "Now, many an English gentleman had made up his mind that staying in London and dabbling with Alchemy was safer than riding 'round the island making war against Cromwell and his New Model Army. So I'd no difficulty lightening my load, and stuffing my purse, in London. Then I nipped up to Oxford, meaning only to pay a call on John Wilkins and pick up some copies of *Cryptonomicon*."

"What is that?" Ben wants to know.

"A very queer old book, dreadfully thick, and full of nonsense," says Godfrey. "Papa uses it to keep the door from blowing shut."

"It is a compendium of secret codes and cyphers that this chap Wilkins had written some years earlier," says Enoch. "In those days, he was Warden of Wadham College, which is part of the University of Oxford. When I arrived, he was steeling himself to make the ultimate sacrifice in the name of Natural Philosophy."

"He was beheaded?" Ben asks

Godfrey: "Tortured?"

Ben: "Mutilated, like?"

"No: he married Cromwell's sister."

"But I thought you said there *was* no Natural Philosophy in those days," Godfrey complains.

"There *was*—once a week, in John Wilkins's chambers at Wadham College," says Enoch. "For that is where the Experimental Philosophical Clubb met. Christopher Wren, Robert Boyle, Robert Hooke, and others you ought to have heard of. By the time I got there, they'd run out of space and moved to an apothecary's shop—a less flammable environment. It was that apothecary, come to think of it, who exhorted me to make the journey north and pay a call on Mr. Clarke in Grantham."

"Have we settled on a year yet?"

"I'll settle on one now, Ben. By the time I reached Oxford, that pendulum-clock I'd seen on the table of Huygens's house in the Hague had been perfected, and set into motion. The first clock worthy of the name. Galileo had timed his experiments by counting his pulse or listening to musicians; but after Huygens we used clocks, which—according to some—told *absolute* time, fixed and invariant. God's time. Huygens published a book about it later; but the clock first began to tick, and the Time of Natural Philosophy began, in the year of Our Lord—"

1655

❦

For between true science and erroneous doctrines,
ignorance is in the middle.

—HOBBES, *Leviathan*

IN EVERY KINGDOM, empire, principality, archbishopric, duchy, and
electorate Enoch had ever visited, the penalty for transmuting base
metals into gold—or trying to—or, in some places, even thinking
about it—was death. This did not worry him especially. It was only
one of a thousand excuses that rulers kept handy to kill inconvenient persons, and to carry it off in a way that made them look
good. For example, if you were in Frankfurt-on-Main, where the
Archbishop-Elector von Schönborn and his minister and sidekick
Boyneburg were both avid practitioners of the Art, you were probably safe.

Cromwell's England was another matter. Since the Puritans had
killed the king and taken the place over, Enoch didn't go around
that Commonwealth (as they styled it now) in a pointy hat with
stars and moons. Not that Enoch the Red had ever been that kind
of alchemist anyway. The old stars-and-moons act was a good way to
farm the unduly trusting. But the need to raise money in the first
place seemed to call into question one's own ability to turn lead
into gold.

Enoch had made himself something of an expert on longevity.
It was only a couple of decades since a Dr. John Lambe had been
killed by the *mobile* in the streets of London. Lambe was a self-styled
sorcerer with high connections at Court. The Mobb had convinced
themselves that Lambe had conjured up a recent thunderstorm
and tornado that had scraped the dirt from graves of some chaps
who had perished in the last round of Plague. Not wishing to end
up in Lambe's position, Enoch had tried to develop the knack of
edging around people's perceptions like one of those dreams that
does not set itself firmly in memory, and is flushed into oblivion by
the first thoughts and sensations of the day.

He'd stayed a week or two in Wilkins's chambers, and attended
meetings of the Experimental Philosophical Clubb. This had been

a revelation to him, for during the Civil War, practically nothing had been heard out of England. The savants of Leipzig, Paris, and Amsterdam had begun to think of it as a rock in the high Atlantic, overrun by heavily armed preachers.

Gazing out Wilkins's windows, studying the northbound traffic, Enoch had been surprised by the number of private traders: adventuresome merchants, taking advantage of the cessation of the Civil War to travel into the country and deal with farmers in the country, buying their produce for less than what it would bring in a city market. They mostly had a Puritan look about them, and Enoch did not especially want to ride in their company. So he'd waited for a full moon and a cloudless night and ridden up to Grantham in the night, arriving before daybreak.

THE FRONT OF CLARKE'S HOUSE was tidy, which told Enoch that Mrs. Clarke was still alive. He led his horse round into the stable-yard. Scattered about were cracked mortars and crucibles, stained yellow and vermilion and silver. A columnar furnace, smoke-stained, reigned over coal-piles. It was littered with rinds of hardened dross raked off the tops of crucibles—the fœces of certain alchemical processes, mingled on this ground with the softer excrement of horses and geese.

Clarke backed out his side-door embracing a brimming chamber-pot.

"Save it up," Enoch said, his voice croaky from not having been used in a day or two, "you can extract much that's interesting from urine."

The apothecary startled, and upon recognizing Enoch he nearly dropped the pot, then caught it, then wished he had dropped it, since these evolutions had set up a complex and dangerous sloshing that must be countervailed by gliding about in a bent-knee gait, melting foot-shaped holes in the frost on the grass, and, as a last resort, tilting the pot when whitecaps were observed. The roosters of Grantham, Lincolnshire, who had slept through Enoch's arrival, came awake and began to celebrate Clarke's performance.

The sun had been rolling along the horizon for hours, like a fat waterfowl making its takeoff run. Well before full daylight, Enoch was inside the apothecary's shop, brewing up a potion from boiled water and an exotic Eastern herb. "Take an amount that will fill the cup of your palm, and throw it in—"

"The water turns brown already!"

"—remove it from the fire or it will be intolerably bitter. I'll require a strainer."

"Do you mean to suggest I'm expected to taste it?"

"Not just *taste* but *drink*. Don't look so condemned. I've done it for months with no effect."

"Other than *addiction,* t'would seem."

"You are too suspicious. The Mahrattas drink it to the exclusion of all else."

"So I'm right about the addiction!"

"It is nothing more than a mild stimulant."

"Mmm . . . not all that bad," Clarke said later, sipping cautiously. "What ailments does it cure?"

"None whatsoever."

"Ah. That's different, then . . . what's it called?"

"*Cha,* or *chai,* or *the,* or *tay.* I know a Dutch merchant who has several tons of it sitting in a warehouse in Amsterdam . . ."

Clarke chuckled. "Oh, no, Enoch, I'll not be drawn into some foreign trading scheme. This tay is inoffensive enough, but I don't think Englishmen will ever take to anything so outlandish."

"Very well, then—we'll speak of other commodities." And, setting down his tay-cup, Enoch reached into his saddle-bags and brought out bags of yellow sulfur he'd collected from a burning mountain in Italy, finger-sized ingots of antimony, heavy flasks of quicksilver, tiny clay crucibles and melting-pots, retorts, spirit-burners, and books with woodcuts showing the design of diverse furnaces. He set them up on the deal tables and counters of the apothecary shop, saying a few words about each one. Clarke stood to one side with his fingers laced together, partly for warmth, and partly just to contain himself from lunging toward the goods. Years had gone by, a Civil War had been prosecuted, and a King's head had rolled in Charing Cross since Clarke had touched some of these items. He imagined that the Continental adepts had been penetrating the innermost secrets of God's creation the entire time. But Enoch knew that the alchemists of Europe were men just like Clarke—hoping, and dreading, that Enoch would return with the news that some English savant, working in isolation, had found the trick of refining, from the base, dark, cold, essentially fœcal matter of which the World was made, the Philosophick Mercury— the pure living essence of God's power and presence in the world—the key to the transmutation of metals, the attainment of immortal life and perfect wisdom.

Enoch was less a merchant than a messenger. The sulfur and antimony he brought as favors. He accepted money in order to pay for his expenses. The important cargo was in his mind. He and Clarke talked for hours.

Sleepy thumping, footfalls, and piping voices sounded from the attic. The staircase boomed and groaned like a ship in a squall. A maid lit a fire and cooked porridge. Mrs. Clarke roused herself and served it to children—too many of them. "Has it been that long?" Enoch asked, listening to their chatter from the next room, trying to tally the voices.

Clarke said, "They're not ours."

"Boarders?"

"Some of the local yeomen send their young ones to my brother's school. We have room upstairs, and my wife is fond of children."

"Are you?"

"Some more than others."

The young boarders dispatched their porridge and mobbed the exit. Enoch drifted over to a window: a lattice of hand-sized, diamond-shaped panes, each pane greenish, warped, and bubbled. Each pane was a prism, so the sun showered the room with rainbows. The children showed as pink mottles, sliding and leaping from one pane to another, sometimes breaking up and recombining like beads of mercury on a tabletop. But this was simply an exaggeration of how children normally looked to Enoch.

One of them, slight and fair-haired, stopped squarely before the window and turned to peer through it. He must have had more acute senses than the others, because he knew that Mr. Clarke had a visitor this morning. Perhaps he'd heard the low murmur of their conversation, or detected an unfamiliar whinny from the stable. Perhaps he was an insomniac who had been studying Enoch through a chink in the wall as Enoch had strolled around the stable-yard before dawn. The boy cupped his hands around his face to block out peripheral sunlight. It seemed that those hands were splashed with colors. From one of them dangled some kind of little project, a toy or weapon made of string.

Then another boy called to him and he spun about, too eagerly, and darted away like a sparrow.

"I'd best be going," Enoch said, not sure why. "Our brethren in Cambridge must know by now that I've been in Oxford—they'll be frantic." With steely politeness he turned aside Clarke's amiable delaying-tactics, declining the offer of porridge, postponing the suggestion that they pray together, insisting that he really needed no rest until he reached Cambridge.

His horse had had only a few hours to feed and doze. Enoch had borrowed it from Wilkins with the implicit promise to treat it kindly, and so rather than mounting into the saddle he led it by the reins down Grantham's high street and in the direction of the school, chatting to it.

He caught sight of the boarders soon enough. They had found stones that needed kicking, dogs that needed fellowship, and a few late apples, still dangling from tree-branches. Enoch lingered in the long shadow of a stone wall and watched the apple project. Some planning had gone into it—a whispered conference between bunks last night. One of the boys had clambered up into the tree and was shinnying out onto the limb in question. It was too slender to bear his weight, but he phant'sied he could bend it low enough to bring it within the tallest boy's jumping-range.

The little fair-haired boy adored the tall boy's fruitless jumping. But he was working on his own project, the same one Enoch had glimpsed through the window: a stone on the end of a string. Not an easy thing to make. He whirled the stone around and flung it upwards. It whipped around the end of the tree-branch. By pulling it down he was able to bring the apple within easy reach. The tall boy stood aside grudgingly, but the fair boy kept both hands on that string, and insisted that the tall one have it as a present. Enoch almost groaned aloud when he saw the infatuation on the little boy's face.

The tall boy's face was less pleasant to look at. He hungered for the apple but suspected a trick. Finally he lashed out and snatched it. Finding the prize in his hand, he looked searchingly at the fair boy, trying to understand his motives, and became unsettled and sullen. He took a bite of the apple as the other watched with almost physical satisfaction. The boy who'd shinnied out onto the tree-limb had come down, and now managed to tease the string off the branch. He examined the way it was tied to the stone and decided that suspicion was the safest course. "A pretty lace-maker you are!" he piped. But the fair-haired boy had eyes only for his beloved.

Then the tall boy spat onto the ground, and tossed the rest of the apple over a fence into a yard where a couple of pigs fought over it.

Now it became unbearable for a while, and made Enoch wish he had never followed them.

The two stupid boys dogged the other one down the road, wide eyes traveling up and down his body, seeing him now for the first time—seeing a little of what Enoch saw. Enoch heard snatches of their taunts—"What's on your hands? What'd you say? Paint!? For what? Pretty pictures? What'd you say? For furniture? I haven't seen any furniture. Oh, *doll* furniture!?"

Being a sooty empiric, what was important to Enoch was not

these tedious details of specifically *how* the boy's heart got broken. He went to the apple tree to have a look at the boy's handiwork.

The boy had imprisoned the stone in a twine net: two sets of helices, one climbing clockwise, the other anti-clockwise, intersecting each other in a pattern of diamonds, just like the lead net that held Clarke's window together. Enoch didn't suppose that this was a coincidence. The work was irregular at the start, but by the time he'd completed the first row of knots the boy had learned to take into account the length of twine spent in making the knots themselves, and by the time he reached the end, it was as regular as the precession of the zodiac.

Enoch then walked briskly to the school and arrived in time to watch the inevitable fight. The fair boy was red-eyed and had porridge-vomit on his chin—it was safe to assume he'd been punched in the stomach. Another schoolboy—there was one in every school—seemed to have appointed himself master of ceremonies, and was goading them to action, paying most attention to the smaller boy, the injured party and presumed loser-to-be of the fight. To the surprise and delight of the community of young scholars, the smaller boy stepped forward and raised his fists.

Enoch approved, so far. Some pugnacity in the lad would be useful. Talent was not rare; the ability to survive having it was.

Then combat was joined. Not many punches were thrown. The small boy did something clever, down around the tall boy's knees, that knocked him back on his arse. Almost immediately the little boy's knee was in the other's groin, then in the pit of his stomach, and then on his throat. And then, suddenly, the tall boy was struggling to get up—but only because the fair-haired boy was trying to rip both of his ears off. Like a farmer dragging an ox by his nose-ring, the smaller boy led the bigger one over to the nearest stone wall, which happened to be that of Grantham's huge, ancient church, and then began to rub his prisoner's face against it as though trying to erase it from the skull.

Until this point the other boys had been jubilant. Even Enoch had found the early stages of the victory stirring in a way. But as this torture went on, the boys' faces went slack. Many of them turned and ran away. The fair-haired boy had flown into a state of something like ecstasy—groping and flailing like a man nearing erotic climax, his body an insufficient vehicle for his passions, a dead weight impeding the flowering of the spirit. Finally an adult man—Clarke's brother?—banged out through a door and stormed across the yard between school and church in the tottering gait of a man unaccustomed to having to move quickly, carrying a cane but not touching the ground with it. He was so angry that he did not utter a word, or try to separate the boys, but simply began to cut air with the cane, like a blind man fending off a bear, as he got close. Soon enough he maneuvered within range of the fair boy and planted his feet and bent to his work, the cane producing memorable whorling noises cut off by pungent whacks. A few brown-nosers now considered it safe to approach. Two of them dragged the fair boy off of his victim, who contracted into a fetal position at the base of the church wall, hands open like the covers of a book to enfold his wrecked face. The schoolmaster adjusted his azimuth as the target moved, like a telescope tracking a comet, but none of his blows seemed to have been actually felt by the fair boy yet—he wore a look of steadfast, righteous triumph, much like Enoch supposed Cromwell must have shown as he beheld the butchering of the Irish at Drogheda.

The boy was dragged inside for higher punishments. Enoch rode back to Clarke's apothecary shop, reining in a silly urge to gallop through the town like a Cavalier.

Clarke was sipping tay and gnawing biscuits, already several pages into a new alchemical treatise, moving crumb-spattered lips as he solved the Latin.

"Who is he?" Enoch demanded, coming in the door.

Clarke elected to play innocent. Enoch crossed the room and found the stairs. He didn't really care about the name anyway. It would just be another English name.

The upstairs was all one odd-shaped room with low adze-marked rafters and rough plaster walls that had once been white-washed. Enoch hadn't visited many children's rooms, but to him it seemed like a den of thieves hastily abandoned and stumbled upon by a plodding constable, filled with evidence of many peculiar, ingenious, frequently unwise plots and machinations suddenly cut short. He stopped in the doorway and steadied himself. Like a good empiric, he had to see all and alter nothing.

The walls were marked with what his eyes first took to be the grooves left behind by a careless plasterer's trowel, but as his pupils dilated, he understood that Mr. and Mrs. Clarke's boarders had been drawing on the walls, apparently with bits of charcoal fetched out of the grate. It was plain to see which pictures had been drawn by whom. Most were caricatures learned by rote from slightly older children. Others—generally closer to the floor—were maps of insight, manifestoes of intelligence, always precise, sometimes beautiful. Enoch had been right in supposing that the boy had excellent senses. Things that others did not see at all, or chose not to register out of some kind of mental obstinacy, this boy took in avidly.

There were four tiny beds. The litter of toys on the floor was generally boyish, but over by one bed there was a tendency toward ribbons and frills. Clarke had mentioned one of the boarders was a girl. There was a dollhouse and a clan of rag dolls in diverse phases of ontogeny. Here there'd been a meeting of interests. There was doll furniture ingeniously made by the same regular mind and clever hands that had woven the net round the stone. The boy had made stalks of grass into rattan tables, and willow twigs into rocking-chairs. The alchemist in him had been at work copying recipes from that old corrupter of curious youths, Bates's *The Mysteries of Nature & Art,* extracting pigments from plants and formulating paints.

He had tried to draw sketches of the other boys while they were sleeping—the only time they could be relied on to hold still and not behave abominably. He did not yet have the skill to make a regular portrait, but from time to time the Muse would take hold of his hand, and in a fortunate sweep of the arm he'd capture something beautiful in the curve of a jawbone or an eyelash.

There were broken and dismantled parts of machines that Enoch did not understand. Later, though, perusing the notebook where the boy had been copying out recipes, Enoch found sketches of the hearts of rats and birds that the boy had apparently dissected. Then the little machines made sense. For what was the heart but the model for the perpetual motion machine? And what was the perpetual motion machine but Man's attempt to make a thing that would do what the heart did? To harness the heart's occult power and bend it to use.

The apothecary had joined him in the room. Clarke looked nervous. "You're up to something clever, aren't you?" Enoch said.

"By that, do you mean—"

"He came your way by chance?"

"Not precisely. His mother knows my wife. I had seen the boy."

"And seen that he had promise—as how could you not."

"He lacks a father. I made a recommendation to the mother. She is steady. Intermittently decent. Quasi-literate . . ."

"But too thick to know what she has begotten?"

"Oh my, yes."

"So you took the boy under your wing—and if he's shown some interest in the Art you have not discouraged it."

"Of course not! He could be the one, Enoch."

"He's not the one," Enoch said. "Not the one you are thinking of. Oh, he will be a great empiricist. He will, perhaps, be the one to accomplish some great thing we have never imagined."

"Enoch, what can you possibly be talking about?"

It made his head ache. How was he to explain it without making Clarke out to be a fool, and himself a swindler? "Something is happening."

Clarke pursed his lips and waited for something a little more specific.

"Galileo and Descartes were only harbingers. Something is happening now—the mercury is rising in the ground, like water climbing up the bore of a well."

Enoch couldn't get Oxford out of his mind—Hooke and Wren and Boyle, all exchanging thoughts so quickly that flames practically leaped between them. He decided to try another tack. "There's a boy in Leipzig like this one. Father died recently, leaving him nothing except a vast library. The boy began reading those books. Only six years old."

"It's not unheard-of for six-year-olds to read."

"German, Latin, and Greek?"

"With proper instruction—"

"That's just it. The boy's teachers prevailed on the mother to lock the child out of the library. I got wind of it. Talked to the mother, and secured a promise from her that little Gottfried would be allowed free run of the books. He taught himself Latin and Greek in the space of a year."

Clarke shrugged. "Very well. Perhaps little Gottfried is the one."

Enoch then should've known it was hopeless, but he tried again: "We are empiricists—we scorn the Scholastic way of memorizing old books and rejecting what is new—and that is good. But in pinning our hopes on the Philosophick Mercury we have decided in advance what it is that we seek to discover, and that is never right."

This merely made Clarke nervous. Enoch tried yet another tack: "I have in my saddlebags a copy of *Principia Philosophica*, the last thing Descartes wrote before he died. Dedicated to young Elizabeth, the Winter Queen's daughter . . ."

Clarke was straining to look receptive, like a dutiful university student still intoxicated from last night's recreations at the tavern. Enoch remembered the stone on the string, and decided to aim for something more concrete. "Huygens has made a clock that is regulated by a pendulum."

"Huygens?"

"A young Dutch savant. Not an alchemist."

"Oh!"

"He has worked out a way to make a pendulum that will always go back and forth in the same amount of time. By connecting it to the internal workings of a clock, he has wrought a perfectly regular time-piece. Its ticks divide infinity, as calipers step out leagues on a map. With these two—clock and calipers—we can measure both extent and duration. And this, combined with the new method of analysis of Descartes, gives us a way to describe Creation and perhaps to predict the future."

"Ah, I see!" Clarke said. "So this Huygens—he is some kind of astrologer?"

"No, no, no! He is neither astrologer nor alchemist. He is something new. More like him will follow. Wilkins, down in Oxford, is trying to bring them together. Their achievements may exceed those of alchemists." If they did not, Enoch thought, he'd be chagrined. "I am suggesting to you that this little boy may turn out to be another one like Huygens."

"You want me to steer him away from the Art?" Clarke exclaimed.

"Not if he shows interest. But beyond that do not steer him at all—let him pursue his own conclusions." Enoch looked at the faces and diagrams on the wall, noting some rather good perspective work. "And see to it that mathematics is brought to his attention."

"I do not think that he has the temperament to be a mere computer," Clarke warned. "Sitting at his pages day after day, drudging out tables of logarithms, cube roots, cosines—"

"Thanks to Descartes, there are other uses for mathematics now," Enoch said. "Tell your brother to show the boy Euclid and let him find his own way."

THE CONVERSATION MIGHT NOT HAVE gone precisely this way. Enoch had the same way with his memories as a ship's master with his rigging—a compulsion to tighten what was slack, mend what was frayed, caulk what leaked, and stow, or throw overboard, what was to no purpose. So the conversation with Clarke might have wandered into quite a few more blind alleys than he remembered. A great deal of time was probably spent on politeness. Certainly it took up most of that short autumn day. Because Enoch didn't ride out of Grantham until late. He passed by the school one more time on his way down towards Cambridge. All the boys had gone home by that hour save one, who'd been made to stay behind and, as punishment, scrub and scrape his own name off the various windowsills and chair-backs where he'd inscribed it. These infractions had probably been noticed by Clarke's brother, who had saved them up for the day when the child would need particular discipline.

The sun, already low at mid-afternoon, was streaming into the open windows. Enoch drew up along the northwest side of the school so that anyone who looked back at him would see only a long hooded shadow, and watched the boy work for a while. The sun was crimson in the boy's face, which was ruddy to begin with from his exertions with the scrub-brush. Far from being reluctant, he seemed enthusiastic about the job of erasing all traces of himself from the school—as if the tumbledown place was unworthy to bear his mark. One windowsill after another came under him and was wiped clean of the name I. NEWTON.

Newtowne, Massachusetts Bay Colony
OCTOBER 12, 1713

> How are these Colonies of the *English* increas'd and improv'd, even to such a Degree, that some have suggested, tho' not for Want of Ignorance, a Danger of their revolting from the *English* Government, and setting up an Independency of Power for themselves. It is true, the Notion is absurd, and without Foundation, but serves to confirm what I have said above of the real Encrease of those Colonies, and of the flourishing Condition of the Commerce carried on there.
>
> —DANIEL DEFOE, *A Plan of the English Commerce*

SOMETIMES IT SEEMS AS IF *everyone's* immigrating to America—sailing-ships on the North Atlantic as thick as watermen's boats on the Thames, more or less wearing ruts in the sea-lanes—and so, in an idle way, Enoch supposes that his appearance on the threshold of the Massachusetts Bay Colony Institute of Technologickal Arts will come as no surprise at all to its founder. But Daniel Waterhouse nearly swallows his teeth when Enoch walks through the door, and it's not just because the hem of Enoch's cloak knocks over a great teetering stack of cards. For a moment Enoch's afraid that some sort of apoplectic climax is in progress, and that Dr. Waterhouse's final contribution to the Royal Society, after nearly a lifetime of service, will be a traumatically deranged cardiac muscle, pickled in spirits of wine in a crystal jug. The Doctor spends the first minute of their interview frozen halfway between sitting and standing, with his mouth open and his left hand on his breastbone. This might be the beginnings of a courteous bow, or a hasty maneuver to conceal, beneath his coat, a shirt so work-stained as to cast aspersions on his young wife's diligence. Or perhaps it's a *philosophick* enquiry, viz. checking his own pulse—if so, it's good news, because Sir John Floyer just invented the practice, and if Daniel Waterhouse knows of it, it means he's been keeping up with the latest work out of London.

Enoch takes advantage of the lull to make other observations and try to judge empirically whether Daniel's as unsound as the faculty of Harvard College would have him believe. From the Doctors' jibes on the ferry-ride, Enoch had expected nothing but cranks and gears. And indeed Waterhouse does have a mechanic's shop in a corner of the—how will Enoch characterize this structure to the Royal Society? "Log cabin," while technically correct, calls to mind wild men in skins. "Sturdy, serviceable, and in no way extravagant laboratory making ingenious use of indigenous building materials." There. But anyway, most of it is given over not to the hard ware of gears, but to softer matters: cards. They are stacked in slender columns that would totter in the breeze from a moth's wings if the columns had not been jammed together into banks, stairways, and terraces, the whole formation built on a layer of loose tiles on the dirt floor to (Enoch guesses) prevent the card-stacks from wicking up the copious ground-water. Edging farther into the room and peering round a bulwark of card-stacks, Enoch finds a writing-desk stocked with blank cards. Ragged gray quills project from inkpots, bent and broken ones crosshatch the floor, bits of down and fluff and cartilage and other bird-wreckage form a dandruffy layer on everything.

On pretext of cleaning up his mess, Enoch begins to pick the spilled cards off the floor. Each is marked at the top with a rather large number, always odd, and beneath it a long row of ones and zeroes, which (since the last digit is always 1, indicating an odd number) he takes to be nothing other then the selfsame number expressed in the binary notation lately perfected by Leibniz.

Underneath the number, then, is a word or short phrase, a different one on each card. As he picks them up and re-stacks them he sees: *Noah's Ark; Treaties terminating wars; Membranophones (e.g., mirlitons); The notion of a classless society; The pharynx and its outgrowths; Drawing instruments (e.g., T-squares); The Skepticism of Pyrrhon of Elis; Requirements for valid maritime insurance contracts; The Kamakura* bakufu; *The fallacy of Assertion without Knowledge; Agates; Rules governing the determination of questions of fact in Roman civil courts; Mummification; Sunspots; The sex organs of bryophytes (e.g., liverwort); Euclidean geometry—homotheties and similitudes; Pantomime; The Election & Reign of Rudolf of Hapsburg; Testes; Nonsymmetrical dyadic relations; the Investiture Controversy; Phosphorus; Traditional impotence remedies; the Arminian heresy;* and—

"Some of these strike one as being too complicated for monads," he says, desperate for some way to break the ice. "Such as this—'The Development of Portuguese Hegemony over Central Africa.' "

"Look at the number at the top of that card," Waterhouse says. "It is the product of five primes: one for *development,* one for *Portuguese,* one for *Hegemony,* one for *Central,* and one for *Africa.*"

"Ah, so it's not a monad at all, but a composite."

"Yes."

"It's difficult to tell when the cards are helter-skelter. Don't you think you should organize them?"

"According to what scheme?" Waterhouse asks shrewdly.

"Oh, no, I'll not be tricked into *that* discussion."

"No linear indexing system is adequate to express the multi-dimensionality of knowledge," Dr. Waterhouse reminds him. "But if each one is assigned a unique number—prime numbers for monads, and products of primes for composites—then organizing them is simply a matter of performing computations . . . *Mr. Root.*"

"Dr. Waterhouse. Pardon the interruption."

"Not at all." He sits back down, finally, and goes back to what he was doing before: running a long file back and forth over a chunk of metal with tremendous sneezing noises. "It is a welcome diversion to have you appear before me, so unlooked-for, so *implausibly well-preserved,*" he shouts over the keening of the warm tool and the ringing of the work-piece.

"Durability is preferable to the alternative—but not always convenient. Less hale persons are forever sending me off on errands."

"Lengthy and tedious ones at that."

"The journey's dangers, discomforts, and tedium are more than compensated for by the sight of you, so productively occupied, and in such good health." Or something like that. This is the polite part of the conversation, which is not likely to last much longer. If he had returned the compliment, Daniel would have scoffed, because no one would say he's well preserved in the sense that Enoch is. He looks as old as he ought to. But he's wiry, with clear, sky-blue eyes, no tremors in his jaw or his hands, no hesitation in his speech once he's over the shock of seeing Enoch (or, perhaps, *anyone*) in his Institute. Daniel Waterhouse is almost completely bald, with a fringe of white hair clamping the back of his head like wind-hammered snow on a tree-trunk. He makes no apologies for being uncovered and does not reach for a wig—indeed, appears not to *own* one. His eyes are large, wide and staring in a way that probably does nothing to improve his reputation. Those orbs flank a hawk-ish nose that nearly conceals the slot-like mouth of a miser biting down on a suspect coin. His ears are elongated and have grown a radiant fringe of lanugo. The imbalance between his organs of input and output seems to say that he sees and knows more than he'll say.

"Are you a colonist now, or—"

"I'm here to see you."

The eyes stare back, knowing and calm. "So it is a social visit! That is heroic—when a simple exchange of letters is so much less fraught with seasickness, pirates, scurvy, mass drownings—"

"Speaking of letters—I've one here," Enoch says, taking it out.

"Great big magnificent seal. Someone dreadfully important must've written it. Can't say how impressed I am."

"Personal friend of Dr. Leibniz."

"The Electress Sophie?"

"No, the other one."

"Ah. What does Princess Caroline want of me? Must be something appalling, or else she wouldn't've sent you to chivvy me along."

Dr. Waterhouse is embarrassed at having been so startled earlier and is making up for it with peevishness. But it's fine, because it seems to Enoch that the thirty-year-old Waterhouse hidden inside the old man is now pressing outward against the loose mask of skin, like a marble sculpture informing its burlap wrappings.

"Think of it as coaxing you forward. Dr. Waterhouse! Let's find a tavern and—"

"We'll find a tavern—after I've had an answer. What does she want of me?"

"The same thing as ever."

Dr. Waterhouse shrinks—the inner thirty-year-old recedes, and he becomes just an oddly familiar-looking gaffer. "Should've known. What other use is there for a broken-down old computational monadologist?"

"It's remarkable."

"What?"

"I've known you for—what—thirty or forty years now, almost as long as you've known Leibniz. I've seen you in some unenviable spots. But in all that time, I don't believe I've ever heard you whine, until just then."

Daniel considers this carefully, then actually laughs. "My apologies."

"Not at all!"

"I thought my work would be appreciated here. I was going to establish what, to Harvard, would've been what Gresham's College was to Oxford. Imagined I'd find a student body, or at least a pro-tégé. Someone who could help me build the Logic Mill. Hasn't worked out that way. All of the mechanically talented sorts are dreaming of steam-engines. Ludicrous! What's wrong with water-wheels? Plenty of rivers here. Look, there's a little one right between your feet!"

"Engines are naturally more interesting to the young."

"You needn't tell me. When I was a student, a *prism* was a won-der. Went to Sturbridge Fair with Isaac to buy them—little miracles wrapped in velvet. Played with 'em for months."

"This fact is now widely known."

"Now the lads are torn every direction at once, like a prisoner being quartered. Or eighthed, or sixteenthed. I can already see it happening to young Ben out there, and soon it'll happen to my own boy. 'Should I study mathematics? Euclidean or Cartesian? Newtonian or Leibnizian calculus? Or should I go the empirical route? Will it be dissecting animals then, or classifying weeds, or making strange matters in crucibles? Rolling balls down inclined planes? Sporting with electricity and magnets?' Against that, what's in my shack here to interest them?"

"Could this lack of interest have something to do with that everyone knows the project was conceived by Leibniz?"

"I'm not doing it his way. His plan was to use balls running down troughs to represent the binary digits, and pass them through mechanical gates to perform the logical operations. Ingenious, but not very practical. I'm using pushrods."

"Superficial. I ask again: could your lack of popularity here be related to that all Englishmen believe that Leibniz is a villain—a plagiarist?"

"This is an unnatural turn in the conversation, Mr. Root. Are you being devious?"

"Only a little."

"You and your Continental ways."

"It's just that the priority dispute has lately turned vicious."

"Knew it would happen."

"I don't think you appreciate just how unpleasant it is."

"You don't appreciate how well I know Sir Isaac."

"I'm saying that its repercussions may extend to here, to this very room, and might account for your (forgive me for mentioning this) solitude, and slow progress."

"Ludicrous!"

"Have you seen the latest flying letters, speeding about Europe unsigned, undated, devoid of even a printer's mark? The anonymous reviews, planted, like sapper's mines, in the journals of the savants? Sudden unmaskings of hitherto unnamed 'leading mathematicians' forced to own, or deny, opinions they have long disseminated in private correspondence? Great minds who, in any other era, would be making discoveries of Copernican significance, reduced to acting as cat's-paws and hired leg-breakers for the two principals? New and deservedly obscure journals suddenly elevated to the first rank of learned discourse, simply because some lackey has caused his latest stiletto-thrust to be printed in its back pages? Challenge problems flying back and forth across the Channel, each one fiendishly devised to prove that Leibniz's calculus is the original, and Newton's but a shoddy counterfeit, or vice versa? Reputations tossed about on points of swords—"

"No," Daniel says. "I moved here to get away from European intrigues." His eyes drop to the Letter. Enoch can't help looking at it, too.

"It is purely an anomaly of fate," Enoch says, "that Gottfried, as a young man, lacking means, seeking a position—anything that would give him the simple freedom to work—landed in the court of an obscure German Duke. Who through intricate and tedious lacework of marryings, couplings, dyings, religious conversions, wars, revolutions, miscarriages, decapitations, congenital feeble-mindedness, excommunications, *et cetera* among Europe's elite—most notably, the deaths of all seventeen of Queen Anne's children—became first in line to the Throne of England and Scotland, or Great Britain as we're supposed to call it now."

"*Some* would call it fate. Others—"

"Let's not get into *that*."

"Agreed."

"Anne's in miserable health, the House of Hanover is packing up its pointed helmets and illustrated beer-mugs, and taking English lessons. Sophie may get to be Queen of England yet, at least for a short while. But soon enough, George Louis will become Newton's King and—as Sir Isaac is still at the Mint—his boss."

"I take your point. It is most awkward."

"George Louis is the embodiment of awkwardness—he doesn't care, and scarcely knows, and would probably think it amusing if he did. But his daughter-in-law the Princess—author of this letter—in time likely to become Queen of England herself—is a friend of Leibniz. And yet an admirer of Newton. She wants a reconciliation."

"She wants a dove to fly between the Pillars of Hercules. Which are still runny with the guts of the previous several peace-makers."

"It's supposed that you are different."

"Herculean, perhaps?"

"Well . . ."

"Do you have any idea why I'm different, Mr. Root?"

"I do not, Dr. Waterhouse."

"The tavern it is, then."

BEN AND GODFREY ARE SENT back to Boston on the ferry. Daniel scorns the nearest tavern—some sort of long-running dispute with the proprietor—so they find the highway and ride northwest for a couple of miles, drawing off to one side from time to time to let drovers bring their small herds of Boston-bound cattle through. They arrive at what used to be the capital of Massachusetts, before the city fathers of Boston out-maneuvered it. Several roads lunge out of the wilderness and collide with one another. Yeomen and drovers and backwoodsmen churn it up into a vortex of mud and manure. Next to it is a College. Newtowne is, in other words, paradise for tavern-keepers, and the square (as they style it) is lined with public houses.

Waterhouse enters a tavern but immediately backs out of it. Looking into the place over his companion's shoulder, Enoch glimpses a white-wigged Judge on a massive chair at the head of the tap-room, a jury empaneled on plank benches, a grimy rogue being interrogated. "Not a good place for a pair of idlers," Waterhouse mumbles.

"You hold *judicial proceedings* in *drinking-houses*!?"

"Poh! That judge is no more drunk than any magistrate of the Old Bailey."

"It is perfectly logical when you put it that way."

Daniel chooses another tavern. They walk through its brick-red door. A couple of leather fire-buckets dangle by the entrance, in accordance with safety regulations, and a bootjack hangs on the wall so that the innkeeper can take his guests' footwear hostage at night. The proprietor is bastioned in a little wooden fort in the corner, bottles on shelves behind him, a preposterous firearm, at least six feet long, leaning in the angle of the walls. He's busy sorting his customers' mail. Enoch cannot believe the size of the planks that make up the floor. They creak and pop like ice on a frozen lake as people move around. Waterhouse leads him to a table. It consists of a single slab of wood sawn from the heart of a tree that must have been at least three feet in diameter.

"Trees such as these have not been seen in Europe for hundreds of years," Enoch says. He measures it against the length of his arm. "Should have gone straight to Her Majesty's Navy. I am shocked."

"There is an exemption to that rule," Waterhouse says, showing for the first time a bit of good humor. "If a tree is blown down by the wind, anyone may salvage it. In consequence of which, Gomer Bolstrood, and his fellow Barkers, have built their colonies in remote places, where the trees are very large—"

"And where freak hurricanoes often strike without warning?"

"And without being noticed by any of their neighbors. Yes."

"Firebrands to furniture-makers in a single generation. I wonder what old Knott would think."

"Firebrands *and* furniture-makers," Waterhouse corrects him.

"Ah, well . . . If my name were Bolstrood, I'd be happy to live anywhere that was beyond the reach of Tories and Archbishops."

Daniel Waterhouse rises and goes over to the fireplace, plucks a couple of loggerheads from their hooks, and thrusts them angrily into the coals. Then he goes to the corner and speaks with the tavern-keeper, who cracks two eggs into two mugs and then begins throwing in rum and bitters and molasses. It is sticky and complicated—as is the entire situation here that Enoch's gotten himself into.

There's a similar room on the other side of the wall, reserved for the ladies. Spinning wheels whirr, cards chafe against wool. Someone begins tuning up a bowed instrument. Not the old-fashioned viol, but (judging from its sound) a violin. Hard to believe, considering where he is. But then the musician begins to play—and instead of a Baroque minuet, it is a weird keening sort of melody—an Irish tune, unless he's mistaken. It's like using watered silk to make grain sacks—the Londoners would laugh until tears ran down their faces. Enoch goes and peers through the doorway to make sure he's not imagining it. Indeed, a girl with carrot-colored hair is playing a violin, entertaining some other women who are spinning and sewing, and the women and the music are as Irish as the day is long.

Enoch goes back to the table, shaking his head. Daniel Waterhouse slides a hot loggerhead into each mug, warming and thickening the drinks. Enoch sits down, takes a sip of the stuff, and decides he likes it. Even the music is beginning to grow on him.

He cannot look in any direction without seeing eyeballs just in the act of glancing away from them. Some of the other patrons actually run down the road to *other* taverns to advertise their presence here, as if Root and Waterhouse were a public entertainment. Dons and students saunter in nonchalantly, as if it's normal to stand up in mid-pint and move along to a different establishment.

"Where'd you get the idea you were escaping from intrigue?"

Daniel ignores this, too busy glaring at the other customers.

"My father, Drake, educated me for one reason alone," Daniel finally says. "To assist him in his preparations for the Apocalypse. He reckoned it would occur in the year 1666—Number of the Beast and all that. I was, therefore, produced in 1646—as always, Drake's timing was carefully thought out. When I came of age, I would be a man of the cloth, with the full university education, well versed in many dead classical languages, so that I could stand on the Cliffs of Dover and personally welcome Jesus Christ back to England in fluent Aramaic. Sometimes I look about myself—" he waves his arm at the tavern "—and see the way it turned out, and wonder whether my father could possibly have been any more wrong."

"I think this is a good place for you," Enoch says. "Nothing here is going according to plan. The music. The furniture. It's all contrary to expectations."

"My father and I took in the execution of Hugh Peters—Cromwell's chaplain—in London one day. We rode straight from that spectacle to Cambridge. Since executions are customarily held at daybreak, you see, an industrious Puritan can view one and yet get in a full day's hard traveling and working before evening prayers. It was done with a knife. Drake wasn't shaken at all by the sight of Brother Hugh's intestines. It only made him that much more determined to get me into Cambridge. We went there and called upon Wilkins at Trinity College."

"Hold, my memory fails—wasn't Wilkins at *Oxford*? Wadham College?"

"Anno 1656 he married Robina. Cromwell's sister."

"*That* I remember."

"Cromwell made him Master of Trinity College in Cambridge. But of course that was undone by the Restoration. So he only served in that post for a few months—it's no wonder you've forgotten it."

"Very well. Pardon the interruption. Drake took you up to Cambridge—?"

"And we called on Wilkins. I was fourteen. Father went off and left us alone, secure in the knowledge that this man—Cromwell's Brother-in-Law, for God's sake!—would lead me down the path of righteousness—perhaps explicate some Bible verses about nine-headed beasts with me, perhaps pray for Hugh Peters."

"You did neither, I presume."

"You must imagine a great chamber in Trinity, a gothickal stone warren, like the underbelly of some ancient cathedral, ancient tables scattered about, stained and burnt alchemically, beakers and retorts clouded with residues pungent and bright, but most of all, *the books*—brown wads stacked like cordwood—more books than I'd ever seen in one room. It was a decade or two since Wilkins had written his great *Cryptonomicon*. In the course of that project, he had, of course, gathered tomes on occult writing from all over the world, compiling all that had been known, since the time of the Ancients, about the writing of secrets. The publication of that book had brought him fame among those who study such things. Copies were known to have circulated as far as Peking, Lima, Isfahan, Shahjahanabad. Consequently more books *yet* had been sent to him, from Portuguese crypto-Kabbalists, Arabic savants skulking through the ruins and ashes of Alexandria, Parsees who secretly worship at the altar of Zoroaster, Armenian merchants who must communicate all across the world, in a kind of net-work of information, through subtle signs and symbols hidden in the margins and the ostensible text of letters so cleverly that a competitor, intercepting the message, could examine it and find nothing but trivial chatter—yet a fellow-Armenian could extract the vital *data* as easy as you or I would read a hand-bill in the street. Secret code-systems of Mandarins, too, who because of their Chinese writing cannot use cyphers as we do, but must hide messages in the position of characters on the sheet, and other means so devious that whole lifetimes must have gone into thinking of them. All of these things had come to him because of the fame of the *Cryptonomicon*, and to appreciate my position, you must understand that I'd been raised, by Drake and Knott and the others, to believe that every word and character of these books was Satanic. That, if I were to so much as lift the cover of one of these books, and expose my eyes to the occult characters within, I'd be sucked down into Tophet just like that."

"I can see it made quite an impression on you—"

"Wilkins let me sit in a chair for half an hour just to soak the place in. Then we began mucking about in his chambers, and set fire to a tabletop. Wilkins was reading some proofs of Boyle's *The Skeptical Chemist*—you should read it sometime, Enoch, by the way—"

"I'm familiar with its contents."

"Wilkins and I were idly trying to reproduce one of Boyle's experiments when things got out of hand. Fortunately no serious damage was done. It wasn't a serious fire, but it accomplished what Wilkins wanted it to: wrecked the mask of etiquette that Drake had set over me, and set my tongue a-run. I must have looked as if I'd gazed upon the face of God. Wilkins let slip that, if it was an actual *education* I was looking for, there was this thing down in London called Gresham's College where he and a few of his old Oxford cronies were teaching Natural Philosophy *directly*, without years and years of tedious Classical nincompoopery as prerequisite.

"Now, I was too young to even think of being devious. Even had I practiced to be clever, I'd have had second thoughts doing it in *that* room. So I simply told Wilkins the truth: I had no interest in religion, at least as a profession, and wanted only to be a natural philosopher like Boyle or Huygens. But of course Wilkins had already discerned this. 'Leave it in my hands,' he said, and winked at me.

"Drake would not hear of sending me to Gresham's, so two years later I enrolled at that old vicar-mill: Trinity College, Cambridge. Father believed that I did so in fulfillment of his plan for me. Wilkins meanwhile had come up with his own plan for my life. And so you see, Enoch, I am well accustomed to others devising hare-brained plans for how I am to live. That is why I have come to Massachusetts, and why I do not intend to leave it."

"Your intentions are your own business. I merely ask that you read the letter," Enoch says.

"What sudden event caused you to be sent here, Enoch? A falling-out between Sir Isaac and a young protégé?"

"Remarkable guesswork!"

"It's no more a guess than when Halley predicted the return of the comet. Newton's bound by his own laws. He's been working on the second edition of the *Principia* with that young fellow, what's-his-name . . ."

"Roger Cotes."

"Promising, fresh-faced young lad, is he?"

"Fresh-faced, beyond doubt," Enoch says, "promising, until . . ."

"Until he made some kind of a misstep, and Newton flew into a rage, and flung him into the Lake of Fire."

"Apparently. Now, all that Cotes was working on—the revised *Principia Mathematica* and some kind of reconciliation with Leibniz—is ruined, or at least stopped."

"Isaac never cast me into the Lake of Fire," Daniel muses. "I was so young and so obviously innocent—he could never think the worst of me, as he does of everyone else."

"Thank you for reminding me! Please." Enoch shoves the letter across the table.

Daniel breaks the seal and hauls it open. He fishes spectacles from a pocket and holds them up to his face with one hand, as if actually fitting them over his ears would imply some sort of binding commitment. At first he locks his elbow to regard the whole letter as a work of calligraphic art, admiring its graceful loops and swirls. "Thank God it's not written in those barbarous German letters," he says. Finally the elbow bends, and he gets down to actually reading it.

As he nears the bottom of the first page, a transformation comes over Daniel's face.

"As you have probably noted," Enoch says, "the Princess, fully appreciating the hazards of a trans-Atlantic voyage, has arranged an insurance policy . . ."

"A posthumous bribe!" Daniel says. "The Royal Society is infested with actuaries and statisticians nowadays—drawing up tables for those swindlers at the 'Change. You must have 'run the numbers' and computed the odds of a man my age surviving a voyage across the Atlantic; months or even years in that pestilential metropolis; and a journey back to Boston."

"Daniel! We most certainly did not 'run the numbers.' It's only reasonable for the Princess to insure you."

"At this amount? This is a pension—a *legacy*—for my wife and my son."

"Do you have a pension now, Daniel?"

"What!? Compared to this, I have nothing." Flicking one nail angrily upon a train of zeroes inscribed in the heart of the letter.

"Then it seems as if Her Royal Highness is making a persuasive case."

Waterhouse has just, at this instant, realized that very soon he is going to climb aboard ship and sail for London. That much can be read from his face. But he's still an hour or two away from admitting it. They will be difficult hours for Enoch.

"Even without the insurance policy," Enoch says, "it would be in your best interests. Natural philosophy, like war and romance, is best done by young men. Sir Isaac has not done any creative work since he had that mysterious catastrophe in '93."

"It's not mysterious to *me*."

"Since then, it's been toiling at the Mint, and working up new versions of old books, and vomiting flames at Leibniz."

"And you are advising me to emulate *that?*"

"I am advising you to put down the file, pack up your cards, step back from the workbench, and consider the future of the revolution."

"What revolution can you possibly be talking about? There was the Glorious one back in '88, and people are nattering on about throwing one here, but . . ."

"Don't be disingenuous, Daniel. You speak and think in a language that did not exist when you and Sir Isaac entered Trinity."

"Fine, fine. If you want to call it a revolution, I won't quibble."

"That revolution is turning on itself now. The calculus dispute is becoming a schism between the natural philosophers of the Continent and those of Great Britain. The British have far more to lose. Already there's a reluctance to use Leibniz's techniques—which are now more advanced, since he actually bothered to disseminate his ideas. Your difficulties in starting the Massachusetts Bay Colony Institute of Technologickal Arts are a symptom of the same ailment. So do not lurk on the fringes of civilization trifling with cards and cranks, Dr. Waterhouse. Return to the core, look at first causes, heal the central wound. If you can accomplish that, why, then, by the time your son is of an age to become a student, the Institute will no longer be a log cabin sinking into the mire, but a campus of domed pavilions and many-chambered laboratories along the banks of the River Charles, where the most ingenious youth of America will convene to study and refine the art of automatic computation!"

Dr. Waterhouse is favoring him with a look of bleak pity usually directed toward uncles too far gone to know they are incontinent. "Or at least I might catch a fever and die three days from now and provide Faith and Godfrey with a comfortable pension."

"There's that added inducement."

To be a European Christian (the rest of the world might be forgiven for thinking) was to build ships and sail them to any and all coasts not already a-bristle with cannons, make landfall at river's mouth, kiss the dirt, plant a cross or a flag, scare the hell out of any indigenes with a musketry demo', and—having come so far, and suffered and risked so much—unpack a shallow basin and scoop up some muck from the river-bottom. Whirled about, the basin became a vortex, shrouded in murk for a few moments as the silt rose into the current like dust from a cyclone. But as that was blown away by the river's current, the shape of the vortex was revealed. In its middle was an eye of dirt that slowly disintegrated from the outside in as lighter granules were shouldered to the outside and cast off. Left in the middle was a huddle of nodes, heavier than all the rest. Blue eyes from far away attended to these, for sometimes they were shiny and yellow.

Now, 'twere easy to call such men stupid (not even broaching the subjects of greedy, violent, arrogant, *et cetera*), for there was something wilfully idiotic in going to an unknown country, ignoring its people, their languages, art, its beasts and butterflies, flowers, herbs, trees, ruins, *et cetera*, and reducing it all to a few lumps of heavy matter in the center of a dish. Yet as Daniel, in the tavern, tries to rake together his early memories of Trinity and of Cambridge, he's chagrined to find that a like process has been going on within his skull for half a century.

The impressions he received in those years had been as infinitely various as what confronted a Conquistador when he dragged his longboat up onto an uncharted shore. *Bewilderment*, in its ancient and literal sense of being cast away in a trackless wild, was the lot of the explorer, and it well described Daniel's state of mind during his first years at Trinity. The analogy was not all that far-fetched, for Daniel had matriculated just after the Restoration, and found himself among young men of the Quality who'd spent most of their lives in Paris. Their clothing struck Daniel's eye much as the gorgeous plumage of tropical birds would a black-robed Jesuit, and their rapiers and daggers were no less fatal than the fangs and talons of jungle predators. Being a pensive chap, he had, on the very first day, begun trying to make sense of it—to get to the bottom of things, like the explorer who turns his back on orang-utans and orchids to jam his pan into the mud of a creek bed. Naught but swirling murk had been the result.

In years since he has rarely gone back to those old memories. As he does now, in the tavern near Harvard College, he's startled to find that the muddy whirl has been swept away. The mental pan has been churning for fifty years, sorting the dirt and sand to the periphery and throwing it off. Most of the memories are simply gone. All that remain are a few wee nuggets. It's not plain to Daniel why *these* impressions have stayed, while others, which seemed as or more important to him at the time they happened, have gone away. But if the gold-panning similitude is faithful, it means that these memories matter more than the ones that have flown. For gold stays in the pan's center because of its density; it has more matter (whatever that means) in a given extent than anything else.

The crowd in Charing Cross, the sword falling silently on the neck of Charles I: this is his first nugget. Then there's nothing until some months later when the Waterhouses and their old family friends the Bolstroods went on a sort of holiday in the country to demolish a cathedral.

Nugget: In silhouette against a cathedral's rose window, a bent, black wraith lumbering, his two arms a pendulum, a severed marble saint's head swinging in them. This was Drake Waterhouse, Daniel's father, about sixty years old.

Nugget: The stone head in flight, turning to look back in surprise at Drake. The gorgeous fabric of the window drawn inwards, like the skin on a kettle of soup when you poke a spoon through it—the glass falling away, the transcendent vision of the window converted to a disk of plain old blue-green English hillside beneath a silver sky. This was the English Civil War.

Nugget: A short but stout man, having done with battering down the gilded fence that Archbishop Laud had built around the altar, dropping his sledgehammer and falling into an epileptic fit on the Lord's Table. This was Gregory Bolstrood, about fifty years old at the time. He was a preacher. He called himself an Independent. His tendency to throw fits had led to rumors that he barked like a dog during his three-hour sermons, and so the sect he'd founded, and Drake had funded, had come to be known as the Barkers.

Nugget: A younger Barker smiting the cathedral's organ with an iron rod—stately pipes being felled like trees, polished boxwood keys skittering across the marble floor. This was Knott Bolstrood, the son of Gregory, in his prime.

BUT THESE ARE ALL FROM his early childhood, before he'd learned to read and think. After that his young life had been well-ordered and (he's surprised to see in retrospect) interesting. Adventurous, even. Drake was a trader. After Cromwell had won and the Civil War ended, he and young Daniel traveled all over England during the 1650s buying the local produce low, then shipping it to Holland where it could be sold high. Despite much of the trade being illegal (for Drake held it as a religious conviction that the State had no business imposing on him with taxes and tariffs, and considered smuggling not just a good idea but a sacred observance), it was all orderly enough. Daniel's memories of that time—to the extent he still has any—are as prim and simple as a morality play penned by Puritans. It was not until the Restoration, and his going off to Trinity, that all became confused again, and he entered into a kind of second toddlerhood.

Nugget: The night before Daniel rode up to Cambridge to begin his four-year Cram Session for the End of the World, he slept in his father's house on the outskirts of London. The bed was a rectangle of stout beams, a piece of canvas stretched across the middle by a zigzag of hairy ropes, a sack of straw tossed on, and half a dozen Dissenting preachers snoring into one another's feet. Royalty was back, England had a King, who was called Charles II, and that King had courtiers. One of them, John Comstock, had drawn up an Act of Uniformity, and the King had signed it—with one stroke of the quill making all Independent ministers into unemployed heretics. Of course they had all converged on Drake's house. Sir Roger L'Estrange, the Surveyor of the Press, came every few days and raided the place, on the suspicion that all those idle Phanatiques must be grinding out handbills in the cellar.

Wilkins—who for a brief while had been Master of Trinity—had secured Daniel a place there. Daniel had phant'sied that he should be Wilkins's student, his protégé. But before Daniel could matriculate, the Restoration had forced Wilkins out. Wilkins had retired to London to serve as the minister of the Church of St. Lawrence Jewry and, in his spare time, to launch the Royal Society. It was a lesson for Daniel in just how enormously a plan could go awry. For Daniel had been living in London, and could have spent as much time as he pleased with Wilkins, and gone to all the meetings of the Royal Society, and learnt everything he might have cared to know of Natural Philosophy simply by walking across town. Instead he went up to Trinity a few months after Wilkins had left it behind forever.

Nugget: On the ride up to Cambridge he passed by roadside saints whose noses and ears had been hammered off years ago by enraged Puritans. Each one of them, therefore, bore a marked resemblance to Drake. It seemed to him that each one turned its head to watch him ride past.

Nugget: A wench with paint on her face, squealing as she fell backwards onto Daniel's bed at Trinity College. Daniel getting an erection. This was the Restoration.

The woman's weight on his legs suddenly doubled as a boy half her age, embedded in a flouncing spray of French lace, fell on top of her. This was Upnor.

Nugget: A jeweled duelling-sword clattering as its owner dropped to hands and knees and washed the floor with a bubbling fan of vomit. "Eehhr," he groaned, rising up to a kneeling position and letting his head loll back on his lace collar. Candle-light shone in his face: a bad portrait of the King of England. This was the Duke of Monmouth.

Nugget: A sizar with a mop and a bucket, trying to clean up the room—Monmouth and Upnor and Jeffreys and all of the other fellow-commoners calling for beer, sending him scurrying down to the cellar. This was Roger Comstock. Related, distantly, to the John Comstock who'd written the Act of Uniformity. But from a branch of the family that was at odds with John's. Hence his base status at Trinity.

Daniel had his own bed at Trinity, and yet he could not sleep. Sharing the great bed in Drake's house with smelly Phanatiques, or sleeping in common beds of inns while traveling round England with his father, Daniel had enjoyed great unbroken slabs of black, dreamless sleep. But when he went off to University he suddenly found himself sharing his room, and even his bed, with young men who were too drunk to stand up and too dangerous to argue with. His nights were fractured into shards. Vivid, exhausting dreams came through the cracks in between, like vapors escaping from a crazed vessel.

His first coherent memory of the place begins on a night like that.

✂

College of the Holy and
Undivided Trinity, Cambridge

1661

☥

> The Dissenters are destitute of all decorations that
> can please the outward Senses, what their Teachers
> can hope for from humane Assistance lies altogether
> in their own endeavours, and they have nothing to
> strengthen their Doctrine with (besides what they
> can say for it) but probity of Manners and exemplary
> Lives.
>
> — *The Mischiefs That Ought Justly*
> *to Be Apprehended from a*
> *Whig-Government,* ANONYMOUS,
> ATTRIBUTED TO BERNARD MANDEVILLE, 1714

SOME SORT OF COMMOTION in the courtyard below. Not the usual
revels, or else he wouldn't have bothered to hear it.

Daniel got out of bed and found himself alone in the chamber.
The voices below sounded angry. He went to the window. The tail
of Ursa Major was like the hand of a cœlestial clock, and Daniel
had been studying how to read it. The time was probably around
three in the morning.

Beneath him several figures swam in murky pools of lanthorn-
light. One of them was dressed as men always had been, in Daniel's
experience, until very recently: a black coat and black breeches
with no decorations. But the others were flounced and feathered
like rare birds.

The one in black seemed to be defending the door from the
others. Until recently, everyone at Cambridge had looked like him,
and the University had been allowed to exist only because a godly
nation required divines who were fluent in Greek and Latin and
Hebrew. He was barring the door because the men in lace and velvet and silk were trying to bring a wench in with them. And hardly
for the first time! But this man, apparently, had seen one wench
too many, and resolved to make a stand.

ෆ

A scarlet boy flourished in the midst of the lanthorn-light—a writhing bouquet of tassles and flounces. His arms were crossed over his body. He drew them apart with a sharp ringing noise. A rod of silver light had appeared in each of his hands—a long one in his right, a short one in his left. He drew into a crouch. His companions were all shouting; Daniel could not make out the words, but the feelings expressed were a welter of fear and joy. The black-clad fellow drew out a sword of his own, something dull and clanging, a heavier spadroon, and the scarlet boy came at him like a boiling cloud, with lightning darting out of the center. He fought as animals fight, with movements too quick for the eye to follow, and the man in black fought as men fight, with hesitations and second thoughts. He had a great many holes in him very soon, and was reduced to a heap of somber, bloody clothing on the green grass of the courtyard, shifting and rocking, trying to find a position that was not excruciatingly painful.

All of the Cavaliers ran away. The Duke of Monmouth picked the wench up over his shoulder like a sack of grain and carried her off at a dead run. The scarlet boy tarried long enough to plant a boot on the dying man's shoulder, turn him over onto his back, and spit something into his face.

All round the courtyard, shutters began to slam closed.

Daniel threw a coat over himself, pulled on a pair of boots, got a lanthorn of his own lit, and hurried downstairs. But it was too late for hurrying—the body was already gone. The blood looked like tar on the grass. Daniel followed one dribble to the next, across the green, out the back of the college, and onto the Backs—the boggy floodplain of the river Cam, which wandered around in back of the University. The wind had come up a bit, making noise in the trees that nearly obscured the splash. A less eager witness than Daniel could have claimed he'd heard nothing, and it would have been no lie.

He stopped then, because his mind had finally come awake, and he was afraid. He was out in the middle of an empty fen, following a dead man toward a dark river, and the wind was trying to blow out his lanthorn.

A pair of naked men appeared in the light, and Daniel screamed.

One of the men was tall, and had the most beautiful eyes Daniel had ever seen in a man's face; they were like the eyes of a painting of the Pieta that Drake had once flung onto a bonfire. He looked towards Daniel as if to say, *Who dares scream?*

The other man was shorter, and he reacted by cringing. Daniel finally recognized him as Roger Comstock, the sizar. "Who's that?" this one asked. "My lord?" he guessed.

"No man's lord," Daniel said. "It is I. Daniel Waterhouse."

"It's Comstock and Jeffreys. What are you doing out here in the middle of the night?" Both of the men were naked and soaked, their long hair draggling and seeping on their shoulders. Yet even Comstock seemed at ease compared to Daniel, who was dry, clothed, and equipped with a lanthorn.

"I might ask the same of you. Where are your clothes?"

Jeffreys now stepped forward. Comstock knew to shut up.

"We doffed our clothing when we swam the river," Jeffreys said, as if this should be perfectly obvious.

Comstock saw the hole in that story as quickly as Daniel did, and hastily plugged it: "When we emerged, we found that we had drifted for some distance downstream, and were unable to find them again in the darkness."

"Why did you swim the river?"

"We were in hot pursuit of that ruffian."

"Ruffian!?"

The outburst caused a narrowing of the beautiful eyes. A look of mild disgust appeared on Jeffreys's face. But Roger Comstock was not above continuing with the conversation: "Yes! Some Phana-tique—a Puritan, or possibly a Barker—he challenged my Lord Upnor in the courtyard just now! You must not have seen it."

"I did see it."

"Ah." Jeffreys turned sideways, caught his dripping penis between two fingers, and urinated tremendously onto the ground. He was staring toward the College. "The window of your and My Lord Monmouth's chamber is awkwardly located—you must have leaned out of it?"

"Perhaps I leaned out a bit."

"Otherwise, how could you have seen the men duelling?"

"Would you call it duelling, or murdering?"

Once again, Jeffreys appeared to be overcome with queasiness at the fact that he was having a conversation of any sort with the likes of Daniel. Comstock put on a convincing display of mock astonishment. "Are you claiming to have witnessed a murder?"

Daniel was too taken aback to answer. Jeffreys continued to jet urine onto the ground; he had produced a great steaming patch of it already, as if he intended to cover his nakedness with a cloud. He furrowed his brow and asked, "Murder, you say. So a man has died?"

"I . . . I should suppose so," Daniel stammered.

"Hmmm. . . . *supposing* is a *dangerous* practice, when you are supposing that an Earl has committed a capital crime. Perhaps you'd better show the dead body to the Justice of the Peace, and allow the coroner to establish a cause of death."

"The body is gone."

"You say *body*. Wouldn't it be *correct* to say, *wounded man*?"

"Well . . . I did not personally verify that the heart had stopped, if that is what you mean."

"Wounded man would be the *correct* term, then. To me, he seemed very much a *wounded* man, and not a *dead* one, when Comstock and I were pursuing him across the Backs."

"Unquestionably not dead," Comstock agreed.

"But I saw him lying there—"

"From your window?" Jeffreys asked, finally done pissing.

"Yes."

"But you are not looking out your window *now*, are you, Waterhouse?"

"Obviously not."

"Thank you for telling me what is *obvious*. Did you leap out of your window, or did you walk down stairs?"

"Down stairs, of course!"

"Can you see the courtyard from the staircase?"

"No."

"So as you descended the stairs, you lost sight of the wounded man."

"Naturally."

"You really haven't the faintest idea, do you, Waterhouse, of what happened in the courtyard during the interval when you were coming down stairs?"

"No, but—"

"And despite this ignorance—ignorance utter, black, and entire—you presume to accuse an Earl, and personal friend of the King, of having committed—what was it again?"

"I believe he said *murder*, sir," Comstock put in helpfully.

"Very well. Let us go and wake up the Justice of the Peace," Jeffreys said. On his way past Waterhouse he snatched the lanthorn, and then began marching back towards the College. Comstock followed him, giggling.

First Jeffreys had to get himself dried off, and to summon his own sizar to dress his hair and get his clothes on—a gentleman could not go and visit the Justice of the Peace in a disheveled state. Meanwhile Daniel had to sit in his chamber with Comstock, who bustled about and cleaned the place with more diligence than he had ever shown before. Since Daniel was not in a talkative mood, Roger Comstock filled in the silences. "Louis Anglesey, Earl of Upnor—pushes a sword like a demon, doesn't he? You'd never guess he's only fourteen! It's because he and Monmouth and all that lot spent the Interregnum in Paris, taking their pushing-lessons at the Academy of Monsieur du Plessis, near the Palais Cardinal. They learned a very French conception of honor there, and haven't quite adjusted to England yet—they'll challenge a man to a duel at the slightest offence—real or phant'sied. Oh, now, don't look so stricken, Mr. Waterhouse—remember that if that fellow he was duelling with is found, and is found to be dead, and his injuries found to be the cause of his death, and those injuries are found to've been inflicted by My Lord Upnor, and not in a duel *per se* but in an unprovoked assault, and if a jury can be persuaded to over-look the faults in your account—in a word, if he is successfully prosecuted for this hypothetical murder—then you won't have to worry about it! After all, if he's guilty, then he can't very well claim you've dishonored him with the accusation, can he? Nice and tidy, Mr. Waterhouse. Some of his friends might be quite angry with you, I'll admit—oh, no, Mr. Waterhouse, I didn't mean it in the way you think. *I* am not your enemy—remember, I am of the Golden, not the Silver, Comstocks."

It was not the first time he'd said something like this. Daniel knew that the Comstocks were a grotesquely large and complicated family, who had begun popping up in minor roles as far back as the reign of King Richard Lionheart, and he gathered that this Silver/Golden dichotomy was some kind of feud between different branches of the clan. Roger Comstock wanted to impress on Daniel that he had nothing in common, other than a name, with John Comstock: the aging gunpowder magnate and arch-Royalist, and now Lord Chancellor, who had been the author of the recent Declaration of Uniformity—the act that had filled Drake's house with jobless Ranters, Barkers, Quakers, *et cetera*. "Your people," Daniel said, "the Golden Comstocks, as you dub them—pray, what are they?"

"I beg your pardon?"

"High Church?" Meaning Anglicans of the Archbishop Laud school, who according to Drake and his ilk were really no different from Papists—and Drake believed that the Pope was literally the Antichrist. "Low Church?" Meaning Anglicans of a more Calvinist bent, nationalistic, suspicious of priests in fancy clothes. "Independents?" Meaning ones who'd severed all ties with the Established Church, and made up their own churches as it suited them. Daniel did not venture any further down the continuum, for he had already shot well beyond Roger Comstock's limits as a theologian.

Roger threw up his hands and said merely, "Because of the unpleasantness with the Silver branch, recent generations of the Golden Comstocks have spent rather a lot of time in the Dutch Republic."

To Daniel, the Dutch Republic meant God-fearing places like Leiden, where the pilgrims had sojourned before going to Massachusetts. But it presently came clear that Roger was talking about Amsterdam. "There are all sorts of churches in Amsterdam. Cheek by jowl. Strange as it must sound, this habit has quite worn off on us over the years."

"Meaning what? That you've become used to preserving your faith despite being surrounded by heretics?"

"No. Rather, it's as if I've got an Amsterdam inside of my head."

"A *what*!?"

"Many different sects and faiths that are always arguing with one another. A Babel of religious disputation that never dies down. I have got used to it."

"You believe *nothing*!?"

Further debate—if listening to Roger's ramblings could be considered such—was cut off by the arrival of Monmouth, who strolled in looking offensively relaxed. Roger Comstock had to make a fuss over him for a while—jacking his boots off, letting his hair down, getting him undressed. Comstock supplied entertainment by telling the tale of chasing the killer Puritan across the Backs and into the River Cam. The more the Duke heard of this story, the more he liked it, and the more he loved Roger Comstock. And yet Comstock made so many ingratiating references to Waterhouse that Daniel began to feel that he was still part of the same merry crew; and Monmouth even directed one or two kindly winks at him.

Finally Jeffreys arrived in a freshly blocked wig, fur-lined cape, purple silk doublet, and fringed breeches, a ruby-handled rapier dangling alongside one leg, and fantastical boots turned down at the tops so far that they nearly brushed the ground. Looking, therefore, twice as old and ten times as rich as Daniel, even though he was a year younger and probably broke. He led the faltering Daniel and the implacably cheerful Comstock down the staircase—pausing there for a while to reflect upon the total impossibility of anyone's seeing the courtyard from it—and across Trinity's great lawn and out the gate into the streets of Cambridge, where water-filled wheel-ruts, reflecting the light of dawn, looked like torpid, fluorescent snakes. In a few minutes they reached the house of the

Justice of the Peace, and were informed that he was at church. Jeffreys therefore led them to an alehouse, where he was soon engulfed in wenches. He caused drink and food to be brought out. Daniel sat and watched him tear into a great bloody haunch of beef whilst downing two pints of ale and four small glasses of the Irish drink known as Usquebaugh. None of it had any effect on Jeffreys; he was one of those who could become staggeringly drunk and yet only wax quieter and calmer.

The wenches kept Jeffreys occupied. Daniel sat and knew fear—not the abstract fear that he dutifully claimed to feel when preachers spoke of hellfire, but a genuine physical sensation, a taste in his mouth, a sense that at any moment, from any direction, a blade of French steel might invade his vitals and inaugurate a slow process of bleeding or festering to death. Why else would Jeffreys have led him to this den? It was a perfect place to get murdered.

The only way to get his mind off it was to talk to Roger Comstock, who continued with strenuous but completely pointless efforts to ingratiate himself. He circled round one more time to the topic of John Comstock, with whom—it could not be said too many times—he had nothing in common. That he had it on good authority that the gunpowder turned out by Comstock's mills was full of sand, and that it either failed entirely to explode, or else caused cannons to burst. Why everyone, save a few self-deluding Puritans, now understood that the defeat of the first King Charles had occurred not because Cromwell was such a great general, but because of the faulty powder that Comstock had supplied to the Cavaliers. Daniel—scared to death—was in no position to understand the genealogical distinctions between the so-called Silver and Golden Comstocks. The upshot was that Roger Comstock seemed, in some way, to want to be his friend, and was trying desperately hard to be just that, and indeed was the finest fellow that a fellow could possibly be, while still having spent the night dumping the corpse of a murder victim into a river.

The ringing of church-bells told them that the Justice of the Peace was probably finished with his breakfast of bread and wine. But Jeffreys, having made himself comfortable here, was in no hurry to leave. From time to time he would catch Daniel's eye and stare at him, daring Daniel to stand up and head for the door. But Daniel was in no hurry, either. His mind was seeking an excuse for doing nothing.

The one that he settled on went something like this: Upnor would be Judged—for good—five years from now when Jesus came back. What was the point of having the secular authorities sit in judgment on him now? If England were still a holy nation, as it had been until recently, then prosecuting Louis Anglesey, Earl of Upnor, would have been a fitting exercise of her authority. But the King was back, England was Babylon, Daniel Waterhouse and the hapless Puritan who'd died last night were strangers in a strange land, like early Christians in pagan Rome, and Daniel would only dirty his hands by getting into some endless legal broil. Best to rise above the fray and keep his eye on the year sixteen hundred and sixty-six.

So it was back to the College of the Holy and Undivided Trinity without saying a word to the Justice of the Peace. It had begun to rain. When Daniel reached the college, the grass had been washed clean.

THE DEAD MAN'S BODY was found two days later, tangled in some rushes half a mile down the Cam. He was a Fellow of Trinity College, a scholar of Hebrew and Aramaic who had been slightly acquainted with Drake. His friends went round making inquiries, but no one had seen a thing.

There was a rowdy funeral service in a primitive church that had been established in a barn five miles from Cambridge. *Exactly* five miles. For the Act of Uniformity stated, among other things, that Independents could not gather churches within five miles of any Established (i.e., Anglican) parish church, and so a lot of Puritans had been busy with compasses and maps lately, and a lot of bleak real estate had changed hands. Drake came up, and brought with him Daniel's older half-brothers, Raleigh and Sterling. Hymns were sung and homilies delivered, affirming that the victim had gone on to his eternal reward. Daniel prayed, rather loudly, to be delivered from the seething den of reptiles that was Trinity College.

Then, of course, he had to suffer advice from his elders. First, Drake took him aside.

Drake had long ago adjusted to the loss of his nose and ears, but all he had to do was turn his face in Daniel's direction to remind him that what he was going through at Trinity wasn't so bad. So Daniel hardly took in a single word of what Drake said to him. But he gathered that it was something along the lines of that coming into one's chambers every night to find a different whore, services already paid for, slumbering in one's bed, constituted a severe temptation for a young man, and that Drake was all in favor of it—seeing it as a way to hold said young man's feet to the eternal fire and find out what he was made of.

Implicit in all of this was that Daniel would pass the test.

He could not bring himself to tell his father that he'd already failed it.

Second, Raleigh and Sterling took Daniel to an extremely rural alehouse on the way back into town and told him that he must be some kind of half-wit, not to mention an ingrate, if he was not in a state of bliss. Drake and his first clutch of sons had made a very large amount of money despite (come to think of it, *because of*) religious persecution. Among that ilk, the entire point of going to Cambridge was to rub elbows with the fine and the mighty. The family had sent Daniel there, at great expense (as they never tired of reminding him), and if Daniel occasionally woke up to find the Duke of Monmouth passed out on top of him, it only meant that all of *their* dreams had come true.

Implicit was that Raleigh and Sterling did *not* believe that the world was coming to an end in 1666. If true, this meant that Daniel's excuse for not ratting on Upnor was void.

The whole incident was then apparently forgotten by everyone at Trinity except Waterhouse and Jeffreys. Jeffreys ignored Daniel for the most part, but from time to time he would, for example, sit across from him and stare at him all through dinner, then pursue him across the lawn afterwards: "I can't stop looking at you. You are fascinating, Mr. Waterhouse, a living and walking incarnation of cravenness. You saw a man murdered, and you did *nothing* about it. Your face glows like a hot branding-iron. I want to brand it into my memory so that as I grow old, I may look back upon it as a sort of Platonic ideal of cowardice.

"I'm going into law, you know. Were you aware that the emblem of justice is a scale? From a beam depend two pans. On one, what is being weighed—the accused party. On the other, a standard weight, a polished gold cylinder stamped with the assayer's mark. You, Mr. Waterhouse, shall be the standard against which I will weigh all guilty cowards.

"What sort of Puritanical sophistry did you gin up, Mr. Waterhouse, to justify your inaction? Others like you got on a ship and sailed to Massachusetts so that they could be apart from us sinners, and live a pure life. I ween you are of the same mind, Mr. Waterhouse, but sailing on a ship across the North Atlantic is not for cowards, and so you are here. I think that you have withdrawn into a sort of Massachusetts of the mind! Your body's here at Trinity, but your spirit has flown off to some sort of notional Plymouth Rock— when we sit at High Table, you phant'sy yourself in a wigwam ripping drumsticks from a turkey and chewing on Indian corn and making eyes at some redskinned Indian lass."

THIS SORT OF THING LED to Daniel's spending much time going for walks in Cambridge's gardens and greens, where, if he chose his route carefully, he could stroll for a quarter of an hour without having to step over the body of an unconscious young scholar, or (in warmer weather) make apologies for having stumbled upon Monmouth, or one of his courtiers, copulating with a prostitute *al fresco*. More than once, he noticed another solitary young man strolling around the Backs. Daniel knew nothing of him—he had made no impression upon the College whatsoever. But once Daniel got in the habit of looking for him, he began to notice him here and there, skulking around the edges of University life. The boy was a sizar— a nobody from the provinces trying to escape from the lower class by taking holy orders and angling for a deaconage in some gale-chafed parish. He and the other sizars (such as Roger Comstock) could be seen descending on the dining-hall after the upper classes— pensioners (e.g., Daniel) and fellow-commoners (e.g., Monmouth and Upnor)—had departed, to forage among their scraps and clean up their mess.

Like a pair of comets drawn together, across a desolate void, by some mysterious action at a distance, they attracted each other across the greens and fells of Cambridge. Both were shy, and so early they would simply fall into parallel trajectories during their long strolls. But in time the lines converged. Isaac was pale as starlight, and so frail-looking that no one would've guessed he'd live as long as he had. His hair was exceptionally fair and already streaked with silver. He already had protruding pale eyes and a sharp nose. There was the sense of much going on inside his head, which he had not the slightest inclination to share with anyone else. But like Daniel, he was an alienated Puritan with a secret interest in natural philosophy, so naturally they fell in together.

They arranged a room swap. Another merchant's son eagerly took Daniel's place, viewing it as a move up the world's ladder. The College of the Holy and Undivided Trinity did not segregate the classes as rigidly as other colleges, so it was permitted for Isaac and Daniel to chum together. They shared a tiny room with a window looking out over the town—for Daniel, a great improvement over the courtyard view, so fraught with bloody memories. Musket-balls had been fired in through their window during the Civil War, and the bullet-holes were still in the ceiling.

Daniel learned that Isaac came from a family prosperous by Lincolnshire standards. His father had died before Newton was even born, leaving behind a middling yeoman's legacy. His mother had soon married a more or less affluent cleric. She did not sound, from Isaac's description, like a doting mum. She'd packed him off to school in a town called Grantham. Between her inheritance from the first marriage and what she'd acquired from the second, she easily could have sent him to Cambridge as a pensioner. But out of miserliness, or spite, or some hostility toward education in general, she'd sent him as a sizar instead—meaning that Isaac was obliged to serve as some other student's boot-polisher and table-waiter. Isaac's dear mother, unable to humiliate her son from a distance, had arranged it so that some other student—it didn't matter which—would do it in her stead. In combination with that Newton was obviously far more brilliant than Daniel was, Daniel was uneasy with the arrangement. Daniel proposed that they make common cause, and pool what they had, and live together as equals.

To Daniel's surprise, Isaac did not accept. He continued to perform sizar's work, without complaint. By any measure, his life was much better now. They'd spend hours, days, in that chamber together, spending candles by the pound and ink by the quart, working their separate ways through Aristotle. It was the life that both of them had longed for. Even so, Daniel thought it strange that Isaac would help him in the mornings with his clothing, and devote a quarter of an hour, or more, to dressing his hair. Half a century later, Daniel could remember, without vanity, that he had been a handsome enough young man. His hair was thick and long, and Isaac learned that if he combed it in a particular way he could bring out a certain natural wave, up above Daniel's forehead. He would not rest, every morning, until he had accomplished this. Daniel went along with it uneasily. Even then, Isaac had the air of a man who could be dangerous when offended, and Daniel sensed that if he declined, Isaac would not take it well.

So it went until one Whitsunday, when Daniel awoke to find Isaac gone. Daniel had gone to sleep well after midnight, Isaac as usual had stayed up later. The candles were all burned down to stubs. Daniel guessed Isaac was out emptying the chamber-pot, but he didn't come back. Daniel went over to their little work-table to look for evidence, and found a sheet of paper on which Isaac had drawn a remarkably fine portrait of a sleeping youth. An angelic beauty. Daniel could not tell whether it was meant to be a boy or a girl. But carrying it to the window and looking at it in day-light, he noticed, above the youth's brow, a detail in the hair. It served as the cryptological key that unlocked the message. Suddenly he recognized himself in that page. Not as he really was, but purified,

61

beautified, perfected, as though by some alchemical refinement—
the slag and dross raked away, the radiant spirit allowed to shine
forth, like the Philosophick Mercury. It was a drawing of Daniel
Waterhouse as he might have looked if he had gone to the Justice
of the Peace and accused Upnor and been persecuted and suffered a Christlike death.

Daniel went down and eventually found Isaac bent and kneeling in the chapel, wracked with agony, praying desperately for the
salvation of his immortal soul. Daniel could not but sympathize,
though he knew too little of sin and too little of Isaac to guess what
his friend might be repenting for. Daniel sat nearby and did a little
praying of his own. In time, the pain and fear seemed to ebb away.
The chapel filled up. A service was begun. They took out the Books
of Common Prayer and turned to the page for Whitsunday. The
priest intoned: "What is required of them who come to the Lord's
Supper?" They answered, "To examine themselves whether they
repent of their former sins, steadfastly purporting to lead a new
life." Daniel watched Isaac's face as he spoke this catechism and
saw in it the same fervor that always lit up Drake's mangled countenance when he really thought he was on to something. Both of
them took communion. *This is the Lamb of God who takes away the
sins of the world.*

Daniel watched Isaac change from a tortured wretch, literally
writhing in spiritual pain, into a holy and purified saint. Having
repented of their former sins—steadfastly purporting to lead new
lives—they went back up to their chamber. Isaac pitched that drawing into the fire, opened up his note-book, and began to write. At
the head of a blank page he wrote *Sins committed before Whitsunday
1662* and then began writing out a list of every bad thing he'd ever
done that he could remember, all the way back to his childhood:
wishing that his stepfather was dead, beating up some boy at
school, and so forth. He wrote all day and into the night. When he
had exhausted himself he started up a new page entitled *Since
Whitsunday 1662* and left it, for the time being, blank.

Meanwhile, Daniel turned back to his Euclid. Jeffreys kept
reminding him that he had failed at being a holy man. Jeffreys did
this because he supposed it was a way of torturing Daniel the Puritan. In fact, Daniel had never wanted to be a preacher anyway, save
insofar as he wanted to please his father. Ever since his meeting
with Wilkins, he had wanted only to be a Natural Philosopher. Failing the moral test had freed him to be that, at a heavy price in self-
loathing. If Natural Philosophy led him to eternal damnation,
there was nothing he could do about it anyway, as Drake the pre-

destinationist would be the first to affirm. An interval of years or even decades might separate Whitsunday 1662 and Daniel's arrival at the gates of Hell. He reckoned he might as well fill that time with something he at least found interesting.

A month later, when Isaac was out of the room, Daniel opened up the note-book and turned to the page headed *Since Whitsunday 1662*. It was still blank.

He checked it again two months later. Nothing.

At the time he assumed that Isaac had simply forgotten about it. Or perhaps he had stopped sinning! Years later, Daniel understood that neither guess was true. Isaac Newton had stopped believing himself capable of sin.

This was a harsh judgment to pass on anyone—and the proverb went *Judge not lest ye be judged*. But its converse was that when you were treating with a man like Isaac Newton, the rashest and cruelest judge who ever lived, you must be sure and swift in your own judgments.

☙

Boston, Massachusetts Bay Colony
OCTOBER 12, 1713

Others apart sat on a Hill retir'd,
In thoughts more elevate, and reason'd high
Of Providence, Foreknowledge, Will and Fate
—MILTON, *Paradise Lost*

LIKE A GOOD CARTESIAN who measures everything against a fixed point, Daniel Waterhouse thinks about whether or not to go back to England while keeping one eye, through a half-closed door, on his son: Godfrey William, the fixed stake that Daniel has driven into the ground after many decades' wanderings. At an arbitrary place on a featureless plain, some would argue, but now the Origin of all his considerations. Sir Isaac would have it that all matter is a sort of permanent ongoing miracle, that planets are held in their orbits, and atoms in their places, by the immanent will of God, and looking at his own son, Daniel can hardly bear to think otherwise. The boy's a coiled spring, the potential for generations of American Waterhouses, though it's just as likely he'll catch a fever and die tomorrow.

In most other Boston houses, a slave woman would be looking after the boy, leaving the parents free to discourse with their visitor. Daniel Waterhouse does not own slaves. The reasons are several. Some of them are even altruistic. So little Godfrey sits on the lap, not of some Angolan negress, but of their neighbor: the daft but harmless Mrs. Goose, who comes into their home occasionally to do the one thing that she apparently *can* do: to entertain children by spouting all manner of nonsensical stories and doggerel that she has collected or invented. Meanwhile Enoch is off trying to make arrangements with Captain van Hoek of the *Minerva*. This has freed Daniel and Faith and the young Rev. Wait Still Waterhouse* to discuss what is the best way to respond to the startling invitation from Princess Caroline of Ansbach. Many words are said, but they make no more impact on Daniel than Mrs. Goose's incoherent narratives about cutlery leaping over cœlestial bodies and sluttish hags living in discarded footwear.

Wait Still Waterhouse says something like, "You're sixty-seven, it's true, but you have your health—many have lived much longer."

"If you avoid large crowds, sleep well, nourish yourself—" Faith says.

"Lon-don Bridge is fal-ling down, fal-ling down, fal-ling down . . . ," sings Mrs. Goose.

"My mind has never felt quite so much like an arrangement of cranks and gears," Daniel says. "I decided what I was going to do quite some time ago."

"But people have been known to change their minds—" says the reverend.

"Am I to infer, from what you just said, that you are a Free Will man?" Daniel inquires. "I really am shocked to find that in a Waterhouse. What are they teaching at Harvard these days? Don't you realize that this Colony was founded by people fleeing from those who backed the concept of Free Will?"

"I don't fancy that the Free Will question really had very much to do with the founding of this Colony. It was more a rebellion against the entire notion of an Established church—be it Papist or Anglican. It is true that many of those Independents—such as our ancestor John Waterhouse—got their doctrine from the Calvinists

---

*Son of Praise-God W., son of Raleigh W., son of Drake—hence, some sort of nephew to Daniel.

in Geneva, and scorned the notion, so cherished by the Papists and the Anglicans, of Free Will. But this alone would not have sufficed to send them into exile."

"I get it not from Calvin but from Natural Philosophy," Daniel says. "The mind is a machine, a Logic Mill. That's what I believe."

"Like the one you have been building across the river?"

"A good deal more effective than that one, fortunately."

"You think that if you made yours better, it could do what the human mind does? That it could have a soul?"

"When you speak of a soul, you phant'sy something above and beyond the cranks and gears, the dead matter, of which the machine—be it a Logic Mill or a brain—is constructed. I do not believe in this."

"Why not?"

Like many simple questions, this one is difficult for Daniel to answer. "Why not? I suppose because it puts me in mind of Alchemy. This soul, this extra thing added to the brain, reminds me of the Quintessence that the Alchemists are forever seeking: a mysterious supernatural presence that is supposed to suffuse the world. But they can never seem to find any. Sir Isaac Newton has devoted his life to the project and has nothing to show for it."

"If your sympathies do not run in that direction, then I know better than to change your mind, at least where Free Will versus Predestination is concerned," says Wait Still. "But I know that when you were a boy you had the privilege of sitting at the knee of men such as John Wilkins, Gregory Bolstrood, Drake Waterhouse, and many others of Independent sympathies—men who preached freedom of conscience. Who advocated Gathered, as opposed to Established, churches. The flourishing of small congregations. Abolition of central dogma."

Daniel, still not quite believing it: "Yes . . ."

Wait Still, brightly: "So what's to stop me from preaching Free Will to *my* flock?"

Daniel laughs. "And, as you are not merely glib, but young, handsome, and personable, converting many to the same creed—including, I take it, my own wife?"

Faith blushes, then stands up and turns around to hide it. In the candle-light, a bit of silver glints in her hair: a hair-pin shaped like a caduceus. She has gotten up on the pretext of going to check on little Godfrey, even though Mrs. Goose has him well in hand.

In a small town like Boston, you'd think it would be impossible to have a conversation about anything without being eavesdropped on. Indeed, the whole place was set up to make it so—they deliver the mail, not to your house, but to the nearest tavern, and if you don't come round and pick it up after a few days the publican will open it up and read it aloud to whomever is in attendance. So Daniel had assumed that Mrs. Goose would be listening in on the whole conversation. But instead she is completely absorbed in her work, as if telling yarns to a boy were more important than this great Decision that Daniel is wrestling with, here at damn near the end of his long life.

"It's quite all right, my dear," Daniel says to the back of Faith's bodice. "Having been raised by a man who believed in Predestination, I'd much rather that my boy was raised by a Free Will woman." But Faith leaves the room.

Wait Still says, "So . . . you believe God has predestined you to sail for England tonight?"

"No—I'm not a Calvinist. Now, you're baffled, Reverend, because you spent too much time at Harvard reading old books about the likes of Calvin and Archbishop Laud, and are still caught up in the disputes of Arminians versus Puritans."

"What should I have been reading, Doctor?" said Wait Still, making a bit too much of a show of flexibility.

"Galileo, Descartes, Huygens, Newton, Leibniz."

"The syllabus of your Institute of Technologickal Arts?"

"Yes."

"Didn't know that you touched on matters of theology."

"That was a bit of a jab—no, no, quite all right! I rather liked it. I'm pleased by the display of backbone. I can see clearly enough that you'll end up raising my son." Daniel means this in a completely non-sexual way—he had in mind that Wait Still would act in some avuncular role—but from the blush on Wait Still's face he can see that the role of stepfather is more likely.

This, then, would be a good time to change the subject to abstract technical matters: "It all comes from first principles. Everything can be measured. Everything acts according to physical laws. Our minds included. My mind, that's doing the deciding, is already set in its course, like a ball rolling down a trough."

"Uncle! Surely you are not denying the existence of souls—of a Supreme Soul."

Daniel says nothing to this.

"Neither Newton nor Leibniz would agree with you," Wait Still continues.

"They're afraid to agree with me, because they are important men, and they would be destroyed if they came out and said it. But no one will bother to destroy *me*."

66

"Can we not influence your mental machine by arguments?" asks Faith, who has returned to stand in the doorway.

Daniel wants to say that Wait Still's best arguments would be about as influential as boogers flicked against the planking of a Ship of the Line in full sail, but sees no reason to be acrimonious—the whole point of the exercise is to be remembered well by those who'll stay in the New World, on the theory that as the sun rises on the eastern fringe of America, small things cast long shadows westwards. "The future is as set as the past," he says, "and the future is that I'll climb on board the *Minerva* within the hour. You can argue that I should stay in Boston to raise my son. Of course, I should like nothing better. I should, God willing, have the satisfaction of watching him grow up for as many years as I have left. Godfrey would have a flesh-and-blood father with many conspicuous weaknesses and failings. He'd hold me in awe for a short while, as all boys do their fathers. It would not last. But if I sail away on *Minerva,* then in place of a flesh-and-blood Dad—a fixed, known quantity—he'll have a phant'sy of one, infinitely ductile in his mind. I can go away and imagine generations of Waterhouses yet unborn, and Godfrey can imagine a hero-father better than I can really be."

Wait Still Waterhouse, an intelligent and decent man, can see so many holes in this argument that he is paralyzed by choices. Faith, a better mother than wife, who has a better son than a husband, encompasses a vast sweep of compromises with a pert nod of the head. Daniel gathers up his son from Mrs. Goose's lap—Enoch calls in a hired coach—they go to the waterfront.

> So I saw in my dream that the man began to run. Now he had not run far from his own door, but his wife and children perceiving it began to cry after him to return: but the man put his fingers in his ears, and ran on crying, "Life, life, eternal life." So he looked not behind him, but fled towards the middle of the plain.
>
> —JOHN BUNYAN, *The Pilgrim's Progress*

MINERVA HAS ALREADY WEIGHED anchor, using the high tide to widen the distance between her keel and certain obstructions near the Harbor's entrance. Daniel is to be rowed out to join her in a pilot's boat. Godfrey, who is half asleep, kisses his old Dad dutifully and watches his departure like a dream—that's good, as he can tailor the memory later to suit his changing demands—like a suit of clothes modified every six months to fit a growing frame. Wait Still stands by Faith's side, and Daniel can't help thinking they make a lovely couple. Enoch, that home-wrecker, remains on the end of the wharf, guiltily apart, his silver hair glowing like white fire in the full moon-light.

A dozen slaves pull mightily at the oars, forcing Daniel to sit down, lest the boat shoot out from under his feet and leave him floundering in the Harbor. Actually he does not sit as much as sprawl and get lucky. From shore it probably looks like a pratfall, but he knows that this ungainly moment will be edited from The Story that will one day live in the memories of the American Water-houses. The Story is in excellent hands. Mrs. Goose has come along to watch and memorize, and she has a creepy knack for that kind of thing, and Enoch is staying, too, partly to look after the physical residue of the Massachusetts Bay Colony Institute of Tech-nologickal Arts, but also partly to look after The Story and see that it's shaped and told to Daniel's advantage.

Daniel weeps.

The sounds of his sniffling and heaving drown out nearly every-thing else, but he becomes aware of some low, strange music: the slaves have begun to sing. A rowing-song? No, that would have a lumbering, yo-ho-ho sort of rhythm, and this is much more com-plicated, with beats in the wrong places. It must be an Africk tune, because they have meddled with some of the notes, made them flatter than they should be. And yet it's weirdly Irish at the same time. There is no shortage of Irish slaves in the West Indies, where these men first fell under the whip, so that might explain it. It is (musicological speculations aside) an entirely sad song, and Daniel knows why: by climbing aboard this boat and breaking down in sobs, he has reminded each one of these Africans of the day when he was taken, in chains, off the coast of Guinea, and loaded aboard a tall ship.

Within a few minutes they are out of view of the Boston wharves, but still surrounded by land: the many islets, rocks, and bony tentacles of Boston Harbor. Their progress is watched by dead men hanging in rusty gibbets. When pirates are put to death, it is because they have been out on the high seas violating Admi-ralty law, whose jurisdiction extends only to the high-tide mark. The implacable logic of the Law dictates that pirate-gallows must, therefore, be erected in the intertidal zone, and that pirate-corpses must be washed three times by the tide before they are cut down. Of course mere death is too good for pirates, and so the sentence normally calls for their corpses to be gibbeted in locked iron cages so that they can never be cut down and given a Christian burial.

New England seems to have at least as many pirates as honest seamen. But here, as in so many other matters, Providence has smiled upon Massachusetts, for Boston Harbor is choked with small islands that are washed by high tides, providing vast resources of pirate-hanging and -gibbeting real estate. Nearly all of it has been put to use. During the daytime, the gibbets are obscured by clouds of hungry birds. But it's the middle of the night, the birds are in Boston and Charlestown, slumbering in their nests of plaited pirate-hair. The tide is high, the tops of the reefs submerged, the supports rising directly out of the waves. And so as the singing slaves row Daniel out on what he assumes will be his last voyage, scores of dessicated and skeletonized pirates, suspended in midair above the moonlit sea, watch him go by, as a ceremonial honor-guard.

It takes better than an hour to catch *Minerva,* just clearing the Spectacle Island shallows. Her hull is barrel-shaped and curves out above them. A pilot's ladder is deployed. The ascent isn't easy. Universal gravitation is not his only opponent. Rising waves, sneaking in from the North Atlantic, bounce him off the hull. Infuriatingly, the climb brings back all manner of Puritanical dogma he's done his best to forget—the ladder becomes Jacob's, the boat of sweaty black slaves Earth, the Ship Heaven, the sailors in the moonlit rigging Angels, the captain none other than Drake himself, ascended these many years, exhorting him to climb faster.

Daniel leaves America, becoming part of that country's stock of memories—the composted manure from which it's sending out fresh green shoots. The Old World reaches down to draw him in: a couple of lascars, their flesh and breath suffused with saffron, asafœtida, and cardamom, lean over the rail, snare his cold pale hands in their warm black ones, and haul him in like a fish. A roller slides under the hull at the same moment—they fall back to the deck in an orgiastic tangle. The lascars spring up and busy themselves drawing up his equipage on ropes. Compared to the little boat with the creaking and splashing of its oars and the grunting of the slaves, *Minerva* moves with the silence of a well-trimmed ship, signifying (or so he hopes) her harmony with the forces and fields of nature. Those Atlantic rollers make the deck beneath him accelerate gently up and down, effortlessly moving his body—it's like lying on a mother's bosom as she breathes. So Daniel lies there spreadeagled for a while, staring up at the stars—white geometric points on a slate, gridded by shadows of rigging, an explanatory network of catenary curves and Euclidean sections, like one of those geometric proofs out of Newton's *Principia Mathematica.*

College of the Holy and Undivided Trinity, Cambridge
1663

An Ideot may be taught by Custom to Write and Read,
yet no Man can be taught Genius.
— *Memoirs of the Right Villanous John Hall, 1708*

DANIEL HAD GONE OUT for a time in the evening, and met with Roger Comstock at a tavern, and witnessed to him, and tried to bring him to Jesus. This had failed. Daniel returned to his chamber to find the cat up on the table with its face planted in Isaac's dinner. Isaac was seated a few inches away. He had shoved a darning-needle several inches into his eyeball.

Daniel screamed from deep down in his gut. The cat, morbidly obese from eating virtually all of Isaac's meals, fell off the table like a four-legged haggis, and trudged away. Isaac did not flinch, which was probably a good thing. Daniel's scream had no other effects on business as usual at Trinity College—those who weren't too impaired to hear it probably assumed it was a wench playing hard-to-get.

"In my dissections of animals' eyes at Grantham, I often marveled at their perfect sphericity, which, in bodies that were otherwise irregular grab-bags of bones, tubes, skeins and guts, seemed to mark them out as apart from all the other organs. As if the Creator had made those orbs in the very image of the heavenly spheres, signifying that one should receive light from the other," Isaac mused aloud. "Naturally, I wondered whether an eye that was *not* spherical would work as well. There are practical as well as theologic reasons for spherical eyes: one, so that they can swivel in their sockets." There was some tension in his voice—the discomfort must have been appalling. Tears streamed down and spattered on the table like the exhaust from a water-clock—the only time Daniel ever saw Isaac weep. "Another practical reason is simply that the eyeball is pressurized from within by the aqueous humour."

"My God, you're not bleeding the humour from your eyeball—?"

"Look more carefully!" Isaac snapped. "Observe—don't imagine."

"I can't bear it."

"The needle is not *piercing* anything—the orb is perfectly intact. Come and see!"

Daniel approached, one hand clamped over his mouth as if he were abducting himself—he did not want to vomit on the open Waste-Book where Isaac was taking notes with his free hand. Upon a closer look he saw that Isaac had inserted the darning-needle not into the eyeball itself but into the lubricated bearing where the orb rotated in its socket—he must've simply pulled his lower eyelid way down and probed between it and the eyeball until he'd found a way in. "The needle is blunt—it is perfectly harmless," Isaac grunted. "If I could trouble you for a few minutes' assistance?"

Now supposedly Daniel was a student, attending lectures and studying the works of Aristotle and Euclid. But in fact, he had over the last year become the one thing, aside from the Grace of God, keeping Isaac Newton alive. He'd long since stopped asking him such annoying, pointless questions as "Can you remember the last time you put food into your mouth" or "Don't you suppose that a nap of an hour or two, once a night, might be good?" The only thing that really worked was to monitor Isaac until he physically collapsed on the table, then haul him into bed, like a grave-robber transporting his goods, then pursue his own studies nearby and keep on eye on him until consciousness began to return, and then, during the moments when Isaac still didn't know what day it was, and hadn't gone off on some fresh train of thought, shove milk and bread at him so he wouldn't starve all the way to death. He did all of this voluntarily—sacrificing his own education, and making a burnt offering of Drake's tuition payments—because he considered it his Christian duty. Isaac, still in theory his sizar, had become his master, and Daniel the attentive servant. Of course Isaac was completely unaware of all Daniel's efforts—which only made it a more perfect specimen of Christlike self-abnegation. Daniel was like one of those Papist fanatics who, after they died, were found to've been secretly wearing hair-shirts underneath their satin vestments.

"The diagram may give you a better comprehension of the design of tonight's experiment," Isaac said. He'd drawn a cross-sectional view of eyeball, hand, and darning-needle in his Waste Book. It was the closest thing to a work of art he had produced since the strange events of Whitsunday last year—since that date, only equations had flowed from his pen.

"May I ask *why* you are doing this?"

"Theory of Colors is part of the Program," Isaac said—referring (Daniel knew) to a list of philosophical questions Isaac had recently written out in his Waste Book, and the studies he had pursued, entirely on his own, in hopes of answering them. Between the two young men in this room—Newton with his Program and Waterhouse with his God-given responsibility to keep the other from killing himself—neither had attended a single lecture, or had any contact with actual members of the faculty, in over a year. Isaac continued, "I've been reading Boyle's latest—*Experiments and Considerations Touching Colors*—and it occurred to me: he uses his eyes to make all of his observations—his eyes are therefore instruments, like telescopes—but does he really understand how those instruments work? An astronomer who did not understand his lenses would be a poor philosopher indeed."

Daniel might have said any number of things then, but what came out was, "How may I assist you?" And it was not just being a simpering toady. He was, for a moment, gobsmacked by the sheer presumption of a mere student, twenty-one years old, with no degree, calling into question the great Boyle's ability to make simple observations. But in the next moment it occurred to Daniel for the first time: What if Newton was right, and all the others wrong? It was a difficult thing to believe. On the other hand, he *wanted* to believe it, because *if* it were true, it meant that in failing to attend so many lectures he had missed precisely *nothing*, and in acting as Newton's manservant he was getting the best education in natural philosophy a man could ever have.

"I need you to draw a reticule on a leaf of paper and then hold it up at various measured distances from my cornea—as you do, I'll move the darning needle up and down—creating greater and lesser distortions in the shape of my eyeball—I say, I'll do that with one hand, and take notes of what I see with the other."

So the night proceeded—by sunrise, Isaac Newton knew more about the human eye than anyone who had ever lived, and Daniel knew more than anyone save Isaac. The experiment could have been performed by anyone. Only one person had actually done it, however. Newton pulled the needle out of his eye, which was blood-red, and swollen nearly shut. He turned to another part of the Waste Book and began wrestling with some difficult math out of Cartesian analysis while Daniel stumbled downstairs and went to church. The sun turned the stained-glass windows of the chapel into matrices of burning jewels.

Daniel saw in a way he'd never seen anything before: his mind was a homunculus squatting in the middle of his skull, peering out through good but imperfect telescopes and listening-horns, gathering observations that had been distorted along the way, as a lens put chromatic aberrations into all the light that passed through it. A man who peered out at the world through a telescope would assume that the aberration was *real,* that the stars actually *looked* like that—what false assumptions, then, had natural philosophers been making about the evidence of their senses, until last night? Sitting in the gaudy radiance of those windows hearing the organ play and the choir sing, his mind pleasantly intoxicated from exhaustion, Daniel experienced a faint echo of what it must be like, *all the time,* to be Isaac Newton: a permanent ongoing epiphany, an endless immersion in lurid radiance, a drowning in light, a ringing of cosmic harmonies in the ears.

Aboard Minerva, *Massachusetts Bay*
OCTOBER 1713

DANIEL BECOMES AWARE that someone is standing over him as he lies on the deck: a stubby red-headed and -bearded man with a lit cigar in his mouth, and spectacles with tiny circular lenses: it's van Hoek, the captain, just checking to see whether his passenger will have to be buried at sea tomorrow. Daniel sits up, finally, and introduces himself, and van Hoek says very little—probably pretending to know less English than he really does, so Daniel won't be coming to his cabin and pestering him at all hours. He leads Daniel aft along *Minerva*'s main deck (which is called the upperdeck, even though, at the ends of the ship, there other other decks above it) and up a staircase to the quarter-deck and shows him to a cabin. Even van Hoek, who can be mistaken for a stout ten-year-old if you see him from behind, has to crouch to avoid banging his head on the subtly arched joists that support the poop deck overhead. He raises one arm above his head and steadies himself against a low beam—touching it not with a hand, but a brass hook.

Even though small and low-ceilinged, the cabin is perfectly all right—a chest, a lantern, and a bed consisting of a wooden box containing a canvas sack stuffed with straw. The straw is fresh, and its aroma will continue to remind Daniel of the green fields of Massachusetts all the way to England. Daniel strips off just a few items of clothing, curls up, and sleeps.

When he wakes up, the sun is in his eyes. The cabin has a small window (its forward bulkhead is deeply sheltered under the poop deck and so it is safe to put panes of glass there). And since they are sailing eastwards, the rising sun shines into it directly—along the way, it happens to beam directly through the huge spoked wheel by which the ship is steered. This is situated just beneath the edge of that same poop deck so that the steersman can take shelter from the weather while enjoying a clear view forward down almost the entire length of *Minerva*. At the moment, loops of rope have been cast over a couple of the handles at the ends of the wheel's spokes and tied down to keep the rudder fixed in one position. No one is at the wheel, and it's neatly dividing the red disk of the rising sun into sectors.

College of the Holy and Undivided Trinity, Cambridge
1664

In the great court of Trinity there was a sundial Isaac Newton didn't like: a flat disk divided by labeled spokes with a gnomon angling up from the center, naïvely copied from Roman designs, having a certain Classical elegance, and always wrong. Newton was constructing a sundial on a south-facing wall, using, as gnomon, a slender rod with a ball on the end. Every sunny day the ball's shadow would trace a curve across the wall—a slightly different curve every day, because the tilt of the earth's axis slowly changed through the seasons. That sheaf of curves made a fine set of astronomical data but not a usable timepiece. To tell time, Isaac (or his faithful assistant, Daniel Waterhouse) had to make a little cross-tick at the place the gnomon's shadow stood when Trinity's bell (always just a bit out of synchronization with King's) rang each of the day's hours. In theory, after 365 repetitions of this daily routine, each of the curves would be marked with ticks for 8:00 A.M., 9:00 A.M., and so on. By connecting those ticks—drawing a curve that passed through all of the eight o'clock ticks, another through all of the nine o'clock ticks, and so on—Isaac produced a second family of curves, roughly parallel to one another and roughly perpendicular to the day curves.

One evening, about two hundred days and over a thousand cross-ticks into this procedure, Daniel asked Isaac why he found sundials so interesting. Isaac got up, fled the room, and ran off in the direction of the Backs. Daniel let him be for a couple of hours and then went out looking for him. Eventually, at about two o'clock in the morning, he found Isaac standing in the middle of Jesus Green, contemplating his own long shadow in the light of a full moon.

"It was a sincere request for information—nothing more—I want you to convey to me whatever it is about sundials I've been too thick-headed to find very interesting."

This seemed to calm Isaac down, though he did not apologize for having thought the worst about Daniel. He said something along the lines of: "Heavenly radiance fills the æther, its rays parallel and straight and, so long as nothing is there to interrupt them, invisible. The secrets of God's creation are all told by those rays, but told in a language we do not understand, or even hear—the direction from which they shine, the spectrum of colors concealed within the light, these are all characters in a cryptogram. The gnomon—look at our shadows on the Green! *We* are the gnomon. We interrupt that light and we are warmed and illuminated by it. By stopping the light, we destroy part of the message without understanding it. We cast a shadow, a hole in the light, a ray of darkness that is shaped like ourselves—some might say that it contains no information save the profile of our own forms—but they are wrong. By recording the stretching and skewing of our shadows, we can attain part of the knowledge hidden in the cryptogram. All we need to make the necessary observations is a fixed regular surface—a plane—against which to cast the shadow. Descartes gave us the plane."

And so from then onwards Daniel understood that the point of this grueling sundial project was not merely to plot the curves, but to understand *why* each curve was shaped as it was. To put it another way, Isaac wanted to be able to walk up to a blank wall on a cloudy day, stab a gnomon into it, and draw all of the curves simply by *knowing* where the shadow *would* pass. This was the same thing as knowing where the sun would be in the sky, and that was the same as knowing where the earth was in its circuit around the sun, and in its daily rotation.

Though, as months went on, Daniel understood that Isaac wanted to be able to do the same thing even if the blank wall happened to be situated on, say, the moon that Christian Huygens had lately discovered revolving around Saturn.

Exactly how this might be accomplished was a question with ramifications that extended into such fields as: Would Isaac (and Daniel, for that matter) be thrown out of Trinity College? Were the Earth, and all the works of Man, nearing the end of a long relentless decay that had begun with the expulsion from Eden and that would very soon culminate in the Apocalypse? Or might things actually be getting *better,* with the promise of *continuing* to do so? Did people have souls? Did they have Free Will?

Aboard Minerva, *Massachusetts Bay*

OCTOBER 1713

> Hereby it is manifest, that during the time men live
> without a common power to keep them all in awe,
> they are in that condition which is called war; and
> such a war, as is of every man, against every man. For
> WAR, consisteth not in battle only, or the act of
> fighting; but in a tract of time, wherein the will to
> contend by battle is sufficiently known.
>
> —HOBBES, *Leviathan*

NOW WALKING OUT ONTO the upperdeck to find *Minerva* sailing steadily eastwards on calm seas, Daniel's appalled that anyone ever doubted these matters. The horizon is a perfect line, the sun a red circle tracing a neat path in the sky and proceeding through an orderly series of color-changes, red-yellow-white. Thus Nature.

Minerva—the human world—is a family of curves. There are no straight lines here. The decks are slightly arched to shed water and supply greater strength, the masts flexed, impelled by the thrust of the sails but restrained by webs of rigging: curve-grids like Isaac's sundial lines. Of course, wherever wind collects in a sail or water skims around the hull it follows rules that Bernoulli has set down using the calculus—Leibniz's version. *Minerva* is a congregation of Leibniz-curves navigating according to Bernoulli-rules across a vast, mostly water-covered sphere whose size, precise shape, trajectory through the heavens, and destiny were all laid down by Newton.

One cannot board a ship without imagining ship-wreck. Daniel envisions it as being like an opera, lasting several hours and proceeding through a series of Acts.

Act I: The hero rises to clear skies and smooth sailing. The sun is following a smooth and well-understood cœlestial curve, the sea is a plane, sailors are strumming guitars and carving *objets d'art* from walrus tusks, *et cetera,* while erudite passengers take the air and muse about grand philosophical themes.

Act II: A change in the weather is predicted based upon readings in the captain's barometer. Hours later it appears in the distance, a formation of clouds that is observed, sketched, and analyzed. Sailors cheerfully prepare for weather.

Act III: The storm hits. Changes are noted on the barometer, thermometer, clinometer, compass, and other instruments—cœlestial bodies are, however, no longer visible—the sky is a boiling chaos torn unpredictably by bolts—the sea is rough, the ship heaves, the cargo remains tied safely down, but most passengers are too ill or worried to think. The sailors are all working without rest—some of them sacrifice chickens in hopes of appeasing their gods. The rigging glows with St. Elmo's Fire—this is attributed to supernatural forces.

Act IV: The masts snap and the rudder goes missing. There is panic. Lives are already being lost, but it is not known how many. Cannons and casks are careering randomly about, making it impossible to guess who'll be alive and who dead ten seconds from now. The compass, barometer, *et cetera,* are all destroyed and the records of their readings swept overboard—maps dissolve—sailors are helpless—those who are still alive and sentient can think of nothing to do but pray.

Act V: The ship is no more. Survivors cling to casks and planks, fighting off the less fortunate and leaving them to drown. Everyone has reverted to a feral state of terror and misery. Huge waves shove them around without any pattern, carnivorous fish use living persons as food. There is no relief in sight, or even imaginable.

—There might also be an Act VI in which everyone was dead, but it wouldn't make for good opera so Daniel omits it.

Men of his generation were born during Act V* and raised in Act IV. As students, they huddled in a small vulnerable bubble of Act III. The human race has, actually, been in Act V for most of history and has recently accomplished the miraculous feat of assembling splintered planks afloat on a stormy sea into a sailing-ship and then, having climbed onboard it, building instruments with which to measure the world, and then finding a kind of regularity in those measurements. When they were at Cambridge, Newton was surrounded by a personal nimbus of Act II and was well on his way to Act I.

But they had, perversely, been living among people who were peering into the wrong end of the telescope, or something, and who had convinced themselves that the opposite was true—that the world had once been a splendid, orderly place—that men had made a reasonably trouble-free move from the Garden of Eden to the Athens of Plato and Aristotle, stopping over in the Holy Land to encrypt the secrets of the Universe in the pages of the Bible, and that everything had been slowly, relentlessly falling apart ever since. Cambridge was run by a mixture of fogeys too old to be considered dangerous, and Puritans who had been packed into the place by Cromwell after he'd purged all the people he *did* consider dangerous. With a few exceptions such as Isaac Barrow, none of them would have had any use for Isaac's sundial, because it didn't look like an *old* sundial, and they'd prefer telling time wrong the Classical way to telling it right the newfangled way. The curves that Newton plotted on the wall were a methodical document of their wrongness—a manifesto like Luther's theses on the church-door.

In explaining why those curves were as they were, the Fellows of Cambridge would instinctively use Euclid's geometry: the earth is a sphere. Its orbit around the sun is an ellipse—you get an ellipse by constructing a vast imaginary cone in space and then cutting through it with an imaginary plane; the intersection of the cone and the plane is the ellipse. Beginning with these primitive objects

---

*In England, the Civil War that brought Cromwell to power, and on the Continent, the Thirty Years' War.

(viz. the tiny sphere revolving around the place where the gigantic cone was cut by the imaginary plane), these geometers would add on more spheres, cones, planes, lines, and other elements—so many that if you could look up and see 'em, the heavens would turn nearly black with them—until at last they had found a way to account for the curves that Newton had drawn on the wall. Along the way, every step would be verified by applying one or the other of the rules that Euclid had proved to be true, two thousand years earlier, in Alexandria, where everyone had been a genius.

Isaac hadn't studied Euclid that much, and hadn't cared enough to study him well. If he wanted to work with a curve he would instinctively write it down, not as an intersection of planes and cones, but as a series of numbers and letters: an algebraic expression. That only worked if there was a language, or at least an alphabet, that had the power of *expressing* shapes without literally *depicting* them, a problem that Monsieur Descartes had lately solved by (first) conceiving of curves, lines, *et cetera*, as being collections of individual points and (then) devising a way to express a point by giving its coordinates—two numbers, or letters *representing* numbers, or (best of all) algebraic expressions that could in principle be evaluated to *generate* numbers. This translated all geometry to a new language with its own set of rules: algebra. The construction of equations was an exercise in translation. By following those rules, one could create new statements that were true, without even having to think about what the symbols referred to in any physical universe. It was this seemingly occult power that scared the hell out of some Puritans at the time, and even seemed to scare Isaac a bit.

By 1664, which was the year that Isaac and Daniel were supposed to get their degrees or else leave Cambridge, Isaac, by taking the very latest in imported Cartesian analysis and then extending it into realms unknown, was (unbeknownst to anyone except Daniel) accomplishing things in the field of natural philosophy that his teachers at Trinity could not even *comprehend*, much less *accomplish*—they, meanwhile, were preparing to subject Isaac and Daniel to the ancient and traditional ordeal of examinations designed to test their knowledge of Euclid. If they failed these exams, they'd be branded a pair of dimwitted failures and sent packing.

As the date drew nearer, Daniel began to mention them more and more frequently to Isaac. Eventually they went to see Isaac Barrow, the first Lucasian Professor of Mathematics, because he was conspicuously a better mathematician than the rest. Also because recently, when Barrow had been traveling in the Mediterranean, the ship on which he'd been passenger had been assaulted by pirates, and Barrow had gone abovedecks with a cutlass and helped fight them off. As such, he did not seem like the type who would really care in what order students learned the material. They were right about that—when Isaac showed up one day, alarmingly late in his academic career, with a few shillings, and bought a copy of Barrow's Latin translation of Euclid, Barrow didn't seem to mind. It was a tiny book with almost no margins, but Isaac wrote in the margins anyway, in nearly microscopic print. Just as Barrow had translated Euclid's Greek into the universal tongue of Latin, Isaac translated Euclid's ideas (expressed as curves and surfaces) into Algebra.

Half a century later on the deck of *Minerva*, that's all Daniel can remember about their Classical education; they took the exams, did indifferently (Daniel did better than Isaac), and were given new titles: they were now scholars, meaning that they had scholarships, meaning that Newton would not have to go back home to Woolsthorpe and become a gentleman-farmer. They would continue to share a chamber at Trinity, and Daniel would continue to learn more from Isaac's idle musings than he would from the entire apparatus of the University.

ONCE HE'S HAD THE OPPORTUNITY to settle in aboard *Minerva*, Daniel realizes it's certain that when, God willing, he reaches London, he'll be asked to provide a sort of affidavit telling what he knows about the invention of the calculus. As long as the ship's not moving too violently, he sits down at the large dining-table in the common-room, one deck below his cabin, and tries to organize his thoughts.

> Some weeks after we had received our Scholarships, probably in the Spring of 1665, Isaac Newton and I decided to walk out to Stourbridge Fair.

Reading it back to himself, he scratches out *probably in* and writes in *certainly no later than.*

Here Daniel leaves much out—it was Isaac who'd announced he was going. Daniel had decided to come along to look after him. Isaac had grown up in a small town and never been to London. To him, Cambridge was a big city—he was completely unequipped for Stourbridge Fair, which was one of the biggest in Europe. Daniel

had been there many times with father Drake or half-brother
Raleigh, and knew what *not* to do, anyway.

> The two of us went out back of Trinity and began to walk
> downstream along the Cam. After passing by the bridge in
> the center of town that gives the City and University their
> name, we entered into a reach along the north side of Jesus
> Green where the Cam describes a graceful curve in the
> shape of an elongated S.

Daniel almost writes *like the integration symbol used in the calculus*.
But he suppresses that, since that symbol, and indeed the term *calculus*, were invented by Leibniz.

> I made some waggish student-like remark about this curve,
> as curves had been much on our minds the previous year,
> and Newton began to speak with confidence and enthusi-
> asm—demonstrating that the ideas he spoke of were not
> extemporaneous speculation but a fully developed theory on
> which he had been working for some time.
>   "Yes, and suppose we were on one of those punts," New-
> ton said, pointing to one of the narrow, flat-bottomed boats
> that idle students used to mess about on the Cam. "And sup-
> pose that the Bridge was the Origin of a system of Cartesian
> coordinates covering Jesus Green and the other land sur-
> rounding the river's course."

No, no, no, no. Daniel dips his quill and scratches that bit out. It
is an anachronism. Worse, it's a Leibnizism. Natural Philosophers
may talk that way in 1713, but they didn't fifty years ago. He has to
translate it back into the sort of language that Descartes would
have used.

> "And suppose," Newton continued, "that we had a rope with
> regularly spaced knots, such as mariners use to log their
> speed, and we anchored one end of it on the Bridge—for
> the Bridge is a fixed point in absolute space. If that rope
> were stretched tight it would be akin to one of the num-
> bered lines employed by Monsieur Descartes in his Geome-
> try. By stretching it between the Bridge and the punt, we
> could measure how far the punt had drifted down-river, and
> in which direction."

Actually, this is not the way Isaac ever would have said it. But Daniel's writing this for princes and parliamentarians, not Natural Philosophers, and so he has to put long explanations in Isaac's mouth.

"And lastly suppose that the Cam flowed always at the same speed, and that our punt matched it. That is what I call a fluxion—a flowing movement along the curve over time. I think you can see that as we rounded the first limb of the S-curve around Jesus College, where the river bends southward, our fluxion in the north-south direction would be steadily changing. At the moment we passed under the Bridge, we'd be pointed northeast, and so we would have a large northwards fluxion. A minute later, when we reached the point just above Jesus College, we'd be going due east, and so our north-south fluxion would be zero. A minute after that, after we'd curved round and drawn alongside Midsummer Commons, we'd be headed southeast, meaning that we would have developed a large southward fluxion—but even that would reduce and tend back towards zero as the stream curved round northwards again towards Stourbridge Fair."

He can stop here. For those who know how to read between the lines, this is sufficient to prove Newton had the calculus—or Fluxions, as he called it—in '65, most likely '64. No point in beating them over the head with it . . .

Yes, beating someone over the head is the *entire* point.

Banks of the River Cam
1665

Almost five thousand years agone, there were pilgrims walking to the Celestial City, as these two honest persons are; and Beelzebub, Apollyon, and
Legion, with their companions, perceiving by the
path that the pilgrims made that their way to the

> City lay through this town of Vanity, they contrived
> here to set up a fair; a fair wherein should be sold all
> sorts of vanity, and that it should last all the year
> long. Therefore at this Fair are all such merchandise
> sold, as houses, lands, trades, places, honours, prefer-
> ments, titles, countries, kingdoms, lusts, pleasures,
> and delights of all sorts, as whores, bawds, wives,
> husbands, children, masters, servants, lives, blood,
> bodies, souls, silver, gold, pearls, precious stones,
> and what not.
>
> And moreover, at this Fair there is at all times to
> be seen jugglings, cheats, games, plays, fools, apes,
> knaves, and rogues, and that of all sorts.
>
> —JOHN BUNYAN, *The Pilgrim's Progress*

IT WAS LESS THAN AN hour's walk to the Fair, strolling along gently
sloped green banks with weeping-willows, beneath whose canopies
were hidden various prostrate students. Black cattle mowed the
grass unevenly and strewed cow-pies along their way. At first the
river was shallow enough to wade across, and its bottom was carpeted with slender fronds that, near the top, were bent slightly
downstream by the mild current. "Now, there is a curve whose fluxion in the downstream direction is nil at the point where it is
rooted in the bottom—that is to say, it rises vertically from the
mud—but increases as it rises."

Here Daniel was a bit lost. "Fluxion seems to mean a flowing
over time—so it makes perfect sense when you apply the word to
the position of a punt on a river, which is, as a matter of fact, flowing over time. But now you seem to be applying it to the shape of
a weed, which is not flowing—it's just standing there sort of
bent."

"But Daniel, the virtue of this approach is that it *doesn't matter*
what the actual physical situation *is,* a curve is *ever a curve,* and
whatever you can do to the curve of a *river* you can do just as
rightly to the curve of a *weed*—we are free from all that old nonsense now." Meaning the Aristotelian approach, in which such
easy mixing of things with obviously different natures would be
abhorrent. All that mattered henceforth, apparently, was what
form they adopted when translated into the language of analysis.
"Translating a thing into the analytical language is akin to what
the alchemist does when he extracts, from some crude ore, a pure
spirit, or virtue, or *pneuma*. The fœces—the gross external forms

of things—which only mislead and confuse us—are cast off to reveal the underlying spirit. And when this is done we may learn that some things that are superficially different are, in their real nature, the same."

Very soon, as they left the colleges behind, the Cam became broader and deeper and instantly was crowded with much larger boats. Still, they were not boats for the ocean—they were long, narrow, and flat-bottomed, made for rivers and canals, but with far greater displacement than the little punts. Stourbridge Fair was already audible: the murmur of thousands of haggling buyers and sellers, barking of dogs, wild strains from bagpipes and shawms whipping over their heads like twists of bright ribbon unwinding in the breeze. They looked at the boat-people: Independent traders in black hats and white neck-cloths, waterborne Gypsies, ruddy Irish and Scottish men, and simply Englishmen with complicated personal stories, negotiating with sure-footed boat-dogs, throwing buckets of mysterious fluids overboard, pursuing domestic arguments with unseen persons in the tents or shacks pitched on their decks.

Then they rounded a bend, and there was the Fair, spread out in a vast wedge of land, bigger than Cambridge, even more noisy, much more crowded. It was mostly tents and tent-people, who were not their kind of people—Daniel watched Isaac gain a couple of inches in height as he remembered the erect posture that Puritans used to set a better example. In some secluded parts of the Fair (Daniel knew) serious merchants were trading cattle, timber, iron, barrelled oysters—anything that could be brought upriver this far on a boat, or transported overland in a wagon. But this wholesale trade *wanted* to be invisible, and *was*. What Isaac *saw* was a *retail* fair whose size and gaudiness was all out of proportion to its importance, at least if you went by the amount of money that changed hands. The larger avenues (which meant sluices of mud with planks and logs strewn around for people to step on, or at least push off against) were lined with tents of rope-dancers, jugglers, play-actors, puppet shows, wrestling-champions, dancing-girls, and of course the speciality prostitutes who made the Fair such an important resource for University students. But going up into the smaller byways, they found the tables and stalls and the cleverly fashioned unfolding wagons of traders who'd brought goods from all over Europe, up the Ouse and the Cam to this place to sell them to England.

Daniel and Isaac roamed for the better part of an hour, ignoring the shouts and pleadings of the retailers on all sides, until finally Isaac stopped, alert, and sidestepped over to a small folding display-case-on-legs that a tall slender Jew in a black coat had set up. Daniel eyed this Son of Moses curiously—Cromwell had re-admitted these people to England only ten years previously, after they'd been excluded for centuries, and they were as exotic as giraffes. But Isaac was staring at a constellation of gemlike objects laid out on a square of black velvet. Noting his interest, the Kohan folded back the edges of the cloth to reveal many more: concave and convex lenses, flat disks of good glass for grinding your own, bottles of abrasive powder in several degrees of coarseness, and prisms.

Isaac signalled that he would be willing to open negotiations over two of the prisms. The lens-grinder inhaled, drew himself up, and blinked. Daniel moved round to a supporting position behind and to the side of Isaac. "You have pieces of eight," the circumcised one said—midway between an assertion and a question.

"I know that your folk once lived in a kingdom where that was the coin of the realm, sir," Isaac said, "but . . ."

"You know nothing—my people did not come from Spain. They came from Poland. You have French coins—the louis d'or?"

"The louis d'or is a beautiful coin, befitting the glory of the Sun King," Daniel put in, "and probably much used wherever you came from—Amsterdam?"

"London. You intend to compensate me, then, with what—Joachimsthalers?"

"As you, sir, are English, and so am I, let us use English means."

"You wish to trade cheese? Tin? Broadcloth?"

"How many *shillings* will buy these two prisms?"

The Hebraic one adopted a haggard, suffering look and gazed at a point above their heads. "Let me see the color of your money," he said, in a voice that conveyed gentle regret, as if Isaac *might* have bought some prisms today, and instead would only get a dreary les-son in the unbelievable shabbiness of English coinage. Isaac reached into a pocket and wiggled his fingers to produce a metallic tromping noise that proved many coins were in there. Then he pulled out a handful and let the lens-grinder have a glimpse of a few coins, tarnished black. Daniel, so far, was startled by how good Isaac was at this kind of thing. On the other hand, he had made a business out of lending money to other students—maybe he had talent.

"You must have made a mistake," said the Jew. "Which is perfectly all right—we all make mistakes. You reached into the wrong pocket and you pulled out your black money*—the stuff you throw to beggars."

"Ahem, er, so I did," Isaac said. "Pardon me—where's the money for paying merchants?" Patting a few other pockets. "By the way, assuming I'm not going to offer you black money, how many shillings?"

"When you say shillings, I assume you mean the new ones?"

"The James I?"

"No, no, James I died half a century ago and so one would not normally use the adjective *new* to describe pounds minted during his reign."

"Did you say *pounds*?" Daniel asked. "A pound is rather a lot of money, and so it strikes me as not relevant to this transaction, which has all the appearances of a shilling type of affair *at most*."

"Let us use the word *coins* until I know whether you speak of the new or the old."

"*New* meaning the coins minted, say, during our lifetimes?"

"I mean the Restoration coinage," the Israelite said, "or perhaps your professors have neglected to inform you that Cromwell is dead, and Interregnum coins demonetized these last three years."

"Why, I believe I *have* heard that the King is beginning to mint new coins," Isaac said, looking to Daniel for confirmation.

"My half-brother in London knows someone who *saw* a gold CAROLUS II DEI GRATIA coin once, displayed in a crystal case on a silken pillow," Daniel said. "People have begun to call them Guineas, because they are made of gold that the Duke of York's company is taking out of Africa."

"I say, Daniel, is it true what they say, that those coins are perfectly circular?"

"They are, Isaac—not like the good old English hammered coins that you and I carry in such abundance in our pockets and purses."

"Furthermore," said the Ashkenazi, "the King brought with him a French savant, Monsieur Blondeau, on loan from King Louis, and that fellow built a machine that mills delicate ridges and inscriptions into the edges of the coins."

"Typical French extravagance," Isaac said.

"The King really did spend more time than was good for him in Paris," Daniel said.

"On the contrary," the forelocked one said, "if someone clips or

---

*Counterfeits made of base metals such as copper and lead.

files a bit of metal off the edge of a round coin with a milled edge, it is immediately obvious."

"That must be why everyone is melting those new coins down as fast as they are minted, and shipping the metal to the Orient . . . ?" Daniel began,

". . . making it impossible for the likes of me and my friend to obtain them," Isaac finished.

"Now there is a good idea—if you can show me coins of a bright silver color—not that black stuff—I'll weigh them and accept them as bullion."

"*Bullion!* Sir!"

"Yes."

"I have heard that this is the practice in China," Isaac said sagely. "But here in England, a shilling is a shilling."

"No matter how little it weighs!?"

"Yes. In principle, yes."

"So when a lump of metal is coined in the Mint, it takes on a magical power of shillingness, and even after it has been filed and clipped and worn down to a mere featureless nodule, it is still worth a full shilling?"

"You exaggerate," Daniel said. "I have here a fine Queen Elizabeth shilling, for example—which I carry around, mind you, as a souvenir of Gloriana's reign, since it is far too fine a specimen to actually *spend*. But as you can see, it is just as bright and shiny as the day it was minted—"

"Especially where it's recently been clipped there along the side," the lens-grinder said.

"Normal, pleasing irregularity of the hand-hammered currency, nothing more."

Isaac said, "My friend's shilling, though magnificent, and arguably worth two or even three shillings in the market, is no anomaly. Here I have a shilling from the reign of Edward VI, which I obtained after an inebriated son of a Duke, who happened to have borrowed a shilling from me some time earlier, fell unconscious on a floor— the purse in which he carried his finest coins fell open and this rolled out of it—I construed this as repayment of the debt, and the exquisite condition of the coin as interest."

"How could it roll when three of its edges are flat? It is nearly triangular," the lens-grinder said.

"A trick of the light."

"The problem with that Edward VI coinage is that for all I knew it might've been issued during the Great Debasement, when, before Sir Thomas Gresham could get matters in hand, prices doubled."

"The inflation was not because the coins were debased, as some believe," Daniel said, "it was because the wealth confiscated from the Papist monasteries, and cheap silver from the mines of New Spain, were flooding the country."

"If you would allow me to approach within ten feet of these coins, it would help me to appreciate their numismatic excellence," the lens-grinder said. "I could even use some of my magnifying-lenses to . . ."

"I'm afraid I would be offended," Isaac said.

"You could inspect this one as closely as you wanted," Daniel said, "and find no evidence of criminal tampering—I got it from a blind innkeeper who had suffered frostbite in the fingertips—had no idea what he was giving me."

"Didn't he think to bite down on it? Like so?" said the Judaic individual, taking the shilling and crushing it between his rear molars.

"What would he have learned by doing that, sir?"

"That whatever counterfeit-artist stamped it out, had used reasonably good metal—not above fifty percent lead."

"We'll choose to interpret that as a wry jest," Daniel said, "the likes of which you could never direct against *this* shilling, which my half-brother found lying on the ground at the Battle of Naseby, not far from fragments of a Royalist captain who'd been blown to pieces by a bursting cannon—the dead man was, you see, a captain who'd once stood guard at the Tower of London where new coins are minted."

The Jew repeated the biting ceremony, then scratched at the coin in case it was a brass clinker japanned with silver paint. "Worthless. But I owe a shilling to a certain vile man in London, a hater of Jews, and I would drive a shilling's worth of satisfaction from slipping this slug of pig-iron into his hand."

"Very well, then—" said Isaac, reaching for the prisms.

"Avid collectors such as you two must also have pennies—?"

"My father hands out shiny new ones as Christmas presents," Daniel began. "Three years ago—" but he suspended the anecdote when he noticed that the lens-grinder was paying attention, not to him, but to a commotion behind them.

Daniel turned around and saw that it was a man, reasonably well-heeled, having trouble walking even though a friend and a servant were supporting him. He had a powerful desire to lie down, it seemed, which was most awkward, as he happened to be wading through ankle-deep mud. The servant slipped a hand between the man's upper arm and his ribs to bear him up, but the man shrieked like a cat who's been mangled under a cart-wheel and convulsed backwards and landed full-length on his back, hurling up a coffin-shaped wave of mud that spattered things yards away.

"Take your prisms," said the merchant, practically stuffing them into Isaac's pocket. He began folding up his display-case. If he felt the way Daniel did, then it wasn't the sight of a man feeling ill, or falling down, that made him pack up and leave, so much as the sound of that scream.

Isaac was walking toward the sick man with the cautious but direct gait of a tightrope-walker.

"Shall we back to Cambridge, then?" Daniel suggested.

"I have some knowledge of the arts of the apothecary." Isaac said, "Perhaps I could help him."

A circle of people had gathered to observe the sick man, but it was a very broad circle, empty except for Isaac and Daniel. The victim appeared, now, to be trying to get his breeches off. But his arms were rigid, so he was trying to do it by writhing free of his clothes. His servant and his friend were tugging at the cuffs, but the breeches seemed to've shrunk onto his legs. Finally the friend drew his dagger, slashed through the cuffs left and right, and then ripped the pant-legs open from bottom to top—or perhaps the force of the swelling thighs burst them. They came off, anyway. Friend and servant backed away, affording Isaac and Daniel a clear vantage point that would have enabled them to see all the way up to the man's groin, if the view hadn't been blocked by black globes of taut flesh stacked like cannonballs up his inner thighs.

The man had stopped writhing and screaming now because he was dead. Daniel had taken Isaac's arm and was rather firmly pulling him back, but Isaac continued to approach the specimen. Daniel looked round and saw that suddenly there was no one within musket range—horses and tents had been abandoned, back-loads of goods spilled on the ground by porters now halfway to Ely.

"I can *see* the buboes expanding even though the body is dead," Isaac said. "The generative spirit lives on—transmuting dead flesh into something else—just as maggots are generated out of meat, and silver grows beneath mountains—why does it bring death sometimes and life others?"

That they lived was evidence that Daniel eventually pulled Isaac away and got him pointed back up the river toward Cambridge. But Isaac's mind was still on those Satanic miracles that had appeared in the dead man's groin. "I admire Monsieur Descartes' analysis, but there is something missing in his supposition that the world is just bits of matter jostling one another like coins shaken in a bag. How could that account for the ability of matter to organize itself into eyes and leaves and salamanders, to transmute itself into alternate forms? And yet it's not simply that matter comes together in good ways—not some ongoing miraculous Creation—for the same process by which our bodies turn meat and milk into flesh and blood can also cause a man's body to convert itself into a mass of buboes in a few hours' time. It might *seem* aimless, but it *cannot* be. That one man sickens and dies, while another flourishes, are characters in the cryptic message that philosophers seek to decode."

"Unless the message was set down long ago and is there in the Bible for all men to read plainly," Daniel said.

Fifty years later, he hates to remember that he ever talked this way, but he can't stop himself.

"What do you mean by that?"

"The year 1665 is halfway over—you know what year comes next. I must to London, Isaac. Plague has come to England. What we have seen today is a harbinger of the Apocalypse."

Aboard Minerva, *off the Coast of New England*

NOVEMBER 1713

DANIEL IS ROUSED by a rooster on the forecastledeck* that is growing certain it's not just imagining that light in the eastern sky. Unfortunately, the eastern sky is off to port this morning. Yesterday it was to starboard. *Minerva* has been sailing up and down the New England coast for the better part of a fortnight, trying to catch a

---

*The forecastledeck is the short deck that, towards the ship's bow, is built above the upperdeck.

wind that will decisively take her out into the deep water, or "off soundings," as they say. They are probably not more than fifty miles away from Boston.

He goes below to the gun deck, a dim slab of sharp-smelling air. When his eyes have adjusted he can see the cannons, all swung around on their low carriages so they are parallel to the hull planking, aimed forwards, lashed in place, and the heavy hatches closed over the gun ports. Now that he cannot see the horizon, he must use the soles of his feet to sense the ship's rolling and pitching—if he waits for his balance-sense to tell him he's falling, it'll be too late. He makes his way aft in very short, carefully planned steps, trailing fingertips along the ceiling, jostling the long ramrods and brushes racked up there for tending the guns. This takes him to a door and thence into a cabin at the stern that's as wide as the entire ship and fitted with a sweep of windows, gathering what light they can from the western sky and the setting moon.

Half a dozen men are in here working and talking, all of them relatively old and sophisticated compared to ordinary seamen—this is where great chests full of good tools are stored, and sheets of potent diagrams nested. A tiller the dimensions of a battering-ram runs straight down the middle of the ceiling and out through a hole in the stern to the rudder, which it controls; the forward end of the tiller is pulled to and fro by a couple of cables that pass up through openings in the decks to the wheel. The air smells of coffee, wood-shavings, and pipe-smoke. Grudging hellos are scattered about. Daniel goes back and sits by one of the windows—these are undershot so that he can look straight down and see *Minerva*'s wake being born in a foamy collision down around the rudder. He opens a small hatch below a window and drops out a Fahrenheit thermometer on a string. It is the very latest in temperature measurement technology from Europe—Enoch presented it to him as a sort of party favor. He lets it bounce through the surf for a few minutes, then hauls it in and takes a reading.

He's been trying to perform this ritual every four hours—the objective being to see if there's anything to the rumor that the North Atlantic is striped with currents of warm water. He can present the data to the Royal Society if-God-willing-he-reaches-London. At first he did it from the upperdeck, but he didn't like the way the instrument got battered against the hull, and he was wearied by the looks of incomprehension on the sailors' faces. The old gaffers back here don't necessarily think he's any less crazy but they don't think less of him for it.

So like a sojourner in a foreign city who eventually finds a coffeehouse where he feels at home, Daniel has settled on this place, and been accepted here. The regulars are mostly in their thirties and forties: a Filipino; a Lascar; a half-African, half-white from the Portuguese city of Goa; a Huguenot; a Cornish man with surprisingly poor English; an Irishman. They're all perfectly at home here, as if *Minerva* were a thousand-year-old ship on which their ancestors had always lived. If she ever sinks, Daniel suspects they'll happily go down with her, for lack of any other place to live. Joined with one another and with *Minerva,* they have the power to travel anywhere on earth, fighting their way past pirates if need be, eating well, sleeping in their own beds. But if *Minerva* were lost, it almost wouldn't make any difference whether it spilled them into the North Atlantic in a January gale, or let them off gently into some port town—either way, it'd be a short, sad life for them after that. Daniel wishes there were a comforting analogy to the Royal Society to be made here, but as that lot are currently trying to throw one of their own number* overboard, it doesn't really work.

A brick-lined cabin is wedged between the upperdeck and the forecastledeck, always full of smoke because fires burn there—food comes out of it from time to time. A full meal is brought to Daniel once a day, and he takes it, usually by himself, sometimes with Captain van Hoek, in the common-room. He's the only passenger. Here it's evident that *Minerva*'s an old ship, because the crockery and flatware are motley, chipped, and worn. Those parts of the ship that *matter* have been maintained or replaced as part of what Daniel's increasingly certain must be a subtle, understated, but fanatical program of maintenance decreed by van Hoek and ramrodded by one of his mates. The crockery and other clues suggest that the ship's a good three decades old, but unless you go down into the hold and view the keel and the ribs, you don't see any pieces that are older than perhaps five years.

None of the plates match, and so it's always a bit of a game for Daniel to eat his way down through the meal (normally something stewlike with expensive spices) until he can see the pattern on the plate. It is kind of an idiotic game for a Fellow of the Royal Society to indulge in, but he doesn't introspect about it until one evening when he's staring into his plate, watching the gravy slosh with the ship's heaving (a microcosm of the Atlantic?), and all of a sudden it's

---

*Baron Gottfried Wilhelm von Leibniz.

☙

The Plague Year

SUMMER 1665

෴

> Th'earths face is but thy Table; there are set
> Plants, cattell, men, dishes for Death to eate.
> In a rude hunger now hee millions drawes
> Into his bloody, or plaguy, or sterv'd jawes.
> —JOHN DONNE, "Elegie on M Boulstred"

DANIEL WAS EATING POTATOES and herring for the thirty-fifth consecutive day. As he was doing it in his father's house, he was expected loudly to thank God for the privilege before and after the meal. His prayers of gratitude were becoming less sincere by the day.

To one side of the house, cattle voiced their eternal confusion—to the other, men trudged down the street ringing handbells (for those who could hear) and carrying long red sticks (for those who could see), peering into court-yards and doorways, and poking their snouts over garden-walls, scanning for bubonic corpses. Everyone else who had enough money to leave London was absent. That included Daniel's half-brothers Raleigh and Sterling and their families, as well as his half-sister Mayflower, who along with her children had gone to ground in Buckinghamshire. Only Mayflower's husband, Thomas Ham, and Drake Waterhouse, Patriarch, had refused to leave. Mr. Ham *wanted* to leave, but he had a cellar in the City to look after.

The idea of leaving, just because of a spot of the old Black Death, hadn't even *occurred* to Drake yet. Both of his wives had died quite a while ago, his elder children had fled, there was no one left to talk sense into him except Daniel. Cambridge had been shut down for the duration of the Plague. Daniel had ventured down here for what he had envisioned as a quick, daring raid on an empty house, and had found Drake seated before a virginal playing old hymns from the Civil War. Having spent most of his good coins, first of all helping Newton buy prisms, and secondly bribing a reluctant coachman to bring him down within walking distance of this pest-hole, Daniel was stuck until he could get money out of Dad—a subject he was afraid to even broach. Since God had pre-destined all events anyway, there was no way for them to avoid the Plague, if that was their doom—and if it *wasn't*, why, no harm in staying there on the edge of the city and setting an example for the fleeing and/or dying populace.

Owing to those modifications that had been made to his head at the behest of Archbishop Laud, Drake Waterhouse made curious percolating and whistling noises when he chewed and swallowed his potatoes and herring.

In 1629, Drake and some friends had been arrested for distrib-uting freshly printed libels in the streets of London. These particu-lar libels inveighed against Ship Money, a new tax imposed by Charles I. But the topic did not matter; if this had happened in 1628, the libels would have been about something else, and no less offensive to the King and the Archbishop.

An indiscreet remark made by one of Drake's comrades after burning sticks had been rammed under his nails led to the discov-ery of the printing-press that Drake had used to print the libels—he kept it in a wagon hidden under a pile of hay. So as he had now been exposed as the master-mind of the conspiracy, Bishop Laud had him, and a few other supremely annoying Calvinists, pilloried, branded, and mutilated. These were essentially practical tech-niques more than punishments. The intent was not to reform the criminals, who were clearly un-reformable. The pillory fixed them in one position for a while so that all London could come by and get a good look at their faces and thereafter recognize them. The branding and mutilation marked them permanently so that the rest of the world would know them.

As all of this had happened years before Daniel had even been born, it didn't matter to him—this was just how Dad had always looked—and of course it had *never* mattered to Drake. Within a few weeks, Drake had been back on the highways of England, buying cloth that he'd later smuggle to the Netherlands. In a country inn, on the way to St. Ives, he encountered a saturnine, beetle-browed chap name of Oliver Cromwell who had recently lost his faith, and seen his life ruined—or so he imagined, until he got a look at Drake, and found God. But that was another story.

The goal of all persons who had houses in those days was to pos-sess the smallest number of pieces of furniture needed to sustain life, but to make them as large and heavy and dark as possible. Accordingly, Daniel and Drake ate their potatoes and herring on a table that had the size and weight of a medieval drawbridge. There was no other furniture in the room, although the eight-foot-high grandfather clock in the adjoining hall contributed a sort of immediate presence with the heaving to and fro of its cannonball-sized pendulum, which made the entire house lean from one side to the other like a drunk out for a brisk walk, and the palpable grinding of its gear-train, and the wild clamorous bonging that exploded from it at intervals that seemed suspiciously random, and that caused flocks of migrating waterfowl, thousands of feet overhead, to collide with each other in panic and veer into new courses. The fur of dust beginning to overhang its Gothick battlements; its internal supply of mouse-turds; the Roman numerals carven into the back by its maker; and its complete inability to tell time, all marked it as pre-Huygens technology. Its bonging would have tried Daniel's patience even if it had occurred precisely on the hour, half-hour, quarter-hour, *et cetera,* for it never failed to make him jump out of his skin. That it conveyed no information whatever as to what the time actually was, drove Daniel into such transports of annoyance that he had begun to entertain a phant'sy of standing at the intersection of two corridors and handing Drake, every time he passed by, a libel denouncing the ancient Clock, and demanding its wayward pendulum be stilled, and that it be replaced with a new Huygens model. But Drake had already told him to shut up about the clock, and so there was nothing he could do.

Daniel was going for days without hearing any other sounds but these. All possible subjects of conversation could be divided into two categories: (1) ones that would cause Drake to unleash a rant, previously heard so many times that Daniel could recite it from memory, and (2) ones that might actually lead to original conversation. Daniel avoided Category 1 topics. All Category 2 topics had already been exhausted. For example, Daniel could not ask, "How is Praise-God doing in Boston?"* because he had asked this on the first day, and Drake had answered it, and since then few letters had arrived because the letter-carriers were dead or running away from London as fast as they could go. Sometimes private couriers would come with letters, mostly pertaining to Drake's business matters but sometimes addressed to Daniel. This would provoke a flurry of conversation stretching out as long as half an hour (not counting

---

*Praise-God W. being the eldest son of Raleigh W., and hence Drake W.'s first grandchild; he had recently sailed to Boston at the age of sixteen to study at Harvard, become part of that City on the Hill that was America, and, if possible, return in glory at some future time to drive Archbishop Laud's spawn from England and reform the Anglican Church once and for all.

rants), but mostly what Daniel heard, day after day, was corpse-collectors' bells, and their creaking carts; the frightful Clock; cows; Drake reading the Books of Daniel and of Revelation aloud, or playing the virginal; and the gnawing of Daniel's own quill across the pages of his notebook as he worked his way through Euclid, Copernicus, Galileo, Descartes, Huygens. He actually learned an appalling amount. In fact, he was fairly certain he'd caught up with where Isaac had been several months previously—but Isaac was up at home in Woolsthorpe, a hundred miles away, and no doubt years ahead of him by this point.

He ate down to the bottom of his potatoes and herring with the determination of a prisoner clawing a hole through a wall, finally revealing the plate. The Waterhouse family china had been manufactured by sincere novices in Holland. After James I had outlawed the export of unfinished English cloth to the Netherlands, Drake had begun smuggling it there, which was easily done since the town of Leyden was crowded with English pilgrims. In this way Drake had made the first of several smuggling-related fortunes, and done so in a way pleasing in the sight of the Lord, viz. by boldly defying the King's efforts to meddle in commerce. Not only that but he had met and in 1617 married a pilgrim lass in Leyden, and he had made many donations there to the faithful who were in the market for a ship. The grateful congregation, shortly before embarking on the *Mayflower,* bound for sunny Virginia, had presented Drake and his new wife, Hortense, with this set of Delft pottery. They had obviously made it themselves on the theory that when they sloshed up onto the shores of America, they'd better know how to make stuff out of clay. They were heavy crude plates glazed white, with an inscription in spidery blue letters:

YOU AND I ARE BUT EARTH.

Staring at this through a miasma of the bodily fluids of herring for the thirty-fifth consecutive day, Daniel suddenly announced, "I was thinking that I might go and, God willing, visit John Wilkins."

Wilkins had been exchanging letters with Daniel ever since the debacle of five years ago, when Daniel had arrived at Trinity College a few moments after Wilkins had been kicked out of it forever.

The mention of Wilkins did not trigger a rant, which meant Daniel was as good as there. But there were certain formalities to be gone through: "To what end?" asked Drake, sounding like a pipe-organ with numerous jammed valves as the words emerged partly from his mouth and partly from his nose. He voiced all questions as if they were pat assertions: *To what end* being said in the same tones as *You and I are but earth.*

"My purpose is to learn, Father, but I seem to've learned all I can from the books that are here."

"And what of the Bible." An excellent riposte there from Drake.

"There are Bibles everywhere, praise God, but only one Reverend Wilkins."

"He has been preaching at that Established church in the city, has he not."

"Indeed. St. Lawrence Jewry."

"Then why should it be necessary for you to leave." As the city was a quarter of an hour's walk.

"The Plague, father—I don't believe he has actually set foot in London these last several months."

"And what of his flock."

Daniel almost fired back, *Oh, you mean the Royal Society?* which in most other houses would have been a *bon mot,* but not here. "They've all run away, too, Father, the ones who aren't dead."

"High Church folk," Drake said self-explanatorily. "Where is Wilkins now."

"Epsom."

"He is with Comstock. What can he possibly be thinking."

"It's no secret that you and Wilkins have come down on opposite sides of the fence, Father."

"The golden fence that Laud threw up around the Lord's Table! Yes."

"Wilkins backs Tolerance as fervently as you. He hopes to reform the church from within."

"Yes, and no man—short of an Archbishop—could be more *within* than John Comstock, the Earl of Epsom. But why should you embroil yourself in such matters."

"Wilkins is not pursuing religious controversies at Epsom—he is pursuing natural philosophy."

"Seems a strange place for it."

"The Earl's son, Charles, could not attend Cambridge because of the plague, and so Wilkins and some other members of the Royal Society are there to serve as his tutors."

"Aha! It is all clear, then. It is all an *accommodation.*"

"Yes."

"What is it that you hope to learn from the Reverend Wilkins."

"Whatever it is that he wishes to teach me. Through the Royal Society he is in communication with all the foremost natural philosophers of the British Isles, and many on the Continent as well."

Drake took some time considering that. "You are asserting that you require my financial assistance in order to become acquainted with a *hypothetical* body of knowledge which you *assume* has come into existence *out of nowhere*, quite recently."

"Yes, Father."

"A bit of an act of faith then, isn't it."

"Not so much as you might think. My friend Isaac—I've told you of him—has spoken of a 'generative spirit' that pervades all things, and that accounts for the possibility of new things being created from old—and if you don't believe me, then just ask yourself, how can flowers grow up out of manure? Why does meat turn itself into maggots, and ships' planking into worms? Why do images of seashells form in rocks far from any sea, and why do new stones grow in farmers' fields after the previous year's crop has been dug out? Clearly some organizing principle is at work, and it pervades all things invisibly, and accounts for the world's ability to have *newness*—to do something other than only decay."

"And yet it decays. Look out the window! Listen to the ringing of the bells. Ten years ago, Cromwell melted down the Crown Jewels and gave all men freedom of religion. Today, a crypto-Papist* and lackey of the Antichrist† rules England, and England's gold goes to making giant punch-bowls for use at the royal orgies, and we of the Gathered Church must worship in secret as if we were early Christians in pagan Rome."

"One of the things about the generative spirit that demands our careful study is that it can go awry," Daniel returned. "In some sense the *pneuma* that causes buboes to grow from the living flesh of plague victims must be akin to the one that causes mushrooms to pop out of the ground after rain, but one has effects we call evil and the other has effects we call good."

"You think Wilkins knows more of this."

"I was actually using it to explain the very *existence* of men like Wilkins, and of this club of his, which he now calls the Royal Society, and of other such groups, such as Monsieur de Montmor's salon in Paris—"

"I see. You suppose that this same spirit is at work *in the minds* of these natural philosophers."

"Yes, Father, and in the very soil of the nations that have

---

*King Charles II of England.
†Usually the Pope, but in this context, King Louis XIV of France.

produced so many natural philosophers in such a short time—to the great discomfiture of the Papists." Reckoning it could not hurt his chances to get in a dig at Popery. "And just as the farmer can rely on the steady increase of his crops, I can be sure that much new work has been accomplished by such people within the last several months."

"But with the End of Days drawing so near—"

"Only a few months ago, at one of the last meetings of the Royal Society, Mr. Daniel Coxe said that mercury had been found running like water in a chalk-pit at Line. And Lord Brereton said that at an Inn in St. Alban's, quicksilver was found running in a saw-pit."

"And you suppose this means—what."

"Perhaps this flourishing of so many kinds—natural philosophy, plague, the power of King Louis, orgies at Whitehall, quicksilver welling up from the bowels of the earth—is a necessary preparation for the Apocalypse—the generative spirit rising up like a tide."

"That much is obvious, Daniel. I wonder, though, whether there is any point in furthering your studies when we are so close."

"Would you admire a farmer who let his fields be overrun with weeds, simply because the End was near?"

"No, of course not. Your point is well taken."

"If we have a duty to be alert for the signs of the End Times, then let me go, Father. For if the signs are comets, then the first to know will be the astronomers. If the signs are plague, the first to know—"

"—will be physicians. Yes, I understand. But are you suggesting that those who study natural philosophy can acquire some kind of occult knowledge—special insight into God's Creation, not available to the common Bible-reading man?"

"Er . . . I suppose that's *quite clearly* what I'm suggesting."

Drake nodded. "That is what I thought. Well, God gave us brains for a reason—*not* to use those brains would be a sin." He got up and carried his plate to the kitchen, then went to a small desk of many drawers in the parlor and broke out all of the gear needed to write on paper with a quill. "Haven't much coin just now," he mumbled, moving the quill about in a sequence of furious scribbles separated by long flowing swoops, like a sword-duel. "There you are."

Mr. Ham pray pay to the bearer one pound I say £1—of that money of myne which you have in your hands upon sight of this Bill

Drake Waterhouse
London

"What is this instrument, Father?"

"Goldsmith's Note. People started doing this about the time you left for Cambridge."

"Why does it say 'the bearer'? Why not 'Daniel Waterhouse'?"

"Well, that's the beauty of it. You could, if you chose, use this to pay a one-pound debt—you'd simply hand it to your creditor and he could then nip down to Ham's and get a pound in coin of the realm. Or he could use it to pay one of *his* debts."

"I see. But in this case it simply means that if I go into the City and present this to Uncle Thomas, or one of the other Hams . . ."

"They'll do what the note orders them to do."

It was, then, a normal example of Drake's innate fiendishness. Daniel was perfectly welcome to flee to Epsom—the seat of John Comstock, the arch-Anglican—and study Natural Philosophy until, literally, the End of the World. But in order to obtain the *means*, he would have to demonstrate his faith by walking all the way across London at the height of the Plague. Trial by ordeal it was.

The next morning: on with a coat and a down-at-heels pair of riding-boots, even though it was a warm summer day. A scarf to breathe through.* A minimal supply of clean shirts and drawers (if he was feeling well when he reached Epsom, he'd send for more). A rather small number of books—tiny student octavo volumes of the usual Continental savants, their margins and inter-linear spaces now caulked with his notes. A letter he'd received from Wilkins, with an enclosure from one Robert Hooke, during a rare spate of mail last week. All went into a bag, the bag on the end of a staff, and the staff over his shoulder—made him look somewhat Vagabondish, but many people in the city had turned to robbery, as normal sources of employment had been shut down, and there were sound reasons to look impoverished and carry a big stick.

Drake, upon Daniel's departure: "Will you tell old Wilkins that I do not think the less of him for having become an Angli-can, as I have the most serene confidence that he has done so in the interest of *reforming* that church, which as you know has been

---

*The consensus of the best physicians in the Royal Society was that plague was not caused by bad air, but had something to do with being crowded together with many other people, especially foreigners (the first victims of the London plague had been Frenchmen fresh off the boat, who'd died in an inn about five hundred yards from Drake's house), however, everyone breathed through scarves anyway.

the steady goal of those of us who are scorned by others as Puritans."

And for Daniel: "I want that you should take care that the plague should not infect you—not the Black Plague, but the plague of Skepticism so fashionable among Wilkins's crowd. In some ways your soul might be safer in a brothel than among certain Fellows of the Royal Society."

"It is not skepticism for its own sake, Father. Simply an awareness that we are prone to error, and that it is difficult to view anything impartially."

"That is fine when you are talking about comets."

"I'll not discuss religion, then. Good-bye, Father."

"God be with you, Daniel."

HE OPENED THE DOOR, trying not to flinch when outside air touched his face, and descended the steps to the road called Holborn, a river of pounded dust (it had not rained in a while). Drake's house was a new (post-Cromwell) half-timbered building on the north side of the road, one of a line of mostly wooden houses that formed a sort of fence dividing Holborn from the open fields on its north, which stretched all the way to Scotland. The buildings across the way, on the south side of Holborn, were the same but two decades older (pre–Civil War). The ground was flat except for a sort of standing wave of packed dirt that angled across the fields, indeed across Holborn itself, not far away, off to his right—as if a comet had landed on London Bridge and sent up a ripple in the earth, which had spread outwards until it had gone just past Drake's house and then frozen. These were the remains of the earth-works that London* had thrown up early in the Civil War, to defend against the King's armies. There'd been a gate on Holborn and a star-shaped earthen fort nearby, but the gate had been torn down a long time ago and the fort blurred into a grassy hummock guarded by the younger and more adventurous cattle.

Daniel turned left, towards London. This was utter madness. But the letter from Wilkins, and the enclosure from Hooke—a Wilkins protégé from his Oxford days, and now Curator of Experiments of the Royal Society—contained certain requests. They were phrased politely. Perhaps not so politely in Hooke's case. They had

---

*Which had been pro-Cromwell.

let Daniel know that he could be of great service to them by fetching certain items out of certain buildings in London.

Daniel could have burned the letter and claimed it had never arrived. He could have gone to Epsom without any of the items on the list, pleading the Bubonic Plague as his excuse. But he suspected that Wilkins and Hooke did not care for excuses any more than Drake did.

By going to Trinity at exactly the wrong moment, Daniel had missed out on the first five years of the Royal Society of London. Lately he had attended a few meetings, but always felt as if his nose were pressed up against the glass.

Today he would pay his dues by walking into London. It was hardly the most dangerous thing anyone had done in the study of Natural Philosophy.

He put one boot in front of the other, and found that he had not died yet. He did it again, then again. The place seemed eerily normal for a short while as long as you ignored the continuous ringing of death-knells from about a hundred different parish churches. On a closer look, many people had adorned the walls of their houses with nearly hysterical pleas for God's mercy, perhaps thinking that like the blood of the lambs on Israel's door-posts, these graffiti might keep the Angel of Death from knocking. Wagons came and went on Holborn only occasionally—empty ones going into town, stained and reeking, with vanguards and rearguards of swooping birds cutting swaths through the banks of flies that surrounded them—these were corpse-wains returning from their midnight runs to the burial-pits and churchyards outside the town. Wagons filled with people, escorted by pedestrians with hand-bells and red sticks, crept out of town. Just near the remains of those earth-works where Holborn terminated at its intersection with the road to Oxford, a pest-house had been established, and when it had filled up with dead people, another, farther away, to the north of the Tyburn gallows, at Marylebone. Some of the people on the wagons appeared normal, others had reached the stage where the least movement caused them hellish buboe-pain, and so even without the bells and red sticks the approach of these wagons would have been obvious from the fusillade of screams and hot prayers touched off at every bump in the road. Daniel and the very few other pedestrians on Holborn backed into doorways and breathed through scarves when these wagons passed by.

Through Newgate and the stumps of the Roman wall, then, past the Prison, which was silent, but not empty. Towards the square-topped tower of Saint Paul's, where an immense bell was being walloped by tired ringers, counting the years of the dead. That old tower leaned to one side, and had for a long time, so that everyone in London had stopped noticing that it did. In these circumstances, though, it seemed to lean more, and made Daniel suddenly nervous that it was about to fall over on him. Just a few weeks ago, Robert Hooke and Sir Robert Moray had been up in its belfry conducting experiments with two-hundred-foot-long pendulums. Now the cathedral was fortified within a rampart of freshly tamped earth, the graves piled up a full yard above ground level.

The old front of the church had become half eaten away by coal-smoke, and a newfangled Classical porch slapped onto it some three or four decades ago. But the new columns were already decaying, and they were marred from where shops had been built between them during Cromwell's time. During those years, Round-head cavalry had pulled the furniture up from the western half of the church and chopped it up for firewood, then used the empty space as a vast stable for nearly a thousand horses, selling their dung as fuel, to freezing Londoners, for 4d a bushel. Meanwhile, in the eastern half Drake and Bolstrood and others had preached three-hour sermons to diminishing crowds. Now King Charles was supposedly fixing the place up, but Daniel could see no evidence that anything had been done.

Daniel went round the south side of the church even though it was not the most direct way, because he wanted to have a look at the south transept, which had collapsed some years ago. Rumor had it that the bigger and better stones were being carted away and used to build a new wing of John Comstock's house on Piccadilly. Indeed, many of the stones had been removed to somewhere, but of course no one was working there now except for gravediggers.

Into Cheapside, where men on ladders were clambering into upper-story windows of a boarded-up house to remove limp, exhausted children who'd somehow outlived their families. Down in the direction of the river, the only gathering of people Daniel had seen: a long queue before the house of Dr. Nathaniel Hodges, one of the only physicians who hadn't fled. Not far beyond that, on Cheapside, the house of John Wilkins himself. Wilkins had sent Daniel a key, which turned out not to be necessary, as his house had already been broken into. Floorboards pried up, mattresses gutted so that the place looked like a barn for all the loose straw and lumber on the floor. Whole ranks of books pawed from the shelves to see if anything was hidden behind. Daniel went round and re-shelved the books, holding back two or three newish ones that Wilkins had asked him to fetch.

Then to the Church of St. Lawrence Jewry.* "Follow the Drain-pipes, find the *Amphib'ns*," Wilkins had written. Daniel walked round the churchyard, which was studded with graves, but had not reached the graves-on-top-of-graves stage—Wilkins's parishioners were mostly prosperous mercers who'd fled to their country houses. At one corner of the roof, a red copper vein descended from the downhill end of a rain-gutter, then ducked into a holed window beneath. Daniel entered the church and traced it down into a cellar where dormant God-gear was cached to expect the steady wheeling of the liturgical calendar (Easter and Christmas stuff, e.g.) or sudden reversals in the prevailing theology (High Church people like the late Bishop Laud wanted a fence round the altar so parish dogs couldn't lift their legs on the Lord's Table, Low Church primitives like Drake didn't; the Rev. Wilkins, more in the Drake mold, had stashed the fence and rail down here). This room hummed, almost shuddered, as if a choir of monks were lurking in the corners intoning one of their chants, but it was actually the buzzing of a whole civilization of flies, so large that many of them seemed to be singing bass—these had grown from the corpses of rats, which carpeted the cellar floor like autumn leaves. It smelled that way, too.

The drain-pipe came into the cellar from a hole in the floor above, and emptied into a stone baptismal Font—a jumbo, total-baby-immersion style of Font—that had been shoved into a corner, probably around the time that King Henry VIII had kicked out the Papists. Daniel guessed as much from the carvings, which were so thick with symbols of Rome that to remove them all would have destroyed it structurally. When this vessel filled with rain-water from the drain-pipe it would spill excess onto the floor, and it would meander off into a corner and seep into the

---

*Which had nothing to do with Jews; it was named partly after its location in a part of the city where Jews had lived before they had been kicked out of England in 1290 by Edward I. For Jews to exist in a Catholic or Anglican country was theoretically impossible because the entire country was divided into parishes, and every person who lived in a given parish, by definition, was a member of the parish church, which collected tithes, recorded births and deaths, and enforced regular attendance at services. This general sort of arrangement was called the *Established Church* and was why dissidents like Drake had no logical choice but to espouse the concept of the *Gathered Church*, which drew like-minded persons from an arbitrary geographical territory. In making it legally *possible* for Gathered Churches to exist, Cromwell had, in effect, re-admitted Jews to England.

earth—perhaps this source of drinking-water had attracted the sick rats.

In any case the top of the font was covered with a grille held down by a couple of bricks—from underneath came contented croaking sounds. A gout of pink shot through an interstice and speared a fly out of midair, paused humming-taut for an instant, then snapped back. Daniel removed the bricks and pulled up the grille and looked at, and was looked at by, half a dozen of the healthiest frogs he'd ever seen, frogs the size of terriers, frogs that could tongue sparrows out of the air. Standing there in the City of Death, Daniel laughed. The generative spirit ran amok in the bodies of rats, whose corpses were transmuted into flies, which gave up their spirit to produce happy blinking green frogs.

Faint ticks, by the thousands, merged into a sound like wind-driven sleet against a windowpane. Daniel looked down to see it was just hordes of fleas who had abandoned the rat corpses and converged on him from all across the cellar, and were now ricocheting off his leather boots. He rummaged until he found a bread-basket, packed the frogs into it, imprisoned them loosely under a cloth, and walked out of there.

Though he could not see the river from here, he could infer that the tide was receding from the trickle of Thames-water that was beginning to probe its way down the gutter in the middle of Poultry Lane, running downhill from Leadenhall. Normally this would be a slurry of paper-scraps discarded by traders at the 'Change, but today it was lumpy with corpses of rats and cats.

He gave that gutter as wide a berth as he could, but proceeded up against the direction of its flow to the edge of the goldsmiths' district, whence Threadneedle and Poultry and Lombard and Cornhill sprayed confusingly. He continued up Cornhill to the highest point in the City of London, where Cornhill came together with Leadenhall (which carried on eastwards, but downhill from here) and Fish Street (downhill straight to London Bridge) and Bishopsgate (downhill towards the city wall, and Bedlam, and the plague-pit they'd dug next to it). In the middle of this intersection a stand-pipe sprouted, with one nozzle for each of those streets, and Thames-water rushed from each nozzle to flush the gutters. It was connected to a buried pipe that ran underneath Fish Street to the northern terminus of London Bridge. During Elizabeth's time some clever Dutchmen had built water-wheels there. Even when the men who tended them were dead or run away to the country, these spun powerfully whenever the tide went out and high water accumulated on the upstream side of the bridge. They were connected to pumps that pressurized the Fish Street pipe and (if you lived on this hill) carried away the accumulated waste, or (if you lived elsewhere) brought a twice-daily onslaught of litter, turds, and dead animals.

He followed said onslaught down Bishopsgate, watching the water get dirtier as he went, but didn't go as far as the wall—he stopped at the great house, or rather compound, that Sir Thomas ("Bad money drives out good") Gresham had built, a hundred years ago, with money he'd made lending to the Crown and reforming the coinage. Like all old half-timbered fabricks it was slowly warping and bending out of true, but Daniel loved it because it was now Gresham's College, home of the Royal Society.

And of Robert Hooke, the R.S.'s Curator of Experiments, who'd moved into it nine months ago—enabling him to do experiments all the time. Hooke had sent Daniel a list of odds and ends that he needed for his work at Epsom. Daniel deposited his frog-basket and other goods on the high table in the room where the Royal Society had its meetings and, using that as a sort of base-camp, made excursions into Hooke's apartment and all of the rooms and attics and cellars that the Royal Society had taken over for storage.

He saw, and rummaged through, and clambered over, slices of numerous tree-trunks that someone had gathered in a bid to demonstrate that the thin parts of the rings tended to point towards true north. A Brazilian compass-fish that Boyle had suspended from a thread to see if (as legend had it) it would do the same (when Daniel came in, it was pointing south by southeast). Jars containing: powder of the lungs and livers of vipers (someone thought you could produce young vipers from it), something called Sympathetic Powder that supposedly healed wounds through a voodoo-like process. Samples of a mysterious red fluid taken from the Bloody Pond at Newington. Betel-nut, camphire-wood, nux vomica, rhino-horn. A ball of hair that Sir William Curtius had found in a cow's belly. Some experiments in progress: a number of pebbles contained in glass jars full of water, the necks of the jars just barely large enough to let the pebbles in; later they would see if the pebbles could be removed, and if not, it would prove that they had grown in the water. Very large amounts of splintered lumber of all types, domestic and foreign—the residue of the Royal Society's endless experiments on the breaking-strength of wooden beams. The Earl of Balcarres's heart, which he had thoughtfully donated to them, but not until he had died of natural causes. A box of stones that various people had coughed up out of their lungs, which the R.S. was saving up to send as a present to the King. Hundreds of wasps' and birds' nests, methodically labeled with the names of the proud patrons who had brought them in. A box of baby vertebrae which had been removed from a large abscess in the side of a woman who'd had a failed pregnancy twelve years earlier. Stored in jars in spirits of wine: various human fœtuses, the head of a colt with a double eye in the center of its forehead, an eel from Japan. Tacked to the wall: the skin of a seven-legged, two-bodied, single-headed lamb. Decomposing in glass boxes: the Royal Society's viper collection, all dead of starvation; some had their heads tied to their tails as part of some sort of Uroburos experiment. More hairballs. The heart of an executed person, superficially no different from that of the Earl of Balcarres. A vial containing seeds that had supposedly been voided in the urine of a maid in Holland. A jar of blue pigment made from tincture of galls, a jar of green made from Hungarian vitriol. A sketch of one of the Dwarves who supposedly inhabited the Canary Islands. Hundreds of lodestones of various sizes and shapes. A model of a giant crossbow that Hooke had designed for flinging harpoons at whales. A U-shaped glass tube that Boyle had filled with quicksilver to prove that its undulations were akin to those of a pendulum.

Hooke wanted Daniel to bring various parts and tools and materials used in the making of watches and other fine mechanisms; some of the stones that had been found in the Earl's heart; a cylinder of quicksilver; a hygroscope made from the beard of a wild oat; a burning-glass in a wooden frame; a pair of deep convex spectacles for seeing underwater; his dew-collecting glass,* and selections from his large collection of preserved bladders: carp, pig, cow, and so on. He also wanted enormous, completely impractical numbers of different-sized spheres of different materials such as lead, amber, wood, silver, and so forth, which were useful in all manner of rolling and dropping experiments. Also, various spare parts for his air-compressing engine, and his Artificial Eye. Finally, Hooke asked him to collect "any puppies, kittens, chicks, or mice you might come across, as the supply hereabouts is considerably diminished."

Some mail had piled up here, despite the recent difficulties, much of it addressed simply "GRUBENDOL London." Following Wilkins's instructions, Daniel gathered it all up and added it to the

---

*A conical glass, wide at the top and pointed on the bottom, which when filled with cold water or (preferably) snow and left outside overnight, would condense dew on its outside; the dew would run down and drip into a receptacle underneath.

pile. But the GRUBENDOL stuff he culled out, and tied up into a packet with string.

Now he was ready to leave London, and wanted only money, and some way to carry all of this stuff. Back down Bishopsgate he went (leaving everything behind at Gresham College, except for the frogs, who demanded close watching) and turned on Threadneedle, which he followed westwards as it converged on Cornhill. Close to their intersection stood a series of row-houses that fronted on both of these streets. As even the illiterate might guess from the men with muskets smoking pipes on the rooftops, all were goldsmiths. Daniel went to the one called HAM BROS. A few trinkets and a couple of gold plates were displayed in a window by the door, as if to suggest that the Hams were still literally in the business of fabricating things out of gold.

A face in a grate. "Daniel!" The grate slammed and latched, the door growled and clanged as might works of ironmongery were slid and shot on the inside. Finally it was open. "Welcome!"

"Good day, Uncle Thomas."

"Half-brother-in-law actually," said Thomas Ham, out of a stubborn belief that pedantry and repetitiveness could through some alchemy be forged into wit. Pedantry because he was technically correct (he'd married Daniel's half-sister) and repetitive because he'd been making the same joke for as long as Daniel had been alive. Ham was more than sixty years old now, and he was one of those who is fat and skinny at the same time—a startling pot-belly suspended from a lanky armature, waggling jowls draped over a face like an edged weapon. He had been lucky to capture the fair Mayflower Waterhouse, or so he was encouraged to believe.

"I was affrighted when I came up the street—thought you were burying people," Daniel said, gesturing at several mounds of earth around the house's foundations.

Ham looked carefully up and down Threadneedle—as if what he was doing could possibly be a secret from anyone. "We are making a Crypt of a different sort," he said. "Come, enter. Why is that basket croaking?"

"I have taken a job as a porter," Daniel said. "Do you have a hand-cart or wheelbarrow I could borrow for a few days?"

"Yes, a very heavy and strong one—we use it to carry lock-boxes back and forth to the Mint. Hasn't moved since the Plague started. By all means take it!"

The parlor held a few more pathetic vestiges of a retail jewelry business, but it was really just a large writing-desk and some books. Stairs led to the Ham residence on the upper floors—dark and silent. "Mayflower and the children are well in Buckinghamshire?" Daniel asked.

"God willing, yes, her last letter quite put me to sleep. Come downstairs!" Uncle Thomas led him through another fortress-door that had been left wedged open, and down a narrow stair into the earth—for the first time since leaving his father's house, Daniel smelled nothing bad, only the calm scent of earth being disturbed.

He'd never been invited into the cellar, but he'd always known about it—from the solemn way it was talked about, or, to be precise, talked *around,* he'd always known it must be full of either ghosts or a large quantity of gold. Now he found it to be absurdly small and homely compared to its awesome reputation, in a way that was heart-warmingly English—but it *was* full of gold, and it was getting larger and less ditch-like by the minute. At the end nearest the base of the stairway, piled simply on the dirt floor, were platters, punch-bowls, pitchers, knives, forks, spoons, goblets, ladles, candlesticks, and gravy-boats of gold—also sacks of coins, boxed medallions stamped with visages of Continental nobles commemorating this or that bat-tle, actual gold bars, and irregular sticks of gold called pigs. Each item was somehow tagged: *367-11/32 troy oz. depos. by my Lord Rochester on 29 Sept. 1662* and so on. The stuff was piled up like a dry-stone wall, which is to say that bits were packed into spaces between other bits in a way calculated to keep the whole formation from col-lapsing. All of it was spattered with dirt and brick-fragments and mortar-splats from the work proceeding at the other end of the cel-lar: a laborer with pick and shovel, and another with a back-basket to carry the dirt upstairs; a carpenter working with heavy timbers, doing something Daniel assumed was to keep the House of Ham from collapsing; and a bricklayer and his assistant, giving the new space a foundation and walls. It was a tidy cellar now; no rats in here.

"Your late mother's candlesticks are, I'm afraid, not on view just now—rather far back in the, er, Arrangement—" said Thomas Ham.

"I'm not here to disturb the Arrangement," Daniel said, pro-ducing the Note from his father.

"Oh! Easily done! Easily and cheerfully done!" announced Mr. Ham after donning spectacles and shaking his jowls at the Note for a while, a hound casting after a scent. "Pocket money for the young scholar—the young divine—is it?"

"Cambridge is very far from re-opening, they say—need to be applying myself elsewhere," Daniel said, merely dribbling small talk behind him as he went to look at a small pile of dirty stuff that was not gold. "What are these?"

"Remains of the house of some Roman that once stood here,"

Mr. Ham said. "Those who follow these things—and I'm sorry to say I *don't*—assure me that something called Walbrook Stream flowed just through here, and spilled into the Thames at the Provincial Governor's Palace, twelve hundred odd years ago—the Roman mercers had their houses along its banks, so that they could ferry goods up and down from the River."

Daniel was using the sole of one boot to sweep loose dirt away from a hard surface he'd sensed underneath. Wee polygons— terra-cotta, indigo, bone-white, beige—appeared. He was looking at a snatch of a mosaic floor. He swept away more dirt and recognized it as a rendering of a naked leg, knee flexed and toe pointed as if its owner were on the run. A pair of wings sprouted from the ankle. "Yes, the Roman floor we'll keep," said Mr. Ham, "as we need a barrier—to discourage clever men with shovels. Jonas, where are the loose bits?"

The digger kicked a wooden box across the floor towards them. It was half-full of small bits of dirty junk: a couple of combs carved out of bone or ivory; a clay lantern; the skeleton of a brooch, jewels long since missing from their sockets; fragments of glazed pottery; and something long and slender: a hairpin, Daniel reckoned, rubbing the dirt away. It was probably silver, though badly tarnished. "Take it, my lad," said Mr. Ham, referring not only to the hairpin but also to a rather nice silver one-pound coin that he had just quarried from his pocket. "Perhaps the future Mrs. Waterhouse will enjoy fixing her coif with a bauble that once adorned the head of some Roman trader's wife."

"Trinity College does not allow us to have wives," Daniel reminded him, "but I'll take it anyway—perhaps I'll have a niece or something who has pretty hair, and who isn't squeamish about a bit of paganism." For it was clear now that the hairpin was fashioned in the shape of a caduceus.

"Paganism? Then we are all pagans! It is a symbol of Mercury— patron of commerce—who has been worshipped in this cellar—and in this city—for a thousand years, by Bishops as well as business-men. It is a cult that adapts itself to any religion, just as easily as quicksilver adopts the shape of any container—and someday, Daniel, you'll meet a young lady who is just as adaptable. Take it." Putting the silver coin next to the caduceus in Daniel's palm, he folded Daniel's fingers over the top and then clasped the fist—chilled by the touch of the metal—between his two warm hands in benediction.

DANIEL PUSHED HIS HAND-CART westwards down Cheapside. He held his breath as he hurried around the reeking tumulus that surrounded St. Paul's, and did not breathe easy again until he'd passed out of Ludgate. The passage over Fleet Ditch was even worse, because it was strewn with bodies of rats, cats, and dogs, as well as quite a few plague-corpses that had simply been rolled out of wagons, and not even dignified with a bit of dirt. He kept a rag clamped over his face, and did not take it off until he had passed out through Temple Bar and gone by the little Watch-house that stood in the middle of the Strand in front of Somerset House. From there he could glimpse green fields and open country between certain of the buildings, and smell whiffs of manure on the breeze, which smelled delightful compared to London.

He had worried that the wheels of his cart would bog down in Charing Cross, which was a perpetual morass, but summer heat, and want of traffic, had quite dried the place up. A pack of five stray dogs watched him make his way across the expanse of rutted and baked dirt. He was worried that they would come after him until he noticed that they were uncommonly fat, for stray dogs.

Oldenburg lived in a town-house on Pall Mall. Except for a heroic physician or two, he was the only member of the R.S. who'd stayed in town during the Plague. Daniel took out the GRUBEN-DOL packet and put it on the doorstep—letters from Vienna, Florence, Paris, Amsterdam, Berlin, Moscow.

He knocked thrice on the door, and backed away to see a round face peering down at him through obscuring layers of green window-glass, like a curtain of tears. Oldenburg's wife had lately died—not of Plague—and some supposed that he stayed in London hoping that the Black Death would carry him off to wherever she was.

On his long walk out of town, Daniel had plenty of time to work out that GRUBENDOL was an anagram for Oldenburg.

Epsom
1665–1666

> By this it appears how necessary it is for any man that
> aspires to true knowledge, to examine the definitions
> of former authors; and either to correct them, where
> they are negligently set down, or to make them him-
> self. For the errors of definitions multiply themselves
> according as the reckoning proceeds, and lead men
> into absurdities, which at last they see, but cannot
> avoid, without reckoning anew from the beginning.
> —HOBBES, *Leviathan*

JOHN COMSTOCK'S SEAT was at Epsom, a short journey from London.
It was large. That largeness came in handy during the Plague,
because it enabled his Lordship to stable a few Fellows of the Royal
Society (which would enhance his already tremendous prestige)
without having to be very close to them (which would disturb
his household, and place his domestic animals in extreme peril).
All of this was obvious enough to Daniel as one of Comstock's servants met him at the gate and steered him well clear of the manor
house and across a sort of defensive buffer zone of gardens and
pastures to a remote cottage with an oddly dingy and crowded look
to it.

To one side lay a spacious bone-yard, chalky with skulls of dogs,
cats, rats, pigs, and horses. To the other, a pond cluttered with the
wrecks of model ships, curiously rigged. Above the well, some sort
of pulley arrangement, and a rope extending from the pulley,
across a pasture, to a half-assembled chariot. On the roof of the
cottage, diverse small windmills of outlandish design—one of them
mounted over the mouth of the cottage's chimney and turned by
the rising of its smoke. Every high tree-limb in the vicinity had
been exploited as a support for pendulums, and the pendulum-
strings had all gotten twisted round each other by winds, and
merged into a tattered philosophickal cobweb. The green space in
front was a mechanical phant'sy of wheels and gears, broken or
never finished. There was a giant wheel, apparently built so that a

man could roll across the countryside by climbing inside it and driving it forward with his feet.

Ladders had been leaned against any wall or tree with the least ability to push back. Halfway up one of the ladders was a stout, fair-haired man who was not far from the end of his natural life span—though he apparently did not entertain any ambitions of actually reaching it. He was climbing the ladder one-handed in hard-soled leather shoes that were perfectly frictionless on the rungs, and as he swayed back and forth, planting one foot and then the next, the ladder's feet, down below him, tiptoed backwards. Daniel rushed over and braced the ladder, then forced himself to look upwards at the shuddering battle-gammoned form of the Rev. Wilkins. The Rev. was carrying, in his free hand, some sort of winged object.

And speaking of winged objects, Daniel now felt himself being tickled, and glanced down to find half a dozen honeybees had alighted on each one of his hands. As Daniel watched in empirical horror, one of them drove its stinger into the fleshy place between his thumb and index finger. He bit his lip and looked up to see whether letting go the ladder would lead to the immediate death of Wilkins. The answer: yes. Bees were now swarming all round— nuzzling the fringes of Daniel's hair, playing crack-the-whip through the ladder's rungs, and orbiting round Wilkins's body in a humming cloud.

Reaching the highest possible altitude—flagrantly tempting the LORD to strike him dead—Wilkins released the toy in his hand. Whirring and clicking noises indicated that some sort of spring-driven clockwork had gone into action—there was fluttering, and skidding through the air—some sort of interaction with the atmosphere, anyway, that went beyond mere falling—but fall it did, veering into the cottage's stone wall and spraying parts over the yard.

"Never going to fly to the moon *that* way," Wilkins grumbled.

"I thought you wanted to be *shot out of a cannon* to the Moon."

Wilkins whacked himself on the stomach. "As you can see, I have far too much *vis inertiae* to be shot out of *anything* to *anywhere*. Before I come down there, are you feeling well, young man? No sweats, chills, swellings?"

"I anticipated your curiosity on that subject, Dr. Wilkins, and so the frogs and I lodged at an inn in Epsom for two nights. I have never felt healthier."

"Splendid! Mr. Hooke has denuded the countryside of small animals—if you hadn't brought him anything, he'd have cut *you* up." Wilkins was coming down the ladder, the sureness of each footfall very much in doubt, massy buttocks approaching Daniel as a spectre of doom. Finally on terra firma, he waved a hundred bees off with an intrepid sweep of the arm. They wiped bees away from their palms, then exchanged a long, warm handshake. The bees were collectively losing interest and seeping away in the direction of a large glinting glass box. "It is Wren's design, come and see!" Wilkins said, bumbling after them.

The glass structure was a model of a building, complete with a blown dome, and pillars carved of crystal. It was of a Gothickal design, and had the general look of some Government office in London, or a University college. The doors and windows were open to let bees fly in and out. They had built a hive inside—a cathedral of honeycombs.

"With all respect to Mr. Wren, I see a clash of architectural styles here—"

"What! Where?" Wilkins exclaimed, searching the roofline for aesthetic contaminants. "I shall cane the boy!"

"It's not the builder, but the tenants who're responsible. All those little waxy hexagons—doesn't fit with Mr. Wren's scheme, does it?"

"Which style do you prefer?" Wilkins asked, wickedly.

"Err—"

"Before you answer, know that Mr. Hooke approaches," the Rev. whispered, glancing sidelong. Daniel looked over toward the house to see Hooke coming their way, bent and gray and transparent, like one of those curious figments that occasionally floats across one's eyeball.

"Is he all right?" Daniel asked.

"The usual bouts of melancholy—a certain peevishness over the scarcity of adventuresome females—"

"I meant is he sick."

Hooke had stopped near Daniel's luggage, attracted by the croaking of frogs. He stepped in and seized the basket.

"Oh, he ever looks as if he's been bleeding to death for several hours—fear for the frogs, not for Hooke!" Wilkins said. He had a perpetual knowing, amused look that enabled him to get away with saying almost anything. This, combined with the occasional tactical master-stroke (e.g., marrying Cromwell's sister during the Interregnum), probably accounted for his ability to ride out civil wars and revolutions as if they were mere theatrical performances. He bent down in front of the glass apiary, pantomiming a bad back; reached underneath; and, after some dramatic rummaging, drew out a glass jar with an inch or so of cloudy brown honey in the bottom. "Mr. Wren provided sewerage, as you can see," he said, giving the jar to Daniel. It was blood-warm. The Rev. now headed in the direction of the house, and Daniel followed.

"You say you quarantined yourself at Epsom town—you must have paid for lodgings there—that means you have pocket-money. Drake must've given it you. What on earth did you tell him you were coming here to do? I need to know," Wilkins added apologetically, "only so that I can write him the occasional letter claiming that you are doing it."

"Keeping abreast of the very latest, from the Continent or whatever. I'm to provide him with advance warning of any events that are plainly part of the Apocalypse."

Wilkins stroked an invisible beard and nodded profoundly, standing back so that Daniel could dart forward and haul open the cottage door. They went into the front room, where a fire was decaying in a vast hearth. Two or three rooms away, Hooke was crucifying a frog on a plank, occasionally swearing as he struck his thumb. "Perhaps you can help me with my book . . ."

"A new edition of the *Cryptonomicon?*"

"Perish the thought! Damn me, I'd almost forgotten about *that* old thing. Wrote it a quarter-century ago. Consider the times! The King was losing his mind—his Ministers being lynched in Parliament—his own drawbridge-keepers locking him out of his own arsenals. His foes intercepting letters abroad, written by that French Papist wife of his, *begging* foreign powers to invade us. Hugh Peters had come back from Salem to whip those Puritans into a frenzy—no great difficulty, given that the King, simply out—*out*—of money, had seized all of the merchants' gold in the Tower. Scottish Covenanters down as far as Newcastle, Catholics rebelling in Ulster, sudden panics in London—gentlemen on the street whipping out their rapiers for little or no reason. Things no better elsewhere—Europe twenty-five years into the Thirty Years' War, wolves eating children along the road in Besançon, for Christ's sake—Spain and Portugal dividing into two separate kingdoms, the Dutch taking advantage of it to steal Malacca from the Portuguese—of *course* I wrote the *Cryptonomicon!* And of course people bought it! But if it was the Omega—a way of hiding information, of making the light into darkness—then the Universal Character is the Alpha—an opening. A dawn. A candle in the darkness. Am I being disgusting?"

"Is this anything like Comenius's project?"

Wilkins leaned across and made as if to box Daniel's ears. "It *is* his project! This was what he and I, and that whole gang of odd

Germans—Hartlib, Haak, Kinner, Oldenburg—wanted to do when we conceived the Invisible College* back in the Dark Ages. But Mr. Comenius's work was burned up in a fire, back in Moravia, you know."

"Accidental, or—"

"*Excellent* question, young man—in Moravia, one never knows. Now, if Comenius had listened to my advice and accepted the invitation to be Master of Harvard College back in '41, it might've been different—"

"The colonists would be twenty-five years ahead of us!"

"Just so. Instead, Natural Philosophy flourishes at Oxford—less so at Cambridge—and Harvard is a pitiable backwater."

"Why didn't he take your advice, I wonder—?"

"The tragedy of these middle-European savants is that they are always trying to apply their *philosophick* acumen in the *political* realm."

"Whereas the Royal Society is—?"

"*Ever so strictly* apolitical," Wilkins said, and then favored Daniel with a stage-actor's hugely exaggerated wink. "If we stayed away from politics, we could be flying winged chariots to the Moon within a few generations. All that's needed is to pull down certain barriers to progress—"

"Such as?"

"Latin."

"*Latin!?* But Latin is—"

"I know, the universal language of scholars and divines, *et cetera, et cetera.* And it *sounds* so lovely, doesn't it. You can say any sort of nonsense in Latin and our feeble University men will be stunned, or at least profoundly confused. That's how the Popes have gotten away with peddling bad religion for so long—they simply say it in Latin. But if we were to unfold their convoluted phrases and translate them into a *philosophical* language, all of their contradictions and vagueness would become manifest."

"Mmm . . . I'd go so far as to say that if a proper philosophical language existed, it would be impossible to express any false concept in it without violating its rules of grammar," Daniel hazarded.

"You have just uttered the most succinct possible definition of it—I say, you're not *competing* with me, are you?" Wilkins said jovially.

"No," Daniel said, too intimidated to catch the humor. "I was merely reasoning by analogy to Cartesian analysis, where false

*Forerunner of the Royal Society.

statements cannot legally be written down, as long as the terms are understood."

"The terms! That's the difficult part," Wilkins said. "As a way to write down the terms, I am developing the Philosophical Language and the Universal Character—which learned men of all races and nations will use to signify ideas."

"I am at your service, sir," Daniel said. "When may I begin?"

"Immediately! Before Hooke's done with those frogs—if he comes in here and finds you idle, he'll *enslave* you—you'll be shovelling guts or, worse, trying the precision of his clocks by standing before a pendulum and counting . . . its . . . alternations . . . all . . . day . . . long."

Hooke came in. His spine was all awry: not only stooped, but bent to one side. His long brown hair hung unkempt around his face. He straightened up a bit and tilted his head back so that the hair fell away to either side, like a curtain opening up to reveal a pale face. Stubble on the cheeks made him look even gaunter than he actually was, and made his gray eyes look even more huge. He said: "Frogs, too."

"Nothing surprises me *now*, Mr. Hooke."

"I put it to you that all living creatures are made out of them."

"Have you considered writing any of this down? Mr. Hooke? Mr. Hooke?" But Hooke was already gone out into the stable-yard, off on some other experiment.

"Made out of *what*??" Daniel asked.

"Lately, every time Mr. Hooke peers at something with his Microscope he finds that it is divided up into small compartments, each one just like its neighbors, like bricks in a wall," Wilkins confided.

"What do these bricks look like?"

"He doesn't call them bricks. Remember, they are hollow. He has taken to calling them 'cells' . . . but you don't want to get caught up in all *that* nonsense. Follow me, my dear Daniel. Put thoughts of cells out of your mind. To understand the Philosophical Language you must know that all things in Earth and Heaven can be classified into forty different genera . . . within each of those, there are, of course, further subclasses."

Wilkins showed him into a servant's room where a writing desk had been set up, and papers and books mounded up with as little concern for order as the bees had shown in building their honeycomb. Wilkins moved a lot of air, and so leaves of paper flew off of stacks as he passed through the room. Daniel picked one up and read it: "Mule fern, panic-grass, hartstongue, adderstongue, moonwort, sea novelwort, wrack, Job's-tears, broomrope, toothwort, scurvy-grass, sowbread, golden saxifrage, lily of the valley, bastard madder, stinking ground-pine, endive, dandelion, sowthistle, Spanish picktooth, purple loose-strife, bitter vetch."

Wilkins was nodding impatiently. "The capsulate herbs, not campanulate, and the bacciferous sempervirent shrubs," he said. "Somehow it must have gotten mixed up with the glandiferous and the nuciferous trees."

"So, the Philosophical Language is some sort of botanical—"

"Look at me, I'm shuddering. Shuddering at the *thought*. Botany! Please, Daniel, try to collect your wits. In this stack we have all of the animals, from the belly-worm to the tyger. Here, the terms of Euclidean geometry, relating to time, space, and juxtaposition. There, a classification of diseases: pustules, boils, wens, and scabs on up to splenetic hypochondriacal vapours, iliac passion, and suffocation."

"Is suffocation a disease?"

"Excellent question—get to work and answer it!" Wilkins thundered.

Daniel, meanwhile, had rescued another sheet from the floor: "Yard, Johnson, dick . . ."

"Synonyms for 'penis,' " Wilkins said impatiently.

"Rogue, mendicant, shake-rag . . ."

"Synonyms for 'beggar.' In the Philosophical Language there will only be one word for penises, one for beggars. Quick, Daniel, is there a distinction between groaning and grumbling?"

"I should say so, but—"

"On the other hand—may we lump genuflection together with curtseying, and give them one name?"

"I—I cannot say, Doctor!"

"Then, I say, there is work to be done! At the moment, I am bogged down in an *endless* digression on the Ark."

"Of the Covenant? Or—"

"The other one."

"How does that enter into the Philosophical Language?"

"Obviously the P.L. must contain one and only one word for every type of animal. Each animal's word must reflect its classification—that is, the words for *perch* and *bream* should be noticeably similar, as should the words for *robin* and *thrush*. But bird-words should be quite different from fish-words."

"It strikes me as, er, *ambitious* . . ."

"Half of Oxford is sending me tedious lists. My—*our*—task is to organize them—to draw up a table of every type of bird and beast in the world. I have entabulated the animals troublesome to other animals—the louse, the flea. Those designed for further transmutation—the caterpillar, the maggot. One-horned sheathed winged insects. Testaceous turbinated exanguious animals—and before you ask, I have subdivided them into those with, and without, spiral convolutions. Squamous river fish, phytivorous birds of long wings, rapacious beasts of the cat-kind—anyway, as I drew up all of these lists and tables, it occurred to me that (going back to Genesis, sixth chapter, verses fifteen through twenty-two) Noah must have found a way to fit all of these creatures into one gopher-wood tub three hundred cubits long! I became concerned that certain *Continental* savants, of an *atheistical* bent, might *misuse* my list to suggest that the events related in Genesis could not have happened—"

"One could also imagine certain Jesuits turning it against you— holding it up as proof that you harbored atheistical notions of your own, Dr. Wilkins."

"Just so! Daniel! Which makes it imperative that I include, in a separate chapter, a complete plan of Noah's Ark—demonstrating not only where each of the beasts was berthed, but also the fodder for the herbivorous beasts, and live cattle for the carnivorous ones, and *more* fodder yet to keep the cattle alive, long enough to be eaten by the carnivores—where, I say, 'twas all stowed."

"Fresh water must have been wanted, too," Daniel reflected.

Wilkins—who tended to draw closer and closer to people when he was talking to them, until they had to edge backwards—grabbed a sheaf of paper off a stack and bopped Daniel on the head with it. "Tend to your Bible, foolish young man! It rained the entire time!"

"Of course, of course—they could've drunk rainwater," Daniel said, profoundly mortified.

"I have had to take some liberties with the definition of 'cubit,' " Wilkins said, as if betraying a secret, "but I think he could have done it with eighteen hundred and twenty-five sheep. To feed the carnivores, I mean."

"The sheep must've taken up a whole deck!?"

"It's not the space they take up, it's all the manure, and the labor of throwing it overboard," Wilkins said. "At any rate—as you can well imagine—this Ark business has stopped all progress cold on the P.L. front. I need you to get on with the Terms of Abuse."

"Sir!"

"Have you felt, Daniel, a certain annoyance, when one of your semi-educated Londoners speaks of 'a vile rascal' or 'a miserable caitiff' or 'crafty knave,' 'idle truant,' or 'flattering parasite'?"

"Depends upon who is calling whom what . . ."

"No, no, no! Let's try an easy one: 'fornicating whore.' "

"It is redundant. Hence, annoying to the cultivated listener."

" 'Senseless fop.' "

"Again, redundant—as are 'flattering parasite' and the others."

"So, clearly, in the Philosophical Language, we needn't have separate adjectives and nouns in such cases."

"How about 'filthy sloven?"

"Excellent! Write it down, Daniel!"

" 'Licentious blade' . . . 'facetious wag' . . . 'perfidious traitor' . . ." As Daniel continued in this vein, Wilkins bustled over to the writing-desk, withdrew a quill from an inkwell, shook off redundant ink, and then came over to Daniel; wrapped his fingers around the pen; and guided him over to the desk.

And so to work. Daniel exhausted the Terms of Abuse in a few short hours, then moved on to Virtues (intellectual, moral, and homiletical), Colors, Sounds, Tastes and Smells, Professions, Operations (viz. carpentry, sewing, alchemy), and so on. Days began passing. Wilkins became fretful if Daniel, or anyone, worked too hard, and so there were frequent "seminars" and "symposia" in the kitchen—they used honey from Christopher Wren's Gothic apiary to make flip. Frequently Charles Comstock, the fifteen-year-old son of their noble host, came to visit, and to hear Wilkins or Hooke talk. Charles tended to bring with him letters addressed to the Royal Society from Huygens, Leeuwenhoek, Swammerdam, Spinoza. Frequently these turned out to contain new concepts that Daniel had to fit into the Philosophical Language's tables.

Daniel was hard at work compiling a list of all the things in the world that a person could own (aquæducts, axle-trees, palaces, hinges) when Wilkins called him down urgently. Daniel came down to find the Rev. holding a grand-looking Letter, and Charles Comstock clearing the decks for action: rolling up large diagrams of the Ark, and feeding-schedules for the eighteen hundred and twenty-five sheep, and stowing them out of the way to make room for more important affairs. Charles II, by the Grace of God of England King, had sent them this letter: His Majesty had noticed that ant eggs were bigger than ants, and demanded to know how *that* was possible.

Daniel ran out and sacked an ant-nest. He returned in triumph carrying the nucleus of an anthill on the flat of a shovel. In the front room Wilkins had begun dictating, and Charles Comstock scribbling, a letter back to the King—not the substantive part (as they didn't have an answer yet), but the lengthy paragraphs of apologies and profuse flattery that had to open it: "With your brilliance you illuminate the places that have long, er, languished in, er—"

"Sounds more like a Sun King allusion, Reverend," Charles warned him.

"Strike it, then! Sharp lad. Read the entire mess back to me."

Daniel slowed before the door to Hooke's laboratory, gathering his courage to knock. But Hooke had heard him approaching, and opened it for him. With an outstretched hand he beckoned Daniel in, and aimed him at a profoundly stained table, cleared for action. Daniel entered the room, upended the ant-nest, set the shovel down, and only then worked up the courage to inhale. Hooke's laboratory didn't smell as bad as he'd always assumed it would.

Hooke ran his hands back through his hair, pulling it away from his face, and tied it back behind his neck with a wisp of twine. Daniel was perpetually surprised that Hooke was only ten years older than he. Hooke just turned thirty a few weeks ago, in June, at about the same time that Daniel and Isaac had fled plaguey Cambridge for their respective homes.

Hooke was now staring at the mound of living dirt on his table-top. His eyes were always focused on a narrow target, as if he peered out at the world through a hollow reed. When he was out in the broad world, or even in the house's front room, that seemed strange, but it made sense when he was looking at a small world on a tabletop—ants scurrying this way and that, carrying egg-cases out of the wreckage, establishing a defensive perimeter. Daniel stood opposite and *looked at,* but apparently did not *see,* the same things.

Within a few minutes Daniel had seen most of what he was going to see among the ants, within five minutes he was bored, within ten he had given up all pretenses and begun wandering round Hooke's laboratory, looking at the remnants of everything that had passed beneath the microscope: shards of porous stone, bits of moldy shoe-leather, a small glass jar labelled WILKINS URINE, splinters of petrified wood, countless tiny envelopes of seeds, insects in jars, scraps of various fabrics, tiny pots labelled SNAILS TEETH and VIPERS FANGS. Shoved back into a corner, a heap of dusty, rusty sharp things: knife-blades, needles, razors. There was probably a cruel witticism to be made here: given a razor, Hooke would sooner put it under his microscope than shave with it.

As the wait went on, and on, and on, Daniel decided that he might as well be improving himself. So with care he reached into the sharp-things pile, drew out a needle, and carried it over to a table where sun was pouring in (Hooke had grabbed all of the south-facing rooms in the cottage, to own the light). There, mounted to a little stand, was a tube, about the dimensions of a piece of writing-paper rolled up, with a lens at the top for looking through, and a much smaller one—hardly bigger than a chick's eye—at the bottom, aimed at a little stand that was strongly illuminated by the sunlight. Daniel put the needle on the stand and peered through the Microscope.

He expected to see a gleaming, mirrorlike shaft, but it was a gnawed stick instead. The needle's sharp point turned out to be a rounded and pitted slag-heap.

"Mr. Waterhouse," Hooke said, "when you are finished with whatever you are doing, I will consult my faithful Mercury."

Daniel stood up and turned around. He thought for a moment that Hooke was asking him to fetch some quicksilver (Hooke drank it from time to time, as a remedy for headaches, vertigo, and other complaints). But Hooke's giant eyes were focused on the Microscope instead.

"Of course!" Daniel said. Mercury, the Messenger of the Gods—bringer of information.

"What think you now of needles?" Hooke asked.

Daniel plucked the needle away and held it up before the window, viewing it in a new light. "Its appearance is almost physically disgusting," he said.

"A razor looks worse. It is all kinds of shapes, except what it should be," Hooke said. "That is why I never use the Microscope any more to look at things that were made by men—the rudeness and bungling of Art is painful to view. And yet things that one would *expect* to look disgusting become beautiful when magnified—you may look at my drawings while I satisfy the King's curiosity."

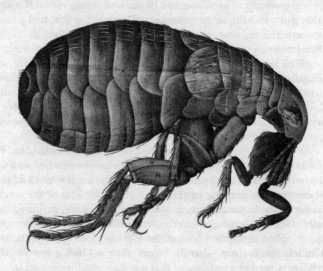

Hooke gestured to a stack of papers, then carried a sample ant-egg over to the microscope as Daniel began to page through them.

"Sir. I did not know that you were an artist," Daniel said.

"When my father died, I was apprenticed to a portrait-painter," Hooke said.

"Your master taught you well—"

"The ass taught me *nothing*," Hooke said. "Anyone who is not a half-wit can learn all there is to know of painting, by standing in front of paintings and *looking* at them. What was the use, then, of being an apprentice?"

"This flea is a magnificent piece of—"

"It is not *art* but a higher form of *bungling*," Hooke demurred. "When I viewed that flea under the microscope, I could see, in its eye, a complete and perfect reflection of John Comstock's gardens and manor-house—the blossoms on his flowers, the curtains billowing in his windows."

"It's magnificent to me," Daniel said. He was sincere—not trying to be a Flattering Parasite or Crafty Knave.

But Hooke only became irritated. "I tell you again. True beauty is to be found in natural forms. The more we magnify, and the closer we examine, the works of Artifice, the grosser and stupider they seem. But if we magnify the natural world it only becomes more intricate and excellent."

Wilkins had asked Daniel which he preferred: Wren's glass apiary, or the bees' honeycomb inside of it. Then he had warned Daniel that Hooke was coming into earshot. Now Daniel understood why: for Hooke there could only be one answer.

"I defer to you, sir."

"Thank you, sir."

"But without seeming to be a Cavilling Jesuit, I should like to know whether Wilkins's urine is a product of Art or Nature."

"You saw the jar."

"Yes."

"If you take the Rev.'s urine and pour off the fluid and examine what remains under the Microscope, you will see a hoard of jewels that would make the Great Mogul swoon. At lower magnification it seems nothing more than a heap of gravel, but with a better lens, and brighter light, it is revealed as a mountain of crystals—plates, rhomboids, rectangles, squares—white and yellow and red ones, gleaming like the diamonds in a courtier's ring."

"Is that true of everyone's urine?"

"It is more true of his than of most people's," Hooke said. "Wilkins has the stone."

"Oh, God!"

"It is not so bad now, but it grows within him, and will certainly kill him in a few years," Hooke said.

"And the stone in his bladder is made of the same stuff as these crystals that you see in his urine?"

"I believe so."

"Is there some way to—"

"To dissolve it? Oil of vitriol works—but I don't suppose that our Reverend wants to have that introduced into his bladder. You are welcome to make investigations of your own. I have tried all of the *obvious* things."

WORD ARRIVED THAT FERMAT had died, leaving behind a theorem or two that still needed proving. King Philip of Spain died, too, and his son succeeded him; but the new King Carlos II was sickly, and not expected to live to the end of the year. Portugal was independent. Someone named Lubomirski was staging a rebellion in Poland.

John Wilkins was trying to make horse-drawn vehicles more efficient; to test them, he had rigged up a weight on a rope, above a well, so that when the weight fell down into the well, it would drag his chariots across the ground. Their progress could then be timed using one of Hooke's watches. That duty fell to Charles Comstock, who spent many days standing out in the field making trials or fixing broken wheels. His father's servants needed the well to draw water for livestock, and so Charles was frequently called out to move the contraption out of the way. Daniel enjoyed watching all of this, out the window, while he worked on Punishments:

PUNISHMENTS CAPITAL
ARE THE VARIOUS MANNERS OF PUTTING MEN
TO DEATH IN A JUDICIAL WAY, WHICH IN SEVERAL
NATIONS ARE, OR HAVE BEEN, EITHER *SIMPLE;* BY

Separation of the parts;
    Head from Body: BEHEADING, strike of one's head
    Member from Member: QUARTERING, Dissecting.
Wound
    At distance, whether
        from hand: STONING, Pelting
        from Instrument, as Gun, Bow, &c.: SHOOTING.
    At hand, either by
        Weight;

       of something else: PRESSING.
       of one's own: PRECIPITATING, Defenestration, casting head-
       long.
    Weapon;
       any way: STABBING
       direct upwards: EMPALING
Taking away necessary Diet: or giving that which is noxious
    STARVING, famishing
    POISONING, Venom, envenom, virulent
Interception of the air
    at the Mouth
       in the air: stifling, smother, suffocate.
       in the Earth: BURYING ALIVE
       in water: DROWNING
       in fire: BURNING ALIVE
    at the Throat
       by weight of a man's own body: HANGING
       by the strength of others: STRANGLING, throttle, choke, suffocate

MIXED OF WOUNDING AND STARVING; THE BODY BEING
    Erect: *CRUCIFYING*
    Lying on a Wheel: *BREAKING ON THE WHEEL*

PUNISHMENTS NOT CAPITAL
ARE DISTINGUISHED BY THE THINGS OR
SUBJECTS RECEIVING DETRIMENT BY THEM,
AS BEING EITHER OF THE *BODY;*
according to the General name; *signifying great pain: TORTURE*
according to special kinds:
    by Striking;
       with a limber instrument: WHIPPING, lashing, scourging, leash-
       ing, rod, slash, switch, stripe, Beadle
       with a stiff instrument: CUDGELLING, bastinado, baste,
       swinge, swaddle, shrubb, slapp, thwack;
    by Stretching of the limbs violently;
       the body being laid along: RACK
       the body lifted up into the Air: STRAPPADO
LIBERTY; OF WHICH ONE IS DEPRIVED, BY
RESTRAINT
into
    a place: IMPRISONMENT, Incarceration, Durance, Custody, Ward,
    clap up, commit, confine, mure, Pound, Pinfold, Gaol, Cage, Set fast

an Instrument: *BONDS, fetters, gyves, shackles, manicles,*
  pinion, chains.
Out of *a place or country, whether*
  with allowance of any other: *EXILE, banishment*
  confinement to one other: *RELEGATION*
REPUTE, WHETHER
  more gently: *INFAMIZATION, Ignominy, Pillory*
  more severely by burning marks in one's flesh: *STIGMATIZA-*
  TION, Branding, Cauterizing
ESTATE; WHETHER
  in part: *MULCT, fine, sconce*
  in whole: *CONFISCATION, forfeiture*
DIGNITY AND POWER; BY DEPRIVING ONE OF
  his degree: *DEGRADING, deposing, depriving*
  his capacity to bear office: *INCAPACITATING, cashier, disable,*
  discard, depose, disfranchize.

As Daniel scourged, bastinadoed, racked, and strappadoed his
mind, trying to think of punishments that he and Wilkins had
missed, he heard Hooke striking sparks with flint and steel, and
went down to investigate.

Hooke was aiming the sparks at a blank sheet of paper. "Mark
where they strike," he said to Daniel. Daniel hovered with a pen,
and whenever an especially large spark hit the paper, he drew a
tight circle around it. They examined the paper under the Microscope, and found, in the center of each circle, a remnant: a more
or less complete hollow sphere of what was obviously steel. "You see
that the Alchemists' conception of heat is ludicrous," Hooke said.
"There is no Element of Fire. Heat is really nothing more than a
brisk agitation of the parts of a body—hit a piece of steel with a
rock hard enough, and a bit of steel is torn away—"

"And that is the spark?"

"That is the spark."

"But why does the spark emit light?"

"The force of the impact agitates its parts so vehemently that it
becomes hot enough to melt."

"Yes, but if your hypothesis is correct—if there is no Element of
Fire, only a jostling of internal parts—then why should hot things
emit light?"

"I believe that light consists of vibrations. If the parts move violently enough, they emit light—just as a struck bell vibrates to produce sound."

Daniel supposed that was all there was to that, until he went with Hooke to collect samples of river insects one day, and they squatted in a place where a brook tumbled over the brink of a rock into a little pool. Bubbles of water, forced beneath the pool by the falling water, rose to the surface: millions of tiny spheres. Hooke noticed it, pondered for a few moments, and said: "Planets and stars are spheres, for the same reason that bubbles and sparks are."

"What!?"

"A body of fluid, surrounded by some different fluid, forms into a sphere. Thus: air surrounded by water makes a sphere, which we call a bubble. A tiny bit of molten steel surrounded by air makes a sphere, which we call a spark. Molten earth surrounded by the Cœlestial Æther makes a sphere, which we call a planet."

And on the way back, as they were watching a crescent moon chase the sun below the horizon, Hooke said, "If we could make sparks, or flashes of light, bright enough, we could see their light reflected off the shadowed part of that moon later, and reckon the speed of light."

"If we did it with gunpowder," Daniel reflected, "John Comstock would be happy to underwrite the experiment."

Hooke turned and regarded him for a few moments with a cold eye, as if trying to establish whether Daniel, too, was made up out of cells. "You are thinking like a courtier," he said. There was no emotion in his voice; he was stating, not an opinion, but a fact.

> The chief Design of the aforementioned Club, was to propagate new Whims, advance mechanic Exercises, and to promote useless, as well as useful Experiments. In order to carry on this commendable Undertaking, any frantic Artist, chemical Operator, or whimsical Projector, that had but a Crotchet in their Heads, or but dream'd themselves into some strange fanciful Discovery, might be kindly admitted, as welcome Brethren, into this teeming Society, where each Member was respected, not according to his Quality, but the searches he had made into the Mysteries of Nature, and the Novelties, though Trifles, that were owing to his Invention: So that a Mad-man, who had beggar'd himself by his Bellows and his Furnaces, in a vain pursuit of the Philosopher's Stone; or the crazy Physician who had wasted his Patrimony, by endeavouring to

> recover that infallible Nostrum, *Sal Graminis*, from
> the dust and ashes of a burnt Hay-cock, were as
> much reverenc'd here, as those mechanic Quality,
> who, to shew themselves *Vertuoso's*, would sit turning
> of Ivory above in their Garrets, whilst their Ladies
> below Stairs, by the help of their He-Cousins, were
> providing Horns for their Families.
>
> —NED WARD, *The Vertuoso's Club*

THE LEAVES WERE TURNING, the Plague in London was worse. Eight thousand people died in a week. A few miles away in Epsom, Wilkins had finished the Ark digression and begun to draw up a grammar, and a system of writing, for his Philosophical Language. Daniel was finishing some odds and ends, viz. Nautical Objects: Seams and Spurkets, Parrels and Jears, Brales and Bunt-Lines. His mind wandered.

Below him, a strange plucking sound, like a man endlessly tuning a lute. He went down stairs and found Hooke sitting there with a few inches of quill sticking out of his ear, plucking a string stretched over a wooden box. It was far from the strangest thing Hooke had ever done, so Daniel went to work for a time, trying to dissolve Wilkins's bladder-gravel in various potions. Hooke continued plucking and humming. Finally Daniel went over to investigate.

A housefly was perched on the end of the quill that was stuck in Hooke's ear. Daniel tried to shoo it away. Its wings blurred, but it didn't move. Looking more closely Daniel saw that it had been glued down.

"Do that again, it gives me a different pitch," Hooke demanded.

"You can hear the fly's wings?"

"They drone at a certain fixed pitch. If I tune this string"—*pluck, pluck*—"to the same pitch, I know that the string, and the fly's wings, are vibrating at the same frequency. I already know how to reckon the frequency of a string's vibration—hence, I know how many times in a second a fly's wings beat. Useful *data* if we are ever to build a flying-machine."

Autumn rain made the field turn mucky, and ended the chariot experiments. Charles Comstock had to find other things to do. He had matriculated at Cambridge this year, but Cambridge was closed for the duration of the Plague. Daniel reckoned that as a *quid pro quo* for staying here at Epsom, Wilkins was obliged to tutor Charles in Natural Philosophy. But most of the tutoring was indistinguishable from drudge work on Wilkins's diverse experiments, many of which (now that the weather had turned) were being conducted in the cottage's cellar. Wilkins was starving a toad in a jar to see if new toads would grow out of it. There was a carp living out of water, being fed on moistened bread; Charles's job was to wet its gills several times a day. The King's ant question had gotten Wilkins going on an experiment he'd wanted to try for a long time: before long, down in the cellar, between the starving toad and the carp, they had a maggot the size of a man's thigh, which had to be fed rotten meat, and weighed once a day. This began to smell and so they moved it outside, to a shack downwind, where Wilkins had also embarked on a whole range of experiments concerning the generation of flies and worms out of decomposing meat, cheese, and other substances. Everyone knew, or thought they knew, that this happened spontaneously. But Hooke with his microscope had found tiny motes on the undersides of certain leaves, which grew up into insects, and in water he had found tiny eggs that grew up into gnats, and this had given him the idea that perhaps all things that were believed to be bred from putrefaction might have like origins: that the air and the water were filled with an invisible dust of tiny eggs and seeds that, in order to germinate, need only be planted in something moist and rotten.

From time to time, a carriage or wagon from the outside world was suffered to pass into the gate of the manor and approach the big house. On the one hand, this was welcome evidence that some people were still alive out there in England. On the other—

"Who is that madman, coming and going in the midst of the Plague," Daniel asked, "and why does John Comstock let him into his house? The poxy bastard'll infect us all."

"John Comstock could not exclude that fellow any more than he could ban air from his lungs," Wilkins said. He had been tracking the carriage's progress, at a safe distance, through a prospective glass. "That is his money-scrivener."

Daniel had never heard the term before. "I have not yet reached that point in the Tables where 'money-scrivener' is defined. Does he do what a goldsmith does?"

"Smite gold? No."

"Of course not. I was referring to this new line of work that goldsmiths have got into—handling notes that serve as money."

"A man such as the Earl of Epsom would not suffer a money-goldsmith to draw within a mile of his house!" Wilkins said indignantly. "A money-scrivener is different altogether! And yet he does something very much the same."

"Could you explain that, please?" Daniel said, but they were interrupted by Hooke, shouting from another room:

"Daniel! Fetch a cannon."

In other circumstances this demand would have posed severe difficulties. However, they were living on the estate of the man who had introduced the manufacture of gunpowder to Britain, and provided King Charles II with many of his armaments. So Daniel went out and enlisted that man's son, young Charles Comstock, who in turn drafted a corps of servants and a few horses. They procured a field-piece from John Comstock's personal armoury and towed it out into the middle of a pasture. Meanwhile, Mr. Hooke had caused a certain servant, who had long been afflicted with deafness, to be brought out from the town. Hooke bade the servant stand in the same pasture, only a fathom away from the muzzle of the cannon (but off to one side!). Charles Comstock (who knew how to do such things) charged the cannon with some of his father's finest powder, shoved a longish fuse down the touch-hole, lit it, and ran away. The result was a sudden immense compression of the air, which Hooke had hoped would penetrate the servant's skull and knock away whatever hidden obstructions had caused him to become deaf. Quite a few window-panes in John Comstock's manor house were blown out of their frames, amply demonstrating the soundness of the underlying idea. But it didn't cure the servant's deafness.

"As you may know, my dwelling is a-throng, just now, with persons from the city," said John Comstock, Earl of Epsom and Lord Chancellor of England.

He had appeared, suddenly and unannounced, in the door of the cottage. Hooke and Wilkins were busy hollering at the deaf servant, trying to see if he could hear anything at all. Daniel noticed the visitor first, and joined in the shouting: "Excuse me! Gentlemen! REVEREND WILKINS!"

After several minutes' confusion, embarrassment, and makeshift stabs at protocol, Wilkins and Comstock ended up sitting across the table from each other with glasses of claret while Hooke and Waterhouse and the deaf servant held up a nearby wall with their arses.

Comstock was pushing sixty. Here on his own country estate, he had no patience with wigs or other Court foppery, and so his silver hair was simply queued, and he was dressed in plain simple riding-and-hunting togs. "In the year of my birth, Jamestown was founded, the pilgrims scurried off to Leyden, and work commenced on the King James version of the Bible. I have lived through London's diverse riots and panics, plagues and Gunpowder Plots. I have escaped from burning buildings. I was wounded at the Battle of Newark and made my way, in some discomfort, to safety in Paris. It was not my last battle, on land or at sea. I was there when His Majesty was crowned in exile at Scone, and I was there when he returned in triumph to London. I have killed men. You know all of these things, Dr. Wilkins, and so I mention them, not to boast, but to emphasize that *if I were living a solitary life* in that large House over yonder, you could set off cannonades, and larger detonations, at all hours of day and night, without warning, and for that matter you could make a pile of meat five fathoms high and let it fester away beneath my bedchamber's window—*and none of it would matter to me.* But as it is, my house is crowded, just now, with Persons of Quality. Some of them are of *royal* degree. Many of them are *female*, and some are of *tender years.* Two of them are *all three.*"

"My lord!" Wilkins exclaimed. Daniel had been carefully watching him, as who wouldn't—the opportunity to watch a man like Wilkins being called on the carpet by a man like Comstock was far more precious than any Southwark bear-baiting. Until just now, Wilkins had *pretended* to be mortified—though he'd done a very good job of it. But now, suddenly, he really *was.*

Two of them are all three—what could *that* possibly mean? Who was royal, female, and of tender years? King Charles II didn't have any daughters, at least *legitimate* ones. Elizabeth, the Winter Queen, had *littered* Europe with princes and princesses until she'd passed away a couple of years ago—but it seemed unlikely that any Continental royalty would be visiting England during the Plague.

Comstock continued: "These persons have come here seeking refuge, as they are terrified *to begin with,* of the Plague and other horrors—including, but hardly limited to, a possible *Dutch* invasion. The violent compression of the air, which you and I might think of as a possible cure for deafness, is construed, by such people, entirely differently . . ."

Wilkins said something fiendishly clever and appropriate and then devoted the next couple of days to abjectly humbling himself and apologizing to every noble person within ear- and nose-shot of the late Experiments. Hooke was put to work making little wind-up toys for the two little royal girls. Meanwhile Daniel and Charles had to dismantle all of the bad-smelling experiments, and oversee their decent burials, and generally tidy things up.

It took days' peering at Fops through hedges, deconstructing carriage-door scutcheons, and shinnying out onto the branches of diverse noble and royal family trees for Daniel to understand what Wilkins had inferred from a few of John Comstock's pithy words

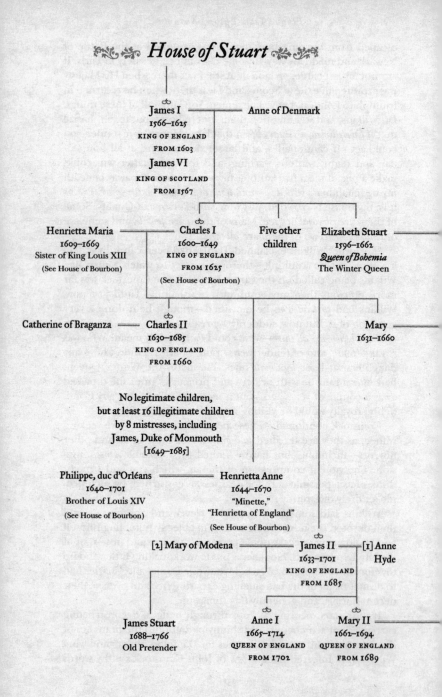

House of Stuart

James I
1566–1625
KING OF ENGLAND
FROM 1603
James VI
KING OF SCOTLAND
FROM 1567

—— **Anne of Denmark**

Henrietta Maria
1609–1669
Sister of King Louis XIII
(See House of Bourbon)

—— **Charles I**
1600–1649
KING OF ENGLAND
FROM 1625
(See House of Bourbon)

Five other children

Elizabeth Stuart
1596–1662
Queen of Bohemia
The Winter Queen

Catherine of Braganza —— **Charles II**
1630–1685
KING OF ENGLAND
FROM 1660

No legitimate children,
but at least 16 illegitimate children
by 8 mistresses, including
James, Duke of Monmouth
[1649–1685]

Mary
1631–1660

Philippe, duc d'Orléans
1640–1701
Brother of Louis XIV
(See House of Bourbon)

—— **Henrietta Anne**
1644–1670
"Minette,"
"Henrietta of England"
(See House of Bourbon)

[2] **Mary of Modena** —— **James II** —— [1] **Anne Hyde**
1633–1701
KING OF ENGLAND
FROM 1685

James Stuart
1688–1766
Old Pretender

Anne I
1665–1714
QUEEN OF ENGLAND
FROM 1702

Mary II
1662–1694
QUEEN OF ENGLAND
FROM 1689

✺✺ ✺ *House of Orange-Nassau* ✺ ✺✺

Frederick V
1596–1632
Elector of the Palatinate
King of Bohemia
The Winter King

William II of Orange
1625–1650

Charles Louis
1617–1680
Elector of the Palatinate

Sophie ——— **Ernst August**
1630–1714   1629–1698
(See House of Welf)   (See House of Welf)

Eleven other siblings

Charles
1651–1685
Elector of the Palatinate

Elisabeth Charlotte
1652–1722
"Liselotte,"
"La Palatine,"
"The Knight of the
Rustling Leaves,"
"Madame"
(See House of Bourbon)

Philippe, duc d'Orléans
1640–1701
Brother of Louis XIV
(See House of Bourbon)

⚭
William III of Orange
1650–1701
Stadholder of the
Dutch Republic
KING OF ENGLAND
FROM 1689

and eyebrow-raisings. Comstock had formal gardens to one side of his house, which for many excellent reasons were off-limits to Natural Philosophers. Persons in French clothes strolled in them. That was not remarkable. To dally in gardens was some people's life-work, as to shovel manure was a stable-hand's. At a distance they all looked the same, at least to Daniel. Wilkins, much more conversant with the Court, spied on them from time to time through a prospective-glass. As a mariner, seeking to establish his bearings at night, will first look for Ursa Major, that being a constellation of exceptional size and brightness, so Wilkins would always commence his obs'v'ns. by zeroing his sights, as it were, on a particular woman who was easy to find because she was twice the size of everyone else. Many furlongs of gaily dyed fabrics went into her skirts, which shewed bravely from a distance, like French regimental standards. From time to time a man with blond hair would come out and stroll about the garden with her, moon orbiting planet. He reminded Daniel, from a distance, of Isaac.

Daniel did not reck who that fellow was, and was too abashed to discover his ignorance by asking, until one day a carriage arrived from London and several men in admirals' hats climbed out of it and went to talk to the same man in the garden. Though first they all doffed those hats and bowed low.

"That blond man who walks in the garden, betimes, on the arm of the Big Dipper—would that be the Duke of York?"

"Yes," said Wilkins—not wishing to say more, as he was breathing shallowly, his eye peeled wide open and bathed in a greenish light from the eyepiece of his prospective-glass.

"And Lord High Admiral," Daniel continued.

"He has many titles," Wilkins observed in a level and patient tone.

"So those chaps in the hats would be—obviously—"

"The Admiralty," Wilkins said curtly, "or some moiety or faction thereof." He recoiled from the scope. Daniel phant'sied he was being proffered a look-see, but only for a moment—Wilkins lifted the instrument out of the tree-crook and collapsed it. Daniel collected that he had seen something Wilkins wished he hadn't.

The Dutch and the English were at war. Because of the Plague, this had been a desultory struggle thus far, and Daniel had forgotten about it. It was midwinter. Cold had brought the Plague to a stand. Months would pass before the weather permitted resumption of the sea-campaign. But the time to lay plans for such campaigns was now. It ought to surprise no one if the Admiralty met with the Lord High Admiral now. It would be surprising if they *didn't*. What struck Daniel was that Wilkins *cared* that he, Daniel, had seen something. The Restoration, and Daniel's Babylonian exile and subjugation at Cambridge, had led him to think of himself as a perfect nobody, except perhaps when it came to Natural Philosophy—and it was more obvious every day that even within the Royal Society he was nothing compared to Wren and Hooke. So why should John Wilkins give a fig whether Daniel spied a flotilla of admirals and collected, from that, that John Comstock was hosting James, Duke of York, brother of Charles II and next in line to the throne?

It must be (as Daniel realized, walking back through a defoliated orchard alongside the brooding Wilkins) because he was the son of Drake. And though Drake was a retired agitator of a defeated and downcast sect, at bay in his house on Holborn, *someone* was still afraid of him.

Or if not of him, then of his sect.

But the sect was shattered into a thousand claques and cabals. Cromwell was gone, Drake was too old, Gregory Bolstrood had been executed, and his son Knott was in exile—

That was it. They were afraid of *Daniel*.

"What is funny?" Wilkins demanded.

"People," Daniel said, "and what goes on in their minds sometimes."

"I say, you're not referring to *me* by that—?—!"

"Oh, perish the thought. I would not mock my betters."

"Pray, who on this estate is *not* your better?"

A hard question that. Daniel's answer was silence. Wilkins seemed to find even that alarming.

"I forget you are a Phanatique born and bred." Which was the same as saying, *You recognize no man as your better, do you?*

"On the contrary, I see now that you have *never* forgotten it."

But something seemed to have changed in Wilkins's mind. Like an Admiral working his ship to windward, he had suddenly come about and, after a few moments' luffing and disarray, was now on an altogether novel tack: "The lady used to be called Anne Hyde— a close relation of John Comstock. So, far from common. Yet too common for a Duke to marry. And yet still too noble to send off to a Continental nunnery, and too fat to move far, in any case. She bore him a couple of daughters: Mary, then Anne. The Duke finally married her, though not without many complications. Since Mary or Anne could conceivably inherit the throne one day, it became a State matter. Various courtiers were talked, bribed, or threatened into coming forward and swearing on stacks of Bibles that they'd fucked Anne Hyde up and down, fucked her in the British Isles and in France, in the Low Countries and the Highlands, in the city and in the country, in ships and palaces, beds and hammocks, bushes, flower-beds, water-closets, and garrets, that they had fucked her drunk and fucked her sober, from behind and in front, from above, below, and both the right and left sides, singly and in groups, in the day and in the night and during all phases of the moon and signs of the Zodiac, whilst also intimating that any number of blacksmiths, Vagabonds, French gigolos, Jesuit provocateurs, comedians, barbers, and apprentice saddlers had been doing the same whensoever they weren't. But despite all of this the Duke of York married her, and socked her away in St. James's Palace, where she's grown like one of our *entomologickal* prodigies in the cellar."

Daniel had heard a good bit of this before, of course, from men who came to the house on Holborn to pay court to Drake—which gave him the odd sense that Wilkins was paying court to *him*. Which could not be, for Daniel had no real power or significance at all, and no prospects of getting any.

It seemed more plausible that Wilkins felt sorry for Daniel, than afraid of him; and as such was trying to shield him from those dangers that were avoidable while tutoring him in how to cope with the rest.

Which meant, if true, that Daniel ought at least to attend to the lesson that Wilkins was trying to give him. The two Princesses, Mary and Anne, would, respectively, be three and one years old now. And as their mother was related to John Comstock, it was entirely plausible that they might be visitors in the house. Which explained Comstock's remark to Wilkins: "Two of them are *all three*." Female, of tender years, and royal.

The burdensome restrictions imposed on their Natural-Philosophic researches by the host made it necessary to convene a very long Symposium in the Kitchen, where Hooke and Wilkins dictated a list (written by Daniel in a loosening hand) of experiments that were neither noisy nor smelly, but (as the evening wore on) increasingly fanciful. Hooke put Daniel to work mending his Condensing Engine, which was a piston-and-cylinder arrangement for compressing or rarefying air. He was convinced that air contained some kind of spirit that sustained both fire and life, which, when it was used up, caused both to be extinguished. So there was a whole range of experiments along the lines of: sealing up a candle and a mouse in a glass vessel, and watching to see what happened (mouse died before candle). They fixed up a huge bladder so that it was leak-proof, and put it to their mouths, and took turns breathing the same air over and over again, to see what would happen. Hooke used his engine to produce a vacuum in a large glass jar, then set a pendulum swinging in the vacuum, and set Charles there to count its swings. On the first really clear night at the onset of winter, Hooke had gone outside with a telescope and peered at Mars: he had found some light and dark patches on its surface, and ever since had been tracking their movements so that he could figure out how long it took that planet to rotate on its axis. He put Charles and Daniel to work grinding better and better lenses, or else bought them from Spinoza in Amsterdam, and they took turns looking at smaller and smaller structures on the moon. But here again, Hooke saw things Daniel didn't. "The moon must have gravity, like the earth," he said.

"What makes you say so?"

"The mountains and valleys have a settled shape to them—no matter how rugged the landforms, there is nothing to be seen, on that whole orb, that would fall over under gravitation. With better lenses I could measure the Angle of Repose and calculate the force of her gravity."

"If the moon gravitates, so must everything else in the heavens," Daniel observed.*

A long skinny package arrived from Amsterdam. Daniel opened it up, expecting to find another telescope—instead it was a straight, skinny horn, about five feet long, with helical ridges and grooves. "What is it?" he asked Wilkins.

Wilkins peered at it over his glasses and said (sounding mildly annoyed), "The horn of a unicorn."

"But I thought that the unicorn was a mythical beast."

"*I've* never seen one."

"Then where do you suppose this came from?"

"How the devil should I know?" Wilkins returned. "All I know is, you can buy them in Amsterdam."

> Kings most commonly, though strong in legions, are
> but weak in Arguments; as they who have ever accus-
> tom'd from the Cradle to use thir will onely as thir

---

*He was not the first person to observe it.

right hand, thir reason alwayes as thir left. Whence
unexpectedly constrain'd to that kind of combat,
they prove but weak and puny Adversaries.
　　　　　—Milton, preface to *Eikonoklastes*

Daniel got used to seeing the Duke of York out riding and hunting with his princely friends—as much as the son of Drake *could*
get used to such a sight. Once the hunters rode past within a bow-
shot of him, near enough that he could hear the Duke talking to
his companion—*in French.* Which gave Daniel an impulse to rush
up to this French Catholic man in his French clothes, who claimed
to be England's next king, and put an end to him. He mastered it
by recalling to mind the way that the Duke's father's head had
plopped into the basket on the scaffold at the Banqueting House.
Then he thought to himself: *What an odd family!*

Too, he could no longer muster quite the same malice towards
these people. Drake had raised his sons to hate the nobility by
wasting no opportunity to point out their privileges, and the way
they profited from those privileges without really being aware of
them. This sort of discourse had wrought extraordinarily, not only
in Drake's sons but in every Dissident meeting-house in the land,
and led to Cromwell and much else; but Cromwell had made
Puritans powerful, and as Daniel was now seeing, that power—as
if it were a living thing with a mind of its own—was trying to pass
itself on to *him,* which would mean that Daniel was a child of privilege too.

The tables of the Philosophical Language were finished: a vast
fine-meshed net drawn through the Cosmos so that everything
known, in Heaven and Earth, was trapped in one of its myriad cells.
All that was needed to identify a particular thing was to give its location in the tables, which could be expressed as a series of numbers.
Wilkins came up with a system for assigning names to things, so
that by breaking a name up into its component syllables, one could
know its location in the Tables, and hence what thing it referred to.

Wilkins drained all the blood out of a large dog and put it into
a smaller dog; minutes later the smaller dog was out chasing sticks.
Hooke built a new kind of clock, using the Microscope to examine
some of its tiny parts. In so doing he discovered a new kind of mite
living in the rags in which these parts had been wrapped. He drew
pictures of them, and then performed an exhaustive three-day
series of experiments to learn what would and wouldn't kill them:
the most effective killer being a Florentine poison he'd been brewing out of tobacco leaves.

Sir Robert Moray came to visit, and ground up a bit of the unicorn's horn to make a powder, which he sprinkled in a ring, and placed a spider in the center of the ring. But the spider kept escaping. Moray pronounced the horn to be a fraud.

Wilkins hustled Daniel out of bed one night in the wee hours and took him on a dangerous nighttime hay-wain ride to the gaol in Epsom town. "Fortune has smiled on our endeavours," Wilkins said. "The man we are going to interview was condemned to hang. But hanging crushes the parts that are of interest to us—certain delicate structures in the neck. Fortunately for us, before the hangman could get to him, he died of a bloody flux."

"Is this going to be a new addition to the Tables, then?" Daniel asked wearily.

"Don't be foolish—the anatomical structures in question have been known for centuries. This dead man is going to help us with the Real Character."

"That's the alphabet for writing down the Philosophical Language?"

"You know that perfectly well. Wake up, Daniel!"

"I ask only because it seems to me you've already come up with *several* Real Characters."

"All more or less arbitrary. A natural philosopher on some other world, viewing a document written in those characters, would think that he were reading, not the Philosophical Language, but the *Cryptonomicon!* What we need is a *systematic* alphabet—made so that the shapes of the characters themselves provide full information as to how they are pronounced."

These words filled Daniel with a foreboding that turned out to be fully justified: by the time the sun rose, they had fetched the dead man from the gaol, brought him back out to the cottage, and carefully cut his head off. Charles Comstock was rousted from bed and ordered to dissect the corpse, as a lesson in anatomy (and as a way of getting rid of it). Meanwhile, Hooke and Wilkins connected the head's wind-pipe to a large set of fireplace-bellows, so that they could blow air through his voice-box. Daniel was detailed to saw off the top of the skull and get rid of the brains so that he could reach in through the back and get hold of the soft palate, tongue, and other meaty bits responsible for making sounds. With Daniel thus acting as a sort of meat puppeteer, and Hooke manipulating the lips and nostrils, and Wilkins plying the bellows, they were able to make the head speak. When his speaking-parts were squished into one configuration he made a very clear "O" sound, which Daniel (very tired now) found just a bit unsettling. Wilkins wrote down an

O-shaped character, reflecting the shape of the man's lips. This experiment went on *all day*, Wilkins reminding the others, when they showed signs of tiredness, that this rare head wouldn't keep forever—as if that weren't already obvious. They made the head utter thirty-four different sounds. For each one of them, Wilkins drew out a letter that was a sort of quick freehand sketch of the positions of lips, tongue, and other bits responsible for making that noise. Finally they turned the head over to Charles Comstock, to continue his anatomy-lesson, and Daniel went to bed for a series of rich nightmares.

Looking at Mars had put Hooke in mind of cœlestial affairs; for that reason he set out with Daniel one morning in a wagon, with a chest of equipment. This must have been important, because Hooke packed it himself, and wouldn't let anyone else near it. Wilkins kept trying to persuade them to use the giant wheel, instead of borrowing one of John Comstock's wagons (and further wearing out their welcome). Wilkins claimed that the giant wheel, propelled by the youthful and vigorous Daniel Waterhouse, could (in theory) traverse fields, bogs, and reasonably shallow bodies of water with equal ease, so they could simply travel in a perfectly straight line to their destination, instead of having to follow roads. Hooke declined, and chose the wagon.

They traveled for several hours to a certain well, said to be more than three hundred feet deep, bored down through solid chalk. Hooke's mere appearance was enough to chase away the local farmers, who were only loitering and drinking anyway. He got Daniel busy constructing a solid, level platform over the mouth of the well. Hooke meanwhile took out his best scale and began to clean and calibrate it. He explained, "For the sake of argument, suppose it really is true that planets are kept in their orbits, not by vortices in the æther, but by the force of gravity."

"Yes?"

"Then, if you do some mathematicks, you can see that it simply would not work unless the force of gravity got weaker, as the distance from the center of attraction increased."

"So the weight of an object should diminish as it rises?"

"And increase as it descends," Hooke said, nodding significantly at the well.

"Aha! So the experiment is to weigh something here at the surface, and then to . . ." and here Daniel stopped, horror-stricken.

Hooke twisted his bent neck around and peered at him curiously. Then, for the first time since Daniel had met him, he laughed out loud. "You're afraid that I'm proposing to lower you,

Daniel Waterhouse, three hundred feet down into the bottom of this well, with a scale in your lap, to weigh something? And that once down there the rope will break?" More laughing. "You need to think more carefully about what I said."

"Of course—it wouldn't work that way," Daniel said, deeply embarrassed on more than one level.

"And why not?" Hooke asked, Socratically.

"Because the scale works by balancing weights on one pan against the object to be weighed, on the other . . . and if it's true that all objects are heavier at the bottom of the well, then both the object, and the weights, will be heavier by the same amount . . . and so the result will be the same, and will teach us nothing."

"Help me measure out three hundred feet of thread," Hooke said, no longer amused.

They did it by pulling the thread off a reel, and stretching it alongside a one-fathom-long rod, and counting off fifty fathoms. One end of the thread Hooke tied to a heavy brass slug. He set the scale up on the platform that Daniel had improvised over the mouth of the well, and put the slug, along with its long bundle of thread, on the pan. He weighed the slug and thread carefully—a seemingly endless procedure disturbed over and over by light gusts of wind. To get a reliable measurement, they had to devote a couple of hours to setting up a canvas wind-screen. Then Hooke spent another half hour peering at the scale's needle through a magnifying lens while adding or subtracting bits of gold foil, no heavier than snowflakes. Every change caused the scale to teeter back and forth for several minutes before settling into a new position. Finally, Hooke called out a weight in pounds, ounces, grains, and fractions of grains, and Daniel noted it down. Then Hooke tied the free end of the thread to a little eye he had screwed to the bottom of the pan, and he and Daniel took turns lowering the weight into the well, letting it drop a few inches at a time—if it got to swinging, and scraped against the chalky sides of the hole, it would pick up a bit of extra weight, and ruin the experiment. When all three hundred feet had been let out, Hooke went for a stroll, because the weight was swinging a little bit, and its movements would disturb the scale. Finally it settled down enough that he could go back to work with his magnifying glass and his tweezers.

Daniel, in other words, had a lot of time to think that day. Cells, spiders' eyes, unicorns' horns, compressed and rarefied air, dramatic cures for deafness, philosophical languages, and flying chariots were all perfectly fine subjects, but lately Hooke's interest had been straying into matters cœlestial, and that made Daniel think about his roommate. Just as certain self-styled philosophers in minor European courts were frantic to know what Hooke and Wilkins were up to at Epsom, so Daniel wanted only to know what Isaac was doing up at Woolsthorpe.

"It weighs the same," Hooke finally pronounced, "three hundred feet of altitude makes no *measurable* difference." That was the signal to pack up all the apparatus and let the farmers draw their water again.

"This proves nothing," Hooke said as they rode home through the dark. "The scale is not precise enough. But if one were to construct a clock, driven by a pendulum, in a sealed glass vessel, so that changes in moisture and baroscopic pressure would not affect its speed . . . and if one were to run that clock in the bottom of a well for a long period of time . . . any difference in the pendulum's weight would be manifest as a slowing, or quickening, of the clock."

"But how would you know that it was running slow or fast?" Daniel asked. "You'd have to compare it against another clock."

"Or against the rotation of the earth," Hooke said. But it seemed that Daniel's question had thrown him into a dark mood, and he said nothing more until they had reached Epsom, after midnight.

THE TEMPERATURE AT NIGHT began to fall below freezing, and so it was time to calibrate thermometers. Daniel and Charles and Hooke had been making them for some weeks out of yard-long glass tubes, filled with spirits of wine, dyed with cochineal. But they had no markings on them. On cold nights they would bundle themselves up and immerse those thermometers in tubs of distilled water and then sit there for hours, giving the tubs an occasional stir, and waiting. When the water froze, if they listened carefully enough, they could hear a faint searing, splintering noise come out of the tub as flakes of ice shot across the surface—then they'd rouse themselves into action, using diamonds to make a neat scratch on each tube, marking the position of the red fluid inside.

Hooke kept a square of black velvet outside so that it would stay cold. When it snowed during the daytime, he would take his microscope outside and spread the velvet out on the stage and peer at any snowflakes that happened to fall on it. Daniel saw, as Hooke did, that each one was unique. But again Hooke saw something Daniel missed: "in any particular snowflake, all six arms are the same—why does this happen? Why shouldn't each of the six arms develop in a different and unique shape?"

"Some central organizing principle must be at work, but—?" Daniel said.

"That is too obvious to even *bother* pointing out," Hooke said. "With better lenses, we could peer into the core of a snowflake and discover that principle at work."

A week later, Hooke opened up the thorax of a live dog and removed all of its ribs to expose the beating heart. But the lungs had gone flaccid and did not seem to be doing their job.

The screaming sounded almost human. A man with an expensive voice came down from John Comstock's house to enquire about it. Daniel, too bleary-eyed to see clearly and too weary to think, took him for a head butler or something. "I shall write an explanation, and a note of apology to him," Daniel mumbled, looking about for a quill, rubbing his blood-sticky hand on his breeches.

"To *whom*, prithee? asked the butler, amused. Though he seemed young for a head-butler. In his early thirties. He was in a linen night-dress. His scalp glistered with a fine carpet of blond stubble, the mark of a man who always wore a periwig.

"The Earl of Epsom."

"Why not write it to the Duke of York?"

"Very well then, I'll write it to him."

"Then why not dispense with writing altogether and simply tell me what the hell you are doing?"

Daniel took this for insolence until he looked the visitor in the face and realized it was the Duke of York in person.

He really ought to bow, or something. Instead of which he jerked. The Duke made a gesture with his hand that seemed to mean that the jerk was accepted as due obeisance and could they please get on with the conversation now.

"The Royal Society—" Daniel began, thrusting that word *Royal* out in front of him like a shield, "has brought a dead dog to life with another's blood, and has now embarked on a study of artificial *breath*."

"My brother is fond of your Society," said James, "or *his* Society I should say, for he made it Royal." This, Daniel suspected, was to explain why he was not going to have them all horsewhipped. "I do wonder at the noise. Is it expected to continue all night?"

"On the contrary, it has already ceased," Daniel pointed out.

The Lord High Admiral preceded him into the kitchen, where Hooke and Wilkins had thrust a brass pipe down the dog's windpipe and connected it to the same trusty pair of bellows they'd used to make the dead man's head speak. "By pumping the bellows they were able to inflate and deflate the lungs, and prevent the dog from asphyxiating," explained Charles Comstock, after the experimenters had bowed to the Duke. "Now it only remains to be seen how long the animal can be kept alive in this way. Mr. Waterhouse and I shall spell each other at the bellows until Mr. Hooke pronounces an end to the experiment."

At the mention of Daniel's family name, the Duke flicked his eyes towards him for a moment.

"If it must suffer in the name of your inquiry, thank Heaven it does so quietly," the Duke remarked, and turned to leave. The others would follow; but the Duke stopped them with a "Do carry on, as you were." But to Daniel he said, "A word, if you please, Mr. Waterhouse," and so Daniel escorted him out onto the lawn half wondering whether he was about to be carved up worse than the dog.

A few moments previously, he'd mastered a daft impulse to tackle his royal highness before his royal highness reached the kitchen, for fear that his royal highness would be disgusted by what was going on in there. But he'd not reckoned on the fact that the Duke, young though he was, had fought in a lot of battles, both at sea and on land. Which was to say that as bad as this business with the dog was, the Duke of York had seen much worse done to *humans*. The R.S., far from seeming like a band of mad ruthless butchers, were dilettantes by his standards. Further grounds (as if any were wanted!) for Daniel to feel queasy.

Daniel really knew of no way to regulate his actions other than to be rational. Princes were taught a thing or two about being rational, as they were taught to play a little lute and dance a passable ricercar. But what drove their actions was their own force of will; in the end they did as they pleased, rational or not. Daniel had liked to tell himself that rational thought led to better actions than brute force of will; yet here was the Duke of York all but rolling his eyes at them and their experiment, seeing naught that was new.

"A friend of mine brought back something nasty from France," his royal highness announced.

It took Daniel a long time to decrypt this. He tried to understand it in any number of different ways, but suddenly the knowledge rumbled through his mind like a peal of thunder through a coppice. The Duke had said: *I have syphilis.*

"Shame, that," Daniel said. For he was not sure, yet, that he had translated it correctly. He must be ever so careful and vague lest this conversation degenerate into a comedy of errors ending with his death by rapier-thrust.

"Some are of the opinion that mercury cures it."

"It is also a poison, though," Daniel said.

Which was common knowledge; but it seemed to confirm, in the mind of James Stuart, Duke of York and Lord High Admiral, that he was talking to just the right chap. "Surely with so many clever Doctors in the Royal Society, working on artificial breath and such, there must be some thought of how to cure a man such as my friend."

And his wife and his children, Daniel thought, for James must have either gotten it from, or passed it on to, Anne Hyde, who had therefore probably given it to the daughters, Mary and Anne. To date, James's older brother the King had not been able to produce any legitimate children. There were plenty of bastards like Monmouth. But none eligible to inherit the throne. And so this nasty thing that James had brought back from France was really a matter of whether the Stuart dynasty was to survive.

This raised a fascinating side question. With a whole cottage full of Royal Society Fellows to choose from, why had James carefully chosen to speak with the one who happened to be the son of a Phanatique?

"It is a sensitive matter," the Duke remarked, "the sort of thing that stains a man's honor, if it is bandied about."

Daniel readily translated this as follows: *If you tell anyone, I'll send someone round to engage you in a duel.* Not that anyone would pay any notice, anyway, if the son of Drake were to level an accusation of moral turpitude against the Duke of York. Drake had been doing such things without letup for fifty years. And so the Duke's strategy was now plain to Daniel: he had chosen Daniel to hear about his syphilis because if Daniel were so foolish as to spread rumors, no one would hear them above the roar of obloquy produced at all times by Drake. In any case, Daniel would not be able to keep it up for very long before he was found in a field outside of London with a lot of rapier wounds in his body.

"You will let me know, won't you, if the Royal Society learns anything on this front?" said James, making to leave.

"So that you can pass the information on to your friend? Of course," Daniel said. Which was the end of that conversation. He returned to the kitchen to get an idea of how much longer the experiment was going to go on.

The answer: longer than any of them really wanted. By the time they were finished, dawn-light was beginning to come in the windows, giving them a premonition of just how ghastly the kitchen was going to look when the sun actually rose. Hooke was sitting crookedly in a chair, shocked and morose, appalled by himself, and Wilkins was hunched forward supporting his head on a smeared fist.

They'd come here supposedly as refugees from the Black Death, but really they were fleeing their own ignorance—they hungered for understanding, and were like starving wretches who had broken into a lord's house and gone on an orgy of gluttonous feasting, wolfing down new meals before they could digest, or even chew, the old ones. It had lasted for the better part of a year, but now, as the sun rose over the aftermath of the artificial breath experiment, they were scattered around, blinking stupidly at the devastated kitchen, with its dog-ribs strewn all over the floor, and huge jars of preserved spleens and gall-bladders, specimens of exotic parasites nailed to planks or glued to panes of glass, vile poisons bubbling over on the fire, and suddenly they felt completely disgusted with themselves.

Daniel gathered the dog's remains up in his arms—messy, but it scarcely mattered—all their clothes would have to be burned anyway—and walked out to the bone-yard on the east side of the cottage, where the remains of all Hooke's and Wilkins's investigations were burned, buried, or used to study the spontaneous generation of flies. Notwithstanding which, the air was relatively clean and fresh out here. Having set the remains down, Daniel found that he was walking directly towards a blazing planet, a few degrees above the western horizon, which could only be Venus. He walked and walked, letting the dew on the grass cleanse the blood from his shoes. The dawn was making the fields shimmer pink and green.

Isaac had sent him a letter: "Require asst. w/obs. of Venus pls. come if you can." He had wondered at the time if this might be something veiled. But standing there in that dew-silvered field with his back to the house of carnage and nothing before him but the Dawn Star, Daniel remembered what Isaac had said years ago about the natural harmony between the heavenly orbs and the orbs we view them with. Four hours later he was riding north on a borrowed horse.

Aboard Minerva,
Plymouth Bay, Massachusetts
NOVEMBER 1713

✣

DANIEL WAKES UP WORRIED. The stiffness in his *masseter* muscles, the aching in his *frontalis* and *temporalis,* tells him he's been worrying about something in his sleep. Still, being worried is preferable to being terrified, which he was until yesterday, when Captain van Hoek finally gave up on the idea of trying to sail *Minerva* into the throat of a gale and turned back to calmer waters along the Massachusetts coast.

Captain van Hoek would probably have called it "a bit of chop" or some other nautical euphemism, but Daniel had gone to his cabin with a pail to catch his vomit, and an empty bottle to receive the notes he'd been scratching out in the last few days. If the weather had gotten any worse, he'd have tossed these down the head. Perhaps some Moor or Hottentot would have found them in a century or two and read about Dr. Waterhouse's early memories of Newton and Leibniz.

The planks of the poop deck are only a few inches above Daniel's face as he lies on his sack of straw. He's learned to recognize the tread of van Hoek's boots on those boards. On a ship it is bad manners to approach within a fathom of the captain, so even when the poop deck is crowded, van Hoek's footsteps are always surrounded by a large empty space. As *Minerva*'s quest for a steady west wind has stretched out to a week and then two, Daniel has learned to read the state of the captain's mind from the figure and rhythm of his movements—each pattern like the steps of a courtly dance. A steady long stride means that all is well, and van Hoek is merely touring the precincts. When he's watching the weather he walks about in small eddies, and when he's shooting the sun with his back-staff he stands still, grinding the balls of his feet against the planks to keep his balance. But this morning (Daniel supposes it is early in the morning, though the sun hasn't come up yet) van Hoek is doing something Daniel's never observed before: flitting back and forth across the poop deck with brisk angry steps, pausing at one rail or another for a few seconds at a time. The sailors, he senses, are mostly awake, but they are all belowdecks shushing one another and tending to small, intense, quiet jobs.

Yesterday they had sailed into Cape Cod Bay—the shallow lake held in the crook of Cape Cod's arm—to ride out the tail end of that northeast gale, and to make certain repairs, and get the ship more winter-ready than it had been. But then the wind shifted round to the north and threatened to drive them against the sandbanks at the southern fringe of said Bay, and so they sailed toward the sunset, and maneuvered the big ship with exquisite care between rocks to starboard and sunken islands to port, and thus entered Plymouth Bay. As night fell they dropped anchor in an inlet, well sheltered from the weather, and (as Daniel supposed) prepared to tarry there for a few days and await more auspicious weather. But van Hoek was obviously nervous—he doubled the watch, and put men to work cleaning and oiling the ship's surprisingly comprehensive arsenal of small firearms.

A distant boom rattles the panes in Daniel's cabin window. He rolls out of bed like a fourteen-year-old and scurries to the exit, flailing one hand over his head in the dark so he won't brain himself on the overhead beam. When he emerges onto the quarter-deck he seems to hear answering fire from all the isles and hillside around them—then he understands that they are merely echoes of the first explosion. With a good pocket-watch he could map their surroundings by the timing of those echoes—

Dappa, the first mate, sits crosslegged on the deck near the wheel, reviewing charts by candle-light. This is an odd place for such work. Diverse feathers and colored ribbons dangle from a string above his head—Daniel supposes it to be a tribal fetish (Dappa is an African) until a fleck of goose-down crawls in a breath of cold air, and he understands that Dappa is trying to guess what the wind will do as the sun rises. He holds up one hand to silence Daniel before Daniel's had a chance to speak. There is shouting on the water, but it is all distant—*Minerva* is silent as a ghost ship. Stepping farther out onto the quarter-deck, Daniel can see yellow stars widely scattered across the water, blinking as they are eclipsed by rolling seas.

"You didn't know what you were getting yourself into," Dappa observes.

"I'll rise to that bait—what have I gotten myself into?"

"You're on a ship whose captain refuses to have anything to do with pirates," Dappa says. "Hates 'em. He nailed his colors to the mast twenty years ago, van Hoek did—he would burn this ship to the waterline before handing over a single penny."

"Those lights on the water—"

"Whaleboats mostly," Dappa says. "Possibly a barge or two. When the sun comes up we may expect to see sails—but before we concern ourselves with those, we shall have to contend with the whaleboats. Did you hear the shouting, an hour ago?"

"I must have slept through it."

"A whaleboat stole up towards us with muffled oars. We let her suppose that we were asleep—waited until she was alongside, then dropped a comet into her."

"Comet?"

"A small cannonball, wrapped in oil-soaked rags and set aflame. Once it lands in such a boat, it's difficult to throw overboard. Gave us a good look, while it lasted: there were a dozen Englishmen in that boat, and one of 'em was already swinging a grappling-hook."

"Do you mean that they were English colonists, or—"

"That's one of the things we aim to find out. After we chased that lot off, we sent some men out in our own whaler."

"The explosion—?"

" 'Twas a grenade. We have a few retired grenadiers in our number—"

"You threw a *bomb* into someone else's boat?"

"Aye, and then—if all went according to plan—our Filipinos— former pearl divers, excellent swimmers—climbed over the gunwales with daggers in their teeth and cut a few throats—"

"But that's *mad*! This is *Massachusetts*!"

Dappa chuckles. "Aye. That it is."

An hour later the sun rises gorgeously over Cape Cod Bay. Daniel is pacing around the ship, trying to find a place where he won't have to listen to the screams of the pirates. Two open boats are now thudding against *Minerva*'s hull: the ship's own longboat, freshly caulked and painted, and the pirate whaler, which was evidently in poor condition even before this morning's action. Splinters of fresh blond wood show where a bench was snapped by the grenade, and an inch or two of blood sloshes back and forth in the bottom as the empty boat is tossed around by a rising wind. Five pirates survived, and were towed back to *Minerva* by the raiding party. Now (judging from the sounds) they are all down in the bilge, where two of *Minerva*'s largest sailors are holding their heads beneath the filthy water. When they are hauled out, they scream for air, and Daniel thinks about Hooke and Wilkins with their poor dogs.

c%

Woolsthorpe, Lincolnshire
SPRING 1666

˜

> He discovereth the depe & secret things: he knoweth
> what is in the darkenes, and the light dwelleth
> with him.
>
> —DANIEL 2:22

FROM ISAAC'S INSTRUCTIONS ("Turn left at Grimethorpe Ruin")
he'd been expecting a few hovels gripping the rim of a wind-
burned scarp, but Woolsthorpe was as pleasant a specimen of English countryside as he'd ever seen. North of Cambridge it was
appallingly flat, a plain scratched with drainage ditches. But
beyond Peterborough the coastal fens fell away and were replaced
by pastures of radiant greenness, like stained-glass windows
infested with sheep. There were a few tall pine trees that made the
place seem farther north than it really was. Another day north, the
country began to roll, and the earth turned brown as coffee, with
cream-colored stone rising out of the soil here and there: once-
irregular croppings rationalized to squared-off block-heaps by the
efforts of quarrymen. Woolsthorpe gave an impression of being
high up in the world, close to the sky, and the trees that lined the
lane from the village all had the same telltale skewage, suggesting
that the place might not be as pleasant all year round as it was on
the morning Daniel arrived.

Woolsthorpe Manor was a very simple house, shaped like a fat *T*
with its crossbar fronting on the lane, made of the soft pale stone
that was used for everything around here—its roof a solid mass of
lichens. It was built sideways to a long slope that rose as it went
northwards, and so, on its southern end, the land fell away from it,
giving it a clear sunny exposure. But this opportunity had been
wasted by the builders, who had put almost no windows there—just
a couple of them, scarcely larger than gun-slits, and one tiny portal
up in the attic that made no sense to Daniel at first. As Daniel
noted while his horse toiled up the hill through the grasping
spring mud, Isaac had already taken advantage of this south-facing
wall by carving diverse sundials into it. Sprawling away from there,

down the hill and away from the lane, were long stables and barns that marked the place as an active farmstead, and that Daniel didn't have to concern himself with.

He turned off the lane. The house was set back from it not more than twenty feet. Set above the door was a coat of arms carved into the stone: on a blank shield, a pair of human thigh-bones crossed. A Jolly Roger, minus skull. Daniel sat on his horse and contemplated its sheer awfulness for a while and savored the dull, throbbing embarrassment of being English. He was waiting for a servant to notice his arrival.

Isaac had mentioned in his letter that his mother was away for a few weeks, and this was perfectly acceptable to Daniel—all he knew of the mother was that she had abandoned Isaac when he'd been three years old, and gone to live with a rich new husband several miles away, leaving the toddler to be raised in this house by his grandmother. Daniel had noticed that there were some families (like the Waterhouses) skilled at presenting a handsome façade to the world, no matter what was *really* going on; it was all lies, of course, but at least it was a convenience to visitors. But there were other families where the emotional wounds of the participants never healed, never even closed up and scabbed over, and no one even bothered to cover them up—like certain ghastly effigies in Papist churches, with exposed bleeding hearts and gushing stigmata. Having dinner or even polite conversation with them was like sitting around the table participating in Hooke's dog experiment—everything you did or said was another squeeze of the bellows, and you could stare right in through the vacancies in the rib cage and see the organs helplessly responding, the heart twitching with its own macabre internal power of perpetual motion. Daniel suspected that the Newtons were one of *those* families, and he was glad Mother was absent. Their coat of arms was a proof, of Euclidean certainty, that he was right about this.

"Is that you, Daniel?" said the voice of Isaac Newton, not very loud. A little bubble of euphoria percolated into Daniel's bloodstream: to re-encounter *anyone*, after so long, during the Plague Years, and find them still alive, was a miracle. He looked uphill. The northern end of the house looked into, and was sheltered by, rising terrain. A small orchard of apple trees had been established on that side. Seated on a bench, with his back to Daniel and to the sun, was a man or woman with long colorless hair spilling down over a blanket that had been drawn round the shoulders like a shawl.

"Isaac?"

The head turned slightly. "It is I."

Daniel rode up out of the mud and into the apple-garden, then dismounted and tethered the horse to the low branch of an apple tree—a garland of white flowers. The petals were coming down from the apple-blossoms like snow. Daniel swung round Isaac in a wide Copernican arc, peering at him through the fragrant blizzard. Isaac's hair had always been pale, and prematurely streaked with gray, but in the year since Daniel had seen him, he'd gone almost entirely silver. The hair fell about him like a hood—as Daniel came around to the front, he was expecting to see Isaac's protruding eyes, but instead he saw two disks of gold looking back at him, as if Isaac's eyes had been replaced by five-guinea coins. Daniel must have shouted, because Isaac said, "Don't be alarmed. I fashioned these spectacles myself. I'm sure you know that gold is almost infinitely malleable—but did you know that if you pound it thin enough, you can see through it? Try them." He took the spectacles off with one hand while clamping the other over his eyes. Daniel bobbled them because they were lighter than he'd expected—they had no lenses, just membranes of gold stretched like drum-heads over wire frames. As he raised them towards his face, their color changed.

"They are blue!"

"It is another clue about the nature of light," Isaac said. "Gold is yellow—it reflects the part of light that is yellow, that is, but allows the remnant to pass through—which being deprived of its yellow part, appears blue."

Daniel was peering out at a dim vision of blue-blossomed apple trees before a blue stone house—a blue Isaac Newton sitting with his back to a blue sun, one blue hand covering his eyes.

"Forgive me their rude construction—I made them in the dark."

"Is there something the matter with your eyes, Isaac?"

"Nothing that cannot heal, God willing. I have been staring into the sun too much."

"Oh." Daniel was semi-dumbstruck by Puritan guilt for having left Isaac alone for so long. It was fortunate he hadn't killed himself.

"I can still work in a dark room, with the spectra that are cast through the prism by the Sun. But the spectra of Venus are too faint."

"Of *Venus*?!"

"I have made observations concerning the nature of Light that contradict the theories of Descartes, Boyle, and Huygens," Isaac said. "I have divided the white light of the Sun into colors, and then recombined these rays to make white light again. I have done the experiment many times, changing the apparatus to rule out possible sources of error. But there is one I have yet to eliminate: the Sun is not a point source of light. Its face subtends a considerable arc in the heavens. Those who will seek to find fault with my work, and to attack me, will claim that this—the fact that the light entering my prism, from different parts of the Sun's disk, strikes it from slightly different angles—renders my conclusions suspect, and therefore worthless. In order to defeat these objections I must repeat the experiments using light, not from the Sun, but from Venus—an almost infinitely narrow point of light. But the light from Venus is so faint that my burned eyes cannot see it. I need you to make the observations with your good eyes, Daniel. We begin tonight. Perhaps you'd care to take a nap?"

The house was divided in half, north/south: the northern part, which had windows but no sunlight, was the domain of Newton's mother—a parlor on the ground floor and a bedchamber above it, both furnished in the few-but-enormous style then mandatory. The southern half—with just a few tiny apertures to admit the plentiful sunlight—was Isaac's: on the ground floor, a kitchen with a vast walk-in fireplace, suitable for alchemical work, and above it a bedchamber.

Isaac persuaded Daniel to lie down in, or at least *on,* his mother's bed for a bit of a nap—then made the mistake of mentioning that it was the same bed in which Isaac had been born, several weeks premature, twenty-four years earlier. So after half an hour of lying in that bed, as rigid as a tetanus victim, looking out between his feet at the first thing Isaac had ever laid eyes on (the window and the orchard), Daniel got up and went outside again. Isaac was still sitting on the bench with a book in his lap, but his gold spectacles were aimed at the horizon. "Defeated them soundly, I should say."

"I beg your pardon?"

"When it started it was close to shore—but it has steadily moved away."

"What on earth can you you talking about, Isaac?"

"The naval battle—we are fighting the Dutch in the Narrow Seas. Can you not hear the sound of the cannons?"

"I've been lying quietly in bed and heard nothing."

"Out here, it is very distinct." Isaac reached out and caught a fluttering petal. "The winds favor our Navy. The Dutch chose the wrong time to attack."

A fit of dizziness came over Daniel just then. Partly it was the thought that James, Duke of York, who a couple of weeks ago had been standing arm's length from Daniel discoursing of syphilis, at this moment stood on the deck of a flagship, firing on, and taking fire from, the Dutch fleet; and the booms rolled across the sea and were gathered in by the great auricle of the Wash, the Boston and the Lynn Deeps, the Long Sand and the Brancaster Roads perhaps serving as the greased convolutions of an ear, and propagated up the channel of the Welland, fanned out along its tributary rivers and rills into the swales and hills of Lincolnshire and into the ears of Isaac. It was partly that, and partly the vision that filled his eyes: thousands of white petals were coming off the apple trees and following the same diagonal path to the ground, their descent skewed by a breeze that was blowing out toward the sea.

"Do you remember when Cromwell died, and Satan's Wind came along to carry his soul to Hell?" Isaac asked.

"Yes. I was marching in his funeral procession, watching old Puritans getting blown flat."

"I was in the schoolyard. We happened to be having a broad-jumping competition. I won the prize, even though I was small and frail. In fact, perhaps I won *because* I was so—I knew that I should have to use my brains. I situated myself so that Satan's Wind was at my back, and then timed my leap so that I left the ground during an especially powerful gust. The wind carried my little body through space like one of these petals. For a moment I was gripped by an emotion—part thrill and part terror—as I imagined that the wind might carry me away—that my feet might never touch the earth again—that I would continue to skim along, just above the ground, until I had circumnavigated the globe. Of course I was just a boy. I didn't know that projectiles rise and fall in parabolic curves. Be those curves ever so flat, they always tend to earth again. But suppose a cannonball, or a boy caught up in a supernatural wind, flew so fast that the centrifugal force (as Huygens has named it) of his motion around the earth just counteracted his tendency to fall?"

"Er—depends on what you assume about the nature of falling," Daniel said. "Why do we fall? In what direction?"

"We fall towards the center of the earth. The same center on which the centrifugal force pivots—like a rock whirled on the end of a string."

"I suppose that if, somehow, you could get the forces to balance just so, you'd keep going round and round, and never fall or fly away. But it seems terrifically improbable—God would have to set it up just so—as He set the planets in their orbits."

"If you make certain assumptions about the force of gravity, and how the weight of an object diminishes as it gets farther away, it's not improbable at all," Isaac said. "It just *happens.* You would keep going round and round forever."

"In a circle?"

"An ellipse."

"An ellipse . . ." and here the bomb finally went off in his head, and Daniel had to sit down on the ground, the moisture of last year's fallen apples soaking through his breeches. "Like a planet."

"Just so—if only we could jump fast enough, or had a strong enough wind at our backs, we could *all* be planets."

It was so pure and obviously Right that it did not occur to Daniel to question Isaac about the details for several hours, as the Sun was going down, and they were preparing for Venus to wheel round into the southern sky. "I have developed a method of fluxions that renders it all perfectly obvious," Isaac said.

Daniel's first thought had been *I have to tell Wilkins* because Wilkins, who had written a novel in which men flew to the moon, would be delighted with Isaac's phrase: *We could all be planets.* But that put him in mind of Hooke, and the experiment at the deep well. Some premonition told him that he had best keep Newton and Hooke in separate cells for now.

Isaac's bedroom might have been designed specifically for doing prism experiments, because one wanted an opening just big enough to admit a ray of light in which to center the prism, but otherwise the room needed to be dark so that the spectrum could be clearly viewed where it struck the wall. The only drawback for Daniel was stumbling over debris. This was the room where Isaac had lived in the years before going to Cambridge. Daniel inferred that they had been lonely years. The floor was cluttered with stuff Isaac had made but been too busy to throw away, and the white plaster walls were covered with graffiti he had sketched with charcoal or scratched with nails: designs for windmills, depictions of birds, geometrickal proofs. Daniel shuffled through the darkness, never lifting a foot off the floor lest it come down on an old piece of doll-furniture or jagged remains of a lens-grinding experiment, the delicate works of a water-clock or the papery skull of a small animal, or a foamy crucible crowned with frozen drips of metal.

Isaac had worked out during which hours of the night Venus would be shining her perfectly unidirectional light on Woolsthorpe Manor's south wall, and he'd done it not only for tonight but for every night in the next several weeks. All of those hours were spoken for: he had planned out a whole program of experiments. It was clear to Daniel that Isaac had been arguing his case against a whole court full of imaginary Jesuits hurling Latin barbs at him from every quarter, objecting to his methods in ways that were often ridiculous—that Isaac fancied himself as a combination of Galileo and St. Anne, but that unlike Galileo he had no intention of knuckling under, and unlike St. Anne he would not end up riddled with his tormentors' arrows—he was getting ready to catch the arrows, and fling them back.

It was the sort of thing that Hooke never bothered with—because for Hooke being right was enough, and he didn't care what anyone else thought of him or his ideas.

When Isaac had got his prisms situated in the window and blown out the candle, Daniel was blind, and painfully embarrassed, for several minutes—he was anxious that, lacking Isaac's acute senses, he would not be able to see the spectrum cast against the wall by the light shining from Venus. "Have due patience," Isaac said with a tenderness Daniel hadn't heard from him in years. The thought stole upon Daniel, as he sat there in the dark with Isaac, that Isaac might have more than one reason for wearing those golden spectacles all the time. They shielded his burnt eyes from the light, yes. But as well, might they hide his burnt heart from the sight of Daniel?

Then Daniel noticed a multicolored blur on the wall—a sliver, red on one end and violet on the other. He said, "I have it."

He was startled by a heavy rustling directly above them, in the attic, a scrabbling of claws.

"What was that?"

"There is a tiny window up there—an invitation for owls to build nests in the attic," Isaac said. "So vermin don't eat the grain stored up there."

Daniel laughed at it. For a moment he and Isaac were boys up past bedtime playing with their toys, the complications of their past forgotten and the perils of the future unthought of.

A deep hooing noise, like the resonant tone of an organ pipe. Then the rustle of feathers as the bird squeezed through the opening, and the rhythm of powerful wings, like the beating of a heart, receding into the sky. The spectrum of Venus flashed off, then on, as the owl momentarily eclipsed the planet. When Daniel looked, he realized that he could now see not only the spectrum from Venus, but tiny, ghostly streaks of color all over the wall: the spectra cast by the stars that surrounded Venus in the southern sky. But spectra were *all* he could see. The earth spun and the ribbons of color migrated across the invisible wall, an inch a minute, pouring across the rough plaster like shining puddles of quicksilver driven before a steady wind, revealing, in gorgeous colors, tiny strips of the pictures that Isaac had drawn and scratched on those walls. Each of the little rainbows showed only a fragment of a picture, and each picture in turn was only part of Isaac's tapestry of sketchings and scratchings, but Daniel supposed that if he stood there through a sufficient number of long cold nights and concentrated very hard, he might be able to assemble, in his mind, a rough conception of the entire thing. Which was the way he had to address Isaac Newton in any case.

> But I did believe, and do still, that the end of our
> City will be with fire and brimstone from above, and
> therefore I have made mine escape.
> —JOHN BUNYAN, *The Pilgrim's Progress*

CAMBRIDGE TRIED TO RESUME that spring, but Daniel and Isaac had only just settled back into their chamber when someone died of the Plague and they had to move out again—Isaac back to Woolsthorpe, Daniel back to a wandering life. He spent some weeks with Isaac working on the colors experiment, others with Wilkins (now back in London, running regular meetings of the Royal Society again) working on the Universal Character manuscript, others with Drake or with his older half-siblings, who'd returned to London at Drake's command, to await the Apocalypse. The Year of the Beast, 1666, was halfway through, then two-thirds. Plague had gone away. War continued, and it was more than just an Anglo-Dutch war now, for the French had made a league with the Dutch against the English. But whatever plans the Duke of York had hatched with his Admirals on that chilly day at Epsom must not have been altogether worthless, because it was going well for them. Drake must be torn between patriotic ardor, and a feeling of disappointment that it showed no sign whatever of developing into an Armageddon sort of war. It was merely a string of naval engagements, and the gist of it was that the English fleet was driving the Dutch and French from the Channel. All in all, there was a failure of events to match up with the program laid out in the Books of Daniel and of Revelation, which forced Drake to re-read them almost every day, working out interpretations new and ever more strained. For Daniel's part, he sometimes went for days without thinking about the End of the World at all.

One evening early in September he was riding back toward London from the north. He'd been up in Woolsthorpe helping Isaac run the numbers on his planetary orbit theory, but with inconclusive results, because they did not know exactly how far from the center of the Earth they were when they stood on the ground and weighed things. He had stopped in at that plague-ridden town of Cambridge to fetch a new book that claimed to specify the crucial figure: how big around was the Earth? and now he was going down to visit his father, who'd sent him an alarming letter, claiming that he had just calculated a different crucial figure: the exact date (early in September, as it happened) that the world would end.

Daniel was still twenty miles outside of the city, riding along in the late afternoon, when a messenger came galloping up the road toward him and shouted, "London has been burning for a day and is burning still!" as he hurtled past.

Daniel knew this, in a way, but he had been denying it. The air had had a burnt smell about it all day long, and a haze of smoke had clung about the trees and the sheltered hollows in the fields. The sun had been a glaring patch that seemed to fill half the southern sky. Now, as the day went on and it sank toward the horizon, it turned orange and then red, and began to limn vast billows and towers of smoke—portents and omens that seemed incomparably vaster than the (still unknown) radius of the Earth. Daniel rode into the night, but not into darkness. A vault of orange light had been thrown about a mile high up into the sky above London. Thuds propagated through the earth—at first he supposed they must be the impacts of buildings falling down, but then they began coming in slow premeditated onslaughts and he reckoned that they must be blowing up whole buildings with powder-kegs, trying to gouge fire-breaks through the city.

At first he'd thought it was impossible for any fire to reach as far as Drake's house outside of town on Holborn, but the number of explosions, the diameter of the arch of light, told him nothing was safe. He was working upstream against a heavy traffic of soot-faced wretches now. It made for slow going, but there was nothing to do about it. The folds of his clothing, and even the porches of his ears, were collecting black grit, nodules and splinters and flakes of charcoal that rained down tickingly on everything.

"Cor, look, it's snowing!" exclaimed a boy with his face turned upwards to catch reflected light. Daniel—not wanting to see it, really—raised his eyes slowly, and found the sky filled with some kind of loose chaff, swirling in slow vortices here and there but heading generally downwards. He grabbed a piece of it from the air: it was page 798 of a Bible, all charred round the margins. He reached again and snared a hand-written leaf from a goldsmith's account-book, still glowing at one corner. Then a handbill—a libel attacking Free Coinage. A personal letter from one Lady to another. They accumulated on his shoulders like falling leaves and he stopped reading them after a while.

It took so long to get there that when he actually saw a house burning by the roadside, he was shocked. Solid beams of flame protruded from the windows, silhouetting people with leather buckets, jewels of water spinning off their rims. Refugees had flooded the fields along Gray's Inn Road and, tired of watching the fire, had begun throwing up shelters out of whatever stuff they could find.

Not far from Holborn, the road was nearly blocked by a rampart of shattered masonry that had spilled across it when buildings to either side had been blown up—even above the smell of burning London, Daniel could detect the brimstone-tang of the gunpowder. Then a building just to his right exploded—to Daniel, an instant's warning, a yellow flare in the corner of his eye, and then gravel embedded in one side of his face (but it felt like that side of his head had simply been sheared off) and deafness. His horse bolted and instantly broke a leg in the rubble-pile, then threw Daniel off—he came down hard on stones and splinters, and got up after lying there for he had no idea how long. There had been more explosions, coming faster now as the main front of the fire drew closer, its heat drawing curtains of steam and smoke out of walls, rooves, and the clothing on the living and dead persons in the street. Daniel took advantage of the fire's light to stumble over the rubble-wall and into a stretch of the road that was still clear, but doomed to burn.

Reaching Holborn, he turned his back to the fire and ran toward the sound of the explosions. Some part of his mind had been doing geometry through all of this, plotting the points of the explosions and extrapolating them, and he was more and more certain that the curve was destined to pass near Drake's house.

There was another rubble-heap on Holborn, so fresh that it was still sledding toward its angle of repose. Daniel charged up it, almost afraid to look down lest he should discover Drake's furniture beneath his feet. But from the top of the heap he obtained a perfect view of Drake's house, still standing, but standing alone now, in a sag-shouldered posture, as the houses to either side of it had been blown up. The walls had begun to smoke, and fire-brands were raining down around it like meteors, and Drake Waterhouse was up on the roof holding a Bible above his head with both hands. He was bellowing something that could not be heard, and did not need to be.

The street below was crowded with an uncommon number of Gentlemen, and better, brandishing swords—their gay courtiers' clothing burnt and blackened—and musketeers, too, looking somewhat unhappy to be standing in such a place with containers of gunpowder strapped to their midsections. Very wealthy and prominent men were looking up at Drake, shouting and pointing at the street, insisting he come down. But Drake had eyes only for the fire.

Daniel turned round to see what his father was seeing, and was nearly slapped to the ground by the heat and the spectacle of it—the Fire. Everything between East and South was flame, and everything below the stars. It fountained and throbbed, jetted and pulsed, and buildings went down beneath it as blades of grass beneath John Wilkins's giant Wheel.

And it was approaching, so fast that it overtook some persons who were trying to run away from it—they were blurring into ghosts of smoke and bursting into flames, their sprinting forms dissolving into light: the Rapture. This had not escaped Drake's notice—he was pointing at it—but the crowd of Court fops below were not interested. To Drake, these particular men had been demons from Hell even *before* London had caught fire, because they were the personal bootlicks of King Charles II, an arch-daemon of King Louis XIV himself. Now, here they were, perversely convened in front of his house.

Daniel had been waving his arms over his head trying to get Drake's attention, but he understood now that he must be an indistinct black shape against a vast glare, the least interesting thing in Drake's panorama.

All of the courtiers had turned inward, attent on the same man—even Drake was looking at him. Daniel caught sight of the Lord Mayor, and thought perhaps *he* was the center of attention—but the Lord Mayor had eyes only to look at another. Sidestepping to a new position on the heap, Daniel finally saw a tall dark man in impossibly glorious clothing and a vast wig, which was shaking from side to side in exasperation. This man suddenly moved forward, seized a torch from a toady, looked up one last time at Drake, then bent down and touched the fire to the street. A bright smoking star rolled across the pavement toward Drake's front door, which had been smashed open.

The man with the torch turned around, and Daniel recognized him as England.

There was a kind of preliminary explosion of humanity away from the house. Courtiers and musketeers formed a crowd behind the King to shield his back from flying harpsichords. Up on the roof, Drake aimed a finger at His Majesty and raised his Bible on high to call down some fresh damnation. From the burning timbers that were now coming down from Heaven like flaming spears hurled by avenging angels, he might have thought, in these moments, that he'd played an important part in Judgment Day. But nothing hit the King.

The spark was climbing the front steps. Daniel plunged forward down the piled house-guts, because he was fairly certain that he could outrun the spark, reach the fuse, and jerk it loose before it touched whatever powder-kegs had been rolled into Drake's parlor. His path was blocked by members of the King's personal bodyguard who were running the other way. They looked at Daniel curiously while Daniel changed course to swing round them. In the corner of his eye he saw one of them understand what Daniel was doing—that slackening of the face, the opening of the features, that came over the faces of students when, suddenly, they knew. This man stepped clear from the group and raised a yawning tube to his shoulder. Daniel looked at his father's house and saw the star snaking down the dark hallway. He was tense for the explosion, but it came from behind him—at the same moment he was bitten in a hundred places and slammed face-down into the street.

He rolled over on his back, trying to snuff the fires of pain burning all over him, and saw his father ascending into heaven, his black clothes changing into a robe of fire. His table, books, and grandfather clock were not far behind.

"Father?" he said.

Which was senseless, if the only kind of sense you heeded was that of Natural Philosophy. Even supposing Drake was alive at the moment Daniel spoke to him—a daring supposition indeed, and not the sort of thing that contributed to a young man's reputation in the Royal Society—he was far away, and getting farther, washed in apocalyptic roar and tumult, beset by many distractions, and probably deaf from the blast. But Daniel had just seen his house exploded and been shot with a blunderbuss in the same instant, and all sense of the Natural-Philosophic kind had fled from him. All that remained to shape his actions was the sentimental logic of a five-year-old bewildered that his father seemed to be leaving him: which was hardly the natural and correct order of things. Moreover, Daniel had another twenty years' important things to say to his father. He had sinned against Drake and would make confession and be absolved, and Drake had sinned against him and must needs be brought to account. Determined to put a stop to this heinous, unnatural leaving, he used the only means of self-preservation that God had granted to five-year-olds: the voice. Which by itself did naught but wiggle air. In a loving home, that could raise alarms and summon help. "Father?" he tried again. But his home was a storm of bricks and a spray of timbers, each tracing its own arc to the smoking and steaming earth, and his father was a glowing cloud. Like a theophany of the Old Testament. But whereas fiery clouds were for YHWH a manifestation, a means of revealing Himself to His children below, this one swallowed Drake up and did not spit him out but made him one with the *Mysterium Tremendum*. He was hidden from Daniel now forever.

cȝ⅄

Aboard Minerva, *Plymouth Bay, Massachusetts*
NOVEMBER 1713

HIS MIND HAS QUITE RUN ahead of his quill; his pen has gone dry, but his face is damp. Alone in his cabin, Daniel indulges himself for a minute in another favorite pastime of five-year-olds. Some say that crying is childish. Daniel—who since the birth of Godfrey has had more opportunities than he should have liked to observe crying—takes a contrary view. Crying *loudly* is childish, in that it reflects a belief, on the cryer's part, that someone is around to hear the noise, and come a-running to make it all better. Crying in absolute silence, as Daniel does this morning, is the mark of the mature sufferer who no longer nurses, nor is nursed by, any such comfortable delusions.

There's a rhythmical chant down on the gundeck that slowly builds and then explodes into a drumming of many feet on mahogany stair-steps, and suddenly *Minerva*'s deck is crowded with sailors, running about and colliding with each other, like a living demonstration of Hooke's ideas about heat. Daniel wonders if

162

perhaps a fire has been noticed down in the powder-magazine, and the sailors have all come up to abandon ship. But this is a highly organized sort of panic.

Daniel pats his face dry, stoppers his ink-well, and goes out onto the quarter-deck, chucking his ink-caked quill overboard. Most of the sailors have already ascended into the rigging, and begun to drop vast white curtains as if to shield landlubber Daniel's eyes from the fleet of sloops and whaleboats that seems now to be converging on them from every cove and inlet on Plymouth Bay. Rocks and trees ashore are moving, with respect to fixed objects on *Minerva*, in a way that they shouldn't. "We're moving—we are adrift!" he protests. Weighing anchor on a ship of *Minerva*'s bulk is a ludicrously complicated and lengthy procedure—a small army of chanting sailors pursuing one another round the giant capstan on the upperdeck, boys scrubbing slime off, and sprinkling sand onto, the wet anchor cable to afford a better purchase for the messenger cable—an infinite loop, passed three times round the capstan, that nimble-fingered riggers are continually lashing alongside the anchor cable in one place and unlashing in another. None of this has even begun to happen in the hour since the sun rose.

"We are adrift!" Daniel insists to Dappa, who's just vaulted smartly off the edge of the poop deck and nearly landed on Daniel's shoulders.

"But naturally, Cap'n—we're all in a panic, don't you see?"

"You are being unduly harsh on yourself and your crew, Dappa—and why are you addressing me as Captain? And how can we be adrift, when we haven't weighed anchor?"

"You're wanted on the poop deck, Cap'n—that's right, just step forward—"

"Let me fetch my hat."

"None of it, Cap'n, we want every pirate in New England—for they're *all* out there, at the moment—to see your white hair shining in the sun, your bald pate, pale and pink, like that of a Cap'n who ain't been abovedecks in years—this way, mind the wheel, sir—that's right—could you dodder just a bit more? Squint into the unaccustomed sunlight—well played, Cap'n!"

"May the Good Lord save us, Mr. Dappa, we've lost our anchors! Some madman has cut the anchor cables!"

"I told you we were in a panic—steady up the stairs, there, Cap'n!"

"Let go my arm! I'm perfectly capable of—"

"Happy to be of service, Cap'n—as is that lopsided Dutchman at the top o' the stairs—"

"Captain van Hoek! Why are you dressed as an ordinary sea-man!? And what has become of our anchors!?"

"Dead weight," van Hoek says, and then goes on to mutter something in Dutch.

"He said, you are showing just the sort of impotent choler that we need. Here, take a spyglass! I've an idea—why don't you peer into the wrong end of it first—then look befuddled, and angry, as if some subordinate had stupidly reversed the lenses."

"I'll have you know, Mr. Dappa, that at one time I knew as much of opticks as any man alive, save one—possibly two, if you count Spinoza—but he was only a *practical* lens-grinder, and generally more concerned with *atheistical* ruminations—"

"Do it!" grunts the one-armed Dutchman. He is still the captain, so Daniel steps to the railing of the poop deck, raises the spyglass, and peers through the objective lens. He can actually *hear* pirates on distant whaleboats laughing at him. Van Hoek plucks the glass from Daniel, spins it around on the knuckles of his only hand, and thrusts it at him. Daniel accepts it and tries to hold it steady on an approaching whaler. But the forward end of that boat is fogged in a bank of smoke, rapidly dispersing in the freshening breeze. For the last few minutes, *Minerva*'s sails have been inflating, frequently with brisk snapping noises, almost like gunshots—but—

"Damn me," he says, "they *fired* on us!" He can see, now, the swivel-gun mounted in the whaleboat's prow, an unsavory-looking fellow feeding a neatly bound cluster of lead balls into its small muzzle.

"Just a shot across the bow," Dappa says. "That panicky look on your face—the gesticulating—perfect!"

"The number of boats is *incredible*—are these all pirating *together*?"

"Plenty of time for explanations later—now's the moment to look stricken—perhaps get wobbly in the knees and clutch your chest like an apoplectic—we'll assist you to your cabin on the upperdeck."

"But my cabin, as you know, is on the quarter-deck . . ."

"Today only, you're being given a complimentary upgrade—Cap'n. Come on, you've been in the sun too long—best retire and break open a bottle of rum."

"DON'T BE MISLED BY THESE exchanges of cannon-fire," Dappa reassures him, thrusting his woolly and somewhat grizzled head into the Captain's cabin. "If this were a true fight, sloops and whaleboats'd be simply exploding all round us."

"Well, if it's *not* a fight, what would you call it when men on ships shoot balls of lead at each other?"

"A game—a dance. A theatrickal performance. Speaking of which—have you practiced your role recently?"

"Didn't seem safe, when grapeshot was flying—but—as it's only an *entertainment*—well . . ." Daniel gets up from his squatting position underneath the Captain's chart-table and sidles over toward the windows, moving in a sort of Zeno's Paradox mode—each step only half as long as the previous. Van Hoek's cabin is as broad as the entire stern of the ship—two men could play at shuttlecocks in here. The entire aft bulkhead is one gently curved window commanding (now that Daniel's in position to see through it) a view of Plymouth Bay: wee cabins and wigwams on the hills, and, on the waves, numerous scuttling boats all flocked with gunpowder-smoke, occasionally thrusting truncated bolts of yellow fire in their general direction. "The critical reaction seems hostile," Daniel observes. Off to his left, a small pane gets smashed out of its frame by what he takes to have been a musket-ball.

"Excellent cringing! The way you raise your hands as if to clap them over your ears, then arrest them in midair, as if already seized in *rigor mortis*—thank God you were delivered into our hands."

"I am meant to believe that all of these goings-on are nothing more than an elaborate manipulation of the pirates' mental state?"

"No need to be haughty—*they* do it to *us*, too. Half of the cannon on those boats are carved out of logs, painted to look real."

A large meteor-like something blows the head door off its hinges and buries itself in an oaken knee-brace, knocking it askew and bending the entire cabin slightly out of shape—wreaking some sort of parallelogram effect on Daniel's Frame o' Reference, so it appears that Dappa's now standing up at an angle—or perhaps the ship's beginning to heel over. "Some of the cannon are, of course, real," Dappa admits before Daniel can score any points there.

"If we are playing with the pirates' minds, what is the advantage in making the ship's captain out as a senile poltroon—which, if I may read 'tween the lines, would appear to be *my* role? Why not fling open every gunport, run out every cannon, make the hills ring with broadsides, set van Hoek up on the poop waving his hook in the air?"

"We'll get round to all that later, in all likelihood. For now we must pursue a multilayered bluffing strategy."

"*Why?*"

"Because we have more than one group of pirates to contend with."

"*What!?*"

"This is why we captured and questioned—"

"*Some* would say tortured—"

"—several pirates before dawn. There are simply too many pirates in this Bay to make sense. Some of them would appear to be mutually hostile. Indeed, we've learned that the traditional, honest, hardworking Plymouth Bay pirates—the ones in the small boats—get over, Cap'n, I say! Two paces over to larboard, if you please!"

Dappa's adverting on something outside the window. Daniel turns round to see a taut manila line dangling vertically just outside—not an unusual sight in and of itself, but it wasn't there a few seconds ago. The stretched line shudders, tattooing a beat on the window-pane. A pair of blistered hands appears, then a broad-brimmed hat, then a head with a dagger clenched in its teeth. Then behind Daniel a tremendous *FOOM* while something unsightly happens to the climber's face—clearly visible through a suddenly absent pane. A gout of smoke roils and rebounds against the panes that are still there, and by the time it's cleared away the pirate is gone. Dappa's in the middle of the cabin holding a hot smoky shooting-iron.

He rummages in van Hoek's chest and pulls out a hook with various straps and stump-cups all a-dangle. "That was one of the sort I was speaking of. Never would've tried anything so foolhardy if the newer breed hadn't brought such hard times down on 'em."

"What newer breed?"

Dappa, wearing a fastidious and disgusted look, threads the hook out through the missing window-pane and catches the dangling pirate-rope, then draws it inside the cabin and severs it with a smart swing of his cutlass. "Lift your head toward the horizon, Cap'n, and behold the flotilla of coasting craft—sloops and topsail schooners, and a ketch—that is forming up there in Plymouth Bay. Half a dozen or more vessels. Strange information glancing from one to the next embodied in pennants, guns, and flashes of sunlight."

"It is because of *them* that the riffraff in the small craft cannot make a living?"

"Just so, Cap'n. Now, if we'd put up a brave front, as you suggested, they'd've known their cause was hopeless, and might've been tempted to make common cause with Teach."

"Teach?"

"Cap'n Edward Teach, the Admiral of yonder pirate-fleet. But as it is, these small-timers have spent themselves in a futile try at seizing *Minerva* before Teach could make sail and form up. Now we can address the Teach matter separately."

"There was a Teach in the Royal Navy—"

"He is the same fellow. He and his men fought on the Queen's side in the War, helping themselves to Spanish shipping. Now that the treaty is signed and we are friendly with Spain, these fellows are at loose ends, and have crossed the Atlantic to seek a home port for American piracy."

"So I ween it's not our cargo that Teach wants, so much as—"

"If we threw every last bale overboard, still he would come after us. He wants *Minerva* for his flagship. And a mighty raider she would be."

There's been no gunfire recently, so Daniel crosses over to the window and watches sail after sail unfurling, Teach's fleet developing into a steady cloud on the bay. "They look like fast ships," he says. "We'll be seeing Teach soon."

"He's easily recognized—according to them we questioned, he's a master of piratical performances. Wears smoking punks twined about his head, like burning dreadlocks, and, at night, burning tapers in his thick black beard. He's got half the people in Plymouth convinced he's the Devil incarnate."

"What think you, Dappa?"

"I think there never was a Devil so fierce as Cap'n van Hoek, when pirates are after his Lady."

Charing Cross
1670

Sir ROBERT MORAY produced a discourse concerning coffee, written by Dr. GODDARD at the King's command; which was read, and the author desired to leave a copy of it with the society.

Mr. BOYLE mentioned, that he had been informed, that the much drinking of coffee produced the palsy.

The bishop of Exeter seconded him, and said, that himself had found it dispose to paralytical effects; which however he thought were caused only in hot constitutions, by binding.

Mr. GRAUNT affirmed, that he knew two gentlemen, great drinkers of coffee, very paralytical.

Dr. WHISTLER suggested, that it might be inquired, whether the same persons took much tobacco.

—THE HISTORY OF THE ROYAL SOCIETY OF LONDON
FOR IMPROVING OF NATURAL KNOWLEDGE,
JAN. 18, 1664/5*

HAVING NO DESIRE to be either palsied, *or* paralytical, Daniel avoided the stuff until 1670, when he got his first taste of it at Mrs. Green's Coffee-House, cunningly sited in the place where the western end of the Strand yawned into Charing Cross. The Church of St. Martin-in-the-Fields lay to the west.† To the east was the New Exchange—this was the nucleus of a whole block of shops. North was Covent Garden, and South, according to rumor and tradition, was the River Thames, a few hundred yards distant—but you couldn't see it because noble Houses and Palaces formed a solid levee running from the King's residence (Whitehall Palace) all the way round the river-bend to Fleet Ditch, where the wharves began.

Daniel Waterhouse walked past Mrs. Green's one summer morning in 1670, a minute after Isaac Newton had done so. It had a little garden in the front, with several tables. Daniel went into it and stood for a moment, checking out his lines of sight. Isaac had risen early, sneaked out of his bedchamber, and taken to the streets without eating any breakfast—not unusual for Isaac. Daniel had followed him out the front door of the (rebuilt, and dramatically enlarged) Waterhouse residence; across Lincoln's Inn Fields, where a few fashionable early risers were walking dogs, or huddling in mysterious conferences; and (coincidentally) right past the very place at Drury Lane and Long Acre where those two Frenchmen had died of the Black Death six years earlier, inaugurating the

---

*I.e., it was already 1665 everywhere except England, where the new year was held to begin on March 25th.
†Though the fields were becoming city streets, so at this point it was more like St. Martin-at-the-edge-of-*a*-field, and soon to be St. Martin-within-visual-range-of-a-very-expensive-field-or-two.

memorable Plague Years. Thence into the dangerous chasm of flying earth and loose paving-stones that was St. Martin's Lane—for
John Comstock, Earl of Epsom, acting in his capacity as Commis-
sioner of Sewers, had decreed that this meandering country cowpath must be paved, and made over into a city street—the axis of a
whole new London.

Daniel had been keeping his distance so that Isaac wouldn't
notice him if he turned around—though you never knew with
Isaac, who had better senses than most wild animals. St. Martin's
Lane was crowded with heavy stone-carts drawn by teams of mighty
horses, just barely under the control of their teamsters, and Daniel
was forced to dodge wagons, and to scurry around and over piles
of dirt and cobbles, in order to keep sight of Isaac.

Once they had reached the open spaces of Charing Cross, and
the adjoining Yard where Kings of Scotland had once come to
humble themselves before their liege-lord in Whitehall, Daniel
could afford to maintain more distance—Isaac's silver hair was easy
to pick out in a crowd. And if Isaac's destination was one of the
shops, coffee-houses, livery stables, gardens, markets, or noblemen's houses lining the great Intersection, why, Daniel could sit
down right about here and spy on him at leisure.

Why he was doing so, Daniel had no idea. It was just that by getting up and leaving so mysteriously, Isaac begged to be followed.
Not that he was doing a good job of being sneaky. Isaac was accustomed to being so much brighter than everyone else that he really
had no idea of what others were or weren't capable of. So when he
got it into his head to be tricky, he came up with tricks that would
not deceive a dog. It was hard not to be insulted—but being
around Isaac was never for the thin-skinned.

They continued to live together at Trinity, though now they
shared a cottage without the Great Gate. They performed experiments with lenses and prisms, and Isaac went to a hall twice a week
and lectured to an empty room on mathematical topics so advanced
that no one else could understand them. So in *that* sense nothing
was different. But lately Isaac had obviously lost interest in optics
(probably because he knew everything about the subject now) and
become mysterious. Then three days ago he had announced, with
studied nonchalance, that he was going to nip down to London for a
few days. When Daniel had announced that he was planning to do
the same—to pay a visit to poor Oldenburg, and attend a Royal Society meeting—Isaac had done a poor job of hiding his annoyance.
But he had at least *tried* to hide it, which was touching.

Then, halfway to London, Daniel (as a sort of experiment) had professed to be shocked that Isaac intended to lodge in an inn. Daniel would not hear of it—not when Raleigh had put so many Waterhouse assets into constructing a large new house on Holborn. At this point Isaac's eyes had bulged even more than usual and he had adopted his suffering-martyr look, and relented only when Daniel mentioned that Raleigh's house was so large, and had so many empty rooms, that Daniel wasn't sure if they would ever *see* each other.

Daniel's hypothesis, based on these observations, was that Isaac was committing Sins Against Nature with someone, but then certain clues (such as that Isaac *never* received any mail) argued against this.

As he stood there in front of the coffee-house, a gentleman* rode out of St. Martin's Lane, reined in his horse, stood up in the stirrups, and surveyed the ongoing low-intensity riot that was Charing Cross, looking anxious until he caught sight of whatever he was looking for. Then he relaxed, sat down, and rode slowly in the general direction of—Isaac Newton. Daniel sat down in that wee garden in front of Mrs. Green's, and ordered coffee and a newspaper.

King Carlos II of Spain was *both* feeble *and* sick, and not expected to live out the year. Comenius was dying, too. Anne Hyde, the Duke of York's wife, was very ill with what everyone assumed to be syphilis. John Locke was writing a constitution for Carolina, Stenka Razin's Cossack rebellion was being crushed in the Ukraine, the Grand Turk was taking Crete away from Venice with his left hand and declaring war on Poland with his right. In London, the fall of pepper prices was sending many City merchants into bankruptcy—while a short distance across the Narrow Seas, the V.O.C.—the Dutch East India Company—was paying out a dividend of 40 percent.

But the *news* was of the doings of the CABAL† and the *courtiers*. John Churchill was one of the few courtiers who actually did things like go to Barbary and go *mano a mano* with heathen corsairs, and so there was plenty concerning him. He and most of the rest of the English Navy were blockading Algiers, trying to do something, at long last, about the Barbary Pirates.

---

*I.e., he had a sword.
†The five men King Charles II had chosen to run England: John Comstock, the Earl of Epsom, Lord Chancellor; Thomas More Anglesey, Duke of Gunfleet, Chancellor of the Exchequer; Knott Bolstrood, who'd been coaxed back from Dutch self-exile to serve as His Majesty's Secretary of State; Sir Richard Apthorp, a banker, and a founder of the East India Company; and General Hugh Lewis, the Duke of Tweed.

The gentleman on horseback had a courtier look about him, though unfashionably battered and frayed. He had nearly ridden Daniel down a few minutes previously when Daniel had emerged from Raleigh's house and foolishly planted himself in the middle of the road trying to catch sight of Isaac. He had the general look of a poor baron from some slaty place in the high latitudes who wanted to make a name for himself in London but lacked the means. He was dressed practically enough in actual boots, rather than the witty allusions to boots worn by young men about town. He wore a dark cassock—a riding garment loosely modeled after a priest's tent-like garment—with numerous silver buttons. He had an expensive saddle on a mediocre horse. The horse thus looked something like a fishwife dressed up in a colonel's uniform. If Isaac was looking for a mistress (or a master or whatever the sodomitical equivalent of a mistress was), he could've done worse and he could've done better.

Daniel had brought a Valuable Object with him—not because he'd expected to use it, but out of fear that one of Raleigh's servants would wreck or steal it. It was in a wooden case buckled shut, which he had set on the table. He undid the buckles, raised the lid, and peeled back red velvet to divulge a tubular device about a foot long, fat enough that you could insert a fist, closed at one end. It was mounted on a wooden sphere the size of a large apple, and the sphere was held in a sort of clamp that gave it freedom to rotate around all axes—i.e., you could set it down on a tabletop and then point the open end of the tube in any direction, which was how Daniel used it. Bored through the tube's wall near the open end was a finger-sized hole, and mounted below this, in the center of the tube, was a small mirror, angled backwards at a concave dish of silvered glass that sealed the butt of the tube. The design was Isaac's, certain refinements and much of the construction were Daniel's. Putting an eye to the little hole, he saw a colored blur. Adjusting a thumbscrew at the mirror end, and thereby collapsing the tube together a bit, he resolved the blur into a chunk of ornamented window-frame with a lace curtain being sucked out of it, down at the other end of Charing Cross. Daniel was startled to realize that he was looking all the way across the Great Court that lay before Whitehall Palace, and peering in through someone's windows—unless he was mistaken, these were the apartments of Lady Castlemaine, the King of England's favorite mistress.

Nudging it round to a slightly different bearing, he saw the end of the Banqueting House, where King Charles I had been beheaded, back when Daniel had been small—Divine Right of Kings

demolished, the Commonwealth founded, Free Enterprise introduced, Drake happy for once, and Daniel sitting on his shoulders,
watching the King's head rock. In those days, all of Whitehall's windows that faced the outside had been bricked up to keep musket-
balls out, and many superstitious fopperies, e.g., paintings and
sculptures, had been crated up and sold to Dutchmen. But now the
windows were windows again, and the artworks had been bought
back, and there wasn't a decapitated King in sight.

So it was not a good time to reminisce about Drake. Daniel
swiveled the Reflecting Telescope around until the ragged plume
in the horseman's hat showed up as a bobbing white blur, like the
tail of a hustling rabbit. Once he'd focused on that, a couple of tiny
adjustments brought Isaac's waterfall of argent hair into view—just
in time, for he was ascending a few steps into a building across
from the Haymarket, along the convergence of traffic that eventually became Pall Mall. Daniel played the telescope around the front
of the building, expecting it to be a coffee-house or pub or inn
where Isaac would await his gentleman friend. But he was completely wrong. To begin with, this place was apparently nothing
more than a town-house. And yet well-dressed men came and went
occasionally, and when they emerged, they (or their servants) were
carrying packages. Daniel reckoned it must be some sort of shop
too discreet to announce itself—hardly unusual in this part of London, but not Isaac's sort of place.

The horseman did not go inside. He rode past the shop once,
twice, thrice, looking at it sidelong—just as baffled as Daniel was.
Then he seemed to be talking to a pedestrian. Daniel recalled,
now, that this rider had been pursued by a couple of servants on
foot. One of these pages, or whatever they were, now took off at a
run, and weaved between hawkers and hay-wains all the way across
Charing Cross and finally vanished into the Strand.

The horseman dismounted, handed the reins to another page,
and made a vast ceremony of unbuttoning his sleeves so that the
cassock devolved into a cloak. He peeled off spatterdashes to reveal
breeches and stockings that were only out-moded by six months to
a year, and then found a coffee-house of his own, just across Pall
Mall from the mysterious shop, along (therefore) the southern
limit of St. James's Fields—one of those Fields that the Church of
St. Martin had formerly been in the middle of. But now houses
were being built all around it, enclosing a little rectangle of farm-
land rapidly being gardenized.

Daniel could do nothing but sit. As a way of paying rent on this
chair, he kept having more coffee brought out. The first sip had

been tooth-looseningly unpleasant, like one of those exotic poisons that certain Royal Society members liked to brew. But he was startled to notice after a while that the cup was empty.

This whole exercise had begun rather early in the day when no one of quality was awake, and when it was too cold and dewy to sit at the outdoor tables anyway. But as Daniel sat and pretended to read his newspaper, the sun swung up over York House and then Scotland Yard, the place became comfortable, and Personages began to occupy seats nearby, and to pretend to read *their* newspapers. He even sensed that in this very coffee-house were some members of the cast of characters he had heard about while listening to his siblings talk over the dinner table. Actually being here and mingling with them made him feel like a theatregoer relaxing after a performance with the actors—and in these racy times, actresses.

Daniel spent a while trying to spy into the upper windows of the mystery-shop with his telescope, because he thought he'd glimpsed silver hair in one of them, and so for a while he was only aware of other customers' comings and goings by their bow-waves of perfume, the rustling of ladies' crinolines, the ominous creaking of their whalebone corset-stays, the whacking of gentlemen's swords against table-legs as they misjudged distances between furniture, the clacking of their slap-soled booties.

The perfumes smelled familiar, and he had heard all of the jokes before, while dining at Raleigh's house. Raleigh, who at this point was fifty-two years old, knew a startling number of dull persons who evidently had nothing else to do but roam around to one another's houses, like mobs of Vagabonds poaching on country estates, and share their dullness with each other. Daniel was always startled when he learned that these people were Knights or Barons or merchant-princes.

"Why, if it isn't Daniel Waterhouse! God save the King!"

"God save the King!" Daniel murmured reflexively, looking up into a vast bursting confusion of clothing and bought hair, within which, after a brief search, he was able to identify the face of Sir Winston Churchill—Fellow of the Royal Society, and father of that John Churchill who was making such a name for himself in the fighting before Algiers.

There was a moment of exquisite discomfort. Churchill had remembered, a heartbeat too late, that the aforementioned King had personally blown up Daniel's father. Churchill himself had many anti-Royalists in his family, and so he prided himself on being a little defter than *that*.

Now Drake's pieces had never been found. Daniel's vague

recollection (vague because he'd just been shot with a blunder-buss, at the time) was that the explosion had flung him in the general direction of the Great Fire of London, so it was unlikely that anything was left of him except for a stubborn film of greasy ash deposited on the linens and windowsills of downwind neighbors. Discovery of shattered YOU AND I ARE BUT EARTH crockery in remains of burnt houses confirmed it. John Wilkins (still distraught over the burning of his Universal Character books in the Fire) had been good enough to preside over the funeral, and only a bridge-builder of his charm and ingenuity could have prevented it from becoming a brawl complete with phalanxes of enraged Phanatiques marching on Whitehall Palace to commit regicide.

Since then—and since most of Drake's fortune had passed to Raleigh—Daniel hadn't seen very much of the family. He'd been working on optics with Newton and was always startled, somehow, to find that the other Waterhouses were doing things when he wasn't watching. Praise-God, Raleigh's eldest son, who had gone to Boston before the Plague, had finally gotten his Harvard degree and married someone, and so everyone (Waterhouses and their visitors alike) had been talking about him—but they always did so mischievously, like naughty children getting away with something, and with occasional furtive glances at Daniel. He had to conclude that he and Praise-God were now the last vestiges of Puritanism in the family and that Raleigh was discreetly admired, among the coffee-house set, for having stashed one of them away at Cambridge and the other at Harvard where they could not interfere in whatever it was that the other Waterhouses were up to.

In this vein: he had gotten the impression, from various tremendously significant looks exchanged across tables at odd times by his half-siblings, their extended families, and their overdressed visitors, that the Waterhouses and the Hams and perhaps a few others had joined together in some kind of vast conspiracy the exact nature of which wasn't clear—but to them it was as huge and complicated as, say, toppling the Holy Roman Empire.

Thomas Ham was now called Viscount Walbrook. All of his gold had melted in the Fire, but none had leaked out of his newly refurbished cellar—when they came back days later they found a slab of congealed gold weighing tons, the World's Largest Gold Bar. None of his depositors lost a penny. Others hastened to deposit their gold with the incredibly reliable Mr. Ham. He began lending it to the King to finance the rebuilding of London. Partly in recognition of that, and partly to apologize for having blown up his father-in-law, the King had bestowed an Earldom on him.

All of which was Context for Daniel as he sat there gazing upon the embarrassed face of Sir Winston Churchill. Now if Churchill had only *asked*, Daniel might have told him that blowing up Drake was probably the correct action for the King to have taken under the circumstances. But Churchill didn't ask, he *assumed*. Which was why he'd never make a real Natural Philosopher. Though the Royal Society would tolerate him as long as he continued paying his dues.

Daniel for his part was aware, now, that he was surrounded by the Quality, and that they were all peering at him. He had gotten himself into a Complicated Situation, and he did not like those. The Reflecting Telescope was resting on the table right in front of him, as obvious as a severed head. Sir Winston was too embarrassed to've noticed it yet, but he *would*, and given that he'd been a member of the Royal Society since before the Plague, he would probably be able to guess what it was—and even if Daniel lied to him about it, the lie would be discovered this very evening when Daniel presented it, on Isaac's behalf, to the Royal Society. He felt an urge to snatch it away and hide it, but this would only make it more conspicuous.

And Sir Winston was only *one* of the people Daniel recognized here. Daniel seemed to have inadvertently sat down along a major game trail: persons coming up from Whitehall Palace and Westminster to buy their stockings, gloves, hats, syphilis-cures, *et cetera* at the New Exchange, just a stone's throw up the Strand, all passed by this coffee-house to get a last fix on what was or wasn't in fashion.

Daniel hadn't moved or spoken in what seemed like ten minutes . . . he was (glancing at the telltale coffee cup here) paralyzed, in fact! Then he solved Sir Winston's etiquette jam by blurting something like "I *say*!" and attempting to stand up, which came out as a palsied spasm of the entire body—he got into a shin-kicking match with his own table and produced a disturbance that sheared cups off their saucers. Everyone looked.

"Ever the diligent Natural Philosopher, Mr. Waterhouse pursues an experiment in Intoxication by Coffee!" Sir Winston announced roundly. Simply *tremendous* laughter and light applause.

Sir Winston was of Raleigh's generation and had fought in the Civil War as a Cavalier—he was a serious man and so was dressed in a way that passed for dignified and understated here, in a black velvet coat, flaring out to just above the knee, with lace handkerchiefs trailing from various openings like wisps of steam, and a yellow waistcoat under that, and God only knew what else beneath the waistcoat—the sleeves of all these garments terminated near the elbows in huge wreaths of lace, ruffles, *et cetera,* and that was to show off his tan kid gloves. He had a broad-brimmed Cavalier-hat fringed with fluffy white stuff probably harvested from the buttocks of some bird that spent a lot of time sitting on ice floes, and a very thin mustache, and a wig of yellow hair, expensively disheveled and formed into bobbling ringlets. He had black stockings fashionably wrinkled up his calves, and high-heeled shoes with bows of a wingspan of eight inches. The stocking/breech interface was presumably somewhere around his knees and was some sort of fantastically complex spraying phenomenon of ribbons and gathers and skirtlets designed to peek out under the hems of his coat, waistcoat, and allied garments.

Mrs. Churchill, for her part, was up to something mordant involving a Hat. It had the general outlines of a Puritan-hat, a Pilgrimish number consisting of a truncated cone mounted on a broad flat brim, but enlivened with colorful bands, trailing ribbons, jeweled badges, curious feathers, and other merchandise—a parody, then, a tart assertion of non-pilgrimhood. Everything from the brim of this hat to the hem of her dress was too complex for Daniel's eye to comprehend—he was like an illiterate savage staring at the first page of an illuminated Bible—but he did notice that the little boy carrying her train was dressed as a Leprechaun (Sir Winston did a lot of business for the King in Ireland).

It was a lot to put on, just to nip out for a cup of coffee, but the Churchills must have known that everyone was going to be fawning over them today because of their gallant son, and decided they ought to dress for it.

Mrs. Churchill was looking over Daniel's shoulder, toward the street. This left Daniel free to stare at her face, to which she had glued several spots of black velvet—which, since the underlying skin had been whitened with some kind of powerful cosmetic, gave her a sort of Dalmatian appearance. "He's here," she said to whomever she was looking at. Then, confused: "Were you expecting your half-brother?"

Daniel turned around and recognized Sterling Waterhouse, now about forty, and his wife of three years, Beatrice, and a whole crowd of persons who'd apparently just staged some type of pillaging-raid on the New Exchange. Sterling and Beatrice were shocked to see him. But they had no choice but to come over, now that Mrs. Churchill had done what she'd done. So they did, cheerfully enough, and then there was a series of greetings and introductions and other formalities (including that all parties congratulated the Churchills on the dazzling qualities of their son John, and promised to say prayers for his safe return from the shores of Tripoli) extending to something like half an hour. Daniel wanted to slash his own throat. These people were doing what they did for a *living*. Daniel *wasn't*.

But he did achieve one insight that would prove useful in later dealings with his own family. Because Raleigh was involved in the mysterious Conspiracy of which Daniel had, lately, become vaguely aware, it probably had something to do with land. Because Uncle Thomas ("Viscount Walbrook") Ham was mixed up in it, it must have something to do with putting rich people's money to clever uses. And because Sterling was involved, it probably had something to do with shops, because ever since Drake had ascended into the flames over London, Sterling had been moving away from Drake's style of business (smuggling, and traveling around cutting private deals away from markets) and towards the newfangled procedure of putting all the merchandise in a fixed building and waiting for customers to transport themselves to it. The whole thing came together complete in Daniel's head when he sat in that coffee-house in Charing Cross and looked at the courtiers, macaronis, swells, and fops streaming in from the new town-houses going up on land that had been incinerated, or that had been open pastures, four years earlier. They were planning some sort of real estate development on the edge of the city—probably on that few acres of pasture out back of the Waterhouse residence. They would put up town-houses around the edges, make the center into a square, and along the square Sterling would put up shops. Rich people would move in, and the Waterhouses and their confederates would control a patch of land that would probably generate more rent than any thousand square miles of Ireland—basically, they would become farmers of rich people.

And what made it extraordinarily clever—as only Sterling could be—was that this project would not even be a *struggle* as such. They would not have to defeat any adversary or overcome any obstacle—merely ride along with certain inexorable trends. All they—all Sterling—had to do was *notice* these trends. He'd always had a talent for noticing—which was why his shops were so highly thought of—so all he needed was to be in the right place to do the necessary noticing, and the right place was obviously Mrs. Green's coffee-house.

But it was the wrong place for Daniel, who only wanted to notice what Isaac was up to. A lively conversation was underway all round him, but it might as well've been in a foreign language—in fact, frequently it was. Daniel divided his time between looking at the telescope and wondering when he could snatch it off the table without attracting attention; staring at the mystery-shop and at the gentleman-rider; fraternal staredowns with Sterling (who was in his red silk suit with silver buttons today, and had numerous scraps of black glued to his face, though not as many as Beatrice); and watching Sir Winston Churchill, who looked equally bored, distracted, and miserable.

At one point he caught Sir Winston gazing fixedly at the telescope, his eyes making tiny movements and focusings as he figured out how it worked. Daniel waited until Sir Winston looked up at him, ready with a question—then Daniel winked and shook his head minutely. Sir Winston raised his eyebrows and looked *thrilled* that he and Daniel now had a small Intrigue of their own—it was like having a pretty seventeen-year-old girl unexpectedly sit on his lap. But this exchange was fully noticed by someone of Sterling's crowd—one of Beatrice's young lady friends—who demanded to know what the Tubular Object was.

"Thank you for reminding me," Daniel said, "I'd best put it away."

"What is it?" the lady demanded.

"A Naval Device," Sir Winston said, "or a model of one—pity the Dutch Fleet when Mr. Waterhouse's invention is realized at full scale!"

"How's it work?"

"This is not the place," said Sir Winston significantly, eyes rattling back and forth in a perfunctory scan for Dutch spies. This caused all of the *other* heads to turn, which led to an important Sighting: an entourage was migrating out of the Strand and into Charing Cross, and someone frightfully significant must be in the middle of it. While they were all trying to figure out *who*, Daniel put the telescope away and closed the box.

"It's the Earl of Upnor," someone whispered, and then Daniel had to look, and see what had become of his former roommate.

The answer: now that Louis Anglesey, Earl of Upnor, was in London, freed from the monastic constraints of Cambridge, and a full twenty-two years of age, he was able to live, and dress, as he pleased. Today, walking across Charing Cross, he was wearing a suit that appeared to've been constructed by (1) dressing him in a blouse with twenty-foot-long sleeves of the most expensive linen; (2) bunching the sleeves up in numerous overlapping gathers on his arms; (3) painting most of him in glue; (4) shaking and rolling him in a bin containing thousands of black silk doilies; and (5) (because King Charles II, who'd mandated, a few years earlier, that all courtiers wear black and white, was getting bored with it, but had not formally rescinded the order) adding dashes of color here and there, primarily in the form of clusters of elaborately gathered and knotted ribbons—enough ribbon, all told, to stretch all the way to whatever shop in Paris where the Earl had bought all of this stuff. The Earl also had a white silk scarf tied round his throat in such a way as to show off its lacy ends. Louis XIV's Croatian mercenaries, *les Cravates,* had made a practice of tying their giant, flapping lace collars down so that gusts of wind would not blow them up over their faces in the middle of a battle or duel, and this had become a fashion in Paris, and the Earl of Upnor, always pushing the envelope, was now doing the *cravate* thing with a scarf instead of an (as of ten minutes ago) outmoded collar. He had a wig that was actually wider than his shoulders, and a pair of boots that contained enough really good snow-white leather that, if pulled on straight, they would have reached all the way to his groin, at which point each one of them would have been larger in circumference than his waist; but he had of course folded the tops down and then (since they were so long) folded them back up again to keep them from dragging on the ground, so that around each knee was a complex of white leather folds about as wide as a bushel-basket, filled with a froth of lace. Gold spurs, beset with jewels, curved back from each heel to a distance of perhaps eight inches. The heels themselves were cherry-red, four inches high, and protected from the muck of Charing Cross by loose slippers whose flat soles dragged on the ground and made clacking noises with each step. Because of the width of his boot-tops, the Earl had to swing his legs around each other with each step, toes pointed, rolling so violently from side to side that he could only maintain balance with a long, encrusted, beribboned walking-stick.

For all that, he made excellent headway, and his admirers in the garden of the coffee-house had only a few moments in which to memorize the details. Daniel secured the Reflecting Telescope and then looked across the square, wanting to regain sight of the strange gentleman who'd been following Isaac.

But that fellow was no longer sitting in the coffee-house opposite. Daniel feared that he'd lost the man's trail—until he happened to glance back at the Earl of Upnor, and noticed that his entourage was parting to admit, and swallow up, none other than the same gentleman rider.

Daniel, unencumbered by sword, giant flaring boots, or clacking boot-protectors, very quickly rose and stepped out of Mrs. Green's without bothering to excuse himself. He did not walk directly towards Upnor, but plotted a course to swing wide around his group, as if going to an errand on the other side of Charing Cross.

As he drew close, he observed the following: the gentleman dismounted and approached the Earl, smiling confidently. Proud of himself, showing big mossy teeth.

While the rider bowed, Upnor glanced, and nodded, at one of his hangers-on. This man stepped in from the side, bending low, and made a sweeping gesture aimed at one of Upnor's boots. Something flew from his hand and struck the top of the boot. In the same moment, this fellow extended his index finger and pointed to it: a neat dollop of brown stuff the size of a guinea coin. Everyone except the Earl of Upnor and the gentleman rider gasped in horror. "What is it?" the Earl inquired.

"Your boot!" someone exclaimed.

"I cannot see it," the Earl said, "the boot-tops obstruct my view." Supporting himself with the walking-stick, he extended one leg out in front of himself and pointed the toe. Everyone in Charing Cross could see it now, including the Earl. "You have got shit on my boot!" he announced. "Shall I have to kill you?"

The rider was nonplussed; he hadn't come close enough to get shit on anyone—but the only other people who could testify to that were the Earl's friends. Looking around, all he could see were the rouged and black-patched faces of the Earl's crowd glowering at him.

"Whyever would you say such a thing, my lord?"

"*Fight a duel with you,* I should say—which would *presumably* mean killing you. Everyone I fight a duel with seems to die—why should you be any exception?"

"Why a . . . duel, my lord?"

"Because to extract an apology from you seems *impossible.* Even my *dog* is apologetic. But you! Why can you not show that you are ashamed of your actions?"

"My actions . . ."

"You have got shit on my boot!"

"My lord, I fear you have been misinformed."

Very ugly noises now from the entourage.

"Meet me tomorrow morning at Tyburn. Bring a second—someone strong enough to carry you away when I'm finished."

The rider finally understood that claiming innocence was getting him nowhere. "But I *can* show that I am ashamed, my lord."

"Really? E'en like a dog?"

"Yes, my lord."

"When my dog gets shit in the wrong place, I rub his nose in it," said the Earl, extending his pointed toe again, so it was nearly in the rider's face.

Daniel was now walking nearly behind the rider, no more than twelve feet distant, and could clearly see a stream of urine form in the crotch of his breeches and pizzle out onto the road. "Please, my lord. I did as you asked. I followed the white-haired man—I sent the message. Why are you doing this to me?"

But the Earl of Upnor fixed his stare on the rider, and raised his boot an inch. The rider bowed his head—lowered his nose toward it—but then the Earl slowly lowered his boot until it was on the ground, forcing the other to bend low, then clamber down onto his knees, and finally to put his elbows into the dirt, in order to put his nose exactly where the Earl wanted it.

Then it was over, and the gentleman rider was running out of Charing Cross with his face buried in his hands, presumably never to be seen in London again—which must have been exactly what the Earl wanted.

The Earl, for his part, shed his entourage at a tavern, and went alone into the same shop as Isaac Newton. Daniel, by that point, wasn't even certain that Isaac was still *in* there. He walked by the front of it once and finally saw a tiny sign in the window: MONSIEUR LEFEBURE—CHYMIST.

Daniel roamed around Charing Cross for the next half an hour, glancing into M. LeFebure's windows from time to time, until he finally caught sight of silver-haired Isaac framed in a window, deep in conversation with Louis Anglesey, the Earl of Upnor, who only nodded, and nodded, and (for good measure) nodded again, rapt.

Much as the sun had burnt its face into Isaac's retinas at Woolsthorpe, this image remained before Daniel long after he had turned his back upon Charing Cross and stalked away. He walked for a long time through the streets, shifting the burden of the telescope from one shoulder to the other from time to time. He was headed generally toward Bishopsgate, where there was a meeting to attend. He was pursued and harried the whole way by a feeling, difficult to identify, until at last he recognized it as a sort of jealousy. He did not know what Isaac was up to in the house/shop/laboratory/salon of M. LeFebure. He suspected Alchemy, Buggery, or some ripe warm concoction thereof: and if not, then a flirtation with same. Which was wholly Isaac's business and not Daniel's. Indeed, Daniel had no interest in either of those pastimes. To feel jealous was, therefore, foolish. And yet he did. Isaac had, somehow, found friends in whom he could confide things he hid from Daniel. There it was, simple and painful as a smack in the gob. But Daniel had friends of his own. He was going to see them now. Some were no less fraudulent, or foolish, than Alchemists. Perhaps Isaac was only giving him his just deserts for that.

Royal Society Meeting, Gresham's College
12 AUGUST 1670

This Club of Vertuoso's, upon a full Night, when some eminent Maggot-monger, for the Satisfaction of the Society, had appointed to demonstrate the Force of Air, by some hermetical Pot gun, to shew the Difference of the Gravity between the Smoak of Tobacco and that of Colts-foot and Bittany, or to try some other such like Experiment, were always compos'd of such an odd Mixture of Mankind, that, like a Society of Ringers at a quarterly Feast, here sat a fat purblind Philosopher next to a talkative Spectacle-maker; yonder a half-witted Whim of Quality, next to a ragged Mathematician; on the other Side a consumptive Astronomer next to a water-gruel Physician; above them, a Transmutator of Metals, next to a Philosopher-Stone-Hunter; at the lower End, a prating Engineer, next to a clumsy-fisted Mason; at the upper End of all, perhaps, an Atheistical Chymist, next to a whimsy-headed Lecturer; and these the learned of the Wise-akers wedg'd here and there with quaint Artificers, and noisy Operators, in all Faculties; some bending beneath the Load of Years and indefatigable Labour, some as thin-jaw'd and heavy-ey'd, with abstemious Living and nocturnal Study as if, like *Pharaoh's* Lean Kine, they were designed by Heaven to warn the World of a Famine; others looking as wild, and disporting themselves as frenzically, as if the Disappointment of their Projects had made them subject to a Lunacy. When they were thus met, happy was the Man that could find out a new Star in the Firmament; discover a wry Step in the Sun's Progress; assign new Reasons for the Spots of the Moon, or add one Stick to the Bundle of Faggots which have been so long burthensome to the back of her old Companion; or, indeed, impart any crooked Secret to the learned Society, that might puzzle their Brains, and disturb their Rest for a Month afterwards, in consulting upon their Pillows how to straiten the Project, that it might appear upright to the Eye of Reason, and the knotty Difficulty to be rectify'd, as to bring Honour to themselves, and Advantage to the Public.

—NED WARD, *The Vertuoso's Club*

AUGUST 12. AT A MEETING of the SOCIETY,

MR. NICHOLAS MERCATOR and MR. JOHN LOCKE were elected and admitted.

The rest of Mr. BOYLE's experiments about light were read, with great satisfaction to the society; who ordered, that all should be registered, and that Mr. HOOKE should take care of having the like experiments tried before the society, as soon as he could procure any shining rotten wood or fish.

Dr. CROUNE brought in a dead parakeet.

Sir JOHN FINCH displayed an asbestos hat-band.

Dr. ENT speculated as to why it is hotter in summer than winter.

Mr. POWELL offered to be employed by the society in any capacity whatever.

Mr. OLDENBURG being absent, Mr. WATERHOUSE read a letter from a PORTUGUESE nobleman, most civilly complimenting the society for its successes in removing the spleens of dogs, without ill effect; and going on to enquire, whether the society might undertake to perform the like operation on his Wife, as she was most afflicted with splenetic distempers.

Dr. ENT was put in mind of an account concerning oysters.

Mr. HOOKE displayed an invention for testing whether a surface is level, consisting of a bubble of air trapped in a sealed glass tube, otherwise filled with water.

The Dog, that had a piece of his skin cut off at the former meeting, being enquired after, and the operator answering, that he had run away, it was ordered, that another should be provided against the next meeting for the grafting experiment.

The president produced from Sir WILLIAM CURTIUS a hairy ball found in the belly of a cow.

THE DUKE OF GUNFLEET produced a letter of Mons. HUYGENS, dated at Paris, mentioning a new observation concerning Saturn, made last spring at Rome by one CAMPANI, viz. that the circle of Saturn had been seen to cast a shadow on the sphere: which observation Mons. HUYGENS looked on as confirming his hypothesis, that Saturn is surrounded by a Ring.

A Vagabond presented himself, who had formerly received a shot into his belly, breaking his guts in two: whereupon one end of the colon stood out at the left side of his belly, whereby he voided all his excrement, which he did for the society.

Mr. POVEY presented a skeleton to the society.

Mr. BOYLE reported that swallows live under frozen water in the Baltic.

Dr. GODDARD mentioned that wainscotted rooms make cracking noises in mornings and evenings.

Mr. WALLER mentioned that toads come out in moist cool weather.

Mr. HOOKE related, that he had found the stars in Orion's belt, which Mons. HUYGENS made but three, to be five.

Dr. MERRET produced a paper, wherein he mentioned, that three skulls with the hair on and brains in them were lately found at Black-friars in pewter vessels in the midst of a thick stone-wall, with certain obscure inscriptions. This paper was ordered to be registered.

Mr. HOOKE made an experiment to discover, whether a piece of steel first counterpoised in exact scales, and then touched by a vigorous magnet, acquires thereby any sensible increase in weight. The event was, that it did not.

Dr. ALLEN gave an account of a person, who had lately lost a quantity of his brain, and yet lived and was well.

Dr. WILKINS presented the society with his book, intitled, An Essay Towards a Real Character and Philosophical Language.

Mr. HOOKE suggested, that it was worth inquiry, whether there were any valves in plants, which he conceived to be very necessary for the conveying of the juices of trees up to the height of sometimes 200, 300, and more feet; which he saw not how it was possible to be performed without valves as well as motion.

Sir ROBERT SOUTHWELL presented for the repository a skull of an executed person with the moss grown on it in Ireland.

THE BISHOP OF CHESTER moved, that Mr. HOOKE might be ordered to try, whether he could by means of the microscopic moss-seed formerly shewn by him, make moss grow on a dead man's skull.

Mr. HOOKE intimated that the experiment proposed by THE BISHOP OF CHESTER would not be as productive of new Knowledge, as a great many others that could be mentioned, if there were time enough to mention them all.

Mr. OLDENBURG being absent, Mr. WATERHOUSE read an extract, which the former had received from Paris, signifying that it was most certain, that Dr. DE GRAAF had unravelled testicles, and that one of them was kept by him in spirit of wine. Some of the physicians present intimating, that the like had been attempted in England many years before, but not with that success, that they could yet believe what Dr. DE GRAAF affirmed.

THE DUKE OF GUNFLEET gave of Dr. DE GRAAF an excellent Character; attesting that, while at Paris, this same Doctor had cured the Duke's son (now the EARL OF UPNOR) of the bite of a venomous *spyder*.

Occasion being given to speak of tarantulas, some of the members said, that persons bitten by them, though cured, yet must dance once a year: others, that different patients required different airs to make them dance, according to the different sorts of tarantulas which had bitten them.

THE DUKE OF GUNFLEET said, that the *Spyder* that had bitten his son in Paris, was not of the *tarantula* sort, and accordingly that the Earl does not under any account suffer any compulsion to dance.

The society gave order for the making of portable barometers, contrived by Mr. BOYLE, to be sent into several parts of the world, not only into the most distant places of England, but likewise by sea into the East and West Indies, and other parts, particularly to the English plantations in Bermuda, Jamaica, Barbados, Virginia, and New England; and to Tangier, Moscow, St. Helena, the Cape of Good Hope, and Scanderoon.

Dr. KING was put in mind of dissecting a lobster and an oyster.

Mr. HOOKE produced some plano-convex spherical glasses, as small as pin-heads, to serve for object-glasses in microscopes. He was desired to put some of them into the society's great microscope for a trial.

THE DUKE OF GUNFLEET produced the skin of a Moor tanned.

Mr. BOYLE remarked, that two very able physicians of his acquaintance gave to a woman desperately sick of the iliac passion above a pound of crude quicksilver which remained several days in her body without producing any fatal symptom; and afterwards dissecting the dead corpse, they found, that part of her gut, where the excrement was stopped, gangrened; but the quicksilver lay all on a heap above it, and had not so much as discoloured the parts of the gut contiguous to it.

Mr. HOOKE was put in mind of an experiment of making a body heavier than gold, by putting quicksilver to it, to see, whether any of it would penetrate into the pores of gold.

Dr. CLARKE proposed, that a man hanged might be begged of the King, to try to revive him; and that in case he were revived, he might have his life granted him.

Mr. WATERHOUSE produced a new telescope, invented by Mr. Isaac NEWTON, professor of mathematics in the university of Cambridge, improving on previous telescopes by contracting the optical path. THE DUKE OF GUNFLEET, Dr. CHRISTOPHER WREN, and Mr. HOOKE, examining it, had so good opinion of it, that they proposed it be shown to the King, and that a description and scheme of it should be sent to Mons. HUYGENS at Paris, thereby to secure this invention to Mr. NEWTON.

The experiment of the opening of the thorax of a dog was suggested. Mr. HOOKE and Mr. WATERHOUSE having made this experiment formerly, begged to be excused for the duration of any such proceedings. Dr. BALLE and Dr. KING made the experiment but did not succeed.

> A fifth Cabal, perhaps, would be a Knot of Mathematicians, who would sit so long wrangling about squaring the Circle, till, with Drinking and Rattling, they were ready to let fall a nauseous Perpendicular from their Mouths to the Chamber-Pot. Another little Party would be deeply engaged in a learned Dispute about Transmutation of Metals, and contend so warmly about turning Lead into Gold, till the Bar had a just Claim to all the Silver in their Pockets . . .
> —NED WARD, *The Vertuoso's Club*

A FEW OF THEM ENDED UP at a tavern, unfortunately called the Dogg, on Broad Street near London Wall. Wilkins (who was the Bishop of Chester now) and Sir Winston Churchill and Thomas More Anglesey, a.k.a. the Duke of Gunfleet, amused themselves using Newton's telescope to peer into the windows of the Navy Treasury across the way, where lamps were burning and clerks were working late. Wheelbarrows laden with lockboxes were coming up every few minutes from the goldsmiths' shops on Threadneedle.

Hooke commandeered a small table, set his bubble-level upon it, and began to adjust it by inserting scraps of paper beneath its legs. Daniel quaffed bitters and thought that this was all a great improvement on this morning.

"To Oldenburg," someone said, and even Hooke raised his head up on its bent neck and drank to the Secretary's health.

"Are we allowed to know *why* the King put him in the Tower?" asked Daniel.

Hooke suddenly became absorbed in table-levelling, the others in viewing a planet that was rising over Bishopsgate, and Daniel reckoned that the reason for Oldenburg's imprisonment was one of those things that everyone in London should simply *know*, it was one of those facts Londoners breathed in like the smoke of sea-coal.

John Wilkins brushed significantly past Daniel and stepped outside, plucking a pipe from a tobacco-box on the wall. Daniel joined him for a smoke on the street. It was a fine summer eve in Bishopsgate: on the far side of London Wall, lunaticks at Bedlam were carrying on vigorous disputes with angels, demons, or the spirits of departed relations, and on this side, the rhythmic yelping of a bone-saw came through a half-open window of Gresham's College as a cabal of Bishops, Knights, Doctors, and Colonels removed the rib-cage from a living mongrel. The Dogg's sign creaked above in a mild river-breeze. Coins clinked dimly inside the Navy's lockboxes as porters worried them up stairs. Through an open window they could occasionally glimpse Samuel Pepys, Fellow of the Royal Society, making arrangements with his staff and gazing out the window, longingly, at the Dogg. Daniel and the Bishop stood there and took it in for a minute as a sort of ritual, as Papists cross themselves when entering a church: to do proper respect to the place.

"Mr. Oldenburg is the heart of the R.S.," Bishop Wilkins began.

"I would give that honor to you, or perhaps Mr. Hooke . . ."

"Hold—I was not finished—I was launching a metaphor. Please remember that I've been preaching to rapt congregations, or at least they are *pretending* to be rapt—in any case, they *sit quietly* while I develop my metaphors."

"I beg forgiveness, and am now pretending to be rapt."

"Very well. Now! As we have learned by doing appalling things to stray dogs, the heart *accepts* blood returning from organs, such as the brain, through veins, such as the jugular. It *expels* blood *toward* these organs through arteries, such as the carotid. Do you remember what happened when Mr. Hooke cross-plumbed the mastiff, and connected his jugular to his carotid? And don't tell me that the splice broke and sprayed blood all around—this I remember."

"The blood settled into a condition of equilibrium, and began to coagulate in the tube."

"And from this we concluded that—?"

"I have long since forgotten. That bypassing the heart is a bad idea?"

"One *might* conclude," said the Bishop helpfully, "that an inert vessel, that merely *accepts* the circulating Fluid, but never *expels* it, becomes a stagnant back-water—or to put it otherwise, that the heart, by forcing it outwards, drives it around the cycle that in good time brings it back in from the organs and extremities. Hallo, Mr. Pepys!" (Shifting his focus to across the way.) "Starting a war, are we?"

"Too easy . . . winding one up, my lord," from the window.

"Is it going to be finished any time *soon*? Your diligence is setting an example for all of us—stop it!"

"I detect the beginnings of a lull . . ."

"Now, Daniel, anyone who scans the History of the Royal Society can see that, at each meeting, Mr. Oldenburg reads several letters from Continental savants, such as Mr. Huygens, and, lately, Dr. Leibniz . . ."

"I'm not familiar with that name."

"You *will* be—he is a mad letter-writer and a protégé of Huygens—a devotee of Pansophism—he has lately been *smothering* us with curious documents. You haven't heard about him because Mr. Oldenburg has been passing his missives round to Mr. Hooke, Mr. Boyle, Mr. Barrow, and others, trying to find someone who can even read them, as a first step towards determining whether or not they are nonsense. But I digress. For every letter Mr. Oldenburg *reads*, he *receives* a dozen—why so many?"

"Because, like a heart, he pumps so many *outwards*—?"

"Yes, precisely. Whole *sacks* of them crossing the Channel—driving the circulation that brings new ideas, from the Continent, back to our little meetings."

"Damn me, and now the King's clapped him in the Tower!" said Daniel, unable to avoid feeling a touch melodramatic—this kind of dialog not being, exactly, his metier.

"Bypassing the heart," said Wilkins, without a trace of any such self-consciousness. "I can already feel the Royal Society coagulating. Thank you for bringing Mr. Newton's telescope. Fresh blood! When can we see him at a meeting?"

"Probably never, as long as the Fellows persist in cutting up dogs."

"Ah—he's squeamish—abhors cruelty?"

"Cruelty to *animals*."

"Some Fellows have proposed that we borrow residents of . . ." said the Bishop, nodding towards Bedlam.

"Isaac might be more comfortable with that," Daniel admitted.

A barmaid had been hovering, and now stepped into the awkward silence: "Mr. Hooke requests your presence."

"Thank God," Wilkins said to her, "I was afraid you were going to complain he had *committed an offense* against your person."

The patrons of the Dogg were backed up against the walls in the configuration normally used for watching bar-fights, viz. forming an empty circle around Mr. Hooke's table, which was (as shown by the bubble instrument) now perfectly level. It was also clean, and empty except for a glob of quicksilver in the middle, with numerous pinhead-sized droplets scattered about in novel constellations. Mr. Hooke was peering at the large glob—a perfect, regular dome—through an optical device of his own manufacture. Glancing up, he twiddled a hog-bristle between thumb and index finger, pushing an invisibly tiny droplet of mercury across the table until it merged with the large one. Then more peering. Then, moving with the stealth of a cat-burglar, he backed away from the table. When he had put a good fathom between himself and the experiment, he looked up at Wilkins and said, "Universal Measure!"

"What!? Sir! You don't say!"

"You will agree," Hooke said, "that *level* is an absolute concept—any sentient person can make a surface level."

"It is in the Philosophical Language," said Bishop Wilkins—this signified *yes*.

Pepys came in the door, looking splendid, and had his mouth open to demand beer, when he realized a solemn ceremony was underway.

"Likewise mercury is the same in all places—in all worlds."

"Agreed."

"As is the number two."

"Of course."

"Here I have created a flat, clean, smooth, level surface. On it I have placed a drop of mercury and adjusted it so that the diameter is exactly two times its height. *Anyone, anywhere* could repeat these steps—the result would be a drop of mercury *exactly* the same size as *this* one. The diameter of the drop, then, can be used as the common unit of measurement for the Philosophical Language!"

The sound of men thinking.

Pepys: "Then you could build a container that was a certain number of those units high, wide, and deep; fill it with water; and have a standard measure of weight."

"Just so, Mr. Pcpys."

"From length and weight you could make a standard pendulum—the time of its alternations would provide a universal unit of time!"

"But water beads up differently on different surfaces," said the Bishop of Chester. "I assume the same sorts of variations occur with mercury."

Hooke, resentful: "The surface to be used could be stipulated: copper, or glass . . ."

"If the force of gravity varies with altitude, how would that affect the height of the drop?" asked Daniel Waterhouse.

"Do it at sea-level," said Hooke, with a dollop of spleen.

"Sea-level varies with the tides," Pepys pointed out.

"What of other planets?" Wilkins demanded thunderously.

"Other *planets*!? We haven't finished with *this* one!"

"As our compatriot Mr. Oldenburg has said: 'You will please to remember that we have taken to task the whole Universe, and that we were obliged to do so by the nature of our Design!' "

Hooke, very stormy-looking now, scraped most of the quicksilver into a funnel, and thence into a flask; departed; and was sighted by Mr. Pepys (peering through the Newtonian reflector) no more than a minute later, stalking off towards Hounsditch in the company of a whore. "He's flown into one of his Fits of Melancholy—we won't see him for two weeks now—then we'll have to reprimand him," Wilkins grumbled.

Almost as if it were written down somewhere in the Universal Character, Pepys and Wilkins and Waterhouse somehow knew that they had unfinished business together—that they ought to be having a discreet chat about Mr. Oldenburg. A triangular commerce in highly significant glances and eyebrow-raisings flourished there in the Dogg, for the next hour, among them. But they could not all break free at once: Churchill and others wanted more details from Daniel about this Mr. Newton and his telescope. The Duke of Gunfleet got Pepys cornered, and interrogated him about dark matters concerning the Navy's finances. Blood-spattered, dejected Royal Society members stumbled in from Gresham's College, with the news that Drs. King and Belle had gotten lost in the wilderness of canine anatomy, the dog had died, and they really needed Hooke— where was he? Then they cornered Bishop Wilkins and talked Royal Society politics—would Comstock stand for election to President again? Would Anglesey arrange to have himself nominated?

BUT LATER—too late for Daniel, who had risen early, when Isaac had—the three of them were together in Pepys's coach, going somewhere.

"I note my Lord Gunfleet has taken up a sudden interest in *Naval*-gazing," said Wilkins.

"As our safety from the Dutch depends upon our Navy," Pepys said carefully, "and most of our Navy is arrayed before the Casbah in Algiers, *many* Persons of Quality share Anglesey's curiosity."

Wilkins only looked amused. "I did not hear him asking you of frigates and cannons," he said, "but of Bills of Exchange, and pay-coupons."

Pepys cleared his throat at length, and glanced nervously at Daniel. "Those who are responsible for *draining* the Navy's coffers, must answer to those who are responsible for *filling* them," he finally said.

Even Daniel, a dull Cambridge scholar, had the wit to know that the coffer-drainer being referred to here was the armaments-maker John Comstock, Earl of Epsom—and that the coffer-filler was Thomas More Anglesey, Duke of Gunfleet, and father of Louis Anglesey, the Earl of Upnor.

"Thus C and A," Wilkins said. "What does the Cabal's second syllable have to say of Naval matters?"

"No surprises from Bolstrood* of course."

"Some say Bolstrood wants our Navy in Africa, so that the Dutch can invade us, and make of us a Calvinist nation."

"Given that the V.O.C.† is paying out dividends of forty percent, I think that there are many new Calvinists on Threadneedle Street."

"Is Apthorp one of them?"

---

*Knott Bolstrood, a Barker and an old friend of Drake's, was rabidly Protestant and anti-French—the King had made him Secretary of State because no one in his right mind could possibly accuse him of being a crypto-Catholic.
†*Vereenigde Oostindische Compagnie,* or Dutch East India Company.

"Those rumors are nonsense—Apthorp would rather build *his* East India Company, than invest in the *Dutch* one."

"So it follows that Apthorp wants a strong Navy, to protect our merchant ships from those Dutch East Indiamen, so topheavy with cannons."

"Yes."

"What of General Lewis?"

"Let's ask the young scholar," Pepys said mischievously.

Daniel was dumbstruck for a few moments—to the gurgling, boyish amusement of Pepys and Wilkins.

The telescope seemed to be watching Daniel, too: it sat in its box across from him, a disembodied sensory organ belonging to Isaac Newton, staring at him with more than human acuteness. He heard Isaac demanding to know what on earth he, Daniel Waterhouse, could possibly be doing, riding across London in Samuel Pepys's coach—pretending to be a man of affairs!

"Err . . . a weak Navy forces us to keep a strong Army, to fight off any Dutch invasions," Daniel said, thinking aloud.

"But with a strong Navy, we can invade the Hollanders!" Wilkins protested. "More glory for General Lewis, Duke of Tweed!"

"Not without French help," Daniel said, after a few moments' consideration, "and my lord Tweed is too much the Presbyterian."

"Is this the same good Presbyterian who enjoyed a secret earldom at the exile court at St. Germaines, when Cromwell ruled the land?"

"He is a Royalist, that's all," Daniel demurred.

What was he doing in this carriage having this conversation, besides going out on a limb, and making a fool of himself? The real answer was known only to John Wilkins, Lord Bishop of Chester, Author of both the *Cryptonomicon* and the *Philosophical Language,* who encrypted with his left hand and made things known to all possible worlds with his right. Who'd gotten Daniel into Trinity College—invited him out to Epsom during the Plague—nominated him for the Royal Society—and now, it seemed, had something else in mind for him. Was Daniel here as an apprentice, sitting at the master's knee? It was shockingly prideful, and radically non-Puritan, for him to think so—but he could come up with no other hypothesis.

"Right, then, it all has to do with Mr. Oldenburg's letters abroad . . ." Pepys said, when some change in the baroscopic pressure (or something) signified it was time to drop pretenses and talk seriously.

Wilkins: "I assumed *that.* Which *one?*"

"Does it matter? All of the GRUBENDOL letters are intercepted and read before he even sees them."

"I've always wondered who does the reading," Wilkins reflected. "He must be very bright, or else perpetually confused."

"Likewise, all of Oldenburg's outgoing mail is examined—you knew this."

"And in some letter, he said something indiscreet—?"

"It is simply that the sheer *volume* of his foreign correspondence—taken together with the fact that he's from Germany—*and* that he's worked as a diplomat on the Continent—and that he's a friend of Cromwell's Puritanickal poet—"

"John Milton."

"Yes . . . finally, consider that no one at court understands even a tenth of what he's saying in his letters—it makes a certain type of person nervous."

"Are you saying he was thrown into the Tower of London on *general principles?*"

"As a precaution, yes."

"What—does that mean he has to stay in there for the *rest of his life?*"

"Of course not . . . only until certain very tender negotiations are finished."

"Tender negotiations . . ." Wilkins repeated a few times, as if further information could thus be pounded out of the dry and pithy words.

And here the discourse, which, to Daniel, had been merely confusing up to this point, plunged into obscurity perfect and absolute.

"I didn't know *he* had a tender bone in his body . . . oh, wipe that smirk off your face, Mr. Pepys, I meant nothing of the sort!"

"Oh, it is known that *his* feelings for *sa soeur* are most affectionate. He's writing letters to her *all the time* lately."

"Does she write back?"

"Minette spews out letters like a *diplomat.*"

"Keeping his *hisness* well acquainted—I am guessing—with all that is new with her beloved?"

"The volume of correspondence is such," Pepys exclaimed, "that His Majesty can never have been so close to the man you refer to as he is today. Hoops of gold are stronger than bands of steel."

Wilkins, starting to look a bit queasy: "Hmmm . . . a good thing, then, isn't it, that *formal* contacts are being made through those two arch-Protestants—"

"I would refer you to Chapter Ten of your 1641 work," said Pepys.

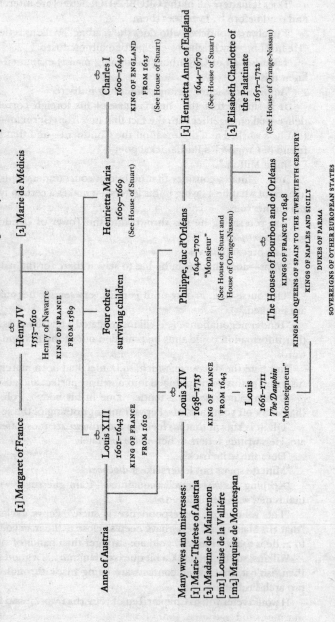

House of Bourbon

The Bourbon-Orléans family tree is infinitely larger, more ramified, and more intertangled than can possibly be shown here, largely owing to the longevity, fertility, and polygamy of Louis XIV. One of the mistresses of Louis XIV produced six children who were made legitimate by fiat, and another produced two.

[1] Margaret of France — Henry IV — [2] Marie de Médicis
1553–1610
Henry of Navarre
KING OF FRANCE
FROM 1589

Charles I
1600–1649
KING OF ENGLAND
FROM 1625
(See House of Stuart)

Anne of Austria — Louis XIII
1601–1643
KING OF FRANCE
FROM 1610

Four other
surviving children

Henrietta Maria
1609–1669
(See House of Stuart)

Many wives and mistresses:
[1] Marie-Thérèse of Austria
[2] Madame de Maintenon
[m1] Louise de la Vallière
[m2] Marquise de Montespan

Louis XIV
1638–1715
KING OF FRANCE
FROM 1643

Philippe, duc d'Orléans
1640–1701
"Monsieur"
(See House of Stuart and
House of Orange-Nassau)

[1] Henrietta Anne of England
1644–1670
(See House of Stuart)

[2] Elisabeth Charlotte of
the Palatinate
1652–1722
(See House of Orange-Nassau)

Louis
1661–1711
The Dauphin
"Monseigneur"

The Houses of Bourbon and of Orléans
KINGS OF FRANCE TO 1848
KINGS AND QUEENS OF SPAIN TO THE TWENTIETH CENTURY
KINGS OF NAPLES AND SICILY
DUKES OF PARMA
SOVEREIGNS OF OTHER EUROPEAN STATES

"Er . . . stupid me . . . I've lost you . . . we're speaking now of Oldenburg?"

"I intended no change in subject—we're still on Treaties."

The coach stopped. Pepys climbed out of it. Daniel listened to the *whack, whack, whack* of his slap-soled boots receding across cobblestones. Wilkins was staring at nothing, trying to decrypt whatever Pepys had said.

Riding in a carriage through London was only a little better than being systematically beaten by men with cudgels—Daniel felt the need for a stretch, and so he climbed out, too, turned round—and found himself looking straight down a lane toward the front of St. James's Palace, a few hundred yards distant. Spinning round a hundred and eighty degrees, he discovered Comstock House, a stupefying Gothick pile heaving itself up out of some gardens and pavements. Pepys's carriage had turned in off of Piccadilly and stopped in the great house's forecourt. Daniel admired its situation: John Comstock could, if he so chose, plant himself in the center of his front doorway and fire a musket across his garden, out his front gate, across Piccadilly, straight down the center of a tree-lined *faux*-country lane, across Pall Mall, and straight into the grand entrance of St. James's, where it would be likely to kill someone very well-dressed. Stone walls, hedges, and wrought-iron fences had been cunningly arranged so as to crop away the view of Piccadilly and neighboring houses, and enhance the impression that Comstock House and St. James's Palace were all part of the same family compound.

Daniel edged out through Comstock's front gates and stood at the margin of Piccadilly, facing south towards St. James's. He could see a gentleman with a bag entering the Palace—probably a doctor coming to bleed a few pints from Anne Hyde's jugular. Off to his left, in the general direction of the river, was an open space—a vast construction site, now—about a quarter of a mile on a side, with Charing Cross on the opposite corner. Since it was night, and no workers were around, it seemed as if stone foundations and walls were growing up out of the ground through some process of spontaneous generation, like toadstools bursting from soil in the middle of the night.

From here, it was possible to see Comstock House in perspective: it was really just one of several noble houses lined up along Piccadilly, facing towards St. James's Palace, like soldiers drawn up for review. Berkeley House, Burlington House, and Gunfleet House were some of the others. But only Comstock House had that direct Palace view down the lane.

He felt a giant door grinding open, and heard dignified murmurings, and saw that John Comstock had emerged from his house, arm in arm with Pepys. He was sixty-three years old, and Daniel thought that he was leaning on Pepys, just a bit, for support. But he had been wounded in battles more than once, so it didn't necessarily mean he was getting feeble. Daniel sprang to the carriage and got Isaac's telescope out of there and had the driver stow it securely on the roof. Then he joined the other three inside, and the carriage wheeled round and clattered out across Piccadilly and down the lane toward St. James's.

John Comstock, Earl of Epsom, President of the Royal Society, and advisor to the King on all matters Natural-Philosophic, was dressed in a Persian vest—a heavy coatlike garment that, along with the Cravate, was the very latest at Court. Pepys was attired the same way, Wilkins was in completely out-moded clothing, Daniel as usual was dressed as a penniless itinerant Puritan from twenty years ago. Not that anyone was looking at him.

"Working late hours?" Comstock asked Pepys, apparently reading some clue in his attire.

"The Pay Office has been extraordinarily busy," Pepys said.

"The King has been preoccupied with concerns of money—*until recently*," Comstock said. "*Now* he is eager to turn his attentions back to his first love—natural philosophy."

"Then we have something that will delight him—a new Telescope," Wilkins began.

But telescopes were not on Comstock's agenda, and so he ignored the digression, and continued: "His Majesty has asked me to arrange a convocation at Whitehall Palace tomorrow evening. The Duke of Gunfleet, the Bishop of Chester, Sir Winston Churchill, you, Mr. Pepys, and I are invited to join the King for a demonstration at Whitehall: Enoch the Red will show us *Phosphorus*."

Just short of St. James's Palace, the carriage turned left onto Pall Mall, and began to move up in the direction of Charing Cross.

"Light-bearer? What's that?" Pepys asked.

"A new elemental substance," Wilkins said. "All the alchemists on the Continent are *abuzz* over it."

"What's it made of?"

"It's not made of *anything*—that's what is meant by *elemental*!"

"What planet is it of? I thought all the planets were spoken for," Pepys protested.

"Enoch will explain it."

"Has there been any movement on the Royal Society's other concern?"

"Yes!" Comstock said. He was looking into Wilkins's eyes, but he made a tiny glance toward Daniel. Wilkins replied with an equally tiny nod.

"Mr. Waterhouse, I am pleased to present you with this order," Comstock said, "from my Lord Penistone,"* producing a terrifying document with a fat wax seal dangling from the bottom margin. "Show it to the guards at the Tower tomorrow evening—and, even as we are at *one* end of London, viewing the Phosphorus Demo', you and Mr. Oldenburg will be convened at the *other* so that you can see to his needs. I know that he wants new strings for his theorbo—quills—ink—certain books—and of course there's an enormous amount of unread mail."

"Unread by GRUBENDOL, that is," Pepys jested.

Comstock turned and gave him a look that must've made Pepys feel as if he were staring directly into the barrel of a loaded cannon.

Daniel Waterhouse exchanged a little glance with the Bishop of Chester. Now they knew who'd been reading Oldenburg's foreign letters: Comstock.

Comstock turned and smiled politely—but not pleasantly—at Daniel. "You're staying at your elder half-brother's house?"

"Just so, sir."

"I'll have the goods sent round tomorrow morning."

The coach swung round the southern boundary of Charing Cross and pulled up before a fine new town-house. Daniel, having evidently out-stayed his relevance, was invited in the most polite and genteel way imaginable to exit the coach, and take a seat on top of it. He did so and realized, without really being surprised, that they had stopped in front of the apothecary shop of Monsieur LeFebure, King's Chymist—the very same place where Isaac Newton had spent most of the morning, and had had an orchestrated *chance encounter* with the Earl of Upnor.

The front door opened and a man in a long cloak stepped out, silhouetted by lamplight from within, and approached the coach. As he got clear of the light shining out of the house, and moved across the darkness, it became possible to see that the hem of his cloak, and the tips of his fingers, shone with a strange green light.

"Well met, Daniel Waterhouse," he said, and before Daniel

---

*None other than Knott Bolstrood, who'd been ennobled, for protocol reasons, when the King had named him Secretary of State—the King had chosen to make him Count Penistone because that way, Bolstrood the ultra-Puritan could not sign his name without writing the word "penis."

could answer, Enoch the Red had climbed into the open door of the coach and closed it behind him.

The coach simply rounded the corner out of Charing Cross, which put them at one end of the long paved plaza before White-hall. They drove directly towards the Holbein Gate, which was a four-turreted Gothic castle, taller than it was wide, that dominated the far end of the space. A huddle of indifferent gables and chimneys hid the big spaces off to their left: first Scotland Yard, which was an irregular mosaic of Wood Yards and Scalding Yards and Cider Houses, cluttered with coal-heaps and wood-piles, and after that, the Great Court of the Palace. On the right—where, during Daniel's boyhood, there'd been nothing but park, and a view towards St. James's Palace—there now loomed a long stone wall, twice as high as a man, and blank except for the gun-slits. Because Daniel was up on top of the carriage he could see a few tree-branches over its top, and the rooves of the wooden buildings that Cromwell had thrown up within those walls to house his Horse Guards. The new King—perhaps remembering that this plaza had once been filled with a crowd of people come to watch his father's head get chopped off—had decided to keep the wall, and the gun-slits, and the Horse Guards.

The Palace's Great Gate went by on the left, opening a glimpse of the Great Court and one or two big halls and chapels at the far end of it, down towards the river. More or less well-dressed pedestrians were going in and out of that gate, in twos and threes, availing themselves of a public right-of-way that led across the Great Court (it was clearly visible, even at night, as a rutted path over the ground) and that eventually snaked between, and through, various Palace Buildings and terminated at Whitehall Stairs, where watermen brought their little boats to pick up and discharge passengers.

The view through the Great Gate was then eclipsed by the corner of the Banqueting House, a giant white stone snuff-box of a building, which was kept dark on most nights so that torch- and candle-smoke would not blacken the buxom goddesses that Rubens had daubed on its ceiling. One or two torches were burning in there to-night, and Daniel was able to look up through a window and catch a glimpse of Minerva strangling Rebellion. But the carriage had nearly reached the end of the plaza now, and was slowing down, for this was an aesthetic cul-de-sac so miserable that it made even horses a bit woozy: the old quasi-Dutch gables of Lady Castlemaine's apartments dead ahead; the Holbein Gate's squat Gothic arch to the right and its medieval castle-towers looming far above their heads; the Italian Renaissance Banqueting House still on their left; and, across from it, that blank, slitted stone wall, which was as close as Puritans had ever come to having their own style of architecture.

The Holbein Gate would lead to King Street, which would take them to a sort of pied-à-terre that Pepys had in that quarter. But instead the driver chivvied his team around a difficult left turn and into a dark downhill passage, barely wider than the coach itself, that cut behind the Banqueting House and drained toward the river.

Now, any Englishman in decent clothing could walk almost anywhere in Whitehall Palace, even passing through the King's antechamber—a practice that European nobility considered to be far beyond vulgar, deep into the realm of the bizarre. Even so, Daniel had never been down this defile, which had always seemed Not a Good Place for a Young Puritan to Go—he wasn't even sure if it had an outlet, and always imagined that people like the Earl of Upnor would go there to molest serving-wenches or prosecute sword-duels.

The Privy Gallery ran along the right side of it. Now technically a gallery was just a hallway—in this case, one that led directly to those parts of Whitehall where the King himself dwelt, and toyed with his mistresses, and met with his counselors. But just as London Bridge had, over time, become covered over with houses and shops of haberdashers and glovers and drapers and publicans, so the Privy Gallery, tho' still an empty tube of air, had become surrounded by a jumbled encrustation of old buildings—mostly apartments that the King awarded to whichever courtiers and mistresses were currently in his favor. These coalesced into a bulwark of shadow off to Daniel's right, and seemed much bigger than they really were because of being numerous and confusing—as the corpse of a frog, which can fit into a pocket, seems to be a mile wide to the young Natural Philosopher who attempts to dissect it, and inventory its several parts.

Daniel was ambushed, several times, by explosions of laughter from candle-lit windows above: it sounded like sophisticated and cruel laughter. The passage finally bent round to the point where he could see its end. Apparently it debouched into a small pebbled court that he knew by reputation: the King, in theory, listened to sermons from the windows of various chambers and drawing-rooms that fronted on it. But before they reached that holy place the driver reined in his team and the carriage stopped. Daniel looked about, wondering why, and saw nothing except for a stone stairway that descended into a vault or tunnel beneath the Privy Gallery.

Pepys, Comstock, the Bishop of Chester, and Enoch the Red climbed out. Down in the tunnel, lights were now being lit. Consequently, through an open window, Daniel could see a banquet laid: a leg of mutton, a wheel of Cheshire, a dish of larks, ale, China oranges. But this room was not a dining-hall. In its corners he could see the gleam of retorts and quicksilver-flasks and fine balances, the glow of furnaces. He had heard rumors that the King had caused an alchemical laboratory to be built in the bowels of Whitehall, but until now, they had only been rumors.

"My coachman will take you back to Mr. Raleigh Waterhouse's residence," Pepys told him, pausing at the lip of the stairway. "Please make yourself comfortable below."

"You are very kind, sir, but I'm not far from Raleigh's, and I could benefit from the walk."

"As you wish. Please give my compliments to Mr. Oldenburg when you see him."

"I shall be honored to do so," Daniel answered, and just restrained himself from saying, *Please give mine to the King!*

Daniel now worked up his courage and walked down into the Sermon Court and gazed up into the windows of the King's chambers, though not for long—he was trying to look as if he came here all the time. A little side passage, under the end of the Privy Gallery, got him into the corner of the Privy Garden, which was a vast space. Another gallery ran along its edge, parallel to the river, and by going down it he could have got all the way to the royal bowling green and thence down into Westminster. But he'd had enough excitement for just now—instead he cut back across the great Garden, heading towards the Holbein Gate. Courtiers strolled and gossiped all round. Every so often he turned around and gazed back towards the river to admire the lodgings of the King and the Queen and their household rising up above the garden with the golden light of many beeswax candles shining out of them.

If Daniel had truly been the man about town that, for a few minutes, he was pretending to be, he'd have had eyes only for the people in the windows and on the garden paths. He'd have strained to glimpse something—a new trend in the cut of Persian vests, or two important Someones exchanging whispers in a shadowed corner. But as it was, there was one spectacle, and one only, that drew his gaze, like Polaris sucking on a lodestone. He turned his back on the King's dwellings and looked south across the garden and the bowling green towards Westminster.

There, mounted up high on a weatherbeaten stick, was a sort of irregular knot of stuff, barely visible as a gray speck in the moonlight: the head of Oliver Cromwell. When the King had come back, ten years ago, he'd ordered the corpse to be dug up from where Drake and the others had buried it, and the head cut off and mounted on a pike and never taken down. Ever since then

Cromwell had been looking down helplessly upon a scene of unbridled lewdness that was Whitehall Palace. And now Cromwell, who had once dandled Drake's youngest son on his knee, was looking down upon him.

Daniel tilted his head back and looked up at the stars and supposed that seen from Drake's perspective up in Heaven it must all look like Hell—and Daniel right in the middle of it.

BEING LOCKED UP in the Tower of London had changed Henry Oldenburg's priorities all around. Daniel had expected that the Secretary of the Royal Society would jump headfirst into the great sack of foreign mail that Daniel had brought him, but all he cared about was the new lute-strings. He'd grown too fat to move around very effectively and so Daniel fetched necessaries from various parts of the half-moon-shaped room: Oldenburg's lute, extra candles, a tuning-fork, some sheet-music, more wood on the fire. Oldenburg turned the lute over across his knees like a naughty boy for spanking, and tied a piece of gut or two around the instrument's neck to serve as frets (the old ones being worn through), then replaced a couple of broken strings. Half an hour of tuning ensued (the new strings kept stretching) and then, finally, Oldenburg got what he really ached for: he and Daniel, sitting face to face in the middle of the room, sang a two-part song, the parts cleverly written so that their voices occasionally joined in chords that resonated sweetly: the curving wall of the cell acting like the mirror of Newton's telescope to reflect the sound back to them. After a few verses, Daniel had his part memorized, and so when he sang the chorus he sat up straight and raised his chin and sang loudly at those walls, and read the graffiti cut into the stone by prisoners of centuries past. Not your vulgar Newgate Prison graffiti—most of it was in Latin, big and solemn as gravestones, and there were astrological diagrams and runic incantations graven by imprisoned sorcerers.

Then some ale to cool the wind-pipes, and a venison pie and a keg of oysters and some oranges contributed by the R.S., and Oldenburg did a quick sort of the mail—one pile containing the latest doings of the Hotel Montmor salon in Paris, a couple of letters from Huygens, a short manuscript from Spinoza, a large pile of ravings sent in by miscellaneous cranks, and a Leibniz-mound. "This damned German will never shut up!" Oldenburg grunted—which, since Oldenburg was himself a notoriously prolix German, was actually a jest at his own expense. "Let me see . . . Leibniz proposes to found a *Societas Eruditorum* that will gather in young Vagabonds and raise them up to be an army of Natural Philosophers to overawe the Jesuits . . . here are his thoughts on free will versus predestination . . . it would be great sport to get him in an argument with Spinoza . . . he asks me here whether I'm aware Comenius has died . . . says he's ready to pick up the faltering torch of Pansophism*. . . . here's a light, easy-to-read analysis of how the bad Latin used by Continental scholars leads to faulty thinking, and in turn to religious schism, war, bad philosophy . . ."

"Sounds like Wilkins."

"Wilkins! Yes! I've considered decorating these walls with some graffiti of my own, and writing it in the Universal Character . . . but it's too depressing. 'Look, we have invented a new Philosophickal Language so that when we are imprisoned by Kings we can scratch a higher form of graffiti on our cell walls.' "

"Perhaps it'll lead us to a world where Kings can't, or won't, imprison us at all—"

"Now you sound like Leibniz. Ah, here are some new mathematical proofs . . . nothing that hasn't been proved already, by Englishmen . . . but Leibniz's proofs are more elegant . . . here's something he has modestly entitled *Hypothesis Physica Nova*. Good thing I'm in the Tower, or I'd never have time to read all this."

Daniel made coffee over the fire—they drank it and smoked Virginia tobacco in clay-pipes. Then it was time for Oldenburg's evening constitutional. He preceded Daniel down a stack of stone pie-wedges that formed a spiral stair. "I'd hold the door and say 'after you,' but suppose I fell—you'd end up in the basement of Broad Arrow Tower crushed beneath me—and I'd be in the pink."

"Anything for the Royal Society," Daniel jested, marveling at how Oldenburg's bulk filled the helical tube of still air.

"Oh, you're more valuable to them than I am," Oldenburg said.

"Poh!"

"I am near the end of my usefulness. You are just beginning. They have great plans for you—"

"Until yesterday I wouldn't've believed you—then I was allowed to hear a conversation—perfectly incomprehensible to me—but it sounded frightfully important."

"Tell me about this conversation."

They came out onto the top of the old stone curtain-wall that joined Broad Arrow Tower to Salt Tower on the south. Arm in arm,

---

*Pansophism was a movement among Continental savants, in which the said Comenius had been an important figure; it had influenced Wilkins, Oldenburg, and others to found the Experimental Philosophical Club and later the Royal Society.

they strolled along the battlements. To the left they could look across the moat—an artificial oxbow-lake that communicated with the Thames—and a defensive glacis beyond that, then a few barracks and warehouses having to do with the Navy, and then the pasture-grounds of Wapping crooked in an elbow of the Thames, dim lights out at Ratcliff and Limehouse—then a blackness containing, among other things, Europe.

"The Dramatis Personae: John Wilkins, Lord Bishop of Chester, and Mr. Samuel Pepys Esquire, Admiral's Secretary, Treasurer of the Fleet, Clerk of Acts of the Navy Board, deputy Clerk of the Privy Seal, Member of the Fishery Corporation, Treasurer of the Tangier Committee, right-hand-man of the Earl of Sandwich, courtier . . . am I leaving anything out?"

"Fellow of the Royal Society."

"Oh, yes . . . thank you."

"What said they?"

"First a brief speculation about who was reading your mail . . ."

"I assume it's John Comstock. He spied for the King during the Interregnum, why can't he spy for the King now?"

"Rings true . . . this led to some double entendres about tender negotiations. Mr. Pepys volunteered—speaking of the King of England, here—'his feelings for *sa soeur* are most affectionate, he's writing many letters to her.' "

"Well, you know that Minette is in France—"

"Minette?"

"That is what King Charles calls Henrietta Anne, his sister," Oldenburg explained. "I don't recommend using that name in polite society—unless you want to move in with me."

"She's the one who's married to the Duc d'Orléans*—?"

"Yes, and Mr. Pepys's lapsing into French was of course a way of emphasizing this. Pray continue."

"My Lord Wilkins wondered whether she wrote back, and Pepys said Minette was spewing out letters like a *diplomat.*"

Oldenburg cringed, and shook his head in dismay. "Very crude work on Mr. Pepys's part. He was letting it be known that this exchange of letters was some sort of diplomatic negotiation. But he did not need to be so coarse with Wilkins . . . he must have been tired, distracted . . ."

"He'd been working late—lots of gold going into the Navy Treasury under cover of darkness."

---

*Philippe, duc d'Orléans, was the younger brother of King Louis XIV of France.

"I know it—behold!" Oldenburg said, and, tightening his arm, swung Daniel round so that both of them were looking west, across the Inmost Ward. They were near Salt Tower, which was the southeastern corner of the squarish Tower complex. The southern wall, therefore, stretched away from them, paralleling the river, connecting a row of squat round towers. Off to their right, planted in the center of the ward, was the ancient donjon: a freestanding building called the White Tower. A few low walls partitioned the ward into smaller quadrangles, but from this viewpoint the most conspicuous structure was the great western wall, built strong to resist attack from the always difficult City of London. On the far side of that wall, hidden from their view, a street ran up a narrow defile between it and a somewhat lower outer wall. Stout piles of smoke and steam were building from that street—which was lined with works for melting and working precious metals. It was called Mint Street. "Their infernal hammers keep me awake—the smoke of their furnaces comes in through the embrasures." Walls hereabouts tended to have narrow cross-shaped arrow-slits called embrasures, which was one of the reasons the Tower made a good prison, especially for fat men.

"So that's why kings live at Whitehall nowadays—to be upwind of the Mint?" Daniel said jestingly.

On Oldenburg's face, perfunctory amusement stamped out by pedantic annoyance. "You don't understand. The Mint's operations are extremely sporadic—it has been cold and silent for months—the workers idle and drunk."

"And now?"

"Now they are *busy* and drunk. A few days ago, as I stood in this very place, I saw a three-master, a man of war, heavily laden, drop anchor just around the river-bend, there. Small boats carrying heavy loads began to put in at the water-gate just there, in the middle of the south wall. On the same night, the Mint came suddenly to life, and has not slept since."

"And gold began to arrive at the Navy Treasury," Daniel said, "making much work for Mr. Pepys."

"Now, let us get back to this conversation you were allowed to hear. How did the Bishop of Chester respond to Mr. Pepys's rather ham-handed revelations?"

"He said something like, 'So Minette keeps his Majesty well acquainted with the doings of her beau?'"

"Now whom do you suppose he meant by that?"

"Her husband—? I know, I know—my naïveté is pathetic."

"Philippe, duc d'Orleans, owns the largest and finest collection of women's underwear in France—his sexual adventures are strictly limited to being fucked up the ass by strapping officers."

"Poor Minette!"

"She knew *perfectly well* when she married him," Oldenburg said, rolling his eyes. "She spent her honeymoon in bed with her new husband's elder brother: King Louis XIV. *That* is what Bishop Wilkins meant when he referred to Minette's *beau.*"

"I stand corrected."

"Pray go on."

"Pepys assured Wilkins that, considering the volume of correspondence, King Charles couldn't help but be very close to the man in question—an analogy was made to hoops of gold . . ."

"Which you took to mean, matrimonial bliss?"

"Even I knew what Pepys meant by *that,*" Daniel said hotly.

"So did Wilkins, I'm sure—how did he seem, then?"

"Ill at ease—he wanted reassurance that 'the two arch-Dissenters' were handling formal contacts."

"It is a secret—but generally known among the sort who rattle around London in private coaches in the night-time—that a treaty with France is being negotiated by the Earl of Shaftesbury, and His Majesty's old drinking and whoring comrade, the Duke of Buckingham. Chosen for the job not because they are skilled diplomats but because not even your late father would ever accuse them of Popish sympathies."

A Yeoman Warder was approaching, making his rounds. "Good evening, Mr. Oldenburg. Mr. Waterhouse."

"Evening, George. How's the gout?"

"Better today, thank you, sir—the cataplasm seemed to work—where did you get the receipt from?" George then went into a rote exchange of code-words with another Beefeater on the roof of Salt Tower, then reversed direction, bade them good evening, and strolled away.

Daniel enjoyed the view until he was certain that the only creature that could overhear them was a spaniel-sized raven perched on a nearby battlement.

Half a mile upstream, the river was combed, and nearly dammed up, by a line of sloppy, boat-shaped, man-made islands, supporting a series of short and none too ambitious stone arches. The arches were joined, one to the next, by a roadway, made of wood in some places and of stone in others, and the roadway was mostly covered with buildings that sprayed in every direction, cantilevered far out over the water and kept from falling into it by makeshift diagonal braces. Far upstream, and far downstream, the river was placid and sluggish, but where it was forced between those starlings (as the man-made islands were called), it was all furious. The starlings themselves, and the banks of the Thames for miles downstream, were littered with wreckage of light boats that had failed in the attempt to shoot the rapids beneath London Bridge, and (once a week or so) with the corpses and personal effects of their passengers.

A few parts of the bridge had been kept free of buildings so that fires could not jump the river. In one of those gaps a burly woman stopped to fling a jar into the angry water below. Daniel could not see it from here, but he knew it would be painted with a childish rendering of a face: this a charm to ward off witch-spells. The water-wheels constructed in some of those arch-ways made gnashing and clanking noises that forced Waterhouse and Oldenburg, half a mile away, to raise their voices slightly, and put their heads closer together. Daniel supposed this was no accident—he suspected they were coming to a part of the conversation that Oldenburg would rather keep private from those sharp-eared Beefeaters.

Directly behind London Bridge, but much farther away round the river-bend, were the lights of Whitehall Palace, and Daniel almost convinced himself that there was a greenish glow about the place tonight, as Enoch the Red schooled the King, and his court, and the most senior Fellows of the Royal Society, in the new Element called Phosphorus.

"Then Pepys got too enigmatic even for Wilkins," Daniel said. "He said, 'I refer you to Chapter Ten of your 1641 work.'"

"The *Cryptonomicon?*"

"So I assume. Chapter Ten is where Wilkins explains steganography, or how to embed a subliminal message in an innocuous-seeming letter—" but here Daniel stopped because Oldenburg had adopted a patently fake look of innocent curiosity. "I think you know this well enough. Now, Wilkins apologized for being thick-headed and asked whether Pepys was speaking, now, of *you.*"

"Ho, ho, ho!" Oldenburg bellowed, the laughter bouncing like cannon-fire off the hard walls of the Inmost Ward. The raven hopped closer to them and screeched, *"Caa, caa, caa!"* Both humans laughed, and Oldenburg fetched a bit of bread from his pocket and held it out to the bird. It hopped closer and reared back to peck it out of the fat pale hand—but Oldenburg snatched it back and said very distinctly, "Cryptonomicon."

The raven cocked its head, opened its beak, and made a long gagging noise. Oldenburg sighed and opened his hand. "I have been trying to teach him words," he explained, "but that one is too much of a mouthful, for a raven." The bird's beak struck the bread out of Oldenburg's hand, and it hopped back out of reach, in case Oldenburg should change his mind.

"Wilkins's confusion is understandable—but Pepys's meaning is clear. There are some suspicious-minded persons upriver" (waving in the general direction of Whitehall) "who think I'm a spy, communicating with Continental powers by means of subliminal messages embedded in what purport to be philosophickal discourses—it being beyond their comprehension that anyone would care as much as I seem to about new species of eels, methods for squaring hyperbolae, *et cetera*. But Pepys was not referring to *that*—he was being ever so much more clever. He was telling Wilkins that the not-very-secret negotiations being carried on by Buckingham and Shaftesbury are like the innocuous-seeming message, being used to conceal the *truly* secret agreement that the two Kings are drawing up, using Minette as the conduit."

"God in Heaven," Daniel said, and felt obliged to lean back against a battlement so that his spinning head wouldn't whirl him off into the moat.

"An agreement whose details we can only guess at—except for this: it causes gold to appear there in the middle of the night." Oldenburg pointed to the Tower's water-gate along the Thames. Discretion kept him from speaking its ancient name: Traitor's Gate.

"Pepys mentioned in passing that Thomas More Anglesey was responsible for filling the Navy's coffers . . . I didn't understand what he meant."

"Our Duke of Gunfleet has much warmer connections with France than anyone appreciates," Oldenburg said—but then refused to say any more.

> And because silver and gold have their value from
> the matter itself; they have first this privilege, that
> the value of them cannot be altered by the power of
> one, nor of a few commonwealths; as being a com-
> mon measure of the commodities of all places. But
> base money, may easily be enhanced, or abased.
> —HOBBES, *Leviathan*

OLDENBURG GENTEELLY KICKED him out not much later, eager to get into that pile of mail. Under the politely curious gaze of the Beefeaters and their semi-tame ravens, Daniel walked down Water Lane, on the southern verge of the Tower complex. He walked past a large rectangular tower planted in the outer wall, above the river, and realized too late that if he'd only turned his head and glanced to the left at that point, he could've looked through the giant arch of Traitor's Gate and out across the river. Too late now—seemed a poor idea to go back. Probably just as well he hadn't gawked—then whoever was watching him would suspect that Oldenburg had mentioned it.

Was he thinking like a courtier now?

The massive octagonal pile of Bell Tower was on his right. As he got past it he dared to look up a narrow buffer between two layers of curtain-walls no more than fifty feet apart. Half of that width was filled up by the Mint's indifferent low houses and workshops. Daniel glimpsed furnace-light radiating from windows, warming high stone walls, making silhouettes of a congestion of carts bringing coal to burn. Men with muskets gazed coolly back at him. Mint workers crossed from building to building in the shambling gait of the exhausted.

Then he was underneath the great arch of the Byward Tower, an elevated building thrown over Water Lane to control the Tower's land approach. A raven perched on a gargoyle and screeched "Cromwell!" at him as he passed through onto the drawbridge that ran from Byward Tower out to Middle Tower, over the moat. Middle Tower gave way to Lion Tower—but the King's menagerie were all asleep and he did not hear the lions roar. From there he crossed over a last little backwater of the moat, over *another* drawbridge, and came into a little walled-in yard called the Bulwark—finally, then, through one last gate and into the world, though he had a lonely stroll over an empty moonlit glacis, past a few scavenging rats and copulating dogs, before he was among buildings and people.

But then Daniel Waterhouse was right in the City of London— slightly confused, as some of the streets had been straightened and simplifed after the Fire. He pulled a fat gold egg from his pocket—one of Hooke's experimental watches, a failed stab at the Longitude Problem, adequate only for landlubbers. It told him that the Phosphorus Demo' was not quite finished at Whitehall, but that it was not too late to call on his in-laws. Daniel did not especially like to just *call* on people—seemed presumptuous to think they'd want to open the door and see *him*—but he knew that this was how men like Pepys got to become men like Pepys. So to the house of Ham.

Lights burned expensively, and a coach and pair dawdled out front. Daniel was startled to discover his own family coat of arms (a castle bestriding a river) painted on the door of this coach. The house was smoking like a heavy forge—it was equipped with over-sized chimneys, projecting tubes of orange light into their own smoke. As Daniel ascended the front steps he heard singing, which faltered but did not stop when he knocked: a very current melody making fun of the Dutch for being so bright, hard-working, and successful. Viscount Walbrook's* butler opened the door and rec-ognized Daniel as a social caller—not, as sometimes happened, a nocturnal customer brandishing a goldsmith's note.

Mayflower Ham, neé Waterhouse—tubby, fair, almost fifty, look-ing more like thirty—gave him a hug that pulled him up on tiptoe. Menopause had finally terminated her fantastically involved and complex relationship with her womb: a legendary saga of irregular bleeding, eleven-month pregnancies straight out of the Royal Soci-ety proceedings, terrifying primal omens, miscarriages, heart-breaking epochs of barrenness punctuated by phases of such explosive fertility that Uncle Thomas had been afraid to come near her—disturbing asymmetries, prolapses, relapses, and just plain lapses, hellish cramping fits, mysterious interactions with the Moon and other cœlestial phenomena, shocking imbalances of all four of the humours known to Medicine plus a few known only to Mayflower, seismic rumblings audible from adjoining rooms—can-cers reabsorbed—(incredibly) three successful pregnancies culmi-nating in four-day labors that snapped stout bedframes like kindling, vibrated pictures off walls, and sent queues of vicars, mid-wives, physicians, and family members down into their own beds, ruined with exhaustion. Mayflower had (fortunately for her!) been born with that ability, peculiar to certain women, of being able to talk about her womb in any company without it seeming inappro-priate, and not only that but you never knew where in a conversa-tion, or a letter, she would launch into it, plunging everyone into a clammy sweat as her descriptions and revelations forced them to consider topics so primal that they were beyond eschatology—even Drake had had to shut up about the Apocalypse when Mayflower had gotten rolling. Butlers fled and serving-maids fainted. The condition of Mayflower's womb affected the moods of England as the Moon ruled the tides.

"How, er . . . *are you?*" Daniel inquired, bracing himself, but she just smiled sweetly, made rote apologies about the house not being finished (but no fashionable house ever *was* finished), and led him

---

*Thomas Ham had been made Viscount Walbrook by the King.

to the Dining-Room, where Uncle Thomas was entertaining Sterling and Beatrice Waterhouse, and Sir Richard Apthorp and his wife. The Apthorps had a goldsmith's shop of their own, and lived a few doors up Threadneedle. The attire was not so aggressively fine, Daniel not so monstrously out of place, as at the coffee-house. Sterling greeted him warmly, as if saying, *Sorry old chap but the other day was business.*

They appeared to be celebrating something. Reference was made to all the work that lay ahead, so Daniel assumed it was some milestone in their grand shop-house-project. He wanted someone to ask him where he'd been, so that he could offhandedly let them know he'd been to the Tower waving around a warrant from the Secretary of State. But no one asked. After a while he realized that they probably would not care if they *did* know. The back door, fronting on Cornhill, kept creaking open, then booming shut. Finally, Daniel caught Uncle Thomas's eye, and, with a look, inquired what on earth was happening back there. A few minutes later, Viscount Walbrook got up, as if to use the House of Office, but tapped Daniel on the shoulder on his way out of the room.

Daniel rose and followed him down a hall—dark except for a convenient red glow at the far end. Daniel couldn't see around the tottering Punchinello silhouette of his host, but he could hear shovels crunching into piles of something, ringing as they flung their loads—obviously coal being fed to a furnace. But sometimes there was the icy trill of a coin falling and spinning on a hard floor.

The hall became sooty and extremely warm, and gave way to a brick-lined room where a laborer, stripped to a pair of drawers, was heaving coal into the open door of the House of Ham's forge—which had been hugely expanded when the house was reconstructed after the Fire. Another laborer was pumping bellows with his feet, climbing an endless ladder. In the old days, this forge had been a good size for baking tarts, which made sense for the sort of goldsmith who made earrings and teaspoons. Now it looked like something that could be used to cast cannon-barrels, and half the weight of the building was concentrated in the chimney.

Several black iron lock-boxes were open on the floor—some full of silver coins and others empty. One of the Hams' senior clerks sat on the floor by one of these in a pond of his own sweat, counting coins into a dish out loud: "Ninety-eight . . . ninety-nine . . . hundred!" whereupon he handed the dish up to Charles Ham (the youngest Ham brother—Thomas being the eldest), who emptied it onto the pan of a scale and weighed the coins against a brass cylinder—then raked them off into a bucket-sized crucible. This was repeated until the crucible was nearly full. Then a glowing door was opened—knives of blue flame probed out into the dark room—Charles Ham donned black gauntlets, heaved a gigantic pair of iron tongs off the floor, thrust them in, hugged, and backed away, drawing out another crucible: a cup shining daffodil-colored light. Turning around very carefully, he positioned the crucible (Daniel could've tracked it with his eyes closed, by feeling its warmth shine on his face) and tipped it. A stream of radiant liquid formed in its lip and arced down into a mold of clay. Other molds were scattered about the floor, wherever there was room, cooling down through shades of yellow, orange, red, and sullen brown, to black; but wherever light glanced off of them, it gleamed silver.

When the crucible was empty, Charles Ham set it down by the scales, then picked up the crucible that was full of silver coins and put it into the fire. Through all of this, the man on the floor never paused counting coins out of the lock-box, his reedy voice making a steady incantation out of the numbers, the coins going *chink, chink, chink.*

Daniel stepped forward, bent down, took a coin out of the lock-box, and angled it to shine fire-light into his eyes, like the little mirror in the center of Isaac's telescope. He was expecting to see a worn-out shilling with a blurred portrait of Queen Elizabeth on it, or an old piece of eight or thaler that the Hams had somehow picked up in a money-changing transaction. What he saw was in fact the profile of King Charles II, very new and crisp, stamped on a limpid pool of brilliant silver—perfect. Shining that way in fire-light, it brought back memories of a night in 1666. Daniel flung it back into the lock-box. Then, not believing his eyes, he thrust his hand in and pulled out a fistful. They were all the same. Their edges, fresh from Monsieur Blondeau's ingenious machine, were so sharp they almost cut his flesh, their mass blood-warm . . .

The heat was too much. He was out in the street with Uncle Thomas, bathing in cool air.

"They are *still warm!*" he exclaimed.

Uncle Thomas nodded.

"From the Mint?"

"Yes."

"You mean to tell me that the coins being stamped out at the Mint are, *the very same night,* melted down into *bullion* on Threadneedle Street?"

Daniel was noticing, now, that the chimney of Apthorp's shop, two doors up the street, was also smoking, and the same was true of diverse other goldsmiths up and down the length of Threadneedle.

Uncle Thomas raised his eyebrows piously.

"Where does it go *then*?" Daniel demanded.

"Only a Royal Society man would ask," said Sterling Waterhouse, who had slipped out to join them.

"What do you mean by that, brother?" Daniel asked.

Sterling was walking slowly towards him. Instead of stopping, he flung his arms out wide and collided with Daniel, embraced him and kissed him on the cheek. Not a trace of liquor on his breath. "No one knows where it goes—that is not the *point*. The point is *that it goes*—it moves—the movement ne'er stops—it is the blood in the veins of Commerce."

"But you must do something with the bullion—"

"We tender it to gentlemen who give us something in return" said Uncle Thomas. "It's like selling fish at Billingsgate—do the fishwives ask where the fish go?"

"It's generally known that silver percolates slowly eastwards, and stops in the Orient, in the vaults of the Great Mogul and the Emperor of China," Sterling said. "Along the way it might change hands hundreds of times. Does that answer your question?"

"I've already stopped believing I saw it," Daniel said, and went back into the house, his thin shoe-leather bending over irregular paving-stones, his dull dark clothing hanging about him coarsely, the iron banister cold under his hand—he was a mote bobbing in a mud-puddle and only wanted to be back in the midst of fire and heat and colored radiance.

He stood in the forge-room and watched the melting for a while. His favorite part was the sight of the liquid metal building behind the lip of the canted crucible, then breaking out and tracing an arc of light down through the darkness.

"Quicksilver is the elementary form of all things fusible; for all things fusible, when melted, are changed into it, and it mingles with them because it is of the same substance with them . . ."

"Who said that?" Sterling asked—keeping an eye on his little brother, who was showing signs of instability.

"Some damned Alchemist," Daniel answered. "I have given up hope, tonight, of ever understanding money."

"It's simple, really . . ."

"And yet it's not simple at all," Daniel said. "It follows simple rules—it obeys logic—and so Natural Philosophy should understand it, encompass it—and I, who know and understand more than almost anyone in the Royal Society, should comprehend it. But I don't. I never will . . . if money is a science, then it is a dark science, darker than Alchemy. It split away from Natural Philosophy millennia ago, and has gone on developing ever since, by its own rules . . ."

"Alchemists say that veins of minerals in the earth are twigs and offshoots of an immense Tree whose trunk is the center of the earth, and that metals rise like sap—" Sterling said, the firelight on his bemused face. Daniel was too tired at first to take the analogy— or perhaps he was underestimating Sterling. He assumed Sterling was prying for suggestions on where to look for gold mines. But later, as Sterling's coach was taking him off towards Charing Cross, he understood that Sterling had been telling him that the growth of money and commerce was—as far as Natural Philosophers were concerned—like the development of that mysterious subterranean Tree: suspected, sensed, sometimes exploited for profit, but, in the end, unknowable.

THE KING'S HEAD TAVERN was dark, but it was not closed. When Daniel entered he saw patches of glowing green light here and there—pooled on tabletops and smeared on walls—and heard Persons of Quality speaking in hushed voices punctuated by out-breaks of riotous giggling. But the glow faded, and then serving-wenches scurried out with rush-lights and re-lit all of the lamps, and finally Daniel could see Pepys and Wilkins and Comstock, and the Duke of Gunfleet, and Sir Christopher Wren, and Sir Winston Churchill, and—at the best table—the Earl of Upnor, dressed in what amounted to a three-dimensional Persian carpet, trimmed with fur and studded with globs of colored glass, or perhaps they were precious gems.

Upnor was explaining phosphorus to three gaunt women with black patches glued all over their faces and necks: "It is known, to students of the Art, that each metal is created when rays from a par-ticular planet strike and penetrate the Earth, *videlicet,* the Sun's rays create gold; the Moon's, silver; Mercury's, quicksilver; Venus's, cop-per; Mars's, iron; Jupiter's, tin; and Saturn's lead. Mr. Root's discov-ery of a new elemental substance suggests there may be another planet—presumably of a green color—beyond the orbit of Saturn."

Daniel edged toward a table where Churchill and Wren were talking past each other, staring ever so thoughtfully at nothing: "It faces to the east, and it's rather far north, isn't it? Perhaps His Majesty should name it New Edinburgh . . ."

"That would only give the Presbyterians ideas!" Churchill scoffed.

"It's not *that* far north," Pepys put in from another table. "Boston is farther north by one and a half degrees of latitude."

"We can't go wrong suggesting that he name it after himself . . ."

"Charlestown? That name is already in use—Boston again."

"His brother then? But Jamestown was used in Virginia."

"What are you talking about?" Daniel inquired.

"New Amsterdam! His Majesty is acquiring it in exchange for Surinam," Churchill said.

"Speak up, Sir Winston, there may be some Vagabonds out in Dorset who didn't hear you!" Pepys roared.

"His Majesty has asked the Royal Society to suggest a new name for it," Churchill added, sotto voce.

"Hmmm . . . his brother sort of conquered the place, didn't he?" Daniel asked. He knew the answer, but couldn't presume to lecture men such as these.

"Yes," Pepys said learnedly, " 'twas all part of York's *Atlantic* campaign—*first* he took several Guinea ports, rich in gold, and richer in slaves, from the Dutchmen, and then it was straight down the trade winds to his next prize—New Amsterdam."

Daniel made a small bow toward Pepys, then continued: "If you can't use his Christian name of James, perhaps you can use his *title* . . . after all, York is a city up to the north on *our* eastern coast—and yet not *too* far north . . ."

"We have already considered that," Pepys said glumly. "There's a Yorktown in Virginia."

"What about 'New York'?" Daniel asked.

"Clever . . . but too obviously derivative of 'New Amsterdam,' " Churchill said.

"If we call it 'New York,' we're naming it after the *city* of York . . . the point is to name it after the *Duke* of York," Pepys scoffed.

Daniel said, "You are correct, of course—"

"Oh, come now!" Wilkins barked, slapping a table with the flat of his hand, splashing beer and phosphorus all directions. "Don't be pedantic, Mr. Pepys. Everyone will understand what it means."

"Everyone who is clever enough to matter, anyway," Wren put in.

"Err . . . I see, you are proposing a more *subtile* approach," Sir Winston Churchill muttered.

"Let's put it on the list!" Wilkins suggested. "It can't hurt to include as many 'York' and 'James' names as we can possibly think up."

"Hear, hear!" Churchill harrumphed—or possibly he was just clearing his throat—or summoning a barmaid.

"As you wish—never mind," Daniel said. "I take it that Mr. Root's Demonstration was well received—?"

For some reason this caused eyes to swivel, ever so briefly, toward the Earl of Upnor. "It went well," Pepys said, drawing closer to Daniel, "until Mr. Root threatened to spank the Earl. Don't look at him, don't look at him," Pepys continued levelly, taking Daniel's arm and turning him away from the Earl. The timing was unfortunate, because Daniel was certain he had just overhead Upnor mentioning Isaac Newton by name, and wanted to eavesdrop.

Pepys led him past Wilkins, who was good-naturedly spanking a barmaid. The publican rang a bell and everyone blew out the lights—the tavern went dark except for the freshly invigorated phosphorus. Everyone said "Woo!" and Pepys wrangled Daniel out into the street. "You know that Mr. Root makes the stuff from urine?"

"So it is rumored," Daniel said. "Mr. Newton knows more of the Art than I do—he has told me that Enoch the Red was following an ancient recipe to extract the Philosophic Mercury from urine, but happened upon phosphorus instead."

"Yes, and he has an entire tale that he tells, of how he found the recipe in Babylonia." Pepys rolled his eyes. "Enthralled the courtiers. Anyway—for this evening's Demo', he'd collected urine from a sewer that drains Whitehall, and boiled it—*endlessly*—on a barge in the Thames. I'll spare you the rest of the details—suffice it to say that when it was finished, and they were done applauding, and all of the courtiers were groping for a way to liken the King's splendor and radiance to that of Phosphorus—"

"Oh, yes, I suppose that would've been obligatory—?"

Wilkins banged out the tavern door, apparently just to *watch* the story being related to Daniel.

"The Earl of Upnor made some comment to the effect that some kingly essence—a royal humour—must suffuse the King's body, and be excreted in his urine, to account for all of this. And when all of the other courtiers were finished agreeing, and marveling at the Earl's *philosophick* acumen, Enoch the Red said, 'In truth, most of this urine came from the Horse Guards—and their horses.'"

"Whereat, the Earl was on his feet! His hand reaching for his sword—to defend His Majesty's honor, of course," Wilkins said.

"What was His Majesty's state of mind?" Daniel asked.

Wilkins made his hands into scale-pans and bobbled them up and down. "Then Mr. Pepys tipped the scales. He related an anecdote from the Restoration, in 1660, when he had been on the boat with the King, and certain members of his household—including the Earl of Upnor, then no more than twelve years old. Also aboard was the King's favorite old dog. The dog shit in the boat. The young Earl kicked at the dog, and made to throw it overboard—but was stayed by the King, who laughed at it, and said, 'You see, in some ways, at least, Kings are like other men!'"

"Did he really say such a thing!?" Daniel exclaimed, and instantly felt like an idiot—

"Of *course* not!" Pepys said, "I merely told the story that way because I thought it would be useful—"

"And was it?"

"The King laughed," Pepys said with finality.

"And Enoch Root inquired, whether it had then been necessary to give the Earl a spanking, to teach him respect for his elders."

"Elders?"

"The dog was older than the Earl—come on, pay attention!" Pepys said, giving Daniel a tremendous frown.

"Strikes me as an unwise thing to have said," Daniel muttered.

"The King said, 'No, no, Upnor has always been a civil fellow,' or some such, and so there was no duel."

"Still, Upnor strikes me as a grudge-holder—"

"Enoch has sent better men than Upnor to Hell—don't trouble yourself about *his* future," Wilkins said. "You need to tend to your own faults, young fellow—excessive sobriety, e.g. . . ."

"A tendency to fret—" Pepys put in.

"Undue chastity—let's back to the tavern!"

HE WOKE UP SOMETIME THE next day on a hired coach bound for Cambridge—sharing a confined space with Isaac Newton, and a load of gear that Isaac had bought in London: a six-volume set of *Theatrum Chemicum,** numerous small crates stuffed with straw, the long snouts of retorts poking out—canisters of stuff that smelled odd. Isaac was saying, "If you throw up again, please aim for this bowl—I'm collecting bile."

Daniel was able to satisfy him there.

"Where Enoch the Red failed, you're going to succeed—?"

"I beg your pardon?"

"Going after the Philosophic Mercury, Isaac?"

"What else is there to do?"

"The R.S. adores your telescope," Daniel said. "Oldenburg wants you to write more on the subject."

"Mmm," Isaac said, lost in thought, comparing passages in three different books to one another. "Could you hold this for a moment, please?" Which was how Daniel came to be a human book-rest for Isaac. Not that he was in any condition to accomplish greater things. In his lap for the next hour was a tome: folio-sized, four inches thick, bound in gold and silver, obviously made centuries

---

*A vast, turgid, incoherent compendium of alchemical lore.

before Gutenberg. Daniel was going to blurt, *This must have been fantastically expensive,* but on closer investigation found a book-plate pasted into it, bearing the arms of Upnor, and a note from the Earl:

Mr. Newton—
May this volume become as treasured by you, as the memory of our fortuitous meeting is to me—

UPNOR.

Aboard Minerva, *Cape Cod Bay, Massachusetts*
NOVEMBER 1713

WHEN THEY'VE MADE it out of Plymouth and into Cape Cod Bay, van Hoek returns to his cabin and becomes Captain once more. He looks rather put out to find the place so discomposed. Perhaps this is a sign of Daniel's being a bitter old Atheistical crank, but he nearly laughs out loud. *Minerva*'s a collection of splinters loosely pulled together by nails, pegs, lashings, and oakum, not even large enough to count as a mote in the eye of the world—more like one of those microscopic eggs that Hooke discovered with his microscope. She floats only because boys mind her pumps all the time, she remains upright and intact only because highly intelligent men never stop watching the sky and seas around her. Every line and sail decays with visible speed, like snow in sunlight, and men must work ceaselessly worming, parceling, serving, tarring, and splicing her infinite network of hempen lines in order to prevent her from falling apart in mid-ocean with what Daniel imagines would be explosive suddenness. Like a snake changing skins, she sloughs away what is worn and broken and replaces it from inner reserves—evoluting as she goes. The only way to sustain this perpetual and necessary evolution is to replenish the stocks that dwindle from her holds as relentlessly as sea-water leaks in. The only way to do *that* is to trade goods from one port to another, making a bit of money on each leg of the perpetual voyage. Each day assails her with hurricanes and pirate-fleets. To go out on the sea and find a *Minerva* is like finding, in the desert, a Great Pyramid blanced upside-down on its tip. She's a baby in a basket—a book in a bonfire. And yet van Hoek has the temerity to appoint his cabin as if it were a gentleman's drawing-room, with delicate weather-glasses, clocks, optickal devices, a decent library, a painting or two, an enamel cabinet stocked with Chinese crockery, a respectable stock of brandy and port. He's got *mirrors* in here, for Christ's sake. Not only that, but when he enters to discover a bit of broken glass on the deck, and small impact-craters here and there, he becomes so outraged that Dappa doesn't need to tell Daniel they'd best leave him alone for a while.

"So the curtain has come down on your performance. Now, a man in your position *might* feel like a barnacle—unable to leave the ship—an annoyance to mariners—but on *Minerva* there is a job for everyone," says Dappa, leading him down the midships staircase to the gundeck.

Daniel's not paying attention. A momentous rearrangement has taken place since Daniel was last here. All of the obstructions that formerly cluttered the space have been moved elsewhere or thrown overboard to create rights-of-way for the cannons. These had been lashed up against the inside of the hull, but now they've been swung round ninety degrees and each aimed at its gunport. As they are maneuvering on Cape Cod Bay, miles from the nearest Foe, those gunports are all closed for now. But like stage-hands laboring in the back of a theatre, the seamen are hard at work with diverse arcane tools, viz. lin-stocks, quoins, gunner's picks, and worming-irons. One man's got what looks like a large magnifying-glass, except without the glass—it's an empty circle of iron on a handle. He sits astride a crate of cannonballs, heaving them out one at a time and passing them through the ring to gauge them, sorting them into other crates. Others whittle and file round blocks of wood, called sabots, and strap cannonballs to them. But anyone carrying a steel blade is distinctly unwelcome near the powder-barrels, because steel makes sparks.

One sailor, an Irishman, is talking to one of the Plymouth whaleboat pirates captured this morning. A cannon is between the two men, and when a cannon is between two men, that is what they talk about. "This is Wapping Wendy, or W.W., or dub-dub as we sometimes dub her in the heat of battle, though you may call her 'darling' or 'love of my life' but never 'Wayward Wendy' as *that* lot—" glowering at the crew of another gun, "Mr. Foote," "—like to defame her."

"Is she? Wayward?"

"She's like any other lass, you must get to know her, and then what might seem inconstant is clearly revealed as a kind of consistency—faithfulness even. And so the first thing you must know about our darling girl is that her bore tends up and to larboard of her centerline. And she's a tight one, is our virginal Wendy, which is why we on the dub-dub crew must keep a sharp eye for undersized balls and husband 'em carefully . . ."

Someone on the crew of "Manila Surprise" nudges that gun's port open for a moment, and sun shines in. But Manila Surprise is on the larboard side of the ship. "We are sailing southwards!?" Daniel exclaims.

"No better way to run before a north wind," Dappa says.

"But in that direction, Cape Cod is only a few miles away! What sort of an escape route is that?"

"As you have reckoned, we shall have to work to windwards *eventually* in order to escape from Cape Cod Bay," Dappa says agreeably. "When we do, Teach's fleet will be tacking along with us. But his ships are fore-and-aft rigged and can sail closer to the wind, and make better headway, than our dear *Minerva,* a square-rigger. Advantage Teach."

"Shouldn't we head north while we can, then?"

"He would catch us in a matter of minutes—his entire fleet together, working in concert. We want to fight Teach's ships one at a time if we can. So southwards it is, for now. Running before the wind in full sail, we are faster than they. So Teach knows that if he pursues us to the south we may lose him. But he also knows that we must wheel about and work northwards before long—so he will spread out a sort of picket-line and wait for us."

"But will Teach not anticipate all of this, and take pains to keep his fleet together?"

"In a well-disciplined fleet, pursuing Victory, that's how it would go. But that is a pirate-fleet, in pursuit of plunder, and by the rules and account-books of piracy, the lion's share goes to the ship that takes the prize."

"Ah—so the captain of each ship has incentive to split away and attack us individually."

"Just so, Dr. Waterhouse."

"But would it not be foolhardy for a little sloop to engage a ship with all—this?" Daniel gestures down the length of the gundeck— a bustling bazaar where cannonballs, sabots, and powder-kegs, lies, promises, and witticisms are being exchanged lustily.

"Not if the ship is undermanned, and the captain a senile poltroon. Now, if you'll just follow me down into the hold—don't worry, I'll get this lantern lit, soon as we are away from the gunpowder—there, that's it. She's a tidy ship, wouldn't you agree?"

"Beg pardon? Tidy? Yes, I suppose, as ships go . . ." says Dr. Waterhouse, finding Dappa, sometimes, too subtle—an excess of quicksilver in the constitution.

"Thank you, sir. But 'tis a disadvantage, when we have to fight with blunderbusses. The virtue of a blunderbuss, as you may know, is to make a weapon out of whatever nails, pebbles, splinters, and fragments might be lying about—but here on *Minerva* we make a practice of sweeping that matter up, and throwing it overboard, several times daily. At times like this we *do* regret that we neglected to hoard it."

"I know more than you imagine of blunderbusses. What do you want me to do?"

"In a little while, one of the men'll be teaching you how to fuze mortar-bombs—but we're not quite ready for that just yet—now I would ask you to go down into the hold and—"

Dr. Waterhouse doesn't believe, until he's down there, what Dappa tells him next. He hasn't seen the hold yet, and reckons it'll be like the shambolic Repository at the Royal Society—but no. The great casks and bales are stacked, and lashed in place, with admirable neatness, and there is even a Diagram tacked to the staircase bulkhead in which the location of each object is specified, and notes made as to what's stored there and when it was done. Underneath, under a subheading labelled BILGE, van Hoek himself has scratched "out-moded china—keep handy."

Dappa has pulled two sailors away from what they've been doing the last half-hour: standing by a gunport carrying on a learned discourse about an approaching pirate-sloop. The sailors considered this to be time well spent, but Dappa felt otherwise. These two spend a minute consulting the Diagram, and Daniel realizes with moderate astonishment that they both know how to read, and interpret figures. They agree that the out-moded china is to be found forward, and so that's where they go—to the most beautiful part of the ship, where many ribs radiate from the up-curving keel, forming an upside-down vault, so it's like being a fly exploring the ceiling of a cathedral. The sailors move a few crates out of the way—they never stop talking, each trying to outdo the other in bloodcurdling yarns about the cruelty of certain infamous pirates. They pull up a hatch that gives access to the bilge, and in no time at all two crates of markedly ugly china have been fetched out.

The crates themselves are handsome productions of clear-grained red cedar, chosen because it won't rot in the wet bilge. Into them the china has been thrown with no packing material between items, so part of Daniel's work is already done. He thanks the two sailors and they look back at him queerly, then return abovedecks. Daniel spreads an old hammock—two yards of sailcloth—on the planking, tips a crate over, and then attacks its spilled contents with a maul.

What is the optimal size (he wonders) of a shard of pottery for firing out of a blunderbuss? When the King's guards shot him before his father's house during the Fire, he was knocked down, bruised, cut, but not really *penetrated*. Probably the larger the better, which makes his job easier—one would like to see great sharp triangles of gaudily-painted porcelain spinning through the air, plunging into pirate-flesh, severing major vessels. But too large and it won't pack into the barrels. He decides to aim for a mean diameter of half an inch, and mauls the plates accordingly, sweeping chunks that are the right size off into small canvas bags, raking bigger ones toward him for more punishment. It is satisfying, and after a while he finds himself singing an old song: the same one he sang with Oldenburg in Broad Arrow Tower. He keeps time with his hammer, and draws out those notes that make the cargo-hold resonate. All round him, water seeps through the cracks between *Minerva*'s hull-planks (for he is well below the water-line) and trickles down merrily into the bilge, and the four-man pumps take it away with a steady suck-and-hiss that's like the systole and diastole of a beating heart.

Gresham's College, Bishopsgate, London
1672

The Inquisitive Jesuit RICCIOLI has taken great pains by 77 Arguments to overthrow the Copernican Hypothesis. . . . I believe this one Discovery will answer them, and 77 more, if so many can be thought of and produced against it.

—ROBERT HOOKE

DANIEL SPENT A GOOD PART of two months on the roof of Gresham's College, working on a hole—making, not mending, one. Hooke could not do it because his vertigo had been acting up, and if it struck while he was on top of the College, he would plunge to the ground like a wormy apple from a tree, his Last Experiment a study into the mysterious power of Gravitation.

For a man who claimed to hate the appearance of sharp things when viewed under a microscope, Hooke spent a great deal of time honing jabs at Inquisitive Jesuits. While Daniel was up on the roof making the hole, and a rain-hatch to cover it, Hooke was safe at ground level, running up and down a gallery. Strapped into his groin was a narrow hard saddle, and projecting from the saddle a strut with a wheel on the end, geared to a clock-work dial: a pedometer of his own design, which enabled him to calculate how much distance he had covered going *nowhere*. The purpose—as he explained to Daniel and diverse other aghast Fellows of the R.S.— was not to get from point A to point B, but to sweat. In some way, sweating would purge his body of whatever caused his headaches, nausea, and vertigo. From time to time, he would stop and refresh himself by drinking a glass of elemental mercury. He had set up a table at one end of the gallery where he stockpiled that and several of Mons. LeFebure's fashionable medicines. There were various sorts of quills, too. Some of them he used to tickle the back of his throat and induce vomiting, others he sharpened, dipped in ink, and used to note down data from his pedometer, or to vent his spleen at Jesuits who refused to admit that the Earth revolved around the Sun, or to sketch out plans for Bedlam, or to write diatribes against Oldenburg, or simply to transact the routine business of the City Surveyor.

The Inquisitive Jesuit Riccioli had pointed out that *if* the heavens were sown with stars, some near and some far, and *if* the Earth were looping round the Sun in a vast ellipse, then the positions of those stars with respect to one another should shift during the course of the year, as trees in a forest changed their relative positions in the eyes of a traveler moving past. But no such parallax had been observed, which proved (to Riccioli, anyway) that the Earth must be fixed in the center of the Universe. To Hooke it only proved that good enough telescopes hadn't been built, nor precise enough measurements made. To obtain the level of magnification he needed, he had to construct a telescope 32 feet long. To annull the light-bending effects of the Earth's atmosphere (which were obvious from the fact that the Sun became an oval when it rose or set), he had to aim it straight up—hence the demand for a vertical shaft to be bored through Gresham's College. Gresham's antique mansion was now like an ancient plaster wall that had been mended so many times it consisted entirely of interlocked patches. It was solid scar tissue. This made the work more interesting for Daniel, and taught him more than he'd ever cared to know about how buildings were put up, and what kept them from falling down.

The goal was to gaze straight *up* into Heaven, and count the miles to the nearest stars. But as Daniel did most of the work during the daytime, he spent most of his idle moments looking *down* into London—six years since the Fire now—but its reconstruction really just getting underway.

Formerly Gresham's College had huddled among buildings of about the same height, but the Fire had burnt almost to its front door, and so now it loomed like a manor house over a devastated fiefdom. If Daniel stood on the ridge of the roof, facing south toward London Bridge half a mile away, everything in his field of view bore marks of heat and smoke. Suppose the city were a giant Hooke-watch, with Gresham's College the central axle-tree, and London Bridge marking twelve o'clock. Then Bedlam was directly behind Daniel at six o'clock. The Tower of London was at about ten o'clock. The easterly wind, and its glacis, had preserved it from the flames. The wedge from the Tower to the Bridge was a tangle of old streets with charred spikes of old church-steeples jutting up here and there, like surveyor's stakes—literally. This to the chagrin of Hooke, who'd presented the City with a plan to rationalize the streets, only to be frustrated by a few such impediments that had survived the flames; for those who opposed his plans used the carbonized steeples as landmarks to shew where streets had once been, and ought to be remade, be they never so narrow and tortuous. The negative space between construction-sites defined new streets now, only a little wider and straighter than the old. Right in the center of this wedge was the place where the Fire had started— an empty moon-crater cordoned off so that Hooke and Wren could build a monument there.

Directly before Daniel, in the wedge from about noon to one o'clock, was the old goldsmiths' district of Threadneedle and Cornhill streets, which converged at the site of the Royal Exchange—all so close that Daniel could hear the eternal flame of buying and selling in the courtyard of the 'Change, fueled by the latest data from abroad, and he could look into the windows of Thomas Ham's house and see Mayflower (like a matron) plumping pillows and (like a schoolgirl) playing leapfrog with William Ham, her youngest child, her dear heart.

The west-bound street formed by the confluence of Threadneedle and Cornhill became Cheapside, which Hooke had insisted on
making much wider than it had been before—eliciting screams of
agony and near-apocalyptic rantings from many—attacks that
Hooke, who cared less than anyone what people thought of him,
was uniquely qualified to ignore. It ran straight as Hooke could
make it to the once and future St. Paul's, now a moraine of blackened stones, congealed roofing-lead, and plague-victims' jumbled
bones. Wren was still working on plans and models for the new
one. The streets limning St. Paul's Churchyard were lined with
printers' shops, including the ones that produced most Royal Society publications, so the trip up and down Cheapside had become
familiar to Daniel, as he went there to fetch copies of Hooke's
Micrographia or inspect the proofs for Wilkins's *Universal Character.*

Raising his sights a notch and gazing over the scab of St. Paul's
(which stood at about two o'clock), he could see Bridewell on the
far side of it—a former Royal palace, now tumbledown, where
whores, actresses, and Vagabond-wenches picked oakum, pounded
hemp, and carried out diverse other character-building chores,
until they had become reformed. That marked the place where the
Fleet River—which was simply a ditch full of shit—intersected the
Thames. Which explained why the Royals had moved out of
Bridewell and ceded it to the poor. The fire had jumped the ditch
easily, and kept eating through the city until a shortage of fuel, and
the King's and Lord Mayor's heroic house-bombing campaign, had
finally drawn a lasso around it. So whenever he did this Daniel
inevitably had to trace the dividing-line between burnt and unburnt
parts of the city from the River up across Fleet Street as far as Holborn (three o'clock). Out back of the place where his father had
been blown up six years ago, a quadrangle had been laid out, lined
with houses and shops, and filled with gardens, fountains, and statues. Others just like it were going up all around, and starting to
crowd in around the edges of those few great Houses along Piccadilly, such as Comstock House. But those developments, and the
great successes they had brought to Sterling and Raleigh, were old
news to Daniel, and didn't command his attention as much as certain strange new undertakings around the edges of the city.

If he turned and looked north over the bones of the old Roman
wall he could look right into Bedlam less than a quarter of a mile
away. It had not been burnt, but the city had hired Hooke to tear it
down and rebuild it anyway, as long as they were rebuilding everything else. The joke being that London and Bedlam seemed to
have exchanged places: for Bedlam had been emptied out and

torn down in preparation for its reconstruction, and was a serene rock-garden now, whereas all of London (save a few special plots such as the Monument site and St. Paul's) was in the throes of building—stones and bricks and timbers moving through the city on streets so congested that watching them fill up in the morning was like watching sausage casings being stuffed with meat. Wrecked buildings being torn down, cellars being dug, mortar being mixed, paving-stones being flung off carts, bricks and stones being chiselled to fit, iron wheel-rims grinding over cobbles—all of it made noise that merged together into a mad grind, like a Titan chewing up a butte.

So: strange enough. But beyond Bedlam, to the north and northeast, and sweeping round beyond the Tower along the eastern skirts of the city, were several artillery-grounds and army camps. These had been busy of late, because of the Anglo-Dutch War. *Not* the same Anglo-Dutch war that Isaac had listened to from his orchard in Woolsthorpe six years ago, for that had concluded in 1667. This was a wholly new and different Anglo-Dutch War, the third in as many decades. This time around, though, the English had finally gotten it right: they were allied with the French. Ignoring all considerations of what was really in the best interests of England, and setting aside all questions of moral rightness (and the current King was rarely troubled and little hindered by either), this seemed like a much better plan than fighting *against* France. Plenty of French gold had entered the country to bring Parliament around to Louis XIV's side, and to pay for a lot of ships to be built. France had an immense army and needed little help from England on land; what Louis had bought, and paid for several times over, was the Royal Navy, and its guns, and its gunpowder.

It was difficult, therefore, for Daniel to make any sense of the project underway northeast of London. Over several weeks Daniel watched a flat parade-ground develop pits and wrinkles, which slowly grew to ditches and mounds, and shaped and resolved themselves (as if he were adjusting the focus of a prospective glass) into sharp neat earthworks. Daniel had never seen such things because, until now, they had not been built in England, but from books and siege-paintings he knew them as ramparts, a bastion, ravelins, and a demilune work. But if this were a preparation for Dutch invasion, it was poorly thought out, because these works stood in isolation, protecting nothing save a pasture with a few dozen befuddled, but extremely well-defended, cows. Nevertheless, guns were mustered out from the Ordnance storehouses in the Tower, and hauled up onto the ramparts by teams of straining oxen—hernias with legs. The cracks of the teamsters' whips and the snorts and bellows of the beasts were carried for miles on a sea breeze all the way across Houndsditch and over the Wall and up the pitched roof of Gresham's College into Daniel's ears. Daniel for his part only stared in amaze.

Nearer the river, in the flat country beyond the Tower, Naval works took over from Military ones: shipyards messy with blond timber from Scotland or Massachusetts, splattered planks drawing themselves up into the curved hulls of ships, dead firs resurrected as masts. Colossal plumes of black smoke spreading downwind, pointing to Comstock-forges where tons of iron were being melted down and poured into subterranean cannon-molds, and windmill-blades rolling on the horizon, turning the gear-trains of mighty Comstock-machines that bored holes down the centers of those cannons.

Which brought Daniel's gaze back to the Tower, where he'd started: the central mystery, where treasure-ships from (as everyone in London now knew) France brought in the gold to be minted into the guineas that paid for all of those ships and cannons, and for the services of England in its new role as a sort of naval auxiliary to France.

ONE DAY, HEARING CHURCH-BELLS RING two o'clock, Daniel descended the ladder through the telescope-shaft. Hooke had gone out to inspect some new pavement, leaving behind nothing but a faint metallic scent of vomit. Daniel walked directly across the street, dodging uncouth traffic of heavy carts. He climbed into Samuel Pepys's carriage and made himself comfortable. Several minutes passed. Daniel looked at passers-by out the window. A hundred yards south, the streets would be a-bustle with brokers of East India stocks and goldsmiths' notes, but this place, tucked up against London wall, was a queer eddy, or backwater, and Daniel observed a jumble of Navy men, Dissident preachers, Royal Society hangers-on, foreigners, and Vagabonds, stirring and shuffling about one another in no steady pattern. It was an inscrutable Gordian knot suddenly cleft by one Chase Scene: a scruffy barefoot boy came bolting up Broad Street, pursued by a bailiff with a cudgel. Glimpsing a side street that ran off to the left, between the Navy Treasury and the Dutch Church, the boy skidded round the corner—paused—considered matters—and freed himself of a burden by heaving a pale brick into the air. It sheared apart, the wind caught it, and it puffed into a cloud of fluttering rectangles, whirling mysteriously round their long axes. By the time Daniel or anyone else thought to look for him, the boy was gone. The bailiff shifted to a straddling gait, as if riding an invisible pony, and began trying to step on all of the libels at once, gathering them in his arms, stuffing them into his pockets. Several members of the Watch stormed up and exchanged monosyllabic gasping noises with the bailiff. They all turned and glared at the façade of the Dutch Church, then went back to rounding up handbills.

Samuel Pepys was preceded by his cologne and his wig, and pursued by a minion embracing a sheaf of giant rolled documents. "I thought it well played, on the boy's part," he said, climbing into the coach and handing Daniel one of the libels.

"An old trick of the trade," Daniel said.

Pepys looked delighted. "Drake put *you* out on the streets?"

"Of course . . . 'twas the common rite of passage for all Waterhouse boys."

The handbill was a cartoon depicting King Louis XIV of France with his breeches piled up round his ankles and hairy buttocks thrust out, shitting an immense turd into the mouth of an English sailor.

"Let's take it to Wilkins! It'll cheer him up enormously," Pepys suggested, and pounded on the ceiling. The coachman drove the horses forward. Daniel made his body go limp so that he would not accrue lacerations from the continual battering onslaughts of the vehicle's benches and bulkheads.

"Did you bring it?"

"I always have it with me," Pepys said, producing an irregular nodule about the size of a tennis ball, "as you have all *your* parts."

"To remind you of your own mortality?"

"Once a man's been cut for the stone, 'tis hardly *necessary*."

"Why, then?"

"It is my conversation-starter of last resort. It gets *anyone* talking: Germans, Puritans, Red Indians . . ." He handed the object to Daniel. It was heavy. Heavy as a stone.

"I cannot believe this came out of your bladder," Daniel said.

"You see? Never fails!" Pepys answered.

But Daniel got no further response from Pepys, who'd already unrolled one of the large documents, creating a screen that divided the carriage in half. Daniel had assumed that they were all diagrams of men-of-war. But when they turned west on Cheapside the sun came in the carriage window and shone through the paper, revealing a grid of numbers. Pepys muttered things to his assistant, who jotted them down. Daniel was left to rotate the bladder-stone in his hand and gaze out at London, so different when seen at street-level. Passing through St. Paul's Churchyard, they saw the whole contents of a printer's shop turned out into the street—several bailiffs, and one of Sir Roger L'Estrange's lieutenants, pawing through stacks of unbound sheets, and holding wood-blocks up to mirrors.

Within a few minutes, anyway, they were at Wilkins's house. Pepys left his assistant and his papers below in the carriage and pounded up stairs holding the bladder-stone in his hand like a questing knight brandishing a fragment of the Cross.

He shook it in Wilkins's face. Wilkins only laughed. But it was good that he did, because his room was otherwise a horror—his dark breeches couldn't conceal that he had been pissing blood, sometimes sooner than he could get to the chamber-pot. He was both wizened and bloated at the same time, if that were possible, and the smell that came out of his flesh seemed to suggest his kidneys weren't keeping up their end of the bargain.

While Pepys exhorted the Bishop of Chester to allow himself to be cut for the stone, Daniel looked about, and was dispirited but not surprised to see several empty bottles from the apothecary shop of Monsieur LeFebure. He gave one a sniff. It was *Elixir Proprietalis LeFebure*—the same stuff Hooke swallowed when headaches had brought him to the brink of suicide—the fruits of LeFebure's researches into certain remarkable properties of the poppy family. It was hugely popular at Court, even among those not afflicted with headaches or the Stone. But when Daniel saw Wilkins go into a bladder spasm—reducing the Lord Bishop of Chester, and Founder of the Royal Society, to a dumb animal for several minutes, convulsing and howling—he decided perhaps Monsieur LeFebure was not such a sinister fellow after all.

When it was over, and Wilkins was Wilkins again, Daniel showed him the handbill, and mentioned L'Estrange's raid on the printing-shop.

"The same men doing the same things as ten years ago," Wilkins pronounced.

From that—*the same men*—Daniel knew that the originator of the handbills, and ultimate target of L'Estrange's raids, must be Knott Bolstrood.

"And that is why I cannot stop what I am doing to be cut for the Stone," Wilkins said.

DANIEL ERECTED A BLOCK AND TACKLE above the Gresham shaft, Hooke put the rebuilding of London on hold for a day, and they put the long telescope into place, Hooke cringing and screaming every time it was bumped, as if the instrument were an extension of his own eyeball.

Meanwhile Daniel could never keep his attention fixed on the heavens, for the warm mutterings and nudgings of London would not leave him alone—notes slipped under his door, raised eyebrows in coffee-shops, odd things witnessed in the street all captured his attention more than they should've. Outside the city, scaffolding rose up from the glacis of those mysterious fortifications, and long benches began to shingle it.

Then, one afternoon, Daniel and all London's Persons of Quality and most of her pickpockets were there, sitting on those benches or milling about in the fields. The Duke of Monmouth rode out, in a Cavalier outfit whose magnificence was such as to refute and demolish every sermon ever preached by a Calvinist—because if those sermons were true, Monmouth ought to be struck dead on the spot by a jealous God. John Churchill—possibly the only man in England handsomer than Monmouth—therefore wore slightly less thrilling clothes. The King of France could not attend this event, as he was so busy conquering the Dutch Republic just now, but a strapping actor pranced out in his stead, dressed in royal ermine, and took up a throne on an artificial hillock, and occupied himself with suitable bits of stage-business, viz. peering at events through a glass; pointing things out to diverse jewelled mistresses draped all about his vicinity; holding out his Sceptre to order his troops forward; descending from his throne to speak a few kind words to wounded officers who were brought up to him on litters; standing up and striking a grave defiant pose during moments of crisis, whilst holding out a steady hand to calm his jittery *femmes*. Likewise an actor had been hired to play the role of D'Artagnan. Since everyone knew what was about to happen to him, he got the most applause when he was introduced—to the visible chagrin of the (real) Duke of Monmouth. In any event: cannons were discharged picturesquely from the ramparts of "Maestricht," and "Dutchmen" struck defiant poses on the battlements, creating among the spectators a *frisson* of righteous anger (how dare those insolent Dutchmen defend themselves!?)—rapidly transmuted into patriotic fervor as, at a signal from "Louis XIV," Monmouth and Churchill led a charge up the slope of the demilune work. After a bit of thrilling swordplay and much spattering-about of stage-blood, they planted French and English flags side by side on the parapet, shook hands with "D'Artagnan," and exchanged all manner of fond and respectful gestures with the "King" on his hillock.

There was an ovation. Daniel could hear nothing else, but he *saw* some odd sort of pratfall directly in front of him: a young man in severe dark clothing, who'd been standing in front of Daniel and blocking his view with a sort of Pilgrim-hat, turned round and splayed his limbs out like a squashed bug, let his head loll back on his white collar, stuck his tongue out, and rolled his eyes back in their sockets. He was mocking the pose of several "Dutch" defenders who were now *hors de combat* up on the demilune. He did not make a very pretty picture. Something was grievously wrong with his face: a dermatological catastrophe about the cheeks.

Behind him, a scene-change was underway: the dead defenders were resurrecting themselves and scurrying round back of the ramparts to prepare for the next act. Likewise the man in front of Daniel now recovered his balance and turned out not to be a dead Dutchman at all, just a young English bloke with a sour look about him. His attire was not just *any* drab garb but the *specific* drab garb worn, nowadays, by Barkers. But (now that Daniel thought about it slightly harder) it was very like the clothing worn by the mock-Dutchmen pretending to defend Maestricht. Come to think of it, those "Dutchmen" had looked a great deal more like English religious Dissenters than they had like actual Dutchmen, who (if the grapevine was to be believed) had long ago ditched their old Pilgrimish togs (which had been inspired by Spanish fashions anyway) and now dressed like everyone else in Europe. So in *addition* to being a re-enactment of the Siege of Maestricht, this show was *also* a parable about well-dressed rakes and blades overcoming dull severe Calvinists in the streets of London town!

The slowness with which Daniel realized all this was infuriating to the young Barker in front of him—who had the cannonball head and mighty jawbone of an authentic Bolstrood.

"Is that Gomer?" Daniel exclaimed, when the ovation had died away into a thrum of thirsty squires calling for beer. Daniel had known the son of Knott Bolstrood as a little boy, but hadn't set eyes on him in at least a decade.

Gomer Bolstrood answered the question by staring Daniel full in the face. On the front of each of his cheeks, just to either side of his nose, was an old wound: a complex of red trenches and fleshy ramparts, curved round into the crude glyph "S.L." These marks had been made by a branding iron in the open-air court before the Sessions House at the Old Bailey, a few moments after Gomer had been pronounced guilty of being a Seditious Libeller.

Gomer Bolstrood could not be more than twenty-five years old, but that munition-like head, combined with those brands, gave him the presence of a much older man. He aimed his chin significantly towards a location off behind the stands.

Gomer Bolstrood, son of His Majesty's Secretary of State Knott, son of ur-Barker Gregory, led Daniel into a Vagabond-camp of tents and wagons set up to serve and support this gala re-enactment. Some of the tents were for the actors and actresses. Gomer led Daniel between a couple of those, which meant fighting their way against a flood tide of "French Mistresses" coming back from the "Sun King's" throne. Even as the sensitive eyes of Isaac Newton had been semi-permanently branded with the image of the solar disk during his colors experiments, so Daniel's retinas were now stamped with a dozen or more cleavages. All of those cleavages must have had heads up above them somewhere—but the only one he *noticed* was speaking to one of the other girls in a French accent. From which he reckoned (in retrospect, somewhat simple-mindedly) that she must be French. But before Daniel could drift off into a full reverie, Gomer Bolstrood had grabbed his upper arm and pulled him 'tween the flaps of an adjoining beer tent.

The beer was Dutch. So was the man sitting at the table. But the *waffle* that the man was eating was indisputably Belgian.

Daniel sat in the chair indicated, and watched the Dutch gentleman eat the waffle for a while. He aimed his eyes in that direction, anyway. The image that still persisted before his eyes was cleavages, and the face of that "French" lass. But after a while this, sadly, faded, and was replaced by a waffle that had been put in front of him on a Delft china plate. And none of your crude heavy Pilgrim-ware, but the good stuff, export-grade.

He sensed an implicit demand that he should Partake. So he dissected a corner from the waffle, put it in his mouth, and began to chew it. It was good. His eyes were adjusting to the dimness of the tent, and he was noticing stacks of handbills piled up in the corners, neatly wrapped up in old proof-sheets. The words on the proof-sheets were in every language save English—these bills had been printed in Amsterdam and brought over on a beer-ship or perhaps a waffle-barge. Every so often the tent-flaps would part, and Gomer, or one of the taciturn, pipe-smoking Dutchmen in the corners, would peer out and thrust a brick of hand-bills through the gap.

"Whaat doo Belgian waffles and the cleavages of those girls haave in common?" said the Dutch Ambassador; for it was none other. He dabbed butter from his lips with a napkin. He was blond, and pyramidal, as if he consumed a lot of beer and waffles. "I saaw you staaring at them," he added, apologetically.

"I haven't the *merest* idea—sir!"

"Negateev Spaace," the Dutch Ambassador intoned, letting those double vowels resonate as only a heavyweight Dutchman could. "Have you heard of thees? It is an *aart woord*. Wee know about *negateev spaace* because we like *peectures soo muuch*."

"Is it anything like negative numbers?"

"Eet ees the spaace between twoo theengs," said the other, and put his hands on his chest and forced his pectorals together to create a poor impression of cleavage. Daniel watched with polite incredulity, and tried not to shudder. The Dutchman plucked a fresh waffle off a plate and held it up by one corner, like a rag soaked with something unpleasant. "Likewise—the waffle of Belgium is shaaped and defiined, not by its own essential naatuure, but by the hot plaates of haard iron that encloose it on toop and boottom."

"Oh, I see—you're making a point about the Spanish Netherlands!"

The Dutch Ambassador rolled his eyes and tossed the waffle back over his shoulder—before it struck the ground, a stout, disconcertingly monkey-like dog sprang into the air and snatched it, and began to masticate it—*literally*—for the sound it made was like a homunculus squatting on the floor muttering, "masticate masticate masticate."

"Traaped between Fraance and the Dutch Republic, the Spanish Netherlands is raapidly consuumed by Louis the Quatorze Bourbon. Fine. But when *Le Roi du Soleil* reaches Maestricht he touches—what?"

"The political and military equivalent of a hot iron plate?"

The Dutch Ambassador probed negative space with a licked finger, seemed to touch something, and drew back sharply, making a sizzling noise through his teeth. Perhaps by Dutch luck, perhaps by some exquisite sense of timing, Daniel felt the atmosphere socking him in the gut. The tent clenched inwards, then inflated. Waffle-irons chattered and buzzed in the dimness, like skeletons' teeth. The monkey-dog scurried under the table.

Gomer Bolstrood pulled back a tent-flap to provide a clear view to the top of the demilune-work, which had been ruptured by detonation of a vast internal store of gunpowder. It looked like a steaming loaf that had been ripped in half. Resurgent Dutchmen were prancing around on the top, trampling and burning those French and English flags. The spectators were on the brink of riot.

Gomer let the tent-flap fall shut again, and Daniel turned his attention back to the ambassador, who had never taken his gaze off of Daniel.

"Maybe Fraance taakes Maestricht—but not so easily—they lose the hero D'Artagnan. The war will be won by us, however."

"I am pleased to know that you will have success in Holland—now will you consider changing your tactics in London?" Daniel said this loudly so that Gomer could share in it.

"In whaat waay?"

"You know what L'Estrange has been doing."

"I know what L'Estrange has been *failing* to do!" the Dutch Ambassador chortled.

"Wilkins is trying to make London like Amsterdam—and I'm not speaking of wooden shoes."

"Many churches—no established religion."

"It is his life's work. He has given up on Natural Philosophy, these last years, to direct all of his energies toward that goal. He wants it because it is best for England—but the High Anglicans and Crypto-Catholics at Court are against anything that smacks of Dissidents. So Wilkins's task is difficult enough—but when those same Dissidents are linked, in the public mind, with the Dutch enemy, how can he hope for success?"

"In a year—when the dead are counted, and the true costs of the war are understood—Wilkins's task will be too easy."

"In a year Wilkins will be dead of the stone. Unless he has it cut out."

"I can recommend a chirurgeon-barber, very speedy with the knife—"

"He does not feel that he can devote several months to recovery, when the pressure is so immediate and the stakes so high. He is just on the verge of success, Mr. Ambassador, and if you would let up—"

"We will let up when the French do," the Ambassador said, and waved at Gomer, who pulled the flap open again to show the demilune being re-conquered by French and English troops, led by Monmouth. To one side, "D'Artagnan" lay wounded in a gap in the wall. John Churchill was supporting the old musketeer's head in his lap, feeding him sips from a flask.

The tent-flap remained open for rather a long time, and Daniel eventually understood that he was being shown the door. As he walked out he caught Gomer's elbow and drew him outside onto the dirt street. "Brother Gomer," he said, "the Dutch are deranged. Understandably. But *our* situation is not so desperate."

"On the contrary," said Gomer, "I say that *you* are in desperate peril, Brother Daniel."

Anyone else would have meant *physical* peril by that, but Daniel had spent enough of his life around Gomer's—which was to say,

Daniel's—ilk to know that Gomer meant the spiritual kind.

"I don't suppose that's just because I was staring at a pretty girl's bosom just now—?"

Gomer did not much fancy the jest. Indeed, Daniel sensed before those words were out of his mouth that they would only confirm Gomer's opinion of him as Fallen, or at best, Falling fast. He tried something else: "Your own father is Secretary of State!"

"Then go and speak to my father."

"The point I am making is that there is no harm—or *peril*, if that is what you want to call it—in employing *tactics*. Cromwell used tactics to win battles, did he not? It did not mean he lacked faith. On the contrary—*not* to use the brains God gave you, and making every struggle into a frontal charge, is sinful—thou shalt not tempt the Lord thy God!"

"Wilkins has the stone," Gomer said. "Whether 'twas placed in his bladder by God, or the Devil, is a question for Jesuits. Anyway, he has it, and shall likely die of it, unless you and your Fellows can gin up a way to transmute it into some watery form that can be pissed out. In dread of his death, you have wrought in your mind this phant'sy that if I, Gomer Bolstrood, leave off distributing handbills in the streets of London, it shall set in motion a lengthy chain of consequences that shall somehow end in Wilkins's suffering some chirurgeon to cut him for the stone, him surviving the operation, and living happily ever after, as the kind father you never had. And *you* say that the *Dutch* are deranged?"

Daniel could not answer. The discourse of Gomer had struck him in the face with no less heat, force, and dumbfounding pain than the branding iron had Gomer's.

"As you phant'sy yourself a master of *tactics*, consider this whorish spectacle we have been witnessing." Gomer waved at the demilune-work. Up on the parapet, Monmouth was planting the French and English flags anew, to the cheers of the spectators, who broke into a lusty chorus of "Pikes on the Dikes" even as "D'Artagnan" breathed his last. John Churchill carried him down the slope of the earthwork in his arms and laid him on a litter where his body was bedecked with flowers.

"Behold the martyr!" Gomer brayed. "Who gave his life for the cause, and is fondly remembered by all the Quality! Now *there* is a tactic for you. I am sorry Wilkins is sick. I would not put him in harm's way on any account, for he was a friend to us. But it is not in my power to keep Death from his door. And when Death does come, 'twill make of him a Martyr—not so romantick as D'Artagnan perhaps—but of more effect in a better cause. Beg your pardon,

Brother Daniel." Gomer stalked away, tearing open the wrapper on a sheaf of libels.

"D'Artagnan" was being carried along the front of the bleachers in a cortege of gorgeously mussed and tousled Cavaliers, and spectators were doing business with roving flower-girls and showering bouquets and blossoms on those heroes living and "dead." But even as petals were fluttering down on the mock-Musketeer, Daniel Waterhouse found slips of paper coming down all around him, carried on a breeze from the bleachers. He slapped one out of the air and was greeted with a cartoon of several French cavaliers gang-raping a Dutch milkmaid. Another showed a cravated musketeer, silhouetted in the light of a burning Protestant church, about to catch a tossed baby on the point of his sword. All around Daniel, and up in the stands, spectators were passing these bills hand-to-hand, sometimes wadding them into sleeves or pockets.

So the matter was complicated. And it only become more so ten minutes later, when, during a bombardment of "Maestricht," a cannon burst in full view of all spectators. Most people assumed it was just a stage-trick until bloody fragments of artillerymen began to shower down all among them, mingling with the continual flurry of handbills.

Daniel walked back to Gresham's College and worked all night with Hooke. Hooke stayed below, gazing up at various stars, and Daniel remained on the roof, looking at a nova that was flaring in the west end of London: a Mobb of people with torches, milling around St. James's Fields and discharging the occasional musket. Later, he learned that they had attacked Comstock House, supposedly because they were furious about the cannon that had burst.

John Comstock himself showed up at Gresham's College the next morning. It took several moments for Daniel to recognize him, so altered was his countenance by shock, by outrage, and even by shame. He demanded that Hooke and the rest drop what they were doing and investigate the remnants of the burst cannon, which he insisted had been tampered with in some way "by mine enemies."

College of the Holy and
Undivided Trinity, Cambridge
1672

✥

There are few things, that are incapable of being
represented by a fiction.

—HOBBES, *Leviathan*

Once More into the Breeches
A COMEDY

DRAMATIS PERSONAE

MEN: MR. VAN UNDERDEVATER, a *Dutchman,* founder of a great
commercial empire in *sow's-ears* and *potatoes'-eyes*
NZINGA, a cannibal Neeger, formerly King of the Congo,
now house-slave to Mr. van Underdevater
JEHOSHAPHAT STOPCOCK, the Earl of BRIMSTONE, an
enthusiast
TOM RUNAGATE, a discharged soldier turned *Vagabond*
THE REV. YAHWEH PUCKER, a Dissident divine
EUGENE STOPCOCK, son of Lord Brimstone, a Captain of
Foot
FRANCIS BUGGERMY, Earl of Suckmire, a *foppish courtier*
DODGE AND BOLT, two of Tom Runagate's accomplices
WOMEN: MISS LYDIA VAN UNDERDEVATER, the daughter and sole
heiress of Mr. van Underdevater, recently returned from
a *Venetian* finishing-school
LADY BRIMSTONE, wife to Jehoshaphat Stopcock
MISS STRADDLE, Tom Runagate's *companion*
SCENE: SUCKMIRE, a rural estate in Kent

ACT I. SCENE I.
SCENE: a Cabin in a Ship at Sea. Thunder heard, flashes of
Lightning seen.

Enter Mr. van Underdevater in dressing-gown, with a lanthorn.

VAN UND: Boatswain!

Enter Nzinga wet, with a Sack.

NZINGA: Here, master, what—

VAN UND: Odd's bodkins! Have you fallen into the tar-pot, boatswain?

NZINGA: It is I, Master—your slave, My Royal Majesty, by the Grace of the tree-god, the rock-god, river-god, and diverse other gods who have slipped my mem'ry, of the Congo, King.

VAN UND: So it is. What have you in the bag?

NZINGA: Balls.

VAN UND: Balls! Sink me! You have quite forgot your Civilizing Lessons!

NZINGA: Of ice.

VAN UND: Thank heavens.

NZINGA: I gathered 'em from the deck—where they are falling like grape-shot—and for this you thank heaven?

VAN UND: Aye, for it means the boatswain is still in possession of all his Parts. Boatswain!

Enter LYDIA in dressing-gown, dishevelled.

LYDIA: Dear father, why do you shout for the boatswain so?

VAN UND: My dear Lydia, I would fain pay him to bring this infernal storm to an end.

LYDIA: But father, the boatswain can't stop a tempest!

VAN UND: Perhaps he knows someone who can.

NZINGA: I know a weather-god in Guinea who can—and at rates very reasonable, as he will accept payment in rum.

VAN UND: Rum! You take me for a half-wit? If this is what the weather-god does when he is *sober*—

NZINGA: Cowrie-shells would do in a pinch. If master would care to despatch My Majesty on the next *southbound* boat, My Majesty would be pleased to broker the transaction—

VAN UND: You prove yourself a shrewd man of commerce. I am reminded of when I traded the holes in a million cannibals' ears, for the eyes of a million potatoes, and beat the market at both ends of the deal—

More thunder.

VAN UND: Too, slow, too slow! Boatswain!

Enter Lord Brimstone.

LORD BRIMSTONE: Here, here, what is this bawling?

LYDIA: Lord Brimstone—your servant.

VAN UND: The price of ending this tempest is too high, the market in Pagan Deities too remote—

LORD B: Then why, sir, do you call for the boatswain?

VAN UND: Why, sir, to tell him to be of good courage and to remain firm in the face of danger.

LYDIA: Oh, too late, father!

VAN UND: What mean you, child?

LYDIA: When the boatswain heard you, he lost what firmness he had, and fled in a panic.

VAN UND: How do you know it?

LYDIA: Why, he upset the hammock altogether, and tumbled me onto the deck!

VAN UND: Lydia, Lydia, I have spent a fortune sending you to that school in Venice, where you have been studying to become a virtuous maiden—

LYDIA: And I have studied hard, Father, but it is ever so difficult!

VAN UND: Has all that money been wasted?

LYDIA: Oh, no, Father, I learned some lovely songs from our dancing-master, Signore Fellatio.

Sings. *

VAN UND: I've heard enough—Boatswain!

Enter Lady Brimstone.

LADY BRIMSTONE: My lord, have you found who is making that dreadful *noise* yet?

LORD B: M'lady, it's that *Dutchman*.

LADY B: So much for idle *investigations*—what have you *done* about it, my lord?

LORD B: Nothing, my lady, for they say that the only way to quiet one of these obstreperous Dutchmen is to drown him.

LADY B: Drown—why, my lord—you're not thinking of throwing him overboard—?

LORD B: Every soul aboard is *thinking* of it, M'lady. But with a Dutchman it isn't necessary, as they live below sea-level to begin with. 'Tis merely a question of getting the sea to go back where the Good Lord put it in the first place—

LADY B: And how d'you propose to effect *that*, my lord?

LORD B: I have been conducting experiments on a novel engine to make windmills turn backwards, and pump water *down-hill*—

---

*Here, a moiety of the audience—mostly Cambridge undergraduates—stood up (if they weren't standing to begin with) and applauded. Admittedly they would've come erect and shown their appreciation for almost any human female recognizable as such who appeared on the grounds of their College, but more so in this case since the role of Lydia was being played by Eleanor (Nell) Gwyn—the King's Mistress.

LADY B: Experiments! Engines! I say the way to put Dutchmen under water's with French gunpowder and English courage!

Whatever the actor playing Lord Brimstone said was like expectorating into the River Amazon. For the true SCENE of these events was Neville's Court* on a spring evening, and the true Dramatis Personae a roll that would've consumed many yards of paper and drams of ink to set it out fully. The script was an unpublished masterwork of courtly and collegiate intrigue, comprising hundreds of more or less clever lines being delivered—mostly *sotto voce*—at the same instant, producing a contrapuntal effect quite intricate but entirely too much for young Daniel Waterhouse to grasp. He had been wondering why persons such as these bothered to go to plays at all, when every day at Whitehall provided more spectacle—now he sensed that they did so because the stories in the theatre were simple, and arrived at fixed conclusions after an hour or two.

Heading up the cast of tonight's performance was King Charles II of England, situated on the upper floor of Trinity's miserable wreck of a library, where several consecutive windows had been opened up and converted into temporary opera-boxes. The Queen, one Catherine of Braganza, a Portuguese princess with a famously inoperative womb, was seated to one side of His Majesty, pretending to understand English as usual. The guest of honor, the Duke of Monmouth (King Charles's son by his mistress Lucy Walter), was on the other side. The windows flanking the King's contained various elements of his court: one was anchored by Louise de Kéroualle, the Duchess of Portsmouth and the King's mistress. Another by Barbara Villiers, a.k.a. Lady Castlemaine, a.k.a. the Duchess of Cleveland, former lover of John Churchill, and the King's mistress.

Moving outwards from the three central windows, there was one all filled up with Angleseys: Thomas More Anglesey and his nearly indistinguishable sons, Philip, now something like twenty-seven years old, and Louis, who was twenty-four, but looking younger. For protocol dictated that, as the Earl of Upnor was visiting his *alma mater*, he had to wear academic robes. Though he'd mobilized a squadron of French tailors to liven them up, they were still academic robes, and the object infesting his wig was unmistakably a mortarboard.

Balancing this Anglesey-window was a window all crowded with Comstocks, specifically the so-called Silver branch of that race: John and his sons Richard and Charles foremost, all dressed likewise in

---

*A grassy quadrangle surrounded by buildings of Trinity College.

robes and mortarboards. Unlike the Earl of Upnor they seemed comfortable dressed that way. Or at least *had* until the play had begun, and the character of Jehoshaphat Stopcock, Lord Brimstone, had come tottering out dressed precisely as they were.

The King's Comedians, performing on a temporary stage that had been erected in Neville's Court, had decided to plow onwards in spite of the fact that no one could hear a word they were saying. "Lord Brimstone" seemed to be upbraiding his wife about something—presumably, her reference to "French gunpowder," as opposed to "English," which, on some other planet, might have been a rhetorical figure, but here seemed very much like a stab at John Comstock. Meanwhile, most of the audience—who, if they had the good fortune to be seated, were seated on chairs and benches arranged in the corner of Neville's Court, beneath the windows of King and Court—were trying to break out into the opening stanza of "Pikes on the Dikes," the most widely plagiarized song in England: a rousing ditty about why it was an excellent idea to invade Holland. But the King held out one hand to silence them. Not that he was lacking in belligerence—but down on the stage, "Lydia van Underdevater" was delivering a line that looked like it was meant to be funny. And the King didn't like it when the buzz of Intrigue drowned out his Mistress.

All of the Comedians suddenly fell down, albeit in dramatickal and actorly ways—and that went double for Nell Gwyn, who wound up draped over a bench with one arm stretched out gracefully, displaying about a square yard of flawless pale armpits and bosoms. The audience were poleaxed. The long-called-for boatswain finally ran in and announced that the ship had run aground in sands just off Castle Suckmire. "Lord Brimstone" sent Nzinga out to fetch his trunk, which arrived with the immediacy that can only happen in stage-plays. The owner pawed through its contents, spilling out a strange mixture of drab out-moded clothing and peculiar equipment, viz. retorts, crucibles, skulls, and microscopes. Meanwhile Lydia was picking up certain of his garments, such as farmers' breeches and cowherds' boots, holding them at arm's length and mugging. Finally, Lord Brimstone stood up, tucking a powder-keg under one arm, and slapping a frayed and bent mortarboard onto his head.

LORD B: What's wanted to move this ship is Gunpowder!

Among the groundlings in their chairs and on the grass, much uneasy shifting and muttering, and tassels flopping this way and that, as mortarboard-wearing scholars turned to each other to enquire as to just who was being made fun of here, or shook their heads, or bowed them low to pray for the souls of the King's Comedians, and of whomever had written this play, and of the King who'd insisted he couldn't make it through a one-night stand at Cambridge without being entertained.

Very different reactions, though, from the windows-cum-opera-boxes: the Duchess of Portsmouth was undone. Her bosom was heaving like a spritsail gone all a-luff, her head was thrown back to expose a whole lot of jewelled throat. These spectacles had already caused diverse groundling scholars to fall out of their chairs. She was being supported by a pair of young blades in huge curled and beribboned wigs, who were wiping tears of mirth away from their eyes with the fingertips of their kid gloves—having already donated their lace hankies to the Duchess.

Meanwhile, mortarboard-wearing gunpowder magnate John Comstock—who'd long opposed the Duchess of Portsmouth's efforts to introduce French fashions to the English court—was managing a thin, oddly distracted smile. The King—who, until tonight anyway, had generally sided with Comstock—was smiling, and the Angleseys were all having the times of their lives.

An elbow to the kidney forced Daniel to stop gaping at the Duchess's efforts to rupture her bodice, and to pay some attention to the rather homelier sight of Oldenburg, who was seated next to him. The hefty German had been released from the Tower as suddenly and as inexplicably as he'd been clapped into it. He glanced down toward the far end of Neville's Court, then frowned at Daniel and said, "Where *is* he? Or at least *it!*" meaning Isaac Newton and his paper on tangents, respectively. Then Oldenburg turned the other way and peeked up round the edge of his mortarboard toward the Angleseys' box, where Louis Anglesey, the Earl of Upnor, had somehow gotten his merriment under control and was giving Oldenburg a Significant Glare.

Daniel was glad to have a pretext for leaving. All through the play he had been trying and trying to suspend his disbelief, but the damned thing just wouldn't suspend. He rose to his feet, bunched his robes up, and sidestepped down a row of chairs, treading on diverse Royal Society feet. Sir Winston Churchill: *Cheers on your boy's Maestricht work, old chap.* Christopher Wren: *Let's get that cathedral up, what, no dilly-dallying!* Sir Robert Moray: *Let's have lunch and talk about eels.* Thank God Hooke had had the temerity to *not* show up—too busy rebuilding London—so Daniel didn't have to step on any of *his* parts. Finally, Daniel was out on open grass. This was really a job for John Wilkins—but the Bishop of Chester was lying on his bed down in London, ill of the stone.

Working his way round back of the stage, Daniel found himself among several wagons that had been used to haul dramaturgickal mysteries up from London. Awnings had been rigged to them and tents pitched in between, so tent-ropes were stretched across the darkness, thick as ship's rigging, and hitched round splintery wooden stakes piercing the (until the actors had shown up, anyway) flawless lawn. Various items of what he could only assume were ladies' undergarments (they were definitely *garments*, but he had never seen their like—Q.E.D.) dangled from the ropes and occasionally surprised the hell out of him by pawing clammily at his face. Daniel had to plot a devious course, then pursue it slowly, to escape the tangle. So it was really—*really*—just an accident that he found the two actresses, doing whatever the hell it was that females do when they excuse themselves and exchange warm knowing looks and go off in pairs. He caught the very end of it: "What should I do w'th'old one?" said a young lady with a lovely voice, and an accent from some part of England with too many sheep.

"Fling it into the crowd—start a riot," suggested the other—an Irish girl.

This touched off fiendish whooping. Clearly no one had taught these girls how to titter.

"But they wouldn't even know what it was," said the girl with the lovely voice, "we are the first women to set *foot* in this place."

"Then neither will they know if you leave it where it lies," the Irish girl answered.

The other now dropped her rural accent and began talking *exactly* like a Cambridge scholar from a good family. "I say, what's this in the middle of my bowling-green? It would appear to be . . . fox-bait!"

More whooping—cut short by a man's voice out of a backstage caravan: "Tess—save some of that for the King—you're wanted on the stage."

The lasses picked up their skirts and exeunted. Daniel glimpsed them as they transited across a gap between tents, and recognized the one called Tess from the "Siege of Maestricht." She was the one he had taken for a Frenchwoman, simply because he'd heard her talking that way. He now understood that she was really an Englishwoman who could talk any way she pleased. This might have been obvious, since she was a professional actress; but it was new to him, and it made her interesting.

Daniel emerged from behind the tent where he'd been (it is fair

to say) lurking, and—purely in a spirit of philosophical inquiry—
approached the spot where Tess of the beautiful voice and many
accents had been (fair to say) squatting.

In a sort of hod projecting above the stage, more gunpowder
was lit off in an attempt to simulate lightning, and it made a pool of
yellow light in front of Daniel for just a moment. Neatly centered
in a patch of grass—grass that was almost phosphorus-green, this
being Spring—was a wadded-up rag, steaming from the warmth of
Tess, bright with blood.

> Of sooty coal the Empiric Alchimist
> Can turn, or holds it possible to turn
> Metals of drossiest Ore to perfet Gold
> As from the Mine.
>
> —MILTON, *Paradise Lost*

IT HAD BEEN A FULL DAY for the King. Or perhaps Daniel was being
naïve to think so—more likely, it was a typical day for the King, and
the only persons feeling exhausted were the Cantabrigians who
had been trying to maintain the pretense that they could keep up
with him. The entourage had appeared on the southern horizon
in mid-morning, looking (Daniel supposed) quite a bit like the
invasion that Louis XIV had recently flung into the Dutch Republic: meaning that it thundered and threw up dust-clouds and consumed oats and generated ramparts of manure like any Regiment,
but its wagons were all gilded, its warriors were armed with jewelled Italian rapiers, its field-marshalls wore skirts and commanded
men, or condemned them, with looks—this fell upon Cambridge,
anyway, with more effect than King Louis had achieved, so far, in
the Netherlands. The town was undone, dissolved. Bosoms everywhere, bare-assed courtiers spilling out of windows, the good Cambridge smell of fens and grass overcome by perfumes, not just of
Paris but of Araby and Rajasthan. The King had abandoned his
coach and marched through the streets of the town accepting the
cheers of the scholars of Cambridge, who had formed up in front
of their several Colleges, robed and arranged by ranks and
degrees, like soldiers drawn up for review. He'd been officially
greeted by the outgoing Chancellor, who had presented him with a
colossal Bible—they said it was possible to see the royal nose wrin-
kling, and the eyes rolling, from half a mile away. Later the King
(and his pack of demented spaniels) had dined at High Table in
the College of the Holy and Undivided Trinity, under the big Holbein portrait of the college's Founder, King Henry VIII. As Fellows,

Daniel and Isaac were accustomed to sitting at High Table, but the town was now stuffed with persons who ranked them, and so they'd been demoted halfway across the room: Isaac in his scarlet robes talking to Boyle and Locke about something, and Daniel shoved off in a corner with several vicars who—in violation of certain Biblical guidelines—plainly did not love one another. Daniel tried to stanch their disputatious drone and to pick up a few snatches of conversation from the High Table. The King had a lot to say about Henry VIII, all of it apparently rather droll.

At first, it was Old Hank's approach to polygamy: so hamhanded it was funny. All of it was veiled in royal wit, of course—he didn't come right out and say anything really, but the point seemed to be: why do people call me a libertine? At least I don't chop their heads off. If Daniel (or any other scholar in this place) had wanted to die instantly, he could have stood up at this point and hollered, "Well, at least *he* eventually got round to producing a legitimate male heir!" but this did not occur.

Several goblets later, the King moved on to some reflections on what a fine and magnificent and (not to put too fine a point on it) *rich* place Trinity College was, and how remarkable it was that such results could have been achieved by Henry VIII merely by defying the Pope, and sacking a few monasteries. So perhaps the coffers of Puritans, Quakers, Barkers, and Presbyterians might go, one day, towards building an even finer College! This was said as a jest, of course—he went on to say that of course he was speaking of *voluntary* contributions. Even so, it made the Dissenters in the room very angry—but (as Daniel later reflected) no more angry, really, than they'd been before. And it was a masterly bit of Catholic-bashing. In other words, all nicely calculated to warm the hearts and ease the fears of all the High Anglicans (such as John Comstock) in the hall. The King had to do a lot of that, because many assumed he was soft on Catholics, and some even thought he *was* one.

In other words, maybe he had just seen a little slice of Court politics as usual, and nothing of consequence had happened. But since John Wilkins had lost the ability to urinate, Daniel's job was to *pay attention* and report all of this to him later.

Then it was off to the chapel where the Duke of Monmouth, now a war hero as well as a renowned scholar and bastard, was installed as Chancellor of the University. After that, finally, the Comedy in Neville's Court.

DANIEL PAUSED IN THE CENTER of a Gothic arch and looked out over a spread of stone steps that led down into the Great Court of

Trinity College: an area about four times the size of Neville's Court. In a strange way it reminded him of the 'Change in London, except that where the 'Change was a daytime place, all a-sparkle with Thomas Gresham's golden grasshoppers and vaulting Mercurys, and crowded with lusty shouting traders, *this* place was Gothickal in the extreme, faintly dusted with the blue light of a half-moon, sparsely populated by robed and/or big-wigged men skulking about the paths and huddling in doorways in groups of two or three. And whereas the 'Change-men made common cause to buy shares in sailing-ships or joint stock companies, and traded Jamaica sugar for Spanish silver, these men were transacting diverse small conspiracies or trading snatches of courtly data. The coming of Court to Cambridge was like Stourbridge Fair—an occasional opportunity for certain types of business, most of which was in some sense occult. He couldn't get in any trouble simply walking direct across the Great Court to the Gate. As a Fellow, he was allowed to tread on the grass. Most of these lurkers and strollers weren't. Not that they cared about the College's pedantic rules, but they preferred shadowy edges, having the courtier's natural affinity for joints and crevices. Across broad open space Daniel strode, so that no one could accuse him of eavesdropping. A line stretched from where he'd come in, to the Gate, would pass direct through a sort of gazebo in the center of the Great Court: an octagonal structure surmounting a little pile of steps, with a goblet-shaped fountain in the middle. Moonlight slanted in among the pillars and gave it a ghastly look—the stone pale as a dead man's flesh, streaked with rivulets of blood, pulsing from arterial punctures. Daniel reckoned it had to be some sort of Papist-style Vision, and was just about to lift up his hands to inspect them for Stigmata when he caught a whiff, and recollected that the fountain had been drained of water and filled with claret wine in honor of the King and of the new Chancellor: a decision that begged to be argued with. But no accounting for taste . . .

"The Africans cannot *propagate*," said a familiar voice, startlingly close.

"What do you mean? They can do so as well as anyone," said a *different* familiar voice. "Perhaps *better!*"

"Not without Neeger *women.*"

"You don't say!"

"You must remember that the planters are short-sighted. They're all *desperate* to get out of Jamaica—they wake up every day expecting to find themselves, or their children, in the grip of some tropical fever. To import *female* Neegers would cost nearly as much as to import males, but the females cannot produce as much sugar—particularly when they are breeding." Daniel had finally recognized this voice as belonging to Sir Richard Apthorp—the second A in the CABAL.

"So they don't import females *at all*?"

"That is correct, sir. And a newly arrived male is only usable for a few years," Apthorp said.

"That explains *much* of the caterwauling that has been emanating lately from the 'Change."

The two men had been sitting together on the steps of the fountain, facing toward the Gate, and Daniel hadn't *seen* them until he'd drawn close enough to *hear* them. He was just getting ready to shift direction, and swing wide around the fountain, when the man who *wasn't* Sir Richard Apthorp stood up, turned around, and dipped a goblet into the fountain—and caught sight of Daniel standing there flat-footed. *Now* Daniel recognized him—he was only too easy to recognize in a dark Trinity courtyard with blood on his hands. "I say!" Jeffreys exclaimed, "is that a new statue over there? A Puritan saint? Oh, I'm wrong, it is moving now—what *appeared* to be a Pillar of Virtue, is revealed as Daniel Waterhouse— ever the keen observer—now making an empiric study of *us*. Don't worry, Sir Richard, Mr. Waterhouse *sees* all and *does* nothing—a model Royal Society man."

"Good evening, Mr. Waterhouse," Apthorp said, managing to convey, by the tone of his voice, that he found Jeffreys embarrassing and tedious.

"Mr. Jeffreys. Sir Richard. God save the King."

"The King!" Jeffreys repeated, raising his dripping goblet and then taking a swallow. "Stand and deliver like a good little scholar, Mr. Waterhouse. Why are Sir Richard's friends in the 'Change making such a fuss?"

"Admiral de Ruyter sailed down to Guinea and took away all of the Duke of York's slave-ports," Daniel said.

Jeffreys—one hand half-covering his mouth, and speaking in a stage-whisper: "Which the Duke of York had stolen from the Dutch, a few years before—but in Africa, who splits hairs?"

"During the years that the Duke's company controlled Guinea, many slaves were shipped to Jamaica—there they made sugar—fortunes were built, and will endure, as long as the attrition of slaves is replaced by new shipments. But the Dutch have now choked off the supply—so I'd guess that Sir Richard's clients at the 'Change can read the implications clearly enough—there must be some turmoil in the commodities markets."

Like a victim of unprovoked Battery looking for witnesses, Jeffreys turned toward Apthorp, who raised his eyebrows and nodded. Now Jeffreys had been a London barrister for some years. Daniel suspected that he knew of these events only as a mysterious influence that caused his clients to go bankrupt. "Some turmoil," Jeffreys said, in a dramatic whisper. "Rather dry language, isn't it? Imagine some planter's family in Jamaica, watching the work-force, and the harvest, dwindle—trying to stay one step ahead of bankruptcy, yellow fever, and slave rebellion—scanning the horizon for sails, praying for the ships that will be their salvation—some turmoil, you call it?"

Daniel could have said, *Imagine a barrister watching his moneybags dwindle as he drinks them away, scanning the Strand for a client who's got the wherewithal to pay his legal bills . . .* but Jeffreys was wearing a sword and was drunk. So he said: "If those planters are in church, and praying, then they've already found salvation. Good evening, gentlemen."

He headed for the Gate, swinging wide round the fountain so that Jeffreys wouldn't be tempted to run him through. Sir Richard Apthorp was applauding him politely. Jeffreys was mumbling and growling, but after a few moments he was able to get words out: "You are the same man as you were—or *weren't*—ten years ago, Daniel Waterhouse! You were ruled by fear *then*—and you'd have England ruled by it *now*! Thank God you are sequestered within these walls, and unable to infect London with your disgusting pusillanimity!"

And more in that vein, until Daniel ducked into the vault of the Great Gate of Trinity College. The gate was a hefty structure with crenellated towers at its four corners: a sort of mock-fortress, just the thing for retreating into when under attack by a Jeffreys. Between it and the side-wall of Trinity's shotgun chapel was a gap in the College's perimeter defenses about a stone's throw wide, patched with a suite of chambers that had a little walled garden in front of it, on the side facing towards the town. These chambers had been used to shield various Fellows from the elements over the years, but lately Daniel Waterhouse and Isaac Newton had been living there. Once those two bachelors had moved in their miserable stock of furniture, there had been plenty of unused space remaining, and so it had become the world's leading alchemical research facility. Daniel knew this, because he had helped build it—*was helping* build it, rather, for it was perpetually under construction.

Entering his home, Daniel pulled his robes close to his body so that they would not catch fire brushing against the glowing dome of the Reverberatory Furnace, wherein flames curled against the ceiling to strike downwards against the target. Then he pulled his skirts up so they wouldn't drag against the heap of coal that (though the room was dark) he knew would be piled on the floor to his right. Or, for that matter, the mound of horse dung on the left (when burnt, it made a gentle moist heat). He maneuvered down a narrow lead among stacks of wooden crates, an egglike flask of quicksilver packed into each one, and came round a corner into another room.

This chamber looked like a miniature city, built by outlandish stone-masons, and just in the act of burning down—for each "building" had a peculiar shape, to draw in the air, channel flame, and carry away fumes in a particular way, and each one was filled with flames. Some of them smoked; some steamed; most gave off queer-smelling vapors. Rather than explaining what the place smelled like, 'twere easier to list what few things could *not* be smelled here. Lumps of gold lay out on tabletops, like butter in a pastry-shop—it being *de rigueur* among the higher sort of Alchemists to show a fashionable contempt for gold, as a way of countering the accusation that they were only in it for the money. Not all operations demanded a furnace, and so there were tables, too, sheathed in peened copper, supporting oil-lamps that painted the round bottoms of flasks and retorts with yellow flame.

Smudged faces turned towards Daniel, sequins of perspiration tumbled from drooping eyebrows. He immediately recognized Robert Boyle and John Locke, Fellows of the Royal Society, but, too, there were certain gentlemen who tended to show up at their garden-gate at perverse hours, robed and hooded—as if they really needed to conceal their identities when the King himself was practicing the Art at Whitehall. Viewing their petulant faces by firelight, Daniel wished they'd kept the hoods on. For, alas, they weren't Babylonian sorcerers or Jesuit warrior-priests or Druidic warlocks after all, but an unmatched set of small-town apothecaries, bored noblemen, and crack-pated geezers, with faces that were either too slack or too spasmodical. One of them was markedly young—Daniel recognized him as Roger Comstock, he of the so-called Golden Comstocks, who'd been a scholar along with Daniel, Isaac, Upnor, Monmouth, and Jeffreys. Isaac had put Roger Comstock to work pumping a bellows, and the strain was showing on his face, but he was not about to complain. Too, there was a small and very trim raptor-faced man with white hair. Daniel recognized him as Monsieur LeFebure, the King's Chymist, who'd introduced John Comstock and Thomas More Anglesey and others—including the King himself—to the Art, when they'd been exiled in St.-Germain during the Cromwell years.

But all of these were satellites, or (like Jupiter's moons) satellites of satellites. The Sun stood at a writing-desk in the center of the room, quill in hand, calmly making notations in a large, stained, yellowed Book. He was dressed in a long splotched smock with several holes burnt through it, though the hem of a scarlet robe could be seen hanging beneath. His head was encased in a sort of leather sack with a windowpane let into it so that he could see out. Where Daniel stood, that rectangle of glass happened to be reflecting an open furnace-door, so instead of the bulging eyes, he saw a brilliant sheet of streaming flame. A breathing-tube, comprising segments of hollow cane plumbed together by the small intestine of some beast, was sewn through the bag. Isaac had tossed it back over his shoulder. It dangled down his back and ran across the floor to Roger Comstock, who pumped fresh air into it with a bellows. So they must be doing something with mercury this evening. Isaac had observed that quicksilver, absorbed into his body, produced effects like those of coffee or tobacco, only more so, and so he used the breathing apparatus whenever he had begun to feel especially twitchy.

The results of some experiment appeared to be cooling down on one of the tables—a crucible hanging in darkness giving off a sullen glow, like Mars—and Daniel reckoned it was as good a time as any to interrupt. He stepped into the middle of the room and held up the bloody rag. "The menstruum of a human female," he announced, "only a few minutes old!"

A bit melodramatic. But these men thrived on it. Why else would they conceal their persons in wizard-cloaks, and their knowledge in occult signs? *Some* of them, anyway, were deeply impressed. Newton turned round and glared significantly at Roger Comstock, who cringed and gave the bellows several brisk strokes. The sack around Isaac's head bulged and whistled. Isaac glared some more. One of the minions rushed up with a beaker. Daniel dropped the moist rag into it. Monsieur LeFebure approached and began to make calm observations in a fifty-fifty French-Latin mix. Boyle and Locke listened politely, the lesser Alchemists formed up in an outer circle, faces strained with the effort of decrypting whatever the King's Chymist was saying.

Daniel turned the other way to see Isaac peeling the wet sack off his head, then gathering his silver hair and holding it atop his skull to let the back of his neck cool down. He was gazing back at Daniel with no particular emotion. Of course he knew that the rag was just a diversionary tactic, but this did not affect him one way or the other.

"There's still time to see the second act of the play," Daniel said. "We're holding an empty seat for you—practically had to use muskets and pikes to keep scheming Londoners from it."

"You are taking the position, then, that God placed me on the earth, and in His wisdom supplied me with the resources that He has, so that I could interrupt my work, and spend my hours, watching a wicked atheistical play?"

"Of course not, Isaac, please don't impute such things to me, not even in private."

They were withdrawing to another room—which, therefore, in a more dignified sort of house would be called the w'drawing room—but here it was a workshop, the floor slick with wood-dust and shavings from a lathe, and a-crackle with failures from the glass-blowing bench, and cluttered with various hand-tools that they'd used to construct everything else. Isaac said nothing, only gazed at Daniel, all patient expectation. "From time to time—perhaps once a day—I prevail upon you to eat something," Daniel pointed out. "Does this mean I believe God put you here to stuff food into your mouth? Of course not. But in order for you to accomplish the work that you, and I, believe God shaped you for, you must put food into your body."

"Is it really your belief that watching *Once More into the Breeches* is comparable to eating?"

"To work, you require certain resources—nutrition is only *one*. A stipend, a workshop, tools, equipment—how do you get *them*?"

"Behold!" Isaac said, sweeping one arm over his empire of tools and furnaces. This caused the cuff of his robe to fly out from under his smock—catching sight of it, he grasped the smock's sleeve with the other hand and yanked it back to reveal the scarlet raiment of the Lucasian Professor of Mathematics. Coming from any other man this would have seemed dramatic and insufferably pompous, but from Isaac it was the simplest and most concise answer to Daniel's question.

"The Fellowship—the chambers—the laboratory—and the Lucasian Chair—all the best that you could hope for. You have all you need—for now. But how did you get those things, Isaac?"

"Providence."

"By which you mean *Divine* Providence. But how—"

"You wish to examine the workings of God's will in the world? I am pleased to hear it. For that is my sole endeavour. You are keeping me from it—let us go back into the other room and pursue an answer to your question together."

"By diverting your attention from those crucibles—for a few hours—you could gain a clearer understanding of, and a more profound gratitude for, what Providence has given you." Devising that sentence had required intense concentration on Daniel's part—he was gratified when it seemed to at least confuse Isaac.

"If there are some *data* I have overlooked, by all means edify me," Isaac said.

"Recall the Fellowship competition of several years ago. You'd been busy doing the work God put you here to do—*instead of* the work that Trinity College *expected* of you—consequently, your prospects seemed bleak—wouldn't you agree?"

"I have always placed my faith in—"

"In God, of course. But don't tell me you weren't worried you'd be sent packing, and live out your days as a gentleman farmer in Woolsthorpe. There were *other* candidates. Men who'd curried favor in the right places, and memorized all of the medieval clap-trap we were expected to know. Do you remember, Isaac, what became of your competitors?"

"One went insane," Isaac recited like a bored scholar. "One passed out in a field from too much drink, caught a fever, and died. One fell down stairs drunk and had to withdraw because of injuries suffered. The fourth—" Here Isaac faltered, which was a rare event for him. Daniel seized the moment by stepping closer and adopting a curious and innocent look.

Isaac looked away and said, "The fourth one *also* fell down stairs drunk and had to withdraw! Now, Daniel, if you're trying to say that this was *incredibly improbable,* and fortunate for me, I have already given you my answer: Providence."

"But *in what form* did Providence exert itself? Some mysterious action at a distance? Or the earthly mechanics of colliding bodies?"

"Now you have quite lost me."

"Do you believe that God stretched out a finger from Heaven, and knocked those two down the staircase? Or did he put someone on Earth who arranged for these things to happen?"

"Daniel—surely you didn't—"

Daniel laughed. "Push them down stairs? No. But I think I know who *did*. You have the wherewithal to work, Isaac, because of certain Powers that Be—which is not to say that Providence isn't working *through* them. But what it all *means* is that you must, from time to time, pause in your labors, and spend a few hours maintaining friendly relations with those Powers."

Isaac had been pacing around the chamber during this lecture, and looking generally skeptical. More than one time he opened his mouth to make some objection. But at about the time Daniel finished, Isaac seemed to notice something. Daniel thought it was one of many papers and note-books scattered upon a certain table. Whatever it might have been, the sight of it caused Isaac to reconsider. Isaac's face slackened, as if the internal flame were being banked. He began stripping off his smock. "Very well," he said, "please inform the others."

The others had already squeezed the rag out into a glass retort and were trying to distill from it whatever generative spirit they supposed must be exuded from a woman's womb. Roger Comstock and the other minions looked crestfallen to learn that Professor Newton would be leaving them, but Locke and Boyle and LeFebure took it in stride. Newton made himself presentable very quickly—this being why academics loved robes, and fops loathed them. A contingent of five Royal Society members—Boyle, Locke, LeFebure, Waterhouse, and Newton—set out across the Great Court of Trinity College. All were in long black robes and mortarboards save Newton, who led the way, a cardinal pursued by a flock of crows, a vivid red mark on the Trinity green.

"I HAVEN'T SEEN *THIS* PLAY," Locke said, "but I have seen one or two from which the story and characters of *this* one were . . . uh . . ."

Newton: "Stolen."

Boyle: "Inspired."

LeFebure: "Appropriated."

Locke: "Adapted, and so I can inform you that a ship has run aground in a storm, near a castle, the seat of a foppish courtier probably named something like Percival Kidney or Reginald Mumblesleeve—"

"Francis Buggermy, according to the Playbill," Daniel put in. Isaac turned around and glared at him.

"So much the better," Locke said. "But of course the fop's in London, never comes to the country—so a Vagabond named Roger Thrust or Judd Vault or—"

"Tom Runagate."

"And his mistress, Madeline Cherry or—"

"Miss Straddle, in this case."

"Are squatting there. Now, seeing a group of castaways from the ship coming ashore, these two Vagabonds dress up in the fop's clothing and impersonate Francis Buggermy and his mistress-of-the-moment—much to the surprise of a withered Puritan Bible-pounder who comes upon the scene—"

"The Reverend Yahweh Pucker," Daniel said.

"The rest we can see for ourselves—"

"Why's that old fellow all charred black?" Boyle demanded, catching sight of a performer up on the stage.

"He's a Neeger slave," Daniel said.

"Which reminds me," Locke put in, "I need to send a message to my broker—time to sell my stock in the Guinea Company, I fear—"

"No, no!" Boyle said, "I mean black as in *charred, burnt,* with smoke coming out of his hair!"

"No such thing was in the version *I* saw," Locke said.

"Oh . . . in an earlier scene, there was a hilarious misadventure, having to do with a keg of gunpowder," Daniel volunteered.

"Er . . . was this comedy written *recently?*"

"Since the . . . um . . . *events?*"

"One can only assume," Daniel said.

Significant chin-stroking and hemming now among the various R.S. Fellows (save Newton), who glanced up towards the Earl of Epsom as they made their way to their seats.

LYDIA: Is this walking, or swimming?

VAN UND: Fine muck—fine hurricanoe—throw up a dike there, and a windmill yonder, and I'll be able to join it to my estates in Flanders.

LYDIA: But it isn't *yours*.

VAN UND: Easily remedied—what's the name of the place?

LYDIA: That pretty boatswain said we were just off a place called Suckmire.

VAN UND: Don't pine for *him,* Lydia—yonder Castle's sure to house some Persons of Quality—why, I spy some now! Halloo!

TOM RUNAGATE: You see, Miss Straddle, they've already marked us as Courtiers. A few stolen rags are as good as Title and Pedigree.

MISS STRADDLE: Aye, Tom, true enough when we're barely within bowshot—but what's to come later?

TOM (*peering through spyglass*): What is to *come?* I have spied one candidate—

STRADDLE: That lass has breeding, my wayward Tom—she'll scorn you as a Vagabond, when she hears your voice—

TOM: I can do a fine accent well as any Lord.

STRADDLE: —and observes your uncouth manners.

TOM: Don't you know that bad manners are high fashion now?

STRADDLE: Stab me!

TOM: 'Tis truth! These fine people insult one another all day long—'tis called wit! Then they poke at one another with swords, and call it honor.

STRADDLE: Then 'tween Wit and Honor, the treasure on that wrack is as good as ours.

VAN UND: Halloo, there, sir! Throw us a line, we are sinking into your garden!

TOM: This one must be daft, he mistakes yonder mud-flat for a garden!

STRADDLE: Daft, or Delft.

TOM: You think he's Dutch!? Then I might levy a rope-climbing toll . . .

STRADDLE: What'll his daughter think of you then?

TOM: 'Tis well considered . . .

Throws rope.

LORD BRIMSTONE: Who's that Frenchman on the sea-wall? Has England been conquered? Heaven help us!

LADY B: He is no Frenchman, my lord, but a good English gentleman in *modern* attire—most likely it is Count Suckmire, and that lady is his latest courtesan.

LORD B: You don't say!

To Miss Straddle. Good day, madam—I'm informed that you are a Cartesian—here stands another!

STRADDLE: What's he on about?

TOM: Never mind—remember what I told you.

LORD B: *Cogito, ergo sum!*

STRADDLE: Air go some? Yes, the air goes some when you flap your jaw, sir—I thought it was a sea-breeze, until I smelled it.

To Tom. Is that the sort of thing?

TOM: Well played, my flower.

LADY B: That whore is most uncivil.

LORD B: No need to be vulgar, my dear—it means she recognizes us as her equals.

ENTER, from opposite, the Rev. Yahweh Pucker, with BIBLE and SHOVEL.

PUCKER: Here's proof the Lord works in mysterious ways—I came expecting to find a ship-wrack, and drownded bodies in need of burying—which service I am ever willing to perform, for a small contribution—group rates available—instead, it is a courtly scene. St. James's Park on a sunny May morn ne'er was so.

TOM: Between the *Dutch* mercer, and the *English* lord, there must
be treasure aplenty on that wrack—if you can divert them in the
Castle, I'll get word to our merry friends—they can steal the
longboat these rowed in on, and go fetch the goods.

STRADDLE: Whilst you salvage the Dutch girl's maidenhead?

TOM: Lost at sea already, I fear.

NOW THERE WAS A CHANGE of scene to the interior of Castle Suckmire. As things were being re-arranged upon the stage, Oldenburg
leaned close and said, "Is that him, then?"

"Yes, that's Isaac Newton."

"Well done—more than one Anglesey will be pleased—how did
you flush him into the open?"

"I am not entirely sure."

"What of the tangents paper?"

"One thing at a time, please, sir . . ."

"I cannot understand his reticence!"

"He's only published one thing in his life—"

"The colors paper!? That was two years ago!"

"For you, two years of interminable waiting—for Isaac, two years
of siege warfare—fending off Hooke on one front, Jesuits on the
other."

"Perhaps if you would only relate to him how you have passed
the last two months—"

Daniel managed not to laugh in Oldenburg's face.

UP ON THE STAGE IN Neville's Court, the plot was thickening, or,
depending on how you liked your plots, expanding into a froth.
Miss Straddle, played by Tess, was flirting with Eugene Stopcock,
an infantry officer, who had rushed in from London to rescue his
shipwrecked parents. Tom Runagate had already been to bed at
least once with Lydia van Underdevater. The courtier Francis Buggermy had showed up incognito and begun chasing the slave
Nzinga around in hopes of verifying certain rumors about the size
of African men.

Isaac Newton was pinching the high bridge of his nose and looking mildly nauseated. Oldenburg was glaring at Daniel, and several
important personages were glaring from On High at Oldenburg.

The play was entering Act V. Soon it would come to an end,
triggering a plan, laid by Oldenburg, in which Isaac was finally
going to be introduced to the King, and to the Royal Society at
large. If Isaac's paper were not brought forth tonight, it never

would be, and Isaac would be known only as an Alchemist who once invented a telescope. So Daniel excused himself and set out across Trinity's courtyards one more time.

The lurkers in the Great Court had thinned out, or perhaps he simply was not paying so much attention to them—he had decided what to do, and that gave him liberty, for the first time in months, to tilt his head back and look up at the stars.

It had turned out that Hooke, with his telescope project, had had much more on his mind than countering the ravings of some pedantic Jesuit. Sitting in the dark hole of Gresham's College, marking down the coordinates of various stars, he'd outlined the rudiments of a larger theory to Daniel: first that all cœlestial bodies attracted all others within their sphere of influence, by means of some gravitating power; second that all bodies put into motion moved forward in a straight line unless acted upon by some effectual power; third that the attractive power became more powerful as the body wrought upon came nearer to the center.

Oldenburg did not yet know the magnitude of Isaac's powers. Not that Oldenburg was stupid—he was anything but. But Isaac, unlike, say, Leibniz the indefatigable letter-writer or Hooke the Royal Society stalwart, did not communicate his results, and did not appear to socialize with anyone save daft Alchemists. And so in Oldenburg's mind, Newton was a clever though odd chap who'd written a paper about colors and then got into a fracas over it with Hooke. If Newton would only mingle with the Fellows a bit, Oldenburg seemed to believe, he would soon learn that Hooke had quite put colors out of his mind and moved on to matters such as Universal Gravitation, which of course would not interest young Mr. Newton in the slightest.

This entire plan was, in other words, an embryonic disaster. But it might not occur for another hundred years that most of the Royal Society, and a King with a passion for Natural Philosophy, would spend a night together in Cambridge, within shouting distance of the bed where Isaac slept and the table where he worked. Isaac had to be drawn out, and it had to happen tonight. If this would lead to open war with Hooke, so be it. Perhaps that was inevitable anyway, no matter what Daniel did in the next few minutes.

DANIEL WAS BACK in the chambers. Roger Comstock, left behind, Cinderella-like, to tidy up and tend the furnaces, had apparently gotten bored and sneaked off to an alehouse, because the candles had all been snuffed, leaving the big room lit only by the furnaces' rosy glow. Here Daniel would've been at a stand, if not for the fact that he lived there, and could find his way round in the dark. He groped a candle out of a drawer and lit it from a furnace. Then he went into the room where he'd conversed with Isaac earlier. Rummaging through papers, trying to find the one about tangents—the first practical fruits of Isaac's old work about fluxions—he was reminded that the sight of something on this table had rattled Isaac, and persuaded him to expose himself to the awful torment of watching a comedy. Daniel kept a sharp eye out, but saw nothing except for tedious alchemical notes and recipes, many signed not "Isaac Newton" but "Jeova Sanctus Unus," which was the pseudonym Isaac used for Alchemy work.

In any case—without solving the eternal mystery of why Isaac did what he did—he spied the tangents paper on the far corner of the table, and stepped forward to reach for it.

The place was suffused with odd sounds, mostly the seething and hissing of diverse fuels burning in the furnaces, and the endless popping and ticking of the wooden wall panels. Another sound, faint and furtive, had reached Daniel's ears from time to time, but that surly porter who bestrides the gate of the conscious mind, spurning most of what is brought in by the senses and admitting only perceptions of Import or Quality, had construed this as a mouse sapping and mining the wall, and shouldered it aside. Now, though, it did come to Daniel's notice, for it grew louder: more rat than mouse. Isaac's tangents paper was in his hand, but he stood still for a few moments, trying to work out where this rat was busy, so that he could come back in daylight and investigate. The sound was resonating in a partition separating this room from the big laboratory with the furnaces, which was not of regular shape, but had several pop-outs and alcoves, built, by men who'd long since passed away, for heaven only knew what reasons: perhaps to encase a chimney here, or add a bit of pantry space there. Daniel had a good idea of what lay on the opposite side of that wall that was making the grinding noises: it was a little sideboard, set into an alcove in the corner of the laboratory, probably used once by servants when that room had been a dining-hall. Nowadays, Isaac used the cabinets below it to store Alchemical supplies. The counter was stocked with mortars, pestles, &c. For certain of the things Isaac worked with had a marked yearning to burst into flame, and so he was at pains to store them in that particular alcove, as far as possible from the furnaces.

Daniel walked as quietly as he could back into the laboratory. He set the tangents paper down on a table and then picked up an iron bar that was lying next to a furnace door for use as a poker. There was more than one way to get rid of rats; but sometimes the best approach was the simplest, viz. ambush and bludgeon. He stalked down an aisle between furnaces, wiggling the poker in his hand. The alcove had been partitioned from the rest of the room by a free-standing screen such as ladies were wont to dress behind, consisting of fabric (now shabby) pleated and hung on a light wooden frame. This was to stop flying sparks, and to shield Isaac's fragile scales and fine powders from gusts of wind coming through open windows or down chimneys.

He faltered, for the gnawing had stopped, as if the rat sensed the approach of a predator. But then it started up again, very loud, and Daniel strode forward, stretched one toe out ahead of him, and kicked the screen out of the way. His poker-hand was drawn back behind his head, poised to ring down a death-blow, and the candle was thrust out before him to find and dazzle the rat, which he guessed would be out on the counter.

Instead he found himself sharing a confined space with another man. Daniel was so astonished that he froze, and sprang several inches into the air, at the same instant, if such a combination were possible, and dropped the poker, and fumbled the candle. He had nearly shoved the flame right into the face of this other chap: Roger Comstock. Roger had been working in the dark with a mortar and pestle and so the sudden appearance of this flame in his face not only startled him half out of his wits, but blinded him as well. And on the heels of those emotions came terror. He dropped what he had been working on: a mortar, containing some dark gray powder, which he had been pouring into a cloth bag at the instant Daniel surprised him. Indeed *drop* did not do justice to Roger's treatment of these two items; gravity was not nearly quick enough. He *thrust* them away, and at the same time flung himself backwards.

Daniel watched the flame of his candle grow to the size of a bull's head, enveloping his hand and arm as far as the elbow. He dropped it. The floor was carpeted with flame that leapt up in a great *FOOM* and disappeared, leaving the place perfectly dark. Not that all flames had gone, for Daniel could still hear them crackling; the darkness was because of dense smoke filling the whole room. Daniel inhaled some and wished he hadn't. This was gunpowder that Roger had been playing with.

Roger was out of the house in five heartbeats, notwithstanding that he did it on his hands and knees. Daniel crawled out after him and stood outside the door long enough to purge his lungs with several deep draughts of fresh air.

Roger had already scuttled across the garden and banged out the gate. Daniel went over to pull it closed, looking out first into the way. Some yards down, a couple of porters, shadowed under the vault of the Great Gate, regarded him with only moderate curiosity. It was *expected* that strange lights and noises would emanate from the residence of the Lucasian Professor of Mathematics. For shadowy figures to flee the building with smoke coming out of their clothes was only a little remarkable. Failing to close the garden gate was an egregious lapse; but Daniel saw to it.

Then, holding his breath, he ventured back in. He found the windows by grope and hauled them open. The flames had caught and spread in the fabric of the toppled screen, but gone no farther, owing to that Isaac suffered very little that was combustible to abide in the furnace-room. Daniel stomped out a few glowing edges.

In a more genteel setting, the smoke would have been accounted as a kind of damage to all the contents of the room that had been darkened and made noisome by it; but in a place such as this, it was nothing.

What had occurred was not an explosion—for the gunpowder, fortunately, had not been confined—but a very rapid burning. The screen was wrecked. The cabinetry in the alcove was blackened. A scale had been blown off the counter and was probably ruined. The mortar that Roger had dropped lay in fat shards at the epicenter of the black burst, making Daniel think of the cannon that had exploded at the "Siege of Maestricht," and other such disasters he had heard about lately aboard ships of the Royal Navy. Surrounding it were burnt scraps of linen—the bag into which Roger had been decocting the gunpowder when Daniel had set fire to it. It was, in other words, the least possible amount of devastation that could possibly result from deflagration of a sack of gunpowder inside the house. That said, this corner of the laboratory was a shambles, and would have to be cleaned up—a task that would fall to Roger anyway. Unless, as seemed likely, Isaac fired him.

One would think that being blown up would throw one's evening's schedule all awry. But all of this had passed very quickly, and there was no reason Daniel could not accomplish the errand that had brought him here. Indeed, the grave problems that had so burdened him on his walk over here were quite forgotten now, and would appear to be perfectly trivial seen against the stunning adventure of the last few minutes. His hand and, to a lesser degree, his face, were raw and red from flash-burns, and he suspected he might have to do without eyebrows for a few weeks. A quick change of robes and a wash were very much in order; no difficulty, as he lived upstairs.

But having done those, Daniel picked up the tangents paper, shook off the black grit that re-punctuated it, and headed out the door. This was no more than a tenth of everything Isaac had accomplished with fluxions, but it was at least a *shred* of evidence— better than nothing—and sufficient to keep most Fellows of the Royal Society in bed with headaches for weeks. The night overhead was clear, the view excellent, the mysteries of the Universe all spread out above Trinity College. But Daniel lowered his sights and plodded toward the cone of steamy light where everyone was waiting.

⚓

London Bridge
1673

⚓

> Once the characteristic numbers of most notions
> are determined, the human race will have a new
> kind of tool, a tool that will increase the power of
> the mind much more than optical lenses helped our
> eyes, a tool that will be as far superior to micro-
> scopes or telescopes as reason is to vision.
>
> —LEIBNIZ, *Philosophical Essays*,
> TRANS. BY ARLEW AND GARBER

NEAR THE MIDPOINT of London Bridge, a bit closer to the City than to Southwark, was a firebreak—a short gap in the row of buildings, like a missing tooth in a crowded jawbone. If you were drifting down-river in a boat, so that you could see all nineteen of the squat piers that held the bridge up, and all twenty of the ragstone arches and wooden drawbridges that let the water through, you'd be able to see that this open space—"the square," it was called—stood directly above an arch that was wider than any of the others— thirty-four feet, at its widest.

As you drew closer to the bridge, and it became more and more obvious that your life was in extreme danger, and your mind, therefore, became focused on practical matters, you'd notice something even more important, namely that the sluice between the starlings—the snowshoe-like platforms of rubble that served as footings for the piers—was also wider, in this place, than anywhere else on the bridge. Consequently the passage through it looked less like a boiling cataract than a river rushing down from mountains during the spring thaw. If you still had the ability to steer for it, you would. And if you were a passenger on this hypothetical boat, and you valued your life, you'd insist that the waterman tie up for a moment at the tip of the starling and let you out, so that you could pick your way over that jammed horde of more or less ancient piles and the in-fill of mucky rubble; take a stair up to the level of the roadway; run across the Square, not forgetting to dodge the carts rushing both ways; descend another stair to the other end of the starling; and then hop, skid, and stagger across it until you reached the end, where your waterman would be waiting to pick you up again if indeed his boat, and he, still existed.

This accounted, anyway, for much that was peculiar about the part of London Bridge called the Square. Persons who went east and west on watermen's boats on the Thames tended to be richer and more important than those who went north and south across the Bridge, and the ones who actually cared enough about their lives, limbs, and estates to bother with climbing out and hiking over the starling tended to be richer and more important yet, and so the buildings that stood atop the Bridge to either side of the Square constituted location! location! location! to the better sort of retailers and publicans.

Daniel Waterhouse spent a couple of hours loitering in the vicinity of the Square one morning, waiting for a certain man on a certain boat. However, the boat he waited for would be coming the other direction: working its way upstream from the sea.

He took a seat in a coffee-house and amused himself watching flushed and sweaty ferry-passengers appear at the head of the stairs, as if they'd been spontaneously generated from the fœtid waters of the Thames. They'd crawl into the nearby tavern for a pint, fortifying themselves for the traversal of the Bridge's twelve-foot-wide roadway, where passengers were crushed between carts a few times a week. If they survived that, then they'd pop into the glover's or the haberdasher's for a bit of recreational shopping, and then perhaps dart into this coffee-house for a quick mug of java. The remainder of London Bridge was getting down at the heels, because much more fashionable shops were being put up in other parts of the city by the likes of Sterling, but the Square was prosperous and, because of the continual threat of boat-wrack and drowning, the merriest part of town.

And in these days it tended to be crowded, especially when ships came across the Channel, and dropped anchor in the Pool, and their Continental passengers were ferried hither in watermen's boats.

As one such boat drew near the Bridge, Daniel finished his coffee, settled his bill, and ventured out onto the street. Cartage and drayage had been baffled by a crowd of pedestrians. They all wanted to descend to the starling on the downstream side, and had formed a sort of bung that stopped not only the stairs but the street as well. Seeing that they were by and large City men, intent on some serious purpose, and not Vagabonds intent on his purse, Daniel insinuated himself into this crowd and was presently drawn in to the top of the stairs and flushed down to the top of the starling along with the rest. He supposed at first that all of these well-dressed men had come to greet specific passengers. But as the boat drew within earshot, they began to shout, not friendly greetings, but questions, in several languages, about the war.

"As a fellow Protestant—albeit Lutheran—it is *my* hoping that England and Holland shall become reconciled and that the war you speak of will no more exist."

The young German was standing up in a boat, wearing French fashions. But as the boat drew closer to the turbulence downstream of the Bridge, he came to his senses, and sat down.

"So much for hopes—now what of your *observations,* sir?" someone fired back—one of a few dozen who had by now crowded onto the starling, trying to get as close to the incoming boats and ferries as they could without falling into the deadly chute. Others were perched up on the edge of the Square, like gargoyles, still others were out on the river in boats plotting intercept courses, like boca-neers in the Caribbean. None of them was having any of this Lutheran diplomacy. None even knew who the young German was—just a passenger on a boat from abroad who was willing to talk. There were several other travelers on the same boat, but all of them ignored the shouting Londoners. If these had information, they would take it to the 'Change, and tell the tale with silver, and propagate it through the chthonic channels of the Market.

"What ship were you on, sir?" someone bellowed.

"*Ste-Catherine,* sir."

"Where did that ship come from, sir?"

"Calais."

"Had you any conversation with Naval persons?"

"A little, perhaps."

"Any news, or rumor, of cannons bursting on English ships?"

"Oh, sometimes it happens. By everyone in the ships of the *melee*, it is seen, for the whole side of the hull is out-blown, and out the bodies fly, or so they say. To all of the sailors, friend and enemy, it is a lesson of mortality, perhaps. Consequently they all talk about it. But in the present war it happens no more than usual, I think."

"Were they Comstock cannons?"

The German took a moment to understand that, without even having set foot on English soil yet, he had talked himself into deep trouble. "Sir! The cannons of my lord Epsom are reckoned the finest in the world."

But no one wanted to hear that kind of talk. The topic had changed.

"Whence came you to Calais?"

"Paris."

"Did you see troops moving on your journey across France?"

"A few ones, exhausted, south-going."

The gentlemen on the starling hummed and vibrated for a few moments, assimilating this. One broke away from the crowd, toiling back towards the stairs, and was engulfed in barefoot boys jumping up and down. He scribbled something on a bit of paper and handed it to the one who jumped highest. This one spun, forced a path through the others, took the stairs four at a time, broke loose onto the Square, vaulted over a wagon, spun a fish-wife, and then began to build speed up the bridge. From here to the London shore was a hundred and some yards, from there to the 'Change was six hundred—he'd be there in three minutes. Meanwhile the interrogation continued: "Did you see Ships of Force in the Channel, *mein Herr*? English, French, Dutch?"

"There was—" and here the man's English gave way. He made a helpless, encompassing gesture.

"Fog!"

"Fog," he repeated.

"Did you hear guns?"

"A few—but very likely they were only signals. Coded *data* speeding through the *fog*, so opaque to light, but so transparent to sound—" and here he lost control of his intellectual sphincters and began to think out loud in French, fortified with Latin, working out a system for sending encrypted data from place to place using explosions, building on ideas from Wilkins's *Cryptonomicon* but marrying them to a practical plan that, in its lavish expenditure of gunpowder, would be sure to please John Comstock. In other words, he identified himself (to Daniel anyway) as Dr. Gottfried Wilhelm Leibniz. The watchers lost interest and began aiming their questions at another boat.

Leibniz set foot on England. He was closely followed by a couple of other German gentlemen, somewhat older, much less talkative, and (Daniel could only suppose) more important. They in turn were pursued by a senior servant who headed up a short column of porters lugging boxes and bags. But Leibniz had burdened himself with a wooden box he would not let go of. Daniel stepped forward to greet them, but was cut off by some brusque fellow who shouldered in to hand a sealed letter to one of the older gentlemen, and whispered to him for a moment in Low-Dutch.

Daniel straightened up in annoyance. As luck would have it, he looked toward the London shore. His eye lingered on a quay just downstream of the Bridge: a jumbled avalanche of blackened rubble left over from the Fire. It *could* have been rebuilt years ago, but hadn't, because it had been judged more important to rebuild other things first. A few men were doing work of a highly intellectual nature, stretching lines about and drawing sketches. One of them—incredibly—just happened to be Robert Hooke, City Surveyor, whom Daniel had quietly abandoned at Gresham's College an hour ago. *Not* so incredibly (given that he was Hooke), he'd noticed Daniel standing there on the starling in the middle of the river, greeting what was quite obviously a foreign delegation, and was therefore glaring and brooding.

Leibniz and the others discussed matters in High-Dutch. The interloper turned round to glance at Daniel. It was one of the Dutch Ambassador's errand-boys-*cum*-spies. The Germans formed some sort of a plan, and it seemed to involve splitting up. Daniel stepped in and introduced himself.

The other Germans were introduced by their *names* but what mattered was their *ancestry:* one of them was the nephew of the Archbishop of Mainz, the other the son of Baron von Boineburg, who was the same Archbishop's Minister. In other words *very* important people in Mainz, hence *rather* important ones in the Holy Roman Empire, which was more or less neutral in the French/English/Dutch broil. It had all the signs of being some sort of peace-brokering mission, i.e.

Leibniz knew who he was, and asked, "Is Wilkins still alive?"

"Yes . . ."

"Thank God!"

"Though very ill. If you would like to visit him I would suggest doing it *now*. I'll escort you gladly, Dr. Leibniz . . . may I have the honor of assisting you with that box?"

"You are very civil," Leibniz said, "but I'll hold it."

"If it contains gold or jewelry, you'd best hold it *tight*."

"Are the streets of London not safe?"

"Let us say that the Justices of the Peace are mostly concerned with Dissenters and Dutchmen, and our cutpurses have not been slow to adapt."

"What this contains is infinitely more valuable than gold," Leibniz said, beginning to mount the stairs, "and yet it cannot be stolen."

Daniel lunged forward in an effort to keep step. Leibniz was slender, of average height, and tended to bend forward when he walked, the head anticipating the feet. Once he had reached the level of the roadway he turned sharply and strode towards the City of London, ignoring the various taverns and shops.

He did not *look* like a monster.

According to Oldenburg, the Parisians who frequented the Salon at the Hotel Montmor—the closest French equivalent to the Royal Society of London—had begun using the Latin word *monstro* to denote Leibniz. This from men who'd personally known Descartes and Fermat and who considered exaggeration an unspeakably vulgar habit. It had led to some etymological researches among some members of the R.S. Did they mean Leibniz was grotesquely misshapen? An unnatural hybrid of a man and something else? A divine warning?

"He lives up this way, does he not?"

"The Bishop has had to move because of his illness—he's at his stepdaughter's house in Chancery Lane."

"Then still we go this way—then left."

"You have been to London before, Dr. Leibniz?"

"I have been studying London-paintings."

"I'm afraid most of those became antiquarian curiosities after the Fire—like street-plans of Atlantis."

"And yet viewing several depictions of even an imaginary city, is enlightening in a way," Leibniz said. "Each painter can view the city from only one standpoint at a time, so he will move about the place, and paint it from a hilltop on one side, then a tower on the other, then from a grand intersection in the middle—all on the same canvas. When we look at the canvas, then, we glimpse in a small way how God understands the universe—for he sees it from every point of view *at once*. By populating the world with so many different minds, each with its own point of view, God gives us a suggestion of what it means to be omniscient."

Daniel decided to step back and let Leibniz's words reverberate, as organ-chords must do in Lutheran churches. Meanwhile they reached the north end of the Bridge, where the racket of the water-wheels, confined and focused in the stone vault of the gatehouse, made conversation impossible. Not until they'd made it out onto dry land, and begun to ascend the Fish Street hill, did Daniel ask, "I note you've already been in communication with the Dutch Ambassador. May I assume that your mission is not entirely *natural-philosophick* in nature?"

"A rational question—in a way," Leibniz grumbled. "We are about the same age, you and I?" he asked, giving Daniel a quick inspection. His eyes were unsettling. Depending on what *kind* of monster he was, either beady, or penetrating.

"I am twenty-six."

"So am I. We were born about sixteen forty-six. The Swedes took Prague that year, and invaded Bavaria. The Inquisition was burning Jews in Mexico. Similar terrible things were happening in England, I assume?"

"Cromwell crushed the King's army at Newark—chased him out of the country—John Comstock was wounded—"

"And we are speaking only of kings and noblemen. Imagine the sufferings of common people and Vagabonds, who possess equal stature in God's eyes. And yet you ask me whether my mission is *philosophick* or *diplomatic,* as if those two things can neatly be separated."

"Rude and stupid I know, but it is my duty to make conversation. You are saying that it should be the goal of all natural philosophers to restore peace and harmony to the world of men. This I cannot dispute."

Leibniz now softened. "Our goal is to prevent the Dutch war from growing into a general conflagration. Please do not be offended by my frankness now: the Archbishop and the Baron are followers of the Royal Society—as am I. They are Alchemists—which I am *not,* except when it is *politic.* They hope that through pursuit of Natural Philosophy I may make contacts with important figures in this country, whom it would normally be difficult to reach through *diplomatic* channels."

"Ten years ago I might have been offended," Daniel said. "Now, there's nothing I'll not believe."

"But my interest in meeting the Lord Bishop of Chester is as pure as any human motive *can* be."

"He will sense that, and be cheered by it," Daniel said. "The last few years of Wilkins's life have been sacrificed entirely to politics— he has been working to dismantle the framework of theocracy, to prevent its resurgence, in the event a Papist ascends to the throne—"

"Or already *has* done so," Leibniz said immediately.

The offhanded way in which Leibniz suggested that King Charles II might be a crypto-Catholic hinted to Daniel that it was common knowledge on the Continent. This made him feel hopelessly dull, naïve, and provincial. He had suspected the King of many crimes and deceptions, but never of baldly lying about his religion to the entire Realm.

He had plenty of time to conceal his annoyance as they were passing through the heart of the city, which had turned into a single vast and eternal building-site even as the normal business of the 'Change and the goldsmiths' shops continued. Paving-stones were whizzing between Daniel and the Doctor like cannonballs, shovels slicing the air around their heads like cutlasses, barrows laden with gold and silver and bricks and mud trundling like munition-carts over temporary walk-ways of planks and stomped dirt.

Perhaps reading anxiety on Daniel's face, Leibniz said, "Just like the Rue Vivienne in Paris," with a casual hand-wave. "I go there frequently to read certain manuscripts in the Bibliothèque du Roi."

"I've been told that a copy of every book printed in France must be sent to that place."

"Yes."

"But it was established in the same year that we had our Fire—so I ween that it must be very small yet, as it's had only a few years to grow."

"A few very good years in mathematics, sir. And it also contains certain unpublished manuscripts of Descartes and Pascal."

"But none of the classics?"

"I had the good fortune to be raised, or to raise myself, in my father's library, which contained all of them."

"Your father was *mathematickally* inclined?"

"Difficult to say. As a traveler comprehends a city only by viewing pictures of it drawn from differing standpoints, I know my father only by having read the books that he read."

"I understand the similitude now, Doctor. The Bibliothèque du Roi then gives you the closest thing that currently exists to God's understanding of the world."

"And yet with a bigger library we could come ever so much closer."

"But with all due respect, Doctor, I do not understand how *this* street could be anything *less* like the Rue Vivienne—we have no such Bibliothèque in England."

"The Bibliothèque du Roi is just a *house,* you see, a house Colbert happened to buy on the Rue Vivienne—probably as an investment, because that street is the center of goldsmiths. Every ten days, from ten in the morning until noon, all of the merchants of Paris send their money to the Rue Vivienne to be counted. I sit there in Colbert's house trying to understand Descartes, working the mathematical proofs that Huygens, my tutor, gives me, and looking out the windows as the street fills up with porters staggering under their back-loads of gold and silver, converging on a few doorways. Are you beginning to understand my riddle now?"

"Which riddle was that?"

"This box! I said it contained something infinitely more valuable than gold, and yet it could not be stolen. Which way do we turn here?"

For they'd come out into the hurricane where Threadneedle, Cornhill, Poultry, and Lombard all collided. Message-boys were flying across that intersection like quarrels from crossbows—or (Daniel suspected) like broad Hints that he was failing to Get.

LONDON CONTAINED A HUNDRED LORDS, bishops, preachers, scholars, and gentlemen-philosophers who would gladly have provided Wilkins with a comfortable sick-bed, but he had ended up in his stepdaughter's home in Chancery Lane, actually rather close to where the Waterhouses lived. The entrance to the place, and the street in front, were choked with sweating courtiers—not the sleek top-level ones but the dented, scarred, slightly too old and slightly too ugly ones who actually got everything done.* They were milling in the street around a black coach blazoned with the arms of Count Penistone. The house was an old one (the Fire had stopped a few yards short of it). It was one of those slump-shouldered, thatch-roofed, half-timbered Canterbury Tales productions, completely out-moded by the gleaming coach and the whip-thin rapiers.

---

*Pepys being a good example—but he wasn't there.

"You see—despite the purity of your motives, you're immersed in politics already," Daniel said. "The lady of the house is Cromwell's niece."

"What!? *The* Cromwell?"

"The same whose skull gazes down on Westminster from the end of a stick. Now, the owner of that excellent coach is Knott Bolstrood, Count Penistone—his father founded a sect called the Barkers, normally lumped in with many others under the pejorative term of Puritans. The Barkers are *gratuitously* radical, however—for example, they believe that Government and Church should have naught to do with each other, and that all slaves in the world should be set free."

"But the gentlemen in front are dressed like courtiers! Are they getting ready to siege the Puritan-house?"

"They are Bolstrood's hangers-on. You see, Count Penistone is His Majesty's Secretary of State."

"I had heard that King Charles the Second made a Phanatique his Secretary of State, but could not believe it."

"Consider it—could Barkers exist in any other country? Save Amsterdam, that is."

"Naturally not!" Leibniz said, lightly offended by the very idea. "They would be extinguished."

"Therefore, whether or not he feels any loyalty toward the King, Knott Bolstrood has no choice but to stand for a free and independent England—and so, when Dissenters accuse the King of being too close to France, His Majesty need only point to Bolstrood as the living credential of his independent foreign policy."

"But it's all a farce!" Leibniz muttered. "All Paris knows England's in France's pocket."

"All London knows it, too—the difference is that we have three dozen theatres here—Paris has only one of them—"

Leibniz's turn, finally, to be baffled. "I don't understand."

"All I am saying is that we happen to *enjoy* farces."

"Why is Bolstrood visiting the niece of Cromwell?"

"He's probably visiting Wilkins."

Leibniz stopped and considered matters. "Tempting. But the protocol is impossible. I cannot enter the house!"

"Of course you can—with me," Daniel said. "Just follow."

"But I must go back and fetch my companions—for I do not have the *standing* to disturb the Secretary of State—"

"I do," Daniel said. "One of my earliest memories is of watching him destroy a pipe organ with a sledgehammer. Seeing me will give him a warm feeling."

Leibniz stopped and looked aghast; Daniel could almost see,

reflected in his eyes, the stained-glass windows and organ-pipes of some fine Lutheran church in Leipzig. "Why would he commit such an outrage!?"

"Because it was in an Anglican cathedral. He would have been about twenty—a high-spirited age."

"Your family were followers of Cromwell?"

"It is more correct to say that Cromwell was a follower of my father—may God rest both of their souls." But now they were in the midst of the courtier-mob, and it was too late for Leibniz to obey his instincts, and run away.

They spent several minutes pushing among progressively higher-ranking and better-dressed men, into the house and up the stairs, and finally entered a tiny low-ceilinged bedchamber. It smelled as if Wilkins had already died, but most of him still lived— he was propped up on pillows, with a board on his lap, and a fine-looking document on the board. Knott Bolstrood—forty-two years old—knelt next to the bed. He turned round to look as Daniel entered. During the ten years Knott had survived on the Common-Side of Newgate Prison, living in a dark place among murderers and lunaticks, he had developed a strong instinct for watching his back. It was as useful for a Secretary of State as it had been for a marauding Phanatique.

"Brother Daniel!"

"My lord."

"You'll do as well as anyone—better than most."

"Do for what, sir?"

"Witnessing the Bishop's signature."

Bolstrood got a quill charged with ink. Daniel wrapped Wilkins's puffy fingers around it. After a bit of heavy breathing on the part of its owner, the hand began to move, and a tangle of lines and curves began to take shape on the page, bearing the same relationship to Wilkins's signature as a ghost to a man. It was a good thing, in other words, that several persons were on hand to verify it. Daniel had no idea what this document was. But from the way it was engrossed he could guess that it was meant for the eyes of the King.

Count Penistone was a man in a hurry, after that. But before he left he said to Daniel: "If you have any stock in the Duke of York's Guinea Company, sell it—for that Popish slave-monger is going to reap the whirlwind." Then, for maybe the second or third time in his life, Knott Bolstrood smiled.

"Show it to me, Dr. Leibniz," Wilkins said, skipping over all of the formalities; he had not urinated in three days and so there was a certain urgency about everything.

Leibniz sat gingerly on the edge of the bed, and opened the box.

Daniel saw gears, cranks, shafts. He thought it might be a new sort of timepiece, but it had no dial and no hands—only a few wheels with numbers stamped on them.

"It owes much to Monsieur Pascal's machine, of course," Leibniz said, "but this one can *multiply* numbers as well as add and subtract them."

"Make it work for me, Doctor."

"I must confess to you that it is not finished yet." Leibniz frowned, tilted the box toward the light, and blew into it sharply. A cockroach flew out and traced a flailing parabola to the floor and scurried under the bed. "This is just a demo'. But when it is finished, it will be *magnifique.*"

"Never mind," Wilkins said. "It uses denary numbers?"

"Yes, like Pascal's—but binary would work better—"

"You needn't tell *me*," Wilkins said, and then rambled for at least a quarter of an hour, quoting whole pages from relevant sections of the *Cryptonomicon.*

Leibniz finally cleared his throat and said, "There are mechanical reasons, too—with denary numbers, too many meshings of gears are necessary—friction and backlash play havoc."

"Hooke! Hooke could build it," Wilkins said. "But enough of machines. Let us speak of Pansophism. Tell me, now—have you met with success in Vienna?"

"I have written to the Emperor several times, describing the French king's Bibliothèque du Roi—"

"Trying to incite his Envy—?"

"Yes—but in his hierarchy of vices, Sloth would appear to reign unchallenged by Envy or anything else. Have you met with success here, my lord?"

"Sir Elias Ashmole is starting a brave library—but he's distracted and addled with Alchemy. I have had to attend to more fundamental matters—" Wilkins said, and gestured weakly toward the door through which Bolstrood had departed. "I believe that binary arithmetickal engines will be of enormous significance—Oldenburg, too, is most eager."

"If I could carry your work forward, sir, I would consider myself privileged."

"Now we are only being polite—I have no time. Waterhouse!"

Leibniz closed up his box. The Bishop of Chester watched the lid closing over the engine, and his eyelids almost closed at the same moment. But then he summoned up a bit more strength. Leibniz backed out of the way, and Daniel took his place.

"My Lord?"

It was all he could get out. Drake had been his father, but John Wilkins really *was* his lord in almost every sense of the word. His lord, his bishop, his minister, his professor.

"The responsibility now falls upon you to make it all happen."

"My Lord? To make *what* happen?"

But Wilkins was either dead or asleep.

THEY STUMBLED THROUGH a small dark kitchen and out into the maze of yards and alleys behind Chancery Lane, where they drew the attention of diverse roosters and dogs. Pursued by their hue and cry, Mr. Waterhouse and Dr. Leibniz emerged into a district of theatres and coffee-houses. Any one of those coffee-houses would have sufficed, but they were close to Queen Street—another of Hooke's paving-projects. Daniel had begun to feel like a flea under the Great Microscope. Hooke subtended about half of the cosmos, and made Daniel feel as if he were flitting from one place of refuge to another, even though he had nothing to hide. Leibniz was hale, and seemed to enjoy exploring a new city. Daniel got them turned back in the direction of the river. He was trying to make out what responsibility, specifically, had just been placed on his shoulders by Wilkins. He realized—after a quarter of an hour of being a very poor conversationalist—that Leibniz might have ideas on the subject.

"You said you wanted to carry Wilkins's work forward, Doctor. *Which* of his projects were you referring to? Flying to the moon, or—"

"The Philosophical Language," Leibniz said, as if this should have been obvious.

He knew that Daniel had been involved in that project, and seemed to take the question as a sign that Daniel wasn't especially proud of it—which was true. Noting Leibniz's respect for the project, Daniel felt a stab of misgivings that perhaps the Philosophical Language had some wonderful properties that he had been too stupid to notice.

"What more is there to be done with it?" Daniel asked. "You have some refinements—additions—? You wish to translate the work into German—? You're shaking your head, Doctor—what is it, then?"

"I was trained as a lawyer. Don't look so horrified, Mr. Waterhouse, it is respectable enough, for an educated man in Germany. You must remember that we don't have a Royal Society. After I was awarded my Doctor of Jurisprudence, I went to work for the

Archbishop of Mainz, who gave me the job of reforming the legal code—which was a Tower of Babel—Roman and Germanic and local common law all mangled together. I concluded that there was little point in jury-rigging something. What was needed was to break everything down into certain basic concepts and begin from first principles."

"I can see how the Philosophical Language would be useful in breaking things down," Daniel said, "but to build them back up, you would need something else—"

"Logic," Leibniz said.

"Logic has a dismal reputation among the higher primates in the Royal Society—"

"Because they associate it with the Scholastic pedants who tormented them in university," Leibniz said agreeably. "I'm not talking about *that* sort of thing! When I say logic, I mean Euclidean."

"Begin with certain axioms and combine them according to definite rules—"

"Yes—and build up a system of laws that is as provable, and as internally consistent, as the theory of conic sections."

"But you have recently moved to Paris, have you not?"

Leibniz nodded. "Part of the same project. For obvious reasons, I need to improve my knowledge of mathematics—what better place for it?" Then his face got a distracted, brooding look. "Actually there was *another* reason—the Archbishop sent me as an emissary, to tender a certain proposal to Louis XIV."

"So today is not the first time you have combined Natural Philosophy with Diplomacy—"

"Nor the last, I fear."

"What was the proposal you set before the King?"

"I only got as far as Colbert, actually. But it was that, instead of invading her *neighbors,* La France ought to make an expedition to Egypt, and establish an Empire there—creating a threat to the Turk's left flank—Africa—and forcing him to move some armies away from his right flank—"

"Christendom."

"Yes." Leibniz sighed.

"It sounds—er—audacious," Daniel said, now on a diplomatic mission of his own.

"By the time I'd arrived in Paris, and secured an appointment with Colbert, King Louis had already flung his invasion-force into Holland and Germany."

"Ah, well—'twas a fine enough idea."

"Perhaps some *future* monarch of France will revive it," Leibniz said. "For the Dutch, the consequences were dire. For me, it was fortuitous—no longer straining at *diplomatic* gnats, I could go to Colbert's house in the Rue Vivienne and grapple with *philosophick* giants."

"I've given up trying to grapple with them," Daniel sighed, "and now only dodge their steps."

They rambled all the way down to the Strand and sat down in a coffee-house with south-facing windows. Daniel tilted the arithmetickal engine toward the sun and inspected its small gears. "Forgive me for asking, Doctor, but is this *purely* a conversation-starter, or—?"

"Perhaps you should go back and ask Wilkins."

"Touché."

Now some sipping of coffee.

"My Lord Chester spoke correctly—in a way—when he said that Hooke could build this," Daniel said. "Only a few years ago, he was a creature of the Royal Society, and he *would* have. Now he's a creature of London, and he has artisans build most of his watches. The only exceptions, perhaps, are the ones he makes for the King, the Duke of York, and the like."

"If I can explain to Mr. Hooke the importance of this device, I'm confident he'll undertake it."

"You don't understand Hooke," Daniel said. "Because you are German, and because you have diverse foreign connections, Hooke will assume you are a part of the Grubendolian cabal—which in his mind looms so vast that a French invasion of Egypt would be only a corner of it."

"Grubendol?" Leibniz said. Then, before Daniel could say it, he continued, "I see—it is an anagram for Oldenburg."

Daniel ground his teeth for a while, remembering how long it had taken *him* to decipher the same anagram, then continued: "Hooke is convinced that Oldenburg is stealing his inventions—sending them overseas in encrypted letters. What is worse, he saw you disembarking at the Bridge, and being handed a letter by a known Dutchman. He'll want to know what manner of Continental intrigues you're mixed up in."

"It's not a secret that my patron is the Archbishop of Mainz," Leibniz protested.

"But you said you were a Lutheran."

"And I am—but one of the Archbishop's objectives is to reconcile the two churches."

"*Here* we say there are *more* than two," Daniel reminded him.

"Is Hooke a religious man?"

"If you mean 'does he go to church,' then no," Daniel admitted, after some hesitation. "But if you mean 'does he believe in God' then I should say yes—the Microscope and Telescope are his stained-glass windows, the animalcules in a drop of his semen, or the shadows on Saturn's rings, are his heavenly Visions."

"Is he like Spinoza, then?"

"You mean, one who says God is nothing more than Nature? I doubt it."

"What does Hooke want?"

"He is busy all day and night designing new buildings, surveying new streets—"

"Yes, and I am busy overhauling the German legal code—but it is not what I *want*."

"Mr. Hooke pursues various schemes and intrigues against Oldenburg—"

"But surely not because he *wants* to?"

"He writes papers, and lectures—"

Leibniz scoffed. "Not a tenth of what he knows is written down, is it?"

"You must keep in mind, about Hooke, that he is poorly understood, partly because of his crookedness and partly because of his difficult personal qualities. In a world where many still refuse to believe in the Copernican Hypothesis, some of Hooke's more forward ideas would be considered grounds for imprisonment in Bedlam."

Leibniz's eyes narrowed. "Is it Alchemy, then?"

"Mr. Hooke despises Alchemy."

"Good!" Leibniz blurted—most undiplomatically. Daniel covered a smile with his coffee-cup. Leibniz looked horrified, fearing that Daniel might be an Alchemist himself. Daniel put him at ease by quoting from Hooke: "'Why should we endeavour to discover Mysteries in that which has no such thing in it? And like Rabbis find out Cabalism, and ænigmas in the Figure, and placing of Letters, where no such thing lies hid: whereas in natural forms . . . the more we magnify the object, the more excellencies and mysteries do appear; and the more we discover the imperfections of our senses, and the Omnipotency and Infinite perceptions of the great Creator.'"

"So Hooke believes that the secrets of the world are to be found in some microscopic process."

"Yes—snowflakes, for example. If each snowflake is unique, then why are the six arms of a *given* snowflake the same?"

"If we assume that the arms grew outwards from the center, then there must be something in that center that imbues each of the six arms with the same organizing principle—just as all oak trees, and all lindens, share a common nature, and grow into the same general shape."

"But to speak of some mysterious *nature* is to be like the Scholastics—Aristotle dressed up in a doublet," Daniel said.

"Or in an Alchemist's robe—" Leibniz returned.

"Agreed. Newton would argue—"

"That fellow who invented the telescope?"

"Yes. He would argue that if you could catch a snowflake, melt it, and distill its water, you could extract some essence that would be the embodiment of its nature in the physical world, and account for its shape."

"Yes—that is a good *distillation,* as it were, of the Alchemists' mental habit—which is to believe that anything we cannot understand must have some physical residue that can in principle be refined from coarse matter."

"Mr. Hooke, by contrast, is convinced that Nature's ways are consonant to man's reason. As the beating of a fly's wings is consonant to the vibration of a plucked string, so that the sound of one, produces a sympathetic resonance in the other—in the same way, every phenomenon in the world can, in principle, be understood by human ratiocination."

Leibniz said, "And so with a sufficiently powerful microscope, Hooke might peer into the core of a snowflake at the moment of its creation and see its internal parts meshing, like gears of a watch made by God."

"Just so, sir."

"And this is what Hooke *wants*?"

"It is the implicit goal of all his researches—it is what he *must* believe and *must* look for, because that is the nature of Hooke."

"Now *you* are talking like an Aristotelian," Leibniz jested.

Then he reached across the table and put his hand on the box, and said something that was apparently quite serious. "What a watch is to *time,* this engine is to *thought.*"

"Sir! You show me a few gears that add and multiply numbers— well enough. But this is not the same as *thought*!"

"What is a number, Mr. Waterhouse?"

Daniel groaned. "How can you ask such questions?"

"How can you *not* ask them, sir? You are a philosopher, are you not?"

"A Natural Philosopher."

"Then you must agree that in the *modern* world, mathematicks is at the heart of Natural Philosophy—it is like the mysterious essence in the core of the snowflake. When I was fifteen years old, Mr. Waterhouse, I was wandering in the Rosenthal—which is a garden on the edge of Leipzig—when I decided that in order to be a Natural Philosopher I would have to put aside the old doctrine of substantial forms and instead rely upon Mechanism to explain the world. This led me inevitably to mathematicks."

"When *I* was fifteen, I was handing out Phanatiqual libels just down the street from here, and dodging the Watch—but in time, Doctor, as Newton and I studied Descartes at Cambridge, I came to share your view concerning the supreme position of mathematics."

"Then I repeat my question: What is a number? And what is it to multiply two numbers?"

"Whatever it is, Doctor, it is different from *thinking*."

"Bacon said, 'Whatever has sufficient differences, perceptible by the sense, is in nature competent to express cogitations.' You cannot deny that numbers are in that sense competent—"

"To *express* cogitation, yes! But to *express* cogitations is not to *perform* them, or else quills and printing-presses would write poetry by themselves."

"Can your mind manipulate this spoon directly?" Leibniz said, holding up a silver spoon, and then setting it down on the table between them.

"Not without my hands."

"So, when you think about the spoon, is your mind manipulating the spoon?"

"No. The spoon is unaffected, no matter what I think about it."

"Because our minds cannot manipulate physical objects—cup, saucer, spoon—instead they manipulate *symbols* of them, which are stored in the mind."

"I will accept that."

"Now, you yourself helped Lord Chester devise the Philosophical Language, whose chief virtue is that it assigns all things in the world positions in certain tables—positions that can be encoded by numbers."

"Again, I agree that numbers can *express* cogitations, through a sort of encryption. But *performing* cogitations is another matter entirely!"

"Why? We add, subtract, and multiply numbers."

"Suppose the number three represents a chicken, and the number twelve the Rings of Saturn—what then is three times twelve?"

"Well, you can't just do it at *random*," Leibniz said, "any more than Euclid could draw lines and circles at random, and come up with theorems. There has to be a formal system of rules, according to which the numbers are combined."

"And you propose building a machine to do this?"

"*Pourquoi non?* With the aid of a machine, truth can be grasped as if pictured on paper."

"But it is still not thinking. Thinking is what angels do—it is a property given to Man by God."

"How do you suppose God gives it to us?"

"I do not pretend to know, sir!"

"If you take a man's brain and distill him, can you extract a mysterious essence—the divine presence of God on Earth?"

"That is called the Philosophick Mercury by Alchemists."

"Or, if Hooke were to peer into a man's brain with a good enough microscope, would he see tiny meshings of gears?"

Daniel said nothing. Leibniz had imploded his skull. The gears were jammed, the Philosophick Mercury dribbling out his ear-holes.

"You've already sided with Hooke, and against Newton, concerning snowflakes—so may I assume you take the same position concerning brains?" Leibniz continued, now with exaggerated politeness.

Daniel spent a while staring out the window at a point far away. Eventually his awareness came back into the coffee-house. He glanced, a bit furtively, at the arithmetical engine. "There is a place in *Micrographia* where Hooke describes the way flies swarm around meat, butterflies around flowers, gnats around water—giving the *semblance* of rational behavior. But he thinks it is all because of internal mechanisms triggered by the peculiar vapors arising from meat, flowers, *et cetera*. In other words, he thinks that these creatures are no more rational than a trap, where an animal seizing a piece of bait pulls a string that fires a gun. A savage watching the trap kill the animal might suppose it to be rational. But the *trap* is not rational—the man who *contrived* the trap is. Now, if you—the ingenious Dr. Leibniz—contrive a machine that gives the *impression* of thinking—is it *really* thinking, or merely reflecting your genius?"

"You could as well have asked: are *we* thinking? Or merely reflecting God's genius?"

"Suppose I *had* asked it, Doctor—what would your answer be?"

"My answer, sir, is both."

"Both? But that's impossible. It has to be one or the other."

"I do not agree with you, Mr. Waterhouse."

"If we are mere mechanisms, obeying rules laid down by God, then all of our actions are predestined, and we are not really thinking."

"But Mr. Waterhouse, you were raised by Puritans, who believe in predestination."

"Raised by them, yes . . ." Daniel said, and let it hang in the air for a while.

"You no longer accept predestination?"

"It does not resonate sweetly with my observations of the world, as a good hypothesis *ought* to." Daniel sighed. "Now I see why Newton has chosen the path of Alchemy."

"When you say he *chose* that path, you imply that he must have *rejected* another. Are you saying that your friend Newton explored the idea of a mechanically determined brain, and rejected it?"

"It may be he explored it, if only in his dreams and nightmares."

Leibniz raised his eyebrows and spent a few moments staring at the clutter of pots and cups on the table. "This is one of the two great labyrinths into which human minds are drawn: the question of free will versus predestination. You were raised to believe in the latter. You have rejected it—which must have been a great spiritual struggle—and become a thinker. You have adopted a modern, mechanical philosophy. But that very philosophy now seems to be leading you back towards predestination. It is most difficult."

"But you claim to know of a third way, Doctor. I should like to hear of it."

"And I should like to tell of it," Leibniz said, "but I must part from you now, and make rendezvous with my traveling companions. May we continue on some other day?"

Aboard Minerva, Cape Cod Bay, Massachusetts

NOVEMBER 1713

HE DISSECTED MORE than his share of dead men's heads during those early Royal Society days, and knows that the hull of the skull is all wrapped about with squishy rigging: haul-yards of tendon and braces of ligament cleated to pinrails on the jawbone and temple, tugging at the corners of spreading canvases of muscle that curve over the forehead and wrap the old Jolly Roger in as many overlapping layers as there are sails on a ship of the line. As Daniel trudges up out of *Minerva*'s bilge, dragging a chinking sack of ammunition behind him, he feels all that stuff tightening up, steadily and inexorably, each stairstep a click of the pawls, as if invisible sailors were turning capstans inside his skull. He's spent the last hour below the water-line—never his favorite place on shipboard, but safe from cannonballs anyway—smashing plates with a hammer and bellowing old songs, and never been so relaxed in all his life. But now he's climbed back up into the center of the hull, just the sort of bulky bull's-eye pirates might aim swivel-guns at if they lacked confidence in their ability to pick off small fine targets from their wave-tossed platforms.

Minerva's got a spacious stairwell running all the way down through the middle of her, just ahead of the mighty creaking trunk of the mainmast, with two flights of stairs spiraling opposite directions so the men descending don't interfere with those ascending—or so doddering Doctors with sacks of pottery-shards do not hinder boys running up from the hold with—what? The light's dim. They appear to be canvas sacks—heavy bulging polyhedra with rusty nails protruding from the vertices. Daniel's glad they're going up the other stairs, because he wouldn't want one of those things to bump into him. It'd be certain death from lockjaw.

Some important procedure's underway on the gundeck. The gunports are all closed, except for one cracked open a hand's breadth on the starboard side—therefore, not far from Daniel when he emerges from the staircase. Several relatively important officers have gathered in a semicircle around this port, as if for a baptism. There's a general commotion of pinging and thudding coming from the hull-planks and the deck above. It could be gunfire. And if it could be, it probably is. Someone grabs the sack from Daniel and drags it to the center of the gundeck. Men with empty blunderbusses converge on it like jackals on a haunch.

Daniel's elbowed hard by a man hauling on a line that enters *Minerva* through a small orifice above the gunport. This has the effect of (1) knocking Daniel down on his bony pelvis and (2) swinging said gunport all the way open, creating a sudden square of light. Framed in it is part of the rigging of a smaller ship, so close that a younger man could easily jump to it. There is a man—a pirate—on that ship pointing a musket in Daniel's direction, but he's struck down by a gaudy spray of out-moded china fragments, fired down from Minerva's upperdeck. "Caltrops away!" says someone, and boys with sacks lunge toward the open gunport and hurl out a tinkling cosmos, down to the deck of the smaller ship. Moments later the same ceremony's repeated through a gunport on the larboard side—so there must be a pirate-vessel *there*, too. The gunports are hauled closed again, sporting new decorations: constellations of lead balls fired into 'em from below.

The screaming/bellowing ratio has climbed noticeably. Daniel (helping himself to his feet, thank you, and hobbling crabwise to a safe haven near the mainmast, to inventory his complaints) reckons that the screaming must originate from shoeless pirates with caltrop-spikes between their metatarsals—until he hears "Fire! Fire!" and notes a curl of smoke invading the gundeck through a cracked gunport, speared on a shaft of sunlight. Then some instinct makes Daniel forget his bruises and sprains—he's up the last flight of stairs, spry as any eight-year-old powder monkey, and out in the sail-dappled sunlight, where he'll happily risk musket-balls.

But it's the pirate-sloop, not *Minerva,* that's on fire. Lines are going slack all over the starboard half of the ship. Each of them happens to terminate in a rusty grappling-hook that's lodged in a ratline or a rail. The pirates are cutting themselves free!

Now comes a general rush of men to larboard, where a whaleboat is still pestering them. *Minerva* rolls that direction on a sea. The whaleboat comes into view, no longer eclipsed by the hull's tumblehome, and a score of muskets and blunderbusses fire down into it at once. Daniel only glimpses the result—appalling—then *Minerva* rolls starboard and hides it from view.

The men throw their weapons into lockers and ascend into the rigging, pursuant to commands from van Hoek, who's up on the poop deck bellowing into a shiny trumpet of hammered brass. There are plenty of men belowdecks who could be making contributions here, but they don't come up. Daniel, beginning to get the hang of pirate-fighting, understands that van Hoek wants to hide the true size of his crew from Teach.

They have been running before a north wind (though it seems to've shifted a few points westwards) for over an hour. The southern limb of Cape Cod is dead ahead, barring their path. But long before reaching the shore, *Minerva* would run aground in coarse brown sand. So they have to come about now and begin to work to windward, towards the open Atlantic. These simple terms—"come about," for example—denote procedures that are as complicated and tradition-bound as the installation of a new Pope. Great big strong men are running toward the bow: the foreyard loosers and furlers, and the headsail loosers and stowers. They take up positions on the forecastledeck or shinny out onto the bowsprit, but politely step aside for the wiry foretopmen who begin their laborious ascent up the fore shrouds to work the topsails and things higher up the foremast. It is a bristling and tangled thicket of nautical detail. Like watching fifty surgeons dissect fifty different animals at once—the kind of stuff that, half a century ago, would've fascinated Daniel, sucked him into this sort of life, made him a sea-captain. But like a captain reefing and striking his sails before too strong a wind, lest it drive his ship onto the shallows, Daniel ignores as much of this as he can get away with, and tries to understand what is happening in its general outlines: *Minerva* is coming round toward the wind. In her wake, a mile abaft, is the sloop, her sails lying a-shiver, leaving the little ship dead in the water, drifting slowly to leeward, as pirates try to beat out flames with sopped canvas whilst not stepping on any of those caltrops. Several miles north of that, four more ships are spread out on the bay, waiting.

A panic of luffing and shivering spreads through *Minerva*'s rig as all the sails change their relationship to the wind, then everything snaps tight, just as the sailors knew it would, and she's running as close-hauled as she can, headed northeast. In just a few minutes she's drawn abeam of that scorched sloop, which is now steaming, rather than smoking, and attempting to make sail. It's obvious that caltrops and flying crockery-shards have deranged the crew, in the sense that no man knows what to do when. So the sloop's movements are inconclusive.

All the more surprising that van Hoek orders a tack, when it isn't really necessary. *Minerva* comes about and sails directly toward the meandering sloop. Several minutes later, *Minerva* bucks once as she rams the sloop amidships, then shudders as her keel drives the wreckage under the sea. Those burly forecastle-men go out with cutlasses and hatchets to cut shreds of the sloop's rigging away from the bowsprit, where it has become fouled. Van Hoek, strolling on the poop deck, aims a pistol over the rail and, in a sudden lily of smoke, speeds a drowning pirate to Hell.

Royal Society Meeting, Gunfleet House
1673

"I RENEW MY OBJECTION—" said Robert Boyle. "It does not seem *respectful* to inventory the contents of our Founder's guts as if they were a few keepsakes left behind in a chest—"

"Overruled," said John Comstock, still President of the Royal Society—just barely. "Though, out of respect for our *remarkably generous* host, I will defer to *him.*"

Thomas More Anglesey, Duke of Gunfleet, was seated at the head of his drawing-room, at a conspicuously new gilt-and-white-enamel table in the *barock* style. Other bigwigs, such as John Comstock, surrounded him, seated according to equally *barock* rules of protocol. Anglesey withdrew a large watch from the pocket of his Persian vest and held it up to the light streaming in through about half an acre of window-glass, exceptionally clear and colorless and bubble-free and recently installed.

"Can we get through it in *fifty seconds?*" he inquired.

Inhalations all round. In his peripheral vision, Daniel saw several old watches being stuffed into pockets—pockets that tended to be frayed, and rimmed with that nameless dark shine. But the Earl of Upnor and—of all people—Roger Comstock (who was sitting next to Daniel) reached into clean bright pockets, took out new watches, and managed to hold them up in such a way that most everyone in the room could see that each was equipped, not just with *two* but *three* hands, the third moving so quickly that you could *see* its progress round the dial—counting the *seconds!*

Many hunched glances, now, toward Robert Hooke, the Hephaestus of the tiny. Hooke managed to look as if he didn't care about how impressed everyone was—which was probably true. Daniel looked over at Leibniz, sitting there with his box on his lap, who had a soulful, distant expression.

Roger Comstock, noting the same thing: "Is that how a German looks before he bursts into tears?"

Upnor, following Roger's gaze: "Or before he pulls out his broadsword and begins mowing down Turks."

"He deserves our credit for showing up at all," Daniel

murmured—hypnotized by the movement of Roger Comstock's second-hand. "Word arrived yesterday—his patron died in Mainz."

"Of embarrassment, most likely," hissed the Earl of Upnor.

A chirurgeon, looking deeply nervous and out of his depth, was chivvied up to the front of the room. It was a big room, this. Its owner, the Duke of Gunfleet, perhaps too much under the spell of his architect, insisted on calling it the *Grand Salon*. This was simply French for *Big Big Room;* but it seemed a little bigger, and ever so much grander, when the French nomenclature was used.

Even under the humble appellation of Big Big Room, it was a bit too big and too grand for the chirurgeon. "Fifty seconds!—?" he said.

There was a difficult interlude, lasting much longer than fifty seconds, as a helpful Fellow tried to explain the idea of fifty seconds to the chirurgeon, who had got stuck on the misconception that they were speaking of $\frac{1}{52}$s—perhaps some idiom from the gambling world?

"Think of minutes of longitude," someone called out from the back of the Big Big Room. "One sixtieth of that sort of a minute is called what?"

"A second of longitude," said the chirurgeon.

"By analogy, then, one sixtieth of a minute of *time* is—"

"A second . . . of time," said the chirurgeon; then was suddenly mortified as he ran through some rough calculations in his head.

"One thirty-six-hundredth of an hour," called out a bored voice with a French accent.

"Time's up!" announced Boyle, "Let us move on—"

"The good doctor may have *another* fifty seconds," Anglesey ruled.

"Thank you, my lord," said the chirurgeon, and cleared his throat. "Perhaps those gentlemen who have been the *patrons* of Mr. Hooke's horologickal researches, and are now the *beneficiaries* of his so ingenious handiwork, will be so kind as to keep me informed, during my presentation of the results of Lord Chester's *post-mortem*, as to the passage of time—"

"I accept that charge—you have already spent twenty seconds!" said the Earl of Upnor.

"Please, Louis, let us show due respect for our Founder, and for this Doctor," said his father.

"It seems *too late* for the former, Father, but I assent to the latter."

"Hear, hear!" Boyle said. This made the chirurgeon falter—but John Comstock stiffened him up with a look.

"Most of Lord Chester's organs were normal for a man of his

age," the chirurgeon said. "In one kidney I found two small stones. In the ureter, some gravel. Thank you."

The chirurgeon sat down very hastily, like an infantryman who has just seen puffs of smoke bloom from the powder-pans of opposing muskets. Buzzing and droning filled the room—suddenly it was like one of Wilkins's glass apiaries, and the chirurgeon a boy who'd poked it with a stick. But the Queen Bee was dead, and there was disagreement as to who was going to be stung.

"It is what I suspected—there was no stoppage of urine," Hooke finally announced, "only pain from small kidney-stones. Pain that induced Lord Chester to take solace in opiates."

Which was as good as flinging a glass of water in the face of Monsieur LeFebure. The King's Chymist stood up. "To have given comfort to the Lord Bishop of Chester in his time of need is the greatest honor of my career," he said. "It would be an infamous shame if any of those *other* medicines he took, led to his demise."

Now a great deal more buzzing, in a different key. Roger Comstock stood up and cut through it: "If Mr. Pepys would be so kind as to show us *his* stone . . ."

Pepys fairly erupted to his feet across the room and shoved a hand into a pregnant pocket.

John Comstock sent both men back down with cast-iron eyes. "It would not be a kindness, Mr., er, Comstock, as we've all *seen* it."

Daniel's turn. "Mr. Pepys's stone is colossal—yet he was able to urinate a *little*. Considering the smallness of the urinary passages, is it not possible that a *small* stone might block urine as well as a *large* one—and perhaps *better*?"

No more buzzing now, but a deep general murmur—the point was awarded, by acclamation, to Daniel. He sat down. Roger Comstock ejaculated compliments all over him.

"I've had stones in the kidney," Anglesey said, "and I will testify that the pain is beyond description."

John Comstock: "Like something meted out by the *Popish Inquisition?*"

"I cannot make out what is going on," said Daniel, quietly, to his neighbor.

"Well, you'd best make it out before you say anything else," Roger said. "Just a suggestion."

"First Anglesey and Comstock are united in disgracing Wilkins's memory—then next moment, at each other's throats over religion."

"Where does that put you, Daniel?" Roger asked.

Anglesey, unruffled: "I'm sure I speak for the entire Royal Society in expressing unbounded gratitude to Monsieur LeFebure for easing Lord Chester's final months."

"The *Elixir Proprietalis LeFebure* is greatly admired at Court—even among young ladies who are *not* afflicted with exquisitely painful disorders," said John Comstock. "Some of them like it so well that they have started a new fashion: going to sleep, and never waking up again."

The conversation had now taken on the semblance of a lawn-tennis match played with sputtering granadoes. There was a palpable shifting of bodies and chairs as Fellows of the R.S. aligned themselves for spectation. Monsieur LeFebure caught Comstock's lob with perfect aplomb: "It has been known since ancient times that syrup of poppies, in even small doses, cripples the judgment by *day* and induces frightful dreams by *night*—would you not agree?"

Here John Comstock, sensing a trap, said nothing. But Hooke answered, "I can attest to that."

"Your dedication to Truth is an example to us all, Mr. Hooke. In *large* doses, of course, the medicine *kills*. The *first* symptom—destruction of judgment—can lead to the *second*—death by overdosing. That is why the *Elixir Proprietalis LeFebure* should only be administered under *my* supervision—and that is why I have personally taken pains to visit Lord Chester several times each week, during the months that his judgment was crippled by the drug."

Comstock was annoyed by LeFebure's resilience. But (as Daniel realized too late) Comstock had *another* goal in sight besides denting LeFebure's reputation, and it was a goal that he shared with Thomas More Anglesey—normally his rival and enemy. A look passed between these two.

Daniel stood. Roger got a grip on his sleeve, but was not in a position to reach his tongue. "I saw Lord Chester several times in his final weeks and saw no evidence that his mental faculties were affected! To the contrary—"

"Lest someone come away with the foolish opinion that you are being *unkind,* Monsieur LeFebure," Anglesey said—shooting a glare at Daniel—"did Lord Chester not consider this mental impairment a fair price to pay for the opportunity to spend a few last months with his family?"

"Oh, he paid that price *gladly,*" Monsieur LeFebure said.

"I collect that this is why we've heard so little from him in the way of Natural Philosophy of late—" Comstock said.

"Yes—and it is why we should overlook any of his more recent, er . . ."

"Indiscretions?"

"Enthusiasms?"

"Impulsive ventures into the *lower* realm of *politics*—"

"His mental powers dimmed—his heart was as pure as ever—and sought solace in well-meaning gestures."

That was all the poisoned eulogies Daniel could stand to hear—then he was out in the garden of Gunfleet House watching a white marble mermaid vomit an endless stream of clear babble into a fish-pond. Roger Comstock was right behind him.

There were marble benches a-plenty, but he could not sit. Rage had taken him. Daniel was not especially susceptible to that passion. But he understood, now, why the Greeks had believed that Furies were angels of a sort, winged-swift, armed with whips and torches, rushing up out of Erebus to goad men unto madness. Roger, watching Daniel pace around the garden, might have convinced himself that his friend's wild lunges and strides were being provoked by invisible lashes, and that his face had been scorched by torches.

"O for a sword," Daniel said.

"Aw, you'd be dead right away if you tried that!"

"I know that, Roger. Some would say there are worse things than being dead. Thank god Jeffreys wasn't in the room—to see me running out of it like a thief!" And here his voice choked and tears rushed to his eyes. For this was the worst part. That in the end he had done nothing—*nothing*—except run out of the *Grand Salon.*

"You're clever, but you don't know what to do," Roger said. "I'm the other way round. We complement each other."

Daniel was annoyed. Then he reflected that to be the complement of a man with as many deficiencies as Roger Comstock was a high distinction. He turned and looked the other up and down, perhaps with an eye towards punching him in the nose. Roger was not so much *wearing* his wig as *embedded* in its lower reaches, and it was *perfect*—the sort of wig that had its own staff. Daniel, even if he were the punching sort, could not bring himself to ruin anything so perfect. "You are too modest, Roger—obviously you've gone out and done *something* clever."

"Oh, you've noticed my attire! I hope you don't think it's foppish."

"I think it's *expensive.*"

"For one of the Golden Comstocks, you mean . . ."

Roger came closer. Daniel kept being cruel to Roger, trying to make him go away, but Roger took it as honesty, implying profound friendship.

"Well, in any case it is certainly an improvement on your appearance the last time I saw you." Daniel was referring to the explosion in the laboratory, which was now far enough in the past that both Daniel and Roger had their eyebrows back. He had not seen Roger since that night because Isaac, upon coming back to find the lab blown up, had fired him, and sent him packing, not just out of the laboratory, but out of Cambridge. Thus had ended a scholarly career that had probably needed to be put out of its misery in any case. Daniel knew not whither their Cinderella had fled, but he appeared to have done well there.

Roger plainly had no idea what Daniel was talking about. "I don't recall that—did you meet me in the street, before I left for Amsterdam? I probably did look wretched then."

Daniel now tried the Leibnizian experiment of rehearsing the explosion in the laboratory from Roger's point of view.

Roger had been working in the dark: a necessity, as any open flame might set fire to the gunpowder. And not much of an inconvenience, since what he'd been up to was dead simple: grinding the powder in a mortar and dumping it into a bag. Both the sound, and the feel of the pestle in his hand, would tell when the powder had been ground to a fine enough consistency for whatever purpose Roger had in mind. So he had worked blind. Light was the one thing he prayed he wouldn't see, for it would mean a spark that would be certain to ignite the powder. Attent on work and worry, he had never known that Daniel had come back to the house—why should he, since he was supposed to be watching a play? And Roger had not yet heard the applause and the distant murmur of voices that would signal its end. Roger had never heard Daniel's approach, for Daniel, who'd phant'sied he was stalking a rat, had been at pains to move as quietly as possible. The heavy fabric screen had blocked the light of Daniel's candle to the point where it was no brighter than the ambient furnace-glow. Suddenly the candle-flame had been in Roger's face. In other circumstances he'd've known it for what it was; but standing there with a sack of gunpowder in his hands, he had taken it for what he'd most dreaded: a spark. He had dropped the mortar and the bag and flung himself back as quick as he could. The explosion had followed in the next instant. He could neither have seen nor heard anything until after he'd fled the building. So there was no ground to suppose he had ever registered as much as the faintest impression of Daniel's presence. He'd not seen Daniel since.

And so Daniel was presented with a choice between telling Roger the truth, and assenting to the lie that Roger had conveniently proffered: namely, that Daniel had spied Roger in the street before Roger had departed for Amsterdam. Telling the truth held no danger, so far as he could see. The lie was attended with a small peril that Roger—who was cunning, in a way—might be dangling it before him as some sort of test.

"I thought you knew," Daniel said, "I was in the laboratory when it happened. Had gone there to fetch Isaac's paper on tangents. Nearly got blown to bits myself!"

Astonishment and revelation came out of Roger's face like sudden flame. But if Daniel had owned a Hooke watch, he would have counted only a few seconds of time before the old look came back down over his face. As when a candle-snuffer pounces on a wild flame and the errant brilliance that had filled one's vision a moment ago is in an instant vanished, the only thing left in its place a dull sight of old silver-work, frozen and familiar.

"I *phant'sied* I'd heard someone moving about in there!" Roger exclaimed. Which was obviously a lie; but it made the conversation move along better.

Daniel was keen to ask Roger what he'd been doing with the gunpowder. But perhaps it would be better to wait for Roger to volunteer something. "So it was to Amsterdam you went, to recuperate from the excitements of that evening," Daniel said.

"Here first."

"Here to London?"

"Here to the Angleseys'. Lovely family. And socializing with them has its benefits." Roger reached up as if to stroke his wig—but dared not touch it.

"What, you're not in their *employ*—?"

"No, no! It's much better. I *know* things. Certain of the Golden Comstocks immigrated—all right, all right, some would say *fled*—to Holland in the last century. Settled in Amsterdam. I went and paid them a visit. From them, I knew that de Ruyter was taking his fleet to Guinea to seize the Duke of York's slave-ports. So I sold my Guinea Company shares while they were still high. Then from the Angleseys I learned that King Looie was making preparations to invade the Dutch Republic—but could never stage a campaign without purchasing grain first—purchasing it you'll never guess *where*."

"No!"

"Just so—the Dutch sold France the grain that King Looie is using to conquer them! At any rate—I took my money from the Guinea Company shares, and took a large position in Amsterdam-grain just before King Looie bid the price up! Voilà! Now I've a

Hooke-watch, a big wig, and a lot on fashionable Waterhouse Square!"

"You own—" Daniel began, and was well on his way to saying *You own some of my family estate!?* when they were interrupted by Leibniz, stalking through a flower-bed, hugging his brain-in-a-box.

"Dr. Leibniz—the Royal Society were quite taken with your Arithmetickal Engine," Roger said.

"But they did not like my *mathematickal* proofs," said one dejected German savant.

"On the contrary—they were acknowledged to be unusually elegant!" Daniel protested.

"But there is no honor in *elegantly* proving a theorem in 1672 that some Scotsman proved *barbarously* in 1671!"

"You could not possibly have known that," Daniel said.

"Happens all the time," said Roger, a-bristle with bogus authority.

"Monsieur Huygens should have known, when he assigned me those problems as exercises," Leibniz grumbled.

"He probably *did*," Daniel said. "Oldenburg writes to him every week."

"It is well-known that GRUBENDOL is a trafficker in foreign intelligence!" announced Robert Hooke, crashing through a laurel bush and tottering onto a marble bench as vertigo seized him. Daniel gritted his teeth, waiting for a fist-fight, or worse, to break out between Hooke and Leibniz, but Leibniz let this jab at Oldenburg pass without comment, as if Hooke had merely farted at High Table.

"Another way of phrasing it might be that Mr. Oldenburg keeps Monsieur Huygens abreast of the latest developments from England," Roger said.

Daniel picked up the thread: "Huygens probably heard about the latest English theorems through that channel, and gave them to you, Doctor Leibniz, to test your mettle!"

"Never anticipating," Roger tidily concluded, "that fortunes of War and Diplomacy would bring you to the *Britannic* shore, where you would innocently present the same results to the Royal Society!"

"Entirely the fault of Oldenburg—who steals my latest watch-designs, and despatches 'em to that same Huygens!" Hooke added.

"Nonetheless—for me to present theorems to the Royal Society—only to have some gentleman in a kilt stand up in the back of the room, and announce that he proved the same thing a year ago—"

"Everyone who matters knows it was innocent."

"It is a blow to my reputation."

"Your reputation will outshine any, when you finish that Arithmetickal Engine!" announced Oldenburg, coming down a path like a blob of mercury in a trough.

"Any *on the Continent,* perhaps," Hooke sniffed.

"But all of the Frenchmen who are competent to *realize* my conception, are consumed with vain attempts to match the work of Mr. Hooke!" Leibniz returned. Which was a reasonably professional bit of flattery, the sort of thing that greased wheels and made reputations in small Continental courts.

Oldenburg rolled his eyes, then straightened abruptly as a stifled belch pistoned up his gorge.

Hooke said, "I have a design for an arithmetickal engine of my own, which I have not had the *leisure* to complete yet."

"Yes—but do you have a design for what you shall *do* with it, when it's finished?" Leibniz asked eagerly.

"Calculate logarithms, I suppose, and outmode *Napier's bones* . . ."

"But why concern yourself with anything so tedious as logarithms!?"

"They are a tool—nothing more."

"And for what purpose do you wish to *use* that tool, sir?" Leibniz asked eagerly.

"If I believed that my answer would remain within the walls of this fair garden, Doctor, I would say—but as matters stand, I fear my words will be carried to Paris with the *swiftness*—though surely not the *grace*—of the winged-footed messenger of the gods." Staring directly at Oldenburg.

Leibniz deflated. Oldenburg stepped closer to him, whilst turning his back on Hooke, and began trying to cheer the Doctor up— which only depressed him more, as being claimed, by Oldenburg, as an ally, would condemn him forever in Hooke's opinion.

Hooke removed a long slim deerskin wallet from his breast pocket and unrolled it on his lap. It contained a neat row of slim objects: diverse quills and slivers of cane. He selected a tendril of whalebone—set the wallet aside—spread his knees wide—leaned forward—inserted the whalebone deep into his throat—wiggled it—and immediately began to vomit up bile. Daniel watched with an empiric eye, until he had made sure the vomit contained no blood, parasites, or other auspices of serious trouble.

Oldenburg was muttering to Leibniz in High-Dutch, of which Daniel could not understand a single word—which was probably why. But Daniel could make out a few names: first of Leibniz's late patron in Mainz, and then of various Parisians, such as Colbert.

He turned round hoping to continue his conversation with Roger, but Roger had quietly removed himself to make way for his distant cousin the Earl of Epsom—who was stalking directly toward Daniel looking as if he would be happy to settle matters with a head-butting duel. "Mr. Waterhouse."

"My Lord."

"You loved John Wilkins."

"Almost as a father, my lord."

"You would have him revered and respected by future generations of Englishmen."

"I pray that Englishmen will have the wisdom and discernment to give Wilkins his due."

"I say to you that those Englishmen will dwell in a country with one Established Church. If, God willing, I have my way, it will be Anglican. If the Duke of Gunfleet has his, it will be the Roman faith. Deciding *which* might require another Civil War, or two, or three. I might kill Gunfleet, Gunfleet might kill me—my sons or grandsons might cross swords with his. And despite these fatal differences, he and I are *as one* in the conviction that no nation can exist without one Established Church. Do you imagine that a few Phanatiques can overcome the combined power of all the world's Epsoms and Gunfleets?"

"I was never one for vain imaginings, my lord."

"Then you admit that England will have an Established Church."

"I confess it is likely."

"Then what does that make those who stand in opposition to an Established Church?"

"I don't know, my lord—eccentric Bishops?"

"On the contrary—it makes them heretics and traitors, Mr. Waterhouse. To change a heretic and a traitor into an eccentric Bishop is no mean task—it is a form of Transmutation requiring many Alchemists—hooded figures working in secret. The last thing they need is for a sorcerer's apprentice to stumble in and begin knocking things over!"

"Please forgive my ineptitude, my lord. I responded impulsively, because I thought he was being attacked."

"*He* was not being attacked, Mr. Waterhouse—*you* were."

DANIEL LEFT ANGLESEY HOUSE and wandered blindly along Piccadilly, realized he was in front of Comstock House, veered away from that, and fled into St. James's Fields—now parted into neat little squares where grass was trying to establish itself on the muck of construction. He sat on a plank bench, and slowly became aware that Roger Comstock had been following him the entire way, and that he'd (presumably) been talking the entire time. But he pointedly declined to bring his breeches into contact with the bench, a splintery improvisation strewn with pasty-flakes, pipe-ashes, and rat-shite.

"What were Leibniz and Oldenburg on about? Is German among the many things that you understand, Daniel?"

"I think it was that Dr. Leibniz has lost his patron, and needs a new one—with any luck, in Paris."

"Oh, most difficult for such a man to make his way in the world without a patron!"

"Yes."

"It seems as if John Comstock is cross with you."

"Very."

"His son is captain of one of the invasion-ships, you know. He is nervous, irritable just now—not himself."

"On the contrary, I think I have just seen the real John Comstock. It's safe to say that my career in the Royal Society is at an end—as long as he remains President."

"Informed opinion is that the Duke of Gunfleet will be president after the next election."

"That's no better—for in their hatred of me, Epsom and Gunfleet are one man."

"Sounds as though *you* need a patron, Daniel. One who sympathizes."

"*Is* there anyone who sympathizes?"

"I do."

This took a while to stop seeming funny, and to percolate inwards. The two of them sat there silently for a while.

Some sort of parade or procession seemed to be headed this general direction from Charing Cross, with beating of drums, and either bad singing or melodious jeering. Daniel and Roger got up and began wandering down towards Pall Mall, to see what it was.

"Are you making me some sort of proposal?" Daniel finally asked.

"I made a penny or two this year—still, I'm far from being an Epsom or a Gunfleet! I put most of my *liquid* capital into buying that parcel of land from your brothers . . ."

"Which one is it?"

"The large one on the corner there, just next to where Mr. Raleigh Waterhouse built *his* house . . . what think you of it, by the way?"

"Raleigh's house? It's, er . . . big, I suppose."

"Would you like to put it in the shade?"

"What can you possibly mean?"

"I want to erect a bigger house. But I didn't study my mathematics at Trinity, as you know only too well, Daniel—I need *you* to design it for me, and oversee the construction."

"But I'm not an architect—"

"Neither was Mr. Hooke, before he was hired to design Bedlam and diverse other great Fabricks—you can bang out a house as well as he, I wager—and certainly better than that block-head who slapped Raleigh's together."

They'd come out into Pall Mall, which was lined with pleasant houses. Daniel was already eyeing their windows and roof-lines, collecting ideas. But Roger kept his eye on the procession, which was nearly upon them: several hundred more or less typical Londoners, albeit with a higher than usual number of Dissident, and even a few Anglican, preachers. They were carrying an effigy, dangling from the top of a long pole: a straw man dressed in ecclesiastical robes, but whorishly colored and adorned, with a huge mitre affixed to his head, and a long bishop's crook lashed to one mitt. The Pope. Daniel and Roger stood to one side and watched for (according to Roger's watch) a hundred and thirty-four seconds as the crowd marched by them and drained out of the street into St. James's Park. They chose a place in clear view of both St. James's Palace and Whitehall Palace, and planted the pole in the dirt.

Soldiers were already headed toward them from the Horse Guards' compound between the two Palaces: a few forerunners on horseback, but mostly formations of infantrymen that had spilled out too hastily to form up into proper squares. These were in outlandish fantastickal attire, with long peaked caps of a vaguely Polish style.* Daniel at first took them for dragoons, but as they marched closer he could see nippled cannonballs—granadoes!— dangling from their ox-hide belts and bandoliers, thudding against their persons with each step.

That detail was not lost on the crowd of marchers, either. After a few hasty words, they held torches to the hem of the Pope's robe and set it afire. Then the crowd burst, granadoe-like. By the time those grenadiers arrived, the procession had been re-absorbed by London. There was nothing for the grenadiers to do but knock the

---

*As King Louis XIV had guards dressed as Croats, so Charles might have Poles; any nation whose survival depended on crossing swords with Turks had a fearsome reputation nowadays.

effigy down and stamp out the flames—keeping them well away from the grenades, of course.

" 'Twas well-conceived," was Roger Comstock's verdict. "Those were Royal Guards—the Duke of York's new regiment. Oh, they're commanded by John Churchill, but make no mistake, they are York's men."

"What on earth do you mean when you say something like this was well-conceived? I mean, you sound like a *connoisseur* sipping the latest port."

"Well, that Mobb could've burnt the Pope anywhere, couldn't they? But they chose here. Why here? Couldn't've chosen a more dangerous place, what with Grenadiers so near to hand. Well, the answer of course is that they wished to send a message to the Duke of York . . . to wit, that if he doesn't renounce his Papist ways, next time they'll be burning *him* in effigy—if not in *person.*"

"Even *I* could see, that night at Cambridge, that Gunfleet and the younger Angleseys are the new favorites at Court," Daniel said. "While Epsom is lampooned in plays, and his house besieged by the Mobb."

"Not so remarkable really, given the rumors . . ."

"What rumors?" Daniel almost added *I am not the sort of person who hears or heeds such things,* but just now it was difficult to be so haughty.

"That our indifferent fortune in the war is chargeable to faulty cannon, and bad powder."

"What a marvellously convenient excuse for failure in war!"

Until that moment Daniel had not heard anyone say aloud that the war was going badly. The very idea that the English and the French together could not best a few Dutchmen was absurd on its face. Yet, now that Roger had mentioned it, there was a lack of good news, obvious in retrospect. Of course people would be looking for someone to blame.

"The cannon that burst at the 'Siege of Maestricht,'" Daniel said, "do you reckon 'twas shoddy goods? Or was it a scheme laid by Epsom's enemies?"

"He has enemies," was all Roger would say.

"*That* I see," said Daniel, "and, too, I see that the Duke of Gunfleet is one of them, and that he, and other Papists, like the Duke of York, are a great power in the land. What I do *not* understand is why those two enemies, Epsom and Gunfleet, a few minutes ago were as one man in heaping obloquy on the memory of John Wilkins."

"Epsom and Gunfleet are like two captains disputing command

of a ship, each calling the other a mutineer," Roger explained. "The ship, in this similitude, is the Realm with its established church—Anglican or Papist, depending on as Epsom's or Gunfleet's faction prevails. There is a third faction belowdecks—dangerous chaps, well organized and armed, but, most unnervingly, under no distinct leader at the moment. When these Dissidents, as they are called, say, 'Down with the Pope!' it is music to the ears of the Anglicans, whose church is founded on hostility to all things Romish. When they say, 'Down with forced Uniformity, let Freedom of Conscience prevail,' it gladdens the hearts of the Papists, who cannot practice their faith under that Act of Uniformity that Epsom wrote. And so at different times both Epsom's and Gunfleet's factions phant'sy the Dissidents as allies. But when the Dissidents question the idea of an Established Church, and propose to make the whole country an Amsterdam, why then it seems to the leaders of both factions that these Dissident madmen are lighting fuzes on powder-kegs *to blow up the ship itself.* And *then* they unite to crush the Dissidents."

"So you are saying that Wilkins's legacy, the Declaration of Indulgence, is a powder-keg to them."

"It is a fuze that might, for all they know, lead to a powder-keg. They must stomp it out."

"Stomping on me as well."

"Only because you presented yourself to be stomped in the stupidest possible way—by your leave, by your leave."

"Well, what *ought* I to've done, when they were attacking him so?"

"Bit your tongue and bided your time," Roger said. "Things can change in a *second.* Behold this Pope-burning! Led by Dissidents, against Papists. If you, Daniel, had marched at the head of that Mobb, why, Epsom would feel you were on his side against Anglesey."

"Just what I need—the Duke of Gunfleet as personal enemy."

"Then prate about Freedom of Conscience! That is the excellence of your position, Daniel—if you would only open your eyes to it. Through nuances and shifts so subtle as to be *plausibly deniable,* you may have *either* Epsom *or* Gunfleet as your ally at any given moment."

"It sounds cavilling and pusillanimous," said Daniel, summoning up some words from the tables of the Philosophick Language.

Without disagreeing, Roger said: "It is the key to achieving what Drake dreamed of."

"How!? When all the power is in the hands of the Angleseys and the Silver Comstocks."

"Very soon you shall see how wrong you are in that."

"Oh? Is there some other source of power I am not aware of?"

"Yes," said Roger, "and your uncle Thomas Ham's cellar is full of it."

"But that gold is not his. It is the sum of his obligations."

"Just so! You have put your finger on it! There is hope for you," Roger said, and stepped back from the bench preparatory to taking leave. "I hope that you will consider my proposal in any event . . . Sir."

"Consider it under consideration, Sir."

"And even if there is no time in your life for houses—perhaps I could beg a few hours for my theatre—"

"Did you say *theatre?*"

"I've bought part interest in one, yes—the King's Comedians play there—we produced *Love in a Tub* and *The Lusty Chirurgeon.* From time to time, we need help making thunder and lightning, as well as demonic apparitions, angelic visitations, impalements, sex-changes, hangings, live births, *et cetera.*"

"Well, I don't know what my family would think of my being involved in such things, Roger."

"Poh! Look at what *they* have been up to! Now that the Apocalypse has failed to occur, Daniel, you must find something to do with your several talents."

"I suppose the least I could to is keep you from blowing yourself to pieces."

"I can hide nothing from you, Daniel. Yes. You have divined it. That evening in the laboratory, I was making powder for the-atrickal squibs. When you grind it finer, you see, it burns faster—more flash, more bang."

"I noticed," Daniel said. Which made Roger laugh; which made Daniel feel happy. And so into a sort of spiral they went. "I've an appointment to meet Dr. Leibniz at a coffee-house in the theatre district later . . . so why don't we walk in that direction now?" Daniel said.

"PERHAPS YOU MIGHT HAVE STUMBLED across my recent mono-graph, *On the Incarnation of God* . . ."

"Oldenburg mentioned it," Daniel said, "but I must confess that I have never attempted to read it."

"During our last conversation, we spoke of the difficulty of rec-onciling a *mechanical* philosophy with free will. This problem has any number of resonances with the *theological* question of incarnation."

"In that both have to do with spiritual essences being infused into bodies that are in essence mechanical," Daniel said agreeably.

All around them, fops and theatre-goers were edging away towards other tables, leaving Leibniz and Waterhouse with a pleasant clear space in the midst of what was otherwise a crowded coffee-house.

"The problem of the Trinity is the mysterious union of the divine and human natures of Christ. Likewise, when we debate whether a mechanism—such as a fly drawn to the smell of meat, or a trap, or an arithmetickal engine—is *thinking* by itself, or merely *displaying the ingenuity* of its creator, we are asking whether or not those engines have, in some sense, been imbued with an *incorporeal principle* or, vulgarly, *spirit* that, like God or an angel, possesses free will."

"Again, I hear an echo of the Scholastics in your words—"

"But Mr. Waterhouse, you are making the common mistake of thinking that we must have Aristotle *or* Descartes—that the two philosophies are irreconcilable. On the contrary! We may accept modern, mechanistic explanations in physics, while retaining Aristotle's concept of self-sufficiency."

"Forgive me for being skeptical of that—"

"It is your *responsibility* to be skeptical, Mr. Waterhouse, no forgiveness is needed. The details of how these two concepts may be reconciled are somewhat lengthy—suffice it to say that I have found a way to do it, by assuming that every body contains an incorporeal principle, which I identify with *cogitatio.*"

"Thought."

"Yes!"

"Where is this principle to be found? The Cartesians think it's in the pineal gland—"

"It is not spread out through space in any such vulgar way—but the *organization* that it causes is distributed throughout the body— it *informs* the body—and we may know that it exists, by observing that information. What is the difference between a man who has just died, and one who is going to die in a few ticks of Mr. Hooke's watch?"

"The Christian answer is that one has a soul, and the other does not."

"And it is a fine answer—it needs only to be translated into a new Philosophical Language, as it were."

"You would translate it, Doctor, by stating that the *living* body is informed by this organizing principle—which is the outward and visible sign that the mechanical body is, for the time being anyway, unified with an incorporeal principle called Thought."

"That is correct. Do you recall our discussion of symbols? You admitted that your mind cannot manipulate a spoon directly— instead it must manipulate a symbol of the spoon, inside the mind.

God could manipulate the spoon directly, and we would name it a miracle. But *created* minds cannot—they need a passive element through which to act."

"The body."

"Yes."

"But you say that *Cogitatio* and *Computation* are the same, Doctor—in the Philosophical Language, a single word would suffice for both."

"I have concluded that they are one and the same."

"But your Engine does computation. And so I am compelled to ask, at what point does it become imbued with the incorporeal principle of Thought? You say that *Cogitatio* informs the body, and somehow organizes it into a mechanical system that is capable of acting. I will accept that for now. But with the Arithmetickal Engine, you are working backwards—constructing a mechanical system in the hopes that it will become impregnated from above—as the Holy Virgin. When does the Annunciation occur—at the moment you put the last gear into place? When you turn the crank?"

"You are too literal-minded," Leibniz said.

"But you have told me that you see no conflict between the notion that the mind is a mechanickal device, and a belief in free will. If that is the case, then there must be some point at which your Arithmetickal Engine will cease to be a collection of gears, and become the body into which some angelic mind has become incarnated."

"It is a false dichotomy!" Leibniz protested. "An incorporeal principle *alone* would not give us free will. If we accept—as we must—that God is omniscient, and has foreknowledge of all events that will occur in the future, then He knows what we will do before we do it, and so—even if we be angels—we cannot be said to have free will."

"That's what I was always taught in church. So the prospects for your philosophy seem dismal, Doctor—free will seems untenable both on grounds of theology and of Natural Philosophy."

"So you say, Mr. Waterhouse—and yet you agree with Hooke that there is a mysterious consonance between the behavior of Nature, and the workings of the human mind. Why should that be?"

"I haven't the faintest idea, Doctor. Unless, as the Alchemists have it, all matter—Nature and our brains together—are suffused by the same Philosophick Mercury."

"A hypothesis neither one of us loves."

"What is *your* hypothesis, Doctor?"

"Like two arms of a snowflake, Mind and Matter grew out of a common center—and even though they grew *independently* and without communicating—each developing according to its own internal rules—nevertheless they grew in perfect harmony, and share the same shape and structure."

"It is rather Metaphysickal," was all Daniel could come back with. "What's the common center? God?"

"God arranged things from the beginning so that Mind could understand Nature. But He did not do this by continual meddling in the development of Mind, and the unfolding of the Universe . . . rather He fashioned the nature of both Mind and Nature to be harmonious from the beginning."

"So, I have complete freedom of action . . . but God knows in advance what I will do, because it is my nature to act in harmony with the world, and God partakes of that harmony."

"Yes."

"It is odd that we should be having this conversation, Doctor, because during the last few days, for the first time in my life, I have felt as if certain possibilities have been set before me, which I may reach out and grasp if I so choose."

"You sound like a man who has found a patron."

The notion of Roger Comstock as patron made Daniel's gorge rise a bit. But he could not deny Leibniz's insight. "Perhaps."

"I am pleased, for your sake. The death of my patron has left *me* with very few choices."

"There must be some nobleman in Paris who appreciates you, Doctor."

"I was thinking rather of going to Leiden to stay with Spinoza."

"But Holland is soon to be overrun . . . you could not pick a worse place to be."

"The Dutch Republic has enough shipping to carry two hundred thousand persons out of Europe, and around the Cape of Good Hope to the furthermost islands of Asia, far out of reach of France."

"That is entirely too phantastickal for me to believe."

"Believe. The Dutch are already making plans for this. Remember, they made half of their land with the labor of their hands! What they did once in Europe, they can do again in Asia. If the last ditch is stormed, and the United Provinces fall under the heel of King Louis, I intend to be there, and I will board ship and go to Asia and help build a new Commonwealth—like the New Atlantis that Francis Bacon described."

"For you, sir, such an adventure might be possible. For me, it can never be anything more than a romance," Daniel said. "Until now, I've always done what I *had* to, and this went along very well with the Predestination that was taught me. But now I may have choices to make, and they are choices of a *practical* nature."

"Whatever acts, cannot be destroyed," said the Doctor.

Daniel went out the door of the coffee-house and walked up and down London for the rest of the day. He was a bit like a comet, ranging outwards in vast loops, but continually drawn back toward certain fixed poles: Gresham's College, Waterhouse Square, Cromwell's head, and the ruin of St. Paul's.

Hooke was a greater Natural Philosopher than he, but Hooke was busy rebuilding the city, and half-deranged with imaginary intrigues. Newton was also greater, but he was lost in Alchemy and poring over the Book of Revelation. Daniel had supposed that there might be an opportunity to slip between those two giants and make a name for himself. But now there was a *third* giant. A giant who, like the others, was distracted by the loss of his patron, and dreams of a free Commonwealth in Asia. But he would not be distracted forever.

It was funny in a painful way. God had given him the desire to be a great Natural Philosopher—then put him on earth in the midst of Newton, Hooke, and Leibniz.

Daniel had the training to be a minister, and the connections to find a nice congregation in England or Massachusetts. He could walk into that career as easily as he walked into a coffee-house. But his ramble kept bringing him back to the vast ruin of St. Paul's—a corpse in the middle of a gay dinner-party—and not just because it was centrally located.

Aboard Minerva, *Cape Cod Bay,* Massachusetts
NOVEMBER 1713

These in thir dark Nativitie the Deep
Shall yield us pregnant with infernal flame,
Which into hallow Engins long and round
Thick-rammed, at th' other bore with touch of fire

Dilated and infuriate shall send forth
From far with thundring noise among our foes
Such implements of mischief as shall dash
To pieces, and oerwhelm whatever stands
Adverse, that they shall fear we have disarmd
The Thunderer of his only dreaded bolt.

—MILTON, *Paradise Lost*

SNATCHING A FEW MINUTES' REST in his cabin between engagements, Daniel's mood is grave. It is the solemnity, not of a man who's involved in a project to kill other men (they've been doing that all day, for Christ's sake!), but of one who's gambling his own life on certain outcomes. Or having it gambled *for* him by a Captain who shows signs of—what's a diplomatic way to put it—having a rich and complicated inner life. Of course, whenever you board ship you put your life in the Captain's hands—*but*—

Someone is *laughing* up there on the poop deck. The gaiety clashes with Daniel's somber mood and annoys him. It's a derisive and somewhat cruel laugh, but not without sincere merriment. Daniel's looking about for something hard and massive to thump on the ceiling when he realizes it's van Hoek, and what has him all in a lather is some sort of technical Dutch concept—the *Zog*.

Trundling noises from the upperdeck,* and all of a sudden *Minerva*'s a different ship: heeling over quite a bit more than she was, but also rolling from side much more ponderously. Daniel infers that a momentous shifting of weights has occurred. Getting up, and going back out on the quarterdeck, he sees it's true: there are several short bulbous carronnades here—nothing more or less than multi-ton blunderbusses, with large-bore, short-range, miserable accuracy. But (not to put too fine a point on it) large bores, into which gunners are shoveling all manner of messy ironmongery: pairs of cannonballs chained together, nails, redundant crowbars, clusters of grapeshot piled on sabots and tied together with ostentatiously clever sailors' knots. Once loaded, the carronnades are being run out to the gunwales—hugely increasing the ship's moment of inertia, accounting for the change in the roll period—

"Calculating our odds, Dr. Waterhouse?" Dappa inquires, descending a steep stair from the poop deck.

"What means *Zog*, Dappa, and why's it funny?"

---

*Which, remember, is one "storey" below the quarterdeck, where Daniel is pretty much giving up on getting any relaxation.

Dappa gets an alert look about him as if it isn't funny at all, and points across half a mile of open water toward a schooner flying a black flag with a white hourglass. The schooner is on the weather bow* parallelling their course but obviously hoping to converge, and grapple, with *Minerva* in the near future. "See how miserably they make headway? We are outpacing them, even though we haven't raised the mainsail."

"Yes—I was going to inquire—*why* haven't we raised it? It *is* the largest sail on the ship, and we *are* trying to go fast, are we not?"

"The mainsail is traditionally raised and worked by the gunners. *Not* raising it will make Teach think we are short-handed in that area, and unable to man all our cannon at one time."

"But wouldn't it be worthwhile to tip our hand, if we could out-run that schooner?"

"We'll outrun her *anyway.*"

"But she *wants* us to draw abeam of her, does she not—that is the entire *point* of being a pirate—so perhaps she has thrown out drogues, and that is why she wallows along so pitiably."

"She doesn't *need* to throw out drogues because of her appalling *Zog.*"

"There it is again—what, I ask, is the meaning of that word?"

"Her wake, look at her wake!" Dappa says, waving his arm angrily.

"Yes—now that we are so, er, unsettlingly close, I can see that her wake's enough to capsize a whaleboat."

"Those damned pirates have loaded so many cannon aboard, she rides far too low in the water, and so she's got a great ugly *Zog.*"

"Is this meant to reassure me?"

"It is meant to answer your question."

"*Zog* is Dutch for 'wake,' then?"

Dappa the linguist smiles yes. Half his teeth are white, the oth-ers made of gold. "And a much better word it is, because it comes from *zuigen* which means 'to suck.'"

"I don't follow."

"Any seaman will tell you that a ship's wake sucks on her stern, holding her back—the bigger the wake, the greater the suck, and the slower the progress. That schooner, Doctor Waterhouse, sucks."

Angry words from van Hoek above—Dappa scurries down to the upperdeck to finish whatever errand Daniel interrupted. Daniel follows him, then goes aft, skirts the capstan, and descends a narrow staircase to the aftmost part of the gundeck. Thence he

---

*That is, ahead of them and off to the side from which the wind is blowing—at about ten o'clock.

enters the room at the stern where he's been in the habit of taking his temperature measurements. He commences a perilous traversal of the room, headed towards that bank of undershot windows. To a landlubber the room would look pleasingly spacious, to Daniel it appears desperately short of handholds—meaning that as the ship rolls, Daniel stumbles for a greater distance, and builds up more speed, before colliding with anything big enough to stop him. In any case, he gets to the windows and looks down into *Minerva*'s *Zog*. She has one, to be sure, but compared to that schooner to windward, *Minerva* hardly sucks at all. The Bernoullis would have a field day with this—

There is also a pirate-ketch converging on them from leeward, in much the same way as the schooner is doing from windward, and Daniel is fairly certain that this ketch doesn't suck much at all. He is certain he saw drogues trailing behind her. *Minerva* is lying dead upon the wind, which is to say, she's as close-hauled as possible—she can fall off to leeward but she cannot turn into the wind any farther. Since the ketch is to leeward—downwind of *Minerva*— falling away from the wind will send *Minerva* straight into the musket-fire and grappling-irons that are no doubt being readied on her decks and fighting-tops. But the ketch, being fore-and-aft rigged, can sail closer to the wind anyway. So even if *Minerva* holds her course, the ketch will be able to cut her off—driving her into the sucking (because heavily armed) schooner.

All of which goes to explain Daniel's second reason for having gone to this room: it's as far from the fighting as he can get without jumping overboard. But he does not find the solace he wants, because from here he can see two *additional* pirate-ships gaining on them from astern, and they seem bigger and better than any of the others.

An explosion, then another, then a lot of them at once—obviously something organized. Daniel's still alive, *Minerva*'s still afloat. He flings open the door to the gundeck but it's dark and quiet, the gunners all convened around the cannons on the larboard side— none of which has been fired. It must have been those carronnades on the upperdeck firing their loads of junk.

Daniel turns round and looks out the window to see the ketch being left behind, fine on the lee quarter.* It is no longer recognizable as a ketch, though—just a hull heaped with tangled, slack rigging and freshly splintered blond wood. One of her guns sparks and something terrible comes out of it, directly towards him—big

---

*At about five o'clock if he were facing toward the bow.

and spreading. He begins to fall down, more out of vertigo than any coherent plan. All the glass in all those windows explodes toward him, driven on a wall of buckshot. Only some of it hits him in the face, and none in the eyes—more luck than a natural philosopher can comfortably account for.

The door's been flung open again, either by the blast of shot or by his falling back into it, so half of him is lying on the gundeck now. Suddenly, radiance warms his tightly closed eyelids. It could be a choir of angels, or a squadron of flaming devils, but he doesn't believe in any of that stuff. Or it could be *Minerva*'s powder magazine exploding—but that would involve loud noises, and the only noises he hears are the creaking and grumbling of gun-carriages being hauled forward. There's a refreshing sea breeze in his nostrils. He takes a big risk and opens his eyes.

All of the gunports on the larboard side have been opened at once, and all of the cannon rolled out. Gunners are hauling on blocks and tackles, slewing their weapons this way or that—others levering the guns' butts up with crowbars and hammering wedges underneath—there are, in short, as many feverish preparations as for a royal wedding. Then fire is brought out, the roll of the ship carefully timed, and Daniel—poor Daniel doesn't think to put his hands over his ears. He hears one or two cannon-blasts before going deaf. Then it's just one four-ton iron tube after another jerking backwards as lightly as shuttlecocks.

He is fairly certain that he is dead now.

Other dead men are around him.

They are lying on the upperdeck.

A couple of sailors are sitting on Daniel's corpse, while another tortures his deceased flesh with a needle. Sewing his dismembered parts back on, closing up the breaches in his abdomen so stuff won't leak out. So *this* is what it felt like to have been a stray dog in the clutches of the Royal Society!

As Daniel is lying flat on his back, his view is mostly skywards, though if he turns his head—an astonishing feat, for a dead man— he can see van Hoek up on the poop deck bellowing through his trumpet—which is aimed nearly straight down over the rail.

"What on earth can he be shouting at?" Daniel asks.

"Apologies, Doctor, didn't know you'd come awake," says a Looming Column of Shadow, speaking in Dappa's voice, and stepping back to block the sun from Daniel's face. "He's parleying with certain pirates who rowed out from Teach's flagship under a flag of truce."

"What do they want?"

"They want you, Doctor."

"I don't understand."

"You're thinking too hard—there's naught *to* understand—it is entirely simple," Dappa says. "They rowed up and said, 'Give us Dr. Waterhouse and all is forgotten.'"

Dr. Waterhouse now ought to spend a long time being dumbstruck. But his stupefaction lasts only a little while. The sensation of nubby silk thread being drawn briskly through fresh holes in his flesh, makes serious reflection all but impossible. "You'll do it—of course," is the best he can come up with.

"Any other captain would—but whoever arranged to put you aboard, must've known about Captain van Hoek's feelings concerning pirates. Behold!" and Dappa steps out of the way to give Daniel an unobstructed view of a sight stranger than anything gawkers would pay to view at St. Bartholomew's Fair: a hammer-handed man climbing up into the rigging of a ship. That is to say that one of his arms is terminated, not by a hand, and not by a hook, but by an actual hammer. Van Hoek ascends to a suitably perilous altitude, up there alongside the colors that fly from the mizzenmast: a Dutch flag, and below it, a smaller one depicting the Ægis. After getting himself securely tangled in the shrouds—weaving limbs through rope so that his body is spliced into the rigging—he begins to pluck nails out of his mouth and drive them through the hem of each flag into the wood of the mast.

It seems, now, that every sailor who's not sitting on Daniel is up in the rigging, unfurling a ludicrously vast array of sails. Daniel notes with approval that the mainsail's finally been hoisted—that charade is over. And now moreover *Minerva*'s height is being miraculously increased as the topmasts are telescoped upwards. An asymptotic progression of smaller and smaller trapezoids spreads out upon their frail-seeming yards.

"It's a glorious gesture for the Captain to make—now that he's sunk half of Teach's fleet," Daniel says.

"Aye, Doctor—but not the better half," Dappa says.

The City of London
1673

> A fifth doctrine, that tendeth to the dissolution of a
> commonwealth, is, *that every private man has an*
> *absolute propriety in his goods; such, as excludeth the right*
> *of the sovereign.*
>
> —HOBBES, *Leviathan*

DANIEL HAD NEVER been an actor on a stage, of course, but when
he went to plays at Roger Comstock's theatre—especially when he
saw them for the fifth or sixth time—he was struck by the sheer
oddity of these men (and women!) standing about on a platform
prating the words of a script for the hundredth time and trying to
behave as if hundreds of persons weren't a few yards away goggling
at them. It was strangely mannered, hollow, and false, and all who
took part in it secretly wanted to strike the show and move on to
something new. Thus London during this the Third Dutch War,
waiting for news of the Fall of Holland.

As they waited, they had to content themselves with such
smaller bits of news as from time to time percolated in from the
sea. All London passed these rumors around and put on a great
pompous show of reacting to them, as actors observe a battle or
storm said to be taking place off-stage.

Queerly—or perhaps not—the only solace for most Londoners
was going to the theatre, where they could sit together in darkness
and watch their own behavior reflected back to them. *Once More*
into the Breeches had become very popular since its Trinity College
debut. It had to be performed in Roger Comstock's theatre after
its first and second homes were set on fire owing to lapses in judgment on the part of the pyrotechnicians. Daniel's job was to simulate lightning-flashes, thunderbolts, and the accidental detonation
of Lord Brimstone without burning down Roger's investment. He
invented a new thunder-engine, consisting of a cannonball rolling
down a Spiral of Archimedes in a wooden barrel, and he abused
his privileges at the world's leading alchemical research facility to
formulate a new variant of gunpowder that made more flash and

less bang. The pyrotechnics lasted for a few minutes, at the beginning of the play. The rest of the time he got to sit backstage and watch Tess, who always dazzled him like a fistful of flash-powder going off right in the face, and made his heart feel like a dented cannonball tumbling down an endless hollow Screw. King Charles came frequently to watch his Nellie sing her pretty songs, and so Daniel took some comfort—or amusement at least—in knowing that he and the King both endured this endless Wait in the same way: gazing at the cheeks of pretty girls.

The small bits of news that *did* come in, while they waited for the *big* one, took various forms at first, but as the war went on they seemed to consist mostly of death-notices. It was not quite like living in London during the Plague; but more than once, Daniel had to choose between two funerals going on at the same hour. Wilkins had been the first. Many more followed, as if the Bishop of Chester had launched a fad.

Richard Comstock, the eldest son of John, and the model for the stalwart if dim Eugene Stopcock in *Breeches,* was on a ship that was part of a fleet that fell under the guns of Admiral de Ruyter at Sole Bay. Along with thousands of other Englishmen, he went to David Jones's Locker. Many of the survivors could now be seen hobbling round London on bloody stumps, or rattling cups on street-corners. Daniel was startled to receive an invitation to the funeral. Not from John, of course, but from Charles, who had been John's fourth son and was now the only one left (the other two had died young of smallpox). After his stint as laboratory assistant during the Plague Year at Epsom, Charles had matriculated at Cambridge, where he'd been tutored by Daniel. He had been well on his way to being a competent Natural Philosopher. But now he was the scion of a great family, and never could be aught else, unless the family ceased to be great, or he ceased being a part of it.

John Comstock got up in front of the church and said, "The Hollander exceeds us in industry, and in all things else, but envy."

King Charles shut down the Exchequer one day, which is to say that he admitted that the country was out of money, and that not only could the Crown not repay its debts, but it couldn't even pay *interest* on them. Within a week, Daniel's uncle, Thomas Ham, Viscount Walbrook, was dead—of a broken heart or suicide, no one save Aunt Mayflower knew—but it scarcely made a difference. This led to the most theatrickal of all the scenes Daniel witnessed in London that year (with the possible exception of the re-enactment of the Siege of Maestricht): the opening of the Crypt.

Thomas Ham's reliable basement had been sealed up by court officials immediately upon the death of its proprietor, and musketeers had been posted all round to prevent Ham's depositors (who had, in recent weeks, formed a small muttering knot that never went away, loitering outside; as others held up libels depicting the atrocities of King Looie's army in Holland, so these held up Goldsmiths's Notes addressed to Thomas Ham) from breaking in and claiming their various plates, candlesticks, and guineas. Legal maneuverings began, and continued round the clock, casting a queer shadow over Uncle Thomas's funeral, and stretching beyond it to two days, then three. The cellar's owner was already in the grave, his chief associates mysteriously unfindable, and rumored to be in Dunkirk trying to buy passage to Brazil with crumpled golden punch-bowls and gravy-boats. But those were rumors. The *facts* were in the famously safe and sturdy Ham Bros. Cellar on Threadneedle.

This was finally unsealed by a squadron of Lords and Justices, escorted by musketeers, and duly witnessed by Raleigh, Sterling, and Daniel Waterhouse; Sir Richard Apthorp; and various stately and important Others. It was three days exactly since King Charles had washed his hands of the royal debts and Thomas Ham had met his personal Calvary at the hands of the Exchequer. That statistic was noted by Sterling Waterhouse—as always, noticer of details *par excellence.* As the crowd of Great and Good Men shuffled up the steps of Ham House, he muttered to Daniel: "I wonder if we shall roll the stone aside and find an empty tomb?"

Daniel was appalled by this dual sacrilege—then reflected that as he was now practically living in a theatre and mooning over an actress every night, he could scarcely criticize Sterling for making a jest.

It turned out not to be a jest. The cellar was empty.

Well—not empty. It was full, now, of speechless men, standing flatfooted on the Roman mosaic.

RALEIGH: "I knew it would be bad. But—my God—there's not even a *potatoe.*"

STERLING: "It is a sort of anti-miracle."

LORD HIGH CHANCELLOR OF THE REALM: "Go up and tell the musketeers to go and get more musketeers."

They all stood there for quite a while. Attempts to make conversation flared sporadically all round the cellar and fizzled like flashes in damp pans. Except—strangely—among Waterhouses. Disaster had made them convivial.

RALEIGH: "Our newest tenant informs me you've decided to turn architect, Daniel."

STERLING: "We thought you were going to be a savant."

DANIEL: "All the other savants are doing it. Just the other day, Hooke figured out how arches work."

STERLING: "I should have thought that was *known* by now."

RALEIGH: "Do you mean to say all existing arches have been built on *guesswork*?"

SIR RICHARD APTHORP: "Arches—and Financial Institutions."

DANIEL: "Christopher Wren is going to re-design all the arches in St. Paul's, now that Hooke has explained them."

STERLING: "Good! Maybe the *new* one won't become all bow-legged and down-at-heels, as the old one did."

RALEIGH: "I say, brother Daniel—don't you have some *drawings* to show us?"

DANIEL: "Drawings?"

RALEIGH: "In the w'drawing room, perhaps?"

Which was a bad pun and a cryptickal sign, from Raleigh the patriarch (fifty-five years comically aged, to Daniel's eyes seeming like a young Raleigh dressed up in rich old man's clothes and stage-makeup), that they were all supposed to Withdraw from the cellar. So they did, and Sir Richard Apthorp came with them. They wound up on the upper floor of Ham House, in a bedchamber—the very same one that Daniel had gazed into from his perch atop Gresham's College. A rock had already come in through a window and was sitting anomalously in the middle of a rug, surrounded by polygons of glass. More were beginning to thud against the walls, so Daniel swung the windows open to preserve the glazing. Then they all retreated to the center of the room and perched up on the bed and watched the stones come in.

STERLING: "Speaking of Guineas, or lack thereof—shame about the Guinea Company, what?"

APTHORP: "Pfft! 'Twas like one of your brother's theatrickal powder-squibs. Sold my shares of it long ago."

STERLING: "What of you, Raleigh?"

RALEIGH: "They owe me money, is all."

APTHORP: "You'll get eight shillings on the pound."

RALEIGH: "An outrage—but better than what Thomas Ham's depositors will get."

DANIEL: "Poor Mayflower!"

RALEIGH: "She and young William are moving in with me anon—and so you'll have to seek other lodgings, Daniel."

STERLING: "What fool is buying the Guinea Company's debts?"

APTHORP: "James, Duke of York."

STERLING: "As I said—what dauntless hero is, *et cetera* . . ."

DANIEL: "But that's nonsense! They are *his own* debts!"

APTHORP: "They are the Guinea Company's debts. But he is winding up the Guinea Company and creating a new Royal Africa Company. He's to be the governor and chief shareholder."

RALEIGH: "What, sinking our Navy and making us slaves to Popery is not sufficient—he's got to enslave all the Neegers, too?"

STERLING: "Brother, you sound more like Drake every day."

RALEIGH: "Being surrounded by an armed mob must be the cause of sounding that way."

APTHORP: "The Duke of York has resigned the Admiralty . . ."

RALEIGH: "As there's nothing left to be Admiral *of* . . ."

APTHORP: "And is going to marry that nice Catholic girl* and compose his African affairs."

STERLING: "Sir Richard, this must be one of those things that you know before anyone else does, or else there would be rioters in the streets."

RALEIGH: "There *are*, you pea-wit, and unless I'm having a Drakish vision, they have set fire to this very house."

STERLING: "I meant they'd be rioting 'gainst the Duke, not our late bro-in-law."

DANIEL: "I personally witnessed a sort of riot 'gainst the Duke the other day—but it was about his religious, not his military, political, or commercial shortcomings."

STERLING: "You left out 'intellectual and moral.'"

DANIEL: "I was trying to be concise—as we are getting a bit short of that spiritous essence, found in *fresh* air, for which fire competes with living animals."

RALEIGH: "The Duke of York! What bootlicking courtier was responsible for naming New York after him? 'Tis a perfectly acceptable *city*."

DANIEL: "If I may change the subject . . . the reason I led us to this room was yonder *ladder*, which in addition to being an excellent Play Structure for William Ham, will also convey us to the roof—where it's neither so hot nor so smoky."

STERLING: "Daniel, never mind what people say about you—you always have your *reasons*."

[Now a serio-comical musical interlude: the brothers Waterhouse break into a shouted, hoarse (because of smoke) rendition of a Puritan hymn about climbing Jacob's Ladder.]

---

*Mary Beatrice d'Este of Modena; for Anne Hyde had been winched into a double-wide grave two years previously.

SCENE: The rooftops of Threadneedle Street. Shouts, shattering of glass, musket-shots heard from below. They gather round the mighty Ham-chimney, which is now venting smoke of burning walls and furniture below.

SIR RICHARD APTHORP: "How inspiring, Daniel, to gaze down the widened and straightened prospect of Cheapside and know that St. Paul's will be rebuilt there anon—'pon *mathematick* principles—so that it's likely to *stay up* for a bit."

STERLING: "Sir Richard, you sound ominously like a *preacher* opening his sermon with a commonplace observation that is soon to become one leg of a tedious and strained *analogy.*"

APTHORP: "Or, if you please, one leg of an arch—the other to be planted, oh, about *here.*"

RALEIGH: "You want to build, what, some sort of triumphal arch, spanning that distance? May I remind you that *first* we want some sort of *triumph*!?"

APTHORP: "It is only a similitude. What Christopher Wren means to do *yonder* in the way of a Church, I mean to do *here* with a *Banca.* And as Wren will use Hooke's principles to build that Church soundly, I'll use modern means to devise a *Banca* that—without in any way impugning your late brother-in-law's illustrious record—will not have armed mobs in front of it burning it down."

RALEIGH: "Our late brother-in-law was ruined, because the King borrowed all of his deposits—presumably at gunpoint—and then declined to pay 'em back—what *mathematick* principle will you use to prevent *that*?"

APTHORP: "Why, the same one that you and your co-religionists have used in order to maintain your faith: tell the King to leave us alone."

RALEIGH: "Kings do not love to be told that, or *anything.*"

APTHORP: "I saw the King yesterday, and I tell you that he loves being bankrupt even less. I was *born* in the very year that the King seized the gold and silver that Drake and the other merchants had deposited in the Tower of London for safekeeping. Do you recall it?"

RALEIGH: "Yes, 'twas a black year, and made rebels of many who only wanted to be merchants."

APTHORP: "Your brother-in-law's business, and the practice of goldsmith's notes, arose as a result—no one trusted the Tower any more."

STERLING: "And after today no one will trust goldsmiths, or their silly notes."

APTHORP: "Just so. And just as the Empty Tomb on Easter led, in the fullness of time, to a Resurrection . . ."

DANIEL: "I am stopping up mine ears now—if the conversation turns Christian, wave your hands about."

THE KNOWLEDGE THAT THE DUTCH had won the war percolated through London invisibly, like Plague. Suddenly everyone had it. Daniel woke up in Bedlam one morning knowing that William of Orange had opened the sluices and put a large part of his Republic under water to save Amsterdam. But he couldn't recall *whence* that knowledge had come.

He and his brothers had worked their way up Threadneedle by assailing one rooftop after another. They'd parted company with Apthorp on the roof of *his* goldsmith's shop, which was still solvent—yet there was an armed mob in front of *it*, too, and in front of the *next* goldsmith's, and the next. Far from *escaping* a riot, they understood, somewhat too late, that they were working their way toward the center of a much *larger* one. The obvious solution was to turn round and go back the way they'd come—but now a platoon of Quakers was coming toward them over the rooftops gripping matchlocks, each Quaker trailing a long thread of smoke from the smoldering punk in his fingers. Looking north across Threadneedle they could see a roughly equivalent number of infantrymen headed over the rooftops of Broad Street, coming from the direction of Gresham's College, and it seemed obvious enough that Quakers and Army men would soon be swapping musket-balls over the heads of the mob of Quakers, Barkers, Ranters, Diggers, Jews, Huguenots, Presbyterians, and other sects down below.

So it was down to the street and into the stone-throwing fray. But when they got down there, Daniel saw that these were not the young shin-kickers and head-butters of Drake's glory days. These were paunchy mercers who simply wanted to know where all of their money had got to. The answer was that it had gone to wherever it goes when markets crash. Daniel kept treading on wigs. Sometimes a hundred rioters would turn around and flee *en bloc* from sudden musket-fire and all of their wigs would fall off at once, as though this were a practiced military drill. Some of the wigs had dollops of brain in them, though, which ended up as pearly skeins on Daniel's shoes.

They pushed their way up Broad Street, away from the 'Change, which seemed to be the center of all disturbance. Those mock-Polish grenadiers were formed up in front of the building that had been the Guinea, and was soon to be the Royal Africa, Company. So the Waterhouses squirted past on the far side of the street, looking back to see whether any of those fatal spheres were trajecting after them. They tried to get in at Gresham's College. But many offices of the City of London had been moved into it after the fire, and so it was shut up and almost as well guarded as the Royal Africa Company.

So they had kept moving north and eventually reached Bedlam, and found an evening's refuge there amid piles of dressed stone and splats of mortar. Sterling and Raleigh had departed the next morning, but Daniel had remained: encamped, becalmed, drained, and feeling no desire to go back into the city. From time to time he would hear a nearby church-bell tolling the years of someone who'd died in the rioting.

Daniel's whereabouts became known, and messengers began to arrive, several times a day, bearing invitations to more funerals. He attended several of them, and was frequently asked to stand up and say a few words—not about the deceased (he scarcely knew most of them), but about more general issues of religious tolerance. In other words, he was asked to parrot what Wilkins would've said, and for Daniel that was easy—much easier than making up words of his own. Out of a balanced respect for his own father, he mentioned Drake, too. This felt like a slow and indirect form of suicide, but after his conversation with John Comstock he did not feel he had much of a life to throw away. He was strangely comforted by the sight of all those pews filled with men in white and black (though sometimes Roger Comstock would show up as a gem of color, accompanied by one or two courtiers who were sympathetic, or at least curious). More mourners would be visible through open doors and windows, filling the church-yard and street.

It reminded him of the time during his undergraduate days when the Puritan had been murdered by Upnor, and Daniel had traveled five miles outside of Cambridge to the funeral, and found his father and brothers, miraculously, there. Exasperating to his mind but comforting to his soul. His words swayed their emotions much more than he wanted, or expected—as two inert substances, mixed in an Alchemist's mortar, can create a fulminating compound, so the invocation of Drake's and Wilkins's memories together.

But this was not what he wanted and so he began to avoid the funerals after that, and stayed in the quiet stone-garden of Bedlam.

Hooke was there, too, for Gresham's College had become too crowded with scheming fops. Bedlam was years away from being done. The masons hadn't even begun work on the wings. But the middle part was built, and on top of it was a round turret with windows on all sides, where Hooke liked to retreat and work, because it was lonely and the light was excellent. Daniel for his part stayed down below, and only went out into the city to meet with Leibniz.

Doctor Gottfried Wilhelm Leibniz picked up the coffee-pot and tipped it into his cup for the third time, and for the third time nothing came out of it. It had been empty for half an hour. He made a little sigh of regret, and then reluctantly stood up. "I beg your pardon, but I begin a long journey tomorrow. First the Channel crossing—then, between Calais and Paris, we shall have to dodge French regiments, straggling home, abject, starving, and deranged."

Daniel insisted on paying the bill, and then followed the Doctor out the door. They began strolling in the direction of the inn where Leibniz had been staying. They were not far from the 'Change. Paving-stones and charred firebrands still littered the unpaved streets.

"Not much divine harmony in evidence, here in London," Daniel said. "I can only hang my head in shame, as an Englishman."

"If you and France had conquered the Dutch Republic, you would have much more to be ashamed of," Leibniz returned.

"When, God willing, you get back to Paris, you can say that your mission was a success: there is no war."

"It was a failure," Leibniz said, "we did not prevent the war."

"When you came to London, Doctor, you said that your philosophick endeavours were nothing more than a cover for diplomacy. But I suspect that it was the other way round."

"My philosophick endeavours were a failure, too," Leibniz said.

"You have gained *one* adherent . . ."

"Yes. Oldenburg pesters me every day to complete the Arithmetickal Engine."

"Make that *two* adherents, then, Doctor."

Leibniz actually stopped in his tracks and turned to examine Daniel's face, to see if he was jesting. "I am honored, sir," he said, "but I would prefer to think of you not as an *adherent* but as a *friend*."

"Then the honor is all mine."

They linked arms and walked in silence for a while.

"Paris!" Leibniz said, as if it were the only thing that could get him through the next few days. "When I get back to the Bibliothèque du Roi, I will turn all of my efforts to mathematics."

"You don't want to complete the Arithmetickal Engine?"

It was the first time Daniel had ever seen the Doctor show annoyance. "I am a philosopher, not a watchmaker. The *philosophickal* problems associated with the Arithmetickal Engine have already been solved . . . I have found my way out of *that* labyrinth."

"That reminds me of something you said on your first day in London, Doctor. You mentioned that the question of free will versus predestination is one of the two great labyrinths into which the mind is drawn. What, pray tell, is the other?"

"The other is the composition of the continuum, or: what is space? Euclid assures us that we can divide any distance in half, and then subdivide each of them into smaller halves, and so on, *ad infinitum.* Easy to say, but difficult to understand . . ."

"It is more difficult for *metaphysicians* than for *mathematicians,* I think," Daniel said. "As in so many other fields, modern mathematics has given us tools to work with things that are infinitely small, or infinitely large."

"Perhaps I am too much of a metaphysician, then," Leibniz said. "I take it, sir, that you are referring to the techniques of infinite sequences and series?"

"Just so, Doctor. But as usual, you are overly modest. You have already demonstrated, before the Royal Society, that you know as much of those techniques as any man alive."

"But to me, they do not resolve our confusion, so much as give us a way to think about how confused we are. For example—"

Leibniz gravitated toward a sputtering lamp dangling from the overhanging corner of a building. The City of London's new program to light the streets at night had suffered from the fact that the country was out of money. But in this riotous part of town, where (in the view of Sir Roger L'Estrange, anyway) any shadow might hide a conspiracy of Dissidents, it had been judged worthwhile to spend a bit of whale-oil on street-lamps.

Leibniz fetched a stick from a pile of debris that had been a goldsmith's shop a week earlier, and stepped into the circle of brown light cast on the dirt by the lamp, and scratched out the first few terms of a series:

$$\frac{\pi}{4} = \frac{1}{1} - \frac{1}{3} + \frac{1}{5} - \frac{1}{7} + \frac{1}{9} - \frac{1}{11} + \frac{1}{13} - \frac{1}{15} + \frac{1}{17} \text{ &c}$$

"If you sum this series, it will slowly converge on pi. So we have a way to *approach* the value of pi—to *reach toward* it, but never to *grasp* it . . . much as the human mind can approach divine things, and gain an imperfect knowledge of them, but never look God in the face."

"It is not necessarily true that infinite series must be some sort of concession to the unknowable, Doctor . . . they can clarify, too! My friend Isaac Newton has done wizardly things with them. He has learned to approximate any curve as an infinite series."

Daniel took the stick from Leibniz, then swept out a curve in the dirt. "Far from *detracting* from his knowledge, this has *extended* his grasp, by giving him a way to calculate the tangent to a curve at any point." He carved a straight line above the curve, grazing it at one point.

A black coach rattled up the street, its four horses driven onwards by the coachman's whip, but veering nervously around piles of debris. Daniel and Leibniz backed into a doorway to let it pass; its wheels exploded a puddle and turned Leibniz's glyphs and Daniel's curves into a system of strange canals, and eventually washed them away.

"Would that *some* of our work last longer than *that*," Daniel said ruefully. Leibniz laughed—for a moment—then walked silently for a hundred yards or so.

"I thought Newton only did Alchemy," Leibniz said.

"From time to time, Oldenburg or Comstock or I cajole him into writing out some of his mathematical work."

"Perhaps I need more cajoling," Leibniz said.

"Huygens can cajole you, when you get back."

Leibniz shrugged violently, as if Huygens were sitting astride his neck, and needed to be got rid of. "He has tutored me well, to this point. But if all he can do is give me problems that have already been solved by some Englishman, it must mean that he knows no more mathematics than I do."

"And Oldenburg is cajoling you—but to do the wrong thing."

"I shall endeavour to have an Arithmetickal Engine built in Paris, to satisfy Oldenburg," Leibniz sighed. "It is a worthy project, but for now it is a project for a mechanic."

They came into the light of another street-lamp. Daniel took advantage of it to look at his companion's face, and gauge his mood. Leibniz looked a good deal more resolute than he had beneath the *previous* street-lamp. "It is childish of me to expect older men to tell me what to do," the Doctor said. "No one *told* me to think about free will versus predestination. I plunged into the middle of the labyrinth, and became thoroughly lost, and then had no choice but to think my way out of it."

"The second labyrinth awaits you," Daniel reminded him.

"Yes . . . it is time for me to plunge into it. Henceforth, that is my only purpose. The next time you see me, Daniel, I will be a mathematician second to none."

From any other Continental lawyer these words would have been laughably arrogant; but they had come from the mouth of the monster.

> I laid the reins upon the neck of my lusts.
> —JOHN BUNYAN, *The Pilgrim's Progress*

DANIEL WAS AWAKENED one morning by a stifled boom, and supposed it was a piece being tested in the Artillery Yard outside of town. Just as he was about to fall back to sleep he heard it again: *thump,* like the period at the end of a book.

Dawn-light had flooded the turret of Bedlam and was picking its way down through struts and lashings, plank-decks and scaffolds, dangling ropes and angling braces, to the ground floor where Daniel lay on a sack of straw. He could hear movements above: not blunderings of thieves or vermin, but the well-conceived, precisely executed maneuvers of birds, and of Robert Hooke.

Daniel rose and, leaving his wig behind, so that the cool air bathed his stubbled scalp, climbed up toward the light, ascending the masons' ladders and ropes. Above his head, the gaps between planks were radiant, salmon-colored lines, tight and parallel as harpsichord-strings. He hoisted himself up through a hatch, rousting a couple of swallows, and found himself within the dome of the turret, sharing a hemispherical room with Robert Hooke. Dust made the air gently luminous. Hooke had spread out large drawings of wings and airscrews. Before the windows he had hung panes of glass, neatly scored with black Cartesian grids, plotted with foreshortened parabolae—the trajectories of actual cannonballs. Hooke liked to watch cannonballs fly from a stand-point next to the cannon, standing inside a contraption he had built, peering through these sheets of glass and tracing the balls' courses on them with a grease-pencil.

"Weigh out five grains of powder for me," Hooke said. He was paying attention to part of a rarefying engine: one of many such piston-and-cylinder devices he and Boyle used to study the expansion of gases.

Daniel went over to a tiny scale set up on a plank between two sawhorses. On the floor next to it was a keg branded with the coat of arms of the Silver Comstocks. Its bung was loose, and peppered with grains of coarse powder. Next to it rested a small cylindrical bag of linen, about the diameter of a fist, plump and round as a full sack of flour. This had once been sewn shut, but Hooke had snipped through the uneven stitches and teased it open. Looking in among the petals of frayed fabric, Daniel saw that it, too, was filled with black powder.

"Would you prefer I take it from the keg, or the little bag?" Daniel asked.

"As I value my eyes, and my Rarefying Engine, take it from the keg."

"Why do you say so?" Daniel drew the loose bung out and found that the keg was nearly full. Taking up a copper spoon that Hooke had left near the scale (copper did not make sparks), he scooped up a small amount of powder from the bung-hole and began sprinkling it onto one of the scale's frail golden pans. But his gaze strayed towards the linen bag. In part this was because Hooke, who feared so little, seemed to think it was a hazard. Too, there was something about this bag that was familiar to him, though he could not place it in his memory.

"Rub a pinch between your fingers," Hooke suggested. "Come, there is no danger."

Daniel probed into the linen bag and got a smudge of the stuff on his fingertips. The answer was obvious. "This is much finer than that in the keg." And that was the clew that reminded him where he had seen such a bag before. The night that Roger Comstock had blown himself up in the laboratory, he had been grinding gunpowder very fine, and pouring it into a bag just like this one. "Where did this come from? A theatre?"

For once Hooke was flummoxed. "What a very odd question for you to ask. Why do you phant'sy such a thing should come from a theatre, of all places?"

"The nature of the powder," Daniel said. "Ground so exceedingly fine." He nodded at the bag, for his hands were busy. Having weighed out five grains of powder from the keg, he poured them from the scale-pan into a cupped scrap of paper and carried it over to Hooke. "Such powder burns much faster than this coarse stuff." He shook the paper for emphasis and it made a sandy rasp. He handed it to Hooke, who poured it into the cylinder of the Rarefying Engine. Some of these engines were wrought of glass, but this was a heavy brass tube about the size of a tobacco-canister: a very small siege-mortar, in effect. Its piston fit into it like a cannonball.

"I am aware of it," Hooke said. "That is why I do not wish to put five grains of it into the Rarefying Engine. Five grains of Comstock's powder burns slow and steady, and drives the piston up in a way that is useful to me. The same weight of that fine stuff from yonder bag would burn in an instant, and explode my apparatus, and me."

"That is why I supposed the bag might have come from a theatre," Daniel said. "Such powder may be unsuitable for the Rarefying Engine, but on the stage it makes a pretty flash and bang."

"That bag," said Hooke, "came from the magazine of one of His Majesty's Ships of War. The practice used to be, and still is on some ships, that powder is introduced into the bore of a cannon by scooping it up out of a keg and pouring it in. Similar to how a musketeer charges the barrel of his weapon. But in the heat of battle, our gunners are prone to mis-measure and to spill the powder on the deck. And to have open containers of powder near active cannon is to tempt disaster. A new practice is replacing the old. Before the battle, when it is possible to work calmly, the powder is carefully measured out and placed into bags, such as that one, which are sewn shut. The bags are stockpiled in the ship's magazine. During battle, as they are needed, they are ferried one at a time to the guns."

"I see," Daniel said, "then the gunner need only slash the bag open and pour its contents into the bore."

Hardly for the first time, Hooke was a bit irked by Daniel's stupidity. "Why waste time opening it with a knife, when fire will open it for you?"

"I beg your pardon?"

"Behold, the diameter of the bag is the same as the bore of the gun. Why open it then? No, the entire bag, sewn shut, is introduced into the barrel."

"The gunners never even see what is inside of it!"

Hooke nodded. "The only powder that the gunners need concern themselves with is the priming-powder that is poured into the touch-hole and used to communicate fire to the bag."

"Then those gunners are trusting the ones who sew up the bags—trusting them with their lives," Daniel said. "If the wrong sort of powder were used—" and he faltered, and went over and dipped his fingers once more into the bag before him to feel the consistency of the powder inside. The difference between it and the Comstock powder was like that between flour and sand.

"Your discourse is strangely like that of John Comstock when he delivered that bag and that keg to me," Hooke said.

"He brought them around *in person*?"

Hooke nodded. "He said he no longer trusted anyone to do it for him."

Whereat Daniel must have looked shocked, for Hooke held up a hand as if to restrain him, and continued: "I understood his state of mind too well. Some of us, Daniel, are prone to a sort of melancholy, wherein we are tormented by phant'sies that other men are secretly plotting to do us injury. It is a pernicious state for a man to fall into. I have harbored such notions from time to time about Oldenburg and others. Your friend Newton shows signs of the same affliction. Of all men in the world, I supposed John Comstock least susceptible to this disorder; but when he came here with this bag, he was very far gone with it, which grieved me more than anything else that has happened of late."

"My lord believes," Daniel guessed, "that some enemy of his has been salting the magazines of Navy ships with bags filled with finely milled powder, such as this one. Such a bag, sewn shut, would look the same, to a gunner, as an ordinary one; but when loaded into the bore, and fired—"

"It would burst the barrel and kill everyone nearby," Hooke said. "Which might be blamed on a faulty cannon, or on faulty powder; but as my lord manufactures *both*, the blame cannot but be laid on him in the end."

"Where did this bag come from?" Daniel asked.

"My lord said it was sent to him by his son Richard, who found it in the magazine of his ship on the eve of their sailing for Sole Bay."

"Where Richard was killed by a Dutch broadside," Daniel said. "So my lord desired that you would inspect this bag and render an opinion that it had been tampered with by some malicious conspirator."

"Just so."

"And have you done so?"

"No one has asked my opinion yet."

"Not even Comstock?"

"Nay, not even Comstock."

"Why would he bring you such evidence in person, and then not ask?"

"I can only guess," Hooke said, "that in the meantime he has come to understand that it does not really matter."

"What an odd thing to think."

"Not really," Hooke said. "Suppose I testified that this bag contained powder that was too fine. What would it boot him? Anglesey—for make no mistake, that's who's behind this—would reply that Comstock had made up this bag in his own cellar, as false evidence to exonerate himself and his faulty cannons. Comstock's son is the only man who could testify that it came from a ship's magazine, and he's dead. There might be other such bags in other magazines, but they are mostly on the bottom of the sea, thanks to Admiral de Ruyter. We have lost the war, and it must be blamed on someone. Someone other than the King and the Duke of York. Comstock has now come to understand that it is being blamed on him."

The daylight had become much more intense in the minutes Daniel had been up here. He saw that Hooke had rigged an articulated rod to the back of the piston, and connected the rod to a system of cranks. Now, by means of a tiny touch-hole in the base of the cylinder, he introduced fire to the chamber. *Thump.* The piston snapped up to the top of the bore much faster than Daniel could flinch away from it. This caused an instant of violent motion in the gear-train, which had the effect of winding a spring that spiraled around in a whirling hoop the size of a dinner-plate. A ratchet stopped this from unwinding. Hooke then re-arranged the gears so that the giant watch-spring was connected, by a string wound around a tapered drum, to the drive-shaft of a peculiar helical object, very light-weight, made of parchment stretched on a frame of steam-bent cane. Like a Screw of Archimedes. The spring unwound slowly, spinning the screw swiftly and steadily. Standing at one end of it, Daniel felt a palpable breeze, which continued for more than a minute—Hooke timed it with his latest watch.

"Properly wrought, and fed with gunpowder at regular intervals, it might generate enough wind to blow itself off the ground," Hooke said.

"Supplying the gunpowder would be difficult," Daniel said.

"I only use it because I *have* some," Hooke said. "Now that Anglesey has been elected President of the Royal Society, I look forward to experimenting with combustible *vapors* in its stead."

"Even if I've moved to Massachusetts by then," Daniel said, "I'll come back to London to watch you fly through the air, Mr. Hooke."

A church-bell began ringing not far away. Daniel remarked that it was a bit early for funerals. But a few minutes later another one started up, and another. They did not simply bong a few times and then stop—they kept pealing in some kind of celebration. But the Anglican churches did not seem to be sharing in the joy. Only the queer churches of Dutchmen and Jews and Dissenters.

LATER IN THE DAY, Roger Comstock appeared at the gates of Bedlam in a coach-and-four. The previous owner's coat of arms had been scraped off and replaced with that of the Golden Comstocks. "Daniel, do me the honor of allowing me to escort you to Whitehall," Roger said, "the King wants you there for the signing."

"Signing of *what?*" Daniel could imagine several possibilities—
Daniel's death warrant for sedition, Roger's for sabotage, or an
instrument of surrender to the Dutch Republic, being three of the
more plausible.

"Why, the Declaration! Haven't you heard? Freedom of conscience for Dissenters of all stripes—almost—just as Wilkins
wanted it."

"That is very good news, if true—but why should His Majesty
want *me* there?"

"Why, next to Bolstrood you are the leading Dissenter!"

"That is *not true.*"

"It doesn't matter," Roger said cheerfully. "He *thinks* it's true—
and after today, it *will* be."

"Why does he think it's true?" Daniel asked, though he already
suspected why.

"Because I have been telling everyone so," Roger answered.

"I haven't clothes fit to wear to a whorehouse—to say nothing of
Whitehall Palace."

"There is very little practical difference," Roger said absent-
mindedly.

"You don't understand. My wig's home to a family of swallows,"
Daniel complained. But Roger Comstock snapped his fingers, and
a valet sprang out of the coach laden with diverse packages and
bundles. Through the open door, Daniel glimpsed women's clothing, too—with women inside of it. Two *different* women. A *thump*
from the turret, a muffled curse from Hooke. "Don't worry, it's
nothing foppish," Roger said. "For a leading Dissident, it is entirely
proper."

"Can the same be said of the *ladies?*" Daniel asked, following
Roger and the valet into Bedlam.

"These aren't *ladies,*" Roger said, and other than that weak jest did
not even try to answer the question. "Do London a favor and take
those damned clothes off. I shall have my manservant burn them."

"The shirt is not so bad," Daniel demurred. "Oh, I agree that it
is no longer fit for wearing. But it might be made into a powder-
bag for the Navy."

"No longer in demand," Roger said, "now that the war is over."

"On the contrary, I say that a great many of them shall have to
be made up now, as so many of the old ones are known to be
defective."

"Hmm, you *are* well-informed, for a political naif. Who has
been filling your head with such ideas? Obviously a supporter of
Comstock."

"I suppose that supporters of Anglesey are saying that the powder-bags are all excellent, and it's Comstock's cannons that were made wrong."

"It is universally known, among the Quality."

"That may be. But it is known among you, and me, and a few other people, that bags were made up, containing powder that was ground fine."

Coincidentally or not, Daniel had reached the point of complete nakedness as he was saying these words. He had a pair of drawers on; but Roger tossed him fresh ones, and averted his gaze. "Daniel! I cannot bear to see you in this state, nor can I listen to any more of your needling suspicious discourse. I will turn my back on you, and talk for a while. When I turn round again, I will behold a new man, as well *informed* as he is *attired*."

"Very well, I suppose I've very little choice."

"None whatsoever. Now, Daniel. You saw me grinding the powder fine, and putting it into the bag, and there is no point in denying it. No doubt you think the worst of me, as has been your wont since we first studied together at Trinity. Have you stopped to ask yourself, how a man in my position could possibly manage to introduce bags of powder into the magazines of a ship of the Royal Navy? Quite obviously it is impossible. Someone else must have done it. Someone with a great deal more power and reach than I can even dream of possessing."

"The Duke of Gunfl—"

"Silence. Silence! And in silence ponder the similitudes between cannons and mouths. The simpleton beholds a cannon and phant'sies it an infallible destroyer of foes. But the veteran artilleryman knows that sometimes, when a cannon speaks, it bursts. Especially when it has been loaded in haste. When this occurs, Daniel, the foe is untouched. He may sense a distant gaseous exhalation, not puissant enough to ruffle his periwig. The eager gunner, *and all his comrades,* are blown to bits. Ponder it, Daniel. And for once in your life, show a trace of discretion. It does not really matter what the gentleman's name was who was responsible for causing those cannons to burst. What matters is that *I had no idea what I was doing.* What do *I*, of all people, know about naval artillery? All I knew was this: I met certain gentlemen at the Royal Society. Presently they became aware that I worked in Newton's laboratory as an assistant. One of them approached me and asked if I might do him a favor. Nothing difficult. He wanted me to grind up some gunpowder very fine and deliver it to him in wee bags. This I did, as you know. I made up half a dozen of those bags over the course of a year. One of them blew up on the spot, thanks to you. Of the other five, I now know that one was smuggled into the 'Siege of Maestricht,' where it caused a cannon to explode in full view of half of London. The other four went to the Royal Navy. One was detected by Richard Comstock, who sent it to his father. One exploded a cannon during a naval engagement against the Dutch. The other two have since found their way into David Jones's Magazine. As to my culpability: I did not understand until recently why the gentleman in question had made such an odd request of me. I did not know, when I was filling those bags, that they would be used to do murder."

Daniel, snaking his limbs through new clothes, believed every word of this. He had long ago lost count of Roger's moral lapses. Roger, he suspected, had broken as many of the ten command-ments and committed as many of the seven deadly sins as it was in his power to do, and was actively seeking ways to break and commit those he had not yet ticked off the list. This had nothing to do with Roger's character. *Someone* was responsible for blowing up those poor gunners, as a ploy to dishonor the Earl of Epsom: as vile an act as Daniel could imagine. Thomas More Anglesey, Duke of Gun-fleet, or one of his sons must have been at the head of the conspir-acy, for as Roger had pointed out, Roger couldn't have done it all himself. The only question then was whether Roger had under-stood what was being done with those powder-bags. The Angleseys would never have told him, and so he'd have had to figure it out on his own. And Roger's career at Trinity gave no grounds to expect dazzling flashes of insight.

Believing in Roger's innocence lifted from Daniel's shoulders an immense weight that he had not been sensible of until it was gone. This felt so good that it triggered a few moments of Puritan-ical self-examination. Anything that felt so good might be a trick of the devil. Was he only *feigning* trust in Roger, *because* it felt good?

"How can you go on associating with those people when you know the atrocious thing they have done?"

"I was going to ask you."

"I beg your pardon?"

"You have been associating with them since the Plague Year, Daniel, at every meeting of the Royal Society."

"But I did not know they were doing murder!"

"On the contrary, Daniel, you have known it ever since that night at Trinity twelve years ago when you watched Louis Anglesey murder one of your brethren." Had he been a rather different sort of chap, Roger might have mentioned this in a cruelly triumphant way. Had he been Drake, he'd have said it sadly, or angrily. But being Roger Comstock, he proffered it as a witticism. He did it so well that Daniel let out a wee snort of amusement before coming to his senses and stifling himself.

The terms of the transaction finally were clear. Why did Daniel refuse to hate Roger? Not out of blindness to Roger's faults, for he saw Roger's moral cowardice as clearly as Hooke peering through a lens at a newt. Not out of Christian forgiveness, either. He refused to hate Roger because Roger saw moral cowardice in Daniel, had done so for years, and yet did not hate Daniel. Fair's fair. They were brothers.

As much as he had to ponder in the way of moral dilemmas vis-à-vis Roger, 'twas as nothing compared to half an hour later, when Daniel emerged, booted, bewigged, cravated, and jacketed, and equipped with a second-hand watch that Roger somehow begged off of Hooke, and climbed into the coach. For one of the women in there was Tess Charter. *Thump.*

When she and the other woman were finished laughing at the look on Daniel's face, she leaned forward and got her fingers all entangled with his. She was shockingly and alarmingly *alive*—somewhat more alive, in fact, than he was. She looked him in the eyes and spoke in her French accent: "Twooly, Daniel, eet eez ze hrole of a lifetime—portraying ze *mistress* of a gentlemen who eez too pure—too spiritual—to sink zee thoughts of zee flesh." Then a middling London accent. "But really I prefer the challenging parts. The ability to do them's what separates me from Nell Gwyn."

"I wonder what separates the *King* from Nell Gwyn?" said the other woman.

"Ten inches of sheepgut with a knot in one end—if the King knows what's good for him!" Tess returned. *Thump.*

This led to more in a similar vein. Daniel turned to Roger, who was sitting next to him, and said, "Sir! What on earth makes you believe I wish to appear to have a mistress?"

"Who said anything about *appearing* to have one?" Roger answered, and when Daniel didn't laugh, gathered himself up and said, "Poh! You could no more show up at Whitehall without a mistress, than at a duel without a sword! Come, Daniel! No one will take you seriously! They'll think you're hiding something!"

"And that he is—though none too effectively," Tess said, eyeing a new convexity in Daniel's breeches.

"I loved your work in *The Dutch Strumpet*," Daniel tried, weakly.

Thus, down London Wall and westwards, ho!—Daniel's every attempt to say anything *serious* pre-empted by a courtly witticism—

more often than not, so bawdy he didn't even *understand* it, any more than Tess would understand the Proceedings of the Royal Society. Every jest followed by exaltations of female laughter and then a radical, and completely irrational, change in subject.

Just when Daniel thought he had imposed a bit of order on the conversation, the coach rattled into the middle of St. Bartholomew's Fair. Suddenly, outside the windows, bears were dancing jigs and hermaphrodites were tottering about on stilts. Devout men and well-bred ladies would avert their eyes from such sights, but Tess and the other woman (another Comedian, who gave every indication of being Roger's *authentic,* not *imaginary,* mistress) had no intentions of averting their gazes from *anything*. They were still chattering about what they'd seen ten minutes later as the coach moved down Holborn. Daniel decided to take his cue from Roger, who rather than trying to *talk* to the ladies merely sat and watched them, face smeared with a village idiot's grin.

They stopped by the corner of Waterhouse Square for ritual adoration of Roger's new lot, and to make sniping comments about Raleigh's house: that soon-to-be-o'ershadowed pile that Raleigh's architect had (it was speculated) blown out of his arse-hole during an attaque of the bloody phlux. The ladies made comments in a similar vein about the attire of the widow Mayflower Ham, who was descending from same, on her way to Whitehall, too.

Then down past any number of fields, churches, squares, *et cetera,* named after St. Giles, and a completely gratuitous detour along Piccadilly to Comstock House, where Roger had the coach stop so that he could spend several minutes savoring the spectacle of the Silver Comstocks moving out of the building that had served as their London seat since the Wars of the Roses. Colossal paintings, depicting scenes of hunting and of naval engagements, had been pulled out and leaned against the wrought-iron fence. Below them was a clutter of smaller canvases, mostly portraits, stripped of their gilded frames, which were going to auction. Making it appear that there was a whole crowd of Silver Comstocks, mostly in outmoded doublets or neck-ruffs, milling about down there and peering out grimly through the fence. "All behind bars where they should've been a hundred years ago!" Roger said, and then laughed at his own jest, loud enough to draw a look from John Comstock himself, who was standing in his forecourt watching some porters maneuver out the door a mainsail-si‿d painting of some Continental Siege. Daniel's eye fixed on this. Partly it was because looking at the Earl of Epsom made him melancholy. But also it was because he had been spending so much time with Leibniz, who often spoke of paintings such as this one when talking about the mind of God. On one piece of canvas, seemingly from one fixed point of view, the artist had depicted skirmishes, sallies, cavalry charges, and the deaths of several of the principals, which had occurred in different places at different times. And this was not the only liberty he had taken with the notion of time and space, for certain events—the digging of a mine beneath a bastion, the detonation of the mine, and the ensuing battle—were shown all together at once. The images stood next to each other like pickled larvae in the Royal Society's collection, sharing the same time for all time, and yet if you let your eye travel over them in the correct order you could make the story unfold within your mind, each event in its proper moment. This great painting did not, of course, stand alone, but was surrounded by all of the other paintings that had been carried out of the house before; its perceptions were ranged alongside others, this little Siege-world nested within a larger array of other things that the House of Comstock during its long history had perceived, and thought worthy to be set down on canvas. Now they were all being aired out and reshuffled, on a gloomy occasion. But to have this moment—the fall of the Silver Comstocks—embedded in so many old ones made it seem less terrible that it might have seemed if it had happened naked, as it were, and all alone in time and space.

THE EARL OF EPSOM TURNED his head and gazed across Piccadilly at his Golden cousin, but showed no particular emotion. Daniel had shrunk far down into the coach, where he hoped he'd be enshrouded in darkness. To him, John Comstock looked almost *relieved*. How bad could it be to live in Epsom and go hunting and fishing every day? That's what Daniel told himself—but later the sadness and haggardness in the Earl's face would appear in his mind's eye at the oddest times.

"Do not become stupid now, just because you are seeing his face," Roger said to him. "That man was a Cavalier. He led cavalry charges against the Parliamentarian foot-soldiers. Do you know what that means? Do you see that great bloody awful painting there of Comstock's great-uncle and his friends galloping after that fox? Replace the fox with a starving yeoman, unarmed, alone, and you have a fair picture of how that man spent the Civil War."

"I know all that," Daniel said. "And yet, and yet, somehow I still prefer him and his family to the Duke of Gunfleet and *his* family."

"John Comstock had to be cleared out of the way, and we had to lose a war, before *anything* could happen," Roger said. "As to Anglesey and his spawn, I love them even less than you do. Do not fret about them. Enjoy your triumph and your mistress. Leave Anglesey to me."

Then to Whitehall where they, and various Bolstroods and Waterhouses and many others, watched the King sign the Declaration. As penned by Wilkins, this document had given freedom of conscience to *everyone*. The version that the King signed today was not quite so generous: it outlawed certain extreme heretics, such as Arians who didn't believe in the Trinity. Nevertheless, it was a good day's work. Certainly enough to justify raising several pints, in several Drury Lane taverns, to the memory of John Wilkins. Daniel's pretend mistress accompanied him on every stage of this epochal pub-crawling campaign, which led eventually to Roger Comstock's playhouse, and, in particular, to a back-room of that playhouse, where there happened to be a bed.

"Who has been making sausages in here?" Daniel inquired. Which sent Tess into a fit of the giggles. She had just about got his new breeches off.

"I should say *you* have made a pretty one!" she finally managed to get out.

"I should say *you* are responsible for making it," Daniel demurred, and then (now that it was in plain view) added: "and it is anything but pretty."

"Wrong on both counts!" said Tess briskly. She stood up and grabbed it. Daniel gasped. She gave it a tug; Daniel yelped, and drew closer. "Ah, so it *is* attached to you. You shall have to accept responsibility for the making of it, then; can't blame the lasses for everything. And as for pretty—" she relaxed her grip, and let it rest on the palm of her hand, and gave it a good look. "You've never seen a *nasty* one, have you?"

"I was raised to believe they were *all* quite nasty."

"That may be true—it is all metaphysickal, isn't it? Quite. But please know some are nastier than others. And that is why we have sausage-casings in a bedchamber."

She proceeded to do something quite astonishing with ten inches of knotted sheepgut. Not that he needed ten inches; but she was generous with it, perhaps to show him a kind of respect.

"Does this mean it is not actually coitus?" Daniel asked hopefully. "Since I am not really touching you?" Actually he was touching her in a lot of places, and vice versa. But where it counted he was touching nothing but sheepgut.

"It is very common for men of your religion to say so," Tess said.

"Almost as common as this irksome habit of talking while you are doing it."

"And what do *you* say?"

"I say that we are not touching, and not having sex, if it makes you feel better," Tess said. "Though, when all is finished, you shall have to explain to your Maker why you are at this moment buggering a dead sheep."

"Please do not make me laugh!" Daniel said. "It hurts somehow."

"What is funny? I simply speak the truth. What you are feeling is not hurting."

He understood then that she was right. Hurting wasn't the word for it.

When Daniel woke up in that bed, sometime in the middle of the following afternoon, Tess was gone. She'd left him a note (who'd have thought she was literate? But she had to read the scripts).

> Daniel,
>   We shall make more sausages later. I am off to act. Yes, it may have slipped your mind that I am an actress.
>   Yesterday I worked, playing the role of mistress. It is a difficult role, because dull. But now it has become fact, not farce, and so I shall not have to act any more; much easier. As I am no longer professionally engaged, pretending to be your mistress, I shall no longer be receiving my stipend from your friend Roger. As I am now your mistress in fact, some small gift would be appropriate. Forgive my forwardness. Gentlemen *know such things*, Puritans *must be instructed*.
>   Tess
> P.S. You want instruction in acting. I shall endeavour to help.

Daniel staggered about the room for some minutes collecting his clothes, and tried to put them on in the right order. It did not escape his notice that he was getting dressed, like an actor, in the backstage of a theatre. When he was done he found his way out among sets and properties and stumbled out onto the stage. The house was empty, save for a few actors dozing on benches. Tess was right. He had found his place now: he was just another actor, albeit he would never appear on a stage, and would have to make up his own lines *ad libitum*.

His role, as he could see plainly enough, was to be a leading Dissident who also happened to be a noted savant, a Fellow of the Royal Society. Until lately he would not have thought this a difficult role to play, since it was so close to the truth. But whatever illusions

Daniel might once have harbored about being a man of God had died with Drake, and been cremated by Tess. He very much phant'sied being a Natural Philosopher, but that simply was not going to work if he had to compete against Isaac, Leibniz, and Hooke. And so the role that Roger Comstock had written for him was beginning to appear very challenging indeed. Perhaps, like Tess, he would come to prefer it that way.

That much had been evident to him on that morning in 1673. But the ramifications had been as far beyond his wits as Calculus would've been to Mayflower Ham. He could not have anticipated that his new-launched career as actor on the stage of London would stretch over the next twenty-five years. And even if he had foreseen that, he could never have phant'sied that, after forty, he would be called back for an encore.

Aboard Minerva, *Cape Cod Bay, Massachusetts*

NOVEMBER 1713

BLACKBEARD IS AFTER *HIM*! Daniel spent the day terrified even *before* he knew this—now's the time to be struck dead with fear. But he is calm instead. Partly it's that the surgeon's not sewing him together any more, and anything's an improvement on *that*. Partly it's that he lost some blood, and drank some rum, during the operation. But those are mechanistic explanations. Despite all that Daniel said to Wait Still concerning Free Will, *et cetera,* on the eve of his departure from Boston, he is not willing to believe, yet, that he is controlled by his balance of humours. No, Daniel is in a better mood (once he's had an hour or two to rest up, anyway) because things are beginning to make sense now. Albeit scantly. Pain scares him, death doesn't especially (he never expected to live so long!), but chaos, and the feeling that the world is not behaving according to rational laws, put him into the same state of animal terror as a dog who's being dissected alive but cannot understand why.

To him the rolling eyes of those bound and muzzled dogs have ever been the touchstone of fear.

"Out for a stroll so soon, Doctor?"

Dappa's evidently recognized him by the tread of his shoes and walking-stick on the quarterdeck—he hasn't taken the spyglass away from his eye in half an hour.

"What about that schooner is so fascinating, Mr. Dappa? Other than that it's full of murderers."

"The Captain and I are having a dispute. I say it is a floaty and leewardly Flemish pirate-bottom. Van Hoek sees idioms in its rigging that argue to the contrary."

"*Bottom* meaning her hull—*floaty* meaning she bobs like a cork, with little below the water-line—which is desirable, I gad, for Flemings and pirates alike, as both must slip into shallow coves and harbors—"

"Perfect marks so far, Doctor."

"*Leewardly,* then, I suppose, means that because of that faintness in the keel, the wind tends to push her sideways through the water whenever she is sailing close-hauled—as she is now."

"And as are we, Doctor."

"*Minerva* has the same defect, I suppose—"

This slander finally induces Dappa to take the spyglass away from his eye. "Why should you assume any such thing?"

"All these Amsterdam-ships are flat-bottomed of necessity, are they not? For entering the Ijsselmeer . . ."

"*Minerva* was built on the Malabar coast."

"Mr. Dappa!"

"I would not dishonor you with jests, Doctor. It is true. I was there."

"But how—"

" 'Tis an awkward time to be telling you the entire Narration," Dappa observes. "Suffice it to say that she is *not* leewardly. Her *apparent* course is as close as it can be to her *true* course."

"And you'd like to know, whether the same is true of yonder schooner," Daniel says. "It is not unlike the problem an astronomer faces, when—imprisoned as he is on a whirling and hurtling planet—he tries to plot the true trajectory of a comet through the heavens."

"Now it's *my* turn to wonder whether *you* are jesting."

"The water is like the Cœlestial Æther, a fluid medium through which all things move. Cape Cod, over yonder, is like the distant, fixed stars—by sighting that church-steeple in Provincetown, the High Land of Cape Cod to the south of it, the protruding mast of yonder wrack, and then by doing a bit of trigonometry, we may plot our position, and by joining one point to the next, draw our trajectory. The schooner, then, is like a comet—also moving through the æther—but by measuring the angles she makes with us and with the church-steeple, *et cetera,* we may find her *true* course; compare it with her *apparent* heading; and easily judge whether she is, or is not, leewardly."

"How long would it take?"

"If you could make sightings, and leave me in peace to make calculations, I could have an answer in perhaps half an hour."

"Then let us begin without delay," Dappa says.

Plotting it out on the back of an old chart in the common room, Daniel begins to understand the urgency. To escape the confines of Cape Cod Bay, they must clear Race Point at the Cape's northernmost tip. Race Point is northeast of them. The wind, for the last few hours, has been steady from northwest by north. *Minerva* can sail six points* from the wind, so she can just manage a northeasterly course. So leaving aside pirate-ships and other complications, she's in a good position to clear Race Point within the hour.

But as a matter of fact there are two pirate-ships paralleling her course, much as the schooner-that-sucked and the ketch were doing earlier. To windward (i.e., roughly northwest of *Minerva*) is a big sloop—Teach's flagship—which has complete freedom of movement under these circumstances. She's fast, maneuverable, well-armed, capable of sailing four points from the wind, and well to the north of the dangerous shallows, hence in no danger of running aground off of Race Point. The schooner, on the other hand, is to leeward, between *Minerva* and the Cape. She can also sail four points from the wind—meaning that she should be able to angle across *Minerva*'s course and grapple with her before Race Point. And if she does, there's no doubt that Teach's sloop will come in along the larboard side at the same moment, so that *Minerva* will be boarded from both sides at once. If that is all true, then *Minerva*'s best course is to turn her stern into the wind, fall upon the schooner, attack, and then come about (preferably before running aground on the Cape) and contend with the sloop.

But if Dappa is right, and the schooner suffers from the defect of leewardliness, then all's not as it seems. The wind will push her sideways, *away* from *Minerva* and *toward* the Race Point shallows— she won't be able to intercept *Minerva* soon enough, and, to avoid running aground, she'll have to tack back to the west, taking her

---

*There are thirty-two points on the compass rose.

out of the action. If that is true, *Minerva*'s best course is to maintain her present close-hauled state and wait for Teach's sloop to make a move.

It's all in the arithmetic—the same sort of arithmetic that Flamsteed, the Astronomer Royal, is probably grinding through at this very moment at the Observatory in Greenwich, toiling through the night in hopes of proving that Sir Isaac's latest calculation of the orbit of the moon is wrong. Except here *Minerva*'s the Earth, that schooner is Luna, and fixed Boston is, of course, the Hub of the Universe. Daniel passes an extraordinarily pleasant half-hour turning Dappa's steady observations into sines and cosines, conic sections and fluxions. Pleasant because it is imbued with the orderliness that taketh away his fear. Not to mention a fascination that makes him forget the throbbing and pulling stitches in his flesh.

"Dappa is correct. The schooner drifts to leeward, and will soon fall by the wayside or run aground," he announces to van Hoek, up on the poop deck. Van Hoek puffs once, twice, thrice on his pipe, then nods and goes into Dutch mutterings. Mates and messenger-boys disseminate his will into all compartments of the ship. *Minerva* forgets about the schooner and bends all efforts to the expected fight against Teach's wicked sloop-of-war.

In another half-hour, the leewardly schooner provides some coarse entertainment by actually running aground at the very knuckle of Cape Cod's curled fist. This is ignominious, but hardly unheard-of; these English pirates have only been in Massachusetts for a couple of weeks and can't expect to have all the sand-banks committed to memory. This skipper would rather run aground in soft sand, and refloat later, than flinch from battle and face Blackbeard Teach's wrath.

Van Hoek immediately has them come about to west by south, as if they were going to sail back to Boston. His intent is to cut behind Teach's stern and fire a broadside up the sloop's arse and along her length. But Teach has too much intelligence for that, and so breaks the other way, turning to the east to get clear of *Minerva*'s broadside, then wearing round to the south, pausing near the grounded schooner to pick up a few dozen men who might come in useful as boarders. After a short time he comes up astern of *Minerva*.

A tacking duel plays out there off of Race Point for an hour or so, Teach trying to find a way to get within musket-range of *Minerva* without being blown apart, van Hoek trying to fire just a single well-considered broadside. There are some paltry exchanges of fire. Teach puts a small hole in *Minerva*'s hull that is soon patched, and a cloud of hurtling junk from one of *Minerva*'s carronnades manages to carry away one of the sloop's sails, which is soon replaced. But with time, even van Hoek's hatred of pirates is worn down by the tedium, and by the need to get away from land while the sun is shining. Dappa reminds him that the Atlantic Ocean is just a mile or two that-a-way, and that nothing stands any more between them and it. He persuades van Hoek that there's no better way to humiliate a pirate than to leave him empty-handed, his decks crowded with boarders who have nothing to throw their grappling-hooks at. To out-sail a pirate, he insists, is a sweeter revenge than to out-fight him.

So van Hoek orders *Minerva* to come about and point herself toward England. The men who've been manning the guns are told to make like Cincinnatus, walking away from their implements of war at the very moment of their victory so that they may apply themselves to peaceful toils: in this case, spreading every last sail that the ship can carry. Tired, smoke-smeared men lumber up into the light and, after a short pause to swallow ladles of water, go to work swinging wide the studdingsail booms. This nearly doubles the width of the ship's mightiest yards. The studdingsails tumble from them and snap taut in the wind. Like an albatross that has endured a long pursuit through a cluttered wilderness, tediously dodging and veering from hazard to hazard, and that finally rises above the clutter, and sees the vast ocean stretching before it, *Minerva* spreads her wings wide, and flies. The hull has shrunk to a mote, dragged along below a giant creaking nebula of firm canvas.

Teach can be seen running up and down the length of his sloop with smoke literally coming out of his head, waving his cutlass and exhorting his crew, but everyone knows that *Queen Anne's Revenge* is a bit crowded, not to mention under-victualled, for a North Atlantic cruise in November.

Minerva accelerates into blue water with power that Daniel can feel in his legs, crashing through the odd rogue swell just as she rammed a pirate-boat earlier today, and, as the sun sets on America, she begins the passage to the Old World sailing large before a quartering wind.

King of the Vagabonds

There is, doubtless, as much skill in pourtraying a Dunghill, as in describing the finest Palace, since the Excellence of Things lyes in the Performance; and Art as well as Nature must have some extraordinary Shape or Quality if it come up to the pitch of Human Fancy, especially to please in this Fickle, Uncertain Age.

— *Memoirs of the Right Villanous John Hall, 1708*

The Mud Below London
1665

⚕

MOTHER SHAFTOE KEPT TRACK of her boys' ages on her fingers, of which there were six. When she ran short of fingers—that is, when Dick, the eldest and wisest, was nearing his seventh summer—she gathered the half-brothers together in her shack on the Isle of Dogs, and told them to be gone, and not to come back without bread or money.

This was a typically East London approach to child-rearing and so Dick, Bob, and Jack found themselves roaming the banks of the Thames in the company of many other boys who were also questing for bread or money with which to buy back their mothers' love.

London was a few miles away, but, to them, as remote and legendary as the Court of the Great Mogul in Shahjahanabad. The Shaftoe boys' field of operations was an infinite maze of brickworks, pig yards, and shacks crammed sometimes with Englishmen and sometimes with Irishmen living ten and twelve to a room among swine, chickens, and geese.

The Irish worked as porters and dockers and coal-haulers during the winter, and trudged off to the countryside in hay-making months. They went to their Papist churches every chance they got and frittered away their silver paying for the services of scribes, who would transform their sentiments into the magical code that could be sent across counties and seas to be read, by a priest or another scrivener, to dear old Ma in Limerick.

In Mother Shaftoe's part of town, that kind of willingness to do a day's hard work for bread and money was taken as proof that the Irish race lacked dignity and shrewdness. And this did not even take into account their religious practices and all that flowed from them, e.g., the obstinate chastity of their women, and the willingness of the males to tolerate it. The way of the mudlarks (as the men who trafficked through Mother Shaftoe's bed styled themselves) was to voyage out upon the Thames after it got dark, find their way aboard anchored ships somehow, and remove items that could be exchanged for bread, money, or carnal services on dry land.

Techniques varied. The most obvious was to have someone climb up a ship's anchor cable and then throw a rope down to his mates. This was a job for surplus boys if ever there was one. Dick, the oldest of the Shaftoes, had learnt the rudiments of the trade by shinnying up the drain-pipes of whorehouses to steal things from the pockets of vacant clothing. He and his little brothers struck up a partnership with a band of these free-lance longshoremen, who owned the means of moving swag from ship to shore: they'd accomplished the stupendous feat of stealing a longboat.

After approaching several anchored ships with this general plan in mind, they learned that the sailors aboard them—who were actually supposed to be on watch for mudlarks—expected to be paid for the service of failing to notice that young Dick Shaftoe was clambering up the anchor cable with one end of a line tied round his ankle. When the captain found goods missing, he'd be sure to flog these sailors, and they felt they should be compensated, in advance, for the loss of skin and blood. Dick needed to have a purse dangling from one wrist, so that when a sailor shone a lantern down into his face, and aimed a blunderbuss at him, he could shake it and make the coins clink together. That was a music to which sailors of all nations would smartly dance.

Of course the mudlarks lacked coins to begin with. They wanted capital. John Cole—the biggest and boldest of the fellows who'd stolen the longboat—hit upon another shrewd plan: they would steal the only parts of ships that could be reached without actually getting aboard first: namely, anchors. They'd then sell them to the captains of ships who had found their anchors missing. This scheme had the added attraction that it might lead to ships' drifting down the current and running aground on oh, say, the Isle of Dogs, at which point their contents would be legally up for grabs.

One foggy night (but all nights were foggy) the mudlarks set off in the longboat, rowing upstream. The mudlark term for a boat's oars was *a pair of wings*. Flapping them, they flew among anchored ships—all of them pointed upriver, since the anchor cables were at their bows, and they weathercocked in the river's current. Nearing the stern of a tubby Dutch *galjoot*—a single-masted trader of perhaps twice their longboat's length, and ten times its capacity—they tossed Dick overboard with the customary rope noosed around his ankle, and a knife in his teeth. His instructions were to swim upstream, alongside the *galjoot*'s hull, towards the bow, until he found her port side anchor cable descending into the river. He was to lash his ankle-rope to said cable, and then saw through the cable above the lashing. This would have the effect of cutting the *galjoot* free from, while making the longboat fast to, the anchor, effecting a sudden and silent transfer of ownership. This accomplished, he was to jerk on the rope three times. The mudlarks would then pull on the rope. This would draw them upstream until they were directly over the anchor, and if they hauled hard enough, the prize would come up off the riverbed.

Dick slopped away into the mist. They watched the rope uncoil, in fits and starts, for a couple of minutes—this meant Dick was swimming. Then it stopped uncoiling for a long while—Dick had found the anchor cable and gone to work! The mudlarks dabbled with rag-swathed oars, flapping those wings against the river's flow. Jack sat holding the rope, waiting for the three sharp jerks that would be Dick's signal. But no jerks came. Instead the rope went slack. Jack, assisted by brother Bob, pulled the slack into the boat. Ten yards of it passed through their hands before it became taut again, and then they felt, not three sharp jerks, exactly, but a sort of vibration at the other end.

It was plain that something had gone wrong, but Jack Cole was not about to abandon a good rope, and so they hauled in what they could, drawing themselves upstream. Somewhere along the flank of the *galjoot*, they found a noose in the rope, with a cold pale ankle lodged in it, and out came poor Dick. The anchor cable was knotted to that same noose. While Jack and Bob tried to slap Dick back into life, the mudlarks tried to pull in the anchor. Both failed, for the anchor was as heavy as Dick was dead. Presently, choleric Dutchmen up on the *galjoot* began to fire blunderbusses into the fog. It was time to leave.

Bob and Jack, who'd been acting as journeyman and apprentice, respectively, to Dick, were left without a Master Rope-Climber to emulate, and with a tendency to have extraordinarily bad dreams. For it was clear to them—if not right away, then eventually—that they had probably caused their own brother's death by drawing the rope taut, thereby pulling Dick down below the surface of the river. They were out of the mudlark trade for good. John Cole found a replacement for Dick, and (rumor had it) gave him slightly different instructions: take your ankle out of the noose *before* you cut the anchor cable.

Scarcely a fortnight later, John Cole and his fellows were caught in the longboat in broad daylight. One of their schemes had succeeded, they'd gotten drunk on stolen grog, and slept right through sunrise. The mudlarks were packed off to Newgate.

Certain of them—newcomers to the judicial system, if not to crime—shared their ill-gotten gains with a starving parson, who came to Newgate and met with them in the Gigger. This was a chamber on the lower floor where prisoners could thrust their faces up to an iron grate and be heard, if they shouted loudly enough, by visitors a few inches away. There, the parson set up a sort of impromptu Bible study class, the purpose of which was to get the mudlarks to memorize the 51st Psalm. Or, failing that, at least the first bit:

Have mercie upon me, o God, according to they loving kindenes: according to the multitude of thy compassions put awaie mine iniquities.

Wash me throughly from mine iniquities, and clense me from my sin. For I knowe mine iniquities, & my sinne is ever before me.

Against thee, against thee onely have I sinned, & done evil in thy sight, that thou maiest be just when thou speakest, and pure when thou judgest.

Behold, I was borne in iniquitie, and in sinne hath my mother conceived me.

Quite a mouthful, that, for mudlarks, but these were more diligent pupils than any Clerke of Oxenford. For on the day that they were marched down the straight and narrow passage to the Old Bailey and brought below the magistrate's balcony, an open Bible was laid in front of them, and they recited these lines. Which, by the evidentiary standards then prevailing in English courts, proved that they could read. Which proved that they were clergymen. Which rendered them beyond the reach of the criminal courts; for clergymen were, by long-hallowed tradition, subject only to the justice of the ecclesiastical courts. Since these no longer existed, the mudlarks were sent free.

It was a different story for John Cole, the oldest of the group. He had been to Newgate before. He had stood in the holding-pen of the Old Bailey before. And in that yard, below that balcony, in the sight of the very same magistrate, his hand had been clamped in a vise and a red-hot iron in the shape of a T had been plunged into the brawn of his thumb, marking him forever as Thief. Which by the evidentiary standards then prevailing, *et cetera,* made it most awkward for him to claim that he was a clergyman. He was sentenced, of course, to hang by the neck until dead at Tyburn.

Bob and Jack did not actually see any of this. They heard the narration from those who had mumbled a few words of Psalm 51 and been released and made their way back to the Isle of Dogs. To this point it was nothing they had not heard a hundred times before from friends and casual acquaintances in the neighborhood. But this time there was a new twist at the end of the story: John Cole had asked for the two surviving Shaftoe boys to meet him at the Triple Tree on the morning of his execution.

They went out of curiosity more than anything. Arriving at Tyburn and burrowing their way through an immense crowd by artful shin-kicking, instep-stomping, and groin-elbowing, they found John Cole and the others on a cart beneath the Fateful Nevergreen, elbows tied behind their backs, and nooses pre-knotted around their throats, with long rope-ends trailing behind them. A preacher—the Ordinary of Newgate—was there, urgently trying to make them aware of certain very important technicalities in the Rules of Eternity. But the condemnees, who were so drunk they could barely stand up, were saying all manner of rude and funny things back to him, faster than he could talk back.

Cole, more solemn than the others, explained to Jack and Bob that when the executioner "turned him off," which was to say, body-checked him off the cart and left him to hang by his neck, Cole would very much appreciate it if Jack could grab his left leg and Bob his right, or the other way round if they preferred, and hang there, pulling him down with their combined weight, so that he'd die faster. In exchange for this service, he told them of a loose board in the floor of a certain shack on the Isle of Dogs beneath which they could find hidden treasure. He laid out the terms of this transaction with admirable coolness, as if he were hanged by the neck until dead every Friday.

They accepted the commission. Jack Ketch was now the man to watch. His office, the gallows, was of admirably simple and spare design: three tall pilings supporting a triangle of heavy beams, each beam long enough that half a dozen men could be hanged from it at once, or more if a bit of crowding could be overlooked.

Jack Ketch's work, then, consisted of maneuvering the cart below a clear space on one of the beams; selecting a loose rope-end; tossing it over the beam; making it fast with a bit of knot-work; and turning off the bloke at the opposing end of the rope. The cart, now one body lighter, could then be moved again, and the procedure repeated.

John Cole was the eighth of nine men to be hanged on that particular day, which meant that Jack and Bob had the opportunity to watch seven men be hanged before the time came for them to discharge their responsibilities. During the first two or three of these hangings, all they really noticed was the obvious. But after they grew familiar with the general outlines of the rite, they began to notice subtle differences from one hanging to the next. In other words, they started to become connoisseurs of the art, like the ten thousand or so spectators who had gathered around them to watch.

Jack noticed very early that men in good clothes died faster. Watching Jack Ketch shrewdly, he soon saw why: when Jack Ketch was getting ready to turn a well-dressed man off, he would arrange the noose-knot behind the client's left ear, and leave some slack in the rope, so that he'd fall, and gather speed, for a moment before being brought up short with an audible crack. Whereas men in ragged clothing were given a noose that was loose around the neck (at first, anyway) and very little room to fall.

Now, John Cole—who'd looked a bit of a wretch to begin with, and who'd not grown any snappier, in his appearance and toilette, during the months he'd languished in the Stone Hold of Newgate—was the shabbiest bloke on the cart, and obviously destined for the long slow kicking style of hanging. Which explained why he'd had the foresight to call in the Shaftoe boys. But it did not explain something else.

"See here," Jack said, elbowing the Ordinary out of the way. He was on the ground below the cart, neck craned to look far up at Jack Ketch, who was slinging John Cole's neck-rope over the beam with a graceful straight-armed hooking movement. "If you've got hidden treasure, why didn't you give it to him?" And he nodded at Jack Ketch, who was now peering down curiously at Jack Shaftoe through the slits in his hood.

"Er—well I din't have it *on* me, did I?" returned John Cole, who was a bit surly in his disposition on the happiest of days. But Jack thought he looked a bit dodgy.

"You could've sent someone to fetch it!"

"How's I to know they wouldn't nick it?"

"Leave off, Jack," Bob had said. Since Dick's demise, he had been, technically, the man of the family; at first he'd made little of it, but lately he was more arrogant every day. "He's s'posed to be saying his prayers."

"Let him pray while he's kicking!"

"He's not going to be doing any kicking, 'cause you and I are going to be hanging on his legs."

"But he's lying about the treasure."

"I can see that, you think I'm stupid? But as long as we're here, let's do a right job of it."

While they argued, Cole was turned off. He sprawled against the sky just above their heads. They dodged instinctively, but of course he didn't fall far. They jumped into the air, gained hand-holds on his feet, and ascended, hand-over-hand.

After a few moments of dangling from the rope, Cole began to kick vigorously. Jack was tempted to let go, but the tremors coming down Cole's legs reminded him of what he'd felt in the rope when poor Dick had been dragged down beneath the river, and he held on by imagining that this was some kind of vengeance. Bob must've had the same phant'sy, for both boys gripped their respective legs like stranglers until Cole finally went limp. When they realized he was pissing himself, they both let go at once and tumbled into the fœtid dust below the gibbet. There was applause from the crowd. Before they'd had time to dust themselves off, they were approached by the sister of the one remaining condemned man— also a slow-hanging wretch, by his looks—who offered them cash money to perform the same service. The coins were clipped, worn, and blackened, but they were coins.

John Cole's loose board turned out not to be loose, and when pried up, to cover shit instead of treasure. They were hardly surprised. It didn't matter. They were prosperous tradesmen now. On the eve of each hanging-day, Jack and Bob could be found in their new place of business: Newgate Prison.

It took them several visits just to understand the place. *Gate* in their usage meant a sort of wicket by which humans could pass through a fence around a hog-yard without having to vault over— not that vaulting was such a difficult procedure, but it was danger-ous when drunk, and might lead to falling, and being eaten by the hogs. So gates they knew.

They had furthermore absorbed the knowledge that in several parts of London town were large fabricks called Gates, viz. Ludgate, Moorgate, and Bishopsgate. They had even passed through Aldgate a few times, that being their usual way of invading the city. But the connexion between gates of that type, and hog-yard-wickets, was most obscure. A gate in the hog-yard sense of the word made no sense unless built in a wall, fence, or other such formal barrier, as its purpose was to provide a means of passage through same. But none of the large London buildings called Gates appeared to have been constructed in any such context. They bestrode important roads leading into the city, but if you didn't want to pass through the actual gate, you could usually find a way round.

This went for Newgate as well. It was a pair of mighty fortress-turrets built on either side of a road that, as it wandered in from the countryside and crossed over Fleet Ditch, was named Holborn. But as it passed between those turrets, the high road was bottle-necked down to a vaulted passageway just wide enough for a four-horse team to squeeze through. Above, a castle-like building joined the turrets, and bridged the road. An iron portcullis made of bars as thick as Jack's leg was suspended within that castle so that it could be dropped down to seal the vault, and bar the road. But it was all show. For thirty seconds of scampering along side streets and alleys would take Jack, or anyone else, to the other side. Newgate was not surrounded by walls or fortifications, but rather by buildings of the conventional sort, which was to say, the half-timbered two- and three-story dwellings that in England grew up as quick and as thick as mushrooms. This Gothick fortress of Newgate, planted in the midst of such a neighborhood, was like a pelvis in a breadbasket.

If you actually did come into the city along Holborn, then when you ducked beneath that portcullis and entered the vaulted passageway beneath Newgate you'd see to the right a door leading into a porter's lodge, which was where new prisoners had their chains riveted on. A few yards farther along, you'd emerge from beneath the castle into the uncovered space of what was now called Newgate Street. To your right you would see a gloomy old building that rose to a height of three or four stories. It had only a few windows, and those were gridded over with bars. This was a separate piece of work from the turret-castle-vault building; rumor had it that it had once done service as an inn for travelers coming into the city along Holborn. But the prison had, in recent centuries, spread up Newgate Street like gangrene up a thigh, consuming several such houses. Most of the doorways that had once welcomed weary travelers were bricked up. Only one remained, at the seam between the castle and the adjoining inn-buildings. Going in there, a visitor could make a quick right turn into the Gigger, or, if he had a candle (for it grew dark immediately), he could risk a trip up or down a stairway into this or that ward, hold, or dungeon. It all depended on what sort of wretch he was coming to visit.

On Jack and Bob's first visit they'd neglected to bring a light, or money with which to buy one, and had blundered down-stairs into a room with a stone floor that made crackling noises beneath their feet as they walked. It was impossible to breathe the air there, and so after a few moments of blind panic they had found their way out and fled back into Newgate Street. There, Jack had noticed that his feet were bloody, and supposed that he must have stepped on broken glass. Bob had the same affliction. But Bob, unlike Jack, was wearing shoes, and so the blood could not have come from him. On careful inspection of the soles of those shoes, the mystery was solved: the blood was not smeared about, but spotted his soles, an array of little bursts. At the center of each burst was a small fleshy gray tube: the vacant corpse of an engorged louse that Bob had stepped on. This accounted for the mysterious crackling noise that they had heard while walking around in that room. As they soon learned, it was called the Stone Hold, and was accounted one of the lowest and worst wards of the prison, occupied only by common felons—such as the late John Cole—who had absolutely no money. Jack and Bob never returned to it.

Over the course of several later sallies into the prison they learned its several other rooms: the fascinating Jack Ketch his Kitchen; the so-called Buggering Hold (which they avoided); the Chapel (likewise); the Press-Yard, where the richest prisoners sat drinking port and claret with their periwigged visitors; and the Black Dogge Tavern, where the cellarmen—elite prisoners who did a brisk trade in candles and liquor—showed a kind of hospitality to any prisoners who had a few coins in their pockets. This looked like any other public house in England save that everyone in the place was wearing chains.

There were, in other words, plenty of lovely things to discover at the time and to reminisce about later. But they were not making these arduous trips from the Isle of Dogs to Newgate simply for purposes of sightseeing. It was a business proposition. They were looking for their market. And eventually, they found it. For in the castle proper, on the north side of the street, in the basement of the turret, was a spacious dungeon that was called the Condemned Hold.

Here, timing was everything. Hangings occurred only eight times a year. Prisoners were sentenced to hang a week or two in advance. And so most of the time there were no condemned people at all in the Condemned Hold. Rather, it was used as a temporary holding cell for new prisoners of all stripes who had been frog-marched to the Porter's Lodge across the street and traded the temporary ropes that bound their arms behind their backs, for iron fetters that they would wear until they were released. After being ironed (as this procedure was called) with so much metal that they could not even walk, they would be dragged across the vault and thrown into the Condemned Hold to lie in the dark for a few days or weeks. The purpose of this was to find out how much money they really had. If they had money, they'd soon offer it to the gaolers in exchange for lighter chains, or even a nice apartment in the Press-Yard. If they had none, they'd be taken to some place like the Stone Hold.

If one paid a visit to the Condemned Hold on a day chosen at random, it would likely be filled with heavily ironed newcomers. These were of no interest to Jack and Bob, at least not yet. Instead, the Shaftoe boys came to Newgate during the days immediately prior to Tyburn processions, when the Condemned Hold was full of men who actually had been condemned to hang. There they performed.

Around the time of their birth, the King had come back to England and allowed the theatres, which had been closed by Cromwell, to open again. The Shaftoe boys had been putting their climbing skills to good use sneaking into them, and had picked up an ear for the way actors talked, and an eye for the way they did things.

So their Newgate performances began with a little mum-show: Jack would try to pick Bob's pocket. Bob would spin round and cuff him. Jack would stab him with a wooden poniard, and Bob would die. Then (Act II) Bob would jump up and 'morphosize into the Long Arm of the Law, put Jack in a hammerlock, (Act III) don a wig (which they had stolen, at appalling risk, from a side-table in a brothel near the Temple), and sentence him to hang. Then (Act IV) Bob would exchange the white wig for a black hood and throw a noose round Jack's neck and stand behind him while Jack would motion for silence (for by this point all of the Condemned Hold would be in a state of near-riot) and clap his hands together like an Irish child going to First Communion, and (Act V) utter the following soliloquy:

John Ketch's rope doth decorate my neck.
    Though rude, and cruel, this garland chafes me not.
    For, like the Necklace of Harmonia,
    It brings the one who wears it life eternal.
    The hangman draweth nigh—he'll turn me off
    And separate my soul from weak'ning flesh.
    And, as I've made my peace with God Almighty,
    My spirit will ascend to Heaven's Door,
    Where, after brief interrogation, Christ will—
Bob steps forward and shoves Jack, then yanks the rope up above Jack's head.
HAWKKH! God's Wounds! The noose quite strangleth me!
    What knave conceived this means of execution?
    I should have bribed John Ketch to make it quick.

But, with so many lordly regicides
Who've lately come to Tyburn to be penalized,
The price of instant, painless death is quite
Inflated—far beyond the humble means
Of common condemnees, who hence must die
As painf'lly as they've lived. God damn it all!
And damn Jack Ketch; the late John Turner; and
The judges who hath sent so many rich men to
The gallows, thereby spurring said inflation.
And damn my frugal self. For, at a cost
That scarce exceeds an evening at the pub,
Might I have hired those exc'llent Shaftoe boys,
Young Jack, and Bob, the elder of the pair,
To dangle from my legs, which lacking ballast,
Do flail most ineffectu'lly in the air,
And make a sort of entertainment for
The *mobile*.

> *Bob removes the noose from Jack's neck.*

But soft! The end approaches—
Earth fades—new worlds unfold before my eyes—
Can this be heaven? It seemeth warm, as if
A brazier had been fir'd 'neath the ground.
Perhaps it is the warmth of God's sweet love
That so envelops me.

> *Bob, dressed as a Devil, approaches with a long pointed Stick.*

How now! What sort
Of angel doth sprout Horns upon his pate?
Where is thy Harp, O dark Seraph?
Instead of which a Pike, or Spit, doth seem
To occupy thy gnarled claws?

DEVIL: I am
The Devil's Turnspit. Sinner, welcome home!

JACK: I thought that I had made my peace with God.
Indeed I had, when I did mount the scaffold.
If I had but died then, at Heaven's Gate
I'd stand. But in my final agony,
I took God's name in vain, and sundry mortal
Sins committed, and thus did damn myself
To this!

DEVIL: Hold still!

> *Devil shoves the point of his Spit up Jack's arse-hole.*

JACK: The pain! The pain, and yet,
It's just a taste of what's to come.

If only I had hired Jack and Bob!
*Jack, by means of a conjuror's trick, causes the point of the spit, smeared
with blood, to emerge from his mouth, and is led away by the Devil, to violent applause and foot-stomping from the Crowd.*

After the applause had died down, Jack, then, would circulate
among the condemned to negotiate terms, and Bob, who was bigger, would watch his back, and mind the coin-purse.

The Continent
LATE SUMMER 1683

> When a woman is thus left desolate and void of
> counsel, she is just like a bag of money or a jewel
> dropt on the highway, which is a prey to the next
> comer.
>
> —DANIEL DEFOE, *Moll Flanders*

JACK HAD KEPT A SHREWD eye on the weather all spring and summer.
It had been perfect. He was living in unaccustomed comfort in
Strasbourg. This was a city on the Rhine, formerly German and, as
of quite recently, French. It lay just to the south of a country called
the Palatinate, which, as far as Jack could make out, was a moth-
eaten rag of land straddling the Rhine. King Looie's soldiers would
overrun the Palatinate from the West, or the Emperor's armies
would rape and pillage it from the East, whenever they couldn't
think of anything else to do. The person in charge of the Palatinate
was called an Elector, which in this part of the world meant a very
noble fellow, more than a Duke but less than a King. Until quite
recently the Electors Palatinate had been of a very fine and noble
family, consisting of too many siblings to keep track of, most quite
magnificent; but since only one (the oldest) could be Elector, all of
the rest of them had gone out of that country, and found better
things to do, or gotten themselves killed in more or less fascinating
ways. Eventually the Elector had died and turned matters over to

his son: an impotent madman named Charles, who liked to stage mock battles around an old Rhine-castle that wasn't good for much else. The fighting was imaginary, but the trenches, siege-works, dysentery, and gangrene were real.

Now Jack had been making a sort of living, for several years, from being a fake soldier in France—a line of work that had been brought to ruin by many tiresome reforms that had recently been introduced to the French Army by one Martinet. When he'd heard about this crazy Elector he'd wasted no time in going to the Palatinate and finding gainful employment as a pretend musketeer.

Not long afterwards, King Louis XIV of France had attacked the nearby city of Strasbourg and made it his, and as frequently happened in sacked cities in those days, there had been a bit of the old Black Death. At the first appearance of buboes in the groins and armpits of the poor, the rich of Strasbourg had boarded up their houses and fled to the country. Many had simply climbed aboard boats and headed downstream on the Rhine, which had naturally taken them past that old wrack of a castle where Jack and others were playing at war for the amusement of the crazy Elector Palatine. One rich *Strasbourgeois,* there, had disembarked from his riverboat and struck up a conversation with none other than Jack Shaftoe. It was not customary for rich men to speak to the likes of Jack, and so the whole business seemed a mystery until Jack noticed that, no matter how he moved about, the rich man always found some pretext to stay well upwind of him.

This rich man had hired Jack and arranged for him to get something called a Plague Pass: a large document in that Gothickal German script with occasional excursions into something that looked like either Latin (when it was desirable to invoke the mercy and grace of God) or French (for sucking up to King Looie, only one rung below God at this point).* By flourishing this at the right times, Jack was able to carry out his mission, which was to go into Strasbourg; proceed to the rich man's dwelling; wash off the red chalk crosses that marked it as a plague-house; pry off the deals he'd nailed over the doors and windows; chase out any squatters; fend off any looters; and live in it for a while. If, after a few weeks, Jack hadn't died of the plague, he was to send word to this rich man in the country that it was safe to move back in.

Jack had accomplished the first parts of this errand in about May, but by the beginning of June had somehow forgotten about

---

*Jack could not read but could infer as much from the types of letters used.

the last. In about mid-June, another Vagabond-looking fellow arrived. The rich man had hired him to go to the house and remove Jack's body so that it wouldn't draw vermin and then live in it for a while and, after a few weeks, if he hadn't died of the plague, send word. Jack, who was occupying the master bedchamber, had accommodated this new fellow in one of the children's rooms, showed him around the kitchen and wine-cellar, and invited him to make himself at home. Late in July, another Vagabond had showed up, and explained he'd been hired to cart away the bodies of the first two, *et cetera, et cetera.*

All spring and summer, the weather was ideal: rain and sun in proportions suitable for the growing of grain. Vagabonds roamed freely in and out of Strasbourg, giving wide berths to those mounds of decomposing plague-victims. Jack sought out the ones who'd come from the east, treated them to the rich man's brandy, conducted broken conversations with them in the zargon, and established two important facts: one, that the weather had been just as fine, if not finer, in Austria and Poland. Two, that Grand Vizier Khan Mustapha was still besieging the city of Vienna at the head of an army of two hundred thousand Turks.

Round September, he and his fellow-squatters found it necessary to depart from that fine house. It did not make him unhappy. Pretending to be dead was not a thing that came naturally to Vagabonds. The population of the house had swollen to a dozen and a half, most of them were tedious people, and the wine-cellar was nearly empty. One night Jack caused the window-shutters to be thrown open and the candles to be lit, and played host and lord over a grand squatters' ball. Vagabond-musicians played raucous airs on shawms and pennywhistles, Vagabond-actors performed a comedy in zargon, stray dogs copulated in the family chapel, and Jack, presiding over all at the head of the table, dressed in the rich man's satin, almost fell asleep. But even through the commotion of the ball, his ears detected the sound of hoofbeats approaching, swords being whisked from scabbards, firelocks being cocked. He was vanishing up the stairs even as the owner and his men were smashing down the door. Sliding down an escape-rope he'd long ago fixed to a balcony's rail, he dropped neatly into the rich man's saddle, still warm from thrashing the master's chubby ass. He galloped to a potter's field on the edge of town where he had stored some provisions against this very sort of event, and took to the road well supplied with salt-cod and biscuit. He rode southwards through the night until the horse was spent, then stripped off its fine saddle and threw it into a ditch, and traded the horse itself to a delighted ferryman for passage east across the Rhine. Finding the Munich road, he struck out for the East.

The barley harvest was underway, and most of it was destined for the same place as Jack. He was able to ride along on barley-carts, and to talk his way across the Neckar and the Danube, by telling people he was off to join the legions of Christendom and beat back the Turkish menace.

This was not precisely a lie. Jack and brother Bob had come to the Netherlands more than once to soldier under John Churchill, who was in the household of the Duke of York. York spent a lot of time abroad because he was Catholic and most everyone in England hated him. But in time he had returned home anyway. John Churchill had gone with him and Bob, dutiful soldier that he was, had gone home with Churchill. Jack had stayed on the Continent, where there were more countries, more Kings, and more wars.

Great big dark mounds were visible off to his right, far away. After they continued to be there for several days in a row, he realized that they must be mountains. He'd heard of them. He had fallen in with a cart-train belonging to a barley-merchant of Augsburg, who was contemptuous of the low grain prices in Munich's great market and had decided to take his goods closer to the place where they were needed. They rode for days through rolling green country, dotted with bent peasants bringing in the barley-harvest. The churches were all Papist, of course, and in these parts they had a queer look, with domes shaped like ripe onions perched atop slender shafts.

Over days those mountains rose up to meet them, and then they came to a river named Salz that pierced the mountain-wall. Churches and castles monitored the valley from stone cliffs. Endless wagon-trains of barley came together, and clashed and merged with the Legions of the Pope of Rome who were coming up from Italy, and Bavarians and Saxons, too: mile-long parades of gentleman volunteers, decorated like knights of old with the Crusaders' red cross, bishops and archbishops with their jeweled shepherd's-hooks, cavalry-regiments that beat the earth as if it were a hollow log—each horseman accompanied by his *cheval de bataille,* a fresh *cheval de marche* or two, a *cheval de poursuite* for hunting stags or Turks, and a *cheval de parade* for ceremonial occasions, and the grooms to care for them. There were armies of musketeers, and finally a vast foaming, surging rabble of barefoot pikemen, marching with their twenty-foot-long weapons angled back over their shoulders, giving those formations the look of porcupines when they are in a mellow and complacent mood and have flattened their quills.

Here the barley-merchant of Augsburg had at last found a market, and might have sold his goods at a handsome profit. But the sight of Christendom at war had inflamed both his avarice and his piety, and he was seized with a passion to ride farther and see what more wonders lay to the east. Likewise Jack, sizing up those pikemen, and comparing their rags and bare feet to his stolen traveling-togs and excellent leather boots, suspected he could strike a better deal closer to Vienna. So they joined together with the general flood and proceeded, in short confused marches, to the city of Linz, where (according to the merchant) there was a very great *Messe*. Jack knew that *Messe* was the German word for a Mass, and reckoned that Herr Augsburg meant to attend church in some great cathedral there.

At Linz they grazed the south bank of the River Danube. In the plain along the river was a fine market that had been swallowed and nearly digested by a vast military camp—but no cathedral. *"Die Messe!"* Herr Augsburg exclaimed, and this was when Jack understood something about the German language: having a rather small number of words, they frequently used one word to mean several different things. *Messe* meant not only a Mass but a trade-fair.

Another army had marched down from the north and was laboriously crossing the Danube here, trickling across Linz's bridges and keeping Linz's watermen busy all day and all night, poling their floats across the stream laden with artillery-pieces, powder-kegs, fodder, rations, luggage, horses, and men. Jack Shaftoe spoke a few words of German. He had picked up quite a bit of French, and of course he knew English and the zargon. These men who had ridden down out of the north did not speak any of those tongues, and he could not guess whether they might be Swedes or Russians or of some other nation. But one day cheering came up from the bridges and the ferries, mingled with the thunder of thousands of war-horses, and from the woods on the north bank emerged the mightiest cavalry that Jack, in all his travels in England, Holland, and France, had ever seen. At its head rode a man who could only be a King. Now this wasn't Jack's first King, as he'd seen King Looie more than once during French military parades. But King Looie was only play-acting, he was like a whoreson actor in a Southwark theatre, got up in a gaudy costume, acting the way he imagined that a warrior King might act. This fellow from the north was no play-actor, and he rode across the bridge with a solemn look on his face that spoke of bitter days ahead for Grand Vizier Khan Mustapha. Jack wanted to know who it was, and finally locating someone who spoke a bit of French he learned that what he was looking at, here, was the army of Poland-Lithuania, and their terrible King was John Sobieski, who had made an alliance with the Holy Roman Emperor to drive the Turks all the way back to Asia, and his mighty, gleaming cavalry were called the Winged Hussars.

Once King John Sobieski and the Winged Hussars had crossed the Danube and made camp, and a *Messe* in the religious sense had been said, and the thrill had died down a little, both Herr Augsburg the barley-merchant and Jack Shaftoe the vagabond-soldier made their own private calculations as to what it all meant for them. Two or (according to rumor) three great cavalry forces were now encamped around Linz. They were the spearheads of much larger formations of musketeers and pikemen, all of whom had to eat. Their rations were carried on wagons and the wagons were drawn by teams of horses. All of it was useless without the artillery, which was, as well, drawn by teams of horses. What it all amounted to, therefore, was the world's richest and most competitive *Messe* for barley. Prices were thrice what they'd been at the crossing of the Salz and ten times what they'd been in Munich. Herr Augsburg, having chosen the moment carefully, now struck, playing John Sobieski's barley-buyers off against those of the Bavarian, Saxon, and Austrian lords.

For his part, Jack understood that no force of cavalry as lordly, as magnificent, as the Winged Hussars could possibly exist, even for a single day, without a vast multitude of especially miserable peasants to make it all possible, and that peasants in such large numbers could never be kept so miserable for so long unless the lords of Poland-Lithuania were unusually cruel men. Indeed, after John Sobieski's vivid crossing of the Danube a gray fog of wretches filtered out of the woods and congealed on the river's northern bank. Jack didn't want to be one of 'em. So he went and found Herr Augsburg, sitting on an empty barley-cart surrounded by his profits: bills of exchange drawn on trading-houses in Genoa, Venice, Lyons, Amsterdam, Seville, London, piled up high on the cart's plankage and weighed down with stones. Mounting up onto the wagon, Jack the Soldier became, for a quarter of an hour, Jack the Actor. In the bad French that Herr Augsburg more or less understood, he spoke of the impending Apocalypse before the gates of Vienna, and of his willingness, nay, eagerness, to die in the midst of same, and his prayerful hope that he might at least take a single Turk down with him, or barring that, perhaps inflict some kind of small wound on a Turk, viz. by jabbing at him with a pointed stick or whatever he might have handy, so that said Turk might be distracted or slowed down long enough for some other soldier of Christendom, armed with a real weapon, such as a musket, to actually take aim at, and slay, that selfsame Turk. This was commingled with a great deal of generally Popish-sounding God-talk and Biblical-sounding quotations that Jack claimed he'd memorized from the Book of Revelation.

In any case it had the desired effect, which was that Herr Augsburg, as his contribution to the Apocalypse, went with Jack to an armaments-market in the center of Linz and purchased him a musket and various other items.

Thus equipped, Jack marched off and offered his services to an Austrian regiment. The captain paid equal attention to Jack's musket and to his boots. Both were impressive in the highest degree. When Jack demonstrated that he actually knew how to load and fire his weapon, he was offered a position. Jack thus became a musketeer.

He spent the next two weeks staring at other men's backs through clouds of dust, and stepping on ground that had already been stepped on by thousands of other men and horses. His ears were filled with the tromping of feet, boots, and hooves; the creaking of overladen barley-carts; nonsensical teamsters' exhortations; marching-songs in unknown languages; and the blowing of trumpets and beating of drums of regimental signal-men desperately trying to keep their throngs from getting all mixed up with alien throngs.

He had a gray-brown felt hat with a gigantic round brim that needed to be pinned up on one or both sides lest it flop down and blind him. More established musketeers had fine feathered brooches for this purpose—Jack made do with a pin. Like all English musketeers, Jack called his weapon Brown Bess. It was of the latest design—the lock contained a small clamp that gripped a shard of flint, and when Jack pulled the trigger, this would be whipped around and skidded hard against a steel plate above the powder-pan, flooding the pan with sparks and igniting it in most cases. Half of the musketeer-formations were impaired by older, flintless weapons called matchlocks. Each of these matchlock-men had to go around with a long fuzzy rope twined through his fingers, one end of which was forever smouldering—as long as it didn't get wet and he remembered to blow on it frequently. Clamped into the same sort of mechanism that held Jack's flint-shard, it would ignite the powder, more often than not, by direct contact.

Jack, like all the other musketeers, had a leather belt over one shoulder whence dangled a dozen thumb-sized and -shaped wooden flasks, each sealed with its own stopper, each big enough to contain one charge of powder for the weapon. They clinked together musically when he walked. There was a powder-horn for refilling these during lulls. At the lowest point of the bandolier was a small pouch containing a dozen lead balls.

A company was a couple of hundred men like Jack walking around packed into a tight square, not because they liked crowds but because this made it harder for an opponent to ride up with an edged weapon and cut pieces off of them. The reason it was harder was because in the center of the square was a smaller square of men carrying extremely long pointed sticks called pikes. The dimensions of the squares and the length of the pikes were worked out so that when the pikes were levelled at the enemy (passing between the surrounding musketeers) their points would project some distance beyond the edge of the formation—provided the musketeers stood close together—discouraging enemy horsemen from simply galloping up and having at the musketeers as they went through their loading rituals, which, even under ideal conditions, seemed to take as long as a Mass.*

That was the general plan. Exactly what would happen when the Turks strung their outlandish recurved bows and began to shower iron-tipped arrows into these formations had not been specified. From Linz onwards, anyway, Jack walked in the midst of such an organization. It made many, many noises, each traceable to something like the wooden powder-flasks. Unlike a company of matchlocks, it did not smolder, nor make huffing and puffing noises.

They turned away from the Danube, leaving it off to their left, and then the formations piled into one another because they were going uphill now, assaulting the tail of that mountain range. The drums and trumpets, muffled now by trees, echoed along

---

*The reason the pikemen didn't protectively surround the musketeers, instead of being surrounded by them, was that even if the musketeers aimed between them, or over their heads, they would get mowed down by errant balls; because if, as frequently happened, a musket ball was a bit too small for its barrel, it would take to bouncing from one side of the barrel to the other as it was propelled out, and might emerge at a sharp, startling sideways angle.

river-valleys as formations split again and again, finding passes over the hills. Jack was frequently confused, but when he wasn't, he sensed that the Poles were on his right, the Bavarians and Saxons on his left.

Compared to the hills of England, these were high, steep, and well-forested. But between them lay broad valleys that made for easy marching, and even when they had to go over hills, instead of between them, the going was easier than it looked—the trees were tall handsome ones with bare white trunks, and what little undergrowth there was had long since been trampled down by others when Jack reached it.

The only way he knew that they'd reached the environs of Vienna was that they stopped marching and began camping. They made a bivouac in a narrow steep valley where the sun rose late and set early. Some of Jack's brothers in arms were impatient to get on with it, but he appreciated that the Army of Christendom had become an immense machine for turning barley into horseshit and that the barley would fast run out. Something had to happen soon.

After they'd bivouacked for two nights, Jack slipped away one morning before dawn and clambered uphill until the ground became level under his feet. He did this partly to get away from the stink of the camp and partly because he wanted to get a look at the city from a high place. Red sunlight was weaving among white tree-trunks as he wandered to a high bluff from which he had a clear view several miles down into the city.

Vienna was a small town dwarfed by its own defenses, in turn engulfed by a larger Turkish city only a few months old. The town itself was, then, the smallest part of what he saw, but it was to the rest as a chalice was to a cathedral. Even from miles off he could see it was a miserable place—actual streets were visible nowhere, just the red tile roofs of long skinny buildings heaped up six and seven stories, wending black crevices between them indicating streets, which he could tell would be sunless trenches, thick with hurtling shit and echoing voices. He could see the foaming stain of the city spreading across the adjacent canal and, farther downstream, into the Danube itself, and from its color he could almost guess that there was a major flux epidemic underway—as indeed there was in the Turkish camp.

Just off-center in the heart of Vienna stood the tallest building Jack had ever seen—a cathedral with a dunce-cap tower topped by a curious symbol, a star wedged in the craw of a crescent moon, like a stick jammed into a shark's mouth. It seemed a prophetic map of the entire scene. Vienna was protected on the north by a canal that split away from the Danube, moated the city on that side, and later rejoined it. The bridges had been wrecked so no one could enter or leave that way. The entire remainder of the city was enveloped by the Turkish camp, narrowest at the two points where it touched the river, and, in the middle, as fat as Vienna itself—therefore, a crescent with the city trapped between its horns. It was a fluttering world of heathenishly colored tents and flags and streamers, with the ruins of Vienna's burnt suburbs poking out here and there like ribs of wrecked ships from a foaming sea.

Between Turkish camp and Christian city was a belt of what a naïve person would identify as empty (albeit curiously sculpted and chiseled) terrain. Jack, a trained professional, by squinting and tilting his head this way and that, could imagine that it was as densely crisscrossed with sight-lines and cannonball-arcs and other geo-metrickal phant'sies of engineers as the space above a ship's deck was with ropes and rigging. For this corridor between camp and fort had been claimed by the engineers—as anyone who stepped into it would learn in as little time as it took a musket-ball to cover the distance. The Engineer-Empire, Jack'd been noticing, waxed as older ones waned. Just as Turks and Franks had their own styles of building, so did Engineers rehearse, again and again, the same shapes: sloping walls, backed up by earth (to deflect and absorb cannonballs) laid out in nested zig-zags, a bastion at each corner from which to shoot at anyone who tried to climb the neighboring stretches of wall. Oh, Vienna had a traditional pre-Engineer wall: a thin curtain of masonry, crenellated on top. But that was nothing but an antiquarian curiosity now, enveloped and shamed by the new works.

Besides that cathedral, there was only one building in Vienna worth a second look, and that was a great big cream-colored, many-windowed building, five stories high and a crossbow-shot in length, constructed right on the edge of the city and rising high above the wall, with wings behind it enclosing courtyards he'd never see. It was obviously the Palace of the Holy Roman Emperor. It had a steep high roof—plenty of attic space—with a row of tiny dormers surmounted by funny copper domes like spiked helmets. Each dormer had a little window, and through one of them (though the distance was very great) Jack convinced himself he could see a figure dressed in white peering out. He wanted to arrange something involving a trapped princess, a dashing rescue, and a reward;

however, in between him and whomever was peering out that window were certain complications, viz. directly below the Palace, a huge bastion was thrust out into the glacis, like a giant's plowshare parting an empty field, and against this very stronghold the Grand Vizier had chosen to mount his attack.

Apparently the Turks had been in too much of a hurry to trundle siege artillery all the way across Hungary and so they were undoing the work of the Engineers one shovel-load at a time. Vienna's walls and bastions had been smooth regular shapes, so the Turks' handiwork was as obvious as a mole-hill in a Duke's bowling-green. They had dug a metropolis of trenches in what had been a perfectly flat glacis. Each trench was surrounded by the dirt that had been flung out of it, giving it the swollen look of an infected wound. A few of these trenches led straight from the heart of the Turkish camp toward the Emperor's Palace, but these were just the great avenue-trenches from which countless street-trenches branched off left and right, running generally parallel to the city's walls, and spaced as closely together as they could be without collapsing. These trenches were as rungs in a horizontal ladder by which the Turks had advanced until they'd reached the foot of the first ravelins: outlying, arrowhead-shaped earthworks between bastions. Here they had gone underground and undermined the ravelins, packed the mines with black powder, and blown them up, creating avalanches where walls had stood—as when molten wax spills from the top of a candle and mars its regular shape with a lumpy cataract. Fresh trenches, then, had been cut across those irregular debris-piles, bringing the Turks into a position whence they could bring musketry to bear on the city walls, to protect their sappers and miners as they advanced, ditch by ditch, across the dry moat. Now they were attacking the great bastion directly before the Palace in the same way. But it was a gradual sort of war, like watching a tree absorb a stone fence, and nothing was happening at the moment.

All well and good; but the question on Jack's mind was: where was the best looting to be found? He chose some likely targets, both in the Turk's camp and in the city of Vienna itself, and committed to memory a few landmarks, so that he could find what he desired when things were smoky and confused.

When he turned to go back to the camp, he discovered that there was another man up on this hill, a stone's throw away: some kind of monk or holy man, perhaps, as he was dressed in a rough sackcloth robe, with no finery. But then the bloke whipped out a sword. It was not one of your needle-thin rapiers, such as fops pushed at each other in the streets of London and Paris, but some kind of relic of the Crusades, a two-handed production with a single crossbar instead of a proper guard—the sort of thing Richard the Lionhearted might've used to slay camels in the streets of Jerusalem. This man went down on one knee in the dirt, and he did it with verve and enthusiasm. You see your rich man kneeling in church and it takes him two or three minutes, you can hear his knees popping and sinews creaking, he totters this way and that, creating small alarums amongst the servants who are gripping his elbows. But this brute knelt easily, even *lustily* if such a thing were possible, and facing toward the city of Vienna, he planted his sword in the ground so that it became a steel cross. The morning light was shining directly into his grizzled face and glinting from the steel of the blade and glowing in some indifferent colored jewels set into the weapon's hilt and crossbar. The man bowed his head and took to mumbling in Latin. The hand that wasn't holding the sword was thumbing through a rosary—Jack's cue to exit stage right. But as he was leaving he recognized the man with the broadsword as King John Sobieski.

LATER IN THE MORNING, a ration of brandy was issued to each man—it being a military axiom that a drunk soldier was an effective soldier. The brandy gave the men, at last, something to gamble with, and so dice and cards came out of pockets. This led to Jack having half a dozen brandy-rations in his belly, and his comrades-in-arms glaring at him suspiciously and muttering foul accusations in barbarous tongues. But then there was more trumpet-blowing and drum-beating and they were up on their feet (Jack barely so), and now another few hours of tromping around staring at the backs of the men in front of them, the horizon in all directions a fur of bayonets and pikes.

Like a storm that has fallen upon the mountains, the companies and regiments drained through trees into ravines and down ravines into valleys, coming together into black thundering floods that foamed out across the plain, finally, and rushed toward Vienna.

The artillery began to fire, first on one side, then the other. But if men were being cut down in swathes by Turkish grape-shot, it was not happening anywhere near Jack. They were moving double-time. They marched from hot, clear air into dust-clouds, then from dust-clouds into permanent banks of gunpowder-smoke.

Then the earth seemed to quail beneath their feet and their entire formation shied back, men piling into one another's backs, and the smoke roiled and parted. Glints of gold and polished brass bobbed through it, and Jack understood that right along their flank, King John Sobieski was charging into the Turks at the head of the Winged Hussars.

Divots of earth continued to rain down for long moments after they had passed. In the Poles' wake, an empty corridor was left across the battlefield, and suddenly there was no man in front of Jack. A yard of open space was more inviting than a pitcher of beer. He couldn't not bolt forward. The other men did likewise. The formation was broken and men of various regiments were simply boiling into the beaten path of the Polish cavalry. Jack followed along, as much out of a desire not to be trampled by the men behind him as to reach the looting. He was listening carefully for the sounds of Turkish cannonades from the front, or the rumble of retreating hussars, coming back toward them in panic, but he heard no such thing. There was plenty of musket-fire, but not in the sputtering waves of organized combat.

He nearly tripped over a severed arm, and saw that it was clad in a curious Oriental fabric. After limbs came bodies—mostly Turkish ones, some clad in vests of fine mail studded with jeweled badges and gold stars. The men around him saw the same thing, and a cheer went up. They were all running now, and they kept getting farther and farther apart, dispersing into some place that, in the dust and smoke, Jack knew as a city, maybe not so great as London, but much bigger, say, than Strasbourg or Munich. It was a city of tents: huge cones supported by central poles and guyed off to the sides with many radiating lines, and curtains hanging down from the rims of the cones to form the walls. The tents were not of rude canvas but of embroidered stuff, all decorated with crescents and stars and spidery words.

Jack ran into a tent and found thick carpet under his feet, a pattern like twining flowers woven into the pile, and then discovered a cat the size of a wolf, with spotted golden fur, chained to a post, a jewelled collar round its neck. He had never seen a cat large enough to eat him before and so he backed out of that tent and continued to wander. At an intersection of great ways, he discovered a tiled fountain with huge golden fish swimming in it. The overflow spilled into a ditch that led to a garden planted with sweet white flowers.

A tree grew in a pot on wheels, its branches burdened with strange fruit and inhabited by emerald-green and ruby-red birds with hooked beaks, which screamed sophisticated curses at him in some tongue he had never heard. A dead Turk with an enormous waxed mustache and a turban of apricot silk lay in a marble bath full of blood. Other pikemen and musketeers wandered about, too flabbergasted to loot.

Jack tripped and landed face-first on red cloth, then stood up to find that he had stepped on a scarlet flag twenty feet on a side, embroidered with swords and heathen letters in gold thread. This was too big to carry away and so he let it lie, and wandered down tent-streets and tent-avenues scattered with collapsible lanterns; wrought-silver incense burners; muskets with stocks inlaid with mother-of-pearl, lapis, and gold; grapefruit-sized hand grenades; turbans clasped with jeweled badges; hand-drums; and vatlike siege mortars, their bombs nearby, half-covered by spiderwebs of fuse. Standards with long horsehair tassels topped by copper cres-cent moons gaping like dead men at the sky. Embroidered quivers and discarded ramrods, both wooden and iron. Stray Bavarian matchlock men ran to and fro, smouldering ropes still tangled in their fingers, glowing red from the wind of their movement so that they appeared as bobbing red sparks in the smoke and dust, trail-ing long wavy tendrils of finer smoke behind them.

Then there was the sound of hooves nearby, coming closer, and Jack spun around and stared into face of a horse, in glowing armor. Above it an armed man in a winged helmet, shouting at him in what he now recognized as Polish, holding up some reins. The reins belonged to a second horse, a *cheval de bataille*, also richly armored and saddled, but in a wholly different style, adorned with crescents rather than crosses, and boxlike metal stirrups. It must be the war-horse of some Turkish lord. The Winged Hussar was thrusting its reins toward Jack and bellowing orders in his thick, sneering language. Jack reached out and accepted a fistful of reins.

Now what? Did this Polish lord want Jack to mount the other horse and ride with him through the camp? Not likely! He was pointing at the ground, repeating the same words over and over until Jack nodded, pretending to understand. Finally he drew his sword and pointed it at Jack's chest and said something very impo-lite and galloped away.

Jack now understood: this Winged Hussar had very grand ambi-tions for the day's looting. He had found this horse early in the day. It was a prize worth keeping, but it would only hinder him if he tried to lead it around. If he tied it to a tree it would be looted by someone else. So he had looked for an armed peasant (to him, anyone on foot would be a peasant) and enlisted him as a sort of flesh-and-blood hitching-post. Jack's job was to stand still holding these reins until the Winged Hussar came back—all day if need be.

Jack had scarcely had time to reflect on the fundamental unsoundness of this plan when a beast darted out of the smoke, headed right for him, then changed direction and ran past. It was the strangest thing Jack had ever seen, certainly one for the Book of Revelation: two-legged, feathered, therefore, arguably, a bird. But taller than a man, and apparently not capable of flight. It ran in the gait of a chicken, pecking the air with each stride to keep its balance. Its neck was as long and bare as Jack's arm and as wrinkled as his Jolly Roger.

A small mob of infantrymen came running after it.

Now, Jack did not have the faintest idea what the giant trotting bird (supposing it was a bird) was. It hadn't occurred to him to chase it, except perhaps out of curiosity. And yet the sight of other men chasing it, working so hard, with such desperate looks on their faces, gave him a powerful urge to do the same. They must be chasing it for a reason. It must be worth something, or else good to eat.

The bird had gone by very fast, easily out-loping the scrambling, miserably shod pursuers. They'd never catch it. On the other hand, Jack was holding the reins of a horse, and (he began to notice) a magnificent horse it was, with a saddle the likes he'd never seen, decorated in golden thread.

It probably had not even occurred to that Winged Hussar that Jack would know how to ride. In his part of the world, a serf could no more ride on horseback than he could speak Latin or dance a minuet. And disobeying the command of an armed lord was even less likely than riding around on a horse.

But Jack was not Polish scum of the earth, barefoot and chained to the land, or even French scum of the earth, in wooden clogs and in thrall to the priest and the tax-farmer, but English scum of the earth in good boots, equipped with certain God-given rights that were (as rumor had it) written down in a Charter somewhere, and armed with a loaded gun. He mounted the horse like a lord, spun it round smartly, reached back and slapped it on the ass, and he was off. In a few moments he had ridden through the middle of that knot of men who were hoping to catch the giant bird. Their only hope had been that their prey would forget that it was being chased, and stop running. Jack had no intention of letting that happen and so he jabbed his boot-heels into his mount's sides and lit out after the bird in a way that was calculated to make it run like hell. Which it did, and Jack galloped after it, far outdistancing his competition. But the bird was astoundingly swift. As it ran, its wings splayed this way and that like an acrobat's balancing-pole. Seeing into those wings from behind, Jack was reminded of decorations he'd seen in the hats of fine French gentlemen, and their mistresses, during military parades: those were the plumes of the, what's it called the, the . . . the ostrich.

The reason for this merry chase was plain now: the ostrich, if caught, could be plucked, and its plumes taken to markets where fine things from exotic lands were sold, and exchanged for silver.

Now, Jack calculated. If he scoured the entire Turkish camp, he might find finer things to loot—but the legions of Christendom were all running wild through this place and others were likely to have found them first. The finest things of all would be taken by lords on horseback, and the musketeers and pikemen would be left to brawl over trifles. The plumes of this ostrich were not the finest prize to be had in this camp, but a bird in the hand was worth two in the bush, and this one was almost in his hand. Ostrich-plumes were small and light, easy to conceal from the prying fingers and eyes of customs men, no burden to carry all the way across Europe if need be. And as the chase continued, his odds only improved, because this ostrich was speeding away from all noise and commotion, tending toward parts of the Grand Turk's camp where nothing was going on. If only it would hold still long enough for him to bring it down with a musket-shot.

The ostrich flailed, squawked, and vanished. Jack reined in his mount and proceeded carefully, and arrived at the lip of a trench. He hadn't the faintest idea where he was, but this trench looked like a big one. He nudged the horse forward, expecting it to balk, but it cheerfully set to work, planting its hooves carefully in the loose earth of the trench's sloping wall and picking its way down. Jack saw fresh ostrich prints in the muck on the bottom, and set the horse to trotting that direction.

Every few yards a smaller trench intersected this one at right-angles. None of these trenches had the palisades of sharpened outward-pointing sticks that the Turks would've installed if they'd been expecting an attack, and so Jack reckoned that these trenches did not belong to the camp's *outer* works, which had been put up to defend it from encircling armies of Christians. These trenches must, instead, be part of the assault against Vienna. The smoke and dust were such that Jack could not see whether the city was ahead of, or behind, him and the ostrich. But by looking at the way that the earth had been piled up to one side of those trenches, to protect the inhabitants from musketballs, any fool could make out in which direction the city lay. The ostrich was going towards Vienna, and so was Jack.

The walls of the big trench steadily became higher and steeper, to the point where they'd had to be shored up with pilings and retaining walls of split logs. Then all of a sudden the walls curved together above him, forming an arch. Jack reined the horse in and stared forward into a dark tunnel, large enough for two or three horsemen to ride abreast. It was cut into the foundation of a steep hill that rose abruptly from generally flat land. Through a momentary parting in the drifting clouds of smoke, Jack looked up and saw the mutilated face of the great bastion looming up above him, and glimpsed the high roof of the Emperor's Palace beyond and above that.

This must be a mine, an enormous one, that the Turks had dug beneath the bastion in the hopes of blowing it to kingdom come. The tunnel floor had been paved with logs that had been mostly driven down into the mud by the weight of oxen and wagons as they hauled dirt out, and gunpowder in. In the mud, Jack could see ostrich-prints. Why should that bird settle for merely burying its head in the sand when it could go wholly underground, and not even have to bend over? Jack did not love the idea of following it, but the die was cast; loot-wise, it was the ostrich or nothing.

As one would expect in any well-organized mining operation, torches were available near the entrance, soaking head-down in a pot of oil. Jack grabbed one, shoved it into the coals of a dying fire until flames emerged, then rode his horse forward into the tunnel.

It had been carefully timbered to keep it from collapsing. The tunnel descended gently for some distance, until it pierced the water table and became a sort of unpleasant mire, and then it began to climb again. Jack saw lights burning ahead of him. He noticed that the floor of the tunnel was striped with a bright line of steaming blood. This triggered what little Jack had in the way of prudent instincts: he threw the torch into a puddle and nudged the horse along at a slow walk.

The lights ahead of him illuminated a space larger than the tunnel: a room that had been excavated, deep underneath— where? Thinking back on the last few minutes' ride, Jack understood that he had covered a considerable distance—he must have passed all the way beneath the bastion—at least as far as the city's inner wall. And as he drew closer to the lights (several large torchières), he could see that the Turks' tunnel-work, and its supporting timbers, were all involved with things that had been planted in the earth hundreds of years ago: tarred pilings, driven in one alongside the next, and footings of mortared stone and of brick. The Turks had burrowed straight through the foundations of something enormous.

Following the rivulet of blood into the illuminated space, Jack saw a few small, bright, billowing tents that had been pitched, for some unfathomable Turkish reason, in the middle of this chamber. Some were standing, others had collapsed into the dirt. A pair of men were striking those gay tents with curt sword-blows. The ostrich stood to one side, cocking its head curiously. The tents tumbled to the floor with blood flying out of them.

There were people in those tents! They were being executed, one by one.

It would be easy to kill the ostrich here with a musket-shot, but this would certainly draw the attention of those Turkish executioners. They were formidable-looking fellows with handsome sabers, the only Turks Jack had laid eyes on today who were actually alive, and the only ones who were in any condition to conduct violence against Christians. He preferred to leave them be.

A saber struck at the top of one of those colorful tents, and a woman screamed. A second blow silenced her.

So, they were all women. Probably one of those famous harems. Jack wondered, idly, whether the mudlarks of East London would ever believe him if he went home and claimed he had seen a live ostrich, and a Turk's harem.

But thoughts of this sort were chased away by others. One of those moments had arrived: Jack had been presented with the opportunity to be stupid in some way that was much more interesting than being shrewd would've been. These moments seemed to come to Jack every few days. They almost never came to Bob, and Bob marveled that two brothers, leading similar lives, could be so different that one of them had the opportunity to be reckless and foolish all the time while the other almost never did. Jack had been expecting such a moment to arrive today. He'd supposed, until moments ago, that it had already come: namely, when he decided to mount the horse and ride after the ostrich. But here was a rare opportunity for stupidity even more flagrant and glorious.

Now, Bob, who'd been observing Jack carefully for many years, had observed that when these moments arrived, Jack was almost invariably possessed by something that Bob had heard about in Church called the Imp of the Perverse. Bob was convinced that the Imp of the Perverse rode invisibly on Jack's shoulder whispering bad ideas into his ear, and that the only counterbalance was Bob himself, standing alongside, counseling good sense, prudence, caution, and other Puritan virtues.*

But Bob was in England.

"Might as well get this over with, then," Jack muttered, and gave his Turkish steed some vigorous heel-digs, and galloped forward. One of the Turks was just raising his saber to strike down the last of the tent-wearing women. And he would've done just that, except that this woman suddenly darted away (as much as a person in such a garment could dart), forcing a postponement of the attack. He shuffled forward—directly into the path of Jack and Jack's horse. They simply rode the Turk down. It was clear that the horse was well-trained in this maneuver—Jack made a mental note to treat the animal kindly.

Then with one hand Jack gave a stiff tug on a rein while unslinging his musket from the opposite shoulder. The horse wheeled around, giving Jack a view of the ground he'd just ridden over. One of the Turks was flattened into the ground, crushed in two or three places under the horse's hooves, and the other was actually striding towards Jack and sort of wiggling his saber in the way of a man limbering up his wrist for a display of swordsmanship. Not wanting to see any such thing, Jack aimed his musket carefully at this Turk and pulled the trigger. The Turk stared calmly into Jack's eyes, up the barrel of the weapon. He had brown hair and green eyes and a bushy mustache flecked with gold, all of which vanished in a smoky flash when the powder in the pan ignited. But the musket did not kick. He heard the *foosh* of the flash in the pan, but not the *boom* of the barrel.

This was known as a hang fire. The fire in the pan had not traveled into the barrel—perhaps the touch-hole had become blocked by a bit of dirt. Nonetheless, Jack kept the weapon aimed in the general direction of the Turk (which involved some guesswork because the Turk was hidden behind the cloud of smoke from the pan). There might still be a slow fire working its way through the touch-hole—the musket was likely to fire, without warning, at any point during the next couple of minutes.

By the time Jack could see again, the Turk had grabbed the horse's bridle with one hand and raised the other to strike. Jack, peering out sidelong through burning eyes, wheeled his musket about to make some kind of barrier between him and the bloody

---

*Not that Bob was a Puritan—far from it—but he was known to talk that way, to demonstrate his superiority over Jack.

saber and felt a mighty shock when the two weapons connected, instantly followed by a hot blast that knocked his hands apart and spat metal into his face. The horse reared up. Under other circumstances, Jack might've been ready for this. As it was, blind, shocked, and burnt, he performed a reverse-somersault down the animal's muscular ass, plunged to the ground, and then rolled away blindly, terrified that the hind hooves might come down on top of him.

At no time during these acrobatics did Jack stop holding the stock of the musket very firmly with his right hand. He staggered up, realized his eyes were clenched shut, buried his face in the crook of his left arm, and tried to wipe away the heat and pain. The raw feel of his sleeve against his eyelids told him that he had been burnt, but not badly. He took the arm away and opened his eyes, then spun around like a drunk, trying to bring the enemy in view. He raised his musket again, to defend himself from any more sword-blows. But it moved far too easily. The weapon had been broken in half only a few inches past the flintlock—a yard of barrel was simply gone.

The female in the tent had already stepped forward and seized the horse's reins and was now speaking to it in soothing tones. Jack couldn't see the second Turk at all, which panicked him for a moment, until he finally saw him on the ground, arms wrapped around his face, rolling from side to side and making muffled cries. That much was good, but the situation was, in general, not satisfactory: Jack had lost his weapon to some sort of accident, and his mount to some Saracen female, and had not acquired any loot yet.

He ran forward to seize the horse's reins, but a glitter on the ground caught his eye: the Turk's sword. Jack snatched it up, then shouldered the woman out of the way, mounted the horse again, and got it turned around to where he could keep a good eye on matters. Where was the damned ostrich? Over there—cornered. Jack rode over to it, cutting the air a few times to learn the balance of the saber. Striking heads off, from the back of a moving horse, was normally a job for highly trained specialists, but only because the neck of a man was a small target. Decapitating an ostrich, which consisted almost entirely of neck, was almost too easy to be satisfying. Jack did the deed with one swift backhand slash. The head fell into the dirt and lay there, eyes open, making swallowing motions. The rest of the ostrich fell down, then climbed up and began to stalk around the chamber with blood spraying out of its severed neck. It fell down frequently. Jack did not especially want to get blood sprayed on him and so he guided the horse away from the bird—but the bird changed direction and came after him! Jack rode the other way and the ostrich once again changed tack and plotted an intercept course.

The woman was laughing at him. Jack glared at her. She stifled herself. Then a voice came out of that tent, saying something in a barbarian tongue. Jack circumvented another blind ostrich-charge, moving the horse around smartly.

"Sir knight, I know none of the tongues of Christendom, save French, English, Qwghlmian, and a dash of Hungarian."

IT WAS THE FIRST TIME that Jack Shaftoe had been called "sir" or mistaken for a knight. He glared meanly at the ostrich, which was staggering around in circles and losing the strength to stand. The woman had meanwhile switched into yet another strange language. Jack interrupted her: "My Qwghlmian is rusty," he announced. "Wandered up to Gttr Mnhrbgh once when I was a boy, as we'd heard a rumor that a Spanish Treasure-Galleon had been wrecked, and pieces of eight scattered up and down the shore, as thick as mussels. But all we found was a few drunken Frenchmen, stealing the chickens and burning the houses."

He was prepared to relate many more dramatic details, but at this point he faltered because there'd been a violent shifting-around of the contents of the tent, exposing, up towards its summit, a complex arrangement of silk handkerchiefs: one tied over the bridge of the nose, hiding everything below, and another tied round the forehead, hiding everything above. Between them, a slit through which a pair of eyes was looking up at him. They were blue eyes. "You are an Englishman!" she exclaimed.

Jack noted that this one was not preceded by a "Sir knight." To begin with, Englishmen were not accorded the respect given naturally to the men of great countries, such as France or Poland-Lithuania. Among Englishmen, Jack's way of speaking, of course, marked him out as No Gentleman. But even if he spoke like an Archbishop, from the nature of the yarn he'd just been relating to her, concerning his scavenging-trip to Qwghlm, it was now obvious that he *had been* at some point an actual Vagabond. Damn it! Not for the first time, Jack imagined cutting his own tongue out. His tongue was admired by that small fraction of mankind who, owing to some want of dignity or wit, were willing to let it be known that they admired any part of Jack Shaftoe. And yet if he had merely held it back, reined it in, this blue-eyed woman might still be addressing him as Sir Knight.

That part of Jack Shaftoe that, up until this point in his life, had kept him alive, counseled him to pull sharply on one rein or the other, wheel the horse around, and gallop away from Trouble here. He looked down at his hands, holding those reins, and noted that they failed to move—evidently, the part of Jack that sought a merry and short life was once again holding sway.

Puritans came frequently to Vagabond-camps bearing the information that at the time of the creation of the Universe—thousands of years ago!—certain of those present had been pre-destined by God to experience salvation. The rest of them were doomed to spend eternity burning in hellfire. This intelligence was called, by the Puritans, the Good News. For days, after the Puritans had been chased away, any Vagabond boy who farted would claim that the event had been foreordained by the Almighty, and enrolled in a cœlestial Book, at the dawn of time. All in good fun. But now here Jack Shaftoe sat astride a Turkish charger, willing his hands to pull one rein or the other, willing his boot-heels to dig into the sides of the beast, so that it would carry him away from this woman, but nothing happened. It must have been the Good News at work.

The blue eyes were downcast. "I thought you were a Knight at first," she said.

"What, in these rags?"

"But the horse is magnificent, and it blocks my view some-what," Trouble said. "The way you fought those Janissaries—like a Galahad."

"Galahad—he's the one who never got laid?" Again with the tongue. Again the sense that his movements were predestined, that his body was a locked carriage running out of control down a hill, directly towards the front entrance of Hell.

"That is one of the few things that *I* have in common with that legendary Knight."

"No!"

"I was *gozde*, which means that the Sultan had taken note of me; but before I was made *ikbal* which means bedded, he gave me to the Grand Vizier."

"Now I am not a learned fellow," said Jack Shaftoe, "but from what little I know of the habits of Turkish Viziers, it is not usual for them to keep beautiful, saucy young blonde slaves about their camps—*as virgins.*"

"Not forever. But there is something to be said for saving a few virgins up to celebrate a special occasion—such as the sacking of Vienna."

"But wouldn't there be plenty of virgins to be rustled in Vienna?"

"From the tales told by the secret agents that the Wazir sent into the city, he feared that there would be none at all."

Jack was inclined to be suspicious. But it was no less plausible for the Vizier, or the Wazir as Blue Eyes called him, to have English virgins than it was for him to have ostriches, giant bejeweled cats, and potted fruit-trees. "These soldiers haven't gotten to you?" asked Jack. He waved the saber around at the dead Turks, inadvertently flicking bullets of blood from the tip.

"They are Janissaries."

"I've heard of 'em," Jack said. "At one point I considered going to Constantinople, or whatever they're calling it now, and joining 'em."

"But what about their Oath of Celibacy?"

"Oh, that makes no difference to me, Blue Eyes—look." He was struggling with his codpiece.

"A Turk would already be finished," the woman said, patiently observing. "They have, in the front of their trousers, a sort of sally-port, to expedite pissing and raping."

"I'm no Turk," he said, finally rising up in the stirrups to afford her a clear view.

"Is it supposed to look like that?"

"Oh, you're a sly one."

"What happened?"

"A certain barber-surgeon in Dunkirk put out the word that he had learnt a cure for the French Pox from a traveling alchemist. My mates and I—we had just got back from Jamaica—went there one night—"

"You had the French Pox?"

"I only wanted a beard trim," Jack said. "My mate Tom Flinch had a bad finger that needed removal. It had bent the wrong way during a naval engagement with French privateers, and begun to smell so badly that no one would sit near him, and he had to take his meals abovedecks. That was why we went, and that was why we were drunk."

"I beg your pardon?"

"We had to get Tom drunk so he'd make less of a fuss when the finger went flying across the barber-shop. The rules of etiquette stated that we must therefore be as drunk as he."

"Pray continue."

"But when we learned that this Barber could also cure the French Pox, why, codpieces were flying around the place like cannonballs."

"So you did have the said Pox."

"So this barber, whose eyes had gotten as big as doubloons, stoked up his brazier and began to heat the irons. While he was performing the amputation of Tom Flinch's digit, the irons were waxing red- and then yellow-hot. Meantimes his young apprentice was mixing up a poultice of herbs, as dictated by the alchemist. Well, to make a long story short, I was the last of the group to have the afflicted member cauterized. My mates were all lying in a heap on the floor, holding poultices over their cocks and screaming, having completed the treatment. The barber and his apprentice tied me into the chair with a large number of stout lines and straps, and jammed a rag into my mouth—"

"They robbed you!?"

"No, no, missy, this was all part of the treatment. Now, the afflicted part of my member—the spot that needed cauterizing, you understand—was on the top, about halfway along. But my Trouser-Snake was all shrunk into m'self by this point, from fear. So the apprentice grasped the tip of my Johnson with a pair of tongs and stretched old One-Eyed Willie out with one hand—holding a candle with the other so that the site of the disease was plainly visible. Then the barber rummaged in his brazier and chose just the right sort of iron—methinks they were all the same, but he wanted to put on a great show of discretion, to justify his price. Just as the barber was lowering the glowing iron into position, what should happen but the tax-man and his deputies smashed down both front and back door at the same instant. 'Twas a raid. Barber dropped the iron."

" 'Tis very sad—a strapping fellow such as you—strong and shapely—buttocks like the shell-halves of an English walnut—a fine set of calves—handsome, after a fashion—never to have children."

"Oh, the barber was too late—I already have two little boys— that's why I'm chasing ostriches and killing Janissaries—got a family to support. And as I still have the French Pox, there's only a few years left before I go crazy and die. So now's the time for building up a handsome legacy."

"Your wife is lucky."

"My wife is dead."

"Too bad."

"Nah, I didn't love her," Jack said bravely, "and after the Barber dropped the iron I'd no practical use for her. Just as I have no practical use for you, Trouble."

"How do you suppose?"

"Well, just take a look. I can't do it."

"Maybe not as the English do. But certain arts have been taught to me from Books of India."

Silence.

"I've never had high regard for book-learning," Jack said, his voice sounding a bit as though a noose were drawing tight around his neck. "Give me practical experience any day."

"I have that, too."

"Aha, but you said you were a virgin?"

"I did my practicing on women."

"What!?"

"You don't think the entire harem just sits around waiting for the master to stiffen up?"

"But what's the point—what is the very *meaning*—of doing it when there is no penis available?"

"It is a question you might even have asked yourself," said Blue Eyes.

Jack had the feeling now—hardly for the first time—that a Change of Subject was urgently called for. He said, "I know that you were lying when you said that I was handsome, when really I'm quite bashed, gouged, pox-marked, rope-burned, weather-tanned, and so on."

"Some women like it," Blue Eyes said, and actually batted her eyelashes. Her eyes, and a few patches of skin in their vicinity, were the only parts of her that Jack could actually see, and this magnified the effect.

It was important that he put up some kind of defense. "You look very young," he said, "and you talk like a girl who is in need of a spanking."

"Books of India," she said coolly, "have entire chapters about that."

Jack began riding the horse around the chamber, inspecting its walls. Scraping away packed earth with one hand, he observed the staves of a barrel, branded with Turkish letters, and with more digging and scraping he found more barrels stacked around it—a whole cache of them, jammed into a niche in the chamber wall and mortared together with dirt.

In the center of the chamber was a pile of timbers and planks where the Turkish carpenters had built the reinforcements to prevent the chamber from caving in. Diverse tools were strewn around, wherever the Turks had dropped them when they'd decided to flee. "Here, make yourself useful, lass, and bring me that axe," Jack said.

Blue Eyes brought him the axe, staring him coolly in the eyes as she handed it over. Jack rose in the stirrups and swung it round so it bit into one of those Turkish kegs. A stave crumpled. Another blow, and the wood gave way entirely, and black powder poured out and hissed onto the ground.

"We're in the cellar of that Palace," Jack said. "Directly above us is the Court of the Holy Roman Emperor, and all around us are his vaults, full of treasure. Do you know what we could get, if we touched this off?"

"Premature deafness?"

"I intend to plug my ears."

"Tons of rock and earth collapsing atop us?"

"We can lay a powder-trail up the tunnel, put fire to it, and watch from a safe distance."

"You don't think that the sudden explosion and collapse of the Holy Roman Emperor's Palace will draw some attention?"

" 'Twas just an idea."

"If you do that, you're going to lose me, brother . . . besides, that is not how you become ennobled. Blowing a hole in the palace floor and slinking in like a rat, with smoke coming out of your clothes . . ."

"I'm supposed to take advice on ennoblement from a *slave*?"

"A slave who has lived in palaces."

"How would you propose to do it, then? If you're so clever— let's hear your plan."

The blue eyes rolled. "Who is noble?"

Jack shrugged. "Noblemen."

"How do most of them get that way?"

"By having noble parents."

"Oh. Really."

"Of course. Is it different in Turkish courts?"

"No different. But from the way you were talking, I thought that, in the courts of Christendom, it had something to do with being clever."

"I don't believe it has any connection at all to cleverness," Jack said, and prepared to relate a story about Charles the Elector Palatine. But before he could do this, Blue Eyes asked:

"Then we don't need a clever plan *at all*, do we?"

"This is an idle conversation, lass, but I am an idle man, and so I don't mind it. You say we do not need any clever plan to become ennobled. But we lack noble birth—so how do you propose to become noble?"

"It's easy. You buy your way in."

"That requires money."

"Let's get out of this hole and get us some money, then."

"How do you propose to do that?"

"I'll need an escort," the slave-girl said. "You have a horse and a sword."

"Blue Eyes, this is a battlefield. Many do. Find a knight."

"I'm a slave," she said. "A knight will take what he wants and then leave me."

"So it's matrimony you're after?"

"Some kind of partnership. Needn't be matrimonial."

"I'm to ride in front, slaying Janissaries, dragons, knights, and you'll tag behind and do—what, exactly? And don't speak to me about Books of India any more."

"I'll handle the money."

"But we have no money."

"That is why you need someone to handle it."

Jack didn't follow, but it sounded clever, and so he nodded sagely, as if he'd taken her meaning very clearly. "What's your name?"

"Eliza."

Rising in his stirrups, doffing his hat, and bowing slightly at the waist. "And I am Half-Cocked Jack at the lady's service."

"Find me a Christian man's clothes. The bloodier the better. I'll pluck the bird."

Erstwhile Camp of Grand Vizier Khan Mustapha

SEPTEMBER 1683

"AND ANOTHER THING—" JACK SAID.

"What, yet *another*!?" said Eliza, in an officer's bloody coat, her head swaddled in ripped shirts, slumped over in the saddle so that her head wasn't far from that of Jack, who was directing the horse.

"If we make it as far as Paris—and that's by no means easily done—and if you've given me so much as a blink of trouble—one cross look, one wifely crossing of the arms—cutting thespian-like asides, delivered to an imaginary audience—"

"Have you had many women, Jack?"

"—pretending to be shocked by what's perfectly normal—

calculated moods—slowness to get underway—murky complaints about female trouble—"

"Now that you mention it, Jack, this *is* my time of the month and I need you to stop right here in the middle of the battlefield for, oh, half an hour should suffice—"

"Not funny at all. Do I look amused?"

"You look like the inside of a handkerchief."

"Then I'll inform you that I don't look amused. We are skirting what's left of Khan Mustapha's camp. Over to the right, captive Turks stand in file in a trench, crossing themselves—that's odd—"

"I can hear them, uttering Christian prayers in a Slavic tongue—those are Janissaries, most likely Serbs. Like the ones you saved me from."

"Can you hear the cavalry-sabers whipping into their necks?"

"Is *that* what that is?"

"Why d'you think they're praying? Those Janissaries are being put to the sword by Polish hussars."

"But why?"

"Ever stumble into a very old family dispute? It wears that face. Some kind of ancient grievance. Some Janissaries must've done something upsetting to some Poles a hundred years ago."

Echelons of cavalry traversed the ruins of the Grand Vizier's camp like ripples snapped across a bedsheet. Though 'twere best not to begin thinking of bedsheets. "What was I just saying?"

"Oh, you were adding another codicil to our partnership agreement. Just like some Vagabond-lawyer."

"That's another thing—"

"*Yet still* another?"

"Don't call me a Vagabond. I may call *myself* one, from time to time, as a little joke—to break the ice, charm the ladies, or whatnot. All in good fun. But you must never direct that notorious epithet my way." Jack noticed that with one hand he was rubbing the base of the other hand's thumb, where a red-hot iron, shaped like a letter V, had once been pressed against his flesh, and held down for a while, leaving a mark that itched sometimes. "But to return to what I was trying to say, before all of your uncouth interruptions—the slightest trouble from you, lass, and I'll abandon you in Paris."

"Oh, horror! Anything but that, cruel man!"

"You're as naïve as a rich girl. Don't you know that in Paris, any woman found on her own will be arrested, cropped, whipped, *et cetera,* by that Lieutenant of Police—King Looie's puissant man, who has an exorbitant scope of powers—a most cruel oppressor of beggars and Vagabonds."

"But you'd know nothing of Vagabonds, O lordly gentleman."

"Better, but still not good."

"Where do you get this stuff like 'notorious epithet' and 'exorbitant scope' and 'puissant'?"

"The thyuhtuh, my dyuh."

"You're an actor?"

"An actor? An *actor*!?" A promise to spank her later was balanced on the tip of his tongue like a ball on a seal's nose, but he swallowed it for fear she'd come back at him with some flummoxing utterance. "Learn manners, child. Sometimes Vagabonds *might*, if in a generous Christian humour, allow actors to follow them around at a respectful distance."

"Forgive me."

"Are you rolling your eyes, under those bandages? I can tell, you know—but soft! An officer is nearby. Judging from heraldry, a Neapolitan count with at least three instances of bastardy in his ancestral line."

Following the cue, Eliza, who fortunately had a deep, unsettlingly hoarse alto, commenced moaning.

"Monsieur, monsieur," Jack said to her, in attempted French, "I know the saddle must pain those enormous black swellings that have suddenly appeared in your groin the last day or two, since you bedded that pair of rather ill-seeming Gypsy girls against my advice—but we must get you to a Surgeon-Barber, or, failing that, a Barber-Surgeon, so that the Turkish ball can be dug out of your brains before there are any more of those shuddering and twitching fits . . ." and so on until the Neapolitan count had retreated.

This led to a long pause during which Jack's mind wandered—though, in retrospect, Eliza's apparently *didn't*.

"Jack, is it safe to talk?"

"For a man, talking to a woman is never precisely safe. But we are out of the camp now, I no longer have to step over occasional strewn body-parts, the Danube is off to the right, Vienna rises beyond that. Men are spreading out to set up camp, queuing before heavily guarded wagons to receive their pay for the day's work—yes, safe as it'll ever be."

"Wait! When will *you* get paid, Jack?"

"Before the battle we were issued rations of brandy, and worthless little scraps of paper with what I take to've been letters inscribed on them, to be redeemed (or so the Captain claimed) in silver at the end of the day. They did not fool Jack Shaftoe. I sold mine to an industrious Jew."

"How much did you get for it?"

"I drove an excellent bargain. A bird in the hand is worth two in the—"

"You got only *fifty percent*!?"

"Not so bad, is it? Think, I'm only getting half of the proceeds from those ostrich plumes—*because of you.*"

"Oh, Jack. How do you suppose it makes me feel when you say such things?"

"What, am I speaking too loudly? Hurting your ears?"

"No . . ."

"Need to adjust your position?"

"No, no, Jack, I'm not speaking of my *body's* feelings."

"Then what the hell are you on about?"

"And, when you say 'one funny look and I'll drop you off among the Poles who brand runaway serfs on the forehead' or 'just wait until King Looie's Lieutenant of Police gets his hands on you . . .'"

"You're only cherry-picking the worst ones," Jack complained. "Mostly I've just threatened to drop you off at nunneries and the like."

"So you *do* admit that threatening to brand me is more cruel than threatening to make me into a nun."

"That's obvious. But—"

"But why be cruel to *any* degree, Jack?"

"Oh, excellent trick. I'll have to remember it. Now who is playing the Vagabond-lawyer?"

"Is it that you feel worried that, perhaps, you erred in salvaging me from the Janissaries?"

"What kind of conversation is this? What place do you come from, where people actually care about how everyone feels about things? What possible bearing could anyone's feelings have on anything that makes a bloody difference?"

"Among harem-slaves, what is there to pass the long hours of the day, except to practice womanly arts, such as sewing, embroidery, and the knotting of fine silk threads into elaborate lace undergarments—"

"Avast!"

"—to converse and banter in diverse languages (which does not go unless close attention is paid to the other's feelings). To partake of schemes and intrigues, to haggle in souks and bazaars—"

"You've already boasted of your prowess there."

"—"

"Was there something else you were going to mention, girl?"

"Well—"

"Out with it!"

"Only what I alluded to before: using all the most ancient and sophisticated practices of the Oriental world to slowly drive one another into frenzied, sweaty, screaming transports of concupiscent—"

"That's quite enough!"

"You asked."

"You led me to ask—schemes and intrigues, indeed!"

"Second nature to me now, I'm afraid."

"What of your first nature, then? No one could look more English."

"It is fortunate my dear mother did not hear that. She took extravagant pride in our heritage—pure Qwghlmian."

"Unadulterated mongrel, then."

"Not a drop of English blood—nor of Celtic, Norse, or what-have-you."

"A hundred percent what-have-you is more likely. At what age were you abducted, then?"

"Five."

"You know your age very clearly," Jack said, impressed. "Of a noble family, are you?"

"Mother maintains that all Qwghlmians—"

"Stay. I already know your ma better than I knew mine. What do you *remember* of Qwghlm?"

"The door of our dwelling, glowing warmly by the light of a merry guano-fire, and all hung about with curious picks and hatchets so that Daddy could chip us out of the place after one of those late June ice-storms, so vigorous and bracing. A clifftop village of simple honest folk who'd light bonfires on moonless nights to guide mariners to safety—Jack, why the noises? Phlegmatical trouble of some kind?"

"They light those fires to *lure* the mariners."

"Why, to trade with them?"

"So that they'll run aground and spill their cargoes on Caesar's Reef, or Viking's Grief, or Saracen's Doom, or Frenchie's Bones, or the Galleon-Gutter, or Dutch-Hammer, or any of the other Hazards to Navigation for which your home is ill-famed."

"Aah—" Eliza said, in melodious tones that nearly struck Jack dead on his feet, "puts a new light on some of their other practices."

"Such as?"

"Going out in the night with great big long knives to 'put stranded sailors out of their suffering . . .'"

"At their own request, I'm sure?"

"Aye, and coming back with chests and bales of goods offered as payment for the service. Yes, Jack, your explanation's much more reasonable—how lovely of my sainted Mummy to shield my tender ears from this awkward truth."

"Now, then, d'you understand why the Kings of England have long suffered—nay, encouraged, and possibly even bribed—the Barbary Corsairs to raid Qwghlm?"

"It was the second week of August. Mother and I were walking on the beach—"

"Wait, you've *beaches* there?"

"In memory, all is golden—perhaps it was a mud-flat. Yes, it was on the way to Snowy Rock, which gleamed a radiant white—" .

"Ha! Even in summer?"

"Not with snow. 'Twas the gifts of seagulls, by which Qwghlm is ever nourished. Mother and I had our slx and sktl—"

"Again?"

"The former is a combined hammering, chopping, scraping, and poking tool consisting of an oyster shell lashed to a thigh-bone."

"Why not use a stick?"

"Englishmen came and took all of the trees. The sktl is a hopper or bucket. We were halfway out to the Rock when we became conscious of a rhythm. Not the accustomed pounding of mountainous waves on jagged rocks—this was faster, sharper, deeper—a beating of savage African drums! North-, not Sub-Saharan, but African anyway, and not typical of the area. Qwghlmian music makes very little use of percussion—"

"It being difficult to make drum-heads of rat-hides."

"We turned towards the sun. Out on the cove—a wrinkled sheet of hammered gold—a shadow like a centipede, its legs swinging fore and aft to the beating of the drum—"

"Wait, a giant bug was walking on water?"

" 'Twas a many-oared coastal raiding-galley of the Barbary Corsairs. We tried to run back towards the shore, but the mud sucked at our bare feet so avidly that we had skwsh for a week thereafter—"

"Skwsh?"

"Heel-hickeys. The pirates launched a long-boat and ran it up on the mud-flat before us, cutting off our escape. Several men—turbaned silhouettes so strange and barbarous to my young eyes—vaulted out and made for us. One of them went straight into quicksand—"

"Haw! Stop! Now, that, as we say in Wapping, is Entertainment!"

"Only a Qwghlmian born and bred could have found her way

across that flat without perishing. In a trice, he'd sunk down to his neck and was thrashing about in exactly the wrong way, hollering certain key verses of the Holy Qur'an."

"And your mother said, 'We could escape now, but we have a Christian duty to this poor sailor; we must sacrifice our freedom to save his life' and you stayed there to help him out."

"No, Mummy said something more like, 'We could try to struggle away through all of this mud, but those darkies have muskets— so I'll pretend to stay behind to help that stupid wog—maybe we can rack up some brown-nosing points.'"

"What a woman!"

"She commandeered an oar and extended it to the trapped sailor. Seeing she'd found solid footing, others made bold to leave the boat and haul this fellow in. Mummy and I were then subjected to a curious sniffing procedure administered by an officer who did not speak English, but who made it plain, by his posture and expressions, that he was embarrassed and apologetic. We were taken aboard the long-boat and then to the galley, and then rowed out to a rendezvous with a forty-gun pirate-galleon cruising offshore. Not some ramshackle barge but a proper ship of the line, captured or perhaps bought, leased, or borrowed from a European navy."

"Where your mother was cruelly used by horny Mahometans."

"Oh, no. These men seemed to be of that sort who only desire women for that which they have in common with men."

"What—eyebrows?"

"No, no!"

"Toenails then? Because—"

"Stop it!"

"But the mercy that your Mum showed to the poor sailor was richly repaid later on, right? When, in a moment of crisis, unlooked-for, he appeared and showed her some favor, and thus saved the day—right?"

"He died a couple of days later, from bad fish, and was tossed overboard."

"Bad fish? On a *ship*? In the *ocean*? I thought those Mussulmen were ever so particular about their victuals."

"He didn't eat it—just touched it while preparing a meal."

"Why would anyone—"

"Don't ask me," Eliza said, "ask the mysterious Personage who subjected my Mummy to his unnatural vice."

"I thought you said—"

"You asked me if she'd been used *by Mahometans*. The Personage was not a Mahometan. Or a Jew. Or any other sort that practices circumcision."

"Er—"

"Would you like to stop, so that I can draw you a picture?"

"No. What sort of man was he, then?"

"Unknown. He never left his cabin in that high-windowed castle at the stern of the ship. It seemed he had a fear of sunlight, or at least of tanning. When Mummy was taken into that place, that curved expanse of glass was carefully shuttered, and the curtains drawn—heavy curtains they were, in a dark green shade like the skin of the *aguacate,* which is a fruit of New Spain. But with thread of gold woven through, here and there, to produce a sparkling effect. Before my mother could react, she was thrown back against the carpet—"

"You mean, *down onto* the carpet."

"Oh, no. For the walls, and even the ceiling, of the cabin were lined, every inch of them, in carpet. Hand-knotted wool, with a most deep and luxurious pile (or so it seemed to Mummy, who'd never seen or touched a carpet before), all in a hue that recalled the gold of fields ripe for harvest—"

"I thought you said it was dark."

"She came back from these trysts with the fibers all over her. And even in the dark she could feel, with the skin of her back, that cunning artisans had sculpted the golden carpet into curious patterns."

"Doesn't sound that bad, so far—that is, by the standards of white women abducted and enslaved by Barbary Corsairs."

"I haven't gotten to the part about the smell yet."

"The world smells bad, lass. Best to hold your nose and get on with it."

"You are a child in the world of bad smells, until—"

"Excuse me. Have you ever been to Newgate Prison? Paris in August? Strasbourg after the Black Death?"

"Think about fish for a moment."

"Now you're on about fish again."

"The only food that the Personage would eat was fish that had gone bad—quite some time ago."

"That's it. No more. I'll not be made a fool of." Jack put his fingers in his ears and sang a few merry madrigal tunes with a great deal of "fa la la" material in them.

A FEW DAYS might have passed here—the road West was long. But in time she inevitably resumed. "The Barbary Corsairs were no less incredulous than you, Jack. But it was evident that the Personage was a man of tremendous power, whose wishes must be obeyed. Every day, some sailor who'd committed an infraction would be sentenced to dress the rotten fish for this man's private table. He'd drop to his knees and beg to be flogged, or keel-hauled, rather than carry out that duty. But always one would be chosen, and sent over the side, and down the ladder—"

"How's that?"

"The fish was ripened in an open long-boat towed far, far behind the ship. Once a day, it would be pulled up alongside, and the luckless sailor would be forced, at pistols drawn, to descend a rope-ladder, clutching a scrap of paper in his teeth on which was inscribed whatever receipt the Personage had selected. Then the tow-rope was hastily paid out again by a gagging team of sailors, and the chef would go to work, preparing the meal on a little iron stove in the long-boat. When he was finished, he'd wave a skull and crossbones in the air and be pulled in until he was just astern. A rope would be thrown out the windows of that gaudy castle— below, the chef would tie it to a basket containing the finished meal. The basket would be drawn up and in through the window. Later, the Personage would ring a bell and a cabin-boy would be heartily bastinadoed until he agreed to go aft to recover the china, and toss it overboard."

"Fine. The cabin smelled bad."

"Oh, this Personage tried to mask it with all the spices and aromatic gums of the East. The place was all a-dangle with small charms, cleverly made in the shape of trees, impregnated with rare perfumes. Incense glowered through the wrought-gold screens of exotic braziers, and crystalline vials of perfumed spirits, dyed the colors of tropical blossoms, sloshed about with great sodden wicks hanging out of 'em to disperse the scent into the air. All for naught, of course, for—"

"The cabin smelled bad."

"Yes. Now, to be sure, Mummy and I had noticed an off odor about the ship from about a mile out, as we were being rowed to it, and had chalked it up to the corsairs' barbarous ways and overall masculinity. We had watched the spectacle of the dinner preparation twice without understanding it. The second time, the chef— who, that day, was the very man Mummy had saved—never waved the Jolly Roger, but seemed to fall asleep in the long-boat. Efforts were made to rouse him by blowing horns and firing cannon-salvos, to no avail. Finally they pulled him in, and the ship's physician descended the rope-ladder, breathing through a compress soaked in a compound of citrus oil, myrrh, spearmint, bergamot, opium, rose-water, camphor, and anise-seed, and pronounced the poor man dead. He had nicked his hand while chopping some week-old squid-meat, and some unspeakable residue had infected his blood and slain him, like a crossbow bolt 'tween the eyes."

"Your description of the Personage's cabin was suspiciously complete and particular," Jack observed.

"Oh, I was taken there, too—after Mummy failed the sniff-test, he flew into a rage, and in desperation they offered me up as a sacrifice. He got no satisfaction from me, as I'd not, at that age, begun to exude the womanly humours that—"

"Stop. Only stop. My life, since I approached Vienna, is become some kind of Bartholomew-Fair geek-baiting."

HOURS, OR A DAY or two, might've passed.

"So, then, I suppose I'm meant to believe that you and dear Mummy were originally taken from the mud-flats simply in hopes that Mummy would pass the sniff-test."

" 'Twas thought she *had* passed it—but the officer who administered that olfactory examination was deceived—his sensorium overwhelmed—by—"

"By the miasma of those Qwghlmian mud-flats and guano-mountains. My God, it is the worst thing I have ever heard—to think I feared that *you* would be appalled by *my* story." Jack waved his arms in the air, gaining the attention of an approaching friar, and shouted: "Which way is Massachusetts? I'm become a Puritan."

"Later in the voyage, finally, the Personage had his way with poor Mummy on one or two occasions, but only because no other choices were available to him, and we did not pass near any more remote settlements where women could be easily abducted."

"Well, c'mon, let's have it—what'd he do in that carpeted castle?"

Eliza then became uncharacteristically shy. Now, by this time they were several days out of Vienna. She had taken off the wounded-officer disguise and was sitting in the saddle with a blanket wrapped around her, covering the tent she'd been wearing the first time Jack had seen her. From time to time she'd offer to dismount and walk, but she was barefoot, and Jack didn't want to be slowed down. Her head, anyway, projected from a vast whorl of fabric, and Jack could therefore turn round and look at it anytime he chose. Generally he didn't, because he knew that only trouble could come of paying undue attention to that visage—its smooth symmetry, its fine set of teeth, and all of those ever-so-important Feelings flickering across it, supple and quick and mesmerizing as fire-light. But at this particular moment he did turn round to look, because her silence was so sudden that he supposed she'd been punched out of the saddle by a stray cannonball. She was there, gazing at some other travelers just ahead of them: four nuns.

They overtook the nuns shortly and left them behind. "Now you can say it," Jack said. But Eliza just set her jaw and gazed into the distance.

A quarter of an hour later they passed the actual nunnery. And a quarter of an hour after *that* suddenly she was back to normal, relating the details of what had gone on behind those aguacate-colored curtains on the carpet of harvest gold. Several odd practices were described—Books of India stuff, Jack suspected.

The high points of Eliza's story were, in sum, curiously synchronized with the appearance of nunneries and towns along their route. At a certain point Jack had heard all he wanted to—a bawdy tale, when told in so much detail, became monotonous, and then started to seem calculated to inspire Feelings of profound guilt and self-loathing in any male listeners who happened to be nearby.

Reviewing his memories of the last few days' journey from Vienna, Jack observed that, when they'd been in open country or forest, Eliza had kept to herself. But whenever they'd neared any kind of settlement, and especially nunneries (which were thick as fleas in this Popish land), the tongue would go into action and reach some highly interesting moment in the tale just as they were passing by the town's gate or the nunnery's door. The story would never resume until they'd passed some distance onwards.

"Next stop: the Barbary Coast. As we'd proven unsatisfactory to the Personage, we were added to the general pool of European slaves there—some tens of thousands of 'em."

"Damn, I'd no idea!"

"Their plight is ignored by all Europe!" Eliza said, and Jack realized too late he'd set her off. A torrential rant ensued. If only her head was still wrapped in those fake bandages—some tightening and knotting and his troubles would be over. Instead, by paying out the reins Jack was able to lead the noble horse, which he'd named, or re-named, Turk, from a distance, much as the Corsair-ship in Eliza's ridiculous fable had towed the unspeakable fish-boat. Snatches and fragments of the Rant occasionally drifted his way. He learned that Mummy had been sold into the harem of an Ottoman military official at the Qasbah of Algiers, and in her copious spare time had founded the Society of Britannic Abductees, which now had branches in Morocco, Tripoli, Bizerta, and Fez; which met on a fortnightly rotation except during Ramadan;

which had bylaws running to several hundred pages, which Eliza had to copy out by hand on filched Ottoman stationery whenever a new chapter was founded . . .

They were close to Linz. Monasteries, nunneries, rich men's houses, and outlying towns came frequently. In the middle of Eliza's sermon about the plight of white slaves in North Africa, Jack (just to see what would happen) slowed, then stopped before the gates of an especially gloomy and dreadful Gothickal convent. Eerie Papist chanting came out of it. Suddenly Eliza was off on a new topic.

"Now, when you started that sentence," Jack observed, "you were telling me about the procedure for amending the bylaws of the Society of Britannic Abductees, but by the time you got to the end of it, you had begun telling me about what happened when the ship packed to the gunwales with Hindoostani dancing-girls ran aground near a castle of the Knights of Malta—you're not *worried* that I'm going to drop you off, or sell you to some farmer, are you?"

"Why should you care about my *feelings*?"

"Now has it never occurred to you that you might be *better off* in a nunnery?"

Clearly it *hadn't*, but now it *did*. A most lovely consternation flooded into her face, and she turned her head, slightly, toward the nunnery.

"Oh, I'll hold up my end of the partnership. Years of dangling from hanged men's feet taught me the value of honest dealings." Jack stopped talking for a moment to stifle his mirth. Then, "Yes, the advantages of being on the road with Half-Cocked Jack are many: no man is my master. I have boots. A sword, axe, and horse, too. I cannot be but chaste. Secret smugglers' roads are all known to me. I know the zargon and the code-signs of Vagabonds, who, taken together, constitute a sort of (if I may speak poetically) network of information, spreading all over the world, functioning smoothly even when damaged, by which I may know which *pays* offer safe haven and passage, and which oppress wandering persons. You could do worse."

"Why then did you say I might be better off there?" Eliza said, nodding toward the great nunnery with its wings curling around toward the road like a beetle's tongs.

"Well, some would say I should've mentioned this to you earlier, but: you've taken up with a man who can be hanged on arrival in most jurisdictions."

"Ooh, you're an infamous criminal?"

"Only some places—but that's not why."

"Why then?"

"I'm *of a particular type.* The Devil's Poor."

"Oh."

"Shames me to say it—but when I was drunk and battle-flushed I showed you my other secret and so now I've no way, I'm sure, to fall any lower in your esteem."

"What is the Devil's Poor? Are you a Satan-worshipper?"

"Only when I fall in among Satan-worshippers. Haw! No, it is an English expression. There are two kinds of poor—God's and the Devil's. God's poor, such as widows, orphans, and recently escaped white slave-girls with pert arses, can and should be helped. Devil's poor are beyond help—charity's wasted on 'em. The distinction 'tween the two categories is recognized in all civilized countries."

"Do you expect to be hanged down there?"

They'd stopped on a hill-top above the Danube's flood-plain. Linz was below. The departure of the armies had shrunk it to a tenth of its recent size, leaving a scar on the earth like the pale skin after a big scab has fallen away. "Things will be loose there just now—many discharged soldiers will be passing through. They can't all be hanged—not enough rope in Austria for that. I count half a dozen corpses hanging from trees outside the city gate, half a dozen more heads on pikes along the walls—low normal, for a town of that size."

"Let's to market, then," Eliza said, peering down into Linz's square with eyes practically shooting sparks.

"Just ride in, find the Street of Ostrich-Plume Merchants, and go from one to the next, playing 'em off against each other?"

Eliza deflated.

"That's the problem with specialty goods," Jack said.

"What's your plan then, Jack?"

"Oh, anything can be sold. In every town is a street where buyers can be found for *anything.* I make it my business to know where those streets are."

"Jack, what sort of price do you suppose we'll fetch at a thieves' market? We could not conceivably do *worse.*"

"But we'll have silver in our pockets, lass."

"Perhaps the reason you're the Devil's Poor is that, having gotten something, you slip into town like a man who *expects* ill-treatment—possibly including capital punishment—and go straight to the thieves' market and sell it to a middleman's middle-man's middleman."

"Please note that I am alive, free, that I have boots, most of my bodily parts—"

"And a pox that'll make you demented and kill you in a few years."

"Longer than I'd live if I went into a town like that one pretending to be a merchant."

"But my point is—as you yourself said—you need to build up a legacy for your boys *now.*"

"Precisely what I just proposed," Jack said. "Unless you've a better idea?"

"We need to find a fair where we can sell the ostrich plumes directly to a merchant of fine clothes—someone who'll take them home to, say, Paris, and sell them to rich ladies and gentlemen."

"Oh, yes. Such merchants are always eager to deal with Vagabonds and slave-girls."

"Oh, Jack—that's simply a matter of dressing *up* instead of *down.*"

"There are sensitive men—touchy blokes—who'd find something disparaging in that remark. But I—"

"Haven't you wondered why, whenever I move, I make all of these rustling and swishing noises?" She demonstrated.

"I'm too much the gentleman to make inquiries about the construction of your undergarments—but since you mentioned it—"

"Silk. I've about a mile of silk wrapped around me, under this black thing. Stole it from the Vizier's camp."

"Silk! I've heard of it."

"A needle, some thread, and I'll be every inch a lady."

"And what will I be? The imbecile fop?"

"My manservant and bodyguard."

"Oh, no—"

"It's just play-acting! Only while we're in the fair! The rest of the time, I'm as ever your obedient slave, Jack."

"Since I know you like to tell fables, I'll play-act with you briefly. Now begging your pardon, but doesn't it take time to sew fine costumes out of Turkish silk?"

"Jack, *many* things take time. This will only take a few weeks."

"A few weeks. And you're aware that you are now in a place that has winters? And that this is October?"

"Jack?"

"Eliza?"

"What does your zargon-network tell you of fairs?"

"Mostly they are in spring or autumn. We want the Leipzig one."

"We do?" Eliza seemed impressed. Jack was gratified by this—a bad sign. No man was more comprehensively doomed than him whose chief source of gratification was making favorable impressions on some particular woman.

"Yes, because it is where goods of the East, coming out of Russia and Turkey, are exchanged for goods of the West."

"For silver, more likely—no one wants Western stuff."

"That's correct, actually. Your elder Vagabonds will tell you that the Parisian merchants are best robbed on the road *to* Leipzig, as that's when they carry silver, whereas on the way *back* they have goods that must be tediously hauled around and fenced. Though your young fellows will take issue with that, and say that no one carries silver anymore—all business is done with bills of exchange."

"At any rate, Leipzig is perfect."

"Except for the small matter that the autumn fair's already over, and we'll have a winter to survive before the next one."

"Keep me alive through that winter, Jack, and come spring, in Leipzig, I'll fetch you ten times what you'd get down *there*."

This was not a proper Vagabond method—making a plan six months in advance. The error was compounded a thousandfold by the prospect of spending so much time with one particular woman. But Jack had already trapped himself by mentioning his sons.

"Still thinking about it?" Eliza asked, some time later.

"Stopped thinking about it long ago," Jack said. "Now I'm trying to remember what I know of the country between here and Leipzig."

"And what have you remembered thus far?"

"Only that we'll see nothing alive that is more than fifty years old." Jack began walking toward a Danube ferry. Turk followed and Eliza rode in silence.

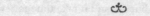

Bohemia

AUTUMN 1683

THREE DAYS NORTH of the Danube, the road focused to a rut in a crowd of scrawny trees that were striving to rise clear from a haze of grasping weeds. The weeds seethed with bugs and stirred with small unseen beasts. Paving-blocks skewed out of pounded ground, forming a sort of shoal that unsettled Turk, who straightened, blinked suspiciously, and slowed. Jack drew the Janissary's sword out of the rolled blanket where it had been hid since Vienna and washed the dried blood off in a creek-bend. When it was clean, he stood in a buttress of sunlight, thigh-deep in brown water, nervously wiping it and swinging it in the air.

"Something troubling you, Jack?"

"Since the Papists slew all the decent folk, this is a country of bandits, haiduks, and Vagabonds—"

"I guessed that. I meant, something about the sword?"

"Can't seem to get it dry—that is, it's dry to the touch, but it ripples like a brook in the sun."

Eliza answered with a scrap of verse:

Watered steel-blade, the world perfection calls,
Drunk with the viper poison foes appals.
Cuts lively, burns the blood whene'er it falls;
And picks up gems from pave of marble halls.

". . . or so says the Poet."

"What manner of poet speaketh such barbarities?" Jack scoffed.

"One who knew more of swords than you. For that is Damascus steel, more than likely. It might be more valuable than Turk and the ostrich plumes summed."

"Save for this defect," Jack said, fitting the ball of his thumb into a notch in the edge, not far from the point. Around it the steel was blackened. "I wouldn't've thought it could happen."

"That's where it cut into your musket's soft belly?"

"Soft? You saw only the wooden stock. But concealed within was an iron ramrod, running the whole length of the weapon through a skinny hole augered into the wood, alongside the musket-barrel itself. This sword cut through the wood—no great feat—but then it must've sliced clean through the ramrod, and then well into the barrel—deep enough to make it weak there. When the powder finally caught, it shoved the ball up only as far as the weak place, and then the barrel burst—that was the end of the Janissary, for he had his face up practically—"

"I saw it. You're rehearsing the story, aren't you, to entertain your friends?"

"I have no friends. It's to cow mine enemies." Jack thought this sounded formidable, but Eliza stared at the horizon and heaved a sigh.

"Or," she said, "it could entice a buyer who was in the market for a legendary blade . . ."

"I know it's difficult, but put all thoughts of markets out of your mind. As the Grand Vizier recently learned, all the riches in the world are of no use if you can't defend 'em. This is wealth, and the means to defend it, combined into one—perfection."

"Do you suppose that a man with a sword and a horse will be defense *enough,* in a place like this?"

"No highwayman of standing would situate himself in a waste."

"Are all the forests of Christendom like this? From Mummy's færy-tales I was expecting great majestic trees."

"Two or three generations ago, 'twas a wheat-field," Jack said, using the sword to harvest a sheaf of overripe stalks growing wild in a sunny break on the bank of the stream. He sheathed the sword and smelled the grain. "The good peasants would come here during the harvest with their dulled whistles slung over their tired shoulders." Before Jack had waded in he had kicked off his boots. He waded around the swirling pool, groping at the bottom with his bare toes, and after a minute bent down, reached in, and brought up a long curved scythe-blade, notched from striking rocks—just a solid crescent of rust now, a few fingers of slimy black wood projecting from the handle-socket. "They would whet their whistles using rocks that had been worn smooth by the river." He brought up one such rock in his other hand and scrubbed it against the blade for a moment, then tossed it up on the bank. "And while they were doing so they might not be above taking a bit of refreshment." Still probing with his feet, he bent down again and produced an earthenware drinking-jug, turned it over, and poured out a green-brown tube of stagnated water. The jug he tossed also onto the bank. Still holding the long rusty arc of the whistle in one hand, he turned round and waded back in search of an exhibit he had detected earlier. He found it again, and nearly fell over, the stream's current dividing round his thigh as he stood flamingo-style and passed the other foot over something down there. "And so went their simple, happy lives—until something intervened—" Jack now swung the whistle-blade slowly and (he liked to suppose) dramatically across the surface of the pool, a pantomime Grim Reaper.

"Plague? Famine?"

"Religious controversy!" Jack said, and produced from the pool a browned human skull, jaw-bone absent, an obvious sword-dent caving in one of the temples. Eliza (he thought) seemed quite struck by his presentation—not by the skull (she'd seen worse) so much as by the cleverness of the performance. He posed with whistle and skull, extending the moment. "Ever seen a morality play?"

"Mummy told me about 'em."

"The intended audience: Vagabonds. The purpose: to impress on their feeble and degenerate minds some idiotic moral."

"What is the moral of your play, Jack?"

"Oh, it could be a number of things: stay the hell out of Europe, for example. Or: when the men with swords come, run away! Especially if they've got Bibles, too."

"Sound advice."

"Even if it means giving up things."

Eliza laughed like a wench. "Ah, now we *are* coming to a moral, I can sense it."

"Laugh all you like at this poor fellow," Jack said, hefting the skull. "If he'd left his wheat-harvest behind, and taken to the road, instead of clinging to his land and his hut like a miser, why he might be alive today."

"Are there such things as fourscore-year-old Vagabonds?"

"Probably not," Jack admitted, "they just *look* twice as old as they are."

THEY WENT NORTH into the dead country of Bohemia, following spoors and traces of old roads, and the trails of the game that had flourished here in the absence of hunters. Jack lamented the loss of Brown Bess, which would have brought down all the deer they might have wanted, or at least scared the hell out of them.

Sometimes they would come down out of the wooded hills to cross over plains—probably old pastures that had grown up into vast thickets. Jack would put Eliza up into the saddle so that thorns, nettles, and bugs wouldn't make a mess of her—not that he cared—but her chief reason for existence was to give him something pleasant to look at. Sometimes he'd put the Damascus blade to the ignoble purpose of hacking through brush. "What do you and Turk see?" he'd say, because all he could see was useless vegetation, gone all brown in preparation for winter.

"To the right, the ground rises to a sort of shelf, high dark hills behind it—on the shelf the walls of a castle, thick and ill-made compared to Moorish ones, which are so elegant—but not thick enough to resist whatever destroying force knocked it down—"

"Artillery, lass—the doom of all ancient forts."

"The Pope's artillery, then, breached the walls in several places—creating spills of rock across the dry-moat. White mortar clings to the dark stones like shards of bleached bone. Then fire burnt out the insides, and took all but a few blackened rafters from the roof—all the windows and gun-ports have spreading smoke-stains above them, as if flames jetted from those openings for hours—it is like an Alchemist's furnace in which a whole town was purified of heresy."

"You have alchemists in Barbary?"

"You have them in Christendom?"

"It is very poetickal—as were the previous half-dozen ruined-castle-descriptions—but I was more interested in practical matters: do you see the smoke of cook-fires anywhere?"

"I'd have mentioned it. Trails in the brush, trampled down by men or horses, I'd have mentioned, too."

"Anything else?"

"To the left a pond—rather shallow-looking."

"Let's go there."

"Turk's been taking us thither—he's thirsty."

They found several such ponds, and after the third or fourth (all of them near ruins) Jack understood that these ponds had been excavated, or at least enlarged and rounded out, by (safe to say) thousands of wretches with picks and shovels. It recalled to his mind some bit of zargon-lore he'd picked up from a gypsy in Paris, who'd ranted to him about lakes, far to the East, but not so far as Romania, where big fish were raised just as herdsman raised beef-cattle in pastures. From the fish skeletons scattered along the shores of these ponds, Jack could see others had been here, harvesting the vestiges of those dead Protestants' clammy flocks. It made his mouth water.

"Why'd the Papists hate this country so much?" Eliza inquired. "Mummy told me there are many Protestant lands."

"It is not the sort of thing I would bother to know about, as a rule," Jack said, "but, as it happens, I've just come from an almost equally ruined land where every peasant knows the tale, and won't leave off telling it. That country is called the Palatinate and its lords, for a few generations anyway, were Protestant heroes. One of those lords married an English girl, name of Elizabeth—the sister of Chuck the First."

"Charles the First—isn't he the one who ran afoul of Cromwell, and got his head chopped off in Charing Cross?"

"The same—and his sister fared little better, as you'll soon see. Because right here in Bohemia, some Protestants got weary of being ruled by Papists, and threw several of 'em out a castle window into a dung-heap, and declared this country free of Popery. But unlike the Dutchmen, who have little use for royalty, these Bohemians couldn't imagine having a country without monarchs.

As Protestant monarchs were in short supply hereabouts, they invited Elizabeth and this Palatine fellow to come here and rule them. Which they did—for a single winter. Then the Pope's legions came up here and made it what it is today."

"What of Elizabeth and her husband?"

"The Winter Queen and the Winter King, as they were called after that, ran away. They couldn't go to the Palatinate because that had likewise been invaded (which is why the people who live there won't shut up about it, even today), so they roamed about like Vagabonds for a while and finally ended up at The Hague, where they sat out the war that had been started by all this."

"Did she have children?"

"She wouldn't *stop* having 'em. My god. To hear people talk, she must've been punching them out, nine and a half months apart, all through the war . . . I cannot remember how many."

"You cannot remember? How long *was* this war?"

"Thirty years."

"Oh."

"She had at least a dozen. The eldest became Elector Palatinate after the war, and the others scattered to the four winds, as far as I know."

"You speak very callously of them," Eliza sniffed, "but I am certain that each bears in his or her heart the memory of what was done to the parents."

"Forgive me, lass, but now I'm confused: are you talking about those Palatine whelps, or yourself?"

"Both," Eliza admitted.

He and Eliza had hit on a new way of subsisting, mostly on wheat. As Jack liked to remind Eliza several times a day, he was not the sort who accumulated possessions. But he had a sharp eye for what might be useful in a pinch, and so had filched a hand-mill from a military baggage-train when the cooks had gone off to loot. Wheat poured into the top would become flour if one only turned the crank a few thousand times. All they needed, then, was an oven. Or so Jack had supposed until one evening between Vienna and Linz when Eliza had thrust a couple of sticks into the ashes of their fire and pulled out a flat blackened disk. Brushed off, it proved to be brown and tan underneath—torn apart, it steamed and smelled more or less like bread. It was, Eliza said, a Mohametan style of bread, requiring no oven, and reasonably good to eat if you didn't mind grinding a few cinders between your teeth. They'd now been eating it for upwards of a month. Compared to real viands it was miserable, compared to starvation it was extremely palatable. "Bread and water, bread and water—it's like being in the brig again. I'm for some fish!" Jack said.

"When were you in a brig?"

"It's just like you to ask. Er, I believe it was after we sailed from Jamaica, but before the pirate attack."

"What were you doing in Jamaica?" Eliza asked suspiciously.

"Worked my extensive military connections to stow away on a ship bringing balls and powder to His Majesty's fortifications there."

"Why?"

"Port Royal. I wanted to see Port Royal, which is to pirates as Amsterdam is to Jews."

"You wanted to become a pirate?"

"I wanted freedom. As a Vagabond, I have it—so long as I keep my wits about me. But a pirate is (or so I thought) like a Vagabond of the seas. They say that all of the seas, put together, are larger than all of the dry land, put together, and I supposed that pirates must be that much freer than Vagabonds. Not to mention a good deal richer—everyone knows that the streets of Port Royal are paved with Spanish silver."

"Are they?"

"Very near, lass. All of the world's silver comes from Peru and Mexico—"

"I know it. We used pieces of eight in Constantinople."

"—and all of it must pass by Jamaica in order to reach Spain. Those Port Royal pirates siphoned off a goodly fraction of it. I reached the place in seventy-six—only a few years since Captain Morgan had personally sacked Portobelo and Panama, and brought all the proceeds back to Port Royal. It was a rich place."

"I'm pleased that you wanted to be a buccaneer . . . I was afraid you had ambitions of being a sugar planter."

"Then, lass, you are the only person in the world who esteems pirates above planters."

"I know that in the Cape Verde Islands and Madeira, all sugar is cultivated by slaves—the same is true in Jamaica?"

"Of course! The Indians all died, or ran away."

"Then better to be a pirate."

"Never mind. A month aboard ship taught me that there's no freedom at all to be had on the high seas. Oh, the ship might be moving. But all water looks the same, and while you wait for land to crawl over the horizon, you're locked up in a box with a lot of insufferable fools. And pirate-ships are no different. There is no end of rules as to how booty and swag are to be collected, valued, and divided among the numerous different classes and ranks of pirates. So after a bad month in Port Royal, trying to keep my arsehole away from randy buccaneers, I sailed for home on a sugar-ship."

Eliza smiled. She did not do this frequently. Jack did not like the effect it had on him when she did. "You have seen much," she said.

"I'm more than twenty years old, lass. An old gaffer like me, in the twilight of his years, has had plenty of time to live a full life, and to see Port Royal and other wonders—you're only a child, you've a good ten or, God willing, twenty years left."

"It was on the sugar-ship that you were thrown into the brig?"

"Yes, for some imagined offense. Then pirates attacked. We were holed by a cannonball. The ship's master saw his profits dissolving. All hands were called on deck, all sins pardoned."

ELIZA WENT ON WITH FURTHER interrogations. Jack heard not a word of it, as he was making observations of this pond, and of the mostly abandoned village that crowded along one shore of it. He paid particular attention to a gossamer-thread of smoke that rose and piled up against some invisible barrier in the atmosphere above. It was coming from a lean-to thrown up against the wall of an old collapsed house. A dog whined somewhere. The scrub between the pond and a nearby forest was scored with various trails cutting purposefully toward water's edge, and the forest itself trapped in a miasma of smoke and vapors.

Jack followed the pond-shore, fish-bones crackling beneath the soles of his boots, until he'd come to the village. A man was dragging a faggot as big as himself down a road toward the lean-to. "No axes—they therefore must burn twigs, instead of cordwood, all winter," Jack said to Eliza, significantly patting the axe that they'd taken from the chamber beneath Vienna.

The man was wearing wooden shoes, and was dressed in rags that had gone the color of ash, and he shimmered in an oily cloud of flies. He was staring lustfully at Jack's boots, with an occasional, sad glance at the sword and the horse, which told him he would never get the boots.

"J'ai besoin d'une cruche," Jack offered.

Eliza was amused. "Jack, we're in Bohemia! Why are you speaking French?"

"Il y a quelques dans la cave de ça—là-bas, monsieur," said the peasant.

"Merci."

"De rien, monsieur."

"You have to look at the shoes," Jack explained airily, after allowing a minute for Eliza's embarrassment to ripen. "No one but a Frenchman wears those sabots."

"But how . . . ?"

"France is a worse than normal place to be a peasant. Some *pays* especially. They know perfectly well there's empty land to the east. As do our dinner guests."

"Guests?"

Jack found a great earthenware jug in a cellar and set Eliza to work dropping pebbles into its open neck until it was so weighed down as to sink. Meanwhile he was working with the contents of his powder-horn, which had been useless weight to him since the destruction of Brown Bess. He tore a long thin strip of linen from a shirt and rolled it in powder until it was nearly black, then sparked one end of it with flint and steel and observed a steady and satisfactory progress of sputtering and smoky flame. The Frenchman's children had come over to watch. They were so infested with fleas that they rustled. Jack made them stay well back. The fuse demonstration was the most wondrous event of their lives.

Eliza was finished with the pebble work. The rest was simple enough. All the remaining supply of gunpowder, plus a piece of new fuse, went into the jug. Jack lit the fuse, dropped it in, jammed a warm candle-stub into the neck to keep water out, and hurled the apparatus as far as he could into the pond, which swallowed it. A few moments later it belched—the water swelled, foamed, and produced a cloud of dry smoke, like a miracle. A minute later the water became lumpy and thick with dead or unconscious fish.

"Dinner is served!" Jack hollered. But the murky forest had already come alive—queues of people were moving down the paths like flame down the fuse. "Up on the horse, lass," Jack suggested.

"Are they dangerous?"

"Depends on what's catching. I have the good fortune to've been born immune and impervious to plague, leprosy, impetigo . . ." but Eliza was up on the horse already, in a performance of a scampering nature that no man alive (excepting sodomites) would not have enjoyed watching. Jack, for lack of other occupations, had taught her what he knew of riding, and she backed Turk off expertly and rode him up onto a little mossy hummock, gaining as much altitude as possible.

"'Twas the Year of our Lord sixteen hundred and sixty-five," Jack said. "I was coming up in the world—having established a thriving business of sorts with brother Bob, providing specialized services to the condemned. My first clew was the scent of brimstone—then heavy yellow smoke of it hanging in the streets, thicker and fouler than the normal fogs of London. People burnt it to purify the air."

"Of what?"

"Then it was wains trundling down streets piled with corpses of rats, then cats, then dogs, then people. Red chalk crosses would appear on certain houses—armed watchmen stood before them to prevent any of the miserable residents from breaking out of those nailed-shut doors. Now, I couldn't've been more than seven. The sight of all those blokes planted in the brimstone-fog, like hero-statues, with pikes and muskets at the ready—churches' bells sounding death-knells all round—why, Bob and I had voyaged to another world without leaving London! Public entertainments were outlawed. Irish even stopped having their Popish feasts, and many absconded. The great hangings at Tyburn stopped. Theatres: shut down for the first time since Cromwell. Bob and I had lost both income and the entertainment to spend it on. We left London. We went to the forest. Everyone did. They were infested. The highwaymen had to pack up and move away. Before we—the Londoners fleeing the Plague—even came into those woods, there had been towns of lean-tos and tree-houses there: widows, orphans, cripples, idiots, madmen, journeymen who'd thought better of their contracts, fugitives, homeless reverends, victims of fire and flood, deserters, discharged soldiers, actors, girls who'd gotten pregnant out of wedlock, tinkers, pedlars, gypsies, runaway slaves, musicians, sailors between sailings, smugglers, confused Irishmen, Ranters, Diggers, Levellers, Quakers, feminists, midwives. The normal Vagabond population, in other words. To this was added, now, any Londoner fleet enough to outrun the Black Death. Now, a year later London burnt to the ground—there was yet another exodus. Same year, the Naval Pay Office went into default—thousands of unpaid sailors joined us. We moved around the South of England like Christmas Carolers from Hell. More'n half of us expected the Apocalypse within a few weeks, so we didn't trouble with planning. We broke down walls and fences, undoing Enclosure, poached game in forests of some extremely worshipful lords and bishops. They weren't happy."

By this time, the Vagabonds had mostly come out into the open. Jack didn't look at them—he knew what they'd be—but rather at Eliza, who'd become anxious. Turk the Horse sensed this and looked askance at Jack, showing a white Mohametan crescent-moon in the eye. Jack knew, then, that, as it was with Turk, so it'd be with every person and beast they met along their way: they'd gladly suffer Eliza to climb on their backs and ride them, they'd feel her feelings as if she were an actress on a Southwark stage, and they'd shoot dirty looks at Jack. He'd only have to find a way to use it.

Eliza breathed easier when she saw that the Vagabonds were just people. If anything they were cleaner and less brutish than those peasants who'd settled in the village, especially after they swam out into the pond to retrieve fish. A couple of Gypsy boys drew a crowd as they struggled to wrestle a prodigious carp, the size of a black-smith, up onto the shore. "Some of these fish must remember the war," Jack mused.

Several people came near, but not too near, to pay their respects to Jack and (more so) Eliza. One was a stringy fellow with pale green eyes staring out of an anatomical complex that looked like anything but a face—his nose was gone, leaving twin vertical air-holes, and his upper lip was missing, and his ears were perforated baby's fists stuck to the sides of this head, and angry words were burnt into his forehead. He came toward them, stopped, and bowed deeply. He had an entourage of more complete persons who obviously loved him, and they all grinned at Eliza, encourag-ing her not to throw up or gallop away screaming.

She was politely aghast. "A leper?" she asked. "But then he wouldn't be so popular."

"A recidivist," Jack said. "When Polish serfs run away, their lords hunt 'em down and brand 'em, or cut off this or that piece—saving the pieces that can do useful work, needless to say—so if they're seen out on the roads again they'll be known as runners. That, lass, is what I mean by the Devil's Poor—one who keeps at it regard-less—who won't be mastered by any man, nor reformed by any church. As you can see, his perseverance has won him a whole Court of admirers."

Jack's gaze had drifted to the lakeshore, where Vagabonds were now scooping guts out of carp-bellies by the double handful, exert-ing a hypnotic power over various mangy dogs. He looked up at Eliza and caught her in the act of examining him. "Trying to pic-ture me without a nose?"

Eliza looked down. He'd never seen her eyes downcast before. It affected him, and made him angry to be affected. "Don't look at me—I'll not be the subject of such investigation. The last person who peered at me that way, from the back of a fine horse, was Sir Winston Churchill."

"Who's that? Some Englishman?"

"A gentleman of Dorsetshire. Royalist. Cromwell's men burnt down his ancestral estate and he squatted in the cinders for ten or fifteen years, siring children and fighting off Vagabonds and wait- ing for the King to come back—that accomplished, he became a man about town in London."

"Then whyever was he peering at you from horseback?"

"In those days of Plague and Fire, Sir Winston Churchill had the good sense to get himself posted to Dublin on the King's business. He'd come back from time to time, suck up to the Royals, and inspect what was left of his country estates. On one of those occa- sions, he and his son came back to Dorset for a visit and rallied the local militia."

"And you happened to be there?"

"I did."

"No coincidence, I presume."

"Bob and I and certain others had come to partake of a charm- ing local custom."

"Clog-dancing?"

"Clubmen—armies of peasants who'd once roamed that part of the country with cudgels. Cromwell had massacred them, but they were still about—we hoped for a revival of the tradition, as Vagabondage of the meek school had become overly competitive in those dark years."

"What did Sir Winston Churchill think of your idea?"

"Didn't want his home burnt again—he'd just gotten a roof on it, finally, after twenty years. He was Lord Lieutenant there- abouts—that's a job that the King gives to the gents with the brownest noses of all—entitled him to command the local militia. Most Lord Lieutenants sit in London all the time, but after the Plague and the Fire, the countryside was in an uproar because of people like me, as I've been explaining, and so they were given the power to search for arms, imprison disorderly persons, and so on."

"Were you imprisoned, then?"

"What? No, we were mere boys, and we looked younger than we were because of not eating enough. Sir Winston decided to carry out a few exemplary hangings, which was the normal means of per- suading Vagabonds to move to the next county. He picked out three men and hanged them from a tree-limb, and as a last favor to them, Bob and I hung from their legs to make 'em perish faster. And in so doing we caught Sir Winston's eye. Bob and I looked sim- ilar, though for all we know we've different fathers. The sight of these two matched urchins plying their trade, with coolness born of experience, was amusing to Sir Winston. He called us over and that was when he (and his son John, only ten years older than meself) gave us that look you were giving me just now."

"And what conclusion did *he* arrive at?"

"I didn't wait for him to arrive at conclusions. I said something like, 'Are you the responsible official here?' Bob'd already made himself scarce. Sir Winston laughed a little too heartily and allowed as how he was. 'Well, I'd like to register a complaint,' I said. 'You said you were going to carry out one or two exemplary hangings. But is this your notion of exemplary? The rope is too thin, the noose is ill-made, the tree-limb is barely adequate to support the burden, and the proceedings were, if I may say so, carried out with a want of pomp and showmanship that'd have the crowd at Tyburn baying for Jack Ketch's blood if he ever staged one so shabbily.'"

"But Jack, didn't you understand that 'exemplary' meant that Sir Winston Churchill was *making an example* of them?"

"Naturally. And just as naturally, Sir Winston began to give me the same tedious explanation I've just now had from you, albeit I interrupted with many more foolish jests—and in the middle of it, young John Churchill happened to glance away and said, 'I say, look, Father, the other chap's going through our baggage.'"

"What—Bob?"

"My performance was a diversion, girl, to keep them looking at me whilst Bob pilfered their baggage-train. Only John Churchill had a lively enough mind to understand what we were doing."

"So . . . what did Sir Winston think of you, then?"

"He had his horsewhip out. But John spoke with him *sotto voce,* and, as I believe, changed his mind—Sir Winston claimed, then, that he'd seen qualities in us Shaftoe boys that would make us useful in a regimental setting. From that moment on we were boot-polishers, musket-cleaners, beer-fetchers, and general errand-boys for Sir Winston Churchill's local regiment. We'd been given the opportunity to prove we were God's, and not the Devil's, Poor."

"So that's where you got your knowledge of matters military."

"Where I *began* to get it. This was a good sixteen years ago."

"And also, I suppose, it's how you became so sympathetic to the likes of these," Eliza said, flicking her blue eyes once toward the Vagabonds.

"Oh. You suppose I arranged this carp-feast out of charity?"

"Come to think of it—"

"I—*we*—need information."

"From *these* people?"

"I have heard that in some cities they have buildings called libraries, and the libraries are full of books, and each book contains a story. Well, I can tell you that there never was a library that had as many stories as a Vagabond-camp. Just as a Doctor of Letters might go to a library to read one of those stories, I need to get a certain tale from one of these people—I'm not sure which one, yet—so I drew 'em all out."

"What sort of tale?"

"It's about a wooded, hilly country, not far north of here, where hot water spills out of the ground year-round and keeps homeless wanderers from freezing to death. You see, lass, if we wanted to survive a northern winter, we should've begun laying in firewood months ago."

Jack then went among the Vagabonds and, speaking in a none too euphonious stew of zargon, French, and sign language, soon got the information he needed. There were many haiduks—runaway serfs who'd made a living preying on the Turks farther east. They understood the tale told by Jack's horse and sword, and wanted Jack to join them. Jack thought it wise to slip away before their friendly invitations hardened into demands. Besides which, the entire scene of motley Vagabonds gutting and mutilating these immense fifty-year-old carp had become almost as strange and apocalyptic as anything they'd seen in the Turk's camp, and they just wanted to put it behind them. Before dark, Jack and Eliza were northbound. That night, for the first time, it got so chilly that they were obliged to sleep curled up next to the fire under the same blanket, which meant Eliza slept soundly and Jack hardly at all.

Bohemia
WINTER OF 1683–1684

FOR THE TWO WEEKS that followed Jack's Christ-like miracle of feeding a thousand Vagabonds from a small bag of gunpowder, he and Eliza talked very little, except about immediate concerns of staying alive. They passed from the rolling country of burnt castles and carp-ponds, with its broad flat valleys, into a mountainous zone farther north, which either had not suffered so badly during the war, or else had recovered faster. From hill-tops and mountain-passes they looked down upon brown fields where haystacks scattered like bubbles on placid ponds, and tidy prosperous towns whose chimneys bristled like so many pikes and muskets brandished against the cold. Jack tried to compare these vistas against the tales the Vagabonds had told him. Certain nights, they were all but certain they were going to perish, but then they'd find a hut, or cave, or even a cleft in the face of some bluff where they could build a nest of fallen leaves and a fire.

Finally one day they came, sudden as an ambush, into a vale where the tree-branches were grizzled with mist, and steam rose from a smelly rill that trickled down a strangely colored and sculpted river-bed. "We're here," Jack said, and left Eliza hidden back in the woods while he rode out into the open to talk to a pair of miners who were working with picks and shovels in the stream, digging up brittle rock that smelled like London in the Plague Years. Brimstone! Jack spoke little German and they spoke no English, but they were thoroughly impressed by his sword, his horse, and his boots, and through grunts and shrugs and signs they made it known they'd make no trouble if he camped for the winter at the headwaters of the hot spring, half a league up the valley.

So they did. The spring emerged from a small cave that was always warm. They could not stay there for very long because of the bad air, but it served as a refuge into which they could retreat, and so kept them alive long enough to reconstitute a tumbledown hut they found on the bank of the steaming creek. Jack cut wood and dragged it back to Eliza, who arranged it. The roof would never keep rain out, but it shrugged off the snow. Jack still had a bit of silver. He used it to buy venison and rabbit from the miners, who set clever snares for game in the woods.

Their first month at the hot springs, then, consisted of small struggles won and forgotten the next day, and nothing passed between them except for the simple plans and affairs of peasants. But eventually things settled to the point where they did not have to spend every moment in toil. Jack did not care one way or the other. But Eliza let it be known that certain matters had been on her mind the entire time.

"Do you *mind*?" Jack was forced to blurt, one day in what was probably December.

"Pay no attention," Eliza snuffled. "Weather's a bit gloomy."

"If the *weather's* gloomy, what're *you*?"

"Just thinking of . . . things."

"Stop thinking then! This hovel's scarcely big enough to lie down in—have some consideration—there's a rivulet of tears running across the floor. Didn't we have a talk, months ago, about female moods?"

"Your concern is ever so touching. How can I thank you?"

"Stop weeping!"

She drew a few deep quivering breaths that made the hut shudder, and then crucified Jack with a counterfeit smile. "The regiment, then—"

"What's this?" Jack asked. "Keeping you alive isn't enough? I'm to provide entertainment as well?"

"You seem reluctant to talk about this. Perhaps you're a bit melancholy, too?"

"You have this clever little mind that never stops working. You're going to put my stories to ill-considered purposes. There are certain details, not really important, in which you'll take an unwholesome interest."

"Jack, we're living like brutes in the middle of the wilderness—what could I possibly do with a story as old as I am? And for God's sake, what else is there to do, when I lack thread and needles?"

"There you go again with the thread and the needles. Where do you suppose a brute in the wilderness would obtain such things?"

"Ask those miners to pick some up when next they go to town. They fetch oats for Turk all the time—why not a needle and thread?"

"If I do that, they'll know I've a woman here."

"You won't for long, if you don't tell me a story, or get me thread and needles."

"All right, then. The part of the story to which you're almost certain to over-react is that, although Sir Winston Churchill was not really an important man, his son John was *briefly* important. He's not any more. Probably never will be again, except in the world of courtiers."

"But you made his father out to be one notch above a Vagabond."

"Yes—and so John never would've reached the high position he did had he not been clever, handsome, brave, dashing, and good in the sack."

"When can you introduce me to him?"

"I know you're just trying to provoke me with that."

"Into what 'high position' exactly did he get?"

"The bed of the favorite mistress of King Charles the Second of England."

A brief pause for pressure to build, and then volcanic laughter from Eliza. Suddenly it was April. "You mean for me to believe that *you*—Half-Cocked 'don't call me a Vagabond' Jack—are personally acquainted with the lover of a mistress of a King?"

"Calm yourself—there are no chirurgeons here, if you should rupture something. And if you knew anything of the world outside of Asiatick Harems, you wouldn't be surprised—the King's *other* favorite mistress is Nell Gwyn—an *actress.*"

"I sensed all along that you were a Person of Quality, Jack. But pray tell—now that I've finally set your tongue in motion—how'd John Churchill get from his papa's regiment in Dorset to the royal sack?"

"Oh, mind you, John was never *attached* to that regiment—just visiting with his Dad. The family lived in London. Jack went to some foppish School there. Sir Winston pulled what few strings were available to him—probably whined about his great loyalty during the Interregnum—and got John appointed as a page to James, the Duke of York—the King's Papist brother—who, last I heard, was up in Edinburgh, going out of his mind and torturing Scotsmen. But back then, of course, round about 1670, the Duke of York was in London, and so John Churchill—being a member of his household—was there, too. Years passed. Bob and I fattened and grew like cattle for the Fair on soldiers' table-scraps."

"And so you did!"

"Don't pretend to admire me—you know my secrets. We plugged away at duties Regimental. John Churchill went to Tangiers for a few years to fight Barbary Pirates."

"Ooh, why couldn't he've rescued *me?*"

"Maybe he will, some day. What I'm getting to, though, is the Siege of Maestricht—a city in Holland."

"That's nowhere near Tangiers."

"Try to follow me here: he came back from Tangiers, all covered in glory. Meantimes Charles II had made a pact with, of all people, that King Looie of France, the arch-Papist, so rich that not only did he bribe the English opposition, but the *other* party, too, just to keep things interesting. So England and France, conjoined, made war, on land and at sea, with Holland. King Looie, accompanied by a mobile city of courtiers, mistresses, generals, bishops, official historians, poets, portrait-painters, chefs, musicians, and the retinues of *those* people, and the retinues' retinues, came up to Maestricht and threw a siege the way common kings throw parties. His camp was not quite as handsomely furnished as the Grand Vizier's before Vienna, but the folk were of higher quality. All the fashionable people of Europe had to be there. And John Churchill was quite fashionable. He came. Bob and I came with him."

"Now, that's where I have trouble following. Why invite two naughty lads?"

"First: we hadn't been naughty *recently.* Second: even the noblest gathering requires someone to empty piss-pots and (if it's a battle) stop musket-balls before they reach the better folk."

"Third?"

"There is no third."

"You lie. I can tell there was a third. Your lips parted, your finger came halfway up, and then you reconsidered."

"Very well then. The third was that John Churchill—courtier, sometime gigolo, fashionable blade-about-town—is the best military commander I have ever seen."

"Oh."

"Though that John Sobieski was not half bad. Anyway—pains me to admit it."

"Obviously."

"But it's true. And being an excellent commander, about to go into a real battle, he had the wit to bring along a few people who could actually get things done for him. It may seem hard for you to believe, but mark my word—whenever serious and competent people need to get things done in the real world, all considerations of tradition and protocol fly out the window."

"What did he suppose you and Bob could get done in the real world?"

"Carry messages across battlefields."

"Was he right?"

"Half right."

"*One* of you succeeded, and the other—"

"I didn't *fail.* I just found more intelligent ways to use my time."

"John Churchill gave you an order, and you refused?"

"No, no, no! It came about as follows. Now—did you pay any attention to the Siege of Vienna?"

"I watched with a keen eye, remember my virginity hung in the balance."

"Tell me how the Grand Vizier did it."

"Dug one trench after another before the walls, each trench a few yards closer than the last. From the foremost, dug tunnels beneath a sort of arrowhead-shaped fortress that lay outside the city—"

"A ravelin, it's called. All modern forts have them, including Maestricht."

"Blew it up. Advanced. And so on."

"That's how all sieges are conducted. Including Maestricht."

"So, then—?"

"All the pick-and-shovel work had been done by the time the swells arrived. The trenches and mines had been dug. Time was ripe to storm a particular outlying work, which an engineer would properly call a demilune, but similar to the ravelins you saw in Vienna."

"A separate fortress just outside of the main one."

"Yes. King Louie wanted that the English gentleman-warriors should, at the conclusion of this battle, either be in his debt, or in their graves, and so he gave to them the honor of storming the demilune. John Churchill and the Duke of Monmouth—King Charles's bastard—led the charge and carried the day. Churchill himself planted the French flag (disgusting to relate) on the parapet of the conquered fort."

"How splendid!"

"I told you he was important *once*. Back they came over the trench-scarred glacis, to our ditch-camp, for a night of celebration."

"So you were never asked to carry messages at all?"

"Next day, I felt the earth turn over, and looked toward that demilune to see fifty French troopers flying into the air. Maestricht's defenders had exploded a vast countermine beneath the demilune. Dutchmen charged into the gap and engaged the survivors in sword- and bayonet-play. They looked sure to retake the demilune and undo Churchill's and Monmouth's glorious deeds. I was not ten feet from John Churchill when it happened. Without a moment's hesitation he was off and running, sword in hand—it was obvious muskets would be useless. To save time, he ran across the surface—ignoring the trenches—exposing himself to musket-fire from the city's defenders, in full view of all those historians and poets watching through jeweled opera glasses from the windows of their coaches, just outside of artillery range. I stood there in amazement at his stupidity, until I realized that brother Bob was right behind him, matching him step-for-step."

"Then?"

"Then I was amazed at Bob's stupidity, too. Placing me, as I need hardly tell you, in an awkward spot."

"Always thinking of yourself."

"Fortunately the Duke of Monmouth appeared before me, that very moment, with a message that he wanted me to take to a nearby company of French musketeers. So I ran down the trench and located Monsieur D'Artagnan, the officer in ch—"

"Oh, stop!"

"What?"

"Even I've heard of D'Artagnan! You don't expect me to believe you—?"

"Is it all right with you if I get on with the story?"

Sigh. "Yes."

"Monsieur D'Artagnan, whom you don't appear to realize was a real human being and not just a figure in romantic legends, ordered his Musketeers forward. *All of us* advanced upon the demilune with conspicuous gallantry."

"I'm enthralled!" said Eliza, only a little sarcastic. At first she would not believe that Jack had actually met the celebrated D'Artagnan, but now that she did she was caught up in the tale.

"Because we did not bother to use the trenches, as *cowards* would've done, we reached the site of the fighting from a direction where the Dutch hadn't bothered to post proper defenses. All of us—French Musketeers, English bastards and gigolos, and Vagabond-messengers—got there at the same instant. But we could only advance through an opening just wide enough to admit one man at a time. D'Artagnan got there first and stood in the path of the Duke of Monmouth himself and begged him in the most gallant and polite French way not to go through that dangerous pass. Monmouth insisted. D'Artagnan consented—but only on the condition that he, D'Artagnan, should go through first. He did just that, and got shot in the head. The others advanced over him and went on to win ridiculous glory, while I stayed behind to look after D'Artagnan."

"He still lived!?"

"Hell no, his brains were all over me."

"But you stayed behind to guard his body—?"

"Actually, I had my eye on some heavy jewelled rings he was wearing."

For half a minute or so, Eliza adopted the pose of someone who'd just herself taken a musket-ball to the head and suffered an injury of unknown severity. Jack decided to move on to more glamorous parts of the tale, but Eliza dug in her heels. "While your brother risked all, you were *looting D'Artagnan's corpse?* I've never heard worse."

"Why?"

"It's so . . . so craven."

"You don't need to make it sound *cowardly*—I was in more danger than Bob was. The musket-balls were going through my *hat.*"

"Still . . ."

"The fighting was *over*. Those rings were the size of *doorknockers*. They would have buried that famed Musketeer with those rings on his fingers—if someone else hadn't looted them first."

"Did you take them, Jack?"

"He'd put them on when he was a younger and thinner man. They were impossible to move. So there I was with my foot planted in his fucking armpit—not the worst place my foot's ever been, but close—bending my fingernails back trying to get this ring up past the rolls of fat that'd grown up around it during his days of wine and women—asking myself whether I shouldn't just cut the damn finger off." Eliza now looked like someone who'd eaten a bad oyster. Jack decided to move on hastily. "When who should show up but brother Bob, with a look of self-righteous horror on his face, like a vicar who's just surprised an altar boy masturbating in the sacristy—or like *you,* for that matter—all dressed up in his little drummer boy outfit—carrying a message—frightfully urgent of course—from Churchill to one of King Looie's generals. He stops to favor me with a lecture about military honor. 'Ach, you don't really *believe* that stuff, do you?' I ask. 'Until today I didn't, Jack, but if you could see what I've seen just now—the feats that those brothers in arms, John Churchill and the Duke of Monmouth and Louis Hector de Villars, have performed—you'd believe.'"

"And then he sped onwards to deliver the message," Eliza said, getting a faraway look in her eye that was somewhat annoying to Jack, who wanted her to remain there in the hut with him. "And John Churchill never forgot Bob's loyalty and bravery."

"Yes—why, just a few months later Bob went to Westphalia with him and campaigned under French generals, as a mercenary, against hapless Protestants, sacking the Palatinate for the hundredth time. Can't remember what that had to do with military honor, exactly."

"*You,* on the other hand—"

"I took a few belts of cognac from D'Artagnan's flask and slunk back to the ditch."

This, at least, brought her back to the here (hut in Bohemia) and now (end of A.D. 1683). She directed the full power of her blue-eyed gaze against him. "You're always making yourself out to be such a ne'er-do-well, Jack—saying you'd have cut D'Artagnan's fingers off—proposing to blow up the Holy Roman Emperor's palace—but I don't think you're as bad as you say you are."

"My deformity gives me fewer chances to be bad than I should prefer to have."

"It is funny you should mention that, Jack. If you could find me a length of sound, unbroken deer or sheep intestine—"

"Why?"

"A Turkish practice—easier to show than explain. And if you could devote a few minutes in the hot spring to making yourself quite a bit cleaner than you are at the moment—the chance to be bad might present itself."

"ALL RIGHT, LET'S REHEARSE IT again. 'Jack, show the gentleman that bolt of the yellow watered silk.' Go on—that's your cue."

"Yes, milady."

"Jack, carry me across yonder mud-puddle."

"With pleasure, milady."

"Don't say 'with pleasure'—sounds naughty."

"As you wish, milady."

"Jack, that is very good—there's been a marked improvement."

"Don't suppose it has anything to do with that you've got your fist lodged in my arse-hole."

Eliza laughed gaily. "Fist? Jack, this is but two fingers. A fist would be more like—this!"

Jack felt his body being turned outside in—there was some thrashing and screaming that was cut short when his head accidentally submerged in the sulfurous water. Eliza got a grip on his hair and hauled his head back up into the cold air with her other hand.

"You're *sure* this is how they do it in India?"

"Would you like to register . . . a *complaint?*"

"Aaugh! Never."

"Remember, Jack: whenever serious and competent people need to get things done in the real world, all considerations of tradition and protocol fly out the window."

There followed a long, long, mysterious procedure—tedious and yet somehow not.

"What're you groping about for?" Jack muttered faintly. "My gall-bladder is just to the left."

"I'm trying to locate a certain *chakra*—should be somewhere around here—"

"What's a *chakra?*"

"You'll know when I find it."

Some time later, she did, and then the procedure took on greater intensity, to say the least. Suspended between Eliza's two hands, like a scale in a market-place, Jack could feel his balance-point shifting as quantities of fluids were pumped between internal

reservoirs, all in preparation for some Event. Finally, the crisis—
Jack's legs thrashed in the hot water as if his body were trying
to flee, but he was staked, impaled. A bubble of numenous light,
as if the sun were mistakenly attempting to rise inside his head.
Some kind of Hindoo apocalypse played out. He died, went to Hell,
ascended into Heaven, was reincarnated as various braying, screech-
ing, and howling beasts, and repeated this cycle many times over.
In the end he was reincarnated, just barely, as a Man. Not a very
alert one.

"Did you get what you wanted?" she inquired. Very close to him.

Jack laughed or wept soundlessly for a while.

"In some of these strange Gothickal German towns," he at last
said, "they have ancient clocks that are as big as houses, all sealed
up most of the time, with a little door where a cuckoo pops out
upon the hour to sing. But once a day, it does something special,
involving more doors, and once a week, something even specialer,
and, for all I know, at the year, decade, and century marks, rows of
great doors, all sealed shut by dust and age, creak open, driven by
sudden descent of ancient weights on rusted chains, and the whole
inner workings of the thing unfold through those openings. Hitherto unseen machines grind into action, strange and surprising
things fly out—flags wave, mechanical birds sing—old pigeon-shit
and cobwebs raining down on spectators' heads—Death comes out
and does a fandango—Angels blow trumpets—Jesus writhes on the
cross and expires—a mock naval battle plays out with repeated discharge of cannons—and would you please take your arm out of my
asshole now?"

"I did a long time ago—you nearly broke it!" Peeling off the knotted length of sheep-gut like an elegant lady removing a silken glove.

"So this is a permanent condition?"

"Stop whining. A few moments ago, Jack, unless my eyes
deceived me, I observed a startlingly large amount of yellow bile
departing your body, and floating away downstream."

"What are you talking about? I didn't barf."

"Think harder, Jack."

"Oh—*that* kind. I should not call it *yellow* but a pearly off-white.
Though it has been years since I saw any. Perhaps it has yellowed
over time, like cheese. Very well! Let's say 'twas yellow."

"Do you know what yellow bile is the humour of, Jack?"

"What am I, a physician?"

"It is the humour of anger and ill-temper. You were carrying a
lot of it around."

"Was I? Good thing I didn't let it affect my behavior."

"Actually I was hoping you might have a change of heart concerning needle and thread."

"Oh, that? I was never opposed to it. Consider it done Eliza."

❧

Leipzig
APRIL 1684

☙

From all I hear of Leibniz he must be very intelligent, and pleasant company in consequence. It is rare to find learned men who are clean, do not stink, and have a sense of humour.

—LISELOTTE IN A LETTER TO SOPHIE,
30 JULY 1705

"JACQUES, SHOW THE GENTLEMAN THAT bolt of the yellow watered silk . . . Jacques? *Jacques!*" Eliza moved on smoothly to some cruel jest about how difficult it was to find reliable and hard-working varlets nowadays, speaking in a French that was too good for Jack to understand. The gentleman in question—evidently a Parisian in the rag trade—took his nose out of Eliza's cleavage long enough to glance up into her eyes and chuckle uncertainly—he sensed a *bon mot* had been issued but he hadn't heard it.

"Cor, he's surprised your tits come wi' a head attached," Jack observed.

"Shut up . . . one of these days, we're going to meet someone who speaks English," Eliza returned, and nodded at the bolt. "Would you please stay awake?"

"Haven't been so awake in half a year—that's the difficulty," Jack said, stooping down to unroll an arm's length of silk, and drawing it through the air like a flag, trying to make it waft. A shaft of sunlight would've been useful. But the only radiant heavenly body shedding light into this courtyard was Eliza's—turned out in one of a few dresses she'd been working on for months. Jack had watched them

413
❧

come together out of what looked to him like scraps, and so the effect on him was not as powerful. But when Eliza walked through the market, she drew such looks that Jack practically had to bind his right arm to his side, lest it fly across his body and whip out the Damascus blade and teach the merchants of Leipzig some manners.

She got into a long difference of opinion with this Parisian, which ended when he handed her an old limp piece of paper that had been written on many times, in different hands, and then collected the bolt of yellow silk from Jack and walked away with it. Jack once again had to restrain his sword-hand. "This kills me."

"Yes. You say that every time."

"You're certain that those scraps are worth something."

"Yes! Says so right here," Eliza said. "Would you like me to read it to you?" A dwarf came by selling chocolates.

"Won't help. Nothing will, but silver in my pocket."

"Are you worried I'm going to cheat you—being that you can't read the numbers on these bills of exchange?"

"I'm worried something'll happen to 'em before we can turn 'em into real money."

"What is 'real' money, Jack? Answer me that."

"You know, pieces of eight, or, how d'you say it, dollars—"

"Th—it starts with a T but it's got a breathy sound behind it—'thalers.'"

"D-d-d-dollars."

"That's a silly name for money, Jack—no one'll ever take you seriously, talking that way."

"Well, they shortened 'Joachimsthaler' to 'thaler,' so why not reform the word even further?"

A KIND OF STEADILY WAXING madness had beset them after a month or so at their hot-springs encampment—Jack had assumed it was the slow-burning fuse of the French Pox finally reaching significant parts of his mind, until Eliza had pointed out they'd been on bread and water and the occasional rasher of carp jerky for months. A soldier's pay was not generous, but put together with what Jack had previously looted from the rich man's house in Strasbourg, it would supply not only Turk with oats but also them with cabbages, potatoes, turnips, salt pork, and the occasional egg—*as long as Jack didn't mind spending all of it*. As his commission-agents, he employed those two brimstone-miners, Hans and Hans. They were not free agents, but employees of one Herr Geidel of Joachimsthal, a nearby town where silver was dug out of the ground. Herr Geidel hired men like Hans and Hans to dig up the ore and refine it into irregular bars, which they took to a mint in the town to be coined into Joachimsthalers.

Herr Geidel, having learned that a strange armed man was lurking in the woods near his brimstone mine, had ridden out with a few musketeers to investigate, and discovered Eliza all alone, at her sewing. By the time Jack returned, hours later, Eliza and Herr Geidel had, if not exactly become friends, then at least recognized each other as being of the same type, and therefore as possible business partners, though it was by no means clear what *kind* of business. Herr Geidel had the highest opinion of Eliza and voiced confidence that she would make out handsomely at the Leipzig Fair. His immediate opinion of Jack was much lower—the only thing Jack seemed to have going for him was that Eliza was willing to partner up with him. Jack, for his part, put up with Herr Geidel because of the flabbergasting nature of what he did for a living: *literally making money.* The first several times this was explained to Jack, he put it down to a translation error. It couldn't be real. "That's all there is? Dig up some dirt, run it through a furnace, stamp a face and some words on it?"

"That's what he seems to be saying," Eliza had answered, puzzled for once. "In Barbary, all the coins were pieces of eight from Spain—I've never been anywhere near a mint. I was about to say 'wouldn't know a mint from a hole in the ground,' but apparently that's just what it *is.*"

When it had gotten warm enough to move, they'd gone down into Joachimsthal and confirmed that it was little more than that. In essence the mint was a brute with a great big hammer and a punch. He was supplied with blank disks of silver—these were not money—put the punch on each one and bashed it with the hammer, mashing the portrait of some important hag, and some incantations in Latin, into it—at which point it *was* money. Officials, supervisors, assayers, clerks, guards, and, in general, the usual crowd of parasitical gentlefolk clustered around the brute with the hammer, but like lice on an ox they could not conceal the simple nature of the beast. The simplicity of money-making had fascinated Jack into a stupor. "Why should we ever leave this place? After all my wanderings I've found Heaven."

"It can't be that easy. Herr Geidel seems depressed—he's branching out into brimstone and other ores—says he can't make any money making money."

"Obvious nonsense. Just trying to scare away competition."

"Did you see all those abandoned mines, though?"

"Ran out of ore," Jack had attempted.

"Then why were the great mining-engines still bestriding the pit-mouths? You'd think they'd've moved them to shafts that were still fruitful."

Jack had had no answer. When next they'd seen Herr Geidel, Eliza had subjected him to a round of brutal questioning that would've gotten Jack into a duel had he done it, but coming from Eliza had only given Herr Geidel a heightened opinion of her. Geidel's French was as miserable as Jack's and so the discussion had gone slowly enough for Jack to follow: for reasons that no one around here fathomed, the Spanish could mine and refine silver in Mexico, and ship it halfway round the world (in spite of the most strenuous efforts by English, Dutch, French, Maltese, and Barbary pirates) cheaper than Herr Geidel and his drinking buddies could produce it in Joachimsthal and ship it a few days' journey to Leipzig. Consequently, only the very richest mines in Europe were still operating. Herr Geidel's strategy was to put idle miners to work digging up brimstone (before the European silver mines had crashed, this never would've worked because they had a strong guild, but now miners were cheap), then ship the brimstone to Leipzig and sell it cheap to gunpowder-makers, in hopes of bringing the cost of gunpowder, and hence of war, down.* Anyway, if war got cheap enough, all hell would break loose, some Spanish galleons might even get sunk, and the cost of silver would climb back to a more wholesome level.

"But won't that also make it cheaper for highwaymen to attack you on the way to Leipzig?" Jack had asked, always working the violent crime angle.

Eliza had given him a look that promised grim penalties the next time she got her hand on the *chakra*. " 'What if war breaks out between here and Leipzig?' is what Jack meant to say."

But Herr Geidel had been completely unfazed. Wars broke out all the time, all over the place, with no effect on the Leipzig Fair. If all of this came to pass, he'd be a rich merchant again. And for five hundred years the Leipzig fairs had operated under a decree from the Holy Roman Emperor stating that as long as the merchants stuck to certain roads and paid a nominal fee to local princes

---

*It turned out that if you did the mathematicks on a typical war, the cost of powder was more important than just about anything else—Herr Geidel insisted that the gunpowder in the arsenal of Venice, for example, was worth more than the annual revenue of the entire city. This explained a lot of oddness Jack had witnessed in various campaigns and forced him to reconsider (briefly) his opinion that all officers were mad.

whose lands they traversed, they could pass freely to and from Leipzig, and must not be molested even if they were traipsing across an active battlefield. They were *above wars*.

"But what if you were carrying gunpowder to sell to the enemy?" Eliza had tried, but for once Herr Geidel had looked impatient and waved her off, as if to say that wars were mere diversions for bored princes, but trade fairs were *serious*.

It turned out to be perfectly all right that Jack had mentioned highwaymen, because Herr Geidel had been doing a lot of thinking on that very subject. His wagon-train had been forming up in the open places of Joachimsthal. Harnessed pairs of draft-horses were being walked down streets by teamsters leaning back to put tension on the traces, talking the animals into place before wagons. Mule-drivers were pretending to be flabbergasted when their animals balked after testing the weight of their loads: the first act of a timeless play that would eventually lead to profanity and violence. Herr Geidel was *not* a rich merchant now, and for the first part of the journey, he would not be taking any of those roads where armed escorts were for hire *anyway,* and so the trip to the Easter fair in Leipzig might be exciting. Herr Geidel had a few men who could go through the motions needed to charge and discharge a musket, but he wouldn't mind adding Jack to his escort, and of course Eliza was welcome to ride along in one of the wagons.

Jack, wotting that Eliza and his boys' inheritance were at stake, had taken this soldiering job more seriously than most. From time to time he had sallied ahead of the cart-train to look for ambushes. Twice he'd found rabbles of unemployed miners loitering sheepishly in narrow parts of the way, armed with pikes and cudgels, and gotten them to disperse by explaining Herr Geidel's plan to restore vigor to the silver mining business. In truth it wasn't his oratory that moved them out of the way so much as that he and his comrades were carrying flintlocks and pistols. Jack, who knew his wretches, could tell at a glance that these men weren't hungry enough, or persuasively led enough, to buy loot with their lives—particularly when the loot was brimstone, which, he reminded them, would be difficult to turn into silver—they'd have to lug it to a fair and sell it, unless there was an Alchemist among them. He did not mention that buried under the rubble of brimstone in one of Herr Geidel's wagons was a chest full of freshly minted Joachimsthalers. He did *think* about mentioning it, and then leading an ambush *himself,* but he knew that in that event he'd ride away without Eliza, the one woman in the world, or at least the only one he personally knew, capable of providing him with carnal satisfaction.

He understood then why Herr Geidel had observed his conversations with Eliza so intently—trying to see whether Jack could be trusted. Apparently he'd concluded Eliza had Jack well in hand. This did not sit well with Jack—but he'd be rid of Herr Geidel soon enough, though not of Eliza.

Anyway, they had ridden north out of those mountains, which Herr Geidel had referred to in his tongue simply as the Ore Range, and into Saxony, about which there was nothing to say except that it was flat. They joined up with a very great and old road that according to Herr Geidel ran from Verona all the way north to Hamburg. Jack was impressed by the mileposts: ten-foot-high stone spikes, each ornately carved with the arms of some dead King, each giving the number of miles to Leipzig. This road was congested with many other merchants' wagon-trains.

In a moist flat basin scribbled all over with the courses of aimless rivers, it intersected another great road that was said to run from Frankfurt to the Orient, and Leipzig *was* that intersection. Jack had most of a day to ramble around and view it from its outskirts, which he did on the general principle of wanting to know where the exits were before entering any confined place. The wagon-trains were backed up for half a mile waiting to get in at the south gate. Leipzig, he found, was smaller and lower-slung than Vienna—a city of several modest spires, not one sky-raking cathedral, which Jack guessed was a sign of its being a Lutheran burg. Of course it was surrounded by the obligatory ramparts and bastions. Outside these were estates and gardens, several of 'em larger than the entire city, all of them belonging not to nobles but to merchants.* Between these estates lay the usual embarrassing swine-crowded suburbs cowering in makeshift barricades that were more like baskets than walls. A few lazily turning mill-wheels took advantage of the nearly imperceptible stirring of the rivers, but millers scarcely ranked above peasants in a town so topheavy with merchants.

JACK AND ELIZA HAD PAID ten pfennigs each at the town gate, then had their silks weighed, and paid duty on them (Eliza had sewn the ostrich-plumes between layers of petticoats, and they were not detected). From the gate a broad street ran north to the center of the town, no more than a musket-shot away. Climbing down from the saddle, Jack was startled by the feel of cobblestones under his

---

*Which Jack could tell by interpreting the coats of arms carved on the gateposts and embroidered on the flags.

feet for the first time in half a year. He was treading on ground that pushed back now, and he knew that his boots needed re-soling. The street was lined with vaulted orifices spewing noise; he felt continually under ambush from left and right, and kept patting his sword-pommel, then hating himself for behaving like a stupid peasant on his first trip to Paris. But Eliza was no less amazed, and kept backing into him, liking to feel his pressure against her back. Queer signs and effigies, frequently in gold leaf, loomed on the fronts of the buildings: a golden snake, a Turk's head, a red lion, a golden bear. So they were a bit like English taverns, which had effigies instead of names, so that people like Jack, who could not read, could know them. But they were not taverns. They were like large town-houses, with many windows, and each had this large vaulted opening giving way to a courtyard full of Bedlam.

Jack and Eliza had kept moving out of an unvoiced fear that if they stopped they'd appear just as lost and stupid as they in fact were. Within a few minutes they'd entered into the town square, and drawn up near a scaffold with the usual selection of dead men hanging from it: a place of comforting familiarity to Jack, even if Eliza did make shrewish comments about the thrumming clouds of flies. Notwithstanding the odd dangling corpse, Leipzig didn't even smell that bad: there was the sewage and smoke of any big town, but it was amazing what a few tons of saffron, cardamom, star anise, and black pepper, distributed round in sacks and bales, would do to freshen a place up.

The town hall ran along one side of the square, and sported Dutch-looking gables above and an arcade of vaulted brown stone at ground level, where well-dressed men were working quietly and intensely. Narrow ditches were incised across the square to channel sewage, and planks had been thrown over them so carts could roll across, or ladies, and fat or lame men, pass over without having to make spectacles of themselves. Jack turned around a couple of times. It was plain that buildings were limited by law to four stories because none (save church towers) had more than that. But clearly the law said nothing about *roofs* and so these were all extremely high and steep—frequently as high as the four-story buildings that supported them—so seen from the street each roof looked like a mountain ridge seen from the valley: a vast terrain densely settled and built up with dormers, towers, gables, cupolas, balconies, and even miniature castles; vegetation (in window-boxes) and statues— not of Jesus or some saint but of Mercury in his winged slippers and hat. Sometimes he was paired against Minerva with her snaky shield, but most of the time Mercury appeared alone and it didn't take a Doctor of Letters to understand that he, and not some dolorous martyr, had been chosen as Patron of Leipzig.

Looking up at vast rooves had been Jack's way to relieve his eyes and mind from the strain of following the action on the ground. There were Eastern men in felt hats with giant rims of rich gleaming fur, talking to long-bearded Jews about racks of animal pelts—the faces of small nasty critters gaping blankly at the sky. Chinese carrying crates of what he had to assume was China, coopers repairing busted casks, bakers hawking loaves, blonde maidens with piles of oranges, musicians everywhere, grinding hurdy-gurdys or plucking at mutant lutes with huge cantilevers projecting asymmetrically from their necks to support thumping bass halyards. Armenian coffee-sellers carrying bright steaming copper and brass tanks on their persons, bored guards with pikes or halberds, turbaned Turks attempting to buy back strange goods that (Jack realized with a shock) had *also* been looted from the Vienna siege-camp—he was amused but, actually, embarrassed and irritated that others had had the same idea. A hookah-smoking area where Turkish boys in pointy-toed slippers scurried from one small table to the next carrying smouldering braziers of ornately wrought silver from which they selected individual coals with silver tongs and placed them carefully atop the hookahs' tobacco-bowls to keep them burning. Everywhere, goods: but here in the square they were in casks, or wrapped up in square bales held together by rope-nets, all marked with curious initials and monograms: trade-marks of diverse merchants.

They'd found a place to stable Turk, then gone down a street, worked up their courage, and entered into one of those broad vaulted portals—wide and high enough for three or four horsemen to ride abreast—and entered the courtyard of one of those buildings. This yard was only some ten by twenty paces, and hemmed in on all sides by the four-story-high walls of the building, which were painted a merry yellow so that what sun did enter the yard cast a symbolic golden radiance on all. The court itself was stuffed with people displaying spices, metal goods, jewels, books, fabric, wine, wax, dried fish, hats, boots, gloves, weapons, and porcelain, frequently standing cheek-to-cheek and talking directly into each other's ears. One whole side of the courtyard, then, gave way to a line of open-sided vaults: an arcade a couple of steps above courtyard level, separated from the courtyard only by a row of stout pillars, and tucked in underneath the actual house. In each vault a grave man in good clothes sat at a mighty desk, or *banca,* with several immense Books, strapped, buckled, and padlocked shut when not in use; an inkwell; quills; and on the floor next to him, a black chest all wrapped about with bronze or iron straps, hinges, chains, and locks of a weight and quality normally seen on arsenal-gates. Sometimes bales and casks of goods were mounded up next to him. More often, the stuff was piled out in the courtyard. Sixty or eighty feet above, stout beams projected from the tops of dormers, thrusting pulleys out over the yard, and by means of ropes through those pulleys, laborers hoisted the goods up for storage in the cavernous attics.

"They are betting prices will rise," Eliza said, observing this, and this was the first inkling Jack received that this was more than a country swap-meet, and that there were layers of cleverness at work here that went far beyond simply knowing how many thalers should buy a tub of butter.

Jack saw so much that was strange in Leipzig, and saw it so fast, that he had to put most of it out of his mind immediately to make room for new material, and didn't remember it until later, when taking a piss or trying to go to sleep, and when he *did* remember it, it seemed so strange to him that he couldn't be sure whether it was a dream, or something that had really happened, or proof that the mines that the French Pox had (he suspected) been patiently excavating under his brain for the last several years, had finally begun to detonate.

There had been, for example, a trip inside one of the factories* to exchange some odd coins that Jack had picked up along his travels and been unable to spend, as no one recognized them. In this room, men sat behind desks with books in whose pages were circular cut-outs made to hold coins—two of each coin, so both heads and tails could be viewed in the same glance, and each coin labeled with various cryptic numbers and symbols in different colors of ink. The money-changer paged steadily through this book until he found a page holding coins just like Jack's, though crisper and shinier. He took out a færy-sized scale made out of gold, whose pans, no larger than dollars, were suspended from its fragile crossbar by blue silken cords. He put Jack's coins on one pan and then, using tweezers, piled featherweight scraps of marked gold foil on the other pan until they balanced. Then he put the scale back into its wooden carrying-case, which was smaller than Eliza's hand; did some calculations; and offered Jack a couple of Leipziger Ratsmarken (Leipzig minted its own coins). Eliza insisted they visit a

---

*As the trading-houses were called, because important men called factors inhabited and ran them.

couple of other money-changers and repeat the ceremony, but the results were always the same. So finally they accepted the Leipziger coins and then watched the money-changer fling Jack's old coins into a box in the corner, half full of assorted coins and fragments of jewelry, mostly black from tarnish. "We'll melt it down," he explained when he saw the look on Jack's face. Eliza, meanwhile, was staring at a wall-chart of exchange rates, reading the names of the coins that had been chalked up there: "Louis d'or, Maximilian d'or, souverain d'or, rand, ducat, Louis franc, Breslau ducat, Schildgroschen, Hohlheller, Schwertgroschen, Oberwehr groschen, Hellengroschen, pfennig, Goldgulden, hal-berspitzgroschen, Engelsgroschen, Real, Ratswertmark, ⅔ thaler, English shilling, ruble, abassid, rupiah . . ."

"Just goes to prove we have to get into the money-making business," Jack said when they left.

"To me it proves that the business is crowded and hard-fought," Eliza said. "Better to get into silver-mining. All the coiners must buy from miners."

"But Herr Geidel would rather have burning splints under his nails than own another silver mine," Jack reminded her.

"It would seem to me *better* to buy into something when it is cheap, and wait for it to become dear," Eliza said. "Think of those trading-houses with their attics."

"We don't have an attic."

"I meant it as a figure of speech."

"So did I. We have no way to purchase a silver mine and sew it into your skirts and carry it round until the price goes up." This sounded to Jack like a sure-fire conversation ender but only produced a thoughtful expression on Eliza's face.

Consequently they found themselves at the Bourse, a small tidy rectangular building of white stone packed with well-dressed men screaming at each other in all the languages of Christendom but bound together by some Pentecostal faith in the Holy Spirit of the Messe that made all tongues one. There were no goods in evidence, only bits of paper, which was so odd that Jack would've stayed up all night wondering over it if he hadn't forgotten immediately in light of later developments. After a brief conversation with a trader who was taking a breather on the edge of the floor, smoking a clay-pipe and quaffing some of that fine golden beer from Pilsen, Eliza returned to Jack with a triumphant and determined look about her that boded ill. "The word is *Kuxen*," she said, "we wish to buy *Kuxen* in a silver mine."

"We *do?*"

"Isn't that what we just decided?" She was joking, perhaps.

"First tell me what *Kuxen* are."

"Shares. The mine is divided in half. Each half into quarters. Each quarter into eighths, and so on—until the number of shares is something like sixty-four or one twenty-eight—that number of shares is then sold. Each share is called a *kux.*"

"And by share, I suppose you mean—?"

"Same as when thieves divvy up their swag."

"I was going to liken it to how sailors partake of a voyage's proceeds, but you stooped lower, faster."

"That man nearly shot beer from his nostrils when I said I wished to invest in a silver mine," Eliza said proudly.

"Always a positive omen."

"He said only one man's even trying to sell them at this fair—the Doctor. We need to talk to the Doctor."

Through involved and tedious investigations that little improved the balance of Jack's humours, they tracked the Doctor down in the general quarter of the *Jahrmarkt,* which (never mind what the German words literally meant) was a fun fair—a sideshow to the *Messe.* "Eeeyuh, I hate these things—loathsome people exhibiting all manner of freakish behaviors—like a morality play depicting my own life."

"The Doctor is in there," Eliza said grimly.

"Why not let's wait until we actually have money to buy kuxen *with?*" Jack pleaded.

"Jack, it is all the same—if we want kuxen, why pass through the intermediate step of exchanging silk or ostrich-plumes for coin, and then coin for kuxen, when we could simply exchange silk or plumes for kuxen?"

"Ow, that one was like a stave to the bridge of the nose. You're saying—"

"I'm saying that at Leipzig all goods—silk, coins, shares in mines—lose their hard dull gross forms and liquefy, and give up their true nature, as ores in an alchemist's furnace sweat mercury—and all mercury is mercury and can be freely swapped for mercury of like weight—indeed cannot be distinguished from it."

"That's lovely, but DO WE REALLY WANT TO OWN SHARES IN A MINE?"

"Oh, who knows?" Eliza said with an airy tossing movement of the hand. "I just like to shop for things."

"And I'm doomed to follow you, carrying your purse," Jack muttered, shifting the burden of silk-bolts from one shoulder to the other.

So to the Fun Fair—indistinguishable (to Jack) from a hospital for the possessed and deformed and profoundly lost: contortionists, rope-walkers, fire-eaters, foreigners, and mystical personalities, a few of whom Jack recognized from Vagabond-camps here and there. They knew the Doctor from his clothing and his wig, about which they'd been warned. He was trying to initiate a philosophickal dispute with a Chinese fortune-teller, the subject of the debate being a diagram on a book-page consisting of a stack of six short horizontal lines, some of which were continuous (—) and others interrupted (– –) The Doctor was trying various languages out on the Chinese man, who only looked more aggrieved and dignified by the moment. Dignity was a clever weapon to use against the Doctor, who did not have very much of it at the moment. On his head was the largest wig Jack had ever seen, a thunderhead of black curls enveloping and dwarfing his head and making him look, from behind, as if a yearling bear-cub had dropped from a tree onto his shoulders and was trying to wrench his head off. His attire was no less formidable. Now, during the long winter, Jack had learned that a dress had more parts, technical zargon, and operating procedures associated with it than a flintlock. The Doctor's outfit mocked any dress: between Leipzig and his skin there had to be two dozen layers of fabric belonging to Christ knew how many separate garments: shirts, waistcoats, vests, and things of which Jack did not know the names. Rank upon rank of heavy, close-spaced buttons, containing, in the aggregate, enough brass to cast a swivel-gun. Straps and draw-strings, lace gushing from the openings around throat and wrists. But the lace needed washing, the wig needed professional maintenance, and the Doctor himself was not, at root, a good-looking man. And despite the attire, Jack ended up suspecting he was not a vain one; he was dressed that way to a purpose. In particular, perhaps, to make himself seem older—when he turned around at the sound of Eliza's voice, it was evident he was no more than about forty years old.

He was up on his three-inch platform heels right away, favoring Eliza with a deep, courtly bow and shortly moving on to hand-kissing. For a minute all was in French that Jack couldn't quite follow, and so he went by appearances: Eliza looked uncharacteristically nervous (though she was trying to be plucky), and the Doctor, a lively and quick sort, was observing with polite curiosity. But there was no drooling or leering. Jack reckoned him for a eunuch or sodomite.

Suddenly the Doctor broke into English—making him the first

person, other than Eliza, whom Jack had heard speaking in the tongue of that remote Isle in a couple of years. "I assumed, from your attire, that you were a fashionable Parisian lady. But I judged too hastily, for I perceive, on closer enjoyment, that you have something that such women typically lack: genuine taste."

Eliza was speechless—flattered by the words, but flustered by the choice of language. The Doctor splayed a hand across his breast and looked apologetic. "Have I made the wrong guess? I thought I detected that the lady's superb French was enlivened and invigorated by the firm sure tread of an Anglo-Saxon cadence."

"Bullseye," Jack said, drawing a raised eyebrow from the Doctor and a glare from Eliza. Now that he knew the Doctor spoke English, it was all Jack could do to limit himself to that one word—he wanted to talk, talk, talk—to make jests* and to voice his opinions on diverse subjects, relate certain anecdotes, *et cetera*. He said "Bullseye" because he was afraid Eliza might try to brazen it out by claiming to be from some odd corner of France, and Jack, who had much experience in brazening, and attempting to sustain elaborate lies, sensed that this would be a losing bet with the annoyingly perceptive Doctor.

"When you have resolved your differences with the Oriental gentleman, I should like to take you up on the subject of *Kuxen*," said Eliza.

A double eye-brow raise greeted this news, causing the topheavy wig to pitch alarmingly. "Oh, I'm free *immediately*," he said, "this Mandarin seems to have no desire to refine his philosophickal position—to disentangle the worthy *science* of number *theory* from the base *superstition* of *numerology*—most unfortunate for him and the rest of his race."

"I am not well versed in any of those subjects," Eliza began, obviously (to Jack) making an heroic bid to change the subject, and obviously (to the Doctor) begging to be given an advanced course of instruction.

"Fortune-tellers frequently make use of a random element, such as cards or tea-leaves," the Doctor began. "This fellow tosses sticks on the ground and reads them, never mind exactly how—all I'm interested in is the end result—a set of half a dozen lines, each of which is either solid or broken. We could do the same thing by flipping six coins—*videlicet . . .*" and here he went into a performance of slapping himself all over, like a man who has a mouse in his

---

*E.g., "Hey, Doc, how many goats were shaved to make that wig?"

clothing, and whenever he detected a coin in one of the manifold pockets of his many garments, he scooped it out and flipped it into the air, letting it clang like a Chinese gong (for the coins tended to be big ones—many of them gold) on the paving-stones. "He's rich," Jack muttered to Eliza, "or connected with rich persons."

"Yes—the clothes, the coins . . ."

"All fakeable."

"How do you know him to be rich, then?"

"In the wilderness, only the most terrible beasts of prey cavort and gambol. Deer and rabbits play no games."

"Very well, then," said the Doctor, bending to peer at the fallen coins. "We have heads, tails, tails, tails, heads, and tails." He straightened up. "To the Chinese mystic this pattern has some great significance which he will, for a small fee, look up in a book, jammed with heathen claptrap, and read to you." The Doctor had forgotten about the coins, and about the circle of fun-fair habitués closing in on it like a noose, each making his best guess (as they lacked scales and books) as to which of them was most valuable. Jack stepped in, using his thumb to nudge his sword a hand's breadth out of its scabbard. Their reaction made it plain they were all keeping one eye on him. He picked up the coins, which he would return to the Doctor in a tremendously impressive display of honesty and sound moral character whenever he snapped out of his rant. "To me, on the other hand, this pattern means: seventeen."

"Seventeen?" Jack and Eliza said in unison—both of them had to step lively, now, to keep pace with the Doctor as he stomped out of the *Jahrmarkt* making good time on those high heels. He wasn't a big man but he had a fine set of calves on him, which his stockings showed off nicely.

"Dyadic, or binary numbers—old news," the Doctor said, waving a hand in the air so that the lace cuff flopped around. "My late friend and colleague Mr. John Wilkins published a cryptographic system based on this more than forty years ago in his great *Cryptonomicon*—unauthorized Dutch editions of it are still available over yonder in the Booksellers' Quarter should you desire. But what I take away from the Chinese method of fortune-telling is the notion of producing *random* numbers by the dyadic technique, and by this Wilkins's system could be incomparably strengthened." All of which was like the baying of hounds to Jack.

"Crypto, graphy . . . writing of secrets?" Eliza guessed.

"Yes—an unfortunate necessity in these times," the Doctor said.

About now, they escaped the closeness of the Fun Fair and stopped in an open square near a church. "Nicolaikirche—I was baptized there," the Doctor said. "*Kuxen!* A topic strangely related to dyadic numbers in that the number of *Kuxen* in a particular mine is always a power of two, *videlicet:* one, two, four, eight, sixteen . . . But that is a mathematical curiosity in which you'll have little interest. I am selling them. Should you buy them? Formerly a prosperous industry, upon which the fortunes of great families such as the Fuggers and Hacklhebers were founded, silver mining was laid low by the Thirty Years' War and the discovery, by the Spaniards, of very rich deposits at Potosí in Peru and Guanajuato in Mexico. Buying *Kuxen* in a European mine that is run along *traditional* lines, as is done in the Ore Range, would be a waste of the lady's money. But my mines or I should say the mines of the House of Brunswick-Lüneburg, which I have been given the responsibility to manage, will be, I think, a better investment."

"Why?" Eliza asked.

"It is *extremely* difficult to explain."

"Oh, but you're so good at explaining things . . ."

"You really must leave the flattery to me, milady, as you are more deserving of it. No, it has to do with certain new sorts of engines, of my own design, and new techniques for extracting metal from ore, devised by a very wise and, as alchemists go, non-fraudulent alchemist of my acquaintance. But a woman of your conspicuous acumen would never exchange her coins—"

"Silk, actually," Jack inserted, turning half round to flash the goods.

"Er . . . lovely silks, then, for *Kuxen* in my mine, just because I *said* these things in a market."

"Probably true," Eliza admitted.

"You would have to inspect the works first. Which I invite you to do . . . we leave tomorrow . . . but if you could exchange your goods for *coin* first it would be—"

"Wait!" Jack said, it being his personal duty to play the role of coarse, armed bumpkin. Giving Eliza the opportunity to say: "Good Doctor, my interest in the subject was just a womanish velleity—forgive me for wasting your time—"

"But why bother talking to me at all then? You must've had some reason. Come on, it'll be fun."

"Where is it?" Jack asked.

"The *lovely* Harz Mountains—a few days' journey west of here."

"That'd be in the general direction of Amsterdam, then?"

"Young sir, when I spied your Turkish sword, I took you for some sort of Janissary, but your knowledge of the lands to the West proves otherwise—even if your East London accent hadn't already given you away."

"Uh, okay, so that's a yes, then," Jack mumbled, leading Eliza a few paces away. "A free ride in the Doctor's train—can't be too much wrong with that."

"He's up to something," Eliza protested.

"So are *we*, lass—it's not a crime."

Eventually she wafted back over to the Doctor and allowed as how she'd be willing to "leave my entourage behind" for a few days, with the exception of "my faithful manservant and bodyguard," and "detour to the Harz Mountains" to inspect the works. They talked, for a while, in French.

"He says a lot in a hurry sometimes," Eliza told Jack as they followed the Doctor, at a distance, down a street of great trading-houses. "I tried to find out approximately what a *kux* would cost—he said not to worry."

"Funny, from a man who claims he's trying to raise money . . ."

"He said that the reason he first took me for Parisian was that ostrich plumes, like the sample in my hat, are in high fashion there just now."

"More flattery."

"No—his way of telling me that we should ask a high price."

"Where's he taking us?"

"The House of the Golden Mercury, which is the factory of the von Hacklheber family."

"We've already been kicked out of there."

"He's going to get us in."

AND THAT HE DID, by means of a mysterious conversation that took place inside the factory, out of their view. This was the biggest courtyard they'd seen in Leipzig: narrow but long, lined with vaulted arcades on both sides, a dozen cranes active at once elevating goods that the von Hacklhebers expected to rise in price, and letting down ones they thought had reached their peak. At the end nearest the street, mounted to the wall above the entry arch, was a skinny three-story-high structure cantilevered outwards over the yard, like balconies on three consecutive floors all merged into one tower. It was enclosed with windows all round except on the top floor, where a golden roof sheltered an open platform and supported a pair of obscenely long-necked gargoyles poised to vomit rain (should it rain) out onto the traders below. "Reminds me of the castle on the butt-end of a galleon," was Eliza's comment, and it wasn't for a few minutes that Jack understood that this was a reminder of the naughty business off Qwghlm years ago, and (therefore) her oblique female way of saying she didn't like it. This despite the gold-plated Mercury, the size of a man, bracketed to it, which seemed to be springing into flight above their heads, holding out a golden stick twined about with snakes and surmounted by a pair of wings. "No, it's a Cathedral of Mercury," Jack decided, trying to get her mind off the galleon. "Your Cathedral of Jesus is cross-shaped. This one takes its plan from that stick in his hand—long and slender—the vaults on the sides like the snakes' loops. The wings of the factory spreading out from the head of it, where is mounted the bishop's pulpit, and all of us believers crowded in below to celebrate the *Messe.*"

Eliza sold the stuff. Jack assumed she sold it well. He knew they were soon to leave Leipzig and so amused himself by looking around. Watching the bales and casks ascend and descend on their ropes, his eye was drawn to a detail: from many of the countless windows that lined the courtyard, short rods projected horizontally into the air, and mounted to their ends, on ball-joints like the one where the thigh-bone meets the pelvis, were mirrors about a foot square, canted at diverse angles. When he first noticed them Jack supposed that they were a clever trick for reflecting sunlight into those many dim offices. But looking again he saw that they shifted frequently, and that their silvered faces were always aimed *down* toward the courtyard. There were scores of them. Jack never glimpsed the watchers who lurked in the dark rooms.

Later he chanced to look up at the highest balcony, and discovered a new gargoyle looking back at him: this was made of flesh and blood, a stout man who hadn't bothered to cover his partly bald, partly grizzled head. He had battled smallpox and won at the cost of whatever good or even bad looks he might ever have had. Quite a few decades of good living had put a lot of weight into his face and drawn the pocked flesh downwards into jowls and wattles and chins, lumpy as cargo nets. He was giving Eliza a look that Jack did not find suitable. Up there on that balcony he was such an arresting presence that Jack did not notice, for a few minutes, that another man, much more finely turned out, was up there, too: the Doctor, talking in the relentless way of one who's requesting a favor, and gesturing so that those white lace cuffs seemed to flit around him like a pair of doves.

Like a couple of peasants huddled together in the Cathedral of Notre Dame, Jack and Eliza performed their role in the Mass and then departed, leaving no sign that they'd ever been there, save perhaps for a evanescent ripple in the coursing tide of quicksilver.

❧

Saxony
LATE APRIL 1684

LEAVING LEIPZIG WITH THE DOCTOR did not happen at any one particular moment—it was a ceremonial procession that extended over a day. Even after Jack and Eliza and Turk the Horse had located the Doctor's entourage, several hours of wandering around the town still awaited them: there was a mysterious call at the von Hacklheber factory, and a stop at the Nicolaikirche so that the Doctor could make devotions and take communion, and then it was over to the University (which like all else in Leipzig was small and serious as a pocket-pistol), where the Doctor simply sat in his carriage for half an hour, chatting with Eliza in French, which was the language he preferred for anything of a high-flown nature. Jack, restlessly circling the carriage—which was chocolate-brown, and painted all over with flowers—put his ear to the window once and heard them talking about some noble lady named Sophie, a second time, a few minutes later, it was dressmaking, then Catholic vs. Lutheran views on transubstantiation . . . Finally Jack pulled the door open. "Pardon the interruption, but I had a notion to go on a pilgrimage to Jerusalem, crawling there and back on my hands and knees, and wanted to make sure that it wouldn't delay our departure . . ."

"Ssh! The Doctor's trying to make a very difficult decision," Eliza said.

"Just *make* it—that's what I say—doesn't get easier if you *think* about it," Jack advised. The Doctor had a manuscript on his lap, and a quill poised above it, a trembling drop of ink ready to break loose, but his hand would not move. His head teetered and tottered through a ponderous arc (or maybe it was the wig that magnified all movements) as he read the same extract over and over, under his breath, each time adopting a different sequence of facial expressions and emphasizing different words, like an actor trying to make sense of some ambiguous verse: should this be read as a jaded pedant? A dim schoolmaster? A skeptical Jesuit? But since the words had been written by the Doctor himself, that couldn't be it—he was trying to imagine how the words would be received by different sorts of readers.

"Would you like to read it out loud, or—"

"It is in Latin," Eliza said.

More waiting. Then: "Well, what *is* the decision that wants making?"

"Whether or not to heave it over the transom of yonder doorway," Eliza said, pointing to the front of one of those Leipziger houses-that-weren't-houses.

"What's it say on that door?"

"*Acta Eruditorum*—it is a journal that the Doctor founded two years ago."

"I don't know what a journal is."

"Like a gazette for savants."

"Oh, so that stack of papers is something he wants to have printed?"

"Yes."

"Well, if *he* founded it, it's *his* journal, so why's he got leeches in his breeches?"

"Ssh! All the savants of Europe will read the words on that page—they must be perfect."

"Then why doesn't he take it with him and work on it some more? This is no place to make anything perfect."

"It has been finished for years," the Doctor said, sounding unusually sad. "The decision: should I publish it *at all?*"

"Is it a good yarn?"

"It is not a narrative. It is a mathematical technique so advanced that only two people in the world understand it," the Doctor said. "When published, it will bring about enormous changes in not only mathematics, but all forms of natural philosophy and engineering. People will use it to build machines that fly through the air like birds, and that travel to other planets, and its very power and brilliance will sweep old, tottering, worn-out systems of thought into the dustbin."

"And you invented it, Doctor?" Eliza asked, as Jack was occupied making finger-twirling movements in the vicinity of his ear.

"Yes—seven or eight years ago."

"And still no one knows about it, besides—"

"Me, and the other fellow."

"Why haven't you told the world about it?"

"Because it seems the other fellow invented it ten years before I did, and didn't tell anyone."

"Oh."

"I've been waiting for him to say something. But it's been almost twenty years since he did it, and he doesn't show the slightest inclination to let anyone else in on it."

"You've waited eight years—why today? It's well after midday," Jack said. "Take it with you—give it another two or three years' thought."

"Why *today*? Because I do not believe God put me on this earth, and gave me either the best or second-best mind currently in existence, so that I could spend my days trying to beg money from the likes of Lothar von Hacklheber, so that I could dig a large hole in the ground," the Doctor said. "I don't want my epitaph to be, 'He brought the price of silver down one-tenth of one percent.'"

"Right! Sounds like a decision to me," Jack said. Reaching into the carriage he gathered up the manuscript, carried it up the walk to the door in question, and heaved it through the transom. "And now, off to the mountains!"

"One more small errand in the Booksellers' Quarter," the Doctor said, "as long as I'm getting myself into trouble."

THE BOOKSELLERS' QUARTER LOOKED AND worked like the rest of Leipzig except all the goods were books: they tumbled out of casks, rose in unsteady stacks, or were arranged into blocks that were wrapped and tied and then stacked into larger blocks. Bent porters carried them around in hods and back-baskets. The Doctor, never one to accomplish anything in a hurry, devoted several minutes to arranging his carriage and escort-train before the widest and clearest of the Book-Fair's exits. In particular he wondered if Jack wouldn't mind mounting Turk and (for lack of a better word) *posing* between the booksellers and the carriage. Jack did so, and was reasonably merry about it, having given up any hope that they'd escape the city before nightfall.

The Doctor squared his shoulders, adjusted numerous subsystems of clothing (today he wore a coat embroidered with flowers, just like the ones painted on his carriage), and walked into the Book-Fair. Jack couldn't see him any more, but he could *hear* him. Not his voice, actually, but rather the effect that the Doctor's appearance had on the overall sound of the fair. As when a handful of salt is thrown into a pot that's about to boil: a hush, then a deep steady building.

The Doctor came running. He moved well for a man on high heels. He was pursued by the booksellers of* Königsberg, Basel, Rostock, Kiel, Florence, Strasbourg, Edinburgh, Düsseldorf, Copenhagen, Antwerp, Seville, Paris, and Danzig, with a second echelon not far behind. The Doctor made it past Jack well before any of them. The sight of a mounted man with a heathen saber brought them to a jagged halt. They contented themselves after that with flinging books: any book that was handy. They gang-tackled porters, molested promotional displays, kicked over casks to get ammunition, and the air above and around Jack grew rather dark with books, as when a flock passes overhead. They fell open on cobblestones and spilled out their illustrative woodcuts: por-traits of great men, depictions of the Siege of Vienna, diagrams of mining-engines, a map of some Italian city, a dissection of the large bowel, vast tables of numbers, musketeer drills, geometers' proofs, human skeletons in insouciant poses, the constellations of the Zodiac, rigging of foreign barkentines, design of alchemical fur-naces, glaring Hottentots with bones in their noses, thirty flavors of Baroque window-frames. This entire scene was carried out with very little bellowing, as if ejection of the Doctor was a routine mat-ter for the booksellers. At the crack of the coachman's whip, they made a few desultory final heaves and then turned back to resume whatever conversations the Doctor had interrupted. Jack for his part adopted a ceremonial rear-guard position behind the Doctor's baggage-cart (inadvertently laden, now, with a few random books). The brittle sparking impacts of horse-shoes and wheel-rims against cobblestones were like heavenly chimes to his Vagabond-ears.

HE COULD NOT GET AN explanation until hours later, when they had put Leipzig's north gate a few miles behind them, and stopped at an inn on the road to Halle. By this time Eliza had been thor-oughly saturated with the Doctor's view of events as well as his gloomy and resentful mood. She stayed in the Ladies' Bedcham-ber, he stayed in the Men's, they met in the Common-Room. "He was born in Leipzig—educated himself in Leipzig—went to school in Leipzig—"

"Why'd he go to school if he educated himself? Which is it?"

"Both. His father was a professor who died when he was very

---

*Just guessing, here.

young—so he taught himself Latin at the same age when you were hanging from dead men's legs."

"That's funny—you know, I tried to teach myself Latin, but what with the Black Death, the Fire, *et cetera* . . ."

"In lieu of having a father, he read his father's library—*then* went to school. And you saw for yourself how they treated him."

"Perhaps they had an excellent reason," Jack said—he was bored, and getting Eliza steamed up would be as good an entertainment as any.

"There is no reason for you to be gnawing at the Doctor's ankles," Eliza said. "He is one of that sort of man who forms very profound *friendships* with members of the gentler sex."

"I saw what sort of friendship he had with you when he was pointing out your gentle bosom to Lothar von Hacklheber," Jack returned.

"There was probably a reason—the Doctor is a tapestry of many threads."

"Which thread brought him to the Book-Fair?"

"For some years he and Sophie have been trying to persuade the Emperor in Vienna to establish a grand library and academy for the entire Empire."

"Who is Sophie?"

"Another one of the Doctor's woman friends."

"What fair did he pick *her* up at?"

Eliza arched her eyebrows, leaned forward, and spoke in a whisper that could etch glass: "Don't speak of her that way—Sophie is none other than the daughter of the Winter Queen herself. She is the Duchess of Hanover!"

"Jeezus. How'd a man like the Doctor end up in such company?"

"Sophie inherited the Doctor when her brother-in-law died."

"What do you mean by that? Is he a slave?"

"He is a librarian. Sophie's brother-in-law hired him in that capacity, and when he died, Sophie inherited the library, and the Doctor along with it."

"But that's not good enough—the Doctor has ambitions—he wants to be the Emperor's librarian?"

"As it is now, a savant in Leipzig may never become aware of a book that's been published in Mainz, and so the world of letters is fragmented and incoherent—not like in England, where all the savants know each other and belong to the same Society."

"What!? A Doctor *here* wants to make things *more like England*?"

"The Doctor proposed to the Emperor that a new decree be drawn up, ordering that all booksellers at the Leipzig and Frankfurt fairs must write up a description of every book they publish, and send these, along with copies of each book, to—"

"Let me guess—to the Doctor?"

"Yes. And then he would make them all part of some vast, hard-to-understand thing he wants to build—he couldn't restrain himself from breaking into Latin here, so I don't know exactly—part library, part academy, part machine."

"Machine?" Jack was imagining a mill-wheel assembled from books.

But they were interrupted by ribald, helpless, snorting laughter from the corner of the Common-Room, where the Doctor himself was sitting on a stool, reading (as they saw when they came over and joined him) one of the hurled books that had lodged in the baggage-cart. As usual their progress across the room, or to be specific *Eliza's*, was carefully tracked by lonely merchants whose eyeballs were practically growing out of their heads on stalks. Jack had at first been surprised, and was now growingly annoyed, that other men were capable of noticing Eliza's beauty—he suspected that they did so in some base way altogether different from how *he* did it.

"I love reading novels," the Doctor exclaimed. "You can understand them without thinking too much."

"But I thought you were a philosopher," Eliza said, apparently having waxed close enough to him now that she could get away with teasing and pouting maneuvers.

"But when philosophizing, one's mind follows its natural inclination—gaining profit along with pleasure—whereas following *another* philosopher's meditations is like stumbling through a mine dug by others—hard work in a cold dark place, and painful if you want to zig where they decided to zag. But this—" holding up the book "—you can read without stopping."

"What's the story about?"

"Oh, all these novels are the same—they are about picaroons—that means a sort of rogue or scoundrel—could be male or female—they move about from city to city like Vagabonds (than whom, however, they are much more clever and resourceful)—getting into hilarious scrapes and making fools—or trying to—out of Dukes, Bishops, Generals, and

". . . Doctors."

Lengthy silence, then, followed by Jack saying, "Errr . . . is this the chapter where I'm supposed to draw my weapon?"

"Oh, stop!" the Doctor said. "I didn't bring you all this way to have an *imbroglio*."

"Why, then?" Jack asked—quickly, as Eliza was still so red-faced he didn't think it would be clever *or* resourceful to give her a chance to speak.

"For the same reason that Eliza sacrificed some of your silk to make some dresses, and thereby fetched a higher price. I need to draw some attention to the mine project—make it seem exciting— fashionable even—so that people will at least think about investing."

"I'm guessing, then," Jack said, "that my role will be to hide behind a large piece of furniture and not emerge until all rich fashionable persons have departed?"

"I gratefully accept your proposal," the Doctor said. "Meanwhile, Eliza—well—have you ever seen how mountebanks ply their trade in Paris? No matter what they are selling, they always have an accomplice in the crowd, attired like the intended victims—"

"That means, like an ignorant peasant," Jack informed Eliza. "And at first this accomplice seems to be the most skeptical person in the whole crowd—asking difficult questions and mocking the entire proceedings—but as it continues he is conspicuously won over, and gladly makes the first purchase of whatever the mountebank is selling—"

"Kuxen, in this case?" Eliza said.

The Doctor: "Yes—and in this case the audience will be made up of Hacklhebers, wealthy merchants of Mainz, Lyons bankers, Amsterdam money-market speculators—in sum, wealthy and fashionable persons from all over Christendom."

Jack made a mental note to find out what a money-market speculator was. Looking at Eliza, he found her looking right back at him, and reckoned that she was thinking the same thing. Then the Doctor distracted her with: "In order to blend in with that crowd, Eliza, we shall only have to find some way to make you seem half as intelligent as you really are, and to dim your natural radiance so that they'll not be blinded by awe or jealousy."

"Oh, Doctor," Eliza said, "why is it that men who desire *women* can never speak such words?"

"You've only been in the presence of men who are in the presence of *you*, Eliza," Jack said, "and how can they pronounce fine words when the heads of their yards are lodged in their mouths?"

The Doctor laughed, much as he'd been doing earlier.

"What's your excuse, Jack?" Eliza responded, eliciting some sort of violent thoracic Incident in the Doctor.

Tears of joy came to Jack's eyes. "Thank God women have no way to rid themselves of the yellow bile," he said.

At this same inn they joined up with a train of small but masty ore-wagons carrying goods that the Doctor had acquired at Leipzig and sent on ahead to wait for them. Some of these were laden with saltpeter from India, others with brimstone from the Ore Range.* The others—though laden only with a few small crates—sagged and screeched like infidels on the Rack. Peering between the boards of same, Jack could see that they contained small earthenware flasks packed in straw. He asked a teamster what was in them: "*Quecksilber*" was the answer.

> *Mammon* led them on,
> *Mammon*, the least erected Spirit that fell
> From heav'n, for ev'n in heav'n his looks and
>   thoughts
> Were always downward bent, admiring more
> The riches of Heav'ns pavement, trod'n Gold,
> Then aught divine or holy else enjoy'd
> In vision beatific; by him first
> Men also, and by his suggestion taught,
> Ransack'd the Center, and with impious hands
> Rifl'd the bowels of thir mother Earth
> For Treasures better hid.
>   —MILTON, *Paradise Lost*

THE ENTIRE TRAIN, amounting to some two dozen wagons, proceeded west through Halle and other cities in the Saxon plain. Giant stone towers with dunce-cap rooves had been raised over city gates so that the burghers could see armies or Vagabond-hordes approaching in time to do something about it. A few days past Halle, the ground finally started to rise up out of that plain and (like one of the Doctor's philosophical books) to channel them this way and that, making them go ways they were not especially inclined to. It was a slow change, but one morning they woke up and it was no longer disputable that they were in a valley, the most beautiful golden valley Jack had ever seen, all pale green with April's first shoots, thickly dotted with haystacks even after cattle had been reducing them all winter long. Broad fells rose gently but steadily from this valley and developed, at length, into shapes colder and more mountainous—ramps built by giants, leading upwards to mysterious culminations. The highest ridge-lines were indented with black shapes, mostly trees; but the Saxons had not

---

*Which they knew because it bore the trademark of none other than Herr Geidel.

been slow to construct watch-towers on those heights that commanded the most sweeping views. Jack couldn't help speculating as to what they were all waiting for. Or perhaps they sparked fires in them at night to speed strange information over the heads of sleeping farmers. They passed a placid lake with what had been a brown stone castle avalanching into it; wind came up and raised goose-bumps on the water, destroying the reflection.

Eliza and the Doctor mostly shared the coach, she amending her dresses according to what he claimed was now in fashion, and he writing letters or reading picaroon-novels. It seemed that Sophie's daughter, Sophie Charlotte, was fixing to marry the Elector of Brandenburg later this year, and the trousseau was being imported direct from Paris, and this gave occasion for them to talk about clothing for *days*. Sometimes Eliza would ride in the seat atop the carriage if the weather was fine, giving the teamsters reason to live another day. Sometimes Jack would give Turk a rest by walking alongside, or riding on, or in, the coach.

The Doctor was always doing *something*—sketching fantastic machines, writing letters, scratching out pyramids of ones and zeroes and rearranging them according to some set of contrived rules.

"What're you doing there, Doc?" Jack asked one time, just trying to be sociable.

"Making some improvements to my Theory of Matter," the Doctor said distantly, and then said no more for three hours, at which time he announced to the driver that he had to piss.

Jack tried to talk to Eliza instead. She'd been rather sulky since the conversation at the Inn. "Why is it you'll perform intimate procedures on one end of me, but you won't kiss the other end?" he asked one evening when she returned his affections with eye-rolling.

"I'm losing blood—the humour of passion— what do you expect?"

"Do you mean that in the normal monthly sense, or—"

"More than usual this month—besides I only kiss people who care about me."

"Aw, whatever made you think otherwise?"

"You know almost nothing about me. So any fond emotions you might have, proceed from lust alone."

"Well, whose fault is that, then? I asked you, months ago, to tell me how you got from Barbary to Vienna."

"You did? I remember no such thing."

"Well, p'r'aps it's just the French Pox going to my brain, lass, but I clearly remember—you gave it a few days' profound thought, hardly speaking, and then said, 'I don't wish to reveal that.' "

"You haven't asked me *recently*."

"Eliza, how'd you get from Barbary to Vienna?"

"Some parts of the story are too sad for me to tell, others too tedious to hear—suffice it to say, that when I reached an age that a horny Moor construes as adulthood, I came, in their minds, to bear the same relationship to my mother as a dividend does to a joint stock corporation—viz. a new piece of wealth created out of the normal functioning of the old. I was liquidated."

"What?"

"Tendered to a Vizier in Constantinople as part of a trade, no different from the trades that sustain the City of Leipzig—you see, a person can also be rendered into a few drops of mercury, and combine with the mysterious international flow of that substance."

"What'd that Vizier have to pay for you? Just curious."

"As of two years ago the price of one me, in the Mediterranean market, was a single horse, a bit slimmer and faster than the one you've been riding around on."

"Seems, er . . . well, *any* price would seem too low, of course—but even so—for Christ's sake . . ."

"But you're forgetting that Turk's an uncommon steed—a bit past his prime, to be sure, and worn round the edges—but, what matters, capable of fathering others."

"Ah . . . so the horse that paid for you was a thoroughbred stallion."

"A strange-looking Arab. I saw it on the docks. It was perfectly white, except for the hooves of course, and its eyes were pink."

"The Berbers are breeders of racehorses?"

"Through the network of the Society of Britannic Abductees, I learned that this stallion was bound, eventually, for *la France*. Someone there is connected to the Barbary pirates—I assume it is the same person who caused me and my mother to be made slaves. Because of that man I shall never see Mum again, for she had a cancer when I left her in Barbary. I will find that man and kill him someday."

Jack counted silently to ten, then said: "Oh, hell, I'll do it. I'm going to die of the French Pox anyway."

"First you have to explain to him *why* you're doing it."

"Fine, I'll try to plan in an extra few hours—"

"It shouldn't take that long."

"No?"

"Why would you kill him, Jack?"

439

"Well, there was your abduction from Qwghlm—perverse goings-on in the ship—years of slavery—forcible separation from an ailing—"

"No, no! That's why *I* want to kill him. Why do *you*?"

"Same reason."

"But *many* are involved in the slave trade—will you kill all of them?"

"No, just—oh, I get it—I want to kill this evil man, whoever he is, because of my fierce eternal pure love for you, my own Eliza."

She did not swoon, but she did get a look on her face that said *This conversation is over,* which Jack took as a sign he was going in the right direction.

Finally, after a couple of days of skirting and dodging, the Doctor gave the word and they turned north and began straightforwardly ascending into what had plainly become a mountain range. At first this was a grassy rampart. Then strange dark hummocks began to pock the fields. At the same time, they began frequently to see pairs of men turning windlasses, like the ones mounted above wells, but this equipment was stouter and grimier, and it brought up not buckets of water but iron baskets filled with black rock. Jack and Eliza had seen it before at Joachimsthal and knew that the dark mounds were the fœces left behind when the metal (copper here) had been smelted out of the ore. Germans called it *schlock.* When they were wet with rain (which was frequently, now), the schlock-heaps glistened and gave back light tinged blue or purple. Men collected the ore from the hand-haspels (as the winches were called) into wheelbarrows and staggered behind them, among schlock-piles, to smoking furnaces tended and stirred by coal-smeared men.

Several times they entered into wooded valleys full of smoke, and followed the traces of dragged logs across the ground until they came to gunpowder-mills. Here, tall whip-thin trees, the trunks hairy with miserable scrawny branches,* were cut and burnt endlessly until they became charcoal. This was taken to a water-powered mill to be ground to dust and mixed with the other ingredients. Men came out of these mills looking all drawn and nervous from never really knowing when they'd be blown up, and the Doctor supplied them with brimstone and saltpeter from the wagons. Teaching Jack that wars, like great rivers, had their well-springs in numerous high remote valleys.

Eliza was beginning to see some of the enormous trees of Mum's færy-tales, though many had blown down and could be

---

Faulbaum, the Germans said, meaning "lazy and rotten tree." They were alders.

viewed only as fists of roots thrust into the air still clutching final handfuls of dirt. The air up here was not still for a moment—it was never rainy, cloudy, or sunny for more than a quarter of an hour at a time—but when they were out of those smoky valleys, it was cold and clear. Their progress was slow, but one time the sky cleared as they came through an open place in the woods (it was clear that Harz was a rock and the forest no more substantial than the film of hop-vines that sometimes grew on an ancient schlock-heap), and then it was obvious that they'd risen to a great height above the plains and valleys. Those schlock-heaps like cowls of robed men in a procession. Patrols of black vultures chased and swirled about one another like ashes ascending a flue. Here and there a tower braced itself on a mountain-top or a conspiracy of trees huddled. Crows raided distant fields for the farmers' seed-corn, and flocks of silver birds wheeled and drilled for some unvoiced purpose on invisible breezes.

So the Doctor decided to cheer them up by taking them down into an old abandoned copper mine.

"Sophie was the first woman to enter a mine," he said helpfully. "You, Eliza, might be the second."

This mine's vein (or the vein-shaped cavity where the vein had once been) was close to the surface and so there was no need to descend numerous ladders in some deep shaft: they pulled up before an old semi-collapsed building, rummaged in a skewed cabinet for lights, sledded down a ramp where once a short staircase had been, and there they were in a tunnel as high as Jack's head and an arm's length wide. Their lights were called kienspans: splits of dry resinous wood about the dimensions of a rapier blade, dipped in some kind of wax or pitch, which burnt enthusiastically, and looked like the flame-swords wielded by Biblical standouts. By this means, they could see that the mine-tunnel was lined with logs and timbers: a hefty post-and-beam lintel every couple of yards, and many horizontal logs, as thick as a person's thigh, laid parallel down the tunnel so as to join each post-and-lintel with the ones before and after it. In this way a long tubular wooden cage was formed, not to keep them in (though it did) but to protect them from a stalled avalanche of loose rubble pressing in from all sides.

The Doctor led them down this tunnel—the entrance quickly lost from view. Frequently, side-tunnels took off to one side or another, but these came up only to mid-thigh on Jack and there was no question of entering them.

Or so he thought until the Doctor stopped before one. The floor all around was strewn with curiously wrought planks, half-moon-shaped pieces of ox-hide, and tabular chunks of black rock. "There is a wonder at the end of this tunnel—no more than half a dozen fathoms back—which you must see."

Jack took it for a joke until Eliza agreed to scurry down the tunnel without hesitation—which meant that according to Rules that applied even to Vagabonds, Jack had to do it first, in order to scout for danger. The Doctor told him that the pieces of ox-hide were called arsch-leders, which was self-explanatory, so Jack put one on. The Doctor then demonstrated the use of the planks, which miners used to protect elbows and forearms from the stony floor when creeping along on their sides. All of this settled, Jack lay down on the floor and crept into it, wielding the plank with one arm and the kienspan with the other. He found it reasonably easy going as long as he didn't think about . . . well, about *anything*.

The kienspan, lunging ahead of him, shed sparks against the end of the tunnel and dazzled him. When his vision settled he found that he was sharing a confined space with a giant black bird—or something—like the ostrich—but with no wings—pawing at the ore, or maybe at Jack's face, with talons bigger than fingers— its long bony neck twisted round almost into a knot, an arrowhead of a skull at the end, jaws open with such . . . big . . . teeth . . .

He only screamed once. Twice, actually, but number two didn't count because it came from smashing his head on the ceiling in a poorly thought-out bid to stand up. He scurried back a couple of fathoms, working on blind fear and pain, stopped, listened, heard nothing but his heart.

Of course it was dead—it was all bones. And the Doctor might be a human oddity in several respects, but he wouldn't send Jack into a monster's lair. Jack retreated slowly, trying not to make his head ache any worse. He could hear the Doctor talking to Eliza: "There are shells scattered upon the mountains! See, this rock has a grain like wood—you can split it into layers—and look at what's between the *strata*! This creature must've been buried in mud— probably the fine dirt that rivers carry—smashed flat, as you can see—its body decomposed leaving a void, later filled in by some other sort of rock—as sculptors cast bronze statues in plaster molds."

"Where do you *get* this stuff? Who told you *that* one?" Jack demanded, a bloody head popping out between their feet, looking up at them.

"I reasoned it out myself," said the Doctor. "*Someone* has to come up with *new* ideas."

Jack rolled over on his belly to find the floor loosely paved with rock-slabs bearing imprints of sundry other Book-of-Revelation fauna. "What river carried this supposed dirt? We're in the middle of a *mountain* of *rock*. There is no *river*," Jack informed the Doctor, after they had gotten Eliza on her way down the tunnel. Jack waited with her traveling-dress slung over his arm while she inched down the tunnel in her knickers and an arsch-leder.

"But there *used* to be," the Doctor said, "Just as there used to be such creatures—" playing his light over impressions of fish with fins too many and jaws too big, swimming creatures shaped like grappling-hooks, dragonflies the size of crossbow-bolts.

"A river in a mountain? I don't think so."

"Then where did the shells come from?"

FINALLY THEY TRAVELED to the rounded top of a mountain where an old stone tower stood, flanked by schlock-heaps instead of bastions. A half-wit could see that the Doctor had been at work here. Rising from the top of the tower was a curious windmill, spinning round sideways like a top instead of rolling like a wheel, so that it didn't have to turn its face into the wind. The base of the tower was protected by an old-fashioned stone curtain-wall that had been repaired recently (they were afraid of being attacked by people who, however, did not have modern artillery). Likewise the gate was new, and it was bolted. A musket-toting engineer opened it for them as soon as the Doctor announced himself, and wasted no time bolting it behind them.

The tower itself was not a fit place for people to lodge. The Doctor gave Eliza a room in an adjoining house. Jack put the fear of God into all the rats he could find in her room, then climbed the stone stair that spiraled* up the inside of the tower. The tower did its part by moaning in wind-gusts like an empty jug when an idler blows over the top. From the windmill at the top a shaft, consisting of tree-trunks linked one to the next with collars and fittings hammered out of iron, dropped through the center of the tower to an engineering works on the dirt floor. The floor, then, was pierced by a large hole that was obviously the mouth of a mine-shaft. An endless chain of buckets had been rigged so that the windmill's power raised them up from the shaft laden with water. As they went round a giant pulley they emptied into a long wooden tray: a mill-race that carried the water out through a small arched portal in the tower wall. Then the empty buckets dove back into the shaft for another go-round. In this way water was drained away from some

—————

*The Doctor: "Actually, it is a helix, not a spiral."

deep part of the mines that would normally be flooded. But up here, the water was a good thing to have. After gathering a bit of head in a system of trenches outside, it powered small mill-wheels that ran bellows and trip-hammers for the smiths, and finally collected in cisterns.

Up top, Jack, who'd wisely spent some of their profits on warm clothes, had a view over a few days' journey in every direction. The mountains (excepting one big one to the north) were not of the craggy sort, but swelling round-topped things separated by bottomless cleavages. The woods were dappled—partly leaf-trees with pale spring growth and partly needle-trees that were almost black. Here and there, pools of pasture-land lay on south-facing slopes, and of snow on north-facing ones. Villages, with their red tile rooves, were strewn about unevenly, like blood-spatters. There was a big one just below, in the gorge that divided this mountain from an even higher one to the north: a bald crag whose summit was crowned with a curious arrangement of long stones. Clouds whipped overhead, as fast and furious as the Winged Hussars, and this made Jack feel as if the tower were eternally toppling. The strangely curved blades of the Doctor's windmill hummed over his head like poorly aimed scimitar-cuts.

"JUST A MINUTE, DOCTOR—with all due respect—you've replaced miners-on-treadwheels with a windmill to pump out the water—but what happens when the wind stops blowing? The water floods back in? Miners are drowned?"

"No, they simply follow the old underground drainage channel, using small ore-boats."

"And how do these miners feel about being replaced by machines, Doctor?"

"The increase in productivity should more than—"

"How easy would it be to slip a *sabot* off one's foot and 'accidentally' let it fall into the gears—"

"Err . . . maybe I'll post guards to prevent any such *sabotage.*"

"*Maybe?* What will these guards cost? Where will they be housed?"

"Eliza—please—if I may just interrupt the rehearsal," the Doctor said, "don't do this job *too* well, I beg of you—avoid saying anything that will make a lasting impression on the, er, audience . . ."

"But I thought the whole idea was to—"

"Yes, yes—but remember drinks will be served—suppose some possible investor feels the need to step out and relieve himself at the climax of the performance, when the scales fall from your eyes and you see that this is, after all, a brilliant opportunity—"

Thus the rehearsal. Eliza performed semi-reclining on a couch, looking pale. Crawling down that cold tunnel probably had not been a good idea for one in her delicate state. It occurred to Jack that, since they had a bit of money now, there was no reason not to go down into the town he'd noticed below, find an apothecary, and buy some kind of potion or philtre that would undo the effects of the bleeding and bring pink back to her cheeks and, in general, the humour of passion back to her veins.

Of this town, which was called Bockboden, the Doctor had had little to say, save for a few mild comments such as "I wouldn't go there," "Don't go there," "It's not a very good place to be in," and "Avoid it." But none of these had been reinforced by the lurid fabrications that a Vagabond would've used to drive the point home. It seemed an orderly town from above, but not dangerously so.

Jack set out on foot, as Turk had been favoring one leg the last day or so, and followed an overgrown path that wound among old schlock-heaps and abandoned furnaces down towards Bockboden. As he went, the idea came to him that if he kept a sharp eye out, he might learn a few more things about the money-making trade, perhaps to include: how to profit therefrom without going through the tedious steps of investing one's own money and waiting decades for the payoff. But the only novel thing he saw on his way into Bockboden was some kind of improvised works, situated well away from dwellings, where foul-smelling steam was gushing from the mouths of iron tubs with Faulbaum-bonfires raging beneath them. It smelled like urine, and so Jack assumed it was a cloth-fulling mill. Indeed, he spied a couple of disgusted workmen pouring something yellow from a cask into one of the boiling-tubs. But there was no cloth in sight. It seemed they were boiling all of this perfectly good urine away to no purpose.

As Jack entered the town, shrewdness came to him belatedly, and he perceived it had not been a good idea—not because anything in particular happened but because of the old terror of arrest, torture, and execution that frequently came upon him in settled places. He reminded himself that he was wearing new clothes. As long as he kept a glove on his hand, where a letter V had been branded years ago, in the Old Bailey, he bore no visible marks of being a Vagabond. Moreover, he was a guest of the Doctor, who must be an important personage hereabouts. So he kept walking. The town gradually embraced and ensnared him. It was all built half-timbered, like most German towns and many English ones—meaning that they began by raising a frame of heavy struts, and then filled in the open spaces between them with whatever they could get. Around here, it looked like they'd woven mats of sticks into the gaps and then slathered them with mud that stiffened as it dried. Each new building borrowed strength, at first, from an older one, i.e., there was hardly an isolated freestanding house in the whole town; Bockboden was a single building of many bodies and tentacles. The frames of the houses—nay, the single frame of the entire town—had probably been level, plumb, and regular at one point, but over centuries it had sagged, warped, and tottered in different ways. The earthen walls had been patched to follow these evolutions. The town no longer looked like something men had built. It looked like the root-ball of a tree, with dirt-colored stuff packed between the roots, and hollowed out to provide a living-place.

Even here there were little schlock-heaps, and dribbles of ore up and down the streets. Jack heard the unsteady ticking of a hand-haspel behind a door. Suddenly the door was rammed open by a wheelbarrow full of rocks, pushed by a man. The man was astonished to find a stranger there staring at him. Jack however did not even have time to become edgy and to adopt an expression of false nonchalance before the miner got an aghast look and made a pitifully abject bowing maneuver, as best he could without letting go the wheelbarrow and precipitating a merry sequence of downhill mishaps. "Apothecary?" Jack said. The man answered in a strangely familiar-sounding kind of German, using his head to point. Behind the door, the hand-haspel stopped ticking for about six heartbeats, then started again.

Jack followed the wheelbarrow-man to the next cross-street, the latter trying to scurry away from him but impeded by his own weight in rocks. Jack wondered whether all of the mines beneath this country might be interconnected so that they all benefited from the Doctor's project of pumping away the ground-water without having to share in the costs. Perhaps that explained why strangers, coming from the direction of the tower, made them so nervous. Not that one really *needed* a reason.

The apothecary shop, at least, stood alone, on the edge of a grassy, schlock-mottled yard, cater-corner from a blackened church. The roof was high and steep as a hatchet-blade, the walls armored in overlapping plates of charcoal-colored slate. Each of its stories was somewhat larger than the one below, and sheltered 'neath the overhangs were rows of carved wooden faces: some faithful depictions of nuns, kings, helmeted knights, hairy wild-men, and beady-eyed Turks, but also angels, demons, lycanthropes, and a goatlike Devil.

Jack entered the place and found no one minding the dispensary window. He began to whistle, but it sounded plaintive and feeble, so he stopped. The ceiling was covered with huge grotesque forms molded in plaster—mostly persons changing into other beings. Some of them he recognized, dimly, from hearing the tales referred to in plays—there was for example the poor sap of a hunter who chanced upon the naked hunt-goddess while she was bathing, and was turned to a stag and torn apart by his own hounds. *That* wretch, caught in mid-metamorphosis, was attached to the ceiling of the dispensary room in life-size.

Perhaps the apothecary was hard of hearing. Jack began to wander about in a loud, obvious, banging way. He entered a big room filled with things he knew it would be a bad idea to touch: glowing tabletop furnaces, murky fluids bubbling in retorts above the flames of spirit-burners, flames as blue as Eliza's eyes. He tried another door and found the apothecary's office—jumping a little when he caught sight of a dangling skeleton. He looked up at the ceiling and found more heavy plaster-works, all of female goddesses: the goddess of dawn, the spring-goddess riding a flowery chariot up out of Hell, the one Europe was named after, the goddess of Love preening in a hand-mirror, and in the center, helmeted Minerva (he knew *some* names at least) with a cold and steady look about her, one arm holding her shield, decorated with the head of a monster whose snaky hair descended almost into the middle of the room.

A big dead fish, all sucked into itself and desiccated, was suspended from a string. The walls were lined with shelves and cabinets dense with professional clutter: diverse tongs, in disturbingly specific shapes; a large collection of mortars and pestles with words on them; various animal skulls; capped cylinders made of glass or stone, again with words on them; a huge Gothickal clock out of whose doors grotesque creatures sallied when Jack least expected it, then retreated before he could turn and really see them; green glass retorts in beautifully rounded shapes that reminded him of female body parts; scales with vast arrays of weights, from cannon-balls down to scraps of foil that could be propelled into the next country by a sigh; gleaming silver rods, which on closer inspection turned out to be glass tubes filled, for some reason, with mercury; some kind of tall, heavy, columnar object, shrouded in heavy fabric and producing internal warmth, and expanding and contracting slowly like a bellows—

"*Guten Tag,* or should I say, good afternoon," it said.

Jack fell back on his ass and looked up at a man, wrapped in a sort of traveling-cloak or monk's robe, standing next to the skeleton. Jack was too surprised to cry out—not least because the man had spoken English.

"How'd you know . . . ?" was all Jack could get out. The man in the robe had a silver robe and a look of restrained amusement nestled in his red beard, which suggested that Jack should wait a minute before leaping up, drawing his sword, and running him through.

". . . that you were an Englishman?"

"Yes."

"You may not know this, but you have a way of talking to yourself as you go about—telling yourself a story about what's happening, or what you suppose is happening—for this reason I already know you are Jack. I'm Enoch. Also, there is something peculiarly English in the way you go about investigating, and amusing yourself with, things that a German or Frenchman would know to be none of his business."

"There's much to think about in that speech," Jack said, "but I don't suppose it's too offensive."

"It's not meant to be offensive at all," Enoch said. "How may I help you?"

"I am here on behalf of a Lady who has gone pale and unsteady from too much feminine, er . . ."

"Menstruation?"

"Yes. Is there anything here for that?"

Enoch gazed out a window at a dim gray sky. "Well—never mind what the apothecary would tell you—"

"You are *not* the apothecary?"

"No."

"Where is he?"

"Down at the town square, where all decent folk should be."

"Well, what does that make you and me then, brother?"

Enoch shrugged. "A man who wants to help his woman, and a man who knows how."

"How, then?"

"She wants iron."

"*Iron?*"

"It would help if she ate a lot of red meat."

"But you said *iron.* Why not have her eat a horseshoe?"

"They are so unpalatable. Red meat contains iron."

"Thank you . . . did you say the apothecary was in the town square?"

"Just that way, a short distance," Enoch said. "There's a butcher there, too, if you want to get her some red meat . . ."

"*Auf wiedersehen,* Enoch."

"Until we meet again, Jack."

And thus did Jack extricate himself from the conversation with the madman (who, as he reflected while walking down the street, had a thing or two in common with the Doctor) and go off in search of someone sane. He could see many people in the square—how would he know which one was the apothecary? Should've asked old Enoch for a description.

Bockboden had convened in a large open ring around a vertical post fixed in the ground and half buried in a pile of faggots. Jack did not recognize the apparatus at first because he was used to England, where the gallows was customary. By the time he'd figured out what was going on, he had pushed his way into the middle of the crowd, and he could hardly turn around and leave without giving everyone the impression that he was soft on witches. Most of them, he knew, had only showed up for the sake of maintaining their reputations, but those sorts would be the *most* likely to accuse a stranger of witchcraft. The *real* witch-haters were up at the front, hollering in the local variant of German, which sometimes sounded maddeningly like English. Jack could not make out what they were saying. It sounded like threats. That was nonsensical, because the witch was about to be killed anyway. But Jack heard snatches like *"Walpurgis"* and *"heute Nacht,"* which he knew meant "tonight" and then he knew that they were threatening not the woman who was about to die, but others in the town they suspected of being witches.

The head of the woman had been shaved, but not recently. Jack could guess, from the length of her stubble, that her ordeal had been going on for about a week. They had been going at her feet and legs with the old wedges-and-sledgehammers trick, and so she would have to be burnt in the seated position. When they set her down on the pile of faggots she winced from the pain of being moved, then leaned back against the stake, seeming glad that she was about to leave Bockboden for good. A plank was nailed into place above her, with a piece of paper on it, on which had been written some sort of helpful information. Meanwhile, a man tied her hands behind the stake—then passed the loose end of the rope around her neck a couple of times, and flung the slack away from the stake: a detail that infuriated the front-row crowd. Someone else stepped up with a big earthenware jug and sloshed oil all around.

Jack, as former execution facilitator, watched with professional interest. The man with the rope pulled hard on it while the fire was started, strangling the woman probably within seconds, and ruining the entire execution in the opinion of some. Most of them watched but didn't see. Jack had found that people watching executions, even if they kept open eyes turned to the entire performance, did not really see the death, and could not remember it later, because what they were really doing was thinking about their own deaths.

But this one affected Jack as if it were Eliza who'd been burnt (the witch was a young woman), and he walked away with shoulders drawn tightly together and watery snot trickling out of his nose. Blurry vision did him no favors vis-à-vis navigation. He walked so fast that by the time he realized he was on the wrong street, the town square—his only star to steer by—was concealed around the bends of Bockboden. And he did not think that aimless wandering, or anything that could be considered suspicious by anyone, was a good idea here. The only thing that was a good idea was to get out of town.

So he did, and got lost in the woods.

⚭

The Harz Mountains
WALPURGISNACHT 1684

☙

> Me miserable! which way shall I flie
> Infinite wrauth, and infinite despaire?
> Which way I flie is Hell; my self am Hell;
> And in the lowest deep a lower deep
> Still threatning to devour me opens wide,
> To which the Hell I suffer seems a Heav'n.
> —MILTON, *Paradise Lost*

JACK SAT ON A DEAD tree in the woods for a time, feeling hungry, and, what was worse, feeling stupid. There was little daylight left and he thought he should use it wisely (he was not above being wise as long as there was no preacher or gentleman *demanding* that he do so). He walked through the trees over a little rise and down into a shallow basin between hills where he was fairly certain he could light a fire without announcing himself to the citizenry of Bockboden. He spent the remainder of the daylight gathering fallen branches and, just as the sun was setting, lit a fire—having learned that the tedious and exacting work of flint, steel, and tinder could be expedited if you simply used a bit of gunpowder in lieu of the tinder. With some pyrotechnics and a cloud of smoke, he had a fire. Now he need only throw sticks on it from time to time and sit there like the lost fool he was until sleep finally caught him unawares. He did not want to think about the witch he'd seen burnt, but it was hard not to. Instead he tried to make himself think about brother Bob, and his two boys, the twins Jimmy and Danny, and his long- and oft-delayed plan to find them a legacy.

He was startled to find three women and a man, their faces all lit up by firelight, standing nearby. They looked as if they had ventured into the woods in the middle of the night expecting to find some *other* vagrant sitting by a fire sleeping.* Jack's first thought might've been *Witch-hunters!* if not for that they'd had longer to react to *him* than he to *them,* and *they* looked worried (they'd noticed the sword)—besides, they were mostly females and they were unarmed, unless the fresh-cut tree-branches that they used as leafy walking-sticks were meant as weapons. At any rate, they turned and hustled off, their sticks giving them the look of a group of stout chamber-maids going off to sweep the forest with makeshift brooms.

After that Jack could not sleep. Another group much like the first came by a few minutes later. This forest was damnably *crowded.* Jack picked up his few belongings and withdrew into the shadows to observe what other moths were attracted to the flame. Within a few minutes, a squadron of mostly women, ranging from girls to hags, had taken over the fire, and stoked it up to a blaze. They'd brought along a black iron kettle that they filled with buckets of water from a nearby creek and set up on the fire to boil. As steam began to rise from the pot—illuminated by firelight down below, vanishing into the cold sky as it ascended—they began to throw in the ingredients of some kind of stew: sacks of some type of fat dark-blue cherries, red mushrooms with white speckles, sprigs of herbs. No meat, or recognizable vegetables, to the disappointment of Jack. But he was hungry enough to eat German food now. The question was: how to secure an invitation to the feast?

In the end, he just went down and got some, which was what

---

*Various pieces of evidence suggested to Jack that he'd been sleeping.

everyone else seemed to be doing. Traffic through this part of the woods had become so heavy that he could not rely on going unnoticed anyway. First he used his sword to cut a leafy branch like everyone else's. None of these persons was armed, and so he stuck the sword and scabbard down his trouser-leg and then, to conceal it better, fashioned a false splint of sticks, and rags torn from his shirt, around the leg so that he would look like a man with a frozen knee, hobbling round with the aid of the staff. Thus disguised, he limped into the firelight and was politely, not to say warmly, greeted by the stew-cookers. One of them offered him a ladle full of the stuff and he swallowed it down fast enough to burn his insides all the way down to his stomach. Probably just as well—it was foul-tasting. On the principle that you never know when you'll find food again, he gestured for more, and they somewhat reluctantly handed him a second ladle, and uneasily watched him drink it. It was as bad as the first, though it had chunks of mushrooms or something on the bottom that might give some nourishment.

He must have *looked* lost, then, because after he'd stood near the fire for a few minutes warming himself the stew-makers began helpfully pointing in the direction that all the other people were migrating. This happened to be generally uphill, which was the way Jack planned to travel anyhow (either it would take him to the Doctor's tower, or to a height-of-land whence he could *see* the tower come morning) and so off he hobbled.

The next time he was really aware of anything (he seemed to be walking and sleeping *at the same time,* though everything had a dreamlike quality now, so the *whole thing* might be a dream) he had evidently covered a couple of miles uphill, judging from that it was much colder and the wind was blowing so hard that he could hear trees being struck down all over, like reports of guns in a battle. Clouds stampeded across the face of a full moon. Occasionally something would rip through the branches overhead and shower him with twigs and brush. Looking up, he saw it was broken-off tree branches, or maybe even small uprooted trees, propelled through the air by the hurricanoe. He was working his way uphill, though not sure why anymore. Others were all around him. The forest was very tall skinny black trees closely packed together like the massed pikes of a military formation, the eruptions of moonlight between fleeing clouds like the bursting of bombs, and Jack heard, or dreamed, the tramping of feet and blowing of trumpets. Forgetting why his leg was splinted, he supposed he must have been wounded in action (possibly in the head as well as the leg) and the wound dressed by a barber. For a while he was almost certain he was still fighting Turks in Vienna and all of the Eliza stuff just a long, elaborate, cruel dream.

But then he was back in the woods above Bockboden. Branches and heavier things were still ripping through space above his head like cannonballs. He looked up at the moon trying to see them, and with the torn clouds streaming by, it was difficult to make out their shapes, but he was fairly certain now that *people* were riding on those branches, as Winged Hussars rode on chargers. They were charging the hilltop! Jack finally stumbled out onto a path that wound up the mountain, and was nearly run over by the *infantry* part of the charge: a river of people with cut branches, and other ornaments, such as the forks farmers used to shovel manure. Forgetting about the splinted leg, Jack wheeled and tried to run with them, but fell, and took a while getting up.

He reached the collection of outcroppings that was the mountain-top somewhat after the main group, but in time to see them chasing away half a dozen musketeers who had apparently been posted there, and who were not welcome. None of them fired his weapon, as they had no desire to kill a few people only to be surrounded by hundreds of their stick-brandishing friends. As this occurred, people farther from the action were shouting threats and offering sour comments in much the same vein as the spectators at the witch-burning had earlier, except that they were using the word *Wächter,* which (Jack's murderously overtaxed mind guessing wildly here) perhaps meant "Watchers."

Battle won, the Hexen (no point in denying it any more) quickly lit up the whole mountain-top with fires (many people had carried faggots on their backs), which burnt with white heat in the continuing wind-blast. Jack hobbled around and looked. He could see that many ages ago a tall stone column had risen from the top of the mountain, bifurcated at the top into what might have been shaped like a pair of goat's horns. It might've looked something like a crossbow standing up on end. But it had been toppled so long ago that it was now covered in moss and dirt. A couple of dozen standing-stones had ringed it; most of them had been toppled as well. The Hexen had led a black goat up onto the ruin of the high column and leashed him there to look out over the whole fiery prospect.

People, frequently naked, danced around those bonfires. Many spring flowers had been brought up and used to decorate rocks, or people. A certain amount of fucking went on, as one would expect, but at least some of it seemed to be *ceremonial* fucking—the participants, actors in a sort of immorality play—the woman always bedecked with garlands of spring wildflowers and the man always donning an eye-patch. Certain small animals might have died unnatural deaths. There was chanting and singing in a language that wasn't exactly German.

Of course, presiding over the entire thing was Satan the Prince of Darkness, or so Jack assumed—as what else would you call a jet-black figure, horned and bearded, maybe a hundred feet high, dancing in the boiling, smoky, cloudy sky just above the summit, sometimes visible and sometimes not, occasionally seen in profile as he lifted his bearded chin to howl, or laugh, at the moon. Jack fully believed this, and knew beyond doubt that every word the preachers had ever said about Lucifer was true. He decided that running away wasn't a bad idea. Choosing the direction he happened to be pointed in at the moment he panicked, he ran. The moon came out a few moments later and showed him he had one or two strides left on rock before he would find himself running in midair—a fantastical gorge plunged straight down for farther than could be seen by moonlight. Jack stopped and turned around, having no other choices, and with a forced and none too sincere calmness, looked at the entire panorama of fire and shadow hoping to find a route that wouldn't take him too near Satan—or actually any of the several Satans of different sizes who seemed to be huddling in council around the mountain-top.

His eye was caught by a tiny black silhouette outlined in a brilliant hairy fringe, elevated above the whole scene: the black goat, tilting its head back to bray. One of the vast Satans duplicated the move precisely. Jack understood that he had been running from shadows of the goat cast against clouds and smoke by the light of the fire.

He sat down at the point where he'd almost hurled himself into the gorge, laughed, and tried to clear his head, and to get his bearings. The cliff, and the somewhat lower bluff across from it, were craggy, with great big shards and flakes of rock angling crazily into the air—and (by the way) exploding the Doctor's idea of how these rocks had been formed, because the grain of these rocks ran straight up and down. Obviously it was the remains of a giant, killed in some antediluvian rock fight, who'd died on his back with his bony fingers thrust up into the air.

Jack drew nearer to a fire, partly because he was cold and

partly because he wanted a closer look at one particular naked girl who was dancing around it—somewhat on the fleshy side and clearly destined to become another broom-wielding hag in the long run, but the least columnar German female Jack had recently seen. By the time he got close enough to have a good look at her, the fire was uncomfortably hot, which should have warned him that the light was very bright, on his face. But he did not consider this important fact at all until he heard the fatal word *Wache!* Turning towards the voice he saw, almost close enough to touch, one of those women who had woken him up earlier in the evening, down below, when he'd been sleeping by his little fire with his sword in view. His sword was exactly what she was looking for, now that she'd gained everyone's attention by uttering their least favorite word. Concealing the weapon in a leg-splint had worked when it was dark, and people were not specifically *looking* for a sword, but here and now it did not work at all—the woman hardly needed do more than glance at Jack before screaming, in a voice that could probably be heard in Leipzig, *"Er ist eine Wache! Er hat ein Schwert!"*

So the party was over for *everyone* and most of all *Jack.* Anyone could've given him a smart shove and sent him into the fire and that would've been the end, or at least an interesting *beginning,* but instead they all ran away from him—but, he had to assume, not for long. The only one who stayed behind was the one who'd fingered him. She hovered out of sword-range giving him a piece of her mind, so furious she was sobbing. Jack had no desire to draw his sword and get these people more angry than they were, but (a) they couldn't possibly get much *more* angry no matter what he did, and (b) he had to get the damn splint off his leg if he were going to do any serious fleeing. And fleeing was the order of the night. So. Out came his dagger. The woman gasped and jumped back. Jack controlled the urge to tell her to shut up and calm down, and slashed through all the rag bands around his leg so that the splint-sticks fell away from him. Then he freed his leg by pulling out the scabbard and sword. The woman now *screamed.* People were running *towards* Jack now, and cries of *"Wächer!"* were making it difficult to hear anything else—Jack had absorbed enough German by now to understand that this meant not "the Watcher" but "the Watchers." They'd made up their minds that Jack must be only one of a whole platoon of armed infiltrators, which of course would be the only way his presence there would make any sense. Because to be here alone was suicide.

Jack ran.

He hadn't been running for long before he understood that the Hexen were generally trying to drive him in the direction of the cliff—an excellent idea. But, as yet, they were not very organized and so there were gaps between them. Jack sallied through one of these and began to lose altitude the slow, safe, and sane way. The commotion had dropped a couple of octaves in pitch. At first it had mostly been shocked females spreading the alarm (which had worked pretty well), and now it was angry males organizing the hunt. Jack had to assume it wasn't the first time they had hunted for large animals in these woods.

Even so, the hunt lasted for perhaps an hour, making its way generally downhill. Jack's only hope was to get out in front of them and flee through the darkness. But they had torches and they knew their way around, and had spread the alarm down the mountain and so no matter what Jack achieved in the way of running, he found himself always surrounded. There were any number of near-escapes that ended in failure. The million poky branches of the alder trees clawed his face and threatened to blind him and caused him to make more noise than he wanted to as he moved about.

Toward the end, he got into situations where he could have escaped, or at least added a few minutes to his life, by killing one or two people. But he didn't—an act of forbearance he wished could have been observed and noted down by some other sort of Watcher, a lurking mystery with a mirror on a stick, so that news of his noble decisions could be provided to Eliza and everyone else who'd ever looked at him the wrong way. Far from earning him universal admiration, this only led to his being surrounded by some half a dozen men with torches, standing just out of sword-range and darting in to sweep flames past his face when they thought they saw an opening. Jack risked a look back over his shoulder and saw no one behind him, which seemed a poor way to surround someone. He wheeled, ran a couple of steps, and hit a wall. A *wall*. Turning back around, he saw a torch-flame headed right for his face and reflexively parried the blow. Another came in from another direction and he parried that, and when the third came in from yet another direction he parried it with the *edge* instead of the *flat* of his blade, and cut the handle of the torch in two. The burning half spun in the air and he snatched it while slashing blindly in the other direction and hurting someone. Now that he'd drawn blood, the other hunters stepped back, knowing that reinforcements were on their way.* Jack, keeping his back to the building, crept sideways, sword in one hand and torch in the other, occasionally taking advantage of the latter's light to glance over his shoulder and gain some knowledge of what he'd run into.

It was an old wooden building. The door was closed by a padlock the size of a ham. Wooden shutters had been pulled shut over the windows and bolted from the inside. A gentleman would've been stymied, but Jack knew that the weakest part of any building was usually the roof—so as soon as he found a wood-pile stacked against the wall, he climbed up it and got up on top, and found clay tiles under his boots. These were thick and heavy, made to withstand hail-storms and tree-branches, but Jack with the strength of panic stomped until a few of them cracked. Fist-sized rocks were pelting down around him now. He stopped one that was trying to roll off, and used it as a hammer. Finally he created a hole through the tiles, threw in the torch, squeezed through feet-first between the wooden laths on which the tiles were mounted, and dropped through, landing on a table. He snatched up the torch lest it set fire to the place, and found himself looking at a portrait of Martin Luther.

His hunters—several dozen by now, he guessed—had surrounded the building and begun pounding, in an exploratory way, on its doors and shutters. The booms in the dark gave Jack a general idea of the building's size and shape. It had several rooms, and

---

*It being one of the many peculiar features of Jack's upbringing that (1) he had a perpetual sparring partner (Bob)—perpetual in the sense that they slept in the same bed at night and, as brothers do, fought all day—against whom he was evenly matched, and (2) at the age when every boy engages in mock sword-fight, he and Bob happened to suddenly find themselves living in a military barracks, where their duels served as free entertainment for large numbers of men who actually *did* know a few things about fighting with swords, and who found the entertainment lacking if it was not well played, both in a *technical* sense (blows had to be delivered and parried in some way that was realistic to their discerning eyes) and in a *dramatic* sense (extra points scored, and extra food thrown in their direction, for enhancements such as hanging by the knees from joists and fighting upside-down, swinging like apes from ropes, etc.). The result being that from a young age the Shaftoe boys had sword-fighting abilities considerably above their station in life (most people like them never came into contact with a sword at all, unless it was with the edge of the blade in the last instant of their life), but limited to the type of sword called the spadroon—a cut-and-thrust weapon—which, they'd been warned, might not be very effective against Gentlemen armed with long slender poky rapiers and trained to insert them deftly through narrow gaps in one's defenses. The Janissary-blade was a rough Mahometan equivalent of a spadroon, therefore, ideally matched to Jack's style, or Bob's for that matter. He waved it around dramatically.

was therefore probably not a church, but not a mere cottage either. No one had tried to pursue him through the hole in the roof and he was certain no one would—they'd burn it. It was inevitable. He could even hear axes thudding into trees out in the forest—more fuel.

This particular room was a rude chapel; the thing he'd landed on, the altar. Next to the Luther portrait was an old and not very good rendition of a woman proffering a chalice with a communion wafer levitating above it, suspended by some ongoing miraculous intervention. It made Jack (who'd had enough, for one night, of accepting mystery drinks from eerie females) shudder. But from having spent too much time lately around miners, he recognized the woman as St. Barbara, patron of men who dug holes in the ground, albeit with all of her Catholic insignia filed off. The rest of the room was striped by plank benches. Jack hopped from one to the next to the back, then went sideways and found a kind of sitting-room with a couple of chairs and one of the towering black iron stoves favored by Germans. Turning on his heel and going the *other* way, he found a very heavy scale dangling from the ceiling; weights for it, the size of cheese-wheels; a cabinet; and, what he most wanted to see, a stairway going *down*.

It was getting smoky in there, and not just from his torch. Jack mauled the cabinet open and grabbed a handful of kienspans. He'd lost his hat while running through the woods and so he stole one of the miners': a conical thing of extremely thick felt that would soften impacts of head against stone. Then he was down the stairs, and none too soon as the old wooden building was burning like gunpowder. They'd make a big fire of it, throwing on whole trees: a fire that could be seen by the burghers of Bockboden, sending those Hexen-hunters a powerful message by which they'd be completely baffled.

The stairway went down for perhaps two dozen steps and then levelled off into a tunnel that went at least as far as Jack's torch (which had consumed most of its fuel) could throw light. He lit a kienspan, which burnt a little brighter, but he still could not see the end of the tunnel, which was good, and to be expected. He began running along in a kind of crouch, not wanting to smash his head on the ceiling timbers, and after a minute, passed by a hand-haspel crammed into a niche in the tunnel wall, its ropes descending into a shaft. A minute later he passed by another, then another, and finally he stopped and decided he should just go down one of those shafts. He'd been down here long enough to stop being so proud of his own cleverness, and he'd begun to worry. The Hexen knew the territory better than he. They couldn't *not* know that the building was a mine entrance, and they must have anticipated that he'd find the tunnel. Perhaps the mine had other entrances, and they'd soon be coming down with torches and dogs and God knows what, as when they hunted burrowing vermin with their sausage-shaped dogs.

One of the hand-haspel's buckets was at the top, the other down below. Jack climbed into the one that was up, and hugged the opposite rope, and by letting it slide through his arms was able to descend smoothly for a short distance: until he relaxed, and the rope slid too fast, and he hugged it tight out of panic, so it burnt him and made him let go, causing the same cycle to repeat, except worse. The only thing that interrupted this round was when, at the halfway mark, the lower bucket came up and caught him under the chin and caused him to let go entirely—which was fine, as he would have been stuck at that point anyway. He dropped, then, with only the empty, ascending bucket as counterweight, and what saved him was that the impact of his chin against same had set it swinging briskly back and forth, its rim biting into the rough wall of the shaft faster and faster as it rose higher and higher, throwing sparks and dislodging fusillades of jagged rock in Jack's direction with every impact, but also slowing his fall with a corresponding series of violent jerks. Jack kept his head down and his kienspan up in case this shaft terminated in water, a possibility he should have considered earlier.

Actually it terminated in rock—the bucket landed unevenly and ejected Jack. Loose bits of stone continued to clatter down from above for a little while and hurt his legs, which was welcome as proof he hadn't been paralyzed. The kienspan still burnt; Jack held it in a death-grip and watched the blue flame pour out of it and turn yellow as it moved sideways along the shaft, contrary to the normal habit of flames, which was to tend *upwards*. Jack kicked the bucket out of the way and did some moving about, and found that there was a rapidly building draft, approaching a breeze, moving toward him along the tunnel. But when he backed up to the other side of the shaft opening in the ceiling, the air was moving the opposite direction. Two flows of air converged at this point and moved up the shaft, starting now to make a certain wailing noise that Jack could not fail to liken to damned souls or whatever. *Now* he understood why the Hexen had gone to work felling trees up above: they knew that with a sufficiently enormous fire they could suck all of the air out of the mine.

He had to find a way out, which did not seem all that likely now, as he'd made the (in retrospect) mistake of going *down* to a lower level. But he chose the direction from which there came the strongest flow of air, and began to move as quickly as he could. The faster he ran into the wind, the more brightly his kienspan burnt. But it burnt less brightly as time went on. He tried lighting a fresh one, but it, too, burnt feebly unless he waved it in the air, and then the light flared up and shone between the heavy bars of the wooden cage that kept the rocks from crushing him on all sides, and cast rapidly moving shadows, sometimes looking like angry faces of mangled giants, or huge ostrich-skeleton-monsters with scimitar teeth: all of which went together neatly with the deafening chorus of moans and wails made by all of the passageways as the breath was sucked out of them.

Around this time Jack also noted that he was on his hands and knees skidding the dully glowing kienspan along the floor. From time to time he'd see the low portal of one of those side-tunnels go by him to the left or right. Going by one of these he felt a strong cool breeze, and the kienspan flared up; but when he went past it, the air became dead and the kienspan went out entirely. He was breathing very fast, but it did him no good. With what strength he still had, he backtracked through absolute darkness until he felt the wind from that side-tunnel on his face. Then he lay down flat on the rock for a while and simply breathed.

Some time later his head was working more clearly and he understood that the flow of air implied an exit somewhere. He groped around on the floor until he found one of those elbow-planks, and then crawled sideways, headed upwind. He followed the air for an amount of time impossible to guess at. The low side-tunnel opened out into a smooth-floored space that seemed to be a natural cave. Here the river of air had been broken up into many trickles curving around rocks and stalagmites (tricky to follow), but (nose to floor, tongue out) he followed them for what seemed like a mile, sometimes standing up and walking through spaces that echoed like cathedrals, sometimes squirming on his belly through spaces so close that his head got wedged between the floor and ceiling. He sloshed through a pond of dead water that froze his legs, climbed up the other shore, and entered a mine-tunnel, then passed through tunnels of low and high ceilings, and up-and-down vertical shafts, so many times that he lost track of how many times he had lost track. He wanted badly to sleep, but he knew that if the fire went out while he slumbered, the air-current would stop and he'd lose the thread that, as with that bloke in the myth, was showing him the way out. His eyes, not satisfied with total darkness, fabricated demon-images from all of the bad things he'd seen or thought he'd seen in the last days.

He heard a bubbling, hissing sound, such as a dragon or Worm might make, but followed it, and the air-current, along a slowly descending tunnel until he came to water's edge. Knocking off a few sparks from his flint and steel he saw that the air he'd been following this whole time was boiling up out of a subterranean lake that filled the tunnel before him and completely blocked his way out. Having nothing else to do, he sat down to die, and fell asleep instead, and had nightmares that were an improvement on reality.

NOISE AND LIGHT, BOTH FAINT, woke him. He refused to take the light seriously: a green glow emanating from the pool (which had stopped bubbling). It was so unearthly that it could only be another of the mind tricks that the broth of the Hexen had been wreaking on him. But the noise, though distant, sounded interesting. Before, it had been drowned out by the seething of the water, but now he could hear a rhythmic hissing and booming sound.

The green light grew brighter. He could see the silhouettes of his hands in front of it.

He'd been dreaming, before he woke up, about the giant water-pipes, the hubbly-bubblies that the Turks smoked in Leipzig. They'd suck on the tube, and smoke from the tobacco bowl would pass *down* through the water and come back upwards into the tube, cooled and purified. The dream had, he guessed, been inspired by the last sound he'd heard before falling asleep, because the cave had made a similar seething and gurgling noise. As he considered it (having no other way to spend the time), he wondered whether the mine might not have acted like a giant water-pipe, and the fire like a giant Turk sucking on its tube, drawing air downwards, through a water-filled sump, from the outside, so that it bubbled up into this tunnel.

Might it be possible, then, that by swimming for some short distance through this water he would come up into the air? Could the green light be the light of sunrise, filtered through greenish pond-scum? Jack began to work up his courage, a procedure he expected would take several hours. He could think only of poor brother Dick who had drowned in the Thames: how he'd swum off all active and pink, and been pulled up limp and white.

He concluded he'd best do the deed *now*, while the witch-brew was still impairing his judgment. So he took off most of his clothes. He could come back for them later if this worked. He took only his sword (in case trouble awaited), flint, and steel, and his miner's hat, which would be good to have if he smashed his head against any underwater ceilings. Then he backed up the tunnel several paces, got a running start downhill, and dove in. The water was murderously cold and he almost screamed out his one lungful of air. He grazed the ceiling once—the light grew brighter—the ceiling wasn't there any more, and so he kicked against the sump's floor and burst up into fresh air! The distance had been only three or four yards.

But the light, though brighter, was not the light of the sun. Jack could tell, by the echoes of the trickling waters and of the murmur of voices, that he was still underground. The strange green light shone from around a nearby bend in the cavern, and glinted curiously off parts of the walls.

Before doing anything else, Jack slipped back into the water, swam back through the sump, retrieved his boots and clothes, and then returned to the glowing cavern. He got dressed and then crept toward the light on hands and knees, trying but failing to control a violent shiver. The glint he'd noticed earlier turned out to come from a patch of clear crystals, the size of fingers, growing out of a wall—diamonds! He had entered into some place of fabulous riches. The walls were fuzzy with gems. Perhaps the light was green because it was shining through a giant emerald?

Then he came round a bend and was nearly struck blind by a smooth disk of brilliant green light, flat on the floor of a roundish chamber. As his eyes adjusted he could see that a circle of persons—or of *something*—stood around the edge, dressed in outlandish and bizarre costumes.

In the center stood a figure in a long robe, a hood drawn over his head, enclosing his face in shadow, though the light shone upwards against chin and cheek-bones to give him a death's-head appearance, and it glinted in his eyes.

A voice spoke out in French—Eliza's voice! She was angry, distressed—the others turned towards her. This was Hell, or Hell's side entrance, and the demons had captured Eliza—or perhaps she was *dead*—dead because of Jack's failure to return with medicine—and she was at this moment being inducted—

Jack plunged forth, drawing his sword, but when he set foot on the green disk it gave way beneath him and he burst *through* it—suddenly he was *swimming* in green light. But there was solid rock underneath. He jumped back up, knee-deep in the stuff, and hollered, "Let her go, ye demons! Take me instead!"

They all screamed and ran away, including Eliza.

Jack looked down to find his clothes saturated with green light.

The hooded figure was the only one left. He sloshed calmly up out of the pool, opened a dark-lantern, took out a burning match, and went round igniting some torchières stuck into the ground all around. Their light was infinitely brighter, and made the green light vanish. Jack was standing in a brown puddle and his clothes were all wet.

Enoch pulled the hood back from his head and said, "What was really magnificent about that entrance, Jack, was that, until the moment you rose up out of the pool all covered in phosphorus, you were invisible—you just seemed to materialize, weapon in hand, with that Dwarf-cap, shouting in a language no one understands. Have you considered a career in the theatre?"

Jack was still too puzzled to take umbrage at this. "Who, or what, were those—?"

"Wealthy gentlefolk who, until just moments ago, were thinking of buying *Kuxen* from Doctor Leibniz."

"But—their freakish attire, their bizarre appearance—?"

"The latest fashions from Paris."

"Eliza sounded distressed."

"She was interrogating the Doctor—demanding to know just what this conjuror's trick, as she called it, had to do with the viability of the mine."

"But why even bother with mining silver, when the walls of this cavern are encrusted with diamonds?"

"Quartz."

"What is the glowing stuff anyway, and while I'm on that subject, what *does* it have to do with the mine?"

"Phosphorus, and nothing. Come, Jack, let's get you out of those wet clothes before you burst into flame." Enoch began leading Jack down a side-passage. Along the way they passed a large item of machinery that was making loud booming and sucking noises as it pumped water out of the mine. Here Enoch prevailed on Jack to strip and bathe.

Enoch said, "I don't suppose that this story shall ever be told in the same admiring way as the Strasbourg Plague House Takeover and the Bohemian Carp Feast."

"What!? How did you know about those?"

"I travel. I talk to Vagabonds. Word gets around. You might be interested to know that your achievements have been compiled into a picaresque novel entitled *L'Emmerdeur,* which has already been burnt in Paris and bootlegged in Amsterdam."

"Stab me!" Jack for the first time began to think that Enoch's friendly behavior toward him might be well-meaning, and not just an extremely subtle form of mockery. Enoch shouldered a six-inch-thick door open and led Jack into a windowless crypt, a vaulted room with a large table in the middle, candles, and a stove, which happened to look exactly like the sort of place Dwarves would inhabit. They sat down and started smoking and drinking. Presently the Doctor came in and joined them. Far from being outraged, he seemed relieved, as if he'd never wanted to be in the mining business anyway. Enoch gave the Doctor a significant look, which Jack was fairly sure meant *I warned you not to involve Vagabonds,* and the Doctor nodded.

"What are the, er, investors doing?" Jack asked.

"Standing up above in the sunlight—the females trying to outdo each other in swooning, the males engaging in a learned dispute as to whether you were an enraged Dwarf come to chase us away from his hoard, or a demon from Hell come to seize us."

"And Eliza? Not swooning I assume."

"She is too busy receiving the compliments, and credentials, of the others, who are all dumbfounded by her acumen."

"Ah, then it's possible she *won't* kill me."

"Far from it, Jack, the girl is blushing, she is radiant, and not in a dipped-in-phosphorus sense."

"Why?"

"Because, Jack, you volunteered to be taken down into eternal torment in place of her. This is the absolute *minimum* (unless I'm mistaken) that any female requires from her man."

"So *that's* what they're all after," Jack mused.

Eliza backed through the door, unable to use her arms, which were hugging a bundle of letters of introduction, visiting-cards, bills of exchange, scraps with scrawled addresses, and small purses a-clink with miscellaneous coinage. "We've missed you, Jack," she said, "where've you been?"

"Running an errand—meeting some locals—partaking of their rich traditions," Jack said. "Can we get out of Germany now, please?"

The Place
SUMMER 1684

Trade, like Religion, is what every Body talks of, but
few understand: The very Term is dubious, and in
its ordinary Acceptation, not sufficiently explain'd.
—DANIEL DEFOE, *A Plan of the English Commerce*

"IF NOTHING HAPPENS IN AMSTERDAM, save that everything going
into it, turns round and comes straight back *out*—"

"Then there must be nothing else *there*," Eliza finished.

Neither one of them had ever been to Amsterdam—yet. But the
amount of stuff moving toward that city, and away from it, on the
roads and canals of the Netherlands, was so vast that it made Leipzig
seem like a smattering of poor actors in the background of a play,
moving back and forth with a few paltry bundles to create the *impression* of commerce. Jack had not seen such bunching-together of
people and goods since the onslaught on Vienna. But that had only
happened once, and this was continuous. And he knew by reputation that what came in and out of Amsterdam over land, compared
to what was carried on ships, was a runny nose compared to a river.

Eliza was dressed in a severe black ensemble with a high stiff white
collar: a prosperous Dutch farmer's wife to all appearances, except
that she spoke no Dutch. During their weeks of almost mortally
tedious westing across the Duchy of Braunschweig-Wolfenbüttel, the
Duchy of Braunschweig-Lüneburg, the Bishopric of Hildesheim,
Duchy of Kalenberg, Landgraviate of something-or-other, County of
Lippe, County of Ravensburg, Bishopric of Osnabrück, County of
Lingen, Bishopric of Münster, and County of Bentheim, she had
mostly gone in man's attire, booted, sworded, and spurred. Not
that anyone really believed she was a man: she was pretending to
be an Italian courtesan on her way to a tryst with a Genoese banker
in Amsterdam. This made hardly any sense at all, but, as Jack had
learned, border guards mostly just wanted something to relieve the
tedium. It was easier to flaunt Eliza than to hide her. Trying to predict when they'd reach the next frontier, and whether the people

on the far side of it would be Protestant or Catholic, and how *serious* about being Prot. or Cath. they'd be, was simply too difficult. Much simpler to be saucily irreligious *everywhere* and, if people got offended, run away. It worked most places. The locals had other concerns: if half the rumors were true, then King Looie—not satisfied with bombarding Genoa, laying siege to Luxembourg, challenging Pope Innocent XI to a staredown, expelling Jewry from Bordeaux, and massing his armies on the Spanish border—had just announced that he owned northwestern Germany. As they happened to *be* in northwestern Germany, this made matters tense, yet fluid, in a way that was not entirely bad for them.

Great herds of scrawny young cattle were being driven across the plain out of the East to be fattened in the manmade pastures of the Netherlands. Commingled with them were hordes of unemployed men going to look for work in Dutch cities—Hollandgänger, they were called. So the borders were easy, except along the frontier of the Dutch Republic, where all the lines of circumvallation ran across their path: not only the natural rivers but walls, ditches, ramparts, palisades, moats, and pickets: some new and crisp and populated by soldiers, others the abandoned soft-edged memories of battles that must have happened before Jack had been born. But after being chased off a time or two, in ways that would probably seem funny when remembered later, they penetrated into Gelderland: the eastern marches of that Republic. Jack had patiently inculcated Eliza in the science of examining the corpses, heads, and limbs of executed criminals that decorated all city gates and border-posts, as a way of guessing what sorts of behavior were most offensive to the locals. What it came down to, here, was that Eliza was in black and Jack was on his crutch, with no weapons, and as little flesh as possible, in sight.

There were tolls everywhere, but no center of power. The cattle-herds spread out away from the high road and into pastures flat as ponds, leaving them and the strewn parades of Hollandgänger to traipse along for a day or two, until they began joining up with other, much greater roads from the south and east: nearly unbroken queues of carts laden with goods, fighting upstream against as heavy traffic coming from the north. "Why not just stop and trade in the middle of the road?" Jack asked, partly because he knew it would provoke Eliza. But she wasn't provoked at all—she seemed to think it was a good question, such as the philosophical Doctor might've asked. "Why indeed? There must be a reason. In commerce there is a reason for *everything*. That's why I like it."

The landscape was long skinny slabs of flat land divided one from the next by straight ditches full of standing water, and what happened on that land was always something queer: tulip-raising, for example. Individual vegetables being cultivated and raised by hand, like Christmas geese, and pigs and calves coddled like rich men's children. Odd-looking fields growing flax, hemp, rape, hops, tobacco, woad, and madder. But queerest of all was that these ambitious farmers were doing things that had nothing to do with farming: in many places he saw women bleaching bolts of English cloth in buttermilk, spreading it out in the fields to dry in the sun. People raised and harvested thistles, then bundled their prickly heads together to make tools for carding cloth. Whole villages sat out making lace as fast as their fingers could work, just a few children running from one person to the next with a cup of water for them to sip, or a bread-crust to snap at. Farmers whose stables were filled, not with *horses,* but with *painters*—young men from France, Savoy, or Italy who sat before easels making copy after copy of land- and sea-scapes and enormous renditions of the Siege of Vienna. These, stacked and bundled and wrapped into cargo-bales, joined the parade bound for Amsterdam.

The flow took them sometimes into smaller cities, where little trade-fairs were forever teeming. Since none of the farmers in this upside-down country grew food, they had to buy it in markets like city people. Jack and Eliza would jostle against rude boers and haggle against farmers' wives with silver rings on their fingers trying to buy cheese and eggs and bread to eat along their way. Eliza saw storks for the first time, building their nests on chimneys and swooping down into streets to snatch scraps before the dogs could get them. Pelicans she liked, too. But the things Jack marveled at—four-legged chickens and two-headed sheep, displayed in the streets by boers—were of no interest to her. She'd seen better in Constantinople.

In one of those towns they saw a woman walking about imprisoned in a barrel with neck- and arm-holes, having been guilty of adultery, and after this, Eliza would not rest, nor let Jack have peace or satisfaction, until they'd reached the city. So they drove themselves onwards across lands that had been ruined a dozen years before, when William of Orange had opened the sluices and flooded the land to make a vast moat across the Republic and save Amsterdam from the armies of King Looie. They squatted in remains of buildings that had been wrecked in that artificial Deluge, and followed canals north, skirting the small camps where canal-pirates, the watery equivalent of highwaymen, squatted round wheezing peat-fires. Too, they avoided the clusters of huts fastened to the canal-banks, where lepers lived, begging for alms by flinging ballasted boxes out at passing boats, then reeling them in speckled with coins.

One day, riding along a canal's edge, they came to a confluence of waters, and turned a perfect right angle and stared down a river that ran straight as a bow-string until it ducked beneath the curvature of the earth. It was so infested with shipping that there seemed to be not enough water left to float a nutshell. Obviously it led straight to Amsterdam.

Their escape from Germany (as that mess of Duchies, Electorates, Landgraviates, Margraviates, Counties, Bishoprics, Archbishoprics, and Principalities was called) had taken much longer than Jack had really wanted. The Doctor had offered to take them as far as Hanover, where he looked after the library of the Duchess Sophia* when he wasn't building windmills atop their Harz silver-mines. Eliza had accepted gratefully, without asking whether Jack might have an opinion on the matter. Jack's opinion would have been *no,* simply because Jack was in the habit of going wherever he wished whenever the mood took him. And accompanying the Doctor to Hanover meant that they could not leave Bockboden until the Doctor had settled all of his business in that district.

"WHAT'S HE WASTING *TODAY* ON?" Jack demanded of Enoch Root one morning. They were riding along a mountain road, followed by a couple of heavy ox-carts. Enoch went on errands like this one every morning. Jack, lacking any other kind of stimulation, had decided to take up the practice.

"Same as yesterday."

"And that is? Forgive an ignorant Vagabond, but I am used to men of *action*—so when the Doctor spends all day, every day, *talking* to people, it seems to me as if he's doing *nothing.*"

"He's *accomplishing* nothing—that's very different from *doing* nothing," Enoch said gravely.

"What's he trying to *accomplish?*"

"He'd persuade the masters of the Duke's mines not to abandon all of his innovations, now that his latest attempt to sell *Kuxen* has gone the way of all the others."

"Well, why should they listen to him?"

"We are going where the Doctor went yesterday," Enoch said, "and heard what he wanted to from the master of a mine."

---

*And of her husband, Duke Ernst August.

"Beggin' yer pardon, guv'nor, but that striketh me not as an answer to my question."

"This entire day will be your answer," Enoch said, and then looked back, significantly, at a heavy cart following behind them, which was laden with quicksilver flasks packed in wooden crates.

They came to a mine like all the others: schlock-heaps, hand-haspels, furnaces, wheelbarrows. Jack had seen it in the Ore Range and he'd seen it in the Harz, but today (perhaps because Enoch had suggested that there was something to be learned) he saw a new thing.

The shards of ore harvested from the veins growing in the earth, were brought together and dumped out in a pile on the ground, then raked out and beaten up with hammers. The fragments were inspected in the light of day by miners too old, young, or damaged to go down into the tunnels, and sorted into three piles. The first was stone with no silver in it, which was discarded. The second was ore rich in silver, which went straight to the furnaces to be (if what Jack had seen in the Ore Range was any guide) crushed between millstones, mixed with burning-lead, shoveled into a chimney-like furnace blown by great mule-powered bellows, and melted down into pigs of crude silver. The third, which Jack had not seen at Herr Geidel's mine, was ore that contained silver, but was not as rich as the other. Geidel would have discarded this as not worth the trouble to refine it.

Jack followed a wagon-load of this down the hill to a flat meadow decorated by curious mounds hidden under oiled canvas tarps. Here, men and women were pounding this low-grade ore in big iron mortars and turning the proceeds out into clattering sieves. Boys shook these to sift out powdered ore, then mixed it with water, salt, and the dross from copper-making to produce a sticky clay. This they emptied into large wooden tubs. Then along came an elder, trailed by a couple of stout boys sweating under heavy backloads that looked familiar: they were the quicksilver-flasks that the Doctor had bought in Leipzig, and that Enoch had delivered to them this very morning. The elder stirred through the mud with his hand, checking its quality and consistency, and, if it was right, he'd hug a flask and draw out the wooden bung and tip it, making a bolt of quicksilver strike into the mud like argent lightning. Barefoot boys went to work stomping the mercury into the mud.

Several such vats were being worked at any one time. Enoch explained to Jack that the amalgam had to be mixed for twenty-four hours. Then the vat was upended to make a heap of the stuff on the ground. At this particular mine, there were dozens of such heaps arrayed across the meadow, each one protected from the rain by a canopy of rugged cloth, and each stuck with a little sign scrawled with information about how long it had been sitting there. "This one was last worked ten days ago—it is due," Enoch told him, reading one of the signs. Indeed, later some of the workers rolled an empty tub up to that pile, shoveled the amalgam into it, added water, and began to work it with their feet again.

Enoch continued to wander about, peeling back canvas to inspect the heaps, and offering suggestions to the elders. Locals had begun filtering out of the woods as soon as visitors had arrived, and were now following him around—greed for knowledge drawing them closer, and fear pushing them back. "This one's got too much quicksilver," he said of one, "that's why it's black." But another was the color of bran. More quicksilver was wanted. Most of them were shades of gray, which was apparently desirable—but Enoch thrust his hand into these to check their warmth. Cold ones needed to have more copper dross added, and overly hot ones needed water. Enoch was carrying a basin, which he used to wash samples of the heaps in water until little pools of silver formed in the bottom. One of the heaps, all of a uniform ash color, was deemed ready. Workers shoveled it into wheelbarrows and took it down to a creek, where a cascade had been set up to wash it. The water carried the ashy stuff away as swirling clouds, and left silvery residue. This they packed into conical bags, like the ones used to make sugar-loaves, and hung them up over pots, rows of them dangling like the tits on a sow, except that instead of producing milk they dripped quicksilver, leaving a gleaming semi-solid mass inside the bags. This they formed into balls, like boys making snowballs, and put them, a few at a time, into crucibles. Over the top of each crucible they put an iron screen, then flipped the whole thing upside-down and placed it over a like crucible, half-buried in the ground, with water in the bottom, so that the two were fitted rim-to-rim, making a capsule divided in half by the iron screen. Then they buried the whole thing in coal and burned it until it was all red-hot. After it cooled, they raked off the ash and took it all apart to reveal that the quicksilver had been liberated from the balls of amalgam and escaped through the screen, to puddle below, leaving above a cluster of porous balls of pure silver metal all stuck together, and ready to be minted into thalers.

Jack spent most of the ride home pondering what he'd seen. He noticed after a while that Enoch Root had been humming in a satisfied way, evidently pleased with himself for having been able to so thoroughly shut Jack up.

"So Alchemy has its uses," Enoch said, noting that Jack was coming out of his reverie.

"You invented this?"

"I improved it. In the old days they used only quicksilver and salt. The piles were cold, and they had to sit for a year. But when dross of copper is added, they become warm, and complete the change in three or four weeks."

"The cost of quicksilver is—?"

Enoch chuckled. "You sound like your lady friend."

"That's the first question she's going to ask."

"It varies. A good price for a hundredweight would be eighty."

"Eighty of *what?*"

"Pieces of eight," Enoch said.

"It's important to specify."

"Christendom's but a corner of the world, Jack," Enoch said. "Outside of it, pieces of eight are the universal currency."

"All right—with a hundredweight of quicksilver, you can make how much silver?"

"Depending on the quality of the ore, about a hundred Spanish marks—and in answer to your next question, a Spanish mark of silver, at the standard level of fineness, is worth eight pieces of eight and six Royals . . ."

"A PIECE OF EIGHT HAS eight *reals*—" Eliza said, later, having spent the last two hours sitting perfectly motionless while Jack paced, leaped, and cavorted about her bedchamber relating all of these events with only modest improvements.

"I know that—that's why it's called a piece of eight," Jack said testily, standing barefoot on the sack of straw that was Eliza's bed, where he had been demonstrating the way the workers mixed the amalgam with their feet.

"Eight pieces of eight plus six royals, makes seventy royals. A hundred marks of silver, then, is worth seven *thousand* royals . . . or . . . eight hundred seventy-five pieces of eight. And the price of the quicksilver needed is—again?"

"Eighty pieces of eight, or thereabouts, would be a *good* price."

"So—those who'd make money need silver, and those who'd make silver need quicksilver—and a piece of eight's worth of quicksilver, put to the right uses, produces enough silver to mint ten pieces of eight."

"And you can re-use it, as they are careful to do," Jack said. "You have forgotten a few other necessaries, by the way—such as a silver mine. Mountains of coal and salt. Armies of workers."

"All gettable," Eliza said flatly. "Didn't you understand what Enoch was telling you?"

"Don't say it!—don't tell me—just wait!" Jack said, and went over to the arrow-slit to peer up at the Doctor's windmill, and down at his ox-carts parked along the edge of the stable-yard. Up and down being the only two possibilities when peering through an arrow-slit. "The Doctor provides quicksilver to the mines whose masters do what the Doctor wants."

"So," Eliza said, "the Doctor has—what?"

"Power," Jack finally said after a few wrong guesses.

"Because he has—what?"

"Quicksilver."

"So that's the answer—we go to Amsterdam and buy quicksilver."

"A splendid plan—if only we had money to buy it *with*."

"Poh! We'll just use someone else's money," Eliza said, flicking something off the backs of her fingernails.

NOW, STARING DOWN THIS CROWDED canal towards the city, Jack saw, in his mind, a map he'd viewed in Hanover. Sophie and Ernst August had inherited their library, not to mention librarian (i.e., the Doctor), when Ernst August's Papist brother—evidently, something of a black sheep—had had the good grace to die young without heirs. This fellow must have been more interested in books than wenches, because his library had (according to the Doctor) been one of the largest in Germany at the time of his demise five years ago, and had only gotten bigger since then. There was no place to put it all, and so it only kept getting shifted from one stable to another. Ernst August apparently spent all of his time either fending off King Louis along the Rhine, or else popping down to Venice to pick up fresh mistresses, and never got round to constructing a permanent building for the collection.

In any event, Jack and Eliza had paused in Hanover for a few days on their journey west, and the Doctor had allowed them to sleep in one of the numerous out-buildings where parts of the library were stored. There had been many books, useless to Jack, but also quite a few extraordinary maps. He had made it his business to memorize these, or at least the parts that were finished. Remote islands and continents splayed on the parchment like stomped brains, the interiors blank, the coastlines trailing off into nowhere and simply ending in mid-ocean because no one had ever sailed farther than that, and the boasts and phant'sies of seafarers disagreed.

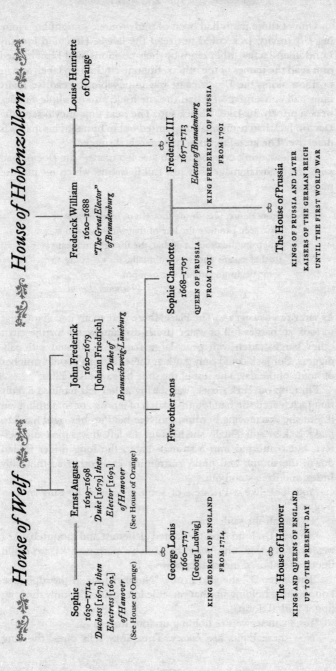

House of Welf ❧ ❧ House of Hohenzollern ❧ ❧

Sophie
1630–1714
Duchess [1679] *then Electress* [1692]
of Hanover
(See House of Orange)

Ernst August
1629–1698
Duke [1679] *then Elector* [1692]
of Hanover
(See House of Orange)

John Frederick
1620–1679
[Johann Friedrich]
Duke of Braunschweig-Lüneburg

Frederick William
1620–1688
"The Great Elector" of Brandenburg

Louise Henriette of Orange

Frederick III
1657–1713
Elector of Brandenburg
KING FREDERICK I OF PRUSSIA
FROM 1701

Sophie Charlotte
1668–1705
QUEEN OF PRUSSIA
FROM 1701

Five other sons

George Louis
1660–1727
[Georg Ludwig]
KING GEORGE I OF ENGLAND
FROM 1714

The House of Hanover
KINGS AND QUEENS OF ENGLAND
UP TO THE PRESENT DAY

The House of Prussia
KINGS OF PRUSSIA AND LATER
KAISERS OF THE GERMAN REICH
UNTIL THE FIRST WORLD WAR

One of those maps had been of trade-routes: straight lines joining city to city. Jack could not read the labels. He could identify London and a few other cities by their positions, and Eliza helped him read the names of the others. But one city had no label, and its position along the Dutch coast was impossible to read: so many lines had converged on it that the city itself, and its whole vicinity, were a prickly ink-lake, a black sun. The next time they'd seen the Doctor, Jack had triumphantly pointed out to him that his map was defective. The arch-Librarian had merely shrugged.

"The Jews don't even bother to give it a name," the Doctor had said. "In their language they just call it *mokum,* which means 'the place.'"

> From desire, ariseth the thought of some means we
> have seen produce the like of that which we aim at;
> and from the thought of that, the thought of means
> to that mean; and so continually, till we come to
> some beginning within our own power.
> —Hobbes, *Leviathan*

As they came closer to The Place, there were many peculiar things to look at: barges full of water (fresh drinking-water for the city), other barges laden with peat, large flat areas infested with salt-diggers. But Jack could only gawk at these things a certain number of hours of the day. The rest of the time he gawked at Eliza.

Eliza, up on Turk's back, was staring at her left hand so fixedly that Jack feared she had found a patch of leprosy, or something, on it. But she was moving her lips, too. She held up her right hand to make Jack be still. Finally she held up the left. It was pink and perfect, but contorted into a strange habit, the long finger folded down, the thumb and pinky restraining each other so that only Index and Ring stood out.

"You look like a Priestess of some new sect, blessing or cursing me."

"D" was all she said.

"Ah, yes, Dr. John Dee, the famed alchemist and mountebank? I was thinking that with some of Enoch's parlor tricks, we could fleece a few bored merchants' wives . . ."

"The letter D," she said firmly. "Number four in the alphabet. Four is this," holding up that versatile left again, with only the long finger folded down.

"Yes, I can see you're holding up four fingers . . ."

"No—these digits are *binary*. The pinky tells ones, the ring finger twos, the long finger fours, the index eights, the thumb six-teens. So when the long finger *only* is folded down, it means four, which means D."

"But you had the thumb and pinky folded down also, just now . . ."

"The Doctor also taught me to encipher these by adding *another* number—seventeen in this case," Eliza said, displaying her right with the thumb and pinky tip-to-tip. Putting her hand back as it had been, she announced, "Twenty-one, which means, in the English alphabet, U."

"But what is the point?"

"The Doctor has taught me to hide messages in letters."

"It's your intention to be *writing letters* to this man?"

"If I do not," she said innocently, "how can I expect to *receive* any?"

"Why would you *want* to?" Jack asked.

"To continue my education."

"Owff!" blurted Jack, and he doubled over as if Turk had kicked him in the belly.

"A guessing-game?" Eliza said coolly. "It's got to be either: you think I'm *already* too educated, or: you hoped it would be something else."

"Both," Jack said. "You've put *hours* into improving your mind— with *nothing* to show for it. I'd hoped you had gotten *financial backing* out of the Doctor, or that Sophie."

Eliza laughed. "I've told you, over and over, that I never came within half a mile of Sophie. The Doctor let me climb a church-steeple that looks down over Herrenhausen, her great garden, so that I could watch while she went out for one of her walks. That's as close as someone like me could ever come to someone like her."

"Why bother, then?"

"It was enough for me simply to lay eyes on her: the daughter of the Winter Queen, and great-granddaughter of Mary Queen of Scots. You would never understand."

"It's just that you are always on about money, and I cannot see how staring at some bitch in a French dress, from a mile away, relates to that."

"Hanover is a poor country anyway—it's not as if they have much money to gamble on our endeavours."

"Haw! If that's poverty, give me some!"

"Why do you think the Doctor is going through such exertions to find investors for the silver mine?"

"Thank you—you've brought me back to my question: what does the Doctor want?"

"To translate all human knowledge into a new philosophical language, consisting of numbers. To write it down in a vast Encyclopedia that will be a sort of machine, not only for finding old knowledge but for making new, by carrying out certain logical operations on those numbers—and to employ all of this in a great project of bringing religious conflict to an end, and raising Vagabonds up out of squalor and liberating their potential energy—whatever *that* means."

"Speaking for myself, I'd like a pot of beer and, later, to have my face trapped between your inner thighs."

"It's a big world—perhaps you and the Doctor can both realize your ambitions," she said after giving the matter some thought. "I'm finding horseback-riding *enjoyable* but ultimately *frustrating*."

"Don't look to *me* for sympathy."

The canal came together with others, and at some point they were on the river Amstel, which took them into the place, just short of its collision with the river Ij, where it had long ago been dammed up by the beaver-like Dutchmen. Then (as Jack the veteran reader of fortifications could see), as stealable objects, lootable churches, and rapable women had accumulated around this Amstel-Dam, those who had the most to lose had created Lines of Circumvallation. To the north, the broad Ij—more an arm of the sea than a proper river—served as a kind of moat. But on the landward side they'd thrown up walls, surrounding Amstel-Dam in a U, the prongs of the U touching the Ij to either side of where the Amstel joined it, and the bend at the bottom of the U crossing the Amstel upstream of the Dam. The dirt for the walls had to come from somewhere. Lacking hills, they'd taken it from excavations, which conveniently filled with ground-water to become moats. But to the avid Dutch there was no moat that could not be put to work as a canal. As the land inside each U had filled up with buildings, newly arrived strivers had put up buildings *outside* the walls, making it necessary to create new, larger Us encompassing the old. The city was like a tree, as long as it lived surrounding its core with new growth. Outer layers were big, the canals widely spaced, but in the middle of town they were only a stone's throw apart, so that Jack and Eliza were always crossing over cleverly counter-weighted drawbridges. As they did so they stared up and down the canals, carpeted with low boats that could skim underneath the bridges, and (on the Amstel, and some larger canals) creaking sloops with collapsible masts. Even the small boats could carry enormous loads below the water-line. The canals and the boats explained, then, why it was possible to move about in Amsterdam at all: the torrent of cargo that clogged roads in the countryside was here transferred to boats, and the streets, for the most part, opened to people.

Long rows of five-story houses fronted on canals. A few ancient timber structures still stood in the middle of town, but almost all of the buildings were brick, trimmed with white and painted over with tar. Jack marvelled like a yokel at the sight of barn doors on the fifth story of a building, opening out onto a sheer drop to a canal. A single timber projected into space above to serve as a cargo hoist. Unlike those Leipziger houses, with storage only in the attic, these were for nothing *but*.

The richest of those warehouse-streets was Warmoesstraat, and when they'd crossed over it they were in a long plaza called Damplatz, which as far as Jack could tell was just the original Dam, paved over. It had men in turbans and outlandish furry hats, and satin-clad cavaliers sweeping their plumed chapeaus off to bow to each other, and mighty buildings, and other features that might have given Jack an afternoon's gawking. But before he could even begin, some kind of phenomenon on the scale of a War, Fire, or Biblical Deluge demanded his attention off to the north. He turned his face into a clammy breeze and stared down the length of a short, fat canal to discover a low brown cloud obscuring the horizon. Perhaps it was the pall of smoke from a fire as big as the one that had destroyed London. No, it was a brushy forest, a leafless thicket several miles broad. Or perhaps a besieging army, a hundred times the size of the Turk's, all armed with pikes as big as pine-trees and aflutter with ensigns and pennants.

In the end, it took Jack several minutes' looking to allow himself to believe that he was viewing all of the world's ships at one time—their individual masts, ropes, and spars merging into a horizon through which a few churches and windmills on the other side of it could be made out as dark blurs. Ships entering from, or departing toward, the Ijsselmeer beyond, fired rippling gun-salutes and were answered by Dutch shore-batteries, spawning oozy smoke-clouds that clung about the rigging of all those ships and seemingly glued them all into a continuous fabric, like mud daubed into a wattle of dry sticks. The waves of the sea could be seen as slow-spreading news.

Once Jack had a few hours to adjust to the peculiarity of Amsterdam's buildings, its water-streets, the people's aggressive cleanliness, their barking language, and their inability to settle on this or that Church, he understood the place. All of its quarters and neighborhoods were the same as in any other city. The knife-grinders might dress like Deacons, but they still ground knives the same way as the ones in Paris. Even the waterfront was just a stupendously larger rendition of the Thames.

But then they wandered into a neighborhood the likes of which Jack had never seen *anywhere*—or rather the neighborhood wandered into *them*, for this was a rambling Mobb. Whereas most of Amsterdam was divided among richer and poorer in the usual way, this roving neighborhood was indiscriminately mixed-up: just as shocking to Vagabond Jack as it would be to a French nobleman. Even from a distance, as the neighborhood came up the street towards Jack and Eliza, he could see that it was soaked with tension. They were like a rabble gathered before palace gates, awaiting news of the death of a King. But as Jack could plainly see when the neighborhood had flowed round them and swept them up, there *were* no palace gates here, nor anything of that sort.

It would have been nothing more than a passing freak of Creation, like a comet, except that Eliza grabbed Jack's hand and pulled him along, so that they became part of that neighborhood for half an hour, as it rolled and nudged its way among the buildings of Amsterdam like a blob of mercury feeling its way through a wooden maze. Jack saw that they were anticipating news, not from some external source, but *from within*—information, or rumors of it, surged from one end of this crowd to the other like waves in a shaken rug, with just as much noise, movement, and eruption of debris as that would imply. Like smallpox, it was passed from one person to the next with great rapidity, usually as a brief furious exchange of words and numbers. Each of these conversations was terminated by a gesture that looked as if it might have been a handshake, many generations in the past, but over time had degenerated into a brisk slapping-together of the hands. When it was done properly it made a sharp popping noise and left the palm glowing red. So the propagation of news, rumors, fads, trends, &c. through this mob could be followed by listening for waves of hand-slaps. If the wave broke over you and continued onwards, and your palm was not red, and your ears were not ringing, it meant that you had missed out on something important. And Jack was more than content to do so. But Eliza could not abide it. Before long, she had begun to ride on those waves of noise, and to gravitate towards places where they were most intense. Even worse, she seemed to understand what was going on. She knew some Spanish, which was the language spoken by many of these persons, especially the numerous Jews among them.

Eliza found lodgings a short distance south and west of the Damplatz. There was an alley just narrow enough for Jack to touch both sides of it at one time, and someone had tried the experiment of throwing a few beams across this gap, between the second, third, and fourth stories of the adjoining buildings, and then using these as the framework of a sort of house. The buildings to either side were being slurped down into the underlying bog at differing rates, and so the house above the alley was skewed, cracked, and leaky. But Eliza rented the fourth story after an apocalyptic haggling session with the landlady (Jack, who had been off stabling Turk, only witnessed the final half-hour of this). The landlady was a hound-faced Calvinist who had immediately recognized Eliza as one who was predestined for Hell, and so Jack's arrival and subsequent loitering scarcely made any impression. Still, she imposed a strict rule against visitors—shaking a finger at Jack so that her silver rings clanked together like links in a chain. Jack considered dropping his trousers as proof of chastity. But this trip to Amsterdam was Eliza's plan, not Jack's, and so he did not consider it meet to do any such thing. They had a place, or rather Eliza did, and Jack could come and go via rooftops and drainpipes.

They lived in Amsterdam for a time.

Jack expected that Eliza would begin to *do* something, but she seemed content to while away time in a coffee-house alongside the Damplatz, occasionally writing letters to the Doctor and occasionally receiving them. The moving neighborhood of anxious people brushed against this particular coffee-house, The Maiden, twice a day—for its movements were regular. They gathered on the Dam until the stroke of noon, when they flocked down the street to a large courtyard called the Exchange, where they remained until two o'clock. Then they spilled out and took their trading back up to the Dam, dividing up into various cliques and cabals that frequented different coffee-houses. Eliza's apartment actually straddled an important migration-route, so that between it and her coffee-house she was never out of earshot.

Jack reckoned that Eliza was content to live off what they had, like a Gentleman's daughter, and that was fine with Jack, who enjoyed spending more than getting. He in the meantime went back to his usual habit, which was to spend many days roaming about any new place he came into, to learn how it worked. Unable to read, unfit to converse with, he learned by watching—and here there was plenty of excellent watching. At first he made the mistake of leaving his crutch behind in Eliza's garret, and going out as an able-bodied man. This was how he learned that despite all of those Hollandgänger coming in from the East, Amsterdam was still ravenous for labor. He hadn't been out on the street for an hour before he'd been arrested for idleness and put to work dredging canals—and seeing all the muck that came off the bottom, he began to think that the Doctor's story of how small creatures got buried in river-bottoms made more sense than he'd thought at first.

When the foreman finally released him and the others from the dredge at day's end, he could hardly climb up onto the wharf for all the men crowded around jingling purses of heavy-sounding coins: agents trying to recruit sailors to man those ships on the Ij. Jack got away from them fast, because where there was such a demand for sailors, there'd be press-ganging: one blunder into a dark alley, or one free drink in a tavern, and he'd wake up with a headache on a ship in the North Sea, bound for the Cape of Good Hope, and points far beyond.

The next time he went out, he bound his left foot up against his butt-cheek, and took his crutch. In this guise he was able to wander up and down the banks of the Ij and do all the looking he wanted. Even here, though, he had to move along smartly, lest he be taken for a vagrant, and thrown into a workhouse to be reformed.

He knew a few things from talking to Vagabonds and from examining the Doctor's expansive maps: that the Ij broadened into an inland sea called Ijsselmeer, which was protected from the ocean by the island called Texel. That there was a good deep-water anchorage at Texel, but between that island and Ijsselmeer lay broad sand-banks that, like the ones at the mouth of the Thames, had mired many ships. Hence his astonishment at the size of the merchant fleet in the Ij: he knew that the *great* ships could not even *reach* this point.

They had driven lines of piles into the bottom of the Ij to seal off the prongs of the U and prevent French or English warships from coming right up to the Damplatz. These piles supported a boardwalk that swung across the harbor in a flattened arc, with drawbridges here and there to let small boats—ferry kaags, Flemish pleyts, beetle-like water-ships, keg-shaped smakschips—into the inner harbor; the canals; and the Damrak, which was the short inlet that was all that remained of the original river Amstel. Larger ships were moored to the outside of this barrier. At the eastern end of the Inner Harbor, they'd made a new island called Oostenburg and put a shipyard there: over it flew a flag with small letters O and C impaled on the horns of a large V, which meant the Dutch East India Company. This was a wonder all by itself, with its ropewalks—skinny buildings a third of a mile long—windmills grinding lead and boring gun-barrels, a steam-house, perpetually obnubilated, for bending wood, dozens of smoking and clanging smithys including two mighty ones where anchors were made, and a small tidy one for making nails, a tar factory on its own wee island so that when it burnt down it wouldn't take the rest of the yard with it. A whole warehouse district of its own. Lofts big enough to make sails larger than any Jack had ever seen. And, of course, skeletons of several big ships on the slanted ways, braced with diagonal sticks to keep 'em from toppling over, and all aswarm with workers like ants on a whale's bones.

Somewhere there must've been master wood-carvers and gilders, too, because the stems and sterns of the V.O.C. ships riding in the Ij were decorated like Parisian whorehouses, with carved statues covered in gold-leaf: for example, a maiden reclining on a couch with one shapely arm draped over a globe, and Mercury swooping down from on high to crown her with the laurel. And yet just outside the picket of windmills and watch-towers that outlined the city, the landscape of pastures and ditches resumed. Mere yards from India ships offloading spices and calico into small boats that slipped through the drawbridges to the Damrak, cattle grazed.

The Damrak came up hard against the side of the city's new weigh-house, which was a pleasant enough building almost completely obscured by a perpetual swarm of boats. On the ground floor, all of its sides were open—it was made on stilts like a Vagabond-shack in the woods—and looking in, Jack could see its whole volume filled with scales of differing sizes, and racks and stacks of copper and brass cylinders engraved with wild snarls of cursive writing: weights for all the measures employed in different Dutch Provinces and the countries of the world. It was, he could see, the third weigh-house to be put up here and still not big enough to weigh and mark all of the goods coming in on those boats. Sloops coming in duelled for narrow water-lanes with canal-barges taking the weighed and stamped goods off to the city's warehouses, and every few minutes a small heavy cart clattered away across the Damplatz, laden with coins the ships' captains had used to pay duty, and made a sprint for the Exchange Bank, scattering wigged, ribboned, and turbaned deal-makers out of its path. The Exchange Bank was the same thing as the Town Hall, and a stone's throw from there was the Stock Exchange—a rectangular courtyard environed by colonnades, like the ones in Leipzig but bigger and brighter.

One afternoon Jack came by the Maiden to pick Eliza up at the end of her hard day's drinking coffee and spending the Shaftoes' inheritance. The place was busy, and Jack reckoned he could slip in the door without attracting any bailiffs. It was a rich airy high-ceilinged place, not at all tavernlike, hot and close, with clever people yammering in half a dozen languages. In a corner table by a window, where northern light off the Ij could set her face aglow, Eliza sat, flanked by two other women, and holding court (or so it seemed) for a parade of Italians, Spaniards, and other swarthy rapier-carrying men in big wigs and bright clothes. Occasionally she'd reach for a big round coffee-pot, and at those moments she'd look just like the Maid of Amsterdam on the stern of a ship— or for that matter, as painted on the ceiling of this very room: loosely draped in yards of golden satin, one hand on a globe, one nipple poking out, Mercury always behind and to the right, and below her, the ever-present Blokes with Turbans, and feather-bedecked Negroes, presenting tributes in the form of ropes of pearls and giant silver platters.

She was flirting with those Genoese and Florentine merchants' sons, and Jack could cope with that, to a point. But they were rich. And this was all she did, every day. He lost the power of sight for a few minutes. But in time his rage cleared away, like the clouds of ash washing away from the amalgam, clearing steadily to reveal a pretty gleam of silver under clear running water. Eliza was staring at him—seeing everything. She glanced at something next to him, telling him to look at it, and then she locked her blue eyes on someone across the table and laughed at a witticism.

Jack followed her look and discovered a kind of shrine against the wall. It was a glass-fronted display case, but all gold-leafed and decked out with trumpet-tooting seraphs, as if its niches had been carved to house pieces of the True Cross and fingernail-parings of Archangels. But in fact the niches contained little heaps of dull everyday things like ingots of lead, scraps of wool, mounds of salt-peter and sugar and coffee-beans and pepper-corns, rods and slabs of iron, copper and tin, and twists of silk and cotton cloth. And, in a tiny crystal flask, like a perfume bottle, there was a sample of quicksilver.

"So, I'm meant to believe that you're transacting business in there?" he asked, once she had extricated herself, and they were out on the Damplatz together.

"You believed that I was doing *what*, then?"

"It's just that I saw no goods or money changing hands."

"They call it *Windhandel.*"

"The wind business? An apt name for it."

"Do you have any idea, Jack, how much quicksilver is stored up in these warehouses all around us?"

"No."

"I do."

She stopped at a place where they could peer into a portal of the Stock Exchange. "Just as a whole workshop can be powered by a mill-wheel, driven by a trickle of water in a race, or by a breath of air on the blades of a windmill, so the movement of goods through yonder Weigh-House is driven by a trickle of paper passing from hand to hand in *there*" (pointing to the Stock Exchange) "and the warm wind that you feel on your face when you step into the Maiden."

Movement caught Jack's eye. He imagined for a moment that it was a watch-tower being knocked down by a sudden burst of French artillery. But when he looked, he saw he'd been fooled for the hundredth time. It was a windmill spinning. Then more movement out on the Ij: a tidal swell coming through and jostling the ships. A dredger full of hapless Hollandgänger moved up a canal, clawing up muck—muck that according to the Doctor would swallow and freeze things that had once been quick, and turn them to stone. No wonder they were so fastidious about dredging. Such an idea must be anathema to the Dutch, who worshipped motion above all. For whom the physical element of Earth was too resistant and inert, an annoyance to traders, an impediment to the fluid exchange of goods. In a place where all things were suffused with quicksilver, it was necessary to blur the transition from earth to water, making out of the whole Republic a gradual shading from one to the other as they neared the banks of the Ij, not entirely complete until they got past the sandbanks and reached the ocean at Texel.

"I must go to Paris."

"Why?"

"Partly to sell Turk and those ostrich plumes."

"Clever," she said. "Paris is retail, Amsterdam wholesale—you'll fetch twice the price there."

"But really it is that I am accustomed to being the one fluid thing in a universe dumb and inert. I want to stand on the stone banks of the Seine, where *here* is solid and *there* is running water and the frontier between 'em is sharp as a knife."

"As you wish," Eliza said, "but I belong in Amsterdam."

"I know it," Jack said, "I keep seeing your picture."

The Dutch Republic
1684

✢

JACK RODE WEST OUT OF Amsterdam, through Haarlem, and then found himself suddenly alone, and perilously close to being under water: autumn rains had submerged the pastures, leaving the walled towns as islands. Soon he reached the line of dunes that fenced the country off from the North Sea. Not even Dutchmen could find a use for this much sand. Turk was unsettled by the change in the ground, but then he seemed to remember how to go on it—perhaps his Turkish master had used to take him for gallops in some Mohametan desert. With a plodding and swimming kind of gait he took Jack up to the crest of a dune. Below them, a mile away, Alp-sized green waves were hurling themselves up onto the sand with monstrous roaring and hissing. Jack sat there and stared until Turk grew annoyed. To the horse it was cold and foreign, to Jack it was just this side of cozy. He was trying to count the years since he'd seen open salt water.

There had been the voyage to Jamaica—but after that, his life (he began to think) had been impossibly confusing. Either that, or else the French Pox had amazed and riddled his memories. He had to count on his fingers. Nay, he had to dismount and use his crutch-tip to draw family trees and maps on the sand.

His return from Jamaica was a good place to start: 1678. He had bedded the fair Mary Dolores, six feet of Irish vigor, and then fled to Dunkirk to avoid a warrant, and then there'd been the penis incident. While he'd been recovering from that, Bob had showed up with news: Mary Dolores was pregnant. Also, that John Churchill fellow, improbably, was *married,* and had been made a Colonel—no, wait, a Brigadier—and had any number of regiments under him now. He was avidly recruiting, and still remembered the Shaftoes—did Jack want a steady job, perhaps, so that he could wed Mary Dolores and raise his offspring?

"Just the sort of tidy plan that Bob would come up with," Jack shouted at the waves, still annoyed, six or seven years later. Turk was becoming edgy. Jack decided to talk to him, as long as he was speaking out loud anyway. Did horses understand what was going on, when you spoke to people who weren't there? "So far, simple enough—but here it becomes very deep," he began. "John Churchill was in the Hague—then he was in Brussels—why? Even a horse can see the contradiction in *that*—but I forget you're an Ottoman horse. All right, then: all of this land—" (stomping the dune for emphasis) "was part of Spain—you heard me—Spain! Then these fucking Dutchmen turned Calvinist and revolted, and drove the Spanish away, down south of the Maas and a bunch of other rivers with hard-to-remember names—past Zeeland, any-way—we'll be seeing more than we want to of those rivers soon. Leaving only a wedge of Papist Spain trapped between the Dutch Republic on its north, and France on its south. This Spain-wedge contains Brussels and Antwerp and a large number of battlefields, basically—it is like the jousting-ground where Europe goes to have its wars. Sometimes the Dutch and the English ally against France, and they have battles in the Spanish Netherlands. Sometimes England and France ally against the Dutch, and they have battles in the Spanish Netherlands. Anyway—at this particular time, I believe, it was England and the Dutch against France, for the rea-son that all England was up in arms against Popery. Importation of French goods had been outlawed—that's why I was in Dunkirk—obvious opportunities for smuggling. And that's also why John Churchill was raising new armies. He went to Holland to parley with William of Orange, who was thought to know more'n anyone about staving off the Catholic hordes, as he'd stopped King Looie at the cost of turning half his country into a moat.

"So far it makes sense, then. But why—an intelligent horse might ask—why was John Churchill *also* in Brussels—part of *Spain's,* and therefore the *Pope's,* dominions? Why, it's because—thanks to the maneuverings of his daddy Winston—ever since John had been just a lad, he'd been in the household of James, King Chuck's brother, the Duke of York. And York—then, and now, first in line for the throne—was, and is today—you'll like this—a fanatical Papist! *Now* do you understand why London was, and probably still is, nervous? The King decided it'd be better if his brother took a long vacation out of the country, and naturally James chose the Catholic city that was closest at hand: Brussels! And John Churchill, being in his household, was obliged to follow him, at least part of the time.

"Anyway—Bob took the King's shilling and I did not. From Dunkirk, he and I rode together through the no-man's-land—which, not to repeat myself, you'll soon be seeing plenty of—by Ypres, Oudenaarde, Brussels, and as far as Waterloo, where we parted ways. I went down to Paris, he went back to Brussels, and probably spent a lot of his time, thereafter, scurrying to and fro carrying messages, as when he was a boy."

During this recital, Jack had been unwinding his crutch: a curved stick with a padded crossbar at the top to go under his armpit, all lashed together with a mile of crude twine. When he'd undone the windings, he was left with two pieces of wood and some rags he'd used for padding. But protruding from the top of the long crutch-pole was the pommel of a Janissary-sword.

He had searched half of the Harz Mountains to find a stick whose curve matched that of the sword. Having found it, he'd split it in half, and hollowed out a space in the middle big enough to contain the scabbard. The pommel and guard still stuck out the top, but when he added the crutch's cross-bar, then swaddled it in rags, and bound all in twine, he had a crutch that seemed innocuous enough—and if a border-guard threatened to unmake it, Jack could always cup a hand under his armpit and complain about the painful black swellings that had recently flared up there.

The crutch was a convenience in settled places where only Gentlemen had the right to bear arms—but between here and northern France, he hoped to see as little of that sort of country as possible. He belted on the sword and strapped the crutch-pole alongside Turk's saddle, and then Jack the crippled vagrant was suddenly Jack the armed rider, galloping down the sea-coast on the back of a Turkish war-horse.

DOWN PAST THE HAGUE, around the Hook of Holland, Jack paid a visit on certain boat-owning fellows of his acquaintance, and learned, from them, that the French had banned the inexpensive cloth coming out of Calicoe in India. Naturally the Dutch were now smuggling it down the coast, and there was a steady traffic of the small cargo-vessels called flutes. Jack's friends ferried him, Turk, and a ton of Calicoe across Zeeland, which was the name the Dutch gave to the huge sandy morass where such rivers as the Maas and the Schelde emptied into the North Sea. But an autumn storm was blowing up in the Channel, and they had to take shelter in a little privateers' cove in Flanders. From there, Jack took advantage of a fortuitous low tide to make a night gallop down the coast to Dunkirk, and the hospitality of the dear old Bomb & Grapnel.

But from Mr. Foot, the proprietor of the *Bomb,* Jack got an earful about how, ever since King Looie had bought Dunkirk from King Chuck, things weren't the same: the French had enlarged the harbor so that it could harbor the big warships of that arch-privateer Jean Bart, and these changes had driven away the small

Channel pirates and smugglers who had once made Dunkirk such a prosperous and merry town.

Disgusted and dismayed, Jack left immediately, striking inland into Artois, where he could still go armed. It was hard up against the frontier of the Spanish Netherlands, and the soldiers who'd been sent up to prosecute King Looie's wars there had not been slow to grasp that there was more to be made by robbing travelers on the London-Paris route—who were still so grateful to've survived the Channel crossing that they practically gave it away—than from dutiful soldiering.

Jack made himself look like one of these highwaymen—no great feat, since he *had been* one for a year or two—and that brought him swift and more or less safe passage down into Picardy: the home of a famous Regiment, which, since they were not there when Jack arrived, he reckoned that they must be up laying waste to the Spanish Netherlands. A few changes in attire (his old floppy musketeer-hat, e.g.) gave him the look of a deserter, or scout, from same.

In one of those Picard villages the church-bell was clanging without letup. Sensing some kind of disorder, Jack rode toward it, across fields crowded with peasants bringing in the harvest. They rotated their crops so that one-third of the fields had wheat, one-third oats, and the remaining third were fallow, and Jack tended to ride across the ones that were fallow. These wretches looked at him with fear that was abject even by the standard of French peasants. Most of them scanned the northern sky, perhaps looking for clouds of smoke or dust, and some dropped to the ground and put their ears against it, listening for hoofbeats, and Jack concluded that it wasn't him *personally* they feared, so much as what might be behind him.

He assessed this village as one where he could get away with being armed, and rode into it, because he needed to buy oats for Turk. The only person he saw was a barefoot boy in coarse dirty linen, visible from the waist down through a low doorway in the base of the bell-tower, his raggedy ass thrusting out rudely with each jerk on the bell-rope.

But then Jack encountered a rider in good but plain clothing who had apparently come up from the direction of Paris. They drew up, a safe distance apart, in the town's deserted market-square, circled round each other once or twice, and then began shouting at each other over the din of the bell, and settled on a mixture of English and French.

Jack: "Why are they ringing the bell?"

"These Catholics think it wards off thunderstorms," said the Frenchman. "Why are they so—?" he then asked and, not trusting his English or Jack's French, pantomimed a furtive cringing peasant.

"They're afraid that I'm a forerunner of the Picardy Regiment, coming home from the wars," Jack guessed. He intended this as a wry jest about the tendency of regiments to "live off the land," as the euphemism went. But it was quite significant to this Huguenot.

"Is it true? Is the regiment coming?"

"How much would it be worth to you?" Jack asked.

Everything about this Huguenot reminded him of the Independent traders of England, who'd ride out to remote districts in harvest-time to buy up goods at better than market price. And both Jack and this trader—who introduced himself as Monsieur Arlanc—understood that the price would drop still further if the sellers believed, rightly or wrongly, that the Picardy Regiment was coming to eat it out from under them.

So there was, inadvertently, a sort of business proposition on the table. Vagabond and Huguenot rode around each other a few more times. All around them, the peasants labored at the harvest. But they were keeping an eye on the two strangers, and soon a village elder came hustling in from the fields on a donkey.

But in the end, Monsieur Arlanc could not bring himself to do it. "We are already hated enough," he said, apparently meaning the Huguenots, "without spreading false panics. These peasants have enough to be afraid of already—that is why my sons and I ride out to such dangerous marches."

"Fine. But incidentally, I don't intend to rob you," Jack said irritably, "you needn't make up phant'sies about your supposed pack of heavily armed sons, just over the rise."

"Tales don't offer sufficient protection in these times, I'm afraid," said Monsieur Arlanc, tucking his cloak back to divulge no fewer than four separate firearms: two conventional pistols, and two more cleverly worked into the handle of a tomahawk and the barrel of a walking-stick respectively.

"Well played, Monsieur—Protestant practicality and French *savoir-faire* united."

"I say, are you sure you'll be all right riding to the Inn at Amiens armed with nothing but a sword? The highways—"

"I do not stay at Inns of the French sort, nor do I generally ride on highways," Jack said. "But if that is *your* habit, and if you are going that way . . ."

So they rode to Amiens together, after purchasing oats from the head man of the village. Jack bought enough to fill Turk's belly, and Monsieur Arlanc bought the rest of the year's harvest (he would send wagons later to take delivery). Jack told no lies—just lounged on the rim of the town well, looking like a Volunteer, as the local deserters and highwaymen were called. After that it was a good stiff ride to Amiens, where there was a large establishment throttling a crossroads: livery stables nearly buried in hay, and paddocks crowded with oxen; queues of empty wagons lining the road (some soon to be hired by M. Arlanc); several smithys, some geared for shoeing horses, others for putting rims on wagon-wheels. As well, harness-shops, and various carpenters specializing in wheels, ox-yokes, cart-frames, and barrel-making. Trains of harvest-laden carts filling the roadway, waiting to be inspected, and to pay tolls. Somewhere, a lodging for traders and travelers that accounted for its being called an Inn. From a distance, it was a great dark smoking knot, clearly recognizable as not Jack's sort of place—he unbelted his sword, slid it back into its concealment in the crutch-pole, and began winding it up again.

"You must come to the Inn, and see that I do in fact have sons," said Monsieur Arlanc. "They are still only boys, but . . ."

"I have never seen my own—I cannot see yours," Jack said. "Besides, I cannot tolerate these French Inns—"

Monsieur Arlanc nodded understandingly. "In your country, goods are free to move on the roads—?"

"—and an Inn is a hospitable place for travelers, not a choke-point."

So he bade good-bye to Monsieur Arlanc, from whom he had learned a thing or two about where in Paris he should sell his ostrich-plumes and his war-horse. In return, the Huguenot had learned some things about phosphorus, silver mines, and Calicoe-smuggling from Jack. Both men had been safer together than they would've been apart.

JACK THE ONE-LEGGED TINKER, leading his plow-horse, smelled Paris half a day before he saw it. The fields of grain gave way to market-gardens crowded with vegetables, and pastures for dairy cattle, and dark, heavy carts came endlessly up the road from the city laden with barrels and tubs of human shit collected from the gutters and stoops, which were worked into the vegetable-fields by peasants using rakes and forks. Parisians seemed to shit more than other humans, or perhaps the garlic in their food made it seem that way—in any case Jack was glad when he got clear of those rank vegetable-fields and entered into the suburbs: endless warrens of straw-roofed huts crowded with misplaced country folk, burning whatever sticks and debris they could rake together to cook their food and ward off the autumn chill, and publicly suffering from various picturesque ailments. Jack didn't stop moving until he reached the perpetual pilgrim-camp around St.-Denis, where almost anyone could get away with loitering for a few hours. He bought some cheese for himself and some hay for Turk from some farmers who were on their way down to the city. Then he relaxed among the lepers, epileptics, and madmen who were hanging around the Basilica, and dozed until a couple of hours before dawn.

When it got light enough to move about, he joined in with the thousands of farmers who came into the city, as they did every morning, bringing vegetables, milk, eggs, meat, fish, and hay into the markets. This crowd was larger than he remembered, and it took longer for them to get into the city. The gate of St.-Denis was impossibly congested, so he tried his luck at the gate of St. Martin, a musket-shot away. By the time he passed under it, dawn-light was glancing prettily off its new stone-work: King Looie as a primordial, naked Hercules leaning insouciantly on a tree-sized club, naked except for a periwig the size of a cloud, and a lion skin slung over one arm so that a flapping corner just covered the royal Penis. Victory was swooping down from Heaven, one arm laden with palm-branches and the other reaching out to slap a laurel-wreath atop that wig. The King's foot rested on the mangled form of someone he'd just apparently beaten the crap out of, and, in the background, a great Tower burnt.

"God damn you, King Looie," Jack muttered, passing under the gate; because he could feel himself cringing. He'd tried to ride across France as fast as he could, specifically to prevent this: but still, it had taken several days. The sheer vastness of it compared to those tiny German principalities, and the component states of the Dutch Republic, was such that by the time you reached Paris, you'd been traveling across this King's dominions for so long that as you passed through the gate you couldn't not cringe beneath his power.

Never mind; he was in Paris. Off to his left the sun was rising over the towers and bastions of the Temple, where those Knights of Malta had their own city within the city—though the old curtain-walls that once enclosed it had lately been torn down. But for the most part his views in all directions were sealed off by vertical walls of white stone: Paris's six- and seven-story buildings rising on either side of the street, funneling the farmers and the fishwives, and the vendors with their loads of flowers, oranges, and oysters into narrow race-ways wherein they jostled sharply for position, all trying to avoid falling into the central gutter. Not far into the city, much of this traffic angled off to the right, toward the great market-place of Les Halles, leaving a (for Paris) clear vista straight down to the Seine and the Île de la Cité.

Jack had developed a suspicion that he was being tailed by an agent of King Looie's Lieutenant of Police, who had unfortunately caught his eye for a moment as he'd gone through the gate. Jack knew not to turn around and look. But by watching the faces of oncoming pedestrians—particularly, scum—he could see that they were surprised by, and then scared of, someone. Jack could hardly slip off into the crowd when he was leading a great big horse, but he could try to make himself not worth following. Les Halles would be a good place for that, so he followed the crowd to the right. The dramatickal option—mounting Turk, producing a weapon— would lead to the galleys. In fact, there were very few roads out of Paris that would *not* end with Jack chained to an oar in Marseille.

Someone behind him came in for brutal tongue-lashings from the fishwives at Les Halles. Jack overheard comparisons between his pursuer's moustache, and the armpit hair of various infidel races. The hypothesis was floated, and generally agreed upon, that this policeman spent rather too much of his time performing oral sex on certain large farm animals infamous for poor hygiene. Beyond that, Jack's French simply was not quick or vile enough. He trolled several times through Les Halles, hoping that the crowd, the smell of yesterday's fish-guts, the fishwives, and sheer boredom would shake this man off his tail, but it didn't work. Jack bought a loaf, so that he could explain why he'd come here, if someone bothered to ask, and to demonstrate that he was not a penniless vagrant, and also because he was hungry.

He put the sun to his back and began to dodge and maneuver through various streets, headed for the Rue Vivienne. The police wanted to arrest him for being in Paris with no business, which normally would have been the case for him. So much so, that he'd forgotten that this time he actually *did* have business.

The streets had begun to congest with strolling retailers: a cheese-seller pushing a large wheel of blue-veined stuff on a sort of wheelbarrow, a mustard-seller carrying a small capped pail and a scoop, numerous *porteurs d'eau,* their stout bodies harnessed into frames all a-dangle with wooden buckets, a butter-seller with baskets of butter-pats strapped to his back. This kind of thing would only get worse, to the point that it would immobilize him. He had to get rid of Turk. No trouble: the horse business was everywhere, he'd already passed by several livery stables, and hay-wains filled narrow streets with their thatched bulk and narcotic fragrance. Jack followed one to a stable and made arrangements to have Turk put up there for a few days.

Then out the other side, and into a large open space: a plaza with (surprisingly enough) a monumental statue of King Looie in the center. On one side of its pedestal, a relief of Looie personally spearheading a cavalry charge across a canal, or perhaps that was the Rhine, into a horizontal forest of muskets. On the other, Looie on the throne with a queue of Kings and Emperors of Europe waiting, crowns in hand, to kneel down and kiss his high-heeled booties.

He must be on the right course, because he was beginning to see a higher class of vendor: sellers of books strolling along holding advertisements over their heads on sign-boards, a candy-man carrying small scales, a seller of *eau-de-vie* carrying a basket of tiny bottles, and a goblet; a seller of pâtés carrying a sort of painter's palette with smudges of different varieties, and many orange-girls: all of them crying the particular cries that belonged to that sort of vendor, like birds with their own distinct calls. Jack was on Rue Vivienne. It was starting to look like Amsterdam: finely-dressed men of many lands, strolling along having serious conversations: making money by exchanging words. But it also looked a bit like the Booksellers' Quarter in Leipzig: whole cart-loads of books, printed but not bound, disappearing into one especially fine House: the King's Library.

Jack crutched his way up one side of the street and down the other until he found the House of the Golden Frigate, adorned with a sculpture of a warship. This had obviously been made by an artisan who'd never come near the ocean, as it was queerly distorted and had an unlikely profusion of gun-decks. But it looked good. An Italian gentleman was there on the front stoop, worrying a hand-wrought iron key of many curious protuberances into a matching keyhole.

"Signor Cozzi?" Jack inquired.

"*Si,*" replied he, looking only a little surprised to be accosted by a one-legged wanderer.

"A message from Amsterdam," Jack said in French, "from your cousin." But this last was unnecessary, as Signor Cozzi had already recognized the seal. Leaving the key jutting from the lock, he broke it open right there and scanned a few lines of beautiful whirling script. A woman with a cask of ink on her back, noting his interest in written documents, shouted a business proposal to him, and before he could deflect it, there was a second woman with a cask of vastly superior and yet far cheaper ink on her back; the two of them got into an argument, and Signor Cozzi took advantage of it to slip inside, beckoning Jack in with a trick of his large brown eyes. Jack could not resist turning around, now, to look behind him for the first time since he had entered the city. He caught sight of a sworded man in a somber sort of cape, just in the act of turning around to slink away: this policeman had spent half the morning tailing a perfectly legitimate banker's messenger. "You are being followed?" Signor Cozzi inquired, as if asking Jack whether he was breathing in and out.

"Not now," Jack answered.

It was another one of those places consisting of *bancas* with large padlocked books, and heavy chests on the floor. "How do you know my cousin?" Cozzi asked, making it clear he wasn't going to invite Jack to take a seat. Cozzi himself sat down behind a desk and began to pull quills out of a little jar and examine their points.

"A lady friend of mine has, uh, made his acquaintance. When he learned, through her, that I was about to journey to Paris, he pressed that letter on me."

Cozzi wrote something down, then unlocked a desk-drawer and began to rummage through it, picking out coins. "It says that if the seal has been tampered with I should send you to the galleys."

"I assumed as much."

"If the seal is intact, and you get it to me within fourteen days of the date it was written, I'm to give you a louis d'or. Ten days gets you two. Fewer than ten, an additional louis d'or for each day you shaved off the trip." Cozzi dropped five gold coins into Jack's hand. "How the hell did you do it? *No one* travels from Amsterdam to Paris in seven days."

"Think of it as a trade secret," Jack said.

"You are dead on your feet—go somewhere and sleep," Cozzi said. "And when you are ready to return to Amsterdam, come to me, and maybe I'll have a message for you to take to my cousin."

"What makes you think I'm going back?"

Cozzi smiled for the first time. "The look in your eye when you spoke of your lady friend. You are mad with love, no?"

"Mad with syphilis, actually," Jack said, "but still mad enough to go back."

WITH THE MONEY HE'D BROUGHT with him, and the money he'd earned, Jack could have stayed somewhere decent—but he didn't know how to find such a place, or how to behave once he found one. The last year had been an education in how little having money really mattered. A rich Vagabond was a Vagabond still, and 'twas common knowledge that King Charles, during the Interregnum, had lived without money in Holland. So Jack wandered across town to the district called the Marais. Movement was now a matter of forcing his body into narrow, ephemeral gaps between other pedestrians—primarily vendors, as of (in some districts) *peaux de lapins* (bundles of rabbit-pelts), baskets (these people carried enormous baskets filled with smaller baskets), hats (small uprooted trees with hats dangling from branch-ends), *linge* (a woman all adrape with lace and scarves), and (as he came into the Marais) *chaudronniers* with pots and pans impaled by their handles on a stick. Vinegar-sellers with casks on wheels, musicians with bagpipes and hurdy-gurdies, cake-sellers with broad flat baskets of steaming confections that made Jack light in the head.

Jack got into the heart of the Marais, found a pissing-corner where he could stand still, and scanned the air above the people's heads for half an hour or so, and listened, until he heard a particular cry. *Everyone* in the street was shouting *something,* usually the name of whatever they were selling, and for the first couple of hours it had just been Bedlam to Jack. But after a while Jack's ear learned to pick out individual voices—something like hearing drum-beats or bugle-calls in battle. Parisians, he knew, had developed the skill to a high degree, just as the Lieutenant of Police could scan a torrent of people coming in through a gate at dawn and pick out the Vagabond. Jack was just able to hear a high-pitched voice crying "*Mort-aux-rats! Mort-aux-rats!*" and then it was easy enough to turn his head and see a long pole, like a pike, being carried at an angle over someone's shoulder, the corpses of a couple of dozen rats dangling from it by their tails, their freshness an unforgeable guarantee that this man had been working *recently.*

Jack shoved his way into the throng, using the crutch now like a burglar's jimmy to widen small openings, and after a few minutes' rattling pursuit caught up with St.-George and clapped him on the shoulder, like a policeman. Many would drop everything and sprint away when so handled, but one did not become a legend in the rat-killer's trade if one was easily startled. St.-George turned around, making the rats on his pole swing wide, like perfectly synchronized pole-dancers at a fun-fair, and recognized him. Calmly, but not coldly. "Jacques—so you *did* escape from those German witches."

"'Twas nothing," Jack said, trying to cover his astonishment, then his pride, that word of this had spread as far as Paris. "They were fools. Helpless. Now, if *you* had been chasing me—"

"Now you have returned to civilization—why?" Steely curiosity being another good rat-killer trait. St.-George had curly hair the color of sand, and hazel eyes, and had probably looked angelic as a boy. Maturity had elongated his cheekbones and (according to legend) other parts of his body in a way that was not so divine—his head was funnel-shaped, tapering to a pair of pursed lips, staring eyes that looked as if they were painted on. "You know that the *passe-volante* trade has been quashed—why are you here?"

"To renew my friendship with you, St.-George."

"You have been riding on horseback—I can smell it."

Jack decided to let this pass. "How can you smell *anything* except man-shit here?"

St.-George sniffed the air. "Shit? Where? Who has been shitting?" This, being a sort of joke, was a signal that Jack could now offer to buy St.-George something, as a token of friendship. After some negotiations, St.-George agreed to be the recipient of Jack's generosity—but not because he *needed* it—only because it was inherent in human nature that one must from time to time give things away, and at such times, one needed someone to give things away *to,* and part of being a good friend was to be that someone, as needed. Then there were negotiations about what Jack was going to buy. St.-George's objective was to figure out how much money Jack was carrying—Jack's was to keep St.-George wanting to know more. In the end, for tactical reasons, St.-George agreed to allow Jack to buy him some coffee—but it had to be from a particular vendor named Christopher.

They were half an hour tracking him down. "He is not a tall man—"

"Hard to find, then."

"But he wears a red fez with a brave golden tassel—"

"He's a Turk?"

"Of course! I told you he sold coffee, didn't I?"

"A Turk named—Christopher?"

"Don't play the clown, Jacques—remember that I know you."

"But—?"

St.-George rolled his eyes, and snapped, "All of the Turks who sell coffee in the streets are actually Armenians dressed up as Turks!"

"I'm sorry, St.-George, I didn't know."

"I should not be so harsh," St.-George admitted. "When you left Paris, coffee was not fashionable yet—not until the Turks fled from Vienna, and left mountains of it behind."

"It's been fashionable in England since I was a boy."

"If it is in England, it is not *fashionable*, but a *curiosity*," St.-George said through clenched teeth.

Onwards they searched, St.-George wending like a ferret through the crowd, passing round, e.g., furniture-sellers carrying fantastic complexes of stools and chairs all roped together on their backs, milk-men with pots on their heads, *d'oublies* carrying unlit lanterns, and bent under enormous dripping barrels of shit; knife-grinders trundling their wheels. Jack had to put the crutch to much rude use, and considered taking out the sword. Eliza had been right—Paris *was* retail—funny she'd known this without ever having set foot in the city, while Jack, who'd lived here, on and off, for years . . .

Best to keep his mind on St.-George. Only the rat-pole prevented Jack from losing him. Though it helped that people were always running out of shops, or shouting from windows, trying to engage his services. The only people who could afford to keep fixed shops were members of a few princely trades, viz. makers of dresses, hats, and wigs. But St.-George treated all men alike, asking them a series of penetrating questions and then firmly sending them home. "Even noblemen and savants are as peasants in their understanding of rats," St.-George said incredulously. "How can I be of service to them when their thinking is so pre-theoretical?"

"Well, as a start, you could get rid of their rats . . ."

"One does not *get rid of* rats! You are no better than these people!"

"Sorry, St.-George. I—"

"Does anyone ever *get rid of* Vagabonds?"

"Individual ones, certainly. But—"

"Individual to *you*—but to a Gentleman, all the same, like rats, *n'est-ce pas*? One must live with rats."

"Except for the ones dangling from your pole—?"

"It is like the exemplary hanging. The heads on the spikes before the city-gates."

"To scare *les autres*?"

"Just so, Jacques. These were, to rats, as you, my friend, are to Vagabonds."

"You are too kind—really, you flatter me, St.-George."

"These were the cleverest—the ones who would find the smallest of holes, who would explore the drain-pipes, who would say to the common rats: 'gnaw through this grate, *mes amis*—it will shorten your teeth to be sure—but once through, such things you will feast on!' These were the savants, the Magellans—"

"And they're dead."

"They displeased me too many times, these did. Many others, I allow to live—to breed, even!"

"No!"

"In certain cellars—unbeknownst to the apothecaries and parfumiers who live above—I have rat seraglios where my favorites are allowed to procreate. Some lines I have bred for a hundred generations. As a breeder of canines creates dogs fierce against strangers, but obedient to the master—"

"You create rats that obey St.-George."

"*Pourquoi non?*"

"But how can you be so certain that the rats are not breeding *you?*"

"I beg your pardon?"

"Your father was *mort-aux-rats,* no?"

"And his father before him. Killed in plagues, may God have mercy on their souls."

"So you believe. But perhaps the rats killed them."

"You anger me. But your theory is not without promise—"

"Perhaps you, St.-George, are the result of a breeding program—you have been allowed to live, and flourish, and have children of your own, because you have a theory that is congenial to the rats."

"Still, I kill very many."

"But those are the stupid ones—without introspection."

"I understand, Jacques. For you, I would serve as *mort-aux-rats* and would do it for free. But these—" he made a flicking gesture at a man in an excellent wig who was trying to call him over to a shop. The man looked crestfallen—temporarily. But then St.-George softened, and moved in the direction of a narrow doorway—more hatch than door—set into the wall of this wig-maker's shop, next to his open shop-window. This suddenly burst open, and a round-bodied five-foot-tall man with a vigorous moustache and curly-toed slippers emerged from a stairway no wider than he was, preceded by a smoking and steaming apparatus of hammered copper that was strapped to his body.

When Christopher (for it was none other) stood in the sun, which he always tried to do, the golden light gleamed off the copper and hung in the steam and glittered off his golden fez-tassel and shone in his embroidered slippers and brass buttons and made him very magnificent, a walking mosque. He switched among French, Spanish, and English in mid-sentence, and he claimed to know all about Jack Shaftoe (whom he addressed as *l'Emmerdeur*), and tried to give him coffee for free. He had just refilled his tanks upstairs, he explained, and was heavy burdened. St.-George had warned that Christopher would make this offer "because he will want to calculate how much money you are carrying," and together they had rehearsed a few scenarios of how the coffee-price negotiation might play out. The plan was that Jack would run their side of the dealings, and that St.-George would hover and, at just the right moment, divulge that Jack was looking for a place to stay. Jack had never said as much to St.-George, but then it was not necessary; this was why one approached St.-George upon one's arrival in the Marais. His work took him into every building—especially to the parts of buildings where people like Jack were apt to stay.

To accept coffee for free was to demean oneself; to overpay was to publicly shame Christopher, by implying that he was the sort of man who cared about something as low and dirty as money; to merely agree on a fair price was to proclaim oneself a simpleton, and accuse Christopher of the same. Arduous haggling, however, laid bare the soul and made the participants blood-brothers. In any event the matter was settled—to the relief of the wig-maker, who stood wringing his hands as this one-legged Vagabond, fat pseudo-Turk, and rat-catcher shouted at each other directly in front of his shop, scaring away business. Meanwhile St.-George was striking a deal of his own with the wig-maker. Jack was too busy to eavesdrop, but he gathered that St.-George was using his influence to get Jack a room, or at least a corner, upstairs.

Just so: after a ceremonial cup of coffee in the street, Jack bid adieu to St.-George (who had immediate responsibilities in the cellar) and to Christopher (who had coffee to vend), stepped through the tiny door, and began to ascend stairs—past the wig-maker's shop on the ground level, and then, on the first story, his dwelling—the fine parts of it anyway, such as parlour and dining-room. Then a story for the family bedchambers. Then a story where his servants had their quarters. Then one he had rented out to a tradesman of lesser rank. As the storys mounted, the quality plunged. In the bottom levels the walls and steps alike were solid stone, but this gave way to wooden steps and plaster walls. As Jack continued to climb, the plaster developed cracks, then began to bulge and flake off the lath. At the same time, the stair-steps became creaky, and began to flex beneath his weight. In the top story there was no plaster on the walls at all, just birds' nests of straw and wattle spanning gaps among timbers. Here, in one large room interrupted by a few struts to shore up the roof, lived Christopher's family: countless Armenians sleeping and sitting on squarish bales of coffee-beans. A ladder in the corner gave access to the roof, whereupon a sort of lean-to shack, called by the grand name of *entresol*, had been improvised. A sailor-hammock hung corner-to-corner. Several bricks were shoved together to form a pad where a fire could be lit. On the tile roof downhill of the entresol, a tissue of brown streakage gave a hint as to where previous occupants had done their shitting and pissing.

Jack vaulted into the hammock and discovered that previous tenants had thoughtfully punched various peep-holes through the adjoining walls. It would be a drafty hovel in winter, but Jack liked it: he had clear views, and open escape-routes, across roof-tops in several directions. The building across the street had a garret, no farther away from Jack's entresol than one room in a house was from another, but separated from him by a crevasse sixty or seventy feet deep. This was more typical of the sort of place Jack would expect to dwell (though he could almost hear St.-George telling him that, now that he was a man of wealth, he must set his sights higher). So he could hear the conversations, and smell the food and the bodies, of the people across the way. But, lying there in his hammock, he got to watch them as if their life were a play, and he in the audience. It appeared to be the usual sort of high-altitude bolt-hole for prostitutes on the run from pimps, runaway servants, women pregnant out of wedlock, and youthful peasants who'd walked to Paris expecting to find something.

Jack tried to nap, but it was the middle of the afternoon and he could not sleep with Paris happening all around him. So he set out across the roof-tops, memorizing the turns he'd take, the leaps he'd make, the crevices he'd hide in, the places he'd stand and fight, if the Lieutenant of Police ever came for him. This led to his tromping over numerous roof-tops, setting off great commotions and panics among many garret-dwellers who lived in fear of raids. Mostly he had the roof-tops to himself. There were a few Vagabondish-looking children moving in packs, and a large number of roof-rats. On almost every block there were tattered ropes, or frail tree-branches, bridging gaps over streets, not strong enough for humans, but enthusiastically used by rats. In other places the ropes lay coiled neatly on roofs, the sticks rested in rain-gutters. Jack reckoned that they must have been put up by St.-George, who used them to channel and control the migrations of rats, as a general might tear down bridges in one part of a disputed territory while improvising new ones elsewhere.

Eventually Jack descended to street-level, and found that he'd arrived in a better part of town, near the river. He headed, without thinking about it, toward his old playground, the Pont-Neuf. The street was a wiser place for him to be—persons who clambered about on roof-tops were not well thought of—but it was dark, and confined between the stone walls of the buildings. Even the view down the street was closed off by balconies jutting out more than halfway across it from either side. The houses all had great arched portals closed off by ironbound fortress-doors. Sometimes a servant would have one open just at the moment Jack happened by. He'd slow down and look through and get a glimpse down a cool shaded passageway into a courtyard lit with sun, half filled in by landslides of flowers, watered by gurgling fountains. Then the door would be shut. Paris to Jack and most others, then, was a network of deep trenches with vertical walls, and a few drafty battlements atop those walls—otherwise, the world's largest collection of closed and locked doors.

He walked by a statue of King Looie as Roman general in stylish Classical armor with exposed navel. On one side of the pedestal, Winged Victory was handing out loaves to the poor, and on the other, an angel with a flaming sword, and a shield decorated with a trinity of fleur-de-lis, backed up by a cross-swinging, chalice-and-wafer-brandishing Holy Virgin, was assaulting and crushing diverse semi-reptilian demons who were toppling backwards onto a mess of books labelled (though Jack could not read, he knew this) with such names as M. Luther, J. Wycliffe, John Hus, John Calvin.

The sky was opening. Sensing he was near the Seine, Jack lunged forward and finally reached the Pont-Neuf. "Pont" was French for an artificial isthmus of stone, spanning a river, with arches beneath to let the water flow through—pylons standing in the flow, dividing it with their sharp blades; atop, a paved street lined with buildings like any other in Paris, so that you wouldn't know you were crossing over a river unless a Parisian told you so. But in this one respect the Pont-Neuf was different: it had no buildings, just hundreds of carved heads of pagan gods and goddesses, and so you could *see* from there. Jack went and did some seeing. Many others had the same idea. Upstream, late-afternoon sunlight set the backs of the buildings on the Pont au Change to glowing; a steady rain of shit flew out of the windows, and was swallowed by the Seine. The river's crisp stone banks were occluded by a permanent jam of small boats and barges. Newly arriving ones attracted surging riots of men hoping to be hired as porters. Some boats carried blocks of stone that had been cut to shape by freemasons working out in the open, somewhere upstream; these boats pulled up along special quays equipped with cranes powered by pairs of large stepped wheels in which men climbed forever without ascending, turning a gear-train that reeled in a cable that passed over a pulley at the end of a tree-sized arm, hoisting the blocks up out of the boats. The entire crane—wheels, men, and all—could be rotated around and the block dropped into a heavy cart.

Elsewhere, the same amount of labor might've made a keg of butter or a week's worth of firewood; here it was spent on raising a block several inches, so that it could be carted into the city and raised by other workers, higher and higher, so that Parisians could have rooms higher than they were wide, and windows taller than the trees they looked out at. Paris was a city of stone, the color of bone, beautiful and hard—you could dash yourself against it and never leave a mark. It was built, so far as Jack could tell, on the principle that there was nothing you couldn't accomplish if you crowded a few tens of millions of peasants together on the best land in the world and then never stopped raping their brains out for a thousand years. Off to the right, as he looked upstream, was the Île de la Cité, crowded and looming with important stuff: the twin, square towers of Notre Dame, and the twin, round towers of the Conciergerie, holding out prospects of salvation and damnation like a mountebank telling him to pick a card, any card. The Palais de Justice was there, too, a white stone monster decorated with eagles, ready to pounce.

A dog ran down the bridge trying to escape from a length of chain that had been tied to its tail. Jack strolled to the other side of the river, shrugging off innumerable mountebanks, beggars, and prostitutes. Turning around, he was able to look downstream and across the river toward the Louvre, where the King had lived until Versailles had gotten finished. In the garden of Tuileries, which was now falling into the long shadow of the city's western wall, trees, planted in neat rows, were being tortured and racked by the King's gardeners for any deviation from correct form.

Jack was leaning back against a stone wall that had been warmed by the sun, when he heard a faint rustling just behind his head. Turning around, he saw the impression of a small creature, crushed flat, and suspended in the rock—a common enough sight in this type of stone, and known to be a trick of Nature, as when animals were born joined at the hip, or with limbs growing out of the wrong places. The Doctor had another theory: that these had been living beings, trapped and immobilized, imprisoned forever. Now with the weight of all the stone in Paris seeming to press down on him, Jack believed it. He heard that faint rustle again, and scanning the wall carefully, finally saw movement there: between a couple of old scallop-shells and fish-bones, he saw a small human figure, half trapped in the stone, and struggling to get out of it. Peering carefully at this creature, no larger than his little finger, he saw that it was Eliza.

Jack turned away and walked back across the Pont-Neuf toward his entresol in the Marais. He tried to stare only at the stone paving-blocks below his feet, but sometimes there were moving creatures trapped in them, too. So he would look up and see peddlers selling human heads—then avert his gaze into the bright sky and see an angel with a flaming sword, like a kienspan, bearing down on the city—then he'd try to concentrate instead on the carved gods' heads that adorned the Pont-Neuf, and they would come alive, and cry out to him for release from this gibbet of stone.

Jack was finally going mad, and it was a small comfort to know that he'd picked the right city for it.

Paris
WINTER OF 1684–1685

THE ARMENIANS LIVING ABOVE THE wig-maker and below Jack did not appear to have any intermediate settings between killing strangers and adopting them into the family. As Jack had come recommended by St.-George, and had further established his *bona fides* by bargaining shrewdly with Christopher over coffee, they could not very well kill him—so: Jack became the thirteenth of thirteen brothers. Albeit something of an estranged, idiot half-brother, who lived in the entresol, came and went at odd times and in odd ways, and did not speak the language. But this did not trouble the matriarch, Madame Esphahnian. *Nothing* troubled her, except for suggestions that anything was troubling her, or *could theoretically* trouble her—if you suggested that anything was troubling her, she would look taken aback, and remind you that she had borne and raised twelve sons—so what, again, was the difficulty? Christopher and the others had learned simply not to bother her. Jack, likewise, quickly got into the habit of entering and leaving his shack via roof-tops so that he would not have to say good-bye to Madame Esphahnian when he left, and hello when he returned. She spoke no English, of course, and just enough French to enable Jack to impregnate her mind with colorful, grotesque misunderstandings whenever he tried to say *anything*.

His stay in Paris was typical of his wanderings: the first day was a great event, but next thing he knew it was a month later, then two months. By the time he thought seriously about leaving, it was not a good time of year to travel northwards. The streets had become even more crowded, now with an influx of hairy firewood-sellers, from parts of France where being torn apart by wild beasts was still a major cause of mortality. The wood-sellers knocked people down like bowling-pins, and were a danger to everyone, especially when they were fighting with each other. The garret-dwellers across the street from Jack began selling themselves as galley-slaves, just to get warm.

The strange visions that had made Jack's first day in Paris so memorable, went away after he had gotten a night's sleep, and usually did not come back unless he got very tired, or drunk. Lying in his hammock and peering across at the garret, he had reason, every day, to thank St.-George for having put him up in a place that did not have so many outbreaks of typhus, sudden raids by the Lieutenant of Police, stillborn babies, and other annoyances: he saw young women—runaway servants—showing up one day only to be dragged out the next, and (he assumed) taken to the city gates to be cropped, whipped, and spat out into the countryside. Either that, or else some private arrangement would be made, and then Jack would be subjected to the sounds and (depending on wind) aromas of some police inspector satisfying himself carnally, in a way no longer attainable to Jack.

He put the ostrich plumes up for sale, and went about it in his favorite way: getting someone else to do it. After he'd been hanging around for a fortnight, and showed no signs of getting ready to leave, Artan (oldest of the Esphahnian brothers who was actually resident there at the time) inquired as to what Jack intended to *do*, actually, in Paris—making it clear that if the answer was "cat-burglary" or "serial rape" the Esphahnians would not think any the less of him—they just needed to *know.* To demonstrate this open-mindedness, Artan brought Jack up to date on the family saga.

It seemed that Jack, here, had blundered into the fourth or fifth act of a drama—neither a comedy nor a tragedy, but a history—that had begun when Monsieur Esphahnian *père* had sailed the first ship of coffee, *ever,* into Marseille in 1644. It was worth a lot of money. The larger Esphahnian family, which was headquartered in Persia, had plowed a lot of their India trading profits into buying this boat-load of beans in Mocha and getting it up the Red Sea and the Nile to Alexandria and thence to France. Anyway—Pa Esphahnian sold the beans, realized a handsome profit, but *realized* it in *reals*—Spanish money—pieces of eight. Why? Because there was an extreme currency shortage in France and he couldn't have taken payment in French money if he'd wanted to—there *was* none. And why was that? Because (and here it was necessary to imagine an Armenian pounding himself on the head with both hands—*imbécile!*) the Spanish mines in Mexico were producing ludicrous amounts of silver—

"Yeah, I know about this," Jack said, but Artan could not be stopped: there were *piles* of silver lying on the ground in Porto Belo, he insisted—consequently its value, compared to that of gold, was plunging—so in Spain (where they used silver money) there was inflation, because it was not worth as much as it *had* been, whereas in France all gold coins were being hoarded, because gold was expected to be worth more in the future. So now Monsieur Esphahnian had lots of rapidly depreciating silver. He should have sailed to the Levant where silver was always in demand, but he didn't. Instead he sailed for Amsterdam expecting to make some kind of unspecified, brilliant commodities deal that would more than recoup his exchange-rate losses. But (as luck would have it) his ship ran aground, and he got his nuts caught in the mangle of the Thirty Years' War. Sweden happened to be just in the act of conquering Holland when Monsieur Esphahnian's ship eased up onto the sandbank and stopped moving; and, to make a long story short, the Esphahnian dynastic fortune was last seen northbound, strapped to the ass of a Swedish pack-horse.

This, by the way, was all first-act material—*before* the first act, really—if it were a play, it would *open* with the young Monsieur Esphahnian, huddled in the beached wreckage of a ship, spewing expository pentameter, gazing miserably off into the audience as he pretended to watch the Swedish column dwindle into the distance.

The upshot, anyway, was that Monsieur Esphahnian, at that point, fell from the graces of his own family. He somehow made his way back to Marseille, collected Madame Esphahnian and her (already!) three sons, and perhaps a daughter or two (daughters tended to be shipped east at puberty), and, in time, drifted as far as Paris (end of Act I), where, ever since, they'd all been trying to work their way off the shit list of the rest of the family in Isfahan. Primarily they did this by retailing coffee, but they would move just about anything—

"Ostrich plumes?" Jack blurted, not really trusting himself to be devious and crafty around such as the Esphahnians. And so at that point the selling of those ostrich plumes, which Jack could've accomplished in a trice a year and a half ago in a thieves' market in Linz, became a global conspiracy, yoking together Esphahnians as far away as London, Alexandria, Mocha, and Isfahan, as letters were sent to all of those places and more inquiring as to what ostrich-plumes were selling for, whether the trend was up or down, what distinguished a Grade A ostrich-plume from a B, how a B could be made to look like an A, *et cetera*. While they waited for the intelligence to come back, Jack had very little to do on the plume front.

His addled brain forgot about Turk for a while. When he finally went back to the livery stable, the owner was just about to sell him off to pay for all the hay he'd been eating. Jack paid the debt, and began to think seriously about how to turn the war-horse into cash.

Now in the old days it was like this: he would go and loiter around the Place Dauphine, which was the sharp downstream tip of the Île de la Cité, spang in the center of the Pont-Neuf. It was the royal execution grounds and so there was always something to see there. Even when there were no executions underway, there were mountebanks, jugglers, puppeteers, fire-eaters; failing that, you could at least gawk at the dangling remains of people who'd been executed *last* week. But on days of big military parades, the aristocrats who were supposedly in command—at least, who were being paid by King Looie to be in command—of various regiments would issue from their *pieds-à-terre* and *hôtels particuliers* on the Right Bank and come across the Pont-Neuf, recruiting vagrants along the way to bring their regiments up to strength. The Place Dauphine would become a vigorous body-market for a few hours.

Rusty firelocks would be passed out, money would change hands, and the new-made regiments would march south over to the Left Bank, to the cheers of the patriotic onlookers. They'd follow those aristocrats' high-stepping chargers out through the city gates, there at the carrefours where the meaner sorts of criminals dangled unconscious from the whipping-posts, and they would come into St. Germain des Pres, outside the walls: a large quadrangle of monks' residences surrounded by open land, where huge fairs of rare goods would sometimes convene. Following the Seine downstream, they'd pass by a few noble families' hotels, but in general the buildings got lower and simpler and gave way to vegetable- and flower-patches tended by upscale peasants. The river was mostly blocked from view by the piles of timber and baled goods that lined the Left Bank. But after a while, it would bend around to the south, and they would cross the green before Les Invalides—surrounded by its own wall and moat—and arrive at the Champs de Mars where King Looie would be, with all of his pomp, having ridden up from Versailles to inspect his troops—which, in those pre-Martinet days, basically meant counting them. So the *passe-volantes* (as people like Jack were called) would stand up (or if unable to stand, prop themselves up on someone who could) and be counted. The aristocrats would get paid off, and the *passe-volantes* would fan out into innumerable Left Bank taverns and bordellos and spend their money. Jack had become aware of this particular line of work during a ride from Dunkirk to Waterloo with Bob, who had spent some time campaigning under John Churchill, alongside the French, in Germany, laying waste to various regions that had the temerity to lie adjacent to *La France*. Bob had complained bitterly that many French regiments had practically zero effective strength because of this practice. To Jack it had sounded like an opportunity only a half-wit would pass up.

In any case, this procedure was the central tent-pole holding up Jack's understanding of how Paris worked. Applied to the problem of selling Turk, it told him that somewhere in the southern part of the Marais, near the river, there lived rich men who had no choice to be in the market for war-horses—or, if they had any brains in their heads at all, for stud-horses capable of siring new ones. Jack talked to the man who managed the livery stable, and he followed hay-wains coming in from the countryside, and he tailed aristocrats riding back from the military parades at the Champs de Mars, and learned that there was a horse-market *par excellence* at the Place Royale.

Now this was one of those places that Jack's kind of person knew only as a void in the middle of the city, sealed off by gates through which an attentive loiterer could sometimes get a flash of sunlit green. By trying to penetrate it from all sides, Jack learnt that it was square, with great barn-doors at the four cardinal compass-points, and high grand buildings rising above each of these gates. Around its fringes were a number of *hôtels*, which in Paris meant private compounds of rich nobles. Twice a week, the gates were jammed solid with carts bringing hay and oats in, and manure out, and an astounding number of fine horses being burnished by grooms. Some horse-trading went on in surrounding streets, but Jack could plainly see that this was little more than a flea-market compared to whatever was going on in the Place Royale.

He bribed a farmer to smuggle him into the place in a hay-wain. When it was safe to get out, the farmer poked him in the ribs with the handle of a pitchfork, and Jack wriggled and slid out onto the ground—the first time he had stood on growing grass since he'd reached Paris.

The Place Royale was found to be a park shaded by chestnut trees (in theory, that is; when Jack saw it the leaves had fallen, and been raked off). In the center was a statue of King Looie's dear old pop, Looie the Thirteenth—on horseback, naturally. The whole square was surrounded by vaulted colonnades, like the trading-courts at Leipzig and the Stock Exchange at Amsterdam, but these were very wide and high, with barn-doors giving way to private courtyards beyond. All of the gates, and all of the arcades, were large enough, not merely for a single rider, but for a coach drawn by four or six horses. It was, then, like a city within the city, built entirely for people so rich and important that they *lived* on horse-back, or in private coaches.

Only that could explain the size of the horse-market that was raging all around him when Jack climbed out of the hay-wain. It was as crowded with horses as the streets of Paris were with people—the only exceptions being a few roped-off areas where the merchandise could prance around and be judged and graded by the buyers. Every horse that Jack saw, he would've remembered as the finest horse he'd ever seen, if he'd encountered it on a road in England or Germany. Here, not only were such horses common, but they were meticulously groomed and brushed almost to the point of being polished, their manes and tails coiffed, and they'd been taught to do tricks. There were horses meant to be saddled, horses in matched sets of two and four and even six, for drawing coaches, and—in one corner—chargers: war-horses for parading beneath the eyes of the King on the Champ de Mars. Jack went thataway and had a look. He did not see a single mount there that he would've traded Turk for, if he were about to ride into battle. But these were in excellent condition and well shod and groomed compared to Turk, who had been languishing in a livery stable for weeks, with only the occasional walk round the stable-yard for exercise.

Jack knew how to fix that. But before he left the Place Royale, he raised his sights for a few minutes, and spent a while looking at the buildings that rose over the park—trying to learn something about his customers-to-be.

Unlike most of Paris, these were brick, which warmed Jack's heart strangely, reminding him of Merry England. The four great buildings rising over the gates at the cardinal points of the compass had enormous steep rooves, two and three stories high, with balconies and lace-curtained dormers, currently all shut up against the cold—but Jack could well imagine how a wealthy horse-fancier would have his Paris pied-à-terre here, so that he could keep an eye on the market by gazing out his windows.

In one of the great squares hereabouts—Jack had lost track of all of them—he'd seen a statue of King Looie riding off to war, with blank spaces on the pedestal to chisel the names of victories he hadn't won yet, and of countries he hadn't captured. Some buildings, likewise, had empty niches: waiting (as everyone in Paris must understand) to receive the statues of the generals who would win those victories for him. Jack needed to find a man whose ambition was to stand forever in one of those niches, and he needed to convince him that he was more likely to win battles with Turk, or Turk's offspring, between his legs. But first he needed to get Turk in some kind of decent physical condition, and that meant riding him.

He was on his way out of the Place Royale, walking under the gate on its south side, when behind him a commotion broke out. The hiss of iron wheel-rims grinding over paving-stones, the crisp footfalls of horses moving in unnatural unison, the shouts of footmen and of bystanders, warning all to make way. Jack was still getting about with the crutch (he daren't let the sword out of his sight, and couldn't bear it openly). So when he didn't move fast enough, a burly servant in powder-blue livery crushed him out of the way and sent him tumbling across the pavement so that his "good" leg plunged knee-deep in a gutter filled with stagnating shit.

Jack looked up and saw the Four Horses of the Apocalypse bearing down on him—or so he imagined for a moment, because it seemed that they all had glowing red eyes. But as they went past, this vision cleared from his mind, and he decided that their eyes, actually, had been pink. Four horses, all white as clouds, save for pink eyes and mottled hooves, harnessed in white leather, pulling a rare coach, sculpted and painted to look like a white sea-shell riding a frothy wave over the blue ocean, all encrusted with garlands and laurels, cherubs and mermaids, in gold.

Those horses put him in mind of Eliza's story; for she had been swapped for one such, back in Algiers.

Jack proceeded crosstown to Les Halles where the fishwives—pretending to be dismayed by the shit on his leg—flung fish-heads at him while shouting some sort of pun on *par fume.*

Jack inquired whether it ever happened that some rich man's servant would come around specifically to purchase *rotten* fish for his master.

It was clear, from the looks on their faces, that he had struck deep with this question—but then, looking him up and down, one of them made a certain guttural jeering noise, and then the fishwives all sneered and told him to hobble back to *Les Invalides* with his ridiculous questions. "I am not a veteran—what idiot goes out and fights battles for rich men?" Jack answered.

They liked that, but were in a cautious mood. "What are you then?" *"Passe-volante!"* "Vagabond!"

Jack decided to try what the Doctor would call an experiment: "Not *any* Vagabond," Jack said, "here stands Half-Cocked Jack."

"L'Emmerdeur!" gasped a younger, and not quite so gorgon-like, fishwife, almost before he'd gotten it out of his mouth.

There was a moment of radical silence. But then the guttural noise again. "You are the fourth Vagabond to make that claim in the last month—"

"And the least convincing—"

"*L'Emmerdeur* is a King among Vagabonds. Seven feet tall."

"Goes armed all the time, like a Gentleman."

"Carries a jeweled scimitar he tore from the hands of the Grand Turk himself—"

"Has magic spells to burn witches and confound Bishops."

"He's not a broken-down cripple with one leg withered and the other dipped in *merde*!"

Jack kicked off his fouled pants, and then his drawers, revealing his Credential. Then, to prove he wasn't really a cripple, he flung the crutch down, and began to dance a bare-assed jig. The fishwives could not decide between swooning and rioting. When they

509

recovered their self-possession, they began to fling handfuls of blackened copper *deniers* at him. This attracted beggars and street-musicians, and one of the latter began to play accompanying music on a *cornemuse* whilst shuffling around racking the worthless coins into a little pile with his feet, and kicking the beggars in the head as necessary.

Having now verified his identity by personal inspection, each of the fishwives had to prance out, shedding glitt'ry showers of fish-scales from their flouncing, gut-stained skirts, and dance with Jack—who had no patience for this, but did take advantage of it to whisper into any ear that came close enough, that if he ever had any money, he'd give some of it to whomever could tell him the name of the noble personage who liked to eat rotten fish. But before he could say it more than two or three times, he had to grab his drawers and run away, because a commotion at the other end of Les Halles told him that the Lieutenant of Police was on his way to make a show of force, and to extract whatever bribes, sexual favors, and/or free oysters he could get from the fishwives in exchange for turning a blind eye to this unforgivable brouhaha.

From there Jack proceeded to the livery stable, got Turk, and also rented two other horses. He rode to the House of the Golden Frigate on Rue Vivienne, and let it be known that he was on his way down to Lyons—any messages?

This made Signor Cozzi very pleased. His place was crowded today with tense Italians scribbling down messages and bills of exchange, and porters hauling what looked like money-boxes down from the attic and up from the cellar, and there was a sparse crowd of street-messengers and competing bankers in the street outside, exchanging speculations as to what was going on in there—what did Cozzi know that no one else did? Or was it just a bluff?

Signor Cozzi scrawled something on a scrap of paper and did not bother to seal it. He came up and lunged for Jack's hand, because Jack was not reaching out fast enough, and shoved the message into his palm, saying, "To Lyons! I don't care how many horses you kill getting there. What are you waiting for?"

Actually Jack was waiting to say he didn't particularly *want* to kill his horse, but Signor Cozzi was not in a mood for sentiment. So Jack whirled, ran out of the building, and mounted Turk. "Watch your back!" someone called after him, "word on the street is that *L'Emmerdeur* is in town!"

"I heard he was *on his way*," Jack said, "at the head of a Vagabond-Army."

It would have been amusing to stay around and continue this, but Cozzi was standing in the doorway glaring at him, and so, riding Turk and leading the rented horses behind him, Jack galloped down Rue Vivienne in what he hoped was dramatic style, and hung the first available left. This ended up taking him right back through Les Halles—so he made a point of galloping through the fish-market, where the police were turning things upside-down searching for a one-legged, short-penised pedestrian. Jack winked at that one young fishwife who'd caught his eye, touching off a thrill that spread like fire through gunpowder, and then he was gone, off into the Marais—right past the Place Royale. He maneuvered round the trundling manure-carts all the way to the Bastille: just one great sweaty rock pocked with a few tiny windows, with grenadiers roaming around on top—the highest and thickest in a city of walls. It sat in a moat fed by a short canal leading up from the Seine. The bridge over the canal was crowded, so Jack rode down to the river and then turned to follow the right bank out of town, and thereby left Paris behind him. He was afraid that Turk would be exhausted already. But when the war-horse saw open fields ahead, he surged forward, yanking on the lead and eliciting angry whinnies from the spare horses following behind.

To Lyons was a long journey, almost all the way to Italy (which was, he reckoned, why the Italian banks were situated there), or, if you wanted to look at it that way, almost all the way to Marseille. The countryside was divided up into innumerable separate *pays* with their own tolls, which were commonly exacted at inns controlling the important cross-roads. Jack, changing horses from time to time, seemed to be racing the whole way against a slippery narrow black coach that scuttled down the road like a scorpion, drawn by four horses. It was a good race, meaning that the lead changed hands many times. But in the end, those inns, and the need to change horse-teams frequently, were too much of an impediment for the coach, and Jack was the first to ride down into Lyons with the news—whatever it was.

Another Genoese banker in vivid clothing received Signor Cozzi's note. Jack had to track him down in a market-place unlike any in Paris, where things like charcoal, bales of old clothing, and rolls of undyed fabric were for sale in large quantities. The banker paid Jack out of his pocket, and read the note.

"You are English?"

"Aye, what of it?"

"Your King is dead." With that the banker went briskly to his office, whence other messengers galloped away within the hour, headed for Genoa and Marseilles. Jack stabled his horses and wandered round Lyons amazed, munching some dried figs he bought at a retail market. The only King he'd ever known was dead, and England was, somehow, a different country now—ruled by a Papist!

✠

The Hague

FEBRUARY 1685

☤

WEE DRIFTS OF wind-skimming snow had already parenthesized the cherry-red platform soles of the French delegation's boots, and inch-long snotcicles had grown from the moustaches of the English delegation. Eliza glided up on her skates, and swirled to a halt on the canal to admire what she took (at first) to be some sort of colossal sculpture group. Of course sculptures did not normally wear clothing, but these Ambassadors and their entourages (a total of eight Englishmen facing off against seven French) had been standing long enough that snow had permeated every pore of their hats, wigs, and coats, giving them the appearance (from a distance) of having been butcherously carved out of a large block of some very low-grade, grayish sculptural medium. Much more lively (and more warmly dressed) was the crowd of Dutchmen who had gathered round to watch, and to stake small wagers on which delegation would first succumb to the cold. A rabble of porters and wood-carriers seemed to have taken the English side, and better-dressed men had gathered round the French, and strode to and fro stamping their feet and blowing into their hands and dispatching swift-skating message-boys towards the States-General and the Binnenhof.

But Eliza was the only girl on skates. So as she came to a stop there on the canal's edge, only a few yards away from, and a foot or two lower than, the two groups of men on the adjoining street, the entire sculpture came to life. Rimes of ice cracked and tinkled as fifteen French and English heads rotated towards her. 'Twas now a standoff of a *different* nature.

☭

The best-dressed man in the French delegation shuddered. They were *all* shivering, but this gentleman *shuddered*. "Mademoiselle," he said, "do you speak French?"

Eliza regarded him. His hat was the size of a washtub, filled with exotic plumes, now crushed under drifts. His boots had the enormous tongues just coming into fashion, erupting from his instep and spreading and curling up and away from the shin—these had filled with snow, which was melting and trickling down inside the boots and darkening the leather from the inside.

"Only when there is some *reason* to, monsieur," she returned.

"What is a reason?"

"How French of you to ask . . . I suppose that when a gentleman, who has been correctly introduced to me, flatters me with a compliment, or amuses me with a witticism . . ."

"I humbly beg Mademoiselle's forgiveness," the Frenchman said, through gray and stiff lips that ruined his pronunciation. "But as you did not arrive with an escort, there was no one to beg for the favor of a decent introduction."

"He is yonder," said Eliza, gesturing half a league down the canal.

"*Mon Dieu,* he flails his limbs like a lost soul tumbling backwards into the Pit," the Frenchman exclaimed. "Tell me, mademoiselle, why does a *swan* venture out on the canals with an *orang-utan?*"

"He claimed he knew how to skate."

"But a lass of your *beauty,* must have heard many brave claims from young men's lips—and one of your *intelligence* must have perceived that all of them were rank nonsense."

"Whereas you, monsieur, are honest and pure of heart?"

"Alas, mademoiselle, I am merely old."

"Not so old."

"And yet I may have perished from *age* or *pneumonia* before your beau struggles close enough to make introductions, so . . . Jean Antoine de Mesmes, comte d'Avaux, your most humble servant."

"Charmed. My name is Eliza . . ."

"Duchess of Qwghlm?"

Eliza laughed at this absurdity. "But how did you know I was Qwghlmian?"

"Your native tongue is English—but you skate like one who was born on ice, *sans* the staggering drunken gait of the Anglo-Saxons who so cruelly oppress your islands," d'Avaux answered, raising his voice so that the English delegation could hear.

"Very clever—but you know perfectly well that I am no Duchess."

"And yet blue blood flows in your veins, I cannot but believe . . ."

"Not half so blue as *yours,* Monsieur, as I cannot but *see.* Why don't you go inside and sit by a warm fire?"

"Now you tempt me cruelly in a *second* way," d'Avaux said. "I must stand here, to uphold the honor and glory of *La France.* But you are bound by no such obligations—why do you go out here, where only harp-seals and polar-bears should be—and in such a skirt?"

"The skirt *must* be short, lest it get caught in the blades of my skates—you see?" Eliza said, and did a little pirouette. Before she'd gotten entirely turned around, a groaning and cracking noise came from the center of the French delegation as a spindly middle-aged diplomat collapsed dizzily to the ground. The men to either side of him crouched down as if to render assistance, but were straightened up by a brisk idiom from d'Avaux. "Once we begin to make exceptions for those who fall—or who *pretend* to—the whole delegation will go down like ninepins," d'Avaux explained, addressing the remark to Eliza, but *intending* it for his entourage. The fallen man contracted to a fœtal position on the pavement; a couple of sword-wearing Dutchmen scurried in with a blanket. Meanwhile a wench came down out of a side-street bearing a large tray, and walked past the French delegation, letting them smell the flip-aroma, and feel the steam, from eight tankards—which she took direct to the Englishmen.

"Exceptions to *what?*" Eliza asked.

"To the rules of diplomatic protocol," d'Avaux answered. "Which state—for example—that when one Ambassador meets another in a narrow way, the junior Ambassador must give way for the senior."

"Ah, so that's it. You're having a dispute as to whether you, or the English Ambassador, has seniority?"

"I represent the Most Christian King,* *that* lot represent King James II of England . . . or so we can only assume, as we have received word that King Charles II has died, but not that his brother has been properly crowned."

"Then it's clear *you* have seniority."

"Clear to you and me, mademoiselle. But *that* fellow has asserted that, since he cannot represent an uncrowned king, he must still be representing the late Charles II, who was crowned in 1651 after the Puritans chopped off the head of his father and predecessor. My King was crowned in 1654."

"But with all due respect to the Most Christian King, monsieur, doesn't that mean that Charles II, if he still lived, would have three years' seniority over him?"

---

*Louis XIV of France.

"A rabble of Scots at Scone tossed a crown at Charles's head," d'Avaux said, "and then he came and lived *here*, begging for handouts from Dutchmen, until 1660 when the cheese-mongers *paid* him to leave. *Practically* speaking, his reign began when he sailed to Dover."

"If we are going to be *practical,* sir," shouted an Englishman, "let us consider that *your* King did not *practically* begin his reign until the death of Cardinal Mazarin on the ninth of March, 1661." He raised a tankard to his lips and quaffed deeply, pausing between gulps to emit little moans of satisfaction.

"At least *my* King is alive," d'Avaux muttered. "You see? And they love to accuse *Jesuits* of sophistry! I say, is your beau wanted by the Guild of St. George?"

Civic order in the Hague was maintained by two Guilds of civic guards. The part of the city around the market and the town hall, where normal Dutchmen lived, was looked after by the St. Sebastian Guild. The St. George Guild was responsible for the Hofgebied, which was the part of the city containing the royal palace, foreign embassies, houses of rich families, and so on. Both Guilds were represented among the crowd of spectators who had gathered round to partake of the spectacle of d'Avaux and his English counterparts freezing to death. So d'Avaux's question was partly intended to flatter and amuse the genteel and aristocratic St. George men—perhaps at the expense of the more plebeian St. Sebastian guards, who seemed to be favoring the English delegation.

"Don't be absurd, monsieur! If he *were*, those brave and diligent men would have apprehended him long ago. Why do you ask such a question?"

"He has covered up his face like some sort of a *volunteer*." Which meant, a soldier-turned-highwayman.

Eliza turned round to see Gomer Bolstrood lurking (there was no other word for it) around a corner of the canal a stone's throw away with a long strip of tartan wrapped over his face.

"Those who live in northerly climes often do this."

"It seems extremely disreputable and in the poorest taste. If your beau cannot tolerate a bit of a sea-breeze—"

"He is not my beau—merely a business associate."

"Then, mademoiselle, you will be free to meet with me here, at this hour, tomorrow, and give me a skating-lesson."

"But, monsieur! From the way you shuddered when you beheld me, I thought you considered such sports beneath your dignity."

"Indeed—but I am an Ambassador, and must submit to any number of degradations . . ."

"For the honor and glory of *la France*?"

"*Pourquoi non?*"

"I hope that they widen the street soon, comte d'Avaux."

"Spring is just around the corner—and when I gaze upon your face, mademoiselle, I feel it is already here."

"'Twas perfectly innocent, Mr. Bolstrood—I thought they were sculpture until eyes turned my way."

They were seated before a fire in a stately hunting-lodge. The place was warm enough, but smoky, and bleak, and entirely too filled with heads of dead animals, who seemed *also* to be turning their eyes Eliza's way.

"You imagine I'm angry, but I'm not."

"What's troubling you, then? I daresay you are the brooding-est fellow I have ever seen."

"These chairs."

"Did I hear you correctly, sir?"

"Look at them," Gomer Bolstrood said, in a voice hollow with despair. "Those who built this estate had no shortage of money, of that you can be sure—but the furniture! It is either stupid and primitive, like this ogre's throne I'm seated on, or else—like yours—raked together out of kindling, with about as much structural integrity as a *faggot*. I could make better chairs in an *afternoon, drunk*, given a *shrub* and a *jackknife*."

"Then I must apologize for having misread you, as I supposed you were angry about that chance encounter, there—"

"My faith teaches me it was inevitable—predestined—that you would enter into a flirtation with the French Ambassador just now. If I'm brooding over *that*, it's not because I'm angry, but because I must understand what it means."

"It means he's a horny old goat."

Gomer Bolstrood shook his colossal head hopelessly, and gazed toward a window. The pane shouted as it was hit by a burst of wind-driven slush. "I pray it did not develop into a riot," he said.

"How much of a riot can eight frozen Englishmen and seven half-dead Frenchmen accomplish?"

"It's the Dutchmen I'm worried about. The commoners and country folk, as always, side with the Stadholder.* The merchants are all Frenchified—and because the States-General are meeting here at the moment, the town's crowded with the latter—all of 'em wearing swords and carrying pistols."

_____
*William of Orange.

"Speaking of Frenchified merchants," Eliza said, "I have some good news for the Client—whoever he is—from the commodities market. It seems that during the run-up to the 1672 war, an Amsterdam banker committed treason against the Republic—"

"Actually any number of 'em did—but pray continue."

"Acting as a cat's-paw for the Marquis de Louvois, this traitor—Mr. Sluys by name—bought up nearly all of the lead in the country to ensure that William's army would be short of ammunition. No doubt Sluys thought the war would be over in a few days, and that King Louis, after planting the French flag on the Damrak, would reward him personally. But of course that is not how it happened. Ever since, Sluys has had a warehouse full of lead, which he's been afraid to sell openly, lest word get out, and an Orangist mob burn his warehouses, and tear him apart, as they did so memorably to the de Witt brothers. But now Sluys *has* to sell it."

"Why?"

"It's been thirteen years. His warehouse has been sinking into the Amsterdam-mud twice as fast as the ones to either side of it, because of the weight of all that lead. The neighbors are beginning to complain. He is taking the whole neighborhood down!"

"So Mr. Sluys should offer an excellent price," Gomer Bolstrood said. "Praise God! The Client will be most pleased. Did this same traitor buy up gunpowder? Matches?"

"All ruined by humidity. But a fleet of Indiamen are expected at Texel any day—they'll be heavy laden with saltpeter, most likely—powder prices are already dropping."

"Probably not dropping *enough* for our purposes," Bolstrood muttered. "Can we buy up saltpeter, and make our own?"

"Sulfur prices are also agreeable, owing to some fortuitous volcanic eruptions in Java," Eliza said, "but proper charcoal is very dear—the Duke of Braunschweig-Lüneburg controls his Faulbaum inventory like a miser counting his coins."

"We may have to capture an arsenal very early in the campaign," Bolstrood said, "God willing."

Talk of campaigns and arsenal-captures made Eliza nervous, so she attempted a change of subject: "When may I have the pleasure of meeting the Client?"

"As soon as we can find him clothed and sober," Bolstrood answered immediately.

"That should be easy, in a Barker."

"The Client is nothing of the sort!" Gomer Bolstrood scoffed.

"How very strange."

"What is strange about it?"

"How came he to oppose Slavery if not through religion?"

"You oppose it, and you're no Calvinist," Bolstrood parried.

"I have personal reasons for feeling as I do. But I phant'sied that the Client was one of your co-religionists. He *does* oppose slavery, does he not?"

"Let us set aside phant'sies, and speak of facts."

"Can't help noticing, sir, that my question is unanswered."

"You appeared at the door of our church in Amsterdam—some felt, like an Angelic visitation—with a most generous donation, and offered to make yourself useful in any way that would further our work 'gainst Slavery. And that is just what you are doing."

"But if the Client is *not* opposed to slavery, how does it further the cause to buy him powder and musket-balls?"

"You may not know that my father—God rest his soul—served as the late King's Secretary of State before he was hounded to exile and death by the Papists who do France's work in England. He submitted to that degradation because he knew that upright men must sometimes treat with the likes of King Charles II for the greater good. In the same way, we who oppose slavery, and Established religion, and in particular all of the abominations and fopperies of the Romish faith, must give our support to any man who might prevent James, Duke of York, from long remaining on the throne."

"James *is* the rightful heir, is he not?"

"As those diplomats just proved, cavilling over the seniority of their Kings," Bolstrood said, "there is no question that cannot be muddled—and powder-smoke muddles things 'specially well. King Louis stamps *Ultima Ratio Regum* on all of his cannon—"

"The last argument of kings."

"You know Latin, too—?"

"I had a Classical education."

"In Qwghlm!?"

"In Constantinople."

THE COMTE D'AVAUX MOVED THROUGH the Hague's canal-network in the gait of a man walking across red-hot coals, but some innate aplomb kept him from falling down even once.

"Would you like to go home now, monsieur?"

"Oh no, mademoiselle—I am enjoying myself," he returned, biting off the syllables one by one, like a crocodile working its way up an oar.

"You dressed more warmly today—is that Russian sable?"

"Yes, but of an inferior grade—a much finer one awaits you—if you get me back alive."

"That is quite unnecessary, monsieur—"

"The entire point of gifts is to be unnecessary." D'Avaux reached into a pocket and pulled out a square of neatly folded black velvet. *"Voilà,"* he said, handing it over to her.

"What is it?" Eliza asked, taking it from his hand, and using the opportunity to grab his upper arm for a moment and steady him.

"A little nothing. I should like you to wear it."

The velvet unfolded into a long ribbon about the width of Eliza's hand, its two ends joined together with a rather nice gold brooch made in the shape of a butterfly. Eliza guessed it was meant to be a sash, and put one arm and her head through it, letting it hang diagonally across her body. "Thank you, monsieur," she said, "how does it look?"

The comte d'Avaux, for once, failed to offer her a compliment. He merely shrugged, as if how it looked was not the point. Which confirmed Eliza's suspicion that a black velvet sash over skating-clothes was rather odd-looking.

"How did you escape your predicament yesterday?" she asked him.

"Made arrangements for the Stadholder to summon the English Ambassador back to the Binnenhof. This compelled him to make a *volte-face:* a maneuver in which the diplomats of perfidious Albion are well practiced. We followed him down the street and made the first available turn. How did you escape *yours*?"

"What—you mean, being out for a skate with a lug?"

"Naturally."

"Tormented him for another half an hour—then returned to his place in the country to transact business. You think I'm a whore, don't you, monsieur? I saw it in your face when I mentioned *business*. Though you would probably say *courtesan*."

"Mademoiselle, in my circles, anyone who transacts business of any sort, on any level, is a whore. Among French nobility, no distinctions are recognized between the finest commerçants of Amsterdam and common prostitutes."

"Is that why Louis hates the Dutch so?"

"Oh no, mademoiselle, unlike these dour Calvinists, we *love* whores—Versailles is aswarm with them. No, we have any number of *intelligent* reasons to hate the Dutch."

"What *sort* of whore do you suppose I am, then, monsieur?"

"That is what I am trying to establish."

Eliza laughed. "Then you should be eager to turn back."

"Non!" The comte d'Avaux made a doddering, flailing turn onto another canal. Something bulky and grim shouldered its way into a

gap ahead of them. Eliza mistook it, at first, for an especially gloomy old brick church. But then she noticed up on the parapet light shining like barred teeth through crenellations, and many narrow embrasures, and realized it had been made for another purpose besides saving souls. The building had tall poky conical spires at the corners, and Gothic decorations along the fronts of the gables that thrust out into the cold air like clenched stone fists. "The Ridderzaal," she said, getting her bearings; for she had gotten quite lost following d'Avaux along the labyrinth of canals that were laced through the Hofgebied like capillaries through flesh. "So we are on the Spij now, going north." A short distance ahead of them, the Spij forked in twain, bracketing the Ridderzaal and other ancient buildings of the Counts of Holland between its branches.

D'Avaux careered into the right fork. "Let us go through yonder water-gate, into the Hofvijver!" Meaning a rectangular pond that lay before the Binnenhof, or palace of the Dutch court. "The view of the Binnenhof rising above the ice will be—er—"

"Magical?"

"Non."

"Magnificent?"

"Don't be absurd."

"Less bleak than anything else we have seen?"

"Now truly you are speaking French," the ambassador said approvingly. "The princeling* is off on another of his insufferable hunting expeditions, but *some* persons of quality are there." He had put on a surprising—almost alarming—burst of speed and was several paces ahead of Eliza now. "They will open the gate for me," he said confidently, tossing the words back over his shoulder like a scarf. "When they do, you put on one of those magnificent *accélérations* and sail past me into the Hofvijver."

"Very devious . . . but why don't you simply ask them to let me through?"

"This will make for a gayer spectacle."

The gate was so close to the Binnenhof that they would nearly pass underneath the palace as they went through. It was guarded by musketeers and archers dressed in blue outfits with lace cravats and orange sashes. When they recognized Jean Antoine de Mesmes, comte d'Avaux, they ventured out onto the ice, skidding on their hard-soled boots, pulled one side of the gate open for him, and bowed—doffing their hats and sweeping the ice with the tips of their orange plumes. The gate was wide enough to admit

—————

*William of Orange.

pleasure-boats during the warmer months, and so Eliza had plenty of room to whoosh past the French Ambassador and into the rectangle of ice that was spread out before William of Orange's palace. It was a maneuver that would have earned her a broad-headed arrow between the shoulder blades if she were a man. But she was a girl in a short skirt and so the guards took her entrance in the spirit intended—as an amusing courtly *plaisanterie* of the comte's devising.

She was going very fast—faster than she needed to, for this had given her an excuse to stretch cold stiff leg-muscles. She'd entered the southeast corner of the Hofvijver, which extended perhaps a hundred yards north–south and thrice that east–west. Slicing up along its eastern bank, she was distracted by musket-fire from open ground off to her right, and had a wild moment of fear that she was about to be cut down by snipers. But not to worry, it was a party of gentlemen honing their markmanship on a target-range spread out between the bank of the pond and an ornate building set farther back. She recognized this, now, as the headquarters of the St. George Guild. Beyond it, wooded land stretched away to the east as far as she could see: the Haagsche Bos, a game-park for the Counts of Holland, where people of all classes went to ride and stroll when the weather was better.

Directly ahead of her was a cobblestone ramp: a street that plunged directly into the water of the pond, when it wasn't frozen, and where horses and cattle could be taken down and watered. She had to lean hard and make a searing turn to avoid it. Swaying her hips from side to side, she picked up a bit of speed as she glided down the long northern shore of the Hofvijver. The south shore, spreading off to her left, was a hodgepodge of brown brick buildings with black slate rooves, many having windows just above the level of the pond, so that she could have skated right up and conversed with people on the inside. But she wouldn't have dared, for this was the Binnenhof, the palace of the Stadholder, William of Orange. Her view of it was obscured, for a time, by a tiny round island planted in the center of the Hofvijver like a half-cherry on a slice of cake. Trees and shrubs grew on it, and moss grew on them, though all was brown and leafless now. But above and behind the Binnenhof she could see the many narrow towers of the Ridderzaal jabbing at the sky like a squadron of knights with lances upright.

That was the end of sightseeing. For as she shot clear of the little island, and curled round to swing back towards d'Avaux, she discovered that she was sharing the ice with a slow-moving clique of skaters. She glimpsed both men and women, finely dressed. To

knock them down would have been bad form. To stop and introduce herself would have been infinitely worse. She spun round to
face towards d'Avaux, skating backwards now, letting her momentum carry her past the group. She carved a long sweeping U round
the west end of the Hofvijver, spun round to face forward again,
built more speed without lifting her skates from the ice, by means
of sashaying hip-movements that took her down the long front of
the Binnenhof, in a serpentine path, and finally stopped just
before running into d'Avaux by planting the blades sideways and
shaving up a glittering wall of ice. Nothing very acrobatic really—
but it was enough to draw applause from Blue Guards, St. George
Guildsmen, and noble skaters alike.

"I learnt defencing at the Academy of Monsieur du Plessis in
Paris, where the finest swordsmen of the world gather to flaunt
their prowess—but none of them can match *your* grace with a pair
of steel blades, mademoiselle," said the prettiest man Eliza had
ever seen, as he was raising her gloved hand to smooch it.

D'Avaux had been making introductions. The gorgeous man
was the Duke of Monmouth. He was escorting a tall, lanky, yet jowly
woman in her early twenties. This was Mary—the daughter of the
new King of England, and William of Orange's wife.

As d'Avaux had announced these names and titles, Eliza had
come close to losing her nerve for the first time in memory. She
was remembering Hanover, where the Doctor had planted her in a
steeple near the Herrenhausen Palace, so that she could gaze
upon Sophie through a field-glass. Yet this d'Avaux—who didn't
know Eliza nearly as well as the Doctor did—had taken her straight
into the Dutch court's inner sanctum. How could d'Avaux introduce her to persons of royal degree—when he didn't have the first
idea who she was in the first place?

In the end it couldn't have been simpler. He had leaned in
towards Monmouth and Mary and said, discreetly: "This is—*Eliza*."
This had elicited knowing nods and winks from the others, and a
little buzz of excitement from Mary's entourage of English servants
and hangers-on. These were apparently not even worth introducing—and that went double for the Negro page-boy and the shivering Javanese dwarf.

"No compliments for *me,* your Grace?" d'Avaux asked, as Monmouth was planting multiple kisses on the back of Eliza's glove.

"On the contrary, monsieur—you are the finest skater of all
France," Monmouth returned with a smile. He still had most of his
teeth. He had forgotten to let go of Eliza's hand.

Mary nearly fell off her skates, partly because she was laughing

at Monmouth's jest a little harder than was really warranted, and
partly because she was a miserable skater (in the corner of Eliza's
eye, earlier, she'd looked like a windmill—flailing without moving). It had been obvious from the first moment Eliza had seen her
that she was infatuated with the Duke of Monmouth. Which to
some degree was embarrassing. But Eliza had to admit that she'd
chosen a likely young man to fall in love with.

Mary of Orange started to say something, but d'Avaux ran her
off the road. "Mademoiselle Eliza has been trying valiantly to teach
me how to skate," he said commandingly, giving Eliza a wet look.
"But I am like a peasant listening to one of the lectures of Monsieur Huygens." He glanced over toward the water-gate through
which he and Eliza had just passed, for the house of the Huygens
family lay very nearby that corner of the palace.

"I should've fallen ever so many times without the Duke to hold
me up," Mary put in.

"Would an Ambassador do as well?" d'Avaux said, and before
Mary could answer, he sidled up to her and nearly knocked her
over. She flailed for the Ambassador's arm and just got a grip on it
in time. Her entourage closed in to get her back on her blades, the
Javanese dwarf getting one hand on each buttock and pushing up
with all his might.

The Duke of Monmouth saw none of this drama, engaged as he
was in a minute inspection of Eliza. He began with her hair,
worked his way down to her ankles, then back up, until he was startled to discover a pair of blue eyes staring back at him. *That* led to
a spell of disorientation just long enough for d'Avaux (who had
pinned Mary's hand between his elbow and ribcage) to say, "By all
means, your Grace, go for a skate, stretch your legs—we novices
will just totter around the Vijver for a few minutes."

"Mademoiselle?" said the Duke, proffering a hand.

"Your grace," said Eliza, taking it.

Ten heartbeats later they were out on the Spij. Eliza let go Monmouth's hand and spun round backwards to see the water-gate
being closed behind them, and, through the bars, Mary of Orange,
looking as if she'd been punched in the stomach, and Jean Antoine
de Mesmes, comte d'Avaux, looking as if he did this kind of thing
several times a day. Once, in Constantinople, Eliza had helped hold
one of the other slave-girls down while an Arab surgeon took out her
appendix. It had taken all of two minutes. She'd been astonished
that a man with a sharp knife and no hesitation about using it could
effect such changes so rapidly. Thus d'Avaux and Mary's heart.

Once they got clear of the Spij the canal broadened and

Monmouth executed a dramatic spin—lots of flesh and bone moving fast—not really graceful, but she couldn't not look. If anything, he was a more accomplished skater than Eliza. He saw Eliza *watching,* and assumed she was *admiring,* him. "During the Interregnum I divided my time between here and Paris," he explained, "and spent many hours on these canals—where did you learn, mademoiselle?"

Struggling across heaving floes to chip gull shit off rocks struck Eliza as a tasteless way to answer the question. She might have come up with some clever story, given enough time—but her mind was too busy trying to fathom what was going on.

"Ah, forgive me for prying—I forget that you are *incognito,*" said the Duke of Monmouth, his eyes straying momentarily to the black sash that d'Avaux had given her. "That, and your coy silence, speak volumes."

"Really? What's in those volumes?"

"The tale of a lovely innocent cruelly misused by some Germanic or Scandinavian noble—was it at the court of Poland-Lithuania? Or was it that infamous woman-beater, Prince Adolph of Sweden? Say nothing, mademoiselle, except that you forgive me my curiosity."

"Done. Now, are you that same Duke of Monmouth who distinguished himself at the Siege of Maestricht? I know a man who fought in that battle—or who was *there,* anyway—and who spoke at length of your doings."

"Is it the Marquis de—? Or the comte d'—?"

"You forget yourself, Monsieur," said Eliza, stroking the velvet sash.

"Once again—please accept my apology," said the Duke, looking wickedly amused.

"You *might* be able to redeem yourself by explaining something to me: the Siege of Maestricht was part of a campaign to wipe the Dutch Republic off the map. William sacrificed half his country to win that war. You fought against him. And yet here you are enjoying the hospitality of that same William, in the innermost court of Holland, only a few years later."

"That's nothing," Monmouth said agreeably, "for only a few years after Maestricht I was fighting by William's side, *against* the French, at Mons, *and* William was *married* to that Mary—who as you must know is the daughter of King James II, formerly the Duke of York, and Admiral of the English Navy until William's admirals blew it out of the water. I could go on in this vein for hours."

"If I had such an enemy I would not rest until he was dead,"

Eliza said. "As a matter of fact, I *do* have an enemy, and it has been a long time since I have rested . . ."

"Who is it?" Monmouth asked eagerly, "the one who taught you to skate and then—"

"It is *another*," Eliza said, "but I know not his name—our encounter was in a dark cabin on a ship—"

"What ship?"

"I know not."

"What flag did it fly?"

"A black one."

"Stab me!"

"Oh, 'twas the typical sort of heathen pirate-galleon—nothing remarkable."

"You were captured by heathen pirates!?"

"Only once. Happens more often than you might appreciate. But we are digressing. I will not rest until my enemy's identity is known, and I've put him in the grave."

"But suppose that when you learn his identity, he turns out to be your great-uncle, *and* your cousin's brother-in-law, *and* your best friend's godfather?"

"I'm only speaking of one enemy—"

"I know. But royal families of Europe are so tangled together that your enemy might bear all of those relations to you *at once*."

"Eeyuh, what a mess."

"On the contrary—'tis the height of civilization," Monmouth said. "It is not—mind you—that we *forget* our grievances. That would be unthinkable. But if our only redress were to put one another into graves, all Europe would be a battleground!"

"All Europe *is* a battleground! Haven't you been paying attention?"

"Fighting at Maestricht and Mons and other places has left me little time for it," Monmouth said drily. "I say to you it could be much worse—like the Thirty Years' War, or the Civil War in England."

"I suppose that is true," Eliza said, remembering all of those ruined castles in Bohemia.

"In the *modern* age we pursue revenge at Court. Sometimes we might go so far as to fight a duel—but in general we wage battles with *wit*, not *muskets*. It does not kill as many people, and it gives ladies a chance to enter the lists—as it were."

"I beg your pardon?"

"Have you ever fired a musket, mademoiselle?"

"No."

"And yet in our conversation you have already discharged any number of *verbal* broadsides. So you see, on the *courtly* battle-ground, women stand on an equal footing with men."

Eliza coasted to a stop, hearing the bells of the town hall chiming four o'clock. Monmouth overshot her, then swooped through a gallant turn and skated back, wearing a silly grin.

"I must go and meet someone," Eliza said.

"May I escort you back to the Binnenhof?"

"No—d'Avaux is there."

"You no longer take pleasure in the Ambassador's company?"

"I am afraid he will try to give me a fur coat."

"That would be terrible!"

"I don't want to give him the satisfaction . . . he has used me, somehow."

"The King of France has given him orders to be as offensive as possible to Mary. As Mary's in love with *me* today . . ."

"Why?"

"Why is she in love with me? Mademoiselle, I am offended."

"I know perfectly well why she is in love with you. I meant, why would the King of France send a Count up to the Hague simply to behave offensively?"

"Oh, the comte d'Avaux does many other things besides. But the answer is that King Louis hopes to break up the marriage between William and Mary—destroying William's power in England—and making Mary available for marriage to one of his French bastards."

"I knew it had to be a family squabble of some sort—it's so mean, so petty, so vicious."

"*Now* you begin to understand!"

"Doesn't Mary love her husband?"

"William and Mary are a well-matched couple."

"You *say* little but *mean* much . . . what *do* you mean?"

"Now it is my turn to be mysterious," Monmouth said, "as it's the only way I can be sure of seeing you again."

He went on in that vein, and Eliza dodged him elaborately, and they parted ways.

But two hours later they were together again. This time Gomer Bolstrood was with them.

A COUPLE OF MILES NORTH of the Hague, the flat polder-land of the Dutch Republic was sliced off by the sea-coast. A line of dunes provided a meager weather-wall. Sheltering behind it, running parallel to the coast, was a strip of land, frequently wooded, but not wilderness, for it had been improved with roads and canals. In that belt of green had grown up diverse estates: the country retreats of nobles and merchants. Each had a proper house with a formal garden. The bigger ones also had wooded game-parks, and hunting-lodges where men could seek refuge from their women.

Eliza still knew little about Gomer Bolstrood and his scheme; but it was obvious enough that he was in league with some merchant or other, who was the owner of one such estate, and that he had gotten permission to use the hunting-lodge as a pied-à-terre. A canal ran along one side of the game-park and connected it—if you knew which turns to take—to the Haagsche Bos, that large park next to the Binnenhof. The distance was several miles, and so it might have been a morning's or an afternoon's journey in the summer. But when ice was on the canals, and skates were on the traveler's feet, it could be accomplished in very little time.

Thus Monmouth had arrived, by himself, incognito. He was seated on the chair that Bolstrood had likened to an ogre's throne, and Eliza and Bolstrood were on the creaking faggot-chairs. Bolstrood tried to make a formal introduction of the Client, but—

"So," Eliza said, "as you were saying a short time ago: fighting battles with muskets and powder is an out-moded practice and . . ."

"It suits my purposes for people to think that I actually *believe* such nonsense," Monmouth said, "and women are ever eager to believe it."

"Why—because in battle, women become swag, and we don't like being swag?"

"I suppose so."

"I've been swag. It didn't suit me. So, for me, your little lecture about modernity was inspiring in a way."

"As I said—women are eager to believe it."

"The two of you are acquainted—?—!" Bolstrood finally forced out.

"As my late Dad so aptly demonstrated, those of us who are predestined to burn in Hell must try to have a *bit* of fun while we are alive," Monmouth said. "Men and women—ones who are not Puritans, anyway—know each other in all sorts of ways!" Regarding Eliza warmly. Eliza gave him a look that was intended to be like a giant icicle thrust through his abdomen—but Monmouth responded with a small erotic quiver.

Eliza said, "If you play into the comte d'Avaux's hands so easily, by diverting your affections from Mary—what use will you be when you sit on the throne of England?"

Monmouth drooped and looked at Bolstrood.

"I didn't tell her, exactly," Gomer Bolstrood protested, "I only told her what commodities we wish to purchase."

"Which was enough to make your plan quite obvious," Eliza said.

"Doesn't matter, I suppose," Monmouth said. "As we cannot make the purchases anyway without putting up some collateral—and in our case the collateral *is* the throne."

"That's not what I was told," Eliza said. "I've been assuming the account would be settled with gold."

"And so it will be—*after.*"

"After what?"

"After we've conquered England."

"Oh."

"But most of England is on our side, so—a few months at most."

"Does most-of-England have *guns?*"

"It's true what he says," put in Gomer Bolstrood. "Everywhere this man goes in England, people turn out into the streets and light bonfires for him, and burn the Pope in effigy."

"So *in addition* to purchasing the required *commodities,* you require a bridge loan, for which your collateral will be—"

"The Tower of London," Monmouth said reassuringly.

"I am a trader, not a shareholder," Eliza said. "I cannot be your financier."

"How can you trade, without being a shareholder?"

"I trade ducat shares, which have one-tenth the value of proper V.O.C. shares and are far more liquid. I hold them—or options—only long enough to eke out a small profit. You will need to skate about forty miles that way, your grace," Eliza said, pointing north-east, "and make connections with Amsterdam moneylenders. There are great men there, princes of the market, who've accumulated stacks of V.O.C. stock, and who will lend money out against it. But as you cannot put the Tower of London in your pocket and set it on the table as security for the loan, you'll need something else."

"We know that," Bolstrood said. "We are merely letting you know that when time comes to effect the transaction, the payment will come, not from us, but—"

"From some credulous lender."

"Not *so* credulous. Important men are with us."

"May I know who those men are?"

A look between Bolstrood and Monmouth. "Not now. Later, in Amsterdam," Bolstrood said.

"This is never going to work—those Amsterdammers have more *good* investments than they know what to do with," Eliza said. "But there might be another way to get the money."

"Where do you propose to get it from, if not the moneylenders of Amsterdam?" Monmouth asked. "My mistress has already pawned all of her jewels—*that* resource is exhausted."

"We can get it from Mr. Sluys," Eliza said, after a long few minutes of staring into the fire. She turned to face the others. The air of the lodge was suddenly cool on her brow.

"The one who betrayed his country thirteen years ago?" Bolstrood asked warily.

"The same. He has many connections with French investors and is very rich."

"You mean to blackmail him, then—?" Monmouth asked.

"Not precisely. First we'll find some *other* investor and tell him of your plan to invade England."

"But the plan is a secret!"

"He'll have every incentive to *keep* it secret—for as soon as he knows, he will begin selling V.O.C. stock short."

"That, 'selling short,' is a bit of zargon I have heard Dutchmen and Jews bandy about, but I know not what it means," Monmouth said.

"There are two factions who war with each other in the market: *liefhebberen* or bulls who want the stock to rise, and *contremines* or bears who want it to fall. Frequently a group of bears will come together and form a secret cabal—they will spread false news of pirates off the coast, or go into the market loudly selling shares at very low prices, trying to create a panic and make the price drop."

"But how do they make money from this?"

"Never mind the details—there are ways of using options so that you will make money if the price falls. It is called short selling. Our investor—once we tell him about your invasion plans—will begin betting that V.O.C. stock will drop soon. And rest assured, it will. Only a few years ago, mere *rumors* about the state of Anglo/Dutch relations were sufficient to depress the price by ten or twenty percent. News of an invasion will plunge it through the *floor.*"

"Why?" Monmouth asked.

"England has a powerful navy—if they are hostile to Holland, they can choke off shipping, and the V.O.C. drops like a stone."

"But *my* policies will be far more congenial to the Hollanders than King James's!" Monmouth protested.

Bolstrood meanwhile had a look on his face as if he were being garrotted by an invisible cord.

Eliza composed herself, breathed deeply, and smiled at Monmouth—then leaned forward and put her hand on his forearm. "Naturally, when it becomes generally understood that your rebellion is going to succeed, V.O.C. stock will soar like a lark in the morning. But *at first* the market will be dominated by ignorant ninehammers who'll foolishly assume that King James will prevail—and that he will be ever so annoyed at the Dutch for having allowed their territory to serve as spring-board for an invasion of his country."

Bolstrood relaxed a bit.

"So at first the market will drop," Monmouth said distractedly.

"Until the *true* situation becomes generally known," Eliza said, patted his arm firmly, and drew back. Gomer Bolstrood seemed to relax further. "During that interval," Eliza continued, "our investor will have the opportunity to reap a colossal profit, by selling the market short. And in exchange for that opportunity he'll gladly buy you all the lead and powder you need to mount the invasion."

"But that investor is *not* Mr. Sluys—?"

"In any short-selling transaction there is a *loser* as well as a *winner*," Eliza said. "Mr. Sluys is to be the loser."

"Why him specifically?" Bolstrood asked. "It could be *any* liefhebber."

"Selling short has been illegal for three-quarters of a century! Numerous edicts have been issued to prevent it—one of them written in the time of the Stadholder Frederick Henry. Now, if a trader is caught short—that is, if he has signed a contract that will cause him to lose money—he can 'appeal to Frederick.'"

"But Frederick Henry died *ages* ago," Monmouth protested.

"It is an expression—a term of art. It simply means to repudiate the contract, and refuse to pay. According to Frederick Henry's edict, that repudiation will be upheld in a court of law."

"But if it's true that there must always be a loser when selling short, then Frederick Henry's decree must've stamped out the practice altogether!"

"Oh, no, your grace—short selling thrives in Amsterdam! Many traders make their living from it!"

"But why don't all of the losers simply 'appeal to Frederick'?"

"It all has to do with how the contracts are structured. If you're clever enough you can put the loser in a position where he dare not appeal to Frederick."

"So it *is* a sort of blackmail after all," Bolstrood said, gazing out the window across a snowy field—but hot on Eliza's trail. "We set Sluys up to be the loser—then if he appeals to Frederick, the entire story comes out in a court of law—including the warehouse full of lead—and he's exposed as a traitor. So he'll eat the loss without complaint."

"But—if I'm following all of this—it relies on Sluys *not knowing* that there is a plan to invade England," Monmouth said. "Otherwise he'd be a fool to enter into the short contract."

"That is certainly true," Eliza said. "We want him to believe that V.O.C. stock will rise."

"But if he's selling us the lead, he'll know we're planning *something*."

"Yes—but he needn't know *what* is being planned, or *when*. We need only manipulate his mental state, so that he has reason to believe that V.O.C. shares are soon to rise."

"And—as I'm now beginning to understand—you are something of a virtuoso when it comes to manipulating men's mental states," Monmouth said.

"You make it sound ever so much more difficult than it really is," Eliza answered. "Mostly I just sit quietly and let the men manipulate themselves."

"Well, if that's all for now," Monmouth said, "I feel a powerful urge to go and practice some self-manipulation in private—unless—?"

"Not today, your grace," Eliza said, "I must pack my things. Perhaps I'll see you in Amsterdam?"

"Nothing could give me greater pleasure."

France

EARLY 1685

> But know that in the Soule
> Are many lesser Faculties that serve
> Reason as chief; among these Fansie next
> Her office holds; of all external things,
> Which the five watchful Senses represent,
> She forms Imaginations, Aerie shapes,
> Which Reason joyning or disjoyning, frames
> All what we affirm or what deny, and call
> Our knowledge or opinion; then retires
> Into her private Cell when Nature rests.

Oft in her absence mimic Fansie wakes
To imitate her; but misjoyning shapes,
Wilde work produces oft, and most in dreams,
Ill matching words and deeds long past or late.
—MILTON, *Paradise Lost*

JACK RODE BETWEEN PARIS and Lyons several times in the early part
of 1685, ferrying news. Paris: the King of England is dead! Lyons:
some Spanish governorships in America are up for sale. Paris: King
Looie has secretly married Mademoiselle de Maintenon, and the
Jesuits have his ear now. Lyons: yellow fever is slaying mine-slaves
by the thousands in Brazil—the price of gold ought to rise.

It was disconcertingly like working for someone—just the sort
of arrangement he'd given up, long ago, as being beneath his dignity. It was, to put it more simply, too much like what Bob did. So
Jack had to keep reminding himself that he was not *actually* doing
it, but *pretending* to do it, so that he could get his horse ready to
sell—then he would tell these bankers to fuck themselves.

He was riding back toward Paris from Lyons one day—an
unseasonably cold day in March—when he encountered a column of three score men shuffling toward him. Their heads were
shaved and they were dressed in dirty rags—though most had
elected to tear up whatever clothes they had, and wrap them
around their bleeding feet. Their arms were bound behind their
backs and so it was easy to see their protruding ribs, mottled with
sores and whip-marks. They were accompanied by some half-
dozen mounted archers who could easily pick off stragglers or
runaways.

In other words, just another group of galley slaves on their way
down to Marseille. But these were more miserable than most. Your
typical galley slave was a deserter, smuggler, or criminal, hence
young and tough. A column of such men setting out from Paris in
the winter might expect to lose no more than half its number to
cold, disease, starvation, and beatings along the way. But this
group—like several others Jack had seen recently—seemed to consist entirely of old men who had no chance whatever of making it
to Marseille—or (for that matter) to whatever inn their guards
expected to sleep in tonight. They were painting the road with
blood as they trudged along, and they moved so slowly that the trip
would take them weeks. But this was a journey you wanted to finish
in as few days as possible.

Jack rode off to the side and waited for the column to pass him by. The stragglers were tailed by a horseman who, as Jack watched, patiently uncoiled his *nerf du boeuf,* whirled it round his head a time or two (to make a scary noise and build up speed), and then snapped it through the air to bite a chunk out of a slave's ear. Extremely pleased with his own prowess, he then said something not very pleasant about the R.P.R. Which made everything clear to Jack, for R.P.R. stood for *Religion Pretendue Réformée,* which was a contemptuous way of referring to Huguenots. Huguenots tended to be prosperous merchants and artisans, and so naturally if you gave them the galley slave treatment they would suffer much worse than a Vagabond.

Only a few hours later, watching another such column go by, he stared right into the face of Monsieur Arlanc—who stared right back at him. He had no hair, his cheeks were grizzly and sucked-in from hunger, but Monsieur Arlanc it was.

There was nothing for Jack to do at the time. Even if he'd been armed with a musket, one of the archers would've put an arrow through him before he could reload and fire a second ball. But that evening he circled back to an inn that lay several miles south of where he'd seen Monsieur Arlanc, and bided his time in the shadows and the indigo night for a few hours, freezing in clouds of vapor from the nostrils of his angry and uncomfortable horses, until he was certain that the guards would be in bed. Then he rode up to that inn and paid a guard to open the gate for him, and rode, with his little string of horses, into the stable-yard.

Several Huguenots were just standing there, stark naked, chained together in the open. Some jostled about in a feeble effort to stay warm, others looked dead. But Monsieur Arlanc was not in this group. A groom shot back a bolt on a stable door and allowed Jack to go inside, and (once Jack put more silver in his pocket) lent him a lantern. There Jack found the rest of the galley slaves. Weaker ones had burrowed into piles of straw, stronger ones had buried themselves in the great steaming piles of manure that filled the corners. Monsieur Arlanc was among these. He was actually snoring when the light from Jack's lantern splashed on his face.

Now the next morning, Monsieur Arlanc set out with his column of fellow-slaves, not very well-rested, but with a belly full of cheese and bread, and a pair of good boots on his feet. Jack meanwhile rode north with his feet housed in some wooden shoes he'd bought from a peasant.

He'd been ready and willing to gallop out of there with Arlanc on one of the spare horses, but the Huguenot had calmly and with the most admirable French logic explained why this would not work: "The other slaves will be punished if I am found missing in the morning. Most of them are my co-religionists and might accept this, but others are common criminals. In order to prevent it, these would raise the alarm."

"I could just kill 'em," Jack pointed out.

Monsieur Arlanc—a disembodied, candlelit head resting on a great misty dung-pile—got a pained look. "You would have to do so one at a time. The others would raise the alarm. It is most gallant of you to make such an offer, considering that we hardly know each other. Is this the effect of the English Pox?"

"Must be," Jack allowed.

"Most unfortunate," Arlanc said.

Jack was irritated to be pitied by a galley slave. "Your sons—?"

"Thank you for asking. When *le Roi* began to oppress us—"

"Who the hell is Leroy?"

"The King, the King!"

"Oh, yeah. Sorry."

"I smuggled them to England. And what of your boys, Jack?"

"Still waiting for their legacy," Jack said.

"Did you manage to sell your ostrich plumes?"

"I've got some Armenians on it."

"I gather you have not parted with the horse yet—"

"Getting him in shape."

"To impress the brokers?"

"Brokers! What do I want with a broker? It's to impress the *customers.*"

Arlanc's head moved in the lantern-light as if he were burrowing into the manure—Jack realized he was shaking his head in that annoying way that he did when Jack had blurted out something foolish. "It is not possible," Arlanc said. "The horse trade in Paris is absolutely controlled by the brokers—a Vagabond can no more ride in and sell a horse at the Place Royale than he could go to Versailles and get command of a regiment—it is simply *not done.*"

If Jack had just arrived in France recently he'd have said, *But that's crazy—why not?* but as it was he knew Arlanc spoke the truth. Arlanc recommended such-and-such a broker, to be found at the House of the Red Cat in the Rue du Temple, but then recollected that this fellow was himself a Huguenot, hence probably dead and certainly out of business.

They ended up talking through the night, Jack feeding him bits of bread and cheese from time to time, and tossing a few morsels to the others to shut them up. By the time dawn broke, Jack had given up his boots as well as his food, which was stupid in a way. But he was riding, and Monsieur Arlanc was walking.

He rode north cold, hungry, exhausted, and essentially barefoot. The horses had not been rested or tended to properly and were in a foul mood, which they found various ways to inflict on Jack. He groggily took a wrong turn and ended up approaching Paris by an unfamiliar route. This got him into some scrapes that did nothing to improve his state of mind. One of these misadventures led to Jack's staying awake through *another* night, hiding from some nobleman's gamekeepers in a wood. The rented horses kept whinnying and so he had no choice but to leave them staked out as decoys, to draw his pursuers while he slipped away with stalwart Turk.

So by the time the sun rose on the next day he was just one step away from being a miserable Vagabond again. He had lost two good horses for which he was responsible, and so all the livery stables and horse-brokers in Paris would be up in arms against him, which meant that selling Turk would be even more thoroughly impossible. So Jack would not get his money, and Turk would not get the life he deserved: eating good fodder and being fastidiously groomed in a spacious nobleman's stable, his only responsibility being to roger an endless procession of magnificent mares. Jack would not get his money, which meant he'd probably never even see his boys, as he couldn't bring himself to show up on their Aunt Maeve's doorstep empty-handed . . . all of Mary Dolores's brothers and cousins erupting to their feet to pursue him through East London with their shillelaghs . . .

It would've made him mad even if he hadn't been afflicted with degeneration of the brain, and awake for the third consecutive day. Madness, he decided, was easier.

As he approached Paris, riding through those vegetable-fields where steam rose from the still-hot shit of the city, he came upon a vast mud-yard, within sight of the city walls, streaked with white quick-lime and speckled with human skulls and bones sitting right out on the surface. Rude crosses had been stuffed into the muck here and there, and jutted out at diverse angles, spattered with the shit of the crows and vultures that waited on them. When Jack rode through it, those birds had, however, all flown up the road to greet a procession that had just emerged from the city-gates: a priest in a long cloak, so ponderous with mud that it hung from his shoulders like chain-mail, using a great crucifix as walking-stick, and occasionally hauling off a dolorous clang on a pot-like bell in the opposite hand. Behind him, a small crowd of paupers employing busted shovels in the same manner as the priest did the crucifix, and then a cart, driven by a couple of starveling mules, laden with a number of long bundles wrapped and sewn up in old grain-sacks.

Jack watched them tilt the wagon back at the blurred brink of an open pit so that the bundles—looked like three adults, half a dozen children, and a couple of babies—slid and tumbled into the ground. While the priest rattled on in rote Latin, his helpers zigzagged showers of quick-lime over the bodies and kicked dirt back into the hole.

Jack began to hear muffled voices: coming from under the ground, naturally. The skulls all around him began to jaw themselves loose from the muck and to rise up, tottering, on incomplete skeletons, droning a monkish sort of chant. But meanwhile those grave-diggers, now pivoting on their shovels, had begun to hum a tune of their own: a jaunty, Irish-inflected hornpipe.

Cantering briskly out onto the road (Turk now positively sashaying), he found himself at the head of a merry procession: he'd become the point man of a flying wedge of Vagabond gravediggers, whose random shufflings had resolved into dazzling group choreography, and who were performing a sort of close-order drill with their shovels.

Behind them went the priest, walloping his bell and walking ahead of the corpse-wain, where the dead people—who had hopped up out of the pit and back into the wagon—but who were still wrapped up in their shrouds—made throaty moaning noises, like organ-pipes to complement the grim churchly droning of the skeletons. Once all were properly arranged on the road, the skeletons finally broke into a thudding, four-square type of church-hymn:

> *O wha-at the Hell was on God's mind,*
> *That sixteen-sixty day,*
> *When he daubed a Vag-a-bond's crude form*
> *From a lump of Thames-side clay?*

> *Since God would ne'er set out to make*
> *A loser of this kind*
> *Jack's life, if planned in Heaven, doth prove*
> *Jehovah's lost His mind.*

Switching to Gregorian chant for the chorus:

> *Quod, erat demonstrandum. Quod, erat demonstrandum . . .*

But at this point, as they were all nearing the city gates, they encountered a southbound column of *galériens,* obviously Huguenots, who were shuffling along in a syncopated gait that made their chains jingle like sleigh-bells; the guards riding behind them cracked their whips in time with a sprightly tune that the Huguenots were singing:

Chained by the necks,
Slaves of Louis the Rex,
You might think that we've lost our freedom,
But the Cosmos,
Like clock-work,
No more than a rock's worth
Of choices, to people, provides!

But now at this point the grave-diggers were greeted by an equal number of fishwives, issuing from the city-gates, who paired up with them, kicked in with trilling soprano and lusty alto voices, and drowned out both the Huguenots and the Skeletons with some sort of merry Celtic reel:

There once was a jolly Vagabond
To the Indies he did sail,
When back to London he did come
He wanted a fe-male.

He found a few in Drury-Lane
In Hounsditch found some more
But cash flow troubles made him long
For a girlfriend, not a whore.

Now Jack he loved the theatre
But didn't like to pay
He met an Irish actress there
While sneaking in one day.

Now the Priest, far from objecting to this interruption, worked it into his solemn hymnody, albeit with a jarring change of rhythm:

He could have gone to make his peace
With Jesus and the Church

Instead he screwed a showgirl
Then he left her in the lurch.

Now God in Heaven ne'er could wish
That Irish lass so ill
Jack's life's proves irrefutably
Th'existence of Free Will

Quod, erat demonstrandum. Quod, erat demonstrandum . . .

And the irrepressible *galériens* seemed to pop their heads into the middle of this scene and take it over with the continuation of their song:

Will he, or nill he,
It's all kinda silly
When predestination prevails!

He can't make decisions
His will just ain't his, and
His destiny runs on fix'd rails!

Now the Priest again:

The Pope would say, that he who blames
The Good Lord for his deeds
Is either cursed with shit for brains
Or is lost 'mong Satan's Weeds.

The former group should take good care
To do as they are told
The latter'd best clean up their act
And come back to the fold.

Quod, erat demonstrandum. Quod, erat demonstrandum . . .

And then the *galériens*, obviously wanting to stay and continue the debate, but driven southward, ever southward, by the guards:

We're off to row boats
Off the Rhone's sunny côtes
Because God, long ago, said we must

If it makes you feel better
You too, Jack, are fettered
By your bodily humours and lusts.

They were now pulled "offstage," as it were, in the following comical way: a guard rode to the front of the column, hitched the end of their chain to the pommel of his saddle, and spurred his horse forward. The tightening chain ran free through the neck-loops of the *galériens* until it jerked the last man in the queue violently forward so that he crashed into the back of the slave in front of him, who likewise was driven forward into the next, *et cetera* in a *chain reaction* as it were, until the whole column had accordioned together and was dragged off toward the Mediterranean Sea.

Now at the same time the rest of the procession burst through the city-gates into lovely Paris. The skeletons, who'd been exceptionally gloomy until this point, suddenly began disassembling themselves and bonking themselves and their neighbors with thigh-bones to produce melodious xylophony. The priest jumped up on the corpse-wain and began to belt out a new melody in a comely, glass-shattering counter-tenor.

Oh, Jaaaack—
Can't say I blame you for feeling like shit
Oh, Jaaaack—
Never seen any one step into it
Like Jaaack—
Corporal punishment wouldn't suffice
The raaack—
Would be too good for you,
Would simply be
Too slaaack—
Even if all of the skin were whipped off of
Your baaack—
Not only evil,
But stupid to boot,
Not charismatic
And not even cute,
The brains that God granted
You now indisput-
ably gone down the tubes
And you don't give a hoot,

You stink!
No getting round it,
It's true, Jack, confound it,
You stink!

And so on; but then here there was a little pause in the music, occasioned by a small and perfectly adorable French girl in a white dress, which Jack recognized as the sort of get-up that young Papists wore to their first communion. Radiant—but gloomy. The priest reined in the mules and vaulted down off the corpse-wain and squatted down next to her.

"Bless me, Father, for I have sinned!" said the little girl.

Awww, gushed all of the skeletons, corpses, grave-diggers, fish-wives, *et cetera,* gathered round in vast circle as if to watch an Irish brawl.

"Believe me, girl, you ain't alone!" hollered a fishwife through cupped hands; the others grinned and nodded supportively.

The priest hitched up his muddy cassock and scooted even closer to the girl, then turned his ear toward her lips; she whispered something into it; he shook his head in sincere, but extremely short-lived dismay; then stood, drawing himself up to his full height, and said something back to her. She put her hands together, and closed her eyes. All of Paris went silent, and every ear strained to listen as she in her high piping voice said a little Papist prayer in Latin. Then she opened her baby blues and looked up in trepidation at the priest—whose stony face suddenly opened up in a big grin as he made the sign of the cross over her. With a great big squeal of delight, the girl jumped up and turned a cartwheel in the street, petticoats a-flying', and suddenly the whole procession came alive again: the priest walking along behind the handspringing girl and the dancers, the wrapped corpses up in the cart swinging their hips in time to the music and uttering pre-verbal *woo! woo!* noises to fill in the chinks in the tune. The grave-diggers and fishwives, plus a number of flower-girls and rat-catchers who joined in along the way, were now dancing to the priest's song in a medley of different dance steps, viz. high-stepping whorehouse moves, Irish stomping, and Mediterranean tarantellas.

When you have been bad
A naughty young lad
Or lass who has had
A man or two sans—marriage,

> *When painting the town*
> *Carousing around*
> *You run a child down*
> *While driving your big—carriage,*

And so on at considerable length, as they had the whole University to parade through, and then the Roman baths at Cluny. As they came over the Petit Pont, about a thousand wretches emerged from the gates of the Hôtel-Dieu—that colossal poorhouse just by Notre Dame, which was where the priest, grave-diggers, and dead persons had all originated—and, accompanied by Notre Dame's organ, boomed out a mighty chorus to ring down the curtain on this entire pageant.

> *Everyone does it—everyone sins*
> *Everyone at the party has egg on their chins*
> *Everyone likes to get, time to time, skin to skin*
> *With a lad or a lass, drink a tumbler of gin.*

> *So confess all your sins and admit you were bad,*
> *It isn't a fashion, nor is it a fad,*
> *It's what the Pope says we should do when we've had*
> *Just a bit too much fun, and we need to be pad-*
> *dled or spanked on the buttocks (unless we enjoy it)*
> *If there's sin in our hearts then it's time to destroy it,*
> *From the poorest of poor all the way to Le Roi, lit-*
> *tle sins or mass murder, if you made the wrong choice it*

> *Is fine if you say so, and change your bad ways*
> *You can do it in private, only God sees your face*
> *In a church or cathedral, your time and your place*
> *What's the payoff? UNDESERVED GRACE!*

This song developed into a sort of round, meant (Jack supposed) to emphasize the cyclical nature of the procedure: some of the wretches, fishwives, *et cetera*, engaging in carnal acts right there in the middle of the street, others rushing, in organized infantry-squares, toward the priest to confess, then turning away to genuflect in the direction of the Cathedral, then charging pall-mall back into fornication. In any case, every skeleton, corpse, wretch, grave-digger, fishwife, street-vendor, and priest now had a specific role to play, and part to sing, except for Jack; and so, one by one, all of Jack's harbingers and outriders peeled away from him, or evaporated into thin air, so that he rode alone (albeit, watched and cheered on by the thousands) into the great Place before the Cathedral of Notre Dame, which was as fine and gorgeous a vision as had ever been seen. For all of King Looie's Regiments were having their colors blessed by some sort of extremely resplendent mitre-wearing Papist authority figure, one or two notches shy of the Pope himself, who stood beneath a canopy of brilliant fleur-de-lis-embroidered cloth that burnt in the sun. The regiments *themselves* were not present—there wouldn't've been room—but their noble commanders were, and their heralds and color-bearers, carrying giant banners of silk and satin and cloth-of-gold: banners meant to be seen from a mile away through squalls of gunpowder-smoke, designed to look resplendent when planted atop the walls of Dutch or German or English cities and to overawe the populace with the glory, might, and, above all, good taste of Leroy. Each one had its own kind of magickal power over the troops of its regiment, and so to see them drawn up here in rows, all together, was like seeing all Twelve of the Apostles sitting round the same table, or something.

As much as Jack hated Leroy, he had to admit it was a hell of a thing to look at—so much so, that he regretted he hadn't arrived sooner, for he only caught the terminal quarter-hour of the ceremony. Then it all broke up. The color-bearers rode off toward their regimental headquarters in the territory outside of the city walls, and the nobility generally rode north over the Pont d'Arcole to the Right Bank where some went down in the direction of the Louvre and others went round back of the Hôtel de Ville toward the Place Royale and the Marais. One of the latter group was wearing an Admiral's hat and riding a white horse with pink eyes—a big one—apparently meant to be some sort of a war-horse.

Jack was not set on what he should do next, but as he (for lack of any other purpose in life) followed this admiral into the narrow streets he began to hear fidgety noises from the walls all around him, like the gnawing of mice, and noticed a lot of radiant dust in the air: on a closer look, he formed the impression that all of the tiny animals trapped in the stones of the city were coming alive and squirming about in their prisons, kicking up dust, as if some invisible tide of quicksilver had seeped up through the walls and brought them back to life; and construing this as an omen, Jack spurred Turk forward with the heels of his wooden *sabots* and, by taking certain back-streets, ducking beneath those jutting balconies, overtook the Admiral on the pink-eyed horse, and rode out into the street in front of him, just short of the entrance to the

Place Royale—in the very street where he'd once been knocked into the shit by (he guessed) the same fellow's servants.

Those servants were now clearing the way for the Admiral and the large contingent of friends and hangers-on riding with him, and so when Jack rode out into the middle of the street, it was empty. A footman in blue livery came toward him, eyeing Jack's wooden shoes and his crutch, and probably sizing him up as a peasant who'd stolen a plowhorse—but Jack gave Turk a little twitch of the reins that meant *I give you leave* and Turk surged toward this man and crushed him straight into the gutter where he ended up stopping turd-rafts. Then Jack drew up to face the Admiral from perhaps half a dozen lengths. Several other footmen were situated in the space between them, but having seen what Turk knew how to do, they were now shrinking back against walls.

The Admiral looked nonplussed. He couldn't stop looking at Jack's shoes. Jack kicked off the *sabots* and they tumbled on the stones with pocking footstep-noises. He wanted to make some kind of insightful point, here, about how the shoe thing was just another example of Frogs' obsession with form over substance—a point worth making here and now, because it related to their (presumed) inability to appreciate what a fine mount Turk was. But in his present state of mind, he couldn't even get that out in *English*.

Someone, anyway, had decided that he was dangerous—a younger man costumed as a Captain of Horse, who now rode out in front of the Admiral and drew his sword, and waited for Jack to do something.

"What'd you pay for that nag?" Jack snarled, and, since he didn't have time to disassemble his crutch, raised it up like a knight's lance, bracing the padded cross-piece against his ribs, and spurred Turk forward with his heels. The cold air felt good rushing over his bare feet. The Captain got a look of dignified befuddlement on his face that Jack would always remember, and the others, behind him, got out of the way in a sudden awkward clocking and scraping of hooves—and then at the last moment this Captain realized he was in an impossible situation, and tried to lean out of the way. The crutch-tip caught him in the upper arm and probably gave him a serious bruise. Jack rode through the middle of the Admiral's entourage and then got Turk turned around to face them again, which took longer than he was comfortable with—but all of those Admirals and Colonels and Captains had to get turned around, *too*, and their horses were not as good as Jack's.

One in particular, a pretty black charger with a bewigged and beribboned aristocrat on top of it, was declining to follow orders, and stood broadside to Jack, a couple of lengths away. "And what do I hear for this magnificent Turkish charger?" Jack demanded, spurring Turk forward again, so that after building up some speed he T-boned the black horse just in the ribcage and actually knocked it over sideways—the horse went down in a fusillade of hooves, and the rider, who hadn't seen it coming, flew halfway to the next *arrondissement*.

"I'll buy it right *now*, Jack," said an English voice, somehow familiar, "if you stop being such a fucking *tosser*, that is."

Jack looked up into a face. His first thought was that this was the handsomest face he had ever seen; his second, that it belonged to John Churchill. Seated astride a decent enough horse of his own, right alongside of Jack.

Someone was maneuvering towards them, shouting in French— Jack was too flabbergasted to consider *why* until Churchill, without taking his eyes off Jack's, whipped out his rapier, and spun it (seemingly over his knuckles) so as to deflect a sword-thrust that had been aimed directly at Jack's heart. Instead it penetrated several inches into Jack's thigh. This hurt, and had the effect of waking Jack up and forcing him to understand that all of this was *really happening*.

"Bob sends greetings from sunny Dunkirk," said Churchill. "If you shut up, there is an infinitesimal chance of my being able to save you from being tortured to death before sundown."

Jack said nothing.

Amsterdam
APRIL 1685

The Art of War is so well study'd, and so equally known in all Places, that 'tis the longest Purse that conquers now, not the longest Sword. If there is any Country whose people are less martial, less enterpris- ing, and less able for the Field; yet if they have but

> more Money than their Neighbors, they shall soon be
> superior to them in Strength, for Money is Power . . .
> —DANIEL DEFOE, *A Plan of the English Commerce*

"IT WAS PHANTASTICKAL in the extreme—Mademoiselle, it was *beyond French*—"

Like a still pond into which a boy has flung a handful of gravel, the Duke of Monmouth's beauty—aglow in the golden light of an Amsterdam afternoon—was now marred by a thought. The eyebrows steepled, the lips puckered, and the eyes might've crossed slightly—it was very difficult to tell, given his and Eliza's current positions: straight out of a Hindoo frieze.

"What is it?"

"Did we actually achieve sexual, er, *congress,* at any point during those, er, proceedings?"

"Poh! What're you, then, some Papist who must draw up a schedule of his sins?"

"You know that I am not, mademoiselle, but—"

"You're the sort who keeps a tally, aren't you? Like a tavern-goer who prides himself on the Ps and Qs chalked up on the wall next his name—save in your case it's wenches."

Monmouth tried to look indignant. But at the moment his body contained, of the yellow bile, less than at any time since infancy, and so even his indignation was flaccid. "I don't think there's anything untoward in wanting to know whom I have, and haven't, rogered! My father—God rest his soul—rogered simply *everyone.* I'm merely the first and foremost of a *legion* of royal bastards! Wouldn't be proper to lose track."

". . . of *your* royal bastards?"

"Yes."

"Then know that no royal bastards can possibly result from what we just did."

Monmouth got himself worked round to a less outlandish position, viz. sitting up and gazing soulfully into Eliza's nipples. "I say, would you like to be a Duchess or something?"

Eliza arched her back and laughed. Monmouth shifted his attention to her oscillating navel, and looked wounded.

"What would I have to do? Marry some syphilitic Duke?"

"Of course not. Be my mistress—when I am King of England. My father made *all* his mistresses into Duchesses."

"Why?"

Monmouth, scandalized: "Elsewise, 'tweren't proper!"

"You already have a mistress."

"It's *common* to have one . . ."

"And *noble* to have *several*?"

"What's the point of being a king if you can't fuck a lot of Duchesses?"

"Just so, sir!"

"Though I don't know if 'fuck' is *le mot juste* for what *we* did."

"What *I* did. You just fidgeted and shuddered."

"Well it's like some modish dance, isn't it, where only one knows the steps. You just have to teach me the other part of it."

"I am honored, Your Grace—does that mean we'll be seeing each other again?"

Monmouth, miffed and slightly buffaloed: "I was *sincere* about making you a Duchess."

"First you have to make yourself a King."

The Duke of Monmouth sighed and slammed back into the mattress, driving out an evoluting cloud of dust, straw-ends, bed-bugs, and mite fœces. All of it hung beautifully in the lambent air, as if daubed on canvas by one of those Brueghels.

"I know it is ever so tiresome," Eliza said, stroking the Duke's hair back from his brow and tucking it neatly behind his ear. "*Later* you'll be slogging round dreadful battlefields. *Tonight* we go to the Opera!"

Monmouth made a vile face. "Give me a battlefield any time."

"William's going to be there."

"Eeeyuh, he's not going to do any tedious *acting*, is he?"

"What, the Prince of Orange—?"

"After the Peace of Breda he put on a ballet, and appeared as Mercury, bringing news of Anglo-Dutch *rapprochement. Embarrassing* to see a rather good warrior prancing about with a couple of bloody goose-wings lashed to his ankles."

"That was a long time ago—he is a grown man, and it is beneath his dignity now. He'll just peer down from his box. Pretend to whisper *bons mots* to Mary, who'll pretend to get them."

"If *he* is coming, we can go late," Monmouth said. "They'll have to search the place for bombs."

"Then we must go early," Eliza countered, "as there'll be that much more time for plots and intrigues."

LIKE ONE WHO HAS ONLY read books and heard tales of a foreign land, and finally goes there and sees the real thing—thus Eliza at the Opera. Not so much for the *place* (which was only a building) as for the *people,* and not so much for the ones with titles and formal ranks (viz. the Raadspensionary, and diverse Regents and Magistrates with their fat jewelled wives) as for the ones who had the power to move the market.

Eliza, like most of that caterwauling, hand-slapping crowd who migrated between the Dam and the Exchange, did not have enough money to trade in actual V.O.C. shares. When she was flush, she bought and sold *ducat* shares, and when she wasn't, she bought and sold options and contracts to buy or sell them. Strictly speaking, ducat shares didn't even exist. They were splinters, fragments, of actual V.O.C. shares. They were a fiction that had been invented so that people who weren't enormously wealthy could participate in the market.

Yet even above the level of those who traded full V.O.C. shares were the princes of the market, who had accumulated large numbers of those shares, and borrowed money against them, which they lent out to diverse ventures: mines, sailing-voyages, slave-forts on the Guinea coast, colonies, wars, and (if conditions were right) the occasional violent overthrow of a king. Such a man could move the market simply by showing his face at the Exchange, and trigger a crash, or a boom, simply by strolling across it with a particular expression on his face, leaving a trail of buying and selling in his wake, like a spreading cloud of smoke from a bishop's censer.

All of those men seemed to be here at the Opera with their wives or mistresses. The crowd was something like the innards of a harpsichord, each person tensed to thrum or keen when plucked. Mostly it was a cacophony, as if cats were lovemaking on the keyboard. But the arrival of certain Personages was a palpable striking of certain chords.

"The French have a word for this: they name it a *frisson*," muttered the Duke of Monmouth behind a kid-gloved hand as they made their way toward their box.

"Like Orpheus, I struggle with a desire to turn around and look behind me—"

"Stay, your turban would fall off."

Eliza reached up to pat the cyclone of cerulean Turkish silk. It was anchored to her hair by diverse heathen brooches, clips, and pins. "Impossible."

"Anyway, why would you want to look behind you?"

"To see what has caused this *frisson*."

"It is *we*, you silly." And for once, the Duke of Monmouth had said something that was demonstrably true. Countless sets of jewelled and gilded opera-glasses had been trained on them, making the owners look like so many goggle-eyed amphibians crowded together on a bank.

"Never before has the Duke's woman been more gloriously attired than *he*," Eliza ventured.

"And never *again*," Monmouth snarled. "I only hope that *your* magnificence does not distract them from what we *want* them to see."

They stood at the railing of their box as they talked, presenting themselves for inspection. For the proscenium where the actors cavorted was only the most obvious of the Opera House's stages, and the story that they acted out was only one of several dramas all going on at once. For example, the Stadholder's box, only a few yards away, was being ransacked by Blue Guards looking for French bombs. *That* had grown tedious, and so now the Duke of Monmouth and his latest mistress had the attention of most everyone. The gaze of so many major V.O.C. shareholders, through so many custom-ground lenses, made Eliza feel like an insect 'neath a Natural Philosopher's burning-glass. She was glad that this Turkish courtesan's get-up included a veil, which hid everything but her eyes.

Even through the veil's narrow aperture, some of the observers might've detected a few moments' panic, or at least anxiety, in Eliza's eyes, as the *frisson* drew out into a general murmur of confusion: opera-goers all nudging one another down below, pointing upwards with flicks of the eyeballs or discreet waftings of gloved and ringed fingers, getting their wigs entangled as they whispered speculations to each other.

It took a few moments for the crowd to even figure out who Eliza's escort *was*. Monmouth's attire was numblingly practical, as if he were going to jump on a war-horse immediately following the Opera and gallop through fen, forest, and brush until he encountered some foe who wanted slaying. Even his sword was a cavalry saber—not a rapier. To that point, at least, the message was clear enough. The question was, in what *direction* would Monmouth ride, and what sorts of heads, specifically, did he intend to be lopping off with that saber?

"I knew it—to expose your navel was a mistake!" the Duke hissed.

"On the contrary—'tis the *keyhole* through which the entire riddle will be *unlocked*," Eliza returned, the t's and k's making her veil ripple gorgeously. But she was not as confident as she sounded, and so, at the risk of being obvious, she allowed her gaze to wander, in what she hoped would be an innocent-seeming way, around the crescent of opera-boxes until she found the one where the comte d'Avaux was seated along with (among other Amsterdammers who

had recently gone on shopping sprees in Paris) Mr. Sluys the traitorous lead-hoarder.

D'Avaux removed a pair of golden opera-glasses from his eyes
and stared Eliza in the face for a ten-count.

His eyes shifted to William's box, where the Blue Guards were
making an *endless* thrash.

He looked at Eliza again. Her veil hid her smile, but the invitation in her eyes was clear enough.

"It's . . . not . . . working," Monmouth grunted.

"It is working *flawlessly*," Eliza said. D'Avaux was on his feet,
excusing himself from the crowd in that box: Sluys, and an Amsterdam Regent, and some sort of young French nobleman, who must
have been of high rank, for d'Avaux gave him a deep bow.

A few moments later he was giving the same sort of bow to the
Duke of Monmouth, and kissing Eliza's hand.

"The *next* time you grace the Opera, mademoiselle, the Blue
Guards will have to search *your* box, too—for you may be sure that
every Lady in this building is shamed by your radiance. None of
them will ever forgive you." But as he was saying these words to
Eliza, his gaze was traveling curiously up and down Monmouth,
searching for clues.

The Duke was wearing several pins and badges that had to be
viewed from close range in order to be properly interpreted: one
bearing the simple red cross of a Crusader, and another with the
arms of the Holy League—the alliance of Poland, Austria, and
Venice that was nudging the wreckage of the Turkish Army back
across Hungary.

"Your Grace," d'Avaux said, "the way East is dangerous."

"The way West is barred forever, to me anyway," Monmouth
replied, "and my presence in Holland is giving rise to all manner of
ugly rumors."

"There is always a place for you in France."

"The only thing I've ever been any good for is fighting—" Monmouth began.

"Not the *only* thing . . . my lord," Eliza said lasciviously. D'Avaux
flinched and licked his lips. Monmouth flushed slightly and continued: "as my uncle* has brought peace to Christendom, I must
seek glory in *heathen* lands."

Something was happening in the corner of Eliza's eye: William

---

*King Louis XIV of France—not really Monmouth's uncle, but the brother of
the widower of the sister of his illegitimate father, as well as the son of the
brother of his grandmother, and many other connexions besides.

and Mary entering their box. Everyone rose and applauded. It was dry, sparse applause, and it didn't last. The comte d'Avaux stepped forward and kissed the Duke of Monmouth on both cheeks. Many of the opera-goers did not see the gesture, but some did. Enough, anyway, to strike a new chord in the audience: a baritone commotion that was soon covered up by the opening strains of the overture.

The ladies and gentlemen of Amsterdam were settling into their seats, but their servants and lackeys still stood in the shadows under the boxes and loges, and some of them were now moving as their masters beckoned to them: stepping forward and cocking their heads to hear whispered confidences, or holding out their hands to accept scribbled notes.

The market was moving. Eliza had moved it with her turban and her navel, and d'Avaux had moved it by showing slightly greater than normal affection for the Duke of Monmouth. Together, these clues could only mean that Monmouth had given up his claim to the English throne and was bound for Constantinople.

The market was moving, and Eliza desperately wanted to be out on the Dam, moving with it—but her place was here for now. She saw d'Avaux return to his box and sit down. Actors had begun to sing down on the stage, but d'Avaux's guests were leaning towards him to whisper and listen. The young French nobleman nodded his head, turned towards Monmouth, crossed himself, then opened his hand as if throwing a prayer to the Duke. Eliza half expected to see a dove fly out of his sleeve. Monmouth pretended to snatch it from the air, and kissed it.

But Mr. Sluys was not in a praying mood. He was thinking. Even in semi-darkness, through a miasma of candle and tobacco smoke, Eliza could read his face: *Monmouth slaying Turks in Hungary means he won't use Holland as a platform to invade England—so there won't be a catastrophe in Anglo-Dutch relations—so the English Navy won't be firing any broadsides at the Dutch merchant fleet—so V.O.C. stock will rise.* Sluys held his right hand up slightly and caressed the air with two fingers. A servant was suddenly draped over his epaulet, memorizing something, counting on his fingers. He nodded sharply, like a pecking gull, and was gone.

Eliza reached up behind her head, untied her veil, and let it fall down onto her bosom. Then she enjoyed the opera.

A hundred feet away, Abraham de la Vega was hiding in the wings with a spyglass, made of lenses ground, to tolerances of a few thousandths of an inch, by his late second cousin, Baruch de Spinoza. Through those lenses, he saw the veil descend. He was nine years old. He moved through the backstage and out of the opera-house like the moon-shadow of a nightingale. Aaron de la Vega, his uncle, was waiting there astride a swift horse.

"Has he offered to make you a Duchess yet?" d'Avaux asked during the intermission.

"He said that he *would have*—had he not renounced his claim to the throne," Eliza said.

D'Avaux was amused by her carefulness. "As your gallant is renewing his Platonic friendship with the Princess, may I escort you to Mr. Sluys's box? I cannot stand to see you neglected."

Eliza looked at the Stadholder's box. Mary was there but William had already sneaked out, leaving the field clear for Monmouth, whose brave resolve to go East and fight the Turk had Mary almost in tears.

"I never even *saw* the Prince," Eliza said, "just glimpsed him scurrying in at the last minute."

"Rest assured, mademoiselle, he is nothing to look at." And he offered Eliza his arm. "If it's *true* that your beau is leaving soon for the East, you'll need new young men to amuse you. Frankly, you are overdue for a change. *La France* did her best to civilize Monmouth, but the Anglo-Saxon taint had penetrated too deeply. He never developed the innate discretion of a Frenchman."

"I'm *mortified* to learn that Monmouth has been indiscreet," Eliza said gaily.

"All of Amsterdam, and approximately half of London and Paris, have learned of your charms. But, although the Duke's descriptions were unspeakably vulgar—when they were not completely incoherent—*cultivated* gentlemen can look beyond ribaldry, and infer that you possess qualities, mademoiselle, beyond the merely gynæcological."

"When you say 'cultivated' you mean 'French'?"

"I know you are teasing me, mademoiselle. You expect me to say 'Why yes, all French gentlemen are cultivated.' But it is not so."

"Monsieur d'Avaux, I'm shocked to hear you say such a thing."

They were almost at the door to Sluys's box. D'Avaux drew back. "Typically only the *worst* sort of French nobility would be in the box that you and I are about to enter, associating with the likes of Sluys—but tonight is an exception."

"Louis le Grand—as he's now dubbed himself—built himself a new château outside of Paris, at a place called Versailles," Aaron de la Vega had told her, during one of their meetings in Amsterdam's narrow and crowded Jewish quarter—which, by coincidence, happened to be built up against the Opera House. "He has moved his entire court to the new place."

"I'd heard as much, but I didn't believe it," Gomer Bolstrood had said, looking more at home among Jews than he ever had among Englishmen. "To move so many people out of Paris—it seems insane."

"On the contrary—it is a master-stroke," de la Vega had said. "You know the Greek myth of Antaeus? For the French nobility, Paris is like the Mother Earth—as long as they are ensconced there, they have power, information, money. But Louis, by forcing them to move to Versailles, is like Hercules, who mastered Antaeus by raising him off the ground and slowly strangling him into submission."

"A pretty similitude," Eliza had said, "but what does it have to do with our putting a short squeeze on Mr. Sluys?"

De la Vega had permitted himself a smile, and looked over at Bolstrood. But Gomer had not been in a grinning mood. "Sluys is one of those rich Dutchmen who craves the approval of Frenchmen. He has been cultivating them since before the 1672 war—mostly without success, for they find him stupid and vulgar. But now it's different. The French nobles used to be able to live off their land, but now Louis forces them to keep a household in Versailles, as well as one in Paris, and to go about in coaches, finely dressed and wigged—"

"The wretches are desperate for lucre," Gomer Bolstrood had said.

AT THE OPERA, before the door to Sluys's box, Eliza said, "You mean, monsieur, the sort of French nobleman who's not content with the old ways, and likes to play the markets in Amsterdam, so he can afford a coach and a mistress?"

"You will spoil me, mademoiselle," d'Avaux said, "for how can I return to the common sort of female—stupid and ignorant—after I have conversed with you? Yes, normally Sluys's box would be *stuffed* with *that* sort of French nobleman. But *tonight* he is entertaining a young man who came by his endowment *properly.*"

"Meaning—?"

"Inherited it—or is going to—from his father, the Duc d'Arcachon."

"Would it be vulgar for me to ask how the Duc d'Arcachon got it?"

"Colbert built our Navy from twenty vessels to three hundred. The Duc d'Arcachon is Admiral of that Navy—and was responsible for much of the building."

The floor around Mr. Sluys's chair was strewn with wadded scraps. Eliza would have loved to smooth some out and read them, but his hard jollity, and the way he was pouring champagne, told her that the evening's trading was going well for him, or so he imagined. "Jews don't go to the Opera—it is against their religion! What a show de la Vega has missed tonight!"

"'Thou shalt not attend the Opera . . . ' Is that in Exodus, or Deuteronomy?" Eliza inquired.

D'Avaux—who seemed uncharacteristically nervous, all of a sudden—took Eliza's remark as a witticism, and produced a smile as thin and dry as parchment. Mr. Sluys took it as stupidity, and got sexually aroused. "De la Vega is still selling V.O.C. stock short! He'll be doing it all night long—until he hears the news tomorrow morning, and gets word to his brokers to stop!" Sluys seemed almost outraged to be making money so easily.

Now Mr. Sluys looked as if he would've been content to drink champagne and gaze 'pon Eliza's navel until any number of fat ladies sang (which actually would not have been long in coming), but some sort of very rude commotion, originating from this very box, forced him to glance aside. Eliza turned to see that young French nobleman—the son of the Duc d'Arcachon—at the railing of the box, where he was being hugged, passionately and perhaps even a little violently, by a bald man with a bloody nose.

Eliza's dear Mum had always taught her that it wasn't polite to stare, but she couldn't help herself. Thus, she took in that the young Arcachon had actually flung one of his legs over the railing, as if he were trying to vault out into empty space. A large and rather good wig balanced precariously on the same rail. Eliza stepped forward and snatched it. It was unmistakably the periwig of Jean Antoine de Mesmes, comte d'Avaux, who must, therefore, be the bald fellow wrestling young Arcachon back from the brink of suicide.

D'Avaux—demonstrating a weird strength for such a refined man—finally slammed the other back into a chair, and had the good grace to so choreograph it that he ended up down on both knees. He pulled a lace hanky from a pocket and stuffed it up under his nose to stanch the blood, then spoke through it, heatedly but respectfully, to the young nobleman, who had covered his face with his hands. From time to time he darted a look at Eliza.

"Has the young Arcachon been selling V.O.C. stock short?" she inquired of Mr. Sluys.

"On the contrary, mademoiselle—"

"Oh, I forgot. He's not the sort who dabbles in markets. But why else would a French duke's son visit Amsterdam?"

Sluys got a look as if something were lodged in his throat.

"Never mind," Eliza said airily, "I'm sure it is *frightfully* complicated—and I'm no good at such things."

Sluys relaxed.

"I was only wondering why he tried to kill himself—assuming that's what he was doing?"

"Étienne d'Arcachon is the politest man in France," Sluys said ominously.

"Hmmph. You'd never know!"

"Sssh!" Sluys made frantic tiny motions with the flesh shovels of his hands.

"Mr. Sluys! Do you mean to imply that this spectacle has something to do with *my* presence in your box?"

Finally Sluys was on his feet. He was rather drunk and very heavy, and stood bent over with one hand gripping the box's railing. "It would help if you'd confide in me that, if Étienne d'Arcachon slays himself in your presence, you'll take offense."

"Mr. Sluys, watching him commit suicide would ruin my evening!"

"Very well. Thank you, mademoiselle. I am in your debt *enormously.*"

"Mr. Sluys—you have no idea."

IT LED TO HUSHED INTRIGUES in dim corners, palmed messages, raised eyebrows, and subtle gestures by candle-light, continuing all through the final acts of the opera—which was fortunate, because the opera was very dull.

Then, somehow, d'Avaux arranged to share a coach with Eliza and Monmouth. As they jounced, heaved, and clattered down various dark canal-edges and over diverse draw-bridges, he explained: "It was Sluys's box. Therefore, he was the host. Therefore, it was his responsibility to make a formal introduction of Étienne d'Arcachon to you, mademoiselle. But he was too Dutch, drunk, and distracted to perform his proper rôle. I never cleared my throat so many times—but to no avail. Monsieur d'Arcachon was placed in an *impossible* situation!"

"So he tried to take his own life?"

"It was the only honourable course," d'Avaux said simply.

"He is the politest man in France," Monmouth added.

"You saved the day," d'Avaux said.

"Oh, that—'twas Mr. Sluys's suggestion."

D'Avaux looked vaguely nauseated at the mere mention of Sluys. "He has much to answer for. This *soirée* had better be *charmante.*"

AARON DE LA VEGA, who was assuredly *not* going to a party tonight, treated balance-sheets and V.O.C. shares as a scholar would old books and parchments—which is to say that Eliza found him sober and serious to a fault. But he could be merry about a few things, and one of them was Mr. Sluys's house—or rather his widening collection of them. For as the first one had pulled its neighbors downwards, skewing them into parallelograms, popping window-panes out of their frames, and imprisoning doors in their jambs, Mr. Sluys had been forced to buy them out. He owned five houses in a row now, and could afford to, as long as he was managing the assets of half the population of Versailles. The one in the middle, where Mr. Sluys kept his secret hoard of lead and guilt, was at least a foot lower than it had been in 1672, and Aaron de la Vega liked to pun about it in his native language, saying it was "*embarazada*," which meant "pregnant."

As the Duke of Monmouth handed Eliza down from the carriage in front of that house, she thought it was apt. For—especially when Mr. Sluys was burning thousands of candles at once, as he was tonight, and the light was blazing from all those conspicuously skewed window-frames—hiding the secret was like a woman seven months pregnant trying to conceal her condition with clever tailoring.

Men and women in Parisian fashions were entering the pregnant house in what almost amounted to a continuous queue. Mr. Sluys—belatedly warming to his rôle as host—was stationed just inside the door, mopping sweat from his brow every few seconds, as if secretly terrified that the added weight of so many guests would finally drive his house straight down into the mud, like a stake struck with a maul.

But when Eliza got into the place, and suffered Mr. Sluys to kiss her hand, and made a turn round the floor, gaily ignoring the venomous stares of pudgy Dutch churchwives and overdressed Frenchwomen—she could see clear signs that Mr. Sluys had brought in mining-engineers, or something, to shore the house up. For the beams that crisscrossed the ceiling, though hidden under festoons and garlands of Barock plasterwork, were uncommonly huge, and the pillars that rose up to support the ends of those beams, though fluted and capitalled like those of a Roman temple, were the size of mainmasts. Still she thought she could detect a pregnant convexity about the ceiling . . .

"Don't come out and say you want to buy lead—tell him only that you want to lighten his burdens—better yet, that you wish to transfer them, forcefully, onto the shoulders of the Turks. Or something along those lines," she said, distractedly, into Monmouth's ear as the first galliard was drawing to a close. He stalked away in a bit of a huff—but he was moving towards Sluys, anyway. Eliza regretted—briefly—that she'd insulted his intelligence, or at least his breeding. But she was too beset by sudden worries to consider his feelings. The house, for all its plaster and candles, reminded her of nothing so much as the Doctor's mine, deep beneath the Harz: a hole in the earth, full of metal, prevented from collapsing in on itself solely by cleverness and continual shoring-up.

Weight could be transferred from lead to floor-boards, and thence into joists, and thence into beams, and from beams into pillars, then down into footings, and thence into log piles whose strength derived from the "stick" (as Dutchmen called it) between them and the mud they'd been hammered into. The final settling of accounts was there: if the "stick" sufficed, the structure above it was a building, and if it didn't, it was a gradual avalanche . . .

"It is very curious, mademoiselle, that the chilly winds of the Hague were balmy breezes to you—yet in this warm room, you alone clutch your arms, and have goosebumps."

"Chilly thoughts, Monsieur d'Avaux."

"And no wonder—your beau is about to leave for Hungary. You need to make some new friends—ones who live in warmer climes, perhaps?"

No. Madness. I belong here. Even Jack, who loves me, said so.

From a corner of the room, clouded with men and pipe-smoke, a trumpeting laugh from Mr. Sluys. Eliza glanced over that way and saw Monmouth plying him—probably reciting the very sentences she'd composed for him. Sluys was giddy with hope that he could get rid of his burden, frantic with anxiety that it might not happen. Meanwhile the market was in violent motion all over Amsterdam as Aaron de la Vega sold the V.O.C. short. It would all lead to an invasion of England. Everything had gone fluid tonight. This was no time to stand still.

A man danced by with an ostrich-plume in his hat, and she thought of Jack. Riding across Germany with him, she'd had nought but her plumes, and his sword, and their wits—yet she'd felt safer then than she did now. What would it take to feel safe again?

"Friends in warm places are lovely to have," Eliza said distractedly, "but there is no one here who would have me, monsieur. You know very well that I am not of noble, or even gentle, birth—I'm too exotic for the Dutch, too common for the French."

"The King's mistress was born a *slave*," d'Avaux said. "Now she is a Marquise. You see, nothing matters *there* save wit and beauty."

"But wit fails and beauty fades, and I don't wish to be a house on piles, sinking into the bog a little each day," Eliza said. "Somewhere I must *stick*. I must have a foundation that does not always move."

"Where on this earth can such a miracle be found?"

"Money," Eliza said. "Here, I can make money."

"And yet this money you speak of is but a chimæra—a figment of the collective imagination of a few thousand Jews and rabble bellowing at one another out on the Dam."

"But in the end I may convert it—bit by bit—into gold."

"Is *that* all you want? Remember, mademoiselle, that gold only has value because some people say it does. Let me tell you a bit of recent history: My King went to a place called Orange—you've heard of it?"

"A principality in the south of France, near Avignon—William's fiefdom, as I understand it."

"My King went to this Orange, this little family heirloom of Prince William, three years ago. Despite William's pretensions of martial glory, my King was able to walk in without a battle. He went for a stroll atop the fortifications. *Le Roi* paused, there along a stone battlement, and plucked out a tiny fragment of loose masonry—no larger than your little finger, mademoiselle—and tossed it onto the ground. Then he walked away. Within a few days, all the walls and fortifications of Orange had been pulled down by *le Roi*'s regiments, and Orange had been absorbed into France, as easily as Mr. Sluys over there might swallow a bit of ripe fruit."

"What is the point of the story, Monsieur, other than to explain why Amsterdam is crowded with Orangish refugees, and why William hates your King so much?"

"Tomorrow, *le Roi* might pick up a bit of Gouda cheese and throw it to his dogs."

"Amsterdam would fall, you are saying, and my hard-earned gold would be loot for some drunken regiment."

"Your gold—and you, mademoiselle."

"I understand such matters far better than you imagine, monsieur. What I do *not* understand is why you pretend to be interested in what happens to me. In the Hague, you saw me as a pretty girl who could skate, and who would therefore catch Monmouth's eye, and make Mary unhappy, and create strife in William's house. And it all came to pass just as you intended. But what can I do for you *now*?"

"Live a beautiful and interesting life—and, from time to time, talk to me."

Eliza laughed out loud, lustily, drawing glares from women who never laughed that way, or at all. "You want me to be your spy."

"No, mademoiselle. I want you to be my friend." D'Avaux said this simply and almost sadly, and it caught Eliza up short. In that moment, d'Avaux spun smartly on the balls of his feet and trapped Eliza's arm. She had little choice but to walk with him—and soon it became obvious that they were walking directly towards Étienne d'Arcachon. In the dimmest and smokiest corner of the room, meanwhile, Mr. Sluys kept laughing and laughing.

Paris
SPRING 1685

Thou hast met with something (as I perceive)
already; for I see the dirt of the Slough of Despond
is upon thee; but that Slough is the beginning of
the sorrows that do attend those that go on in that
way; hear me, I am older than thou!
—JOHN BUNYAN, *The Pilgrim's Progress*

JACK WAS BURIED up to his neck in the steaming manure of the white, pink-eyed horses of the duc d'Arcachon, trying not to squirm as a contingent of perhaps half a dozen maggots cleaned away the dead skin and flesh surrounding the wound in his thigh. This itched, but did not hurt, beyond the normal wholesome throbbing. Jack had no idea how many days he'd been in here, but from listening to the bells of Paris, and watching small disks of sunlight prowl around the stable, he guessed it might be five in the afternoon. He heard boots approaching, and a padlock negotiating with its key. If that lock were the only thing holding him in this stable, he would've escaped long ago; but as it was, Jack was chained by the neck to a pillar of white stone, with a few yards of slack so that he could, for example, bury himself in manure.

The bolt shot and John Churchill stepped in on a tongue of

light. In contrast to Jack, he was *not* covered in shit—far from it! He was wearing a jeweled turban of shimmering gold cloth, and robes, with lots of costume jewelry; old scuffed boots, and a large number of weapons, viz. scimitar, pistols, and several granadoes. His first words were: "Shut up, Jack, I'm going to a fancy-dress ball."

"Where's Turk?"

"I stabled him," Churchill said, pointing with his eyes toward an adjacent stable. The duc had several stables, of which this was the smallest and meanest, and used only for shoeing horses.

"So the ball you mean to attend is *here.*"

"At the Hotel d'Arcachon, yes."

"What're you supposed to be—a Turk? Or a Barbary Corsair?"

"Do I look like a Turk?" Churchill asked hopefully. "I understand you have personal knowledge of them—"

"No. Better say you're a Pirate."

"A breed of which *I* have personal knowledge."

"Well, if you hadn't fucked the King's mistress, he wouldn't have sent you to Africa."

"Well, I *did,* and *he* did—send me there, I mean—and I came back."

"And now he's dead. And you and the duc d'Arcachon have something to talk about."

"What is that supposed to mean?" Churchill asked darkly.

"Both of you have been in contact with the Barbary Pirates— that's all I meant."

Churchill was taken aback—a small pleasure and an insignificant victory for Jack. "You are well-informed," he said. "I should like to know whether *everyone in the world* knows of the duc d'Arcachon's intercourse with Barbary, or is it just that you are special?"

"Am I, then?"

"They say *l'Emmerdeur* is King of the Vagabonds."

"Then why didn't the duc put me up in his finest apartment?"

"Because I have gone to such extravagant lengths to prevent him from knowing who you are."

"So *that's* why I'm still alive. I was wondering."

"If they knew, they would tear you apart with iron tongs, over the course of several days, at the Place Dauphine."

"No better place for it—lovely view from there."

"Is that all you have for me, in the way of thanks?"

Silence. Gates were creaking open all round the Hotel d'Arcachon as it mobilized for the ball. Jack heard the hollow grumbling of barrels being rolled across stone courtyards, and (since his nose had stopped being able to smell shit) he could smell birds roasting, and buttery pastries baking in ovens. There were less agreeable odors, too, but Jack's nose sought out the good ones.

"You could at least answer my question," Churchill said. "Does everyone know that the duc has frequent dealings with Barbary?"

"Some small favor would be appropriate at this point," Jack said.

"I can't let you go."

"I was thinking of a pipe."

"Funny, so was I." Churchill went to the stable door and flagged down a boy and demanded *des pipes en terre* and *du tabac blond* and *du feu*.

"Is King Looie coming to the duc's fancy-dress ball, too?"

"So it is rumored—he has been preparing a costume in great secrecy, out at Versailles. Said to be of a radically shocking nature. *Impossibly* daring. All the French ladies are aflutter."

"Aren't they *always*?"

"I wouldn't know—I've taken a sound, some would say stern, English bride: Sarah."

"What's *she* coming as? A nun?"

"Oh, she's back in London. This is a diplomatic mission. Secret."

"You stand before me, dressed as you are, and say that?"

Churchill laughed.

"You take me for an imbecile?" Jack continued. The pain in his leg was most annoying, and shaking away flies had given his neck a cramp, as well as raw sores from the abrasion of his iron collar.

"You are only *alive* because of your recent imbecility, Jack. *L'Emmerdeur* is known to be clever as a fox. What you did was so stupid that it has not occurred to anyone, yet, that you could be he."

"So, then . . . in France, what's considered suitable punishment for an imbecile who does something stupid?"

"Well, naturally they were going to kill you. But I seem to have convinced them that, as you are not only a rural half-wit, but an *English* rural half-wit, the whole matter is actually *funny*."

"Funny? Not likely."

"The duc de Bourbon hosted a dinner party. Invited a certain eminent writer. Became annoyed with him. Emptied his snuff-box into the poor scribbler's wine when he wasn't looking, as a joke. The writer drank the wine and died of it—hilarious!"

"What fool would drink wine mixed with snuff?"

"That's not the point of the story—it's about what French nobility do, and don't, consider to be funny—and how I saved your life. Pay attention!"

"Let's set aside *how,* and ask: *why* did you save my life, guv'nor?"

"When a man is being torn apart with pliers, there's no telling what he'll blurt out."

"Aha."

"The last time I saw you, you were ordinary Vagabond scum. If there happened to be an old connexion between the two of us, it scarcely mattered. *Now* you are *legendary* Vagabond scum, a pica-roon, much talked of in salons. *Now* if the old link between us came to be widely known, it would be inconvenient for me."

"But you *could* have let that other fellow run me through with his rapier."

"And probably *should* have," Churchill said ruefully, "but I wasn't thinking. It is very odd. I saw him lunging for you. If I had only stood clear and allowed matters to take their natural course, you'd be dead. But some impulse took me—"

"The Imp of the Perverse, like?"

"Your old companion? Yes, perhaps he leapt from your shoulder to mine. Like a perfect imbecile, I saved your life."

"Well, you make a most splendid and gallant perfect imbecile. Are you going to kill me now?"

"Not directly. You are now a *galérien*. Your group departs for Marseille tomorrow morning. It's a bit of a walk."

"I know it."

Churchill sat on a bench and worried off one boot, then the other, then reached into them and pulled out the fancy Turkish slippers that had become lodged inside, and drew the slippers on. Then he threw the boots at Jack and they lodged in the manure, temporarily scaring away the flies. At about the same time, a stable-boy came in carrying two pipes stuffed with tobacco, and a taper, and soon both men were puffing away contentedly.

"I learned of the duc's Barbary connexions through an escaped slave, who seems to consider the information part of a closely guarded personal secret," Jack said finally.

"Thank you," said Churchill. "How's the leg, then?"

"Someone seems to've poked it with a sword . . . otherwise fine."

"Might need something to lean on." Churchill stepped outside the door for a moment, then returned carrying Jack's crutch. He held it crosswise between his two hands for a moment, weighing it. "Seems a bit *heavy* on this end—a *foreign* sort of crutch, is it?"

"Exceedingly foreign."

"Turkish?"

"Don't toy with me, Churchill."

Churchill spun the crutch around and chucked it like a spear so that it stuck in the manure-pile. "Whatever you're going to do, do it *soon* and then get the hell out of France. The road to Marseille will take you, in a day or two, through the *pays* of the Count of Joigny."

"Who's that?"

"That's the fellow you knocked off his horse. Notwithstanding my earlier reassuring statements, he *does not* find you amusing—if you enter his territory . . ."

"Pliers."

"Just so. Now, as insurance, I have a good friend lodging at an inn just to the north of Joigny. He is to keep an eye on the road to Marseille, and if he sees you marching down it, he is to make sure that you never get past that inn alive."

"How's he going to recognize me?"

"By that point, you'll be starkers—exposing your most distinctive feature."

"You really *are* worried I'll make trouble for you."

"I told you I'm here on a diplomatic mission. It is important."

"Trying to work out how England is to be divvied up between Leroy and the Pope of Rome?"

Churchill puffed on his pipe a few times in a fine, but not altogether convincing, display of calmness, and then said, "I *knew* we'd reach this point in the conversation, Jack—the point where you accused me of being a traitor to my country and my religion—and so I'm ready for it, and I'm actually *not* going to cut your head off."

Jack laughed. His leg hurt a great deal, and it itched, too.

"Through no volition of my own, I have for many years been a member of His Majesty's household," Churchill began. Jack was confused by this until he recollected that "His Majesty" no longer meant Charles II, but James II, the whilom Duke of York. Churchill continued: "I suppose I could reveal to you my innermost thoughts about what it's like to be a Protestant patriot in thrall to a Catholic King who loves France, but life is short, and I intend to spend as little of it as possible standing in dark stables apologizing to shit-covered Vagabonds. Suffice it to say that it's better for England if *I* do this mission."

"Suppose I do get away, before Joigny . . . what's to prevent me from telling everyone about the longstanding connexions between the Shaftoes and the Churchills?"

"No one of Quality will ever believe a word you say, Jack, unless you say it while you are being expertly tortured . . . it's only when you are stretched out on some important person's rack that you are dangerous. Besides, there is the Shaftoe legacy to think of." Churchill pulled out a little purse and jiggled it to make the coins ring.

"I *did* notice that you'd taken possession of my charger, without *paying* for it. Very bad form."

"The price in here is a fair one—a handsome sum, even," Churchill said. Then he pocketed the purse.

"Oh, come on—!"

"A naked *galérien* can't carry a purse, and these French coins are too big to stuff up even *your* asshole, Jack. I'll make sure your spawn get the benefit of this, when I'm back in England."

"Get *it,* or get *the benefit of* it? Because there is a slipperiness in those words that troubles me."

Churchill laughed again, this time with a cheerfulness that really made Jack want to kill him. He got up and plucked the empty pipe from Jack's mouth, and—as stables were notoriously inflammable, and he did not wish to be guilty of having set fire to the duc's—went over to the little horseshoe-forge, now cold and dark, and whacked the ashes out of the pipes. "Try to concentrate. You're a galley slave chained to a post in a stable in Paris. Be troubled by *that.* Bon voyage, Jack."

Exit Churchill. Jack had been meaning to advise him not to sleep with any of those French ladies, and to tell him about the Turkish innovation involving sheep-intestines, but there hadn't been time—and besides, who was he to give John Churchill advice on fucking?

Equipped now with boots, a sword, and (if he could just reach it, and slay a few stable-boys) a horse, Jack began considering how to get the damned chain off his neck. It was a conventional slave-collar: two iron semicircles hinged together on one side and with a sort of hasp on the other, consisting of two loops that would align with each other when the collar was closed. If a chain was then threaded through the loops, it would prevent the collar from opening. This made it possible for a single length of chain to secure as many collars, and hence slaves, as could be threaded onto it, without the need for expensive and unreliable padlocks. It kept the ironmongery budget to a minimum and worked so handily that no French Château or German Schloss was without a few, hanging on a wall-peg just in case some persons needed enslaving.

The particular chain that went through Jack's collar-hasp had a circular loop—a single oversized link—welded to one end. The chain had been passed around the stone pillar and its narrow end threaded through this loop, then through Jack's collar, and finally one of the duc's smiths had heated up the chain-end in the stable's built-in forge, and hammered an old worn-out horseshoe onto it, so it could not be withdrawn. Typical French extravagance! But the duc had an infinite fund of slaves and servants, so it cost him nothing, and there was no way for Jack to get it off.

The tobacco-embers from the pipes had formed a little mound on the blackened hearth of the forge and were still glowing, just barely. Jack squirmed free of the manure-pile and limped over to the forge and blew on them to keep them alive.

Normally this whole place was swarming with stable-boys, but now, and for the next hour or two, they'd be busy with ball duty: taking the horses of the arriving guests and leading them to stalls in the duc's better stables. So a fire in this hearth would be detectable only as a bit of smoke coming out of a chimney, which was not an unusual sight on a cool March evening in seventeenth-century Paris.

But he was getting ahead of himself. This was a long way from being a fire. Jack began looking about for some tinder. Straw would be perfect. But the stable-boys had been careful not to leave anything so tinderlike anywhere near the forge. It was all piled at the opposite end of the stable, and Jack's chain wouldn't let him go that far. He tried lying flat on the floor, with the chain stretched out taut behind him, and reaching out with the crutch to rake some straw towards him. But the end of the crutch came a full yard short of the goal. He scurried back and blew on the tobacco some more. It would not last much longer.

His attention had been drawn to the crutch, which was bound together with a lot of the cheapest sort of dry, fuzzy twine. Perfect tinder. But he'd have to burn most of it, and then he'd have no way to hold the crutch together, and therefore to conceal the existence of the sword—so, if the attempt failed tonight, he was doomed. In that sense 'twere safer to wait until tomorrow, when they'd take the chain off of him. But only to chain him up, he supposed, to a whole file of other *galériens*—doddering Huguenots, most likely. And he wasn't about to wait for *that*. He must do it now.

So he unwound the crutch and frizzed the ends of the twine and put it to the last mote of red fire in the pipe-ashes, and blew. The flame almost died, but then one fiber of twine warped back, withered, flung off a little shroud of steam or smoke, then became a pulse of orange light: a tiny thing, but as big in Jack's vision as whole trees bursting into flames in the Harz.

After some more blowing and fidgeting he had a morsel of yellow flame on the hearth. While supplying it more twine with one hand, he rummaged blindly for kindling, which ought to be piled up somewhere. Finding only a few twigs, he was forced to draw the sword and shave splints off the crutch-pole. This didn't last long, and soon he was planing splinters off pillars and beams, and chopping up benches and stools. But finally it was big and hot enough to ignite coal, of which there was plenty. Jack began tossing handfuls of it into his little fire while pumping the bellows with the other hand. At first it just lay in the fire like black stones, but then the sharp, brimstony smell of it came into the stable, and the fire became white, and the heat of the coal annihilated the remaining wood-scraps, and the fire became a meteor imprisoned in a chain—for Jack had looped the middle part of his chain around it. The cold iron poisoned the fire, sucked life from it, but Jack heaped on more coal and worked the bellows, and soon the metal had taken on a chestnut color which gave way to various shades of red. The heat of the blaze first dried the moist shit that was all over Jack's skin and then made him sweat, so that crusts of dung were flaking off of him.

The door opened. *"Où est le maréchal-ferrant?"* someone asked.

The door opened *wider*—wide enough to admit a horse—then did just that. The horse was led by a Scot in a tall wig—or maybe *not*. He was wearing a kiltlike number, but it was made of red *satin* and he had some sort of ridiculous contrivance slung over one shoulder: a whole pigskin, sewn up and packed with straw to make it look as if it had been inflated, with trumpet-horns, flutes, and pennywhistles dangling from it: a caricature of a bagpipe. His face was painted with blue woad. Pinned to the top of his wig was a tam-o'-shanter with an approximate diameter of three feet, and thrust into his belt, where a gentleman would sheathe his sword, was a sledgehammer. Next to that, several whiskey-jugs holstered.

The horse was a prancing beauty, but it seemed to be favoring one leg—it had thrown a shoe on the ride over.

"Maréchal-ferrant?" the man repeated, squinting in his direction. Jack reckoned that he, Jack, was visible only as a silhouette against the bright fire, and so the collar might not be obvious. He cupped a hand to his ear—smiths were notorious for deafness. That seemed to answer the question—the "Scot" led his horse toward the forge, nattering on about a *fer à cheval* and going so far as to check his pocket-watch. Jack was irritated. *Fer* meant "iron," *fer à cheval* as he knew perfectly well meant "horseshoe." But he had just understood that the English word "farrier" must be derived

somehow from this—even though "horseshoe" was completely different. He was aware, vaguely—from watching certain historical dramas, and then from roaming round *la France* listening to people talk—that French people had conquered England at least one time, and thereby confused the English language with all sorts of words such as "farrier," and "mutton," which common folk now used all the time without knowing that they were speaking the tongue of the conquerors. Meanwhile, the damned French had a tidy and proper tongue in which, for example, the name of the fellow who put shoes on horses was clearly related to the word for horseshoe. Made his blood boil—and now that James was King, Katie bar the door!

"Quelle heure est-il?" Jack finally inquired. The "Scot" without pausing to wonder why a *maréchal-ferrant* would need to know the time went once again into the ceremony of withdrawing his pocket-watch, getting the lid open, and reading it. In order to do this he had to turn its face towards the fire, and then he had to twist himself around so that he could see it. Jack waited patiently for this to occur, and then just as the "Scot" was lisping out something involving *sept* Jack whipped the chain out of the fire and got it round his neck.

It was stranglin' time in gay Paree. Most awkwardly, the red-hot part of the chain ended up around the throat of the "Scot," so Jack could not get a grip on it without first rummaging in the tool-box for some tongs. But it had already done enough damage, evidently, that the "Scot" could not make any noise.

His horse was another matter: it whinnied, and backed away, and showed signs of wanting to buck. That was a problem, but Jack had to take things one at a time here. He solved the tong problem and murdered the "Scot" in a great sizzling cloud of grilled neck-flesh—which, he felt sure, must be a delicacy in some part of France. Then he peeled the hot chain off, taking some neck parts with it, and tossed it back into the fire. Having settled these matters, he turned his attention—somewhat reluctantly—to the horse. He was dreading that it might have run out through the open sta-ble doors and drawn attention to itself in the stable-yard beyond. But—oddly—the stable-doors were now *closed*, and were being bolted shut, by a slender young man in an assortment of not very good clothes. He had evidently seized the horse's reins and tied them to a post, and had the presence of mind to toss a grain-sack over its head so that it could not see any more of the disturbing sights that were now so abundant in this place.

Having seen to these matters, the gypsy boy—it was certainly a gypsy—turned to face Jack, and made a somber, formal little bow.

He was barefoot—had probably gotten here by clambering over rooftops.

"You must be Half-Cocked Jack," he said, as if this weren't funny. Speaking in the zargon.

"Who are you?"

"It does not matter. St.-George sent me." The boy came over, stepping carefully around the glowing coals that had been scattered on the floor when Jack had whipped out the chain, and began to work the bellows.

"What did St.-George tell you to do?" asked Jack, throwing on more coal.

"To see what kind of help you would need, during the entertainment."

"What entertainment would that be?"

"He did not tell me *everything*."

"Why should St.-George care so much?"

"St.-George is angry with you. He says you have shown poor form."

"What are you going to tell him?"

"I will tell him," the gypsy boy said, and here he smiled for the first time, "that *l'Emmerdeur* does not need his help."

"That's just it," Jack said, and grabbed the bellows-handle. The boy turned and ran across the stable and vanished through an opening up in the eaves that Jack hadn't known was there.

While the chain heated, Jack amused himself by going through his victim's clothing and trying to guess how many gold coins were in his purse. After a couple of minutes (by the pocket-watch, which lay open on the floor) Jack reached into the fire with the tongs and drew out a length of yellow-hot chain. Before it could cool he draped it across an anvil, then smashed it with a heavy chisel-pointed hammer, and then he was free. Except that a yard of hot chain still dangled from his neck, and he could not pull it through his neck-loop without burning himself. So he quenched it in a trough of water. But then he found that in breaking it he'd smashed the last link, and broadened it, so it would no longer pass through the neck-loop. He did not want to spend the time to heat the chain back up, so he was stuck with the collar, and an arm's length of chain, for now. No matter, really. It was dark outside, he would be seen only as a silhouette, and he needed only that it be a respectable type of silhouette—a shape that people would not discharge weapons at without thinking twice. So he yanked the wig (now wrecked and burnt, but still a wig) off the dead "Scot" and put it on—discarding, however, the unwieldy tam-o'-shanter. He pulled on the boots that John Churchill had donated, and took the long cape that the "Scot" had been wearing. Also his gloves—an old habit to cover the V branded on his thumb. Finally he pilfered the saddle from the horse—it was a magnificent saddle—and carried it out into the stable-yard.

The sight of a supposed Person of Quality toting his own saddle was anomalous, and even if it weren't, Jack's dragging one leg, brandishing a scimitar, and muttering out loud in vulgar English also cast uncertainty on his status as a French nobleman. But, as he'd hoped, most of the stable-boys were busy in the main courtyard. The guests were now arriving in force. He barged into the next stable, which was dimly lit by a couple of lanterns, and came face-to-face with a stable-boy who, in an instant, became the most profoundly confused person Jack had ever seen.

"Turk!" Jack called, and was answered by a whinny from several stalls down the line. Jack sidled closer to the stable-boy and allowed the saddle to slide off his shoulders. The boy caught it out of habit, and seemed relieved to have been given a specific job. Then Jack, using his sword as a pointing-device, got him moving in the direction of Turk.

The boy now understood that he was being asked to help steal a horse, and stiffened up in a way that was almost penile. It took no end of prodding to get him to heave the saddle onto Turk's back. Then Jack socked him in the chin with the guard of the sword, but failed to knock him out. In the end, he had to drag the fool over to a convenient place by the entrance and push him down and practically draw him a picture of how to go about pretending he'd been surprised and knocked unconscious by the English villain.

Then back to Turk, who seemed pleased to see him. As Jack tightened the girth, and made other adjustments, the war-horse's sinews became taut and vibrant, like the strings of a lute being tuned up. Jack checked his hooves and noted that Churchill had gotten some expert *maréchal-ferrant* to shoe him. "You and me both," Jack said, slapping his new boots so that the horse could admire them.

Then he put one of those boots into a stirrup, threw his leg over the saddle, and was hurtling across the duc's stable-yard before he could even get himself situated properly. Turk wanted out of here as badly as *he* did. Jack had intended to look for a back exit, but Turk was having none of that, and took him *out* the way Churchill had ridden him *in:* straight through a gate into what Jack reckoned must be the main courtyard of the Hôtel d'Arcachon.

Jack sensed quite a few people, but couldn't really see them because he was dazzled by all of the light: giant torchières like bon-fires on pikes, and lanterns strung on colored ropes, and the light of thousands of lanterns and tapers blasting out through the twenty-foot-high windows that constituted most of the front wall of a large noble House directly in front of him. A hundred sperm whales must have given up their bodily fluids to light the lanterns. And as for the tapers in those chandeliers, why, even over the smells of cuisine, fashionable perfume, wood-smoke, and horse-manure, Jack's nose could detect the fragrance of honey-scented Mauritanian beeswax. All of this sweet-smelling radiance glanced wetly off a large fountain planted in the middle of the court: various Neptunes and Naiads and sea monsters and dolphins cleverly enwrithed to form a sup-port for a naval frigate all speckled with fleurs-de-lis. Wreckage of Dutch and English ships washed up on shores all around, forming benches for French people to put their buttocks on.

The force of the light, and Jack's hauling back on the reins, had taken the edge off of Turk's impetuous charge for the exit, but not quite soon enough: the fact remained that Turk, and thus Jack, had effectively burst into the couryard at a near-gallop and then stood agape for several seconds, almost as if *demanding* to be noticed. And they *had* been: little knots of Puritans, Færy-Queens, Persians, and Red Indians were looking at them. Jack gave the war-horse an encouraging nudge, while holding fast to the reins so he wouldn't bolt.

Turk began following a groomed gravel path among flower-beds, which Jack hoped would take them round the fountain even-tually and to a place where they could at least *see* the way out. But they were moving directly toward the light rushing from those banks of windows. Through them Jack saw an immense ballroom, with white walls garlanded with gold, and white polished marble floors where the nobility, in their fancy-dress, were dancing to music from a consort stuffed into a corner.

Then—like anyone else coming towards a grand party—Jack glanced down at his own person. He had been counting on dark-ness, but had blundered into light, and was shocked at how clearly his shit-covered rags and neck-iron stood out.

He saw a man inside who'd been in the duc's entourage the other day. Not wanting to be recognized, Jack turned up the collar of the stolen cape, and drew it round to conceal the bottom half of his face.

A few small clusters of party-goers had formed in the lawn between the front of the house and the fountain, and *all* conversa-tion had been suspended so that all faces could turn to stare at Jack. But they did not raise a hue and cry. They stared for a remarkably long time, as if Jack were a new and extremely expensive sculpture that had just been unveiled. Then Jack sensed a contagious thrill, a *frisson* like the one that had run through the fishmarket at Les Halles when he'd galloped through it. There was a strange pattering noise. He realized they were *applauding* him. A serving-girl flashed away into the ballroom, hitching up her skirts as she ran, to spread some news. The musicians stopped playing, all faces turned to the windows. The people on the lawn had converged toward Jack, while maintaining a certain respectful distance, and were bowing and curtseying, very low. A pair of footmen practically sprawled out onto the grass in their anxiety to hurl the front doors open. Framed in the arch was a porky gentleman armed with a long Trident, which naturally made Jack flinch when he saw it— this fellow, Jack suspected, was the duc d'Arcachon, dressed up as Neptune. But then the duc held the weapon out towards him, resting crossways on his outstretched hands—*offering* it to Jack. Neptune then backed out of the way, still doubled over in a deep bow, and beckoned him into the ballroom. Inside, the party-goers had formed up in what he instinctively recognized as a gauntlet to whip all the skin off his back—but then understood must actually be a pair of lines to *receive* him!

Everything seemed to point to that he was expected to ride into the ballroom on horseback, which was unthinkable. But Jack had become adept (or so he believed) at distinguishing things that were really happening from the waking dreams or phant'sies that came into his head more and more frequently of late, and, reckoning that this was one of the latter, he decided to enjoy it. Accordingly, he now rode Turk (who was extremely reluctant) right past the duc and into the ballroom. Now *everyone* bowed low, giving Jack the opportunity to look down a large number of white-powdered cleavages. A trumpeter played some sort of fanfare. One cleavage in particular Jack was afraid he might fall into and have to be winched out on a rope. The lady in question, noticing Jack's fixed stare, seemed to think that he was staring at least partly at the string of pearls around her neck. Something of a complicated nature occurred inside her head, and then she blushed and clasped both hands to her black-spotted face and squealed and said something to the effect of "No, no, please, not my jewels . . . Emmerdeur," and then she unclasped the pearls from behind her neck; clasped them back together into a loop; *threw* it over the point of Jack's sword, like a farm girl playing ring-toss at the fair; and then expertly swooned back into the waiting arms of her escort: a satyr with a two-foot-long red leather penis.

Another woman shrieked, and Jack raised his weapon in case he was going to have to kill her—but all he saw was another mademoiselle going into the same act—she ran up and pinned a jeweled brooch to the hem of his cloak, muttering *"pour les Invalides,"* then backed away curtseying before Jack could say what was on his mind, which was: *If you want to give this away to charity, lady, you came to the wrong bloke.*

Then they were *all* doing it, the thing was a sensation, the ladies were practically elbowing each other to get near and decorate Jack's clothes and his sword, and Turk's bridle, with jewelry. The only person *not* having a good time was a certain handsome young Barbary Pirate who stood at the back of the crowd, red-faced, staring at Jack with eyes that, had they been pliers . . .

A stillness now spread across the ballroom like a blast of frigid air from a door blown open by a storm. Everyone seemed to be looking toward the entrance. The ladies were backing away from Jack in hopes of getting a better view. Jack sat up straight in the saddle and got Turk turned around, partly to see what everyone else was staring at and partly because he had the sense it would soon be time to leave.

A *second* man had ridden into the ballroom on horseback. Jack identified him, at first, as a Vagabond recently escaped from captivity—no doubt well-deserved captivity. But of course it was really some nobleman *pretending* to be a Vagabond, and his costume was *much better* than Jack's—the chain around his neck, and the broken fetters on his wrists and ankles, appeared to've been forged out of *solid gold,* and he was brandishing a gaudy jeweled scimitar, and wearing a conspicuous, diamond-studded, but comically tiny codpiece. Behind him, out in the courtyard, was a whole entourage: Gypsies, jeweled and attired according to some extremely romantic conception of what it was to be a gypsy; ostrich-plume-wearing Moors; and fine ladies dressed up as bawdy Vagabond-wenches.

Jack allowed the cape to fall clear of his face.

There followed the longest period of silence that he had ever known. It was so long that he could have tied Turk's reins to a candelabra and curled up under the harpsichord for a little nap. He could have run a message down to Lyons during this silence (and, in retrospect, probably *should* have). But instead he just sat there on his horse and waited for something to happen, and took in the scene.

Silence made him aware that the house was a hive of life and activity, even when all of the Persons of Quality were frozen up like statues. There was the normal dim clattering of the kitchen, for example. But his attention was drawn to the ceiling, which was

(a) a hell of a thing to look at, and (b) making a great deal of noise—he thought perhaps a heavy rain had begun to thrash the roof, partly because of this scrabbling, rushing noise that was coming from it, and partly because it was leaking rather badly in a number of places. It had been decorated both with plaster relief-work and with paint, so that if you could lie on your back and stare at it you would see a vast naval Tableau: the gods of the four winds at the edges of the room, cheeks all puffed as they blew out billowy plaster clouds, and the Enemies of France angling in from various corners, viz. English and Dutch frigates riding the north wind, Spanish and Portuguese galleons the south, as well as pirates of Barbary and Malta and the Turk, and the occasional writhing sea-monster. Needless to say, the center was dominated by the French Navy in massive three-dimensional plasterwork, guns pointing every which way, and on the poop-deck of the mightiest ship, surrounded by spyglass-toting Admirals, stood a laurel-wreath-crowned Leroy, one hand fingering an astrolabe and the other resting on a cannon. And as if to add even greater realism, the entire scene was now running and drizzling, as if there really were an ocean up above it trying to break through and pay homage to the living King who had just rode in. From this alarming leakage, and from the rustling noise, Jack naturally suspected a sudden violent storm coming through a leaky roof. But when he looked out the windows into the courtyard he saw no rain. Besides (he remembered with some embarrassment), the Hôtel d'Arcachon was not some farmhouse, where the ceiling was merely the underside of the roof. Jack well knew, from having broken into a few places like this, that the ceiling was a thin shell of plaster troweled over horizontal lath-work, and that there would be a crawl space above it, sandwiched between ceiling and roof, with room for dull, dirty things like chandelier-hoists and perhaps cisterns.

That was it—there must be a cistern full of collected rainwater up there, which must have sprung a leak—in fact, had probably been encouraged to do so by St.-George or one of his friends, just to create a distraction that might be useful to Jack. The water must be gushing out across the top of the plaster-work, percolating down between the laths, saturating the plaster, which was darkening in several large irregular patches—gathering storm-clouds besetting the French Navy and darkening the sea from robin's-egg blue to a more realistic iron-gray. Gray, and heavy, and no longer flat and smooth—the ceiling was swelling and bulging downwards. In several places around the room, dirty water had begun to spatter down onto the floor. Servants were fetching mops and buckets, but dared not interrupt the Silence.

Turk complained of something, and Jack looked down to discover that the satyr with the very long, barbed, red leather penis had sidled up and grabbed Turk's bridle.

"That's an *incredibly* bad idea," Jack said in English (there was no point in even *trying* his French among *this* crowd). He said it *sotto voce*, not wanting to officially break the Silence, and indeed most people could not hear him over the odd scrabbling noises and muffled squeaks emanating from above. The squeaks might be the sound of lath-nails being wrenched out of old dry joists by the growing weight of the ceiling. Anyway, it was good that Jack glanced down, because he also noticed John Churchill striding round the back of the crowd, examining the flintlock mechanism on a pistol, very much in the manner of an experienced slayer of men who was looking forward to a moment soon when he'd fire the weapon. Jack didn't have a firearm, only a sword, freighted with jewelry at the moment. He shoved its tip through the satin lining of the riding-cloak, cutting a small gash, and then allowed all of the goods to avalanche into it.

The satyr responded in better English than Jack would ever speak: "It is a *dreadful* thing for me to have done—life is not long enough for me to make sufficient apologies. Please know that I have simply tried to make the best of an awkward—"

But then he was interrupted by King Louis XIV of France, who, in a mild yet room-filling voice, delivered some kind of witticism. It was only a sentence, or phrase, but it said more than any bishop's three-hour Easter homily. Jack could scarcely hear a word, and wouldn't't've understood it anyway, but he caught the word Vagabond, and the word *noblesse*, and inferred that something profoundly philosophical was being said. But not in a dry, fussy way— there was worldly wisdom here, there was irony, a genuine spark of wit, droll but never vulgar. Leroy was amused, but would never be so common as to laugh aloud. *That* was reserved for the courtiers who leaned in, on tiptoe, to hear the witticism. Jack believed, just for a moment, that if John Churchill—who had no sense of humor at all—had not been homing in on him with that loaded pistol, all might have been forgiven, and Jack might have stayed and drunk some wine and danced with some ladies.

He could not move away from Churchill when the satyr was gripping Turk's bridle. "Are you going to make me cut that off?" he inquired.

"I freely confess that I deserve no better," said the satyr. "In fact—I am so humiliated that I must do it myself, to restore my, and my father's, honor." Whereupon he pulled a dagger from his belt and began to saw through the red leather glove on the hand that was gripping the bridle—attempting to cut off his left hand with his right. In doing so he probably saved Jack's life, for this spectacle—the man sawing at his own arm, blood welling out of the glove and dribbling onto the white floor—stopped Churchill in his curly-toed tracks, no more than a fathom away. It was the only time Jack had ever seen Churchill hesitate.

There was a ripping and whooshing noise from one end of the room. The East Wind had been split open by a sagging crevice that unloaded a sheet of dirty, lumpy water onto the floor. A whole strip of ceiling, a couple of yards wide, peeled away now, like a plank being ripped away from the side of a boat. It led straight to the French Navy—half a ton of plaster, bone dry—which came off in a single unified fleet action and seemed to hang in space for a moment before it started accelerating toward the floor. Everyone got out of the way. The plaster exploded and splayed snowballs of damp crud across the floor. But stuff continued to rain down from above, small dark lumps that, when they struck the floor, shook themselves and took off running.

Jack looked at Churchill just in time to see the flint whipping round on the end of its curved arm, a spray of sparks, a preliminary bloom of smoke from the pan. Then a lady blundered in from one side, not paying attention to where she was going because she had realized that there were rats in her wig—but she didn't know how many (Jack, at a quick glance, numbered them at three, but more were raining down all the time and so he would've been loath to commit himself to a specific number). She hit Churchill's arm. A jet of fire as long as a man's arm darted from the muzzle of Churchill's pistol and caught Turk in the side of the face, though the ball apparently missed. The polite satyr was lucky to be alive—it had gone off inches from his head.

Turk was stunned and frozen, if only for a moment. Then a Barbary pirate-galley, driven downwards by a gout of water/rat slurry, exploded on the floor nearby. Some of the water, and some of the rats, poured down on Turk's neck—and then he detonated. He tried to rear up and was held down by the satyr's bloody but steadfast clutch, so he bucked—fortunately Jack saw this coming—and then kicked out with both hind-legs. Anyone behind him would've been decapitated, but the center of the ballroom had been mostly given over to rats now. A few more of those bucks and Jack would be flung off. He needed to let Turk run. But Churchill was now trying to get round the satyr to lay a second hand on Turk's bridle. "This is the worst fucking party I've ever been to!" Jack said, whirling his sword-arm around like a windmill.

"Sir, I am sorry, but—"

The polite satyr did not finish the apology, because Jack delivered a cut to the middle of his forearm. The blade passed through sweetly. The dangling hand balled itself into a fist and maintained its grip on the bridle, even as the now one-armed satyr was falling back on top of Churchill. Turk sensed freedom and reared up. Jack looked down at Churchill and said, "Next time you want one of my horses—pay in *advance*, you rogue!"

Turk tried to bolt for the front door, but his hard *fers de cheval* slipped and scrabbled on the marble, and he could not build up speed. A sea-monster came down across his path, shedding a hundred rats from its crushed entrails. Turk wheeled and scrambled off toward a crowd of ladies who were doing a sort of tarantella, inspired by the belief that rats were scaling their petticoats. Then, just as Jack was convinced that the charger was going to crush the women under his hooves, Turk seemed to catch sight of a way out, and veered sideways, his hooves nearly sliding out from under him, and made for a doorway set into the back corner of the ballroom. It was a low doorway. Jack had little time to react—seeing the lintel headed for his face, decorated in the middle with a plaster d'Arcachon coat of arms,* and not wanting to have it stamped on his face forever, he flung himself backwards and fell off the horse.

He managed to get his right foot, but not his left, out of the stirrup, and so Turk simply dragged him down the ensuing corridor (which had a smooth floor, but not smooth enough for Jack). Nearly upside-down, Jack pawed desperately against that floor with the hand that wasn't gripping the sword, trying to pull himself sideways so that Turk's hooves wouldn't come down on him. Time and again his hand slammed down onto the backs of rats, who all seemed to be fleeing down this particular corridor—drawn by some scent, perhaps, that struck them as promising. Turk outpaced the rats, of course, and was making his own decisions. Jack knew that they were passing into diverse rooms because the thresholds barked his hips and ribs and he got fleeting views of servants' breeches and skirts.

But then, suddenly, they were in a dimly lit room, alone, and Turk wasn't running anymore. Nervous and irritable to be sure,

---

*A quartering of elements old (fleurs-de-lis, denoting their ancient connections to the royal family) and new (Negro-heads in iron neck-collars).

though. Jack cautiously wiggled his left foot. Turk startled, then looked at him.

"Surprised to see me? I've been with you the whole way—loyal friend that I am," Jack announced. He got his boot out of that stirrup and stood. But there was no time for additional banter. They were in a pantry. Squealing noises heralded the approach of the rats. Pounding of boots was not far behind, and where there were boots, there'd be swords. There was a locked door set into the wall, opposite to where they had come in, and Turk had gone over to sniff at it curiously.

If this was not a way out, Jack was dead—so he went over and pounded on it with the pommel of his sword, while looking significantly at Turk. It was a stout door. Curiously, the crevices between planks had been sealed with oakum, just like a ship's planking, and rags had been stuffed into the gaps round the edges.

Turk wheeled around to face away from it. Jack hopped out of the way. The war-horse's hindquarters heaved up as he put all weight on his forelegs, and then both of his rear hooves smashed into the door with the force of cannonballs. The door was half caved in, and torn most of the way loose from its upper hinge. Turk gave it a few more, and it disappeared.

Jack had sunk to his knees by that point, though, and wrapped a manure-plastered sleeve up against his nose and mouth, and was trying not to throw up. The stench that had begun to leak from the room beyond, after the first blow, had nearly felled him. It nearly drove Turk away, too. Jack just had the presence of mind to slam the other door and prevent the horse's fleeing into the hallway.

Jack grabbed the candle that was the pantry's only illumination, and stepped through, expecting to find a sepulchre filled with ripe corpses. But instead it was just another small kitchen, as tidy a place as Jack had ever seen.

There was a butcher's block in the center of the room with a fish stretched out on it. The fish was so rotten it was bubbling.

At the other end of this room was a small door. Jack opened it and discovered a typical Parisian back-alley. But what he *saw* in his mind's eye was the moment, just a few minutes ago, when he had ridden right past the duc d'Arcachon while carrying an unsheathed sword. One twitch of the wrist, and the man who (as he now knew) had taken Eliza and her mother off into slavery would be dead. He could run back into the house now, and have a go at it. But he knew he'd lost the moment.

Turk planted his head in Jack's back and shoved him out the

door, desperate to reach the comparative freshness of a Paris alley choked with rotting kitchen-waste and human excrement. Back inside, Jack could hear men battering at the pantry door.

Turk was eyeing him as if to say, *Shall we?* Jack mounted him and Turk began to gallop down the alley without being told to. The alarm had gone up. So as Jack thundered out into the Place Royale, sparks flying from his mount's new shoes, the wind blowing his cape out behind him—in other words, cutting just the silhouette he'd intended—he turned round and pointed back into the alley with his sword and shouted: *"Les Vagabonds! Les Vagabonds anglaises!"* And then, catching sight of the bulwark of the Bastille rising above some rooftops, under a half-moon, and reckoning that this would be a good place to pretend to summon reinforcements—not to mention a way out of town—he got Turk pointed in that direction, and gave him free rein.

Amsterdam
1685

> Must businesse thee from hence remove?
> Oh, that's the worst disease of love,
> The poore, the foule, the false, love can
> Admit, but not the busied man.
> He which hath businesse, and makes love, doth doe
> Such wrong, as when a maryed man doth wooe.
> —JOHN DONNE, "Breake of Day"

"WHO IS YOUR GREAT BIG tall, bearded, ill-dressed, unmannerly, harpoon-brandishing, er—?" asked Eliza, and ran out of adjectives. She was peering out the windows of the *Maiden* coffee-house at a loitering Nimrod who was blotting out the sun with an immense, motley fur coat. The management had been reluctant to let even *Jack* come into the place, but they had drawn the line at the glaring wild man with the harping-iron.

"Oh, him?" Jack asked, innocently—as if there were more than one such person who owned that description. "That's Yevgeny the Raskolnik."

"What's a Raskolnik?"

"Beats me—all I know is they're all getting out of Russia as fast as they can."

"Well, then . . . how did you *meet* him?"

"I've no idea. Woke up in the Bomb & Grapnel—there he was, snuggled up against me—his beard thrown over my neck like a muffler."

Eliza shuddered exquisitely. "But the Bomb & Grapnel's in Dunkirk . . ."

"Yes?"

"How'd you get there from Paris? Weren't there adventures, chases, duels—?"

"Presumably. I've no idea."

"What of the leg wound?"

"I was fortunate to engage the services of a fine, lusty crew of maggots along the way—they kept it clean. It healed without incident."

"But how can you simply forget about a whole week's journey?"

"It's how my mind works now. As in a play, where only the most dramatic parts of the story are shown to the audience, and the tedious bits assumed to happen offstage. So: I gallop out of the Place Royale; the curtain falls, there is a sort of intermission; the curtain rises again, and I'm in Dunkirk, in Mr. Foot's finest bedchamber, upstairs of the Bomb & Grapnel, and I'm with Yevgeny, and stacked around us on the floor are all of his furs and skins and amber."

"He's some sort of commodities trader, then?" Eliza asked.

"No need to be waspish, lass."

"I'm simply trying to work out how he found his way into the drama."

"I've no idea—he doesn't speak a word of *anything*. I went down stairs and asked the same question of Mr. Foot, the proprietor, a man of parts, former privateer—"

"You've told me, and told me, and told me, about Mr. Foot."

"He said that just a week or two earlier, Yevgeny had rowed a longboat into the little cove where the Bomb & Grapnel sits."

"You mean—rowed ashore from some ship that had dropped anchor off Dunkirk."

"No—that's just it—he came from *over the horizon*. Rode a swell up onto the beach—dragged the longboat up as far as it would go—collapsed on the threshold of the nearest dwelling, which happened to be the old Bomb. Now, Mr. Foot has been lacking for customers these last few years—so, instead of throwing him back like a fish, as he might've done in the B & G's heyday, and discovering, furthermore, that the longboat was filled to the gunwales with Arctic valuables, he toted it all upstairs. Finally he rolled Yevgeny himself onto a cargo net, and hoisted him up through the window with a block and tackle—thinking that when he woke up, he might know how to obtain more of the same goods."

"Yes, I can see his business strategy very clearly."

"There you go again. If you'd let me finish, you wouldn't judge of Mr. Foot so harshly. At the cost of many hours' backbreaking labor, he gave a more or less Christian burial to the remains—"

"*Which*? There has been no discussion of *remains*."

"I may've forgotten to mention that Yevgeny was sharing the long-boat with several comrades who'd all succumbed to the elements—"

"—or possibly Yevgeny."

"The same occurred to me. But then, as the Good Lord endowed me with more *brains*, and less *bile*, than *some*, I reckoned that if this had been the case, the Raskolnik would've thrown the victims overboard—especially after they waxed gruesome. Mr. Foot—and I only tell you this, lass, in order to clear Yevgeny's name—said that the meatier parts of these corpses had been picked clean to the bone by seagulls."

"Or by a peckish Yevgeny," Eliza said, lifting a teacup to her lips to conceal a certain triumphal smile, and looking out the window toward the furry Russian, who was whiling away the time by puffing on a rude pipe and honing the flukes of his harping-iron with a pocket-whetstone.

"Making a good character for my Raskolnik friend—though he truly has a heart of gold—will be impossible when, tidy and stylish girl that you are, you are gaping at his rude exterior form. So let us move on," Jack said. "Next thing Mr. Foot knows, I show up, all decorated with baubles from France, nearly as spent as Yevgeny. So he took me in, in the same way. And finally, a French gentleman approached him and let it be known that he'd like to purchase the Bomb & Grapnel—proving the rule that things tend to happen in threes."

"Now you've amazed me," Eliza said. "What do those events have in common with each other, that you should conceive of them as a group of three?"

"Why, just as Yevgeny and I were wandering lost—yet, in possession of things of great value—Mr. Foot was cast out into the wilderness—I am making a similitude, here—"

"Yes, you have the daft look you always get, when you are."

"Dunkirk's not the same since Leroy bought it from King Chuck. It is a great *base navale* now. All the English, and other, privateers who used to lodge, drink, gamble, and whore at the Bomb & Grapnel have signed on with Monsieur Jean Bart, or else sailed away to Port Royal, in Jamaica. And despite these troubles, Mr. Foot had something of value: the Bomb & Grapnel itself. An opportunity began to take shape in Mr. Foot's mind, like a stage-ghost appearing from a cloud of smoke."

"Much as a profound sense of foreboding is beginning to take shape in my bosom."

"I had a vision in Paris, Eliza—rather of a complex nature—there was considerable singing and dancing in it, and ghastly and bawdy portions in equal measure."

"Knowing you as I do, Jack, I'd expect nothing less from one of your visions."

"I'll spare you the details, most of which are indelicate for a lady of your upbringing. Suffice it to say that on the strength of this heavenly apparition, and other signs and omens, such as the Three Similar Events at the Bomb & Grapnel, I have decided to give up Vagabonding, and, along with Yevgeny and Mr. Foot, to go into Business."

Eliza faltered and shrank, as if a large timber, or something, had snapped inside of her.

"Now why is it," Jack said, "then when I suggest you reach in and grab me by the *chakra*, it's nothing to you, and yet, when the word *business* comes out of my mouth, you get a wary and prim look about you, like a virtuous maiden who has just had lewd proposals directed her way by a bawdy Lord?"

"It's nothing. Pray continue," Eliza said, in a colorless voice.

But Jack's nerve had faltered. He began to digress. "I'd hoped brother Bob might be in town, as he commonly traveled in John Churchill's retinue. And indeed Mr. Foot said he had been there very recently, inquiring after me. But then the Duke of Monmouth had surprised them all by coming to Dunkirk incognito, to meet with certain disaffected Englishmen, and proceeding inland toward Brussels in haste. Bob, who knows that terrain so well, had been dispatched by one of Churchill's lieutenants to follow him and report on his doings."

At the mention of the Duke of Monmouth, Eliza began to look Jack in the face again—from which he gathered that one of two things might be the case: either she was looking for a romantic fling with a claim (highly disputable) to the English throne, or else she numbered political intrigues among her interests now. Indeed, when he had surprised her by coming into the Maiden, she'd been writing a letter with her right hand while doing that binary arithmetic on her left, according to the Doctor's practice.

At any rate—as long as he had her attention—he decided to strike. "And that is when I was made aware, by Mr. Foot, of the Opportunity."

Eliza's face became a death mask, as when a physician says, *Please sit down* . . .

"Mr. Foot has many contacts in the shipping industry—"

"Smugglers."

"Most shipping is smuggling to some degree," Jack said learnedly. "He had received a personal visit from one Mr. Vliet, a Dutch fellow who was in the market for a seaworthy vessel of moderate size, capable of crossing the Atlantic with a cargo of such-and-such number of tons. Mr. Foot was not slow in securing the *God's Wounds,* a well-broken-in double-topsail brig."

"Do you even know what that *means?*"

"It is both square, and fore-and-aft rigged, hence well-suited for running before the trade winds, or plying the fickle breezes of coastlines. She has a somewhat lopsided but seasoned crew—"

"And only needed to be victualled and refitted—?"

"Some capital was, of course, wanted."

"So Mr. Vliet went to Amsterdam and—?"

"To *Dunkirk* went Mr. Vliet, and explained to Mr. Foot, who then explained to me and, as best he could, Yevgeny, the nature of the proposed trading voyage: of lapidary simplicity, yet guaranteed to be lucrative. We agreed to cast in our lots together. Fortunately, it is not difficult to sell goods quickly in Dunkirk. I liquidated the jewelry, Yevgeny sold his furs, whale-oil, and some fine amber, and Mr. Foot has sold the Bomb & Grapnel to a French concern."

"It seems a farfetched way for this Mr. Vliet to raise money," Eliza said, "when there is a large and extremely vigorous capital market right here in Amsterdam."

This was (as Jack figured out later, when he had much time to consider it) Eliza's way of saying that she thought Mr. Vliet was a knave, and the voyage not fit for persons in their right minds to invest in. But having been in Amsterdam for so long, she said it in the zargon of bankers.

"Why not just sell the jewels and give the money to your boys?" she continued.

"Why not invest it—as they have no immediate need for money—and, in a few years, give them quadruple the amount?"

"Quadruple?"

"We expect no less."

Eliza made a face as if she were being forced to swallow a whole English walnut. "Speaking of money," she murmured, "what of the horse, and the ostrich plumes?"

"That noble steed is in Dunkirk, awaiting the return of John Churchill, who has voiced an intention of buying him from me. The plumes are safe in the hands of my commission-agents in Paris," Jack said, and gripped the table-edge with both hands, expecting a thorough interrogation. But Eliza let the matter drop, as if she couldn't stand to come any nearer to the truth. Jack realized she'd *never* expected to see him, or the money, again—that she'd withdrawn, long ago, from the partnership they'd formed beneath the Emperor's palace in Vienna.

She would not look him in the eye, nor laugh at his jokes, nor blush when he provoked her, and he thought that chill Amsterdam had frozen her soul—sucked the humour of passion from her veins. But in time he persuaded her to come outside with him. When she stood up, and the Maiden's proprietor helped her on with a cape, she looked finer than ever. Jack was about to compliment her on her needle-work when he noticed rings of gold on her fingers, and jewels round her neck, and knew she probably had not touched needle and thread since reaching Amsterdam.

"*Windhandel,* or gifts from suitors?"

"I did not escape slavery to be a whore," she answered. "*You* might wake up next to a Yevgeny and jest about it—I would be of a different mind."

Yevgeny, unaware that he was being abused in this way, followed them through the scrubbed streets of the town, thumping at the pavement with the butt of his harping-iron. Presently they came to a southwestern district *not* so well scrubbed, and began to hear a lot of French and Ladino, as Huguenots and Sephardim had come to live here—even a few Raskolniks, who stopped Yevgeny to exchange rumors and stories. The houses became cracked and uneven, settling into the muck so fast you could practically see them moving, and the canals became narrow and scummed-over, as if rarely troubled by commerce.

They walked up such a street to a warehouse where heavy sacks were being lowered into the hold of a sloop. "There it is—our Commodity," Jack said. "Good as—and in some parts of the world, preferable to—gold."

"What is it—hazelnuts?" Eliza asked. "Coffee beans?" Jack had no particular reason to keep the secret from her, but this was the first time she'd shown any interest at all in his venture, and he wanted to make it last.

The sloop's hold was full. So even as Jack, Eliza, and Yevgeny were approaching, the lines were cast off and sails raised, and she began to drift down the canal ahead of a faint breeze, headed for the inner harbor, a few minutes' walk away.

They followed on foot. "You have insurance?" she asked.

"Funny you should ask," Jack said, and at this Eliza rolled her eyes, and then slumped like one of those sinking houses. "Mr. Foot says that this is a great adventure, but—"

"He means that you have made Mr. Vliet a loan *à la grosse aventure*, which is a typical way of financing trading-voyages," Eliza said. "But those who make such loans always buy insurance—*if they can find anyone to sell it to them*. I can point you to coffee-houses that specialize in just that. But—"

"How much does it cost?"

"It depends on *everything*, Jack, there is no one fixed price. Are you trying to tell me you don't have enough money left to buy insurance?"

Jack said nothing.

"If so, you should withdraw now."

"Too late—the victuals are paid for and stowed in the hold of *God's Wounds*. But perhaps there is room for one more investor."

Eliza snorted. "What's come over you? Vagabonding you do very well, and you cut a fine figure doing it. But investing—it's not your *métier*."

"I wish you had mentioned that before," Jack said. "From the first moment Mr. Foot mentioned it to me, I saw this trading-voyage as a way I might become worthy in your eyes." Then Jack nearly toppled into a canal, as recklessly telling the truth had given him an attack of giddiness. Eliza, for her part, looked as if she'd been butt-stroked by Yevgeny's harpoon—she stopped walking, planted her feet wide, and crossed her arms over her bodice as if nursing a stomach-ache; looked up the canal with watery eyes for a moment; and sniffled once or twice.

Jack ought to've been delighted. But all he felt, finally, was a dull sense of doom. He hadn't told Eliza about the rotten fish or the pink-eyed horses. He *certainly* had not mentioned that he could have killed, but had idiotically spared, the villain who had once made her a slave. But he knew that someday she would find out, and when that happened, he did not want to be on the European continent.

"Let me see the ship," she said finally.

They came round a bend and were greeted by one of those sudden surprising Amsterdam-vistas, down the canal to the ship-carpeted Ijsselmeer. Planted on the Ij-bank was the Herring-Packers' Tower, a roundish brick silo rising above a sloppy, fragrant quay where three vessels were tied up: a couple of hulks that were shuttling victuals out to bigger ships in the outer harbor, and *God's Wounds,* which looked as if she were being disassembled. All her hatches were removed for loading, and what remained had a structurally dubious look—especially when great sweating barrels of herring, and these mysterious sacks from the warehouse, were being dropped into it.

But before Jack could really dwell on the topic of sea-worthiness, Eliza—moving with a decisiveness he could no longer muster—had gone out onto the quay, her skirts sweeping up all manner of stuff that she would later regret having brought home. A sack had split open and spilled its contents, which snapped, crackled, and popped beneath the soles of her shoes as she drew up close. She bent over and thrust her hand into the hole, somewhat like doubting Thomas, and raised up a handful of the cargo, and let it spill in a colorful clinking shower.

"Cowrie shells," she said distractedly.

Jack thought, at first, that she was dumbfounded—probably by the brilliance and magnificence of the plan—but on a closer look he saw that she was showing all the symptoms of thinking.

"Cowrie shells to you," Jack said. "In Africa, this is money!"

"Not for long."

"What do you mean? Money's money. Mr. Vliet has been sitting on this hoard for twenty years, waiting for prices to drop."

"A few weeks ago," said Eliza, "news arrived that the Dutch had acquired certain isles, near India, called the Maldives and Laccadives, and that vast numbers of cowrie shells had been found there. Since that news arrived, these have been considered worthless."

It took Jack some time to recover from this.

He had a sword, and Mr. Vliet, a pudgy flaxen-haired man, was just a stone's throw away, going over some paperwork with a ship's victualer, and it was natural to imagine simply running over and inserting the tip of the sword between any two of Mr. Vliet's chins and giving it a hard shove. But this, he supposed, would simply have proved Eliza's point (viz. that he was not cut out to be a businessman), and he did not want to give her such satisfaction. Jack wasn't going to get the kind of satisfaction *he* had been craving for the last six months, and so why should *she* get any? As a way of keeping his body occupied while the mind worked, he helped roll some barrels over the plank to the deck of the ship.

"Now I understand the word *Windhandel* in a new way," was all that he could come up with. "This is real," he said, slapping a barrel-head, "and this" (stomping the deck of *God's Wounds*) "is real, and these" (lofting a double handful of cowrie shells) "are real, and all of them every bit as real, *now,* as they were, ten minutes ago, or before this rumor arrived from the Maldives and the Laccadives . . ."

"The news came over land—faster than ships normally travel, when they have to round the Cape of Good Hope. So it is possible that you will reach Africa in advance of the great cargo-ships of cowrie-shells that, one can only presume, are headed that way now from the Maldives."

"Just as Mr. Vliet had it planned, I'm sure."

"But when you get to Africa, what will you buy with your cowrie-shells, Jack?"

"Cloth."

"*Cloth!?*"

"Then we sail west—there is said to be a great market for African cloth in the West Indies."

"Africans do not export cloth, Jack. They import it."

"You must be mistaken—Mr. Vliet is very clear on this—we will sail to Africa and exchange our cowrie-shells for *pieces of India,* which as I'm sure you know means India cloth, and then carry it across the Atlantic . . ."

"A *piece of India* is an expression meaning a male African slave between fifteen and forty years of age," Eliza said. "India cloth—just like cowrie shells—is money in Africa, Jack, and Africans will sell other Africans for one piece of it."

Now a silence nearly as long as the one at the duc d'Arcachon's party. Jack standing on the slowly moving deck of the *God's Wounds,* Eliza on the quay.

"You are going into the slave trade," she said, in a dead voice.

"Well . . . I had no idea, until *now.*"

"I believe you. But now you have to get off that boat and walk away."

This was a superb idea, and part of Jack was thrilled by it. But the Imp of the Perverse prevailed, and Jack decided to take Eliza's suggestion in a negative and resentful spirit.

"And simply *throw away* my investment?"

"Better than throwing away your immortal soul. You threw away the ostrich plumes and the horse, Jack, I know you did—so why not do the same now?"

"This is more valuable *by far*."

"What about the other item you looted from the Grand Vizier's camp, Jack?"

"What, the sword?"

Eliza shook her head no, looked him in the eye, and waited.

"I remember that item," Jack allowed.

"Will you throw her away, too?"

"She is far more valuable, true . . ."

"*And* worth more money," Eliza put in slyly.

"You're not proposing to sell yourself—?"

Eliza went into a strange amalgam of laughing and crying. "I mean to say that I have already made more money than the plumes, sword, and horse were *worth*, and stand to make far more, soon—and so if it is money that concerns you, walk away from the *God's Wounds* and stay with me, here in Amsterdam—soon you'll forget this ship ever existed."

"It does not seem respectable—being supported by a woman."

"When in your life have *you* ever cared about *respect*?"

"Since people began to respect me."

"I am offering you safety, happiness, wealth—and *my* respect," Eliza said.

"You would not respect me for *long*. Let me take this one voyage, and get my money back, then—"

"One voyage for *you*. Eternal wretchedness for the Africans you'll buy, and their descendants."

"Either way I've lost my Eliza," Jack said with a shrug. "So that makes me something of an authority when it comes to eternal wretchedness."

"Do you want your life?"

"*This* life? Not especially."

"Get off the boat, if you want to have a life at all."

Eliza had noticed what Jack hadn't, which was that *God's Wounds* had finished being loaded. The hatch-covers were back in place, the herring was paid for (in silver coins, not cowrie-shells), and the sailors were casting off lines. Only Mr. Vliet, and Yevgeny, remained on the quay—the former haggling with an apothecary over a medicine-chest, and the latter being blessed by an outlandish Raskolnik priest in a towering hat. This scene was so curious that it diverted Jack's attention completely, until all of the sailors began to holler. Then he looked at *them*. But *they* were all looking at some apparently horrid spectacle on the quay, putting Jack suddenly in fear that ruffians, or something, were assaulting Eliza.

Jack turned around just in time to discover that Eliza had seized the harpoon, which Yevgeny had left leaning against a stack of crates, and was just in the act of launching it toward Jack. She was not, of course, a professional harpooneer, but she had the womanly knack of aiming for the heart, and so the weapon came at him straight as Truth. Jack, recalling a dim bit of sword-fighting lore from his Regimental days, twisted sideways to present a narrower target, but lost his balance and fell toward the mainmast and threw out his left arm to break his fall. The broad flukes of the harpoon made a slashing attack across the breadth of his chest and glanced off a rib, or something, so that its point struck his forearm and passed sideways through the narrow space between the two bones and buried itself in the mast—pinning him. He felt all of this before he saw it because he was looking for Eliza. But she'd already turned her back on him and was walking away, not even caring whether she had hit him or not.

Amsterdam
JUNE 1685

D'AVAUX AND A PAIR OF tall, uncommonly hard-bitten "valets" saw her to the brink of a canal, not far from the Dam, that ran westwards toward Haarlem. A vessel was tied up there, accepting passengers, and from a distance Eliza thought it a tiny one, because it had an amusing toylike look, with the stem and the stern both curved sharply upwards—giving it the profile of a fat boy doing a bold belly-flop. But as they drew closer she saw it was a large (albeit lightly built) ship, at least twenty yards long, and narrower of beam than she'd expected—a crescent moon.

"I do not mean to belabor you with tedious details—that sort of thing is the responsibility of Jacques, here, and Jean-Baptiste . . ."

"*These* are coming with me!?"

"The way to Paris is not devoid of perils, mademoiselle," d'Avaux said drily, "even for the *weak* and the *innocent*." Then he turned his head in the direction of the still lightly smoking wrack of Mr. Sluys's string of houses, only a musket-shot away along this very canal.

"Evidently you think I am *neither*," Eliza sniffed.

"Your practice of harpooning sailors along the waterfront would make it difficult for even the most *lubrique* to harbor illusions as to your true nature—"

"You've heard about that?"

"Miracle you weren't arrested—here, in a city where *kissing* someone is a misdemeanour."

"Have you had me followed, monsieur?" Eliza looked indignantly at Jacques and Jean-Baptiste, who pretended, for the time being, to be deaf and blind, and busied themselves with a cartload of rather good luggage. She'd never seen most of these bags before, but d'Avaux had implied, more than once, that they and their contents all belonged to her.

"Men will ever follow you, mademoiselle, you'd best *adapt*. In any event—setting aside the odd harpooning—in this town are certain busybodies, scolds, and *cancaniers* who insist that you were involved in the financial implosion of Mr. Sluys; the invasion fleet that sailed for England, from Texel, the other day, flying the Duke of Monmouth's colors; and the feral mob of Orangist patriots who, some say, set Mr. Sluys's dwelling afire. I, of course, do not believe in any of these nonsenses—and yet I worry about you—"

"Like a fretful uncle. Oh, how dear!"

"So. This *kaag* will take you, and your escorts—"

"Over the Haarlemmermeer to Leiden, and thence to Den Briel via the Hague."

"How did you guess?"

"The coat of arms of the City of Den Briel is carved on the taffrail, there, opposite that of Amsterdam," Eliza said, pointing up at the stern. D'Avaux turned to look, and so did Jacques and Jean-Baptiste; and in the same moment Eliza heard behind her a weird sighing, whistling noise, like a bagpipe running out of wind, and was jostled by a passing boer headed for the gangplank. As this rustic clambered up onto the *kaag* she saw his oddly familiar hump-backed profile, and caught her breath for a moment. D'Avaux turned to peer at her. Something told Eliza that this would be an awkward time to make a fuss, and so she let her mouth run: "She carries more sail than the usual canal-barge—presumably for crossing the Haarlemmermeer. She is a slender vessel, made to pass through that narrow lock between Leiden and the Hague. And yet she's too flimsy to traverse Zeeland's currents and tides—she could never afford the insurance."

"Yes," d'Avaux said, "at Den Briel you must transfer to a *more insurable* ship that will take you to Brussels." He was looking at Eliza queerly—so suspicious! The boer, meanwhile, had disappeared into the clutter of passengers and cargo on the *kaag*'s deck. "From Brussels you will travel over land to Paris," d'Avaux continued. "The inland route is less comfortable during summer—but much *safer* during an armed rebellion against the King of England."

Eliza sighed deeply, trying to hold in her mind the phant'sy of a million slaves being released from bondage. But it was a frail gauzy construction ripped apart by the strong summer-light of Amsterdam, the hard clear shapes of black buildings and white windows. "My lovely Dukie," she said, "so impetuous."

"Étienne d'Arcachon—who asks about you, by the way, in every one of his letters—suffers from a similar fault. In *his* case it is tempered by breeding and intelligence; yet he has lost a hand to a Vagabond because of it!"

"Oh, nasty Vagabonds!"

"They say he is recovering as well as can be expected."

"When I get to Paris, I'll send you news of him."

"Send me news of *everything*, especially what does not *appear* to be news," d'Avaux insisted. "If you can learn to read the comings and goings at Versailles as well as you do the taffrails and insurance-policies of Dutch boats, you'll be running France in a trice."

She kissed the cheeks of the comte d'Avaux and he kissed hers. Jacques and Jean-Baptiste escorted her up the plank and then, as the *kaag* began to drift down the canal, busied themselves storing her luggage away in the small cabin d'Avaux had procured for her. Eliza meanwhile stood at the *kaag*'s railing, along with many other passengers, and enjoyed the view of Amsterdam's canal-front. When you were on dry land in that city you could never slow down, never stop moving, and so it was strange and relaxing to be so close to it, yet so still and placid—like a low-flying angel spying on the doings of men.

Too, that she was escaping cleanly from Amsterdam, after all that had happened of late, was something akin to a miracle. D'Avaux was right to wonder why she had not been arrested for the matter of the harpoon. She had stumbled away from the scene— the Herring Packers' Tower—weeping with anger at Jack. But soon anger had been shouldered aside by fear as she'd realized she was being followed, rather obviously, by several parties at once. Looking back wouldn't've done her any good and so she'd kept walking, all the way across the Dam and then through the Exchange, which was as good a place as any to lose pursuers—or at least to remind them that they could be doing more profitable things with their time. Finally she'd gone to the Maiden and sat by a window for several hours, watching—and had seen very little. A couple of tall loiterers, whom she now knew to've been Jacques and Jean-Baptiste, and one lolling Vagabond-beggar, identifiable by his humpbacked posture and insistent hacking cough.

The *kaag* was being towed in the direction of Haarlem by a team of horses on the canal-bank, but on deck the crew were making preparations to swing her side-boards down into the water and deploy her clever folding mast, so that they could hoist a sail or two. The horses faltered as they came to a section of pavement that was broken and blackened, and ridged with trails of lead that had flowed molten from Mr. Sluys's house, and spread across the paving-stones in glowing rivers that had divided and combined as they crept toward the bank. Finally the streams of molten lead had plunged gorgeously over the stone quay and dropped into the canal, where they'd flung up a column of steam that dwarfed and enveloped the pillar of smoke from Mr. Sluys's burning houses. By that time, of course, those who'd set the fire had long since disappeared. It was up to the *drost* to interrogate the very few witnesses and to figure out whether it had really been done by infuriated Orangers, taking revenge on Sluys for backing the French, or by arsonists in the pay of Mr. Sluys. Sluys had lost so much, so fast, in the recent crash of V.O.C. stock* that his only way of getting any liquidity would have been to set fire to everything he still owned and then make claims against those who'd been rash enough to sell him insurance. This morning—three days since the fire—salvagers in the pay of those insurers were busy with pry-bars and hoists, pulling congealed rivulets and puddles of lead from the canal.

She heard that whining sound next to her again, but it suddenly crescendoed, as if a cart-wheel were rolling over that leaky bagpipe and forcing the last bit of air through its drones. Then it broke open into a croaking, hacking laugh. That humpbacked boer had taken up a spot on the *kaag*'s rail not far from Eliza, and was

---

*It dropped from 572 to 250 when word of Monmouth's rebellion spread.

watching the salvagers. "The Duke of Monmouth's rebellion has made lead a valuable commodity again," he said (Eliza could understand that much Dutch, anyway). "It's as valuable as gold."

"I beg your pardon, *meinheer,* but—though it's true the price of lead has risen—it is nowhere near as valuable as gold, or even silver." Eliza said this in stumbling Dutch.

The wheezing boer startled her by coming back in passable English. "That depends on *where you are.* An army, surrounded by the enemy, running low on balls, will happily exchange coins of gold for an equal weight of lead balls."

Eliza didn't doubt the truth of this, but it struck her as an oddly bleak point of view, and so she broke off the conversation, and spoke no more to that boer as the *kaag* passed through a water-gate in Amsterdam's western wall and entered flat Dutch countryside, diced by drainage ditches into pea-green bricks that were arrayed by the canal-side as if on a table in the market. The other passengers likewise gave the fellow a wide berth, partly because they didn't want to catch whatever was afflicting his lungs, and mostly because they tended to be prosperous mercers and farmers coming back from Amsterdam with bags of gold and silver coins; they did not want to come anywhere near a man who would contemplate using florins as projectiles. The boer seemed to understand this all too well, and spent the first couple of hours of the voyage regarding his fellow-passengers with a glum knowingness that verged on contempt, and that would have earned him a challenge to a duel in France.

Aside from that, he did nothing noteworthy until much later in the day, when, all of a sudden, he murdered Jacques and Jean-Baptiste.

It came about like this: the *kaag* sailed down the canal to Haarlem, where it stopped to pick up a few more passengers, and then it raised more sails and set out across the Haarlemmermeer, a fairly sizable lake ventilated by a stiff maritime breeze. The fresh air had an obvious effect on the boer. The pitiable wheezing and hacking stopped with miraculous speed. His ribcage no longer labored with each breath. He stood up straighter, bringing him to average height, and seemed to shed a decade or two. He now appeared to be in his mid-thirties. He lost his dour expression and, instead of lurking at the stern glowering at the other passengers, began striding round the deck almost cheerfully. By the time he'd made several laps around the deck, all the other passengers had gotten used to this, and paid him no mind—which is how he was able to walk up behind Jacques, grab both of his ankles, and pitch him overboard.

This happened so quickly, and with so little ado, that it might have been easy to believe it had never happened at all. But Jean-Baptiste believed it, and rushed at the boer with sword drawn. The boer had no sword, but the Antwerp merchant standing nearby had a perfectly serviceable one, and so the boer simply yanked it out of the owner's scabbard and then dropped neatly into a defencing stance.

Jean-Baptiste stopped to think, which probably did him no good, and much harm. Then he charged anyway. The pitching of the *kaag* ruined his attack. When he actually stumbled close enough to cross swords with the boer, it was obvious that Jean-Baptiste was the inferior swordsman—miserably so. But even setting aside these differences, the boer would have prevailed anyway, because to him, killing other men in close combat was as kneading dough was to a baker. Jean-Baptiste considered it to be an important matter, requiring certain formalities. A ring of dark windmills, ranged around the shore of the Haarlemmermeer, looked on like grim Dutch eminences, chopping the air. Rather soon, Jean-Baptiste had a couple of feet of bloody steel protruding from his back, and a jeweled hilt fixed to his chest like an awkward piece of jewelry.

That was all that Eliza was allowed to take in before the gunny sack descended over her head, and was made snug—but not tight—around her neck. Someone hugged her around the knees and lifted her feet off the deck while another caught her by the armpits. She feared, only for a moment, that she was about to be thrown overboard like Jacques (and—to judge from a booming splash audible through the gunny sack—Jean-Baptiste). As she was being carried belowdecks she heard a terse utterance in Dutch, then, all around the *kaag*, a storm of thudding and rustling: passengers' knees hitting the deck, and hats being whipped off their heads.

When the sack came off her head, she was in her little cabin with two men: a brute and an angel. The brute was a thick-set boer, who had managed the gunny sack and borne most of her weight. He was immediately dismissed and sent out by the angel: a blond Dutch gentleman, so beautiful that Eliza was more inclined to be jealous of, than attracted to, him. "Arnold Joost van Keppel," he explained curtly, "page to the Prince of Orange." He was looking at Eliza with the same coolness as she was showing him—obviously he had little interest in women. And yet rumor had it that William kept an English mistress—so perhaps he was the sort who could love *anything*.

William, Prince of Orange, Stadholder, Admiral-General, and Captain-General of the United Provinces, Burgrave of Besançon, and Duke or Count or Baron of diverse other tiny fragments of Europe,* entered the cabin a few minutes later, ruddy and unshaven, slightly blood-flecked, and, in general, looking anything but Dutch. As d'Avaux never got tired of pointing out, he was a sort of European mongrel, with ancestors from all corners of the Continent. He looked as comfortable in that rough boer's get-up as Monmouth had in Turkish silk. He was too excited and pleased with himself to sit down—which anyway would have led to a tedious welter of protocol, since there was only one place to sit in this cabin, and Eliza had no intention of vacating it. So William shooed Arnold Joost van Keppel out of the place, then braced his shoulder against a curving overhead knee-brace and remained on his feet. "My god, you're but a child—not even twenty yet? That's in your favor—it excuses your foolishness, while giving hope that you may improve."

Eliza was still too angry about the gunny sack to speak, or even to give any sign that she'd heard him.

"Don't delay writing a thank-you note to the Doctor," said William, "if it weren't for him, you'd be on a slow boat to Nagasaki."

"You are acquainted with Doctor Leibniz?"

"We met at Hanover about five years ago. I traveled there, and to Berlin—"

"Berlin?"

"A town in Brandenburg, of little significance, save that the Elector has a palace there. I have various relations among the Electors and Dukes of that part of the world—I was making the rounds, you see, trying to bring them into an alliance against France."

"Evidently, without success—?"

"*They* were willing. Most *Dutchmen* were, too—but *Amsterdam* was not. In fact, the Regents of Amsterdam were plotting with your friend d'Avaux to go over to the French so that Louis could wield their fleet against England."

"*Also* without success, or someone would've heard about it."

"I like to flatter myself that *my* efforts in northern Germany— aided to no small degree by your friend Doctor Leibniz—and

---

*E.g., Nassau, Katsenellenbogen, Dietz, Vianden, Meurs.

d'Avaux's exertions here, produced a stalemate," William announced. "I was pleased to have fared so well, and Louis was furious to have made out so poorly."

"Is that the reason he raped Orange?"

This made William of Orange very angry, which Eliza considered to be fair exchange for the gunny sack. But he mastered his rage, and answered in a tight voice: "Understand: Louis is not like us—he does not trifle with *reasons*. He *is* a reason. Which is why he must be destroyed."

"And it's *your* ambition to do the destroying?"

"Humor me, girl, by using the word 'destiny' instead of 'ambition.'"

"But you don't even have control over your own territory! Louis has Orange, and here in Holland you skulk about in disguise, for fear of French dragoons—"

"I am not here to rehearse these facts with you," William said, now much calmer. "You are right. Furthermore, I cannot dance or write poetry or entertain a company at dinner. I'm not even a particularly good general, never mind what my supporters will tell you. All I know is that nothing that opposes me endures."

"France seems to be enduring."

"But I will see to it that France's ambitions fail, and in some small way, you will help me."

"Why?"

"You should be asking *how*."

"Unlike *le Roi*, I need reasons."

William of Orange thought it was amusing that she thought she needed reasons, but killing a couple of French dragoons had put him into a playful mood. "The Doctor says you hate slavery," he offered. "Louis wants to enslave all of Christendom."

"Yet, all of Africa's great slave-forts belong to the Dutch or the English."

"Only because the duc d'Arcachon's navy is still too incompetent to take them away from us," William returned. "Sometimes in life it is necessary to do things *incrementally*, and that goes double for a Vagabond girl-child who is trying to do away with a universal institution such as slavery."

Eliza said, "How remarkable that a Prince would dress up like a farmer and go on a boat-trip only to edify a Vagabond girl-child."

"You glorify yourself. First: as you have already pointed out, I always go incognito in Amsterdam, for d'Avaux has assassins all over the city. Second: I was going back to the Hague anyway, since your lover's invasion of England has imposed certain obligations on me. Third: I have got rid of your escorts, and brought you to this cabin, not to edify you or anyone else, but to intercept the messages d'Avaux hid in your baggage."

Eliza now felt her face getting hot. William eyed her bemusedly for a few moments, and decided, perhaps, not to press his advantage. "Arnold!" he shouted. The cabin door opened. Through it, Eliza could see her things spread out all over the deck, stained with tar and bilge-water, some of the more complicated garments ripped into pieces. The luggage given to her by d'Avaux had been broken up into fragments, now being peeled apart layer by layer. "Two letters so far," Arnold said, stepping into the cabin and, with a little bow, handing over sheets covered with writing.

"Both encyphered," William observed. "No doubt he's had the wit to change over to a new code since last year."

Like a rock that had been struck by a cannon-ball, Eliza's mind split into a few large independent pieces about now. One piece understood that the existence of these letters made her a French spy in the eyes of Dutch law, and presumably gave William the right to inflict any imaginable punishment on her. Another part was busily trying to figure out what d'Avaux's plan had been (this seemed an over-elaborate way of mailing some letters!—or perhaps not?), and yet a third part seemed to be carrying on polite conversation without really thinking (maybe not such a good idea, but—). "What happened last year?"

"I had d'Avaux's *previous* dupe arrested. The messages *he* was carrying to Versailles were deciphered by my cryptologist. They had to do with all the fine things Sluys and certain Amsterdam Regents were doing on behalf of Louis."

This remark, at least, gave Eliza something to think about other than Doom and Rage. "Étienne d'Arcachon was visiting Sluys several weeks ago—but apparently *not* to discuss investments . . ."

"She stirs—the eyelids flutter—I do believe she is about to Wake Up, sire," said Arnold Joost van Keppel.

"Would you get that man out of my cabin now, please?" said Eliza to William, with evenness that surprised everyone. William made some subliminal gesture and van Keppel was gone, the door closed—though the shredding and seam-popping noises now redoubled.

"Is he going to leave me with *any* clothing *at all*?"

William considered it. "No—except for one garment—the one you are wearing now. You will sew this letter into the corset, after Arnold has made a copy. When you arrive in Paris—exhausted, dishevelled, sans escort or luggage—you'll have a magnificent tale to tell, of how the cheesemongers molested you, slew your traveling-companions, rifled your bags—and yet you'll be able to produce one letter that you cleverly secreted in your undergarments."

"It is a beautiful romance."

"It will create a sensation at Versailles—much better, for you, than if you'd showed up fresh and well-dressed. Duchesses and Countesses will pity you, instead of fearing you, and take you under their wings. It is such an excellent plan that I wonder why d'Avaux didn't come up with it himself."

"Perhaps d'Avaux never *intended* for me to find a place in the French court. Perhaps I was to deliver these messages, and then be discarded."

This remark was meant to be a self-pitying trifle. William was supposed to object vehemently. Instead he seemed to weigh it seriously—which did nothing to steady Eliza's nerves.

"Did d'Avaux introduce you to anyone?" he asked thoughtfully.

"That same Étienne d'Arcachon."

"Then d'Avaux has plans for you—and I know what they are."

"You have a smug look about you, O Prince, and I don't doubt that you have read Monsieur d'Avaux's mind, just as you'll read those letters. But since you have me at such a disadvantage, I would fain know of *your* plans for me."

"Doctor Leibniz has taught you cyphers that put these French ones quite to shame," said William, rattling d'Avaux's letter. "Use them."

"You want me to spy for you, at Versailles."

"Not only for *me* but for Sophie and all of the others who oppose Louis. For now, that's how you can be useful. Later, perhaps, I will require something else."

"*Now* I am in your power—but when I reach France, and those Duchesses begin fawning over me, I'll have all of *le Roi*'s armies and navies to protect me . . ."

"So how can I trust you, girl-child, not to tell the *entire* tale to the French, and become a double-agent?"

"Just so."

"Isn't it sufficient that Louis is repellent, and I stand for freedom?"

"Perhaps . . . but you'd be foolish if you trusted me to act accordingly . . . and I won't spy for a fool."

"Oh? You did for Monmouth."

Eliza gasped. "Sir!"

"You should not *joust* if you are afraid to be punched out of the saddle, girl-child."

"Monmouth is no scholar, admitted—but he's a fine warrior."

"He is *adequate*—but he's no John Churchill. You don't really believe he'll overthrow King James, do you?"

"I wouldn't have abetted him if I didn't think so."

William laughed very grimly. "Did he offer to make you a Duchess?"

"Why does everyone ask me that?"

"He addled your brain when he did that. Monmouth is doomed. I have six English and Scottish regiments garrisoned in the Hague, as part of a treaty with England . . . as soon as I get there, I'll send them back across the narrow seas to help put down Monmouth's rebellion."

"But why!? James is almost a *vassal* to Louis! You should be supporting Monmouth!"

"Eliza, did Monmouth skulk about Amsterdam incognito?"

"No, he cut a brave swath."

"Did he continually watch his back for French assassins?"

"No, he was carefree as a jay-bird."

"Were bombs with sputtering fuses found in his carriage?"

"No bombs—only bon-bons."

"Is d'Avaux an intelligent man?"

"Of course!"

"Then—since he must have known what Monmouth was planning—as you made it so obvious—why did he make no effort to assassinate *Monmouth?*"

Nothing from poor Eliza.

"Monmouth has landed, of all places, in Dorset—John Churchill's home ground! Churchill is riding out from London to engage him, and when that happens the rebellion will be crushed. My regiments will arrive much too late . . . I despatch them only for the sake of appearances."

"Don't you want a Protestant King of England?"

"Of course! In order to defeat Louis, I'll need Britain."

"You say it ever so casually."

"It is a simple truth." William shrugged. Then, an idea. "I rather like simple truths. Arnold!"

Once again, Arnold was in the cabin—he'd found another two letters. "Sire?"

"I need a witness."

"A witness to what, sire?"

"This girl fears that I'd be a fool to trust her, as matters stand. She is a Qwghlmian girl . . . so I'm going to make her Duchess of Qwghlm."

"But . . . Qwghlm is part of the King of England's domains, sire."

"That's just the point," William said. "This girl will be a duchess, *secretly*, and in name only, until such time as I sit upon the Throne of England . . . at which time she'll become a duchess *in fact*. So I can trust her to take my side—and she won't think I'm a fool for doing so."

"It's either this, or the slow boat to Nagasaki?" Eliza asked.

"It's not *so very* slow," Arnold said. "By the time you arrive, you should still have one or two teeth remaining."

Eliza ignored this, and kept her gaze on William's eyes. "On your knees!" he commanded.

Eliza gathered her skirts—the only intact clothes she had left—rose from her chair, and fell to her knees in front of the Prince of Orange, who said: "You cannot be ennobled without a ceremony that demonstrates your submission to your new liege-lord. This has been the tradition since ancient times."

Arnold drew a small-sword from its sheath and held it out in both hands, making it available to the Prince; but not without striking several braces, bulkheads, and items of furniture with elbows, hilt, sword-tip, *et cetera*, for the cabin was tiny and crowded. The Prince watched with sour amusement. "Sometimes the lord taps the vassal on the shoulder with his sword," he allowed, "but there is no room in here to wield such a weapon safely; besides, I am trying to make a Duchess here, not a Knight."

"Would you prefer a dagger, my lord?" Arnold asked.

"Yes," said the Prince, "but don't concern yourself with it, I have one handy." Whereupon he peeled his belt open with a quick movement of the hand, and dropped his breeches. A hitherto concealed weapon popped up into view, so close to Eliza's face that she could feel its heat. It was neither the longest nor the shortest such blade she had ever seen. She was pleased to note that it was clean—a Dutch virtue—and well-maintained. It oscillated with the beating of the Prince's heart.

"If you are going to tap me on the shoulder with that, you are going to have to step a bit closer, my lord," Eliza said, "for, as splendid as it is, it does not compete with the other for length."

"On the contrary, you shall have to approach closer to me," said the Prince. "And as you know perfectly well, it is not your shoulder that I am aiming for: neither the left one, nor the right, but a softer and more welcoming berth in between. Do not feign ignorance, I know your history, and that you learned this and many other practices in the *Harim* of the Sultan."

"There, I was a slave. Here, it is how I become a Duchess?"

"As it was with Monmouth, and as it shall be in France, so it is here and now," William said agreeably. His hand came down on the top of her head, and grabbed a handful of hair. "Perhaps you can teach Arnold a trick or two. Arnold, witness carefully." William pulled Eliza forward. Eliza's eyes clenched shut. What was about to happen wasn't so very bad, in and of itself; but she couldn't stand to have that other man watching.

"There now," the Prince said, "ignore *him*. Open your eyes, and stare into mine, boldly, as befits a Duchess."

Coast of Europe and of Northern Africa
1685

And Midas joyes our Spanish journeys give,
We touch all gold, but find no food to live.
And I should be in the hott parching clyme,
To dust and ashes turn'd before my time.
To mew me in a Ship, is to inthrall
Mee in a prison, that weare like to fall;
Or in a Cloyster; save that there men dwell
In a calme heaven, here in a swaggering hell.
Long voyages are long consumptions,
And ships are carts for executions.
Yea they are Deaths; Is't not all one to flye
Into an other World, as t'is to dye?
—JOHN DONNE, "Elegie XX: Loves Warre"

JACK SOBBED FOR THE FIRST time since he'd been a boy, and brother Dick had been pulled up, all stiff and white, from the Thames.

The crew was not especially surprised. The moment of a ship's departure was commonly a time for the colorful venting of emotions, and that went double or triple for young women being left behind at dockside. Mr. Vliet was obviously worried that it would lead to some kind of legal ensnarements, and fled over the plank onto the ship, followed shortly by the duly blessed and sacramentalized Yevgeny. *God's Wounds* cast off without any ceremonies and skulked out of the harbor into the Ijsselmeer, where the sails were raised to drive her through ragged, swelling seas. Yevgeny came and planted a giant mukluk against the mast and pulled his harpoon out of it, and of Jack's arm, muttering in what sounded like embarrassment. One of the crew, who was said to have some experience as a barber-surgeon, stoked up the galley-fire to heat some irons. As Jack had been slashed deeply across the chest, as well as pierced through the forearm, there was much cauterizing to be done. Half the ship's crew, it seemed, sat on Jack to make him be still while the irons were applied, reheated, applied, reheated, seemingly all the way across the Ijsselmeer. At the beginning of this interminable cattle-branding, Jack screamed for mercy. Some of the men who were sitting on him looked disgusted and some looked amused, but none looked merciful—which made sense when Jack recalled he was on a slaver-ship. So after that he just screamed until he lost his voice and could hear only the wet sizzle of his own flesh.

When it was done, Jack sat, wrapped in blankets, out on the bowsprit, as sort of a Vagabond-wretch-figurehead, and smoked a pipe that Yevgeny had brought him. Queerly, he felt nothing at all. Big merchant ships, locked into huge air-filled boxes to lift them higher in the water, were being towed over the sand-banks, which were all cluttered with old spidery wrecks. Beyond that, the rhythm of the ocean subtly changed, as before a play, when a frilly overture gives way to the booming music of a Tragedy or History. It got darker and palpably colder, and those ships were set free from their boxes, and began to spread cloth before the wind, like canvasmerchants displaying their wares to an important buyer. The offerings were grudgingly accepted—the sails filled with air, became taut and smooth, and the ships accelerated toward the sea. Later, they came to Texel, and all the sailors paused in their chores to view the immense Ships of the Line of the Dutch Navy riding on the huge waves of the North Sea, their flags and banners swirling like colored smoke-clouds and their triple gun-decks frowning at England.

Then finally they were at sea, bringing a certain kind of solace to Jack, who felt that he must be a condemned man, now, on every scrap of dry land in the world. They put in briefly at Dunkirk to recruit a few more hands. His brother Bob came out to visit Jack, who was in no condition to leave the ship, and they exchanged a few stories, which Jack forgot immediately. This last encounter with his brother was like a dream, a sweeping-together of fragments, and he heard someone telling Bob that Jack was not in his right mind.

Then south. Off St.-Malo they were overhauled and boarded by French privateers, who only laughed when they learned of the worthless cargo, and let them go with only token pilfering. But one of these Frenchmen, as he left the deck of *God's Wounds*, walked up to Mr. Vliet, who cringed. And in response to that cringing, more than anything else, the privateer slapped the Dutchman on the side of the head so hard that he fell down.

Even with his mind impaired in several ways, Jack understood that this action was more damaging to his investment than if the French had fired a broadside of cannonballs through their hull. The sailors became more surly after that, and Mr. Vliet began to spend most of his time closeted in his wardroom. The only thing that kept *God's Wounds* from becoming an ongoing mutiny was Mr. Foot, who (with Yevgeny as his muscle) became the real captain of the ship after that, stepping easily into the role, as if his twenty-year hiatus tending bar at the Bomb & Grapnel had never happened.

Following the coast, they rounded the various capes of Brittany and then steered a southwesterly rhumb-line across the Bay of Biscay, coming in view of the Galician coast after a number of anxious days. Jack did not really share in the anxiety because his wounds had become infected. Between the fevers, and the relentless bleedings meted out by the ship's barber to cure them, he lacked the faintest idea of where they were, and sometimes even forgot he was aboard ship. Mr. Vliet refused to move from the best wardroom, which was probably a savvy position for him to take, as there was sentiment among the crew for tossing him overboard. But he was the only man on the ship who knew how to navigate. So Jack was tucked into a hammock belowdecks, peering up day after day at blue needles of light between the deck-planks, hearing little but the merry clink of cowrie-shells being sifted to and fro by the ship's pitching and rolling.

When he finally got well enough to come abovedecks again, it was hot, and the sun was higher in the sky than he'd ever seen it. He was informed that they had, for a time, dropped anchor in the harbor of Lisbon, and since moved on. Jack regretted missing that, for there was said to be a very great Vagabond-camp outside that city, and if he'd managed to slip away, he might be on dry land again, reigning as Vagabond-king. But that was only the crack-pated phant'sy of a condemned man chained by the neck to a wall, and he soon made himself forget it.

According to Mr. Vliet, who spent hours taking measurements with a backstaff and making laborious calculations with numbers and tables, they had passed through the latitude of Gibraltar, and so the land they glimpsed off to port from time to time was Africa. But the Slave Coast was yet far, far to the south, and many weeks of sailing lay ahead of them.

But he was wrong about that. Later on the same day there was a commotion from the lookouts, and coming abovedecks Jack and the others saw two strange vessels approaching from abaft, seeming to crawl across the water on countless spindly legs. These were galleys, the typical warships of the Barbary Corsairs. Mr. Vliet watched them through his spyglass for a time, making certain geometrickal calculations on a slate. Then he commenced vomiting, and retreated to his cabin. Mr. Foot broke open some chests and began to pass out rusty cutlasses and blunderbusses.

"But why fight for cowrie-shells?" one of the English sailors asked. "It'll be just like the Frenchies at St.-Malo."

"They are not hunting us for what is in our hold," Mr. Foot explained. "Do you think *free* men would pull oars like that?"

Now Jack was not the first or last man aboard *God's Wounds* to question the wisdom of nailing their colors to the mast, but when he understood that those Barbary Corsairs intended to make galley-slaves out of them, his view changed. As when powder-smoke is driven away from a battle by a sea-breeze, he saw with clarity that he would die that day. He saw also that the arrival of the corsairs was fortunate for him, since his death was not long in coming *anyway,* and better to die in fighting for his liberty, than in scheming to take away some other man's.

So he went down belowdecks and opened up his sea-chest and took out his Janissary-sword in its gaudy sheath, and brought it up abovedecks. The crew had formed up into a few distinct clusters, obviously the beginnings of mutinous conspiracies. Jack climbed up onto the prow of a longboat that was lashed to the deck, and from there vaulted up onto the roof of a pilot-house that stood just aft of the foremast. From this height, he had a view up and down the length of *God's Wounds* and was struck (as usual) by what a narrow sliver of a thing she was. And yet she, or any other European cargo-vessel, was a wallowing pig compared to those galleys, which slid over the top of the water like Dutch ice-skates hissing over the top of a frozen canal. They had enormous saffron-colored triangular sails to drive them forward as well as the oars, and they were approaching in single file from directly astern, so that *God's Wounds*'s few paltry cannon could not fire a broadside. There was a single swivel-gun astern that might have pelted the lead galley with a tangerine-sized cannonball or two, but the men near it were arguing, instead of loading the weapon.

"What a world!" Jack hollered.

Most everyone looked at him.

"Year after year at home, chopping wood and drawing water and going to church, nothing to divert us save the odd hailstorm or famine—and yet all a man need do is board ship and ride the wind for a few days, and what've you got? Barbary Corsairs and pirate-galleys off the coast of Morocco! Now, Mr. Vliet, he has no taste for adventure. But as for myself, I would rather cross swords with corsairs than pull oars for them—so I'm for fighting!" Jack pulled out the Janissary-sword, which, compared to Mr. Foot's pitted relics, burnt and glittered beneath the African sun. Then he flung the scabbard away. It *fup-fup-fupped* off to port and then stopped in midair and dove vertically into the waves. "*This* is the only thing they're going to get from Half-Cocked Jack!"

This actually wrung a cheer from the approximately half of the crew who'd made up their minds to fight anyway. The other half only looked embarrassed on Jack's behalf. "Easy for you to say—everyone knows you're dying," said one of the latter group, one Henry Flatt, who until this moment had been on easy terms with Jack.

"And yet I'll live longer'n *you*," Jack said, then jumped down from the pilot-house and began to approach Flatt—who stood and watched dumbly at first, perhaps not aware that all of his fellows had fled to other parts of the ship. When Jack drew closer, and turned sideways, and bent his knees, and showed Flatt the edge of his blade, Flatt went *en garde* for just a moment, then seemed to come to his senses, backpedaled several yards, then simply turned and ran. Jack could hear men laughing—satisfying in a way, but, on second thought, vexing. This was serious work, not play-acting. The only way to make these half-wits understand that weighty matters were at stake was probably to kill someone. So Jack cornered Flatt up at the bow, and pursued him, actually, out onto the very bowsprit, weaving and dodging around the points of the inner jib, the outer jib, and the flying jib, all of which were quivering and snapping in the wind as no one was paying attention to keeping them trimmed. Finally the wretch Flatt was perched on the tip of the bowsprit, gripping the last available line* to keep from being tossed away by the routine pitching of the ship. With the other hand he raised a cutlass in a feeble

---

*The flying jib downhaul.

threat. "Be killed now by a Christian or in ten minutes by a heathen—it's all one to me—but if you choose to be a slave, your life is worthless, and I'll flick you into the ocean like a turd," Jack said.

"I'll fight," Flatt said. Jack could see plainly that he was lying. But everyone was watching now—not just the crew of *God's Wounds,* but a startlingly large crowd of armed men who had emerged onto the decks of the galleys. Jack had to observe proper form. So he made a great show of turning his back on Henry Flatt, and began to work his way back down the bowsprit, with the intent of whirling around and striking Flatt down when Flatt inevitably came after him. In fact, he was just about to do so when he saw Mr. Foot swinging his cutlass at a taut line that had been made fast to a pinrail at the bow: the sheet that held the obtuse corner of the flying jib, and transferred all of its power into the frame of the ship. The jib went slack above him. Jack dove, and grabbed at a line. He heard a sort of immense metallic fart as the shivering canvas wrapped around Flatt like a shroud, held him for a moment, and then dropped him into the sea, where he was immediately driven under by the onrushing hull.

Jack nearly fell overboard himself, as he ended up dangling by a rope with one hand, maintaining a grip on the sword with the other—but Yevgeny's big hand seized his forearm and hauled him up to safety.

That is, if *this* could be considered safety: the two galleys, which until now had been idling along in single file, had, during the dispute with Flatt, forked apart so that they could come up on both flanks of *God's Wounds* at the same time. For some minutes it had been possible to hear, from those galleys, a faint musick: an eerie chaunt sung by many voices, in a strange keening melody, that, somewhat like an Irish tune, struck Jack's English ears as being Not from Around Here. Though, come to think of it, it probably *was* from around here. Anyway, it was a strange alien melody sung in some barbarous tongue. And until very recently, it had been sung slowly, as the crashing of the galleys' many oar-blades into the brine had served as the drum-beat marking the time.

But now that the galleys had got themselves sorted out into parallel courses, they emitted a sudden fusillade of snapping noises— Jack thought, some sort of outlandish gunfire. Immediately the singing grew louder. Jack could just make out the heathen syllables:

Havah nagilah, Havah nagilah, Havah nagilah, v'nism'chah!
Havah nagilah, Havah nagilah, Havah nagilah, v'nism'chah.

"It is like the bagpipes of the Scots," he announced, "a sort of shrill noise that they make before battle, to cover the sound of their knees knocking together."

One or two men laughed. But even these were shushed by others, who were now listening intently to the song of the corsairs. Rather than proceeding to a steady beat, as good Christian music always did, it seemed to be getting faster.

Uru, uru achim
Uru achim b'lev sa me ach!
Uru achim b'lev sa me ach!
Uru achim b'lev sa me ach!
Uru achim b'lev sa me ach!
Havah nagilah . . .

It was most certainly getting faster; and as the oars bit into the water on each beat of the song, this meant that they were now *rowing* as well as *singing* faster. And indeed the gap between the bow of the foremost galley, and the stern of *God's Wounds,* was getting rapidly narrower.

Uru, uru achim
Uru achim b'lev sa me ach!
Uru achim b'lev sa me ach!
Uru achim b'lev sa me ach!
Uru achim b'lev sa me ach!
Havah nagilah.
Havah nagilah, Havah nagilah, Havah nagilah, v'nism'chah!
Havah nagilah, Havah nagilah, Havah nagilah, v'nism'chah.

The corsairs were singing and rowing with abandon now, easily coming up along both flanks, maintaining just enough distance to give their oars the freedom to claw at the waves. Even not counting the unseen oar-slaves, the number of men aboard was insane, reckless, as if a whole pirate-city had crowded into each galley.

The one to port came alongside soonest, its sails and rigging struck and furled for the attack, its rail, and the poop deck, crowded with corsairs, many of them swinging grappling-hooks on the ends of ropes, others brandishing boarding-ladders with vicious curved spikes on the ends. Jack—and all of the others aboard *God's Wounds*—saw, and understood, the same thing at the same time. They *saw* that almost none of the fighting men were

Arabs except for the *agha* shouting the orders. They were, instead, white men, black Africans, even a few Indians. They *understood* that all of them were Janissaries, which is to say non-Turks who did the Turks' fighting for them.

Having understood *that,* they would not be slow to grasp that becoming a Barbary Corsair might, for men such as them, constitute a fine opportunity.

Jack, being half a step quicker than the average sea-scum, understood this a moment sooner than anyone else, and decided that he would blurt it out, so that everyone would think it had been his idea. He picked up a grappling-hook and coil of rope that had been rattling around in the bottom of the weapons-chest, and returned to his former podium atop the pilot-house, and hollered, "All right! Who's for turning Turk?"

A lusty cheer came up from the crew. It seemed to be unanimous, with the single exception of Yevgeny, who as usual had no idea what was being said. While the others were all shaking hands and congratulating one another, Jack clenched his sword in his teeth, tossed the rope-coil over his shoulder, and began ascending the ladderlike web of rigging—the fore shrouds, so called—that converged on the fore-top: a platform about halfway up the mast. Reaching it, he jammed the point of the sword into the planking, and regarded the galleys from above. The singing had sped up into a frenzy now, and the movements of the oars were beginning to get into disarray, as not all of the slaves could move their implements fast enough!

Uru, uru achim
Uru achim b'lev sa me ach!
Uru achim b'lev sa me ach!
Uru achim b'lev sa me ach!
Uru achim b'lev sa me ach!
Havah nagilah . . .

Uru achim b'lev sa me ach
Uru achim b'lev sa me ach
Uru achim b'lev sa me ach
Uru achim b'lev sa me ach

Both of the galleys had moved half a length ahead of *God's Wounds* now. Upon a signal from one of the *aghas,* both suddenly folded their oars and steered inwards, falling back and converging on *God's Wounds*. The oar-slaves collapsed onto their benches, and the only thing that kept all of them from landing flat on their backs was that they were packed into the hull too tightly to lie down.

"You men are only seeing the turbans and jewels and polished weapons of the Janissaries!" Jack hollered. "I can see the slaves pulling the oars now—she's a coffin packed with half-dead wretches. Did you hear those snapping noises before? 'Twas not gunfire—'twas the long bullwhips of the slave-drivers! I see a hundred men with fresh stripes torn from their backs, slumped over their oars. We'll all be slaves in half an hour's time—unless we show the *agha* that we know how to fight, and deserve to be Janissaries instead!"

As Jack was delivering this oration, he was laying his rope-coil out on the planking of the fore-top, so it would unfurl cleanly. A grappling-hook flung from the rail of the port galley nearly struck him in the face. Jack ducked and shrugged. It bit into the planking at his feet, which popped and groaned as some Janissary put his weight on the attached line. Jack jerked his sword loose and chopped through it, sending a corsair down to be crushed between the converging hulls of the two ships.

The engagement, which had been miraculously quiet—almost serene—until now, became a cacophony of booms as the Barbary pirates fired all of their guns. Then it became silent again, as no one would have time to reload before it was all over. Jack's view below was temporarily clouded by smoke. He was looking almost level across to the port galley's tall mainmast, which had a narrow crow's nest near the top. It was an obvious target for a grappling-hook and indeed Jack snagged it on the first throw—then, pulling the slack out of the line, was almost torn off the fore-top as the ships rocked in opposite directions and their masts suddenly spread apart. Jack decided to construe this as an opportunity, and quickly wrapped the rope round his left forearm several times. The next movement of the ships ripped him off the fore-top, putting a few thousand splinters into his abdomen, and sent him plunging into space. The rope broke his fall, by nearly pulling his arm off. He whizzed across the middle of the galley in an instant, seeing just a blur of crimson and saffron, and a moment later found himself hanging out over the blue ocean, ponderously changing direction. Looking back the way he'd just come, and was shortly to go again, he saw a few non-combatants staring back at him curiously—including one of those slave-drivers. When Jack's next pendulum-swing took him back over the galley's deck, he reached out with the sword and cut that man's head in two. But the impact of sword on skull sent him spinning round, out of control. Flailing, he swung back over the deck of *God's Wounds* and slammed into the base of the foremast hard enough to knock the wind out of his lungs and make him let go of the rope. He slid to the deck and looked around at a number of men's legs—but not legs he recognized. The whole ship was covered with Janissaries, and Jack was the only one who'd done any fighting at all.

The one exception to that rule was Yevgeny, who had got the gist of Jack's stirring first speech, but not understood the more pragmatic second one. Accordingly, he had harpooned the *rais*, or captain of the starboard galley, right through the throrax.

This and other statistics of the battle (such as it was) were conveyed to Jack by Mr. Foot later, after they had been stripped of all clothes and possessions and moved onto a galley, where a blacksmith was stoking up his forge and making ready to weld fetters around narrow parts of their bodies.

The corsairs rifled the holds of *God's Wounds* in all of about fifteen minutes, and obviously lacked enthusiasm for the cowrie shells. The only captive who wasn't transferred to a galley was Mr. Vliet, who had been ferreted out of the bilge, where he had concealed himself. The Dutchman was brought up abovedecks, stripped naked, and tied over a barrel. An African was roundly fucking him now.

"What was all that nonsense you were raving from the fore-top?" Mr. Foot asked. "No one could understand a word you were saying. We were all just looking at each other—" Mr. Foot pantomimed a bewildered shrug.

"That you'd all better show what magnificent fighters you were," Jack summarized, "or else they'd have you chained up straight off."

"Hmph," Mr. Foot said, too diplomatic to point out that it hadn't worked in Jack's case. Though a few discreet winks from some of the bleeding sunburned wretches told Jack that his partial decapitation of that one slave-driver might make him as popular among galley-slaves as he'd formerly been among Vagabonds.

"Why should you care?" Mr. Foot asked a few minutes later, as the anal violation of his erstwhile business partner showed no sign of coming to a climax any time soon. The barrel supporting Mr. Vliet had slowly worked its way across the deck of *God's Wounds* until it lodged against a rail, and was now booming like a drum. "You're not long for this world anyway."

"If you ever visit Paris, you can take this question up with St.-George, *mort-aux-rats*," Jack said. "He taught me a few things about correct form. I have a reputation, you know—"

"So they say."

"I hoped that you, or one of the *younger* men, might show some valor, and become a Janissary, and one day make his way back to Christendom, and tell the tale of my deeds 'gainst the Barbary Corsairs. So that all would know how my story came out, and that it came out well. That's all."

"Well, next time enunciate," Mr. Foot said, "because we literally could not make out a word you were saying."

"Yes, yes," Jack snapped—hoping he would not be chained to the same oar as Mr. Foot, who was already becoming a bore. He sighed. "That is one prodigious butt-fucking!" he marveled. "Like something out of the Bible!"

"There's no butt-fucking in the Good Book!" said the scandalized Mr. Foot.

"Well, how should I know?" Jack said. "Back off! Soon, I'll be in a place where everyone reads the Bible all the time."

"Heaven?"

"Does it sound like heaven to you?"

"Well, it appears they are leading me off to a different oar, Jack," Mr. Foot said. Indeed, a dead man was being cut loose from an oar at the stern, and Mr. Foot was being signalled for. "So if we never speak again—as seems likely—Godspeed!"

"Godspeed? *Godspeed!* What kind of a thing is that to say to a fucking *galley slave?*" were Jack's last words, or so he supposed, to Mr. Foot.

Mr. Vliet was being pushed overboard by a couple of Janissaries. Jack heard the splash just as he was sitting down on the shit-stained bench where he would row until he died.

BOOK THREE

Odalisque

In all times kings, and persons of sovereign
authority, because of their independency, are in
continual jealousies, and in the state and posture
of gladiators; having their weapons pointing, and
their eyes fixed on one another; that is, their
forts, garrisons, and guns upon the frontiers of
their kingdoms; and continual spies upon their
neighbors; which is a posture of war.

—HOBBES, *Leviathan*

✣

Whitehall Palace

⚱

LIKE A HORSEMAN WHO REINS in a wild stallion that has borne him, will he, nill he, across several counties; or a ship's captain who, after scudding before a gale through a bad night, hoists sail, and gets underway once more, navigating through unfamiliar seas— thus Dr. Daniel Waterhouse, *anno domini* 1685, watching King Charles II die at Whitehall Palace.

Much had *happened* in the previous twelve years, but nothing was really *different*. Daniel's world had been like a piece of *caout- chouc* that stretched but did not rupture, and never changed its true shape. After he'd gotten his Doctorate, there'd been nothing for him at Cambridge save lecturing to empty rooms, tutoring dull courtiers' sons, and watching Isaac recede further into the murk, pursuing his quest for the Philosophic Mercury and his occult studies of the Book of Revelation and the Temple of Solomon. So Daniel had moved to London, where events went by him like musket-balls.

John Comstock's ruin, his moving out of his house, and his with-drawal from the Presidency of the Royal Society had seemed epochal at the time. Yet within weeks Thomas More Anglesey had not only been elected President of the Royal Society but also bought and moved into Comstock's house—the finest in London, royal palaces included. The upright, conservative arch-Anglican had been replaced with a florid Papist, but nothing was really dif-ferent—which taught Daniel that the world was full of powerful men but as long as they played the same roles, they were as inter-changeable as second-rate players speaking the same lines in the same theatre on different nights.

All of the things that had been seeded in 1672 and 1673 had spent the next dozen years growing up into trees: some noble and well-formed, some curiously gnarled, and some struck down by lightning. Knott Bolstrood had died in exile. His son Gomer now lived in Holland. Other Bolstroods had gone over the sea to New England. This was all because Knott had attempted to indict Nell Gwyn as a prostitute in 1679, which had seemed sensational at the time. The older King Charles II had grown, the more frightened London had become of a return to Popery when his brother James ascended to the throne, and the more the King had needed to keep a nasty bleak Protestant—a Bolstrood—around to reassure them. But the more power Bolstrood acquired, the more he was able to whip people up against the Duke of York and Popery. Late in 1678, they'd gotten so whipped up that they'd commenced hanging Catholics for being part of a supposed Popish Plot. When they'd begun running low on Catholics, they had hanged Protestants for doubting that such a Plot existed.

By this point Anglesey's sons Louis, the Earl of Upnor, and Philip, Count Sheerness, had gambled away most of the family's capital anyway, and had little to lose except their creditors, so they had fled to France. Roger Comstock—who had been ennobled, and was now the Marquis of Ravenscar—had bought Anglesey (formerly Comstock) House. Instead of moving in, he had torn it down, plowed its gardens under, and begun turning it into "the finest piazza in Europe." But this was merely Waterhouse Square done bigger and better. Raleigh had died in 1678, but Sterling had stepped into his place just as easily as Anglesey had stepped into John Comstock's, and he and the Marquis of Ravenscar had set about doing the same old things with more capital and fewer mistakes.

The King had dissolved Parliament so that it could not murder any more of his Catholic friends, and had sent James off to the Spanish Netherlands on the "out of sight, out of mind" principle, and, for good measure, had gotten James's daughter Mary wedded to the Protestant Defender himself: William of Orange. And in case none of that sufficed, the Duke of Monmouth (who was Protestant) had been encouraged to parade around the country, tantalizing England with the possibility that he might be de-bastardized through some genealogical sleight-of-hand, and become heir to the throne.

King Charles II could still dazzle, entertain, and confuse, in other words. But his alchemical researches beneath the Privy Gallery had come to naught; he could not make gold out of lead. And he could not levy taxes without a Parliament. The surviving goldsmiths in Threadneedle Street, and Sir Richard Apthorp in his new Bank, had been in no mood to lend him anything. Louis XIV had given Charles a lot of gold, but in the end the Sun King turned out to be no different from any other exasperated rich in-law: he had begun finding ways to make Charles suffer in lieu of paying interest. So the King had been forced to convene Parliament. When he had, he had found that it was controlled by a City of London/friends of Bolstrood alliance (Foes of Arbitrary Government, as they styled themselves) and that the first item on their list had been, not to raise taxes, but rather to exclude James (and every other Catholic) from the throne. This Parliament had instantly become so unpopular with those who loved the King that the whole assembly—wigs, wool-sacks, and all—had had to move up to Oxford to be safe from London mobs whipped up by Sir Roger L'Estrange—who'd given up trying to suppress others' libels, and begun printing up his own. Safe (or so they imagined) at Oxford, these Whigs (as L'Estrange libelled them) had voted for Exclusion, and cheered for Knott Bolstrood as he proclaimed Nellie a whore.

A crier marching up Piccadilly had related this news to Daniel as he and Robert Hooke had stood in what had once been Comstock's and then Anglesey's ballroom and was by that point a field of Italian marble rubble open to a fine blue October sky. As a work table they had been using the capital of a Corinthian column that had plunged to earth when the column had been jerked out from under it by Ravenscar's merry Irish demolition men. The capital had half-embedded itself in the soil and now rested at a convenient angle; Hooke and Waterhouse had unrolled large sheets and weighed down the corners with stray bits of marble: tips of angels' wings and shards of acanthus leaves. These were surveyor's plats laying out Ravenscar's scheme to embed a few square blocks of Cartesian rationality on the pot-bound root-ball that was the London street system. Surveyors and their apprentices had stretched cords and hammered in stakes plotting the axes of three short parallel streets that, according to Roger, would sport the finest shops in London: one was labeled Anglesey, one Comstock, and one Ravenscar. But that afternoon, Roger had showed up, armed with an inky quill, and scratched out those names and written in their stead Northumbria,* Richmond,† and St. Alban's.‡

A month after that there'd been no Parliament and no more Bolstroods in Britain. James had come home from exile, Monmouth

---

*The Duke of Northumbria was the bastard son of Charles II by his mistress Barbara Palmer, *nee* Villiers, Duchess of Castlemaine.

†The Duke of Richmond was the bastard son of Charles II by his mistress Louise de Kéroualle, Duchess of Portsmouth.

‡The Duke of St. Alban's was the bastard son of Charles II by his mistress Nell Gwyn, the nubile comedienne and apple-woman.

had been removed from the King's service, and England had become, effectively, a department of France, with King Charles openly accepting a hundred thousand pounds a year, and most of the politicians in London—Whigs and Tories alike—receiving bribes from the Sun King as well. Quite a few Catholics who'd been tossed into the Tower for supposed involvement in the Popish Plot had been released, making room for as many Protestants who had supposedly been involved in a Rye House Plot to put Monmouth on the throne. Just like many Popish Plotters before them, these had promptly begun to "commit suicide" in the Tower. One had even managed the heroic feat of cutting his own throat all the way to the vertebrae!

So Wilkins's work had been undone, at least for a while. Thirteen hundred Quakers, Barkers, and other Dissenters had been clapped into prison. Thus had Daniel spent a few months in a smelly place listening to angry men sing the same hymns he'd been taught as a boy by Drake.

It had been—in other words—a reign. Charles II's reign. He was the King, he loved France and hated Puritans and was always long on mistresses and short on money, and nothing ever really changed.

Now Dr. Waterhouse was standing on the King's Privy Stairs: a rude wooden platform clinging to a sheer vertical wall of limestone blocks that plunged straight into the Thames. All of the Palace buildings that fronted on the river were built this way, so as he gazed downriver, keeping watch for the boat that carried the chirurgeons, he found himself sighting down a long, continuous, if somewhat motley wall, interrupted by the occasional window or mock bastion. Three hundred feet downstream, a dock was thrust out into the river, and several intrepid watermen were walking to and fro on it in the lock-kneed gait of men trying to avoid freezing to death. Their boats were tied up alongside, awaiting passengers, but the hour was late, the weather cold, the King was dying, and no Londoners were availing themselves of the old right-of-way that ran through the Palace.

Beyond that dock, the river curved slowly around to the right, towards London Bridge. As the midday twilight had faded to an ashy afternoon, Daniel had seen a boat shove off from the Old Swan: a tavern at the northern end of the bridge that drew its clientele from those who did not like to gamble their lives by penetrating its turbulent arches. The boat had been struggling upstream ever since, and it was close enough now that, with the aid of the spyglass in Daniel's pocket, he could see it carried only two passengers.

Daniel had been remembering the night in 1670 when he'd come to Whitehall in Pepys's carriage, and wandered around the Privy Garden trying to act natural. At the time he'd thought it was cheeky and romantic, but now, remembering that he had ever been that fatuous made him grind his teeth, and thank God that the only witness had been Cromwell's severed head.

Recently he had spent a lot of time at Whitehall. The King had decided to relax his grip just a bit, and had begun letting a few Barkers and Quakers out of prison, and had decided to nominate Daniel as a sort of unofficial secretary for all matters having to do with mad Puritans: Knott Bolstrood's successor, that is, with all the same burdens, but much less power. Of Whitehall's two thousand or so rooms, Daniel had probably set foot in a few hundred—enough to know that it was a dirty, mildewed jumble, like the map of the inside of a courtier's mind, a slum in all but name. Whole sections had been taken over by the King's pack of semi-feral spaniels, who'd become inbred even by Royal standards and thus hare-brained even by Spaniel standards. Whitehall Palace was, in the end, a House: the house of a Family. It was a very strange old family. As of one week ago Daniel had already been somewhat better acquainted with that Family than anyone in his right mind would *want* to be. And *now,* Daniel was waiting here on the Privy Stairs only as an excuse to get out of the King's bedchamber—nay, his very *bed*—and to breathe some air that did not smell like the royal body fluids.

After a while the Marquis of Ravenscar came out and joined him. Roger Comstock—the least promising, and so far the most successful, of the men Daniel had gone to Cambridge with—had been in the north when the King had fallen ill on Monday. He was overseeing the construction of his manor house, which Daniel had designed for him. The news must've taken a day or two to reach him, and he must've set out immediately: it was now Thursday evening. Roger was still in his traveling-clothes, looking more drab than Daniel had ever seen him—almost Puritanical.

"My lord."

"Dr. Waterhouse."

From the expression on Roger's face, Daniel knew that he had stopped by the King's bedchamber first. In case there was any doubt of that, Roger tucked the long skirts of his coat behind him, clambered down onto both knees, bent forward, and threw up into the Thames.

"Will you please excuse me."

"Just like College days."

"I didn't imagine that a man could contain so many fluids and whatnot in his entire body!"

Daniel nodded toward the approaching boat. "Soon you'll witness fresh marvels."

"I could see from looking at His Majesty that the physicians have been quite busy?"

"They have done their utmost to hasten the King's departure from this world."

"Daniel! Lower your voice, I say," Roger huffed. "Some may not understand your sense of humor—if that is the correct word for it."

"Funny you should bring up the subject of Humours. It all began with an apoplectical fit on Monday. The King, hardy creature that he is, might've recovered—save that a Doctor happened to be in the very room, armed with a full complement of lancets!"

"Ugh! Worse luck!"

"Out came a blade—the Doctor found a vein—the King bade farewell to a pint or two of the Humour of Passion. But of course, he's always had plenty of that to go round—so he lived on through Tuesday, and had the strength to fend off the gathering swarm of Doctors on into yesterday. Then, alas, he fell into an epileptical fit, and all of the Doctors burst in at once. They'd been camped in his anterooms, arguing as to which humours, and how much of 'em, needed to be removed. After going for a whole night and a day without sleep, a sort of competition had arisen among them as to who advocated the most heroic measures. When the King—after a valorous struggle—finally lost his senses, and could no longer keep 'em at bay, they fell on him like hounds. The Doctor who had been insisting that the King suffered from an excess of blood, had his lancet buried in the King's left jugular before the others had even unpacked their bags. A prodigious quantity of blood spewed forth—"

"I believe I saw it."

"Stay, I'm only beginning. The Doctor who had diagnosed an excess of *bile*, now pointed out that said imbalance had only been worsened by the loss of so much *blood*, and so he and a pair of bulky assistants sat the King up in bed, hauled his mouth open, and began tickling his gorge with diverse feathers, scraps of whalebone, *et cetera*. Vomiting ensued. Now, a third Doctor, who had been insisting, most tiresomely, that all the King's problems were owed to an accumulation of *colonic* humours, rolled his Majesty over and shoved a prodigious long-necked calabash up the Royal Anus. In went a mysterious, very expensive fluid—out came—"

"Yes."

"Now a fourth Doctor set to work cupping him all over to draw out other poisons through the skin—hence those gargantuan hickeys, ringed by circular burns. The *first* doctor was now in a panic, seeing that the adjustments made by the *other* three had led to an excess of blood—it being all *relative,* you know. So he opened the *other* jugular, promising to let out just a little. But he let out quite a bit. The other doctors became indignant now, and demanded the right to repeat all of *their* treatments. But here's where I stepped in, and, exercising—some would say, abusing—my full authority as Secretary of the Royal Society, recommended a purging of *Doctors* rather than *humours* and kicked them out of the bedchamber. Threats were made against my reputation and my life, but I ejected them anon."

"But I heard news, as I came into London, that he was on the mend."

"After the Sons of Asclepius were finished with him, he did not really move for a full twenty-four hours. Some might've construed this as sleeping. He lacked the strength to pitch a fit—some might call it recovery. Occasionally I'd hold an ice-cold mirror in front of his lips and the reflection of the King's face would haze. In the middle of the day today, he began to stir and groan."

"His Majesty can scarcely be blamed for *that!*" Roger said indignantly.

"Nevertheless, more physicians got to him, and diagnosed a fever. They gave him a royal dose of the Elixir Proprietalis LeFebure."

"Now that must've improved the King's mood *to no end!*"

"We can only speculate. He has gotten worse. The sorts of Doctors who prescribe powders and elixirs have, consequently, fallen from favor, and the bleeders and purgers are upon us!"

"Then I'll add my weight as President, to yours as Secretary, of the Royal Society, and we'll see how long we can keep the lancets in their sheathes."

"Interesting point you raise there, Roger. . . ."

"Oh, Daniel, you have got that Waterhousian brooding look about you now, and so I fear you do not mean a *literal* point, as in *lancets*—"

"I was thinking—"

"Help!" Roger cried, waving his arms. But the watermen on yonder dock had all turned their backs on the Privy Stairs to watch the approach of the boat carrying those chirurgeons.

"D'you recall when Enoch Root made phosphorus from horse

urine? And the Earl of Upnor made a fool of himself supposing that it must have come from *royal* piss?"

"I'm *terrified* that you're about to say something *banal*, Daniel, about how the King's blood, bile, *et cetera* are no different from *yours*. So is it all right with you if I just *stipulate* that Republicanism makes *perfect sense*, seems to work well in Holland, and thereby *exempt* myself from this part of the conversation?"

"That is not precisely where I was going," Daniel demurred. "I was thinking about how easily your cousin was replaced with Anglesey—how disappointingly little difference it made."

"Before you corner yourself, Daniel, and force me to drag you out *as usual*, I would discourage any further usage of this similitude."

"Which similitude?"

"You are about to say that Charles is like Comstock and James is like Anglesey and that it will make no difference, in the end, which one is king. Which would be a dangerous thing for you to say— because the House where Comstock and Anglesey lived has been *razed* and *paved over*." Roger jerked his head upwards towards Whitehall. "Which is not a fate we would wish on *yonder* house."

"But that is not what I was saying!"

"What were you saying, then? Something *not* obvious?"

"As Anglesey replaced Comstock, and Sterling replaced Raleigh, I replaced Bolstrood, in a way . . ."

"Yes, Dr. Waterhouse, we live in an orderly society and men replace each other."

"*Sometimes*. But some *can't* be replaced."

"I don't know that I agree."

"Suppose that, God forbid, Newton died. Who would replace him?"

"Hooke, or maybe Leibniz."

"But Hooke and Leibniz are *different*. I put it to you that some men really have unique qualities and cannot be replaced."

"Newtons come along so rarely. He is an exception to any rule you might care to name—really a very cheap rhetorical tactic on your part, Daniel. Have you considered running for Parliament?"

"Then I should have used a different example, for the point I'm wanting to make is that all round us, in markets and smithys, in Parliament, in the City, in churches and coal-mines, there are persons whose departure really *would* change things."

"Why? What makes these persons different?"

"It is a very profound question. Recently Leibniz has been refining his system of metaphysics—"

"Wake me up when you are finished."

"When I first saw him at Lion Quay these many years ago, he was showing off his knowledge of London, though he'd never been here before. He'd been studying views of the city drawn by diverse artists from differing points of view. He went off on a rant about how the city itself has one form but it is perceived in different ways by each person in it, depending on their unique situation."

"Every *sophomore* thinks this."

"That was more than a dozen years ago. In his *latest* letter to me he seems to be leaning towards the view that the city does *not* have one absolute form *at all* . . ."

"Obvious nonsense."

". . . that the city is, in some sense, the result of the sum total of the perceptions of it by all of its constituents."

"I knew we never should have let him into the Royal Society!"

"I am not explaining it very well," Daniel admitted, "because I do not quite understand it, yet."

"Then why are you belaboring me with it *now* of all times?"

"The salient point has to do with perceptions, and how different parts of the world—different souls—perceive all of the other parts—the other souls. Some souls have perceptions that are confused and indistinct, as if they are peering through poorly ground lenses. Whereas others are like Hooke peering through his Microscope or Newton through his Reflecting Telescope. They have superior perceptions."

"Because they have better opticks!"

"No, even without lenses and parabolic mirrors, Newton and Hooke see things that you and I don't. Leibniz is proposing a strange inversion of what we normally mean when we describe a man as distinguished, or unique. Normally when we say these things, we mean that the man himself stands out from a crowd in some way. But Leibniz is saying that such a man's uniqueness is rooted in his ability to perceive *the rest of the universe* with unusual clarity—to distinguish one thing from another more effectively than ordinary souls."

Roger sighed. "All I know is that Dr. Leibniz has been saying some very rude things about Descartes lately—"

"Yes, in his *Brevis Demonstratio Erroris Memorabilis Cartesii et Aliorum Circa Legem Naturalem*—"

"And the French are up in arms."

"You said, Roger, that you would add your weight as President, to mine as Secretary, of the Royal Society."

"And I shall."

"But you flatter me by saying so. Some men *are* interchangeable, yes. Those two chirurgeons could be replaced with any other two, and the King would still die this evening. But could I—could *anyone*—fill *your* shoes so easily, Roger?"

"Why, Daniel, I do believe this is the first time in your life you've actually exhibited something akin to *respect* for me!"

"You are a man of parts, Roger."

"I am touched and of course I agree with the point you were trying to make—whatever the hell it might have been."

"Good—I am pleased to hear you agree with me in believing that James is no replacement for Charles."

Before Roger could recover—but after he mastered his anger—the boat was in earshot and the conversation, therefore, over.

"Long live the King, m'Lord, and *Doctor* Waterhouse," said one Dr. Hammond, clambering over the boat's gunwale onto the Privy Stairs. Then they all had to say it.

Hammond was followed by Dr. Griffin, who *also* greeted them with "Long live the King!" which meant that they all had to say it *again*.

Daniel must have said it with a noticeable lack of enthusiasm, for Dr. Hammond gave him a sharp look—then turned toward Dr. Griffin as if trolling for eyewitnesses. "It is very good that you have come in time, m'Lord," said Hammond to Roger Comstock, "as, between Jesuits on the one hand, and Puritans on t'other" (squirting long jets of glowing vitriol out of the pupils of his eyes, here, at Daniel), "some would say the King has had enough of bad advice."

Now Roger tended to say things after long pauses. When he'd been a clownish sizar at Trinity, this had made him seem not very intelligent; but now that he was a Marquis, and President of the Royal Society, it made him seem exceedingly sober and grave. So after they'd all climbed up the steps to the balcony that led into the part of Whitehall called the King's Apartments, he said: "A King's *mind* should never want for the counsel of learned *or* pious men, just as his *body* should never want for a bountiful supply of the diverse *humours* that sustain life and health."

Waving an arm at the shambling Palace above them, Dr. Hammond said to Roger, "This place is such a bazaar of rumor and intrigue, that your presence, m'Lord, will go far towards quelling any *whisperings* should the worst happen which Almighty God forbid." Favoring Daniel with another fearsome over-the-shoulder glare, as he followed the Marquis of Ravenscar into the King's Apartments.

"It sounds as if *some* have already gone far beyond *whispering*," Daniel said.

"I'm certain that Dr. Hammond is solely concerned with pre-serving *your* reputation, Dr. Waterhouse," Roger said.

"What—it's been nigh on twenty years since His Majesty blew up my father—do people suppose I am still nursing a grudge?"

"That's not it, Daniel—"

"On the contrary! Father's departure from this plane was so brisk, so hot—leaving behind no physical remains—that it has been a sort of balm to my spirit to sit up with the King, night after night, imbrued in the royal gore, breathing it into my lungs, sop-ping it up with my flesh, and many other enjoyments besides, that I missed out on when my Father ascended . . ."

The Marquis of Ravenscar and the two other Doctors had slowed almost to a standstill and were now exchanging deeply sig-nificant looks. "Yes," Roger finally said, after another grand pause, "too much sitting up, in such a fœtid atmosphere, is not healthful for one's body, mind, or spirit . . . perhaps an evening's rest is in order, Daniel, so that when these two good Doctors have restored the King to health, you'll be ready to offer his Majesty your con-gratulations, as well as to re-affirm the profound loyalty you har-bor, and have always harbored, in your breast, notwithstanding those events of two decades hence, which some would say have already been alluded to more than enough . . ."

He did not finish this sentence for a quarter of an hour. Before putting it to a merciful death, he'd managed to work in several enco-niums for both Drs. Hammond and Griffin, likening one to Ascle-pius and the other to Hippocrates, while not failing to make any number of cautiously favorable remarks about every other Doctor who had come within a hundred yards of the King during the last month. He also (as Daniel noted, with a kind of admiration) was able to make it clear, to all present, just what a morbid catastrophe it would be if the King died and turned England over into the hands of that mad Papist the Duke of York whilst, practically in the same phrases—with the same *words*—asserting that York was really such a splendid fellow that it was almost imperative that all of them rush straight-away to the King's Bedchamber and smother Charles II under a mattress. In a sort of recursive fugue of dependent clauses he was, similarly, able to proclaim Drake Waterhouse to've been the finest Englishman who'd ever boiled beef whilst affirm-ing that blowing him up with a ton of gunpowder had been an absolute touchstone of (depending on how you looked at it) monarchical genius that made Charles II such a colossal figure, (or) rampant despotism that augured so favorably for his brother's reign.

All of this as Daniel and the physicians trailed behind Roger through the leads, halls, galleries, antechambers, and chapels of Whitehall, rupturing stuck doors with shoulder-thrusts and beating back tons of dusty hangings. The Palace must have been but a single building at some point, but no one knew which bit had been put up first; anyway, other buildings had been scabbed onto that first one as fast as stones and mortar could be ferried in, and galleries strung like clothes-lines between wings of it that were deemed too far apart; this created courtyards that were, in time, subdivided, and encroached upon by new additions, and filled in. Then the builders had turned their ingenuity to bricking up old openings, and chipping out new ones, then bricking up the new ones and re-opening the old, or making newer ones yet. In any event, every closet, hall, and room was claimed by one nest or sect of courtiers, just as every snatch of Germany had its own Baron. Their journey from the Privy Stairs to the King's Bedchamber would, therefore, have been fraught with difficult border-crossings and protocol disputes if they'd made it in silence. But as the Marquis of Ravenscar was leading them surely through the maze, he went on, and on, with his Oration, a feat akin to threading needles while galloping on horseback through a wine cellar. Daniel lost track of the number of claques and cabals they burst in on, greeted, and left behind; but he did notice a lot of Catholics about, and more than a few Jesuits. Their route took them in a sort of jagged arc circumventing the Queen's Apartments, which had been turned into a sort of Portuguese nunnery quite a long time ago, furnished with prayer-books and ghastly devotional objects; yet it buzzed with its own conspiracies. Whenever they spied a door ajar, they heard brisk steps approaching it from the opposite side and saw it slammed and locked in their faces. They passed by the King's little chapel, which had been turned into a base-camp for this Catholic invasion, which didn't really surprise Daniel but would have ignited riots over nine-tenths of England had it been widely known.

Finally they arrived at the door to the King's Bedchamber, and Roger startled them all by finishing his sentence. He somehow contrived to separate Daniel from the physicians, and spoke briefly to the latter before showing them in to see the patient.

"What'd you tell them?" Daniel asked, when the Marquis came back.

"That if they unsheathed their lancets, I'd have their testicles for tennis-balls," Roger said. "I have an errand for you, Daniel: go to the Duke of York and report on his brother's condition."

Daniel took a breath, and held it. He could scarcely believe, all of a sudden, how tired he was. "I could say something obvious here, such as that *anyone* could do that, and *most* would do it better than *I,* and then you'd answer with something that'd make me feel a bit dim, such as—"

"In our concern for the *previous* king we must not forget to maintain good relations with the *next.*"

" 'We' meaning—in this case—?"

"Why, the Royal Society!" said Roger, miffed to have been asked.

"Righto. What shall I tell him?"

"That London's finest physicians have arrived—so it shouldn't be much longer."

HE MIGHT HAVE SHIELDED HIMSELF from the cold and the wind by walking up the length of the Privy Gallery, but he'd had quite enough of Whitehall, so instead he went outside, crossed a couple of courts, and emerged at the front of the Banqueting House, directly beneath where Charles I had had his head lopped off, lo these many years ago. Cromwell's men had kept him prisoner in St. James's and then walked him across the Park for his decapitation. Four-year-old Daniel, sitting on Drake's shoulders in the plaza, had watched every one of the King's steps.

This evening, thirty-nine-year-old Daniel would be retracing that King's final walk—except backwards.

Now, Drake, twenty years ago, would have been the first to admit that most of Cromwell's work had been rolled back by the Restoration. But at least Charles II was a Protestant—or had the decency to pretend to be one. So Daniel oughtn't to make too much of an omen out of this walk—God forbid he should start thinking like Isaac, and find occult symbols in every little thing. But he couldn't help imagining that time was being rolled back even farther now, even past the reign of Elizabeth, all the way back to the days of Bloody Mary. In those days John Waterhouse, Drake's grandfather, had fled over the sea to Geneva, which was a hornets' nest of Calvinists. Only after Elizabeth was on the throne had he returned, accompanied by his son Calvin—Drake's father—and many other English and Scottish men who thought the way he did about religion.

In any event, now here was Daniel crossing the old Tilt Yard and descending the stairs into St. James's Park, going to fetch the man who had all the earmarks of the next Bloody Mary. James, the Duke of York, had lived at Whitehall Palace with the King and Queen until the tendency of Englishmen to riot and burn large objects in the streets at the least mention of his name had given the

King the idea to pack him off to places like Brussels and Edin-burgh. Since then he'd been a political comet, spending almost all of his time patrolling the liminal dusk, occasionally swooping back to London and scaring the hell out of everyone until the blaze of bonfires and burning Catholic churches drove him off into the darkness. After the King had finally lost patience, suspended Par-liament, kicked out all the Bolstroods, and thrown the remaining Dissenters into jail, James had been suffered to come back and set-tle his household—but at St. James's Palace.

From Whitehall it was five minutes' walk across several gardens, parks, and malls. Most of the big old trees had been uprooted by the Devil's Wind that had swept over England on the day Cromwell had died. As a lad wandering up and down Pall Mall handing out libels, Daniel had watched new saplings being planted. He was dis-mayed, now, to see how large some of them had grown.

In spring and summer, royals and courtiers wore ruts in the paths that wound between these trees, going out for strolls that had become ritualized into processions. Now the terrain was empty, an unreadable clutter of brown and gray: a crust of frozen mud float-ing on a deep miasma of bog and horse-manure. Daniel's boots kept breaking through and plunging him into the muck. He learned to avoid stepping near the crescent-shaped indentations that had been made a few hours ago by the hooves of John Churchill's regiment of Guards drilling and parading on this ground, galloping hither and yon and cutting the heads off of straw men with sabers. Those straw men had not been dressed up as Whigs and Dissenters, but even so the message had been clear enough, for Daniel and for the crowds of Londoners gathered along the limit of Charing Cross burning bonfires for their King.

One Nahum Tate had recently translated into English a hundred-and-fifty-year-old poem by the Veronese astronomer Hieronymus Fracastorius, entitled (in the original) *Syphilis, Sive Morbvs Gallicvs* or (as Tate had it) *"Syphilis: or, a poetical history of the French Disease."* Either way, the poem told the tale of a shepherd named Syphilus who (like all shepherds in old myths) suffered a miserable and perfectly undeserved fate: he was the first person to be struck down by the disease that now bore his name. Inquiring minds might wonder why Mr. Tate had troubled himself to trans-late, at this moment, a poem about a poxy shepherd that had lan-guished in Latin for a century and a half without any Englishman's feeling its lack: a poem about a disease, by an astronomer! Certain Londoners of a cynical turn of mind believed that the answer to this riddle might be found in certain uncanny similarities between the eponymous shepherd and James, the Duke of York. Viz. that all of said Duke's lovers, mistresses, and wives ended up with the said pestilence; that his first wife, Anne Hyde, had apparently died of it; that Anne Hyde's daughers, Mary and Anne, both had difficulties with their eyes, and with their wombs; that the Duke had obvious sores on his face and that he was either unbelievably stupid or out of his fucking mind.

Now (as Daniel the Natural Philosopher understood only too well) people had a habit of over-burdening explanations, and to do so was a bad habit—a kind of superstition. And yet the parallels between Syphilus the Shepherd and James the Heir to the English Throne were hard to ignore—and as if that weren't enough, Sir Roger L'Estrange had recently been leaning on Nahum Tate, asking him to perhaps find some *other* mildewy old Latin poems to translate. And everyone *knew* that L'Estrange was doing so, and understood why.

James was Catholic, and wanted to be a Saint, and that all fit together because he had been born in the Palace *of St. James's* some fifty-two years ago. It had always been his true home. In his tender years he'd been taught princely rudiments in this yard: fencing and French. He had been spirited up to Oxford during the Civil War, and more or less raised himself from that point on. Occasionally Dad would swing by and swoop him up and take him off to some battle-front to get creamed by Oliver Cromwell.

James had spent quite a bit of time hanging about with his cousins, the offspring of his aunt Elizabeth (the Winter Queen), a fecund but hapless alternate branch of the family. When the Civil War had been lost, he'd gone back to St. James's and lived there as a pampered hostage, wandering about this park and mounting the occasional boyish escape attempt, complete with encyphered letters spirited out to loyal confederates. One of those letters had been intercepted, and John Wilkins had been called in to decypher it, and Parliament had threatened to send James off to live in the decidedly less hospitable Tower. Eventually he'd slipped out across this park, disguised himself as a girl, and fled down the river and across the sea to Holland. Therefore he'd been out of the country when his father had been marched across this park to have his head lopped off. As the English Civil War had slowly ground to a halt, James had grown into a man, bouncing around between Holland, the Island of Jersey, and St. Germain (a royal suburb of Paris) and busying himself with the princely pastimes of riding, shooting, and screwing high-born Frenchwomen. But as Cromwell had continued to crush the Royalists at every turn, not only in

England but Ireland and France as well, James had finally run out of money and become a soldier—a rather good one—under Marshal Turenne, the incomparable French general.

AS HE TRUDGED ALONG Daniel occasionally swiveled his head to gaze north across Pall Mall. The view was different every time, as per the observations of Dr. Leibniz. But when the parallax of the streets was just right, he could see between the bonfires built there by nervous Protestants, up the lengths of the streets-named-after-royal-bastards, and all the way up to the squares where Roger Comstock and Sterling Waterhouse were putting up new houses and shops. Some of the larger ones were being made with great blocks of stone taken from the rubble of John Comstock's house—blocks that Comstock, in turn, had salvaged from the collapsed south transept of Old St. Paul's. Lights were burning in windows up there, and smoke drifting from chimneys. Mostly it was the mineral smoke of coal, but on the north wind Daniel caught the occasional whiff of roasting meat. Crunching and squelching across this wasted park, stepping over stuffed heads that had been lopped from straw men a few hours before, had given Daniel his appetite back. He wanted to be up there with a tankard in one hand and a drumstick in the other—but here he was, doing the sort of thing that he did. Which was what, exactly?

St. James's Palace was getting close, and he really ought to have an answer before he got there.

AT SOME POINT CROMWELL HAD, improbably, formed an alliance with the French, and then young James had had to go north to an impoverished, lonely, boring existence in the Spanish Netherlands. In the final years before the Restoration he'd knocked about Flanders with a motley army of exiled Irish, Scottish, and English regiments, picking fights with Cromwell's forces around Dunkirk. After the Restoration he'd come into his hereditary title of Lord High Admiral, and taken part in some rousing and bloody naval engagements against the Dutch.

However: the tendency of his siblings to die young, and the failure of his brother Charles to produce a legitimate heir, had made James the only hope for continuance of his mother's bloodline. While Mother had been living a good life in France, her sister-in-law, the Winter Queen, had been kicked around Europe like a stuffed pig's bladder at a county fair. Yet Elizabeth had pumped out babies with inhuman efficiency and Europe was bestrewn with her offspring. Many had come to naught, but her daughter Sophie seemed to have bred true, and was carrying on the tradition with seven surviving children. So, in the royal propagation sweepstakes, Henrietta Maria of France, the mother of James and Charles, seemed to be losing, in the long run, to the miserable Winter Queen. James was her only hope. And consequently, during James's various adventures she had used all of her wiles and connexions to keep him out of danger—leaving James with a simmering feeling of never having destroyed as many armies or sunk as many fleets as he *could* have.

Stymied, he'd spent much of the time since about 1670 doing—what, exactly? Mining Africa for gold, and, when that failed, Negroes. Trying to persuade English noblemen to convert to Catholicism. Sojourning in Brussels, and then in Edinburgh, where he had made himself useful by riding out to wild parts of Scotland to suppress feral Presbyterians in their rustic conventicles. Really he had been wasting his time, just waiting.

Just like Daniel.

A dozen years had flown by, dragging him along like a rider with one foot caught in the stirrup.

What did it mean? That he had best take matters in hand and get his life in order. Find something to do with his allotted years. He had been too much like Drake, waiting for some Apocalypse that would never come.

The prospect of James on the throne, working hand-in-glove with Louis XIV, was just sickening. This was an emergency, every bit as pressing as when London had burnt.

The realizations just kept coming—or rather they'd all appeared in his mind at once, like Athena jumping out of his skull in full armor, and he was merely trying to sort them out.

Emergencies called for stern, even desperate measures, such as blowing up houses with kegs of gunpowder (as King Charles II had personally done) or flooding half of Holland to keep the French out (as William of Orange had done). Or—dare he think it—overthrowing Kings and chopping their heads off as Drake had helped to. Men such as Charles and William and Drake seemed to take such measures without hesitation, while Daniel was either (a) a miserably pusillanimous wretch or (b) wisely biding his time.

Maybe this was why God and Drake had brought him into this world: to play some pivotal role in this, the final struggle between the Whore of Babylon, a.k.a. the Roman Catholic Church, and Free Trade, Freedom of Conscience, Limited Government, and diverse other good Anglo-Saxon virtues, which was going to commence in about ten minutes.

> Romanists now swarming at Court with greater
> confidence than had ever been seen since the
> Reformation.
>
> — *John Evelyn's Diary*

ALL OF THESE THOUGHTS terrified him so profoundly as to nearly bring him to his knees before the entrance of St. James's Palace. This wouldn't have been as embarrassing as it sounded; the courtiers circulating in and out of the doors, and the Grenadier Guards washing their hands in the blue, wind-whipped flames of torchières, probably would have pegged him as another mad Puritan taken in a Pentecostal fit. However, Daniel remained on his feet and slogged up stairs and into the Palace. He made muddy footprints on the polished stone: making a mess of things as he went and leaving abundant evidence, which seemed a poor beginning for a conspirator.

St. James's was roomier than the suite in Whitehall where James had formerly dwelt, and (as Daniel only now apprehended) this had given him the space and privacy to gather his own personal Court, which could simply be marched across the Park and swapped for Charles's at the drop of a crown. They'd seemed a queer swarm of religious cultists and second-raters. Daniel now cursed himself for not having paid closer attention to them. *Some* of them were players who'd end up performing the same roles and prattling the same dialogue as the ones they were about to replace, but (if Daniel's ruminations on the Privy Stairs were not completely baseless) *others* had unique perceptions. It would be wise for Daniel to identify these.

As he worked his way into the Palace he began to see fewer Grenadier Guards and more shapely green ankles scissoring back and forth beneath flouncing skirts. James had five principal mistresses, including a Countess and a Duchess, and seven secondary mistresses, typically Merry Widows of Important Dead Men. Most of them were Maids of Honour, i.e., members of the ducal household, therefore entitled to loiter around St. James's all they wanted. Daniel, who made a sporting effort to keep track of these things, and who could easily list the King's mistresses from memory, had entirely lost track of the Duke's. But it was known empirically that the Duke would pursue any young woman who wore green stockings, which made it much easier to sort things out around St. James's, just by staring at ankles.

From the mistresses he could learn nothing, at least, until he learned their names and gave them further study. What of the courtiers? Some could be described exhaustively by saying "courtier" or "senseless fop," but others had to be known and understood in the full variety of their perceptions. Daniel recoiled from the sight of a fellow who, if he had not been clad in the raiments of a French nobleman, might have been taken for a shakerag. His head seemed to have been made in some ghastly Royal Society experiment by taking two different men's heads and dividing them along the centerline and grafting the mismatched halves together. He jerked frequently to one side as if the head-halves were fighting a dispute over what they should be looking at. From time to time the argument would reach some impasse and he'd stand frozen and mute for a few seconds, mouth open and tongue exploring the room. Then he'd blink and resume speaking again, rambling in accented English to a younger officer—John Churchill.

The better half of this strange Frenchman's head looked to be between forty and fifty years of age. He was Louis de Duras, a nephew of Marshal Turenne but a naturalized Englishman. He had, by marrying the right Englishwoman and raising a lot of revenue for Charles, acquired the titles Baron Throwley, Viscount Sondes, and the Earl of Feversham. Feversham (as he was generally called) was Lord of the Bedchamber to King Charles II, which meant that he really ought to have been over in Whitehall just now. His failure to be there might be seen as proof that he was grossly incompetent. But he was also a Commander of Horse Guards. This gave him an excuse for being here, since James, as a highly unpopular but healthy king-to-be, needed a lot more guarding than Charles, a generally popular king at death's door.

Around a corner and into another hall, this one so chilly that steam was coming from people's mouths as they talked. Daniel caught sight of Pepys and veered towards him. But then a wind-gust, leaking through an ill-fitting window-frame, blew a cloud of vapor away from the face of the man Pepys was talking to. It was Jeffreys. His beautiful eyes, now trapped in a bloated and ruddy face, fixed upon Daniel, who felt for a moment like a small mammal paralyzed by a serpent's hypnotic glare. But Daniel had the good sense to look the other way and duck through an opportune doorway into a gallery that connected several of the Duke's private chambers.

Mary Beatrice d'Este, a.k.a. Mary of Modena—James's second wife—would be sequestered back in these depths somewhere, presumably half out of her mind with misery. Daniel tried not to think of what it would be like for her: an Italian princess raised midway between Florence, Venice, and Genoa, and now stuck *here, forever,* surrounded by the mistresses of her syphilitic husband, surrounded in turn by Protestants, surrounded in turn by cold water, her only purpose in life to generate a male child so that a Catholic could succeed to the throne, but her womb barren so far.

Looking quite a bit more cheerful than that was Catherine Sedley, Countess of Dorchester, who'd been rich to begin with and had now secured her pension by producing two of James's innumerable bastard sons. She was not an attractive woman, she was not Catholic, and she hadn't even bothered to pull on green stockings—yet she had some mysterious unspecified hold over James exceeding that of any of his other mistresses. She was strolling down the gallery *tête-à-tête* with a Jesuit: Father Petre, who among other duties was responsible for bringing up all of James's bastards to be good Catholics. Daniel caught a moment of genuine amusement on Miss Sedley's face and guessed that the Jesuit was relating some story about her boys' antics. In this windowless gallery, lit feebly by some candles, Daniel could not have been more than a dim apparition to them—a pale face and a lot of dark clothing—a Puritan Will-o'-the-wisp, the sort of bad memory that forever haunted the jumpy Royals who'd survived the Civil War. The affectionate smiles were replaced by alert looks in his direction: was this an invited guest, or a Phanatique, a *hashishin?* Daniel was grotesquely out of place. But his years at Trinity had made him accustomed to it. He bowed to the Countess of Dorchester and exchanged some sort of acrid greeting with Father Petre. These people did not like him, did not want him here, would never be friendly to him in any sense that counted. And yet there was a symmetry here that unnerved him. He'd seen wary curiosity on their faces, then recognition, and now polite masks had fallen over their covert thoughts as they wondered why he was here, and tried to fit Daniel Waterhouse into some larger picture.

But if Daniel had held a mirror up to his own face he'd have seen just the same evolution.

He was one of them. Not as powerful, not as highly ranked—in fact, completely unranked—but he was *here, now,* and for these people that was the only sort of rank that amounted to anything. To be here, to smell the place, to bow to the mistresses, was a sort of initiation. Drake would have said that merely to set foot in such people's houses and show them common courtesy was to be complicit in their whole system of power. Daniel and most others had scoffed at such rantings. But now he knew it was true, for when the Countess had acknowledged his presence and known his name,

Daniel had felt important. Drake—if he'd had a grave—would have rolled over in it. But Drake's grave was the air above London.

An ancient ceiling beam popped as the Palace was hit by another gust.

The Countess was favoring Daniel with a knowing smile. Daniel had had a mistress, and Miss Sedley knew it: the incomparable Tess Charter, who had died of smallpox five years ago. Now he *didn't* have a mistress, and Catherine Sedley probably knew *that,* too.

He had slowed almost to a stop. Steps rushed toward him from behind and he cringed, expecting a hand on his shoulder, but two courtiers, then two more—including Pepys—divided around him as if he were a stone in a stream, then converged on a large Gothic door whose wood had turned as gray as the sky. Some protocol of knocking, throat-clearing, and doorknob-rattling got underway. The door was opened from inside, its hinges groaning like a sick man.

St. James's was in better upkeep than Whitehall, but still just a big old house. It was quite a bit shabbier than Comstock/Anglesey House. But that House had been brought down. And what had brought it down had not been revolution, but the movings of markets. The Comstocks and Angleseys had been ruined, not by lead balls, but by golden coins. The neighborhood that had been built upon the ruins of their great House was now crowded with men whose vaults were well-stocked with that kind of ammunition.

To mobilize those forces, all that was needed was some of that kingly ability to decide, and to act.

He was being beckoned forward. Pepys stepped toward him, holding out one hand as if to take Daniel's elbow. If Daniel were a Duke, Pepys would be offering sage advice to him right now.

"What should I say?" Daniel asked.

Pepys answered immediately, as if he'd been practicing the answer for three weeks in front of a mirror. "Don't fret so much over the fact that the Duke loathes and fears Puritans, Daniel. Think instead of those men that the Duke loves: Generals and Popes."

"All right, Mr. Pepys, I am thinking of them . . . and it is doing me no good."

"True, Roger may have sent you here as a sacrificial lamb, and the Duke may see you as an assassin. If he does, then any attempt you make to sweeten and dissemble will be taken the wrong way. Besides, you're no good at it."

"So . . . if my head's to be removed, I should go lay my head on the chopping-block like a man . . ."

"Belt out a hymn or two! Kiss Jack Ketch and forgive him in advance. Show these fops what you're made of."

"Do you *really* think Roger sent me here to . . ."

"Of course not, Daniel! I was being *jocular.*"

"But there is a certain tradition of killing the messenger."

"Hard as it might be for you to believe, the Duke admires certain things about Puritans: their sobriety, their reserve, their flinty toughness. He saw Cromwell fight, Daniel! He saw Cromwell mow down a generation of Court fops. He has not forgotten it."

"What, you're suggesting I'm to emulate *Cromwell* now!?"

"Emulate *anything* but a courtier," said Samuel Pepys, now gripping Daniel's arm and practically shoving him through the doorway.

Daniel Waterhouse was now in the Presence of James, the Duke of York.

The Duke was wearing a blond wig. He had always been pale-skinned and doe-eyed, which had made him a bonny youth, but a somewhat misshapen and ghastly adult. A dim circle of courtiers ringed them, hemming into their expensive sleeves and shuffling their feet. The occasional spur jingled.

Daniel bowed. James seemed not to notice. They looked at each other for a few moments. Charles would already have made some witty remark by this point, broken the ice, let Daniel know where he stood, but James only looked at Daniel expectantly.

"How is my brother, Dr. Waterhouse?" James asked.

Daniel realized, from the way he asked it, that James had no idea just how sick his brother really was. James had a temper; everyone knew it; no one had the courage to tell him the truth.

"Your brother will be dead in an hour," Daniel announced.

Like a barrel's staves being drawn together in a cooper's shop, the ring of courtiers tensed and drew inwards.

"He has taken a turn for the worse, then!?" James exclaimed.

"He has been at death's door the whole time."

"Why was this never said plainly to me until this instant?"

The correct answer, most likely, was that it *had* been, and he simply hadn't gotten it; but no one could say this.

"I have no idea," Daniel answered.

Roger Comstock, Samuel Pepys, and Daniel Waterhouse were in the antechamber at Whitehall.

"He said, 'I am surrounded by men who are afraid to speak truth to my face.' He said, 'I am not as complicated as my brother—not complicated enough to be a king.' He said, 'I need your help and I know it.'"

"He said all of that!?" Roger blurted.

"Of course not," Pepys scoffed, "but he *meant* it."

The antechamber had two doors. One led to London, and half of London seemed to be gathered on the other side of it. The other door led to the King's bedchamber, where, surrounding the bed of the dying monarch, were James, Duke of York; the Duchess of Portsmouth, who was Charles's primary mistress; Father Huddlestone, a Catholic priest; and Louis de Duras, the Earl of Feversham.

"What else did he say?" Roger demanded. "Or more to the point, what else did he *mean*?"

"He is dim and stiff, and so he needs someone clever and flexible. Apparently I have a reputation for being both."

"Splendid!" Roger exclaimed, showing a bit more merriment than was really appropriate in these circumstances. "You have Mr. Pepys to thank for it—the Duke trusts Mr. Pepys, and Mr. Pepys has been saying good things about you."

"Thank you, Mr. Pepys . . ."

"You're welcome, Dr. Waterhouse!"

". . . for telling the Duke that I have a cowardly willingness to bend my principles."

"As much as it offends me to tell such beastly lies about you, Daniel, I'm willing to do it, as a personal favor to a good friend," Pepys answered instantly.

Roger ignored this exchange, and said: "Did his royal highness ask you for any advice?"

"I told him, as we trudged across the park, that this is a Protestant country, and that he belongs to a religious minority. He was astounded."

"It must have come as a grievous shock to him."

"I suggested that he turn his syphilitic dementia into an asset—it shows off his humane side while providing an excuse for some of his behavior."

"You didn't really say that!"

"Dr. Waterhouse was just seeing if you were paying attention, m'Lord," Pepys explained.

"He told me he had syphilis twenty years ago at Epsom," Daniel said, "and the secret—it was a secret in those days—did not get out *immediately*. Perhaps this is why he trusts me."

Roger had no interest whatever in such old news. His eyes were trained to the opposite corner of the room, where Father Petre was shoulder-to-shoulder with Barrillon, the French Ambassador.

One of the doors opened. Beyond it, a dead man was lying in a stained bed. Father Huddlestone was making the sign of the cross, working his way through the closing stanzas of the rite of extreme unction. The Duchess of Portsmouth was weeping into a hanky and the Duke of York—no, the King of England—was praying into clasped hands.

The Earl of Feversham tottered out and steadied himself against the doorjamb. He looked neither happy nor sad, but vaguely lost. This man was now Commander in Chief of the Army. Paul Barrillon had a look on his face as if he were sucking on a chocolate truffle and didn't want anyone to know. Samuel Pepys, Roger Comstock, and Daniel Waterhouse shared an uneasy look.

"M'Lord? What news?" Pepys said.

"What? Oh! The King is dead," Feversham announced. His eyes closed and he leaned his head on his upraised arm for a moment, as if taking a brief nap.

"Long live . . ." Pepys prompted him.

Feversham awoke. "Long live the King!"

"Long live the King!" everyone said.

Father Huddlestone finished the rite and turned towards the door. Roger Comstock chose that moment to cross himself.

"Didn't know you were Catholic, m'lord," Daniel said.

"Shut up, Daniel! You know I'm a Freedom of Conscience man—have I ever troubled you about *your* religion?" said the Marquis of Ravenscar.

Versailles
SUMMER 1685

For the market is against our sex just now; and if a young woman has beauty, birth, breeding, wit, sense, manners, modesty, and all to an extreme, yet if she has not money she's nobody, she had as good want them all; nothing but money now recommends a woman; the men play the game all into their own hands.

—DANIEL DEFOE, *Moll Flanders*

To M. le comte d'Avaux
12 July 1685
Monseigneur,

As you see I have encyphered this letter according to your instructions, though only you know whether this is to protect it from the eyes of Dutch spies, or your rivals at Court. Yes, I have discovered that you have rivals.

On my journey I was waylaid and ill-used by some typically coarse, thick Dutchmen. Though you would never have guessed it from their looks and manners, these had something in common with the King of France's brother: namely, a fascination with women's undergarments. For they went through my baggage thoroughly, and left it a few pounds lighter.

Shame, shame on you, monseigneur, for placing those letters among my things! For a while I was afraid that I would be thrown into some horrid Dutch work-house, and spend the rest of my days scrubbing sidewalks and knitting hose. But from the questions they asked me, it soon became obvious that they were perfectly baffled by this French cypher of yours. To test this, I replied that I could read those letters as well as *they* could; and the dour looks on the faces of my interrogators demonstrated that their incompetence had been laid bare, and my innocence proved, in the same moment.

I will forgive you, monseigneur, for putting me through those anxious moments if you will forgive me for believing, until quite recently, that you were utterly mad to send me to Versailles. For how could a common girl such as I find a place in the most noble and glorious palace in the world?

But now I know things and I understand.

There is a story making the rounds here, which you must have heard. The heroine is a girl, scarcely better than a slave—the daughter of a ruined petty noble fallen to the condition of a Vagabond. Out of desperation this waif married a stunted and crippled writer in Paris. But the writer had a *salon* that attracted certain Persons of Quality who had grown bored with the insipid discourse of Court. His young wife made the acquaintance of a few of these noble visitors. After he died, and left this girl a penniless widow, a certain Duchess took pity on her, brought her out to Versailles, and made her a governess to some of her illegitimate children. This Duchess was none other than the *maîtresse déclarée* to the

King himself, and her children were royal bastards. The story goes that King Louis XIV, contrary to the long-established customs of Christian royalty, considers his bastards to be only one small step beneath the Dauphin and the other *Enfants de France*. Protocol dictates that the governess of *les Enfants de France* must be a duchess; accordingly, the King made the governess of his bastards into a marquise. In the years since then, the King's *maîtresse déclarée* has gradually fallen from favor, as she has grown fat and histrionic, and it has been the case for some time that when the King went every day to call upon her at one o'clock in the afternoon, just after Mass, he would simply walk through her apartment without stopping, and go instead to visit this widow—the Marquise de Maintenon, as she was now called. Finally, Monseigneur, I have learned what is common knowledge at Versailles, namely that the King secretly married the Marquise de Maintenon recently and that she is the Queen of France in all but name.

It is plain to see that Louis keeps the powerful of France on a short leash here, and that they have nothing to do but gamble when the King is absent and ape his words and actions when he is present. Consequently every Duke, Count, and Marquis at Versailles is prowling through nurseries and grammar-schools, disrupting the noble children's upbringing in the hunt for nubile governesses. No doubt you knew this when you made arrangements for me to work as a governess to the children of M. le comte de Béziers. I cringe to think what awful debt this poor widower must have owed you for him to consent to such an arrangement! You might as well have deposited me in a bordello, Monseigneur, for all the young blades who prowl around the entrance of the count's apartment and pursue me through the gardens as I try to carry out my nominal duties—and not because of any native attractiveness I may possess but simply because it is what the King did.

Fortunately the King has not seen fit to grace me with a noble title yet or I should never be left alone long enough to write you letters. I have reminded some of these loiterers that Madame de Maintenon is a famously pious woman and that the King (who could have any woman in the world, and who ruts with disposable damsels two or three times a week) fell in love with her because of her intelligence. This keeps most of them at bay.

I hope that my story has provided you with a few

moments' diversion from your tedious duties in the Hague, and that you will, in consequence, forgive me for not saying anything of substance.

> Your obedient servant,
> Eliza

P.S. M. le comte de Béziers' finances are in comic disarray—he spent fourteen percent of his income last year on wigs, and thirty-seven percent on interest, mostly on gambling debts. Is this typical? I will try to help him. Is this what you wanted me to do? Or did you want him to remain helpless? That is easier.

> My dark and cloudy words they do but hold
> The truth, as cabinets enclose the gold.
> —JOHN BUNYAN, *The Pilgrim's Progress*

To Gottfried Wilhelm Leibniz
4 August 1685
Dear Doctor Leibniz,

Difficulty at the beginning* is to be expected in any new venture, and my move to Versailles has been no exception. I thank God that I lived for several years in the *harim* of the Topkapi Palace in Constantinople, being trained to serve as a consort to the Sultan, for only this could have prepared me for Versailles. Unlike Versailles, the Sultan's palace grew according to no coherent plan, and from the outside looks like a jumble of domes and minarets. But seen from the inside both palaces are warrens of stuffy windowless rooms created by subdividing other rooms. This is a mouse's-eye view, of course; just as I was never introduced to the domed pavilion where the Grand Turk deflowers his slave-girls, so I have not yet been allowed to enter the Salon of Apollo and view the Sun King in his radiance. In both Palaces I have seen mostly the wretched closets, garrets, and cellars where courtiers dwell.

Certain parts of this Palace, and most of the gardens, are open to anyone who is decently dressed. At first this meant they were closed to me, for William's men ripped up all of my clothes. But after I arrived, and word of my adventures

---

*☷☶ The name of Hexagram 3 of the *I Ching*, or 010001, that being the encryption key for the subliminal message embedded in the script of this letter.

began to circulate, I received cast-offs from noblewomen who either sympathized with my plight or needed to make room in their tiny closets for next year's fashions. With some needle-work I have been able to make these garments over into ones that, while not quite fashionable, will at least not expose me to ridicule as I lead the son and daughter of M. le comte de Béziers through the gardens.

To describe this place in words is hopeless. Indeed I believe it was meant to be so, for then anyone who wants to know it must come here in person, and that is how the King wants it. Suffice it to say that here, every dram of water, every leaf and petal, every square inch of wall, floor, and ceiling bear the signature of Man; all have been thought about by superior intellects, nothing is accidental. The place is pregnant with Intention and wherever you look you see the gaze of the architects—and by extension, Louis—staring back at you. I am contrasting this to blocks of stone and beams of wood that occur in Nature and, in most places, are merely harvested and shaped a bit by artisans. Nothing of that sort is to be found at Versailles.

At Topkapi there were magnificent carpets everywhere, Doctor, carpets such as no one in Christendom has ever seen, and all of them were fabricated thread by thread, knot by knot, by human hands. That is what Versailles is like. Buildings made of plain stone or wood are to this place what a sack of flour is to a diamond necklace. Fully to describe a routine event, such as a conversation or a meal, would require devoting fifty pages to a description of the room and its furnishings, another fifty to the clothing, jewelry, and wigs worn by the participants, another fifty to their family trees, yet another to explaining their current positions in the diverse intrigues of the Court, and finally a single page to setting down the words actually spoken.

Needless to say this will be impractical; yet I hope you will bear with me if I occasionally go on at some length with florid descriptions. I know, Doctor, that even if you have not seen Versailles and the costumes of its occupants, you have seen crude copies of them in German courts and can use your incomparable mind to imagine the things I see. So I will try to restrain myself from describing every little detail. And I know that you are making a study of family trees for Sophie, and have the resources in your library to investigate the genealogy of any petty nobleman I might mention. So I will try to show restraint there as well. I will try to explain the current state of Court intrigue, since you have no way of knowing about such things. For example, one evening two months ago, my master M. le comte de Béziers was given the honor of holding a candle during the King's going-to-bed ceremony, and consequently was invited to all the best parties for a fortnight. But lately his star has been in eclipse, and his life has been very quiet.

If you are reading this it means you detected the key from the I Ching. *It appears that French cryptography is not up to the same standard as French interior decoration; their diplomatic cypher has been broken by the Dutch, but as it was invented by a courtier highly thought of by the King, no one dares say anything against it. If what they say about Colbert is true, he never would have allowed such a situation to arise, but as you know he died two years ago and cyphers have not been upgraded since. I am writing in that broken cypher to d'Avaux in Holland on the assumption that everything I write will be decyphered and read by the Dutch. But as is probably obvious already, I write to you on the assumption that your cypher affords us a secure channel.*

Since you employ the Wilkins cypher, which uses five plaintext letters to encrypt one letter of the actual message, I must write five words of drivel to encypher one word of pith, and so you may count on seeing lengthy descriptions of clothing, etiquette, and other tedious detail in future letters.

I hope I do not seem self-important by presuming that you may harbor some curiosity concerning *my* position at Court. Of course I am a nothing, invisible, not even an ink-speck in the margin of the Register of Ceremonies. But it has not escaped the notice of the nobles that Louis XIV chose most of his most important ministers (such as Colbert, who bought one of your digital computers!) from the middle class, and that he has (secretly) married a woman of low degree, and so it is fashionable in a way to be seen speaking to a commoner if she is clever or useful.

Of course hordes of young men want to have sex with me, but to relate details would be repetitious and in poor taste.

Because M. le comte de Béziers' bolt-hole in the south wing is so uncomfortable, and the weather has been so fine, I have spent several hours each day going on walks with my two charges, Beatrice and Louis, who have 9 and 6 years of age, respectively. Versailles has vast gardens and parks, most of which are deserted except when the King goes to hunt or promenade, and then they are crowded with courtiers. Until very recently they were also filled with common people who would come all the way from Paris to see the sights, but these pressed around the King so hotly, and made such a shambles of the statues and waterworks, that recently the King banned the *mobile* from all of his gardens.

As you know, it is the habit of all well-born ladies to cover their faces with masks whenever they venture out of doors, so that they will not be darkened by the sun. Many of the more refined men do likewise—the King's brother Philippe, who is generally addressed as Monsieur, wears such a mask, though he frets that it smears his makeup. On such warm days as we have had recently, this is so uncomfortable that the ladies of Versailles, and by extension their attendants, households, and gallants, prefer simply to remain indoors. I can wander for hours through the park with Beatrice and Louis in train and encounter only a few other people: mostly gardeners, occasionally lovers on their way to trysts in secluded woods or grottoes.

The gardens are shot through with long straight paths and avenues that, as one steps into certain intersections, provide sudden unexpected vistas of fountains, sculpture groups, or the château itself. I am teaching Beatrice and Louis geometry by having them draw maps of the place.

If these children are any clue as to the future of the nobility, then France as we know it is doomed.

Yesterday I was walking along the canal, which is a cross-shaped body of water to the west of the château; the long axis runs east–west and the crossbar north–south, and since it is a single body of water its surface is, of course, level, that being a known property of water. I put a needle in one end of a cork and weighted the other end (with a corkscrew, in case you are wondering!) and set it afloat in the circular pool where these canals intersect, hoping that the needle would point vertically upwards—trying (as you have no doubt already perceived) to acquaint Beatrice and Louis with the idea of a third spatial dimension perpendicular to the other two. Alas, the cork did not float upright. It drifted away and I had to lie flat on my belly and reach out over the water to rake it in, and the sleeves of my hand-me-down dress became soaked with water. The whole time I was preoccupied with the whining of the bored children, and with my own passions as well—for I must tell you that tears were running down my sunburned cheeks as I remembered the many lessons I was taught, as a young girl in Algiers, by Mummy and by the Ladies' Volunteer Sodality of the Society of Britannic Abductees.

At some point I became aware of voices—a man's and a woman's—and I knew that they had been conversing nearby for quite some time. With all of these other concerns and distractions I had taken no note of them. I lifted my head to gaze directly across the canal at two figures on horseback: a tall magnificent well-built man in a vast wig like a lion's mane, and a woman, built something like a Turkish wrestler, dressed in hunting clothes and carrying a riding crop. The woman's face was exposed to the sun, and had been for a long time, for she was tanned like a saddlebag. She and her companion had been talking about something else, but when I looked up I somehow drew the notice of the man; instantly he reached up and doffed his hat to me, from across the canal! When he did, the sun fell directly on his face and I recognized him as King Louis XIV.

I simply could not imagine any way to recover from this indignity, and so I pretended I had not seen him. As the crow flies we were not far apart, but by land we were far away—to reach me, the King and his Diana-like hunting-companion would have had to ride west for some distance along the bank of the canal; circumnavigate the large pool at that end; and then go the same distance eastwards along the opposite bank. So I convinced myself that they were far away and I pretended not to see them; God have mercy on me if I chose wrong. I tried to cover my embarrassment by ranting to the children about Descartes and Euclid.

The King put his hat back on and said, "Who is she?"

I closed my eyes and sighed in relief; the King had decided to play along, and act as if we had not seen each other. Finally I had coaxed the floating cork back into my hands. I drew myself up and sat on the brink of the canal with my skirts spread out around me, in profile to the King, and quietly lectured the children.

Meanwhile I was praying that the woman would not know my name. But as you will have guessed, Doctor, she was none other than his majesty's sister-in-law, Elisabeth Charlotte, known to Versailles as Madame, and known to Sophie—her beloved aunt—as Liselotte.

Why didn't you tell me that the Knight of the Rustling Leaves was a clitoriste? *I suppose this should come as no surprise given*

*that her husband Philippe is a homosexual, but it caught me some-
what off guard. Does she have lovers? Hold, I presume too much;
does she even know what she is?*

She gazed at me for a languid moment; at Versailles, no
one of importance speaks quickly and spontaneously, every
utterance is planned like a move in a chess game. I knew
what she was about to say: "I do not know her." I prayed for
her to say it, for then the King would know that I was not a
person, did not exist, was no more worthy of his attention
than a fleeting ripple in the surface of the canal. Then finally
I heard Madame's voice across the water: "It looks like that
girl who was duped by d'Avaux and molested by the Dutchmen, and showed up dishevelled and expecting sympathy."

*It strikes me as unlikely that Liselotte could have recognized me
in this way without another channel of information; did you write a
letter to her, Doctor? It is never clear to me how much you are acting
on your own and how much as a pawn—or perhaps I should say
"knight" or "rook"—of Sophie.*

These cruel words would have brought me to tears if I'd
been one of those rustic countesses who flock to Versailles to
be deflowered by men of rank. But I had already seen
enough of this place to know that the only truly cruel words
here are "She is nobody." And Madame had not said that.
Consequently, the King had to look at me for a few moments
longer.

Louis and Beatrice had noticed the King, and were
frozen with a mixture of awe and terror—like statues of
children.

Another one of those pauses had gone by. I heard the
King saying, "That story was told in my presence." Then he
said, "If d'Avaux would only put his letters into the bodice of
some poxy old hag he could be assured of absolute secrecy,
but what Dutchman would not want to break the seal on *that*
envelope?"

"But, Sire," said Liselotte, "d'Avaux is a Frenchman—and
what Frenchman *would*?"

"He is not as refined in his tastes as he would have you
think," the King returned, "and *she* is not as coarse as *you*
would have *me* think."

At this point little Louis stepped forward so suddenly that
I was alarmed he would topple into the Canal and oblige me
to swim; but he stopped on the brink, thrust out one leg, and
bowed to the King just like a courtier. I pretended now to

notice the King for the first time, and scrambled to my feet. Beatrice and I made curtseys across the canal. Once more the King acknowledged us by doffing his hat, perhaps with a certain humorous exaggeration.

"I see that look in your eye, *vôtre majesté*," said Liselotte.

"I see it in yours, Artemis."

"You have been listening to gossip. I tell you that these girls of low birth who come here to seduce noblemen are like mouse droppings in the pepper."

"Is *that* what she wants us to believe? How banal."

"The best disguises are the most banal, Sire."

This seemed to be the end of their strange conversation; they rode slowly away.

The King is said to be a great huntsman, but he was riding in an extremely stiff posture—I suspect he is suffering from hemorrhoids or possibly a bad back.

I took the children back straightaway and sat down to write you this letter. For a nothing like me, today's events are the pinnacle of honor and glory, and I wanted to memorialize them before any detail slipped from my memory.

To M. le comte d'Avaux
1 September 1685
Monseigneur,

I have as many visitors as ever (much to the annoyance of M. le comte de Béziers), but since I got a deep tan and took to wearing sackcloth and quoting from the Bible a lot, they are not as interested in romance. Now they come asking me about my Spanish uncle. "I am sorry that your Spanish uncle had to move to Amsterdam, mademoiselle," they say, "but it is rumored that hardship has made him a wise man." The first time some son of a marquis came up to me spouting such nonsense I told him he must have me mixed up with some other wench, and sent him packing! But the next one dropped your name and I understood that he had in some sense been dispatched by you—or, to be more precise, that his coming to me under the delusion of my having a wise Spanish uncle was a consequence or ramification of some chain of events that had been set in motion by you. On that assumption, I began to play along, quite cautiously, as I did not know what sort of game might be afoot. From the way this fellow talked I soon understood that he believes me to be a sort of crypto-Jew, the bastard offspring of a swarthy Spanish

Kohan and a butter-haired Dutchwoman, which might actually seem plausible as the sun has bleached my hair and darkened my skin.

These conversations are all the same, and their particulars are too tedious to relate here. Obviously you have been spreading tales about me, Monseigneur, and half the petty nobles of Versailles now believe that I (or, at any rate, my fictitious uncle) can help them get out from under their gambling debts, pay for the remodeling of their châteaux, or buy them splendid new carriages. I can only roll my eyes at their avarice. But if the stories are to be believed, their fathers and grandfathers used what money they had to raise private armies and fortify their cities against the father and grandfather of the present King. I suppose it's better for the money to go to dressmakers, sculptors, painters, and *chefs de cuisine* than to mercenaries and musket-makers.

Of course it is true that their gold would fetch a higher rate of return wisely invested in Amsterdam than sitting in a strong-box under their beds. The only difficulty lies in the fact that I cannot manage such investments from a closet in Versailles while at the same time teaching two motherless children how to read and write. My Spanish uncle is a fiction of yours, presumably invented because you feared that these French nobles would never entrust their assets to a woman. This means that I must do the work personally, and this is impossible unless I have the freedom to travel to Amsterdam several times a year . . .

To Gottfried Wilhelm Leibniz
12 Sept. 1685

This morning I was summoned to the comparatively spacious and splendid apartments of a Lady in Waiting to the Dauphine, in the South Wing of the palace adjacent to the apartments of the Dauphine herself.

The lady in question is the duchesse d'Oyonnax. She has a younger sister who is the marquise d'Ozoir and who happens to be visiting Versailles with her daughter of nine years.

The girl seems bright but is half dead with asthma. The marquise ruptured something giving birth to her and cannot have any more children.

The d'Ozoirs are one of the rare exceptions to the general rule that all French nobles of any consequence must dwell at Versailles—but only because the Marquis has responsibilities at Dunkirk. In case you have not been properly maintaining your family trees of the European nobility, Doctor, I will remind you that the Marquis d'Ozoir is the bastard son of the duc d'Arcachon.

Who, when he was a stripling of fifteen, begat the future marquis off his grandmama's saucy maid-companion—the poor girl had been dragooned into teaching the young Duke his first love-lesson.

The duc d'Arcachon did not actually take a wife until he was twenty-five, and she did not produce a viable child (Étienne d'Arcachon) for three years after that. So the bastard was already a young man by the time his legitimate half-brother was born. He was shipped off to Surat as an aide to Boullaye and Beber, who tried to establish the French East India Company there around 1666.

But as you may know the French E.I.C. did not fare quite as well as the English and Dutch have done. Boullaye and Beber began to assemble a caravan in Surat but had to depart before all preparations had been made, because the city was in the process of falling to the Mahratta rebels. They traveled into the interior of Hindoostan, hoping to establish trade agreements. As they approached the gates of a great city, a delegation of banyans—the richest and most influential *commerçants* of that district—came out to greet them, carrying small gifts in bowls, according to the local custom. Boullaye and Beber mistook them for beggars and thrashed them with their riding-whips as any self-respecting upper-caste Frenchmen would do when confronted by panhandling Vagabonds on the road.

The gates of the city were slammed in their faces. The French delegation were left to wander through the hinterland like out-castes. Quickly they were abandoned by the guides and porters they had hired at Surat, and began to fall prey to highwaymen and Mahratta rebels. Eventually they found their way to Shahjahanabad, where they hoped to beg for succor from the Great Mogul Aurangzeb, but they were informed he had retired to the Red Fort at Agra. They traveled to Agra only to be told that the officials they needed to prostrate themselves before, and to shower with gifts, in order to gain access to the Great Mogul, were stationed in Shahjahanabad. In this way they were shuttled back and forth along one of Hindoostan's most dangerous roads until Boullaye had been strangled by dacoits and Beber had succumbed to disease (or perhaps it was the other way round) and most of their expedition had fallen victim to more or less exotic hazards.

The bastard son of the duc d'Arcachon survived all of them, made his way out to Goa, talked his way aboard a Portuguese ship bound for Mozambique, and pursued a haphazard course to the slave coast of Africa, where finally he spied a French frigate flying the coat of arms of the Arcachon family: fleurs-de-lis and Neeger-heads in iron collars. He persuaded some Africans to row him out to that ship in a long-boat and identified himself to her captain, who of course was aware that the duc's illegitimate son was lost, and had been ordered to keep an ear to the ground for any news. The young man was brought aboard the ship.

And the Africans who had brought him out were rewarded with baptisms, iron jewelry, and a free trip to Martinique to spend the rest of their lives working in the agricultural sector.

This led to a career running slaves to the French West Indies. During the course of the 1670s the young man amassed a modest fortune from this trade and purchased, or was rewarded by the King with, the title of Marquis. Immediately he settled in France and married. For several reasons he and his wife have not established themselves near Versailles. For one thing, he is a bastard whom the duc d'Arcachon prefers to keep at arm's length. For another, his daughter has asthma and needs to breathe sea-air. Finally, he has responsibilities along the sea-coast. You may know, Doctor, that the people of India believe in the perpetual reincarnation of souls; likewise, the French East India Company might be thought of as a soul or spirit that goes bankrupt every few years but is always re-incarnated in some new form. Recently it has happened one more time. Naturally many of its operations are centered at Dunkirk, le Havre, and other sea-ports, and so that is where the Marquis and his family spend most of their time. But the Marquise comes to visit her sister the duchesse d'Oyonnax frequently, and brings the daughter with her.

As I mentioned, Oyonnax is a lady-in-waiting to the Dauphine, which is looked on as an extremely desirable position. The Queen of France died two years ago, and had been estranged from the King for many years at the time of her death. The King has Mme. de Maintenon now, but she is not officially his wife. Therefore, the most important woman at

Versailles *not really, but nominally, according to the rules of precedence* is the Dauphine, wife of the King's eldest son and heir
apparent. Competition among the noble ladies of France for
positions in her household is intense . . .

*So intense that it has resulted in no fewer than four poisonings. I
do not know if the sister of d'Ozoir poisoned anyone herself, but it is
generally understood that she did allow her naked body to be used as
a living altar during black masses held at an abandoned country
church outside of Versailles. This was before the King became aware
that his court was infested with homicidal Satanists, and instituted
the* chambre ardente *to investigate these doings. She was indeed
among the 400-odd nobles arrested and interrogated, but nothing
was ever proved against her.*

All of which is to say that Mme. la duchesse d'Oyonnax is
a great lady indeed, who entertains her sister Mme. la marquise d'Ozoir in grand style.

When I entered her salon I was surprised to see my
employer, M. le comte de Béziers, seated on a stool so low
and tiny it seemed he was squatting on his haunches like a
dog. And indeed he had hunched his shoulders and was gazing sidelong at the Marquise like an old peasant's cur anticipating the descent of the cudgel. The Duchess was in an
armchair of solid silver and the Marquise was in a chair without arms, also in silver.

I remained standing. Introductions were made—here I
elide all of the tedious formalities and small talk—and the
Marquise explained to me that she had been looking for a
tutor to educate her daughter. The girl already has a governess, mind you, but that woman is quite close to being illiterate and consequently the child's mental development has
been retarded *or perhaps she is simply an imbecile.* Somehow she
had settled on me as being the most likely candidate *this is
the work of d'Avaux.*

I was *pretended to be* astonished, and went on at some
length protesting the decision on grounds that I was not
equal to such a responsibility. I wondered aloud who would
look after poor little Beatrice and Louis. M. le comte de
Béziers gave me the happy news that he'd found an opportunity in the south and would soon be leaving Versailles.

*You may not know that one of the only ways for a French noble-
man to make money without losing caste is by serving as an officer
on a merchant ship. Béziers has taken such a position on a French
E.I.C. vessel that will be sailing out of the Bassin d'Arcachon come*

spring, bound for the Cape of Good Hope; points east; and if I'm any judge of such matters, David Jones's Locker.

Although, if Mme. de Maintenon opens her school for poor girls of the French nobility at St. Cyr next year *her personal obsession—St. Cyr lies within sight of Versailles, to the southwest, just beyond the walls,* then Beatrice might be shipped there to be groomed for life at Court.

Under the circumstances I could hardly show the tiniest degree of reluctance, let alone decline this offer, and so I write you this letter from my new lodging in an attic room above the Duchess's apartments. Only God in Heaven knows what new adventures await me now! The Marquise hopes to remain at Versailles until the end of the month *the King will spend October at Fontainebleu as is his custom, and there is no point remaining at Versailles when he is not here* and then repair to Dunkirk. I shall, of course, go with her. But I will certainly write another letter to you before then.

To M. le comte d'Avaux
25 September 1685

It is two weeks since I entered the service of the Marquis and the Marquise d'Ozoir, and another week until we leave for Dunkirk, so this is the last letter I will send from Versailles.

If I am reading your intentions correctly, I'll remain in Dunkirk only as long as it takes to walk across the gangplank of a Holland-bound ship. If that comes to pass, any letters I send after today will reach Amsterdam after I do.

When I came down here some months ago, I stopped over in Paris for a night and witnessed the following from my window: in the market-square before that *pied-à-terre* where you were so kind as to let me stay, some common people had erected a cantilever, a beam projecting out into space, like the cranes used by merchants to hoist bales up into their warehouses. On the pavement beneath the end of this beam they kindled a bonfire. A rope was thrown over the end of the beam.

These preparations had drawn a crowd and so it was difficult for me to see what happened next; but from the laughter of the crowd and the thrashing of the rope, I inferred that some antic, hilarious struggle was taking place on the street. A stray cat dashed away and was half-heartedly pursued by a couple of boys. Finally the other end of the rope was drawn tight, hoisting a great, lumpy sack into the air; it swung to and fro high above the fire. I guessed it was full of some sausages to be cooked or smoked.

Then I saw that something was moving inside the sack.

The rope was let out and the writhing bag descended until its underside glowed red from the flames underneath. A horrible yowling came out of it and the bag began to thrash and jump. I understood now that it was filled with dozens of stray cats that had been caught in the streets of Paris and brought here to amuse the crowd. And believe me, Monseigneur, they were amused.

If I had been a man, I could have ridden out into that square on horseback and severed that rope with a sword-blow, sending those poor animals down to perish quickly in the roaring flames. Alas, I am not a man, I lack a mount and a sword, and even if I had all of these I might lack courage. In all my life I have only known one man brave or rash enough to do such a deed, but he lacked moral fiber and probably would have reveled in the spectacle along with all those others. All I could do was to close up the shutters and plug my ears; though as I did, I noticed that many windows around the square were open. Merchants and persons of quality were watching it, too, and even bringing their children out.

During the dismal years of the Fronde Rebellion, when the young Louis XIV was being hounded through the streets of Paris by rebellious princes and starving mobs, he must have witnessed one of these cat-burnings, for at Versailles he has created something similar: all the nobles who tormented him when he was a scared little mouse have been rounded up and thrown into this bag and suspended in the air; and the King holds the end of the rope. I am in the sack now, Monseigneur, but as I am only a kitten whose claws have not grown in, all I can do is remain as close as possible to much bigger and more dangerous cats.

Mme. la duchesse d'Oyonnax runs her household like a Ship of the Line: everything trim, all the time. I have not been out of doors since I entered the service of her sister. My tan has faded, and all of the patched-together clothes in my wardrobe have been torn up for rags and replaced with better. I will not call it finery, for it would never do to outshine these two sisters in their own apartment. But neither would it do to embarrass them. So I will venture to say that the Duchess no longer cringes and grimaces when she catches sight of me.

In consequence I am now catching the eyes of the young

blades again. If I still served M. le comte de Béziers I would never get a moment's peace, but Mme. la duchesse d'Oyonnax has claws—some would say, poison-tipped ones—and fangs. So the lust of the courtiers has been channelled into spreading the usual rumors and speculations about me: that I am a slut, that I am a prude, that I am a Sapphist, that I am an untutored virgin, that I am a past mistress of exotic sexual practices. An amusing consequence of my notoriety is that men come to call on the Duchess at all hours, and while most of them only want to bed me, some bring bills of exchange or little purses of diamonds, and instead of whispering flattery and lewd suggestions they say, "What rate of return could this bring in Amsterdam?" I always answer, "Why, it all depends on the whim of the King; for do the markets of Amsterdam not fluctuate according to the wars and treaties that only His Majesty has the power to make?" They think I am only being coy.

Today the King came to see me; but it is not what you think.

I had been warned of His Majesty's coming by the cousin of the Duchess: a Jesuit priest named Édouard de Gex, who has come here on a visit from the *pays* in the southeast where this family maintains its ancestral seat. Father Édouard is a very pious man. He had been invited to play a minor role in the King's getting-out-of-bed ceremony, and had overheard a couple of courtiers speculating as to which man would claim my maidenhead. Then another offered to wager that I didn't *have* a maidenhead, and yet another wagered that if I did it would be claimed by a woman, not a man—two likely candidates being the Dauphine, who is having an affair with her maid, and Liselotte.

At some point, according to Father Édouard, the King took notice of this conversation and inquired as to what lady was being talked about. "It is no lady, but the tutor of the daughter of the d'Ozoirs," said one of them; to which the King replied, after a moment's thought, "I have heard of her. They say she is beautiful."

When Father Édouard told me this story I understood why not a single young courtier had come sniffing around after me that day. They thought the King had conceived an interest in me, and were now afraid to come anywhere near!

Today the Duchess, the Marquise, and all their household

took the unusual measure of attending Mass at half past noon. I was left alone in the apartment under the pretext that I needed to pack some things for the upcoming journey to Dunkirk.

At one o'clock the chapel bells rang, but my mistresses did not return to the apartment. Instead a gentleman—the most famous chirurgeon in Paris—let himself in through the servants' entrance, followed by a retinue of assistants, as well as a priest: Father Édouard de Gex. Moments later King Louis XIV of France entered *solus* through the front, slamming a gilded door in the faces of his courtiers, and greeted me in a very polite way.

The King and I stood in a corner of the Duchess's salon and (as bizarre as this must sound) exchanged trivial conversation while the surgeon's assistants worked furiously. Even one who is as unschooled in Court etiquette as I knew that in the presence of the King no other person may be acknowledged, and so I pretended not to notice as the assistants dragged the massive silver chairs to the edges of the room, rolled up the carpets, laid down canvas drop-cloths, and carried in a heavy wooden bench. The chirurgeon was arranging some very unpleasant-looking tools on a side table, and muttering occasional commands; but all of this took place in nearly perfect silence.

"D'Avaux says you are good with money," the King said.

"I say d'Avaux is good at flattering young ladies," I answered.

"It is an error for you to feign modesty when you are talking to me," the King said, firmly but not angrily.

I saw my error. We use humility when we fear that someone will consider us a rival or a threat; and while this may be true of common or even noble men, it can never be true of *le Roi* and so to use humility in His Majesty's presence is to imply that the King shares the petty jealousies and insecurities of others.

"Forgive me for being foolish, Sire."

"Never; but I forgive you for being inexperienced. Colbert was a commoner. He was good with money; he built everything you see. He did not know how to speak to me at first. Have you ever experienced a sexual climax, mademoiselle?"

"Yes."

The King smiled. "You have learned quickly how to answer my questions. That pleases me. You will please me more by now making the sounds that you made when you had this climax. You may have to make those sounds for a long time—possibly a quarter of an hour."

I must have clutched my hands together in front of my bosom, or put on some such show of girlish anxiety. The King shook his head and smiled in a knowing way. "To see a certain *déshabille,* in a quarter of an hour, would please me—only that it might be glimpsed, through the door, by the ones who wait in the gallery." The King nodded toward the door through which he had entered. "Now if you will excuse me, mademoiselle. You may begin at any time." He turned away from me, doffing his coat and handing it to one of the chirurgeon's assistants as he moved toward the heavy bench, now draped in white linen, that sat in the middle of the room on a carpet of sailcloth. The chirurgeon and his assistants closed in on the King like flies on a piece of meat. Suddenly—to my indescribable shock—the King's breeches were down around his ankles. He lay down on his stomach on the bench. For a moment I fancied he was one of those men who likes to be struck on the buttocks. But then he spread his legs apart, bracing his feet against the floor to either side of the bench, and I saw a frightful purplish swelling in the crevice of his buttocks.

"Father Édouard," the King said quietly, "you are among the most learned men of France. Even among your fellow Jesuits you are respected as one to whom no detail is unnoticed. Since I cannot view the operation, you will please me by paying the closest attention, and telling me the story later, so that I will know whether this chirurgeon is to be counted a friend or an enemy of France."

Father Édouard nodded and said something I could not hear.

"Your Majesty!" the chirurgeon exclaimed. "To perfect my skills, I have performed a hundred of these operations, in the last six months, since I was made aware of your complaint—"

"Those hundred are not of interest to me."

Father Édouard had noticed me standing in the corner. I prefer not to speculate what sort of expression was on my face! He locked his dark eyes on mine—he is a handsome man—and then glanced significantly toward the door, through which I could hear a low hubbub of ribald conversation among the dozen or so courtiers biding their time.

I moved closer to that door—not too close—and let out a throaty sigh. "Mmm, *Vôtre Majesté!*" The courtiers outside began shushing one another. In my other ear I heard a faint ringing noise as the chirurgeon picked a knife up off his table.

I let out a groan.

So did the King.

I let out a scream.

So did the King.

"Oh, gentle, it is my first time!" I shouted, as the King shouted curses at the chirurgeon, muffled by a silken pillow Father Édouard was holding to his face.

So it went. For a while I continued screaming as if suffering great discomfort, but as the minutes wore on, I changed over to moans of pleasure. It seemed to go on for much longer than a quarter of an hour. I lay down on a rolled-up carpet and tore at my own clothes, pulled the ribbons and braids from my hair, and breathed as heavily as I could, to make my face flushed and sweaty. Towards the end, I closed my eyes: partly to block out the hellish things I was beginning to see in the middle of the room, and partly to play my role more convincingly. Now I could clearly hear the courtiers in the gallery.

"She's a screamer," said one of them admiringly. "I like that, it makes my blood hot."

"It is most indiscreet," said another scornfully.

"The mistress of a King does not *have* to be discreet."

"Mistress? He'll throw her away soon, then where will she be?"

"In my bed, I hope!"

"Then you had best invest in a set of earplugs."

"He had best learn to fuck like a King before he'll need them!"

A drop of moisture struck me on the forehead. Fearing that it was a splash of blood, I opened my eyes and looked vertically upwards into the face of Father Édouard de Gex. He was indeed all spattered with the blood royal, but what had fallen on me was a bead of sweat from his brow. He was glaring straight down into my face. I have no idea how long he had been watching me thus. I glanced over towards the bench and saw blood everywhere. The chirurgeon was sitting on the floor, drained. His assistants were packing rags between the King's buttocks. To stop all of a sudden would be to give the ruse away, and so I closed my eyes again and brought myself to a screaming—if simulated—climax, then exhaled one long last moan, and opened my eyes again.

Father Édouard was still standing there above me, but his eyes were closed and his face slack. It is an expression I have seen before.

The King was standing up, flanked between a pair of assistants who stood ready to catch him if he should faint. He was deathly pale and tottering from side to side, but—somewhat incredibly—he was alive, and awake, and buttoning up his own breeches. Behind him other assistants were bundling up the bloody sheets and drop-cloths and rushing them out through the back door.

Here is what the King said to me as he was leaving:

"Nobles of France enjoy my esteem and confidence as a birthright, and make themselves common by their failures. Commoners may earn my esteem and confidence by pleasing me, and thereby ennoble themselves. You may please me by showing discretion."

"What of d'Avaux?" I asked.

"You may tell him everything," said the King, "so that he may feel pride, inasmuch as he is my friend, and fear, inasmuch as he is my foe."

Monseigneur, I do not know what His Majesty meant by this, but I am sure you do . . .

To Gottfried Wilhelm Leibniz
29 September 1685
Doctor,

The season has turned and brought a noticeable darkening of the light.* In two days the sun will sink farther beneath the southern horizon as I journey with Mme. la marquise d'Ozoir to Dunquerque at the extreme northern limit of the King's realm *and thence God willing to Holland*. I have heard that the sun has been shining very hot in the South, in the country of Savoy *more on this later*.

The King is at war—not only with the Protestant heretics who infest his realms, but with his own doctors. A few weeks ago he had a tooth pulled. Any tooth-puller chosen at random from the Pont-Neuf could have handled this operation, but d'Aquin, the King's doctor, got it wrong, and the resulting wound became abscessed. D'Aquin's solution to this problem was to pull out every last one of the King's upper teeth.

---

* ☰ ☷ Darkening of the Light: Hexagram 36 of the *I Ching*, or 000101.

But while he was doing this he somehow managed to rip out part of the King's palate, creating a horrendous wound which he then had to close up by the application of red-hot irons. Nonetheless, it too abscessed and had to be cauterized several more times. *There is another story, too, concerning the King's health, which I will have to tell you some other time.*

It is nearly beyond comprehension that a King should suffer so, and if these facts were generally known among the peasantry they would doubtless be misconstrued as an omen of Divine misfavor. In the corridors of Versailles, where most *but not all!* of the King's sufferings are common knowledge, there are a few weak-minded ninehammers who think this way; but fortunately this château has been graced, for the last few weeks, by the presence of Father Édouard de Gex, a vigorous young Jesuit of a good family *when Louis seized the Franche-Comté in 1667 this family betrayed their Spanish neighbors and flung open their gates to his army; Louis has rewarded them with titles* and a great favorite of Mme. de Maintenon, who looks to him as a sort of spiritual guide. Where most of our fawning courtier-priests would prefer to avoid the theological questions raised by the King's sufferings, Father Édouard has recently taken this bull by the horns, and both asked and answered these questions in a most forthright and public way. He has given lengthy homilies at Mass, and Mme. de Maintenon has arranged for his words to be printed and distributed around Versailles and Paris. I will try to send you a copy of his booklet. The gist of it is that the King is France and that his ailments and sufferings are reflections of the condition of the realm. If various pockets of his flesh have become abscessed it is a sort of carnal metaphor for the continued existence of heresy within the borders of France—meaning, as everyone knows, the R.P.R., the *religion prétendue réformée,* or Huguenots as they are known by some. The points of similarity between R.P.R. communities and suppurating abscesses are many, viz. . . .

Forgive this endless homily, but I have much to tell and am weary of writing endless descriptions of gowns and jewels to cover my traces. This family of Fr. de Gex, Mme. la duchesse d'Oyonnax, and Mme. la marquise d'Ozoir have long dwelt in the mountains of Jura between Burgundy and the southern tip of the Franche-Comté. It is a territory where many things come together and accordingly it is a sort of cornucopia of enemies. For generations they looked on with envy as their neighbor the Duke of Savoy reaped a harvest of wealth and power by virtue of sitting astride the route joining Genoa and

Lyons—the financial aorta of Christendom. And from their châteaux in the southern Jura they can literally gaze down into the cold waters of Lake Geneva, the wellspring of Protestantism, where the English Puritans fled for refuge during the reign of Bloody Mary and where the French Huguenots have enjoyed a safe haven from the repressions of their Kings. I have seen much of Father Édouard lately because he pays frequent visits to the apartments of his cousines, and I have witnessed in his dark eyes a hatred of the Protestants that would make your flesh crawl if you saw it.

This family's opportunity finally came when Louis conquered the Franche-Comté, as I said, and they have not failed to take full advantage of it. Last year brought them more good fortune: the Duke of Savoy was forced to take as his wife Anne Marie, the daughter of Monsieur by his first wife, Minette of England, and hence the niece of King Louis XIV. So the Duke—hitherto independent—became a part of the Bourbon family, and subject to the whims of the patriarch.

Now Savoy also borders on that troublesome Lake and it has long been the case that Calvinist proselytizers would come up the valleys to preach to the common folk, who have followed the example of their Duke in being independent-minded and have been receptive to the rebel creed.

You can almost finish the story yourself now, Doctor. Father Édouard has been telling his disciple, Mme. de Maintenon, all about how Protestants have been running rampant in Savoy, and spreading the infection to their R.P.R. brethren in France. De Maintenon repeats all of this to the suffering King, who even in the best of times has never hesitated to be cruel to his subjects, or even his own family, for the good of the realm. But these are not the best of times for the King—there has been a palpable darkening of the light, which is why I chose this hexagram as my encryption key. The King has told the Duke of Savoy that the "rebels" as he considers them are not merely to be suppressed—they are to be exterminated. The Duke has temporized, hoping that the King's mood will improve as his ailments heal. He has proffered one excuse after another. But very recently the Duke made the error of claiming that he cannot carry out the King's commands because he does not have enough money to mount a military campaign. Without hesitation the King generously offered to undertake the operation out of his own pocket.

As I write this Father Édouard is preparing to ride south as chaplain of a French army with Maréchal de Catinat at its head. They will go into Savoy whether the Duke likes it or not, and enter the valleys of the Protestants and kill everyone they see. Do you know of any way to send warnings to that part of the world?

The King and all who know of his late sufferings take comfort in the understanding that Father Édouard has brought us: namely that the measures taken against the R.P.R., cruel as they might seem, are more painful to the King than to anyone; but that this pain must be endured lest the whole body perish.

I must go—I have responsibilities below. My next letter will come from Dunquerque, God willing.

Your most affectionate student and servant,

Eliza

London

SPRING 1685

> Philosophy is written in this immense book that stands ever open before our eyes (I speak of the Universe), but it cannot be read if one does not first learn the language and recognize the characters in which it is written. It is written in mathematical language, and the characters are triangles, circles, and other geometrical figures, without the means of which it is humanly impossible to understand a word; without these philosophy is confused wandering in a dark labyrinth.
>
> —GALILEO GALILEI, *Il Saggiatore* (THE ASSAYER) IN *Opere*, V. 6, P. 197, TRANSLATION BY JULIAN BARBOUR

THE AIR IN THE COFFEE-HOUSE made Daniel feel as if he'd been buried in rags.

Roger Comstock was peering down the stem of his clay pipe like a drunken astronomer drawing a bead on something. In this case the target was Robert Hooke, Fellow of the Royal Society, visible only barely (because of gloom and smoke) and sporadically (because of table-flitting patrons). Hooke had barricaded himself behind a miniature apothecary shop of bottles, purses, and flasks, and was mixing up his dinner: a compound of mercury, iron filings, flowers of sulfur, purgative waters from diverse springs, many of which were Lethal to Waterfowl; and extracts of several plants, including the rhubarb and the opium poppy. "He is still alive, I see," Roger mused. "If Hooke spent any more time lingering at Death's door, Satan himself would have the man ejected for vagrancy. Yet just as I am wondering whether I can make time for his funeral, I learn from Sources that he is campaigning like a French regiment through every whorehouse in Whitechapel."

Daniel could think of nothing to add.

"What of Newton?" Roger demanded. "You *said* he was going to *die*."

"Well, I was the only way he ever got food," Daniel said weakly. "From the time we began rooming together until my ejection in '77, I kept him alive like a nursemaid. So I had good reasons for making that prediction."

"Someone else must have been bringing him food since then—one of his students?"

"He *has* no students," Daniel pointed out.

"*But he must eat,*" Roger countered.

Daniel glimpsed Hooke stirring up his concoction with a glass rod. "Perhaps he has concocted the *Elixir Vitae* and is immortal now."

"Judge not lest ye be judged! I believe that is your third helping of *usquebaugh*," Roger said sternly, glaring at the amber dram in front of Daniel. Daniel reached out to guard it in the curled fingers of his left hand.

"I am entirely serious," Roger continued. "Who looks after him?"

"Why does it matter, as long as *someone* does?"

"It matters who the someone is," Roger said. "You told me that when he was a student Newton would lend out money, and keep track of his loans like a Jew!"

"Actually I believe that Christian lenders *also* prefer to be paid back . . ."

"Never mind, you know what I mean. In the same way, Daniel, if someone is providing for Newton's upkeep and maintenance, they may be expecting favors in return."

Daniel sat up straighter. "You think it's the esoteric brotherhood."

Roger raised his eyebrows in a cruel parody of innocence. "No, but evidently *you* think so."

"For a while Upnor was trying to get his barbs into Isaac," Daniel admitted, "but that was a long time ago."

"Let me remind you that among people who *keep track* of debts—as opposed to *forgiving* 'em—'a long time ago' means 'lots and lots of compound interest.' Now, you told me he vanishes several weeks out of each year."

"Not necessarily for sinister purposes. He has land in Lincolnshire that needs looking after."

"*You* made it sound sinister, when you told me of it."

Daniel sighed, forsook his dram, clamped his temples between the thumb and fingertips of one hand. All he could see now was his pink palm—cratered from smallpox, now. The disease had converted perhaps a quarter of Tess's body to pustules, and removed most of the skin from her face and torso, before she'd finally given up the ghost. "To be quite honest with you, I do not care," he said. "I tried to hold him back. Tried to turn his attention toward astronomy, dynamics, physics—natural philosophy as opposed to unnatural theology. I failed; I left; here I am."

"You left? Or were ejected?"

"I misspoke."

"Which time?"

"I meant it in a sort of metaphorical way, when I used the word 'ejected.' "

"You are a damned liar, Daniel!"

"What did you say!?"

"Oh, sorry, I was speaking in a sort of metaphorical way."

"Try to understand, Roger, that the circumstances of my break with Isaac were—are—complicated. As long as I try to express it with a single verb, *videlicet,* 'to leave,' 'to be ejected,' I'll be in some sense a liar, and inasmuch as a liar, damnable."

"Give me more verbs, then," said Roger, catching the eye of a serving-girl and giving her a look that meant *I have him going now, keep it coming and keep the sleeve-tuggers away from us.* Then he leaned forward, looming in an alarming way through the smoke above the table, catching the light of a candle on the underside of his chin. "It is sixteen seventy-six!" Roger thundered. "Leibniz has come to London for the second time! Oldenburg is furious with him because he has failed to bring the digital computer, as promised! Instead Leibniz has devoted the last four years to fooling around with mathematics in Paris! Now he is asking extremely awkward questions about some maths work that Newton did years ago. Something mysterious is afoot—Newton has you, Doctor Waterhouse, copying out papers and encrypting arcane mathematical formulae—Oldenburg is beside himself—Enoch Root is mixed up in it somehow—there are *rumors* of letters, and even conversations, between Newton and

Leibniz. Then Oldenburg dies. Not long afterwards there is a fire in your chambers at Trinity, and many of Newton's alchemical papers go up in particolored flames. Then you move to London and refuse to say why. What is the correct verb? 'To leave' or 'to be ejected?' "

"There was simply no room for me there—my bed took up space that could have been used for another furnace."

"To conspire? To plot?"

"The mercury fumes were making me jumpy."

"To burn? To torch?"

Daniel now gripped the arms of his chair, threatening to get up and leave. Roger held up a hand. "I'm President of the Royal Society—it is my duty to be curious."

"I'm Secretary, and it is my duty to hold it all together when the President is being a fool."

"Better a fool in London than fuel in Cambridge. You will forgive me for wondering what went on."

"Since you're pretending to be a Catholic now, you may expect cheap grace from your French priests, but not from me."

"You are showing the self-righteousness I associated with upright men who've secretly done something very wrong—which is not to assert that you have any dark secrets, Daniel, only that you *act* that way."

"Does this conversation have any purpose other than to make me want to kill you, Roger?"

"I simply want to know what the hell Newton is doing."

"Then why harry me with these questions about what happened in '77?"

Roger shrugged. "You won't talk about *now,* so I thought I would try my luck with *then.*"

"Why the sudden interest in Isaac?"

"Because of *De Motu Corporum in Gyrum.* Halley says it is stupendous."

"No doubt."

"He says that it is only a sketch for a vast work that is consuming all of Newton's energies now."

"I am pleased that Halley has an explanation for the orbit of his comet, and even more pleased that he has taken over responsibility for the care and feeding of Isaac. What do you want of me?"

"Halley is blinded by comet-light," Roger scoffed. "If Newton decides to work out the mysteries of gravity and of planetary motion then Halley cares not why—he is a happy astronomer! And with Flamsteed around to depress the statistics, we need more happiness in the astronomical profession."

In *anno domini* 1674, the Sieur de St. Pierre (a French courtier, never mind the details) had been at some excellent Royal soiree when Louise de Kéroualle and her cleavage had hove into view above the rim of his goblet. Like most men who found themselves in her presence, the Sieur had been seized by an unaccountable need to impress her, somehow, some way. Knowing that Natural Philosophy was a big deal at the Court of Charles II, he had employed the following gambit: he had remarked that one could solve the problem of finding the Longitude by plotting the motions of the moon against the stars and using the heavens as a big clock. Kéroualle had relayed this to the King during some sort of Natural-Philosophic pillow talk, and his majesty had commissioned four Fellows of the Royal Society (the Duke of Gunfleet, Roger Comstock, Robert Hooke, and Christopher Wren) to find out if such a thing were really possible. They had asked one John Flamsteed. Flamsteed was the same age as Daniel. Too sickly to attend school, he had stayed home and taught himself astronomy. Later his health had improved to the point where he'd been able to attend Cambridge and learn what could be taught there, which was not much, at the time. When he had received this inquiry from the aforementioned four Fellows of the Royal Society, he had been just finishing up his studies, and looking for something to do. He had shrewdly written back saying that the proposal of the Sieur de St. Pierre, though it might be possible in theory, was perfectly absurd in practice, owing to a want of reliable astronomical data—*which could only be remedied by a lengthy and expensive research program.* It was the first and the last politic thing that Flamsteed had ever done. Without delay Charles II had appointed him Astronomer Royal and founded the Royal Observatory.

Flamsteed's temporary quarters, for the first couple of years, were in the Tower of London, atop the round turret of the White Tower. He made his first observations there while a permanent facility was being constructed on a patch of disused royal property at Greenwich.

Henry VIII, not satisfied with six wives, had maintained any number of mistresses, storing them, when not in use, in a sort of bolt-hole on the top of a hill above Greenwich Palace. His successors had not shared his appetites, and so the royal fuck-house had largely fallen into ruin. The foundations, however, were still sound. Atop them, Wren and Hooke, working in a hurry, and on a tiny budget, had built some apartments, which served as plinth for an octagonal salt-box. Atop that was a turret, an allusion in miniature to the Norman turrets of the Tower of London. The apartments were for Flamsteed to live in. The octagon above was constructed essentially so that the court-fop contingent of the Royal Society would have a place to go and peer learnedly through telescopes. But because it had been built on the foundations of Henry VIII's hilltop love shack, the whole building was oriented the wrong way. To make real observations, it had been necessary to construct an alienated limestone wall in the garden out back, oriented north–south. This was partly sheltered by a sort of roofless shack. Bolted to it were a pair of Hooke-designed quadrants, one looking north and the other looking south, each equipped with a sighting-tube. Flamsteed's life, thereafter, consisted of sleeping all day, then going out at night, leaning against this wall, peering through the sighting-tubes at stars swinging past, and noting their positions. Every few years, the work was enlivened by the appearance of a comet.

"What was Newton doing one year ago, Daniel?"

"Sources tell me he was calculating the precise date and hour of the Apocalypse, based upon occult shreds of data from the Bible."

"We must have the same sources," Roger said agreeably. "How much do *you* pay them?"

"I say things to them in return. It is called having conversations, and for some it is payment enough."

"You must be right, Daniel. For, several months ago, Halley shows up and has a conversation with Newton: 'Say, old chap, what about comets?' And Newton drops the Apocalypse and turns to Euclid. Within a few months he's got *De Motu* out."

"He worked out most of it in '79, during his *last* feud with Hooke," Daniel said, "and mislaid it, and had to work it out a second time."

"What—Doctor Waterhouse—do alchemy, the Apocalypse, and the elliptical orbits of heavenly bodies have in common? Other than that Newton is obsessed with all of them."

Daniel said nothing.

"*Anything? Everything? Nothing?*" Roger demanded, and slapped the edge of the table. "Is Newton a billiard ball or a comet?"

"I beg your pardon?"

"Oh, come here, Daniel," Roger clucked, going into sudden motion. Rather than standing up first, *then* walking, he lowered his wig, raised his hindquarters, and lunged off into the crowd like a bull, and in spite of bulk, middle age, gout, and drink, forged a path through the coffee-house faster than Daniel could follow. When Daniel next caught sight of Roger, the Marquis was shouldering his way past a fop. The fop was gripping a wooden implement shaped vaguely like a long-handled flour-scoop, and taking aim at a painted wooden sphere at rest on a green baize firmament. "Behold!" Roger exclaimed, and shoved at the ball with his bare hand. It rolled into another ball and stopped; the second ball rolled away. The fop was gripping his stick with both hands and winding up to break it over Roger's head, when Roger adroitly turned his back on the table, giving the fop a clear view of his face. The stick fell from the fop's hands. "Excellent shot, m'Lord," he began, "though not wholly in line with the spirit or the letter of the rules . . ."

"I am a Natural Philosopher, and my Rules are the God-given Rules of the Universe, not the arbitrary ones of your insipid sport!" Roger thundered. "The ball transfers its *vis viva* into another ball, the quantity of motion is conserved, all is more or less orderly." Roger now opened one hand to reveal that he had snatched another ball. "Or, I may toss it into the air thus—" he did so "—and it describes a Galilean trajectory, a parabola." The ball plonked down squarely into a mug of chocolate, halfway across the room; its owner recovered quickly, raising the mug to Roger's health. "But comets adhere to no laws, they come from God only knows where, at unpredictable times, and streak through the cosmos on their own unfathomable trajectories. So, I ask you, Daniel: Is Newton like a comet? Or, like a billiard ball, is he following some rational trajectory I have not the wit to understand?"

"I understand your question now," Daniel said. "Astronomers used to explain the seeming retrograde movements of the planets by imagining a phantastic heavenly axle-tree fitted out with crystalline spheres. *Now* we know that in fact the planets move in smooth ellipses and that retrograde motion is an *illusion* created by the fact that we are making our observations from a moving platform."

"Viz. the Earth."

"If we could see the planets from some fixed frame of reference, the retrograde motion would disappear. And you, Roger, observing Newton's wandering trajectory—one year devising new receipts for the Philosophic Mercury, the next hard at work on Conic Sections—are trying to figure out whether there might be some Reference Frame within which all of Isaac's moves make some kind of damned sense."

"Spoken like Newton himself," Roger said.

"You want to know whether his recent work on gravitation is a change of subject, or merely a new point of view—a new way of perceiving the same old Topic."

"*Now* you are talking like Leibniz," Roger said grumpily.

"And with good reason, for Newton and Leibniz are both working on the same problem, and have been since at least '77," Daniel said. "It is the problem that Descartes could not solve. It comes down to whether the collisions of those billiard balls can be explained by geometry and arithmetic—or do we need to go beyond pure thought and into Empirical and/or Metaphysical realms?"

"Shut up," Roger said, "I'm working on a murderous headache *as it is.* I do not want to hear of metaphysics." He seemed partly sincere—but he was keeping one eye on someone who was coming up behind Daniel. Daniel turned around and came face to face with—

"Mr. Hooke!" Roger said.

"M'lord."

"You, sir, taught this fellow to make thermometers!"

"So I did, m'lord."

"I was just explaining to him that I wanted him to go up to Cambridge and gauge the heat of that town."

"The entire country seems warm to me, m'lord," said Hooke gravely, "in particular the eastern limb."

"I hear that the warmth is spreading to the West country."

"Here is a *pretext,*" said the Marquis of Ravenscar, stuffing a sheaf of papers into Daniel's right hip pocket, "and here is something for you to peruse on your journey—the latest from Leipzig." He shoved something rather heavier into the left pocket. "Good night, fellow Philosophers!"

"Let us go and walk in the streets of London," Hooke said to Daniel. He did not need to add: *Most of which I laid out personally.*

"RAVENSCAR HATED HIS COUSIN John Comstock, ruined him, bought his house, and tore it down," Hooke said, as if he'd been backed into a corner and forced to admit it, "but learned from him all the same! Why did John Comstock back the Royal Society in its early days? Because he was curious as to Natural Philosophy? Perhaps. Because Wilkins talked him into it? In part. But it cannot have escaped your notice that most of our experiments in those days—"

"Had something to do with gunpowder. Obviously."

"*Roger* Comstock owns no gunpowder-factories. But his interest in the doings of our Society is no less pragmatic. Make no mistake. The French and the Papists are running the country now—are they running Newton?"

Daniel said nothing. After years of sparring with Hooke over gravitation, Isaac had soared far beyond Hooke's reach since Halley's visit.

"I see," Daniel said finally. "Well, I must go north anyway, to play at being the Puritan Moses."

"It would be worth an excursion to Cambridge, then, in order to—"

"In order to clear Newton's name of any scurrilous accusations that might be made against him by jealous rivals," Daniel said.

"I was going to say, in order to disentangle him from the foreign supporters of a doomed King," Hooke said. "Good night, Daniel." And with a few dragging steps he was swallowed up in the sulfurous fog.

THE ENTIRE COUNTRY SEEMS WARM *to me . . . in particular the eastern limb*. Hooke might throw accusations carelessly, but not words. Among men who peered through telescopes, "limb" meant the edge of a heavenly body's disk, such as the moon's crescent when it was illumined from the side. Setting out to the northeast the next day, Daniel glanced at a map of Essex, Suffolk, and Norfolk and noticed that they formed a semicircular limb, bounded by the Thames on the south and the Wash on the north, and in between them, bulging eastwards into the North Sea. A bright light kindled above the Hague would shine a hundred nautical miles across the sea and light up that entire sweep of coastline, setting it aglow like a crescent moon, like the alchemist's symbol for silver. Silver was the element of the Moon, the complement and counterpart of the Sun, whose element was gold. And as the Sun King was now pouring much gold into England, the possible existence of a silvery lunar crescent just to the north of London had import. Roger had no patience with alchemical suppositions and superstitions, but politics he knew well.

The fifty-second parallel ran directly from Ipswich to the Hague, so any half-wit with a backstaff and an ephemeris could sail unerringly from one to the other and back. Daniel knew the territory well—the North Sea infiltrated the Suffolk coast with so many spreading rays of brackish water that when you gazed east at sunrise the terrain seemed to be crazed with rivers of light. It was impossible to travel up the coast proper. The road from London was situated ten to twenty miles inland, running more or less straight from Chelmsford to Colchester to Ipswich, and everything to the right side—between it and the sea—was hopeless, from the point of view of a King or anyone else who wanted to rule it: a long strip of fens diced up by estuaries and therefore equally impassable to horses and boats, easier to reach from Holland than from London. *Staying* there wasn't so bad, and staying out was even better, but *movement* was rarely worth the trouble. Objects would not move in a resistive medium unless impelled by a powerful force—ergo, any travelers in that coastal strip had to be smugglers, drawn by profit and repulsed by laws, shipping England's rude goods to Holland and importing Holland's finished ones. So Daniel, like his brothers Sterling and Oliver and Raleigh before him, had spent much time in this territory as a youth, loading and unloading flat-bottomed Dutch boats lurking beneath weeping willows in dark river-courses.

The first part of the journey was like being nailed, with several other people, into a coffin borne through a coal-mine by epileptic pallbearers. But at Chelmsford some passengers got out of the carriage and thereafter the way became straight and level enough that Daniel could attempt to read. He took out the printed document that Roger had given him in the coffee-house. It was a copy of *Acta Eruditorum,* the scholarly rag that Leibniz had founded in his home town of Leipzig.

Leibniz had been trying for a long time to organize the smart Germans. The smart Britons tended to see this as a shabby mockery of the Royal Society, and the smart Frenchmen viewed it as a mawkish effort by the Doctor (who'd been living in Hanover since '77) to hold up a flawed and tarnished mirror to the radiant intellectual life of Paris. While Daniel (reluctantly) saw some justice in these opinions, he suspected that Leibniz was *mostly* doing it simply because it was a good idea. At any rate *Acta Eruditorum* was Leibniz's (hence Germany's) answer to *Journal des Savants,* and it tended to convey the latest and best ideas coming from Germany—i.e., whatever Leibniz had been thinking about lately.

This particular issue had been printed several months earlier and contained an article by Leibniz on mathematics. Daniel began skimming it and right away saw distinctly familiar terms—the likes of which he had not glimpsed since '77—

"Stab me in the vitals," Daniel muttered, "he's finally done it!"

"Done what!?" demanded Exaltation Gather, who was sitting across from Daniel hugging a large box full of money.

"Published the calculus!"

"And what, pray tell, is that, Brother Daniel? Other than something that grows on one's teeth." The hoard of coins in Exaltation Gather's strong-box made dim muffled chinking noises as the carriage rocked from side to side on its Suspension—one of those annoyingly good French ideas.

"New mathematics, based upon the analysis of quantities that are infinitesimal and evanescent."

"It sounds very *metaphysical*," said the Reverend Gather. Daniel looked up at him. No one and nothing had ever been less metaphysical than he. Daniel had grown up in the company of men like this and for a while had actually considered them to be normal-looking. But several years spent in London coffee-houses, theatres, and royal palaces had insensibly altered his tastes. Now when he gazed upon a member of a Puritan sect he always cringed inside. Which was just the effect that the Puritans were aiming for. If the Rev. Gather's Christian name had been Exultation his garb would have been wildly inappropriate. But Exaltation it was, and for these people exaltation was a grim business.

Daniel had finally convinced King James II that His Majesty's claims to support all religious dissidents would seem a lot more convincing if he would take Cromwell's skull down from the stick where it had been posted all through Charles II's quarter-century-long reign, and put it back in the Christian grave with the rest of Cromwell. To Daniel and certain others, a skull on a stick was a conspicuous object and the request to take it down wholly reasonable. But His Majesty and every courtier within earshot had looked startled: they'd forgotten it was there! It was part of the London landscape, it was like the bird-shit on a windowpane you never notice. Daniel's request, James's ensuing decree, and the fetching down and re-interment of the skull had only drawn attention to it. Attention, in a modern Court, meant cruel witticisms, and so it had been a recent vogue to address wandering Puritan ministers as "Oliver," the joke being that many of them—being wigless, gaunt, and sparely dressed—looked like skulls on sticks. Exaltation Gather looked so much like a skull on a stick that Daniel almost had to physically restrain himself from knocking the man down and shoveling dirt on him.

"Newton seems to agree with you," Daniel said, "or else he's afraid that some Jesuit will *say* so, which amounts to the same thing."

"One need not be a Jesuit to be skeptical of vain imaginings—" began the now miffed Gather.

"*Something* must be there," Daniel said. "Look out the window, yonder. That fen is divided into countless small plots by water-courses—some natural, some carved out by industrious farmers. Each rectangle of land could be made into two smaller ones—just drag a stick across the muck and the water will fill up the scratch in the ground, like the æther filling the void between particles of matter. Is that metaphysical yet?"

"Why no, it is a good similitude, earthy, concrete, like something from the Geneva Bible. Have you looked into the Geneva Bible recently, or—"

"What happens then if we continue subdividing?" Daniel asked. "Is it the same all the way down? Or is it the case that *something happens* eventually, that we reach a place where no further subdivision is possible, where fundamental properties of Creation are brought into play?"

"Er—I have no idea, Brother Daniel."

"Is it vanity for us to consider the question? Or did God give us brains for a reason?"

"No religion, with the possible exception of Judaism, has ever been more favorably disposed towards education than ours," said Brother Exaltation, "so that question is answered before 'twas asked. But we must consider these, er, infinitesimals and evanescents in a way that is rigorous, pure, free from heathenish *idolatry* or French *vanity* or the metaphysical infatuations of the Papists."

"Leibniz agrees—and the result of applying just the approach you have prescribed, in the mathematical realm, is here, and it is called the calculus," said Daniel, patting the document on his knee.

"Does Brother Isaac agree?"

"He did twenty years ago, when he *invented* all of this," Daniel said. "Now I have no idea."

"I have heard from one of our brethren in Cambridge that Brother Isaac's comportment in church has raised questions as to his faith."

"Brother Exaltation," said Daniel sharply, "before you spread rumors that may get Isaac Newton thrown into prison, let's see about getting a few of our brethren *out*—shall we?"

IPSWICH HAD BEEN A CLOTH port forever, but that trade had fallen on hard times because of the fatal combination of cheap stuff from India and Dutch shipping that could bring it to Europe. It was the prototype of the ridiculously ancient English town, situated at the place where the River Orwell broadened into an estuary, the obvious spot where anyone from a cave-man to a Cavalier would drive a stake into the muck and settle. Daniel judged that the gaol had been the first structure to go up, some five or six thousand years ago perhaps, and that the rats had moved in a week or two later. Ipswich was the county seat, and so when Charles II had whimsically decided to enforce the Penal Laws, all of Suffolk's most outstanding Quakers, Barkers, Ranters, Congregationalists, Presbyterians, and the odd Jew had been rounded up and been deposited here. They might just as well have been released a month ago, but it was important to the King that Daniel, his chosen representative, come out and handle the matter in person.

The carriage pulled up in front of the gaol and Exaltation Gather sat in it nervously gripping his strong-box while Daniel went inside and scared the gaoler half to death by brandishing a tablecloth-sized document with a wax seal as big as a man's heart dangling from it. Then Daniel went into the gaol, interrupting a prayer meeting, and spouted an oration he'd already used in half a dozen other gaols, a wrung-out rag of a speech so empty and banal that he had no idea whether he was making any sense at all, or just babbling in tongues. The startled, wary looks on the faces of the imprisoned Puritans suggested that they were extracting *some* meaning from Daniel's verbalizations—he had no idea *what* exactly. Daniel did not really know how his speech was being interpreted until later. The prisoners had to be released one at a time. Each of them had to pay the bill for his meals and other necessaries—and many had been here for years.

Hence Exaltation Gather and his box of money. The King's gesture would fall flat if half the prisoners remained in pokey for debts accumulated during their (unjust and un-Christian) imprisonment and so the King had (through Daniel) encouraged special collections to be taken up in sympathetic churches and had (though this was supposed to be grievously secret) supplemented that money with some from his own reserves to make sure it all came off well. In practice it meant that the nonconformists of London and the King of England had used Exaltation Gather's strong-box as a dust-bin for disposal of all their oldest, blackest, lightest in weight, most clipped, worn, filed-down, and adulterated coins. The true value of each one of these objects had to be debated between the gaoler of Ipswich on one hand, and on the other, Exaltation Gather and any recently freed Puritans who (a) were sharp when it came to money and (b) enjoyed verbal disputes—i.e., all of them.

Daniel staged an orderly retreat to a church-yard with a view down to the harbor, where the sound of the argument was partly masked by the rushing and slapping of the surf. Various Puritans found him, and lined up to give him pieces of their minds. This went on for most of the day—but as an example, Edmund Palling came up and shook Daniel's hand.

Edmund Palling was a perpetual old man. So it had always

seemed to Daniel. Admittedly his strategy of radical hairlessness made it difficult to guess his age. But he'd seemed an old man running around with Drake during the Civil War, and as an old man he had marched in Cromwell's funeral procession. As an old trader he had frequently showed up at Stourbridge Fair peddling this or that, and had walked into Cambridge to inflict startling visitations on Daniel. Old Man Palling had attended the memorial service for Drake, and during his years living in London, Daniel had occasionally bumped into this elderly man on the streets of London.

Now here he was: "Which is it, Daniel, stupid or insane? You know the King."

Edmund Palling was a sensible man. He was, as a matter of fact, one of those Englishmen who was so sensible that he was daft. For as any French-influenced courtier could explain, to insist on everything's being reasonable, in a world that *wasn't*, was, in itself, unreasonable.

"Stupid," Daniel said. Until now he had been every inch the Court man, but he could not dissimulate to such as Edmund Palling. To be with this old man was to be thrown back four decades, to a time when it had become common for ordinary sensible Englishmen to speak openly the widely agreed-upon, but previously unmentionable fact that monarchy was a load of rubbish. The fact that, since those days, the Restoration had occurred and that Europe was in fact ruled by great Kings was of no consequence. At any rate, Daniel felt perfectly at home and at peace among these men, which was a bit alarming given that he was a close advisor to King James II. He could no more defend that King, or any monarch, to Edmund Palling than go to a meeting of the Royal Society and assert that the Sun revolved around the Earth.

Edmund Palling was fascinated, and nodded sagely. "Some have been saying insane, you know—because of the syphilis."

"Not true."

"That is extraordinary, because *everyone* is convinced he has syphilis."

"He *does*. But having gotten to know His Majesty reasonably well, Mr. Palling, it is my opinion, as Secretary of the Royal Society, that when he, er . . ."

"Does something that is just amazingly ludicrous."

"As some would say, Mr. Palling, yes."

"Such as letting us out of gaol in the hopes that we'll not perceive it as a cynical ploy, and supposing that we'll rally about his standard as if he really gives a farthing for Freedom of Conscience!"

"Without staking myself to any position concerning what you've just said, Mr. Palling, I would encourage you to look towards mere stupidity in your quest for explanations. Not to rule out fits of syphilitic insanity *altogether,* mind you . . ."

"What's the difference then? Or is it a distinction without a difference?"

"*This* sort of thing," Daniel said, waving towards the Ipswich gaol, "is *stupidity.* By contrast, a fit of syphilitic insanity would lead to results of a different character entirely: spasms of arbitrary violence, mass enslavements, beheadings."

Mr. Palling shook his head, then turned toward the water. "One day soon the sun will rise from across yonder sea and chase the fog of stupidity and the shadows of syphilitic insanity away."

"Very poetic, Mr. Palling—but I have met the Duke of Monmouth, I have roomed with the Duke of Monmouth, I have been vomited on by the Duke of Monmouth, and I am telling you that the Duke of Monmouth is no Charles II! To say nothing of Oliver Cromwell."

Mr. Palling rolled his eyes. "Very well, then—if Monmouth fails I'm on the next ship to Massachusetts."

STRETCH A LINE, and another intersecting it, and rotate the former about the latter and it will sweep out a cone. Now shove this cone through a plane (fig. 1) and mark every point on the plane where the cone touches it. Commonly the result is an ellipse (fig. 2), but if the cone's slope is parallel to the plane it makes a parabola (fig. 3), and if it's parallel to the axis it makes a two-part curve called a hyperbola (fig. 4).

An interesting feature of all of these curves—the ellipse, the parabola, and the hyperbola—was that they were generated by straight things, viz. two lines and a plane. An interesting feature of the hyperbola was that far away its legs came very close to being straight lines, but near the center there was dramatic curvature.

Greeks, e.g., Euclid, had done all of these things long ago and discovered various more or less interesting properties of conic sections (as this family of curves was called) and of other geometric constructions such as circles and triangles. But they'd done so as an exploration of pure thought, as a mathematician might compute the sum of two numbers. Every assertion that Euclid, *et al.,* made concerning geometry was backed up by a chain of logical proofs that could be followed all the way back to a few axioms that were obviously true, e.g., "the shortest distance between two points is a straight line." The truths of geometry were *necessary* truths; the human mind could imagine a universe in which Daniel's name was

LIBRI I. CONICORVM APOLLONII

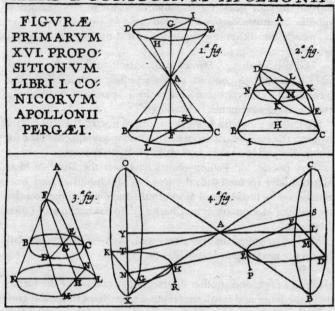

FIGVRÆ PRIMARVM XVI. PROPOSITIONVM LIBRI I. CONICORVM APOLLONII PERGÆI.

David, or in which Ipswich had been built on the other side of the Orwell, but geometry and math *had* to be true, there was no conceivable universe in which 2 + 3 was equal to 2 + 2.

Occasionally one discovered correspondences between things in the real world and the figments of pure math. For example: Daniel's trajectory from London to Ipswich had run in nearly a straight line, but after every one of the Dissenters had been let out of gaol, Daniel had executed a mighty change in direction and the next morning began riding on a rented horse towards Cambridge, following a trajectory that became straighter the farther he went. He was, in other words, describing a hyperbolic sort of path across Essex, Suffolk, and Cambridgeshire.

But he was not doing so *because* it was a hyperbola, or (to look at it another way) it was not a hyperbola because he was doing so. This was simply the route that traders had always taken, going from market to market as they traveled up out of Ipswich with wagonloads of imported or smuggled goods. He could have followed a *zigzag* course. That it looked like a hyperbola when plotted on a map of England was *luck*. It was a *contingent* truth.

It did not *mean* anything.

In his pocket were some notes that his patron, the good Marquis of Ravenscar, had stuffed into his pocket with the explanation "Here is a pretext." They'd been written out by John Flamsteed, the Astronomer Royal, apparently in response to inquiries sent down by Isaac. Daniel dared not unwrap and read this packet—the uncannily sensitive Isaac would smell Daniel's hand-prints on the pages, or something. But the cover letter was visible. Wedged into the chinks between its great blocks of Barock verbiage were a few dry stalks of information, and by teasing these out and plaiting them together Daniel was able to collect that Newton had requested information concerning the comet of 1680; a recent conjunction of Jupiter and Saturn; and the ebb and flow of tides in the ocean.

If any other scholar had asked for data on such seemingly disparate topics he'd have revealed himself to be a crank. The mere fact that Isaac was thinking about all of them at the same time was as good as proof that they were all related. Tides obviously had something to do with the moon because the formers' heights were related to the latter's phase; but what influence could connect the distant sphere of rock to every sea, lake, and puddle on the earth? Jupiter, orbiting along an inside track, occasionally raced past Saturn, lumbering along on the outer boundary of the solar system. Saturn had been seen to slow down as Jupiter caught up with it, then to speed up after Jupiter shot past. The distance separating Jupiter from Saturn was, at best, two thousand times that between the moon and the tides; what influence could span such a chasm? And comets, almost by definition, were above and outside of the laws (whatever they might be) that governed moons and planets— comets were not astronomical bodies, or indeed natural phenomena at all, so much as metaphors for the alien, the exempt, the transcendent—they were monsters, thunderbolts, letters from God. To bring them under the jurisdiction of any system of natural laws was an act of colossal hubris and probably asking for trouble.

But a few years earlier a comet had come through inbound, and a bit later an outbound one had been tracked, each moving on a different line, and John Flamsteed had stuck his neck out by about ten miles and asked the question, What if this was not *two* comets but one?

The obvious rejoinder was to point out that the two lines were different. One line, one comet; two lines, two comets. Flamsteed, who was as painfully aware of the vagaries and limitations of observational astronomy as any man alive, had answered that comets *didn't* move along lines and *never had;* that astronomers had observed only short segments of comets' trajectories that might actually be relatively straight excerpts of vast curves. It was known, for example, that most of a hyperbola was practically indistinguishable from a straight line—so who was to say that the supposed two comets of 1680 might not have been one comet that had executed a sharp course-change while close to the Sun, and out of astronomers' view?

In some other era this would have ranked Flamsteed with Kepler and Copernicus, but he was living now, and so it had made him into a sort of data cow to be kept in a stall in Greenwich and milked by Newton whenever Newton became thirsty. Daniel was serving in the role of milk-maid, rushing to Cambridge with the foaming pail.

There was much in this that demanded the attention of any European who claimed to be educated.

(1) Comets passed freely through space, their trajectories shaped only by (still mysterious) interactions with the Sun. If they moved on conic sections, it was no accident. A comet following a precise hyperbolic trajectory through the æther was a completely different thing from Daniel's *just happening* to trace a roughly hyperbolic course through the English countryside. If comets and planets moved along conic sections, it had to be some kind of *necessary* truth, an intrinsic feature of the universe. It *did* mean something. What exactly?

(2) The notion that the Sun exerted some centripetal force on the planets was now becoming pretty well accepted, but by asking for data on the interactions of moon and sea, and of Jupiter and Saturn, Isaac was as much as saying that these were all of a piece, that *everything* attracted *everything*—that the influences on (say) Saturn of the Sun, of Jupiter, and of Titan (the moon of Saturn that Huygens had discovered) were different only insofar as they came from different directions and had different magnitudes. Like the diverse goods piled up in some Amsterdam merchant's warehouse, they might come from many places and have different values, but in the end all that mattered was how much gold they could fetch on the Damplatz. The gold that paid for a pound of Malabar pepper was melted and fused with the gold that paid for a boatload of North Sea herring, and all of it was simply gold, bearing no trace or smell of the fish or the spice that had fetched it. In the case of Cœlestial Dynamics, the gold—the universal medium of exchange, to which everything was reduced—was force. The force exerted on Saturn by the Sun was no different from that exerted by Titan. In the end, the two forces were added together to make a vector, a combined resultant force bearing no trace of its origins. It was a powerful kind of alchemy because it took the motions of

heavenly bodies down from inaccessible realms and brought them within reach of men who had mastered the occult arts of geometry and algebra. Powers and mysteries that had been the exclusive province of Gods, Isaac was now arrogating to himself.

A SAMPLE CONSEQUENCE OF THIS alchemical fusing of forces would be that a comet fleeing the Sun on the out-bound limb of a hyperbola, traveling an essentially straight line, would, if it happened to pass near a planet, be drawn towards it. The Sun was not an absolute monarch. It did not have any special God-given power. The comet did not have to respect its force more than the forces of mere planets—in fact, the comet could not even perceive these two influences as being separate, they'd already been converted to the universal currency of force, and fused into a single vector. Far from the Sun, close to the planet, the latter's influence would predominate, and the comet would change course smartly.

And so did Daniel, after riding almost straight across the fenny country northeast of Cambridge for most of a day, and traversing the pounded, shit-permeated mud flat where Stourbridge Fair was held, suddenly swing round a bend of the Cam and drop into an orbit whose center was a certain suite of chambers just off to the side of the Great Gate of Trinity College.

Daniel still had a key to the old place, but he did not want to go there just yet. He stabled his horse out back of the college and came in through the rear entrance, which turned out to be a bad idea. He knew that Wren's library had started building, because Trinity had dunned him, Roger, and everyone else for contributions. And from the witty or despairing status reports that Wren gave the R.S. at every meeting, he was aware that the project had stopped and started more than once. But he hadn't thought about the practical consequences. The formerly smooth greens between the Cam and the back of the College were now a rowdy encampment of builders, their draft-animals, and their camp-followers (and not just whores but itinerant publicans, tool-sharpeners, and errand-boys, too). So there was a certain amount of wading through horse-manure, wandering into blind alleys that had once been bowling-greens, tripping over hens, and declining more or less attractive carnal propositions before Daniel could even get a clear view of the library.

Most of Cambridge had fallen into twilight while Daniel had been seeking a route through the builders' camp. Not that it made much of a difference, since the skies had looked like hammered lead all day. But the upper story of the Wren Library was high enough to look west into tomorrow's weather, which would be fine and clear. The roof was mostly on, and where it wasn't, its shape was lofted by rafters and ridge-beams of red oak that seemed to resonate in the warm light of the sunset, not merely blocking the rays but humming in sympathy with their radiance. Daniel stood and looked at it for a while because he knew that any moment of such beauty could never last, and he wanted to describe it to the long-suffering Wren when he got back to London.

The bell began to toll, calling the Fellows to the dining hall, and Daniel slogged forward through the Library's vacant arches and across Neville's Court just in time to throw on a robe and join his colleagues at the High Table.

The faces around that table were warmed by port and candle-light, and exhibiting a range of feelings. But on the whole they looked satisfied. The last Master who'd tried to enforce any discipline on the place had suffered a stroke while hollering at some rowdy students. There was no preventing students and faculty from drawing weighty conclusions from such an event. His replacement was a friend of Ravenscar, an Earl who'd showed up reliably for R.S. meetings since the early 1670s and reliably fallen asleep halfway through them. He came up to Cambridge only when someone more important than he was there. The Duke of Monmouth was no longer Chancellor; he'd been stripped of all such titles during one of his banishments, and replaced by the Duke of Tweed—a.k.a. General Lewis, the L in Charles II's CABAL.

Not that he or any other Chancellor made any difference. The college was run by the Senior Fellows. Twenty-five years earlier, just at the moment Daniel and Isaac had entered Trinity, Charles II had kicked out the Puritan scholars who had nested there under Wilkins and replaced 'em with Cavaliers who could best be described as gentlemen-scholars—in that order. While Daniel and Isaac had been educating themselves, these men had turned the college into their own personal termite-mound. Now they were Senior Fellows. The High Table diet of suet, cheese, and port had had its natural effect, and it was a toss-up as to whether their bodies or their minds had become softer.

No one could recollect the last time Isaac had set foot in this Hall. His lack of interest was looked on as proving not that something was wrong with Trinity but that something was wrong with Isaac. And in a way, this was just; if a College's duty was to propagate a certain way of being to the next generation, this one was working perfectly, and Isaac would only have disrupted the place by bothering to participate.

The Fellows seemed to know this (this was how Daniel thought of them: not as a roomful of individuals but as The Fellows, a sort of hive or flock, an aggregate. The question of aggregates had been vexing Leibniz to no end. A flock of sheep consisted of several individual sheep and was a flock only by convention—the quality of flockness was put on it by humans—it existed only in some human's mind as a perception. Yet Hooke had found that the human body was made up of cells—therefore, just as much an aggregate as a flock of sheep. Did this mean that the body, too, was just a figment of perception? Or was there some unifying influence that made those cells into a coherent body? And what of High Table at Trinity College? Was it more like a flock of sheep or a body? To Daniel it seemed very much like a body at the moment. To carry out the assignment given him by Roger Comstock he'd have to interrupt that mysterious unifying principle somehow, disaggregate the College, then cut a few sheep from the flock). The aggregate called Trinity noticed that Isaac only came to church once a week, on Sunday, and his behavior in the chapel was raising Trinity's eyebrows, though unlike Puritans these High Church gentles would never come out and say what they were thinking about religion. That was all right with Daniel, who knew perfectly well what Newton was doing and what these men were thinking about it.

But later, after Daniel and several of the Fellows had filed out of the Hall and gone upstairs to a smaller room, to sit around a smaller table and drink port, Daniel used this as a sort of lure, dragging it through the pond to see if anything would rise up out of the murk and snap at it: "Given the company Newton's been known to keep, I can't help but wonder if he has become attracted to Popery."

Silence.

"Gentlemen!" Daniel continued, "there's nothing *wrong* with it. Remember, our King is a Catholic."

There were thirteen other men in the room. Eleven of them found his remark to be in unspeakably poor taste (which was true) and said nothing. Daniel did not care; they'd forgive him on grounds that he'd been drinking and was well-connected. One of them understood immediately what Daniel was up to: this was Vigani, the alchemist. If Vigani had been following Isaac as closely, and listening to him as intently, as he had followed and listened to Daniel this evening, he would know a lot. For now, the ends of his mustache curled up wickedly and he hid his amusement in a goblet.

But one man, the youngest and drunkest in the room—a man who'd made no secret of the fact that he desperately wanted to get into the Royal Society—rose to the bait.

"I'd sooner expect all of Mr. Newton's nocturnal visitors to convert to *his* brand of religion than *he* to *theirs!*"

This produced a few stiff chuckles, which only encouraged him. "Though God help 'em if they tried to get back into France afterwards—considering what King Louis does to Huguenots, imagine what kind of welcome he'd give to a full-blown—"

"To say nothing of Spain with the Inquisition," said Vigani drolly. Which was a heroic and well-executed bid to change the topic to something so banal as to be a complete waste of breath—after all, the Spanish Inquisition had few defenders locally.

But Daniel had not endured years among courtiers without developing skills of his own. "I'm afraid we'll have to wait for an English Inquisition to find out what our friend was just about to say!"

"*That* should be coming along any day now," someone muttered.

They were beginning to break ranks! But Vigani had recovered: "Inquisition? Nonsense! Freedom of Conscience is the King's byword—or so Dr. Waterhouse has been telling everyone."

"I have been a mere conduit for what the King says."

"But you have just come from releasing a lot of Dissenters from prison, have you not?"

"Your knowledge of my pastimes is uncanny, sir," Daniel said. "You are correct. There are plenty of empty cells available just now."

"Shame to waste 'em," someone offered.

"The King will find some use for those vacancies," predicted someone else.

"An easy prediction to make. Here's a more difficult: what will that King's name be?"

"England."

"I meant his Christian name."

"You're assuming he's going to be a Christian, then?"

"You're assuming he's one now?"

"Are we speaking of the King who lives in Whitehall, or the one who has been spotted in the Hague?"

"The one in Whitehall has been *spotted* ever since his years in France: spotted on his face, on his hands, on his—"

"Gentlemen, gentlemen, this room is too warm and close for your wit, I beg you," said the most senior of the Fellows present, who looked as if he might be on the verge of having a stroke of his own. "Dr. Waterhouse was merely enquiring about his old friend, our colleague, Newton—"

"Is this the version we're all going to relate to the English Inquisition?"

"You are merry, too merry!" protested the Senior Fellow, now red in the face, and not with embarrassment. "Dr. Newton might serve as an example to you, for he goes about his work with *gravity*, and it is *sound* work in geometry, mathematics, astronomy . . ."

"Eschatology, astrology, alchemy . . ."

"No! No! Ever since Mr. Halley came up to enquire on the subject of Comets, Newton has had many fewer visitors from outside, and Signore Vigani has had to seek companionship in the Hall."

"I need only *enter* the Hall and companionship is *found*," said Vigani smoothly, "there is never *seeking*."

"Please excuse me," Daniel said, "it sounds as if Newton might welcome a visitor."

"He might welcome a crust of bread," someone said, "lately he has been scratching in his garden like a peckish hen."

> I cannot choose but condemn those Persons, who suffering themselves to be too much dazzled with the Lustre of the noble Actions of the Ancients, make it their Study to Extol them to the Skies; without reflecting, that these later Ages have furnished us with others more Heroick and Wonderful.
>
> — GEMELLI CARERI

PASSING THROUGH the Great Gate, he borrowed a lantern from a porter and exited onto a walkway that led to the street, hemmed in by crenellated walls. The wall to his left had a narrow gate let into it. Using his old key, Daniel opened the lock on this gate and stepped through into a sizable garden. It was laid out as a grid of gravel walkways with squares of greenery between. Some of the squares were planted with small fruit trees, others with shrubs or grass. To his left a line of taller trees screened the windows of the row of chambers that filled the space between the Great Gate and the Chapel. The buds in their branches were just evolving to nascent leaves, and where light shone from Isaac's windows they glowed like stopped explosions, phosphorus-green. But most of the windows were dark, and the stars above the muzzles of the chimneys were sharp and crystalline, not blurred by heat or dimmed by smoke. Isaac's furnaces were cold, the stuff in their crucibles congealed. Their heat had all gone into his skull.

Daniel let his lantern-hand fall to his side so that the light shone across the gravel path from the altitude of his knee. This made Isaac's chicken-scratchings stand out in high relief.

Every one had started the same way: with Isaac slashing the toe of his shoe, or the point of his stick, across the ground to make a curve. Not a specific curve—not a circle or a parabola—but a representative curve. Everything in the universe was curved, and those curves were evanescent and fluxional, but with this gesture Isaac snatched a particular curve—it didn't matter which—down from the humming cosmos, like a frog flicking its tongue out to filch a gnat from a swarm. Once trapped in the gravel, it was frozen and helpless. Isaac could stand and look at it for as long as he wanted, like Sir Robert Moray gazing at a stuffed eel in a glass box. After a while Isaac would begin to slash straight lines into the gravel, building up a scaffold of rays, perpendiculars, tangents, chords, and normals. At first this would seem to grow in a random way, but then lines would intersect with others to form a triangle, which would miraculously turn out to be an echo of another triangle in a different place, and this fact would open up a sort of sluice-gate that would free information to flood from one part of the diagram to another, or to leap across to some other, completely different diagram—but the results never came clear to Daniel's mind because here the diagram would be aborted and a series of footsteps—lunar craters in the gravel—would plot Isaac's hasty return to his chambers, where it could be set down in ink.

Daniel followed these footsteps into the chambers he had once shared. The ground floor was cluttered with alchemical droppings, but not as dangerous as usual, since everything was cold. Daniel shone his lantern around one quiet room and then another. Everything that gave light back was hard mineral stuff, the inert refractory elements to which nature always returned: crusty crucibles, sooty retorts, corroded tongs, black crystals of charcoal, globs of quicksilver trapped in floor-cracks, a box of golden guineas left open next to a window as if to prove to all passers-by that the man who lived here cared nothing for gold.

On a desk he saw letters in Latin from gentlemen in Prague, Naples, St.-Germain, addressed to JEOVA SANCTUS UNUS. Through gaps between them Daniel saw parts of a large drawing that had been pinned down to the surface of the table. It looked like a floor plan of a building. Daniel moved some papers and books out of the way to expose more of it. He was wondering whether Isaac—like Wren, Hooke, and Daniel himself—had gone into Architecture.

Isaac appeared to be designing a square, walled court with a rectangular structure in the middle. Sweeping a trapezoid of lantern-light over a block of writing, Daniel read the following: *The same God gave the dimensions of the Tabernacle to Moses and Temple with its Courts to David & Ezekiel & altered not the proportion of the areas but only doubled them in the Temple . . . So then Solomon and Ezekiel agree, and are double to Moses.*

"I am only trying to recover what Solomon knew," Isaac said.

Knowing that the lantern would blind Isaac's burnt eyes, Daniel raised it up and blew it out before turning around. Isaac had come in silence down a stone staircase. His atelier on the first story had candles burning, and these warmed the stone behind Isaac with orange light. He was a black silhouette robed in a dressing-gown, his head cloaked with silver. He had not grown any heavier since College days, which was no surprise if the rumors about his dining habits were to be credited.

"I can't help but wonder if you—perhaps even *I*—don't know a hell of a lot more about practically every subject than Solomon ever did," Daniel said.

Isaac said nothing for a moment, but something about his silhouette looked wounded, or sad.

"It's right there in the Bible, Daniel. First chapter: the Garden of Eden. Last chapter: the Apocalypse."

"I know, I know, the world started out perfectly good and has gotten worse and worse since then, and the only question is how bad will it get before God brings down the curtain. I was raised to believe that this tendency was as fixed and unavoidable as gravity, Isaac. But the Apocalypse did not come in 1666."

"It will occur not long after 1867," Isaac said. "That is the year when the Beast will fall."

"Most Anglican cranks are guessing 1700 for the demise of the Catholic Church."

"It is not the only way that the Anglicans are wrong."

"Could it be, Isaac, that things are getting *better,* or at worst remaining more or less *the same,* rather then getting *worse* all the time? Because I really think you may know certain things that never entered Solomon's head."

"I am working out the System of the World upstairs," Isaac said offhandedly. "It is not beyond reason to think that Solomon and other ancients knew that System, and encrypted it in the design of their Temples."

"But according to the Bible those designs were given to them directly by God."

"But go outside and look up at the stars and you see God trying to give you the same thing, if only you will pay attention."

"If Solomon knew all of this, why didn't he just come out and say, 'The sun is in the middle of the solar system and planets go round about it in ellipses?'"

"I believe he did say so, in the design of his temple."

"Yes, but why are God and Solomon alike so damned oblique in everything? Why not just come out and say it?"

"It is good that you do not waste my time with tedious letters," Isaac said. "When I read a letter I can follow the words, but I cannot fathom the mind, of him who sent it. It is better that you come to visit me in the night-time."

"Like an alchemist?"

"Or an early Christian in pagan Rome . . ."

"Scratching curves in the dust?"

". . . or any Christian who dares oppose the idolators. If you were to use me thus in a letter, I would conclude you were in the employ of the Beast, as some say you are."

"What, merely for suggesting that the world does something other than rot?"

"Of course it rots, Daniel. There is no perpetual motion machine."

"Except for the heart."

"The heart rots, Daniel. Sometimes it even begins to rot while its owner still lives."

Daniel dared not follow that one up. After a silence Isaac continued, in a throatier voice: "Where do we find God in the world? That is all I want to know. I have not found Him yet. But when I see anything that does *not* rot—the workings of the solar system, or a Euclidean proof, or the perfection of gold—I sense I am drawing nearer to the Divine."

"Have you found the Philosophick Mercury yet?"

"In '77, Boyle was certain he had it."

"I remember."

"I agreed with him for a short time—but it was wishful thinking. I am seeking it in geometry now—or rather I am seeking it where geometry fails."

"Fails?"

"Come upstairs with me Daniel."

DANIEL RECOGNIZED THE first proof as easily as his own signature. "Objects governed by a centripetal force conserve angular momentum and sweep out equal areas in equal times."

"You have read my *De Motu Corporum in Gyrum*?"

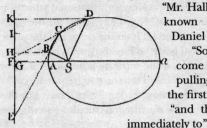

"Mr. Halley has made its contents known to the Royal Society," Daniel said drily.

"Some supporting lemmas come out of this," Isaac said, pulling another diagram over the first.

"and thence we can move on immediately to"

"That is the great one," Daniel said. "If the centripetal force is governed by an inverse-square law, then the body moves on an ellipse, or at any rate a conic section."

"I would say, 'That heavenly bodies *do* move on conic sections proves the inverse-square law.' But we are only speaking of fictions, so far. These proofs only apply to infinitesimal concentrations of mass, which do not exist in the real world. *Real* heavenly bodies possess geometry—they comprise a vast number of tiny particles arranged in the shape of a sphere. If Universal Gravitation exists, then each of the motes that make up the Earth attracts every other, and attracts the moon as well, and vice versa. And each of the moon's particles attracts the water in Earth's oceans to create tides. But how does the spherical geometry of a planet inform its gravity?"

Isaac produced another sheet, much newer-looking than the rest.

Daniel did not recognize this one. At first he thought it was a diagram of an eyeball, like the ones Isaac had made as a student. But Isaac was speaking of planets, not eyes.

A few awkward moments followed.

"Isaac," Daniel finally said, "*you* can draw a diagram like this one and say, 'Behold!' and the proof is finished. *I* require a bit of explanation."

"Very well." Isaac pointed to the circle in the middle of the diagram. "Consider a spherical body—actually an aggregate of countless particles, each of which produces gravitational attraction according to an inverse square law." Now he reached for the nearest handy object—an inkwell—and set it on the corner of the page, as far away from the "spherical body" as it could go. "What is felt by a satellite, here, on the outside, if the separate attractions of all of those particles are summed and fused into one aggregate force?"

"Far be it from me to tell you how to do physics, Isaac, but this strikes me as an ideal problem for the integral calculus—so why are you solving it geometrically?"

"Why not?"

"Is it because Solomon didn't have the calculus?"

"The calculus, as *some* call it, is a harsh method. I prefer to develop my proofs in a more geometric way."

"Because geometry is ancient, and everything ancient is good."

"This is idle talk. The result, as anyone can see from contemplating my diagram, is that a spherical body—a planet, moon, or star—having a given quantity of matter, produces a gravitational attraction that is the same as if all of its matter were concentrated into a single geometric point at the center."

"The *same*? You mean *exactly* the same?"

"It is a geometrical proof," Isaac merely said. "That the particles are spread out into a sphere *doesn't make any difference* because the geometry of the sphere is what it is. The gravity is the same."

Daniel now had to locate a chair; all the blood in his legs seemed to be rushing into his brain.

"If that is true," he said, "then everything you proved *before* about point objects—for example that they move along conic section trajectories—"

"Applies without alteration to spherical bodies."

"To *real things*." Daniel had a queer vision just then of a shattered Temple reconstituting itself: fallen columns rising up from the rubble, and the rubble re-aggregating itself into cherubim and seraphim, a fire sparking on the central altar. "You've done it then . . . created the System of the World."

"*God* created it. I have only *found* it. Rediscovered what was forgot. Look at this diagram, Daniel. It is *all here,* it is Truth made manifest, *epiphanes*."

"Now you said before that you were looking for God where Geometry failed."

"Of course. There is no *choice* in this," Isaac said, patting his diagram with a dry hand. "Not even God could have made the world otherwise. The only God here—" Isaac slammed the page hard "—is the God of Spinoza, a God that is everything and therefore nothing."

"But it seems as if you've explained everything."

"I've not explained the inverse square law."

"You've a proof right there saying that if gravity follows an inverse square law, satellites move on conic sections."

"And Flamsteed says that they do," Isaac said, yanking the sheaf of notes out of Daniel's hip pocket. Ignoring the cover letter, he tore the ribbon from the bundle and began to scan the pages. "Therefore gravity does indeed follow an inverse square law. But we may only say so because it is consistent with Flamsteed's observations. If tonight Flamsteed notices a comet moving in a spiral, it shows that all my work is wrong."

"You're saying, why do we need Flamsteed at all?"

"I'm saying that the fact that we do need him proves that God is making choices."

"Or has made them."

This caused a sort of queasy sneer to come across Isaac's face. He closed his eyes and shook his head. "I am not one of those who believes that God made the world and walked away from it, that He has no further choices to make, no ongoing presence in the world. I believe that He is everywhere, making choices all the time."

"But only because there are certain things you have not explained yet with geometric proofs."

"As I told you, I seek God where Geometry fails."

"But perhaps there is an undiscovered proof for the inverse square law. Perhaps it has something to do with vortices in the æther."

"No one has been able to make sense of vortices."

"Some interaction of microscopic particles, then?"

"Particles traversing the distance from the Sun to Saturn and back, at infinite speed, without being hindered by the æther?"

"You're right, it is impossible to take seriously. What is *your* hypothesis, Isaac?"

"*Hypothesis non fingo.*"

"But that's not really true. You begin with a hypothesis—I saw several of them scratched in the gravel out there. Then you come up with one of these diagrams. I cannot explain how you do that part, unless God is using you as a conduit. When you are finished, it is no longer a hypothesis but a demonstrated truth."

"Geometry can never explain gravity."

"Calculus then?"

"The calculus is just a convenience, a short-hand way of doing geometry."

"So what is beyond geometry is also beyond calculus."

"Of course, by definition."

"The inner workings of gravity, you seem to be saying, are beyond the grasp, or even the reach, of Natural Philosophy. To whom should we appeal, then? Metaphysicians? Theologians? Sorcerers?"

"They are all the same to me," Isaac said, "and I am one."

Beach North of Scheveningen
OCTOBER 1685

IT WAS AS IF WILLIAM of Orange had searched the world over to find the place most different from Versailles, and had told Eliza to meet him there. At Versailles, everything had been designed and made by men. But here was nothing to see but ocean and sand. Every grain of sand had been put where it was by waves that formed up in the ocean according to occult laws that might have been understood by the Doctor, but not by Eliza.

She had dismounted and was leading her horse northwards up the beach. The sand was hard-packed and solid and wet, speckled all over with cockle shells in colors and patterns of such profusion and variety that they must have given the first Dutchmen the idea to go out into the sea and bring back precious things from afar. They made a welcome contrast against the extreme flatness and sameness of beach, water, and misty sky, and exerted a hypnotic effect on her. She forced herself to look up from time to time. But the only feature of the view that ever changed was the signatures of foam deposited on the beach by the waves.

Each breaker, she supposed, was as unique as a human soul. Each made its own run up onto the shore, being the very embodiment of vigor and power at the start. But each slowed, spread thin, faltered, dissolved into a hissing ribbon of gray foam, and got buried under the next. The end result of all their noisy, pounding, repetitive efforts was the beach. Seen through a lens, the particular arrangement of sand-grains that made up the beach presumably was complicated, and reflected the individual contributions of every single wave that had ended its life here; but seen from the level of Eliza's head it was unspeakably flat, an "abomination of desolation in a dark place," as the Bible would put it.

She heard a ripping noise behind her and turned around to look to the south, toward the dent in the beach, several miles distant, that formed the harbor of Scheveningen. The last time she'd looked back, a few minutes ago, there had been nothing between her and the anchorage but a few clam-diggers. But now there was a sail on the sand: a triangle of canvas, stretched drum-tight by the wet wind off the sea. Below it hovered a spidery rig of timbers with spoked wagon-wheels at their ends. One wheel was suspended in the air by the heeling of the vehicle. Taken together with the speed of its progress up the beach, this created the impression that it was flying. The wheel spun slowly in the air, dripping clots of wet sand from its rim, which was very wide so that it rolled over, instead of cutting into, the sand and its gay mosaic of cockle shells. The opposite wheel was scribing a long fat track down the beach, slaloming between the dark hunched forms of the diggers; though, a hundred yards in its wake, this trace had already been erased by the waves.

A fishing-boat had eased in to shore as the tide ebbed, pulled up her sideboards, and allowed herself to be stranded there. The fishermen had chocked her upright with baulks of wood, brought their catch up out of the hold, and laid it out on the sand, creating a little fish-market that would last until the tide flowed in again, chased away the customers, and floated the boat. People had carried baskets out from town, or driven out in carriages, to carry out disputes with the fishermen over the value of what they'd brought back from the deep.

Some of them turned to look at the sand-sailer. It rushed past Eliza, moving faster than any horse could gallop. She recognized the man operating the tiller and manipulating the lines. Some of the fish-buyers did, too, and a few of those bothered to doff their hats and bow. Eliza mounted her horse and rode in pursuit.

The view inland was blocked by dunes. Not dunes such as Eliza had once seen in the Sahara, but hybrids of dunes and hedges. For these were covered by, and anchored in, vegetation that was light green in the lower slopes, but in other places deepened to a bluish cast, and formed up into great furry dark eyebrows frowning at the sea.

A mile or so north of where the fishing-boat had been beached, the sight-line from the town was severed by a gradual bend in the coastline, and a low spur flung seawards by a dune. From here, the only sign that Holland was a settled country was a tall watchtower with a conical roof, built atop a dune, perhaps half a mile distant. The sand-sailer had come to rest, its sheets loosened so that the sail reached and weathercocked.

"I am probably meant to ask, 'Where is your Court, O Prince, your entourage, your bodyguards, your train of painters, poets, and historians?' Whereupon you'd give me a stern talking-to about the decadence of France."

"Possibly," said William, Prince of Orange and Stadholder of the Dutch Republic. He had extricated himself from the canvas seat of the sailer and was standing on the beach facing out to sea, layers of sand-spattered leather and spray-soaked wool giving his body more bulk than it really had. "Or perhaps I like to go sand-sailing by myself, and your reading so much into it is proof you've been too long at Versailles."

"Why is this dune here, I wonder?"

"I don't know. Tomorrow it may not be. Why do you mention it?"

"I look at all these waves, spending so much effort to accomplish so little, and wonder that from time to time they can raise something as interesting as a dune. Why, this hill of sand is equivalent to Versailles—a marvel of ingenuity. Waves from the Indian Ocean, encountering waves of Araby off the Malabar Coast, must gossip about this dune, and ask for the latest tidings from Scheveningen."

"It is normal for women, at certain times of the month, and in certain seasons of the year, to descend into moods such as this one," the prince mused.

"A fair guess, but wrong," Eliza said. "There are Christian slaves in Barbary, you know, who expend vast efforts to accomplish tiny goals, such as getting a new piece of furniture in their *banyolar* . . ."

"Banyolar?"

"Slave-quarters."

"What a pathetic story."

"Yes, but it is all right for them to achieve meager results because they are in a completely hopeless and desperate situation," Eliza said. "In a way, a slave is fortunate, because she has more head-room for her dreams and phant'sies, which can soar to dizzying heights without bumping up 'gainst the ceiling. But the ones who live at Versailles are as high as humans can get, they practically have to go about stooped over because their wigs and head-dresses are scraping the vault of heaven—which consequently seems low and mean to them. When they look up, they see, not a vast beckoning space above, but rather—"

"The gaudy-painted ceiling."

"Just so. You see? There is no head-room. And so, for one who has just come from Versailles, it is easy to look at these waves, accomplishing so little, and to think that no matter what efforts we put forth in our lives, all we're really doing is rearranging the sand-grains in a beach that in essence never changes."

"Right. And if we're really brilliant, we can cast up a little dune or hummock that will be considered the Eighth Wonder of the World."

"Just so!"

"Lass, it's very poetic, albeit in a bleak Gothic sort of way, but, begging your pardon, I look up and I don't see the ceiling. All I see is a lot of damned Frenchmen looking down their noses at me from a mile high. I must pull them all down to my level, or draw myself up to theirs, before I can judge whether I have succeeded in making a dune, or what-have-you. So let us turn our attentions thither."

"Very well. There is little to hold our attention *here.*"

"What do you imagine was the point of the King's admonition, at the end of your most recent letter?"

"What—you mean, what he said to me after his operation?"

"Yes."

"Fear me inasmuch as you are my foe, be proud inasmuch as my friend? That one?"

"Yes, that one."

"Seems self-explanatory to me."

"But why on earth would the King feel the need to deliver such a warning to d'Avaux?"

"Perhaps he has doubts as to the count's loyalty."

"That is inconceivable. No man could be more his King's creature than d'Avaux."

"Perhaps the King is losing his grip, and perceiving enemies where none exist."

"Very doubtful. He has too many real enemies to indulge himself so—and besides, he is very far from losing his grip!"

"Hmph. None of *my* explanations is satisfactory, it seems."

"Now that you are out of France you must shed the habit of pouting, my Duchess. You do it exquisitely, but if you try it on a Dutchman he'll only want to slap you."

"Will you share *your* explanation with me, if I promise not to pout?"

"Obviously the King's admonition was intended for someone other than the comte d'Avaux."

This left Eliza baffled for a minute.. William of Orange fussed with the rigging of his sand-sailer while she turned it over in her head. "You are saying then that the King knows my letters to d'Avaux are being decyphered and read by Dutch agents . . . and that his warning was intended for *you*. Have I got it right?"

"You are only starting to get it right . . . and this is becoming tedious. So let me explain it, for until you understand this, you will be useless to me. Every letter posted abroad from Versailles, whether it originates from you, or Liselotte, or the Maintenon, or some chambermaid, is opened by the Postmaster and sent to the *cabinet noir* to be read."

"Heavens! Who is in the *cabinet noir?*"

"Never mind. The point is that they have read all of your letters to d'Avaux and conveyed anything important to the King. When they are finished they give the letters back to the Postmaster, who artfully re-seals them and sends them north . . . *my* Postmaster then re-opens them, reads them, re-seals them, and sends them on to d'Avaux. So the King's admonition could have been intended for anyone in that chain: d'Avaux (though probably not), me, my advisors, the members of his own *cabinet noir* . . . or *you*."

"Me? Why would he want to admonish a little nothing like me?"

"I simply mention you for the sake of completeness."

"I don't believe you."

The Prince of Orange laughed. "Very well. Louis' entire system is built on keeping the nobility poor and helpless. Some of them enjoy it, others don't. The latter sort look for ways of making money. To whatever degree they succeed, they threaten the King. Why do you think the French East India Company fails time and again? Because Frenchmen are stupid? They are not stupid. Or rather, the stupid ones get despatched to India, because Louis wants that company to fail. A port-city filled with wealthy *commerçants*—a London or an Amsterdam—is a nightmare to him."

"Now, some of those nobles who desire money have turned their attentions toward Amsterdam and begun to engage the services of Dutch brokers. This was how your former business associate, Mr. Sluys, made his fortune. The King is pleased that you ruined Sluys, because he took some French counts down with him, and they serve as object lessons to any French nobles who try to build fortunes in the market of Amsterdam. But now you are being approached, yes? Your 'Spanish Uncle' is the talk of the town."

"You can't possibly expect me to believe that the King of France views *me* as a threat."

"Of course not."

"*You*, William of Orange, the Protestant Defender, are a threat."

"I, William, whatever titles you wish to hang on me, am an *enemy*, but not a *threat*. I may make war on him, but I will never imperil him, or his reign. The only people who can do that are all living at Versailles."

"Those dreadful dukes and princes and so on."

"And duchesses and princesses. Yes. And insofar as you might help these do mischief, you are to be watched. Why do you imagine d'Avaux put you there? As a favor? No, he put you there to be watched. But insofar as you may help Louis maintain his grip, you are a tool. One of many tools in his toolbox—but a strange one, and strange tools are commonly the most useful."

"If I am so useful to Louis—your enemy—then what am I to *you*?"

"To date, a rather slow and unreliable pupil," William answered.

Eliza heaved a sigh, trying to sound bored and impatient. But she could not help shuddering a bit as the air came out of her—a premonition of sobs.

"Though not without promise," William allowed.

Eliza felt better, and hated herself for being so like one of William's hounds.

"None of what I have written in any of my letters to d'Avaux has been of any use to you at all."

"You have only been learning the ropes, so far," William said, plucking like a harp-player at various lines and sheets in the rigging of his sand-sailer. He climbed aboard and settled himself into the seat. Then he drew on certain of those ropes while paying out others, and the vehicle sprang forward, rolling down the slope of the dune, and building speed back towards Scheveningen.

ELIZA MOUNTED HER HORSE and turned around. The wind off the sea was in her face now, like a fine mixture of ice and rock salt fired out of blunderbusses. She decided to cut inland to get out of the weather. Riding up over the crest of the dune was something of a project, for it had grown to a considerable height here.

In the scrubby plants of the beach—shrubs as tall as a man, with wine-colored leaves and red berries—spiders had spun their webs. But the mist had covered them with strings of gleaming pearls so that she could see them from a hundred feet away. So much for being stealthy. Though a stealthy human, crouching among those same shrubs to look down on the beach, would be perfectly invisible. Farther up the slopes grew wind-raked trees inhabited by raucous, irritable birds, who made it a point to announce, to all the world, that Eliza was passing through.

Finally she reached the crest. Not far away was an open sea of grass that would take her to the polders surrounding the Hague. To reach it, she'd have to pass through a forest of scrubby gnarled trees with silvery gray foliage, growing on the lee side of the dune. She stopped for a moment there to get her bearings. From here she could see the steeples of the Hague, Leiden, and Wassenaar, and dimly make out the etched rectangles of formal gardens in private compounds built in the countryside along the coast.

As she rode down into the woods the susurration of the waves was muted, and supplanted by the hissing of a light, misty rain against the leaves. But she did not enjoy the sudden peace for very long. A man in a hooded cloak rose up from behind one of those trees and clapped his hands in the horse's face. The horse reared. Eliza, completely unready, fell off and landed harmlessly in soft sand. The cloaked man gave the horse a resounding slap on the haunches as it returned to all fours, and it galloped off in the direction of home.

This man stood with his back to Eliza for a moment, watching the horse run away, then looked up at the crest of the dune, and down the coast to that distant watch-tower, to see if anyone had seen the ambuscade. But the only witnesses were crows, flapping into the air and screaming as the horse charged through their sentry-lines.

Eliza had every reason to assume that something very bad was planned for her now. She had barely seen this fellow coming in the corner of her eye, but his movements had been brisk and forceful—those of a man accustomed to action, without the affected grace of a gentleman. This man had never taken lessons in dancing or fencing. He moved like a Janissary—like a soldier, she corrected herself. And that was rather bad news. A fair proportion of the murder, robbery, and rape committed in Europe was the work of soldiers who had been put out of work, and just now there were thousands of those around Holland.

Under the terms of an old treaty between England and Holland, six regiments of English and Scottish troops had long been stationed on Dutch soil, as a hedge against invasion from France (or, much less plausibly, the Spanish Netherlands). A few months earlier, when the Duke of Monmouth had sailed to England and mounted his rebellion, his intended victim, King James II, had sent word from London that those six regiments were urgently required at home. William of Orange—despite the fact that his sympathies lay more with Monmouth than with the King—had complied without delay, and shipped the regiments over. By the time they had arrived, the rebellion had been quashed, and there had been nothing for them to do. The King had been slow to send them back, for he did not trust his son-in-law (William of Orange) and suspected that those six regiments might one day return as the vanguard of a Dutch invasion. He had wanted to station them in France instead. But King Louis—who had plenty of his own regiments—had seen them as an unnecessary expense, and William had insisted that the treaty be observed. So the six regiments had come back to Holland.

Shortly thereafter, they had been disbanded. So now the Dutch countryside was infested with unpaid and unled foreign soldiers. Eliza guessed that this was one of them; and since he had not bothered to steal her horse, he must have other intentions.

She rolled onto her elbows and knees and gasped as if she'd had the wind knocked out of her. One arm was supporting her head, the other clutching at her abdomen. She was wearing a long cape that had spread over her like a tent. Propping her forehead against her wrist, she gazed upside-down into the hidden interior of that tent, where her right hand was busy in the damp folds of her waist-sash.

One of the interesting bits of knowledge she had picked up in the Topkapi Palace was that the most feared men in the Ottoman Empire were not the Janissaries with their big scimitars and muskets, but rather the *hashishin:* trained murderers who went unarmed except for a small dagger concealed in the waistband. Eliza did not have the skills of a *hashishin,* but she knew a good idea when she saw one, and she was never without the same kind of weapon. To whip it out now would be a mistake, though. She only made sure it was ready to hand.

Then she lifted her head, pushed herself up to a kneeling position, and gazed at her attacker. At the same moment, he turned to face her and threw back his hood to reveal the face of Jack Shaftoe.

ELIZA WAS PARALYZED for several moments.

Since Jack was almost certainly dead by now, it would be conventional to suppose that she was looking upon his ghost. But this was the reverse of the truth. A ghost ought to be paler than the original, a drawn shadow. But Jack—at least, the Jack she'd most recently seen—had been like the ghost of *this* man. This fellow was heavier, steadier, with better color and better teeth . . .

"Bob," she said.

He looked slightly startled, then made a little bow. "Bob Shaftoe it is," he said, "at your service, Miss Eliza."

"You call knocking me off my horse being at my service?"

"You *fell* off your horse, begging your pardon. I apologize. But I did not wish that you would gallop away and summon the Guild."

"What are you doing here? Was your regiment one of those that was disbanded?"

His brain worked. Now that Bob had begun talking, and reacting to things, his resemblance to Jack was diminishing quickly. The physical similarity was strong, but this body was animated by a different spirit altogether. "I see Jack told you something of me—but skipped the details. No. My regiment still exists, though it has a new name now. It's guarding the King in London."

"Then why're you not with it?"

"John Churchill, the commander of my regiment, sends me on odd errands."

"This one must be very odd indeed, to bring you to the wrong shore of the North Sea."

"It is a sort of salvage mission. No one expected the regiments here to be disbanded. I am trying to track down certain sergeants and corporals who are well thought of, and recruit them into the service of my master before they get hanged in Dutch towns for stealing chickens, or press-ganged on India ships, or recruited by the Prince of Orange . . ."

"Do I looked like a grizzled sergeant to you, Bob Shaftoe?"

"I am laying that charge to one side for a few hours to speak to you about a private matter, Miss Eliza. The time it will take to walk back to the Hague should suffice."

"Let's walk, then, I am getting cold."

Dorset
JUNE 1685

꧁

> I never justify'd cutting off the King's Head, yet the
> Disasters that befel Kings when they begun to be
> Arbitrary, are not without their use, and are so many
> Beacons to their Successors to mark out the Sands
> which they are to avoid.
>
> — *The Mischiefs That Ought Justly*
> *to Be Apprehended from a*
> *Whig-Government,* ANONYMOUS,
> ATTRIBUTED TO BERNARD MANDEVILLE, 1714

IF POOR JACK'S RAVINGS have any color of truth in them, then you
have been among Persons of Quality. So you have learnt how
important Family is to such people: that it gives them not only name
but rank, a house, a piece of land to call home, income and food,
and that it is the windowpane through which they look out and perceive the world. It brings them troubles, too: for they are born heirs
to superiors who must be obeyed, roofs that want fixing, and diverse
local troubles that belong to them as surely as their own names.

Now, in place of "Persons of Quality" substitute "common men
of soldier type" and in place of "Family" say "Regiment," and you
will own a fair portrait of my life.

You seem to've spent a lot of time with Jack and so I'll spare you
the explanation of how two mudlark boys found themselves in a
regiment in Dorset. But my career has been like his in a mirror,
which is to say, all reversed.

The regiment he told you of was like most old English ones,
which is to say, 'twas *militia*. The soldiers were common men of the
shire and the officers were local gentlemen, and the big boss was a
Peer, the Lord Lieutenant—in our case, Winston Churchill—who
got the job by living in London, wearing the right clothes, and saying the right things.

Those militia regiments once came together to form Cromwell's New Model Army, which defeated the Cavaliers, slew the
King, abolished Monarchy, and even crossed the Channel to rout

the Spaniards in Flanders. None of this was lost on Charles II. After he came back, he made a practice of keeping *professional* soldiers on his payroll. They were there *to keep the militias in check*.

You may know that the Cavaliers who brought Charles II back made their landfall in the north and came down from Tweed, crossing the Cold Stream with a regiment under General Lewis. That regiment is called the Coldstream Guards, and General Lewis was made the Duke of Tweed for his troubles. Likewise King Charles created the Grenadier Guards. He probably would have abolished the militia altogether if he could have—but the 1660s were troublous times, what with Plague and Fire and bitter Puritans roaming the country. The King needed his Lords Lieutenant to keep the people down— he granted 'em the power to search homes for arms and to throw troublesome sorts in prison. But a Lord Lieutenant could not make use of such powers save through a local militia and so the militias endured. And 'twas during those times that Jack and I were plucked out of a Vagabond-camp and made into regimental boys.

A few years later John Churchill reached an age—eighteen years—when he was deemed ready to accept his first commission, and was given a regiment of Grenadier Guards. It was a new regiment. Some men and armaments and other necessaries were made available to him, but he had to raise the rest himself, and so he did the natural thing and recruited many soldiers and non-commissioned officers from his father's militia regiment in Dorset—including me and Jack. For there is a difference 'twixt Families and Regiments, which is that the latter have no female members and cannot increase in the natural way—new members must be raised up out of the soil like crops, or if you will, taxes.

Now I'll spare you a recitation of my career under John Churchill, as you've no doubt heard a slanderous version of it from brother Jack. Much of it consisted of long marches and sieges on the Continent—very repetitive—and the rest has been parading around Whitehall and St. James, for our nominal purpose is to guard the King.

Lately, following the death of Charles II, John Churchill spent some time on the Continent, going down to Versailles to meet with King Louis and biding in Dunkirk for a time to keep a weather eye on the Duke of Monmouth. I was there with him and so when Jack came through aboard his merchant-ship full of cowrie-shells I went out to have a brotherly chat with him.

Here the tale could turn ghastly. I'll not describe Jack. Suffice it to say I have seen better and worse on battle-fields. He was far gone with the French Pox and not of sound mind. I learnt from him about you. In particular I learnt that you have the strongest possible aversion to Slavery—whereof I'll say more anon. But first I must speak of Monmouth.

There was a Mr. Foot aboard *God's Wounds,* one of those pleasant and harmless-seeming fellows to whom anyone will say anything, and who consequently knows everyone and everything. While I was waiting for Jack to recover his senses I passed a few hours with him and collected the latest gossip—or, as we say in the military, intelligence—from Amsterdam. Mr. Foot told me that Monmouth's invasion-force was massing at Texel and that it was certainly bound for the port of Lyme Regis.

When I was finished saying my good-byes to poor Jack I went ashore and tried to seek out my master, John Churchill, to give him this news. But he had just sailed for Dover, London-bound, and left orders for me to follow on a slower boat with certain elements of the regiment.

Now I've probably given you the impression that the Grenadier Guards were in Dunkirk, which is wrong. They were in London guarding the King. Why was I not with my regiment? To answer I would have to explain what I am to John Churchill and what he is to me, which would take more time than it would be worth. Owing to my advanced age—almost thirty—and long time in service, I am a very senior non-commissioned officer. And if you knew the military this would tell you much about the peculiar and irregular nature of my duties. I do the things that are too difficult to explain.

Not very clear, is it? Here is a fair sample: I ignored my orders, cast off my uniform, borrowed money on my master's good name, and took passage on a west-bound ship that brought me eventually to Lyme Regis. Before I embarked I sent word to my master that I was making myself useful in the West, where I had heard that some Vagabonds wanted hanging. As I'm certain you have perceived, this was both a prophecy of what was soon to come, and a reminder of events long past. Monmouth had set sail for Dorset because it was a notorious hotbed of Protestant rebellion. Ashe House, which was the seat of the Churchill family, looked down into the harbor of Lyme Regis, which had been the site of a dreary siege during the Civil War. Some of the Churchills had been Roundheads, others Cavaliers. Winston had taken the Cavalier side, had brought this riotous place to heel, and he and his son had been made important men for their troubles. Now Monmouth—John's old comrade-in-arms from Siege of Maestricht days—was coming to make a bloody mess of the place. It would make Winston look either foolish or disloyal in the eyes of the rest of Parliament, and it would cast doubts on John's loyalty.

For some years, John has been in the household of the Duke of York—now King James II—but his wife Sarah is now Lady of the Bedchamber to the Duke's daughter, the Princess Anne: a Protestant who might be Queen someday. And among those Londoners who whisper into each other's ears for a living, this has been taken to mean that John's merely putting on a show of loyalty to the King, biding his time until the right moment to betray that Papist and bring a Protestant to the throne. Nothing more than Court gossip—but if Monmouth used John's very home ground as the beach-head of a Protestant rebellion, how would it look?

Monmouth's little fleet dropped anchor in the harbor of Lyme Regis two days after I had arrived. The town was giddy—they thought Cromwell had been re-incarnated. Within a day, fifteen hundred men had rallied to his standard. Almost the only one who did not embrace him was the Mayor. But I had already warned him to keep his bags packed and horses saddled. I helped him and his family slip out of town, following covert trails of Vagabonds, and he despatched messengers to the Churchills in London. This way Winston could go to the King and say, "My constituents are in rebellion and here is what my son and I are doing about it" rather than having the news sprung on him out of the blue.

It would be a week at the earliest before my regiment could come out from London—which amounts to saying that Monmouth had a week to raise his army, and that I had a week in which to make myself useful. I waited in a queue in the market-square of Lyme Regis until the clerk could prick my name down in his great book; I told him I was Jack Shaftoe and under that name I joined Monmouth's army. The next day we mustered in a field above the town and I was issued my weapon: a sickle lashed to the end of a stick.

The next week's doings were of some moment to John Churchill, when I told him the tale later, but would be tedious to you. There is only one part you might take an interest in, and that is what happened at Taunton. Taunton is an inland town. Our little army reached it after several days' straggling through the countryside. By that time we were three thousand strong. The town welcomed us even more warmly than Lyme Regis; the school girls presented Monmouth with a banner they had embroidered for him, and served us meals in a mess they had set up in the town square. One of these girls—a sixteen-year-old named Abigail Frome . . .

Shall I devote a thousand words, or ten thousand, to how I fell in love with Abigail Frome? "I fell in love with her" does not do it justice, but ten thousand words would be no better, and so let us leave it at that. Perhaps I loved her because she was a rebel girl, and my heart was with the rebellion. My mind could see it was doomed, but my heart was listening to the Imp of the Perverse. I had chosen the name of Jack Shaftoe because I reckoned my brother was dead by now and would not be needing it. But being "Jack Shaftoe" had awakened a lust I had long forgotten: I wanted to go a-vagabonding. And I wanted to take Abigail Frome with me.

That was true the first and possibly the second day of my infatuation. But in between those long sunny June days were short nights of broken and unrestful sleep, when fretful thoughts would dissolve into strange dreams that would end with me shocked upright in my bed, like a sailor who has felt his ship hit a reef, and who knows he ought to be doing somewhat other than just lying there. I'd not bedded the girl or even kissed her. But I believed we were joined together now, and that I needed to make preparations for a life altogether different. Vagabonding and rebellion could not be part of that life—they are fit for men, but men who try to bring their women and children along on that life are bastards plain and simple. If you spent any time on the road with Jack, you will take my meaning.

So my Vagabond-passion for this rebel girl made me turn against the rebellion finally. I could flirt with one or the other but not with both; and flirting with Abigail was more rewarding.

Now came word that the militia—my old regiment of local commoners—was being called up to perform its stated function, namely, to put down the rebellion. I deserted my rebel regiment, crept out of Taunton, and went to the mustering-place. Some of the men were ready to throw in their lot with Monmouth, some were loyal to the King, and most were too scared and amazed to do anything. I rallied a company of loyal men, little better than stragglers, and marched them to Chard, where John Churchill had at last arrived and set up an encampment.

This is as good a time as any to mention that while sneaking through the rebel lines at Taunton I had been noticed—not by the sentry, a dozing farmhand, but by his dog. The dog had come after me and seized me by the leg of my breeches and held me long enough for the farmer to come after me with a pitchfork. As you can see, I had let things get out of hand. It was because I have a fatuous liking for dogs, and always have, ever since I was a mudlark boy and Persons of Quality would call me a dog. I had removed the sickle from the end of my stick and left it in Taunton, but the stick I still had, so I raised it up and brought the butt down smartly between the dog's brown eyes, which I remember clearly glaring up at me. But it was a dog of terrier-kind and would on no account loosen its bite. The farmer thrust at me with his pitchfork. I spun away. One tine of the fork got under the skin of my back and tunneled underneath for about a hand's breadth and then erupted somewhere else. I made a backhand swing of my stick and caught him across the bridge of the nose. He let go the pitchfork and put his hands to his face. I pulled the iron out of my flesh, raised it up above the dog, and told the farmer that if he would only call the damned creature off I would not have to spill any blood here, other than my own.

He saw the wisdom of this. But now he had recognized me. "Shaftoe!" he said, "have you lost your nerve so soon?" I recognized him now as a fellow I had passed time with while we waited in the queue in Lyme Regis to enlist in Monmouth's army.

I am accustomed to the regular and predictable evolutions of the march, the drill, and the siege. Yet now within a few days of my conceiving a boyish infatuation with Abigail Frome, I had worked my way round to one of those farcical muddles you see in the fourth act of a comedy. I was forsaking the rebellion in order to forge a new life with a rebel lass, who had fallen in love, not with me, but with my brother, who was dead. I who have slain quite a few men had been caught and recognized because I would not hurt a mongrel. And I who was—if I may say so—doing something that demanded a whiff of courage or so, and that demonstrated my loyalty, would now be denounced as a coward and traitor, and Abigail would consider me in those terms forever.

A civilian—by your leave—would have been baffled, amazed. My soldier's mind recognized this immediately as a screw-up, a cluster-fuck, a Situation Normal. This sort of thing happens to us all the time, and generally has worse consequences than a pretty girl deciding that she despises you. Fermented beverages and black humor are how we cope. I extricated myself without further violence. But by the time I made my way into the camp of John Churchill, the pitchfork-wound on my back had suppurated, and had to be opened up and aired out by a barber. I could not see it myself, but all who gazed upon it were taken a-back. Really 'twas a shallow wound, and it healed quickly once I became strong enough to fend off the barber. But that I had staggered into the camp bleeding and feverish at the head of a column of loyal militia troops was made into something bigger than it really was. John Churchill heaped praise and honor upon me, and gave me a purse of money. When I related the entire tale to him, he laughed and mused, "I am doubly indebted to your brother now—he has furnished me with an excellent horse and a vital piece of intelligence."

Jack tells me you are literate and so I will let you read about the details of the fighting in a history-book. There are a few particulars

I will mention because I doubt that historians will consider them meet to be set down in print.

The King declined to trust John Churchill, for the reasons I stated earlier. Supreme command was given to Feversham, who despite his name is a Frenchman. Years ago Feversham undertook to blow up some houses with gunpowder, supposedly to stop a fire from spreading, but really, I suspect, because he was possessed of that urge, common to all men, to blow things up for its own sake. Moments after he satisfied that urge, he was brained by a piece of flying debris, and left senseless. His brain swelled up. To make room for it, the chirurgeons cut a hole in his skull. You can imagine the details for yourself—suffice it to say that the man is a living and breathing advertisement for the Guild of Wigmakers. King James II favors him, which, if you knew nothing else about His Majesty, would give you knowledge sufficient to form an opinion about his reign.

It was this Feversham who had been placed in command of the expedition to put down the Duke of Monmouth's rebellion, and he who received credit for its success, but it was John Churchill who won the battles, and my regiment, as always, that did the fighting. The Duke of Grafton came out at the head of some cavalry and did battle with Monmouth at one point. The engagement was not all that important, but I mention it to add some color to the story, for Grafton is one of Charles II's bastards, just like Monmouth himself!

The campaign was made exciting only by Feversham's narcolepsy. That, combined with his inability to come to grips with matters even when he was awake, made it seem for a day or two as if Monmouth had a chance. I spent most of the time lying on my stomach recovering from the pitchfork-wound. And I count myself fortunate in that, because I had, and have, no love for the King, and I liked those rustic Nonconformists with their sickles and blunderbusses.

In the end Monmouth deserted those men even as they were fighting and dying for him. We found him cowering in a ditch. He was shipped off to the Tower of London and died groveling.

The farmers and tradesmen of Lyme Regis and Taunton who had made up Monmouth's army were Englishmen through and through, which is to say not only were they level-headed decent sensible moderate folk, but they could not conceive of, and did not know about, any other way of being. It simply did not occur to them that Monmouth would abandon them and try to flee the island. But it had occurred to me, because I had spent years fighting on the Continent.

Likewise they never imagined the repression that followed. Living in that open green countryside or settled in their sleepy market-towns, they had no understanding of the feverish minds of the Londoners. If you go to a lot of plays, as Jack and I used to do, you notice, soon enough, that the playwrights only have so many stories to go around. So they use them over and over. Oftimes when you sneak into a play that has just opened, the characters and situations will seem oddly familiar, and by the time the first scene has played out, you will recall that you've already seen this one several times before—except that it was in Tuscany instead of Flanders, and the schoolmaster was a parson, and the senile colonel was a daft admiral. In like manner, the high and mighty of England have the story of Cromwell stuck in their heads, and whenever anything the least bit upsetting happens—especially if it's in the country, and involves Nonconformists—they decide, in an instant, that it's the Civil War all over again. All they want is to figure out which one is playing the role of Cromwell, and put his head on a stick. The rest must be put down. And so it will continue until the men who run England come up with a new story.

Worse, Feversham was a French nobleman to whom peasants (as he construed these people) were faggots to be stuffed into the fireplace. By the time he was finished, every tree in Dorset had dead yeomen, wheelwrights, coopers, and miners hanging from its branches.

Churchill wanted no part of this. He got himself back to London as directly as possible, along with his regiments—myself included. Feversham had not been slow to spread tales of the glorious fight. He had already made himself into a hero, and every other part of the tale was likewise made into something much grander than it really was. The ditch in which we captured Monmouth was swollen, by the tale-tellers, into a raging freshet called the Black Torrent. The King was so taken with this part of the story that he has given my regiment a new name: we are now, and forever, the King's Own Black Torrent Guards.

Now at last I can speak to you of slavery, which according to Jack is a practice on which you harbor strong opinions.

The Lord Chief Justice is a fellow name of Jeffreys, who was reputed for cruelty and bloody-mindedness even in the best of times. He has spent his life currying favor with the Cavaliers, the Catholics, and the Frenchified court, and when King James II came to the throne Jeffreys got his reward and became the highest judge of England. Monmouth's rebellion brought a whiff of blood on the west wind, and Jeffreys followed it like a slavering hound and established a Court of Assizes in that part of the country. He has executed no fewer than four hundred persons—that is, four hundred in addition to those slain in battle or strung up by Feversham. In some parts of the Continent, four hundred executions would go nearly unnoticed, but in Dorset it is reckoned a high figure.

As you can see, Jeffreys has been ingenious in finding grounds for putting men to death. But there are many cases where not even he could justify capital punishment, and so instead the defendants were sentenced to slavery. It says something about his mind that he considers slavery a lighter punishment than death! Jeffreys has sold twelve hundred ordinary West Country Protestants into chattel slavery in the Caribbean. They are on their way to Barbados even now, where they and their descendants will chop sugar cane forever among neegers and Irishmen, with no hope of ever knowing freedom.

The girl I love, Abigail Frome, has been made a slave. All the schoolgirls of Taunton have been. For the most part these girls have not been sold to sugar plantations; they would never survive the voyage. Instead they have been parceled out to various courtiers in London. Lord Jeffreys gives 'em away like oysters in a pub. Their families in Taunton then have no choice but to buy them back, at whatever price their owners demand.

Abigail is now the property of an old college chum of Lord Jeffreys: Louis Anglesey, the Earl of Upnor. Her father has been hanged and her mother died years ago; of her cousins, aunts, and uncles, many have been sent to Barbados, and the ones who remain do not have the money to buy Abigail back. Upnor has amassed heavy gambling debts, which drove his own father to bankruptcy and forced him to sell his house years ago; now Upnor hopes to repay some of those debts by selling Abigail.

It goes without saying that I want to kill Upnor. One day, God willing, I shall. But this would not help Abigail—she'd only be inherited by Upnor's heirs. Only money will buy her freedom. I think that you are skilled where money is concerned. I ask you now to buy Abigail. In return, I give you myself. I know you hate slavery and do not want a slave, but if you do this for me I will be your slave in all but name.

As BOB SHAFTOE HAD TOLD his story, he had led Eliza through a maze of paths through the lee woods, which he appeared to know quite well. Before long they had reached the edge of a canal that ran from the city out to the shore at Scheveningen. This canal was not lined with sharp edges of stone, as in the city, but was soft and sloping at the edges, and in some places lined with rushes. Cows stood chewing on these, and watched Bob and Eliza walk by, interrupting him from time to time with their weird, pointless lamentations. As they had drawn closer to the Hague, Bob had begun to show uncertainty at certain canal-intersections, and Eliza had stepped into the lead. The scenery did not change very much, except that houses and small feeder canals become more frequent. Woods appeared to their left side, and continued for some distance. The Hague sneaked up on them. For it was not a fortified city, and at no point did they pass through anything like a wall or gate. But suddenly Eliza turned to the right on the bank of another canal—a proper stone-edged one—and Bob realized that they had penetrated into something that could be called a neighborhood. And not just any neighborhood, but the Hofgebied. Another few minutes' walk would take them to the very foundations of the Binnenhof.

In the woods by the sea, it might have been foolhardy for Eliza to speak frankly; but here she could summon the St. George Guild from their clubhouse with a shout. "Your willingness to repay me is of no account," she told Bob.

This was a cold answer, but it was a cold day, and William of Orange had treated her coldly, and Bob Shaftoe had knocked her off her horse. Now Bob looked dismayed. He was not accustomed to being beholden to anyone save his master, John Churchill, and now he was in the power of two girls not yet twenty: Abigail, who owned his heart, and Eliza, who (or so he imagined) had it in her power to own Abigail. A man more accustomed to helplessness would have put up more of a struggle. But Bob Shaftoe had gone limp, like the Janissaries before Vienna when it had come clear to them that their Turkish masters were all dead. All he could do was look with watery eyes at Eliza and shake his head amazed. She kept walking. He had no choice but to follow.

"I was taken a slave just like your Abigail," Eliza said. " 'Twas as if Mummy and I'd been plucked off the beach by a rogue wave and swallowed by the Deep. No man came forward to ransom *me*. Does that mean it was *just* that I was so taken?"

"Now you're talking *nonsense*. I don't—"

"If 'tis evil for Abigail to be a slave—as I believe—then your offer of service to me is neither here nor there. If *she* should be free, all the *others* should be as well. That you're willing to do me a *favor* or two should not advance her to the head of the queue."

"I see, now you're making it into a grand moral question. I am a soldier and we have good reasons to be suspicious of those."

They had entered into a broad square on the east side of the Binnenhof, called the Plein. Bob was looking about alertly. A stone's throw from here was a guard-house that served as a gaol; he might have been wondering whether Eliza was trying to lead him straight into it.

But instead she stopped in front of a house: a large place, grand after the Barock style, but a little odd in its decorations. For atop the chimneys, where one would normally expect to see crosses or statues of Greek gods, there were armillary spheres, weathercocks, and swivel-mounted telescopes. Eliza fished in the folds of her waistband, nudged the stiletto out of the way, found the key.

"What's this, a convent?"

"Don't be absurd, do I look like some French mademoiselle who stays at such places?"

"A rooming-house?"

"It is the house of a friend. A friend of a friend, really."

Eliza swung the key round on the end of the red ribbon to which she had tied it. "Come in," she finally said.

"Beg pardon?"

"Come inside this house with me that we may continue our conversation."

"The neighbors—"

"Nothing that could happen here could possibly faze this gentleman's neighbors."

"What of the gentleman himself?"

"He is asleep," Eliza said, unlocking the front door. "Be quiet."

"Asleep, at noon?"

"He stirs at night—to make observations of the stars," Eliza said, glancing upwards. Mounted to the roof of the house, four stories above their heads, was a wooden platform with a tubular device projecting over the edge—too frail to shoot cannonballs.

The first floor's main room might have been grand, for its generous windows looked out over the Plein and the Binnenhof. But it was cluttered with the debris of lens- and mirror-grinding—always messy, sometimes dangerous—and with thousands of books. Though Bob would not know this, these were not only about Natural Philosophy but history and literature as well, and nearly all of them were in French or Latin.

To Bob these artifacts were only moderately strange, and he learned to overlook them after a few moments' nervous glancing around the room. What really paralyzed him was the omnipresent noise—not because it was loud, but because it *wasn't*. The room contained at least two dozen clocks, or sub-assemblies of clocks, driven by weights or springs whose altitude or tension stored enough energy, summed, to raise a barn. That power was restrained and disciplined by toothy mechanisms of various designs: brass insects creeping implacably around the rims of barbed wheels, constellations of metal stars hung on dark stolid axle-trees, all marching or dancing to the beat of swinging plumb-bobs.

Now a man in Bob Shaftoe's trade owed his longevity, in part, to his alertness—his sensitivity to (among other things) significant noises. Even the dimmest recruits could be relied on to notice the *loud* noises. A senior man like Bob was supposed to scrutinize the *faint* ones. Eliza got the impression that Bob was the sort of bloke who was forever shushing every man in the room, demanding absolute stillness so that he could hold his breath and make out whether that faint sporadic itching was a mouse in the cupboard, or enemy miners tunnelling under the fortifications. Whether that distant rhythm was a cobbler next door or an infantry regiment marching into position outside of town.

Every gear and bearing in this room was making the sort of sound that normally made Bob Shaftoe freeze like a startled animal. Even after he'd gotten it through his head that they were all clocks, or studies for clocks, he was hushed and intimidated by a sense of being surrounded by patient mechanical life. He stood at attention in the middle of the big room, hands in his pockets, blowing steam from his mouth and darting his eyes to and fro. These clocks were made to tell time precisely and nothing else. There were no bells, no chimes, and certainly no cuckoos. If Bob was waiting for such entertainments, he'd wait until he was a dusty skeleton surrounded by cobweb-clogged gears.

Eliza noted that he had shaved before going out on this morning's strange errand, something that would never have entered Jack's mind, and she wondered how it all worked—what train of thoughts made a man say, "I had better scrape my face with a blade before undertaking this one." Perhaps it was some sort of a symbolic love-offering to his Abigail.

"It is all a question of pride, isn't it?" Eliza said, stuffing a cube of peat into the iron stove. "Or honor, as you'd probably style it."

Bob looked at her instead of answering; or maybe his look was his answer.

"Come on, you don't have to be *that* quiet," she said, setting a kettle on the stove to heat.

"What Jack and I have in common is an aversion to begging," he said finally.

"Just as I thought. So, rather than beg Abigail's ransom from me, you are proposing a sort of financial transaction—a loan, to be paid back in service."

"I don't know the words, the terms. Something like that is what I had in mind."

"Then why me? You're in the Dutch Republic. This is the financial capital of the world. You don't need to seek out one particular lender. You could propose this deal to anyone."

Bob had clutched a double handful of his cloak and was wringing it slowly. "The confusions of the financial markets are bewildering to me—I prefer not to treat with *strangers* . . . "

"What am I to you if not a stranger?" Eliza asked, laughing. "I am *worse* than a stranger, I threw a spear at your brother."

"Yes, and that is what makes you *not* a stranger to me, it is how I *know* you."

"It is proof that I hate slavery, you mean?"

"Proof of that and of other personal qualities—qualities that enter into this matter."

"I am no Person of Quality, or of qualities—do not speak to me of that. It is proof only that my hatred of slavery makes me do irrational things—which is what you are asking me to do now."

Bob lost his grip on his cloak-wad and sat down unsteadily on a stack of books.

Eliza continued, "She threw a harpoon at my brother—she'll throw some money at me—is that how it goes?"

Bob Shaftoe put his hands over his face and began to cry, so quietly that any sounds he made were drowned out by the whirring and ticking of the clocks.

Eliza retreated into the kitchen, and went back to a cool corner where some sausage-casings had been rolled up on a stick. She unrolled six inches—on second thought, twelve—and cut it off. Then she tied a knot in one end. She fit the little sock of sheep-gut over the handle of a meat-axe that was projecting firmly into the air above a chopping-block, then, with her fingertips, coaxed the open end of it to begin rolling up the handle. Once it was started, with a quick movement of her hand she rolled the whole length up to make a translucent torus with the knotted end stretched across the middle like a drum-head. Gathering her skirts up one leg, she tucked the object into the hem of her stocking, which came up to about mid-thigh, and finally went back into the great room where Bob Shaftoe was weeping.

There was not much point in subtlety, and so she forced her way in between his thighs and stuffed her bosom into his face.

After a few moment's hesitation he took his hands away from between his wet cheeks and her breasts. His face felt cold for a moment, but only a moment. Then she felt his hands locking together behind the small of her back, where her bodice was joined to her skirt.

He held her for a moment, not weeping anymore, but thinking. Eliza found that a bit tedious and so she left off stroking his hair and began going to work on his ears in a way he would not tolerate for long. Then, finally, Bob knew what to do. She could see that for Bob, knowing what to do was always the hard part, and the doing was easy. All those years Vagabonding with Jack, Bob had been the older and wiser brother preaching sternly into Jack's one ear while the Imp of the Perverse whispered into the other, and it had made him a stolid and deliberate sort. But having made up his mind, he was a launched cannonball. Eliza wondered what the two of them had been like, partnered together, and pitied the world for not allowing it.

Bob cinched an arm around the narrowest part of her waist and hoisted her into the air with a thrust of rather good thigh-muscles. Her head grazed a dusty ceiling-beam and she ducked and hugged his head. He yanked a blanket from a couch; the books that had been scattered all over the blanket ended up differently scattered on the couch. Carrying Eliza and dragging the blanket, he trudged in a mighty floorboard-popping cadence to an elliptical dining-table scattered with the remains of a scholarly dinner: apple-peels and gouda-rinds. Making a slow orbit of this he flipped the corners of the tablecloth into the center. Gathering them together turned the tablecloth into a bag of scraps, which he let down gently onto the floor. Then he broadcast the blanket onto the table, slapped it once with his palm to stop it from skimming right off, and rolled Eliza's body out into the middle of the woolly oval.

Standing above her, he'd already begun fumbling with his breeches, which she deemed premature—so bringing a knee up smartly between his thighs and pulling down on a grabbed handful of his hair, she obliged him to get on top of her. They lay there for a while with thighs interlocked, like fingers of two hands clutching each other, and Eliza felt him get ready as she was getting ready. But long after that they ground away at each other, as if Bob could somehow force his way through all those layers of masculine and feminine clothing. They did this because it felt good, and they were together in a cold echoing house in the Hague and had no other demands on their time. Eliza learned that Bob was not a man who felt good very often and that it took him a long time to relax. His whole body was stiff at first, and it took a long time for that stiff-ness to drain out of his limbs and his neck, and concentrate in one particular Member, and for him to agree that this did not all have to happen in an instant. At the beginning his face was planted between her breasts, and his feet were square on the floor, but inch by inch she coaxed him upwards. At first he showed a fighting man's reluctance to sever his connection with the ground, but in time she made it understood that additional delights were to be found toward the head of the table, and so he kicked his boots off and got his knees, and eventually his toes, up on the tabletop.

For a long time then they were face-to-face, which Eliza thought was as pleasant as this was likely to get. But after a while she got Bob to raise his chin and entrust her with his throat. While she was exploring that terrain she was undoing the top few buttons of his shirt, pulling it down off his shoulders as she did so, pinning his arms to his sides and exposing his nipples.

She locked her right knee behind his left, then shoved her tongue through a protective nest of hair, found his right nipple, and carefully nipped it. He twisted up and away from her. Pulling down hard on his trapped knee she drew her left leg up, planted her foot on the raised blade of his pelvis, and shoved. Bob rolled over onto his back. She came up from under him and wound up sitting on his thighs. A hard yank down on his breeches freed his erect penis while binding his thighs together. She pulled the knotted sheepgut from her stocking, stripped it down over him, straddled him, and sat down hard. He was distracted with pretending to be angry, and the sudden pleasure ambushed him. The sudden pain astonished her, for this was the first time a man had ever been inside Eliza. She let out an angry yell and tears spurted from her eyes; she shoved clenched fists into her eye-sockets and tried to control her leg-muscles, which were convulsively trying to climb up and off of him. She felt that he was rocking her up and down, which made her angry, but her knees were grinding steadily into the hard wood of the table, and so the sensation of movement must arise from light-headedness: a swoon that needed to be fought off.

She did not want him looking up at her like this and so she fell forward and struck the table to either side of his head with the flats of both palms, then bowed her head so that her hair fell down in a curtain, hiding her face, and everything below his chest, from Bob's view. Not that he was doing a lot of sightseeing; he had apparently decided that there were worse situations he could be in.

She moved up and down on him for a while, very slowly, partly because she was in pain and partly because she did not know how close he might be to reaching his climax—all men were different, a particular man would be different according to the time of day, and the only way to judge it was by the rhythm of his breathing (which she could hear) and the slackness of his face (which she could monitor through a narrow embrasure between dangling locks of hair). By those measures, she was nowhere near finished, and a lengthy and painful grind awaited her. But finally he came complete, in a long ordeal of back-arching and head-thumping.

He took the first breath, the one that meant he was finished, and opened his eyes. She was staring directly back at him.

"I hurt like hell," she announced. "I have inflicted this on myself as a demonstration."

"Of *what?*" he asked, bewildered, stuporous, but pleased with himself.

"To show you what I think of honor, as you style it. Where was Abigail just now?"

Bob Shaftoe now tried to become angry, without much success. An Englishman of higher class would have huffed "Now see here!" but Bob set his jaw and tried to sit up. He had more success in that— at first—because Eliza was not a large girl. But then from behind the dazzling hair curtain came a hand, and the hand was holding a small Turkish dagger—very nice, a wriggling blade of watered steel— which closed on his left eyeball and obliged him to lie flat again.

"The demonstration is very important," Eliza said—or growled, rather, for she really was very uncomfortable. "You come with high talk of honor and expect me to swoon and buy Abigail back for you. I have heard many men speak of honor while ladies are in the room, and then seen them abandon all thought of it when the lusts and terrors of the body overcame their noble pretensions. Like cavaliers throwing down their polished armor and bright battle-flags to flee a charging Vagabond-host. You are no worse—but no better. I will not help you because I am touched by your love for Abigail or stirred by your prating about honor. I will help you because I wish to be somewhat more than another wave spreading and spending itself on a godforsaken beach. Monsieur Mansart may build kingly châteaux to prove that he once existed, and you may marry your Abigail and raise up a clan of Shaftoes. But if I am to make a mark on this world, it will have something to do with slavery. I will help you only insofar as it serves that end. And buying the freedom of one maiden does not serve it. But Abigail may be of use to me in other ways . . . I shall have to think on it. While I think, she'll be a slave to this Upnor. If she remembers you at all, it will be as a turncoat and a coward. You will be a miserable wretch. In the fullness of melancholy time, perhaps you'll come to see the wisdom of my position."

Now the conversation—if it could be called that—was interrupted by a mighty throat-clearing from the opposite end of the room, gallons of air shifting dollops of phlegm out of the main channel. "Speaking of Positions," said a husky Dutch voice, "would you and your gentleman friend please find a different one? For since you've made *sleep* quite impossible I should like to *eat*."

"With pleasure, *meinheer,* I would, but your lodger has a poniard at my eye," said Bob.

"You are much cooler in dealing with men than with women," Eliza observed, *sotto voce*.

"A woman such as you has never seen a man in a cool condition, unless you were spying on him through a knot-hole," Bob returned.

More throat-clearing from the owner: a hearty, grizzled man in his middle fifties, with all that that implied in the way of eyebrows. He had hoisted one of them like a furry banner and was peering out from under it at Eliza; typically for an astronomer who did his best seeing through a single eye. "The Doctor warned me to expect odd callers . . . but not *business transactions*."

"Some would call me a whore, and some *shall*," Eliza admitted, giving Bob a sharp look, "but in this case you are assuming too much, Monsieur Huygens. The *transaction* we are discussing is not related to the *act* we have performed . . ."

"Then why do both at the same time? Are you in *such* a hurry? Is this how it is done in Amsterdam?"

"I am trying to clear this fellow's mind so that he can think straighter," said Eliza, straightening up herself as she said it, for her back was getting tired and her bodice was griping her stomach.

Bob knocked her dagger-hand aside and sat up violently, throwing her into a backward somersault. She'd have landed on her head except that he caught her upper arms in his hands and spun her over—or something rather complicated and dangerous—all she knew was that, when it was over, she was dizzy, and her heart had skipped a few beats, her hair was in her face and her dagger-hand was empty. Bob was behind her, using her as a screen while he pulled his breeches up with one hand. His other hand had a grip on her laces, which he was exploiting as a sort of bridle. "You should never have straightened your arm," he explained quietly, "It tells the opponent that you are unable to make a thrust."

Eliza thanked him for the fencing-lesson by pirouetting in a direction calculated to bend his fingers backwards. He cursed, let go of her laces, and yanked his breeches up finally.

"Mr. Huygens, Bob Shaftoe of the King's Own Black Torrent Guards. Bob, meet Christiaan Huygens, the world's foremost Natural Philosopher."

"Hooke would *bite* you for saying so . . . Leibniz is brighter than I . . . Newton, though *confused,* is said to be talented. So let us say only that I am the foremost Natural Philosopher *in this room*," Huygens said, taking a quick census of the occupants: himself, Bob, Eliza, and a skeleton hanging in the corner.

Bob had not noticed the skeleton before, and its sudden inclusion in the conversation made him uneasy. "I beg your pardon, sir, 'twas disgraceful—"

"Oh, stop!" Eliza hissed, "he is a Philosopher, he cares not."

"Descartes used to come up here when I was a young man, and sit at that very table, and drink too much and discourse of the Mind-Body Problem," Huygens mused.

"Problem? What's the problem? I don't see any problem," Bob muttered parenthetically, until Eliza crowded back against him and planted a heel on his instep.

"So Eliza's attempt to clarify your mental processes by purging you of imbalancing humours could not have been carried out in a more appropriate location," Huygens continued.

"Speaking of humours, what am I to do with this?" Bob muttered, dangling a narrow bulging sac from one finger.

"Put it in a box and post it to Upnor as a down payment," Eliza said.

The sun had broken through as they spoke, and golden light suddenly shone into the room from off the Plein. It was a sight to gladden most any Dutch heart; but Huygens reacted to it strangely, as if he had been put in mind of some tiresome obligation. He conducted a poll of his clocks and watches. "I have a quarter of an hour in which to break my fast," he remarked, "and then Eliza and I have work to do on the roof. You are welcome to stay, Sergeant Shaftoe, though—"

"You have already been more than hospitable enough," Bob said.

HUYGENS'S WORK CONSISTED OF STANDING very still on his roof as the clock-towers of the Hague bonged noon all around him, and squinting into an Instrument. Eliza was told to stay out of his way, and jot down notes in a waste-book, and hand him small necessaries from time to time.

"You wish to know where the sun is at noon—?"

"You have it precisely backwards. *Noon is* when the sun is in a particular place. Noon has no meaning otherwise."

"So, you wish to know when noon is."

"It is now!" Huygens said, and glanced quickly at his watch.

"Then all of the clocks in the Hague are wrong."

"Yes, including all of mine. Even a well-made clock drifts, and must be re-set from time to time. I do it here whenever the sun shines. Flamsteed will be doing it in a few minutes on top of a hill in Greenwich."

"It is unfortunate that a person may not be calibrated so easily," Eliza said.

Huygens looked at her, no less intensely than he had been peering at his instrument a moment earlier. "Obviously you have some specific person in mind," he said. "Of persons I will say this: it is difficult to tell when they are running *aright* but easy to see when something has gone *awry*."

"Obviously *you* have someone in mind, Monsieur Huygens," Eliza said, "and I fear it is I."

"You were referred to me by Leibniz," Huygens said. "A shrewd judge of intellects. Perhaps a bit less shrewd about *character*, for he always wants to think the best of everyone. I made some inquiries around the Hague. I was assured by persons of the very best quality that you would not be a political liability. From this I presumed that you would know how to behave."

Suddenly feeling very high and exposed, she took a step back, and reached out with a hand to steady herself against a heavy telescope-tripod. "I am sorry," she said. "It was stupid, what I did down there. I *know* it was, for I *do* know how to behave. Yet I was not always a courtier. I came to this place in my life by a roundabout path, which shaped me in ways that are not always comely. Perhaps I should be ashamed. But I am more inclined to be defiant."

"I understand you better than you suppose," Huygens said. "I was raised and groomed to be a diplomat. But when I was thirteen years old, I built myself a lathe."

"Pardon me, a what?"

"A lathe. Down below, in this very house. Imagine my parents' consternation. They had taught me Latin, Greek, French, and other languages. They had taught me the lute, the viol, and the harpsichord. Of literature and history I had learned everything that was in their power to teach me. Mathematics and philosophy I learned from Descartes himself. But I built myself a lathe. Later I taught myself how to grind lenses. My parents feared that they had spawned a tradesman."

"No one is more pleased than I that matters turned out so well for you," Eliza said, "but I am too thick to understand how your story is applicable to my case."

"It is all right for a clock to run fast or slow at times, so long as it is calibrated against the sun, and set right. The sun may come out only once in a fortnight. It is enough. A few minutes' light around noon is all that you need to discover the error, and re-set the clock—provided that you bother to go up and make the observation. My parents somehow knew this, and did not become overly

715

concerned at my strange enthusiasms. For they had confidence that they had taught me how to know when I was running awry, and to calibrate my behavior."

"Now I think I understand," Eliza said. "It remains only to apply this principle to *me*, I suppose."

"If I come down in the morning to find you copulating on my table with a foreign deserter, as if you were some sort of Vagabond," Huygens said, "I am annoyed. I admit it. But that is not as important as what you do next. If you posture defiantly, it tells me that you have not learned the skill of recognizing when you are running awry, and correcting yourself. And you must leave my house in that case, for such people only go further and further astray until they find destruction. But if you take this opportunity to consider where you have gone wrong, and to adjust your course, it tells me that you shall do well enough in the end."

"It is good counsel and I thank you for it," Eliza said. "In principle. But in practice I do not know what to make of this Bob."

"There is something that you must settle with him, or so it would appear to me," Huygens said.

"There is something that I must settle with the world."

"Then by all means apply yourself to it. Then you are welcome to stay. But from now on please go to your bedchamber if you want to roger someone."

The Exchange
[*Between Threadneedle and Cornhill*]

SEPTEMBER 1686

> I find that men (as high as trees) will write
> Dialogue-wise; yet no man doth them slight
> For writing so; indeed if they abuse
> Truth, cursed be they, and the craft they use
> To that intent; but yet let truth be free
> To make her sallies upon thee, and me,
> Which way it pleases God.
>
> —JOHN BUNYAN, *The Pilgrim's Progress*

DRAMATIS PERSONAE

DANIEL WATERHOUSE, a Puritan.

SIR RICHARD APTHORP, a former Goldsmith, proprietor of
   Apthorp's Bank.

A DUTCHMAN.

A JEW.

ROGER COMSTOCK, Marquis of Ravenscar, a courtier.

JACK KETCH, chief Executioner of England.

A HERALD.

A BAILIFF.

EDMUND PALLING, an old man.

TRADERS.

APTHORP'S MINIONS.

APTHORP'S HANGERS-ON AND FAVOR-SEEKERS.

JACK KETCH'S ASSISTANTS.

SOLDIERS.

MUSICIANS.

Scene: A court hemmed in by colonnades.
Discover DANIEL WATERHOUSE, seated on a Chair amid scuffling
and shouting TRADERS. Enter SIR RICHARD APTHORP, with
Minions, Hangers-on, and Favor-seekers.

APTHORP: It couldn't be—Dr. Daniel Waterhouse!

WATERHOUSE: Well met, Sir Richard!

APTHORP: Sitting in a chair, no less!

WATERHOUSE: The day is long, Sir Richard, my legs are tired.

APTHORP: It helps if you keep moving—which is the whole point
   of the 'Change, by the by. This is the Temple of Mercury—not
   of Saturn!

WATERHOUSE: Did you think I was being Saturnine? Saturn is
   Cronos, the God of Time. For your truly Saturnine character you
   had better look to Mr. Hooke, world's foremost clockmaker . . .
      Enter Dutchman.

DUTCHMAN: Sir! Our Mr. Huygens taught your Mr. Hooke everything he knows!
      Exits.

WATERHOUSE: Different countries revere the same gods under
   different names. The Greeks had Cronos, the Romans Saturn.
   The Dutch have Huygens and we have Hooke.

APTHORP: If you are not Saturn, what are you, then, to bide in a
   chair, so gloomy and pensive, in the middle of the 'Change?

WATERHOUSE: I am he who was born to be his family's designated participant in the Apocalypse; who was named after the strangest book in the Bible; who rode Pestilence out of London and Fire into it. I escorted Drake Waterhouse and King Charles from this world, and I put Cromwell's head back into its grave with these two hands.

APTHORP: My word! Sir!

WATERHOUSE: Of late I have been observed lurking round White-hall, dressed in black, affrighting the courtiers.

APTHORP: What brings Lord Pluto to the Temple of Mercury?

Enter Jew.

JEW: By're leave, by're leave, Señor—pray—where stands the *tablero?*

Wanders off.

APTHORP: He sees that you have a Chair, and hopes you know where is the Table.

WATERHOUSE: That would be *mesa*. Perhaps he means *banca*, desk . . .

APTHORP: Every other man in this 'Change, who is seated upon a chair, is in front of such a *banca*. He wants to know where yours has got to!

WATERHOUSE: I meant that perhaps he is looking for the bank.

APTHORP: You mean, me?

WATERHOUSE: That is the new title you have given your gold-smith's shop now, is it not? A bank?

APTHORP: Why, yes; but why doesn't he just ask for me then?

WATERHOUSE: Señor! A moment, I beg you!

Jew returns with a paper.

JEW: Like this, like this!

APTHORP: What is he holding up there, I do not have my spec-tacles.

WATERHOUSE: He has drawn what a Natural Philosopher would identify as a Cartesian coordinate plane, and what *you* would style a ledger, and scrawled words in one column, and numerals in the next.

APTHORP: *Tablero*—he means the board where the prices of some-thing are billed. Commodities, most likely.

JEW: Commodities, yes!

WATERHOUSE: 'Sblood, it's right over there in the corner, is the man blind?

APTHORP: Rabbi, do not take offense at my friend's irritable tone, for he is the Lord of the Underworld, and known for his moods. Here in Mercury's temple all is movement, flux—which is why we name it the 'Change. Knowledge and intelligence flow like the running waters spoken of in the Psalms. But you have made the mistake of asking Pluto, the God of Secrets. Why is Pluto here? 'Tis something of a mystery—I myself was startled to see him just now, and supposed I was looking at a ghost.

WATERHOUSE: The *tablero* is over yonder.

JEW: That is all!?

APTHORP: You have come from Amsterdam?

JEW: Yes.

APTHORP: How many commodities are billed on the *tablero* in Amsterdam now?

JEW: This number . . .

Writes.

APTHORP: Daniel, what has he written there?

WATERHOUSE: Five hundred and fifty.

APTHORP: God save England, the Dutchmen have a *tablero* with near six hundred commodities, and we've a plank with a few dozen.

WATERHOUSE: No wonder he did not recognize it.

Exit Jew in the direction of said Plank, rolling his eyes and scoffing.

APTHORP (TO MINION): Follow that Kohan and learn what he is on about—he knows something.

Exit Minion.

WATERHOUSE: Now who is the God of Secrets?

APTHORP: You are, for you still have not told me why you are here.

WATERHOUSE: As Lord of the Underworld, I customarily sit enthroned in the Well of Souls, where departed spirits whirl about me like so many dry leaves. Arising this morning at my lodgings in Gresham's College and strolling down Bishopsgate, I chanced to look in 'tween the columns of the 'Change here. It was deserted. But a wind-vortex was picking up all the little scraps of paper dropped by traders yesterday and making 'em orbit round past all of the *bancas* like so many dry leaves . . . I became confused, thinking I had reached Hell, and took my accustomed seat.

APTHORP: Your discourse is annoying.

Enter Marquis of Ravenscar, magnificently attired.

RAVENSCAR: "The hypothesis of vortices is pressed with many difficulties!"

WATERHOUSE: God save the King, m'lord.

APTHORP: God save the King—and damn all riddlers—m'lord.

WATERHOUSE: 'Twere redundant to damn Pluto.

RAVENSCAR: He's damning me, Daniel, for prating about vortices.

APTHORP: The mystery is resolved. For now I perceive that the two of you have arranged to meet here. And since you are speaking of vortices, m'lord, I ween it has to do with Natural Philosophy.

RAVENSCAR: I beg leave to disagree, Sir Richard. For 'twas this fellow in the chair who chose the place of our meeting. Normally we meet in the Golden Grasshopper.

APTHORP: So the mystery endures. Why the 'Change today, then, Daniel?

WATERHOUSE: You will see soon enough.

RAVENSCAR: Perhaps it is because we are going to *exchange* some documents. Voilà!

APTHORP: What is that you have whipped out of your pocket m'lord, I do not have my spectacles.

RAVENSCAR: The latest from Hanover. Dr. Leibniz has favored you, Daniel, with a personalized and autographed copy of the latest *Acta Eruditorum*. Lots of mathematickal incantations are in here, chopped up with great stretched-out S marks—extraordinary!

WATERHOUSE: Then the Doctor has finally dropped the other shoe, for that could only be the Integral Calculus.

RAVENSCAR: Too, some letters addressed to you personally, Daniel, which means they've only been read by a few dozen people so far.

WATERHOUSE: By your leave.

APTHORP: Good heavens, m'lord, if Mr. Waterhouse had snatched 'em any quicker they'd've caught fire. One who dwells in the Underworld ought to be more cautious when handling Inflammable Objects.

WATERHOUSE: Here, m'lord, fresh from Cambridge, as promised, I give you Books I and II of *Principia Mathematica* by Isaac Newton—have a care, some would consider it a valuable document.

APTHORP: My word, is that the cornerstone of a building, or a manuscript?

RAVENSCAR: Err! To judge by weight, it is the former.

APTHORP: Whatever it is, it is too long, too long!

WATERHOUSE: It explains the System of the World.

APTHORP: Some sharp editor needs to step in and take that wretch in hand!

RAVENSCAR: Will you just look at all of these damned illustrations . . . do you realize what this will cost, for all of the woodcuts?

WATERHOUSE: Think of each one of them as saving a thousand pages of tedious explanations full of great stretched-out S marks.

RAVENSCAR: None the less, the cost of printing this is going to *bankrupt* the Royal Society!

APTHORP: So that is why Mr. Waterhouse is seated at a chair, with no *banca*—it is a symbolic posture, meant to express the financial condition of the Royal Society. I very much fear that I am to be asked for money at this point. Say, can either one of you hear a word I am saying?

Silence.

APTHORP: Go ahead and read. I don't mind being ignored. Are those documents terribly fascinating, then?

Silence.

APTHORP: Ah, like a salmon weaving a devious course up-torrent, slipping round boulders and leaping o'er logs, my assistant is making his way back to me.

Enter Minion.

MINION: You were right concerning the Jew, Sir Richard. He wants to purchase certain commodities in large amounts.

APTHORP: At this moment on a Board in Amsterdam, those commodities must be fetching a higher price than is scribbled on our humble English Plank. The Jew wants to buy low here, and sell high there. Pray tell, what sorts of commodities are in such high demand in Amsterdam?

MINION: He takes a particular interest in certain coarse, durable fabrics . . .

APTHORP: Sailcloth! Someone is building a navy!

MINION: He specifically does not want sailcloth, but cheaper stuff.

APTHORP: Tent cloth! Someone is building an army! Come, let us go and buy all the war-stuff we can find.

Exit Apthorp and entourage.

RAVENSCAR: So this is the thing Newton's been working on?

WATERHOUSE: How could he have produced that without working on it?

RAVENSCAR: When I work on things, Daniel, they come out in disjoint parts, a lump at a time; this is a unitary whole, like the garment of Our Saviour, seamless . . . what is he going to do in Book III? Raise the dead and ascend into Heaven?

WATERHOUSE: He is going to solve the orbit of the moon, provided Flamsteed will part with the requisite *data*.

RAVENSCAR: If Flamsteed doesn't, I'll see to it he parts with his fingernails. God! Here's a catchy bit: "To every action there is an equal and opposite reaction . . . if you press a stone with your finger, the finger is also pressed by the stone." The perfection of this work is obvious even to me, Daniel! How must it look to you?

WATERHOUSE: If you are going down that road, then ask rather how it looks to Leibniz, for he is as far beyond me as I am beyond you; if Newton is the finger, Leibniz is the stone, and they press against each other with equal and opposite force, a little bit harder every day.

RAVENSCAR: But Leibniz has not read it, and you have, so there would be little point in asking him.

WATERHOUSE: I have taken the liberty of conveying the essentials to Leibniz, which explains why he is writing so many of these damned letters.

RAVENSCAR: But certainly Leibniz would not dare to challenge a work of such radiance!

WATERHOUSE: Leibniz is at the disadvantage of not having seen it. Or perhaps we should count this as an advantage, for anyone who sees it is dumbfounded by the brilliance of the geometry, and it is difficult to criticize a man's work when you are down on your knees shielding your eyes.

RAVENSCAR: You believe that Leibniz has discovered an error in one of these proofs?

WATERHOUSE: No, proofs such as Newton's cannot have errors.

RAVENSCAR: Cannot?

WATERHOUSE: As a man looks at an apple on a table and says, "There is an apple on the table," you may look at these geometrical diagrams of Newton's and say, "Newton speaks the truth."

RAVENSCAR: Then I'll convey a copy to the Doctor forthwith, so that he may join us on his knees.

WATERHOUSE: Don't bother. Leibniz's objection lies not in what Newton has done but in what he has *not* done.

RAVENSCAR: Perhaps we can get Newton to do it in Book III, then, and remove the objection! You have influence with him . . .

WATERHOUSE: The ability to annoy Isaac is not to be confused with influence.

RAVENSCAR: We will convey Leibniz's objections to him directly, then.

WATERHOUSE: You do not grasp the nature of Leibniz's objections. It is not that Newton left some corollary unproved, or failed to follow up on some promising line of inquiry. Turn back, even before the Laws of Motion, and read what Isaac says in his introduction. I can quote it from memory: "For I here design only to give a mathematical notion of these forces, without considering their physical causes and seats."

RAVENSCAR: What is wrong with that?

WATERHOUSE: Some would argue that as Natural Philosophers we are *supposed* to consider their physical causes and seats! This morning, Roger, I sat in this empty courtyard, in the midst of a whirlwind. The whirlwind was invisible; how did I know 'twas here? Because of the motion it conferred on innumerable scraps of paper, which orbited round me. Had I thought to bring along my instruments I could have taken observations and measured the velocities and plotted the trajectories of those scraps, and if I were as brilliant as Isaac I could have drawn all of those data together into a single unifying picture of the whirlwind. But if I were Leibniz I'd have done none of those things. Instead I'd have asked, *Why is the whirlwind here?*

ENTR'ACTE

Noises off: A grave Procession ascending Fish Street Hill, coming from the TOWER OF LONDON.

Traders exhibit startlement and dismay as the Procession marches into the Exchange, disrupting Commerce.

Enter first two platoons of the King's Own Black Torrent Guards, armed with muskets, affixed to the muzzles whereof are long stabbing-weapons in the style recently adopted by the French Army, and nominated by them bayonets. *Leveling these, the soldiers clear all traders from the center of the 'Change, and compel them to form up in concentric ranks, like spectators gathered round an impromptu Punchinello-show at a fair.*

Enter now trumpeters and drummers, followed by a HERALD bellowing legal gibberish.

As drummers beat a slow and dolorous cadence, enter JACK KETCH in a black hood. The assembled traders are silent as the dead.

Jack Ketch walks slowly into the center of the empty space and stands with arms folded.

Enter now a wagon drawn by a black horse and loaded with faggots and jars, flanked by the ASSISTANTS of Jack Ketch. Assistants pile the wood on the ground and then soak it with oil poured from the jars.

Enter now BAILIFF carrying a BOOK bound up in chains and pad-locks.

JACK KETCH: In the name of the King, stop and identify yourself!

BAILIFF: John Bull, a bailiff.

JACK KETCH: State your business.

BAILIFF: It is the King's business. I have here a prisoner to be bound over for execution.

JACK KETCH: What is the prisoner's name?

BAILIFF: *A History of the Late Massacres and Persecutions of the French Huguenots; to which is appended a brief relation of the bloody and atrocious crimes recently visited upon blameless Protestants dwelling in the realms of the Duke of Savoy, at the behest of King Louis XIV of France.*

JACK KETCH: Has this prisoner been accused of a crime?

BAILIFF: Not only accused, but justly convicted, of spreading con-
tumacious falsehoods, attempting to arouse civil discord, and
leveling many base slanders against the good name of The Most
Christian King Louis XIV, a true friend of our own King and a
loyal ally of England.

JACK KETCH: Vile crimes, indeed! Has a sentence been pronounced?

BAILIFF: Indeed, as I mentioned before, it has been ordered by
Lord Jeffreys that the prisoner is to be bound over to you for
immediate execution.

JACK KETCH: Then I'll welcome him as I did the late Duke of
Monmouth.

*Jack Ketch advances toward the Bailiff and grips the end of the chain.
The bailiff drops the Book and dusts off his hands. To a slow cadence of
muffled drums, Jack Ketch marches to the wood-pile, dragging the book
across the pavement behind him. He heaves the book onto the top of the pile,
steps back, and accepts a torch from an assistant.*

JACK KETCH: Any last words, villainous Book? No? Very well, then
to hell with thee!

Lights the fire.

*Traders, Soldiers, Musicians, Executioner's Staff, &c. watch silently as
the Book is consumed by the flames.*

*Exeunt Bailiff, Herald, Executioners, Musicians, and Soldiers, leaving
behind a smouldering heap of coals.*

*Traders resume commerce as if nothing had happened, save for
EDMUND PALLING, an old man.*

PALLING: Mr. Waterhouse! From the fact that you are the only
one who brought something to sit on, may I assume you knew
that this shameful poppet-show would disgrace the 'Change
today?

WATERHOUSE: That would appear to be the unspoken message.

PALLING: *Unspoken* is an interesting word . . . what of the truths
that were *spoken* in the late Book, concerning the persecutions
of our brethren in France and Savoy? Have they now been
unspoken because the pages were burnt?

WATERHOUSE: I have heard many a sermon in my life, Mr. Palling,
and I know where this one is bound . . . you're going to say that
just as the immortal spirit departs the body to be one with God,
so the contents of the late Book are now going to wherever its
smoke is distributed by the four winds . . . say, weren't you
Massachusetts-bound?

PALLING: I am only bating until I have raised money for the passage, and would probably be finished by now if Jack Ketch had not muddied and stirred the subtle currents of the market.

Exits.

Enter Sir Richard Apthorp.

APTHORP: Burning books . . . is that not a favorite practice of the *Spanish Inquisition?*

WATERHOUSE: I have never been to Spain, Sir Richard, and so the only way I know that they burn books is because of the vast number of books that have been published on the subject.

APTHORP: Hmmm, yes . . . I take your meaning.

WATERHOUSE: I beg of you, do not say 'I take your meaning' with such ponderous significance . . . I do not wish to be Jack Ketch's next guest. You have asked, sir, over and over, why I am sitting here in a chair. Now you know the answer: I came to see justice done.

APTHORP: But you knew 'twould happen—you had aught to do with it. Why did you set it in the 'Change? At Tyburn tree, during one of the regularly scheduled Friday hangings, 'twould've drawn a much more appreciative crowd—why, you could burn a whole *library* there and the Mobb would be stomping their feet for an encore.

WATERHOUSE: They don't read books. The point would've been lost on 'em.

APTHORP: If the point is to put the fear of God into *literate* men, why not burn it at Cambridge and Oxford?

WATERHOUSE: Jack Ketch hates to travel. The new carriages have so little leg-room, and his great Axe does not fit into the luggage bins . . .

APTHORP: Could it be because College men do not have the money and power to organize a rebellion?

WATERHOUSE: Why, yes, that's it. No point intimidating the weak. Threaten the dangerous.

APTHORP: To what end? To keep them in line? Or to put thoughts of rebellion into their minds?

WATERHOUSE: Your question, sir, amounts to asking whether I am a turncoat against the cause of my forebears—corrupted by the fœtid atmosphere of Whitehall—or a traitorous organizer of a secret rebellion.

APTHORP: Why, yes, I suppose it does.

WATERHOUSE: Then would you please ask easier questions or else go away and leave me alone? For whether I'm a back-stabber or a Phanatique, I am in either case no longer a scholar to be trifled with. If you must ply someone with such questions, ask them of yourself; if you insist on an answer, unburden your secrets to me before you ask me to trust you with mine. Assuming I have any.

APTHORP: I think that you do, sir.

Bows.

WATERHOUSE: Why do you doff your hat to me thus?

APTHORP: To honor you, sir, and to pay my respects to him who made you.

WATERHOUSE: What, Drake?

APTHORP: Why, no, I refer to your Mentor, the late John Wilkins, Lord Bishop of Chester—or as some would say, the living incarnation of Janus. For that good fellow penned the *Cryptonomicon* with one hand and the *Universal Character* with the other; he was a good friend of high and mighty Cavaliers at the same time he was wooing and marrying Cromwell's own sister; and, in sum, was Janus-like in diverse ways I'll not bother enumerating to you. For you are truly his pupil, his creation: one moment dispensing intelligence like a Mercury, the next keeping counsel like Pluto.

WATERHOUSE: Mentor was a guise adopted by Minerva, and her pupil was great Ulysses, and so by hewing to a strict Classical interpretation of your words, sir, I'll endeavour not to take offense.

APTHORP: Endeavour and succeed, my good man, for no offense was meant. Good day.

Exits.

Enter Ravenscar, carrying Principia Mathematica.

RAVENSCAR: I'm taking this to the printer's straightaway, but before I do, I was pondering this Newton/Leibniz thing . . .

WATERHOUSE: What!? Jack Ketch's performance made no impression on you at all?

RAVENSCAR: Oh, that? I assume you arranged it that way in order to buttress your position as the King's token Puritan bootlick—whilst in fact stirring rebellious spirits in the hearts and minds of the rich and powerful. Forgive me for not tossing out a compliment. Twenty years ago I'd have admired it, but by my current standards it is only a modestly sophisticated ploy. The matter of Newton and Leibniz is much more interesting.

WATERHOUSE: Go ahead, then.

RAVENSCAR: Descartes explained, years and years ago, that the planets move round the sun like slips of paper caught up in a wind-vortex. So Leibniz's objection is groundless—there is no mystery, and therefore Newton did not gloss over any problems.

WATERHOUSE: Leibniz has been trying to make sense of Descartes' dynamics for years, and finally given up. Descartes was wrong. His theory of dynamics is beautiful in that it is purely geometrical and mathematical. But when you compare that theory to the world as it really is, it proves an unmitigated disaster. The whole notion of vortices does not work. There is no doubt that the inverse square law exists, and governs the motions of all heavenly bodies along conic sections. But it has nothing to do with vortices, or the cœlestial æther, or any of that other nonsense.

RAVENSCAR: What brings it about, then?

WATERHOUSE: Isaac says it is God, or God's presence in the physical world. Leibniz says it has to be some sort of interaction among particles too tiny to see . . .

RAVENSCAR: Atoms?

WATERHOUSE: Atoms—to make a long story short and leave out all the good bits—could not move and change fast enough. Instead Leibniz speaks of monads, which are more fundamental than atoms. If I try to explain we'll both get headaches. Suffice it to say, he is going at it hammer and tongs, and we will hear more from him in due course.

RAVENSCAR: That is very odd, for he avers in a personal letter to me that, having published the Integral Calculus, he'll now turn his attention to genealogical research.

WATERHOUSE: That sort of work entails much travel, and the Doctor does his best work when he's rattling round the Continent in his carriage. He can do both things, and more, at the same time.

RAVENSCAR: In the decision to study history, some will see an admission of defeat to Newton. I myself cannot understand why he should want to waste his time digging up ancient family trees.

WATERHOUSE: Perhaps I'm not the only Natural Philosopher who can put together a "moderately sophisticated ploy" when he needs to.

RAVENSCAR: What on earth are you talking about?

WATERHOUSE: Dig up some ancient family trees, stop assuming that Leibniz is a defeated ninehammer, and consider it. Put your *philosophick* acumen to use: know, for example, that the children of syphilitics are often syphilitic themselves, and unable to bear viable offspring.

RAVENSCAR: Now you are swimming out into the deep water, Daniel. Monsters are there—bear it in mind.

WATERHOUSE: 'Tis true, and when a man has got to a point in his life when he needs to slay a monster, like St. George, or be eaten by one, like Jonah, I think that is where he goes a-swimming.

RAVENSCAR: Is it your intention to slay, or be eaten?

WATERHOUSE: I have already been eaten. My choices are to slay, or else be vomited up on some bit of dry land somewhere— Massachusetts, perhaps.

RAVENSCAR: Right. Well, before you make me any more alarmed, I'm off to the printer's.

WATERHOUSE: It may be the finest errand you ever do, Roger.

Exit Marquis of Ravenscar.
Enter Sir Richard Apthorp solus.

APTHORP: Woe. Bad tidings and alarums! Fear for England . . . O miserable island!

WATERHOUSE: What can possibly have happened, in the Temple of Mercury, to alter your mood so? Did you lose a lot of money?

APTHORP: No, I made a lot, buying low and selling high.

WATERHOUSE: Buying what?

APTHORP: Tent-cloth, saltpeter, lead, and other martial commodities.

WATERHOUSE: From whom?

APTHORP: Men who knew less than I did.

WATERHOUSE: And you sold it to—?

APTHORP: Men who knew more.

WATERHOUSE: A typical commercial transaction, all in all.

APTHORP: Except that I acquired knowledge as part of the bargain. And the knowledge fills me with dread.

WATERHOUSE: Share it with Pluto, then, for he knows all secrets, and keeps most of 'em, and basks in Dread as an old dog lies in the sun.

APTHORP: The buyer is the King of England.

WATERHOUSE: Good news, then! Our King is bolstering our defences.

APTHORP: But why d'you suppose the Jew braved the North Sea to come and buy it here?

WATERHOUSE: Because 'tis cheaper here?

APTHORP: It *isn't*. But he saves money to buy it in England, because then there are no expenses for shipping. For these war-like commodities are supposed to be delivered, not to some foreign battle-ground, but *here*—to England—which is where the King intends to use 'em.

WATERHOUSE: That is extraordinary, since there are no foreigners here to practise war upon.

APTHORP: Only Englishmen, as far as the eye can see!

WATERHOUSE: Perhaps the King fears a foreign invasion.

APTHORP: Does it give you comfort to think so?

WATERHOUSE: To think of being invaded? No. To think of the Coldstream Guards, the Grenadiers, and the King's Own Black Torrent
Guards fighting foreigners, 'stead of Englishmen, why yes.

APTHORP: Then it follows, does it not, that all good Englishmen
should bend their efforts to bringing it about.

WATERHOUSE: Let us now choose our words carefully, for Jack
Ketch is only just round the corner.

APTHORP: No man has been choosing his words more carefully
than you, Daniel.

WATERHOUSE: *Lest native arms fraternal blood might shed,*
For want of alien foes and righteous broil,
We'd fain see foreign canvas off our shores,
And English towns beset by armèd Boers.
Our soldiers, if they love by whom they're led,
May then let foreign blood on English soil.
And if they don't, and let their colors fall,
Their leader never was their King at all.

Versailles
1687

To d'Avaux, March 1687

Monseigneur,

Finally, a real spring day—my fingers have thawed out and
I am able to write again. I would like to be out enjoying the
flowers, but instead I am despatching letters to tulip-land.

You will be pleased to know that as of last week there are
no beggars in France. The King has declared beggary illegal.
The nobles who live at Versailles are of two minds concerning this. Of course they all agree that it is magnificent. But
many of them are scarcely above beggars themselves, and so
they are wondering whether the law applies to them.

Fortunately—for those who have daughters, anyway—
Mme. de Maintenon has got her girls' school open at St.-Cyr,
just a few minutes' ride from the château of Versailles. This
has complicated my situation a little. The girl I have supposedly been tutoring—the daughter of the Marquise d'Ozoir—
has begun attending the school, which makes my position
redundant. So far, there has been no talk of letting me go. I
have been putting my free time to good use, making two trips
to Lyons to learn about how commerce works in that place.
But apparently Édouard de Gex has been spreading tales of
my great skills as a tutor to the Maintenon, who has begun
making noises about bringing me to St.-Cyr as a teacher.

Did I mention that the teachers are all nuns?

De Maintenon and de Gex are so shrouded in outward
Godliness that I cannot make out their motives. It is almost
conceivable that they believe, sincerely, that I am a good candidate for the convent—in other words, that they are too
detached from worldly matters to understand my true function here. Or perhaps they know full well that I am managing
assets for twenty-one different French nobles, and they wish
to neutralize me—or bring me under their control by threatening to do so.

To business: returns for the first quarter of 1687 have
been satisfactory, as you know since you are a client. I pooled
all of the money into a fund and invested it mostly through
sub-brokers in Amsterdam, who specialize in particular commodities or species of V.O.C. derivatives. We are still making
money on India cloth, thanks to King Louis who made it
contraband and thereby drove up the price. But V.O.C.
shares fell after William of Orange declared the League of
Augsburg. William may be full of bluster about how the
Protestant alliance is going to rein in the power of France,
but his own stock market seems to take an extremely dim
view of the project! As does the court here—*tout le monde*
finds it tremendously amusing that William, and Sophie of
Hanover, and a grab-bag of other frostbitten Lutherans
believe they can stand up to *La France*. There is brave talk
about how Father de Gex and Maréchal de Catinat, who suppressed the Protestants in Savoy with such force, ought now
to ride North and and give the same treatment to the Dutch
and the Germans.

For now it is my rôle to set aside any personal feelings I
may have concerning politics, and to think only of how this

might affect markets. My footing here is soft—I am like a mare galloping down a mucky beach, afraid to falter, out of fear that she may be treading on quicksand. With markets in Amsterdam fluctuating hourly, I cannot really manage assets from Versailles—the day-to-day buying and selling is carried out by my associates in the north.

But French nobles will not be seen doing business with Dutch hereticks and Spanish Jews. So I am a sort of figure-head, like the pretty mermaid on the bow of a ship that is laden with other people's treasure and manned by swarthy corsairs. The only thing to be said in favor of being a figure-head is that the position gives one an excellent view ahead, and plenty of time to think. Help me, Monseigneur, to have as clear a view as possible of the seas we are about to plow up. I cannot help but think that in a year or two I shall be forced to gamble all of my clients' assets on the outcome of great events. Investing round the time of Monmouth's rebellion was not difficult because I knew Monmouth, and knew how it would come out. But I know William, too—not as well—but well enough to know I cannot gamble against him with certainty. Monmouth was a hobbyhorse and William is a stallion. Experience gained riding the first can only misinform me as to what it shall be like to ride the second.

So inform me, Monseigneur. Tell me things. You know your intelligence will be safe in transit, because of the excellence of this cypher, and you know it will be safe with me, for I have no friends here to whisper it to.

> Only small minds want always to be right.
> —LOUIS XIV

To d'Avaux, June 1687
Monseigneur,

When I complained that Fr. de Gex and Mme. de Maintenon were trying to make me over into a nun, I never imagined you would respond by making me out to be a whore! Mme. la duchesse d'Oyonnax has practically had to post Swiss guards at the entrance of her apartments to keep the young blades away from me. What sorts of rumors have you been spreading? That I am a nymphomaniac? That a thousand *louis d'or* will go to the first Frenchman who beds me?

At any rate, now I have some idea as to who belongs to the *cabinet noir.* One day, all of a sudden, Fr. de Gex was very cool to me, and Étienne d'Arcachon, the one-armed son of the Duke, called on me to say that he did not believe any of the rumors that were being spread about me. I think I was meant to be bowled over by his nobility—with him, it is difficult to tell. For on the one hand he is so excessively polite that some affirm he is not in his right mind, and on the other (though he has no other!) he saw me at the opera with Monmouth and knows some of my history. Otherwise why would a Duke's son even give the time of day to a common servant?

The only circumstance under which a man of his rank and a woman of mine could ever be seen conversing with each other is a fancy-dress ball, when ranks are of no account and all the normal rules of precedence are suspended for a few hours. The other evening, Étienne d'Arcachon escorted me to one at Dampierre, the château of the duc de Chevreuse. He dressed as Pan and I as a Nymph. Here any proper Court lady would devote several pages to describing the costumes, and the intrigues and machinations that went into their making, but since I am not a proper Court lady and you are a busy man, I will leave it at that—pausing only to mention that Étienne had a special prosthetic hand carved out of boxwood and strapped to his stump. The hand was gripping a silver Pan-pipe all twined about with ivy (emerald leaves, of course, and ruby berries) and from time to time he would raise this to his lips and pipe a little melody that he had Lully compose for him.

As we rode in the carriage to Dampierre, Étienne mentioned to me, "You know, our host the duc de Chevreuse is the son-in-law of a commoner: Colbert, the late Contrôleur-Général, who built Versailles among other accomplishments."

As you know, this is not the first such veiled remark that has been directed my way by a Frenchman of high rank. The first time it happened I became ever so excited, thinking I was about to be ennobled at any minute. Then for a time I affected a cynical view, supposing that this was like a snatch of meat dangled high above a dog's nose to make it do tricks. But on this evening, riding to the splendid château of Dampierre on the arm of a future Duke, the burden of my low rank lifted for a few hours by a mask and costume, I phant'sied that Étienne's remark really meant something, and that if I could use my skills to achieve some great accomplishment, I might be rewarded as Colbert had been.

Pretend now that I have dutifully described all of the costumes, the table-settings, the food, and the entertainments that the duc de Chevreuse had brought together at Dampierre. This will spare enough pages to make a small book. At first the mood was somewhat gloomy, for Mansart—the King's architect—was there, and he had just received news that the Parthenon in Athens has been blown up. Apparently the Turks had been using it as a powder-magazine and the Venetians, who are trying to bring that city back into Christendom, bombarded it with mortars and touched off a great explosion. Mansart—who had always harbored an ambition of making a pilgrimage to Athens to see that building with his own eyes—was inconsolable. There was some blustery talk from Étienne to the effect that he would personally lead a squadron of his father's Mediterranean fleet to Athens to take that city back into Christendom. This was a *faux pas* of sorts because Athens is not actually located on the water. Therefore it led to a few moments' awkward silence.

I decided to strike. No one knew who I was, and even if they found out, my status and my reputation (thanks to you!) could scarcely sink lower. "So gloomy are we because of this news from abroad," I exclaimed, "and yet what is news but words, and what are words but air?"

Now this produced only a few titters because everyone was assuming that I was just another empty-headed Duchess who had read too much Pascal. But I had their attention (if you could see my gown, Monseigneur, you would know I had their attention; my face was hidden, everything else was getting a good airing-out).

I continued, "Why should we not conjure up some news more to our liking, and throw our enemies the Dutchmen into a gloomy mood, so that we may be infused with gaiety and joy?"

Now most of them were nonplussed, but several took an interest—including one chap who was dressed up as Orion after he had been blinded by Oenopion, so that his mask had blood running out of the eye-sockets. Orion asked me to say more, and so I did: "Here, we are susceptible to emotion, because we are people of great feeling and passion, and accordingly we are saddened by the destruction of the Parthenon, for we value beauty. In Amsterdam, they have investments instead of emotions, and all they value is their precious V.O.C. stock. We could destroy all the treasures of the Classical world and they would not care; but if they hear bad news that touches the V.O.C., they are plunged into despair—or rather the price of the stock falls, which amounts to the same thing."

"Since you appear to know so much about it, tell us what would be the worst news they could hear," said blind Orion.

"Why, the fall of Batavia—for that is the linch-pin of their overseas empire."

By now Orion had come face-to-face with me and we were in the middle of a ring of costumed nobles who were all leaning forward to listen. For it was obvious to everyone that the man dressed as Orion was none other than the King himself. He said, "The doings of the cheese-mongers are a vulgar muddle to us—trying to understand them is like watching muddy English peasants at one of their shin-kicking contests. If it is so easy to bring about a crash in the Amsterdam market, why doesn't it crash all the time? For anyone could spread such a rumor."

"And many do—it is very common for a few investors to get together and form a cabal, which is a sort of secret society that manipulates the market for profit. The machinations of these cabals have grown exceedingly complex, with as many moves and variations as dance steps. But at some point they all rely upon spreading false news into the ears of credulous investors. Now these cabals form and join, split and vanish like clouds in the summer sky, and so the market has become resistant to news, especially bad news; for most investors now assume that any bad news from abroad is false information put out by a cabal."

"Then what hope have we of convincing these skeptical heretics that Batavia has fallen?" asked Orion.

"My answering your question is complicated somewhat by the fact that everyone here is wearing a disguise," I said, "but it would not be unreasonable to suppose that the Grand Admiral of the French Navy (the duc d'Arcachon) and the *Contrôleur* of the French East India Company (the Marquis d'Ozoir) are present, and able to hear my words. For men of such eminence, it would be no great thing to make it believed and understood, from the top to the bottom of the French naval and merchant fleets, and in every port from Spain to

Flanders, that a French expeditionary force had rounded the Cape of Good Hope and fallen suddenly upon Batavia and seized it from the V.O.C. The news would spread north up the coast like fire along a powder-trail, and when it reached the Damplatz—"

"The Damplatz is the powder-keg," Orion concluded. "This plan has beauty, for it would require little risk or expenditure from us, yet would cause more damage to William of Orange than an invasion by fifty thousand of our dragoons."

"While at the same time bringing profit to anyone who knew in advance, and who took the right positions in the market," I added.

Now, Monseigneur, I know for a fact that on the next morning Louis XIV went on a trip to his lodge at Marly, and invited the Marquis d'Ozoir and the duc d'Arcachon to join him.

Speaking for myself, I have spent all the time since talking to French nobles who are desperate to know what "the right position" is. I have lost track of the number of times I have had to explain the concept of selling short, and that when V.O.C. stock falls it tends to bring about a rise in commodity prices as capital flies from one to the other. Above all, I've had to make it clear that if a lot of Frenchmen, new to the markets, suddenly sell the V.O.C. short while investing in commodities futures, it will make it obvious to the Dutch that a cabal has formed at the court of the Sun King. That (in other words) the ground-work must be laid with great care and subtlety—which amounts to saying that I must do it.

In any event, a lot of French gold is going to be making its way north in the next week. I will send details in another letter.

> The diligent *Dutch* seeing the Easiness of the managing and curing the Berry, and how that Part had no Dependence, either upon the Earth, the Air, the Water, or anything else more there, than in another Place, took the Hint, and planted the Coffee Tree in the Island of *Java,* near their City of *Batavia,* there it thrives, bears, and ripens every jot as well as at *Mocha;* and now they begin to leave off the Red Sea, and bring 20 to 30 Tons of Coffee, at a time, from *Batavia,* in the Latitude of 5 Deg. S.
> —DANIEL DEFOE, *A Plan of the English Commerce*

To Leibniz, August 1687

Doctor,

Increase is the order of the day here;* the gardens, orchards, and vineyards are buried in their own produce and the country roads crowded with wagons bringing it to market. France is at peace, her soldiers at home, mending and building *and getting maidens pregnant out of wedlock so that there will be a next generation of soldiers*. New construction is going on all over Versailles, and many here have become modestly wealthy *or at least paid off part of their gambling debts* in the wake of the stock market crash in Amsterdam.

I am sorry not to have written in so many weeks. This cypher is extremely time-consuming and I have been too busy with all of the machinations surrounding the "fall of Batavia."

Mme. la duchesse d'Oyonnax threw a garden party the other evening; the highlight was a re-enactment of the Fall of Batavia—which, as everyone knows by now, never really happened—played out on the Canal. A fleet of French "frigates," no bigger than rowboats, and trimmed and decorated phantastically, like dream-ships, besieged a model "Batavia" built on the brink of the canal. The Dutchmen in the town were drinking beer and counting gold until they fell asleep. Then the dream-fleet made its attack. The Dutchmen were alarmed at first, until they woke up and understood it had all been a dream . . . but when they returned to their counting-tables, they found that their gold was really gone! The vanishing of the gold was accomplished through some sleight-of-hand so that everyone in the party was completely surprised. Then the dream-fleet cruised up and down the canal for the better part of an hour, and everyone crowded along the banks to admire it. Each vessel represented some virtue that is representative of *la France*, e.g., Fertility, Martial Prowess, Piety, *et cetera, et cetera*, and the captain of each one was a Duke or Prince, dressed up in costumes to match. As they drifted up and down the Canal they threw the captured coins in showers of gold into the ranks of the party-goers.

The Dauphin wore a golden frock embroidered with . . . *I have seen this man Upnor now. He enjoys a high rank in the court of James II and has many friends in France, for he was a boy here during the time of Cromwell. Everyone wants to hear about his*

---

* ☷☳ Increase: Hexagram 42 of the *I Ching*, or 110001.

Protestant slave-girl and he is not slow to talk about her. He is too well-bred to gloat openly, but it is obvious that he takes great pleasure in owning her. Here, the enslavement of rebels in England is likened to the French practice of sending Huguenots to the galleys, and rated as more humane than simply killing them all as was done in Savoy. I had not been sure whether to credit Bob Shaftoe's tale and so I was quite startled to see Upnor in the flesh, and to hear him talking about this. It seems shameful to me—a scandal that the guilty would wish to hide from the world. But to them it is nothing. While sympathizing with poor Abigail Frome, I rejoice that this has come to pass. If the slavers had shown more discretion and continued to take their victims only from black Africa, no one would notice or care—why, I am as guilty as the next person of putting sugar in my coffee without considering the faraway Negroes who made it for me. For James and his ilk to take slaves from Ireland entails more risk, even when they are criminals. But to take English girls from farm-towns is repugnant to almost everyone (the population of Versailles excepted) and an invitation to rebellion. After listening to Upnor I am more certain than ever that England will soon rise up in arms—and James apparently agrees with me, for word has it that he's built great military camps on the edge of London and lavished money on his prize regiments. I fear only that in the chaos and excitement of rebellion, the people of that country will forget about the Taunton schoolgirls and what they signify about slavery in general . . . the tiller and rudder of which were all overgrown with living grape-vines.

Forgive me this endless description of the various Dukes and their dream-boats, I look back over the preceding several pages and see I quite forgot myself.

To Leibniz, October *1687*
Doctor,

Family, family, family* is all anyone wants to talk about. Who is talking to me, you might ask, given that I am a commoner? The answer is that in certain recesses of this immense château there are large salons that are given over entirely to gambling, which is the only thing these nobles can do to make their lives interesting. In these places the usual etiquette is suspended and everyone talks to everyone. Of course the trick is gaining admission to such a salon in the first place—but after my success with the "Fall of Batavia"

---

* ☰☷ Family: Hexagram 37 of the *I Ching,* or 110101.

some of these doors were opened to me (back doors, anyway—I must come in through the servants' entrances) and so it is not unusual for me now to exchange words with a Duchess or even a Princess. But I don't go to these places as often as you might think, for when you are there you have no choice but to gamble, and I don't enjoy it *I loathe it and the people who do it is more accurate. But some of the men who will read this letter are heavy gamblers and so I will be demure.*

More and more frequently people ask me about my family. Someone has been spreading rumors that I have noble blood in my veins! I hope that during your genealogical research you can turn up some supporting evidence . . . turning me into a Countess should be easy compared to making Sophie an Electress. *Enough people here now depend on me that my status as a commoner is awkward and inconvenient. They need a pretext to give me a title so that they can have routine conversations with me without having to set up elaborate shams, such as fancy-dress balls, to circumvent the etiquette.*

Just the other day I was playing basset with M. le duc de Berwick, who is the bastard of James II by Arabella Churchill, sister of John. This places him in excellent company since as you know this means his paternal grandmother was Henrietta Maria of France, the sister of Louis XIII . . . *again, forgive the genealogical prattle. Will you please sort out everything to do with sorcerers, alchemists, Templars, and Satan-worshippers? I know that you got your start in life by bamboozling some rich alchemists into thinking you actually believed their nonsense. And yet you appear to be a sincere friend of the man called Enoch the Red, who is apparently an alchemist of note. From time to time, his name comes up around a gambling table. Most are nonplussed but certain men will cock an eyebrow or cough into a hand, exchange tremendously significant looks, et cetera, conspicuously trying not to be conspicuous. I have observed the same behaviors in connection with other subjects that are of an esoteric or occult nature. Everyone knows that Versailles was infested with Satan-worshippers, poisoners, abortionists, et cetera, in the late 1670s and that most but not all of them were purged; but this only makes it seem murkier and more provocative now. The father of the Earl of Upnor—the Duke of Gunfleet—died suddenly in those days, after drinking a glass of water at a garden party thrown by Mme. la duchesse d'Oyonnax, whose own husband died in similar fashion a fortnight later, leaving all his titles and possessions to her. There is not a man or woman here who does not suspect poisoning in these and other cases. Upnor and*

Oyonnax would probably come in for closer scrutiny if there weren't so many other poisonings to distract people's attention. Anyway, Upnor is obviously one of those gentlemen who takes an interest in occult matters, and keeps making dark comments about his contacts at Trinity College in Cambridge. I am tempted to dismiss all of this as a faintly pathetic hobby for noble toffs bored out of their minds by the ingenious tedium, the humiliating inconsequence, of Versailles. But since I have picked out Upnor as an enemy I would like to know if it amounts to anything . . . can he cast spells on me? Does he have secret brethren in every city? What is Enoch Root?

I am going to spend much of the winter in Holland and will write to you from there.

Eliza

Bank of Het Kanaal,
Between Scheveningen and the Hague

DECEMBER 1687

No man goes so high as he who knows not where he
is going.

—CROMWELL

"WELL MET, BROTHER WILLIAM," SAID Daniel, getting a boot up on the running-board of the carriage, vaulting in through the door, and surprising the hell out of a dumpling-faced Englishman with long stringy dark hair. The passenger snatched the hem of his long black frock coat and drew it up; Daniel could not tell whether he was trying to make room, or to avoid being brushed against by Daniel. Both hypotheses were reasonable. This man had spent a lot more time in ghastly English prisons than Daniel had, and learned to get out of other men's way. And Daniel was mud-spattered from riding, whereas this fellow's clothes, though severe and dowdy, were immaculate. Brother William had a tiny mouth that was pursed sphincter-tight at the moment.

"Recognized your arms on the door," Daniel explained, slamming it to and reaching out the window to give it a familiar slap. "Flagged your coachman down, reckoning we must be going to the same lodge to see the same gentleman."

"When Adam delved and Eve span, who *then* was the Gentleman?"

"Forgive me, I should have said chap, bloke . . . how are things in your Overseas Possession, Mr. Penn? Did you ever settle that dispute with Maryland?"

William Penn rolled his eyes and looked out the window. "It will take a hundred years and a regiment of Surveyors to settle it! At least those damned Swedes have been brought to heel. Everyone imagines that, simply because I own the Biggest Pencil in the World, that my ticket is punched, my affairs settled once and for all . . . but I tell you, Brother Daniel, that it has been nothing but troubles . . . if it is a sin to lust after worldly goods, *videlicet* a horse or a door-knocker, then what have I got myself into *now*? It is a whole new universe of sinfulness."

"'Twas either accept Pennsylvania, or let the King continue owing you sixteen thousand pounds, yes?"

Penn did not take his gaze away from the window, but squinted as if trying to hold back a mighty volume of flatulence, and shifted his focal point to a thousand miles in the distance. But this was coastal Holland and there was nothing out that window save the Curvature of the World. Even pebbles cast giant shadows in the low winter sun. Daniel could not be ignored.

"I am chagrined, appalled, mortified that you are here! You are *not welcome,* Brother Daniel, you are a problem, and obstacle, and if I were not a pacifist I would beat you to death with a rock."

"Brother William, meeting as we so often do at Whitehall, in the King's Presence, to have our lovely chats about Religious Toleration, it is most difficult for us to hold frank exchanges of views, and so I am pleased you've at last found this opportunity to hose me down with those splenetic humours that have been so long pent up."

"I am a plain-spoken fellow, as you can see. Perhaps *you* should say what you mean more frequently, Brother Daniel—it would make everything so much simpler."

"It is easy for you to be that way, when you have an estate the size of Italy to go hiding in, on the far side of an ocean."

"That was unworthy of you, Brother Daniel. But there is some truth in what you say . . . it is . . . distracting . . . at the oddest times . . . my mind drifts, and I find myself wondering what is happening on the banks of the Susquehanna . . ."

"Right! And if England becomes completely unlivable, you have someplace to go. Whereas *I* . . ."

Finally Penn looked at him. "Don't tell me you haven't considered moving to Massachusetts."

"I consider it every day. Nonetheless, most of my constituency does not have that luxury available and so I'd like to see if we can avoid letting Olde Englande get any more fouled up than 'tis."

Penn had disembarked from a ship out at Scheveningen less than an hour ago. That port-town was connected to the Hague by several roads and a canal. The route that Penn's driver had chosen ran along a canal-edge, through stretches of Dutch polder-scape and fields where troops drilled, which extended to within a few hundred yards of the spires of the Binnenhof.

The carriage now made a left turn onto a gravel track that bordered an especially broad open park, called the Malieveld, where those who could afford it went riding when the weather was pleasant. No one was there today. At its eastern end the Malieveld gave way to the Haagse Bos, a carefully managed forest laced through with riding-paths. The carriage followed one of these through the woods for a mile, until it seemed that they had gone far out into the wild. But then suddenly cobblestones, instead of gravel, were beneath the wheel-rims, and they were passing through guarded gates and across counterweighted canal-bridges. The formal gardens of a small estate spread around them. They rolled to a stop before a gate-house. Daniel glimpsed a hedge and the corner of a fine house before his view out the carriage-window was blocked by the head, and more so by the hat, of a captain of the Blue Guards. "William Penn," said William Penn. Then, reluctantly, he added: "And Dr. Daniel Waterhouse."

THE PLACE WAS BUT A small lodge, close enough to the Hague to be easily reached, but far enough away that the air was clean. William of Orange's asthma did not trouble him when he was here, and so, during those times of the year when he had no choice but to stick at the Hague, this was where he abided.

Penn and Waterhouse were ushered to a parlor. It was a raw day outside, and even though a new fire was burning violently on the hearth, making occasional lunges into the room, neither Penn nor Waterhouse made any move to remove his coat.

There was a girl there, a petite girl with large blue eyes, and Daniel assumed she was Dutch at first. But after she'd heard the two visitors conversing in English she addressed them in French, and explained something about the Prince of Orange. Penn's

French was much better than Daniel's because he had spent a few years exiled to a Protestant college (now extirpated) in Saumur, so he exchanged a few sentences with the girl and then said to Daniel: "The sand-sailing is excellent today."

"Could've guessed as much from the wind, I suppose."

"We'll not be seeing the Prince for another hour."

The two Englishmen stood before the fire until well browned on both sides, then settled into chairs. The girl, who was dressed in a rather bleak Dutch frock, set a pan of milk there to heat, then busied herself with some kitchen-fuss. It was now Daniel's turn to be distracted, for there was something in the girl's appearance that was vaguely disturbing or annoying to him, and the only remedy was to look at her some more, trying to figure it out; which made the feeling worse. Or perhaps better. So they sat there for a while, Penn brooding about the Alleghenies and Waterhouse trying to piece together what it was that provoked him about this girl. The feeling was akin to the nagging sense that he had met a person somewhere before but could not recall the particulars. But that was not it; he was certain that this was the first time. And yet he had that same unscratchable itch.

She said something that broke Penn out of his reverie. Penn fixed his gaze upon Daniel. "The girl is offended," he said. "She says that there may be women, of an unspeakable nature, in Amsterdam, who do not object to being looked at as you are looking at *her;* but how dare you, a visitor on Dutch soil, take such liberties?"

"She said a lot then, in five words of French."

"She was pithy, for she credits me with wit. I am discursive, for I can extend you no such consideration."

"You know, merely knuckling under to the King, simply because he waves a Declaration of Indulgence in front of your eyes, is no proof of wit—some would say it proves the opposite."

"Do you really want another Civil War, Daniel? You and I both grew up during such a war—*some* of us have elected to move on— *others* want to re-live their childhoods, it seems."

Daniel closed his eyes and saw the image that had been branded onto his retinas thirty-five years ago: Drake hurling a stone saint's head through a stained-glass window, the gaudy image replaced with green English hillside, silvery drizzle reaching in through the aperture like the Holy Spirit, bathing his face.

"I do not think you see what we can make of England now if we only try. I was brought up to believe that an Apocalypse was coming. I have not believed that for many years. But the people who believe in that Apocalypse are my people, and their way of thinking is my way. I have only just come round to a new way of looking at this, a new view-point, as Leibniz would have it. Namely that there is something to the *idea* of an Apocalypse—a sudden changing of all, an overthrow of old ways—and that Drake and the others merely got the *particulars* wrong, they fixed on a date certain, they, in a word, *idolized*. If idolatry is to mistake the symbol for the thing symbolized, then that is what they did with the symbols that are set down in the Book of Revelation. Drake and the others were like a flock of birds who all sense that something is nigh, and take flight as one: a majestic sight and a miracle of Creation. But they were confused, and flew into a trap, and their revolution came to naught. Does that mean that they were mistaken to have spread their wings at all? No, their senses did not deceive them . . . their higher minds did. Should we spurn them forever because they erred? Is their legacy to be laughed at only? On the contrary, I would say that we might bring about the Apocalypse now with a little effort . . . not precisely the one they phant'sied but the same, or better, in its effects."

"You really should move to Pennsylvania," Penn mused. "You are a man of parts, Daniel, and certain of those parts, which will only get you half-hanged, drawn, and quartered in London, would make you a great man in Philadelphia—or at least get you invited to a lot of parties."

"I've not given up on England just yet, thank you."

"England may prefer that you give up, rather than suffer another Civil War, or another Bloody Assizes."

"Much of England sees it otherwise."

"And you may number me in that party, Daniel, but a scattering of Nonconformists does not suffice to bring about the changes you seek."

"True . . . but what of the men whose signatures are on these letters?" said Daniel, producing a sheaf of folded parchments, each one be-ribboned and wax-sealed.

Penn's mouth shrank to the size of a navel and his mind worked for a minute. The girl came round and served chocolate.

"For you to surprise me in this way was not the act of a gentleman."

"When Adam delved and Eve span . . ."

"Shut up! Do not trifle with me. Owning Pennsylvania does not make me any better than a Vagabond in the eyes of God, Daniel, but it serves as a reminder that I'm not to be trifled and toyed with."

"And that, Brother William, is why I nearly killed myself to cross the North Sea on the front of a wind-storm, and galloped through frost and muck to intercept you—*before* you met with your next King." Daniel drew out a Hooke-watch and turned its ivory face toward the fire-light. "There is still time for you to write a letter of your own, and put it on the top of this stack, if you please."

"I WAS GOING TO ASK, do you have any idea how many people in Amsterdam want to kill you . . . but by coming up here, you seem to've answered the question: no," said William, Prince of Orange.

"You had fair warning in my letter to d'Avaux, did you not?"

"It barely reached me in time . . . the brunt of the blow was absorbed by some big shareholders there, whom I held off from warning."

"Francophiles."

"No, the bottom has quite fallen out of *that* market, very few Dutchmen are selling themselves to the French nowadays. My chief enemies nowadays are what you would call Dutchmen of limited vision. At any rate, your Batavia charade caused no end of head-aches for me."

"Establishing a first-rate intelligence source at the Court of Louis XIV cannot come cheaply."

"That insipid truism can be turned around easily: when it comes so dear, then I demand first-rate intelligence. What did you learn from the two Englishmen, by the way?" William glanced at a dirty spoon and flared his nostrils. A Dutch houseboy, fairer and more beautiful than Eliza, bustled over and began to clear away the gleam-ing, crusted evidence of a long chocolate binge. The clattering of the cups and spoons seemed to irritate William more than gunfire on a battlefield. He leaned back deep into his armchair, closed his eyes, and turned his face toward the fire. To him the world was a dark close cellar with a net-work of covert channels strung through it, frail and irregular as cobwebs, transmitting faint cyphers of intel-ligence from time to time, and so a fire broadcasting clear strong radiance all directions was a sort of miracle, a pagan god manifest-ing itself in a spidery Gothick chapel. Eliza did not speak until the boy was finished and the room had gone quiet again and the folds and creases in the prince's face had softened. He was a couple of years shy of forty, but time spent in sun and spray had given him the skin, and battles had given him the mentality, of an older man.

"Both believe the same things, and believe them sincerely," Eliza said, referring to the two Englishmen. "Both have been tested by suffering. At first I thought the fat one had been corrupted. But the slender one did not think so."

"Maybe the slender one is naïve."

"He is not naïve in *that* way. No, those two belong to a common sect, or something—they knew and recognized each other. They dislike each other and work at cross-purposes but betrayal, corruption, any straying from whatever common path they have chosen, these are inconceivable. Is it the same sect as Gomer Bolstrood?"

"No and yes. The Puritans are like Hindoos—impossibly various, and yet all of a type."

Eliza nodded.

"Why are you so fascinated by the Puritans?" William asked.

It was not asked in a friendly way. He suspected her of some weakness, some occult motive. She looked at him like a little girl who had just been run over by a cart-wheel. It was a look that would cause most men to fall apart like stewed chickens. It didn't work. Eliza had noticed that William of Orange had a lot of gorgeous boys around him. But he also had a mistress, an Englishwoman named Elizabeth Villiers, who was only moderately beautiful, but famously intelligent and witty. The Prince of Orange would never make himself vulnerable by relying on one sex or the other; any lust he might feel for Eliza he could easily channel towards that houseboy, as Dutch farmers manipulated their sluice-gates to water one field instead of another. Or at least that was the message he wanted to convey, by keeping the company he did.

Eliza sensed that she had quite inadvertently gotten into danger. William had found an inconsistency in her, and if it weren't explained to his satisfaction, he'd brand her as Enemy. And while Louis XIV kept his enemies in the gilded cage of Versailles, William probably had more forthright ways of dealing with his.

The truth wasn't so bad after all. "I think they are interesting," she said, finally. "They are so different from anyone else. So peculiar. But they are not ninehammers, they are formidable in the extreme; Cromwell was only a prelude, a practice. This Penn controls an estate that is stupefyingly vast. New Jersey is a place of Quakers, too, and different sorts of Puritans are all over Massachusetts. Gomer Bolstrood used to say the most startling things . . . overthrowing monarchy was the *least* of it. He said that Negroes and white men are equal before God and that all slavery everywhere must be done away with, and that his people would never let up until everyone saw it their way. 'First we'll get the Quakers on our side, for they are rich,' he said, 'then the other Nonconformists, then the Anglicans, then the Catholics, then all of Christendom.'"

William had turned his gaze back to the fire as she spoke, signalling that he believed her. "Your fascination with Negroes is very odd. But I have observed that the best people are frequently odd in one way or another. I have got in the habit of seeking them out, and declining to trust anyone who has no oddities. Your queer ideas concerning slavery are of no interest to me whatever. But the fact that you harbor queer ideas makes me inclined to place some small amount of trust in you."

"If you trust my judgment, the slender Puritan is the one to watch," Eliza said.

"But he has no vast territories in America, no money, no followers!"

"That is *why*. I would wager he had a father who was very strong, probably older brothers, too. That he has been checked and baffled many times, never married, never enjoyed even the small homely success of having a child, and has come to that time in his life when he must make his mark, or fail. This has become all confused, in his thinking, with the coming rebellion against the English King. He has decided to gamble his life on it—not in the sense of living or dying, but in the sense of making something of his life, or not."

William winced. "I pray you never see that deep into *me*."

"Why? Perhaps 'twould do you good."

"Nay, nay, you are like some Fellow of the Royal Society, dissecting a living dog—there is a placid cruelty about you."

"About *me*? What of *you*? To fight wars is *kindness*?"

"Most men would rather be shot through with a broad-headed arrow than be *described* by you."

Eliza could not help laughing. "I do not think my description of the slender one is at all cruel. On the contrary, I believe he will succeed. To judge from that pile of letters, he has many powerful Englishmen behind him. To rally that many supporters while remaining close to the King is very difficult." Eliza was hoping, now, that the Prince would let slip some bit of information about *who* those letter-writers were. But William perceived the gambit almost before she uttered the words, and looked away from her.

"It is very dangerous," he said. "Rash. Insane. I wonder if I should trust a man who conceives such a desperate plan."

A bit of a silence now. Then one of the logs in the fireplace gave way in a cascading series of pops and hisses.

"Are you asking me to do something about it?"

More silence, but this time the burden of response was on William. Eliza could relax, and watch his face. His face showed that he did not like being put in this position.

"I have something important for you to do at Versailles," he admitted, "and cannot afford to send you to London to tend to

Daniel Waterhouse. But, where he is concerned, you might be more useful in Versailles anyway."

"I don't understand."

William opened his eyes wide, took a deep breath, and sighed it out, listening clinically to his own lungs. He sat up straighter, though his small hunched body was still overwhelmed by the chair, and looked alertly into the fire. "I can tell Waterhouse to be careful and he will say, 'yes, sire,' but it is all meaningless. He will not really be careful until he has something to live for." William looked Eliza straight in the eye.

"You want me to give him that?"

"I cannot afford to lose him, and the men who put their signatures on these letters, because he suddenly decides he cares not whether he lives or dies. I want him to have some reason to care."

"It is easily done."

"Is it? I cannot think of a pretext for getting the two of you in the same room together."

"I have another oddity, sire: I am interested in Natural Philosophy."

"Ah yes, you stay with Huygens."

"And Huygens has another friend in town just now, a Swiss mathematician named Fatio. He is young and ambitious and *desperate* to make contacts with the Royal Society. Daniel Waterhouse is the Secretary. I'll set up a dinner."

"That name Fatio is familiar," William said distantly. "He has been pestering me, trying to set up an audience."

"I'll find out what he wants."

"Good."

"What of the other thing?"

"I beg your pardon?"

"You said you had something important for me to do at Versailles."

"Yes. Come to me again before you leave and I'll explain it. Now I am tired, tired of talking. The thing you must do there for me is pivotal, everything revolves around it, and I want to have my wits about me when I explain it to you."

> M. Descartes had found the way to have his conjectures and fictions taken for truths. And to those who read his *Principles of Philosophy* something happened like that which happens to those who read novels which please and make the same impression as true stories. The novelty of the images of his

little particles and vortices are most agreeable.
When I read the book . . . the first time, it seemed
to me that everything proceeded perfectly; and
when I found some difficulty, I believe it was my
fault in not fully understanding his thought. . . .
But since then, having discovered in it from time to
time things that are obviously false and others that
are very improbable, I have rid myself entirely of
the prepossession I had conceived, and I now find
almost nothing in all his physics that I can accept
as true. . . .

—HUYGENS, P. 186 OF WESTFALL'S 1971
The Concept of Force in Newton's Physics:
The Science of Dynamics in
the Seventeenth Century

CHRISTIAAN HUYGENS SAT at the head of the table, the perihelion
of the ellipse, and Daniel Waterhouse sat at the opposite end, the
aphelion. Nicolas Fatio de Duilliers and Eliza sat across from each
other in between. A dinner of roast goose, ham, and winter vegetables was served up by various members of a family that had long
been servants in this house. Eliza was the author of the seating
plan. Huygens and Waterhouse must not sit next to each other or
they'd fuse together and never say a word to the others. This way
was better: Fatio would only want to talk to Waterhouse, who would
only want to talk to Eliza, who would pretend she had ears only for
Huygens, and so the guests would pursue each other round the
table clockwise, and with a bit of luck, an actual conversation might
eventuate.

It was near the time of the solstice, the sun had gone down in
the middle of the afternoon, and their faces, lit up by a still-life of
candles thrust into wax-crusted bottles, hung in the darkness like
Moons of Jupiter. The ticking of Huygens's clock-work at the other
end of the room was distracting at first, but later became part of
the fabric of space; like the beating of their hearts, they could hear
it if they wanted to, its steady process reassured them that all was
well while reminding them that time was moving onwards. It was
difficult to be uncivilized in the company of so many clocks.

Daniel Waterhouse had arrived first and had immediately apologized to Eliza for having taken her for a house-servant earlier. But
he had not dropped the other shoe and asked what she *really* was.
She'd accepted his apology with tart amusement and then
declined to offer any explanation. This was light flirtation of the

most routine sort—at Versailles it would have elicited a roll of the eyes from anyone who had bothered to notice it. But it had been more than enough to plunge Waterhouse into utter consternation. Eliza found this slightly alarming.

He had tried again: "Mademoiselle, I would be less than . . ."

"Oh, speak English!" she'd said, in English. This had practically left him senseless: first, with surprise that she could speak English at all, then with alarm that she'd overheard his entire conversation with William Penn. "Now, what was it you were saying?"

He scrambled to remember what he had been saying. In a man half his age, to've been so flustered would have been adorable. As it stood, she was dismayed, wondering what would happen to this man the first time some French-trained countess got her talons into him. William had been right. Daniel Waterhouse was a Hazard to Navigation.

"Err . . . I'd be less than honest if, er . . ." he winced. "It sounded gallant in French. Pompous in English. I was wondering . . . the state of international relations being so troublous and relations 'tween the sexes more so, and etiquette being an area in which I am weak . . . whether there was any pretext at all under which I might converse with you, or send letters, without giving offense."

"Isn't this dinner good enough?" she'd asked, flirtatiously mock-offended, and just then Fatio had arrived. In truth, she'd seen him coming across the Plein, and adjusted her timing accordingly. Waterhouse was obliged to stand off to one side and stew and draw up a great mental accompt of his failures and shortcomings while Eliza and Fatio enacted a greeting-ritual straight out of the Salon of Apollo at Versailles. This had much in common with a courtly dance, but with overtones of a duel; Eliza and Fatio were probing each other, emanating signals coded in dress, gesture, inflection, and emphasis, and watching with the brilliant alertness of sword-fighters to see whether the other had noticed, and how they'd respond. As one who'd lately come from the Court of the Sun King, Eliza held the high ground; the question was, what level of esteem should she accord Fatio? If he'd been Catholic, and French, and titled, this would have been settled before he came in the door. But he was Protestant, Swiss, and came from a gentle family of no particular rank. He was in his early twenties, Eliza guessed, though he tried to make himself older by wearing very good French clothes. He was not a handsome man: he had giant blue eyes below a high domelike forehead, but the lower half of his face was too small, his nose stuck out like a beak, and in general he had the exhausting intensity of a trapped bird.

At some point Fatio had to tear those eyes away from Eliza and begin the same sort of dance-*cum*-duel with Waterhouse. Again, if Fatio had been a Fellow of the Royal Society, or a Doctor at some university, Waterhouse would have had some idea what to make of him; as it was, Fatio had to conjure his credentials and *bona fides* out of thin air, as it were, by dropping names and scattering references to books he'd read, problems he'd solved, inflated reputations he had punctured, experiments he had performed, creatures he had seen. "I had half expected to see Mr. Enoch Root here," he said at one point, looking about, "for a (ahem) gentleman of my acquaintance here, an *amateur* of (ahem) chymical studies, has shared with me a rumor—only a rumor, mind you—that a man owning Root's description was observed, the other day, debarking from a canal-ship from Brussels." As Fatio stretched this patch of news thinner and thinner, he flinched his huge eyes several times at Waterhouse. Certain French nobles would have winked or stroked their moustaches interestedly; Waterhouse offered up nothing but a basilisk-stare.

That was the last time Fatio had anything to say concerning Alchemy; from that point onwards it was strictly mathematics, and the new work by Newton. Eliza had heard from both Leibniz and Huygens that this Newton had written some sort of discourse that had left all of the other Natural Philosophers holding their heads between their knees, and quite dried up the ink in their quills, and so she was able to follow Fatio's drift here. Though from time to time he would turn his attention to Eliza and revert to courtly posturing for a few moments. Fatio prosecuted all of these uphill strugglings with little apparent effort, which spoke well of his training, and of the overall balance of his humours. At the same time it made her tired just to watch him. From the moment he came in the door he controlled the conversation; everyone spent the rest of the evening reacting to Fatio. That suited Eliza's purposes well enough; it kept Daniel Waterhouse frustrated, which was how she liked him, and gave her leisure to observe. All the same, she wondered what supplied the energy to keep a Fatio going; he was the loudest and fastest clock in the room, and must have an internal spring keyed up very tight. He had no sexual interest whatever in Eliza, and that was a relief, for she could tell that he would be relentless and probably tiresome in wooing.

Why didn't they just eject Fatio and have a peaceful dinner? Because he had genuine merit. Confronted by a nobody so desperate to establish his reputation, Eliza's first impulse (and Waterhouse's, too, she inferred) was to assume he was a *poseur*. But he was not. Once he figured out that Eliza wasn't Catholic he had interesting things to say concerning religion and the state of French society. Once he figured out that Waterhouse was no alchemist, he began to discourse of mathematical functions in a way that snapped the Englishman awake. And Huygens, when he finally woke up and came downstairs, made it obvious by his treatment of Fatio that he rated him as an equal—or as close to equal as a man like Huygens could ever have.

"A man of my tender age and meager accomplishments cannot give sufficient honor to the gentleman who once dined at this table—"

"Actually Descartes dined here *many* times—not just *once*!" Huygens put in gruffly.

"—and set out his proposal to explain physical reality with mathematics," Fatio finished.

"You would not speak of him that way unless you were about to say something against him," Eliza said.

"Not against him, but some of his latter-day followers. The project that Descartes started is finished. Vortices will never do! I am surprised that Leibniz still holds out any hope for them."

Everyone sat up straighter. "Perhaps you have heard from Leibniz more recently than I have, sir," Waterhouse said.

"You give me more credit than I deserve, Doctor Waterhouse, to suggest that Doctor Leibniz would communicate his freshest insights to *me*, before despatching them to the *Royal Society*! Please correct me."

"It is not that Leibniz has any particular attachment to vortices, but that he cannot bring himself to believe in any sort of mysterious action at a distance." Hearing this, Huygens raised a hand momentarily, as if seconding a motion. Fatio did not fail to notice. Waterhouse continued, "Action at a distance is a sort of occult notion—which may appeal to a certain sort of mentality—"

"But not to those of us who have adopted the Mechanical Philosophy that Monsieur Descartes propounded at this very table!"

"In that very chair, sir!" said Huygens, pointing at Fatio with a drumstick.

"I have my own Theory of Gravitation that should account for the inverse square relation," Fatio said. "As a stone dropped into water makes spreading ripples, so a planet makes concentric disturbances in the cœlestial æther, which press upon its satellites . . ."

"Write it down," Waterhouse said, "and send it to me, and we will print it alongside Leibniz's account, and may the better one prevail."

"Your offer is gratefully accepted!" Fatio said, and glanced at

Huygens to make sure he had a witness. "But I fear we are boring Mademoiselle Eliza."

"Not at all, Monsieur, any conversation that bears on the Doctor is of interest to me."

"Is there any topic that does not relate to Leibniz in some way?"

"Alchemy," Waterhouse suggested darkly.

Fatio, whose chief object at the moment was to draw Eliza into the conversation, ignored this. "I can't but wonder whether we may discern the Doctor's hand in the formation of the League of Augsburg."

"I would guess not," Eliza said. "It has long been Leibniz's dream to re-unite the Catholic and Lutheran churches, and prevent another Thirty Years' War. But the League looks to me like a *preparation* for war. It is not the conception of the Doctor, but of the Prince of Orange."

"The Protestant Defender," Fatio said. Eliza was accustomed to hearing that phrase drenched in French sarcasm, but Fatio uttered it carefully, like a Natural Philosopher weighing an unproven hypothesis. "Our neighbors in Savoy could have used some defending when de Catinat came through with his dragoons. Yes, in this matter I must disagree with the Doctor, as well-meaning as he is . . . we do need a Defender, and William of Orange will make a good one, provided he stays out of the clutches of the French." Fatio was staring at Eliza while he said this.

Huygens chuckled. "That should not be difficult, since he never leaves Dutch soil."

"But the coast is long, and mostly empty, and the French could put a force ashore anywhere they pleased."

"French fleets do not sail up and down the Dutch coast without drawing attention," Huygens said, still amused by the idea.

Continuing to watch Eliza, Fatio replied, "I said nothing about a *fleet*. A single *jacht* would suffice to put a boat-load of dragoons on the beach."

"And what would those dragoons do against the might of the Dutch army?"

"Be destroyed, if they were stupid enough to encamp on the beach and wait for that army to mobilize," Fatio answered. "But if they happened to light on the particular stretch of beach where William goes sand-sailing, at the right time of the morning, why, they could redraw the map, and rewrite the future history, of Europe in a few minutes' work."

Now nothing could be heard for a minute or so except the clocks. Fatio still held Eliza fast with his vast eyes, giant blue lenses that seemed to take all the light in the room. What might they not have noticed, and what might the mind in back of them not know?

On the other hand, what tricks could the mind not conjure up, and with those eyes, whom couldn't he draw into his snares?

"It is a clever conceit, like a chapter from a picaroon-romance," Eliza said. Fatio's high brow shriveled, and the eyes that had seemed so penetrating a moment ago now looked pleading. Eliza glanced toward the stairs. "Now that Fatio has provided us with entertainment, will you elevate us, Monsieur Huygens?"

"How should I translate that word?" Huygens returned. "The last time one of your guests became elevated in my house, I had to look the other way."

"Elevate us to the roof, where we may see the stars and planets, and then elevate our minds by showing us some new phenomenon through your telescope," Eliza answered patiently.

"In company such as this we must all elevate one another, for I carry no advantage on these men," Huygens said. This triggered a long tedious volley of self-deprecations from Fatio and Waterhouse. But soon enough they all got their winter coats on and labored up a staircase devious and strait, and emerged into starlight. The only clouds in this sky were those that condensed in front of their lips as they breathed. Huygens lit up a clay pipe. Fatio, who had assisted Huygens before, took the wraps off the big Newtonian reflector with the tense precision of a hummingbird, keeping an ear cocked toward Huygens and Waterhouse, who were talking about optics, and an eye on Eliza, who was strolling around the parapet enjoying the view: to the east, the Haagse Bos, woolly and black with trees. To the south, the smoking chimneys and glowing windows of the Hofgebied. To the west, the windy expanse of the Plein, stretching to the Grenadier's Gate on the far side, which controlled access to the Binnenhof. A lot of wax and whale-oil was being burnt there tonight, to illuminate a soiree in the palace's Ballroom. To the young ladies who had been invited, it must have seemed never so glamorous. To Huygens it was a damnable nuisance, for the humid air snared the radiance of all those tapers and lamps, and glowed faintly, in a way that most people would never notice. But it ruined the seeing of his telescope.

Within a few minutes the two older men had gotten embroiled in the work of aiming the telescope at Saturn: a body that would show up distinctly no matter how many candles were burning at the Binnenhof. Fatio glided over to keep Eliza company.

"Now let us set aside formalities and speak directly," she said.

"As you wish, Mademoiselle."

"Is this notion of the *jacht* and the dragoons a phant'sy of yours or—"

"Say if I am wrong: on mornings when the weather is not perfectly abominable, and the wind is off the sea, the Prince of Orange goes to his boat-house on the beach at Scheveningen at ten o'clock, chooses a sand-sailer, and pilots it northwards up the beach to the dunes near Katwijk—though on a clear day he'll venture as far as Noordwijk—then turns round and is back in Scheveningen by midday."

Not wanting to give Fatio the satisfaction of telling him he was right, Eliza answered, "You have made a study of the Prince's habits?"

"No, but Count Fenil has."

"Fenil—I have heard his name in the salon of the Duchess of Oyonnax—he originates in that place where Switzerland and Savoy, Burgundy, and the Piedmont are all convolved, yes?"

"Yes."

"And he is Catholic, and a Francophile."

"He is Savoyard in name, but he saw very early that Louis XIV would eclipse the Duke of Savoy, and swallow up his dominions, and so he became more French than the French, and served in the army of Louvois. That alone should prove his *bona fides* to the King of France. But after the recent show of force by the French Army next door to his lands, Fenil evidently feels some further demonstration of his loyalty is needed. So he has devised the plan I mentioned, of abducting William from the beach and carrying him back to France in chains."

They had now paused at a corner where they could look out over the Plein toward the Binnenhof. To Eliza this had seemed grand (at least by European standards) when d'Avaux had taken her skating there. Now that she'd grown accustomed to Versailles, it looked like a woodshed. Lit up for this evening's fête, it was as grand as it would ever be. William Penn would be there, and various members of the diplomatic corps—including d'Avaux, who had invited her to attend it on his arm. She had accepted, then changed her mind so that she could organize the present dinner. D'Avaux had not been happy about it and had asked questions that were difficult to answer. Once d'Avaux had recruited her, and sent her down to Versailles, their relationship had changed to that of lord and vassal. He had allowed her to see his hard, cruel, vengeful aspects, mostly as an implicit warning of what would come if she disappointed him. Eliza supposed it must have been d'Avaux who had supplied intelligence to Fenil concerning William's routine.

It had been a mild winter so far, and the Hofvijver, in front of the Binnenhof, was a black rectangle, not yet frozen, reflecting gleams of candlelight from the party as gusts of wind wrinkled its surface. Eliza recalled her own abduction from a beach, and felt like crying. Fatio's yarn might or might not be true, but in combination with some cutting remarks that d'Avaux had made to her earlier, it had put real melancholy into her heart. Not connected with any one particular man, or plan, or outcome, but melancholy like the black water that ate up the light.

"How do you know the mind of M. le comte de Fenil?"

"I was visiting my father at Duillier—our seat in Switzerland—a few weeks ago. Fenil came on a visit. I went for a stroll with him and he told me what I have told you."

"He must be an imbecile to talk about it openly."

"Perhaps. Inasmuch as the purpose is to enhance his prestige, the more he talks about it, the better."

" 'Tis an outlandish plan. Has he suggested it to anyone who could realize it?"

"Indeed, he proposed it to the Maréchal Louvois, who wrote back to him and directed him to make preparations."

"How long ago?"

"Long enough, mademoiselle, for the preparations to have been made by now."

"So you have come here to warn William?"

"I have been striving to warn him," Fatio said, "but he will not grant me an audience."

"It is very strange, then, that you should approach *me*. What makes you believe that *I* have the ear of the Prince of Orange? I live at Versailles and I invest money for members of the Court of the King of France. I journey up this way from time to time to consult with my brokers, and to meet with my dear friend and client the comte d'Avaux. What on earth makes you believe that I should have any connection to William?"

"Suffice it to say, I know that you do," Fatio returned placidly.

"Who else knows?"

"Who knows that bodies in an inverse square field move on conic sections? Who knows that there is a division between the Rings of Saturn?"

"Anyone who reads *Principia Mathematica,* or looks through a telescope, respectively."

"And who has the wit to understand what he has read, or seen."

"Yes. Anyone can possess Newton's book, few can understand it."

"Just so, mademoiselle. And likewise anyone may observe you, or listen to gossip about you, but to interpret those *data* and know the truth requires gifts that God hoards jealously and gives out to very few."

"Have you learned much of me, then, from talking to your brethren? For I know that they are to be found in every Court, Church, and College, and that they know each other by signs and code-words. Please do not be coy with me, Fatio, it is ever so tedious."

"Coy? I would not dream of so insulting a woman of your sophistication. Yes, I tell you without reserve that I belong to an esoteric brotherhood that numbers many of the high and the mighty among its members; that the very *raison d'être* of that brotherhood is to exchange information that should not be spread about promiscuously; and that I have learned of you from that source."

"Are you saying that my lord Upnor, and every other gentleman who pisses in the corridors of Versailles, knows of my connexion to William of Orange?"

"Most of them are *poseurs* with very limited powers of understanding. Do not change your plans out of some phant'sy that they will penetrate what I have penetrated," Fatio said.

Eliza, who did not find this a very satisfying answer, said nothing. Her silence caused Fatio to get that pleading look again. She turned away from him—the only alternative being to scoff and roll her eyes—and gazed down into the Plein. There something caught her eye: a long figure darkly cloaked, silver hair spilling out onto his shoulders. He had lately emerged from the Grenadiers' Gate, as if he had just excused himself from the party. A gust of steam flourished from his mouth as he shouted, "How is the seeing tonight?"

"Much better than I should like," returned Eliza.

"Bad, very bad, Mr. Root, because of our troublesome neighbor!"

"Do not be disheartened," said Enoch the Red, "I believe that Pegasus, to-night, shall be adorned by a *meteor;* turn your telescope thither."

Eliza and Fatio both turned and looked towards the telescope, which was situated cater-corner from them, meaning that Huygens and Waterhouse could neither hear nor see Enoch Root. When they turned back around, Root had turned his back on them, and was vanishing into one of the many narrow side-streets of the Hofgebied.

"Most disappointing! I was going to invite him up here . . . he must have come from the fête at the Binnenhof," Fatio said.

Eliza finished the thought herself: *Where he was hobnobbing with my brethren of the Dutch court—the same ones who cannot keep their mouths shut concerning you, Eliza.*

Fatio looked toward Polaris. "It is half past midnight, never mind what the church-bells say . . ."

"How can you tell?"

"By reading the positions of the stars. Pegasus is far to the west, there. It shall descend beneath the western horizon within two hours. A miserable place to make observations! And in any case, meteors come and go too quickly for one to aim a telescope at 'em . . . what did he mean?"

"Is this a fair sample of the esoteric brotherhood's discourse? No wonder that Alchemists are famed mostly for blowing up their own dwellings," Eliza said, feeling somewhat relieved to get this glimpse into the mystery, and to find nothing but bafflement there.

They spent the better part of an hour looking at, and arguing about, the gap in Saturn's rings, which was named after Cassini, the French royal astronomer, and which Fatio could explain mathematically. Which was to say that Eliza was cold, bored, and ignored. Only one person could peer into the telescope's eyepiece at a time, and these men quite forgot their manners, and never offered her a turn.

Then Fatio persuaded the others to point the telescope into Pegasus, or those few stars of it that had not yet been drowned in the North Sea. The search of Pegasus was not nearly so interesting to them as Saturn had been, and so they let Eliza look all she wanted, sweeping the instrument back and forth, hoping to catch the predicted meteor.

"Have you found something, Mademoiselle?" Fatio asked at one point, when he noticed Eliza's stiff fingers pawing at the focusing-screw.

"A cloud, just peeking over the horizon."

"Weather as fine as today's could never last," said Huygens, in a fair sample of Dutch pessimism; for the weather had been wretched.

"Does it have the appearance of a rain-cloud or . . ."

"That is what I am trying to establish," Eliza said, trying to bring it into focus.

"Enoch was having you on a bit," Huygens said, for the others had by now told him the story of Enoch's enigmatic turn in the Plein. "He felt his joints aching and knew a change in the weather was in the offing! And he knew it would come out of Pegasus since that is in the west, and that is where the wind is from. Very clever."

"A few wisps of cloud, indeed . . . but what I first mistook for heavy rain-clouds, is actually a ship under sail . . . taking advantage of the moon-light to raise her sails, and make a run up the coast," Eliza said.

"Cloth-smugglers," Waterhouse predicted, "coming in from round Ipswich." Eliza stepped back and he took a turn at the eye-piece. "No, I'm wrong, 'tis the wrong sail-plan for a smuggler."

"She is rigged for speed, but proceeding cautiously just now," Huygens pronounced. Then it was Fatio's turn: "I would wager she is bringing contraband from France—salt, wine, or both." And so they continued, more and more tediously, until Eliza announced that she was going down to bed.

SHE WAS AWAKENED BY THE tolling of a church-bell. For some reason she felt it was terribly important to count the strokes, but she woke up too late to be sure. She had left her long winter coat across the foot of her bed to make her toes a little warmer and she now sat up and snatched it and drew it round her shoulders in one quick movement, before the chill could rush through the porous linen of her nightgown. She swung her feet out of bed, poked at the pair of rabbit-pelt slippers on the floor to chase away any mice that might be using them as beds, and then pushed her feet into them.

For in somewhat the same way as rodents may quietly set up house-keeping in one's clothing during the hours of darkness, an idea had established itself in Eliza's mind while she had been asleep. She did not become fully conscious of this idea until a few minutes later when she went into the great room to stoke up the fire, and saw all of Huygens's clocks reading the same time: a few minutes past nine o'clock in the morning.

She looked out a window over the Plein and saw high white clouds. From the myriad chimneys of the Binnenhof, plumes of smoke trailed eastwards before a steady onshore breeze. Perfect day for sand-sailing.

She went to the door of Huygens's bedchamber and raised a fist, then held off. If she were wrong, it were foolish to disturb him. If she were right, it were foolish to spend a quarter of an hour waking him up and trying to convince him.

Huygens kept only a few horses here. The riding-fields of the Malieveld and the Koekamp lay only a musket-shot from the house, and so when he or any of his guests felt like going riding, they need only stroll to one of the many livery-stables that surrounded those places.

Eliza ran out a back door of the house, nearly knocking down a Dutch woman out sweeping the pavement, and took off round the corner running in her rabbit-slippers.

Then she faltered, remembering she'd not brought any money.

"Eliza!" someone shouted.

She turned around to see Nicolas Fatio de Duilliers running up the street after her.

"Do you have money?" she called.

"Yes!"

Eliza ran away from him and did not stop until she reached the nearest livery stable, a couple of hundred long strides away, far enough to get her heart pounding and her face flushed. By the time Fatio caught up with her she had wrapped up a negotiation with the owner; the Swiss mathematician came in the gate just in time to see Eliza thrusting a finger at him and shouting, "and *he* pays!"

Saddling the horses would take several minutes. Eliza felt on the verge of throwing up. Fatio was agitated, too, but breeding was at war with common sense in him, and breeding prevailed; he attempted to make conversation.

"I infer, Mademoiselle, that you too have received some communication from Enoch the Red on this morning?"

"Only if he came and whispered in my ear while I was sleeping!"

Fatio didn't know what to make of that. "I encountered him a few minutes ago at my usual coffee-house . . . he elaborated on his cryptic statement of last night . . ."

"What we saw last night was enough for me," Eliza answered. A sleepy stable-boy dropped a saddle, and instead of bending to pick it up, tried to make some witty comment. The owner was doing sums with a quill-pen that wouldn't hold its ink. Tears of frustration came to Eliza's eyes. "Damn it!"

"RIDING BARE-BACK IS LIKE RIDING, only more so," Jack Shaftoe had said to her once. She preferred to remember Jack as little and as infrequently as possible, but now this memory came to her. Until the day they had met underneath Vienna, Eliza had never ridden a horse. Jack had taken obvious pleasure in teaching her the rudiments, more so when she seemed uncertain, or fell off, or let Turk run away with her. But after she had become expert, Jack had turned peevish and haughty, and lost no opportunity to remind her that riding well in a saddle was no accomplishment, and that until one learned to ride bare-back, one didn't know how to ride at all. Jack knew all about it, of course, because it was how Vagabonds stole horses.

Choosing the proper mount was of the utmost importance (he had explained). Given a string or stable of horses to choose from, one wanted to pick a mount with a flat back, and yet not too wide-bodied or else it wouldn't be possible to get a good grip with the knees. The wither, or bony hump at the base of the neck, should not be too large (which would make it impossible to lie flat while galloping) nor too small (which gave no purchase for the hands), but somewhere in between. And the horse should be of a compliant disposition, for at some point it was bound to happen that the horse-thief would become disarranged on the horse's back, as the outcome of some bump or swerve, and then it would be entirely up to the horse whether the Vagabond would be flung off into space or coaxed back into balance.

Now it might have been pure chance that Eliza's favorite horse in this stable—the mare she asked for by name whenever she called—possessed a flat but not overly broad back, a medium-sized wither, and a sweet disposition. Or perhaps Jack Shaftoe's advice on the finer points of horse-thievery had subtly informed her choice. At any rate, the mare's name was Vla ("cream"), and Eliza rated it as unlikely she would ever try to pitch Eliza off her bare back. The stable-boy was attempting to saddle up a different mare, but Vla was in a stall only a few paces away.

Eliza walked over and opened the gate to that stall, greeting Vla by name, and then stepped forward until her nose was caressing the mare's, and breathed very gently into Vla's nostrils. This prompted Vla to raise her enormous head slightly, trying to draw closer to that warmth. Eliza cupped the mare's chin in her hand and exhaled into those nostrils again, and Vla responded with a little shudder of gratitude. Giant overlapping slabs of muscle twitched here and there, coming awake. Eliza now stepped into the stall, trailing a hand along the mare's side, and then used the stall's side-planks as a ladder, climbing to a level from which she was able to dive across Vla's back. Then, by gripping that convenient medium-sized wither with one hand, she was able to spin herself round on her belly and get her legs wrapped around Vla's body—this required pulling the narrow skirts of her nightgown up round her hips, but her coat hung down to either side and covered her legs. Her bare buttocks, thighs, and calves were pressed directly against the mare's body, which was exquisitely warm. Vla took this all calmly enough. She did not respond the first time Eliza pinched her bottom, but on the second pinch she walked out into the stable-yard, and when Eliza told her what a good girl she was and pinched her a third time she broke into a trot that nearly bounced Eliza straight off. Eliza flung herself full-length onto the mare's back and neck, and buried her face in the mane, and clenched a hank of the coarse hair in her teeth. All her attention was concentrated for those few moments on not falling off. The next time she looked around, they had trotted out into the street, pursued none too effectively by a few grooms and stable-hands who still could not make out whether they were witnessing a bizarre mishap or a criminal act.

They were headed northwards along the edge of the riding-ground called Koekamp, which was limned on this side by the big canal that ran straight to Scheveningen. Vla wanted to turn her nose out of the stinging sea-wind and stray off into the Koekamp, which was what she did for a living. Every time her nose bent that way, Eliza gave her a sharp reprimand, and a dig on that side with her foot. So progress was balky, and relations between horse and rider were tense, as long as the Koekamp and then the Malieveld beckoned to their right. But once they had ridden clear of such temptations, Vla seemed to understand that they were riding up the canal to Scheveningen, and settled down noticeably. Another pinch caused Vla to break into a canter, which was both smoother and faster. Very soon after that Eliza was galloping down the canal-side hollering "Make way in the name of the Stadholder!" whenever she saw anyone in the way. But this was rarely, for by now they were out in open country, and cows were more common than people.

Jack had been right, she decided—remaining on the back of a galloping horse without benefit of saddle was a question of balance, and of anticipating the horse's movements, while also relying on some cooperation from the horse! Soon Vla began to sweat, which made her slippery, and then Eliza had to abandon all pretense of holding on by brute force and rely entirely on a very complicated and ever-changing sort of sympathy between her and the mare.

Fatio did not catch up with her until she was most of the way to Scheveningen. They were being pursued, at a distance, by two men who were presumably members of the St. George Guild. As long as these did not draw close enough to loose any pistol-balls in their direction, they did not especially care. It could all be explained later.

"The ship . . . we saw . . ." Eliza shouted, forcing out the occasional word when not gasping for breath or being jolted by the mare. " 'Twas the *jacht*?"

"The same. . . . It is . . . *Météore*, the flagship . . . of the Duc . . . d'Arcachon! We may . . . assume it . . . to be full . . . of dragoons!" Fatio returned.

Behind them, someone had begun blowing a horn from the top of a watch-tower in the Hague. It was a signal to the sheriff in Scheveningen, who was answerable to the town council of the Hague; very soon Fatio and Eliza would find out how diligent this sheriff was, and how well he had organized his watchmen.

They reached the boat-house at Scheveningen at ten minutes past ten o'clock. As they approached, Eliza saw a sand-sailer out on the beach, being worked on by a ship-wright, and cried "Aha!" thinking they'd arrived in time. But then she noticed wheel-tracks in the sand, and followed them north up the beach until she saw another sailer, already a mile away, heeled over by the sea-breeze.

The boat-house was not really a single house, but a horseshoe-shaped compound of diverse sheds, shacks, and workshops scabbed on to one another, crammed with distracting detail: tools, forges, lathes, lofts. . . . Eliza got lost in that detail for a few moments, then turned around to look behind them, and discovered a landscape of pandemonium in their wake: breathless Guildsmen from the Hague, Blue Guards, marines from ships in the harbor, enraged members of Scheveningen's Watch, all seemingly contending with one another to lay hands first on Fatio—who was trying to explain everything in French. He was throwing unreadable looks at Eliza, half pleading for assistance, half wanting to defend her from the mob.

"Fire guns!" Eliza shouted in Dutch. "The Prince is in danger." Then she explained what she could, in what little Dutch she had. Nodding his head the whole time was the Captain of the Blue Guards, who, she collected, had always taken a dim view of the Prince's beach-sailing anyway. At some point he decided he had heard plenty. He fired a pistol in the air to silence the crowd and tossed the empty, smoking weapon to a guardsman, who tossed him a loaded one back. Then he uttered a few words in Dutch and everyone scattered.

"What did he say, mademoiselle?" Fatio asked.

"He said, 'Guards, ride! Watchmen, fire! Sailors, launch! Others, get out of the way!' "

Fatio watched in fascination: a squadron of mounted Blue Guards took off hell-for-leather up the beach, galloping in pursuit of the Prince. Sailors were sprinting down towards the waterfront, the gunners on the harbor batteries were loading their cannons. Anyone with a loaded firearm was shooting in the air; but the Prince, far away in a cosmos of wind and surf, could not hear them. "I suppose we belong in the category of 'others,' " Fatio said, a bit dejectedly. "It will be all right, I suppose . . . those cavalrymen will catch up to him anon."

The sun had found a rift in the high clouds and illuminated veils of steam rising from the sweaty coats of their horses. "They'll never catch him," Eliza demurred, "in this wind he can out-sail them with ease."

"Perhaps the Prince will take notice of *that*!" Fatio said, startled by a ragged volley of cannon-fire.

"He'll only assume it is a salute, for some ship approaching the harbor."

"What can we do, then?"

"Follow orders. Leave," Eliza said.

"Then pray tell why are you dismounting?"

"Fatio, you are a gentleman," Eliza called over her shoulder, kicking off the rabbit-pelts and stepping barefoot across the sand towards the other sailer. "You grew up near Lake Geneva. Do you know how to sail?"

"Mademoiselle," said Fatio, dismounting, "on a rig of this plan I can out-sail a *Dutchman*. I want only one thing."

"Name it."

"The craft will heel over. The sail will spill wind and I will lose speed. Unless I had someone small, nimble, tenacious, and very brave, to lean out of the vehicle on the windward side, and act as a counterweight."

"Let us go and defend the Defender then," Eliza said, climbing aboard.

THEY COULD NOT POSSIBLY BE moving as fast as it *seemed*, or so Eliza told herself until they caught up with the squadron of Blue Guards. With a twitch of the tiller Fatio could have veered round them as if they were standing still. Instead he let out the main-sheet and spilled a huge dollop of air, causing the sailer to drop to what felt like a slow walking pace—and yet they were staying abreast of the galloping Guards. The sailer dropped back onto all three wheels and Eliza, leaning way out on what had been the high side, nearly planted her head in the sand. Fortunately she was gripping with both hands a line that Fatio had hitched round the mast, and by pulling hard on this she was able to draw herself up faster than the zooming sand could lunge at her. And now she had a few moments to wipe spray and grit out of her face, and to tie her hair into a sodden knot that lay cold and rough against her neck. Fatio had got the attention of some of the Blue Guards by gesticulating and shouting in a hotch-potch of languages. Something came flying towards them, tumbling end-over-end, plopped into the mainsail, and slid down the curved canvas into Fatio's lap: a musket. Then another, flung by a different Guard, whirled just over their heads and embedded itself barrel-first in the sand, surf swirling around its stock, and fell away aft. Now a pistol came flying toward them and Eliza, finally ready, was able to reach up and slap it out of the air with one hand.

Instantly Fatio hauled in on the sheet and the sailer hurled itself forward. He got in front of the foremost of the Guards and then veered up away from the surf onto drier and firmer sand. Eliza had had time to shove the pistol into her coat-sash now, and to get that rope wrapped securely round her hands; Fatio hauled the sheet in recklessly, and the sailer bit so fiercely into the wind that it nearly capsized. One of its wheels was spinning in the air, flinging sand and water at Eliza, who clambered over its rim, planted both of her bare feet on the end of the axle, and let the rope slither through her numb hands until she was leaning back almost horizontally and gazing (when she could see anything) at the undercarriage of the sand-sailer.

It occurred to her to wonder whether they were now traveling faster than any human beings had ever gone. For a minute she fancied it was so—then the Natural Philosopher in her weighed in with the observation that ice-boats had less friction to contend with and probably went even faster.

Then why was she so exhilarated? Because despite the cold and the danger and the uncertainty of what they might find at the end of the journey, she had a kind of freedom here, a wildness she had not known since her Vagabond days with Jack. All the cares and intrigues of Versailles were forgotten.

Craning her neck around, she was able to look out to sea. There was the normal clutter of coastal traffic, but mostly these vessels had triangular sails. The square-rigged *jacht* of the duc d'Arcachon should be conspicuous. Indeed, she thought she could see a square-rigger standing off several leagues from shore, a short distance to the north—that must be *Météore*! The longboat would have come in at dawn and been hauled up on the beach so that the Prince would not notice it until too late.

Fatio had been raving for some minutes about the Bernoullis— Swiss mathematicians, therefore friends and colleagues of his. "Sailmakers of a hundred years ago phant'sied that sails worked as literal wind-bags, which is why ships in old pictures all have a big-bellied appearance that is very odd to our modern eyes, as if they need to be taken in . . . now we have learned that sails develop force by virtue of air-currents to either side, shaping, and shaped by, the curve of the canvas . . . but we understand not the *particulars* . . . the Bernoullis are making this their field of specialization . . . soon we'll be able to use my calculus to loft sails according to *rational* principles. . . ."

"*Your* calculus!?"

"Yes . . . and it will enable us to attain speeds even . . . better . . . than . . . *this*!"

"I see him!" Eliza shouted.

Fatio's view ahead was blocked by sail and rigging, but Eliza was in the clear, and she could see the top of William's mast protruding above a low hummock of sand and beach-scrub. The Prince's sailer was heeled over, but not so much as theirs, since he lacked a human counter-weight. He was perhaps half a mile ahead. Halfway between them, but coming up on them rapidly, was the said hummock, which (Eliza realized) was just the sort of visual obstacle behind which the dragoons would want to set up their ambuscade. And indeed she could see the mast of William's sailer swinging up to vertical as he faltered and lost speed . . .

"It is happening now," she shouted.

"Would you like me to stop and let you off, mademoiselle, or—"

"Don't be foolish."

"Very well!" Fatio now steered the sailer in a slashing arc around the end of the hummock. In that moment a mile of open beach was revealed to them.

Straight ahead and alarmingly close was a longboat, still cluttered with branches that had been laid over it as camouflage. This had just been dragged out of a hiding place on the north face of the hummock and was now being hauled and shoved down toward the water by half a dozen hefty French dragoons. At the moment its keel was slicing directly across the tracks that had been laid in the sand by William's sailer a few seconds ago. It was cutting off the Prince's line of retreat—and it barred Eliza and Fatio's advance. Fatio jerked on the tiller and steered up-slope, round behind the boat. Eliza could only hold her rope. She clenched her teeth so that she would not bite off her tongue, and kept her eyes closed through a series of jolts. The wheels that were on the ground plunged across the furrow that had been cut by the longboat's keel, and the one that was in the air smashed into the head of a startled dragoon and felled him like a statue.

The trim of the sails and balance of the vehicle were now all awry, and there was some veering and bouncing as Fatio brought matters in hand again. Sheer speed was not as important as it had been, and so Eliza put her whole weight on the hand-rope, raised her knees, and swung inwards far enough to plant her feet near the mast of the sailer. Fatio settled into a slower pace. They both looked up the beach.

A bow-shot ahead of them, another contingent of half a dozen dragoons were running in pursuit of the Prince of Orange's sand-sailer. This had come to a stop before a barrier consisting of a chain stretched along a row of pilings that the Frenchmen had apparently pounded into the sand. The ambushers all had their backs to Eliza and Fatio, and their attention fixed upon the Prince, who had clambered out of his sailer and turned round to face the attackers.

William strode free of his sailer, shrugged his cape off into the sand, reached round himself, and drew his sword.

Fatio sailed into the line of dragoons, taking two of them, including their captain, from behind. But this was the end of his and Eliza's sand-sailing career, for the vehicle planted its nose in the sand and tumbled over smartly. Eliza landed face-first in wet sand and sensed wreckage slamming down near her, but nothing touched her save a few snarled wet ropes. Still, these were an impediment to getting up. When she struggled to her feet, all water-logged, sand-covered, cold, and battered, she discovered that she'd lost the pistol; and by the time she'd pulled it up out of the sand, the action at this end of the beach was over—William's sword, which had been bright a moment ago, was red now, and two dragoons were lying on sand clutching at their vitals. Another was being held at bay by Fatio with his musket, and the sixth member of the squad was running toward the longboat, waving his arms over his head and shouting.

The longboat was in the surf now, ready to convey the dragoons and their prisoner back out to *Météore*. After a short discussion, four of the men who'd dragged it down the beach detached themselves and took off running towards the stopped sand-sailers while another stayed behind to mind the boat's bow-rope. The sixth member of that contingent was still face-down in the sand with a wheel-track running over his back.

Eliza had not been noticed yet.

She crouched down behind the broken frame of the sand-sailer and devoted a few moments to examining the firing-mechanism of the pistol, trying to brush out the sand while leaving some powder in the pan.

Hearing a scream, she looked up to see that William had simply walked up to the captured dragoon and run him through with his sword. Then the prince took the musket from Fatio, dropped to one knee, took careful aim, and fired toward the five dragoons now running toward them.

Not a one of them seemed to take any notice.

Eliza lay down on her belly and began crawling south down the beach. In a moment the dragoons ran past her, about ten paces off to her left. As she'd hoped, none of them noticed her. They had eyes only for the two men, William and Fatio, who now stood, swords drawn, back to back, waiting.

Eliza clambered to her feet and shed her long heavy coat. Before boarding the sand-sailer at Scheveningen, she'd borrowed Fatio's dagger and used it to slit the skirt of her nightgown and cut off the bottom few inches, freeing her legs. She sprinted toward the longboat. She was dreading the sound of pistols or muskets, which would mean that the dragoons had decided to drop William and Fatio on the spot. But she heard nothing except surf. The Frenchmen must have orders to bring the Prince back alive. Fatio was unknown to them and wholly expendable, but they could not shoot at him without hitting William of Orange.

The solitary dragoon holding the longboat's bow-rope watched, dumbfounded, as Eliza ran towards him. Even if he hadn't been dumbfounded there was nothing he could have done save stand there; if he dropped the rope, the boat would be lost, and he lacked the strength to beach it unaided. As Eliza drew closer she observed that this fellow had a pistol stuck in his waistband. But since the troughs of the waves were around his hips, and the crests wrapped themselves around his chest, the weapon was no cause for concern.

Eliza planted herself on the shore, took out the pistol, cocked the hammer, and took dead aim at the dragoon from perhaps ten paces. "This may fire or it may not," she said in French. "You have until I count to ten to decide whether you'll gamble your life and your immortal soul on it. One . . . two . . . three . . . did I mention I'm on the rag? Four . . ."

He lasted until seven. It was not the pistol that concerned him so much as her overall jaggedness, the look in her eye. He dropped the rope in the sea, raised his hands, and sidled up onto the beach, keeping well clear of Eliza, then turned and took off running toward the other group. 'Twas not a bad play. If he'd stayed, the pistol might have fired, and he'd be dead and they'd lose the boat for certain. But there was a good chance that they could get it back from Eliza if he got help from the others.

Eliza let the hammer down gently, tossed the pistol into the longboat, waded out a few steps, reached up over her head to grip the boat's transom, and hauled herself up. After a few kicks she was able to get an ankle hooked over the top of the transom, and then she brought herself up out of the water and rolled sideways over the stern and dropped into the bottom of the boat.

Her first view was of a caulked sea-chest. Pulling herself up on it, she saw that it was one of several massive lockers that rested on the deck. Presumably they contained weapons. But if it came to gun-play they were all lost.

The weapons she *needed* were oars, and these were lying out in plain sight on the boat's simple plank benches. She tried to snatch one up and was dismayed to find it was twice as long as she was tall, too heavy and unwieldy to be snatched; but at any rate she heaved it up off the benches and rotated its blade down into the water. Standing in the stern, where the water under the keel was shallowest, she stabbed down through the surf and into the firm sand. The longboat was reluctant to move, and one who had not recently familiarized herself with the contents of Isaac Newton's *Principia Mathematica* might have given up. But the elemental precepts of that work were certain laws of motion that stated that, if she pushed on the oar, the boat *had* to move; at first it might move too slowly to be perceived, but it *had* to be moving. Eliza ignored the unreliable evidence of her senses, which were telling her that the boat was not moving at all, and pushed steadily with all her might. Finally she felt the oar's angle change as the boat moved out from shore.

The moment she pulled the oar out, wind and surf began pushing her back, sapping the *vis inertiae* she had imparted to the longboat. She planted the oar a second time. The water seemed very little deeper than the first time around.

She wanted in the worst way to look up the beach, but looking would not do any good. Only getting the boat clear of the beach would serve their purposes. And so she waited until she had planted the oar half a dozen times, and doubled her distance from the surf-line, before she dared to look up.

Fatio was down. A dragoon was sitting on him, holding something near his head. William was at bay, sword still drawn, but surrounded by four dragoons who were leveling guns at him. One of these seemed, from his stance and his gestures, to be talking to the Prince—negotiating terms of surrender, Eliza guessed. The dragoon who had been left behind to hold the longboat's bow-rope had finally reached the others and was gesticulating, trying to get their attention. The ones who surrounded William ignored him, but the one who was sitting on Fatio took notice, and looked at Eliza.

Eliza glanced toward shore and perceived that the surf had pushed her back in a few yards; the water below the longboat was only waist-deep. In a hurry now, she planted the oars in their locks, sat down, and began to row. Her first several strokes were useless, as the seas, summing and subtracting chaotically, exposed the blades of one or both oars so that they flailed and skittered across the surface. But the dragoons were re-deploying themselves with admirable coolness and she decided she'd better learn from their example. She half-stood and raised the oar-handles high, driving the blades deep, and fell back, thrusting with her legs and arching her body backwards, and felt the boat move. Then she did it again.

Fatio was unguarded and unmoving. William was bracketed between two dragoons who were leveling muskets at his head. The remaining four Frenchmen had run down the beach and were now staring at Eliza across perhaps fifty feet of rough water. One of them had already stripped off most of his clothes, and as Eliza stood up for another oar-stroke she saw him race out into the surf several paces and dive in. The remaining three knelt in the sand, aimed their muskets at the boat, and waited for Eliza to show herself again.

By crouching in the bilge she could remain out of their line of fire—but she couldn't row the longboat.

A hand gripped the gunwale. Eliza smashed it with the butt of the pistol and it went away. But a minute later it reappeared, bleeding, somewhere else—followed by another hand, then elbows, then a head. Eliza aimed the pistol between the blinking eyes and pulled the trigger; the flint whipped around and cast off a feeble spark but nothing further happened. She turned the weapon around, thinking to smash him on the head, but he raised a hand to parry the blow, and she thought better of it. Instead she stood up, gripped the handles of a gun-chest, heaved it up off the deck, and, just as he was whipping one leg over the gunwale, launched it into his face with a thrust of her hips. He fell off the boat. The dragoons on the shore opened fire and splintered a bench, but they missed Eliza. Still, the sight of those craters of fresh clean wood that had been torn into the benches crushed any sense of relief she might have felt over getting rid of the swimmer.

She had an opportunity now to pull on the oars several times while the dragoons re-loaded. As she stood up for an oar-stroke, movement caught her eye off to the south. She turned that way to see a dozen of the Prince's Blue Guards cresting the hummock, or circumventing it along the beach, all riding at a dead gallop on foaming and exhausted chargers. As they took in the scene ahead they stood up in their stirrups, raised sabers high, and erupted in shouts of mixed indignation and triumph. Disgustedly, the French dragoons all flung their weapons down into the sand.

"You must not come near me now for a good long while," said William of Orange. "I shall make arrangements to spirit you out of this place, and my agents shall spread some story or other that shall account for your whereabouts this morning."

The Prince paused, distracted by shouts from the far side of a dune. One of the Blue Guards ran up onto its crest and announced he had found fresh horse-tracks. A rider had tarried for some time recently there (the manure of his horse was still warm) and smoked some tobacco, and then galloped away only moments ago (the sand disturbed by his horse's hooves was still dry). On hearing this news three of the Blue Guards spurred their horses into movement and took off in pursuit. But those mounts were exhausted, whereas the spy's had been well rested—everyone knew the pursuit would be bootless.

" 'Twas d'Avaux," William said. "He would be here, so that he could come out of hiding and taunt me after I had been put in chains."

"Then he knows about me!"

"Perhaps, and perhaps not," said the Prince, showing a lack of concern that did nothing for Eliza's peace of mind. He glanced curiously at Fatio, who was sitting up now, having a bloody head-wound bandaged. "Your friend is a Natural Philosopher? I shall endow a chair for him at the university here. You, I will proclaim a Duchess, when the time is right. But now you must return to Versailles, and make love to Liselotte."

"*What!?*"

"Do not put on this show of outrage, it is very tedious. You know what I am, I think, and so you must know what *she* is."

"But *why?*"

"That is a more intelligent question. What you have just witnessed here, Eliza, is the spark that ignites the pan, that fires the musket, that ejects the ball, that fells the king. If you do nothing else today, fix that clearly in your mind. Now I have no choice but to make Britain mine. But I shall require troops, and I dare not pull so many of them from my southern marches while Louis menaces me there. But if, as I expect, Louis decides to enlarge his realms at the expense of the Germans, he'll draw off his forces on his Dutch flank, and free me to send mine across the North Sea."

"But what has this to do with Liselotte?"

"Liselotte is the grand-daughter of the Winter Queen—who, some say, sparked the Thirty Years' War by accepting the crown of Bohemia. At any rate the said Queen spent most of those Thirty Years just yonder, in the Hague—my people sheltered her, for Bohemia was by then a shambles, and the Palatinate, which was rightfully hers, had fallen to the Papists as a spoil of that war. But when the Peace of Westphalia was finally signed, some forty years ago now, the Palatinate was returned to that family; the Winter Queen's eldest son, Charles Louis, became Elector Palatine. Various of his siblings, including Sophie, moved there, and set up housekeeping in Heidelberg Castle. Liselotte is the daughter of that same Charles Louis, and grew up in that household. Charles Louis died a few years ago and passed the crown to the brother of Liselotte, who was demented—he died not long ago conducting a mock-battle at one of his Rhine-castles. Now the succession is in dispute. The King of France has very chivalrously decided to take the side of Liselotte, who, after all, is his sister-in-law now."

"It is very adroit," Eliza said. "By extending a brotherly hand to Madame, *Le Roi* can add the Palatinate to France."

"Indeed, it would be a pleasure to watch Louis XIV go about his work, if he were not the Antichrist," William said. "I cannot help Liselotte and I can do nothing for the poor people of the Palatinate. But I can make France pay for the Rhine with the British Isles."

"You need to know if *Le Roi* intends to move his regiments away from your borders, towards the Rhine."

"Yes. And no one is in a better position to know that than Liselotte—if not precisely a *pawn,* she is a sort of captured *queen,* on France's side of the board."

"If the stakes are that high, then I suppose the least I can do is contrive some way to get close to Liselotte."

"I don't want you to get close to her, I want you to *seduce* her, I want you to make her your *slave.*"

"I was trying to be delicate."

"My apologies!" William said with a courtly bow, looking her up and down. Covered in salt and sand, and wrapped up in a bloody dragoon-coat, Eliza couldn't have looked delicate at all. William looked as if he were on the verge of saying as much. But he thought better of it, and looked away.

"You have ennobled me, my prince. It was done some years ago. You have grown used to thinking of me as a noblewoman, even if that is only a secret between you and me. To Versailles I am still a commoner, and a foreigner to boot. As long as this remains true you may be assured that Liselotte will have nothing to do with me."

"*In public.*"

"Even in private! Not everyone there is as much of a hypocrite as you seem to think."

"I did not say it would be easy. This is why I am asking *you* to do it."

"As I said, I am willing to give it a try. But if d'Avaux has seen me here today, going back to Versailles would seem unwise."

"D'Avaux prides himself on playing a deep and subtle game, and that is his weakness," William announced. "Besides, he depends on your financial advice. He will not crush you *immediately.*"

"*Later*, then?"

"He'll *try* to," William corrected her.

"And he will succeed."

"No. For by that point you will be the mistress of Madame—Liselotte—the King's sister-in-law. Who has her rivals and her weaknesses, true—but who is of infinitely higher rank than d'Avaux."

Versailles
EARLY 1688

To Leibniz, February 3, 1688

Doctor,

Madame has graciously offered to send this letter to Hanover along with some others that her friend is carrying personally to Sophie, and so I'll dispense with the cypher.

You may wonder why Madame is offering such courtesies to me now, since in the past she has always viewed me as a mouse turd in the pepper.

It seems that as the King of France was rising one day recently, he remarked, to the nobles who were attending his getting-out-of-bed ceremony, that he had heard that "the woman from Qwghlm" was secretly of noble blood.

It was a secret even to me until an hour or so later, when I heard someone calling for "Mademoiselle la comtesse de la Zeur," which (as I slowly figured out) is their way of trying to pronounce Sghr. As you may know, my island is a well-known Hazard to Navigation, recognizable, to terrified sailors, by its three towers of rock, which we denote by that name. Evidently some courtier, who had been so reckless as to sail within view of Qwghlm at some point, remembered this detail and concocted a title for me. To the Court ladies here, especially those of ancient families, it has a savage ring to it. Fortunately there are many foreign princesses here who do not have such exacting standards, and they have already sent minions around to invite me to parties.

Of course Kings may ennoble commoners whenever they

please, and so it isn't clear to me why someone has gone to the trouble of making me out to be a *hereditary* noble. Here is a clue, though: Father Édouard de Gex has been asking me questions about the Qwghlmian Church, which is not technically Protestant in that it was founded before the Roman Catholic Church was established (or at least before anyone notified the Qwghlmians). The Father speaks of going to visit Qwghlm to seek out proofs that our faith is really no different from his and that the two should be merged.

Meanwhile I keep hearing expressions of sympathy from various French nobles, who cluck their tongues over the barbaric occupation of my homeland by England. In fact, every Qwghlmian would be pleased if Englishmen *did* come and occupy our Island, for presumably they would bring some food and warm clothes. I suspect that Louis knows he may soon see a sworn enemy sitting on the throne of England, and is making ready to out-flank that foe by shoring up relations with places such as Ireland, Scotland, and that flyspeck of rock where I was born. It has been ages since Qwghlm had hereditary nobles (nine hundred years ago the Scots rounded them all up and sealed them into a cave with some bears), but now they have decided I am one. Mother would have been so proud!

According to the date at the top of your last letter, you penned it while you were paying a visit to Sophie's daughter at the Court of Brandenburg around the time of Christmas. Please tell me what Berlin is like! I know that many Huguenots have ended up there. It is strange to consider that only a few years ago Sophie and Ernst August were offering their daughter's hand in marriage to Louis XIV. Yet now Sophie Charlotte is Electress of Brandenburg instead, and (if the rumors are to be believed) presiding over a salon of religious dissidents and free-thinkers in Berlin. If the marriage had gone the other way she would bear a measure of responsibility for putting the very same men to death or slavery. I can't help but suppose she is happier where she is.

They say that Sophie Charlotte participates in the discussions of those savants with ever so much poise and confidence. I can't help but suppose that this is because she grew up around you, Doctor, and listened to the conversations you had with her mother. Now that I am reckoned a Countess, and am considered fit to exchange chit-chat with Madame, I have begged her to tell me what you and Sophie talk about at Hanover. But she only rolls her eyes and claims that erudite talk makes no sense to her. I believe that she has spent too much time around self-styled Alchemists, and suspects that all such talk is rubbish.

⚕

The Star Chamber, Westminster Palace
APRIL 1688

⚕

> For to accuse, requires less eloquence, such is man's nature, than to excuse; and condemnation, than absolution more resembles justice.
>
> —HOBBES, *Leviathan*

"HOW DOES THE SAYING GO? 'All work and no play . . . a dull boy," said a disembodied voice. It was the only perception that Daniel's brain was receiving at the moment. Vision, taste, and the other senses were dormant, and memory did not exist. This made it possible for him to listen with more-than-normal acuteness to the voice, and to appreciate its fine qualities—of which there were many. It was a delicious voice, belonging to an upper-class man who was used to being listened to, and who liked it that way.

"This boy's lucubrations have made him very dull indeed, he is a very sluggard!" the voice continued.

A few men chuckled, and shifted bodies sheathed in silk. The sounds echoed from a high and hard ceiling.

Daniel's mind now recollected that it was attached to a body. But like a regiment that has lost contact with its colonel, the body had not received any orders in a long time. It had gone all loose and discomposed, and had stopped sending signals back to headquarters.

"Give him more water!" commanded the beautiful voice.

Daniel heard boots moving on a hard floor to his left, felt blunt pressure against numbed lips, heard the rim of a bottle crack against one of his front teeth. His lungs began to fill up with some sort of beverage. He tried to move his head back but it responded sluggishly, and something cold hit him on the back of the neck hard enough to stop him. The fluid was flooding down his chin now and trickling under his clothes. His whole thorax clenched up trying to cough the fluid out of his lungs, and he tried to move his head forward—but now something cold caught him across the throat. He coughed and vomited at the same moment and sprayed hot humours all over his lap.

"These Puritans cannot hold their drink—really one cannot take them anywhere."

"Save, perhaps, to Barbados, my Lord!" offered up another voice.

Daniel's eyes were bleary and crusted. He tried raising his hands to his face, but halfway there each one of them collided with a bar of iron that was projecting across space. Daniel groped at these, but dire things happened to his neck when he did, and so he ended up feeling around them to paw at his eyes and wipe grit and moisture away from his face. He could make out now that he was sitting on a chair in the middle of a large room; it was night, and the place was lit up by only a modest number of candles. The light gleamed from white lace cravats round the throats of several gentlemen who were arranged round Daniel in a horseshoe.

The light wasn't bright enough, and his vision wasn't clear enough, to make sense of this ironmongery that was about his neck, so he had to explore that with his hands. It seemed to be a band of iron bent into a neck-ring. From four locations equally spaced around its circumference rods of iron projected outwards like spokes from a wheel-hub, to a radius of perhaps half a yard, where each split into a pair of back-curved barbs, like the flukes of grappling-hooks.

"While you were sleeping off the effects of M. LeFebure's draught, I took the liberty of having you fitted out with new neck-wear," said the voice, "but as you are a Puritan, and have no use for vanity, I called upon a *blacksmith* instead of a *tailor*. You'll find that this is all the mode in the sugar plantations of the Caribbean."

The barbs sticking out behind had gotten lodged in the back of the chair when Daniel had unwisely tried to sit forward. Now he gripped the ones in front and pushed himself back hard, knocking the rear ones free. Momentum carried him and the collar back; his spine slammed into the chair and the collar kept moving and tried to shear his head off. He ended up with his head tilted back, gazing almost straight up at the ceiling. His first thought was that candles had somehow been planted up there, or burning arrows shot at random into the ceiling by bored soldiery, but then his eyes focused and he saw that the vault had been decorated with painted stars that gleamed in the candle-light from beneath. Then he knew where he was.

"The Court of Star Chamber is in session—Lord Chancellor Jeffreys presiding," said another excellent voice, husky with some kind of precious emotion. And what sort of man got choked up over *this*?

Now just as Daniel's senses had recovered one at a time, beginning with his ears, so his mind was awakening piece-meal. The part of it that warehoused ancient facts was, at the moment, getting along much better than the part that did clever things. "Nonsense . . . the Court of Star Chamber was abolished by the Long Parliament in 1641 . . . five years before I was *born*, or *you* were, Jeffreys."

"I do not recognize the self-serving decrees of that rebel Parliament," Jeffreys said squeamishly. "The Court of Star Chamber was ancient—Henry VII convened it, but its procedures were rooted in Roman jurisprudence—consequently, 'twas a model of clarity, of effiency, unlike the time-encrusted monstrosity of Common Law, that staggering, cobwebbed Beast, that senile compendium of folk-lore and wives' tales, a scabrous Colander seiving all the chunky bits out of the evanescent flux of Society and compacting 'em into legal head-cheese."

"Hear, hear!" said one of the other Judges, who apparently felt that Jeffreys had now encompassed everything there was to be said about English Common Law. Daniel assumed they must all be judges, at any rate, and that they'd been hand-picked by Jeffreys. Or, more like it, they'd simply gravitated to him during his career, they were the men that he always saw, whenever he troubled to glance around him.

Another one of them said, "The late Archbishop Laud found this Chamber to be a convenient facility for the suppression of Low Church dissidents, such as your father, Drake Waterhouse."

"But the entire point of my father's story is *that he was not suppressed*—Star Chamber cut his nose and his ears off and it only made him more formidable."

"Drake was a man of exceptional strength and resilience," Jeffreys said. "Why, he haunted my very nightmares when I was a boy. My father told me tales of him as if he were a bogey-man. I know that you are no Drake. Why, you stood by and watched one of your own kind be murdered, under your window, at Trinity, by my lord Upnor, twenty-some years ago, and you did *nothing*—nothing! I remember it well, and I know that you do as well, Waterhouse."

"Does this sham have a purpose, other than to reminisce about College days?" Daniel inquired.

"Give him a *revolution*," Jeffreys said.

The fellow who had poured water into Daniel's mouth earlier—some sort of armed bailiff—stepped up, grabbed one of the four grappling-hooks projecting from Daniel's collar, and gave it a wrench. The whole apparatus spun round, using Daniel's neck as an axle, until he could get his arms up to stop it. A simpler man would have guessed—from the sheer amount of pain involved—that his head had been half sawed away. But Daniel had dissected enough necks to know where all the important bits were. He ran a few quick experiments and concluded that, as he could swallow, breathe, and wiggle his toes, none of the main cables had been severed.

"You are charged with perverting the English language," Jeffreys proclaimed. "To wit: that on numerous occasions during idle talk in coffee-houses, and in private correspondence, you have employed the word 'revolution,' heretofore a perfectly innocent and useful English word, in an altogether new sense, conceived and propagated by you, meaning radical and violent overthrow of a government."

"Oh, I don't think violence need have anything to do with it."

"You admit you are guilty then!"

"I know how the *genuine* Star Chamber worked . . . I don't imagine this *sham* one is any different . . . why should I dignify it by pretending to put up a defense?"

"The defendant is guilty as charged!" Jeffreys announced, as if, by superhuman effort, he'd just brought an exhausting trial to a close. "I shan't pretend to be surprised by the outcome—while you were asleep, we interrogated several witnesses—all agreed you have been using 'revolution' in a sense that is not to be found in any treatise of Astronomy. We even asked your old chum from Trinity . . ."

"Monmouth? But didn't you chop his head off?"

"No, no, the other one. The Natural Philosopher who has been so impertinent as to quarrel with the King in the matter of Father Francis . . ."

"Newton!?"

"Yes, that one! I asked him, 'You have written all of these fat books on the subject of Revolutions, what does the word signify to you?' He said it meant one body moving about another—he uttered *not a word* about politics."

"I cannot believe you have brought Newton into this matter."

Jeffreys abruptly stopped playing the rôle of Grand Inquisitor, and answered in the polite, distracted voice of the busy man-about-town: "Well, I had to grant him an audience anyway, on the Father Francis matter. He does not know you are here. . . . just as you, evidently, did not know he was in London."

In the same sort of tone, Daniel replied, "Can't blame you for finding it all just a bit bewildering. Of course! You'd assume that Newton, on a visit to London, would renew his acquaintance with me, and other Fellows of the Royal Society."

"I have it on good authority he has been spending time with that damned Swiss traitor instead."

"Swiss traitor?"

"The one who warned William of Orange of the French dragoons."

"Fatio?"

"Yes, Fatio de Duilliers."

Jeffreys was absent-mindedly patting his wig, puzzling over this fragment re Newton. The sudden change in the Lord Chancellor's affect had engendered, in Daniel, a giddiness that was probably dangerous. He had been trying to stifle it. But now Daniel's stomach began to shake with suppressed laughter.

"Jeffreys! Fatio is a *Swiss* Protestant who warned the *Dutch* of a *French* plot, on *Dutch* soil . . . and for this you call him a traitor?"

"He betrayed Monsieur le comte de Fenil. And now this traitor has moved to London, for he knows that his life is forfeit anywhere on the Continent . . . anywhere Persons of Quality observe a decent respect for justice. But here! London, England! Oh, in other times his presence would not have been tolerated. But in these parlous times, when such a man comes and takes up residence in our city, no one bats an eye . . . and when he is seen buying alchemical supplies, and talking in coffee-houses with our foremost Natural Philosopher, no one thinks of it as scandalous."

Daniel perceived that Jeffreys was beginning to work himself up into another frenzy. So before the Lord Chancellor completely lost his mind, Daniel reminded him: "The real Star Chamber was known for pronouncing stern sentences, and executing them quickly."

"True! And if this assembly had such powers, your nose would be lying in the gutter, and the rest of you would be on a ship to the West Indies, where you would chop sugar cane on my plantation for the rest of your life. As it stands, I cannot punish you until I've convicted you of something in the common-law court. Shouldn't be all that difficult, really."

"How do you suppose?"

"Tilt the defendant back!"

The Star Chamber's bailiffs, or executioners or whatever they were, converged on Daniel from behind, gripped the back of his chair, and yanked, raising its front legs up off the floor and leaving Daniel's feet a-dangle. His weight shifted from his buttocks to his back, and the iron collar went into motion and tried to fall to the floor. But it was stopped by Daniel's throat. He tried to raise his hands to take the weight of the iron off his wind-pipe, but Jeffreys' henchmen had anticipated that: each of them had a spare hand that he used to pin one of Daniel's hands down to the chair. Daniel could see nothing but stars now: stars painted on the ceiling when his eyes were open, and other stars that zoomed across his vision when his eyes were closed. The face of the Lord Chancellor now swam into the center of this firmament like the Man in the Moon.

Now Jeffreys had been an astonishingly beautiful young man, even by the standards of the generation of young Cavaliers that had included such Adonises as the Duke of Monmouth and John Churchill. His eyes, in particular, had been of remarkable beauty—perhaps this accounted for his ability to seize and hold the young Daniel Waterhouse with his gaze. Unlike Churchill, he had not aged well. Years in London, serving as solicitor general to the Duke of York, then as a prosecutor of supposed conspirators, then Lord Chief Justice, and now Lord Chancellor, had put leaves of lard on him, as on a kidney in a butcher-stall. His eyebrows had grown out into great gnarled wings, or horns. The eyes were beautiful as ever, but instead of gazing out from the fair unblemished face of a youth, they peered out through a sort of embrasure, between folds of chub below and snarled brows above. It had probably been fifteen years since Jeffreys could list, from memory, all the men he had murdered through the judicial system; if he hadn't lost count while extirpating the Popish Plot, he certainly had during the Bloody Assizes.

At any rate Daniel could not now tear his eyes away from those of Jeffreys. In a sense Jeffreys had planned this spectacle poorly. The drug must have been slipped into Daniel's drink at the coffee-house and Jeffreys's minions must have abducted him after he'd fallen asleep in a water-taxi. But the elixir had made him so groggy that he had failed to be afraid until this moment.

Now, *Drake* wouldn't have been afraid, even fully awake; he'd sat in this room and defied Archbishop Laud to his face, knowing what they would do to him. Daniel had been brave, until now, only insofar as the drug had made him stupid. But now, looking up into the eyes of Jeffreys, he recalled all of the horror-stories that had emanated from the Tower as this man's career had flourished: Dissidents who "committed suicide" by cutting their own throats to the vertebrae; great trees in Taunton decorated with hanged men, dying slowly; the Duke of Monmouth having his head gradually hacked off by Jack Ketch, five or six strokes of the axe, as Jeffreys looked on with those eyes.

The colors were draining out of the world. Something white and fluffy came into view near Jeffreys's face: a hand surrounded by a lace cuff. Jeffreys had grasped one of the hooks projecting up from Daniel's collar. "You say that your revolution does not have to involve any violence," he said. "I say you must think harder about the nature of revolution. For as you can see, this hook is on top now. A different one is on the bottom. True, we can raise the low one up by a simple *revolution—*" Jeffreys wrenched the collar around, its entire weight bearing on Daniel's adam's apple—giving Daniel every reason to scream. But he made no sound other than a pitiable attempt to suck in some air. "Ah, but observe! The one that was *high* is now *low*! Let us raise it up then, for it does not love to be low." Jeffreys wrenched it back up. "Alas, we are back to where we started; the high is high, the low is low, and what's the point of having a revolution at all?" Jeffreys now repeated the demonstration, laughing at Daniel's struggle for air. "Who could ask for a better career!" he exclaimed. "Slowly decapitating the men I went to college with! We made Monmouth last as long as 'twas possible, but the axe is imprecise, Jack Ketch is a butcher, and it ended all too soon. But this collar is an excellent device for a gradual sawing-off, I could make *him* last for *days!*" Jeffreys sighed with delight. Daniel could not see any more, other than a few pale violet blotches swimming in turbulent gray. But Jeffreys must have signalled the bailiffs to right the chair, for suddenly the weight of the collar was on his collarbones and his efforts to breathe were working. "I trust I have disabused you of any ludicrous ideas concerning the true nature of revolutions. If the low are to be made high, Daniel, then the high must be made low—but the high *like* to be high—and they have an army and a navy. 'Twill never occur without violence. And 'twill fail given enough time, as your father's failed. Have you quite learnt the lesson? Or shall I repeat the demonstration?"

Daniel tried to say something: namely to beg that the demonstration *not* be repeated. He had to because it hurt too much and might kill him. To beg for mercy was utterly reasonable—and the act of a coward. The only thing that prevented him from doing it was that his voice-box was not working.

"It is customary for a judge to give a bit of a scolding to a guilty man, to help him mend his ways," Jeffreys reflected. "That part of the proceedings is now finished—we move on to Sentencing. Concerning this, I have Bad News, and Good News. 'Tis an ancient custom to give the *recipient* of Bad and Good News, the choice of which to hear first. But as Good News for me is Bad for you, and vice versa, allowing you to make the choice will only lead to confusion. So: the Bad News, for me, is that you are correct, the Star Chamber has not been formally re-constituted. 'Tis just a pastime for a few of us Senior Jurists and has no legal authority to carry out sentences. The Good News, for me, is that I can pronounce a most severe sentence upon *you* even without legal authority: I sentence you, Daniel Waterhouse, to be Daniel Waterhouse for the remainder of your days, and to live, for that time, every day with the knowledge of your own disgusting cravenness. Go! You disgrace this Chamber! Your father was a vile man who deserved what he got here. But you are a disfigurement of his memory! Yes, that's right, on your feet, about face, march! Get out! Just because *you* must live with yourself does not mean *we* must be subjected to the same degradation! Out, out! Bailiffs, throw this quivering mound of shite out into the gutter, and pray that the piss running down his legs will wash him down into the Thames!"

THEY DUMPED HIM like a corpse in the open fields upriver from Westminster, between the Abbey and the town of Chelsea. When they rolled him out the back of the cart, he came very close to losing his head, as one of the collar-hooks caught in a slat on the wagon's edge and gave him a jerk at the neck so mighty it was like to rip his soul out of his living body. But the wood gave way before his bones did, and he fell down into the dirt, or at least that was what he inferred from evidence near to hand when he came to his senses.

His desire at this point was to lie full-length on the ground and weep until he died of dehydration. But the collar did not permit lying down. Having it round his neck was a bit like having Drake stand over him and berate him for not getting up. So up he got, and stumbled round and wept for a while. He reckoned he must be in Hogs-den, or Pimlico as men in the real estate trade liked to name it: not the country and not the city, but a blend of the most vile features of both. Stray dogs chased feral chickens across a landscape that had been churned up by rooting swine and scraped bald by scavenging goats. Nocturnal fires of bakeries and breweries shot rays of ghastly red light through gaps in their jumble-built walls, spearing whores and drunks in their gleam.

It could have been worse: they could have dumped him in a place with vegetation. The collar was designed to prevent slaves from running away by turning every twig, reed, vine, and stalk into a constable that would grab the escapee by the nape as he ran by. As Daniel roamed about, he explored the hasp with his fingers and found it had been wedged shut with a carven peg of soft wood which had been hammered through the loops. By worrying this back and forth he was able to draw it out. Then the collar came loose on his neck and he got it off easily. He had a dramatical impulse to carry it over to the river-bank and fling it into the Thames, but then coming to his senses he recollected that there was a mile of dodgy ground to be traversed before he reached the edge of Westminster, and any number of dogs and Vagabonds who might need to be beaten back in that interval. So he kept a grip on it, swinging it back and forth in the darkness occasionally, to make himself feel better. But no assailant came for him. His foes were not of the sort that could be struck down with a rod of iron.

ON THE SOUTHERN EDGE of the settled and civilized part of Westminster, a soon-to-be-fashionable street was under construction. It was the latest project of Sterling Waterhouse, who was now Earl of Willesden, and spent most of his days on his modest country estate just to the northwest of London, trying to elevate the self-esteem of his investors.

One of the people who'd put money into this Westminster street was the woman Eliza, who was now Countess of Zeur. Eliza occupied something like fifty percent of all Daniel's waking thoughts now. Obviously this was a disproportionate figure. If it'd been the case that Daniel continually come up with *new and original* thoughts on the subject of Eliza, then he might have been able to justify thinking about her ten or even twenty percent of the time. But all he did was think the same things over and over again. During the hour or so he'd spent in the Star Chamber, he'd scarcely thought of her at all, and so now he had to make up for that by thinking about nothing else for an hour or so.

Eliza had come to London in February, and on the strength of personal recommendations from Leibniz and Huygens, she had talked her way into a Royal Society meeting—one of the few women ever to attend one, unless you counted Freaks of Nature brought in to display their multiple vaginas or nurse their two-headed babies. Daniel had escorted the Countess of Zeur into Gresham's College a bit nervously, fearing that she'd make a spectacle of herself, or that the Fellows would get the wrong idea and use her as a subject for vivisection. But she had dressed and behaved modestly and all had gone well. Later Daniel had taken her out to Willesden to meet Sterling, with whom she gotten along famously. Daniel had known they would; six months earlier both had been commoners, and now they strolled in what was to become Sterling's French garden, deciding where the urns and statues ought to go, and compared notes as to which shops were the best places to buy old family heirlooms.

At any rate, both of them now had money invested in this attempt to bring civilization to Hogs-den. Even Daniel had put a few pounds into it (not that he considered himself much of an investor; but British coinage had only gotten worse in the last twenty years, if that was imaginable, and there was no point in keeping your money that way). To prevent the site from being ravaged every night by the former inhabitants (human and non-), a porter was stationed there, in a makeshift lodge, with a large number of more or less demented dogs. Daniel managed to wake all of them up by stumbling over the fence at 3:00 A.M. with his neck half sawn through. Of course the porter woke up last, and didn't call the dogs off until half of Daniel's remaining clothes had been torn away. But by that point in the evening, those clothes could not be accounted any great loss.

Daniel was happy just to be recognized by someone, and made up the customary story about having been set upon by blackguards. To this, the porter responded with the obligatory wink. He gave Daniel ale, an act of pure kindness that brought fresh tears to Daniel's eyes, and sent his boy a-running into Westminster to summon a hackney-chair. This was a sort of vertical coffin suspended on a couple of staves whose ends were held up by great big taciturn men. Daniel climbed into it and fell asleep.

When he woke up it was dawn, and he was in front of Gresham's College, on the other end of London. A letter was waiting for him from France.

THE LETTER BEGAN,

> Is the weather in London still quite dismal? From the vantage point of Versailles, I can assure you that spring approaches London. Soon, I will be approaching, too.

Daniel (who was reading this in the College's entrance hall) stopped there, stuffed the letter into his belt, and stumbled into the penetralia of the Pile. Not even Sir Thomas Gresham his own self would be able to find his way around the place now, if he should come back to haunt it. The R.S. had been having its way with the building for almost three decades and it was just about spent. Daniel scoffed at all talk of building a new Wren-designed structure and moving the Society into it. The Royal Society was not reducible to an inventory of strange objects, and could not be re-located by transporting that inventory to a new building, any more than a man could travel to France by having his internal organs cut out and packed in barrels and shipped across the Channel. As a geometric proof contained, in its terms and its references, the whole history of geometry, so the piles of stuff in the larger Pile that was Gresham's College encoded the development of Natural Philosophy from the first meetings of Boyle, Wren, Hooke, and Wilkins up until to-day. Their arrangement, the order of stratifications, reflected what was going on in the minds of the Fellows (predominantly Hooke) in any given epoch, and to move it, or to tidy it up, would have been akin to burning a library. Anyone who could not find what he needed there, didn't deserve to be let in. Daniel felt about the place as a Frenchman felt about the French language, which was to say that it all made perfect sense once you understood it, and if you didn't understand it, then to hell with you.

He found a copy of the *I Ching* in about a minute, in the dark, and carrying it over to where rosy-fingered Dawn was clawing desperately at a grime-caked window, found the hexagram 19, *Lin*, Approach. The book went on at length concerning the bottomless significance of this symbol, but the only meaning that mattered to Daniel was 000011, which was how the pattern of broken and unbroken lines translated to binary notation. In decimal notation this was 3.

It would have been perfectly all right for Daniel to have crawled up to his garret atop the College and fallen asleep, but he felt that having been stupefied with opium for a night and a day ought to have enabled him to catch up on his sleep, and events in the Star Chamber and later in Hogs-den had got him rather keyed up. Any one of these three things sufficed to prevent sleep: the raw wounds around his neck, the commotion of the City coming awake, and his beastly, uncontrollable lust for Eliza. He went up-stairs to a room that was optimistically called the Library, not because it had books (every room did) but because it had windows. Here he spread out Eliza's letter on a table all streaked and splotched with disturbing stains. Next to it he set down a rectangle of scrap paper (actually a proof of a woodcut intended for Volume III of Newton's *Principia Mathematica*). Examining the characters in Eliza's letter one by one, he assigned each to either the 0 alphabet or the 1 alphabet and wrote a corresponding digit on the scrap paper, arranging them in groups of five. Thus

D O C T O R W A T E R H O U S E
0 1 1 0 0 0 0 1 0 0 1 0 0 0 0 0

The first group of binary digits made the number 12, the second 4, the next 16, and the one after that 6. So writing these out on a new line, and subtracting a 3 from each, he got

```
12  4   16  6
 3  3    3  3
_____
 9  1   13  3
```

Which made the letters

I A M C

The light got better as he worked.

Leibniz was building a splendid library in Wolfenbüttel, with a high rotunda that would shed light down onto the table below . . .

His forehead was on the table. Not a good way to work. Not a good way to sleep either, unless your neck was so torn up as to make lying down impossible, in which case it was the *only* way to sleep. And Daniel *had* been sleeping. The pages under his face were a sea of awful light, the unfair light of noon.

"Truly you are an inspiration to all Natural Philosophers, Daniel Waterhouse."

Daniel sat up. He was stiff as a grotesque. He could feel and hear the scab-work on his neck cracking. Seated two tables away, quill in hand, was Nicolas Fatio de Duilliers.

"Sir!"

Fatio held up a hand. "I do not mean to disturb you, there is no need for—"

"Ah, but there is a need for me to express my gratitude. I have not seen you since you saved the life of the Prince of Orange."

Fatio closed his eyes for a moment. " 'Twas like a conjunction of planets, purely fortuitous, reflecting no distinction on me, and let us say no more of it."

"I learned only recently that you were in town—that your life was in danger so long as you remained on the Continent. Had I known as much earlier, I'd have offered you whatever hospitality I could—"

"And if I were worthy of the title of gentleman, I'd have waited for that offer before making myself at home here," Fatio returned.

"Isaac of course has given you the run of the place and that is splendid."

Daniel now noticed Fatio gazing at him with a penetrating, analytical look that reminded him of Hooke peering through a lens. From Hooke it was not objectionable, somehow. From Fatio it was mildly offensive. Of course Fatio was wondering how Daniel knew that he'd been hobnobbing with Isaac. Daniel could have told him the story about Jeffreys and the Star Chamber, but it would only have confused matters more.

Fatio now appeared to notice, for the first time, the damage to Daniel's neck. His eyes saw all, but they were so big and luminous that it was impossible for him to conceal what he was gazing at; unlike the eyes of Jeffreys, which could secretly peer this way and that in the shadow of their deep embrasures, Fatio's eyes could never be used discreetly.

"Don't ask," Daniel said. "You, sir, suffered an honorable wound on the beach. I've suffered one, not so honorable, but in the same cause, in London."

"Are you quite all right, Doctor Waterhouse?"

"Splendid of you to inquire. I am fine. A cup of coffee and I'll be as good as new."

Whereupon Daniel snatched up his papers and repaired to the coffee-house, which was full of people and yet where he felt more privacy than under the eyes of Fatio.

The binary digits hidden in the subtleties of Eliza's handwriting became, in decimal notation,

$$4 \quad 16 \quad 6 \quad 18 \quad 16 \quad 12 \quad 17 \quad 10$$

which when he subtracted 3 from each (that being the key hidden in the *I Ching* reference) became

$$9 \quad 1 \quad 13 \quad 3 \quad 15 \quad 13 \quad 9 \quad 14 \quad 7 \cdots$$

which said,

I AM COMING . . .

THE FULL DECIPHERMENT took a while, because Eliza provided details concerning her travel plans, and wrote of all she wanted to do while she was in London. When he was finished writing out the message he came alive to the fact that he had sat for a long time, and consumed much coffee, and needed to urinate in the worst way. He could not recall the last time he had made water. And so he went back to a sort of piss-hole in the corner of the tiny court in back of the coffeehouse.

Nothing happened, and so after about half a minute he bent forward as if bowing, and braced his forehead against the stone wall. He had learned that this helped to relax some of the muscles in his lower abdomen and make the urine come out more freely. That stratagem, combined with some artful shifting of the hips and deep breathing, elicited a few spurts of rust-colored urine. When it ceased to work, he turned round, pulled his garments up around his waist, and squatted to piss in the Arab style. By shifting his center of gravity just so, he was able to start up a kind of gradual warm seepage that would provide relief if he kept it up for a while.

This gave him lots of time to think of Eliza, if spinning phant'sies could be named thinking. It was plain from her letter that she expected to visit Whitehall Palace. Which signified little, since any person who was wearing clothes and not carrying a lighted grana-doe could go in and wander about the place. But since Eliza was a Countess who dwelt at Versailles, and Daniel (in spite of Jeffreys) a sort of courtier, when she said she wanted to visit Whitehall it meant that she expected to stroll and sup with Persons of Quality. Which could easily be arranged, since the Catholic Francophiles who made up most of the King's court would fall all over themselves making way for Eliza, if only to get a look at the spring fashions.

But to arrange it would require planning—again, if the dreaming of fatuous dreams could be named planning. Like an astronomer plotting his tide-tables, Daniel had to project the slow wheeling of the seasons, the liturgical calendar, the sessions of Parliament and the progress of various important people's engagements, terminal diseases, and pregnancies into the time of the year when Eliza was expected to show up.

His first thought had been that Eliza would be here at just the right time: for in another fortnight the King was going to issue a new Declaration of Indulgence that would make Daniel a hero, at least among Nonconformists. But as he squatted there he began to count off the weeks, tick, tick, tick, like the drops of urine detaching themselves one by one from the tip of his yard, and came aware that it would be much longer before Eliza actually got here—she'd be arriving no sooner than mid-May. By that time, the High Church priests would have had several Sundays to denounce Indulgence from their pulpits; they'd say it wasn't an act of Christian toleration at all, but a stalking-horse for Popery, and Daniel Waterhouse a dupe at best and a traitor at worst. Daniel might have to go *live* at Whitehall around then, just to be safe.

It was while imagining *that*—living like a hostage in a dingy chamber at Whitehall, protected by John Churchill's Guards—that Daniel recalled another datum from his mental ephemeris, one that stopped up his pissing altogether.

The Queen was pregnant. To date she'd produced no children at all. The pregnancy seemed to have come on more suddenly than human pregnancies customarily did. Perhaps they'd been slow to announce it because they'd expected it would only end in yet another miscarriage. But it seemed to have taken, and the size of her abdomen was now a matter of high controversy around White-hall. She was expected to deliver in late May or early June—just the same time that Eliza would be visiting.

Eliza was using Daniel to get inside the Palace so that she, Eliza, could know as early as possible whether King James II had a legitimate heir, and adjust her investments accordingly. This should have been as obvious as that Daniel had a big stone in his bladder, but somehow Daniel managed to finish what he was doing and go back into the coffee-house without becoming aware of either.

The only person who seemed to understand matters was Robert Hooke, who was in the same coffee-house. He was *talking*, as usual, to Sir Christopher Wren. But he had been *observing* Daniel, this whole time, through an open window. He had the look on his face of a man who was determined to speak plainly of unpleasant facts, and Daniel managed to avoid him.

Versailles
JULY 1688

To d'Avaux
Monsieur,

As you requested, I have changed over to the new cypher. To me it seems preposterous to imagine that the Dutch had broken the old one and read all of your letters! But, as always, you are the soul of discretion, and I will follow whatever precautions you demand of me.

It was good that you wrote me that lovely, if vaguely

sarcastic, letter of congratulations on the occasion of my being accorded my rightful hereditary title (since we are now of equal rank—whatever doubts you may harbor as to the legitimacy of my title—I hope you are not offended that I address you as Monsieur instead of Monseigneur now). Until your letter arrived, I had not heard from you in many months. At first, I assumed that the Prince of Orange's vulgar over-reaction to the so-called abduction attempt had left you isolated in the Hague, and unable to send letters out. As months went by, I began to worry that your affection for your most humble and obedient servant had cooled. Now I can see that this was all just idle phant'sy—the sort of aimless fretting to which my sex is so prone. You and I are as close as ever. So I will try to write a good letter and entice you to write me back.

Business first: I have not tallied the numbers for the second quarter of 1688, and so please keep what follows in confidence from the other investors, but I am confident that we have made out better than anyone suspects. True, V.O.C. stock has been performing miserably, and yet the market has been too volatile to make a winning proposition out of selling it short or playing derivatives. Yet a few things—all in London, strangely enough—have saved our investments from disaster. One is traffic in commodities, particularly silver. England's coinage is becoming more debased every day, counterfeiters are a plague on the land, and, not to bore you with details, this entails flows of gold and silver in and out of that island from which we can profit if we make the right bets.

You may wonder how I can possibly know which bets to make, living as I do in Versailles. Let me ease your concerns by explaining to you that I have made two visits to London since I last saw you, one in February and one in May, around the time that the son of King James II was born. The second visit was mandatory, of course, for everyone knew that the Queen of England was pregnant, and that the future of Britain and of Europe hinged upon her producing a legitimate male heir. The markets in Amsterdam were bound to react strongly to any news from Whitehall and so I had to be there. I have seduced an Englishman who is close to the King—so close that he was able to get me into Whitehall during the time that the Queen went into labor. Since this is a business report, Monsieur, I'll say no more here; but allow me to mention that there are certain peculiarities surrounding the delivery of this infant with which I'll entertain you some other time.

The Englishman is a figure of some note in the Royal Society. He has an older half-brother who makes money in more ways than I can enumerate. The family has old connections to the goldsmith's shops that used to be situated around Cornhill and Threadneedle, and newer connections to the *banca* that was set up by Sir Richard Apthorp after Charles II put many of the goldsmiths out of business. If you are not familiar with a *banca*, it means something akin to a goldsmith, except that they have dropped any pretense of goldsmithing *per se;* they are financiers dealing in metal and paper. Odd as it might sound, this type of business actually makes sense, at least in the context of London, and Apthorp is doing well by it. It was through this connexion that I became aware of the trends in silver and gold mentioned earlier, and was able to make the right bets, as it were.

Lacking the refinement of the French, the English have no equivalent of Versailles, so the high and mighty, the adherents of diverse religions, *commerçants*, and Vagabonds are all commingled in London. You've spent time in Amsterdam, which may give you some idea of what London is like, except that London is not nearly as well organized. Much of the mixing takes place in coffee-houses. Surrounding the 'Change are diverse coffee- and chocolate-houses that, over time, have come to serve specific clientele. Birds of a feather flock together and so those who trade in East India Company stocks go to one place and so forth. Now as the overseas trade of England has waxed, the business of under-writing ships and other risky ventures has become a trade of some significance in and of itself. Those who are in the market for insurance have recently begun going to Lloyd's Coffee-house, which has, for whatever reason, become the favorite haunt of the underwriters. This arrangement works well for buyer and seller alike: the buyer can solicit bids from diverse underwriters simply by strolling from table to table, the sellers can distribute the risks by spontaneously forming associations. I hope I am not boring you to death, Monsieur, but it is a fascinating thing to watch, and you yourself have now made a bit of money from this quarter, which you can use to buy yourself a picaroon-romance if my discourse is too tedious. *Tout le monde* at Versailles agree that *L'Emmerdeur in Barbary* is a good read, and I have it on high authority that a copy was spied in the King's bedchamber.

Enough of business; now, gossip.

Madame deigns to recognize me now that I am known to be a Countess. For the longest time, she regarded me as a parasite, a strangling vine, and so I expected she would be the last person at Court to accept me as a noblewoman. But she astonished me with a welcome that was courteous and almost warm, and begrudged me a few moments' polite conversation, when I encountered her in the gardens the other day. I believe her previous coldness toward me came from two reasons. One is that like all the other foreign royals, *la Palatine* (as Liselotte is sometimes referred to here) is insecure about her rank, and tends to exalt herself by belittling those whose bloodlines are even more questionable than hers. This is not an attractive feature but it is all too human! The second reason is that her chief rival at Court is de Maintenon, who came up from a wretched state to become the unofficial Queen of France. And so whenever Madame sees a woman at Court who has aspirations, it reminds her of the one she hates.

Many nobles of ancient families sneer at me because I handle money. Liselotte is not, however, one of these. On the contrary, I believe it explains why she has accepted me.

Now that I have spent two years in the household of Mme. la duchesse d'Oyonnax, surrounded by the very type of ambitious young woman Madame despises so much, I can understand why she takes such care to avoid them. Those girls have very few assets: their names, their bodies, and (if they are lucky enough to have been born with any) their wits. The first of these—their names, and the pedigrees attached—suffice to get them in the gates. They are like an invitation to the ball. But most of those families have more liabilities than assets. Once one of those girls has found a position in some household at Versailles, she has only a few years to make arrangements for the remainder of her life. She is like a plucked rose in a vase. Every day at dawn she looks out the window to see a gardener driving a wagon loaded with wilted flowers that are taken out to the countryside to be used for mulch, and the similitude to her own future is clear. In a few years she will be outshined, at all the parties, by younger girls. Her brothers will inherit any assets the family might have. If she can marry well, as Sophie did, she may have a life to look forward to; if not, she will be shipped off to some convent, as two of Sophie's beautiful and brilliant sisters were. When that desperation is combined with the heedless irresponsible nature of young persons generally, cruelty becomes mundane.

It's only reasonable for Madame to want to avoid young women of that type. She has always assumed that I was one of them—having no way to distinguish me from the others. But lately, as I mentioned, she has become aware that I handle investments. This sets me apart—it tells her that I have interests and assets outside of the intrigues of Court and so am not as dangerous as the others. In effect, she is treating me as if I had just married a rich handsome Duke, and gotten all my affairs in order. Instead of a cut rose in a vase, I am a rose-bush with living roots in rich soil.

Or perhaps I'm reading too much into a brief conversation!

She asked me if the hunting was good on Qwghlm. Knowing how much she loves to hunt, I told her it was miserable, unless throwing stones at rats qualified—and how, pray tell, was the hunting here at Versailles? Of course I meant the vast game parks that the King has constructed around the château, but Liselotte shot back, "Indoors or out?"

"I have seen game taken indoors," I allowed, "but only through trapping or poisoning, which are common *peasant* vices."

"Qwghlmians are more accustomed to the *outdoor* life?"

"If only because our dwellings keep getting blown down, madame."

"Can you ride, mademoiselle?" she asked.

"After a fashion—for I learned *bareback* style," I answered.

"There are no saddles where you come from?"

"In olden days there were, for we would suspend them from tree-branches overnight, to prevent them from being eaten by small creatures in the night-time. But then the English cut down the trees, and so now it is our custom to ride bareback."

"I should like to see that," she returned, "but it is hardly proper."

"We are guests in the King's house and must abide by his standards of propriety," I said dutifully.

"If you can ride well in a saddle *here,* I shall invite you to St. Cloud—that is *my* estate, and you may abide by *my* rules there."

"Do you think Monsieur would object?"

"My husband objects to *everything* I do," she said, "and so he objects to *nothing.*"

In my next letter, I'll let you know whether I passed the riding-test, and got the invitation to St. Cloud.

And I will send the quarterly figures as well!

Eliza de la Zeur

Tower of London
SUMMER AND AUTUMN 1688

> Therefore it happeneth commonly, that such as value themselves by the greatness of their wealth, adventure on crimes, upon hope of escaping punishment, by corrupting public justice, or obtaining pardon by money, or other rewards.
> —HOBBES, *Leviathan*

NOW AS ENGLAND WAS A country of fixed ways, they imprisoned him in the same chamber where they had put Oldenburg twenty years before.

But some things changed even in England; James II was peevish and fitful where his older brother had been merry, and so Daniel was kept closer than Oldenburg had been, and allowed to leave the chamber to stroll upon the walls only rarely. He spent all his time in that round room, encircled by the eldritch glyphs that had been scratched into the stone by condemned alchemists and sorcerers of yore, and pathetic Latin plaints graven by Papists under Elizabeth.

Twenty years ago he and Oldenburg had made idle jests about carving new graffiti in the Universal Character of John Wilkins. The words he had exchanged with Oldenburg still seemed to echo around the room, as if the stone were a telescope mirror that forever recurved all information towards the center. The idea of the Universal Character now seemed queer and naïve to Daniel, and so it didn't enter his mind to begin scratching at the stone for the first fortnight or so of his imprisonment. He reckoned that it would take a long time to make any lasting mark, and he assumed he would not live long enough. Jeffreys could only have put him in here to kill him, and when Jeffreys set his mind to killing someone there was no stopping him, he did it the way a farmer's wife plucked a chicken. But no specific judicial proceedings were underway—a sign that this was not to be a *judicial* murder (meaning a stately and more or less predictable one), but the *other* kind.

It was marvelously *quiet* at the Tower of London, the Mint being shut down at the moment, and people never came to visit him, and this was good—rarely was a murder victim afforded such an opportunity to get his spiritual house in order. Puritans did not go to confession or have a special sacrament before dying, as Papists did, but even so, Daniel supposed there must be a bit of tidying-up he could do, in the dusty corners of his soul, before the men with the daggers came.

So he spent a while searching his soul, and found nothing there. It was as sparse and void as a sacked cathedral. He did not have a wife or children. He lusted after Eliza, Countess de la Zeur, but something about being locked up in this round room made him realize that she neither lusted after nor particularly liked him. He did not have a career to speak of, because he was a contemporary of Hooke, Newton, and Leibniz, and therefore predestined for rôles such as scribe, amanuensis, sounding-board, errand-boy. His thorough training for the Apocalypse had proved a waste, and he had gamely tried to redirect his skills and his energies towards the shaping of a secular Apocalypse, which he styled Revolution. But prospects for such a thing looked unfavorable at the moment. Scratching something on the wall might enable him to make a permanent mark on the world, but he would not have time.

All in all, his epitaph would be: DANIEL WATERHOUSE 1646–1688 SON OF DRAKE. It might have made an ordinary man just a bit melancholy, this, but something about its very bleakness appealed to the spirit of a Puritan and the mind of a Natural Philosopher. Suppose he'd had twelve children, written a hundred books, and taken towns and cities from the Turks, and had statues of himself all over, and *then* been clapped in the Tower to have his throat cut? Would matters then stand differently? Or would these be meaningless distractions, a clutter of vanity, empty glamour, false consolation?

Souls were created somehow, and placed in bodies, which lived for more or fewer years, and after that all was faith and speculation. Perhaps after death was nothing. But if there was *something*, then Daniel couldn't believe it had anything to do with the earthly things that the body had done—the children it had spawned, the gold it had hoarded—except insofar as those things altered one's soul, one's state of consciousness.

Thus he convinced himself that having lived a bleak spare life had left his soul no worse off than anyone else's. Having children, for example, might have changed him, but only by providing insights that would have made it easier, or more likely, to have accomplished some *internal* change, some transfiguration of the spirit. Whatever growth or change occurred in one's soul *had* to be internal, like the metamorphoses that went on inside of cocoons, seeds, and eggs. External conditions might help or hinder those changes, but could not be strictly *necessary*. Otherwise it simply was not *fair*, did not make *sense*. Because in the end every soul, be it never so engaged in the world, was like Daniel Waterhouse, alone in a round room in a stone tower, and receiving impressions from the world through a few narrow embrasures.

Or so he told himself; either he would be murdered soon, and learn whether he was right or wrong, or be spared and left to wonder about it.

On the twentieth day of his imprisonment, which Daniel reckoned to be August 17th, 1688, the perceptions coming in through his embrasures were of furious argument and wholesale change. The soldiers he'd been glimpsing out in the yard were gone, replaced by others, in different uniforms. They looked like the King's Own Black Torrent Guards, but that couldn't be, for they were a household regiment, stationed at Whitehall Palace, and Daniel couldn't imagine why they would be uprooted from their quarters there and moved miles down-river to the Tower of London.

Unfamiliar men came to empty his chamber-pot and bring him food—better food than he'd become accustomed to. Daniel asked them questions. Speaking in Dorsetshire accents, they said that they were indeed the King's Own Black Torrent Guards, and that the food they were bringing him had been piling up for quite some time in a porter's lodge. Daniel's friends had been bringing it. But the men who'd been running the Tower until yesterday—a distinctly inferior foot regiment—had not been delivering it.

Daniel then moved on to questions of a more challenging nature and the men stopped supplying answers, even after he shared a few oysters with them. When he became insistent, they allowed as how they would relay his questions to their sergeant, who (as they warned him) was very busy just now, taking an inventory of the prisoners and of the Tower's defenses.

It was two days before the sergeant came to call on Daniel. They were trying days. For just when Daniel had convinced himself that his soul was a disembodied consciousness in a stone tower, perceiving the world through narrow slits, he had been given oysters. They were of the best: Roger Comstock had sent them. They made his body happy when he ate them, and affected his soul much more than seemed proper, for a disembodied consciousness. Either his theory was wrong, or the seductions of the world were more powerful than he'd remembered. When Tess had got the smallpox she'd got it bad, and the pustules had all joined together and her whole skin had fallen off, and her guts had shot out of her anus into a bloody pile on the bed. After that she had somehow remained alive for a full ten and a half hours. Considering the carnal pleasures she had brought him during the years she'd been his mistress, Daniel had taken this the same way Drake would've: as a cautionary parable about fleshly delights. Better to perceive the world as Tess had during those ten and a half hours than as Daniel had while he'd been fucking her. But the oysters were extraordinarily good, their flavor intense and vaguely dangerous, their consistency clearly sexual.

Daniel shared some with the sergeant, who agreed that they were extraordinary but had little else to say—most of Daniel's questions caused him to go shifty-eyed, and some even made him cringe. Finally he agreed to take the matter up with *his* sergeant, giving Daniel a nightmare vision of some endless regression of sergeants, each more senior and harder to reach than the last.

Robert Hooke showed up with a firkin of ale. Daniel assaulted it in much the same way as the murderers would him. "I was apprehensive that you would spurn my gift, and pour it into the Thames," Hooke said irritably, "but I see that the privations of the Tower have turned you into a veritable *satyr.*"

"I am developing a new theory of bodily perceptions, and their intercourse with the soul, and this is *research,*" said Daniel, quaffing vigorously. He huffed ale-foam out of his whiskers (he'd not shaved in weeks) and tried to adopt a searching look. "Being condemned to die is a mighty stimulus to philosophick ratiocination, all of which is however wasted at the instant the sentence is carried out— fortunately I've been spared—"

"So that you may pass on your insights to *me,*" Hooke finished dourly. Then, with ponderous tact: "My memory has become faulty, pray just write it all down."

"They won't allow me pen and paper."

"Have you asked again recently? They would not allow me, or anyone, to visit you until today. But with the new regiment, a new regimen."

"I've been scratching on yonder wall instead," Daniel announced, waving at the beginnings of a geometric diagram.

Hooke's gray eyes regarded it bleakly. "I spied it when I came in," he confessed, "and supposed 'twas something very *ancient* and *time-worn*. Very *recent* and *in progress* would never have crossed my mind."

Daniel was flummoxed for a few moments—just long enough for his pulse to rouse, his face to flush, and his vocal cords to constrict. "It is difficult not to take that as a *rebuke*," he said. "I am merely trying to see if I can reconstruct one of Newton's proofs from memory."

Hooke looked away. The sun had gone down a few minutes ago. A westerly embrasure reflected in his eyes as an identical pair of vertical red slits. "It is a perfectly defensible practice," he admitted. "If I'd spent more of my youth learning geometers' tricks and less of it looking at things, and learning how to see, perhaps I'd have written the *Principia* instead of him."

This was an appalling thing to say. Envy was common as pipe-smoke at Royal Society meetings, but to voice it so baldly was rare. But then Hooke had never cared, or even noticed, what people thought of him.

It took a few moments for Daniel to collect himself, and to give Hooke's utterance the ceremonial silence it demanded. Then he said, "Leibniz has much to say on the subject of *perceptions* which I have but little understood until recently. And you may love Leibniz or not. But consider: Newton has thought things that no man before has ever thought. A great accomplishment, to be sure. Perhaps the greatest achievement any human mind has ever made. Very well—what does that say of Newton, and of us? Why, that his mind is framed in such a way that it can out-think anyone else's. So, all hail Isaac Newton! Let us give him his due, and glorify and worship whatever generative force can frame such a mind. Now, consider Hooke. Hooke has perceived things that no man before has ever perceived. What does that say of Hooke, and of us? That Hooke was framed in some special way? No, for just look at you, Robert—by your leave, you are stooped, asthmatic, fitful, beset by aches and ills, your eyes and ears are no better than those of men who've not perceived a thousandth part of what you have. Newton makes his discoveries in geometrickal realms where our minds cannot go, he strolls in a walled garden filled with wonders, to which he has the only key. But you, Hooke, are cheek-by-jowl with all of humanity in the streets of London. *Anyone* can look at the things you have looked at. But in those things *you* see what no one else has. You are the millionth human to look at a spark, a flea, a raindrop, the moon, and the first to see it. For anyone to say that this is less remarkable than what Newton has done, is to understand things in but a hollow and jejune way, 'tis like going to a Shakespeare play and remembering only the sword-fights."

Hooke was silent for a time. The room had gone darker, and he'd faded to a gray ghost, that vivid pair of red sparks still marking his eyes. After a while, he sighed, and the sparks winked out for a few moments.

"I shall *have* to fetch you quill and paper, if this is to be the nature of your discourse, sir," he said finally.

"I am certain that in the fullness of time, the opinion I have just voiced will be wide spread among learned persons," Daniel said. "This may not however elevate your stature during the years you have remaining; for fame's a weed, but repute is a slow-growing oak, and all we can do during our lifetimes is hop around like squirrels and plant acorns. There is no reason why I should conceal my opinions. But I warn you that I may express them all I like without bringing you fame or fortune."

"It is enough you've expressed them to *me* in the aweful privacy of this chamber, sir," Hooke returned. "I declare that I am indebted to you, and will repay that debt one day, by giving you something of incalculable value when you least expect it. A pearl of great price."

LOOKING AT THE MASTER SERGEANT made Daniel feel old. From the way that lower ranks had alluded to this man, Daniel had expected some sort of graybearded multiple amputee. But under the scars and weathering was a man probably no more than thirty years of age. He entered Daniel's chamber without knocking or introducing himself, and inspected it as if he owned the place, taking particular care to learn the field of fire commanded by each of its embrasures. Moving sideways past each of those slits, he seemed to envision a fan-shaped territory of dead enemies spread across the ground beyond.

"Are you expecting to fight a war, sergeant?" said Daniel, who'd been scratching at some paper with a quill and casting only furtive dart-like glances at the sergeant.

"Are you expecting to start one?" the sergeant answered a minute later, as if in no especial hurry to respond.

"Why do you ask me such an odd question?"

"I am trying to conjure up some understanding of how a Puritan gets himself clapped in Tower just *now*, at a time when the only friends the King *has* are Puritans."

"You have forgotten the Catholics."

"No, sir, the *King* has forgotten 'em. Much has changed since you were locked up. *First* he locked up the Anglican bishops for refusing to preach toleration of Catholics and Dissenters."

"I know that much—I was a free man at the time," Daniel said.

"But the whole country was like to rise up in rebellion, Catholic churches were being put to the torch just for sport, and so he let 'em go, just to quiet things down."

"But that is very different from forgetting the Catholics, sergeant."

"Ah but *since*—since you've been immured here—why, the King has begun to fall apart."

"So far I've learned nothing remarkable, sergeant, other than that there is a sergeant in the King's service who actually knows how to use the word 'immured.' "

"You see, no one believes his son is really his son—that's what has him resting so uneasy."

"What on earth do you mean?"

"Why, the story's gotten out that the Queen was never pregnant at all—just parading around with pillows stuffed under her dress—and that the so-called Prince is just a common babe snatched from an orphanage somewhere, and smuggled into the birth-chamber inside a warming-pan."

Daniel contemplated this, dumbfounded. "I saw the baby emerge from the Queen's vagina with my own eyes," he said.

"Hold on to that memory, Professor, for it may keep you alive. No one in England thinks the child is anything but a base smuggled-in changeling. And so the King is retreating on every front now. Consequently the Anglicans no longer fear him, while the Papists cry that he has abandoned the only true faith."

Daniel pondered. "The King wanted Cambridge to grant a degree to a Benedictine monk named Father Francis, who was viewed, around Cambridge, as a sort of stalking-horse for the Pope of Rome," he said. "Any news of him?"

"The King tried to insinuate Jesuits and such-like *everywhere*," said the sergeant, "but has withdrawn a good many of 'em in the last fortnight. I'd wager Cambridge can stand down, for the King's power is ebbing—ebbing halfway to France."

Daniel now went silent for a while. Finally the sergeant resumed speaking, in a lower, more sociable tone: "I am not learned, but I've been to many plays, which is where I picked up words like 'immured,' and it oftimes happens—especially in your newer plays—that a player will forget his next line, and you'll hear a spear-carrier or lutenist muttering 'im a prompt. And in that spirit, I'll now supply you with your next line, sir: something like 'My word, these are disastrous tidings, my King, a true friend to all Nonconformists, is in trouble, what shall become of us, how can I be of service to his Majesty?'"

Daniel said nothing. The sergeant seemed to have become provoked, and could not now contain himself from prowling and pacing around the room, as if Daniel were a specimen about whom more could be learned by peering at it from diverse angles. "On the other hand, perhaps you are not a run-of-the-mill Nonconformist, for you are in the Tower, sir."

"As are you, sergeant."

"I have a key."

"Poh! Do you have permission to leave?"

This shut him up for a while. "Our commander is John Churchill," he said finally, trying a new tack. "The King no longer entirely trusts him."

"I was wondering when the King would begin to doubt Churchill's loyalty."

"He needs us close, as we are his best men—yet not so close as the Horse Guards, hard by Whitehall Palace, within musket-shot of his apartments."

"And so you have been moved to the Tower for safe-keeping."

"You've got mail," said the sergeant, and flung a letter onto the table in front of Daniel. It bore the address: GRUBENDOL LONDON.

It was from Leibniz.

"It *is* for you, isn't it? Don't bother denying it, I can see it from the look on your face," the sergeant continued. "We had a devil of a time working out who it was supposed to be given to."

"It is intended for whichever officer of the Royal Society is currently charged with handling foreign correspondence," Daniel said indignantly, "and at the moment, that is my honor."

"You're the one, aren't you? You're the one who conveyed certain letters to William of Orange."

"There is no incentive for me to supply an answer to that question," said Daniel after a brief interval of being too appalled to speak.

"Answer this then: do you have friends named Bob Carver and Dick Gripp?"

"Never heard of them."

"That's funny, for we have come upon a page of written instructions, left with the warder, saying that you're to be allowed no visitors at all, except for Bob Carver and Dick Gripp, who may show up at the oddest hours."

"I do not know them," Daniel insisted, "and I beg you not to let them into this chamber under any circumstances."

"That's begging a lot, Professor, for the instructions are written out in my lord Jeffreys's own hand, and signed by the same."

"Then you must know as well as I do that Bob Carver and Dick Gripp are just murderers."

"What I *know* is that my lord Jeffreys is Lord Chancellor, and to disobey his command is an act of rebellion."

"Then I ask you to rebel."

"You first," said the sergeant.

Hanover, August 1688

Dear Daniel,

I haven't the faintest idea where you are, so I will send this to good old GRUBENDOL and pray that it finds you in good health.

Soon I depart on a long journey to Italy, where I expect to gather evidence that will sweep away any remaining cobwebs of doubt that may cling to Sophie's family tree. You must think me a fool to devote so much effort to genealogy, but be patient and you'll see there are good reasons for it. I'll pass through Vienna along the way, and, God willing, obtain an audience with the Emperor and tell him of my plans for the Universal Library (the silver-mining project in the Harz has failed—not because there was anything wrong with my inventions, but because the miners feared that they would be thrown out of work, and resisted me in every imaginable way—and so if the Library is to be funded, it will not be from silver mines, but from the coffers of some great Prince).

There is danger in any journey and so I wanted to write down some things and send them to you before leaving Hanover. These are fresh ideas—green apples that would give a stomach-ache to any erudite person who consumed them. On my journey I shall have many hours to recast them in phrasings more pious (to placate the Jesuits), pompous (to impress the scholastics), or simple (to flatter the salons), but I trust you will forgive me for writing in a way that is informal and plain-spoken. If I should meet with some misfortune along the way, perhaps you or some future Fellow of the Royal Society may pick up the thread where I've dropped it.

Looking about us we can easily perceive diverse Truths, viz. that the sky is blue, the moon round, that humans walk on two legs and dogs on four, and so on. Some of those truths are brute and geometrickal in nature, there is no imaginable way to avoid them, for example that the shortest distance between any two points is a straight line. Until Descartes, everyone supposed that such truths were few in number, and that Euclid and the other ancients had found almost all of them. But when Descartes began his project, we all got into the habit of mapping things into a space that could be described by numbers. We now cross two of Descartes' number-lines at right angles to define a coordinate plane, to which we have given the name Cartesian coordinates, and this conceit appears to be catching on, for one can hardly step into a lecture-room anywhere without seeing some professor drawing a great + on the slate. At any rate, when we all got into the habit of describing the size and position and speed of everything in the world using numbers, lines, curves, and other constructions that are familiar, to erudite men, from Euclid, I say, then it became a sort of vogue to try to explain all of the truths in the universe by geometry. I myself can remember the very moment that I was seduced by this way of thinking: I was fourteen years old, and was wandering around in the Rosenthal outside of Leipzig, ostensibly to smell the blooms but really to prosecute a sort of internal debate in my own mind, between the old ways of the Scholastics and the Mechanical Philosophy of Descartes. As you know I decided in favor of the latter! And I have not ceased to study mathematics since.

Descartes himself studied the way balls move and collide, how they gather speed as they go down ramps, *et cetera,* and tried to explain all of his data in terms of a theory that was purely geometrical in nature. The result of his lucubrations was classically French in that it did not square with reality but it was very beautiful, and logically coherent. Since then our friends Huygens and Wren have expended more toil towards the same end. But I need hardly tell you that it is Newton, far beyond all others, who has vastly expanded the realm of truths that are geometrickal in nature. I truly believe that if Euclid and Eratosthenes could be brought back to life they would prostrate themselves at his feet and (pagans that they were) worship him as a god. For their geometry treated mostly simple abstract shapes, lines in the sand, while Newton's lays down the laws that govern the very planets.

I have read the copy of *Principia Mathematica* that you so kindly sent me, and I know better than to imagine I will find any faults in the author's proofs, or extend his work into any realm he has not already conquered. It has the feel of something finished and complete. It is like a dome—if it were not whole, it would not stand, and because it is whole, and does stand, there's no point trying to add things on to it.

And yet its very completeness signals that there is more work to be done. I believe that the great edifice of the *Principia Mathematica* encloses nearly all of the geometrickal truths that can possibly be written down about the world. But every dome, be it never so large, has an inside and an outside, and while Newton's dome encloses all of the geometrickal truths, it excludes the other kind: truths that have their sources in fitness and in final causes. When Newton encounters such a truth—such as the inverse square law of gravity—he does not even consider trying to understand it, but instead says that the world simply *is* this way, because that is how God made it. To his way of thinking, any truths of this nature lie outside the realm of Natural Philosophy and belong instead to a realm he thinks is best approached through the study of alchemy.

Let me tell you why Newton is wrong.

I have been trying to salvage something of value from Descartes' geometrickal theory of collisions and have found it utterly devoid of worth.

Descartes holds that when two bodies collide, they should have the same quantity of motion after the collision as they had before. Why does he believe this? Because of empirical observations? No, for apparently he did not make any. Or if he did, he saw only what he wanted to see. He believes it because he has made up his mind in advance that his theory must be *geometrickal,* and geometry is an austere discipline—there are only certain quantities a geometer is allowed to measure and to write down in his equations. Chief among these is extension, a pompous term for "anything that can be measured with a ruler." Descartes and most others allow time, too, because you can measure time with a pendulum, and you can measure the pendulum with a ruler. The distance a body travels (which can be measured with a ruler) divided by the time it took covering it (which can be measured with a pendulum, which can be measured with a ruler) gives speed. Speed figures into Descartes' calculation of Quantity of Motion—the more speed, the more motion.

Well enough so far, but then he got it all wrong by treating Quantity of Motion as if it were a scalar, a simple directionless number, when in fact is is a vector. But that is a minor lapse. There is plenty of room for vectors in a system with two orthogonal axes, we simply plot them as arrows on what I call the Cartesian plane, and lo, we have geometrickal constructs that obey geometrickal rules. We can add their components geometrickally, reckon their magnitudes with the Pythagorean Theorem, &c.

But there are two problems with this approach. One is relativity. Rulers move. There is no fixed frame of reference for measuring extension. A geometer on a moving canal-boat who tries to measure the speed of a flying bird will get a different number from a geometer on the shore; and a geometer riding on the bird's back would measure no speed at all!

Secondly: the Cartesian Quantity of Motion, mass multiplied by velocity (mv), is not conserved by falling bodies. And yet by doing, or even imagining, a very simple experiment, you can demonstrate that mass multiplied by the *square* of velocity (mv^2) *is* conserved by such bodies.

This quantity mv^2 has certain properties of interest. For one, it measures the amount of work that a moving body is capable of doing. Work is something that has an absolute meaning, it is free from the problem of relativity that I mentioned a moment ago, a problem unavoidably shared by all theories that are founded upon the use of rulers. In the expression mv^2 the velocity is squared, which means that it has lost its direction, and no longer has a geometrickal meaning. While mv may be plotted on the Cartesian plane and subjected to all the tricks and techniques of Euclid, mv^2 may not be, because in being squared the velocity v has lost its directionality and, if I may wax metaphysical, transcended the geometrickal plane and gone into a new realm, the realm of Algebra. This quantity mv^2 is scrupulously conserved by Nature, and its conservation may in fact be considered a law of the universe—but it is outside Geometry, and excluded from the dome that Newton has built, it is another contingent, non-geometrickal truth, one of many that have been discovered, or will be, by Natural Philosophers. Shall we then say, like Newton, that all such truths are made arbitrarily by God? Shall we seek such truths in the occult? For if God has laid these rules down arbitrarily, then they are occult by nature.

To me this notion is offensive; it seems to cast God in the rôle of a capricious despot who desires to hide the truth from us. In some things, such as the Pythagorean Theorem, God may not have had any choice when He created the world. In others, such as the inverse square law of gravity, He may have had choices; but in such cases, I like to believe he would have chosen wisely and according to some coherent plan that our minds—insofar as they are in God's image—are capable of understanding.

Unlike the Alchemists, who see angels, demons, miracles, and divine essences everywhere, I recognize nothing in the world but bodies and minds. And nothing in bodies but certain observable quantities such as magnitude, figure, situation, and changes in these. Everything else is merely said, not understood; it is sounds without meaning. Nor can anything in the world be understood clearly unless it is reduced to these. Unless physical things can be explained by mechanical laws, God cannot, even if He chooses, reveal and explain nature to us.

I am likely to spend the rest of my life explaining these ideas to those who will listen, and defending them from those who won't, and anything you hear from me henceforth should probably be viewed in that light, Daniel. If the Royal Society seems inclined to burn me in effigy, please try to explain to them that I am trying to extend the work that Newton has done, not to tear it down.

Leibniz

P.S. I know the woman Eliza (de la Zeur, now) whom you mentioned in your most recent letter. She seems to be attracted to Natural Philosophers. It is a strange trait in a woman, but who are we to complain?

"DR. WATERHOUSE."

"Sergeant Shaftoe."

"Your visitors have arrived—Mr. Bob Carver and Mr. Dick Gripp."

Daniel rose from his bed; he had never come awake so fast. "Please, I beg you, Sergeant, do not—" he began, but he stopped there, for it had occurred to him that perhaps Sergeant Shaftoe's mind was already made up, the deed was all but done, and that Daniel was merely groveling. He got to his feet and shuffled over the wooden floor towards Bob Shaftoe's face and his candle, which hung in darkness like a poorly resolved binary star: the face a dim reddish blob, the flame a burning white point. The blood dropped from Daniel's head and he tottered, but did not hesitate. He'd be nothing more than a bleating voice in the darkness until he entered the globe of light balanced on that flame; if Bob Shaftoe had thoughts of letting the murderers into this room, let him look full on Daniel's face first. The brilliance of the light was governed by an inverse square law, just like gravity.

Shaftoe's face finally came into focus. He looked a little sea-sick. "I'm not such a black-hearted bastard as'd admit a pair of hired killers to spit a helpless professor. There is only one man alive whom I hate enough to wish such an end on him."

"Thank you," Daniel said, drawing close enough now that he could feel the candle's faint warmth on his face.

Shaftoe noticed something, turned sideways to Daniel, and cleared his throat. This was not your delicate pretentious upper-class 'hem but an honest and legitimate bid to dislodge an actual phlegm-ball that had sprung into his gorge.

"You've noticed me pissing myself, haven't you?" Daniel said. "You imagine that it's your fault—that you put such a terror into me, just now, that I could not hold my urine. Well, you did have me going, it is true, but that's not why piss is running down my leg. I have the stone, Sergeant, and cannot make water at times of my own choosing, but rather I leak and seep like a keg that wants caulking."

Bob Shaftoe nodded and looked to have been somewhat relieved of his burden of guilt. "How long d'you have then?"

He asked the question so offhandedly that Daniel did not get it for a few moments. "Oh—you mean, *to live?*" The Sergeant nodded. "Pardon me, Sergeant Shaftoe, I forget that your profession has put you on such intimate terms with death that you speak of it as sea-captains speak of wind. How long have I? Perhaps a year."

"You could have it cut out."

"I have seen men cut for the stone, Sergeant, and I'll take death, thank you very much. I'll wager it is worse than anything you may have witnessed on a battlefield. No, I shall follow the example of my mentor, John Wilkins."

"Men have been cut for the stone, and lived, have they not?"

"Mr. Pepys was cut nigh on thirty years ago, and lives still."

"He walks? Talks? Makes water?"

"Indeed, Sergeant Shaftoe."

"Then, by your leave, Dr. Waterhouse, being cut for the stone is *not* worse than anything I have seen on battlefields."

"Do you know how the operation is performed, Sergeant? The incision is made through the perineum, which is that tender place between your scrotum and your anus—"

"If it comes down to swapping blood-curdling tales, Dr. Waterhouse, we shall be here until this candle has burnt down, and all to no purpose; and if you really intend to die of the stone, you oughtn't to be wasting that much time."

"There is nothing to do, here, *but* waste time."

"That is where you are wrong, Dr. Waterhouse, for I have a lively sort of proposition to make you. We are going to help each other, you and I."

"You want money in exchange for keeping Jeffreys's murderers out of my chamber?"

"That's what I should want, were I a base, craven toad," Bob Shaftoe said. "And if you keep mistaking me for that sort, why, perhaps I *shall* let Bob and Dick in here."

"Please forgive me, Sergeant. You are right in being angry with me. It is only that I cannot imagine what sort of transaction you and I could . . ."

"Did you see that fellow being whipped, just before sundown? He would've been visible to you out in the dry-moat, through yonder arrow-slit."

Daniel remembered it well enough. Three soldiers had gone out, carrying their pikes, and lashed them together close to their points, and spread their butts apart to form a tripod. A man had been led out shirtless, his hands tied together in front of him, and the rope had then been thrown over the lashing where the pikes were joined, and drawn tight so that his arms were stretched out above his head. Finally his ankles had been spread apart and lashed fast to the pikes to either side of him, rendering him perfectly immobile, and then a large man had come out with a whip, and used it. All in all it was a common rite around military camps, and went a long way towards explaining why people of means tried to live as far away from barracks as possible.

"I did not observe it closely," Daniel said, "I am familiar with the general procedure."

"You might've watched more carefully had you known that the man being whipped calls himself Mr. Dick Gripp."

Daniel was at a loss for words.

"They came for you last night," said Bob Shaftoe. "I had them clapped into separate cells while I decided what to do with 'em. Talked to 'em separately, and all they gave me was a deal of hot talk. Now. Some men are entitled to talk that way, they have been ennobled, in a sense, by their deeds and the things they have lived through. I did not think that Bob Carver and Dick Gripp were men of that kind. Others may be suffered to talk that way simply because they entertain the rest of us. I once had a brother who was like that. But not Bob and Dick. Unfortunately I am not a magistrate and have no power to throw men in prison, compel them to answer questions, *et cetera*. On the other hand, I am a sergeant, and have the power to recruit men into the King's service. As Bob and Dick were clearly idle fellows, I recruited them into the King's Own Black Torrent Guards on the spot. In the next instant, I perceived that I'd made a mistake, for these two were discipline problems, and wanted chastisement. Using the oldest trick in the book, I had Dick—who struck me as the better man—whipped directly in front of Bob Carver's cell window. Now Dick is a strong bloke, he is unbowed, and I may keep him in the regiment. But Bob feels about *his* chastisement—which is scheduled for dawn—the same way you feel about being cut for the stone. So an hour ago he woke up his guards, and they woke me, and I went and had a chat with Mr. Carver."

"Sergeant, you are so industrious that I almost cannot follow everything you are about."

"He told me that Jeffreys personally ordered him and Mr. Gripp to cut your throat. That they were to do it slow-like, and that they were to explain to you, while you lay dying, that it had been done by Jeffreys."

"It is what I expected," Daniel said, "and yet to hear it set out in plain words leaves me dizzy."

"Then I shall wait for you to get your wits back. More to the point, I shall wait for you to become angry. Forgive me for presuming to instruct a fellow of your erudition, but at a moment like this, you are supposed to be angry."

"It is a very odd thing about Jeffreys that he can treat people abominably and never make them angry. He influences his victims' minds strangely, like a glass rod bending a stream of water, so that we feel we deserve it."

"You have known him a long time."

"I have."

"Let's kill him."

"I beg your pardon?"

"Slay, murder. Let us bring about his death, so he won't plague you any more."

Daniel was shocked. "It is an extremely fanciful idea—"

"Not in the least. And there is something in your tone of voice that tells me you like it."

"Why do you say 'we'? You have no part in my problems."

"You are high up in the Royal Society."

"Yes."

"You know many Alchemists."

"I wish I could deny it."

"You know my lord Upnor."

"I do. I've known him as long as I've known Jeffreys."

"Upnor owns my lady love."

"I beg your pardon—did you say he *owns* her?"

"Yes—Jeffreys sold her to him during the Bloody Assizes."

"Taunton—your love is one of the Taunton schoolgirls!"

"Just so."

Daniel was fascinated. "You are proposing some sort of pact."

"You and I'll rid the world of Jeffreys and Upnor. I'll have my Abigail and you'll live your last year, or whatever time God affords you, in peace."

"I do not mean to quail and fret, Sergeant—"

"Go ahead! My men do it all the time."

"—but may I remind you that Jeffreys is the Lord Chancellor of the Realm?"

"Not for long," Shaftoe answered.

"How do you know?"

"He's as much as admitted it, by his actions! You were thrown in Tower why?"

"For acting as go-between to William of Orange."

"Why, that is treason—you should've been half-hanged, drawn, and quartered for it! But you were kept alive why?"

"Because I am a witness to the birth of the Prince, and as such, may be useful in attesting to the legitimacy of the next King."

"If Jeffreys has now decided to kill you, what does that signify then?"

"That he is giving up on the King—my God, on the entire *dynasty*—and getting ready to flee. Yes, I understand your reasoning now, thank you for being so patient with me."

"Mind you, I'm not asking you to take up arms, or do anything else that ill suits you."

"Some would take offense at that, Sergeant, but—"

"E'en though my chief grievance may lie with Upnor, the first cause of it was Jeffreys, and I would not hesitate to swing my spadroon, if he should chance to show me his neck."

"Save it for Upnor," Daniel said, after a brief pause to make up his mind. In truth, he'd long since made it up; but he wanted to put on a show of thinking about it, so that Bob Shaftoe would not view him as a man who took such things lightly.

"You're with me, then."

"Not so much that *I* am with *you* as that *we* are with most of *England,* and England with us. You speak of putting Jeffreys to death with the strength of your right arm. Yet I tell you that if we must rely on your arm, strong as it is, we would fail. But if, as I believe, England is with us, why, then we need do no more than find him and say in a clear voice, 'This fellow here is my lord Jeffreys,' and his death will follow as if by natural law, like a ball rolling down a ramp. This is what I mean when I speak of revolution."

"Is that a French way of saying 'rebellion'?"

"No, rebellion is what the Duke of Monmouth did, it is a petty disturbance, an aberration, predestined to fail. Revolution is like the wheeling of stars round the pole. It is driven by unseen powers, it is inexorable, it moves all things at once, and men of discrimination may understand it, predict it, benefit from it."

"Then I'd best go find a man of discrimination," muttered Bob Shaftoe, "and stop wasting the night with a hapless wretch."

"I simply have not understood, until now, how *I* might benefit from the revolution. I have done all for England, naught for myself, and I have lacked any organizing principle by which to shape my plans. Never would I have dared to imagine I might strike Jeffreys down!"

"As a mudlark, Vagabond soldier, I am always at your service, to be a bringer of base, murderous thoughts," said Bob Shaftoe.

Daniel had receded to the outer fringes of the light and worried a candle out of a bottle on his writing-table. He hustled back and lit it from Bob's candle.

Bob remarked, "I've seen lords die on battlefields—not as often as I'd prefer, mind you—but enough to know it's not like in paintings."

"Paintings?"

"You know, where Victory comes down on a sunbeam with her tits hanging out of her frock, waving a laurel for said dying lord's brow, and the Virgin Mary slides down on another to—"

"Oh, yes. *Those* paintings. Yes, I believe what you say." Daniel had been working his way along the curving wall of the Tower, holding the candle close to the stone, so that its glancing light would deepen the scratchings made there by prisoners over the centuries. He stopped before a new one, a half-finished complex of arcs and rays that cut through older graffiti.

"I do not think I shall finish this proof," he announced, after gazing at it for a few moments.

"We'll not leave tonight. You shall likely have a week—maybe more. So there's no cause for breaking off work on whatever that is."

"It is an ancient thing that used to make sense, but now it has been turned upside-down, and seems only a queer, jumbled bag of notions. Let it bide here with the other old things," Daniel said.

Château Juvisy
NOVEMBER 1688

From Monsieur Bonaventure Rossignol, Château Juvisy
To His Majesty Louis XIV, Versailles
21 November 1688
Sire,

It was my father's honor to serve your majesty and your majesty's father as cryptanalyst to the Court. Of the art of decipherment, he endeavoured to teach me all that he knew. Moved by a son's love for his father as well as by a subject's ardent desire to be of service to his King, I strove to learn as much as my lesser faculties would permit; and if, when my father died six years ago, he had imparted to me a tenth part of what he knew, why then it sufficed to make me more nearly fit to serve as your majesty's cryptanalyst than any man in Christendom; a measure, not of *my* eminence (for I cannot claim to possess any) but of my father's, and of the degraded condition of cryptography in the uncouth nations that surround France as barbarian hordes once hemmed in mighty Rome.

Along with some moiety of his knowledge, I have inherited the salary your beneficent majesty bestowed upon him, and the château that Le Nôtre built for him at Juvisy, which your majesty knows well, as you have more than once

RHINE
VALLEY

honored it with your presence, and graced it with your wit, as you journeyed to and from Fontainebleau. Many affairs of state have been discussed in the *petit salon* and the garden; for your father of blessed memory, and Cardinal Richelieu, also were known to ennoble this poor house with their presences during the days when my father, by deciphering the communications passing into and out of the fortifications of the Huguenots, was helping to suppress the rebellions of those heretics.

Than your majesty no monarch has been more keenly alive to the importance of cryptography. It is only to this acuity on your majesty's part, and not to any intrinsic merit of mine, that I attribute the honors and wealth that you have showered upon me. And it is only because of your majesty's oft-demonstrated interest in these affairs that I presume to pick up my quill and to write down a tale of cryptanalysis that is not without certain extraordinary features.

As your majesty knows, the incomparable château at Versailles is adorned by several ladies who are indefatigable writers of letters, notably my friend Madame de Sévigné; *la Palatine;* and Eliza, the Countess de la Zeur. There are many others, too; but we who have the honor of serving in your majesty's *cabinet noir* spend as much time reading the correspondence of these three as of all the other ladies of Versailles combined.

My narrative chiefly concerns the Countess de la Zeur. She writes frequently to M. le comte d'Avaux in the Hague, using the approved cypher to shield her correspondence from my Dutch counterparts. As well she carries on a steady flow of correspondence to certain Jews of Amsterdam, consisting predominantly of numbers and financial argot that, read, cannot be decyphered, and decyphered, cannot be understood, unless one is familiar with the workings of that city's commodities markets, as vulgar as they are complex. These letters are exceptionally pithy, and of no interest to anyone save Jews, Dutchmen, and other persons who are motivated by money. Her most voluminous letters by far go to the Hanoverian savant Leibniz, whose name is known to your majesty—he made a computing machine for Colbert some years ago, and now toils as an advisor to the Duke and Duchess of Hanover, whose exertions on behalf of united Protestantism have been the cause of so much displeasure to your majesty. Ostensibly the letters of the Countess de la Zeur to this Leibniz consist of interminable descriptions of the magnificence of Versailles and its inhabitants. The sheer volume and consistency of this correspondence have caused me to wonder whether it was not a channel of encrypted communications; but my poor efforts at finding any hidden patterns in her flowery words have been unavailing. Indeed, my suspicion of this woman is grounded, not on any flaw in her cypher—which, assuming it exists at all, is a very good one—but on what little understanding I may claim to possess of human nature. For during my occasional visits to Versailles I have sought this woman out, and engaged her in conversation, and found her to be highly intelligent, and conversant with the latest work of mathematicians and Natural Philosophers both foreign and domestic. And of course the brilliance and erudition of Leibniz is acknowledged by all. It is implausible to me that such a woman could devote so much time to writing, and such a man so much time to reading, about hair.

Perhaps two years ago, M. le comte d'Avaux, on one of his visits to your majesty's court, sought me out, and, knowing of my position in the *cabinet noir,* asked many pointed questions about the Countess's epistolary habits. From this it was plain enough that he shared some of my suspicions. Later he told me that he had witnessed with his own eyes an incident in which it was made obvious that this woman was an agent of the Prince of Orange. D'Avaux at this time mentioned a Swiss gentleman of the name of Fatio de Duilliers, and intimated that he and the Countess de la Zeur were in some way linked.

D'Avaux seemed confident that he knew enough to crush this woman. Instead of doing so outright, he had decided that he could better serve your majesty by pursuing a more complex and, by your majesty's leave, risky strategy. As is well known, she makes money for many of your majesty's vassals, including d'Avaux, by managing their investments. The price of liquidating her outright would be high; not a consideration that would ever confound your majesty's judgment, but telling among men of weak minds and light purses. Moreover, d'Avaux shared my suspicion that she was communicating over some encrypted channel with Sophie and, through Sophie, with William, and hoped that if I were to achieve a cryptological break of this channel the *cabinet noir* might thereafter read her despatches without her being aware of it; which would be altogether more beneficial to

France and pleasing to your majesty than locking the woman up in a nunnery and keeping her incommunicado to the end of her days, as she deserves.

There had been during the first part of this year a sort of flirtation between the Countess de la Zeur and *la Palatine*, which appeared to culminate in August when the Countess accepted an invitation from Madame to join her (and your majesty's brother) at St. Cloud. Everyone who knew of this assumed that it was a common, albeit Sapphic, love affair: an interpretation so obvious that it ought by its nature to have engendered more skepticism among those who pride themselves on their sophistication. But it was summer, the weather was warm, and no one paid it any heed. Not long after her arrival at St. Cloud, the Countess sent a letter to d'Avaux in the Hague, which has subsequently found its way back to my writing desk. Here it is.

St. Cloud
AUGUST 1688

Eliza, Countess de la Zeur, to d'Avaux
16 August 1688
Monsieur,

Summer has reached its pinnacle here and for those, such as Madame, who like to hunt wild animals, the best months lie in the future. But for those, such as Monsieur, who prefer to hunt (or be hunted by) highly cultivated humans, this is the very best time of the year. So Madame endures the heat, and sits with her lap-dogs and writes letters, while Monsieur's only complaint is that the torrid weather causes his makeup to run. St. Cloud is infested with young men, aficionados of fencing, who would give anything to sheathe their blades in his scabbard. To judge from the noises emanating from his bedchamber, his chief lover is the Chevalier de Lorraine. But when the Chevalier is spent, the Marquis d'Effiat is never far behind; and behind him (as it were) is a whole queue of handsome cavaliers. In other words, here as at Versailles, there is a strict pecking-order (though one must imagine a different sort of pecking), and so most of these young blades can never hope to be anything more than ornaments. Yet they are continually lustful like any other men. Since they cannot satiate themselves on Monsieur inside the château, they practice on one another in the gardens. One cannot go for a stroll or a ride without breaking into the middle of a tryst. And when these young men are interrupted, they do not slink away meekly, but (emboldened by the favor shown them by Monsieur) upbraid one in the most abusive way imaginable. Wherever I go, my nose detects the humour of lust wafted on every draught and breeze, for it is spilled about the place like wine-slops in a tavern.

Liselotte has been putting up with this for seventeen years now, ever since the day when she crossed over the Rhine, never to cross back. And so it's no wonder that she ventures out into society only rarely, and prefers the company of her dogs and her ink-well. Madame has been known to grow very attached to members of her household—she used to have a lady-in-waiting named Théobon who was a great comfort to her. But the lovers of Monsieur—who are supported by him, and who have nothing to do all day long but hatch plots— began to whisper vile rumors into Monsieur's ear, and caused him to send this Théobon away. Madame was so angry that she complained to the King himself. The King reprimanded Monsieur's lovers but balked at intervening in the household affairs of his own brother, and so Théobon has presumably ended up in a convent somewhere, and will never return.

From time to time they entertain guests here, and then, as you know, protocol dictates that everyone dress up in the sort of costume known as *en manteau*, which is even stiffer and less comfortable (if you can imagine it) than dressing *en grand habit* as is done at Versailles. As an ambassador, you see women dressed in that manner all the time, but as a man, you never see machinations that go on in ladies' private chambers for hours ahead of time, to make them look that way. Dressing *en manteau* is an engineering project at least as complicated as rigging a ship. Neither can even be contemplated without a large and well-trained crew. But Madame's household has been reduced to a skeleton crew by the ceaseless petty intrigues of the lovers of Monsieur. And in any case she has no patience with female vanities. She is old enough, and foreign enough, and intelligent enough, to understand that Fashion (which lesser women view as if it were Gravity) was merely an invention, a device. It was devised by Colbert as a way to neutralize those Frenchmen and Frenchwomen who, because of their wealth and independence, posed the greatest threat to the King. But Liselotte, who might have been formidable, has already been neutralized by marrying Monsieur and joining the royal family. The only thing that prevents her country from being annexed to France is a dispute as to whether she, or another descendant of the Winter Queen, should succeed her late brother.

At any rate, Liselotte refuses to play the game that Colbert devised. She has a wardrobe, of course, and it includes several costumes that are worthy of the names *grand habit* and *manteau*. But she has had them made up in a way that is unique. In Madame's wardrobe, all the layers of lingerie, corsetry, petticoats, and outer garments that normally go on one at a time are sewn together into a single construct, so heavy and stiff that it stands by itself, and slit up the back. When Monsieur throws a grand party, Liselotte plods naked into her closet and walks into one of these and stands for a few moments as a lady-in-waiting fastens it in the back with diverse buttons, hooks, and ties. From there she goes straight to the party, without so much as a glance in the mirror.

I will complete this little portrait of life at St. Cloud with a story about dogs. As I mentioned, *la Palatine,* like Artemis, is never far from her pack of dogs. Of course these are not swift hounds, but tiny lap-dogs that curl up on her feet in the winter to keep her toes warm. She has named them after people and places she remembers from her childhood in the Palatinate. They scurry about her apartments all day long, getting into absurd feuds and controversies, just like so many courtiers. Sometimes she herds them out onto the lawn and they run around in the sunshine interrupting the *amours* of Monsieur's hangers-on, and then the peace of these exquisite gardens is broken by the angry shouts of the lovers and the yelps of the dogs; the cavaliers, with their breeches down around their ankles, chase them out from their trysting-places, and Monsieur comes out onto his balcony in his dressing-gown and damns them all to hell and wonders aloud why God cursed him to marry Liselotte.

The King has a pair of hunting-dogs named Phobos and

Deimos who are very aptly named, for they have been fed on the King's own table-scraps and have grown enormous. The King has indulged them terribly and so they want discipline, and feel they are entitled to attack whatever strikes their fancy. Knowing how much Liselotte loves hunting and dogs, and knowing how lonely and isolated she is, the King has tried to interest her in these beasts—he wants Liselotte to think of Phobos and Deimos as her own pets and to look upon them with affection, as the King does, so that they can go hunting for large game in the east when the season comes around. So far this is nothing more than a proposal. Madame is more than a little ambivalent. Phobos and Deimos are too big and unruly to be kept at Versailles any more, and so the King prevailed upon his brother to keep them at St. Cloud, in a paddock where they can run around loose. The beasts have long since killed and eaten all of the rabbits who used to dwell in that enclosure, and now they devote all their energies to searching for weak places in the fence where they might tunnel out or jump over and go marauding in the territory beyond. Recently they broke through the southeast corner and got loose in the yard beyond and killed all the chickens. That hole has been repaired. As I write this I can see Phobos patrolling the northern fence-line, looking for a way to jump over into the neighboring property, which is owned by another nobleman who has never had good relations with my hosts. Meanwhile Deimos is working on an excavation under the eastern wall, hoping to tunnel through and run amok in the yard where Madame exercises her lapdogs. I have no idea which of them will succeed first.

Now I must lay down my pen, for some months ago I promised Madame that I would one day give her a demonstration of bareback riding, Qwghlmian-style, and now the time is finally at hand. I hope that my little description of life at St. Cloud has not struck you as overly vulgar, but since you, like any sophisticated man, are a student of the human condition, I thought you might be fascinated to learn what peasant-like noise and rancor prevail behind the supremely elegant façade of St. Cloud.

Eliza, Countess de la Zeur

Your majesty will already have perceived that Phobos and Deimos are metaphors for the armed might of France; their chicken-killing escapade is the recent campaign in which your majesty brought the rebellious Protestants of Savoy to heel; and the question of where they might attack next, a way of saying that the Countess could not guess whether your majesty intended to strike north into the Dutch Republic or east into the Palatinate. Just as obviously, these sentences were written as much for William of Orange—whose servants would read the letter before it reached d'Avaux—as for the recipient.

Perhaps less transparent is the reference to bareback riding. I would have assumed it signified some erotic practice, except that the Countess is never so vulgar in her letters. In time I came to understand that it was meant literally. As hard as it might be for your majesty to believe, I have it on the authority of several of Monsieur's friends that Madame and the Countess de la Zeur did indeed go riding that day, and moreover that the latter requested that no saddle be placed on her horse. They rode off into the park thus, escorted by two of Madame's young male cousins from Hanover. But when they returned, the Countess's horse was bare, not only of saddle, but of rider, too; for, as the story went, she had fallen off after the horse had been startled, and suffered an injury that made it impossible for her to ride back. This had occurred near the banks of the river. Fortunately they had been able to summon a passing boat, which had taken the injured Countess upriver to a nearby convent that is generously supported by Madame. There, or so the story went, the Countess would be tended to by the nuns until her bones had mended.

Needless to say, no one but the smallest child would believe such a story; everyone assumed the obvious, which is that the Countess had become pregnant and that her period of recuperation in the nunnery was to last only long enough for her to arrange an abortion, or to deliver the baby. I myself gave it no further thought until I received a communication from d'Avaux several weeks later. This was, of course, encyphered. I enclose the plaintext, shorn of pleasantries, formalities, and other impedimenta.

French Embassy, the Hague
17 SEPTEMBER 1688

From Jean Antoine de Mesmes, comte d'Avaux
French Embassy, the Hague
To Monsieur Bonaventure Rossignol
Château Juvisy, France
Monsieur Rossignol,

You and I have had occasion to speak of the Countess de la Zeur. I have known for some time that her true allegiance lay with the Prince of Orange. Until today she has been at pains to conceal this. Now she has at last run her true colors up the mast. Everyone believes she is in a nunnery near St. Cloud having a baby. But today, below the very battlements of the Binnenhof, she disembarked from a canal-boat that had just come down from Nijmegen. Most of the heretics who came pouring out of it had originated from much farther upstream, for they are people of the Palatinate who, knowing that an invasion was imminent, have lately fled from that place as rats are said to do from a house in the moments before an earthquake. To give you an idea of their quality, among them were at least two Princesses (Eleanor of Saxe-Eisenach and her daughter Wilhelmina Caroline of Brandenburg-Ansbach), as well as any number of other persons of rank; though as much could never have been guessed from their degraded and bedraggled appearance. Consequently the Countess de le Zeur—who was even more dishevelled than most—attracted less notice than is her wont. But I know that she was there, for my sources in the Binnenhof inform me that the Prince of Orange ordered a suite to be made available to her, for a stay of indefinite duration. Previously she has been coy about her dealings with the said Prince; today she lives in his house.

I shall have more to say on this later, but for now I should like to ask the rhetorical question of how this woman was able to get from St. Cloud to the Hague, via the Rhine, in one month, during the preparations for a war, without anyone's having noticed? That she was working as a spy for the Prince of Orange is too obvious to mention; but where did she go, and what is she now telling William in the Binnenhof?

> Yours in haste,
> d'Avaux

Rossignol to Louis XIV Continued
NOVEMBER 1688

Your majesty will already have understood how fascinated I was by this news from d'Avaux. The letter had reached me after a considerable delay, as, owing to the war, d'Avaux had been forced to show some ingenuity in finding a way to have it delivered to Juvisy. I knew that I could not expect to receive any more, and to attempt to respond in kind would have been a waste of paper. Accordingly, I resolved to travel in person, and *incognito*, to the Hague. For to be of service to your majesty is my last thought as I go to bed in the night-time and my first upon waking in the morning; and it was plain that where this matter was concerned I was useless so long as I remained at home.

Of my journey to the Hague, much could be written in a vulgar and sensational vein, if I felt that I could better serve your majesty by producing an entertainment. But it is all beside the point of this report. And as better men than I have sacrificed their lives in your service with no thought of fame, or of reward beyond a small share in the glory of *la France*, I do not think it is meet for me to relate my tale here; after all, what an Englishman (for example) might fancy to be a stirring and glorious adventure is, to a gentleman of France, altogether routine and unremarkable.

I arrived in the Hague on the 18th of October and reported to the French embassy, where M. le comte d'Avaux saw to it that what remained of my clothing was burned in the street; that the body of my manservant was given a Christian burial; that my horse was destroyed so that he would not infect the others; and that my pitchfork-wounds and torch-burns were tended to by a French barber-surgeon who dwells in that city. On the following day I began my investigation, which naturally was erected upon the solid foundation that had been laid by d'Avaux during the weeks since his letter to me. As it happened, it was on this very day—the 19th of October, *anno domini* 1688—that an unfortunate change in the wind made it possible for the Prince of Orange to set sail for England at the head of five hundred Dutch ships. As distressing as this event was for the small colony of French in the Hague, it militated to our advantage in that the heretics who engulfed us were so beside themselves (for to them, invading other countries is a new thing, and a tremendous adventure) that they paid me little heed as I went about my work.

My first task, as I have suggested, was to familiarize myself with all that d'Avaux had learned of the matter during the previous weeks. The Hofgebied, or diplomatic quarter of the Hague, may not contain as many servants and courtiers as its counterpart in France, but there are more than enough; those who are *venal,* d'Avaux has bought, and those who are *venereal,* he has compromised in one way or another, so that he may know practically anything he wishes to of what goes on in that neighborhood, provided only that he has the diligence to interview his sources, and the wit to combine their fragmentary accounts into a coherent story. Your majesty will in no way be surprised to learn that he had done so by the time of my arrival. D'Avaux imparted to me the following:

First, that the Countess de la Zeur, unlike all of the other refugees on the canal-ship, had not taken it all the way from Heidelberg. Rather, she had embarked at Nijmegen, filthy and exhausted, and accompanied by two young gentlemen, also much the worse for wear, whose accents marked them as men of the Rhineland.

This in itself told me much. It had already been obvious that on that August day at St. Cloud, Madame had made some arrangement to spirit the Countess aboard a boat on the Seine. By working its way upstream to Paris, such a vessel could take the left fork at Charenton and go up the Marne deep into the northeastern reaches of your majesty's realm, within a few days' overland journey of Madame's homeland. It is not the purpose of this letter to cast aspersions on the loyalty of your sister-in-law; I suspect that the Countess de la Zeur, so notorious for her cunning, had preyed upon Madame's natural and humane concern for her subjects across the Rhine, and somehow induced her to believe that it would be beneficial to despatch the Countess on a sightseeing expedition to that part of the world. Of course this would take the Countess into just that part of France where preparations for war would be most obvious to a foreign spy.

Your majesty during his innumerable glorious campaigns has devoted many hours to studying maps, and contemplating all matters of logistics, from grand strategy down to the smallest detail, and will recollect that there is no direct connection by water from the Marne to any of the rivers that flow down into the Low Countries. The Argonne Forest, however, nurses the headwaters, not only of the Marne, but also of the Meuse, which indeed passes to within a few miles of Nijmegen. And so, just as d'Avaux had already done before me, I settled upon the working hypothesis that after taking a boat from St. Cloud up the Marne, the Countess had disembarked in the vicinity of the Argonne—which as your majesty well knows was an active theatre of military operations during these weeks—and made some sort of overland journey that had eventually taken her to the Meuse, and via the Meuse to Nijmegen where we have our first report of her from d'Avaux's informants.

Second, all who saw her on the Nijmegen-Hague route agree that she had practically nothing with her. She had no luggage. Her personal effects, such as they were, were stored in the saddlebag of one of her German companions. Everything was soaked through, for in the days before her appearance at Nijmegen the weather had been rainy. During the voyage on the canal-ship, she and the two Germans emptied the saddlebags and spread out their contents on the deck to dry. At no time were any books, papers, or documents of any kind observed, and no quills or ink. In her hands she carried a small bag and an embroidery frame with a piece of crewel-work mounted on it. There was nothing else. All of this is confirmed by d'Avaux's informants in the Binnenhof. The servants who furnished the Countess's suite there insist that nothing came off the canal-boat save:

(Item) The dress on the Countess's back. Mildewed and creased from (one assumes) a lengthy journey in the bottom of a saddlebag, this was torn up for rags as soon as she peeled it off. Nothing was hidden beneath.

(Item) A set of boy's clothing approximately the Countess's size, badly worn and filthy.

(Item) The embroidery frame and crewel-work, which had been ruined by repeated soakings and dryings (the colors of the thread had run into the fabric).

(Item) Her handbag, which turned out to contain nothing but a scrap of soap, a comb, an assortment of rags, a sewing-kit, and a nearly empty coin-purse.

Of the items mentioned, all were removed or destroyed save the coins, the sewing-kit, and the embroidery project. The Countess showed a curiously strong attachment to the latter, mentioning to the servants that they were not to touch it, be it never so badly damaged, and even keeping it under her pillow when she slept, for fear that it might be taken away by mistake and used as a rag.

Third, after she had recuperated for a day, and been supplied with presentable clothing, she went to the forest-hut of the Prince of Orange that is out in the wilderness nearby, and met with him and his advisors on three consecutive days. Immediately thereafter the Prince withdrew his regiments from the south and set in motion his invasion of England. It is said that the Countess produced, as if by sorcery, a voluminous report filled with names, facts, figures, maps, and other details difficult to retain in the memory.

So much for d'Avaux's work. He had given me all that I could have asked for as a cryptologist. It remained only for me to apply Occam's Razor to the facts that d'Avaux had amassed. My conclusion was that the Countess had made her notes, not with ink on paper, but with needle and thread on a work of embroidery. The technique, though extraordinary, had certain advantages. A woman who is forever writing things down on paper makes herself extremely conspicuous, but no one pays any notice to a woman doing needle-work. If a person is suspected of being a spy, and their possessions searched, paper is the first thing an investigator looks for. Crewel-work will be ignored. Finally, paper-and-ink documents fare poorly in damp conditions, but a textile document would have to be unraveled thread by thread before its information was destroyed.

By the time of my arrival in the Hague, the Countess had vacated her chambers in the Binnenhof and moved across the Plein to the house of the heretic "philosopher" Christiaan Huygens, who is her friend. On the day of my arrival she departed for Amsterdam to pay a call on her business associates there. I paid a cat-burglar, who has done many such jobs for d'Avaux in the past, to enter the house of Huygens, find the embroidery, and bring it to me without disturbing anything else in the room. Three days later, after I had conducted an analysis detailed below, I arranged for the same thief to put the embroidery back just where he had found it. The Countess did not return from her sojourn to Amsterdam until several days afterwards.

It is a piece of coarsely woven linen, square, one Flemish ell on a side. She has left a margin all round the edges of about a hand's breadth. The area in the center, then, is a square perhaps eighteen inches on a side: suitable for an *opus pulvinarium* or cushion-cover. This area has been almost entirely covered in crewel-work. The style is called grospoint, a technique that is popular among English peasants, overseas colonists, and other rustics who amuse themselves sewing naïve designs upon the crude textiles they know how to produce. As it has been superseded, in France, by petitpoint, it may be unfamiliar to your majesty, and so I will permit myself the indulgence of a brief description. The fabric or matrix is always of a coarse weave, so that the warp and weft may be seen by the naked eye, forming a regular square grid à la Descartes. Each of the tiny squares in this grid is covered, during the course of the work, by a stitch in the shape of a letter *x*, forming a square of color that, seen from a distance, becomes one tiny element of the picture being fashioned. Pictures formed in this manner necessarily have a jagged-edged appearance, particularly where an effort has been made to approximate a curve; which explains why such pieces have been all but banished from Versailles and other places where taste and discrimination have vanquished sentimentality. In spite of which your majesty may easily envision the appearance of one of these minute *x*-shaped stitches when viewed closely: one leg running from northwest to southeast, as it were, and the other southwest to northeast.

The two legs cross in the center. One must lie over the other. Which lies on top is a simple matter of the order in which they were laid down. Some embroiderers are creatures of habit, always performing the stitches in the same sequence, so that one of the legs invariably lies atop the other. Others are not so regular. As I examined the Countess's work through a magnifying lens, I saw that she was one of the latter—which I found noteworthy, as she is in other respects a person of the most regular and disciplined habits. It occurred to me to wonder whether the orientations of the overlying legs might be a hidden vector of information.

The pitch of the canvas's weave was about twenty threads per inch. A quick calculation showed that the total number of threads along each side would be around 360, forming nearly 130,000 squares.

A single square by itself could only convey a scintilla of information, as it can only possess one of two possible states: either the northwest-southeast leg is on top, or the southwest-northeast. This might seem useless; as how can one write a message in an alphabet of only two letters?

Mirabile dictu, there is a way to do just that, which I had recently heard about because of the loose tongue of a gentleman who has already been mentioned: Fatio de Duilliers. This Fatio fled to England after the Continent became a hostile place for him, and befriended a prominent English Alchemist by the name of Newton. He has become a sort of Ganymede to Newton's Zeus, and follows him wherever he can; when they are perforce separated, he prates to anyone who will listen about his close relationship to the great man. I know this from Signore Vigani, an Alchemist who is at the same college with Newton and so is often forced to break bread with Fatio. Fatio is prone to irrational jealousy, and he endlessly schemes to damage the reputation of anyone he imagines may be a rival for Newton's affections. One such is a Dr. Waterhouse, who shared a room with Newton when they were boys, and for all I know buggered him; but the facts do not matter, only Fatio's imaginings. In the library of the Royal Society, Fatio recently happened upon Dr. Waterhouse sleeping over some papers on which he had been working out a calculation consisting entirely of ones and zeroes—a mathematical curiosity much studied by Leibniz. Dr. Waterhouse woke up before Fatio could get a closer look at what he had been doing; but as the document in question appeared to be a letter from abroad, he inferred that it might be some sort of cryptographic scheme. Not long after, he went to Cambridge with Newton and let this story drop at High Table so that all could know how clever he was, and that Waterhouse was certainly a dolt and probably a spy.

From my records of the *cabinet noir* I knew that the Countess de la Zeur had sent a letter to the Royal Society at the same time, and that she has had business contacts with the brother of Dr. Waterhouse. And I have already mentioned her suspiciously voluminous and inane correspondence with Leibniz. And so once again applying Occam's Razor I formulated the hypothesis that the Countess uses a cypher, probably invented by Leibniz, based upon binary arithmetic, which is to say consisting of ones and zeroes: an alphabet of two letters, perfectly suited to representation in cross-stitch embroidery, as I have explained.

I enlisted a clerk from the Embassy, who had keen eyesight, to go over the embroidery stitch by stitch, marking down a numeral 1 for each square in which the northwest-to-southeast leg lay on top, and a 0 otherwise. I then applied myself to the problem of breaking the cypher.

A series of binary digits can represent a number; for example, 01001 is equal to 9. Five binary digits can represent up to 32 different numbers, sufficient to encypher the entire Roman alphabet. My early efforts assumed that the Countess's cypher was of that sort; but alas, I found no intelligible message, and no patterns tending to give me hope that my fortunes would ever change.

Presently I departed from the Hague, taking the transcript of ones and zeroes with me, and bought passage on a small ship down the coast to Dunquerque. Most of the crew on this vessel were Flemish, but there were a few who looked different from the rest and who spoke to one another in a pithy, guttural tongue unlike any I had ever heard. I asked where they were from—for they were redoubtable seamen all—and they answered with no little pride that they were men of Qwghlm. At this moment I knew that Divine Providence had led me to this boat. I asked them many questions concerning their extraordinary language and their way of writing: a system of runes that is as primitive as an alphabet can possibly be and yet be

worthy of the name. It contains no vowels, and sixteen con-
sonants, several of which cannot be pronounced by anyone
who was not born on that rock.

As it happens, an alphabet of sixteen letters is perfectly
suited to translation into a binary cypher, for only four
binary digits—or four stitches of embroidery—are required
to represent a single letter. The Qwghlmian language is
almost unbelievably pithy—one of these people can say with
a few grunts, gags, and stutters what would take a Frenchman
several sentences—and little known outside of that God-
cursed place. Both of which made it perfectly suited to the
purposes of the Countess, who need communicate, in this
case, only with herself. In sum, the Qwghlmian language
need not be encyphered, for it is already a nearly perfect
cypher to begin with.

I tried the experiment of breaking down the transcribed
1s and os into groups of four and translating each group into
a number between 1 and 16, and shortly began to see patterns of the sort that give a cryptographer great confidence
that he is progressing rapidly to a solution. Upon my return
to Paris I was able to find in the *Bibliothèque du Roi* a scholarly
work about Qwghlmian runes, and thereby to translate the
list of numbers into that alphabet—some 30,000 runes in all.
A cursory comparison of the results against the word-list in
the back of this tome suggested that I was on the correct
path to a full solution; but to translate it was beyond my powers. I consulted with Father Édouard de Gex, who has lately
taken an interest in Qwghlm, hoping to convert it to the
True Faith and make it a thorn in the side of the heretics. He
referred me to Father Mxnghr of the Society of Jesus in
Dublin, who is a Qwghlmian born and bred, and known to
be absolutely loyal to your majesty as he travels frequently to
Qwghlm, at great risk, to baptize the people there. I sent him
the transcript and he replied, some weeks later, with a translation of the text into Latin that ran to almost forty thousand
words; which is to say that it requires more than one word in
Latin to convey what is signified by a single rune in
Qwghlmian.

This text is so pithy and fragmentary as to be nearly
unreadable, and makes use of many curious word substitu-
tions—"gun" written as "England stick" and so on. Much of
its bulk consists of tedious lists of names, regiments, places,
et cetera, which are of course staples of espionage, but of little

interest now that the war has begun and everything become
fluid. Some of it, however, is personal narrative that she
apparently set down in crewel when she was bored. This
material solves the riddle of how she got from St. Cloud to
Nijmegen. I have taken the liberty of translating it into a
more elevated style and redacting it into a coherent, if
episodic narrative, which is copied out below for your
majesty's pleasure. From place to place I have inserted a note
supplying additional information about the Countess's activ-
ities which I have gleaned from other sources in the meantime. At the end, I have attached a postscript as well as a note
from d'Avaux.

> If I had to read romances for long stretches at a
> time, I should find them tiresome; but I only read
> three or four pages in the mornings and evenings
> when I sit (by your leave) on my close-stool, and
> then it is neither fatiguing nor dull.
> —LISELOTTE IN A LETTER TO SOPHIE,
> 1 MAY 1704

JOURNAL ENTRY
17 AUGUST 1688

Dear reader,

There is no way for me to guess whether this scrap of linen will, on purpose or through some calamity, be destroyed; or be made into a cushion; or,
by some turn of events, fall under the scrutiny of some clever person and be
decyphered, years or centuries from now. Though the fabric is new, clean,
and dry as I sew these words into it, I cannot but expect that by the time anyone reads them, it will have become streaked with rain or tears, mottled and
mildewed from age and damp, perhaps stained with smoke or blood. In any
event I congratulate you, whoever you may be and in whatever era you may
live, for having been clever enough to read this.

Some would argue that a spy should not keep a written account of her
actions lest it fall into the wrong hands. I would answer that it is my duty to
find out detailed information, and supply it to my lord, and if I do not learn
more than I can recite from memory, then I have not been very industrious.

On 16 August 1688, I met Liselotte von der Pfalz, Elisabeth Charlotte,
duchesse d'Orleans, who is known to the French Court as Madame or La
Palatine, and to her loved ones in Germany as the Knight of the Rustling
Leaves, at the gate of a stable on her estate at St. Cloud on the Seine, just

downstream of Paris. She ordered her favorite hunting-horse brought out and saddled, while I went from stall to stall and selected a mount that would be suitable for riding bareback; that being the outward purpose of the expedition. Together we rode off into the woods that line the bank of the Seine for some miles in the neighborhood of the château. We were accompanied by two young men from Hanover. Liselotte maintains close relations with her family in that part of the world, and from time to time some nephew or cousin will be sent out to join her household for a time, and be "finished" in the society of Versailles. The personal stories of these boys are not devoid of interest, but, reader, they do not pertain to my narration, and so I will tell you only that they were German Protestant heterosexuals, which meant that they could be trusted within the environment of St. Cloud, if only because they were utterly isolated.

In a quiet backwater of the Seine, shielded from view by overhanging trees, a small flat-bottomed boat was waiting. I climbed aboard and burrowed under a tangle of fishing-nets. The boatman shoved off and poled the craft out into the main stream of the river, where we shortly made rendezvous with a larger vessel making its way upstream. I have been on it ever since. We have already passed up through the middle of Paris, keeping to the north side of the Île de la Cité. Just outside the city, at the confluence of the rivers Seine and Marne, we took the left fork, and began to travel up the latter.

JOURNAL ENTRY
20 AUGUST 1688

For several days we have been working our languid way up the Marne. Yesterday we passed through Meaux, and [as I believed] left it many miles behind us, but today we came again close enough to hear its church-bells. This is because of the preposterous looping of the river, which turns in on itself like the arguments of Father Édouard de Gex. This vessel is what they call a *chaland*, a long, narrow, cheaply made box with but a single square sail that is hoisted whenever the wind happens to come from astern. But most of the time the mast is used only as a hitching-place for tow-ropes by which the *chaland* is pulled against the current by animals on the banks.

My captain and protector is Monsieur LeBrun, who must live in mortal terror of Madame, for whenever I venture near the gunwale or do anything else the least bit dangerous he begins to sweat, and holds his head in his hands as if it were in danger of falling off. Mostly I sit on a keg of salt near the stern and watch France go by, and observe traffic on the river. I wear the clothes of a boy and keep my hair under my hat, which is sufficient to hide my sex from men on other boats and on the riverbank. If anyone hails me, I smile and say nothing, and after a few moments they falter and take me for an imbecile, perhaps a son of M. LeBrun who has been hit on the head. The lack of activity suits me, for I have been menstruating most of the time I've been on the chaland, and am in fact sitting on a pile of rags.

It is obvious that this countryside produces abundant fodder. In a few weeks' time the barley will be ripe and then it will be easy to march an army through here. If an invasion of the Palatinate is being planned, the armies will come from the north [for they are stationed along the Dutch border] and the food will come from here; so there is nothing for a spy to look for, except, perhaps, shipments of certain military stocks. The armies would carry many of their own supplies with them, but it would not be unreasonable to expect that certain items, such as gunpowder, and especially lead, might be shipped up the river from arsenals in the vicinity of Paris. For to move a ton of lead in wagons requires teams of oxen, and many more wagon-loads of fodder, but to move the same cargo in the bilge of a *chaland* is easy. So I peer at the *chalands* making their way upriver and wonder what is stored down in their holds. To outward appearances they are all carrying the same sort of cargo as the *chaland* of M. LeBrun, viz. salted fish, salt, wine, apples, and other goods that originated closer to where the Seine empties into the sea.

JOURNAL ENTRY
25 AUGUST 1688

Sitting still day after day has its advantages. I am trying to view my surroundings through the eye of a Natural Philosopher. A few days ago I was gazing at another *chaland* making its way up-stream about a quarter of a mile ahead of us. One of the boatmen needed to reach a lashing on the mast that was too high for him. So he gripped the rim of a large barrel that was standing upright on the deck, tipped it back towards himself, and rolled it over to where he wanted it, then climbed up onto its end. From the way he managed this huge object and from the sound that it made under his feet, I could tell that it must be empty. Nothing terribly unusual in and of itself, since empty barrels are commonly shipped from place to place. But it made me wonder whether there was any outward sign by which I could distinguish between a *chaland* loaded as M. LeBrun's is, and one that had a few tons of musket-balls in the bilge with empty barrels above to disguise the true nature of its cargo from spies?

Even from a distance it is possible to observe the sideways rocking of one of these *chalands* by watching the top of its mast——for being long, the mast magnifies the small movements of the hull, and being high, it can be seen from far off.

I borrowed a pair of wooden shoes from M. LeBrun and set both of them afloat in the stagnant water that has accumulated in the bilge. Into one of these, I placed an iron bar, which rested directly upon the sole of the shoe. Into the other, I packed an equal weight of salt, which had spilled out of a fractured barrel. Though the weights of the shoes' cargoes were equal, the distributions of those weights were not, for the salt was evenly distributed through the whole volume of the shoe, whereas the iron bar was concentrated in its "bilge." When I set the two shoes to rocking, I could easily observe that the one laden with iron rocked with a slower, more ponderous motion, because all of its weight was far from the axis of the movement.

After re-uniting M. LeBrun with his shoes I returned to my position on the deck of the *chaland*, this time carrying a watch that had been given to me by Monsieur Huygens. First I timed one hundred rockings of the *chaland* I was on, and then I began to make the same observation of other *chalands* on the river. Most of them rocked at approximately the same frequency as the one of M. LeBrun. But I noticed one or two that rocked very slowly. Naturally I then began to scrutinize these *chalands* more carefully, whensoever they came into view, and familiarized myself with their general appearance and their crews. Somewhat to my disappointment, the first one turned out to be laden with quarried stones. Of course, no effort had been made to conceal the nature of its cargo. But later I saw one that had been filled up with barrels.

M. LeBrun really does think I am an imbecile now, but it is of no concern as I shall not be with him for very much longer.

JOURNAL ENTRY
28 AUGUST 1688

I have now passed all the way across Champagne and arrived at St.-Dizier, where the Marne comes very near the frontier of Lorraine and then turns southwards. I need to go east and north, so here is where I disembark. The journey has been slow, but I have seen things I would have overlooked if it had been more stimulating, and to sit in the sun on a slow boat in quiet country has hardly been a bad thing. No matter how strongly I hold to my convictions, I feel my resolve weakening after a few weeks at Court. For the people there are so wealthy, powerful, attractive, and cocksure that after a while it is impossible not to feel their influence. At first it induces a deviation too subtle to detect, but eventually one falls into orbit around the Sun King.

The territory I have passed through is flat, and unlike western France, it is open, rather than being divided up into hedgerows and fences. Even without a map one can sense that a vast realm lies beyond to the north and east. The term "fat of the land" is almost literal here, for the grain-fields are ripening before my eyes, like heavy cream rising up out of the very soil. As one born in a cold stony place, I think it looks like Paradise. But if I view it through the eyes of a man, a man of power, I see that it demands to be invaded. It is spread thick with the fodder and fuel of war, and war is bound to come across it in one direction or the other; so best have it go away from you at a time of your choosing than wait for it to darken the horizon and come sweeping towards you. Anyone can see that France will ever be invaded across these fields until she extends her border to the natural barrier of the Rhine. No border embedded in such a landscape will endure.

Fortune has presented Louis with a choice: he can try to maintain his influence over England, which is a very uncertain endeavour and does not really add to the security of France, or he can march on the Rhine, take the Palatinate, and secure France against Germany forever. It seems obvious that this is the wiser course. But as a spy it is not my charge to advise Kings how they *ought* to rule, but to observe how they *do*.

St.-Dizier, where I am about to disembark, is a river-port of modest size, with some very ancient churches and Roman ruins. The dark forest Argonne rises up behind it, and somewhere through those woods runs the border separating France from Lorraine. A few leagues farther to the east lies the vale of the river Meuse, which runs north into the Spanish Netherlands, and then becomes convolved with the shifting frontiers that separate Spanish, Dutch, and German states.

Another ten leagues east of the Meuse lies the city of Nancy, which is on the river Moselle. That river likewise flows north, but it sweeps eastwards after skirting the Duchy of Luxembourg, and empties into the Rhine between Mainz and Cologne. Or at least that is what I recollect from gazing at the maps in the library at St. Cloud. I did not think it politic to take any of them with me!

Continuing east beyond Nancy toward the Rhine, then, the maps depicted twenty or thirty leagues of jumbled and confused territory: an archipelago of small isolated counties and bishoprics, crumbs of land that belonged to the Holy Roman Empire until the Thirty Years' War. Eventually one reaches Strasbourg, which is on the Rhine. Louis XIV seized it some years ago. In some sense this event created me, for the plague and chaos of Strasbourg drew Jack there, and later the prospects of a fine barley-harvest and its inevitable result——war——drew him to Vienna where he met me. I wonder if I will complete the circle by journeying as far as Strasbourg now. If so, I shall complete another circle at the same time, for it was from that city that Liselotte crossed into France seventeen years ago to marry Monsieur, never to return to her homeland.

JOURNAL ENTRY
30 AUGUST 1688

At St.-Dizier I changed back into the clothes of a gentlewoman and lodged at a convent. It is one of those convents where women of quality go to live out their lives after they've failed, or declined, to get married. In its ambience it is closer to a bordello than a nunnery. Many of the inmates are not even thirty years old, and never so lusty; when they cannot sneak men inside, they sneak out, and when they cannot sneak out, they practice on one another. Liselotte knew some of these girls when they were at Versailles and has continued to correspond with them. She sent letters ahead telling them that I was a sort of shirt-tail relative of hers, a member of her household, and that I was traveling to the Palatinate to pick up certain art-objects and family curios that Liselotte was supposed to have inherited upon the death of her brother, but which had been the subject of lengthy haggling and disputation with her half-siblings. Since it is inconceivable for a woman to undertake such a journey herself, I was to bide at the convent in St.-Dizier until my escort arrived: some minor nobleman of the Palatinate who would journey to this place with horses and a carriage to collect me, then convey me northeastwards across Lorraine, and the incomprehensible tangle of borders east of it, to Heidelberg. My identity and mission are false, but the escort is real——for needless to say, the people of the Palatinate are as eager to know their fate as their captive Queen, Liselotte.

As of this writing my escort has not arrived, and no word has been heard of him. I am anxious that they have been detained or even killed, but for now there is nothing for me to do but go to Mass in the morning, sleep in the afternoon, and carouse with the nuns in the night-time.

I was making polite conversation with the Mother Superior, a lovely woman of about threescore who turns a blind eye to the young women's comings and goings. She mentioned in passing that there are iron works nearby, and this caused me to doubt my own judgment concerning those slow-rolling *chalands*. Perhaps they were only carrying iron, and not lead. But later I went out on the town with some of the younger girls, and we passed within view of the river-front, where a *chaland* was being unloaded. Barrels were being rolled off and stacked along the quay, and heavy ox-carts were standing by waiting. I asked these girls if this was typical, but they affect complete ignorance of practical matters and were of no use at all.

Later I claimed I was tired, and went to my allotted cell as if to sleep. But instead I changed into my boy-clothes and sneaked out of the convent using one of the well-worn escape-routes used by nuns going to trysts in the town. This time I was able to get much closer to the quay, and to observe the *chaland* from between two of the barrels that had been taken from it earlier. And indeed I saw small but massive objects being lifted up out of its bilge and loaded onto those ox-carts. Overseeing the work was a man whose face I could not see, but of whom much could be guessed from his clothing. About his boots were certain nuances that I had begun to notice in the boots of Monsieur's lovers shortly before my departure from St. Cloud. His breeches——

No. By the time anyone reads these words, fashions will have changed, and so it would be a waste of time for me to enumerate the details——suffice it to say that everything he wore had to have been sewn in Paris within the last month.

My observations were cut short by the clumsiness of a few Vagabonds who had crept down to the quay hoping to pilfer something. One of them leaned against a barrel, assuming it was full and would support his weight, but being empty it tilted away from him and then, when he sprang back, came down with a hollow boom. Instantly the courtier whipped out his sword and pointed it at me, for he had spied me peering at him between barrels, and several men came running towards me. The Vagabonds took off at a run and I followed them, reasoning that they would know better than I how to disappear into this town. And indeed by vaulting over certain walls and crawling down certain gutters they very nearly disappeared from me, who was but a few paces behind them.

Eventually I followed them as far as a church-yard, where they had set up a little squat in a tangle of vines growing up the side of an ancient mausoleum. They made no effort either to welcome me or to chase me away, and so I hunkered down in the darkness a few paces off, and listened to them mutter. Much of their zargon was incomprehensible, but I could discern that there were four of them. Three seemed to be making excuses, as if resigned to whatever fate awaited them. But the fourth was frustrated, he had the energy to be critical of the others, and to desire some improvement in their situation. When this one got up and stepped aside for a piss, I rose and drew a little closer to him and said, "Meet me alone at the corner of the convent where the ivy grows," and then I darted away, not knowing whether he might try to seize me.

An hour later I was able to observe him from the parapet of the convent. I threw him a coin and told him that he would receive ten more of the same if he would follow the ox-carts, observe their movements, and report back to me in three days. He receded into the darkness without saying a word.

The next morning the Mother Superior delivered a letter to one of the girls, explaining that it had been left at the gate the night before. The recipient took one look at the seal and exclaimed, "Oh, it is from my dear cousin!" She opened it with a jerk and read it then and there, pronouncing half the words aloud, as she was barely literate. The import seemed to be that her cousin had passed through St.-Dizier the night before but very much regretted he'd not been able to stop in for a visit, as his errand was very pressing; however, he expected to be in the area for some time, and hoped that he would have the opportunity to see her soon.

When she pulled the letter open, the disc of wax sealing it shut popped off and rolled across the floor under a chair. As she was reading the letter I went over and picked it up. The coat of arms pressed into that seal was one I did not fully recognize, but certain elements were familiar to me from my time at Versailles——I could guess that he was related to a certain noble family of Gascony, well known for its military exploits. It seemed safe to assume he was the gentleman I'd spied on the quay the night before.

JOURNAL ENTRY
2 SEPTEMBER 1688

> CRYPTANALYST'S NOTE: *In the original, the section below contains considerable detail about the cargoes being unloaded from the* chalands *at St.-Dizier, and the coats of arms and insignias of persons that the Countess observed there, all of which were no doubt of greater interest to the Prince of Orange than they can be to your majesty. I have elided them.* ——*B.R.*

A slow three days at the convent of St.-Dizier have given me more than enough time to catch up on my embroidery! With any luck my Vagabond will come back tonight with news. If I have received no word from the Palatinate by tomorrow I shall have little choice but to strike out on my own, though I have no idea how to manage it.

I have tried to make what use I could of this fallow time, as I did on the *chaland*. During the days I have tried to make conversation with Eloise, the girl who received the letter. This has been difficult because she is not very intelligent and we have few interests in common. I let it be known that I have been at Versailles and St. Cloud recently. In time, word reached her of this, and she began to sit near me at meals, and to ask if I knew this or that person there, and what had become of so-and-so. So at last I have learned who she is, and who her well-dressed cousin is: the Chevalier d'Adour, who has devoted his last several years to currying favor with Maréchal Louvois, the King's commander-in-chief. He distinguished himself in the recent massacres of Protestants in the Piedmont and, in sum, is the sort who might be entrusted with a mission of some importance.

In the evenings I have tried to keep an eye on the river-front. Several more *chalands* have been unloaded there, in the same style as the first.

JOURNAL ENTRY
5 SEPTEMBER 1688

Suddenly so much happened I could not tend to my embroidery for a few days. I am catching up on it now, in a carriage on a bumpy road in the Argonne. This type of writing has more advantages to a peripatetic spy than I appreciated at first. It would be impossible for me to write with pen and ink here. But needlework I can just manage.

To say it quickly, my young Vagabond came back and earned his ten silver pieces by informing me that the heavy ox-carts carrying the cargo from the *chalands* were being driven east, out of France and into Lorraine, circumventing Toul and Nancy on forest tracks, and then continuing east to Alsace, which is France again [the Duchy of Lorraine being flanked by France to both east and west]. My Vagabond had been forced, for lack of time, to turn round and come back before he could follow the carts all the way to their destination, but it is obvious enough that they are bound towards the Rhine. He heard from a wanderer he met on the road that such carts were converging from more than one direction on the fortress of Haguenau, which lately had been a loud and smoky place. This man had fled the area because the troops had been press-ganging any idlers they could find, putting them to work chopping down trees——little ones for firewood and big ones for lumber. Even the shacks of the Vagabonds were being chopped up and burnt.

After hearing this news I did not sleep for the rest of the night. If my recollection of the maps was right, Haguenau is on a tributary of the Rhine, and is part of the *barrière de fer* that Vauban built to protect France from the Germans, Dutch, Spanish, and other foes. Supposing that I was right in thinking that the cargo was lead; then the meaning of what I'd just been told was that it was being melted down at Haguenau and made into musket- and cannonballs. This would explain the demand for firewood. But why did they also require lumber? I guessed it was to build barges that could carry the ammunition down to the Rhine. The current would then take them downstream into the Palatinate in a day or two.

Certain things I had noticed at Court now became imbued with new meanings. The Chevalier de Lorraine——lord of the lands over which the ox-carts passed en route to Haguenau——has long been the most senior of Monsieur's lovers, and the most cruel and implacable of Madame's tormentors. In theory he is a vassal of the Holy Roman Emperor, of which Lorraine is still a tributary state, but in practice he has become completely surrounded by France——one cannot enter or leave Lorraine without traveling over territory that is ruled from Versailles. This explains why he spends all his time in the French Court instead of Vienna.

Conventional wisdom has it that the duc d'Orleans was raised to be effeminate and passive so that he would never pose a threat to his older brother's kingship. One might suppose that the Chevalier de Lorraine, who routinely penetrates Monsieur, and who rules his affections, has thereby exploited a vulnerability in the ruling dynasty of France. That, again, is the conventional wisdom at Court. But now I was seeing it in a different light. One cannot penetrate without being encompassed, and the Chevalier de Lorraine is encompassed by Monsieur just as his territory has been encompassed by France. Louis invades and penetrates, his brother seduces and surrounds, they share a common will, they complement each other as brothers should. I see a homosexual who makes a sham marriage and spurns his wife for the love of a man. But Louis sees a brother who will fight a sham war in the Palatinate, supposedly to defend his wife's claim on that territory, while using his lover's fiefdom as a highway to transport matériel to the front.

When these three——Monsieur, Madame, and the Chevalier——were packed off to St. Cloud on short notice a few weeks ago, I assumed it was because the King had grown sick of their squabbling. But now I perceive that the King thinks in metaphors, and that he had to put them all together, like animals in a baiting-ring, to bring their conflict to a head, before undertaking his military campaign. Just as the domestic squabbles of Jupiter and Juno were thought by the Romans to be manifested in thunderstorms, so the squalid triangle of St. Cloud will be manifested as war in the Palatinate. Louis' empire, which now is interrupted in the Argonne, will be extended across and down the Rhine, as far as Mannheim and Heidelberg, and when domestic tranquillity is finally restored to St. Cloud, France will be two hundred miles wider, and the *barrière de fer* will run across burnt territory where German-speaking Protestants used to dwell.

All of this came together in my head in an instant, but then I lay awake until dawn fretting over what I should do. Weeks before, I had made up a little metaphor of my own, concerning two dogs named Phobos and Deimos, and put it in a letter to d'Avaux in the hopes that the Prince of Orange's spies would read it, and understand its message. At the time I'd thought myself very clever. But now my metaphor seemed childish and inane compared to that of Louis. Worse, its message was ambiguous——for its entire point was that I could not be sure, yet, whether Louvois intended to attack northwards into the Dutch Republic, or draw back, wheel round to the east, and launch himself across the Rhine. Now I felt sure I knew the answer, and needed to get word to the Prince of Orange. But I was stuck in a convent in St.-Dizier and had nothing to base my report on, save Vagabond hearsay, as well as a conviction in my own mind that I had understood the mentality of the King. And even this might evaporate like dew in a few hours, as the fears of the night-time so often do in the morning.

I was on the verge of becoming a Vagabond myself, and striking out on the eastern road, when a spattered and dusty carriage pulled up in front of the convent, just before morning Mass, and a gentleman knocked on the door and asked for me under the false name I'd adopted.

That gentleman and I were on our way as soon as his team could be fed and watered. He is Dr. Ernst von Pfung, a long-suffering gentleman scholar of Heidelberg. When he was a boy, his homeland was occupied and ravaged by the Emperor's armies; at the end of the Thirty Years' War, when the Palatinate was handed over to the Winter Queen in the peace settlement, his family helped them establish their royal household in what remained of Heidelberg Castle. So he has known Sophie and her siblings for a long time. He got all of his education, including a doctorate of jurisprudence, at Heidelberg. He served as an advisor to Charles Louis [the brother of Sophie, and father of Liselotte] when he was Elector Palatine, and later tried to exert some sort of steadying influence on Liselotte's elder brother Charles when he succeeded to the Electoral throne. But this Charles was daft, and only wanted to conduct mock-sieges at his Rhine castles, using rabble like Jack as his "soldiers." At one of these, he caught a fever and died, precipitating the succession dispute on which the King of France now hopes to capitalize.

Dr. von Pfung, whose earliest and worst memories are of Catholic armies burning, raping, and pillaging his homeland, is beside himself with worry that the same thing is about to happen all over again, this time with French instead of Imperial troops. The events of the last few days have done nothing to reassure him.

Between Heidelberg and the Duchy of Luxembourg, the Holy Roman Empire forms a hundred-mile-wide salient that protrudes southwards into France, almost as far as the River Moselle. It is called the Saarland and Dr. von Pfung, as a petty noble of the Empire, is accustomed to being able to travel across it freely and safely. As it gets closer to Lorraine, this territory becomes fragmented into tiny principalities. By threading his way between them Dr. von Pfung had intended to make safe passage to Lorraine, which is technically part of the Empire. A brief transit across Lorraine would have brought him across the French border very close to St.-Dizier.

Fortunately Dr. von Pfung has the wisdom and foresight one would expect in a man of his maturity and erudition. He had not simply assumed that his plan would work out, but had sent riders out a few days in advance to scout the territory. When they had not returned, he had set out anyway, hoping for the best; but very shortly he had met one of them on the road, returning with gloomy tidings. Certain obstacles had been discovered, of a complicated nature that Dr. von Pfung declined to explain. He had ordered a volte-face and ridden south down the east bank of the Rhine as far as the city of Strasbourg, where he had crossed over into Alsace, and from there he made his way as fast as he could. As a gentleman he is entitled to bear arms, and he has not been slow to take advantage of that right, for in addition to the rapier on his hip he has a pair of pistols and a musket inside the carriage.

We are accompanied by two out-riders: young gentlemen similarly armed. At every inn and river-crossing they have had to force their way through by bluff and bluster, and the strain is showing on Dr. von Pfung's face; after we left the precincts of St.-Dizier he very courteously excused himself, removed his wig to reveal a bald pate fringed with gray, leaned back next to an open window, and rested his eyes for a quarter of an hour.

The journey has left him *suspecting* much but *knowing* nothing, which puts him in the same predicament as I. When he had revived, I put a suggestion to him: "I hope you will not think me forward, Doctor, but it seems to me that vast consequences balance on the intelligence that we collect, or fail to, in the next days. You and I have each used all the craft and wit that we could muster, and only skirted the matter. Could it be that we must now relax our grip on Subtlety, and fling our arms around Courage, and strike for the heart of this thing?"

Contrary to what I had expected, these words eased and softened the face of Dr. von Pfung. He smiled, revealing a finely carven set of teeth, and nodded once, in a sort of bow. "I had already resolved to gamble my life on it," he admitted. "If I have seemed nervous or distracted to you, it is because I could not see my way clear to risking *yours* as well. And it makes me uneasy still, for you have much more life ahead of you than I do. But——"

"Say no more, we must not waste our energies on this sort of idle talk," I said. "It is decided——we'll roll the dice. What of your escorts?"

"Those young men are officers of a cavalry regiment——probably the first to be cut down when Louvois invades. They are men of honor."

"Your driver?"

"He has been in the service of my family his whole life and would never permit me to journey, or to die, alone."

"Then I propose we strike out for the Meuse, which ought to lie two or three days' hard riding east of here, on the far side of the forest Argonne."

As quickly as that, Dr. von Pfung rapped on the ceiling and instructed the driver to keep the sun on his right hand through most of the coming day. The driver naturally fell onto those eastward roads that seemed most heavily traveled, and so we ended up following the deep wheel-ruts that had been scored across the ground by the heavy ox-carts in preceding days.

We'd not been on the road for more than a few hours before we overtook a whole train of them, laboring up a long grade between the valleys of the Marne and the Ornain. By taking advantage of occasional wide places in the road, our driver was able to pass these carts one at a time. Peering out through the carriage windows, Dr. von Pfung and I could now plainly see that the carts were laden with pigs of a gray metal that might have been iron—— but as there was not a speck of rust on any of them, they must have been lead. Reader, I hope you will not think me silly and girlish if I confess that I was pleased and excited to see my suspicions borne out and my cleverness proven at last. But a glance at the face of Dr. von Pfung crushed any such emotions, for he looked like a man who has returned home in the night-time to discover flames and smoke billowing from the windows of his own house.

At the head of the train rode a French cavalry officer, looking as if he had just been condemned to serve a hundred-year stint in Purgatory. He made no effort to hail us and so we quickly left him and his column far to the rear. But our hopes of making up for lost time were quashed by the nature of the terrain. The Argonne is a broad ridge running from north to south, directly across our path, and in many places the ground drops away into deep rivercourses. Where the terrain is level, it is densely forested. So one has no choice but to follow the roads and to make use of the fords and bridges provided, be they never so congested and tumbledown.

But the sight of that miserable young officer had given me an idea. I asked Dr. von Pfung to close his eyes, and made him promise not to peek. This intimidated him to such a degree that he simply climbed down out of the carriage and walked alongside it for a while. I changed out of the drab habit of the nunnery and into a dress I had brought along. At Versailles this garment would scarce have been fit to mop the floor with. Here in the Argonne Forest, though, it rated as a significant Fire Hazard.

A few hours later, as we descended into the valley of a smaller river called the Ornain, we overtook another train of lead-bearing ox-carts, which was picking its way down the grade with an infinity of cursing, collisions, and splintering wood. Just as before, there was a young officer riding at the head. He looked every bit as miserable as the first one——until I popped out of the carriage window, and almost out of my dress. Once he got over his astonishment, he almost wept with gratitude. It made me happy to give this poor man such pleasure, and by nothing more than putting on a dress and opening a window. His mouth fell open in a way that reminded me of a fish; so I resolved to go fishing. "Excuse me, Monsieur, but can you tell me where I might find my uncle?"

At this his mouth opened a little wider, and his face reddened. "Mademoiselle, I am ever so sorry, but I do not know him."

"That is impossible! Every officer knows him!" I tried.

"Pardon me, Mademoiselle, but you have mistaken my meaning. No doubt, your uncle is a great man whose name I would recognize, and honor, if I heard it——but I am too foolish and ignorant to know who *you* are, and consequently I do not know *which* great man has the privilege of being your uncle."

"I thought you would know who I was!" I pouted. The officer looked extremely dismayed. "I am——" Then I turned around and slapped Dr. von Pfung lightly on the arm. "Stop it!" Then, to the officer: "My chaperone is an old fart who will not allow me to introduce myself."

"Indeed, Mademoiselle, for a young lady to introduce herself to a young man would be unpardonable."

"Then we shall have to conduct our conversation *incognito,* and say it never happened——as if it were a lovers' tryst," I said, leaning a bit farther out the window, and beckoning him to ride a little closer. I was afraid he would swoon and get himself wrapped around the axle of our carriage. He maintained his balance with some effort, though, and drew so close that I was able to reach out and steady myself by putting my hand on the pommel of his saber. In a lower voice I continued: "You have probably guessed that my uncle is a man of very high rank who has been sent out to these parts to execute the will of the King, in coming days."

The officer nodded.

"I was on my way up from Oyonnax, returning to Paris, when I learned he was in these parts, and I have decided to find his camp and pay him a surprise visit, and neither you nor my chaperone nor anyone else can prevent it! I just need to know where to find his headquarters."

"Mademoiselle, is your uncle the Chevalier d'Adour?"

I adopted the look of one who has been gagged with the handle of a spoon.

"Of course not, I didn't really think so . . . neither are you of the House of Lorraine, I gather, or you would not need directions . . . is it Étienne d'Arcachon? No, forgive me, he has no siblings and could not have a niece. But I see from the softening of your beautiful face, Mademoiselle, that I am drawing nearer the truth. The only one in these parts who is above the young Arcachon in rank is the Maréchal de Louvois himself. And I do not know whether he has yet come south from the Dutch front . . . but when he does, you may look for him along the banks of the Meuse. Provided, that if you ask for him there, and learn that he has already disembarked, you will have to follow his track eastwards into the Saarland."

That conversation occurred the day before yesterday, and we have done nothing since then but toil eastwards through the woods. It has had the air of a funeral procession, for as soon as Dr. von Pfung heard the name of Louvois, all doubt vanished that the Palatinate was to be invaded. But the officer who uttered that name might have been guessing, or passing on a baseless rumor, or telling me what he thought I wanted to hear. We must see this thing through and view incontrovertible evidence with our own eyes.

As I write this we are descending another long tedious grade into what must be the valley of the Meuse. From here that river flows up through the Ardennes and across the Spanish Netherlands into the territory along the Dutch border where the best regiments of the French Army have long been encamped to menace William's flank and pin down the Dutch Army.

CRYPTANALYST'S NOTE: *At this point the account becomes badly disjointed. The countess blundered into the midst of your majesty's army and had an adventure, which she did not have the leisure to write*

down. Later, as she was fleeing north in the direction of Nijmegen, she
made a few cryptic notes as to what had happened. These are intermin-
gled with more lengthy espionage reports listing the regiments and officers
she observed moving south to join your majesty's forces along the Rhine. I
have been able to reconstruct the Countess's actions, and thereby to make
some sense of her notes, by interviewing several of the persons who saw her
in the French camp. The narrative that follows is incomparably more dis-
cursive than what appears in her needlework but I believe that it is accu-
rate, and I hope that it will be more informative, and therefore more
pleasing, to your majesty than the original. At the same time, I have
removed all of the Countess's tedious lists of battalions, et cetera.

—*B.R.*

JOURNAL ENTRY
7 SEPTEMBER 1688

I am riding north post-haste and can only jot down a few words during pauses
to change horses. The carriage is lost. The driver and Dr. von Pfung are dead.
I am traveling with the two cavalrymen from Heidelberg. As I write these
words we are in a village beside the Meuse, near Verdun I believe. Now I'm
told we must ride again.

It is later, and I think we are near where France, the Duchy of Luxembourg, and the Spanish Netherlands come together. We have had to strike up
away from the Meuse and into the forest. Between here and Liège, which lies
some hundred miles to the north, the river does not run in a direct line, but
makes a lengthy excursion to westward, running for much of the way through
French lands. This makes it perfectly suited to serve as a conduit for French
military traffic from the north, but bad for us. Instead we shall attempt to
traverse the Ardennes [as these woods are called] northwards.

JOURNAL ENTRY
8 SEPTEMBER 1688

Catching our breath and rubbing our saddle-sores along a riverbank while
Hans looks for a ford. Will try to explain as I go along.

When we at last reached the Meuse, three days ago [had to count on my
fingers, as it seems nearer three weeks!], we immediately saw the evidence we
had been looking for. Thousands of ancient trees felled, valley full of smoke,
landing-stages improvised on the riverbank. Vanguards of the regiments

from the Dutch front had come upriver, made rendezvous with officers sent out from Versailles, and begun preparations to receive the regiments themselves.

For many hours Dr. von Pfung did not say a word. When he did, only slurred meaningless sounds came from his mouth, and I understood that he had suffered a stroke.

I asked him if he wanted to turn back and he only shook his head no, pointed to me, and then pointed north.

Everything had fallen apart. Until that moment I had presumed that we were operating according to some coherent plan of Dr. von Pfung's, but now in retrospect I understood that we had been plunging into danger heedlessly, like a man carried into a battlefield by a wild horse. I could not think at all for a while. I am ashamed to report that because of this failure we blundered into the camp of a cavalry regiment. A captain rapped on the door of the carriage and demanded that we explain ourselves.

It was already obvious to them that most of our party were German-speaking, and it would not take long for them to understand that Dr. von Pfung and the others were of the Palatinate; this would mark us as enemy spies and lead to the worst imaginable consequences.

During my long journey up the Marne on the *chaland* I had had plenty of time to imagine bad outcomes, and had concocted and rehearsed several false stories to tell my captors in the event I should be caught spying. But looking into the face of that captain, I was no more able to tell tales than the stricken Dr. von Pfung. The problem lay in that this operation was on a much vaster scale than either Liselotte or I had imagined, and many more people of Court rank were involved; for all I knew, some Count or Marquis might be nearby, with whom I had dined or danced at Versailles, and who would recognize me the moment I got out of the carriage. To adopt some made-up name and elaborate some tale would amount to confessing that I was a spy.

So I told the truth. "Do not look to this man to make introductions, for he has suffered a stroke, and lost the faculty of speech," I said to the astonished captain. "I am Eliza, Countess de la Zeur, and I am here in the service of Elisabeth Charlotte, the Duchess of Orleans and rightful inheritor of the Palatinate. It is in her name you are about to invade that land. It is she whom my escorts serve, for they are Court officials of Heidelberg. And it is she who has sent me here, as her personal representative, to look into your operations and ensure that the right thing is done."

This bit of nonsense, "that the right thing is done," was a list of dead words I tacked on to the end of the sentence because I did not know what to say, and was losing my nerve. For even when I stood beneath the Emperor's palace in Vienna, waiting to feel the blade of a Janissary's scimitar biting into my neck, I had not felt so uncertain as I did there. But I think the very vagueness of my words had a great effect on this captain, for he stepped back from the window and bowed deeply, and proclaimed that he would send word of my arrival to his superiors without delay.

Hans has come back saying he has found a place where we may attempt to ford this river and so I will only narrate that in due course, word of our arrival was passed up the chain of command until it reached a man whose rank at Court was high enough that he could entertain me without violating any rules of precedence. That man turned out to be Étienne d'Arcachon.

JOURNAL ENTRY
10 SEPTEMBER 1688

They think we are somewhere around Bastogne. Have been unable to do needlework for some while as our day-to-day affairs have pressed in on us sorely. The Ardennes Forest is crowded with Vagabonds and highwaymen [and, some say, witches and goblins] at the best of times. To these have now been added a large number of deserters from the French regiments that are being moved southwards. They jump off the slow-moving barges and wade to the bank and infiltrate the forest. We have had to move carefully and to post watches all night long. I am making these notes on my watch. To sit by a crackling fire would be folly and so I am perched up in the fork of a tree, wrapped up in blankets, sewing by moonlight.

Men who have weathered terrible trials are wont to have dull and useless children to demonstrate their power, as rich Arabs grow their fingernails long. So with the duc d'Arcachon and his only legitimate son, Étienne. The Duke survived the bad dream of the Fronde Rebellion and built a navy for the King. Étienne has chosen a career in the Army; this is his notion of youthful rebellion.

It is said of some men that "he would cut off his right arm before doing thus-and-such." Of Étienne, it used to be said that he would sacrifice a limb before violating the smallest rule of etiquette. But now people say, rather, that he actually *did* cut off his right arm out of politeness, for several years ago something happened at a party to that general effect——accounts vary, for I get the impression it was in some way disgraceful to his family. At any rate the details are unknown to me, but the tale rings true. He has become a great patron of woodcarvers and silversmiths, whom he pays to make artificial hands for him. Some of them are shockingly lifelike. The hand he extended to help me down out of the carriage was carved of ivory with fingernails fashioned from mother-of-pearl. When we dined on roast grouse in his quarters, he had switched to a hand of carven ebony, permanently gripping a serrated

845

knife, which he used to cut his meat, though it looked as if it would have made an excellent weapon, too! And after dinner, when he undertook to seduce me, he wore a special hand carved out of jade, with an extremely oversized middle finger. That digit was, in fact, a perfect reproduction of a man's erect phallus. As such it was nothing I had not already seen in various private "art" collections in and around Versailles, for lords, and even ladies, love to have such things in their private chambers, as proof of their sophistication, and many of their rooms are veritable Shrines to the god Priapus. But I was caught unawares by a hidden feature of this hand: it must have been hollow, and stuffed with clockwork, for when Étienne d'Arcachon tripped a hidden lever, it suddenly came alive, and began to hum and buzz like a hornet in a bottle. Inside, it seemed, was a coil spring that had been tightly wound in advance.

I need hardly tell you, reader, that events of the past few days had left me rather tightly wound myself, and I can assure you that the tension was gone from my body long before it was gone from the spring.

You may despise me for having reveled in fleshly pleasure while Dr. von Pfung was laid out with a stroke, but to have been pent up in a stifling carriage with a dying man for all that time had left me with a ravening to partake of life. I closed my eyes at the moment of climax and fell back onto the bed, exhausting my lungs in a long cry, and feeling all tension drain from my body. Étienne executed some deft maneuver of which I was scarcely aware. When I opened my eyes, I found that the jade phallus had been withdrawn and replaced by a real one, that of Étienne d'Arcachon. Again, you may well doubt my judgment in allowing myself to be taken in this way. That is your prerogative. Indeed, to marry such a man would be a grievous error. But in looking for a lover, one could do worse than a man who is clean, extremely polite, and has a madly vibrating jade phallus for a right forefinger. The warmth of his trunk felt good against my thighs; it did not occur to me to object; before I could really consider my situation, I realized that he was already climaxing inside of me.

JOURNAL ENTRY
12 SEPTEMBER 1688

Still in the damnable Ardennes, creeping northwards, pausing from time to time to observe the movements of the French battalions. These woods cannot possibly go on much farther. At least we have grown accustomed to the territory now, and know how to make our way. But at times we seem to move no faster than mice chewing their way through wood.

When I woke up in the bed of Étienne d'Arcachon the next morning, he had, in typical fashion, already left; but somewhat less typically, he had written me a love-poem and left it on the bedside table.

> Some ladies boast of ancient pedigrees
> And prate about their ancestors a lot
> But cankers flourish on old family trees
> Whose mossy trunks do oft conceal rot.

> My lady's blood runs pure as mountain streams
> So I don't care if her high rank was bought
> Her beauty lends fresh vigor to my dreams
> Of children free of blemish and of blot.

His quarters was a little château on the east bank of the Meuse. Out the window I could see Belgian river-boats——variously leased, borrowed, bought, or commandeered——coming upstream, their decks crowded with French soldiers. I dressed and went downstairs to find Dr. von Pfung's carriage-driver waiting for me.

The night before, I had explained my friend's plight to Étienne d'Arcachon, who had made arrangements for his own personal physician to administer treatment. Having personally witnessed the violence inflicted upon no less a personage than the King of France himself by the Royal Physician, I had assented to this with some ambivalence. Indeed, Dr. von Pfung's driver now informed me that the poor man had been bled twice during the night and was now very weak. He had signalled his desire to return to the Palatinate without delay, in hopes that he might look upon Heidelberg Castle one last time before he went to his long home.

The driver and I both understood that this would be impossible. According to the tale I had told my host, we were there as forward observers representing Liselotte. If that were true, we should either stay with the main body, or retire westwards towards St. Cloud——never run ahead of the invasion force. Yet Dr. von Pfung wanted to do just that, whereas I needed to strike out for the north and inform the Prince of Orange that his southern flank was soon to be free of French troops. And so we devised a plan, which was that our little group would leave that day on the pretext of taking Dr. von Pfung back to the west, but that when conditions were right, the carriage would break eastwards towards Heidelberg while I would go north accompanied by the two cavalrymen [who have imposing names and titles but whom I now call by their Christian names, Hans and Joachim]. When eyebrows were raised about this later, as seemed more than likely, I would claim that the others had turned out to be Protestant spies, working for William of Orange, and that I had been borne along against my will.

The plan unfolded correctly at first; we crossed the Meuse again as if going back into the west, but then began to make our way northwards up the bank, fighting against an increasing stream of south-bound military traffic. For since the boats were coming up against the river's current, most of them were drawn by teams of animals on the banks.

After we had traveled north for about half a day we came to a ferry, where we resolved to part ways. I went into the carriage and kissed Dr. von Pfung and said some words to him——though all words, especially ones improvised in haste, seemed inadequate, and the doctor managed to say more with his eyes and his one good hand than I did with my entire faculties. I changed once again into a man's clothes, hoping to pass myself off as a page to Hans and Joachim, and mounted a pony we'd borrowed from the stables of Étienne d'Arcachon. After some haggling with the ferryman——who was loath to venture across through the regimental traffic——the carriage was driven onto the ferry, its wheels were chocked, the horses hobbled, and the short voyage across the Meuse began.

They had almost reached the eastern bank when they were hailed by a French officer on one of the south-bound vessels. He had perceived, through his spyglass, Dr. von Pfung's coat of arms painted on the door of the carriage, and recognized him as coming from the Palatinate.

Now, the driver had a letter from Étienne d'Arcachon giving him permission to travel *west*——but he had now been observed crossing the Meuse *eastwards*. His only hope was therefore to make a run for it. That is what he attempted to do when the ferry reached the east bank. The only available road ran parallel to the bank for some distance before turning away from the river into a village. He therefore had to drive along in full view of all the boats crowding the river, whose decks were thronged with French musketeers. Some of the boats were armed with swivel-guns as well. By this time a hue and cry had gone up among the boats, and there was plenty of time for them to load their guns as the carriage disembarked from the ferry. The officer had traded his spyglass for a saber, which he raised high, then brought down as a signal. Instantly, the French boats were completely obscured in clouds of powder-smoke. The valley of the Meuse was filled with flocks of birds that erupted from the trees, startled by the sound of the guns. The carriage was reduced to splinters, the horses torn apart, and the fates of the brave driver and his stricken passenger perfectly obvious.

I could have tarried on the spot and wept for a long time, but on this bank were several locals who had seen us arrive in the company of the carriage, and it would not be long before one of them sold that intelligence to the Frenchmen on the river. So we struck out for the north, beginning the journey that continues even as I write these words.

JOURNAL ENTRY
13 SEPTEMBER 1688

The peasants around here say that the lord of the manor is a Bishop. This gives me hope that we are now in the Bishopric of Liège, not terribly far from one of the outlying tendrils of the Dutch Republic. Hans and Joachim have been having a long discussion in German, which I understand but meagerly. One thinks he ought to strike out alone to the East, go to the Rhine, and then double back to the South and warn the Palatinate. The other fears it is too late; there is nothing they can do now for their homeland; it is better to seek revenge by throwing all of their energies behind the Protestant Defender.

Later. The dispute was resolved as follows: we shall ride north past French lines to Maestricht and take passage on a canal-boat down the river to Nijmegen, where the Meuse and the Rhine almost kiss each other. That is some hundred miles north of here, yet it may be a quicker way to reach the Rhine than to cut east cross-country through God knows what perils and complications. In Nijmegen, Hans and Joachim can get the latest news from passengers and boatmen who have lately come down the Rhine from Heidelberg and Mannheim.

It did not take long, once we left our camp near Liège, to pass out of the zone of French military control. We rode over an area of torn-up ground that, until a few days ago, was the permanent camp of a French regiment. Ahead of us are a few French companies left along the border as a façade. They stop and interrogate travelers trying to come in, but ignore those like us who are only trying to pass out towards Maestricht.

JOURNAL ENTRY
15 SEPTEMBER 1688

On a canal-boat bound from Maestricht to Nijmegen. Conditions not very comfortable, but at least we do not have to ride or walk any more. Am renewing my acquaintance with soap.

JOURNAL ENTRY
16 SEPTEMBER 1688

I am in a cabin of a canal-ship making its way west across the Dutch Republic. I am surrounded by slumbering Princesses.

The Germans have a fondness for faery-tales, or *Märchen* as they call them, that is strangely at odds with their orderly dispositions. Ranged in parallel with their tidy Christian world is the *Märchenwelt*, a pagan realm of romance, wonders, and magical beings. *Why* they believe in the *Märchenwelt* has ever been a mystery to me; but I am closer to understanding it today than I was yesterday. For yesterday we reached Nijmegen. We went direct to the bank of the Rhine and I began looking for a canal-boat bound in the direction of Rotterdam and the Hague. Hans and Joachim meanwhile canvassed travelers debarking from boats lately come from upstream. I had no sooner settled myself in a comfortable cabin on a Hague-bound canal-ship when Joachim found me; and he had in tow a pair of characters straight out of the *Märchenwelt*. They were not gnomes, dwarves, or witches, but Princesses: one full-grown [I believe she is not yet thirty] and one pint-sized [she has told me three different times that she is five years old]. True to form, the little one carries a doll that she insists is *also* a princess.

They do not look like princesses. The mother, whose name is Eleanor, has something of a regal bearing. But this was not obvious to me at first, for when they joined me, and Eleanor noticed a clean bed [mine] and saw that Caroline——for that is the daughter's name——was under my watch, she fell immediately into [my] bed, went to sleep, and did not awaken for some hours, by which time the boat was well underway. I spent much of that time chatting with little Caroline, who was at pains to let me know she was a princess; but as she made the same claim of the dirty lump of stuffed rags she bore around in her arms, I did not pay it much mind.

But Joachim insisted that the disheveled woman snoring under my blankets was genuine royalty. I was about to chide him for having been deluded by mountebanks, when I began to recollect the tales I had been told of the Winter Queen, who after being driven out of Bohemia by the Pope's legions, wandered about Europe as a Vagabond before finding safe haven at the Hague. And my time at Versailles taught me more than I wished to know about the desperate financial straits in which many nobles and royals live their whole lives. Was it really so unthinkable that three Princesses——mother, daughter, and doll——should be wandering about lost and hungry on the Nijmegen riverfront? For war had come to this part of the world, and war rends the veil that separates the everyday world from the *Märchenwelt*.

By the time Eleanor woke up, I had mended the doll, and I had been looking after little Caroline for long enough that I felt responsible for her, and would have been willing to snatch her away from Eleanor if the latter had proved, upon awakening, to be some sort of madwoman [this is by no means my usual response to small children, for at Versailles, playing my role as governess, I had been put in charge of many a little snot-nose whose names I have long since forgotten. But Caroline was bright, and interesting to talk to, and a welcome relief from the sorts of people I had been spending time with for the last several weeks].

When Eleanor had arisen, and washed, and eaten some of my provisions, she told a story that was wild but, by modern standards, plausible. She claims to be the daughter of the Duke of Saxe-Eisenach. She married the Margrave of Brandenburg-Ansbach. The daughter is properly called Princess Wilhelmina Caroline of Ansbach. But this Margrave died of smallpox a few years ago and his title passed to a son by an earlier wife, who had always considered Eleanor to be a sort of wicked stepmother [this being a *Märchen,* after all] and so cast her and little Caroline out of the *Schloß.* They drifted back to Eisenach, Eleanor's place of birth. This is a place on the edge of the Thüringer Wald, perhaps two hundred miles east of where we are now. Her position in the world at that time, a few years ago, was the reverse of mine: she had a lofty title, but no property at all. Whereas I had no titles other than Slave and Vagabond, but I did have some money. At any rate, she and Caroline were suffered to dwell in what sounds like a family hunting-lodge in the Thüringer Wald. But she does not seem to have been much more welcome in Eisenach than she had been at Ansbach following the death of her husband. And so, while spending part of each year at Eisenach, it has been her practice to roam about and pay extended visits to shirttail relatives all over northern Europe, moving from time to time lest she wear out her welcome in any one place.

Recently she paid a brief visit to Ansbach in an effort to patch things up with her hostile stepson. Ansbach is within striking distance of Mannheim on the Rhine, and so she and Caroline next went there to look in on some cousins who had shown them charity in the past. They arrived, naturally, at the worst possible moment, a few days ago, just as the French regiments were swarming over the Rhine on the barges built at Haguenau, and bombarding the defensive works. Someone there had the presence of mind to pack them on a boat full of well-heeled refugees, bound down the river. And so they passed quickly out of the area of danger, though they continued to hear cannon-fire for a day or more, echoing up the valley of the Rhine. They reached Nijmegen without incident, though the boat was so crowded with refugees——some of them with suppurating wounds——that she was unable to take more than the occasional catnap. When they debarked, Joachim——who is a Person of Quality in the Palatinate——recognized them as they stumbled down the gangplank, and brought them to me.

Now the current of the Rhine slowly flushes us, and a lot of other war-flotsam, downstream towards the sea. I have oft heard French and Germans alike speak disparagingly of the Netherlands, likening the country to a gutter that collects all the refuse and fœces of Christendom, but lacks the vigor to force it out to sea, so that it piles up in a bar around Rotterdam. It is a cruel and absurd way to talk about a noble and brave little country. Yet as I look on my condition, and on that of the Princesses, and review our recent travels [blundering about in dark and dangerous parts until we stumbled upon running water, then drifting downstream], I can recognize a kind of cruel truth in that slander.

We shall not, however, let ourselves be flushed out to sea. At Rotterdam we divert from the river's natural course and follow a canal to the Hague. There the Princesses can find refuge, just as did the Winter Queen at the end of her wanderings. And there I shall try to deliver a coherent report to the Prince of Orange. This bit of embroidery is ruined before it was finished, but it contains the information that William has been waiting for. When I have finished my report I may make it into a pillow. Everyone who sees it will wonder at my foolishness for keeping such a dirty, stained, faded thing around the house. But I will keep it in spite of them. It is an important thing to me now. When I started it, I only intended to use it to record details of French troop movements and the like. But as the weeks went on and I frequently found myself with plenty of time on my hands to tend to my needle-work, I began to record some of my thoughts and feelings about what was going on around me. Perhaps I did this out of boredom; but perhaps it was so that some part of me might live on, if I were killed or made a captive along the way. This might sound like a foolish thing to have done, but a woman who has no family and few friends is forever skirting the edges of a profound despair, which derives from the fear that she could vanish from the world and leave no trace she had ever existed; that the things she has done shall be of no account and the perceptions she has formed [as of Dr. von Pfung for example] shall be swallowed up like a cry in a dark woods. To write out a full confession and revelation of my doings, as I've done here, is not without danger; but if I did not do so I would be so drowned in melancholy that I would do nothing at all, in which event my life truly would be of no account. This way, at least, I am part of a story, like the ones Mummy used to tell me in the *banyolar* in Algiers, and like the ones that were told by Shahrazad, who prolonged her own life for a thousand and one nights by the telling of tales.

But given the nature of the cypher that I am using, chances are that you, reader, will never exist, and so I cannot see why I should continue running this needle through the dirty old cloth when I am so tired, and the rocking of the boat invites me to close my eyes.

Rossignol to Louis XIV Continued
NOVEMBER 1688

Your majesty will have been dismayed by the foregoing tale of treason and perfidy. If it were generally known, I fear it would do grave damage to the reputation of your majesty's sister-in-law the duchesse d'Orléans. She is said to be prostrate with grief, and ungrateful for all that your majesty's legions have done in order to secure her rights in the Palatinate. Out of a gentleman's respect for her rank, and humane compassion for her feelings, I have been as discreet as possible with this intelligence which could only bring her further suffering if it were known. I have shared the foregoing account only with your majesty. D'Avaux has importuned me for a copy, but I have deflected his many requests and will continue to do so unless your majesty instructs me to send the document to him.

In the weeks that I have spent in the decypherment of this document, Phobos and Deimos have been unleashed on the east bank of the Rhine. The lead that the Countess so assiduously followed to the banks of the Meuse has been conveyed in bulk to the Palatinate, and ended its long journey traveling at inconceivable velocities through the bodies and the buildings of heretics. Half the young blades of Court have quit Versailles to go hunting in Germany, and many of them write letters, which it is my duty to read. I am told that Heidelberg Castle burnt brilliantly for days, and that everyone is looking forward to repeating the experiment in Mannheim. Philippsburg, Mainz, Speier, Trier, Worms, and Oppenheim are scheduled for later in the year. As winter draws on, your majesty will be troubled to learn of all the brutality. You will draw your forces back, and give Louvois a firm scolding for having acted so excessively. Historians will record that the Sun King cannot be held responsible for all of the unpleasantness.

From your majesty's many excellent sources in England, your majesty will know that the Prince of Orange is now there, commanding an army made up not only of Dutchmen, but of the English and Scottish regiments that were stationed on Dutch soil by treaty; Huguenot scum who filtered up from France; mercenaries and freebooters from Scandinavia; and Prussians who've been lent to the cause by Sophie Charlotte— the daughter of the cursed Hanoverian bitch Sophie.

All of which only seems to prove that Europe is a chess-board. Even your majesty cannot gain (say) the Rhine without sacrificing (say) England. Likewise, whatever Sophie and William may gain from their ceaseless machinations they'll have to pay for in the end. And as for the Countess de la Zeur, why, the new King of England might make her Duchess of Qwghlm, but in return your majesty will no doubt see to it that her sacrifices are commensurate.

M. le comte d'Avaux has redoubled his surveillance of the Countess in the Hague. He has received assurances from the laundresses who work in the house of Huygens that she has not bled a single drop of menstrual blood in the nearly two months she's been there. She is pregnant with a bastard of Arcachon. She is therefore now a part of the family of France, of which your majesty is the patriarch. As it is become a family matter, I will refrain from any further meddling unless your majesty instructs me otherwise.

> I have the honour to be, your majesty's
> humble and obedient servant,
> Bonaventure Rossignol

Sheerness, England

11 DECEMBER 1688

Then the Kings countenance was changed, and his thoghts troubled him, so that the joyntes of his loines were loosed, and his knees smote one against the other.

—DANIEL 5:6

ON ANY OTHER DAY, DANIEL did not have a thing in common with anyone else at the Court of St. James. Indeed, that was the very reason he was allowed to bide there. Today, though, he had two things in common with them. One, that he had spent most of the preceding night, and most of this day, traipsing all over Kent trying to figure out where the King had got to. And two, that he stood in utmost need of a pint.

Finding himself alone on a boat-flecked mudflat, and happening on a tavern, he entered it. The only thing he sought in that place was that pint and maybe a banger. In additition to which, he found James (by the Grace of God King of England, Scotland, Ireland, and the occasional odd bit of France) Stuart being beaten up by a couple of drunken English fishermen. It was just the sort of grave indignity absolute monarchs tried at all costs to avoid. In normal times, procedures and safeguards were in place to prevent it. One could imagine one of the ancient Kings of England, say, your Sven Forkbeard, or your Ealhmund the Under-King of Kent, wandering into an inn somewhere and throwing a few punches. But barroom brawling had been pushed off the bottom of the list of Things Princes Should Know How to Do during the great Chivalry vogue of five centuries back. And it showed: King James II had a bloody nose. To be fair, though, he'd been having an epic one for weeks. As past generations sang of Richard Lionheart's duels against Saladin before Jerusalem, future ones would sing of James Stuart's nosebleed.

It was, in sum, not a scenario that had ever been contemplated by the authors of the etiquette-books that Daniel had perused when he'd gone into the Courtier line of work. He'd have known just how to address the King during a masque at the Banqueting House or a hunt in a royal game-park. But when it came to breaking up a royal bar-fight in a waterfront dive at the mouth of the Medway, he was at a loss, and could only order himself that pint, and consider his next move.

His Majesty was standing up to the treatment surprisingly well. Of course, he'd fought in battles on land and at sea; no one had ever accused him of being a ninehammer. And this altercation was really more of a cuffing and slapping about: not so much fight as improvised entertainment by and for men who got out to Punchinello shows only infrequently. This was a very old tavern, half sunk into the riverside muck, and the ceiling was so close to the floor that the fishermen scarcely had room to draw their fists back properly. There were flurries of jabs that failed to connect with any part of the King's body. The blows that did land were open-handed, roundhouse slaps. Daniel sensed that if the King would only stop flinching, say something funny, and buy a round for the house, everything would change. But if he were that sort of King he wouldn't have ended up here in the first place.

At any rate Daniel was immensely relieved that it was not a serious beating. Otherwise he would've been obliged to draw the sword hanging from his belt, which he had no idea how to use. King James II most certainly *would* know what to do with it, of course. As Daniel plunged his upper lip through the curtain of foam on his pint, he had a moment's phant'sy of unbelting the weapon and tossing it across the room to the sovereign, who'd snatch it from the air, whip it out, and commence slaying subjects. Then Daniel could perhaps embroider 'pon his deed by smashing a bit of crockery over someone's head—better yet, sustain an honorable wound or two. This would guarantee him a free, all-expenses paid, but strictly one-way trip to France, where he'd probably be rewarded with an English earldom that he'd never be able to visit, and get to lounge around in James's exile court all day.

This phant'sy did not last for very long. One of the King's attackers had felt something in His Majesty's coat-pocket and yanked it out: a crucifix. A moment of silence. Those here who were conscious enough to see the object, felt obliged to give it due reverence; either because it was an emblem of Our Lord's passion, or because it was made predominantly out of gold. Through the tavern's atmosphere, which had approximately the mass and consistency of aspic, the artifact gleamed attractively, and even cast off a halo. Descartes had abhorred the idea of a vacuum, and held that what we took to be empty space was really a plenum, a solidly packed ocean of particles, swirling and colliding, trading and trafficking in a fixed stock of movement that had been imparted to the universe at its creation by the Almighty. He must have come up with that idea in a tavern like this one; Daniel wasn't sure a pistol-ball would be able to dig a tunnel through this air from one side of the room to the other.

"What's this, then!?" the fellow holding up the crucifix wanted to know.

James II looked suddenly exasperated. "Why, it is a crucifix!"

Another blank moment passed. Daniel had completely let go of the idea of being an exiled earl at Versailles, and was now feeling uncomfortably rabble-like himself, and strongly tempted to go and take a poke at His Majesty—if only for the sake of Drake, who'd never have hesitated.

"Well, if you're *not* a bleeding Jesuit spy, then why're you bearing this bit o' idolatry about!?" demanded the fellow with the quick hands, shaking the crucifix just out of the King's reach. "Didjer *loot* it? Didjer steal this holy object from a burnin' church, didjer?"

They had no idea who he was. At this the scene made sense for the first time. Until then Daniel had wondered just *who* was suffering from syphilitic hallucinations around here!

James had surprised all London by galloping away from White-hall Palace after midnight. Someone had caught sight of him hurling the Great Seal of the Realm into the Thames, which was not a wholly usual thing for the Sovereign to do, and with that he'd pelted off into the night, east-bound, and no person of gentle or noble rank had seen him since, until the moment Daniel had blundered into this tavern in search of refreshment.

Mercifully, the urge to sprint over and take a swing at the royal gob had passed. A semi-comatose man, slumped on a bench against the wall, was eyeing Daniel in a way that was not entirely propitious. Daniel reflected that if it was considered meet and proper for a well-heeled stranger to be beaten up and robbed on the mere suspicion that he was a Jesuit, things might not go all that well for Daniel Waterhouse the Puritan.

He drained about half the pint and turned round in the middle of the tavern so that his cloak fell open, revealing the sword. The weapon's existence was noted, with professional interest, by the tavernkeeper, who didn't look directly at it; he was one of those blokes who used peripheral vision for everything. Give him a spyglass, he'd raise it to his ear, and see as much as Galileo. His nose had been broken at least twice and he'd endured a blowout fracture of the left eye-socket, which made it seem as if his face were a clay effigy squirting out between the fingers of a clenching fist. Daniel said to him, "Let your friends understand that if serious harm comes to that gentleman, there lives a witness who'll tell a tale to make a judge's wig uncurl."

And then Daniel stepped out onto a deal boardwalk that might've answered to the name of *verandah* or *pier,* depending on whence you looked at it. In theory boats of shallow draught might be poled up to it and made fast, in practice they'd been drawn up on the muck about a horseshoe-throw away from the crusty ankles of its pilings. The tracks of the boatmen were swollen wounds in the mudflat, and spatterings across the planks. Half a mile out, diverse ships were riding at anchor in the wide spot where the Medway exhausted into the Thames. It was low tide! James, the sea-hero, the Admiral who'd fought the Dutch, and occasionally beaten 'em, who'd made Isaac Newton's ears ring with the distant roar of his cannons, had galloped out from London at exactly the wrong moment. Like King Canute, he would have to wait for the tide. It was simply too awful. Exhausted from the ride, left with no choice but to kill a few hours, the King must've wandered into this tavern—and why not? Every place he'd ever entered into, people had served him on bended knee. But James, who did not drink and did not curse, who stuttered, who couldn't speak the English of fishermen, might as well have been in a Hindoo temple. He'd switched to a dark wig from the usual blond one, and it had been knocked from his head early in the scuffle, revealing a half-bald head, thin yellow-white hair in a Caesar cut, shellacked to his pocked pate by sweat and grease. Wigs enabled one to avert one's attention from the fact of the wearer's age. Daniel had seen an odd-looking chap, fifty-five years old, lost.

Daniel was beginning to feel he had more in common with this syphilitic Papist despot than with the people of Sheerness. He did not like where his feelings were taking him. So he had his feet take him elsewhere—to what passed for the high street of Sheerness, to an inn, where an uncommon number of well-dressed gentlemen were milling about, wringing their hands and kicking at the chickens. These men, Daniel included, had come out from London post-haste, only a few hours behind their fleeing King, on the presumption that if the Sovereign had left London, then they must all be missing something important by tarrying in the city. Wrong!

He went in and told the tale to Ailesbury, the Gentleman of the Bedchamber, then turned to leave; but practically ended up with spur-marks in his back, as every courtier wanted to be first on the spot. In the stable-yard a horse was brought out for Daniel. Climbing into the saddle, and ascending to the same plane as all the other equestrians, he noted diverse faces turned his way, none of them looking very patient. So without sharing in any of the sense of romantic drama that animated all of the others, he rode out into the street, and led them on a merry gallop back down to the river. To uninformed bystanders, it must have looked like a Cavalier hunting-party pursuing a Roundhead, which Daniel hoped was no prefiguring of events to follow.

When they reached the tavern, an astounding number of Persons of Quality packed themselves inside, and commenced making stentorian announcements. One might've expected drunks and ne'er-do-wells to flood out through windows and trap-doors, like mice fleeing when the lantern is lit, but not a soul left the building, even after it was made known that they were all in the Presence. There seemed, in other words, to be a general failure, among the waterfront lowlives of Sheerness, to really take the notion of monarchy seriously.

Daniel lingered outside for a minute or two. The sun was setting behind a gapped cloud-front and shoving fat rays of gaudy light across the estuary of the Medway: a big brackish sump a few miles across, with a coastline as involuted as a brain, congested with merchant and naval traffic. Most of the latter huddled sheepishly down at the far end, behind the chain that was stretched across the river, below the sheltering guns of Upnor Castle. James had for some reason expected William of Orange's fleet to attack there, in the worst possible place. Instead the Protestant Wind had driven the Dutchman all the way to Tor Bay, hundreds of miles to the west—almost Cornwall. Since then the Prince had been marching steadily eastwards. English regiments marched forth to stand in his path, only to defect and about-face. If William was not in London yet, he would be soon.

The waterfront people were already reverting to a highly exaggerated Englishness: womenfolk were scurrying toward the tavern, hitching up their skirts to keep 'em out of the muck, so that they glissaded across the tidelands like bales on rails. They were bringing victuals to the King! They hated him and wanted him gone. But that was no reason to be inhospitable. Daniel had reasons to tarry—he felt he should go in and say good-bye to the King. And, to be pragmatic, he was fairly certain he could be charged with horse-thievery if he turned this mount towards London.

On the other hand, he had another hour of twilight, and the

low tide could cut a few hours off the time it would take him to work his way round the estuary, cross the river, and find the high road to London. He had the strongest feeling that important things were happening there; and as for the King, and his improvised Court here at Sheerness: if the local pub scum couldn't bring themselves to take him seriously, why should the Secretary of the Royal Society? Daniel aimed his horse's backside at the King of England and then spurred the animal forward into the light.

Since the time of the Babylonian astronomers, solar eclipses had from time to time caused ominous shadows to fall upon the land. But England in winter sometimes afforded its long-suffering populace a contrary phenomenon, which was that after weeks of dim colorless skies, suddenly the sun would scythe in under the clouds after it had seemed to set, and wash the landscape with pink, orange, and green illumination, clear and pure as gems. Empiricist though he was, Daniel felt free to ascribe meaning to this when it went his way. Ahead all was clear light, as if he were riding into stained glass. Behind (and he only bothered to look back once) the sky was a bruise-colored void, the land a long scrape of mud. The tavern rose up from the middle of the waste on a sheave of pilings that leaned into each other like a crowd of drunks. Its plank walls pawed a bit of light out of the sky, its one window glowed like a carbuncle. It was the sort of grotesque sky-scape that Dutchmen would come over to paint. But come to think of it, a Dutchman *had* come over and painted it.

Most travelers would take little note of Castle Upnor. It was but a stone fort, built by Elizabeth a hundred years ago, but looking much older—its vertical stone walls obsolete already. But since the Restoration it had been the nominal seat of Louis Anglesey, the Earl of Upnor, and owner of the fair Abigail Frome (or at least Daniel presumed she was fair). As such it gave Daniel the shudders; he felt like a little boy riding past a haunted house. He'd have gone wide of it if he could, but the ferry next to it was by far the most expeditious way of crossing the Medway, and this was no time to let superstition take him out of his way. The alternative would've been to ride a few miles up the east bank to the huge naval shipyard of Chatham, where there were several ways of getting across. But passing through a naval base did not seem the most efficient way of getting around, during a foreign invasion.

He pretended to give his horse a few minutes' rest at the ferry landing, and did what half-hearted spying he could. The sun was positively down now and everything was dark blue on a backdrop of even darker blue. The Castle fronted on the west bank of the river and was buried in its own shadow. However, lights were burning in some of the windows, and particularly in the outbuildings. A sharp two-masted vessel was anchored in the dredged channel nearby.

When the Dutch had sailed up here in '67 and, over the course of a leisurely three-day rampage, stolen some of Charles II's warships and burned diverse others, Castle Upnor had acquitted itself reasonably well, declining to surrender and taking pot-shots at any Dutchmen who'd come anywhere near close enough. The Earl of Upnor, whose travails with gambling debts and Popish Plot hysteria still lay in the future, had picked up some reflected luster. But to have one's chief Navy Yard infested with Dutchmen was embarrassing even to a foreign-policy slut like Charles II. So modern defenses with proper earthworks had since been put up in the neighborhood, and Upnor had been demoted to the status of a giant powder-magazine, sort of an outlying gunpowder depot for the Tower of London—the unspoken message being that no one cared if it blew up. Powder-barges came hither frequently from the Tower and moored in the place claimed, tonight, by that two-master. Daniel knew only a little of ships, but even a farmer could see that this one had several cabins astern, well-appointed with windows, and lights burning behind their drawn curtains and closed shutters. Louis Anglesey hardly ever came to this place, as why should any Earl in his right mind go to a dank stone pit to sit upon powder-kegs? And yet in times of trouble there were worse places to bolt. Those stone walls might not stop Dutch cannonballs, but they would keep Protestant mobs at bay for weeks, and the river was only a few steps away; once he stepped off the quay and boarded his boat, Upnor was as good as in France.

There were a few watchmen posted about the place, hugging their pikes to their chests so they could keep their hands stuffed into their armpits, shooting the breeze, mostly gazing outwards towards the Roman road, occasionally turning round to enjoy some snatch of domestic comedy playing itself out within the walls. Potato peels and chicken feathers were bobbing in the river's backwaters, and he caught whiffs of yeast on the breeze. There was, in other words, a functioning household there. Daniel decided that Upnor was not here at the moment, but that he was expected. Perhaps not tonight, but soon.

He left Castle Upnor behind him and went back to riding around England by himself in the dark, which seemed to be how he had spent half of his life. Now that he'd crossed over the Medway there were no real barriers between him and London, which was something like twenty-five miles away. Even if there hadn't been a Roman road to follow, he probably would have been able to find the route by riding from one fire to the next. The only hazard was that some mob might take him for an Irishman. That Daniel bore no resemblance to an Irishman was of no account— rumors had spread that James had shipped in a whole legion of Celtic avengers. No doubt many an Englishman would agree, tonight, that strange riders should be burnt first and identified on the basis of their dental peculiarities after the ashes had cooled.

So it was boredom and terror, boredom and terror, all the way. The boring bits gave Daniel some leisure to ponder the quite peculiar family curse he seemed to be living under, namely, this marked tendency to be present at the demise of English Kings. He'd literally seen Charles I's head roll, and he'd watched Charles II being done in by his physicians, and now this. If the next Sovereign knew what was good for him, he'd make sure Daniel was assigned, by the Royal Society, to spend the rest of his life taking daily measurements of the baroscopic pressure in Barbados.

The last bit of his route ran within view of the river, which was a pleasant sight, a snaking constellation of ships' lanterns. By contrast the flat countryside was studded with pylons of streaming fire that warmed Daniel's face from half a mile away, like the first uncontrollable flush of shame. Mostly these were simply bonfires, which were the only way Englishmen had of showing emotion. But in one town that he rode through, the Catholic church was being not merely burnt but pulled down, its very bricks prised apart by men with sharpened bars—men made orange by the fire-light, not people he recognized, any more, as countrymen.

The river attracted him. At first he told himself that it did so because it was cool and serene. When he got finally to Greenwich he turned aside from the road and rode onto the lumpy pasture of the Park. He couldn't see a damned thing, which was funny because the place was supposed to be an Observatory. But he kept to a policy of insisting that his horse go the way it *didn't* want to—which meant uphill. This had more than a little in common with trying to get a large and basically prosperous country to revolt.

A saltbox of a building perched on the edge of a precipice in the midst of this little range of hills out in the middle of nowhere: a house, queer-looking and haunted. Haunted by philosophers. Its pedestal—a brick of living-space—was surrounded by trees in a way that obscured the view out its windows. Any other tenant would have chopped them down. But Flamsteed had let them grow; they made no difference to him, as he slept all day, and his nights were devoted to looking not out but up.

Daniel reached a place where he could see the light of London shining through gaps among trees. The lambent sky was dissected by the spidery black X of the sixty-foot refracting telescope, supported by a mast scavenged from a tall ship. As he neared the crest he diverted to the right, instinctively avoiding Flamsteed, who exerted a mysterious repulsive force all his own. He was likely to be awake, but unable to make observations because of the light in the sky, therefore more irritable than usual, perhaps scared. His apartment's windows had solid wooden shutters that he had clapped shut for safety. He was holed up in one of the tiny rooms, probably unable to hear anything save the ticking of diverse clocks. Upstairs, in the octagonal saltbox, were two Hooke-designed, Tompion-built clocks with thirteen-foot pendulums that ticked, or rather clunked, every two seconds, slower than the human heartbeat, a hypnotic rhythm that could be felt everywhere in the building.

Daniel led his horse on a slow traverse round the top of the hill. Below, along the riverbank, the brick ruins of Placentia, the Tudor palace, swung gradually into view. Then the new stone buildings that Charles II had begun to put up there. Then the Thames: first the Greenwich bend, then a view straight upriver all the way into the east end. Then all of London was suddenly unrolled before him. Its light shone from the wizened surface of the river, interrupted only by the silhouettes of the anchored ships. If he had not long ago seen the Fire of London with his own eyes, he might have supposed that the whole city was ablaze.

He had entered into the upper reaches of a little wood of oak and apple trees that gripped the steepest part of the hill. Flamsteed's apartments were only a few yards above and behind him along the Prime Meridian. The fragrance of fermenting apples was heady, for Flamsteed had not bothered to collect them as they dropped from the trees during the autumn. Daniel did not bother to tie his horse, but let it forage there, getting fed and drunk on the apples. Daniel moved to a place where he could see London between trees, dropped his breeches, squatted down on his haunches, and began experimenting with various pelvic settings in hopes of allowing some urine to part with his body. He could feel the boulder in his bladder, shifting from side to side like a cannon-ball in a poke.

London had never been so bright since it had burned to the ground twenty-two years ago. And it had never *sounded* thus in all its ages. As Daniel's ears adjusted themselves to this quiet hill-top he could hear a clamor rising up from the city, not of guns or of cart-wheels but of human voices. Sometimes they were just babbling, each to his own, but many times they came together in dim choruses that swelled, clashed, merged, and collapsed, like waves of a tide probing and seeking its way through the mazy back-waters of an estuary. They were singing a song, *Lilliburlero,* that had become universal in the last few weeks. It was a sort of nonsense-song but its meaning was understood by all: down with the King, down with Popery, out with the Irish.

If the scene in the tavern hadn't made it clear enough, the very appearance of the city tonight told him that the thing had happened—the thing that Daniel had been calling the Revolution. The Revolution was done, it had been Glorious, and what made it glorious was that it had been an anticlimax. There'd been no Civil War this time, no massacres, no trees bent under the weight of hanged men, no slave-ships. Was Daniel flattering himself to suppose that this could be put down to his good work?

All his upbringing had taught him to expect a single dramatic moment of apocalypse. Instead this had been slow evolution spread all round and working silently, like manure on a field. If anything important had happened, it had done so in places where Daniel *wasn't*. Buried in it somewhere was an inflection point that later they'd point to as the Moment It All Happened.

He was not such an old tired Puritan that he didn't get joy out of it. But its very anticlimactitude, if that was a word, its diffuseness, was a sort of omen to him. It was like being an astronomer, up in that tower behind him, at the moment that the letter arrived from the Continent in which Kepler mentioned that the earth was not, in fact, at the center of the universe. Like that astronomer, Daniel had much knowledge, and only *some* of it was wrong—but *all* of it had to be gone over now, and re-understood. This realization settled him down a bit. As when a queer wind-gust comes down chimney and fills a room of merry-makers with smoke, and covers the pudding with a black taste. He was not quite ready for life in this England.

Now he understood why he'd felt so attracted to the river earlier: not because it was serene, but because it had the power to take him somewhere else.

He left the horse there, with an explanatory note for Flamsteed, who'd be apoplectic. He walked down to the Thames and woke up a waterman he knew there, a Mr. Bhnh, the patriarch of a tiny

Qwghlmian settlement lodged in the south bank. Mr. Bhnh had grown so accustomed to the nocturnal crossings of Natural Philosophers that someone had nominated him, in jest, as a Fellow of the Royal Society. He agreed to convey Daniel across to the Isle of Dogs on the north bank.

Of late, reductions in the cost of window-glass, and improvements in the science of architecture, had made it possible to build whole blocks of shops with large windows facing the street, so that fine goods could be set out in view of passers-by. Shrewd builders such as Sterling (the Earl of Willesden) Waterhouse and Roger (the Marquis of Ravenscar) Comstock had built neighborhoods where courtiers went to do just that. The noun "shop" had been verbed; people went "shopping" now. Daniel of course never lowered himself to this newfangled vice—except that as he crossed the river he seemed to be doing it with ships. And he was a discriminating shopper. The watermen's boats, the smacks and barges of the estuary were beneath his notice altogether, and the coasting vessels—anything with a fore-and-aft rig—were scarcely more than impediments. He raised his eyes up out of the clutter to scan for the great ships thrusting their yards up, like High Church priests exalting the sacraments above the rabble, into the sky where the wind blew straight and brave. The sails hung from those yards like vestments. There were not many such ships in the Pool tonight, but Daniel sought them all out and appraised each one shrewdly. He was shopping for something to take him away; he wanted to voyage out of sight of land for once in his life, to die and be buried on another continent.

One in particular caught his eye: trim, clean-lined, and sharply managed. She was taking advantage of the in-coming tide to make her way up-stream, ushered forward by a faint southerly breeze. The movement of the air was too faint for Daniel to feel it, but the crew of this ship, *Hare,* had seen flickers of life in the streamers dangling from her mastheads, and spread out her topsails. These stopped a bit of air. They stopped some of the fire-light from the city, too, projecting long prismatic shadows off into the void. The sails of *Hare* hovered above the black river, glowing like curtained windows. Mr. Bhnh tracked them for half a mile or so, taking advantage of the lead that the great ship forced among the smaller vessels. "She's fitted out for a long voyage," he mused, "probably sailing for America on the next tide."

"Would I had a grapnel," Daniel said, "I'd climb aboard like a pirate, and stow away on her."

This startled Mr. Bhnh, who was not used to hearing such

flights of fancy from his clientele. "Are you going to America, Mr. Waterhouse?"

"Someday," Daniel allowed, "there is tidying-up to do in this country yet."

Mr. Bhnh was loath to discharge Daniel in the fiery wilds of East London, which tonight was thronged with drunken mudlarks lighting out in torrid pursuit of real or imaginary Jesuits. Daniel gave no heed to this good man's worries. He had made it all the way from Sheerness without any trouble. Even in the tavern there, he had been left alone. Those who took any notice of him at all, soon lost their interest, or (strange to relate) lost their nerve and looked away. For Daniel carried now the unstudied nonchalance of a man who knew he'd be dead in a year no matter what; people seemed to smell the grave about him, and were happy to leave him alone.

On the other hand, a man with little time to live, and no heirs, need not be so miserly. "I shall give you a pound if you take me direct to the Tower," Daniel said. Then, observing a wary look on Mr. Bhnh's face, he teased his purse open and tossed a handful of coins beside the boat's lantern until he found one that shone a little, and was nearly round. In the center was a battered and scratched plop of silver that with careful tilting and squinting and use of the imagination could be construed as a portrait of the first King James, who had died sixty-some odd years ago, but who was held to have managed the Mint competently. The waterman's hand closed over this artifact and almost as quickly Daniel's eyelids came to with an almost palpable slamming noise. He was remotely aware of massive wool blankets being thrown over his body by the solicitous Mr. Bhnh, and then he was aware of nothing.

> For the King of the North shal returne, and shal set
> forthe a greater multitude then afore, and shal
> come forthe (after certeine yeres) with a mightie
> armie, & great riches.
>
> And at the same time there shal manie stand up
> against the King of the South: also the rebellious
> children of thy people shal exalte them selves to
> establish the vision, but they shal fall.
>
> So the King of the North shal come, and cast up
> a mounte, & take the strong citie: and the armes of
> the South shal not resist, neither his chosen people,
> neither shal there be anie strength to withstand.
>
> —DANIEL 11:13–15

HAVING GONE TO SLEEP in that boat on that night he should on no account have been surprised to wake up in the same boat on the same night; but when it happened he was perfectly a-mazed, and had to see and understand everything afresh. His body was hot on the top and cold on the bottom, and on the whole, not happy with its management. He tried closing and opening his eyes a few times to see if he could conjure up a warm bed, but a mightier conjuration had been wrought on him, and condemned him to this place and time. To call it nightmarish was too easy, for it had all the detail, the lively perversity that nightmares wanted. London—burning, smoking, singing—was still all around. However, he was confronted by a sheer wall of stone that rose up out of the Thames, and was thickly jacketed in all of the unspeakables that flowed in it. Atop that wall was a congeries of small buildings, hoists, large guns, a few relatively small and disciplined bonfires, armed men, but snarls of running boys, too. There was the smell of coal, iron, and sulfur, reminding Daniel of Isaac's laboratory. And because the sense of smell is plumbed into the mind down in the cellar, where dark half-formed notions lurk and breed, Daniel entertained a momentary phant'sy that Isaac had come to London and set his mind to the acquisition of temporal power, and constructed a laboratory the size of Jerusalem.

Then he perceived stone walls and towers rising up behind this wharf, and taller ones rising up behind them, and an even higher fort of pale stone above and behind those, and he understood that he lay before the Tower of London. The roar of the artificial cataracts between the starlings of London Bridge, off to his left, confirmed it.

The wharf-wall was pierced by an arch whose floor was a noisome back-water of the Thames. The boat of Mr. Bhnh was more or less keeping station before that arch, though the current was flowing one way and the tide striving against it, so they were being ill-used by marauding vortices and pounced upon by rogue waves. The waterman, in other words, was using every drowning-avoidance skill he'd practised in the rocky flows off Qwghlm, and more than earning his pound. For in addition to duelling those currents he had been prosecuting a negotiation with a figure who stood on the top of the wharf, just above the arch. That man in turn was exchanging shouts through a speaking trumpet with a periwigged gentleman up on the parapet of the wall behind: a crenellated medieval sort of affair with a modern cannon poking out through each slot, and each cannon conspicuously manned.

Some of the men on the wharf were standing near enough to bonfires that Daniel could make out the colors of their garments. These were the Black Torrent Guards.

Daniel rose up against the gravity of many stout damp blankets, his body reminding him of every injustice he had dealt it since he had been awakened, twenty-four hours ago, with news that the King had gone on the lam. "Sergeant!" he hollered to the man on the wharf, "please inform yonder officer that the escaped prisoner has returned."

THE KING'S OWN BLACK TORRENT Guards had gone into the west country with King James just long enough for their commander, John Churchill, to sneak away from camp and ride to join up with William of Orange. This might have surprised some of the Guards, but it had not surprised Daniel, for almost a year ago he had personally conveyed letters from John Churchill, among others, to the Prince of Orange in the Hague; and though he hadn't read those letters, he could guess what they had said.

Within a few days, Churchill and his regiment had been back in London. But if they'd hoped to be stationed back at their old haunt of Whitehall, they'd been disappointed. William, still trying to sort out his newly acquired Kingdom, was posting his own Dutch Blue Guards at the royal palaces of Whitehall and St. James, and was happy to keep Churchill and the Black Torrent Guards at arm's length in the Tower—which needed defending in any case, as it housed the Royal Mint, and controlled the river with its guns, and was the chief arsenal of the Realm.

Now Daniel was known, to the men of that regiment, as a wretch who'd been imprisoned there by King James II; one cheer for Daniel! Jeffreys had sent murderers to slay him—two cheers! And he had arrived at some untalked-about agreement with Sergeant Bob: three cheers! So in the last weeks before his "escape" Daniel had become a sort of regimental mascot—as Irish regiments kept giant wolf-hounds, this one had a Puritan.

And so the long and the short of it was that Mr. Bhnh was suffered to bring his boat through that tunnel under the wharf. After they passed under the arch, the sky appeared again briefly, but a good half of it was occulted by that out-thrust bulwark: St. Thomas's Tower, a fortress unto itself, grafted to the outer wall of the Tower complex, straddling another stone arch-way paved with fœtid moat-water. Their progress was barred by a water-gate filling that arch. But as they approached, the gates were drawn open, each vertical bar leaving an arc of oily vortices in its wake. Mr. Bhnh hesitated, as any sane man would, and tilted his head back for a moment, in case he never got a chance to see the sky again. Then he probed for the bottom with his pole.

"This is my family coat of arms, such as it is," Daniel remarked, "a stone castle bestriding a river."

"Don't say that!" Mr. Bhnh hissed.

"Why ever not?"

"We are entering into Traitor's Gate!"

PAST THE NARROW APERTURE OF THE Gate lay a pool vaulted over with a vast, fair stone arch. Some engineer had lately constructed a tide-driven engine there for raising water to a cistern in some higher building back in the penetralia of the citadel, and its fearsome grinding—like a troll gnashing its teeth in a cave—appalled Mr. Bhnh more than anything he'd seen all night. He took his leave gladly. Daniel had disembarked onto some ancient slime-covered stairs. He ascended, carefully, to the level of the Water Lane, which ran between the inner and outer fortifications. This had become the scene of a makeshift camp: several hundred Irish people at least were here, taking their ease on blankets or thin scatterings of straw, smoking pipes if they were lucky, playing hair-raising plaints on penny-whistles. No celebratory bonfires here: just a few brooding cook-fires setting kettle-bottoms aglow, and begrudging faint red warmth on the hands and faces of the squatters. There had to be a rational explanation for their being here, but Daniel could not conjure one up. But that was what made city life interesting.

Bob Shaftoe approached, harried by a couple of boys who were running around barefoot even though this was December. He ordered them away gruffly, even a bit cruelly, and as they turned to run off, Daniel got a look at one of their faces. He thought he saw a familial resemblance to Bob.

Sergeant Shaftoe was headed down the lane in the direction of the Byward Tower, which was the way out to London. Daniel fell into step beside him and in a few paces they'd left the water-engine far enough behind that they could talk without shouting.

"I was ready to set off without you," Bob said somewhat bitterly.

"For where?"

"I don't know. Castle Upnor."

"He's not there yet. I'd wager he's still in London."

"Let's to Charing Cross, then," Bob said, "as I think he has a house near there."

"Can we get horses?"

"You mean, is the Lieutenant of the Tower going to supply you, an escaped prisoner, with a free horse—?"

"Never mind, there are other ways of getting down the Strand. Any news concerning Jeffreys?"

"I have impressed 'pon Bob Carver the grave importance of his providing useful information to us concerning that man's whereabouts," Bob said. "I do not think his fear was affected; on the other hand, he has a short memory, and London contains many diversions to-night, most appealing to a man of his character."

Passing through the Byward Tower they came out into the open and began to traverse the causeway over the moat: first a plank bridge that could be moved out of the way, then a stone ramp onto the permanent causeway. Here they encountered John Churchill, smoking a pipe in the company of two armed gentlemen whom Daniel recognized well enough that he could have recalled their names, had it been worth the effort. Churchill broke away from them when his eyes fell on Daniel, and pursued for a few steps, glaring at Bob Shaftoe in a way that meant "keep walking." So Daniel ended up isolated in mid-causeway, face to face with Churchill.

"In truth I have no idea whether you're about to embrace and thank me, or stab me and shove me into the moat," Daniel blurted, because he was nervous, and too exhausted to govern his tongue.

Churchill appeared to take Daniel's words with utmost gravity— Daniel reckoned he must've said something terribly meaningful, out of blind luck. Daniel had encountered Churchill many times at Whitehall, where he had always been surrounded by a sort of aura or nimbus of Import, of which his wig was only the innermost core. You could feel the man coming. He had never been more important than he was tonight—yet here on this causeway all that remained of his aura was his wig, which stood sore in need of maintenance. It was easy to see him as Sir Winston's lad, a Royal Society whelp who had gone to sojourn in the world of affairs.

"So it'll be for everyone, from now on," Churchill said. "The old schemes by which we reckoned a man's virtue have now been o'erthrown along with Absolute Monarchy. Your Revolution is pervasive. It is tricky, too. I don't know whether you will run afoul of its tricks in the end. But if you do, it shall not be by my hand . . ."

"Your face seems to say, '*provided* . . .'"

"Provided you continue to be the enemy of my enemies—"

"Alas, I've little choice."

"So you say. But when you walk through yonder gate," Churchill said, pointing toward the Middle Tower at the end of the causeway, which was visible only as a crenellated cutout in the orange sky, "you'll find yourself in a London you no longer know. The changes wrought by the Fire were nothing. In *that* London, loyalty and allegiance are subtle and fluxional. 'Tis a chessboard with not only black and white pieces, but others as well, in diverse shades. You're a Bishop, and I'm a Knight, I can tell that much by our shapes, and the changes we have wrought on the board; but by fire-light 'tis difficult to make out your true shade."

"I have been awake for twenty-four hours and cannot follow your meaning when you speak in figures."

"It is not that you are tired, but that you are a Puritan and a Natural Philosopher; neither group is admired for its grasp of the subtle and the ambiguous."

"I am defenseless against your japes. But as we are not within earshot of anyone, please avail yourself of this opportunity to speak plainly."

"Very well. I know many things, Mr. Waterhouse, because I make it my business to converse with fellows like those—we trade news as fervidly as traders swapping stocks on the 'Change. And one thing I know is that Isaac Newton is in London to-night."

It struck Daniel as bizarre that John Churchill should even know who Isaac was. Until Churchill continued, "Another thing I know is that Enoch turned up in our city a few days ago."

"Enoch the Red?"

"Don't act like an imbecile. It makes me distrustful, as I know you are not one."

"I take such a dim view of the Art that my heart denies what my mind knows."

"That is just the sort of thing you would say if you were one of them, and wished to hide it."

"Ah. Now I perceive what you meant with your talk of chesspieces and colors—you think I am hiding the red robes of an Alchemist beneath these weeds?! What a thought!"

"You'd have me just *know* that the notion is absurd? Pray tell, sir, how should I *know* it? I'm not learned as you are, I'll admit it; but no one has yet accused me of being stupid. And I say to you that I do not know whether you are mixed up in Alchemy or no."

"It is vexing to you," Daniel thought aloud, "not to follow it."

"More than that, it is *alarming*. In a given circumstance, I know what a soldier will do, what a Puritan will do, what a French cardinal or a Vagabond will do—certain ones excepted—but the motives of the esoteric brotherhood are occult to me, and I do not love that. And as I look forward to being a man of moment in the new order—"

"Yes, I know, I know." Daniel sighed and tried to gather himself. "Really, I think you make too much of them. For never have you seen such a gaggle of frauds, fops, ninehammers, and mountebanks."

"Which of these is Isaac Newton?"

The question was like a bung hammered into Daniel's gob.

"What of King Charles II? Which was His Majesty, ninehammer or mountebank?"

"I have to go and talk to them anyway," Daniel finally said.

"If you can penetrate that cloud, Mr. Waterhouse, I shall consider myself obliged to you."

"*How* obliged?"

"What is on your mind?"

"If an earl dies on a night such as this, might it be overlooked?"

"Depends on the earl," Churchill said evenly. "There will be someone, somewhere, who'll not be of a mind to overlook it. You must never forget that."

"I entered from the river tonight," Daniel said.

"This is an oblique way of saying, you came in through the Traitor's Gate—?"

Daniel nodded.

"I arrived from the land, as you can see, but there shall be many who shall say that I passed through the same portal as you."

"Which puts us in the same boat," Daniel proclaimed. "Now they say that there's no honor among thieves—I wouldn't know— but perhaps there may be a kind of honor among traitors. If I'm a traitor, I'm an honorable one; my conscience is clear, if not my reputation. So now I am holding my hand out to you, John Churchill, and you may stand there eyeing it all night long if you please. But if you would care to stand behind me and shore me up as I look into this question of Alchemy, I should like it very much if you took that hand in yours and shook it, as a gentleman; for as you have noticed the esoteric brotherhood is powerful, and I cannot work against it without a brotherhood of sorts to stand with me."

"You have entered into contracts before, Mr. Waterhouse?" asked Churchill, still appraising Daniel's out-stretched hand. Daniel could sense Bob Shaftoe looking at them from one end of the causeway.

"Yes, as when working as an architect, *et cetera*."

"Then you know every contract involves obligations *reciprocal.* I might agree to 'shore you up' when you are undermined—but in return I may call upon you from time to time."

Daniel's hand did not move.

"Very well, then," said Churchill, reaching out across smoke, damp, and dark.

CHARING CROSS was strewn with bonfires. But it was the green one that caught Daniel's eye.

"M'Lord Upnor's town-house lies *this* way," shouted Bob Shaftoe, pointing insistently in the direction of Piccadilly.

"Work with me, Sergeant," Daniel said, "as if I were a guide taking you on a hunt for strange game of which you know nothing." They began to push their way across the vast cosmos of the square, which was crowded with dark matter: huge mobs pressing in round bonfires, singing *Lilliburlero,* and diverse knaves who'd come up out of Hogs-den to prey upon 'em, and patchwork mutts fighting over anything that escaped the attention of the knaves. Daniel lost sight of the green flames for a while and was about to give up when he saw red flames shooting up in the same place—not the usual orange-red but an unnatural scarlet. "If we should become separated, I shall meet you at the northern end of the Tilt-Yard where King Street loses itself in the Cross."

"Right you are, Guv."

"Who was that boy I saw you talking to before the Bulwark, as we were leaving the Tower?"

"A messenger from Bob Carver."

"Ah, what news from him?"

"The house of Jeffreys is boarded up, and dark."

"If he went to the trouble of having it boarded up, then he's done a proper job."

"It's as we reckoned it, these many weeks ago, Guv," Bob answered, "Jeffreys planned his departure well."

"Well for *us.* If he fled in a panic, how would we find him? Has Mr. Carver any other news?"

"The intent was not to supply us with news, so much as to impress on us what a hard-working and diligent bloke he is."

"That's what I was afraid of," Daniel said, distracted by a rage of blue flame up ahead.

"Fireworks?" Bob guessed.

"Some plan their departures better than others," Daniel answered.

Finally they reached the southwestern margin of the square,

where King Street bent round into Pall Mall, and the view of the park and the Spring Garden was screened by an arc of town-houses that seemed to bulge out into Charing Cross, like a dam holding back pressure behind. The bonfire that kept changing its color was planted before those houses, a bow-shot away. This one was not surrounded by any crowd. This might've been because the true center of drinking, singing, and sociability lay elsewhere, up towards Haymarket, or perhaps it could be laid to the fact that this fire sputtered evilly and let off vile smells. Daniel fell into orbit round it, and saw books, maps, and wooden boxes being dismantled and dissolved in the flames. A chest was being devoured, and small glass phials spilled out of it a few at a time, bursting in the heat to release jets of vapor that sometimes exploded in brilliant-colored flames.

Bob Shaftoe nudged him and pointed toward one of the townhouses. The front door was being held open by a servant. Two younger servants were lugging a portmanteau out and down the front steps. The lid was half open and papers and books were spilling out. The servant who had held the door open let it fall to and then scurried after the others, picking up what they'd let drop, and stuffing it all together in a great wad, a double armload, which rested comfortably on his belly as he waddled across the dirt towards the fire. It looked as if he were planning to fling himself headlong into the particolored inferno, but he stopped just short and with a final grand belly-thrust projected the load of goods into the flames. A moment later the other two caught up with him and heaved the portmanteau right into perdition. The fire dimmed for a minute, seeming taken aback, but then the flames began to get their teeth into the new load of fuel, and to whiten as they built heat.

Still circling round, Daniel stopped to stare at a map, drawn with inks of many colors upon excellent vellum. The hottest part of the fire was behind it, so the light shone through the empty places on the map—which were many, as it was a map of some mostly uncharted sea, the voids decorated with leviathans and dreadlocked cannibals. There was a scattering of islands literally gilded onto the page with some sort of golden ink, labelled "Ye Islands of King Solomon." As Daniel gazed at them, the ink finally burst into flames and burnt like trails of gunpowder; the words vanished from the world but were committed to his memory in letters of fire.

"It is the house of M. LeFebure," Daniel explained, walking towards it with Bob in tow. "Mark those three great windows above the entrance, glowering blood-red as the light shines through their curtains. Once I spied on Isaac Newton through those windows, using his own telescope."

"What was he doing?"

"Making the acquaintance of the Earl of Upnor—who wanted to meet him so badly that he'd made arrangements for him to be followed."

"What is that house, then? A den of sodomites?"

"No. It has been the chief nest of Alchemists in the city ever since the Restoration. I've never set foot in it, but I go there now; if I fail to come out, go to the Tower and tell your master the time has come to make good on his end of our contract."

The big-bellied servant had seen Daniel approaching and was standing warily at the door. "I am here to join them," Daniel snapped, brushing past into the entrance hall.

The place had been decorated in the Versailles way, all magnificent, as expensive as possible, and calculated to overawe the Persons of Quality who came here to buy powders and philtres from M. LeFebure. He was not here, having fled the country already. This went a long way toward explaining the fact that the house, tonight, was about as elegant as a fish-market. Servants, and two gentlemen, were bringing goods down from the upper floors, and up from the cellar, dumping them out on tables or floors, and messing through them. After a few moments Daniel realized that one of the gentleman was Robert Boyle and the other Sir Elias Ashmole. Nine things out of ten were tossed in the general direction of the entrance to be hauled out to the fire. The rest were packed in bags and boxes for transport. Transport *where,* was the question. In the kitchen, a cooper was at work, sealing ancient books up inside of barrels, which suggested a sea-voyage was contemplated by someone.

Daniel ascended the stairs, moving purposefully, as if he actually knew his way around the place. In fact, all he had to go on was vague memories of what he'd spied through the telescope twenty years ago. If they served, the room where Upnor and Newton had met was dark-paneled, with many books. Daniel had been having odd dreams about that room for two decades. Now he was finally about to enter it. But he was dead on his feet, so exhausted that everything was little different from a dream anyway.

At least a gross of candles were burning in the stairs and the upstairs hall: little point in conserving them now. Cobwebby candelabras had been dragged out of storage, and burdened with mismatched candles, and beeswax tapers had been thrust into frozen wax-splats on expensive polished banisters. A painting of Hermes Trismegistus had been pulled down from its hook and used to prop open the door of a little chamber, a sort of butler's pantry at the top of the stairs, which was mostly dark; but enough light spilled in from the hall that Daniel could see a gaunt man with a prominent nose, and large dark eyes that gave him a sad preoccupied look. He was conversing with someone farther back in the room, whom Daniel could not see. He had crossed his arms, hugging an old book to himself with an index finger thrust into it to save his place. The big eyes turned Daniel's way and regarded him without surprise.

"Good morning, Dr. Waterhouse."

"Good morning, Mr. Locke. And welcome back from Dutch exile."

"What news?"

"The King is run to ground at Sheerness. And what of you, Mr. Locke, shouldn't you be writing us a new Constitution or something?"

"I await the pleasure of the Prince of Orange," said John Locke patiently. "In the meantime, this house is no worse a place to wait than any other."

"It is certainly better than where I have been living."

"We are all in your debt, Dr. Waterhouse."

Daniel turned round and walked five paces down the hall, moving now towards the front of the house, and paused before the large door at the end.

He could hear Isaac Newton saying, "What do we know, truly, of this Viceroy? Supposing he *does* succeed in conveying it to Spain—will he understand its true value?"

Daniel was tempted to stand there for a while listening, but he knew that Locke's eyes were on his back and so he opened the door.

Opposite were the three large windows that looked over Charing Cross, covered with scarlet curtains as big as mainsails, lit up by many tapers in sconces and candelabras curiously wrought, like vine-strangled tree-branches turned to solid silver. Daniel had a dizzy sensation of falling into a sea of red light, but his eyes adjusted, and with a slow blink his balance recovered.

In the center of the room was a table with a top of black marble shot through with red veins. Two men were seated there, looking up at him: on Daniel's left, the Earl of Upnor, and on his right, Isaac Newton. Posed nonchalantly in the corner of the room, pretending to read a book, was Nicolas Fatio de Duilliers.

Daniel immediately, for some reason, saw this through the suspicious eyes of a John Churchill. Here sat a Catholic nobleman who was more at home in Versailles than in London; an Englishman of Puritan upbringing and habits, lately fallen into heresy, the smartest man in the world; and a Swiss Protestant famous for having saved

William of Orange from a French plot. Just now they'd been interrupted by a Nonconformist traitor. These differences, which elsewhere sparked duels and wars, counted for naught here; their Brotherhood was somehow above such petty squabbles as the Protestant Reformation and the coming war with France. No wonder Churchill found them insidious.

Isaac was a fortnight shy of his forty-sixth birthday. Since his hair had gone white, his appearance had changed very little; he never stopped working to eat or drink and so he was as slender as he had always been, and the only symptom of age was a deepening translucency of his skin, which brought into view tangles of azure veins strewn around his eyes. Like many College dwellers he found it a great convenience to hide his clothing—which was always in a parlous state, being not only worn and shabby but stained and burnt with diverse spirits—underneath an academic robe; but his robe was scarlet, which made him stand out vividly at the College, and here in London all the more so. He did not wear it in the street, but he was wearing it now. He had not affected a wig, so his white hair fell loose over his shoulders. Someone had been brushing that hair. Probably not Isaac. Daniel guessed Fatio.

For the Earl of Upnor it had been a challenging couple of decades. He'd been banished once or twice for slaying men in duels, which he did as casually as a stevedore picked his nose. He had gambled away the family's great house in London and been chased off to the Continent for a few years during the most operatic excesses of the so-called Popish Plot. He had, accordingly, muted his dress somewhat. To go with his tall black wig and his thin black moustache he was wearing an outfit that was, fundamentally, black: the *de rigueur* three-piece suit of waistcoat, coat, and breeches, all in the same fabric—probably a very fine wool. But the whole outfit was crusted over with embroidery done in silver thread, and thin strips of parchment or something had been involved with the needle-work to lift it off the black wool underneath and give it a three-dimensional quality. The effect was as if an extremely fine network of argent vines had grown round his body and now surrounded him and moved with him. He was wearing riding-boots with silver spurs, and was armed with a Spanish rapier whose guard was a tornadic swirl of gracefully curved steel rods with bulbous ends, like a storm of comets spiraling outwards from the grip.

Fatio's attire was relatively demure: a many-buttoned sort of cassock, a middling brown wig, a linen shirt, a lace cravat.

They were only a little surprised to see him, and no more than normally indignant that he'd burst in without knocking. Upnor showed no sign of wanting to run him through with that rapier. Newton did not seem to think that Daniel's appearing here, now, was any more bizarre than any of the other perceptions that presented themselves to Isaac in a normal day (which was probably true), and Fatio, as always, just observed everything.

"Frightfully sorry to burst in," Daniel said, "but I thought you'd like to know that the King's turned up in Sheerness—not above ten miles from Castle Upnor."

The Earl of Upnor now made a visible effort to prevent some strong emotion from assuming control of his face. Daniel couldn't be certain, but he thought it was a sort of incredulous sneer. While Upnor was thus busy, Daniel pressed his advantage: "The Gentleman of the Bedchamber is in the Presence as we speak, and I suppose that other elements of Court will travel down-river tomorrow, but for now he has nothing—food, drink, a bed are being improvised. As I rode past Castle Upnor yesterday evening, it occurred to me that you might have the means, there, to supply some of His Majesty's wants—"

"Oh yes," Upnor said, "I have all."

"Shall I make arrangements for a messenger to be sent out then?"

"I can do it myself," said the Earl.

"Of course I am aware, my lord, that you have the power to dispatch messages. But out of a desire to make myself useful I—"

"No. I mean, I can deliver the orders myself, for I am on my way to Upnor at daybreak."

"I beg your pardon, my lord."

"Is there anything else, Mr. Waterhouse?"

"Not unless I may be of assistance in this house."

Upnor looked at Newton. Newton—who'd been gazing at Daniel—seemed to detect this in the corner of his eye, and spoke: "In this house, Daniel, a vast repository of alchemical lore has accumulated. Nearly all of it is garbled nonsense. Some of it is true wisdom—secrets that ought rightly to be *kept* secret from them in whose hands they would be dangerous. Our task is to sort out one from the other, and burn what is useless, and see to it that what is good and true is distributed to the libraries and laboratories of the adept. It is difficult for me to see how you could be of any use in this, since you believe that *all* of it is nonsense, and have a well-established history of incendiary behavior in the presence of such writings."

"You continue to view my 1677 actions in the worst possible light."

"Not so, Daniel. I am aware that you thought you were showering favors on me. Nonetheless, I say that what happened in 1677 must be looked on as permanently disqualifying you from being allowed to handle alchemical literature around open flames."

"Very well," said Daniel. "Good night, Isaac. M'Lord. Monsieur." Upnor and Fatio were both looking a bit startled by Isaac's cryptic discourse, so Daniel bowed perfunctorily and backed out of the room.

They resumed their previous conversation as if Daniel were naught more than a servant who'd nipped in to serve tea. Upnor said, "Who can guess what notions have got into his head, living for so many years in that land, over-run with the cabals of crypto-Jews, and Indians sacrificing each other atop Pyramids?"

"You could just write him a letter and ask him," suggested Fatio, in a voice so bright and reasonable that it annoyed even Daniel, who was rapidly backing out of earshot. He could tell, just from this, that Fatio was no alchemist; or if he was, he was new to it, and not yet inculcated to make everything much more obscure and mysterious than it needed to be.

He turned around finally, and nearly bumped into a fellow whom he identified, out of the corner of his eye, as a merry monk who had somehow got grievously lost: it was a robed figure gripping a large stoneware tankard that he had evidently taken out on loan from one of the local drinking establishments. "Have a care, Mr. Waterhouse, you look too little, for listening so well," said Enoch Root affably.

Daniel started away from him. Locke was still standing there embracing his book; Root was the chap he'd been talking to earlier. Daniel was caught off guard for a few moments; Root took advantage of the lull to down a mouthful of ale.

"You are very rude," Daniel said.

"What did you say? Root?"

"*Rude,* to drink alone, when others are present."

"Each man finds his own sort of rudeness. Some burst into houses, and conversations, uninvited."

"I was bearing important news."

"And I am celebrating it."

"Aren't you afraid that drink will shorten your longevity?"

"Is longevity much on your mind, Mr. Waterhouse?"

"It is on the mind of every man. And I am a man. Who or what are *you?*"

Locke's eyes had been going back and forth, as at a tennis

match. Now they fixed on Enoch for a while. Enoch had got a look as if he were trying to be patient—which was not the same as being patient.

"There's a certain unexamined arrogance to your question, Daniel. Just as Newton presumes that there is some absolute space by which all things—comets even!—are measured and governed, you presume it is all perfectly natural and pre-ordained that the earth should be populated by men, whose superstitions ought to be the ruler by which all things are judged; but why might I not ask of you, 'Daniel Waterhouse, who or what are you? And why does Creation teem with others like you, and what is your purpose?' "

"I'll remind you, sirrah, that All Hallows' Eve was more than a month since, and I am not of a humour to be baited with hobgoblin-stories."

"Nor am I of a humour to be rated a hobgoblin or any other figment of the humane imagination; for 'twas God who imagined me, just as He did you, and thereby brought us into being."

"Your tankard brims over with scorn for our superstitions and imaginings; yet here you are, as always, in the company of Alchemists."

"You might have said, 'Here you are in the center of the Glorious Revolution conversing with a noted political philosopher,'" Root returned, glancing at Locke, who flicked his eyes downward in the merest hint of a bow. "But I am never credited thus by you, Daniel."

"I have only seen you in the company of alchemists. Do you deny it?"

"Daniel, I have only seen *you* in the company of alchemists. But I am aware that you do other things. I know you have oft been at Bedlam with Hooke. Perhaps you have seen priests there who go to converse with madmen. Do you suppose those priests to be mad?"

"I'm not sure if I approve of the similitude—" Locke began.

"Stay, 'tis just a figure!" Root laughed rather winningly, reaching out to touch Locke's shoulder.

"A faulty one," Daniel said, "for you *are* an alchemist."

"I am *called* an Alchemist. Within living memory, Daniel, everyone who studied what I—and *you*—study was called by that name. And most persons even today observe no distinction between Alchemy and the younger and more vigorous order of knowledge that is associated with your club."

"I am too exhausted to harry you through all of your evasions. Out of respect for your friends Mr. Locke, and for Leibniz, I shall give you the benefit of the doubt, and wish you well," Daniel said.

"God save you, Mr. Waterhouse."

"And you, Mr. Root. But I say this to you—and you as well, Mr. Locke. As I came in here I saw a map, lately taken from this house, burning in the fire. The map was empty, for it depicted the ocean—most likely, a part of it where no man has ever been. A few lines of latitude were ruled across that vellum void, and some legendary isles drawn in, with great authority, and where the mapmaker could not restrain himself he drew phantastickal monsters. That map, to me, is Alchemy. It is good that it burnt, and fitting that it burnt tonight, the eve of a Revolution that I will be so bold as to call my life's work. In a few years Mr. Hooke will learn to make a proper chronometer, finishing what Mr. Huygens began thirty years ago, and then the Royal Society will draw maps with lines of longitude as well as latitude, giving us a grid—what we call a Cartesian grid, though 'twas not his idea—and where there be islands, we will rightly draw them. Where there are none, we will draw none, nor dragons, nor sea-monsters—and that will be the end of Alchemy."

" 'Tis a noble pursuit and I wish you Godspeed," Root said, "but remember the poles."

"The poles?"

"The north and south poles, where your meridians will come together—no longer parallel and separate, but converging, and all one."

"That is nothing but a figment of geometry."

"But when you build all your science upon geometry, Mr. Waterhouse, figments become real."

Daniel sighed. "Very well, perhaps we'll get back to Alchemy in the end—but for now, no one can get near the poles—unless you can fly there on a broom, Mr. Root—and I'll put my trust in geometry and not in the books of fables that Mr. Boyle and Sir Elias are sorting through below. 'Twill work for me, for the short time I have remaining. I have not time to-night."

"Further errands await you?"

"I would fain bid a proper farewell to my dear old friend Jeffreys."

"He is an old friend of the Earl of Upnor as well," Enoch Root said, a bit distractedly.

"This I know, for they cover up each other's murders."

"Upnor sent Jeffreys a box a few hours ago."

"Not to his house, I'll wager."

"He sent it in care of the master of a ship in the Pool."

"The name of the ship?"

"I do not know it."

"The name of the messenger, then?"

Enoch Root leaned over the baluster and peered down the middle of the stairwell. "I do not know that, either," he said, then shifted his tankard to the other hand so that he could reach out. He pointed at a young porter who was just on his way out the door, bearing another pile of books to the bonfire. "But it was *him.*"

HARE RODE AT ANCHOR, LANTERNS a-blaze, before Wapping: a suburb crooked in an elbow of the Thames just downstream of the Tower. If Jeffreys had already boarded her, there was nothing they could do, short of hiring a pirate-ship to overhaul her when she reached blue water. But a few minutes' conversation with the watermen loitering round the Wapping riverfront told them that no passengers had been conveyed to that ship yet. Jeffreys must be waiting for something; but he would wait close by, within view of *Hare,* so that he could bolt if he had to. And he would choose a place where he could get strong drink, because he was a drunkard. That narrowed it down to some half a dozen taverns, unevenly spaced along the riverbank from the Tower of London down to Shadwell, mostly clustered around the stairs and docks that served as gate-ways 'tween the Wet and the Dry worlds. Dawn was approaching, and any normal business ought to've been closed half a dozen hours ago. But these dockside taverns served an irregular clientele at irregular hours; they told time by the rise and fall of the tides, not by the comings and goings of the sun. And the night before had been as wild as any in England's history. No sane tavernkeeper would have his doors closed now.

"Let's be about it smartly then, guv'nor," said Bob Shaftoe, striding off the boat they'd hired near Charing Cross and lighting on King Henry's Stairs. "This may be nigh on the longest night of the year, but it can't possibly be much longer; and I believe that my Abigail awaits me at Upnor."

This was a gruff way of speaking to a tired sick old Natural Philosopher, yet an improvement on the early days in the Tower, when Bob had been suspicious and chilly, or recent times when he'd been patronizing. When Bob had witnessed John Churchill shaking Daniel's hand on the Tower causeway a few hours earlier, he'd immediately begun addressing him as "guv'nor." But he'd persisted in his annoying habit of asking Daniel whether he was tired or sick until just a quarter of an hour ago, when Daniel had insisted that they shoot one of the flumes under London Bridge rather than take the time to walk around.

It was the first time in Daniel's life that he'd run this risk, the second time for Bob, and the fourth time for the waterman. A hill of water had piled up on the upstream side of the bridge and was finding its way through the arches like a panicked crowd trying to bolt from a burning theatre. The boat's mass was but a millionth part of it, and was of no account whatever; it spun around like a weathercock at the brink of the cataract, bashed against the pilings below Chapel Pier hard enough to stave in the gunwale, spun round the opposite way from the recoil, and accelerated through the flume sideways, rolling toward the downstream side so that it scooped up a ton or so of water. Daniel had imagined doing this since he'd been a boy, and had always wondered what it would be like to look up and see the Bridge from underneath; but by the time he thought to raise his gaze outside the narrow and dire straits of the boat, they'd been thrust half a mile downstream and were passing right by the Traitor's Gate once more.

This act had at last convinced Bob that Daniel was a man determined to kill himself this very night, and so he now dispensed with all of the solicitous offers; he let Daniel jump off the boat under his own power, and did not volunteer to bear him piggy-back up King Henry's Stairs. Up they trudged into Wapping, river-water draining in gallons from their clothes, and the waterman—who'd been well paid—was left to bail his boat.

They tried four taverns before they came to the Red Cow. It was half wrecked from the past night's celebrations, but efforts were underway to shovel it out. This part of the riverfront was built up only thinly, with one or two strata of inns and warehouses right along the river, crowding in against a main street running direct to the Tower a mile away. Beyond that 'twas green fields. So the Red Cow offered Daniel juxtapositions nearly as strange as what he'd witnessed in Sheerness: viz. one milkmaid, looking fresh and pure as if angels had just borne her in from a dewy Devonshire pasture-ground, carrying a pail of milk in the back door, stepping primly over a peg-legged Portuguese seaman who'd passed out on a heap of straw embracing a drained gin-bottle. This and other particulars, such as the Malay-looking gent smoking bhang by the front door, gave Daniel the feeling that the Red Cow merited a thoroughgoing search.

As on a ship when exhausted sailors climb down from the yards and go to hammocks still warm from the men who replace them, so the late-night drinkers were straggling out, and their seats being taken by men of various watery occupations who were nipping in for a drink and a nibble.

But there was one bloke in the back corner who did not move.

He was dark, saturnine, a lump of lead on a plank, his face hidden in shadow—either completely unconscious or extremely alert. His hand was curled round a glass on the table in front of him, the pose of one who needs to sit for many hours, and who justifies it by pretending he still nurses his drink. Light fell onto his hand from a candle. His thumb was a-tremble.

Daniel went to the bar at the opposite corner of the room, which was little bigger than a crow's nest. He ordered one dram, and paid for ten. "Yonder bloke," he said, pointing with his eyes, "I'll lay you a quid he is a common man—common as the air."

The tavernkeeper was a fellow of about three score, as pure-English as the milkmaid, white-haired and red-faced. "It'd be thievery for me to take that wager, for you've only seen his clothes—which *are* common—while I've heard his voice—which is anything but."

"Then, a quid says he has a disposition sweet as clotted cream."

The tavernkeeper looked pained. "It slays me to turn your foolish bets away, but again, I have such knowledge to the contrary as would make it an unfair practice."

"I'll bet you a quid he has the most magnificent set of eyebrows you've ever seen—eyebrows that would serve for pot-scrubbers."

"When he came in he kept his hat pulled down low, and his head bowed—I didn't see his eyebrows—I'd say you've got yourself a wager, sir."

"Do you mind?"

"Be at your ease, sir, I'll send my boy round to be the judge of it—if you doubt, you may send a second."

The tavernkeeper turned and caught a lad of ten years or so by the arm, bent down, and spoke to him for a few moments. The boy went directly to the man in the corner and spoke a few words to him, gesturing toward the glass; the man did not even deign to answer, but merely raised one hand as if to cuff the boy. A heavy gold ring caught the light for an instant. The boy came back and said something in slang so thick Daniel couldn't follow.

"Tommy says you owe me a pound then," the tavernkeeper said.

Daniel sagged. "His eyebrows were not bushy?"

"That wasn't the wager. His eyebrows *are* not bushy, that was the wager. *Were* not bushy, that's neither here nor there!"

"I don't follow."

"I've a blackthorn shillelagh behind this counter that was witness to our wager, and it says you owe me that quid, never mind your weasel-words!"

"You may let your shillelagh doze where it is, sir," Daniel said, "I'll let you have that quid. I only ask that you explain yourself."

"Bushy eyebrows he might have had yesterday, for all I know," the tavernkeeper said, calming down a little, "but as we speak, he has no eyebrows at all. Only stubble."

"He cut them off!"

"It is not *my* place to speculate, sir."

"Here's your pound."

"Thank you, sir, but I would prefer one of full weight, made of silver, not this counterfeiter's amalgam . . ."

"Stay. I can give you better."

"A better coin? Let's have it then."

"No, a better circumstance. How would you like this place to be famous, for a hundred years or more, as the place where an infamous murderer was brought to justice?"

Now it was the tavernkeeper's turn to deflate. It was clear from his face that he'd much rather not have any infamous murderers at all in the house. But Daniel spoke encouraging words to him, and got him to send the boy running up the street toward the Tower, and to stand at the back exit with the shillelagh. A look sufficed to get Bob Shaftoe on his feet, near the front door. Then Daniel took a fire-brand out of the hearth and carried it across the room, and finally waved it back and forth so that it flared up and filled the dark corner with light.

"Damned be to Hell, you shit, Daniel Waterhouse! Traitorous, bastard whore, pantaloon-pissing coward! How dare you impose on a nobleman thus! By what authority! I'm a baron, as you are a sniveling turncoat, and William of Orange is no Cromwell, no Republican, but a *prince*, a nobleman like me! He'll show me the respect I merit, and *you* the contempt you deserve, and 'tis *you* who'll feel Jack Ketch's blade on his neck, and die like a whipped bitch in the Tower as you should've done!"

Daniel turned to address the other guests in the tavern—not so much the comatose dregs of last night as the breakfasting sailors and watermen. "I apologize for the disruption," he announced. "You have heard of Jeffreys, the Hanging Judge, the one who decorated trees in Dorset with bodies of ordinary Englishmen, who sold English schoolgirls into chattel slavery?"

Jeffreys got to his feet, knocking his table over, and made for the closest exit, which was at the rear; but the tavernkeeper raised the shillelagh in both hands and wound up like a woodman preparing to swing his axe at a tree. Jeffreys shambled to a stop and reversed direction, heading for the front of the room. Bob Shaftoe let him build to full speed, and let him enjoy a few seconds' hope, before side-stepping in front of the doorway and whipping a dagger out of his boot. It was all Jeffreys could do to stop before impaling himself on it; and the casual look on Bob's face made it clear he would not have turned the point aside.

The men in the tavern had all got to their feet now and begun reaching into their clothes, betraying locations of various daggers, coshes, and other necessaries. But they did this because they were confused, not because they'd formed any clear intentions. For that, they were still looking to Daniel.

"The man I speak of, whose name you have all heard, the man who is responsible for the Bloody Assizes and many other crimes besides—judicial murders, for which he has never dreamed he would be made to pay, until this moment—George Jeffreys, Baron of Wem, is *he.*" And Daniel pointed his finger like a pistol into the face of Jeffreys, whose eyebrows would have shot up in horror, if he still had any. As it was, his face was strangely devoid of expression, of its old power to stir Daniel's emotions. Nothing he could do with that face could now make Daniel fear him, or pity him, or be charmed by him. This was attributing more power to a set of eyebrows than was really sensible, and so it had to be something else instead; some change in Jeffreys, or in Daniel.

The daggers and coshes had begun to come out—not to be used, but to keep Jeffreys hemmed in. Jeffreys was speechless for the first time since Daniel had known him. He could not even curse.

Daniel met Bob's eyes, and nodded. "Godspeed, Sergeant Shaftoe, I hope you rescue your princess."

"So do I," Bob said, "but whether I live or die in the attempt, do not forget that I have helped you; but you have not helped me yet."

"I have not forgotten it, nor will I ever. Chasing armed men cross-country is not something I am very good at, or I would come with you now. I await a chance to return the favor."

"It is not a favor, but one side of a contract," Bob reminded him, "and all that remains is for us to choose the coin in which I shall be repaid." He turned and bolted into the street.

Jeffreys looked around, taking a quick census of the men and weapons closing in around him, and finally turned his gaze on Daniel: not fierce any more, but offended, and bewildered—as if asking why? Why go to the trouble? I was running away! What is the point of this?

Daniel looked him in the eye and said the first thing that entered his mind:

"You and I are but earth."

Then he walked out into the city. The sun was coming up now, and soldiers were running down the street from the Tower, led by a boy.

Venice
JULY 1689

> The *Venetian* Republick began thus; a despicable
> Croud of People flying from the Fury of the *Barbar-*
> *ians* which over-run the *Roman* Empire, took Shelter
> in a few inaccessible Islands of the *Adriatic* Gulph . . .
> THEIR City we see raised to a prodigious Splen-
> dour and Magnificence, and their rich Merchants
> rank'd among the ancient Nobility, and all this by
> Trade.
>
> —DANIEL DEFOE, *A Plan of the English Commerce*

To Eliza, Countess de la Zeur and Duchess of Qwghlm
From G. W. Leibniz
July 1689
Eliza,

Your misgivings about the Venetian Post Office have once again proved unfounded—your letter reached me quickly and without obvious signs of tampering. Really, I think that you have been spending too much time in the Hague, for you are becoming as prim and sanctimonious as a Dutch-woman. You need to come here and visit me. Then you would see that even the most debauched people in the world have no difficulty delivering the mail on time, and doing many other difficult things besides.

As I write these words I am seated near a window that looks out over a canal, and two gondoliers, who nearly collided a minute ago, are screaming murderous threats at each other. This sort of thing happens all the time here. The Venetians have even given it a name: "Canal Rage." Some say that it is a new phenomenon—they insist that gondoliers never used to scream at each other in this way. To them it is a symptom of the excessively rapid pace of change in the modern world, and they make an analogy to poisoning by quicksilver, which has turned so many alchemists into shaky, irritable lunatics.

The view from this window has changed very little in hundreds of years (God knows that my room could use some maintenance), but the letters scattered across my table (all delivered punctually by Venetians) tell of changes the like of which the world has not seen since Rome fell and the Vagabond Emperor moved his court to this city. Not only have William and Mary been crowned at Westminster (as you and several others were so kind as to inform me), but in the same post I received word from Sophie Charlotte in Berlin that there is a new Tsar in Russia, named Peter, and that he is as tall as Goliath, as strong as Samson, and as clever as Solomon. The Russians have signed a treaty with the Emperor of China, fixing their common border along some river that does not even appear on the maps—but from all accounts, Russia now extends all the way to the Pacific, or (depending on which set of maps you credit) to America. Perhaps this Peter could march all the way to Massachusetts without getting his feet wet!

But Sophie Charlotte says that the new Tsar's gaze is fixed westwards. She and her incomparable mother are already scheming to invite him to Berlin and Hanover so that they can flirt with him in person. I would not miss that for the world; but Peter has many rivals to crush and Turks to slay before he can even consider such a journey, and so I should have plenty of time to make my way back from Venice.

Meanwhile *this* city looks to the east—the Venetians and the other Christian armies allied with them continue to press the Turks back, and no one here will talk about anything else but the news that came in the latest post, or when the next post is expected. For those of us more interested in philosophy, it makes for tedious dinners! The Holy League have taken Lipova, which as you must know is the gateway to Transylvania, and there is hope of driving the Turks all the way to the Black Sea before long. And in a month I'll be able to write you another letter containing the same sentence with a different set of incomprehensible place names. Woe to the Balkans.

Pardon me if I seem flippant. Venice seems to have that effect on me. She finances her wars the old-fashioned way, by levying taxes on trade, and this naturally limits their scope. By contrast, the reports I hear from England and from France are most disquieting. First you tell me that (according to your sources at Versailles) Louis XIV is melting down the silver furniture in the *Grands Appartements* to pay for the raising of an even vaster army (or perhaps he wanted to redecorate). Next, Huygens writes from London that the Government there has hit upon the idea of financing the Army and Navy by creating a national debt—using all of England as collateral, and levying a special tax that is earmarked for paying it back. I can scarcely picture the upheaval that these innovations must have created in Amsterdam! Huygens also mentioned that the ship he took across the North Sea was crowded with Amsterdam Jews who appeared to be bringing their entire households and estates with them to London. No doubt some of the silver that used to be part of Louis' favorite armchair has by this route made its way via the *ghetto* of Amsterdam to the Tower of London where it has been minted into new coins bearing the likeness of William and Mary, and then been sent out to pay for the building of new warships at Chatham.

Thus far, in these parts, Louis' declaration of war against England seems to have had little effect. The duc d'Arcachon's navy is dominant in the Mediterranean, and is rumored to have taken many Dutch and English merchantmen around Smyrna and Alexandria, but there have not been any pitched sea-battles that I know of. Likewise, James II is said to have landed in Ireland whence he hopes to launch attacks on England, but I have no news thence.

My chief concern is for you, Eliza. Huygens gave me a good description of you. He was touched that you and those royals you have befriended—the Princess Eleanor and little Caroline—went to the trouble of seeing him off on his voyage to London, especially given that you were quite enormously pregnant at the time. He used various astronomical metaphors to convey your roundness, your hugeness, your radiance, and your beauty. His affection for you is obvious, and I believe he is a touch saddened that he is not the father (who *is*, by the way? Remember I am in Venice, you may tell me *anything* and I cannot be shocked by it).

At any rate—knowing how strongly you are attracted to the financial markets, I fret that the recent upheavals have drawn you into the furor of the Damplatz, which would be no place for one in a delicate condition.

But there is little point in my worrying about it now, for by this time you must have entered into your confinement, and you and your baby must have emerged dead or alive, and gone to the nursery or the grave; I pray both of you are in the nursery, and whenever I see a picture of the Madonna and child (which in Venice is about three times a minute) I phant'sy it is a fair portrait of you and yours.

Likewise I send my prayers and best wishes to the Princesses. Their story was pathetic even before they were made into refugees by the war. It is good that in the Hague they have found a safe harbor, and a friend such as you to keep them company. But the news from the Rhine front—Bonn and Mainz changing hands, &c.—suggests that they shall not soon be able to return to that place where they were living out their exile.

You ask me a great many questions about Princess Eleanor, and *your* curiosity has aroused *mine;* you remind me of a merchant who is considering a momentous transaction with someone she does not know very well, and who is casting about for references.

I have not met Princess Eleanor, only heard strangely guarded descriptions of her beauty (e.g., "she is the most beautiful German princess"). I did know her late husband, the Margrave John Frederick of Brandenburg-Ansbach. As a matter of fact I was thinking of him the other day, because the new Tsar in Russia is frequently described in the same terms as were once applied to Eleanor's late husband: forward-thinking, modern-minded, obsessed with securing his country's position in the new economic order.

Caroline's father went out of his way to welcome Huguenots or anyone else he thought had unusual skills, and tried to make Ansbach into a center of what your friend and mine, Daniel Waterhouse, likes to call the Technologickal Arts. But he wrote novels too, did the late John Frederick, and you know of my shameful weakness for those. He loved music and the theatre. It is a shame that smallpox claimed him, and a crime that his own son made Eleanor feel so unwelcome there that she left town with little Caroline.

Beyond those facts, which are known to all, all I can offer you concerning these two Princesses is gossip. However, *my* gossip is copious, and of the most excellent quality. For Eleanor figures into the machinations of Sophie and Sophie Charlotte, and so her name is mentioned from time to time in the letters that fly to and fro between Hanover and Berlin. I do believe that Sophie and Sophie Charlotte are trying to organize some sort of North German super-state. Such a thing can never exist without princes; German Protestant princes and princesses are in short supply, and getting shorter as the war goes on; beautiful princesses who lack husbands are, therefore, exceptionally precious.

If precious Eleanor were rich she could command, or at least influence, her own destiny. But because her falling-out with her stepson has left her penniless, her only assets are her body and her daughter. Because her body has shown the ability to manufacture little princes, it is enfeoffed to larger powers. I shall be surprised if a few years from now, your friend Princess Eleanor is not dwelling in Hanover or Brandenburg, married to some more or less hideous German royal. I would advise her to seek out one of the madly eccentric ones, as this will at least make her life more interesting.

I hope that I do not sound callous, but these are the facts of the matter. It is not as bad as it sounds. They are in the Hague. They will be safe there from the atrocities being committed against Germans by the army of Louvois. More dazzling cities exist, but the Hague is perfectly serviceable, and a great improvement over the rabbit-hutch in the Thüringer Wald where, according to gossip, Eleanor and Caroline have been holed up for the last few years. Best of all, as long as they remain in the Hague, Princess Caroline is being exposed to *you*, Eliza, and learning how to be a great woman. Whatever may befall Eleanor at the hands of those two redoubtable match-makers, Sophie and Sophie Charlotte, Caroline will, I believe, learn from you and from them how to manage her affairs in such a way that, when she reaches a marriageable age, she shall be able to choose whatever Prince and whatever Realm are most suitable to her. And this will provide comfort to Eleanor in her old age.

As for Sophie, she will never be satisfied with Germany alone—her uncle was King of England and she would be its Queen. Did you know she speaks perfect English? So here I am, far away from home, trying to track down every last one of her husband's ancestors among the Guelphs and the Ghibellines. Ah, Venice! Every day I get down on my knees and thank God that Sophie and Ernst August are not descended from people who lived in some place like Lipova.

At any rate, I hope you, Eleanor, Caroline, and, God willing, your baby are all well, and being looked after by officious Dutch nurses. Do write as soon as you feel up to it.

Leibniz

P.S. I am so annoyed by Newton's mystical approach to force that I am developing a new discipline to study that subject alone. I am thinking of calling it "dynamics," which derives from the Greek word for force—what do you think of the name? For I may know Greek backwards and forwards, but *you* have taste.

The Hague
AUGUST 1689

Dear Doctor,

"Dynamics" makes me think not only of force, but of Dynasties, which use forces, frequently concealed, to maintain themselves—as the Sun uses forces of a mysterious nature to make the planets pay court to him. So I think that the name has a good ring to it, especially since you are becoming such an expert on Dynasties new and old, and are so adept at balancing great forces against each other. And insofar as words are names for things, and naming gives a kind of power to the namer, then you are very clever to make your objections to Newton's work a part of the very name of your new discipline. I would only warn you that the frontier between "ingenious" (which is held to be a good quality) and "clever" (which is looked at a-skance) is as ill-defined as most of the boundaries in Christendom are today. Englishmen are particularly distrustful of cleverness, which is odd, because they are so clever, and they are wont to draw the boundary in such a way as to encompass all the works of Newton (or any other Englishman) in the country called "ingenious" while leaving you exiled to "clever." And the English must be attended to because they seem to be drawing all the maps. Huygens went to be among the Royal Society because he felt it was the only place in the world (outside of whatever room *you* happen to be in) where he could have a conversation that would not bore him to death. And despite the never-ending abuse from Mr. Hooke, he never wants to leave.

I have been slow to write about myself. This is partly because the very existence of this letter proves, well enough, that I live. But it is also because I can hardly bring myself to write about the baby—may God have mercy on his little soul. For by now, he is with the angels in Heaven.

After several false starts my labor began in the evening of the 27th of June, which I think was extremely late—certainly I felt as if I had been pregnant for two years! It was early the next morning that my bag of waters broke and poured out like a flood from a broken dam.* Now things became very busy at the Binnenhof as the apparatus of labor and delivery swung into action. Doctors, nurses, midwives, and clergy were summoned, and every gossip within a radius of five miles went to the highest state of alert.

As you have guessed, the incredibly tedious descriptions of labors and deliveries that follow are nothing but the vessel for this encrypted message. But you should read them anyway because it took me several drafts and a gallon of ink to put into words one one-hundredth of the agony, the endless rioting in my viscera as my body tried to rip itself open. Imagine swallowing a melon-seed, feeling it grow in your belly to full size, and then trying to vomit it up through the same small orifice. Thank God the baby is finally out. But pray for God to help me, for I love him.

Yes, I say "love," not "loved." Contrary to what is written in the unencrypted text, the baby lives. But I get ahead of myself.

For reasons that will shortly become obvious, you must destroy this letter.

That is, if I don't destroy it first by dissolving the words with my tears. Sorry about the unsightly blotching.

To the Dutch and the English, I am the Duchess of Qwghlm. To the French, I am the Countess de la Zeur. But neither a Protestant Duchess nor a French Countess can get away with bearing and rearing a child out of wedlock.

My pregnancy I was able to conceal from all but a few, for once I began to show, I ventured out in public only rarely. For the most part I confined myself to the upper storys of the house of Huygens. So it

---

* ☰ Break-through: Hexagram 43 of the *I Ching*, or 011111.

has been a tedious spring and summer. The Princesses of Ansbach, Eleanor and Caroline, have been staying as honored guests of the Prince of Orange at the Binnenhof, which as you know is separated from the Huygens house by only a short distance. Almost every day they strolled across the square to pay a call on me. Or rather Eleanor strolled, and Caroline sprinted ahead. To give a curious six-year-old the run of such a place, cluttered as it is with Huygens's clocks, pendulums, lenses, prisms, and other apparatus, is a joy for the little one and a deadly trial for all adults within the sound of her voice. For she can ask a hundred questions about even the least interesting relic that she digs up from some corner. Eleanor, who knows practically nothing of Natural Philosophy, quickly wearied of saying "I don't know" over and over again, and became reluctant to visit the place. But I had nothing better to do with my time as the baby grew, and was hungry for their company, and so attended closely to Caroline and tried as best I could to give some answer to every one of her questions. Perceiving this, Eleanor got in the habit of withdrawing to a sunny corner to do embroidery or write a letter. Sometimes she would leave Caroline with me and go out riding or attend a soiree. So the arrangement worked out well for all three of us. You mentioned to me, Doctor, that the late Margrave John Frederick, Caroline's father, had a passion for Natural Philosophy and Technologickal Arts. I can now assure you that Caroline has inherited this trait; or perhaps she has dim memories of her father showing off his fossil collection or his latest pendulum-clock, and so feels some communion with his departed soul when I show her the wonders of Huygens's house. If so it is a tale that will seem familiar to you, who knew your father only by exploring his library.

Thus Eliza and Caroline. But too Eliza and Eleanor have been talking, late at night, when Caroline is asleep in her bedchamber in the Binnenhof. We have been talking about Dynamics. Not the dynamics of rolling balls on inclined planes, but the dynamics of royal and noble families. She and I are both a little bit like mice scurrying around on a bowling-green, trying not to be crushed by the rolling and colliding balls. We must understand dynamics in order to survive.

Only a few months before I became pregnant, I visited London. I was at Whitehall Palace with Daniel Waterhouse when the son of James II—now Pretender to the throne—was supposedly born. Was Mary of Modena really pregnant, or only stuffing pillows under her dress? If she was pregnant, was it really by the syphilitic King James II, or was a healthy stud brought in to the royal apartments to father a robust heir? Supposing she was really pregnant, did the baby survive childbirth? Or was the babe brought forth from that room really an orphan, smuggled into Whitehall in a warming-pan, and triumphantly brought forth so that the Stuart line could continue to reign over England? In one sense it does not matter, since that king is deposed, and that baby is being reared in Paris. But in another sense it matters very much, for the latest news from across the sea is that the father has taken Derry, and is on the march elsewhere in Ireland, trying to win his kingdom back for his son. All because of what did or did not happen in a certain birthing-room at Whitehall.

But I insult your intelligence by belaboring this point. Have you found any changelings or bastards in Sophie's line? Probably. Have you made these facts known? Of course not. But burn this anyway, and sift the ashes into that canal you are always writing about, making sure beforehand that there are no ill-tempered gondoliers beneath your window.

As a Christian noblewoman, never married, I could not be pregnant, and could not have a child. Eleanor knew this as well as I. We talked about it for hours and hours as my belly grew larger and larger.

My pregnancy was hardly a secret—various servants and women of the household knew—but I could deny it later. Gossips would know I was lying, but in the end, they are of no account. If, God forbid, the baby was stillborn, or died in infancy, then it would be as if it had never happened. But if the baby throve, then matters would be complicated.

Those complications did not really daunt me. If there was one thing I learned at Versailles, it was that Persons of Quality have as many ways of lying about their affairs, perversions, pregnancies, miscarriages, births, and bastards as sailors have of tying knots. As the months of my pregnancy clunked past, ponderous but inexorable, like one of Huygens's pendulums, I had some time to consider which lie I would choose to tell when my baby was born.

Early, when my belly was just a bit swollen, I considered giving the baby away. As you know, there are plenty of well-funded "orphanages" where illegitimate children of the Quality are raised. Or if I searched long enough I might find some decent mother and father who were barren, and would be more than happy to welcome a healthy infant into their house.

But on the first day that the baby began to kick inside of me, the idea of giving him away faded to an abstraction, and shortly vanished from my mind.

When I reached my seventh month, Eleanor sent to Eisenach for a certain Frau Heppner. Frau Heppner arrived some weeks later, claiming to be a nurse who would look after Princess Caroline and *teach her the German language. And this she did; but in truth, Frau Heppner is a midwife. She delivered Eleanor, and has delivered many other noble and common babies since then. Eleanor said that she was loyal and that her discretion could be relied on.*

The Binnenhof, though far from luxurious by the standards of French palaces, contains several suites of apartments, each appointed in such a way that a royal house guest can dwell there in the company of her ladies-in-waiting, Lady of the Bedchamber, &c. As you will understand from my earlier letters, Princess Eleanor did not have enough of a household to occupy a suite fully; she had a couple of servants who had come out from Eisenach, and two Dutch girls who'd been assigned to her, by William's household staff, as an act of charity. And now she had Frau Heppner. This still left an empty room in her suite. And so, when Frau Heppner was not giving Caroline lessons, she began organizing the bedsheets and other necessaries of the midwife's art, making that extra room into a birthing-chamber.

The plan was that when I went into labor I would be carried across the square into the Binnenhof in a sedan-chair, and taken direct to Eleanor's suite. We practiced this, if you can believe such a thing: I hired a pair of brawny Dutchmen to serve as porters, and once a day, during the final weeks of my pregnancy, had them carry me from Huygens's house to the Binnenhof, not stopping or slowing until they had set the sedan chair down inside Eleanor's bedchamber.

These dress rehearsals seemed a good idea at the time, because I did not know the strength of my enemy, and the number of his spies in the Binnenhof. In retrospect, I was telling him everything about my plan, and giving him all he needed to lay a perfect ambush.

But again I get ahead of myself. The plan was that Frau Heppner would preside over the delivery. If the baby died and I lived, no word of it need ever leave that chamber. If I died and the infant lived, it would become a ward of Eleanor, and inherit my wealth. If both I and the baby survived, then I would recuperate for a few weeks and then move to London as soon as the obvious symptoms of childbirth were gone from my body. I would bring the infant along with me, and pass it off as an orphaned niece or nephew, the sole survivor of some massacre in the Palatinate. There is no shortage of massacres to choose from, and no want of Englishmen who would be eager to credit such a tale be it never so patchy—particularly if the tale came from a Duchess who had been of great service to their new King.

Yes, it all sounds absurd. I never would have dreamed such things went on if I had not gone to Whitehall and seen (from a distance) the retinue of high and mighty persons gathered there for no

*reason other than to stand in the Queen's bedchamber and stare
fixedly at her vagina all day, like villagers at a magic-show, determined to catch the magician out in some sleight-of-hand.*

*I supposed that my own vagina, so humble and common, would
never draw such a large and distinguished audience. So by making
some simple arrangements ahead of time, I should be able to adjust
matters to my satisfaction after it was over.*

*You may refer to the plaintext now, doctor, to become acquainted
with all of the delightful sensations that preoccupied me during my
first several hours of labor (I assume it was several hours; at first
'twas dark outside and then light). When my bag of waters broke, and
I knew that the time had come, I sent word for the porters. Between
contractions, I made my way carefully downstairs and climbed into
the sedan chair, which was kept waiting in a room at the side of the
house, at street-level. Once I was inside the box, I closed the door, and
drew the curtains across the little windows, so that curious eyes
should not look in on me as I was taken across the square. The darkness and confinement did not really trouble me, considering that the
baby inside my womb had been living with far worse for many weeks,
and had suffered it patiently, aside from a few kicks.*

*Presently I heard the familiar voices of the porters outside, and
felt the sedan being lifted into the air, and rotated around in the
street for the short journey to the Binnenhof. This passed without
incident. I believe that I may have dozed a little bit. Certainly I lost
track of the twists and turns, after a while, as they carried me down
the long galleries of the Binnenhof. But soon enough I felt the sedan
being set down on a stone floor, and heard the porters walking away.*

*I reached up, flipped the door-latch, and pushed it open, expect-
ing to see the faces of Frau Heppner, Eleanor, and Caroline.*

*Instead I was looking at the face of Dr. Alkmaar, the court physi-
cian, a man I had seen once or twice, but never spoken to.*

*I was not in Eleanor's apartment. It was an unfamiliar bed-
chamber, somewhere else in the Binnenhof. A bed was ready—ready
for me!—and a steaming vat of water rested on the floor, and piles of
torn sheets had been put in position. There were some women in the
room, whom I knew a little, and a young man I'd never seen at all.*

*It was a trap; but so shocking that I did not know what to do.
Would that I could tell you, Doctor, that I kept my wits about me,
and perceived all that was going on, and jumped out of the sedan
chair and ran down the gallery to freedom. But in truth, I was perfectly dumbfounded. And at the moment that I found myself in this
unfamiliar room, I was taken by a strong contraction, which made
me helpless.*

By the time that the pangs had subsided, I was lying in that bed; Dr. Alkmaar and the others had pulled me out of the sedan chair. The porters were long since gone. Whoever had arranged this ambush—and I had a good idea of who it was—had either paid them to take me to the wrong room, or somehow talked them into believing that this was what I wanted. I had no way to send out a message. I could scream for help, but women in labor always scream for help. There was plenty of help already in the room.

Dr. Alkmaar was far from being a warm person, but he was reputed competent and (almost as important) loyal. If he spied on me (which was only to be expected) he would tell my secrets to William of Orange, who knows my secrets anyway. Dr. Alkmaar was assisted by one of his pupils (the young man) and by two girls who had no real business being in this room. When I had arrived in the Hague almost nine months before, in a canal-boat with Eleanor and Caroline, William had tried to furnish me with the rudiments of a household, befitting my exalted rank. The Prince of Orange did this not because I desired it but because it is how things are done, and it seemed absurd to have a Duchess in residence at a royal palace who was bereft of servants and staff. He sent me two young women. Both were daughters of minor nobles, serving time at Court, awaiting husbands, and wishing they were at Versailles instead. Since being spied on by members of one's household is the staple of palace intrigue, I had been careful to have all of my conversations with Eleanor in places where neither of these two girls could possibly overhear us. Later I had moved to Huygens's house, dismissed them from my service, and forgotten about them. But by some narrow definition of Court protocol, they were still technically members of my household, whether I wanted them or not. My fogged mind, trying to make sense of these events, cast that up as an explanation.

Again refer to plaintext for description of various agonies and indignities. The point, for purposes of this narration, is that when the worst fits came over me, I was not really conscious. If you doubt it, Doctor, eat some bad oysters and then try doing some of your calculus at the moment your insides try to turn themselves inside out.

At the conclusion of one of these fits I gazed down through half-closed eyes at Dr. Alkmaar, who was standing between my thighs with his sleeve rolled up and his armhairs plastered to his skin by some sort of wetness. I inferred that he had been inside me, doing a little exploration."

"It's a boy," he announced, more for the benefit of the spectators than for me—I could tell from the way they looked at me that they thought I was asleep or delirious.

I opened my eyes slightly, thinking that it was all over, wanting to see the baby. But Dr. Alkmaar was empty-handed and he was not smiling.

"How do you know?" asked Brigitte—one of those two girls who made up my household. Brigitte looked like she belonged in a Dutch farm-yard operating a butter churn. In Court dress she looked big and out of place. She was harmless.

"He is trying to come out buttocks-first," Dr. Alkmaar said distractedly.

Brigitte gasped. Despite the bad news, I took comfort from this. I had found Brigitte tedious and stupid because of her sweetness. Now, she was the only person in the room feeling sympathy for me. I wanted to get out of bed and hug her, but it did not seem practical.

Marie—the other girl—said, "That means both of them will die, correct?"

Now, Doctor, since I am writing this letter, there is no point in my trying to keep you in suspense—obviously I did not die. I mention this as a way of conveying something about the character of this girl Marie. In contrast to Brigitte, who was always warm (if thick-seeming), Marie had an icy soul—if a mouse ran into the room, she would stomp it to death. She was the daughter of a baron, with a pedigree pieced together from the dribs, drabs, fag-ends, and candle-stubs of diverse Dutch and German principalities, and she struck me (by your leave) as one who had issued from a family where incest was practiced often and early.

Dr. Alkmaar corrected her: "It means I must reach up and rotate the baby until it is head-down. The danger is that the umbilical cord will squirt out while I am doing this, and get throttled later. The chief difficulty is the contractions of her uterus, which bear down on the infant with more strength than my arms, or any man's, can match. I must wait for her womb to relax and then try it."

So we waited. But even in the intervals between my contractions, my womb was so tense that Dr. Alkmaar could not budge the infant. "I have drugs that might help," he mused, "or I could bleed her to make her weaker. But it would be better to wait for her to become completely exhausted. Then I might have a better chance."

More delay now—for them it was a matter of standing around waiting for time to pass, for me it was to be a victim of bloody murder and then to return to life again, over and over; but a lower form of life each time.

By the time the messenger burst in, I could only lie there like a sack of potatoes and listen to what was said.

"Doctor Alkmaar! I have just come from the bedside of the Chevalier de Montluçon!"

"And why is the new ambassador in bed at four in the afternoon?"

"He has suffered an attack of some sort and urgently requires your assistance to bleed him!"

"I am occupied," said Dr. Alkmaar, after thinking about it. But I found it disturbing that he had to mull it over in this way.

"A midwife is on her way to take over your work here," said the messenger.

As if on cue, there was a knock at the door. Showing more vitality than she had all day, Marie dashed over and flung it open to reveal a certain crone of a midwife, a woman with a very mixed reputation. Peering out through a haze of eyelashes I could see Marie throwing her arms around the midwife's neck with a little cry of simulated joy, and muttering something into her ear. The midwife listened and said something back, listened and said something back, three times before she ever turned her colorless gray eyes towards me, and when she did, I felt death reaching for me.

"Tell me more of the symptoms," said Dr. Alkmaar, beginning to take an interest in this new case. The way he was looking at me—staring without seeing—I sensed he was giving up.

I mustered the strength to lever myself up on one elbow, and reached out to grab the bloody cravat around Dr. Alkmaar's neck. *"If you think I am dead, explain this!"* I said, giving him a violent jerk.

"It will be hours before you will have become exhausted enough," he said. *"I shall have time to go and bleed the Chevalier de Montluçon—"*

"Who will then suffer another attack, and then another!" I replied. *"I am not a fool. I know that if I become so exhausted that you are able to turn the baby around in my womb, I shall be too weak to push her out. Tell me of the drug you mentioned before!"*

"Doctor, the French Ambassador may be dying! The rules of precedence dictate that—" began Marie, but Dr. Alkmaar held up one hand to stay her. To me, he said, *"It is but a sample. It relaxes certain muscles for a time, then it wears off."*

"Have you experimented with it yet?"

"Yes."

"And?"

"It made me unable to hold in my urine."

"Who gave it to you?"

"A wandering alchemist who came to visit two weeks ago."

"A fraud or—"

"He is well reputed. He remarked that, with so many pregnant women in the house, I might have need of it."

"'Twas the Red?"

Dr. Alkmaar's eyes darted from side to side before he answered with a very slight nod.

"Give me the drug."

It was some sort of plant extract, very bitter, but after about a quarter of an hour it made me go all loose in the joints, and I became light-headed even though I had not lost that much blood yet. So I was not fully conscious when Dr. Alkmaar did the turning, and that suited me, as it was not anything I wanted to be conscious of. My passion for Natural Philosophy has its limits.

I heard him saying to the midwife, "Now the baby is head down, as it should be. God be praised, the cord did not emerge. The baby is crowning now, and when the drug wears off in a few hours, the contractions will resume and, God willing, she will deliver normally. Know that she is delivering late; the baby is well-developed; as frequently occurs in such cases, it has already defecated inside the womb."

"I have seen it before," said the midwife, a little bit insulted.

Dr. Alkmaar did not care whether she was insulted or not: "The baby has got some of it into his mouth. There is danger that when he draws his first breath he shall aspirate it into his lungs. If that happens he shall not live to the end of the week. I was able to get my finger into the little one's mouth and clear out a good deal of it, but you must remember to hold him head-down when he emerges and clear the mouth again before he inhales."

"I am in debt to your wisdom, Doctor," said the midwife bitterly.

"You felt around in his mouth? The baby's mouth?" Marie asked him.

"That is what I have just said," Dr. Alkmaar replied.

"Was it . . . normal?"

"What do you mean?"

"The palate . . . the jaw . . . ?"

"Other than being full of baby shit," said Dr. Alkmaar, picking up his bag of lancets and handing it to his assistant, "it was normal. Now I go to bleed the French Ambassador."

"Take a few quarts for me, Doctor," I said. Hearing this weak jest, Marie turned and gave me an indescribably evil look as she closed the door behind the departing Doctor.

The crone took a seat next to me, used the candle on the nightstand to light up her clay-pipe, and set to work replacing the air in the room with curls of smoke.

The words of Marie were an encrypted message that I had understood as soon as it had reached my ears. Here is its meaning:

Nine months ago I got into trouble on the banks of the Meuse. As a means of getting out of this predicament I slept with Étienne d'Arcachon, the scion of a very ancient family that is infamous for passing along its defects as if they were badges and devices on its coat of arms. Anyone who has been to the royal palaces in Versailles, Vienna, or Madrid has seen the cleft lips and palates, the oddly styled jaw-bones, and the gnarled skulls of these people; King Carlos II of Spain, who is a cousin to the Arcachons in three different ways, cannot even eat solid food. Whenever a new baby is born into one of these families, the first thing everyone looks at, practically before they even let it breathe, is the architecture of the mouth and jaw.

I was pleased to hear that my son would be free of these defects. But that Marie had asked proved that she had an opinion as to who the father was. But how could this be possible? "It is obvious," you might say, "this Étienne d'Arcachon must have boasted, to everyone who would listen, of his conquest of the Countess de la Zeur, and nine months was more than enough time for the gossip to have reached the ears of Marie." But you do not know Étienne. He is an odd duck, polite to a fault, and not the sort to boast. And he could not know that the baby in my womb was his. He knew only that he'd had a single opportunity to roger me (as Jack would put it). But I traveled for weeks before and weeks after in the company of other men; and certainly I had not impressed Étienne with my chastity!

The only possible explanation was that Marie—or, much more likely, someone who was controlling her—had read a deciphered version of my personal journal, in which I stated explicitly that I had slept with Étienne and only Étienne.

Clearly Marie and the midwife were working as cat's-paws of some Frenchman or other of high rank. M. le comte d'Avaux had been recalled to Versailles shortly after the Revolution in England, and this Chevalier de Montluçon had been sent out to assume his role. But Montluçon was a nobody, and there was no doubt in my mind that he was a meat marionette whose strings were being pulled by d'Avaux, or some other personage of great power at Versailles.

Suddenly I felt sympathy with James II's queen, for here I was flat on my back in a foreign palace with a lot of strangers gazing fixedly at my vagina.

Who had arranged this? What orders had been given to Marie?

Marie had made it obvious that one of her tasks was to find out whether the baby was sound.

Who would care whether Étienne's bastard child had a well-formed skull?

Étienne had written me a love poem, if you can call it that:

Some ladies boast of ancient pedigrees
And prate about their ancestors a lot
But cankers flourish on old family trees
Whose mossy trunks do oft conceal rot.

My lady's blood runs pure as mountain streams
So I don't care if her high rank was bought
Her beauty lends fresh vigor to my dreams
Of children free of blemish and of blot.

Étienne d'Arcachon wanted healthy children. He knew that his line had been ruined. He needed a wife of pure blood. I had been made a Countess; but everyone knew that my pedigree was fake and that I was really a commoner. Étienne did not care about about that—he had nobility enough in his family to make him a Duke thrice over. And he did not really care about me, either. He cared about one thing only: my ability to breed true, to make children who were not deformed. He, or someone acting on his behalf, was controlling Marie. And Marie was now effectively controlling me.

That explained Marie's unseemly curiosity about what Dr. Alkmaar had felt when he had put his fingers into the baby's mouth. But what other tasks might Marie have been given?

The baby trying to escape from my womb, healthy as he might be, could never be anything other than Étienne's bastard: a trivial embarrassment to him (for many men had bastards) but a gross one to me.

I had bred true, and proved my ability to make healthy Arcachon babies. When Étienne heard this news, he would want to marry me, so that I could make other babies who were not bastards. But what did it all portend for today's baby, the inconvenient and embarrassing bastard? Would he be sent to an orphanage? Raised by a cadet branch of the Arcachon family? Or—and forgive me for raising this terrible image, but this is the way my mind was working—had Marie been ordered to make certain that the child was stillborn?

I looked around the room between contractions and thought of the possibilities. I had to get away from these people and deliver my baby among friends. A day of labor had left me too weak to get up, so I could hardly get up and run away from them.

But perhaps I could rely upon the strength of some, and the weakness of others. I have already mentioned that Brigitte was built like a stallion. And I could tell she was good. Sometimes I am not the best

*judge of character, it is true, but when you are in labor, confined
with certain people for what seems like a week, you come to know
them very well.*

"Brigitte," I said, "it would do my heart good if you would get up
and find Princess Eleanor."

Brigitte squeezed my sweaty hand and smiled, but Marie spoke
first: "Dr. Alkmaar has strictly forbidden visitors!"

"Is Eleanor far away?" I asked.

"Just at the other end of the gallery," Brigitte said.

"Then go there quickly and tell her I shall have a healthy baby boy
very soon."

"That is by no means assured yet," Marie pointed out, as Brigitte
stormed out of the room.

Marie and the midwife immediately went into the corner, turned
their backs to me, and began to whisper. I had not anticipated this,
but it suited my purposes. I reached over to the nightstand and
wrenched the candle out of its holder. The nightstand had a lace tablecloth draped over it. When I held the flame of the candle beneath its
fringe, it caught fire like gunpowder. By the time Marie and the midwife had turned around to see what was happening, the flames had
already spread to the fringe of the canopy over my bed.

This is what I meant when I said I must rely on the weakness of
some, for as soon as Marie and the midwife perceived this, it was a
sort of wrestling-match between the two of them to see which would be
out the door first. They did not even bother to cry "Fire!" on their way
out of the building. This was done by a steward who had been walking up the gallery with a basin of hot water. When he saw the smoke
boiling out of the open door, he cried out, alerting the whole palace,
and ran into the room. Fortunately he had the presence of mind to
keep the basin of water steady, and he flung its whole contents at the
biggest patch of flames that caught his eye, which was on the canopy.
This scalded me but did not really affect the most dangerous part of
the fire, which had spread to the curtains.

Mind you, I was lying on my back staring up through the tattered and flaming canopy, watching a sort of thunder-storm of
smoke-clouds clashing and gathering against the ceiling. Quickly it
progressed downwards, leaving a diminishing space of clear air
between it and the floor. All I could do was wait for it to reach my
mouth.

Then suddenly Brigitte was filling the doorway. She dropped into
a squat so that she could peer under the smoke and lock her eyes on
mine. Did I call her stupid before? Then I withdraw the accusation,
for after a few heartbeats she got a fierce look on her face, stomped

forward, and gripped the end-seam of my mattress—a flat sack of feathers—with both hands. Then she kicked off her shoes, planted her bare feet against the floor, and flung herself backwards towards the door. The mattress was practically ripped out from under me— but I came with it, and shortly felt the foot of the bed sliding under my spine. My buttocks fell to the floor and my head rapped against the bed-frame, both cushioned only a little by the mattress. I felt something giving way inside my womb. But it hardly mattered now. It felt as if my whole body were coming apart like a ship dashed on rocks— each contraction another sea heaving me apart. I have a distinct memory of the stone floor sliding along inches from my eyes, boots of the staff running the other way with buckets and blankets, and— gazing forward, between my upraised knees—the huge bare feet and meaty calves of Brigitte flashing out from under her bloody skirt hem, left-right-left-right, as implacably she dragged me on the mattress down the length of the gallery to where the air was clear enough for me to see the frescoes on the ceiling. We came to a stop underneath a fresco of Minerva, who peered down at me from under the visor of her helmet, looking stern but (as I hoped) approving. Then the door gave way under Brigitte's pounding and she dragged me straight into Eleanor's bedchamber.

Eleanor and Frau Heppner were sitting there drinking coffee. Princess Caroline was reading a book aloud. As you might imagine, they were all taken aback; but Frau Heppner, the midwife, took one look at me, muttered something in German, and got to her feet.

Eleanor's face appeared above me. "Frau Heppner says, 'At last, the day becomes interesting!'"

People who are especially bad, and know that they are, such as Father Édouard de Gex, may be drawn to religion because they harbor a desperate hope that it has some power to make them virtuous— to name their demons and to cast them out. But if they are as clever as he is, they can find ways to pervert their own faith and make it serve whatever bad intentions they had to begin with. Doctor, I have come to the conclusion that the true benefit of religion is not to make people virtuous, which is impossible, but to put a sort of bridle on the worst excesses of their viciousness.

I do not know Eleanor well. Not well enough to know what vices may be lurking in her soul. She does not disdain religion (as did Jack, who might have benefited from it). Neither does she cling to it morbidly, like Father Édouard de Gex. This gives me hope that in her case religion will do what it is supposed to do, namely, stay her hand when she falls under the sway of some evil impulse. I have no choice but to believe that, for I let her take my baby. The child passed straightaway from the midwife's hands to Eleanor's arms, and she gathered it to her bosom as if she knew what she was doing. I did not try to fight this. I was so exhausted I could scarcely move, and afterwards I slept as if I did not care whether I ever woke up or not.

In the plaintext version of my story of labor and delivery, Doctor, I tell the version that everyone at the Binnenhof believes, which is that because of the disgraceful cowardice of Marie and of that midwife, my baby died, and that I would have died, too, if brave Brigitte had not taken me to the room where the good German nurse, Frau Heppner, saw to it that the afterbirth was removed from my womb so that the bleeding stopped, and thereby saved my life.

That is all nonsense. But one paragraph of it is true, and that is where I speak of the physical joy that comes over one's body when the burden it has borne for nine months is finally let go—only to be replaced a few moments later by a new burden, this one of a spiritual nature. In the plaintext story it is a burden of grief over the death of my child. But in the real story—which is always more complicated—it is a burden of uncertainty, and sadness over tragedies that may never happen. I have gone back to live by myself at the house of Huygens, and the baby remains at the Binnenhof in the care of Frau Heppner and Eleanor. We have already begun to circulate the story that he is an orphan, born to a woman on a canal-boat on the Rhine as she escaped from a massacre in the Palatinate.

It seems likely that I shall live. Then I will take up this baby and try to make my way to London, and build a life for both of us there. If I should sicken and die, Eleanor will take him. But sooner or later, whether tomorrow or twenty years from now, he and I shall be separated in some way, and he shall be out in the world somewhere, living a life known to me only imperfectly. God willing, he will outlive me.

In a few weeks or months, there shall be a parting of ways here at the Hague. The baby and I will go west. Eleanor and Caroline will journey east and enjoy the hospitality, and take part in the schemes of, the women whom you serve.

When, God willing, I reach London I shall write you a letter. If you receive no such letter, it means that while I was recuperating I fell victim to some larger scheme of d'Avaux. He may or may not want the baby dead. He certainly wants me at Versailles, where I shall be none the less in his power for being the unwilling wife of Étienne d'Arcachon. The next few weeks, when I am too weak to move, are the most dangerous time.

There remain only two loose ends to clear up: one, if Étienne is the father, why is the baby flawless? And two, if my cypher has been broken, and my private writings are being read by the cabinet noir, why am I telling you all of these secrets?

Actually there is a third loose end, of a sort, which may have been troubling you: why would I sleep with Étienne in the first place, when I had my pick of ten million horny Frenchmen?

All three of these loose ends may be neatly tied up by a single piece of information. During my time at Versailles I got to know Bonaventure Rossignol, the King's cryptanalyst. Rossignol, or Bon-bon as I like to call him (hello, Bon-bon!) was sent out to the Rhine front last autumn during the build-up to the invasion of the Palatinate. When I blundered in to the middle of it all, and got into trouble, Bon-bon became aware of it within a few hours, for he was reading everyone's despatches, and came galloping—literally—to my rescue. It is difficult to tell the story right under present circumstances, and so I'll jump to the end of it, and admit that his gallantry made my blood hot in a way I had never known before. It seems very crude and simple when I set it down thus, but at root it is a crude and simple thing, no? I attacked him. We made love several times. It was very sweet. But we had to devise a way out for me. Choices were few. The best plan we could come up with was that I seduced Étienne d'Arcachon, or rather stood by numbly in a sort of out-of-body trance while he seduced me. This I then parlayed into an escape north. I wrote it all down in a journal. When I got to the Hague, d'Avaux became aware of the existence of that journal and prevailed upon the King's cryptanalyst to translate it—which he did, though he left out all the best parts, namely, those passages in which he himself played the romantic hero. He could not make me out to be innocent, for d'Avaux already knew too much, and too many Frenchmen had witnessed my deeds. Instead Bon-bon contrived to tell the story in such as way as to make me into the paramour of Étienne: the true-breeding woman of his, and his family's, dreams.

I must stop writing now. My body wants to suckle him, and when at night I hear him cry out from across the square, my breasts let down a thin trickle of milk, which I then wash away with a heavier flood of tears. If I were a man, I'd say I was unmanned. As I am a woman, I'll say I am over-womanned. Good-bye. If when you go back to Hanover you meet a little girl named Caroline, teach her as well as you have taught Sophie and Sophie Charlotte, for I prophesy that she will put both of them in the shade. And if Caroline is accompanied by a little orphan boy, said to have been born on the Rhine, then you shall know his story, and who is his father, and what became of his mother.

Eliza

Bishopsgate

OCTOBER 1689

> Thou art too narrow, wretch, to comprehend
> Even thy selfe: yea though thou wouldst but bend
> To know thy body. Have not all soules thought
> For many ages, that our body'is wrought
> Of Ayre, and Fire, and other Elements?
> And now they thinke of new ingredients,
> And one Soule thinkes one, and another way
> Another thinkes, and 'tis an even lay.
> Knowst thou but how the stone doth enter in
> The bladders cave, and never break the skinne?
> —JOHN DONNE, *Of the Progresse of the Soule,*
> *The Second Anniversarie*

THE VISITOR—FIFTY-SIX YEARS old, but a good deal more vigorous than the host—feigned aloofness as he watched his bookish minions fan out among the stacks, boxes, shelves, and barrels that now constituted the personal library of Daniel Waterhouse. One of them strayed towards an open keg. His master warned him away with a barrage of clucking, harrumphing, and finger-snaps. "We must assume that anything Mr. Waterhouse has placed in a barrel, is bound for Boston!"

But when the assistants had all found ways to make themselves busy cataloguing and appraising, he turned towards Daniel and foamed up like a bottle of champagne. "Can't *say* what an *immense* pleasure it is to see you, old chap!"

"Really, I do not think my countenance is all that pleasing at the moment, Mr. Pepys, but it is extraordinarily decent of you to fake it so vigorously."

Samuel Pepys straightened up, blinked once, and parted his lips as if to follow up on the *Conversational Opportunity* Daniel had just handed him. The hand trembled and crept toward the Pocket where the Stone had lurked these thirty years. But some gentlemanly instinct averted him; he'd not crash the conversation onto that particular *Hazard* just yet. "I'd have thought you

908

would be in Massachusetts by now, from the things the Fellows were saying."

"I should have begun making my preparations immediately following the Revolution," Daniel admitted, "but I delayed until after Jeffreys had his enounter with Mr. Jack Ketch at the Tower—by then, 'twas April, and I discovered that in order to leave London I should have to liquidate my life—which has proved much more of a bother than I had expected. Really, 'tis much more expedient simply to drop dead and let one's mourners see to all of these tedious dispositions." Daniel waved a hand over his book-stacks, which were dwindling rapidly as Pepys's corps of librarian-mercenaries carried them towards their master and piled them at his feet. Pepys glanced at the cover of each and then flicked his eyes this way or that to indicate whether they should be returned, or taken away; the latter went to a hard-bitten old computer who had set himself up with a lap-desk, quill, and inkwell, and was scratching out a bill of particulars.

Daniel's remark on the convenience of dropping dead laid a *second* grievous temptation in the way of Mr. Pepys, who had to clench his fist to keep it from stabbing into the pocket. Fortunately he was distracted by an assistant who held before him a large book of engravings of diverse fishes. Pepys frowned at it for a moment. Then he recognized and rejected in the same instant, with revulsion. The R.S. had printed too many copies of it several years ago. Ever since, Fellows had been fobbing copies off on each other, trying to use them as legal tender for payment of old debts, employing them as doorstops, table-levelers, flower-presses, *et cetera*.

Daniel was not normally a cruel man, but he had been laid flat by nausea for days, and could not resist tormenting Pepys yet a third time: "Thy judgment is swift and remorseless, Mr. Pepys. Each book goes to thy left hand or thy right. When a ship founders in a hurricano, and Saint Peter is suddenly confronted with a long queue of soggy souls, not even he could despatch 'em to their deserved places as briskly as thee."

"You are toying with me, Mr. Waterhouse; you have penetrated my deception, you know why I have come."

"Not at all. How goes it with you since the Revolution? I have heard nothing of you."

"I am retired, Mr. Waterhouse. Retired to the life of a gentleman scholar. My aims now are to assemble a library to rival Sir Elias Ashmole's, and to try to fill the void that shall be left by your departure from the day-to-day affairs of the Royal Society."

"You must have been tempted to plunge into the new Court, the new Parliament—"

"Not in the slightest."

"Really?"

"To move in those circles is a bit like swimming. Swimming with rocks in one's pockets! It demands ceaseless exertions. To let up is to die. I bequeath that sort of life to younger and more energetic strivers, like your friend the Marquis of Ravenscar. At my age, I am happy to stand on dry land."

"What about those rocks in your pockets?"

"I beg your pardon?"

"I am giving you a cue, Mr. Pepys—the segue you have been looking for."

"Ah, well done!" said Pepys, and in a lunge he was by Daniel's bedside, holding the auld Stone right up in his face.

Daniel had never seen it quite this close before, and he noticed now that it had a pair of symmetrically placed protrusions, like little horns, where it had begun growing up into the ureters leading down from Pepys's kidneys. This made him queasy and so he shifted his attention to Pepys's face, which was nearly as close.

"BEHOLD! My Death—premature, senseless, avoidable Death—mine, and *yours,* Daniel. But I hold mine in my hand. Yours is lodged thereabouts—do not flinch, I shall not lay hands on you—I wish only to demonstrate, Daniel, that *thy* Stone is only two inches or so from my hand when I hold it thus. *My* Stone is *in* my hand. A distance of only two inches! Yet for me that small interval amounts to thirty years of added life—three decades and God willing one or two more, of wenching, drinking, singing, and learning. I beg you to make the necessary arrangements, Daniel, and have that rock in your bladder moved two inches to your pocket, where it may lodge for another twenty or thirty years without giving you any trouble."

"They are a very significant two inches, Mr. Pepys."

"Obviously."

"During the Plague Year, when we lodged at Epsom, I held candles for Mr. Hooke while he dissected the bodies of diverse creatures—humans included. By then I had enough skill that I could dissect *most* parts of *most* creatures. But I was always baffled by necks, and by those few inches around the bladder. Those parts had to be left to the superior skill of Mr. Hooke. All those orifices, sphincters, glands, frightfully important bits of plumbing—"

At the mention of Hooke's name, Pepys brightened as if he had been put in mind of something to say; but as Daniel's anatomy lesson drew on, his expression faded and soured.

"I of course *know this,*" Pepys finally said, cutting him off.

"Of course."

"I know it of my own knowledge, and I have had occasion to review and refresh my mastery of the subject whenever some dear friend of mine has died of the Stone—John Wilkins comes to mind—"

"That is low, a very low blow, for you to mention him now!"

"He is gazing down on you from Heaven saying, 'Can't wait to see you up here Daniel, but I don't mind waiting another quarter-century or so, by all means take your time, have that Stone out, and finish your work.'"

"I really think you cannot possibly be any more disgraceful now, Mr. Pepys, and I beg you to leave a sick man alone."

"All right . . . let's to the pub then!"

"I am unwell, thank you."

"When's the last time you ate solid food?"

"Can't remember."

"Liquid food, then?"

"I've no incentive to take on liquids, lacking as I do the means of getting rid of 'em."

"Come to the pub anyway, we are having a going-away party for you."

"Call it off, Mr. Pepys. The equinoctial gales have begun. To sail for America now were foolish. I have entered into an arrangement with a Mr. Edmund Palling, an old man of my long acquaintance, who has for many years longed to migrate to Massachusetts with his family. It has been settled that in April of next year we shall board the *Torbay*, a newly built ship, at Southend-on-Sea; and after a voyage of approximately—"

"You'll be dead a week from now."

"I know it."

"Perfect time for a going-away party then." Pepys clapped his hands twice. Somehow this caused loud thumping noises to erupt in the hall outside.

"I cannot walk to your carriage, sir."

"No need," Pepys said, opening the door to reveal two porters carrying a sedan-chair—one of the smallest type, little more than a sarcophagus on sticks, made so that its occupant could be brought from the street all the way into a house before having to climb out, and therefore popular among shy persons, such as prostitutes.

"Ugh, what will people think?"

"That the Fellows of the Royal Society are entertaining someone extremely mysterious—business as usual!" Pepys answered. "Do not think of *our* reputations, Daniel, they cannot sink any lower; and we shall have plenty of time, after you are gone, to sort that out."

Under a flood of mostly non-constructive criticism from Mr. Pepys, the two porters lifted Daniel up out of his bed, turning gray-green as they worked. Daniel remembered the odor that had filled Wilkins's bedchamber during his final weeks, and supposed that he must smell the same way now. His body was as light and stiff as a fish that has been dried on a rack in the sun. They put him into that black box and latched the door on him, and Daniel's nostrils filled with the scent of perfumes and powders left behind by the usual clientele. Or maybe that was what ordinary London air smelt like compared to his bed. His Reference Frame began to tilt and sway as they maneuvered him down-stairs.

They took him north beyond the Roman wall, which was the wrong way. But inasmuch as Daniel was facing his own death, it seemed illogical to fret over something as inconsequential as being kidnapped by a couple of sedan-chair carriers. When he wrenched his rigid neck around to peer out through the screened aperture in the back of the box, he saw Pepys's coach stealing along behind.

As they maneuvered through streets and alleys, diverse views, prospects, and more or less pathetic spectacles presented themselves. But one large, newly-completed, stone building with a cupola kept presenting itself square in their path, closer and closer. It was Bedlam.

Now at this point any other man in London would have commenced screaming and trying to kick his way out, as he'd have realized that he was about to be sent into that place for a stay of unknown duration. But Daniel was nearly unique among Londoners in that he thought of Bedlam not solely as a dumping-ground for lunatics but also as the haunt of his friend and colleague Mr. Robert Hooke. Calmly he allowed himself to be carried in through its front door.

That said, he was a bit relieved when the porters turned away from the locked rooms and conveyed him towards Hooke's office under the cupola. The howls and screams of the inmates faded to a sort of dim background babble, then were drowned out by more cheerful voices coming through a polished door. Pepys scurried round in front of the sedan chair and flung that door open to reveal *everyone:* not only Hooke, but Christiaan Huygens, Isaac Newton, Isaac's little shadow Fatio, Robert Boyle, John Locke, Roger Comstock, Christopher Wren, and twenty others—mostly Royal Society regulars, but a few odd men out such as Edmund Palling and Sterling Waterhouse.

They took him out of his sedan chair like a rare specimen being unpacked from its shipping-crate and held him up to accept several waves of cheers and toasts. Roger Comstock (who, since England's Adult Supervision had all run away to France, was becoming more terribly important every day) stood up on Hooke's lens-grinding table (Hooke became irate, and had to be restrained by Wren) and commanded silence. Then he held up a beaker of some fluid that was more transparent than water.

"We all know of Mr. Daniel Waterhouse's high regard and admiration for Alchemy," Roger began. This was made twice as funny by the exaggerated pomposity of his voice and manner; he was using his speaking-to-Parliament voice. After the laughter and Parliamentary barking noises had died down, he continued, just as gravely: "Alchemy has created many a miracle in our time, and I am assured, by some of its foremost practitioners, that within a few years they will have accomplished what has, for millennia, been the paramount goal of every Alchemist: namely, to bring us *immorality*!"

Roger Comstock now affected a look of extreme astonishment as the room erupted into true Bedlam. Daniel could not help glancing over at Isaac, who was the last man in the world to find anything amusing in a joke about Alchemy or immorality. But Isaac smiled and exchanged a look with Fatio.

Roger cupped a hand to his ear and listened carefully, then appeared taken aback. "What!? You say, instead, *immortality*?" Now he waxed indignant, and pointed a finger at Boyle. "Sirrah, my solicitor will call upon you in the morning to see about getting my money back!"

The audience had now been rendered completely helpless, which was the way Roger liked his audiences. They could only wait for him to continue, which he was only too happy to do: "The Chymists have accomplished smaller miracles along their way. Among those who frequent drinking establishments—or so I am told—it is known, empirically, that spiritous liquors are frequently contaminated by unwanted and unwholesome by-products. Of these, the most offensive by far is *water*, which gorges the bladder and obliges the drinker to step outside, where he is subject to cold, rain, wind, and the disapproving glares of neighbors and passers-by until such time as the bladder has become empty—which in the case of our Guest of Honor may be as long as a fortnight!"

"I can only say in my defense that I have time to sober up during those fortnights," Daniel returned, "and when I go back inside I find that you have left all the glasses empty, my lord."

Roger Comstock answered, "It is true. I give the contents of those glasses to our Alchemical brethren, who use them in their lucubrations. They have learnt how to remove water from wine and produce the pure spirit. But this is beginning to sound like a *theologickal* discourse, and so let me turn to *practical* matters." Roger hoisted the beaker up above his head. "Pray, gentlemen, extinguish all smoking materials! We do not wish to set fire to Mr. Hooke's edifice. The inmates will be so terrified that they will be driven sane, to a man. I hold in my hand the pure spirit I spoke of, and it could burn the place down like Greek fire. It will remain a grave hazard until our Guest of Honor has been so prudent as to sequester it in his belly. Cheers to you, Daniel; and rest assured that this libation will surely go to your head, but not a drop of it will trouble your kidneys!"

Under the center of the cupola they had set up a very stout oaken chair on a platform like a throne, which Daniel thought extremely considerate, as it put his head at or above the level of everyone else's. It was the first time in ages he'd been able to talk to anyone without feeling as if he were being peered down at. Once he was mounted in that chair, and wedged more or less upright by a few pillows, he did not have to move anything save his jaw and his drinking-arm. The others came round in ones and twos to pay court to him.

Wren spoke of the progress building the great Dome of St. Paul's. Edmund Palling related details of the voyage to Massachusetts planned for April. Hooke, when not arguing with Huygens about clocks (and fending off bawdy puns on "horology" from Roger Comstock), discoursed of his work on artificial muscles. He did not say that they were for use in flying machines, but Daniel already knew it. Isaac Newton was living in London now, sharing lodgings with Fatio, and had become Member of Parliament for Cambridge. Roger was bursting with scandalous gossip. Sterling was devising some sort of plot with Sir Richard Apthorp, some colossal scheme for financing the eternal follies of Government. Spain might have mines in America and France might have an infinite supply of taxable peasants, but Sterling and Sir Richard seemed to think that England could overcome her lack of both with some metaphysical sleight-of-hand. Huygens came over and told him the melancholy news that the Countess de la Zeur had got pregnant out of wedlock, then lost her baby. In a way, though, Daniel was pleased to hear that she was getting on with her life. He had dreamed once of proposing marriage to her. Looking at his condition now, it was hard to imagine a worse idea.

But thinking about her put him into a sort of reverie from which he did not return. He did not lose consciousness at any one certain point; consciousness slowly leaked out of him, rather, over the course of the evening. Every friend who came to greet him raised his glass, and Daniel raised his beaker in return. The liquor did not trickle down his throat but raced like panic across his mucous membranes, burning his eye-sockets and his eustachian tubes, and seeping direct from there into his brain. His vision faded. The babble and roar of the party put him gently to sleep.

The quiet woke him up. The quiet, and the light. He phant'sied for a moment that they had carried him out to face the Sun. But there were several suns ranged about him in a constellation. He tried to raise first one arm, then the other, to shield his eyes from the glare, but neither limb would move. His legs, too, were frozen in place.

"Perhaps you imagine you are having a cerebral anomaly, a near-death, or even a post-death, experience," said a voice quietly. It emanated from down low, between Daniel's knees. "And that several arch-angels are arrayed before you, burning your eyes with their radiance. In that case I would be a shade, a poor gray ghost, and the screams and moans you hear from far off would be the complaints of other departed souls being taken off to Hell."

Hooke was indeed too dim to see clearly, for the lights were behind him. He was sorting through some instruments and tools on a table that had been set in front of the chair.

Now that Daniel had stopped looking into the bright lights, his eyes had adjusted well enough to see what was restraining him: white linen cord, miles of it, spiraled around his arms and legs, and cunningly interwoven into a sort of custom-built web or net. This was clearly the work of the meticulous Hooke, for even Daniel's fingers and thumbs had been individually laced down, knuckle by knuckle, to the arms of this chair, which were as massive as the timbers of a gun-carriage.

His mind went back to Epsom during the Plague Year, when Hooke would sit in the sun for an hour watching through a lens as a spider bound up a horse-fly with whorls of gossamer.

The other detail that caught his eye was the gleaming of the small devices that Hooke was sorting out on the table. In addition to the various magnifiers that Hooke always had with him, there was the crooked probe that would be inserted up the length of the patient's urethra to find and hold the stone. Next to it was the lancet for making the incision through the scrotum and up into the bladder. Then a hook for reaching up through that opening and pulling the stone down and out between the testicles, and an assortment of variously sized and shaped rakes for scraping the inside of the bladder and probing up into the ureters to find and withdraw any smaller stones that might be a-building in the crannies.

There was the silver pipe that would be left in his urethra so that the uproar of urine, blood, lymph, and pus would not be dammed up by the inevitable swelling, and there was the fine sheep-gut for sewing him back together, and the curved needles and pliers for drawing it through his flesh. But for some reason none of these sights perturbed him so much as the scale standing by at the end of the table, its polished brass pans flashing inscrutable signals to him as they oscillated on the ends of their gleaming chains. Hooke, ever the empiricist, would of course weigh the stone when it came out.

"In truth you are still alive and will be for many years—more years than I have remaining. There are some who die of shock, it is true, and perhaps that is why all of your friends wished to come and pass time time with you before I started. But, as I recollect, you were shot with a blunderbuss once, and got up and walked away from it. So I am not afraid on that 'count. The bright lights you see are sticks of burning phosphorus. And I am Robert Hooke, than whom no man was ever better suited to perform this work."

"No, Robert."

Hooke took advantage of Daniel's plea to jam a leather strap into his mouth. "You may bite down on that if you wish, or you may spit it out and scream all you like—this is Bedlam, and no one will object. Neither will anyone take heed, or show mercy. Least of all Robert Hooke. For as you know, Daniel, I am utterly lacking in the quality of mercy. Which is well, as it would render me perfectly incompetent to carry out this operation. I told you a year ago, in the Tower, that I would one day repay your friendship by giving you something—a pearl of great price. Now the time has come for me to make good on that promise. The only question left to answer is how much will that pearl weigh, when I have washed your blood off it and let it clatter onto the pan of yonder scale. I am sorry you woke up. I shall not insult you by suggesting that you relax. Please do not go insane. I will see you on the other side of the Styx."

When he and Hooke and Wilkins had cut open live dogs during the Plague Year, Daniel had looked into their straining brown eyes and tried to fathom what was going on in their minds. He'd decided, in the end, that *nothing* was, that dogs had no conscious minds, no thought of past or future, living purely in the moment, and that this made it worse for them. Because they could neither look forward to the end of the pain, nor remember times when they had chased rabbits across meadows.

Hooke took up his blade and reached for Daniel.

Dramatis Personae

MEMBERS OF THE NOBILITY went by more than one name: their family surnames and Christian names, but also their titles. For example, the younger brother of King Charles II had the family name Stuart and was baptized James, and so might be called James Stuart; but for most of his life he was the Duke of York, and so might also be referred to, in the third person anyway, as "York" (but in the second person as "Your Royal Highness"). Titles frequently changed during a person's lifetime, as it was common during this period for commoners to be ennobled, and nobles of lower rank to be promoted. And so not only might a person have several names at any one moment, but certain of those names might change as he acquired new titles through ennoblement, promotion, conquest, or (what might be considered a combination of all three) marriage.

This multiplicity of names will be familiar to many readers who dwell on the east side of the Atlantic, or who read a lot of books like this. To others it may be confusing or even maddening. The following Dramatis Personae may be of help in resolving ambiguities.

If consulted too early and often, it may let cats out of bags by letting the reader know who is about to die, and who isn't.

The compiler of such a table faces a problem similar to the one that bedeviled Leibniz when trying to organize his patron's library. The entries (books in Leibniz's case, personages here) must be arranged in a linear fashion according to some predictable scheme. Below, they are alphabetized by name. But since more than one name applies to many of the characters, it is not always obvious where the entry should be situated. Here I have sacrificed consistency for ease of use by placing each entry under the name that is most commonly used in the book. So, for example, Louis-François de

Lavardac, duc d'Arcachon, is under "A" rather than "L" because he is almost always called simply the duc d'Arcachon in the story. But Knott Bolstrood, Count Penistone, is under "B" because he is usually called Bolstrood. Cross-references to the main entries are spotted under "L" and "P," respectively.

Entries that are relatively reliable, according to scholarly sources, are in Roman type. Entries in *italics* contain information that is more likely to produce confusion, misunderstanding, severe injury, and death if relied upon by time travelers visiting the time and place in question.

❧

ANGLESEY, LOUIS: 1648–. *Earl of Upnor. Son of Thomas More Anglesey. Courtier and friend of the Duke of Monmouth during the Interregnum and, after the Restoration, at Trinity College, Cambridge.*

ANGLESEY, PHILLIP: 1645–. *Count Sheerness. Son of Thomas More Anglesey.*

ANGLESEY, THOMAS MORE: 1618–1679. *Duke of Gunfleet. A leading Cavalier and a member of Charles II's court in exile during the Interregnum. After the Restoration, one of the A's in Charles II's CABAL (which see). Relocated to France during the Popish Plot troubles, died there.*

ANNE I OF ENGLAND: 1665–1714. Daughter of James II by his first wife, Anne Hyde.

APTHORP, RICHARD: 1631–. *Businessman and banker. One of the A's in Charles II's CABAL (which see). A founder of the Bank of England.*

D'ARCACHON, DUC: 1634–. *Louis-François de Lavardac. A cousin to Louis XIV. Builder, and subsequently Admiral, of the French Navy.*

D'ARCACHON, ÉTIENNE: 1662–. *Étienne de Lavardac. Son and heir of Louis-François de Lavardac, duc d'Arcachon.*

D'ARTAGNAN, CHARLES DE BATZ-CASTELMORE: C. 1620–1673. French musketeer and memoirist.

ASHMOLE, SIR ELIAS: 1617–1692. Astrologer, alchemist, autodidact, Comptroller and Auditor of the Excise, collector of curiosities, and founder of Oxford's Ashmolean Museum.

D'AVAUX, JEAN-ANTOINE DE MESMES, COMTE: French ambassador to the Dutch Republic, later an advisor to James II during his campaign in Ireland.

BOLSTROOD, GOMER: 1645–. *Son of Knott. Dissident agitator, later an immigrant to New England and a furniture maker there.*

BOLSTROOD, GREGORY: 1600–1652. *Dissident preacher. Founder of the Puritan sect known as the Barkers.*

BOLSTROOD, KNOTT: 1628–1682. *Son of Gregory. Ennobled as Count Penistone and made Secretary of State by Charles II. The B in Charles II's CABAL (which see).*

BOYLE, ROBERT: 1627–1691. Chemist, member of the Experimental Philosophical Club at Oxford, Fellow of the Royal Society.

VON BOYNEBURG, JOHANN CHRISTIAN: 1622–1672. An early patron of Leibniz in Mainz.

CABAL, THE: unofficial name of Charles II's post-Restoration cabinet, loosely modeled after Louis XIV's Conseil d'en-Haut, which is to say that each member had a general area of responsibility, but the boundaries were vague and overlapping (see table, p. 920).

CAROLINE, PRINCESS OF BRANDENBURG-ANSBACH: 1683–1737. Daughter of Eleanor, Princess of Saxe-Eisenach.

CASTLEMAINE, LADY: see Villiers, Barbara.

CATHERINE OF BRAGANZA: 1638–1705. Portuguese wife of Charles II of England.

CHARLES I OF ENGLAND: 1600–1649. Stuart king of England, decapitated at the Banqueting House after the victory of Parliamentary forces under Oliver Cromwell.

CHARLES II OF ENGLAND: 1630–1685. Son of Charles I. Exiled to France and later the Netherlands during the Interregnum. Returned to England 1660 and re-established monarchy (the Restoration).

CHARLES LOUIS, ELECTOR PALATINATE: 1617–1680. Eldest surviving son of the Winter King and Queen, brother of Sophie, father of Liselotte. Re-established his family in the Palatinate following the Thirty Years' War.

CHARLES, ELECTOR PALATINATE: 1651–1685. Son and heir to Charles Louis. War-gaming enthusiast. Died young of disease contracted during a mock siege.

CHESTER, LORD BISHOP OF: see Wilkins, John.

CHURCHILL, JOHN: 1650–1722. Courtier, warrior, duellist, cocksman, hero, later Duke of Marlborough.

CHURCHILL, WINSTON: Royalist, Squire, courtier, early Fellow of the Royal Society, father of John Churchill.

CLEVELAND, DUCHESS OF: see Villiers, Barbara.

COMENIUS, JOHN AMOS (JAN AMOS KOMENSKY): 1592–1670. Moravian Pansophist, an inspiration to Wilkins and Leibniz among many others.

The CABAL

Responsible party	General area[s] of responsibility	Corresponding roughly to formal position of*
C COMSTOCK, JOHN (EARL OF EPSOM)	(Early in the reign) domestic affairs and justice. Later retired	Lord High Chancellor
A ANGLESEY, LOUIS (DUKE OF GUNFLEET)	(Early) the Exchequer and (covertly) foreign affairs, especially vis-a-vis France. Later Apthorp came to dominate the former. After Comstock's retirement, but before the Popish Plot, domestic affairs, and the Navy.	Various, including Lord High Admiral
B BOLSTROOD, KNOTT (COUNT PENISTONE)	Foreign affairs (ostensibly)	Secretary of State
A APTHORP, SIR RICHARD	Finance	Chancellor of the Exchequer
L LEWIS, HUGH (DUKE OF TWEED)	Army	Marshal, or (though no such position existed at the time) Defense Minister

*But sometimes they formally held these positions and sometimes they didn't.

☙

COMSTOCK, CHARLES: 1650–1708. *Son of John. Student of Natural Philosophy. After the retirement of John and the death of his elder brother, Richard, an immigrant to Connecticut.*

COMSTOCK, JOHN: 1607–1685. *Leading Cavalier, and member of Charles II's court in exile in France. Scion of the so-called Silver branch of the Comstock family. Armaments maker. Early patron of the Royal Society. After the Restoration, the C in Charles II's CABAL (which see). Father of Richard and Charles Comstock.*

COMSTOCK, RICHARD: 1638–1673. *Eldest son and heir of John Comstock. Died at naval battle of Sole Bay.*

COMSTOCK, ROGER: 1646–. *Scion of the so-called Golden branch of the Comstock family. Classmate of Newton, Daniel Waterhouse, the Duke of Monmouth, the Earl of Upnor, and George Jeffreys at Trinity College, Cambridge, during the early 1660s. Later, a successful developer of real estate, and Marquis of Ravenscar.*

DE CRÉPY: *French family of gentlemen and petty nobles until the Wars of Religion in France, during which time they began to pursue a strategy of aggressive upward mobility. They intermarried in two different ways with the older but declining de Gex family. One of them (Anne Marie de Crépy, 1653–) married the much older duc d'Oyonnax and survived him by many years. Her sister (Charlotte Adélaide de Crépy 1656–) married the Marquis d'Ozoir.*

CROMWELL, OLIVER: 1599–1658. Parliamentary leader, general of the anti-Royalist forces during the English Civil War, scourge of Ireland, and leading man of England during the Commonwealth, or Interregnum.

CROMWELL, ROGER: 1626–1712. Son and (until the Restoration) successor of his much more formidable father, Oliver.

EAUZE, CLAUDE: see *d'Ozoir, Marquis.*

ELEANOR, PRINCESS OF SAXE-EISENACH: D. 1696. Mother (by her first husband, the Margrave of Ansbach) of Caroline, Princess of Brandenburg-Ansbach. Late in life, married to the Elector of Saxony.

ELISABETH CHARLOTTE: 1652–1722. Liselotte, *La Palatine.* Known as Madame in the French court. Daughter of Charles Louis, Elector Palatinate, and niece of Sophie. Married Philippe, duc d'Orléans, the younger brother of Louis XIV. Spawned the House of Orléans.

EPSOM, EARL OF: see *Comstock, John.*

FREDERICK V, ELECTOR PALATINATE: 1596–1632. King of Bohemia ("Winter King") briefly in 1618, lived and died in exile during the Thirty Years' War. Father of many princes, electors, duchesses, etc., including Sophie.

FREDERICK WILLIAM, ELECTOR OF BRANDENBURG: 1620–1688. Known as the Great Elector. After the Thirty Years' War created a standing professional army, small but effective. By playing the great powers of the day (Sweden, France, and the Hapsburgs) against each other, consolidated the scattered Hohenzollern fiefdoms into a coherent state, Brandenburg-Prussia.

DE GEX: *A petty-noble family of Jura, which dwindled until the early seventeenth century, when the two surviving children of Henry, Sieur de Gex (1595–1660), Francis and Louise-Anne, each married a member of the more sanguine family de Crépy. The children of Francis carried on the de Gex name. Their youngest was Édouard de Gex. The children of Louise-Anne included Anne Marie de Crépy (later duchesse d'Oyonnax) and Charlotte Adélaide de Crépy (later marquise d'Ozoir).*

DE GEX, FATHER ÉDOUARD: 1663–. *Youngest offspring of Marguerite Diane de Crépy (who died giving birth to him) and Francis de Gex, who was thirty-eight years old and in declining health. Raised at a school and orphanage in Lyons by Jesuits, who found in him an exceptionally gifted pupil. Became a Jesuit himself at the the age of twenty. Was posted to Versailles, where he became a favorite of Mademoiselle. de Maintenon.*

GREAT ELECTOR: see Frederick William.

GUNFLEET, DUKE OF: see *Anglesey, Thomas More.*

GWYN, NELL: 1650–1687. Fruit retailer and comedienne, one of the mistresses of Charles II.

HAM, THOMAS: 1603–. *Money-goldsmith, husband of Mayflower Waterhouse, leading man of Ham Bros. Goldsmiths. Created Earl of Walbrook by Charles II.*

HAM, WILLIAM: 1662–. *Son of Thomas and Mayflower.*

HENRIETTA ANNE: 1644–1670. Sister of Charles II and James II of England, first wife of Philippe, duc d'Orléans, Louis XIV's brother.

HENRIETTA MARIA: 1609–1669. Sister of King Louis XIII of France, wife of King Charles I of England, mother of Charles II and James II of England.

HOOKE, ROBERT: 1635–1703. Artist, linguist, astronomer, geometer, microscopist, mechanic, horologist, chemist, optician, inventor, philosopher, botanist, anatomist, etc. Curator of Experiments for the Royal Society, Surveyor of London after the fire. Friend and collaborator of Christopher Wren.

HUYGENS, CHRISTIAAN: 1629–1695. Great Dutch astronomer, horologist, mathematician, and physicist.

HYDE, ANNE: 1637–1671. First wife of James, Duke of York (later James II). Mother of two English queens: Mary (of William and Mary) and Anne.

JAMES I OF ENGLAND: 1566–1625. First Stuart king of England.

JAMES II OF ENGLAND: 1633–1701. Duke of York for much of his early life. Became King of England upon the death of his brother in 1685. Deposed in the Glorious Revolution, late 1688–early 1689.

JAMES VI OF SCOTLAND: see James I of England.

JEFFREYS, GEORGE: 1645–1689. Welsh gentleman, lawyer, solicitor general to the Duke of York, lord chief justice, and later lord chancellor under James II. Created Baron Jeffreys of Wem in 1685.

JOHANN FRIEDRICH: 1620–1679. Duke of Braunschweig-Lüneburg, book collector, a patron of Leibniz.

JOHN FREDERICK: see Johann Friedrich.

KÉROUALLE, LOUISE DE: 1649–1734. Duchess of Portsmouth. One of the mistresses of Charles II.

KETCH, JACK: Name given to executioners.

LAVARDAC: *A branch of the Bourbon family producing various hereditary dukes and peers of France, including the duc d'Arcachon* (see).

LeFEBURE: French alchemist/apothecary who moved to London at the time of the Restoration to provide services to the Court.

LEIBNIZ, GOTTFRIED WILHELM: 1646–1716. Refer to novel.

LESTRANGE, SIR ROGER: 1616–1704. Royalist pamphleteer and (after the Restoration) Surveyor of the Imprimery, hence chief censor for Charles II. Nemesis of Milton. Translator.

LEWIS, HUGH: 1625–. *General. Created Duke of Tweed by Charles II after the Restoration, in recognition of his crossing the River Tweed with his regiment (thenceforth called the Coldstream Guards) in support of the resurgent monarchy. The L in Charles II's CABAL (which see).*

LISELOTTE: *see* Elisabeth Charlotte.

LOCKE, JOHN: 1632–1704. Natural Philosopher, physician, political advisor, philosopher.

DE MAINTENON, MME.: 1635–1719. Mistress, then second and last wife of Louis XIV.

MARY: 1662–1694. Daughter of James II and Anne Hyde. After the Glorious Revolution (1689), Queen of England with her husband, William of Orange.

MARY OF MODENA: 1658–1718. Second and last wife of James II of England. Mother of James Stuart, aka "the Old Pretender."

MAURICE: 1621–1652. One of the numerous princely offspring of the Winter Queen. Active as a Cavalier in the English Civil War.

DE MESMES, JEAN-ANTOINE: see d'Avaux.

MINETTE: see Henrietta Anne.

MONMOUTH, DUKE OF (JAMES SCOTT): 1649–1685. Bastard of Charles II by one Lucy Walter.

MORAY, ROBERT: C. 1608–1673. Scottish soldier, official, and courtier, a favorite of Charles II. Early Royal Society figure, probably instrumental in securing the organization's charter.

NEWTON, ISAAC: 1642–1727. Refer to novel.

OLDENBURG, HENRY: 1615–1677. Emigrant from Bremen. Secretary of the Royal Society, publisher of the *Philosophical Transactions,* prolific correspondent.

d'Oyonnax, Anne Marie de Crépy, duchesse: 1653–. *Lady in Waiting to the Dauphine, Satanist, poisoner.*

d'Ozoir, Charlotte Adélaide de Crépy, marquise: 1656–. *Wife of Claude Eauze, Marquis d'Ozoir.*

d'Ozoir, Claude Eauze, marquis: 1650–. *Illegitimate son of Louis-François de Lavardac, duc d'Arcachon, by a domestic servant, Luce Eauze. Traveled to India in late 1660s as part of ill-fated French East India Company expedition. In 1674, when noble titles went on sale to raise funds for the Dutch war, he purchased the title Marquis d'Ozoir using a loan from his father secured by revenues from his slaving operations in Africa.*

Penistone, Count: see *Bolstrood, Knott.*

Pepys, Samuel: 1633–1703. Clerk, Administrator to the Royal Navy, Member of Parliament, Fellow of the Royal Society, diarist, man about town.

Peters, Hugh: 1598–1660. Fulminant Puritan preacher. Spent time in Holland and Massachusetts, returned to England, became Cromwell's chaplain. Poorly thought of by Irish for his involvement with massacres at Drogheda and Wexford. For his role in the regicide of Charles I, executed by Jack Ketch, using a knife, in 1660.

Philippe, duc d'Orléans: 1640–1701. Younger brother of King Louis XIV of France. Known as Monsieur to the French Court. Husband first of Henrietta Anne of England, later of Liselotte. Progenitor of the House of Orléans.

Portsmouth, Duchess of: see *Kéroualle, Louise de.*

Qwghlm: *Title bestowed on Eliza by William of Orange.*

Ravenscar, Marquis of: see *Comstock, Roger.*

Rossignol, Antoine: 1600–1682. "France's first full-time cryptologist" (David Kahn, *The Codebreakers,* which buy and read). A favorite of Richelieu, Louis XIII, Mazarin, and Louis XIV.

Rossignol, Bonaventure: d. 1705. Cryptanalyst to Louis XIV following the death of his father, teacher, and collaborator Antoine.

Rupert: 1619–1682. One of the numerous princely offspring of the Winter Queen. Active as a Cavalier in the English Civil War.

de Ruyter, Michiel Adriaanszoon: 1607–1676. Exceptionally gifted Dutch admiral. Particularly effective against the English.

von Schönborn, Johann Philipp: 1605–1673. Elector and Archbishop of Mainz, statesman, diplomat, and early patron of Leibniz.

SHEERNESS, COUNT: see *Anglesey, Phillip.*

SOPHIE: 1630–1714. Youngest daughter of the Winter Queen. Married Ernst August, who later became duke of Braunschweig-Lüneburg. Later the name of this principality was changed to Hanover, and Ernst August and Sophie elevated to the status of Elector and Electress. From 1707 onwards, she was first in line to the English throne.

SOPHIE CHARLOTTE: 1668–1705. Eldest daughter of Sophie. Married Frederick III, elector of Brandenburg and son of the Great Elector. In 1701, when Brandenburg-Prussia was elevated to the status of a kingdom by the Holy Roman Emperor, she became the first Queen of Prussia and spawned the House of Prussia.

STUART, ELIZABETH: 1596–1662. Daughter of King James I of England, sister of Charles I. Married Frederick, Elector Palatinate. Proclaimed Queen of Bohemia briefly in 1618, hence her sobriquet "the Winter Queen." Lived in exile during the Thirty Years' War, mostly in the Dutch Republic. Outlived her husband by three decades. Mother of many children, including Sophie.

STUART, JAMES: 1688–1766. Controversial but probably legitimate son of James II by his second wife, Mary of Modena. Raised in exile in France. Following the death of his father, styled James III by the Jacobite faction in England and "the Old Pretender" by supporters of the Hanoverian succession.

UPNOR, EARL OF: see *Anglesey, Louis.*

VILLIERS, BARBARA (LADY CASTLEMAINE, DUCHESS OF CLEVELAND): 1641–1709. Indefatigable mistress of many satisfied Englishmen of high rank, including Charles II and John Churchill.

WALBROOK, EARL OF: see *Ham, Thomas.*

WATERHOUSE, ANNE: 1649–. *Née Anne Robertson. English colonist in Massachusetts. Wife of Praise-God Waterhouse.*

WATERHOUSE, BEATRICE: 1642–. *Née Beatrice Durand. Huguenot wife of Sterling.*

WATERHOUSE, CALVIN: 1563–1605. *Son of John, father of Drake.*

WATERHOUSE, DANIEL: 1646–. *Youngest (by far) child of Drake by his second wife, Hortense.*

WATERHOUSE, DRAKE: 1590–1666. *Son of Calvin, father of Raleigh, Sterling, Mayflower, Oliver, and Daniel. Independent trader, political agitator, leader of Pilgrims and Dissidents.*

WATERHOUSE, ELIZABETH: 1621–. *Née Elizabeth Flint. Wife of Raleigh Waterhouse.*

WATERHOUSE, EMMA: 1656–. *Daughter of Raleigh and Elizabeth.*

WATERHOUSE, FAITH: 1689–. *Née Faith Page. English colonist in Massachusetts. (Much younger) wife of Daniel, mother of Godfrey.*

WATERHOUSE, GODFREY WILLIAM: 1708–. *Son of Daniel and Faith in Boston.*

WATERHOUSE, HORTENSE: 1625–1658. *Née Hortense Bowden. Second wife (m. 1645) of Drake Waterhouse, and mother of Daniel.*

WATERHOUSE, JANE: 1599–1643. *Née Jane Wheelwright. A pilgrim in Leiden. First wife (m. 1617) of Drake, mother of Raleigh, Sterling, Oliver, and Mayflower.*

WATERHOUSE, JOHN: 1542–1597. *Devout early English Protestant. Decamped to Geneva during reign of Bloody Mary. Father of Calvin Waterhouse.*

WATERHOUSE, MAYFLOWER: 1621–. *Daughter of Drake and Jane, wife of Thomas Ham, mother of William Ham.*

WATERHOUSE, OLIVER I: 1625–1646. *Son of Drake and Jane. Died in Battle of Newark during English Civil War.*

WATERHOUSE, OLIVER II: 1653–. *Son of Raleigh and Elizabeth.*

WATERHOUSE, PRAISE-GOD: 1649–. *Eldest son of Raleigh and Elizabeth. Immigrated to Massachusetts Bay Colony. Father of Wait Still Waterhouse.*

WATERHOUSE, RALEIGH: 1618–. *Eldest son of Drake, father of Praise-God, Oliver II, and Emma.*

WATERHOUSE, STERLING: 1630–. *Son of Drake. Real estate developer. Later ennobled as Earl of Willesden.*

WATERHOUSE, WAIT STILL: 1675–. *Son of Praise-God in Boston. Graduate of Harvard College. Congregational preacher.*

WEEM, WALTER: 1652–. *Husband of Emma Waterhouse.*

WHEELWRIGHT, JANE: see *Waterhouse, Jane.*

WILHELMINA CAROLINE: see Caroline, Princess of Brandenburg-Ansbach.

WILKINS, JOHN (BISHOP OF CHESTER): 1614–1672. Cryptographer. Science fiction author. Founder, first chairman, and first secretary of the Royal Society. Private chaplain to Charles Louis, Elector Palatinate. Warden of Wadham (Oxford) and Master of Trinity (Cambridge). Prebendary of York, Dean of Ripon, holder of many other ecclesiastical appointments. Friend of Nonconformists, Supporter of Freedom of Conscience.

WILLESDEN, EARL OF: see *Waterhouse, Sterling.*

WILLIAM II OF ORANGE: 1626–1650. Father of the better-known William III of Orange. Died young (of smallpox).

WILLIAM III OF ORANGE: 1650–1702. With Mary, daugher of James II, co-sovereign of England from 1689.

WINTER KING: see Frederick V.

WINTER QUEEN: see Stuart, Elizabeth.

WREN, CHRISTOPHER: 1632–1723. Prodigy, Natural Philosopher, and Architect, a member of the Experimental Philosophical Club and later Fellow of the Royal Society.

YORK, DUKE OF: The traditional title of whomever is next in line to the English throne. During much of this book, James, brother to Charles II.

DE LA ZEUR: *Eliza was created Countess de la Zeur by Louis XIV.*

**Order further Neal Stephenson titles
from your local bookshop, or have them delivered
direct to your door by Bookpost**

☐	**Cryptonomicon**	0 09 941067 2	£8.99
☐	**The Confusion**	0 09 941069 9	£8.99
☐	**The System of the World**	0 09 946336 9	£8.99

Free post and packing
Overseas customers allow £2 per paperback

Phone: 01624 677237

Post: Random House Books
c/o Bookpost, PO Box 29, Douglas, Isle of Man IM99 1BQ

Fax: 01624 670923

email: bookshop@enterprise.net

Cheques (payable to Bookpost) and credit cards accepted

Prices and availability subject to change without notice.
Allow 28 days for delivery.
When placing your order, please state if you do not wish to receive any
additional information.

www.randomhouse.co.uk/arrowbooks

a r r o w b o o k s